THE MARK TWAIN PAPERS

AUTOBIOGRAPHY OF MARK TWAIN

VOLUME 1

The Mark Twain Project is an editorial and
publishing program of The Bancroft Library,
working since 1967 to create a comprehensive
critical edition of everything Mark Twain wrote.

This volume is the first one in that edition to
be published simultaneously in print and as an
electronic text at http://www.marktwainproject.org.
The textual commentaries for all Mark Twain
texts in this volume are published *only* there.

AUTOBIOGRAPHY OF MARK TWAIN

VOLUME 1

HARRIET ELINOR SMITH, EDITOR

Associate Editors

Benjamin Griffin

Victor Fischer

Michael B. Frank

Sharon K. Goetz

Leslie Diane Myrick

Mark Twain

A publication of the Mark Twain Project
of The Bancroft Library

UNIVERSITY OF CALIFORNIA PRESS

BERKELEY   LOS ANGELES   LONDON

Frontispiece: Photograph by Albert Bigelow Paine, 25 June 1906, Upton House, Dublin, New Hampshire

University of California Press, one of the most distinguished university presses in the United States, enriches lives around the world by advancing scholarship in the humanities, social sciences, and natural sciences. Its activities are supported by the UC Press Foundation and by philanthropic contributions from individuals and institutions. For more information, visit http://www.ucpress.edu.

University of California Press
Berkeley and Los Angeles, California

University of California Press, Ltd.
London, England

Library of Congress Cataloging-in-Publication Data

Twain, Mark, 1835–1910
  [Autobiography]
  Autobiography of Mark Twain, Volume 1 / editor: Harriet Elinor Smith ;
associate editors: Benjamin Griffin, Victor Fischer, Michael B. Frank, Sharon K. Goetz, Leslie Diane Myrick
    p. cm. — (The Mark Twain Papers)
  "A publication of the Mark Twain Project of The Bancroft Library."
  Includes bibliographical references and index.
  ISBN 978-0-520-26719-0 (cloth : alk. paper)
  1. Twain, Mark, 1835–1910. 2. Authors, American—19th century—Biography. I. Smith, Harriet Elinor. II. Griffin, Benjamin, 1968– III. Fischer, Victor, 1942– IV. Frank, Michael B. V. Goetz, Sharon K. VI. Myrick, Leslie Diane. VII. Bancroft Library. VIII. Title.
  PS1331.A2 2010
  818'.4'0924—dc22   2009047700
Manufactured in the United States of America

19 18 17 16 15 14 13 12 11 10
10 9 8 7 6 5 4 3

This book is printed on Natures Book, which contains 30% post-consumer waste and meets the minimum requirements of ANSI/NISO Z39.48–1992 (R 1997) (*Permanence of Paper*).

Editorial work for this volume has been supported
by a generous gift to the Mark Twain Project of
The Bancroft Library from the

KORET FOUNDATION

and by matching and outright grants from the

NATIONAL ENDOWMENT
FOR THE HUMANITIES,
an independent federal agency.

Without that support, this volume could not
have been produced.

The Mark Twain Project at the University of California, Berkeley, gratefully acknowledges generous support from the following, for editorial work on the *Autobiography of Mark Twain* and for the acquisition of important new documents:

The University of California, Berkeley, Class of 1958
Members of the Mark Twain Luncheon Club
The Barkley Fund
The Mark Twain Foundation

The Beatrice Fox Auerbach Foundation Fund at the
    Hartford Foundation for Public Giving
Lawrence E. Brooks
Helen Kennedy Cahill
Kimo Campbell
Virginia Robinson Furth
The Herrick Fund
The Hofmann Foundation
The House of Bernstein, Inc.
Robert and Beverly Middlekauff
The Renee B. Fisher Foundation
The Benjamin and Susan Shapell Foundation
Jeanne and Leonard Ware
Patricia Wright, in memory of Timothy J. Fitzgerald

and

The thousands of individual donors over the past fifty years
who have helped sustain the ongoing work
of the Mark Twain Project.

The publication of this volume has been made possible by a gift to the University of California Press Foundation by

WILSON GARDNER COMBS

FRANK MARION GIFFORD COMBS

in honor of

WILSON GIFFORD COMBS
BA 1935, MA 1950, University of California, Berkeley

MARYANNA GARDNER COMBS
MSW 1951, University of California, Berkeley

University of California Press
gratefully acknowledges the support of

John G. Davies

and the Humanities Endowment Fund
of the UC Press Foundation

CONTENTS

LIST OF MANUSCRIPTS
AND DICTATIONS

Except for the subtitle "Random Extracts from It" (which Clemens himself enclosed in brackets), bracketed titles have been editorially supplied for works that Clemens left untitled.

AUTOBIOGRAPHY OF MARK TWAIN

ACKNOWLEDGMENTS

Intensive editorial work on the *Autobiography of Mark Twain* began some six years ago and will continue for several more years. But the collective skills and expertise that have allowed us to solve the daunting problems posed by this manuscript came gradually into existence over four decades of editorial work on Mark Twain. We therefore thank the National Endowment for the Humanities, an independent federal agency, both for its three most recent outright and matching grants over the last six years, and for its patient, generous, and uninterrupted support of the Mark Twain Project since 1966. At the same time and with the same fervor, we thank the Koret Foundation for its recent generous grant in support of editorial and production work on the *Autobiography,* all of which has gone (or will go) to satisfy the matching component of the Endowment's recent grants to the Project.

For additional continuing support of work on the *Autobiography* and for help in acquiring important original documents for the Mark Twain Papers, we thank those institutions and individuals listed on page ix. The Mark Twain Project has been sustained over the years in so many ways by so many people that we are obliged, with regret, to thank them as one large group rather than by individual names. For donations to sustain our work, ranging from five dollars to five million dollars, we here thank all our loyal and generous supporters. Without their support, the Project would long ago have ceased to exist, and would certainly not be completing work on the *Autobiography* at this time.

Recent efforts have been made to create an endowment to support the present and future work of the Mark Twain Project, and we want to acknowledge those efforts here. First and foremost we thank all the members of the University of California, Berkeley, Class of 1958, led by Roger and Jeane Samuelsen, Edward H. Peterson, and Don and Bitsy Kosovac, who recently created an endowment of $1 million dedicated to the Mark Twain Project. We thank each and every member of the Class for their far-seeing wisdom and generosity. To that endowment fund we may now add, with renewed gratitude, contributions from the estate of Phyllis R. Bogue and the estate of Peter K. Oppenheim.

Instrumental in all recent fund-raising for the Project has been the Mark Twain Luncheon Club, organized ten years ago by Ira Michael Heyman, Watson M. (Mac) Laetsch, and Robert Middlekauff. Their leadership has been unflagging and indispensable, and we thank them for it and for a thousand other forms of help. We also thank all of the Club's nearly one hundred members for their loyal financial and moral support of the Project, and on their behalf we extend thanks to the several dozen speakers who have agreed to address the Luncheon Club members over the years. Our thanks also go to Dave Duer, director of development in the Berkeley University Library, for his continuing wise and judicious counsel, and for his unprecedented efforts to raise financial support for the Project. Last but not least we want to thank the Berkeley campus as a whole for granting the Project relief from indirect costs on its several grants from the Endowment. We are grateful for this and all other forms of support from our home institution.

We thank the staff of the University Library and The Bancroft Library at Berkeley, especially Thomas C. Leonard, University Librarian; Charles Faulhaber, the James D. Hart Director of The Bancroft Library; and Peter E. Hanff, its Deputy Director, all of whom serve on the Board of Directors of the Mark Twain Project. To them and to the other members of the Board—Jo Ann Boydston, Laura Cerruti, Don L. Cook, Frederick Crews, Michael Millgate, George A. Starr, G. Thomas Tanselle, and Lynne Withey—we are indebted for multiple forms of moral and intellectual support.

Scholars and archivists at other institutions have been vital to editorial work on this volume. Barbara Schmidt, an independent scholar who maintains an invaluable website (www.twainquotes.com) for Mark Twain research, tops our list when it comes to information and documentation freely and generously volunteered. For this particular volume she also provided us with photocopies of important original documents not previously known to us. Kevin Mac Donnell, an expert dealer and collector of Mark Twain documents, has as always been generous in sharing his extensive collection. Photographs and other documentation were also provided by the following, to whom we express our thanks: Lee Brumbaugh of the Nevada Historical Society, Reno; Christine Montgomery of The State Historical Society of Missouri, Columbia; Patti Philippon of the Mark Twain House and Museum, Hartford; and Henry Sweets of the Mark Twain Boyhood Home and Museum, Hannibal. At our own university, we are grateful to Dan Johnston of the Digital Imaging Laboratory for generating superb digital files from negatives of rare photographs. We would also like to thank the following archivists who generously assisted us in our research: Louise A. Merriam of the Andersen Library, University of Minnesota; Eva Guggemos of the Beinecke Library at Yale University; and Kathleen Kienholz of the American Academy of Arts and Letters, New York. Patricia Thayer Muno and James R. Toncray contributed important information about their families.

We are grateful for the tireless help of Kathleen MacDougall, our highly skilled copy editor and project manager at UC Press, who contributed much to the accuracy of the editorial matter and was a guiding hand at every stage of the production process. We thank Sandy Drooker, who designed the book and the dust jacket with her usual consummate skill. As of old, we again thank Sam Rosenthal, who expertly supervised the printing and binding process, and Laura Cerruti, our sponsoring editor, whose enthusiasm and support for this edition were essential to its publication.

All volumes produced by the Mark Twain Project are the products of complex and sustained collaboration. The student employees listed on page iii as Contributing Editors carried out much of the preliminary work of transcribing, proofreading, and collating the source documents that form the basis of the critical text. Associate editors Benjamin Griffin, Victor Fischer, and Michael B. Frank contributed to every aspect of the editorial work. They carried out original research for and drafted much of the annotation, and helped with the painstaking preparation and checking required to produce accurate texts, apparatus, and index. Associate editors Sharon K. Goetz and Leslie Diane Myrick brought their unmatched technical expertise and innovative programming to bear on the challenge of publishing this edition simultaneously in print and on Mark Twain Project Online (www.marktwainproject.org). None of us would be able to edit as we do without the Project's administrative assistant, Neda Salem, who skillfully held the bureaucracy at bay and patiently answered the myriad requests for information and copies of documents which the Project receives from scholars and the general public.

We wish to express special gratitude to my colleague Lin Salamo, who retired from the Project before this volume was completed. After more than two decades of dedicated editorial work, she contributed to this edition what is arguably her most significant professional accomplishment—reassembling and analyzing the hundreds of typescript pages that make up the Autobiographical Dictations. Her research was the indispensable key to our new understanding of Mark Twain's plan for his autobiography.

H. E. S.

INTRODUCTION

Between 1870 and 1905 Mark Twain (Samuel L. Clemens) tried repeatedly, and at long intervals, to write (or dictate) his autobiography, always shelving the manuscript before he had made much progress. By 1905 he had accumulated some thirty or forty of these false starts—manuscripts that were essentially experiments, drafts of episodes and chapters; many of these have survived in the Mark Twain Papers and two other libraries. To some of these manuscripts he went so far as to assign chapter numbers that placed them early or late in a narrative which he never filled in, let alone completed. None dealt with more than brief snatches of his life story.

He broke this pattern in January 1906 when he began almost daily dictations to a stenographer. He soon decided that these Autobiographical Dictations would form the bulk of what he would call the *Autobiography of Mark Twain*. Within a few months he reviewed his accumulation of false starts and decided which to incorporate into the newer dictation series and which to leave unpublished. By the time he had created more than two hundred and fifty of these almost daily dictations (and written a final chapter in December 1909, about the recent death of his daughter Jean), he had compiled more than half a million words. He declared the work done, but insisted that it should not be published in its entirety until a hundred years after his death, which occurred less than four months later, on 21 April 1910.

This belated success with a project that had resisted completion for thirty-five years can be traced to two new conditions. First, he had at last found a skilled stenographer who was also a responsive audience—Josephine S. Hobby—which encouraged him to embrace dictation as the method of composition, something he had experimented with as early as 1885. Second, and just as important, dictating the text made it easier to follow a style of composition he had been drifting toward for at least twenty years. As he put it in June 1906, he had finally seen that the "right way to do an Autobiography" was to "start it at no particular time of your life; wander at your free will all over your life; talk only about the thing which interests you for the moment; drop it the moment its interest threatens to pale, and turn your talk upon the new and more interesting thing that has intruded itself into your mind meantime."[1]

Combining dictation and discursiveness in this bold way was unexpectedly liberating, in large part because it produced not a conventional narrative marching inexorably toward the grave, but rather a series of spontaneous recollections and comments on the present as well as the past, arranged simply in the order of their creation. The problem of method had been solved. It was also liberating to insist on posthumous publication, but that idea had been around from

---

1. "The Latest Attempt," one of the prefaces written to introduce the final form of the autobiography; see p. 220.

the start and was closely tied to Clemens's ambition to tell the whole truth, without reservation. As he explained to an interviewer in 1899: "A book that is not to be published for a century gives the writer a freedom which he could secure in no other way. In these conditions you can draw a man without prejudice exactly as you knew him and yet have no fear of hurting his feelings or those of his sons or grandsons." Posthumous publication was also supposed to make it easier for Clemens to confess even shameful parts of his own story, but that goal proved illusory. In that same 1899 interview he admitted that a "man cannot tell the whole truth about himself, even if convinced that what he wrote would never be seen by others."[2]

But if delaying publication failed to make him into a confessional autobiographer, it did free him to express unconventional thoughts about religion, politics, and the damned human race, without fear of ostracism. In January 1908 he recalled that he had long had "the common habit, in private conversation with friends, of revealing every private opinion I possessed relating to religion, politics, and men"—adding that he would "never dream of *printing* one of them."[3] The need to defer publication of subversive ideas seemed obvious to him. "We suppress an unpopular opinion because we cannot afford the bitter cost of putting it forth," he wrote in 1905. "None of us likes to be hated, none of us likes to be shunned."[4] So having the freedom to speak his mind (if not confess his sins) was still ample justification for delaying publication until after his death.

Seven months after he began the Autobiographical Dictations in 1906, however, Clemens did permit—indeed actively pursued—partial publication of what he had so far accumulated. He supervised the preparation of some twenty-five short extracts from his autobiographical manuscripts and dictations for publication in the *North American Review,* each selection deliberately tamed for that time and audience, and each prefaced by a notice: "No part of the autobiography will be published in book form during the lifetime of the author."[5] But not long after Clemens died, his instruction to delay publication for a hundred years began to be ignored—first in 1924 by Albert Bigelow Paine, Mark Twain's official biographer and first literary executor, then in 1940 by Paine's successor, Bernard DeVoto, and most recently by Charles Neider in 1959.

Each of these editors undertook to publish only a part of the text, and none ventured to do so in the way that Clemens actually wanted it published. Paine began his two-volume edition with all but a handful of the manuscripts and dictations carried out before 1906, as well as several texts that were probably never part of those early experiments. He arranged all of them "in accordance with the author's wish . . . in the order in which they were written, regardless of the chronology of events."[6] It now seems clear that Paine's understanding of "the author's

---

2. "Mark Twain's Bequest," London *Times,* 23 May 1899, 4, in Scharnhorst 2006, 334. All of the abbreviations and short forms of citation used in these notes are fully defined in References.

3. AD, 13 Jan 1908.

4. "The Privilege of the Grave," written in 1905, published in SLC 2009, 56.

5. These words came at the end of the editorial note that preceded each of the twenty-five selections in the *Review.*

6. *MTA,* 1:1. The following pre-1906 writings published by Paine in the autobiography did not meet the criteria for inclusion in this edition: "Jane Lampton Clemens" (1890; published in *Inds,* 82–92), "Macfarlane" (1894–95; published in *WIM,* 76–78), and "Henry H. Rogers *(Continued)*" (1909) (*MTA,* 1:115–25, 143–47, 256–65).

wish" was mistaken: Clemens never intended to include all those false starts, let alone in chronological order; he intended only the dictations begun in 1906 to be published that way. But having chosen this course, Paine then had space for only a relative handful of the dictations. And on top of that, he felt obliged to suppress or even alter certain passages without notice to the reader. He eventually acknowledged that he had published only about one-third of what he regarded as the whole text.[7]

DeVoto was critical of Paine's acceptance of "the arrangement Mark Twain originally gave" the dictations, "interspersed as they were with trivialities, irrelevancies, newspaper clippings, and unimportant letters—disconnected and without plan." Instead he chose to print only passages that Paine had left unpublished, drawn from "the typescript in which everything that Mark wanted in his memoirs had been brought together" (that is, the Autobiographical Dictations begun in 1906). DeVoto then arranged the selections by topic, "omitting trivialities and joining together things that belonged together." And he said with great satisfaction that he had "modernized the punctuation by deleting thousands of commas and dashes, and probably should have deleted hundreds more." He was confident that he had "given the book a more coherent plan than Mark Twain's" and he was unapologetic about having "left out" what seemed to him "uninteresting."[8]

Neider, too, was unhappy with Paine's acceptance of Mark Twain's plan to publish the autobiography "not in chronological order but in the sequence in which it was written and dictated. What an extraordinary idea! As though the stream of composition time were in some mysterious way more revealing than that of autobiographical time!"[9] Neider had permission from the Mark Twain Estate to combine some thirty thousand words from the unpublished dictations with what Paine and DeVoto had already published. Like DeVoto, he omitted what he disliked, and was also obliged to exclude portions that Clara Clemens Samossoud (Clemens's daughter, by then in her eighties) disapproved of publishing. He then (figuratively) cut apart and rearranged the texts he had selected so that they approximated a conventional, chronological narrative—exactly the kind of autobiography Mark Twain had rejected.

The result of these several editorial plans has been that no text of the *Autobiography* so far published is even remotely complete, much less completely authorial. It is therefore the goal of the present edition to publish the complete text as nearly as possible in the way Mark Twain intended it to be published after his death. That goal has only recently become attainable, for the simple reason that no one knew which parts of the great mass of autobiographical manuscripts and typescripts Mark Twain intended to include. In fact, the assumption had long

---

7. Paine told a reporter in 1933 that the "complete autobiography . . . would fill about six volumes, including the two already published, and probably would not be made public for 'many, many years'" ("Canard Blasted by Biographer of Mark Twain," New York *Herald Tribune,* 8 July 1933, clipping in CU-MARK).

8. "Introduction," *Mark Twain in Eruption,* edited by Bernard DeVoto (New York: Harper and Brothers, 1940), vi–ix; hereafter *MTE.*

9. "Introduction," *The Autobiography of Mark Twain, Including Chapters Now Published for the First Time,* arranged and edited, with an introduction and notes, by Charles Neider (New York: Harper and Brothers, 1959), ix, xvi, xx–xxiii; hereafter *AMT.*

prevailed that Mark Twain did not decide what to put in and what to leave out—that he left the enormous and very complicated manuscript incomplete and unfinished.

That assumption was wrong. Although Mark Twain left no specific instructions (not even documentation for the instructions that Paine professed to follow), hidden within the approximately ten file feet of autobiographical documents are more than enough clues to show that he had in fact decided on the final form of the *Autobiography,* and which of the preliminary experiments were to be included and which omitted. This newly discovered and unexpected insight into his intentions is itself a story worth telling, and it is told for the first time in this introduction.

Three printed volumes are planned for this edition, which will also be published in full at *Mark Twain Project Online (MTPO)*. Exhaustive documentation of all textual decisions will *only* be published online.[10] This first volume begins with the extant manuscripts and dictations that must now be regarded as Clemens's preliminary efforts to write the autobiography and that he reviewed and rejected (but did not destroy) in June 1906. They are arranged arbitrarily in the order of their date of composition, solely because Clemens himself never specified any order. Some of these texts he explicitly labeled "autobiography," and some are judged to be part of his early experiments on other grounds, always explained in the brief headnotes that introduce them. We include those preliminary texts for which the evidence is reasonably strong, without asserting that there were no others.

The *Autobiography of Mark Twain* proper begins on p. 201 in this volume, starting with the several prefaces Clemens created in June 1906 to frame the early manuscripts and dictations he had selected as opening texts, followed by his almost daily Autobiographical Dictations from 9 January through the end of March 1906—all that will fit into this volume. The dictations are arranged in the chronological order of their creation because that is how Clemens instructed his editors to publish them. The remaining volumes in this edition will include all the dictations he created between April 1906 and October 1909, likewise arranged chronologically, the whole concluding with the "Closing Words of My Autobiography," a manuscript about the death of his youngest daughter, Jean.

PRELIMINARY MANUSCRIPTS AND DICTATIONS

Autobiographical Fiction and Fictional Autobiography

Autobiography as a literary form had a special fascination for Mark Twain. Long before he had given serious thought to writing his own, he had published both journalism and fiction that were, in the most straightforward way, autobiographical. From the earliest juvenilia in his brother's Hannibal, Missouri, newspaper (1851–53) to his personal brand of journalism in Nevada and California (1862–66), he played endlessly with putting himself at the center of

10. *MTPO* (http://www.marktwainproject.org) is an open access website maintained by the Mark Twain Project in order to make all of its editions available online. *Autobiography of Mark Twain* is the first work to be published there simultaneously with the print edition, and the first to publish the textual apparatus only in electronic form.

what he wrote. Twenty years and nine books later, in October 1886, he acknowledged (and oversimplified) the result: "Yes, the truth is, my books are simply autobiographies. I do not know that there is an incident in them which sets itself forth as having occurred in my personal experience which did not so occur. If the incidents were dated, they could be strung together in their due order, & the result would be an autobiography."[11] He was thinking of his travel books and personal narratives—*The Innocents Abroad, Roughing It, A Tramp Abroad,* and *Life on the Mississippi*—the only books up to that point in which he set forth anything "as having occurred" in his own experience. To be sure he also made extensive fictional use of that experience. The factual basis of characters and situations in works like *The Gilded Age, The Adventures of Tom Sawyer,* and *Adventures of Huckleberry Finn* has been thoroughly documented, and the autobiographical content is obvious in dozens of shorter works like "The Private History of a Campaign That Failed" and "My First Lie and How I Got Out of It," even when they are not entirely factual.[12]

More germane to Clemens's thinking about his own autobiography is his interest in fictional autobiography—that is, fictions in the shape and form of an autobiography. *Mark Twain's (Burlesque) Autobiography* was written in late 1870 and published in pamphlet form in March 1871. Mark Twain tells us that his own parents were "neither very poor nor conspicuously honest," and that almost all of his ancestors were born to be hanged—and for the most part *were* hanged. An even briefer "burlesque" called simply "An Autobiography" appeared in the *Aldine* magazine in April 1871: "I was born November 30th, 1835. I continue to live, just the same."[13] The whole sketch takes fewer than two hundred words and pointedly leaves the reader as ignorant of the facts as before.

Burlesque implies familiarity with genuine autobiographies, despite what Clemens told William Dean Howells in 1877 ("I didn't know there *were* any but old Franklin's & Benvenuto Cellini's"). Benjamin Franklin's didactic bent made him a lifelong target of Mark Twain's ridicule. But he thought Cellini's autobiography the "most entertaining of books," and he admired the daring frankness of Jean-Jacques Rousseau's *Confessions* and Giovanni Giacomo Casanova's *Mémoires,* as well as Samuel Pepys's *Diary,* which Paine said was the book Clemens "read and quoted most."[14]

In 1871 he proposed writing "an Autobiography of Old Parr, the gentleman who lived to be 153 years old," but apparently he never did so.[15] In the summer of 1876 he wrote four hundred pages of a work he was then calling "Huck Finn's Autobiography." And in March 1877, he told Howells he was writing such a work about his own older brother: "I began Orion's autobiography yesterday & am charmed with the work. I have started him at 18,

---

11. 8 Oct 1886 to Kate Staples, NN-BGC.

12. SLC 1869a, 1872, 1880a, 1883, 1873–74, 1876, 1885a, 1885b, 1899e.

13. SLC 1871a, 1871c.

14. Howells had asked for suggestions for a series of "Choice Biographies." 6 June 1877 to Howells, *Letters 1876–1880;* "The Late Benjamin Franklin," SLC 1870c; Gribben 1980, 1:134, 241–43, 2:539–40; *MTB,* 3:1538.

15. 18 Aug 1871 to OLC, *L4,* 446–47. He may have been reading Henry Wilson's *Wonderful Characters; Comprising Memoirs and Anecdotes of the Most Remarkable Persons of Every Age and Nation* (1854). Among its subjects was Thomas Parr, who reputedly lived from 1483 to 1635.

printer's apprentice, soft & sappy, full of fine intentions & shifting religions & not aware that he is a shining ass." He assigned various real incidents of Orion's life and aspects of his character to an apprentice named Bolivar, and wrote more than a hundred pages before abandoning the project.[16]

In 1880, Orion's decision to write a real autobiography prompted Clemens to suggest that he instead "write two books which it has long been my purpose to write, but I judge they are so far down on my docket that I shan't get to them in this life. I think the subjects are perfectly new. One is 'The Autobiography of a Coward,' & the other 'Confessions of a Life that was a Failure.'" The object here was not burlesque, but rather a kind of thought experiment to test the difficulty of telling the whole truth in an autobiographical narrative—in this case, by shielding it behind a deliberate fiction.

> My plan was simple—to take the absolute facts of my own life & tell them simply & without ornament or flourish, exactly as they occurred, with this difference, that I would turn every courageous action (if I ever performed one) into a cowardly one, & every success into a failure. You can do this, but only in one way; you must *banish* all idea of an audience—for ~~no man~~ ˌfew menˌ can straitly & squarely confess shameful things to others—you must tell your story *to yourself,* & to no other; you must not use your own name, for *that* would keep you from telling shameful things, too.

Another version of this scheme Clemens said was more difficult, to "tell the story of an abject coward who is *unconscious* that he is a coward," and to do the same for "an unsuccessful man."

> In these cases the titles I have suggested would not be used. This latter plan is the one I should use. I should *confine* myself to *my own* actual experiences (to invent would be to fail) & I would name everybody's actual name & locality & describe his character & actions unsparingly, then *change* these names & localities *after the book was finished.* To use fictitious names, & localities while writing is a befogging & confusing thing.

The inspiration for both of these ideas was obviously two autobiographies that Clemens admired.

> The supremest charm in Casanova's Memoires (they are not printed in English) is, that he frankly, flowingly, & felicitously tells the dirtiest & vilest & most contemptible things on himself, without ever suspecting that they are other than things which the reader will admire & applaud. . . . Rousseau confesses to masturbation, theft, lying, shameful treachery, & attempts made upon his person by Sodomites. But he tells it as a man who is *perfectly aware* of the shameful nature of these things, whereas your coward & your Failure should be happy & sweet & unconscious, ˌ ~~of their own contemptibility.~~[17]

16. 9 Aug 1876 and 23? Mar 1877 to Howells, *Letters 1876–1880.* The manuscript is unfinished and untitled; Paine titled it "Autobiography of a Damned Fool" (SLC 1877b).

17. 26 Feb 1880 to OC, *Letters 1876–1880.* Clemens would remember and rehearse his advice to Orion in his Autobiographical Dictation of 23 February 1906; see the note at 378.25–27 for a fuller account of Orion's autobiography, which is now lost.

Clemens himself seems not to have attempted what he urged Orion to try, but it is obvious he was thinking about the challenge of writing with the perfect frankness he admired in these writers. The question of how fully he could tell the truth about himself, and especially to what extent he could confess what he regarded as his own shameful behavior, occupied him off and on throughout work on the *Autobiography*.

The First Attempts (1876 and 1877)

Clemens's plan to write his own autobiography is more or less distinct from these fictional uses of the form. The first indication that he had such a plan survives only in the report of a conversation that took place when he was forty. Mrs. James T. Fields and her husband were visiting the Clemenses in Hartford. She recorded in her diary that at lunch, on 28 April 1876, Clemens

> proceeded to speak of his Autobiography which he intends to write as fully and sincerely as possible to leave behind him—His wife laughingly said, she should look it over and leave out objectionable passages—No, he said very earnestly almost sternly, *you* are not to edit it—it is to appear as it is written with the whole tale told as truly as I can tell it—I shall take out passages from it and publish as I go along, in the Atlantic and elsewhere, but I shall not limit myself as to space and at whatever ever age I am writing about even if I am an infant and an idea comes to me about myself when I am forty I shall put that in. Every man feels that his experience is unlike that of anybody else and therefore he should write it down—he finds also that everybody else has thought and felt on some points precisely as he has done, and therefore he should write it down.[18]

This remarkable statement shows that Clemens was already committed to several ideas that would govern the autobiography he worked on over the next thirty-five years. The notion is already present that publication must be posthumous, a requirement linked to the ambition to have "the whole tale told as truly as I can tell it," without censoring himself or allowing others to do it for him. He also plans to publish selections from the narrative while still alive, withholding the rest "to leave behind him." He will not limit himself "as to space," but will be as digressive and discursive as he likes, even ignoring chronology when it suits him. These cardinal points are clearly interrelated: absolute truth telling would be made easier by knowing that his own death would precede publication, and discursiveness (quite apart from his natural preference for it) would help to disarm his own impulse toward self-censorship. But it would take another thirty years to actually apply these various ideas to a real autobiography.

Just a year or so later, sometime in 1877, Clemens seems actually to have begun writing, prompted (as he recalled in 1904) by a conversation with his good friend John Milton Hay. Hay "asked if I had begun to write my autobiography, and I said I hadn't. He said that I ought to begin at once" (since the time to begin was at age forty, and Clemens was already forty-two).

> I had lost two years, but I resolved to make up that loss. I resolved to begin my autobiography at once. I did begin it, but the resolve melted away and disappeared in a week and

18. Annie Adams Fields Papers, diary entry for 28 Apr 1876, MHi, published in Howe 1922, 250–51.

I threw my beginning away. Since then, about every three or four years I have made other beginnings and thrown them away. Once I tried the experiment of a diary, intending to inflate that into an autobiography when its accumulation should furnish enough material, but that experiment lasted only a week; it took me half of every night to set down the history of the day, and at the week's end I did not like the result.[19]

In late November 1877 Clemens listed "My Autobiography" among other projects in his notebook, reminding himself to "Publish scraps from my Autobiography occasionally." He did indeed write an eleven-page manuscript at this time which he intended as the first chapter of an autobiography—very likely the "beginning" that in 1904 he remembered having thrown away. He titled it merely "Chapter 1," but it is commonly known as "Early Years in Florida, Missouri," the title Paine assigned it.[20] It begins, "I was born the 30th of November, 1835"—the same way Clemens began his *Aldine* burlesque in 1871—and it goes on to reminisce briefly about his early memories of childhood in that "almost invisible village of Florida, Monroe county, Missouri." Like "The Tennessee Land" (the only extant autobiographical fragment that was written earlier, in 1870) it ends somewhat abruptly, exactly as if the author's interest had "melted away and disappeared."

If Clemens did, as he says, make successive attempts to write the autobiography "every three or four years" after 1877, few are known to survive.[21] What we have instead are such things as his advice in 1880 to Orion about *his* autobiography: "Keep in mind what I told you—when you recollect something which belonged in an earlier chapter, do not go back, but jam it in *where you are*. Discursiveness does not hurt an autobiography in the least."[22]

Clemens took between three and seven years to complete almost all of his major books. He required that much time chiefly because he always encountered stretches during which he was unable to proceed, and composition came to a complete halt. Since at least 1871 he had found it necessary, when his "tank had run dry" in this way, to "pigeonhole" his manuscripts. And he learned to resume work on them only after the "tank" had been refilled by "unconscious and profitable cerebration."[23] But the time he spent on his earlier books is brief compared with the nearly four decades it took him to finish his autobiography. Its construction was certainly punctuated by long interruptions as well, but for somewhat different reasons. Until January

19. See "John Hay," note at 223.27–28, for a discussion of the possible date of this conversation. No such "diary" is known to survive, but some of the texts written in Vienna in 1898 have the look of diary entries. See "Four Sketches about Vienna."

20. *N&J2,* 50–51; *MTA,* 1:7.

21. In 1940 DeVoto published a manuscript about Joseph H. Twichell's encounter with a profane ostler which he described as "one of the random pieces that preceded Mark's sustained work on the *Autobiography,*" suggesting that it was "probably written in the 1880s and at one time formed part of a long manuscript—I cannot tell which one" (*MTE,* 366–72). But this anecdote was not part of any draft of the autobiography. It was written for *Life on the Mississippi* (1883) and removed from the manuscript before publication.

22. 6 May 1880 to OC, *Letters 1876–1880.*

23. AD, 30 Aug 1906. Clemens said that he made this discovery while writing *The Adventures of Tom Sawyer,* but there is good reason to suppose that he experienced the same difficulty in 1871 while writing *Roughing It,* even though he did not then know to "pigeonhole" the manuscript until the "tank" had refilled itself. See *RI 1993,* 823.

1906, the tank seemed to "run dry" after relatively brief stints of writing, or dictating, because he grew dissatisfied with his method of composing the work, or with its overall plan, or both.

General Grant and James W. Paige (1885 and 1890)

In the spring of 1885 Clemens made his first attempt at doing an autobiography for which more than a few pages survive. He had some previous experience with dictating letters and brief memoranda to a secretary, but he had never tried it for literary composition.[24] Now he decided that it might be a good way to work on the autobiography. In late March he wrote in his notebook:

> Get short-hander in New York & begin my autobiography at once & continue it straight through the summer.
>
> Which reminds me that Susie, aged 13, (1885), has begun to write my biography—solely of her own motion—a thing about which I feel proud & gratified. At breakfast this morning I intimated that if I seemed to be talking on a pretty high key, in the way of style, it must be remembered that my biographer was present. Whereupon Susie struck upon the unique idea of having me sit up & purposely *talk* for the biography![25]

At about the same time, he realized that dictation might be of help to his friend Ulysses S. Grant. Grant had written several articles for the *Century Magazine*'s series on the Civil War. In the spring of 1885, when he was dying of throat cancer, Grant was close to completing the manuscript of the first volume of his two-volume *Memoirs*. Clemens had recently secured them for his own publishing house, Charles L. Webster and Co., confident they would earn large profits both for Grant's family and for himself. As a frequent visitor to Grant's New York house, Clemens knew that Grant feared dying before he could finish his book. He suggested that Grant hire a stenographer to ease his task. Grant at first demurred, but later hired a former secretary, Noble E. Dawson. On 29 April Clemens visited Grant on his first day of dictation and learned that it "was a thorough success."[26]

No doubt encouraged by Grant's experience, in early May Clemens asked his friend and former lecture manager James Redpath to serve as his stenographer. He liked and respected

24. Back in 1873 he had hired Samuel C. Thompson to accompany him to England as his secretary. Thompson was a novice at shorthand, and he was dismissed almost immediately when Clemens became dissatisfied with this "first experience in dictating." He later explained, "I remember that my sentences came slow & painfully, & were clumsily phrased, & had no life in them—certainly no humor." It also did not help that he found Thompson to be a humorless and unpleasant companion (*N&J1*, 517–18, Thompson's notebook is on 526–71; "To Rev. S. C. Thompson," SLC 1909a, 12). A later experiment with dictation came in the spring of 1882 when Clemens hired Roswell Phelps, a trained stenographer, to accompany him and James Osgood on their trip down the Mississippi. Phelps recorded Clemens's (and others') remarks at the time, but Clemens did not dictate to him when writing *Life on the Mississippi* (*N&J2*, 516–18, Phelps's notebook is transcribed on 521–74).

25. *N&J3*, 112. Clemens would eventually reproduce much of Susy's biography in the final form of his autobiography, beginning with AD, 7 Feb 1906.

26. Grant 1885a, 1885b, 1885c, and 1886; "Grant's Last Stand," Philadelphia *Inquirer,* 6 Feb 1894, unknown page; AD, 26 Feb 1906.

Redpath, who had been a journalist and knew shorthand. On 4 May 1885 Redpath replied to Clemens's proposal: "Now about the auto. When I do work by the week, I charge $100 a week for the best I can do. I have had a run of ill-luck lately but I found that that was what I averaged. It w^d take you much less time than you think. I get you word for word & it takes a long time to write out." Clemens accepted these terms and urged Redpath to come to Hartford soon. "I think we can make this thing blamed enjoyable." It is clear that he was beginning to intuit the need for a responsive, human audience when dictating—something he articulated quite clearly six years later in a letter to Howells.[27]

The two men began working together sometime in mid-May and continued for several weeks. In the six dictations that survive, Clemens traced the history of his friendship with Grant, then talked about his own protégé, the young sculptor Karl Gerhardt, who had a commission to create a bust of Grant. In the longest of these dictations he launched into a detailed account of how he had acquired the right to publish Grant's *Memoirs,* defending his tactics and countering newspaper insinuations that he had acted unethically.

Clemens probably stopped dictating shortly before Grant died on 23 July 1885.[28] In July and August (and possibly earlier) Clemens read over some of the typescripts that Redpath had created from his stenographic notes, adding his own corrections here and there but making few changes in wording. He found the result far from satisfactory, as he implied in a letter to Henry Ward Beecher:

> I will enclose some scraps from my Autobiography—scraps about Gen. Grant—they may be of some trifle of use, & they may not—they at least verify known traits of his character. My Autobiography is pretty freely dictated, but my idea is to jack-plane it a little before I die, some day or other; I mean the rude construction & rotten grammar. It is the only dictating I ever did, & it was most troublesome & awkward work.[29]

Redpath's work as an amanuensis was unskillful. None of his stenographic notes are known to survive, but his typescripts are manifestly ill-prepared—full of typing errors, struck-over characters, and extraneous marks—and his numerous penciled corrections create punctuation that is in no way characteristic of Clemens's own habits.

No manuscripts for the autobiography written between 1885 and 1890 have survived, but the project was certainly not forgotten. In late 1886 as he worked on *A Connecticut Yankee in King Arthur's Court,* Clemens wrote to Mary Mason Fairbanks: "I fully expect to write one other book besides this one; two others, in fact, if one's autobiography may be called a book—in fact mine will be nearer a library." His 1876 plan for a work not limited "as to space" was evidently alive and well. And in August 1887, two years after halting the Grant Dictations,

27. Redpath to SLC, 4 May 1885, CU-MARK; 5 May 1885 to Redpath, MiU-H. See 4 Apr 1891 to Howells, NN-BGC, in *MTHL,* 2:641, quoted below in the section on the Florentine Dictations. Clemens's earlier letter containing the proposal that Redpath accepted has not been found.

28. 17 June 1885 to Pond, NN-BGC; 12 Sept 1885 to Redpath, CU-MARK.

29. 11 Sept 1885 to Beecher, draft in CU-MARK. Beecher was then preparing a eulogy for Grant to be delivered in Boston on 22 October 1885, and had written Clemens for biographical information; in particular, he wanted to know if Grant had been "a drunkard for a time" (Beecher to SLC, 8 Sept 1885, CU-MARK).

Clemens wrote to his nephew, "I want a *perfect* copy of Fred Grant's letter, for my Autobiography. I was supposing I had about finished the detailed private history of the Grant Memoirs, but doubtless more than one offensive chapter must be added yet, if Fred Grant lives." A few months earlier he told another correspondent, "No, I'll leave those details in my autobiography when I die, but they won't answer for a speech."[30]

Then, in December 1887, Orion wrote to ask his brother's permission to reveal "something of your boyhood" in an upcoming interview with a local journalist. He listed a few "points" he wanted to offer:

> I thought of mentioning Grandpa and Grandma Casey; some younger and older characteristics of ma (fondness for or tenderness for animals, &c.); pa's studying law under Cyrus Walker; their marriage and removal to Tennessee; pa's treatment of the strange preacher about the cow; his facing down the old bully, Frogg; his settling a dispute before him as justice of the peace with a mallet; your philosophical dissatisfaction with your lack of a tail; your sleep-walking and entrance into Mrs. Ament's room; your year's schooling; your quitting at 11; your work in my office; your first writing for the paper (Jim Wolf, the wash-pan and the broom); your going to Philadelphia at 17 . . . ; your swimming the river and back; ma's complaint that you broke up her scoldings by making her laugh; Pa's death; his sharp pen writing for the paper; her present age and vigor; fondness for theatre.[31]

Clemens had already used a number of these "points" in published work. His making wicked fun of Jim Wolf's pointless rescue of a wash-pan and broom from the threat of a fire next door was in fact his "first writing" for Orion's Hannibal newspaper, "A Gallant Fireman" (1851).[32] And in the first chapter of *Tom Sawyer* Aunt Polly (based on Jane Clemens) had mildly complained that Tom knew that if he could "make me laugh," her anger toward him would disappear. Still, Clemens refused Orion's request:

> I have never yet allowed an interviewer or biography-sketcher to get out of me any circumstance of my history which I thought might be worth putting some day into my AUTObiography. . . .
>
> I have been approached as many as five hundred times on the biographical-sketch lay, but they never got anything that was worth printing.[33]

Clemens would make use of only a few of these "points" in the autobiography. But his stinginess about letting others reveal the raw materials of his history is certainly understandable,

30. 16 Nov 1886 to Fairbanks, CSmH, in *MTMF,* 258; 3 Aug 1887 to Webster, NN-BGC; 3 and 4 Feb 1887 to Smith, ODaU (the "details" referred to have not been identified). Clemens returned to the topic of Grant's *Memoirs* in the Autobiographical Dictations for 6 February, 28 May, 1 June, and 2 June 1906. The last of these included remarks about Fred Grant, but not his letter of 22 July 1887 (TS in CU-MARK), which disputed the accuracy of the financial statement from the Webster Company accountant.

31. OC to SLC, 5 Dec 1887, typed copy of the original letter made by or for Paine, given to the Mark Twain Papers by Anne E. Cushman in 2004. The typescript reads "your mark in my office," clearly a mistranscription.

32. SLC 1851.

33. 8 Dec 1887 to OC, NPV.

and it may suggest that at this time in 1887 he still intended to write an autobiography that would include these anecdotes from his early life.

By the fall of 1890, Clemens had been investing money in the typesetting machine invented by James W. Paige for almost ten years (since 1881). It was, however, still not completed. The relevance of this project to his autobiography was inescapable, and in the "closing days" of that year he began to write "The Machine Episode," an unsparing account of the way Paige had charmed and beguiled him into an enormous investment without having yet achieved a salable product. By the time Clemens added the second part to this self-revealing account, in the winter of 1893–94, Paige had still not perfected the machine but was about to sign a new, more satisfactory contract for it. Left in a rather unfinished state, the manuscript was very likely among those Clemens reviewed in 1906 before deciding to omit it from the final form. He did return to the subject in an Autobiographical Dictation of 2 June 1906.

Vienna (1897 and 1898)

Clemens's hopes for the Paige typesetting machine were finally crushed in December 1894, and the bankruptcy of Webster and Company earlier that year had placed its debts solely on his shoulders. In the summer of 1895, in order to repay them, he, Olivia, and Clara undertook a lecture tour around the world (Susy and Jean stayed at home), which ended when they arrived in England on 31 July 1896. The family landed at Southampton and then traveled to Guildford, where they learned that Susy was ill in Hartford. "A fortnight later Mrs. Clemens and Clara sailed for home to nurse Susy," Clemens recalled in 1906, and "found her in her coffin in her grandmother's house." Within weeks of this calamity Clemens wrote his friend Henry H. Rogers that he intended to "submerge myself & my troubles in work." In the last week of September 1896 he reminded himself to "Write my autobiography in full & with remorseless attention to facts & proper names."[34] But he still needed to finish the book about his around-the-world lecture tour.[35] The family spent the winter and spring of 1897 in London while Clemens wrote *Following the Equator,* which would be published in November.

In the summer of 1897 they retreated to Switzerland, and in late September they moved to Vienna. Two autobiographical manuscripts were begun that fall, "Travel-Scraps I" and a much longer sketch called "My Autobiography [Random Extracts from It]." "Travel-Scraps I" appears to be unfinished, or at least not quite ready for the typist, since Clemens made a tentative revision of its title, in pencil ("~~Travel~~-Scraps. ˎfrom Autobiog.ˎ") and the manuscript itself still has two sets of page numbers (1–20 and 1–28). It was probably written soon after Clemens arrived in Vienna, for it is largely a complaint about London's cab drivers and its postal service, things that would naturally have been on his mind since the spring.

On the evidence of the paper and ink used, "My Autobiography [Random Extracts from

34. AD, 4 June 1906; 20 Sept 1896 to Rogers, Salm, in *HHR,* 237; Notebook 39, TS p. 4, CU-MARK.

35. On 1 November he again wrote Rogers: "After I finish the present subscription book, I shall go straight on & clear out my skull. There are several books in there, & I mean to dig them out, one after the other without stopping. . . . One of them—my Autobiography—should be sold by subscription, I judge" (1 Nov 1896 to Rogers, Salm, in *HHR,* 243–44).

It]" was begun about the same time, but probably not completed until 1898. Clemens identified the text as "From Chapter II."[36] (The first page of this manuscript is reproduced in facsimile in figure 1.) It begins as a history of the Clemens and Lampton relatives and ancestors and, more briefly, the despised Tennessee land. But it meanders, without apology, into an anecdote about an incident in Berlin in 1891, and it ends with an evocative description of Clemens's idyllic summers on his uncle's farm near Florida, Missouri. This typical combination of early memories and later experiences helps to make clear why Clemens would reject the idea of a completely chronological narrative: his preference for juxtaposing related events from different times deeply resisted that way of organizing his story. At the same time, labeling the sketch "From Chapter II" implied that most of what it contained would come early in the autobiography, as would befit a review of ancestors. The chapter number suggests that while he was not writing about his experiences in the order of their occurrence, he was still making an attempt to assign chapter numbers that respected chronology.

Before Clemens completed "Random Extracts" in 1898, he wrote several more sketches for the autobiography between February and June of that year, grouped here under the supplied title "Four Sketches about Vienna": "Beauties of the German Language," "Comment on Tautology and Grammar," "A Group of Servants" (the only one that Paine did not include in his edition), and "A Viennese Procession." These were not reminiscences but rather more like entries in a diary, with each piece prefaced by a date. None of these sketches would be included in his final plan, but he did eventually include another manuscript written at this time, "Dueling," in the Autobiographical Dictation of 19 January 1906.

Two further sketches were written in the fall of 1898 and also later inserted into the final structure of autobiographical dictations. The first was "Wapping Alice," a tale deemed unsuitable for magazine publication, which was based on an actual event. It joined a growing collection of manuscripts that Clemens would eventually draw on for what he called "fat"—"old pigeon-holed things, of the years gone by, which I or editors didn't das't to print"—that he would use to enlarge the bulk of the *Autobiography*.[37] More than a year after he began dictating his autobiography in 1906, he inserted "Wapping Alice" in the Autobiographical Dictation of 9 April 1907.

The second sketch was "My Debut as a Literary Person," which he dated *"October 1, 1898"* and labeled "Chapter XIV." The revision of this manuscript reflects a season of discouragement about the autobiography, a mood that shows up sporadically during the winter of 1898–99. Just below the title he first inserted a footnote: "This is Chapter XIV of my unfinished Autobiography and the way it is getting along it promises to remain an unfinished one." Then he changed "unfinished" to "unpublished" and canceled the words following "Autobiography." When the sketch appeared in the *Century Magazine* for November 1899, it omitted any reference to his autobiography. Still, it is the first "chapter" to be published in fulfillment of his long-held plan to publish selections from it.[38]

36. Paine published it as "Early Days" (*MTA,* 1:81–115).
37. 17 June 1906 to Howells, NN-BGC, in *MTHL,* 2:811.
38. Clemens evidently revised the title again on the typescript (now lost) that he sent to the *Century*. See the editorial headnote to this manuscript.

My Autobiography

=

[Random Extracts from it.]

=

We are no other than a moving row
Of Magic Shadow-shapes that come & go
  Round with the Sun-illumined Lantern held
In Midnight by the Master of the Show;

But helpless Pieces of the Game He plays
Upon this Chequer-board of Nights & Days;
  Hither & thither moves, & checks, & slays,
And one by one back in the Closet lays.

From Chapter II.

=

x x x x So much for the earlier days, &
the New England branch of the Clemenses.
The other brother settled in the South, & is
remotely responsible for me. He has
collected his reward generations ago,
whatever it was. He went South with

FIGURE 1. The first page of the manuscript of "My Autobiography [Random Extracts from It]."
Clemens deleted the epigraph shown here—two stanzas from *The Rubáiyát of Omar Khayyám*—
and "From Chapter II" when revising the forty-four-page typescript (now lost) that was made from
the manuscript; they are therefore omitted from the present text. Two notes at the top were written
by Paine: "Vienna | 1897–8" and "no 109" (a filing designation). Rosamond Chapman, DeVoto's
assistant, wrote "Publ. *Auto*, 81ff "—where Paine published the text.

Clemens's unsettled attitude toward his "unfinished" autobiography is clear, but not readily explained. On 10 October 1898, even as he was preparing "My Debut" for magazine publication, he told Edward Bok, editor of the *Ladies' Home Journal,*

> A good deal of the Autobiography is written, but I never work on it except when a reminiscence of some kind crops up in a strong way & in a manner forces me; so it is years too early yet to think of publishing—except now & then at long intervals a single chapter, maybe. I intend to do that, someday. But it would not answer for your Magazine. Indeed a good deal of it is written in too independent a fashion for a magazine. One may publish a *book* & print whatever his family shall approve & allow to pass, but it is the Public that edit a Magazine, & so by the sheer necessities of the case a magazine's liberties are rather limited. For instance: a few days ago I wrote Chapter XIV—"My Debut as a Literary Person"—my wife edited it, approved it (with enthusiasm—this is unusual), & said send it to you & retire the "Platonic Sweetheart." It was a good idea, & I said I would. But on my way to the village postoffice with it I remembered that it contained a sentence of nine words which you would have to drive a blue pencil through—so that blocked that scheme.[39]

A month later, in a more ambitious frame of mind, he wrote to Rogers that he now planned to "take up my uncompleted Autobiography & finish it, & let Bliss and Chatto each make $15,000 out of it for me next fall (as they did with the Equator-book)." But almost immediately he changed his mind about the need for money, and concluded that he would "never write the Autobiography till I'm in a hole. It is best for me to *be* in a hole sometimes, I reckon." Then, just a few days later, he wrote again to Rogers: "I have resumed my Autobiography, and I suppose I shall have Vol. 1 done by spring time. ~~I hope so~~ I expect so." And at last, in February 1899, still trying to find a magazine publisher for "My Debut," he told *Century* editor Richard Watson Gilder: "I have abandoned my Autobiography, & am not going to finish it; but I took a reminiscent chapter out of it ~~some time ago & & had it copyrighted~~ & had it type-written, thinking it would make a readable magazine article."[40] So within the span of a few months he claimed that a "good deal" of the autobiography was written; that he would never finish it until he was "in a hole"; that he expected to have the first volume "done by spring time"; and that he had "abandoned" it altogether. He was obviously struggling with how, or even whether, to proceed with a work that had been in and out of the pigeonhole for twenty years.

Innumerable Biographies (1898 and 1899)

It is difficult to be entirely sure, but Clemens seems to have become discouraged at least in part over his inability to be completely frank and self-revealing, after the fashion of Rousseau and Casanova. His solution was, at least temporarily, to recast the autobiography as a series of

39. 10 Oct 1898 to Bok, ViU. The "too independent" words may have been "the bowels of some of the men virtually ceased from their functions" (143.35–36). Clemens had sent Bok "My Platonic Sweetheart" on 2 September, but Bok rejected it and soon Clemens himself decided against publishing it (Notebook 40, TS p. 32, CU-MARK; *HHR,* 365 n. 1, 373 n. 3).

40. 6 and 7 Nov 1898 and 12 Nov 1898 to Rogers (2nd of 2), Salm, in *HHR,* 374, 376; 25 Feb 99 to Gilder, CtY-BR.

thumbnail biographies of people he had met over the years. Several autobiographical manuscripts written in Vienna—"Horace Greeley," "Lecture-Times," and "Ralph Keeler"—are character sketches that were part of this reconception, one that he also relied on to some extent in 1904. The Vienna portraits recall men and women whom he knew in his days on the lyceum circuit in the early 1870s. The new plan probably owed something to the idea of a lecture he wrote back then called "Reminiscences of Some un-Commonplace Characters I Have Chanced to Meet." He delivered this lecture, which he said covered his "whole acquaintance—kings, humorists, lunatics, idiots & all," only twice. No text of it is known to survive, but in Vienna he evidently resurrected its premise.[41] In an interview for the London *Times* in May 1899 the reporter explained:

> Mr. Clemens has kindly given me permission to telegraph to *The Times* some particulars of a pet scheme of his to which he has already devoted a great deal of his time and which will occupy a great part of the remainder of his life. In some respects it will be unparalleled in the history of literature. It is a bequest to posterity, in which none of those now living and comparatively few of their grandchildren even will have any part or share. This is a work which is only to be published 100 years after his death as a portrait gallery of contemporaries with whom he has come into personal contact. These are drawn solely for his own pleasure in the work, and with the single object of telling the truth, the whole truth and nothing but the truth, without malice, and to serve no grudge, but, at the same time, without respect of persons or social conventions, institutions, or pruderies of any kind.

Clemens even spelled out exactly why he had abandoned his original plan for an autobiography: "You cannot lay bare your private soul and look at it. You are too much ashamed of yourself. It is too disgusting. For that reason I confine myself to drawing the portraits of others." And in an interview after he returned to London, he said again that the new idea had actually supplanted his earlier ideas for the autobiography:

> I'm not going to write autobiography. The man has yet to be born who could write the truth about himself. Autobiography is always interesting, but howsoever true its facts may be, its interpretation of them must be taken with a great deal of allowance. In the innumerable biographies I am writing many persons are represented who are not famous today, but who may be some day.[42]

If this switch to biographical portraits signaled frustration over the puzzle of how to tell even the shameful truths, his interest in it was still relatively brief. We have no indication that he wrote any further portraits until 1904, and by 1906 the character-sketch idea had fallen entirely out of favor. For about a year Clemens seems not to have added anything to his accumulation of autobiographical "chapters." In the fall of 1899 he moved his family to London, and for about a year seems to have taken leave of the autobiography.

41. *L4:* 27 June 1871 to OC (2nd of 2), 414; 15 Oct 1871 to OLC, 472 n. 1; 17 Oct 1871 to OLC, 475 n. 1; 24 Oct 1871 to Redpath, 478.

42. "Mark Twain's Bequest," datelined "Vienna, May 22," London *Times,* 23 May 1899, 4, in Scharnhorst 2006, 332–34; Curtis Brown 1899.

Scraps and Chapters (1900 to 1903)

Clemens's use of the terms "Scraps" and "Extracts" (as well as "Random") in 1897–98 suggests that he was looking for a way to label "chapters" which, while not themselves strictly chronological, might still have been parts of some coherent narrative sequence. In the fall of 1900 he used the term "Scraps" in the titles of three more sketches for the autobiography: "Travel-Scraps II," "Scraps from My Autobiography. Private History of a Manuscript That Came to Grief," and "Scraps from My Autobiography. From Chapter IX." Only one of these made it into the final form: "Travel-Scraps II" continued the 1897 recital of grievances about London's telephones and postal system and was ultimately inserted in the Autobiographical Dictation for 27 February 1907. "Scraps from My Autobiography. Private History of a Manuscript That Came to Grief" was much longer. It concerned a recent experience with T. Douglas Murray, an amateur historian, who had invited Clemens to write an introduction for an English translation of Joan of Arc's trial records. Clemens submitted his draft, and wrote Murray: "When I send the Introduction, I must get you to do two things for me—knock the lies out of it & purify the grammar (which I think stinks, in one place.)"[43] Murray took this invitation all too literally and proceeded to revise the text extensively, making the language more formal, even pretentious. Enraged by this tampering, Clemens proceeded to draft a reply in the shape of a scathing letter to Murray, which of course he never sent, preparing it instead for the autobiography.[44] The third manuscript, also excluded from the final form, nevertheless illustrates a rather different dynamic, namely the persistent reluctance or inability to break entirely free from the chronological structure of conventional autobiography. The manuscript was titled (as revised) "~~Selections~~ ₐScrapsₐ from my Autobiography. ~~Passages f~~From Chapter IX." Paine thought it was written "about 1898" but it was in fact written in 1900, as one reference in the text makes clear. The assignment of a chapter number is something that it shares with only a handful of other manuscripts, summarized in the following list.

Chap I	Written in 1877. Describes Clemens's home until aged 4, when the family moved to Hannibal.
Chap II	Written in 1897–98. "My Autobiography [Random Extracts from It]." Clemens aged 7 to 12.
Chap IV	Written in 1903. "Scraps from My Autobiography. From Chapter IV." Transcribed in ADs, 1 and 2 Dec 1906. Clemens aged 14.
Chap IX	Written in 1900. "Scraps from My Autobiography. From Chapter IX." Clemens aged 14, 38, and 61.
Chap XII	Not found, but written after 1898 since it refers to Vienna. Clemens aged 62. Mentioned in chapter XVII.
Chap XIV	Written in 1898. "My Debut as a Literary Person." Clemens aged 30.

43. 3 Sept 1899 to Murray, CU-MARK.

44. The text was not included in the final form and, like the third manuscript written in 1900, is therefore published in the "Preliminary Manuscripts and Dictations" section of this volume.

Chap XVII   Written in 1903. "From Chapter XVII." Transcribed in AD, 3 Dec 1906. Clemens aged 62.

Although some additional numbered chapters may have been written and subsequently lost or destroyed, it is highly unlikely that in 1903, when Clemens labeled a text "Chapter XVII," he had actually written seventeen chapters. But the numbers assigned to the chapters that do survive correspond roughly to the chronology of their topics, even though they do not accurately reflect the lapse of time: Clemens was fourteen in both Chapter IV and Chapter IX, but between Chapter IX and Chapter XIV he aged from fourteen to thirty, and then to age sixty-two by Chapter XVII. Still, this rough approximation is exactly what one would expect if the chapter numbers were only *estimates,* intended to place the chapters in approximate chronological order. Together they again suggest that although he was not writing about his life in the order of its occurrences, he was still trying to maintain an overall chronology, even as late as 1903.

The text numbered "Chapter IX" ("Scraps from My Autobiography," written in 1900) is suggestive in a related way. The chapter number would place it relatively early in his life. It recounts two stories from Clemens's youth, when he was fourteen (1849–50), but it concludes each story with much later events—the first in Calcutta in 1896 when he was sixty-one, and the second in London in 1873 when he was thirty-eight. In both cases it seems that to follow the stories to what Clemens regarded as their natural conclusion, it was necessary to skip over several decades of his life. So whatever else "Chapter IX" was in 1900, it was not a purely chronological account—even though the chapter number placed it toward the beginning of the narrative.

A similar tension occurs in the two manuscripts with chapter numbers written in 1903 but revised in 1906 after Clemens had settled on discursiveness as the principle for the whole autobiography: both were inserted into the dictations for 1, 2, and 3 December 1906. In 1903 he titled the first one "Scraps from My Autobiography. From Chapter IV," and began it with a marginal date ("1849–51"). It concerns his youthful encounters with mesmerism in Hannibal. The second 1903 manuscript, paginated separately but probably written at the same time (they share the same ink and paper), brought this story to its conclusion. It is another story about mesmerism, in which a haughty aristocrat is embarrassed by being hypnotized and ordered to undress, in retaliation for his incredulity. Clemens originally titled it "From Chapter XVII." But when he decided to use the manuscripts in the December dictations, he removed all reference to chapter numbers. So the first mesmerism story was originally assigned to Chapter IV, and its natural conclusion to Chapter XVII, separated by some twelve putative chapters. Their revision shows that in 1903 Clemens was still wrestling with the compulsion to maintain some semblance of his life's chronology, while in 1906, when he made the manuscripts into one continuous narrative, he had clearly shed that compulsion.

On 15 October 1900 the family arrived in New York City, where they soon rented a house at 14 West 10th Street. "Jean is learning to type-write," Clemens wrote a friend, "& presently I'll dictate & thereby save some scraps of time."[45] Jean's new skill may have prompted Clemens

45. 31 Dec 1900 to MacAlister, ViU.

to think again of dictating, rather than writing, the autobiography. There were other temptations as well. The president of Harper and Brothers, George Harvey, was clearly interested in the prestige that would flow from having the rights to publish the autobiography, even though it would not actually appear until long after both men had died. On 17 October 1900 Harvey proposed to Rogers (who was acting as Clemens's agent) to "publish the memoirs in the year 2000" and suggested that Clemens "insert a clause in his will to the effect that the memoirs shall be sealed without reading by his executors, and deposited with a trust company."

> The agreement would, of course, provide for publication in whatever modes should then be prevalent, that is, by printing as at present, or by use of phonographic cylinders, or by electrical method, or by any other mode which may then be in use, any number of which would doubtless occur to his vivid imagination, and would form an interesting clause in the agreement.[46]

Harvey was in fact eager to make Harper and Brothers into Clemens's exclusive American publisher, and on 14 November, after much discussion, he proposed a rate of twenty cents a word for the exclusive serial rights to anything he might write in the next year, as well as the exclusive right to publish all of his books in the same period. One week later Clemens wrote to Harvey, "Let us add the 100-year book to the arrangements again, & make it definite; for I am going to dictate that book to my daughter, with the certainty that as I go along I shall grind out chapters which will be good for magazine & book to-day, & not need to wait a century." Nothing dictated to Jean at this time has been found, but Clemens soon agreed to Harvey's "proposal regarding the publication of my memoirs 100 years hence," although no formal contract for the autobiography was signed at this time.[47]

In August 1902, Olivia's health grew alarmingly worse. Despite temporary improvements, it continued to decline, and in 1903, on the recommendation of her doctors, Clemens decided to take the family to Italy. In early November they settled into the Villa di Quarto near Florence. In addition to Clemens himself, the travelers included Olivia, Clara, and Jean. Three employees were also with them: longtime family servant Katy Leary, a nurse for Olivia, and Isabel V. Lyon, who had been hired in 1902 as Olivia's secretary but had since assumed more general duties.

The Florentine Dictations (1904)

During his eight-month stay in Florence Clemens made unusual progress on the autobiography, in large part because of a renewed enthusiasm for dictation as a method of composition. He had experimented with mechanical methods of transferring words to paper ever since the

46. Harvey for Harper and Brothers to Rogers, 17 Oct 1900, CU-MARK. For Harvey's biography, see AD, 12 Jan 1906, note at 267.35.

47. Harvey for Harper and Brothers to SLC, 14 Nov 1900, CU-MARK (the term of this 14 November letter agreement was "between this date and January 1st, 1902"); 20 Nov 1900 to Harvey, MH-H; SLC *per* Harvey to Harvey, 26 Nov 1900, Harper and Row archives, photocopy in CU-MARK.

dictations to Redpath in 1885. In 1888 he tried (and failed) to get access to one of Thomas Edison's recording phonographs.[48] Then in 1891 he suffered an attack of rheumatism in his right arm and, compelled by the necessity of working on his current book *(The American Claimant),* he did briefly experiment with the phonograph. "I feel sure I can dictate the book into a phonograph if I don't have to yell. I write 2,000 words a day; I think I can dictate twice as many," he wrote to Howells on 28 February. But by 4 April he had concluded that the machine "is good enough for mere letter-writing" but

> you can't write literature with it, because it hasn't any ideas & it hasn't any gift for elaboration, or smartness of talk, or vigor of action, or felicity of expression, but is just matter-of-fact, compressive, unornamental, & as grave & unsmiling as the devil. I filled four dozen cylinders in two sittings, then found I could have said about as much with the pen & said it a deal better. Then I resigned. I believe it could teach one to dictate literature to a phonographer—& some time I will experiment in that line.[49]

His expectation in December 1900 of relying on Jean to type up dictated autobiography at last became a reality in January 1904, when he tried dictating once more, but not to a machine. According to Isabel Lyon,

> About January 14, Mr. Clemens began to dictate to me. His idea of *writing* an autobiography had never proved successful, for to his mind autobiography is like narrative & should be spoken. At Mrs. Clemens's suggestion we tried, and Mr. Clemens found that he could do it to a charm. In fact he loves the work. But we have had to stop for he has been ill, Mrs. Clemens has been very ill, & I too have taken a weary turn in bed.[50]

Lyon did not know shorthand and so took down Clemens's words in full, then gave Jean her record to be typed. Shortly after he had begun to dictate, Clemens wrote to Howells on 16 January:

> I've struck it! And I will give it away—to you. You will never know how much enjoyment you have lost until you get to dictating your autobiography; then you will realize, with a pang, that you might have been doing it all your life if you had only had the luck to think of it. And you will be astonished (& charmed) to see how like *talk* it is, & how real it sounds, & how well & compactly & sequentially it constructs itself, & what a dewy & breezy & woodsy freshness it has, & what a darling & worshipful absence of the signs of starch, & flatiron, & labor & fuss & the other artificialities! Mrs. Clemens is an exacting

48. In May 1888, having "spent an hour & a half" with one of Thomas Edison's recently marketed phonographs "with vast satisfaction," he tried to leverage his friendship with Edison to secure two of the machines "*immediately,* instead of having to wait my turn. Then all summer long I could use one of them in Elmira, N. Y., & express the wax cylinders to my helper in Hartford to be put into the phonograph here & the contents transferred to paper by typewriter." At the end of July, however, when the machines failed to arrive, he canceled the order (25 May 1888 to Edison, NjWoE; SLC *per* Whitmore to the North American Phonograph Company, 30 July 1888, CU-MARK).

49. SLC 1892; SLC and OLC to Howells, 28 Feb 1891, NN-BGC, in *MTHL,* 2:637; 4 Apr 1891 to Howells, NN-BGC, in *MTHL,* 2:641.

50. Lyon 1903–6, entry for 28 Feb 1904. Clemens actually began dictating earlier than 14 January; see "Villa di Quarto": "I am dictating these informations on this 8th day of January 1904" (233.12–13).

critic, but I have not talked a sentence yet that she has wanted altered. There are little slips here & there, little inexactnesses, & many desertions of a thought before the end of it has been reached, but these are not blemishes, they are merits, their removal would take away the naturalness of the flow & banish the very thing—the nameless something—which differentiates real narrative from artificial narrative & makes the one so vastly better than the other—the subtle something which makes good talk so much better than the best imitation of it that can be done with a pen.

It seems that he recognized Lyon's lack of shorthand as an advantage, for he went on to urge Howells to try this method, but "with a long-hand scribe, not with a stenographer. At least not at first. Not until you get your hand in, I should say. There's a good deal of waiting, of course, but that is no matter; soon you do not mind it." More important even than the leisurely pace was the scribe's role as audience: "Miss Lyons does the scribing, & is an inspiration, because she takes so much interest in it. I dictate from 10. 30 till noon. The result is about 1500 words. Then I am a free man & can read & smoke the rest of the day, for there's not a correction to be made."

Dictation proved so congenial, in fact, that his opinion of the drafts and experiments he had written over the years now began to change. He continued to Howells:

> I've a good many chapters of Auto—written with a pen from time to time & laid away in envelops—but I expect that when I come to examine them I shall throw them away & do them over again with my mouth, for I feel sure that my quondam satisfaction in them will have vanished & that they will seem poor & artificial & lacking in color....
>
> One would expect dictated stuff to read like an impromptu speech—brokenly, catchily, repetitiously, & marred by absence of coherence, fluent movement, & the happy things that didn't come till the speech was done—but it isn't so.[51]

Howells replied to this letter on 14 February, shrewdly raising a familiar issue (clearly not for the first time)—the difficulty of telling the whole truth:

> I'd like immensely to read your autobiography. You always rather bewildered me by your veracity, and I fancy you may tell the truth about yourself. But *all* of it? The black truth, which we all know of ourselves in our hearts, or only the whity-brown truth of the pericardium, or the nice, whitened truth of the shirtfront? Even *you* wont tell the black heart's-truth. The man who could do it would be famed to the last day the sun shone upon.[52]

Clemens had of course already reached the same skeptical conclusion. He answered Howells:

> Yes, I set up the safeguards, in the first day's dictating—taking this position: that an Autobiography is the truest of all books; for while it inevitably consists mainly of extinctions of the truth, shirkings of the truth, partial revealments of the truth, with hardly an instance of plain straight truth, the remorseless truth *is* there, between the lines, where

51. 16 Jan 1904 to Howells, MH-H, in *MTHL*, 2:778–79.
52. Howells to SLC, 14 Feb 1904, CU-MARK, in *MTHL*, 2:781.

the author-cat is raking dust upon it which hides from the disinterested spectator neither it nor its smell (though I didn't use that figure)—the result being that the reader knows the author in spite of his wily diligences.[53]

What those "safeguards" were remains unknown, since no copy of the "first day's dictating" has survived. The most one can say is that Clemens seems to have moved on from his despair at not being able to tell "the black heart's-truth," rationalizing that that truth would emerge anyway, in spite of all his attempts to suppress it. In a dictation made in late January 1904 he hinted at the disinhibiting nature of talk:

> Within the last eight or ten years I have made several attempts to do the autobiography in one way or another with a pen, but the result was not satisfactory, it was too literary. . . .
>
> With a pen in the hand the narrative stream is a canal; it moves slowly, smoothly, decorously, sleepily, it has no blemish except that it is all blemish. It is too literary, too prim, too nice; the gait and style and movement are not suited to narrative.

Two years later, in mid-June 1906, he would look back on this time in 1904 as the moment he discovered free-wheeling, spoken narrative as "the right way to do an Autobiography."[54]

Only six Florentine Dictations are known to survive. Three of them are portraits of friends or acquaintances—"John Hay," "Robert Louis Stevenson and Thomas Bailey Aldrich," and "Henry H. Rogers"—presumably products of the "portrait gallery" concept. Two are reminiscences: "Notes on 'Innocents Abroad'" and a sketch (untitled) recalling his first use of the typewriter. The sixth is a complaint about the Villa di Quarto, the family's current residence near Florence.[55] It is the longest and the least polished, an extended diatribe about the rented villa and especially its hated owner, the Countess Massiglia. Clemens concluded it by inserting an 1892 manuscript about the Villa Viviani, where the Clemenses had lived during an earlier, more enjoyable stay in Florence. Despite that moderating addition, the 1904 dictation is replete with fiery insults to the countess—so much so that when, in May and June 1906, Clemens considered publishing selections of autobiography with S. S. McClure, he marked in blue pencil the offending passages on Jean's typescript and wrote (on the verso of page 2), "Leave out that blue-penciled ˏpassageˏ (& *all* blue-penciled passages₍₎] in the *first* edition," and added, "Restore them in later editions."[56]

It is clear that there were Florentine Dictations that have not survived, at least not as originally dictated. In August 1906 Clemens said that he had created more than a dozen "little biographies," of which we have almost none.

---

53. 14 Mar 1904 to Howells, NN-BGC, in *MTHL*, 2:782.

54. "John Hay," 224.26–39; "The Latest Attempt," 220.17.

55. Lyon's longhand notes for these dictations are presumed lost, and one of only two typescripts by Jean Clemens to survive is the first part (twenty-one pages) of the "Villa di Quarto" dictation. With that exception, all the Florentine Dictations are preserved only in typed copies made in 1906 from Jean's (now lost) typescripts. The dictation about the typewriter was published under the heading "From My Unpublished Autobiography" in *Harper's Weekly* for 18 March 1905, and Clemens later inserted it in AD, 27 Feb 1907 (SLC 1905c).

56. See the Textual Commentary for "Villa di Quarto," *MTPO*.

By my count, estimating from the time when I began these dictations two years ago, in Italy, I have been in the right mood for competently and exhaustively feeding fat my ancient grudges in the cases of only thirteen deserving persons—one woman and twelve men. It makes good reading. Whenever I go back and re-read those little biographies and characterizations it cheers me up, and I feel that I have not lived in vain. The work was well done. The art of it is masterly. I admire it more and more every time I examine it. I do believe I have flayed and mangled and mutilated those people beyond the dreams of avarice.[57]

Only one such Florentine Dictation is known to survive: Clemens certainly "flayed" the Countess Massiglia in "Villa di Quarto." We can only guess who the "deserving" men were by considering other evidence. For example, in a letter of 29 January 1904 Clemens vented his anger toward Henry A. Butters, head of the American Plasmon Company, whom he held responsible for his investment losses: "As soon as I get back we will pull Butters into Court, & I guess we can jail him. . . . ~~He occupies space enough in my Autobiography to pay back all he & his pimp have robbed me of.~~"[58] But no such text from 1904 or earlier survives, and Butters is mentioned only in passing in the later Autobiographical Dictations. (On 31 October 1908, for example, Clemens described him as "easily the meanest white man, and the most degraded in spirit and contemptible in character I have ever known.") There are others who might have received harsh treatment in now-lost dictations from 1904 whose portraits were then "done over" between January and August 1906. Clemens scattered a few sarcastic remarks about Charles L. Webster in the early 1906 dictations, then excoriated him at length in the one for 29 May 1906. Other candidates include Daniel Whitford, Clemens's attorney; James W. Paige, inventor of the failed typesetter; and of course Bret Harte.[59]

The Copyright Extension Gambit (1904 to 1909)

When Olivia died suddenly on 5 June 1904, Clemens's interest in his autobiography quite naturally evaporated, and in the next year and a half he wrote only one short sketch for it, "Anecdote of Jean." But before Olivia died, his new enthusiasm for dictating the autobiography gave rise to a scheme to provide income for the family he thought would survive him (he was then sixty-eight). In the same January letter to Howells in which he enthused about dictation he described this new idea: "If I live two years this Auto will cover many volumes, but they will not be published independently, but only as *notes* (copyrightable) to my existing books. Their purpose is, to add 28 years to the life of the existing books. I think the notes will add 50% of matter to each book, & be some shades more readable than the book itself."[60]

This notion was still alive almost a year after Clemens had begun his dictations to Josephine

57. AD, 6 Aug 1906.
58. 29 Jan 1904 to Stanchfield, CU-MARK.
59. See the ADs of 26 May (Whitford), 2 June (Paige), and 14 June 1906 (Bret Harte).
60. 16 Jan 1904 to Howells, MH-H, in *MTHL*, 2:779.

Hobby in January 1906. In December of that year he spoke of it to a reporter, who then summarized it in the New York *Times:*

> As soon as the copyright expires on one of his books Mark Twain or his executors will apply for a new copyright on the book, with a portion of the autobiography run as a footnote. For example, when the copyright on "Tom Sawyer" expires, a new edition of that book will be published. . . . About one third of this new edition of "Tom Sawyer" will be autobiography, separated from the old text only by the rules or lines. The same course will be followed with each book, as the copyright expires.
>
> So far as possible the part of the autobiography will be germane to the book in which it appears. . . .
>
> He is confirmed in this by the experience of Sir Walter Scott, from whom he got the germ of his idea. Scott kept his copyrights alive by publishing new editions with commentaries. . . . He believes his scheme will insure a copyright of eighty-four years instead of forty-two, and, as he said the other day: "The children are all I am interested in; let the grandchildren look out for themselves.[61]

It is difficult to know just how serious Clemens was about this scheme because it was never put to the test. On 24 December 1909, in "Closing Words of My Autobiography," he explained that the

> reason that moved me was a desire to save my copyrights from extinction, so that Jean and Clara would always have a good livelihood from my books after my death. . . .
>
> That tedious long labor was wasted. Last March Congress added fourteen years to the forty-two-year term, and so my oldest book has now about fifteen years to live. I have no use for that addition, (I am seventy-four years old), poor Jean has no use for it now, Clara is happily and prosperously married and has no use for it.

Because of that change in the law, he evidently told Clara much the same thing. She protested, and he replied on 23 February 1909:

> Maybe I ought to have said "half-wasted." Bless your heart I put in two or three years on that Autobiography in order to add 28 years to my book-lives. Congress has ˄now˄ gone & added 14 of the 28; & the law is now in such a sane shape that Congress can be persuaded presently, without difficulty, to add another 14. . . .
>
> My child, I wasn't doing the Autobiography in the world's interest, but only in yours & Jean's.[62]

Still, it is clear that extending his copyrights had never been his primary motive for creating the *Autobiography.*

61. "Twain's Plan to Beat the Copyright Law," New York *Times,* 12 Dec 1906, 1. The then current copyright law granted protection for twenty-eight years, with one extension of fourteen, for a total term of forty-two years. Clemens thought that if the autobiographical notes were attached to a book at the end of its term, they would create a new publication with its own term of forty-two years, for an overall total of eighty-four years.

62. 21, 22, and 23 Feb 1910 to CC, photocopy in CU-MARK. The "Copyright Act of 1909" passed both houses of Congress on 4 March 1909.

AUTOBIOGRAPHY OF MARK TWAIN

The Autobiographical Dictations Begin (January 1906)

Clemens, his two daughters, Katy Leary, and Isabel Lyon accompanied Olivia's body back to America in July 1904. They buried her at Quarry Farm, and Clara entered a rest home in New York City while Clemens, Jean, and Lyon spent the rest of the month in a rented summer home in Lee, Massachusetts. On 10 August Clemens went to New York and soon signed a three-year lease for a town house at 21 Fifth Avenue, which he and Jean occupied in December 1904 after it was renovated and furnished.

One year later, in January 1906, work on the autobiography had been at a standstill for eighteen months. A catalyst was needed to revive the enthusiasm of 1904, and on the night of 3 January it arrived in the form of Albert Bigelow Paine. Paine was an experienced writer and editor who in 1904 had published a biography of Thomas Nast which Clemens admired. On that January evening Paine attended a dinner in honor of Clemens, hosted by The Players club, and happened to be seated "nearly facing" him. Three days later he called at 21 Fifth Avenue and asked to write Mark Twain's biography. After brief preliminaries Clemens turned to him and said: "When would you like to begin?" Paine went on to suggest that a stenographer be hired to take notes of what Clemens said in response to the biographer's questions. Clemens said that he thought he would "enjoy dictating to a stenographer, with some one to prompt me and to act as audience," and he offered Paine office room and access to "a trunkful or two" of his manuscripts, notes, and letters. "Whatever you need will be brought to you. We can have the dictation here in the morning, and you can put in the rest of the day to suit yourself. You can have a key and come and go as you please."[63]

It was agreed that work should begin on 9 January. On that Saturday morning, Paine arrived accompanied by a stenographer, Josephine S. Hobby. The procedure for working on the biography was promptly decided, but Clemens

> proposed to double the value and interest of our employment by letting his dictations continue the form of those earlier autobiographical chapters, begun with Redpath in 1885, and continued later in Vienna and at the Villa Quarto. He said he did not think he could follow a definite chronological program; that he would like to wander about, picking up this point and that, as memory or fancy prompted, without any particular biographical order. It was his purpose, he declared, that his dictations should not be published until he had been dead a hundred years or more—a prospect which seemed to give him an especial gratification.[64]

Josephine Hobby was an experienced stenographer and an excellent typist, known to Paine for about eight years. She had previously worked for Charles Dudley Warner and Mary Mapes Dodge and was currently employed by the Century Company, which, since 1899, had also

---

63. *MTB,* 3:1260–64. The following account of the history of the Autobiographical Dictation series is founded upon and greatly indebted to the ground-breaking research of Lin Salamo, an editor at the Mark Twain Project until 2009.

64. *MTB,* 3:1266.

employed Paine as an editor of *St. Nicholas,* a magazine for young people. Hobby charged one dollar per hour of dictation and five cents per hundred words of typescript. She began immediately with a transcription of the morning's conversation. "We will try this," Clemens told Paine, "see whether it is dull or interesting, or whether it will bore us and we will want to commit suicide. I hate to get at it. I hate to begin, but I imagine that if you are here to make suggestions from time to time, we can make it go along, instead of having it drag." He proposed a schedule of four or five days a week, for roughly two hours each morning.[65] Clemens talked while Hobby took him down in shorthand and Paine listened appreciatively. For these early sessions, Paine recalled, Clemens usually dictated from bed, "clad in a handsome silk dressing-gown of rich Persian pattern, propped against great snowy pillows."[66]

Before Clemens was done dictating in 1909, he and Hobby, along with three other typists, generated more than five thousand pages of typescript. That enormous body of material has, since Clemens's death, constituted the largest part of the manuscript known as the "Autobiography." But probably since DeVoto's time as editor of the Mark Twain Papers, anyone who consulted that file was likely to be puzzled by two things. First, most of the Autobiographical Dictations between January and August 1906 were filed in folders—one per dictation—containing between two and four separate, distinct typed copies of essentially the same text. No one understood the purpose of the duplicates. Second, the differences (if any) between these various "duplicates" were not obvious or readily intelligible: pagination differed, seemingly without pattern; some contained handwritten authorial revisions, while others were unmarked; and many were extensively marked by at least half a dozen different (mostly unidentified) hands, in addition to the author's. These documents constituted the central puzzle confronting anyone who set out to publish the *Autobiography of Mark Twain.*

The First Typescript (TS1)

A first step in solving the puzzle was to find reliable ways of distinguishing between the several, nearly identical typed copies in any given folder. The paper used, specific characteristics of the typewriter and habits of the typist, and of course the unexplained differences in pagination proved to be essential pieces of evidence. The very first typescript Hobby created from her stenographic notes was eventually isolated and identified in this way, and it is called hereafter TS1 (for typescript 1). Each of the other typescripts (sometimes with carbon copies as well) were similarly identified, and are herein referred to by number (TS2, TS3, and TS4). Once they were physically distinguishable in this way, it became possible to see that the (understandable) fashion in which daily dictations were filed had in fact long obscured why there *were* different typed copies.[67] It was in turn possible to decide, on the basis of meticulous collation,

---

65. AD, 9 Jan 1906; Lyon 1906, entry for 25 May; *MTB,* 3:1266.

66. *MTB,* 3:1267.

67. If TS1 through TS4 had been preserved in the way they were doubtless left to Paine—as four stacks of consecutively numbered pages—it would long ago have been obvious that each was a discrete sequence. But the pages of each typescript were distributed into individual folders labeled by the date of the relevant dictation, blocking that simple insight.

which was copied from which, and to begin to make some sense of the various differences between them.

By 18 January Hobby had settled on a standard format for each session: she recorded the time spent on dictation and a word count at the top left of the first page, with the page number centered, and the date of dictation at the right, usually followed by a summary of the contents. Hobby marked in pencil any errors she had failed to correct on the machine. The typescript then went to Clemens for correction and revision. TS1 would total roughly twenty-six hundred consecutively numbered pages, beginning at page 1 with the dictation of 9 January 1906 and ending with the dictation of 14 July 1908, which Hobby completed shortly before leaving Clemens's employment. Two later stenographer-typists produced another hundred or so pages of typescript, which did not continue the TS1 pagination sequence.[68]

Hobby soon agreed to give up her job with the Century Company in order to work for Clemens exclusively during the summer and possibly longer. On 13 March Lyon commented in her journal, "Mr. Clemens finds her entirely to his liking & he says 'it is a case of established competency' which is saying a great deal—for she is a good audience, is sympathetic & very appreciative."[69] By 8 April Hobby had transcribed her notes through the end of the 28 March 1906 dictation.

Despite the risk of somehow losing TS1, a unique copy (there was no carbon copy at this point), Clemens allowed Clara to carry away and read about five hundred pages, through the end of the 16 March dictation. He also lent Twichell three days' dictation, probably those for 23, 26, and 27 March. On 8 April, Lyon recorded that "Mr. Twichell is here—Mrs., too—& Mr. T. thinks the auto. MS. is absorbingly interesting." He presumably returned the three dictations at that time. The same day Clemens took the entire 28 March dictation (Orion's misadventure with Dr. Meredith's "old-maid sisters") up to lunch with Howells at the Hotel Regent. Howells returned the pages by the next day's mail:

> I want to see every word of the 578 pages before this, which is one of the humanest and richest pages in the history of man. If you have gone this gate [*i.e.,* gait] all through you have already gone farther than any autobiographer ever went before. You are nakeder than Adam and Eve put together, and truer than sin. But—but—but you really *mustn't* let Orion have got into the bed. I know he did, but—

Lyon noted that Clara had written "enthusiastically about it too," but her letter has not been found. Clemens replied to her in Atlantic City, two days before she was supposed to return the pages to him:

> I am so glad, you dear ashcat! so glad the auto interests you; I was so afraid it wouldn't. I couldn't guess as to how it might read, for I have purposely refrained from reading a line of it myself, lest I should find myself disappointed & throw up the job. I wanted it to gather

68. The two later employees were Mary Louise Howden (who began in October 1908) and William Edgar Grumman (who began in February 1909). They worked during a period when work on the autobiography was drawing to a close, and their combined typescripts totaled only slightly more than a hundred pages.

69. Lyon 1906, entry for 13 Mar.

age before I should look at it, so that it would read to me as it would to a stranger—then I could judge it intelligently. However, as Twichell wanted to experiment with it I took the last 3 days instalments & corrected them—& in this way I found out that I was doing well enough for an apprentice who was an unpractised learner in the art of dictating to a stenographer. Twichell's verdict is, that the interest doesn't flag. That's all I want. I only want to interest the reader, he can go elsewhere for profit & instruction.[70]

On 11 April Clemens took a break from his dictating routine, and did not resume until 21 May, after he, Jean, and Lyon were settled for the summer in the isolated Upton House near the village of Dublin, New Hampshire. Clemens arrived there on 15 May; Paine and Hobby arrived a few days later and found quarters nearby. Paine reported, "We began in his bedroom, as before, but the feeling there was depressing." He described the view from the verandah of the Upton House as "one of the most beautiful landscape visions on the planet," and reported that Clemens soon saw the opportunity it presented: "I think we'll do our dictating out here hereafter. It ought to be an inspiring place." Lyon occasionally recorded Clemens's (and her own) impatience with the "old-maidish whims" and slowness of the "Hobby horse," but for the most part the morning sessions seem to have been remarkably amicable.[71] Lyon described one of them in her journal:

> There was a long—a 3 hour dictation this morning, when M^r· Clemens used letters as a subject. . . . It was beautiful to hear the laughter from the porch; the King's rich laugh, the biographer's falsetto delight & the stenographer's chirping gurgle—it made a lovely song. I stole out to sit on a wicker thing in the hall & watch & listen. The King in white—the biographer in soft grey & the stenographer in dark blue, with a kitten in her lap.[72]

In late May Clemens also began in earnest the job of reading and correcting the four months' accumulation of TS1, which by then consisted of over seven hundred pages (through the dictation for 11 April). He revised the typescript in black ink, only rarely in pencil, making relatively few changes in wording—at least after the first ten dictations—and he consistently made a smattering of changes or corrections to spelling, punctuation, and paragraphing. For the most part Hobby seems to have learned, directly or indirectly from Clemens, how he preferred to spell and punctuate. Inevitably there were mistakes, especially in proper names ("Katie" instead of "Katy," "Susie" instead of the preferred "Susy," "Twitchell" instead of "Twichell"). And with a backlog of hundreds of pages typed before he began his review, Clemens inevitably found repetitive errors. Lyon noted in her journal:

> Day after day M^r· Clemens is harassed and tormented when he is reading the dictated matter by continually coming across Hobby blunders, & the worst one—the most exasperating one is where she invariably corrects M^r· Clemens, writing "one thousand" or "one hundred," where he has said "*a* thousand", or "a hundred." Today it passed the limit of his

---

70. Lyon 1906, entries for 8 and 9 Apr; Howells to SLC, 8 Apr 1906, CU-MARK, in *MTHL,* 2:803–4 (which misidentifies the typescript pages lent to Howells); 8 Apr 1906 to CC, MoPlS and CU-MARK.

71. Lyon 1906, entries for 15 May, 20 May, 25 May, and 21 June; *MTB,* 3:1307–8.

72. Lyon 1906, entry for 29 Aug. "The King" was the pet name that Lyon and Paine used for Clemens.

endurance. Through his tightly shut teeth he damned that "hell-fired word" until he was tired; & then he went for "that idiot!"—"that devilish woman! I'd like some one to take her out & have her scalped and gutted!"—[73]

He had found (and corrected) over two dozen instances of this trivial but irritating error. One can only hope that he alerted Hobby to her mistake in a less ferocious mood.

S. S. McClure and Syndication

Clemens's correction and revision of TS1 was given a special impetus by S. S. McClure, founder of McClure's Syndicate and *McClure's Magazine,* who offered to pay Clemens a dollar per word for the right to syndicate fifty thousand words from the autobiography. As Clemens reviewed Hobby's typescripts and some of his pre-1906 texts, he began noting likely candidates for McClure's proposed syndication. For instance, the blue-penciled notation "M^c" is written at the top of the first page of the 1904 "Villa di Quarto" typescript, and the same or a similar notation can be seen on several other pages of TS1 prepared between January and March 1906. Still other dictations were marked "*Not* for MC."

Clemens was not, however, free to accept McClure's bid. He had signed an exclusive contract with Harper and Brothers on 22 October 1903, which prohibited his publishing with another firm any of his "books, writings or works now existing or which may hereafter be created." It further stipulated that all "miscellaneous articles accepted for magazines or periodicals shall be paid for at the rate of thirty cents a word." Even so, on 27 May Clemens kept Lyon busy for two hours taking notes while he outlined "a course of action to be followed out in his scheme of breaking away from the Harper Contract & selling 50000 words to McClure for $50000.^{00} to be syndicated." His interest in publishing with McClure was more than financial, however. He had an express desire to see the selections "go into the papers—even into the Hearst papers—to reach his 'submerged clientele.'"[74] He further explained to Rogers,

> I'd like to see a lot of this stuff in print before I die—but not the *bulk* of it, oh no! I am not desiring to be crucified yet. Howells *thinks* the Auto will outlive the Innocents Abroad a thousand years, & I *know* it will. I would like the literary world to see (as Howells says) that the *form* of this book is one of the most memorable literary inventions of the ages. And so it is. It ranks with the steam engine, the printing press & the electric telegraph. I'm the only person who has ever found out the right way to build an autobiography.

Rogers, however, did not favor accepting McClure's offer. Believing that the Harper contract was "so valuable that they would seize the opportunity of breaking the arrangement if it were possible," he urged Clemens not to "think of anything that will vitiate" it.[75]

---

73. Lyon 1906, entry for 20 June. Hobby's stenographic record apparently did not make a distinction between "a" and "one."

74. Lyon 1906, entry for 27 May; *HHR,* 697. See "Robert Louis Stevenson and Thomas Bailey Aldrich" for Clemens's comments on "submerged renown."

75. 17 June 1906 to Rogers, Salm, in *HHR,* 611; Rogers to SLC, 4 June 1906, CU-MARK, in *HHR,* 608.

"The Final (and Right) Plan" (June 1906)

On 10 June Clemens wrote to a friend, "I've stopped dictating—tired of it. I've stopped reading autobiography & admiring it—tired to death of it!"[76] Clemens's lack of enthusiasm must have been merely a passing mood, however, since he did not in fact stop dictating or "reading autobiography." From 11 to 14 June he dictated every day (as well as on six more days before the end of the month), while he continued to read and revise TS1, working his way through the backlog of over nine hundred pages by 21 June. And it was also at this time that he decided to return to a task that he had begun the previous winter but suspended in May: reviewing his earlier manuscripts, including his preliminary attempts at autobiography. On 8 June he sent Paine to the house at 21 Fifth Avenue to fetch the cache of manuscripts that he had gathered together for use in the biography as well as for his copyright scheme.[77] Many years later, Lyon annotated a copy of Paine's edition where "The Tennessee Land" began, explaining that "in the winter of 1905–6" Clemens pursued his idea of using "autobiographical notes to be added to each volume on its copyright expiration, thus creating a new volume with its new copyright to be extended for 14 years. . . . He asked me for the notes he wrote in 1870 & later—& here is the beginning." It is also likely that at about the same time she heard Clemens read the manuscript of what Paine titled "Early Years in Florida, Missouri." She noted in Paine's edition, "Mr Clemens called for this MS. which he read aloud to me; often deeply moved by memories his voice momentarily lost in emotion."[78]

Paine arrived back in Dublin on the thirteenth with a "small steamer trunk" of manuscripts. On 22 June Lyon wrote in her journal:

> . . . & then after luncheon we sat on the porch & M^r. Clemens read the very first autobiography beginning, ~~a bit~~ written many years ago ˄about 1879˄—44 typewritten pages, & telling of his boyhood days, & the farm, & ~~the joys of living in~~ It is a beautiful ~~bit of poetry—it is full of pictures & the afternoon was very very lovely~~ ˄He was deeply moved as he read on & on.˄[79]

Clemens may have been considering which of his early reminiscences he liked well enough to add to the autobiography, if only to enlarge its bulk. A few days earlier (17 June) he had written a long letter to Howells in which he referred to yet another way to expand his text, this one taking advantage of posthumous publication:

> There's a good deal of "fat." I've dictated, (from Jan. 9) 210,000 words, & the "fat" adds about 50,000 more.
> The "fat" is old pigeon-holed things, of the years gone by, which I or editors didn't das't to print. For instance, I am dumping in the little old book which I read to you in Hartford

76. 10 June 1906 to Teller, NN-BGC.

77. Lyon 1906, entries for 8 June and 21 June.

78. Pages 3 and 7 of Lyon's copy of Paine's *Autobiography,* quoted courtesy of Kevin MacDonnell, its owner. Lyon made her notes in 1947 or 1948.

79. Paine to Lyon, 11 June 1906, CU-MARK; Lyon 1906, entries for 13 and 22 June. Lyon's date (1879) for this typescript was wrong; she may have intended to write "1897," which would have been about right.

about 30 years ago & which you said "publish—& ask Dean Stanley to furnish an introduction; he'll do it." "(Captain Stormfield's Visit to Heaven.") It reads quite to suit me, without altering a word, now that it isn't to see print until I am dead.

And, in a postscript, he added: "I've written a short Preface. I like the title of it: 'Spoken from the Grave.' It will prepare the reader for the solemnities within."[80]

The manuscript of this preface (whose subtitle is "As from the Grave") and a draft of the title page survive in the Mark Twain Papers, as does a typed copy of the title page, on which Clemens drafted a series of notes specifying restrictions and conditions for publishing the autobiography. He then decided to add to his short "Preface" by enlarging on these notes. Addressing his "editors, heirs and assigns," he dwelt at facetious length on how successive editions could include more and more of his (supposedly shocking) "sound and sane expressions of opinion."

It is now clear that by the time Clemens read aloud the "44 typewritten pages . . . telling of his boyhood days, & the farm" on 22 June, he had already decided to use that sketch to begin the *Autobiography*. He wrote a one-page preface called "An Early Attempt" to introduce it, then followed that with a single page instruction: "Here insert the 44 old type-written pages." This "old" typescript has been lost, but we now know that it was a typed copy of the manuscript he called "My Autobiography [Random Extracts from It]," written in Vienna in 1897–98. It is not known when this (now missing) typescript was prepared, but it was probably no later than 1900.[81]

At about the same time he also decided to further illustrate the evolution of his ideas about autobiography by including some of the dictations produced in Florence in 1904. To frame these he wrote a matching preface called "The Latest Attempt," characterizing them as examples of "the right way" to do an autobiography. And he made one more change, adding "The Final (and Right) Plan" and an epigraph ("What a wee little part of a person's life . . . ").[82] The result was a three-part preface, concluding with the "Preface. As from the Grave" (divided into three sections), followed by the introductory note "Here begin the Florentine Dictations."

The present edition prints this extensive front matter, complete and in the sequence that

80. 17 June 1906 to Howells, NN-BGC, in *MTHL*, 2:811; Lyon 1906, entry for 14 June. The sketch Clemens referred to here was "Captain Stormfield's Visit to Heaven," a manuscript written as early as 1868 and several times revised. Among the "fat" must have been other unfinished or unpublished manuscripts he later inserted into the autobiography, motivated at least in part by his copyright renewal scheme: "Down the Rhone," known as "The Innocents Adrift," written in 1891 (see the Textual Commentary for "Villa di Quarto" at *MTPO*); and "Wapping Alice," written in 1898. See the ADs of 6 June and 9 Apr 1906. Many other such "nonautobiographical" manuscripts were ultimately inserted in the Autobiographical Dictations.

81. Hobby had already begun to retype the forty-four pages, but her typescript (TS2) is also now missing. Collation of the manuscript against another 1906 typescript (TS4) derived from the "old" lost typescript shows that Clemens had revised it (see the next section: "Two More Typescripts: TS2 and TS4"). TS4 has "[1900]" typed at the top, which suggests that the lost typescript included this date.

82. The first draft of the epigraph was inscribed by Clemens in a small calendar notebook for "November, 1901" and identified on the cover as "Autobiography" (CU-MARK). Other notes by Clemens indicate that he was using it in early 1902. The 1906 version, which survives only in a typescript, shows that he revised it on a document that is now missing.

Clemens intended, for the first time. All of the material was known to Paine (his penciled page numbers are on the manuscript pages). But he apparently realized that it interfered with his own plan for the autobiography: a sequence of early sketches and the Florentine Dictations in the order of their composition, followed by a selection of the Autobiographical Dictations from January through April 1906. He included the epigraph and the first section of "As from the Grave" at the beginning of his first volume, placing "The Latest Attempt" before the Florentine Dictations but calling it "Author's Note." He omitted entirely "An Early Attempt" and the second and third sections of "Preface. As from the Grave."[83] The prefatory pages, all in the Mark Twain Papers, are shown in sequence on the facing page and reproduced in facsimile in figures 2–13.

Since the "44 old type-written pages" are admittedly lost, how can we be sure that they were in fact a copy of "My Autobiography [Random Extracts from It]"? And how can we tell which of the six surviving Florentine Dictations were intended to follow "As from the Grave"?

The multiple typescripts of the January–August 1906 dictations hold the answer to both questions.

Two More Typescripts: TS2 and TS4

In his postscript to the 17 June letter to Howells, Clemens had said: "I think Miss Lyon told you the reason we couldn't send you the Autobiography—there's only one typed copy, & we had to have it for reference, to guard against repetitions. The making of a second copy is now begun; & so, we can presently begin to mail batches of it to you."[84] TS1 had been begun without any provision for a carbon copy. But Howells's and Twichell's interest in seeing the text earlier in April, and McClure's interest in late May, made it increasingly clear that duplicates were vitally needed—hence the decision to begin a carbon copy of TS1 from that point, certainly no later than 11 June.[85] But that still left more than eight hundred pages of dictation in a unique copy, much of which had been revised.

Clemens's postscript shows that by 17 June "a second copy" had been commissioned. In fact, not one but two typed copies of TS1 were begun in mid- to late June, soon after the various prefaces had been created: the first typed by Hobby (TS2) and the second by an unidentified typist (TS4). These sequences are distinguishable by their differences in pagination and by minute differences in their typists' styles. Collation demonstrates that TS2 and TS4 were both copied independently from the recently revised TS1, not one from the other. Both TS2 and TS4 originally began with the "Random Extracts" text, but both omit the "Early Attempt" preface written for it. TS4 includes the other three-part preface and four of the Florentine Dictations ("John Hay," "Notes on 'Innocents Abroad,'" "Robert Louis Stevenson and Thomas Bailey Aldrich," and "Villa di Quarto"), and TS2 originally did so as well. But only parts of TS2 for these early texts survive: gaps in it (shown by missing page numbers) cannot always be certainly reconstructed, but all surviving evidence shows that the missing pages were identical in content to

---

83. For details, see the Appendix "Previous Publication" (pp. 663–67).
84. 17 June 1906 to Howells, NN-BGC, in *MTHL,* 2:811.
85. The first *surviving* carbon copy of TS1 is of the 11 June 1906 dictation.

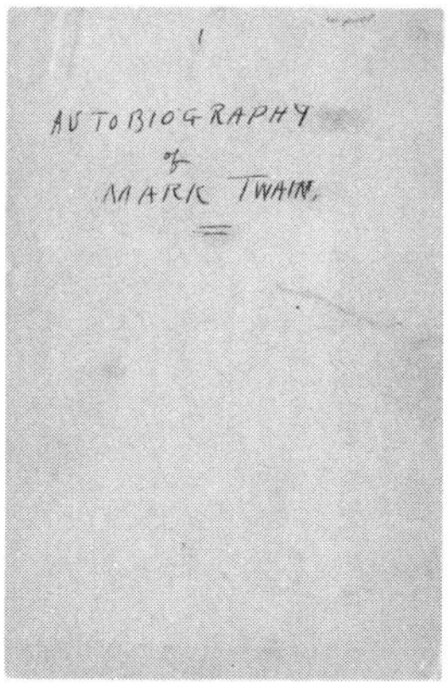

1

AUTOBIOGRAPHY
of
MARK TWAIN.

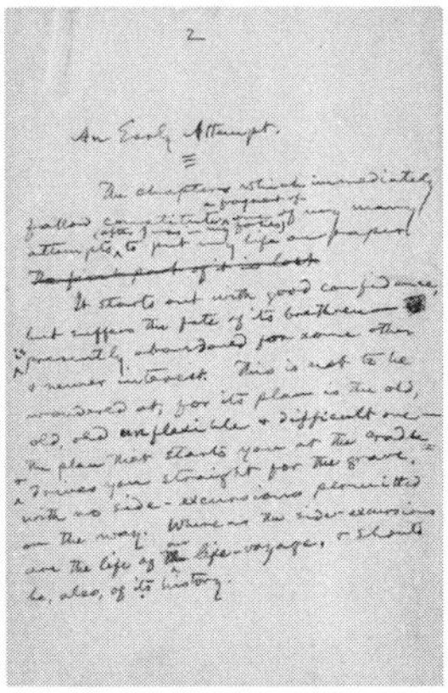

2

An Early Attempt.

The chapters which immediately follow constitute a fragment of one of my many attempts to put my life on paper—the fragment of one of them.

It starts out with good confidence, but suffers the fate of the rest—generally abandoned for some other & newer interest. This is not to be wondered at, for its plan is the old, old, old, inflexible & difficult one—the plan that starts you at the cradle & drives you straight for the grave, with no side-excursions permitted on the way. Whereas the side-excursions are the life of our life-voyage, & should be, also, of its history.

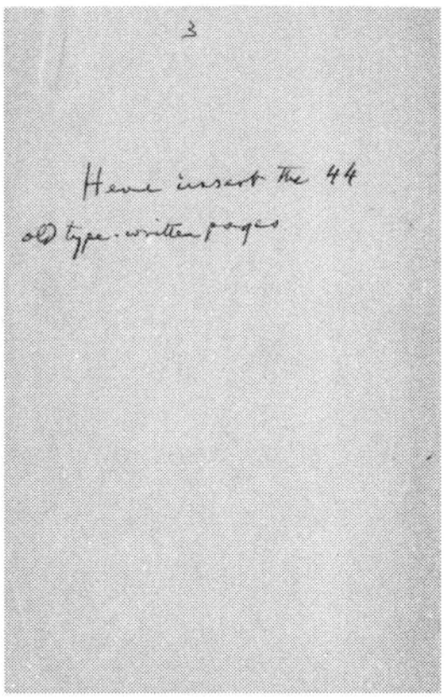

3

Here insert the 44 old type-written pages

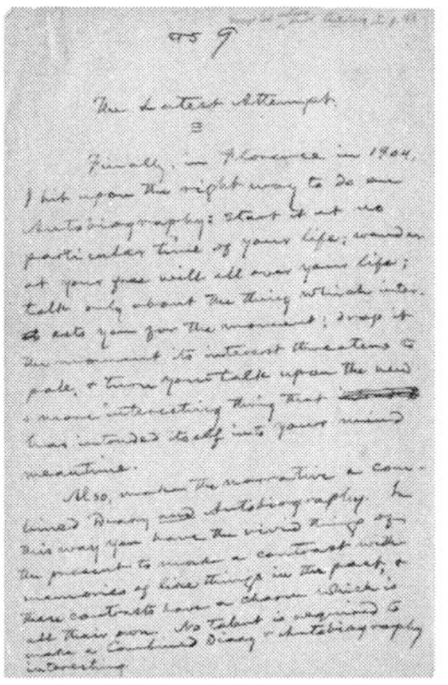

9

The Latest Attempt.

Finally, in Florence in 1904, I hit upon the right way to do an Autobiography: start it at no particular time of your life; wander at your free will all over your life; talk only about the thing which interests you for the moment; drop it the moment its interest threatens to pale, & turn your talk upon the new & more interesting thing that has intruded itself into your mind meantime.

Also, make the narrative a combined Diary and Autobiography. In this way you have the vivid things of the present to make a contrast with memories of like things in the past, & these contrasts have a charm which... all their own. So talked is combined Diary & Autobiography interesting

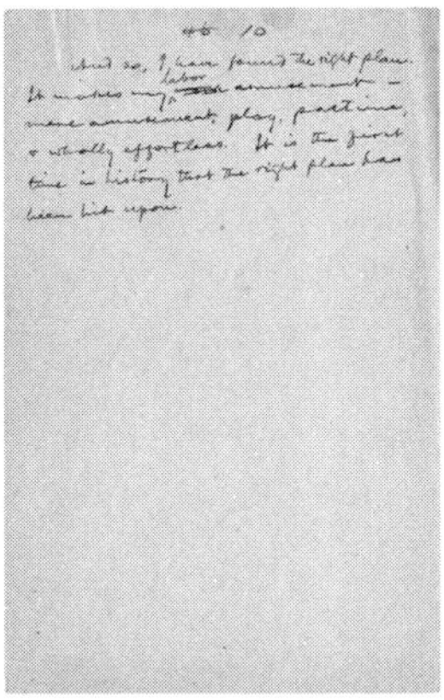

---

44 10

and so, I have found the right plan. It makes my... amusement, play, pastime, & wholly effortless. It is the first time in history that the right plan has been hit upon.

---

47 11

The Final (& Right) Plan.

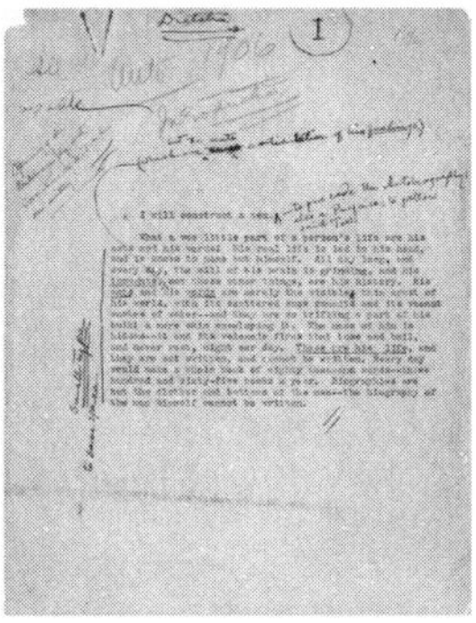

1

[typewritten inserted page, with handwritten annotations]

I will construct a text...

When a new little part of a person's life are his acts and his words... All his long, and every day, the will of his acts is growing, and the lines which are those inner things, are his history. But out of the whole can surely the making him out of ... now. With its positive very should and the change of the acts of every... to trifling ... to build a man with everything... The man of his in labored out the reason I find that tame and tell, and never ... night nor day. There are his acts, and they are not written, and I must be written. Every day would make a good task of dying the man... and out the matter and bottom of the remote biography of the ... man himself cannot be written.

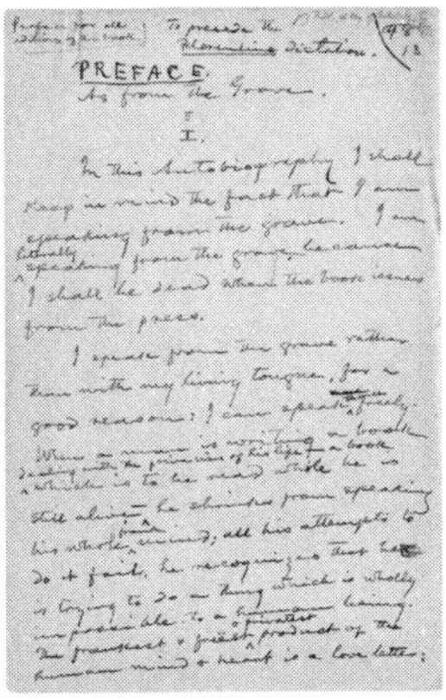

---

48 12

PREFACE.
As from the Grave.

I.

In this Autobiography I shall keep in mind the fact that I am speaking from the grave. I am literally speaking from the grave, because I shall be dead when the book issues from the press.

I speak from the grave rather than with my living tongue, for a good reason: I can speak freely.

When a man is writing a book dealing with the privacies of his life—a book which is to be read while he is still alive—he shrinks from speaking his whole frank mind; all his attempts to do it fail, he recognizes that he is trying to do a thing which is wholly impossible to a human being. The frankest & freest product of the human mind & heart is a love-letter.

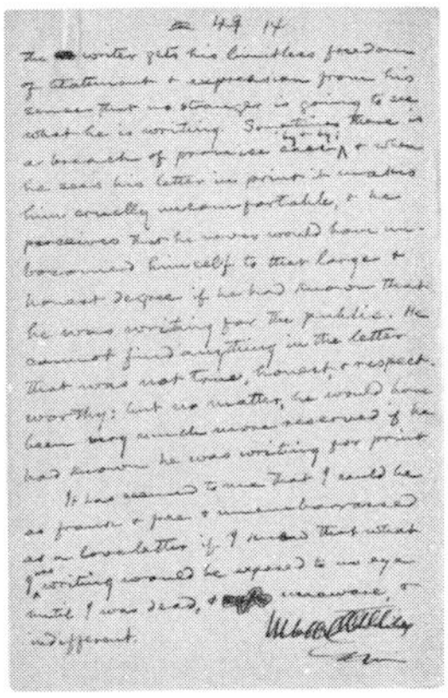

---

44 14

The writer gets his limitless freedom of statement & expression from his sense that no stranger is going to see what he is writing. Sometimes there is a breach of promise case, & when he sees his letter in print he is uncomfortable, & he perceives that he never would have unbosomed himself to that large & honest degree if he had known that he was writing for the public. He cannot find anything in the letter that was not true, honest, & respect-worthy; but no matter, he would have been very much more reserved if he had known he was writing for print.

It has seemed to me that I could be as frank & free & unembarrassed as a love-letter if I knew that what I was writing would be exposed to no eye until I was dead, & unaware, & indifferent.

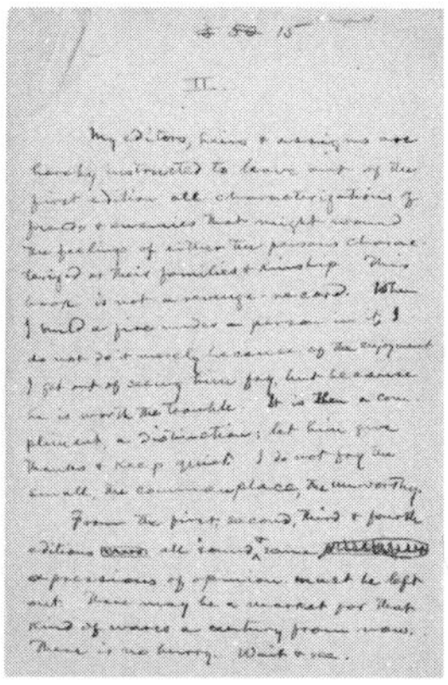

[signature]

---

44 15

II.

My editors, heirs & assigns are hereby instructed to leave out of the first edition all characterizations of friends & enemies that might wound the feelings of either the persons characterized or their families & kinship. This book is not a revenge-record. When I build a fire under a person in it I do not do it merely because of the enjoyment I get out of seeing him fry, but because he is worth the trouble. It is then a compliment, a distinction; let him give thanks & keep quiet. I do not fry the small, the commonplace, the unworthy.

From the first, second, third & fourth editions all... expressions of opinion must be left out. There may be a market for that kind of wares a century from now. There is no hurry. Wait & see.

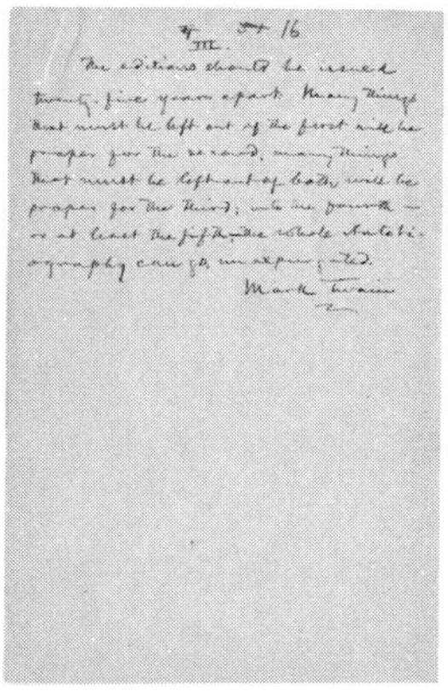

---

44 16

III.

The editions should be issued twenty-five years apart. Many things that must be left out of the first will be proper for the second; many things that must be left out of both will be proper for the third; so on, so forth—or at least the fiftieth whole Autobiography can get in unexpurgated.

Mark Twain

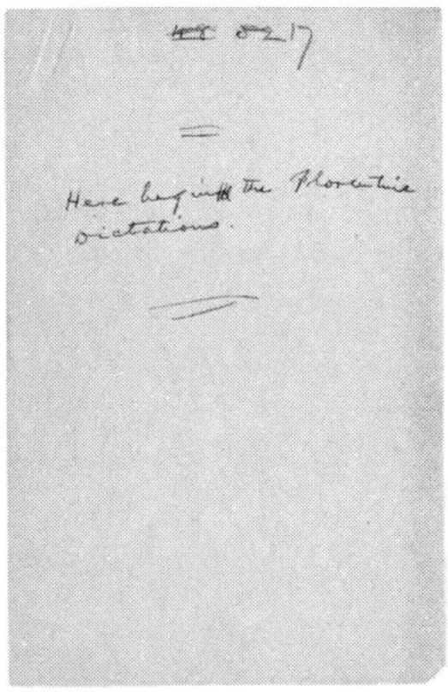

---

44 17

Here begins the Florentine Dictations.

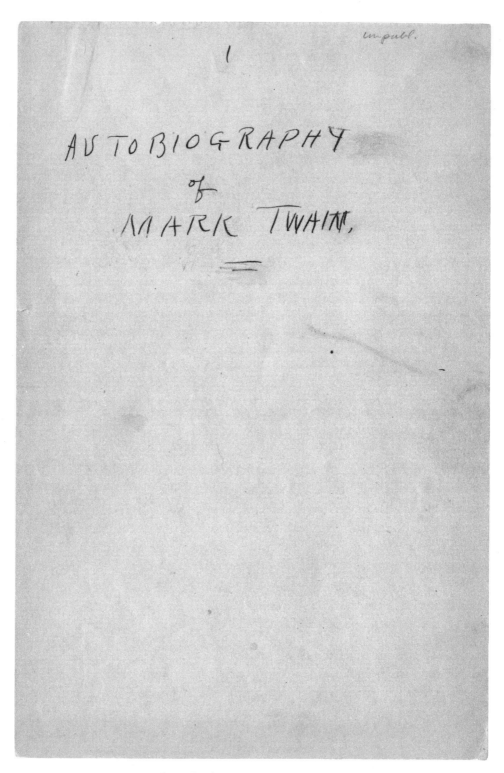

FIGURE 2. Manuscript page 1, Clemens's title page.

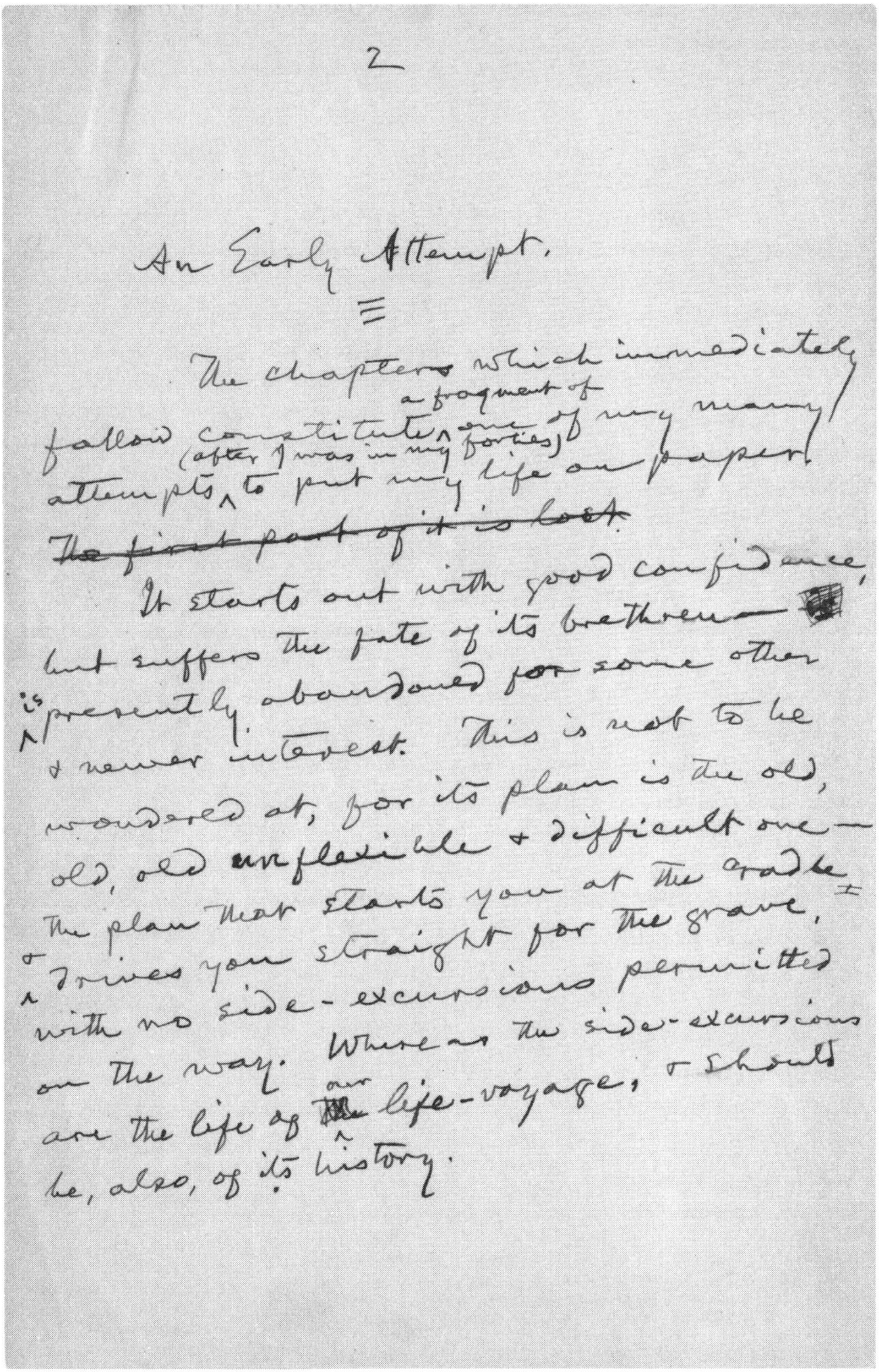

2

An Early Attempt.

The chapters which immediately
follow constitute a fragment of one of my many
(after I was in my forties)
attempts, to put my life on paper.
~~The first part of it is lost.~~

It starts out with good confidence,
but suffers the fate of its brethren —
is presently abandoned for some other
& newer interest. This is not to be
wondered at, for its plan is the old,
old, old unflexible & difficult one —
the plan that starts you at the cradle
& drives you straight for the grave,
with no side-excursions permitted
on the way. Whereas the side-excursions
are the life of our life-voyage, & should
be, also, of its history.

FIGURE 3. Manuscript page 2, the "Early Attempt" preface introducing the "44 old type-written pages."

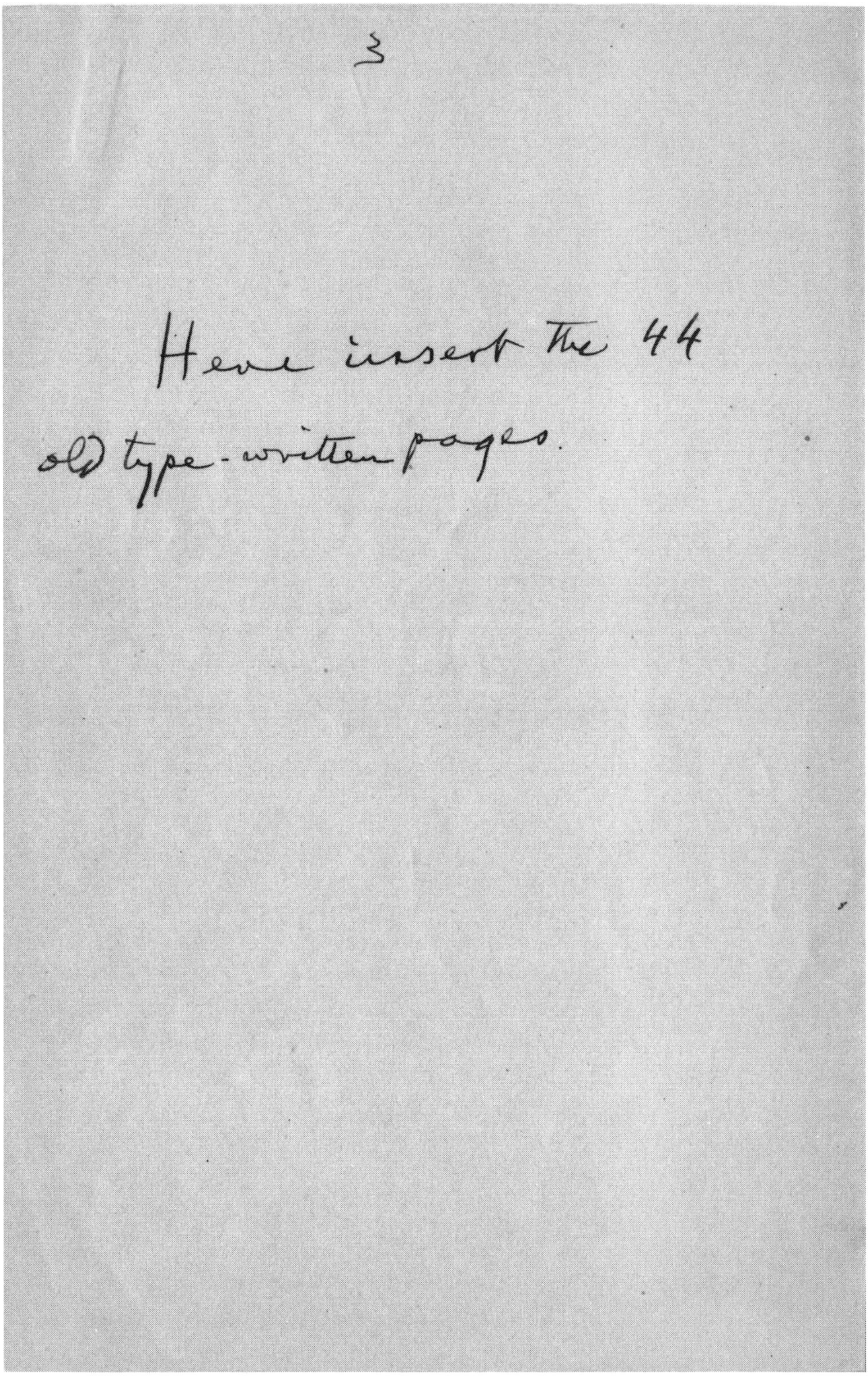

3

Here insert the 44 old type-written pages.

FIGURE 4. Manuscript page 3, the instruction to insert what has now been identified as "My Autobiography [Random Extracts from It]."

Except last sentence publ. Autobiog. I, p. 193

45 9

The Latest Attempt.
≡

Finally, in Florence in 1904, I hit upon the right way to do an Autobiography: start it at no particular time of your life; wander at your free will all over your life; talk only about the thing which interests you for the moment; drop it the moment its interest threatens to pale, & turn your talk upon the new & more interesting thing that has intruded itself into your mind meantime.

Also, make the narrative a combined Diary and Autobiography. In this way you have the vivid things of the present to make a contrast with memories of like things in the past, & these contrasts have a charm which is all their own. No talent is required to make a Combined Diary & Autobiography interesting.

FIGURE 5. Manuscript page 45, the first page of "The Latest Attempt" preface, numbered to continue the sequence after the inserted forty-four-page typescript. (The page number 9, and the numbers 10–17 on the following pages, were all added by Paine in pencil and were not part of Clemens's plan.)

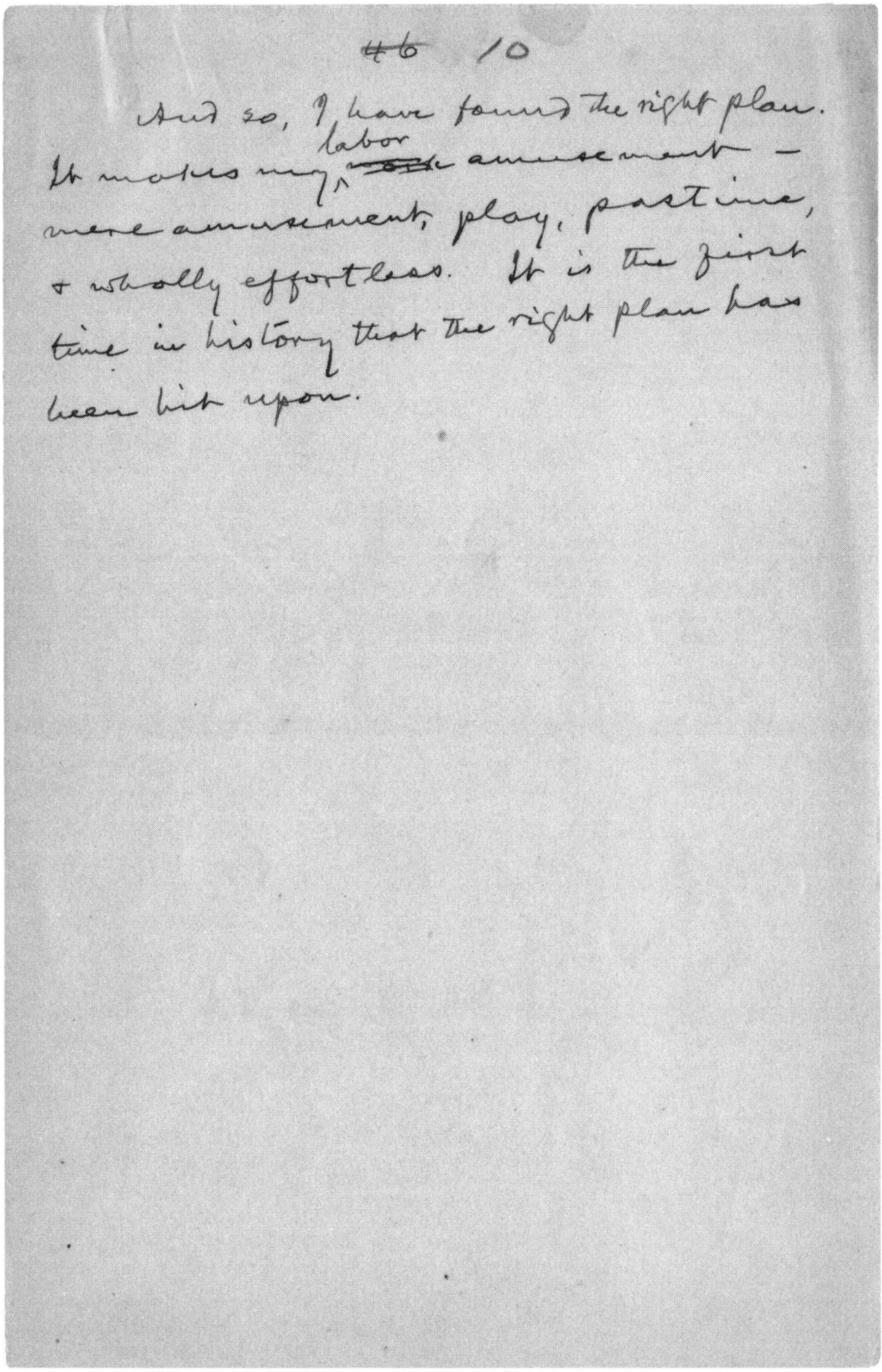

~~46~~ 10

And so, I have found the right plan. It makes my ~~work~~ labor amusement — mere amusement, play, pastime, & wholly effortless. It is the first time in history that the right plan has been hit upon.

FIGURE 6. Manuscript page 46, the second page of "The Latest Attempt" preface.

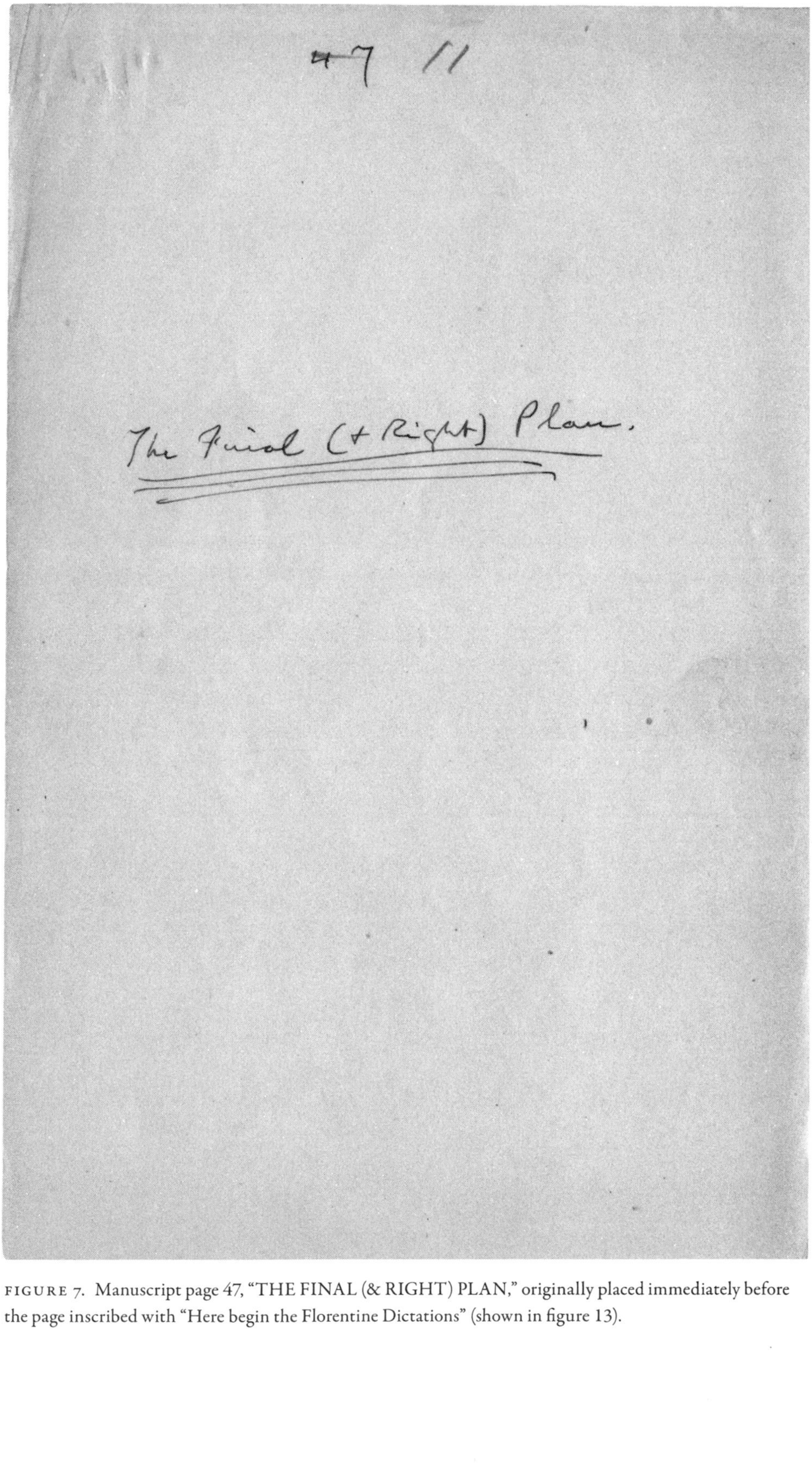

The Final (& Right) Plan.

FIGURE 7. Manuscript page 47, "THE FINAL (& RIGHT) PLAN," originally placed immediately before the page inscribed with "Here begin the Florentine Dictations" (shown in figure 13).

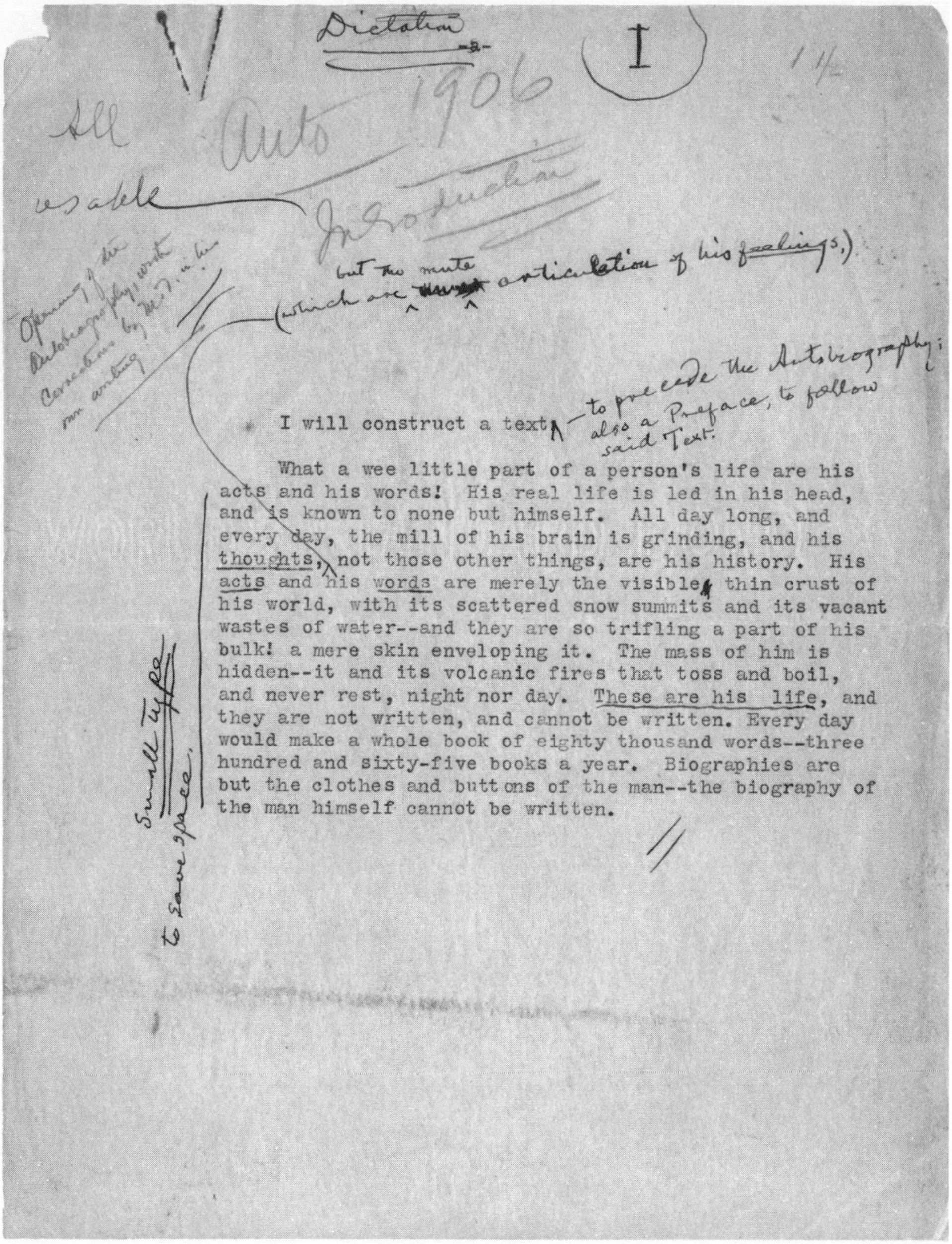

Dictation

1906

All usable

Auto

Introduction

(which are but ~~the mute~~ articulation of his feelings.)

I will construct a text —to precede the Autobiography; also a Preface, to follow said Text.

What a wee little part of a person's life are his acts and his words! His real life is led in his head, and is known to none but himself. All day long, and every day, the mill of his brain is grinding, and his thoughts, not those other things, are his history. His acts and his words are merely the visible thin crust of his world, with its scattered snow summits and its vacant wastes of water--and they are so trifling a part of his bulk! a mere skin enveloping it. The mass of him is hidden--it and its volcanic fires that toss and boil, and never rest, night nor day. These are his life, and they are not be written, and cannot be written. Every day would make a whole book of eighty thousand words--three hundred and sixty-five books a year. Biographies are but the clothes and buttons of the man--the biography of the man himself cannot be written.

Small type to save space.

FIGURE 8. The typed epigraph. In an earlier version, Clemens had deleted the title "A Text For All Biographies," and added, "I will construct a text"; here he inserted "to precede the Autobiography; also a Preface, to follow said Text" and "(which are but the mute articulation of his *feelings*.)" He placed the page after "THE FINAL (& RIGHT) PLAN," where it was transcribed in TS4. Clemens wrote "All usable" and "SMALL TYPE to save space" in the margin. The circled "I" in the top margin may have been written by either Clemens or Paine. The other writing on the page is Paine's.

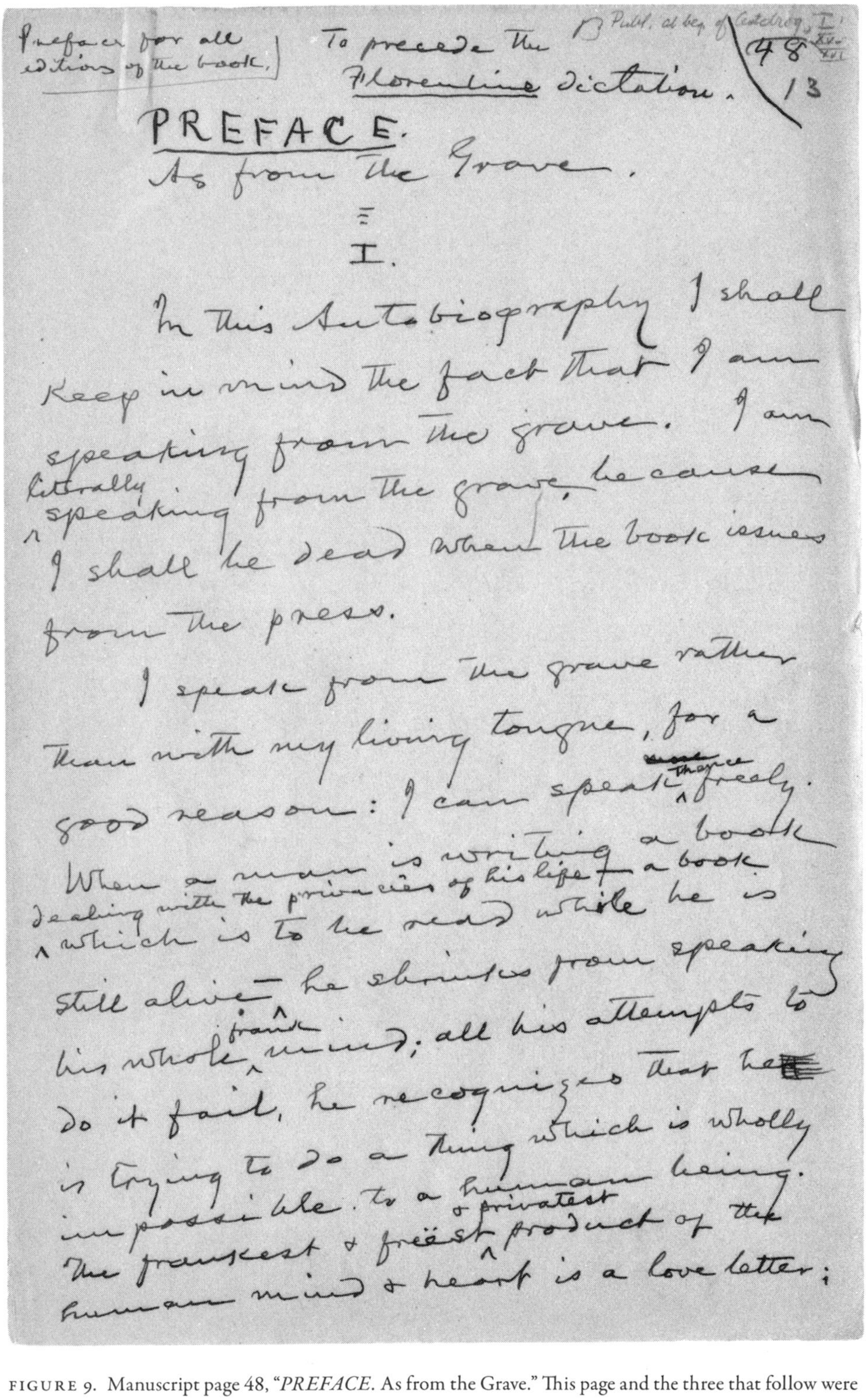

Preface for all editions of the book.) To precede the Florentine dictation.

B Publ. at beg of Autobiog, I

48

13

PREFACE.

As from the Grave.

I.

In this Autobiography I shall keep in mind the fact that I am speaking from the grave. I am literally speaking from the grave, because I shall be dead when the book issues from the press.

I speak from the grave rather than with my living tongue, for a good reason: I can speak thence freely. When a man is writing a book dealing with the privacies of his life—a book which is to be read while he is still alive—he shrinks from speaking his whole frank mind; all his attempts to do it fail, he recognizes that he is trying to do a thing which is wholly impossible to a human being. The frankest & freest & privatest product of the human mind & heart is a love letter;

FIGURE 9. Manuscript page 48, "*PREFACE.* As from the Grave." This page and the three that follow were first numbered 1–4. When Clemens inserted them into the sequence after page 47, he renumbered them 48–51. He moved the page originally numbered 48, containing "Here begin the Florentine Dictations," to the end and renumbered it 52 (figure 13).

the writer gets his limitless freedom
of statement & expression from his
sense that no stranger is going to see
what he is writing. Sometimes there is
a breach of promise case by & by; & when
he sees his letter in print it makes
him cruelly uncomfortable, & he
perceives that he never would have unbosomed himself to that large &
honest degree if he had known that
he was writing for the public. He
cannot find anything in the letter
that was not true, honest, & respect-
worthy; but no matter, he would have
been very much more reserved if he
had known he was writing for print.

It has seemed to me that I could be
as frank & free & unembarrassed
as a love-letter if I knew that what
I was writing would be exposed to no eye
until I was dead, & unaware, &
indifferent.

FIGURE 10. Manuscript page 49, the second page of "As from the Grave," first numbered 2 and later changed to 49. Clemens initially ended the preface at the bottom of this page, then canceled his signature and added two more sections.

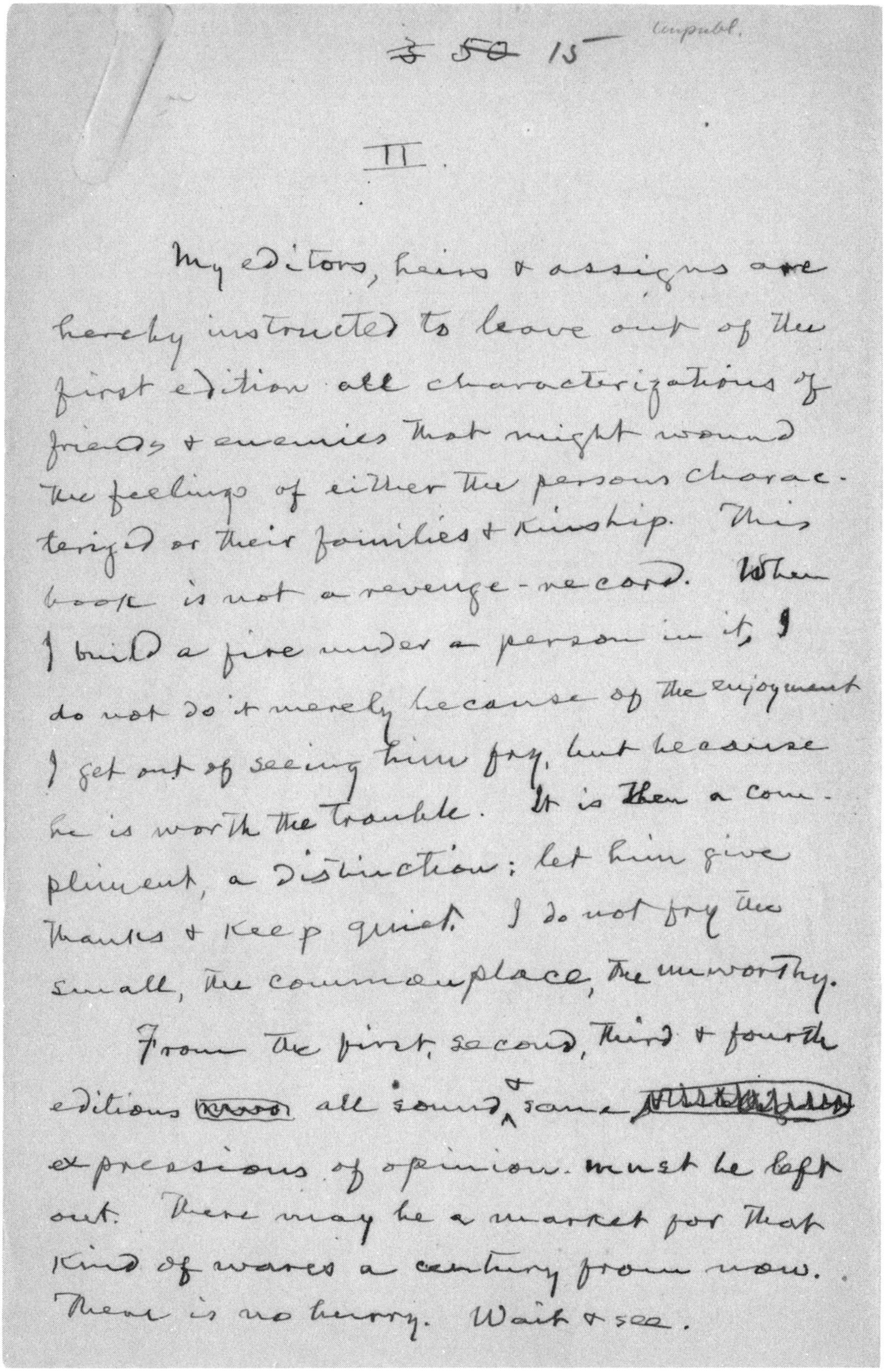

II.

My editors, heirs & assigns are hereby instructed to leave out of the first edition all characterizations of friends & enemies that might wound the feelings of either the persons characterized or their families & kinship. This book is not a revenge-record. When I build a fire under a person in it, I do not do it merely because of the enjoyment I get out of seeing him fry, but because he is worth the trouble. It is then a compliment, a distinction: let him give thanks & keep quiet. I do not fry the small, the commonplace, the unworthy.

From the first, second, third & fourth editions ~~known~~ all ~~sound~~ sound, ^& same~~ ~~xxxxxxxxx~~ expressions of opinion. must be left out. There may be a market for that kind of wares a century from now. There is no hurry. Wait & see.

FIGURE 11. Manuscript page 50, section II of "As from the Grave," which Clemens first numbered 3 and later changed to 50.

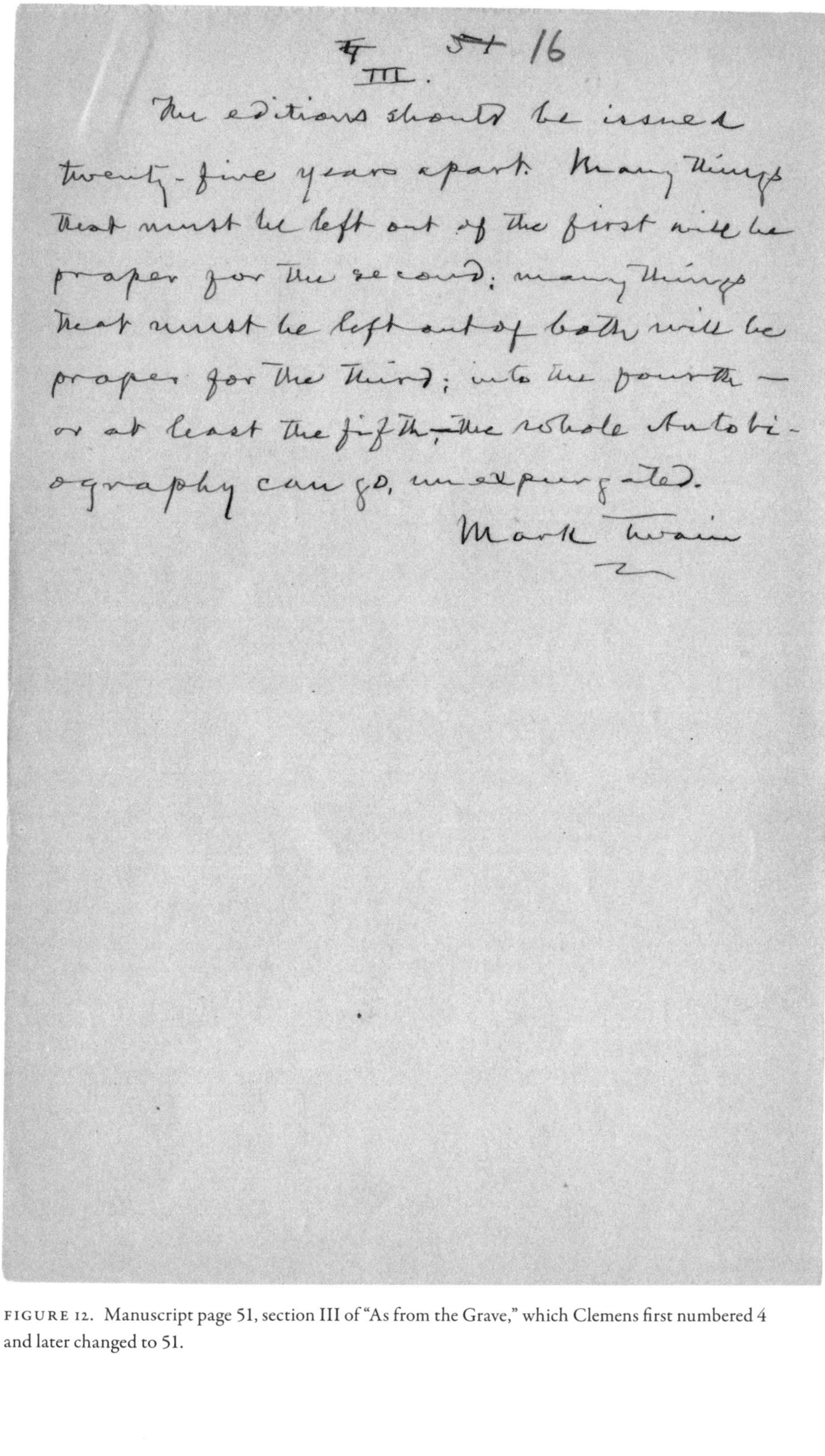

III.

The editions should be issued twenty-five years apart. Many things that must be left out of the first will be proper for the second; many things that must be left out of both will be proper for the third; into the fourth — or at least the fifth, the whole Autobiography can go, unexpurgated.

Mark Twain

FIGURE 12. Manuscript page 51, section III of "As from the Grave," which Clemens first numbered 4 and later changed to 51.

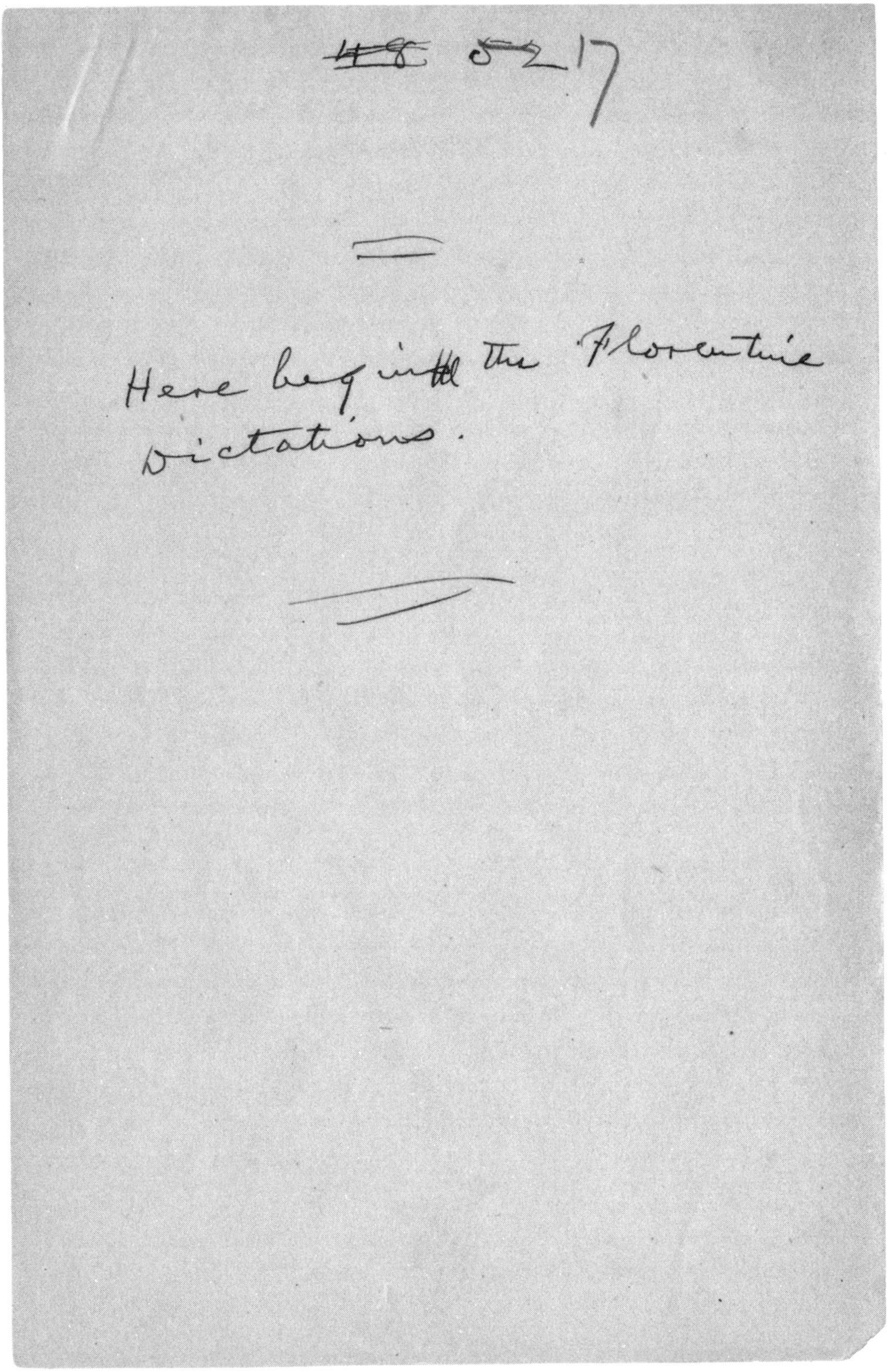

FIGURE 13. Manuscript page 52, "Here begin the Florentine Dictations," which Clemens first numbered 48 and later changed to 52 when he inserted the four-page *"PREFACE. As from the Grave."*

those of TS4, which is the only complete record of these initial elements in Clemens's plan. This conjecture explains why the page numbers for the January–August 1906 dictations in TS2 and TS4 are different from each other and consistently higher than the page numbers of TS1 for the corresponding dictation. TS1 *begins* with the Autobiographical Dictation of 9 January, having been started *before* Clemens decided to include any of the early material.[86]

We now understand why there are often two, three, or even four nearly identical typescripts for the January through August 1906 Autobiographical Dictations. The resolution of this first part of the textual mystery shows, among other things, that TS1 is the primary source for the text of those dictations, and that when parts of TS1 are lost, the missing text can be reliably restored from either TS2 or TS4, because they were created by copying TS1 before the losses occurred. Our understanding of the typescripts also helps to explain the multiple inscriptions on so many of their pages: they are the traces left behind by the editors and typists who collaborated with Clemens in 1906–9, and by the editors who published parts of the autobiography after his death, from Paine to DeVoto. The four typescript pages reproduced in facsimile in figures 14–17 illustrate some of the many hands that had to be identified and, above all, distinguished from Clemens's own hand.

The *North American Review* (August and September 1906)

To recapitulate: by 21 June Clemens had read through and corrected all of TS1 that Hobby had so far typed (over nine hundred pages, probably through the dictation for 20 June 1906).[87] He had reviewed his earlier manuscripts and selected at least those he wanted to begin with (he would later select several more, inserting them in later dictations). And he had written the title page and the several prefaces to frame those early pieces and introduce the 1906 dictations. Hobby began to create TS2, and an unidentified typist started TS4, probably as soon as Hobby made the revised TS1 available.

With all that in train, Clemens left Dublin on 26 June to be away for a month, in Boston and New York City, occasionally visiting Henry Rogers at his home in Fairhaven, Massachusetts, and joining him on his yacht, the *Kanawha*. Following Rogers's advice, he met several times with the Harper executives and lawyers in order to resolve their mutual disagreements about the recent republication of *Mark Twain's Library of Humor*. While in New York he also met with S. S. McClure and left with him some pages from the dictations about Susy—probably those of 2–7 February. McClure wrote Clemens about them on 2 July:

> This is not a business letter it is a love-letter. I read the wonderful chapters of your autobiography all are wonderful, but the chapters about the dear dear child are the finest I have ever read in literature
>
> I wept & loved & suffered & enjoyed

86. The only large difference between TS2 and TS4 is the placement of "John Hay." In TS4 it precedes "The Latest Attempt" and other prefaces, but it apparently followed them in TS2. The TS2 order is adopted in the present edition on the assumption that TS4 was in error. See the Textual Commentary for "The Latest Attempt" preface, *MTPO*.

87. Lyon 1906, entry for 21 June.

D

-178-

Instalment:
I. Whittier Banquet.
II. The $3-Dog.

1 h. 40 min. Original
Abt. 4,200 wds.

Jan. 11, 1906.

Chapters from My Autobiography—XXV
By Mark Twain
Prefatory note as usual

Begin on next page.

Stop on p. 197.

15½ pages.
Half of it small type.
Say 8 pages of the Review.

leave out.

I received the following letter some days ago, from Mrs. Laura K. Hudson:

"287 Quincy St.,
Jan. 3d, '06.

Mr. Samuel L. Clemens.

My dear Sir:-

Some twenty years ago we were in the first years of our married life; the first two small instalments of a growing family kept us severely domestic and my husband and I used to spend our happy evenings together, he reading aloud from magazine or book and I meanwhile sewing and listening. One evening he read from one of the New York papers the report of some function-- I have a hazy idea it was a Press Club dinner or other jamboree--during which "Mark Twain" read aloud a paper which to me seemed the best and funniest thing our great favorite had ever written. And now that the growing family has gotten its growth and has grown very fond of "Mark Twain" I have searched high and low in every collection of his works for this delightful bit of fun, but always in vain. May I therefore apply to Mr. Clemens for some help?

It was about a miner in his mountain-hut; to whom come three men for food and a night's shelter. They give their names as Longfellow, Holmes and Whittier; and the way they are described--the last-mentioned with "double-chins way down to his stomach"-- by the miner who tells the story, and the high-flown quotations from their own writings which they give in answer to the miner's very gruff and to-the-point questions are fun of the funniest kind. The miner stands it until in an-

* Copyright, 1906, by Harper & Brothers. All Rights Reserved

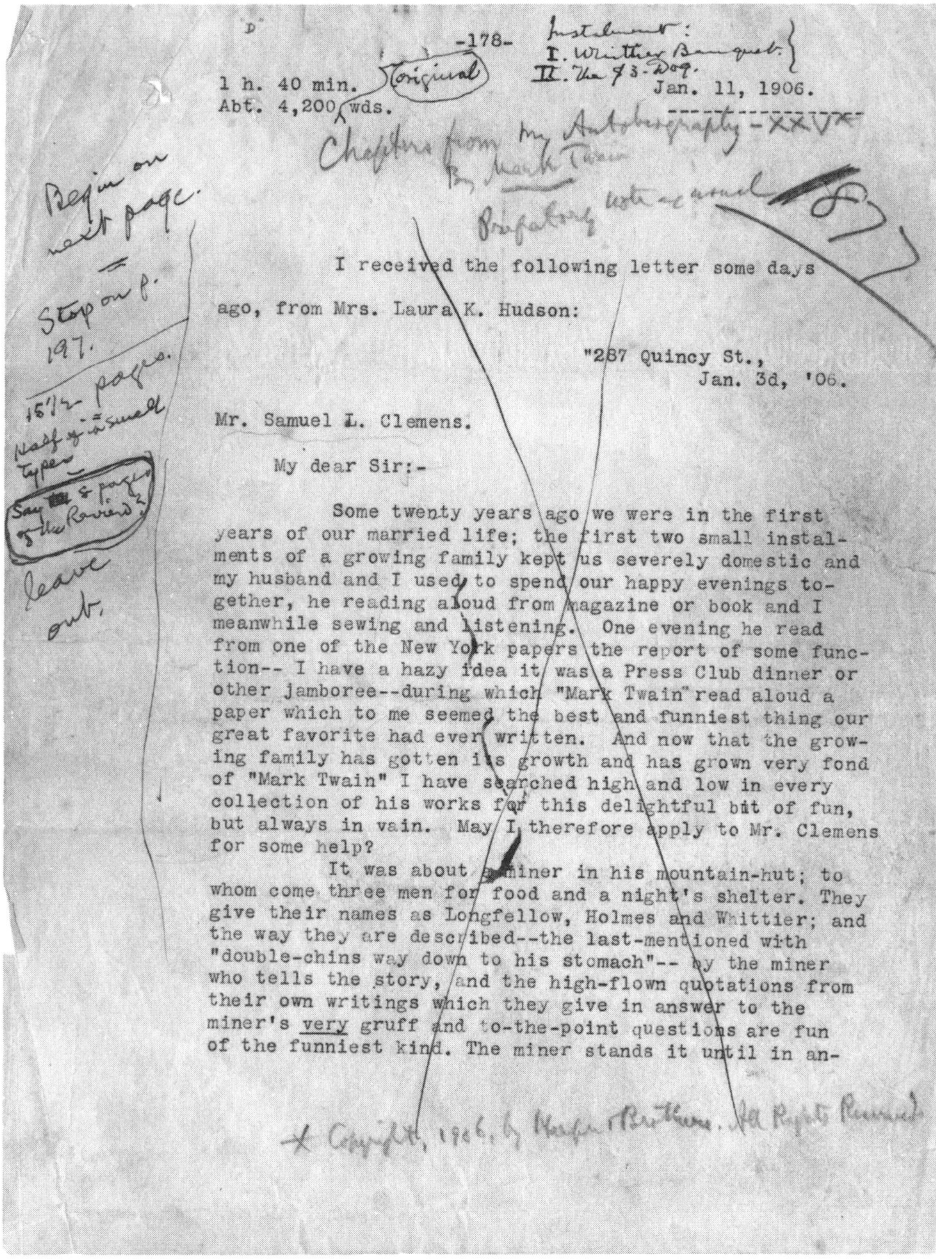

FIGURE 14. The first page of the Autobiographical Dictation of 11 January 1906 (TS2, 178). Clemens wrote in ink at the top of the page and in the left margin, and crossed out the entire page. The "$3-Dog" (which he suggested as part "II" of a *Review* installment) is from AD, 3 Oct 1907. David Munro, a *Review* editor, wrote the title, the author's name, and an instruction to include the "Prefatory note as usual." "1877" is in an unidentified hand. The excerpt was published in December 1907 (NAR 25), typeset directly from this page.

1 h. 40 min. dic.   -199-
Abt. 3,400 wds.

Jan. 12, 1906.

This talk about Mr. Whittier's seventieth
birthday reminds me that my own seventieth arrived re-
cently--that is to say, it arrived on the 30th of November, but Col. Harvey was not able to celebrate it on
that date because that date had been preempted by the
President to be used as the usual and perfunctory Thanksgiving Day, a function which originated in New England
two or three centuries ago when those people recognized
that they really had something to be thankful for--an-
nually, not oftener-- if they had succeeded in exterminating their neighbors, the Indians, during the previous
twelve months instead of getting exterminated by their
neighbors the Indians. Thanksgiving Day became a habit,
for the reason that in the course of time, as the years
drifted on, it was perceived that the exterminating had
ceased to be mutual and was all on the white man's side,
consequently on the Lord's side, consequently it was
proper to thank the Lord for it and extend the usual

FIGURE 15. The first page of the Autobiographical Dictation of 12 January 1906 (TS2, 199). Clemens noted in ink in the left margin: "None of this is printable while I am alive. It is too personal. . . . Leave it till I am dead, then print *all* of it some day. SLC." In pencil in the right margin, he wrote, "USE ONLY THE DREAM." Stenographer Josephine Hobby wrote "Auto. Part" in the center and Harvey, editor of the *Review,* wrote inclusive page numbers "199 to 242" at the top right. Paine, who in early 1907 helped Clemens prepare a section for publication in the *Review,* wrote in the top left corner, and later added (in blue pencil), "Copied for use"—referring to another typescript, TS3, prepared from this one to serve as printer's copy for the excerpt, which was published in the *Review* for 19 April 1907 (NAR 16).

1 h. 40 min. dic.
Abt. 2,200 wds.

Corrected
941 words

Follow Susy's spelling & punctuation always! SLC

233

[Wednesday, March 7, 1906.

¶Susie's biography.—John Hay incident--giving the young
girl the French novel.—Susie & her father escort Mrs.
Clemens to train, then go over Brooklyn Bridge.—On the
way to Vassar they discuss German profanity.—Mr. Clemens
tells of the sweet and profane German nurse.—The arrival
at Vassar & the dreary reception--told by Susie--the
reading, etc. Mr. Clemens's opinion of girls.—He is to
talk to the Barnard girls this afternoon.¶

~~To return to Susie's biography--~~

From Susy's Biography.

¶The next day mamma planned to take the four-
o'clock car back to Hartford. We rose quite early that
morning and went to the Vienna Bakery and took breakfast
there.   From there we went to a German bookstore and
bought some German books for Clara's birthday.

~~From Susy's Biography~~

¶Then mamma and I went to do some shopping and
papa went to see General Grant.   After we had finnished
doing our shopping we went home to the hotel together.

I was walking down it too, that morning, and I overtook
Hay and asked him what the trouble was.   He turned a
lusterless eye upon me and said:

"My case is beyond cure. In the most innocent way

FIGURE 16. The first page of the Autobiographical Dictation of 7 March 1906 (TS1, 419). Clemens wrote
"Follow Susy's spelling & punctuation always. SLC" at the top left; inserted the head "*From Susy's Biography*"
(twice); and noted that the extracts were to be set "solid" (i.e., with reduced line spacing). Another typescript,
TS3, was prepared from this one to serve as printer's copy for an excerpt published in the *Review* for 16 November 1906 (NAR 6). The rest of the writing is by Paine, who used this typescript to prepare his 1924 edition (*MTA*, 2:166–72), from which he omitted all of page 420 and most of page 421. He cut a strip from the
bottom of page 421 and pasted it to this page (covering part of the text), crossed out the second heading for
Susy's biography, and altered Clemens's "solid" to "smaller."

tell

has taught me, long ago, that if I ~~would~~ a boy's story,
or anybody else's, it is never worth printing; it comes
from the head, not the heart, and always goes into the
waste-basket.   To be successful, and worth printing,
imagined
the boy would have to tell his story _himself_, and let
me act merely as his amanuensis.   I did not tell the
"Horse's Tale," the horse told it himself, through me.
If he hadn't done that it wouldn't have been told at all.
When a tale tells itself there is no trouble about it;
there are no hesitancies, no delays, no cogitations, no
attempts at invention; there is nothing to do but hold
the pen and let the story talk through it and say, after
its own fashion, what it desires to say.

       Mr. Howells began the composite tale. He held the
pen, and through it the father delivered his chapter--
therefore it was well done.   A lady followed Howells,
and furnished the old-maid sister's chapter. This lady
is of high literary distinction, she is nobly gifted,
she has the ear of the nation, and her novels and stories
are among the best that the country has produced, but
she did not tell those tales, she merely held the pen
and they told themselves--of this I am convinced. I am

FIGURE 17. The fourth page of the Autobiographical Dictation of 29 August 1906 (TS1, 1092). All of the revisions are in pencil, but only some of them are Clemens's: DeVoto added his own before he published the dictation in _Mark Twain in Eruption_ (243). They can all be correctly identified by examining the text of TS4, which followed only Clemens's markings, and DeVoto's book, which followed all of them. Clemens made no changes in the punctuation; he wrote "tell" and "imagined," and underlined "I," "himself," and "she" to italicize them.

These chapters should be issued soon in a little book. It would be a classic for a thousand years, & it could later be published in the large book. I am off to Chicago tomorrow & back on the 9ᵗʰ   I wish I could print this wonderful thing in McClure's Magazine. It would civilize a nation. It will uplift the Sunday press.

Finally, with Harvey's return from England in mid-July, the troublesome *Library of Humor* problem was resolved and Clemens was able to return to Dublin on 25 July.[88]

Clemens had already published several essays in Harvey's *North American Review:* "To the Person Sitting in Darkness" and "To My Missionary Critics" (1901) as well as his satirical commentary on Christian Science (1902–3). His first impulse had been to sell Harvey selections from the autobiography to go into *Harper's Weekly* (which Harvey also edited), a much more widely read journal than the *Review.* But when Harvey finally made the twice-postponed visit to Dublin, arriving late on 31 July, he had big plans for the *Review.*[89] He promptly immersed himself in the autobiography, and by the time he left Dublin on 4 August he and Clemens had agreed on what would become a sixteen-month series in the *Review.* "I like *this* arrangement," Clemens confided to his friend Mary Rogers (Henry's daughter-in-law), even as Harvey departed, "& so will Mr. Rogers; but he didn't much like the idea of McClure's newspaper syndicate, & I ceased to like it myself & stopped the negociations before I left New York."[90] As Clemens wrote to Clara on 3 August, he was impressed by Harvey's "great plan: to turn the North American Review into a *fortnightly* the 1ˢᵗ of Sept, introduce into it a purely *literary* section, of high class, & in other ways make a great & valuable periodical of it." He was also clearly flattered by Harvey's response to his text:

> He was always icily indifferent to the Autobiography before, but thought he would like to look at it now, so I told him to come up. He arrived 3 days ago, & has now carefully read close upon a hundred thousand words of it (there are 250,000). He says it is the "greatest book of the age," & has in it "the finest literature."
>
> He has done some wonderful editing; for he has selected 5 instalments of 5,000 words each; & although these are culled from here & there & yonder, he has made each seem to have been written by itself—& without altering a word. At 10,000 words a month we shall place about 110,000 or 120,000 words before the public in 12 months....
>
> To-morrow Harvey will carry away one full set of the MSS to Howells & get him to help select instalments. I can't do the selecting myself. The instalments will come to me in galley-proofs for approval, but I guess I will pass them on to you for final judgment after I have examined them.[91]

---

88. McClure to SLC, 2 July 1906, CU-MARK; 4 June 1906 to Duneka, MFai; 17 June 1906 to Rogers, MFai, in *HHR,* 611–13; Lyon 1906, entry for 25 July; Harvey to SLC, 4 June 1906, CU-MARK; McClure to SLC, 2 July 1906, CU-MARK; 3 Aug 1906 to CC, photocopy in CU-MARK.

89. Mott 1938, 219–20, 256–57; Johnson 1935, 73, 205, 268; SLC 1902d, 1903b–d; Lyon 1906, entry for 31 July.

90. 4 and 5 Aug 1906 to Rogers, NNC, in Leary 1961, 39.

91. 3 Aug 1906 to CC, photocopy in CU-MARK. If Howells did help make selections, no sign of it has survived.

Not only did Harvey "carefully read close upon a hundred thousand words" of the autobiography's 250,000, but by the time he left Dublin on 4 August he had read the remaining 150,000 words, encompassing the pre-1906 material and all the dictations through the end of June.[92]

A Composite Typescript: TS3

Harvey's "wonderful editing" was exactly as Clemens characterized it: he selected excerpts and patched them together to create five installments, essentially without "altering a word." Domestic anecdotes were a principal theme. He used the moving description of Olivia, and of Susy and her death, with nearly all the excerpts from Susy's biography of her father that were quoted in the February and March dictations. Other favored topics included Clemens's amusing misdeeds, such as his swearing about the missing shirt buttons; Susy's charming eccentricities of spelling; Clemens's puzzlement over the "spoon-shaped drive"; and the challenges of the burglar alarm at the Hartford house. Harvey also included the recollections of Hannibal, such as the story of "playing bear" from "Scraps from My Autobiography. From Chapter IX" (which Clemens had omitted from his plan for the *Autobiography*), the dreadful anticholera "Pain-Killer," and Orion's 3:00 A.M. call on a young lady. Harvey did not share Howells's squeamishness about Orion climbing (by mistake) into bed with the "middle-aged maiden sisters" (as they were called in the *North American Review* text): he included that episode without apparent concern. He rejected material with less broad appeal, such as the death of Patrick McAleer (the Clemenses' beloved coachman), and omitted Clemens's excursions into political commentary—the massacre of the "rebellious" Moro people in the Philippines and the treatment of Mrs. Morris, who had been thrown out of the White House. Harvey's penciled notations on the typescripts, such as "Begin," "End," and "Continue," show that Clemens's own participation in the selection process was probably much smaller than has previously been supposed.[93]

Since Harvey drew each *Review* installment from several different daily dictations, Hobby was now charged with creating yet another typescript to serve as printer's copy, working "under high pressure" to get it ready in time for the first chapter of the series, in the issue slated for 1 September. This composite typescript, called TS3, was typed from the start with a carbon copy, and was paginated independently of the three other ongoing sequences.[94] Hobby managed to complete two batches of TS3, of some two dozen pages each, in time for Clemens to revise them lightly and give them to Harvey when he left Dublin on 4 August. She immediately set to work typing a third large batch of TS3 (sixty-three pages), which Clemens agreed to send off "as soon as finished." These three batches of TS3 were intended for installments 1–5 in the *Review.* Because TS2 had at that time been completed only through 12 February, Harvey also

92. 7 Aug 1906 to Teller, NN-BGC.

93. See Michael J. Kiskis's "Afterword" in the facsimile edition of the *North American Review* installments (SLC 1996), 10–20. Other critical studies of the autobiography include Cox 1966, Krauth 1999, Robinson 2007, and Kiskis's "Introduction" to SLC 1990.

94. 3 Aug 1906 to CC, photocopy in CU-MARK. Because the TS3 batches contained excerpts from several different Autobiographical Dictations, the way they were filed in the Mark Twain Papers also created a confusing anomaly until their function was understood.

asked that the "copy of complete dictation beginning with Feb. 13 as it proceeds" be forwarded to him.[95]

Clemens soon revised and returned the proof for the first installment, first to Clara for her approval, and then to the *Review* editors. But no sooner had he done so than a new decision was made: an excerpt from the first half of "My Autobiography [Random Extracts from It]," the text that he had just recently chosen to begin the *Autobiography,* would now lead off the series. It has not been discovered who made this late change, or why, but by the end of August Clemens had read galley proofs for this "Virginia-Clemens" installment, as he called it in a letter to Mary Rogers.[96]

The first issue of "Chapters from My Autobiography" appeared on 7 September, accompanied by a statement that would be repeated before each installment:

> PREFATORY NOTE.—Mr. Clemens began to write his autobiography many years ago, and he continues to add to it day by day. It was his original intention to permit no publication of his memoirs until after his death; but, after leaving "Pier No. 70," he concluded that a considerable portion might now suitably be given to the public. It is that portion, garnered from the quarter-million of words already written, which will appear in this REVIEW during the coming year. No part of the autobiography will be published in book form during the lifetime of the author.—EDITOR N.A.R.

In the "Editor's Diary" section of the same issue Harvey "let go all holts," as Clemens might say, in an announcement of the upcoming series:

> The proverbial irony of fate was never more clearly marked than by the fact that the life of the world's greatest humorist has consisted of a succession of personal tragedies. . . . But in his breast there lived a spirit which rose triumphant over all depressing emotions, and still continues, after half a century, to make joy for more millions of human beings the world over than any other now existing. An attempt, even by one accomplished in the art, to analyze the character of this unique human genius would be futile. Its phases are too multifarious. There is humor pre-eminent, wit unexcelled, philosophy rare, if uneven; repugnance, often violent, to wrong in any form; instinctive and invariable, though occasionally ill-timed, revolt against oppression of humanity whether by God or man; all supplemented by the reasonableness of a comrade, the kindliness of a friend, the devotion of a lover and the sweetness of a child. . . . It is a wonderful autobiography that he is writing,—wonderful, because of the variety of experiences it depicts, wonderful because of its truth, its sincerity, its frankness, its unhesitating and unrestricted human feeling. . . . We have read perhaps a quarter of the million of words which will finally be written, and are convinced that a life story of such surpassing interest was never told before.[97]

95. Harvey to SLC, 3 or 4 Aug 1906, CU-MARK. Harvey carried away TS3 typescripts of selections intended for installments 1 and 5, and the third batch in progress was for installments 2, 3, and 4.

96. 25–28 Aug 1906 to Rogers, NNC, in Leary 1961, 53. By the time the early installments were published, they had been further rearranged. Harvey's note to Clemens of 3 or 4 Aug 1906, listing the batches of TS3 he was taking with him (CU-MARK), referred to installments "No. 1" and "No. 5," which ultimately became installments 3 and 2, respectively; his "Nos. 2, 3 & 4" became 4, 5, and 6.

97. Harvey 1906, 442–43. Clemens used the expression "pier No. 70" in his speech at his seventieth birthday dinner (see the Appendix, pp. 657–61).

Reading the above in proof, Clemens facetiously professed himself "troubled" and suggested to Mary Rogers that she write a letter of protest to Harvey, even providing her with a text. She was to say that Harvey's "prodigal, even extravagant" praises "sounded cold & indifferent" to him. "He is almost morbidly fond of compliments, & he realizes that these are good ones, but thinks they are over-cautious & thin. When we of the family butter him we do not do it with a knife, we use a trowel."[98]

Harvey's first round of selections, the second through sixth installments, appeared in the *Review* between 21 September and 16 November. According to Clemens, during his August visit he had actually earmarked a total of twenty-four selections—"a year's lot"—drawing on the dictations of January, March, and April 1906, "John Hay," and the second part of the "Random Extracts" sketch for installments 7–8 and 10–13, published through 1 March 1907.[99] Later material, from the dictations of October 1906 through February 1907, began to appear in installments 14 and 15, published on 15 March and 5 April 1907. Hobby made only one additional batch of TS3, for installment 16, published 19 April 1907. Apart from the dictation of 21 May 1906 ("My experiences as an author . . . "), which had been used in installment 2, no material from the dictations of May through August 1906 was published in the *Review*.[100] In those months Clemens dictated some rather stringent comments about religion, business, and various of his associates—comments he had no intention of publishing during his lifetime. Besides, there were soon so many excerpts stockpiled that the making of further selections could be safely postponed.

This basic work flow remained in place for the next sixteen months. Clemens continued to revise his typescripts, censoring or "softening" them as needed. For example, he deleted the phrase "'Stud' Williams was his society name"; altered "Plasmon thieves" to "Plasmon buccaneers"; changed his description of "Dr. Meredith's two ripe old-maid sisters" to "Dr. G.'s two middle-aged maiden sisters"; altered "a dying parishioner" to "a fictitious ailing parishioner"; and deleted "God forgive me."[101] The revised typescripts were sent to the *Review* and marked for house style by editor David A. Munro; after typesetting, the typescripts were returned to Clemens along with the galley proofs ready for correction. The editorial relationship was easygoing: Munro and Harvey offered very few substantive revisions, and Clemens often took a joking tone in his responses. He occasionally addressed remarks to Munro in the margins of the printer's copy or the galley proofs; pressing matters might be handled by mail and telegram and, conceivably, by telephone.[102]

98. 25–28 Aug 1906 to Rogers, NNC, in Leary 1961, 45–46.

99. 4 and 5 Aug 1906 to Rogers, NNC, in Leary 1961, 39. Installment 9, published on 4 Jan 1907, was based on ADs from December 1906, which consisted largely of manuscript material.

100. There were twenty-five *Review* installments in all. See the Appendix "Previous Publication" (pp. 666–67) for a list of all the excerpts and a summary of their contents.

101. See the ADs of 9 Jan, 8 Feb, 28 Mar, 12 Jan, and 9 Feb 1906.

102. For example, on the printer's copy for NAR 6 Clemens noted, "I think a date necessary now and then. I think they should be let into the *margin,* David. | M.T." He had begun adding such marginal dates to guide the reader through his nonchronological narrative when preparing "Scraps from My Autobiography. From Chapter IX" for NAR 2, but Munro had ignored them; they are adopted in this edition. And on the galley proofs of NAR 7 Clemens wrote, "David, if you don't send stamped & addressed envelops with these things I'll have your scalp! With love, Mark" (ViU; see the Textual Commentaries for the ADs of 26 Feb and 5 Mar 1906, *MTPO*). For Munro's biography see AD, 16 Jan 1906, note at 284.7.

Critical Reception and "Sunday Magazine" (1906 to 1908)

Between September and December 1906 brief excerpts from the early *North American Review* "Chapters from My Autobiography" appeared in several newspapers, accompanied by a scattering of complimentary remarks. The New York *Times,* for example, reprinted the passage from the first installment (excerpted from "My Autobiography [Random Extracts from It]") in which Clemens identified James Lampton as the real Colonel Sellers, commenting that the passage was "noteworthy" as an example of "honest self-revelation." Two weeks later the *Times* remarked that the second installment, the "story of how G. W. Carleton refused Mr. Clemens's first book and twenty years afterward called himself for so doing 'the prize ass of the nineteenth century,'" was "a good story."[103] Other reprinted passages included the Florentine Dictation about Robert Louis Stevenson; the emotional descriptions of Olivia and Susy; the humorous episode about the burglar alarm in the Hartford house; and the essay about dueling.[104] A reviewer in the Louisville, Kentucky, *Courier-Journal* (possibly its editor, Clemens's lifelong friend and distant relative Henry Watterson) called the autobiography "delightful," and while conceding that Clemens did not claim to be "strictly speaking a historian," went on to correct the inaccuracies in his account of Jeremiah and Sherrard Clemens.[105] The Washington *Post* characterized the installments as "filled with his gentle humor," and an editor of *Pearson's Magazine* noted:

> It is the old Mark Twain that speaks to us again, not the solemn reformer and critic whose heavy essays have so long afflicted a good-natured and affectionate public.... We see him frolicking with the creatures of his fancy, stirring the dust of their droll adventures and wagging his venerable head at their quaint sayings. And then we see him kneeling beside the graves of his wife and child, recalling their every look and word, and we forget the world's great humorist, knowing only the father, the husband, the true American gentleman.[106]

None of the notices of the autobiography found in contemporary newspapers and journals, however, offered any substantial critical commentary or analysis, and after the early months of 1907, the installments received little attention.

For all Clemens's insistence on publishing the *Autobiography* only long after his death, the excerpts in the *North American Review* were surprisingly important to him. Just how important became clear only when he realized how few readers had actually seen the magazine text. On 30 July 1907, nine months after the installments began, Lyon made the following entry in her journal:

---

103. New York *Times:* "Topics of the Week," 15 Sept 1906, BR568, and 29 Sept 1906, BR602; see AD, 21 May 1906.

104. See the ADs of 1 Feb, 2 Feb, 5 Feb, 8 Feb, and 19 Jan 1906.

105. "Mark Twain's Memory," Louisville (Kentucky) *Courier-Journal*, 20 Nov 1906, 6; see the explanatory notes for the "Random Extracts" sketch.

106. "Mark Twain Declares That His Wife Made Him Swear off Swearing," Washington *Post,* 16 Dec 1906, B8; "The Two Sides of It," *Pearson's Magazine,* Jan 1907, 117; this journal was an American affiliate of the British journal of the same name, devoted to literature, politics, and the arts.

Evidently the N.A. Review is on very shaky legs, for the Colonel asked Mᵣ Clemens to wait for the autobiographical monies that are due him; to wait until the first of the year, for funds are low & he must borrow if he pays. It annoyed the King—for it is, as he says, "doing business through sentimental channels[ⁿ]—& he doesn't like it atall. And it isn't fair to the King.[107]

One result of this problem was that between 27 October 1907 and 27 September 1908 the *North American Review* chapters were reprinted, with newly commissioned illustrations, as a series in the weekly "Sunday Magazine," a supplement that was syndicated in many large-circulation newspapers. Harvey himself proposed the syndication, but he implied that greater circulation was his only concern, not how much money it made. Lyon noted on 6 September 1907 that Harvey

> got the King's consent—his glad consent—to syndicate the autobiography in newspapers throughout the country & so the King will reach his "submerged clientele." It will not bring him in a penny though. If any one gets anything it will be the Harpers & they will not get much for the newspapers do not pay much for matter—no matter how great—which has been already published. It will be a good advertisement for the King's books though.[108]

Clemens hoped that this syndication would expose his work to a very different class of readers. He was undoubtedly pleased, and he even praised his portrait by F. Luis Mora that accompanied the first installment reprinted in "Sunday Magazine."[109] Many years later, on 28 October 1941, the artist John Thomson Willing, who was the art editor of the Associated Sunday Magazines at the time of the syndication, wrote to an unidentified correspondent in response to a "request for Mark Twain stories":

> I had charge of the serial issuing of his autobiography in the Sunday Magazine[,] a supplement to many important papers and aggregating nearly two million copies a week. This autobiography was first begun in The North American Review, edited by George Harvey,—published by Harper Bros   Mr Clemens was much dissatisfied by the limited circulation of this Review and so arranged for the larger distribution of the newspapers. When I showed him the initial copy of our magazine with the heading *Autobiography of Mark Twain* as the title he turned to me and said "Barkis, you have left something out. It should have added *'Hitherto confidentially circulated'*"—referring to its having run in the Review—[110]

Autobiography as Literature (1909)

Not surprisingly, in 1907 and 1908 the intensity of Clemens's interest in adding to the autobiography gradually abated. In each successive year the number of dictations declined by half,

---

107. Lyon 1907, entry for 30 July.

108. Lyon 1907, entry for 9 Sept.

109. See Schmidt 2009b for a detailed comparison of the syndicated texts with those in the *North American Review*, access to almost all the illustrations, and a record of newspapers known to have carried "Sunday Magazine."

110. Willing to Unidentified, 28 Oct 1941, photocopy in CU-MARK; Clemens's words to Willing were a pun on the catch-phrase "Barkis is willing" from *David Copperfield* (chapter 5).

they became briefer, and the proportion of inserted clippings and other documents grew larger. By 1908 much of what he produced for the autobiography was actually original manuscript that he *labeled* as dictation. When on 24 December 1909 he wrote that because of Jean's death "this Autobiography closes here," he had in fact produced fewer than twelve new pages of typescript in the previous eight months.

In 1910, after Clemens's death, Howells reported in *My Mark Twain* that at some point Clemens had "suddenly" told him he was no longer working on the autobiography, although Howells was unclear whether Clemens "had finished it or merely dropped it; I never asked." He also recalled that at the outset of his work Clemens had intended the autobiography to be "a perfectly veracious record of his life and period," but he now admitted that "as to veracity it was a failure; he had begun to lie, and that if no man ever yet told the truth about himself it was because no man ever could."[111] Of course, by 1904 Clemens had already convinced himself, by experiment, that an autobiography "consists mainly of extinctions of the truth," even if "the remorseless truth *is* there, between the lines." And in April 1906 he had said in one of his dictations,

> I have been dictating this autobiography of mine daily for three months; I have thought of fifteen hundred or two thousand incidents in my life which I am ashamed of, but I have not gotten one of them to consent to go on paper yet. I think that that stock will still be complete and unimpaired when I finish these memoirs, if I ever finish them. I believe that if I should put in all or any of those incidents I should be sure to strike them out when I came to revise this book.[112]

We have seen that in 1898 Clemens had been so discouraged by this insight that he (temporarily) decided to change the very nature of his autobiography. But there is good reason to suppose that by the time of his death he had reached a more enlightened understanding of what his or anyone else's autobiography could accomplish. In mid-1909 he was asked whether his remarks about the Tennessee land as published in the *North American Review* were true. "Yes," he replied, "literarily they are true, that is to say they are a product of my impressions—recollections. As sworn testimony they are not worth anything; they are merely literature."[113]

A hundred years have now passed since Clemens's death. It certainly seems fitting that his plan for publishing the *Autobiography of Mark Twain* in its entirety should just now be recovered from his vast accumulation of papers, and that the *Autobiography*'s standing and value as "literature" be at last recognized. This edition, prepared by his editors (if not his "heirs and assigns"), relies on the eloquent evidence of historical documents to understand and carry out his wishes for this, his last major literary work. His long-standing plan to speak as truthfully as possible "from the grave" is no longer just a plan. And as Colonel Harvey predicted more

111. Howells 1910, 93–94.

112. AD, 6 Apr 1906.

113. Clemens was giving a deposition as a plaintiff in a lawsuit involving the land ("Interrogatories for Saml. L. Clemens," filed 3 April 1909, and "Deposition S.L. Clemens," filed 11 June 1909, U.S. National Archives and Records Administration 1907–9; copies of these documents provided courtesy of Barbara Schmidt).

than a hundred years ago, the *Autobiography* is being published both as printed volumes and "by electrical method," a fact that would no doubt have appealed to Mark Twain's "vivid imagination."[114]

Harriet Elinor Smith
Mark Twain Project, Berkeley

114. For Harvey's 17 Oct 1900 draft of publishing terms for Clemens's "memoirs in the year 2000," see p. 19 above. For details of the textual policy and practices applied throughout this edition, see "Note on the Text," pp. 669–79.

PRELIMINARY MANUSCRIPTS
AND DICTATIONS

1870–1905

Clemens wrote this manuscript, now in the Mark Twain Papers, sometime in 1870, leaving it incomplete and without a title (but with space for one on the first page). It is the earliest extant manuscript that might fairly be called a draft chapter for his autobiography, although he did not explicitly identify it as such. He evidently planned to publish it in some way, for he changed the reference to his father's nemesis from "Ira Stout" to "Ira ———."

The text has never been accurately published before. Albert Bigelow Paine did include it in *Mark Twain's Autobiography* under the title he gave it, "The Tennessee Land," but he silently omitted the anecdote at the end of the third paragraph (beginning with "A venerable lady . . . ") and changed Clemens's description of his father as a "candidate for county judge, with a certainty of election" to say instead that he "had been elected to the clerkship of the Surrogate Court" (*MTA,* 1:3–6; neither description is accurate: see the Appendix "Family Biographies," p. 654). Charles Neider reprinted the text from the manuscript, restoring the anecdote omitted by Paine but adopting Paine's changed description of John Marshall Clemens; he also made dozens of his own omissions and changes, and he appended two paragraphs from "My Autobiography [Random Extracts from It]," written in Vienna in 1897–98 (*AMT,* 22–24). Clemens returned to the subject of the Tennessee land in that manuscript and in the Autobiographical Dictation of 5 April 1906.

John Marshall Clemens's land purchases and the family's subsequent sales of the land have been only partly documented from independent sources. The extant grants, deeds, and bills of sale are incomplete, but it was also the case that contradictory or inaccurate deeds often led to disputed claims. Orion Clemens referred to one cause of such conflict in a letter to his brother on 7 July 1869, alleging that "Tennessee grants the same land over and over again to different parties" (OC to SLC, 7 July 1869, CU-MARK, quoted in 3? July 1869 to OC, *L3,* 279 n. 1 [bottom]; for family correspondence on the subject from 1853 to 1870, see *L1, L2, L3,* and *L4*).

[The Tennessee Land]

The monster tract of land which our family own in Tennessee, was purchased by my father a little over forty years ago. He bought the enormous area of seventy-five thousand acres at one purchase. The entire lot must have cost him somewhere in the neighborhood of four hundred dollars. That was a good deal of money to pass over at one payment in those days—at least it was so considered away up there in the pineries and the "Knobs" of the Cumberland Mountains of Fentress county, East Tennessee. When my father paid down that great sum, and turned and stood in the courthouse door of Jamestown, and looked abroad over his vast possessions, he said: "Whatever befalls me, my heirs are secure; I shall not live to see these acres turn to silver and gold, but my children will." Thus, with the very kindest intentions in the world toward us, he laid the heavy curse of prospective wealth upon our shoulders. He went to his grave in the full belief that he had done us a kindness. It was a woful mistake, but fortunately he never knew it.

He further said: "Iron ore is abundant in this tract, and there are other minerals; there are thousands of acres of the finest yellow pine timber in America, and it can be rafted down Obeds river to the Cumberland, down the Cumberland to the Ohio, down the Ohio to the Mississippi, and down the Mississippi to any community that wants it. There is no end to the tar, pitch and turpentine which these vast pineries will yield. This is a natural wine district, too; there are no vines elsewhere in America, cultivated or otherwise, that yield such grapes as grow wild here. There are grazing lands, corn lands, wheat lands, potato lands, there are all species of timber—there is everything in and on this great tract of land that can make land valuable. The United States contain fourteen millions of inhabitants; the population has increased eleven millions in forty years, and will henceforth increase faster than ever; my children will see the day that immigration will push its way to Fentress county, Tennessee, and then, with seventy-five thousand acres of excellent land in their hands, they will become fabulously wealthy."

Everything my father said about the capabilities of the land was perfectly true—and he could have added with like truth, that there were inexhaustible mines of coal on the land, but the chances are that he knew very little about the article, for the innocent Tennesseeans were not accustomed to digging in the earth for their fuel. And my father might have added to the list of eligibilities, that the land was only a hundred miles from Knoxville, and right where some future line of railway leading south from Cincinnati could not help but pass through it. But he never had seen a railway, and it is barely possible that he had not even heard of such a thing. Curious as it may seem, as late as eight years ago there were people living close to James-town who never had heard of a railroad and could not be brought to believe in steamboats. They do not vote for Jackson in Fentress county, they vote for Washington. A venerable lady of that locality said of her son: "Jim's come back from Kaintuck and fotch a stuck-up gal with him from up thar; and bless you they've got more new-fangled notions, massy *on* us! Common log house ain't good enough for *them*—no indeedy!—but they've tuck 'n' gaumed the inside of theirn all over with some kind of nasty disgustin' truck which they say is all the go in Kain-tuck amongst the upper hunky, and which they calls it *plarsterin'!*"

My eldest brother was four or five years old when the great purchase was made, and my eldest sister was an infant in arms. The rest of us—and we formed the great bulk of the family—came afterwards, and were born along from time to time during the next ten years. Four years after the purchase came the great financial crash of '34, and in that storm my father's fortunes were wrecked. From being honored and envied as the most opulent citizen of Fentress county—for outside of his great landed possessions he was considered to be worth not less than three thousand five hundred dollars—he suddenly woke up and found himself reduced to less than one-fourth of that amount. He was a proud man, a silent, austere man, and not a person likely to abide among the scenes of his vanished grandeur and be the target for public commiseration. He gathered together his household and journeyed many tedious days through wilderness solitudes, toward what was then the "Far West," and at last pitched his tent in the almost invis-ible little town of Florida, Monroe county, Missouri. He "kept store" there several years, but had no luck, except that I was born to him. He presently removed to Hannibal, and prospered somewhat, and rose to the dignity of justice of the peace, and was candidate for county judge, with a certainty of election, when the summons came which no man may disregard. He had been doing tolerably well, for that age of the world, during the first years of his residence in Hannibal, but ill fortune tripped him once more. He did the friendly office of "going security" for Ira ——, and Ira —— walked off and deliberately took the benefit of the new bankrupt law—a deed which enabled him to live easily and comfortably along till death called for him, but a deed which ruined my father, sent him poor to his grave, and condemned his heirs to a long and discouraging struggle with the world for a livelihood. But my father would brighten up and gather heart, even upon his death-bed, when he thought of the Tennessee land. He said that it would soon make us all rich and happy. And so believing, he died.

We straightway turned our waiting eyes upon Tennessee. Through all our wanderings and all our ups and downs for thirty years they have still gazed thitherward, over intervening continents and seas, and at this very day they are yet looking toward the same fixed point, with the hope of old habit and a faith that rises and falls, but never dies.

After my father's death we reorganized the domestic establishment, but on a temporary basis, intending to arrange it permanently after the land was sold. My brother borrowed five hundred dollars and bought a worthless weekly newspaper, believing, as we all did, that it was not worth while to go at anything in serious earnest until the land was disposed of and we could embark intelligently in something. We rented a large house to live in, at first, but we were disappointed in a sale we had expected to make (the man wanted only a part of the land and we talked it over and decided to sell all or none,) and we were obliged to move to a less expensive one.

Paine published this manuscript, with typical errors and omissions, under a title he contrived for it, "Early Years in Florida, Missouri" (*MTA*, 1:7–10). The text itself shows that Clemens wrote it in 1877, heading it simply "Chap. 1" (omitted by Paine). Neider copied Paine's version (errors and all), but he left off the last sixty words and inserted three paragraphs from "My Autobiography [Random Extracts from It]," two after the first sentence and one at the end (*AMT*, 1–3). It seems likely that the manuscript was the "beginning," or one of the beginnings, of an autobiography that Clemens made in response to prodding from his friend John Milton Hay (see "John Hay"). The manuscript was doubtless part of the Mark Twain Papers on which Paine drew for the biography and other works, but in about 1920 he gave the manuscript to the American Academy of Arts and Letters, where it now resides.

[Early Years in Florida, Missouri]

Chapter 1

I was born the 30th of November, 1835, in the almost invisible village of Florida, Monroe county, Missouri. I suppose Florida had less than three hundred inhabitants. It had two streets, each a couple of hundred yards long; the rest of the avenues mere lanes, with rail fences and corn fields on either side. Both the streets and the lanes were paved with the same material— tough black mud, in wet times, deep dust in dry.

Most of the houses were of logs—all of them, indeed, except three or four; these latter were frame ones. There were none of brick, and none of stone. There was a log church, with a puncheon floor and slab benches. A puncheon floor is made of logs whose upper surfaces have been chipped flat with the adze. The cracks between the logs were not filled; there was no carpet; consequently, if you dropped anything smaller than a peach, it was likely to go through. The church was perched upon short sections of logs, which elevated it two or three feet from the ground. Hogs slept under there, and whenever the dogs got after them during services, the minister had to wait till the disturbance was over. In winter there was always a refreshing breeze up through the puncheon floor; in summer there were fleas enough for all.

A slab bench is made of the outside cut of a saw-log, with the bark side down; it is supported on four sticks driven into augur-holes at the ends; it has no back, and no cushions. The church was twilighted with yellow tallow candles in tin sconces hung against the walls. Week-days, the church was a schoolhouse.

There were two stores in the village. My uncle, John A. Quarles, was proprietor of one of them. It was a very small establishment, with a few rolls of "bit" calicoes in half a dozen shelves, a few barrels of salt mackerel, coffee, and New Orleans sugar behind the counter, stacks of brooms, shovels, axes, hoes, rakes, and such things, here and there, a lot of cheap hats, bonnets and tin-ware strung on strings and suspended from the walls; and at the other end of the room was another counter with bags of shot on it, a cheese or two, and a keg of powder; in front of it a row of nail kegs and a few pigs of lead; and behind it a barrel or two of New Orleans molasses and native corn whisky on tap. If a boy bought five or ten cents' worth of anything, he was entitled to half a handful of sugar from the barrel; if a woman bought a few yards of calico she was entitled to a spool of thread in addition to the usual gratis "trimmins;" if a man bought a trifle, he was at liberty to draw and swallow as big a drink of whisky as he wanted.

Everything was cheap: apples, peaches, sweet potatoes, Irish potatoes, and corn, ten cents a bushel; chickens ten cents apiece, butter six cents a pound, eggs three cents a dozen, coffee and sugar five cents a pound, whisky ten cents a gallon. I do not know how prices are out there in interior Missouri now, (1877,) but I know what they are here in Hartford, Connecticut. To wit: apples, three dollars a bushel; peaches five dollars; Irish potatoes (choice Bermudas), five dollars; chickens a dollar to a dollar and a half apiece according to weight; butter forty-five to sixty cents a pound, eggs fifty to sixty cents a dozen; coffee forty-five cents a pound; sugar about the same; native whisky four or five dollars a gallon, I believe, but I can only be certain concerning the sort which I use myself, which is Scotch and costs ten dollars a gallon when you take two gallons—more when you take less.

Thirty and forty years ago, out yonder in Missouri, the ordinary cigar cost thirty cents a hundred, but most people did not try to afford them, since smoking a pipe cost nothing in that tobacco-growing country. Connecticut is also given up to tobacco raising, to-day, yet we pay ten dollars a hundred for Connecticut cigars and fifteen to twenty-five dollars a hundred for the imported article.

At first my father owned slaves, but by and by he sold them, and hired others by the year from the farmers. For a girl of fifteen he paid twelve dollars a year and gave her two linsey-wolsey frocks and a pair of "stogy" shoes—cost, a modification of nothing; for a negro woman of twenty-five, as general house servant, he paid twenty-five dollars a year and gave her shoes and the aforementioned linsey-wolsey frocks; for a strong negro woman of forty, as cook, washer, etc., he paid forty dollars a year and the customary two suits of clothes; and for an able bodied man he paid from seventy-five to a hundred dollars a year and gave him two suits of jeans and two pairs of "stogy" shoes—an outfit that cost about three dollars. But times have changed. We pay our German nursemaid $155 a year; Irish housemaid, $150; Irish laundress, $150; negro woman, as cook, $240; young negro man, to wait on door and table, $360; Irish coachman, $600 a year, with gas, hot and cold water, and dwelling consisting of parlor, kitchen and two bed-rooms, connected with the stable, free.

THE GRANT DICTATIONS

The following six typed dictations, known ever since Paine published them (out of order) in 1924 as "The Grant Dictations" (*MTA,* 1:13–70), are now in the Mark Twain Papers. They were all created in May and June 1885; Clemens dictated to his friend and colleague James Redpath, who transcribed his shorthand notes on an all-capitals typewriter (for Redpath see "Lecture-Times," note at 148.8). Redpath then reviewed the typescripts, adding punctuation but overlooking many errors, and passed them on to Clemens, who lightly revised and corrected them. They make up the earliest known substantial body of texts that Clemens said were intended for his autobiography. The subjects he covered were all of recent date, and all touch on one aspect or another of his relationship with Ulysses S. Grant, who was by then dying of throat cancer. The six dictations are here printed for the first time in the order they were created.

- "The Chicago G.A.R. Festival" is about Clemens's experience, including his toast to "The Babies," when Grant was honored at the convention of the Grand Army of the Republic in 1879. This is the only one of the six Grant dictations that Neider chose to reprint, and he followed Paine's text in all of its details (*AMT,* 241–45).
- "A Call with W.D. Howells on General Grant" treats three seemingly unrelated topics: Grant's help for the father of William Dean Howells, Grant's appreciation of George Horatio Derby (John Phoenix), and Clemens's own efforts to persuade Grant to write his memoirs. The title adopted here was supplied by Paine.
- "Grant and the Chinese" describes Grant's efforts to preserve a program for educating Chinese students in the United States.
- "Gerhardt" (previously unpublished) is about the frustration that Clemens's protégé, the sculptor Karl Gerhardt, experienced in competing to make a statue of Nathan Hale. Gerhardt also made a commercially successful bust of Grant, discussed in the fifth dictation, "About General Grant's Memoirs."
- "About General Grant's Memoirs," a long and detailed account of how Clemens secured the contract for Grant's *Personal Memoirs,* was written to some extent in response to newspaper comments insinuating that he had done so unethically. Paine published the first section and part of the third as continuous text, and made the middle section into a separate dictation, which he titled "Gerhardt and the Grant Bust"; he also omitted the newspaper clippings at the end of this section.
- "The Rev. Dr. Newman" is about Grant's spiritual adviser during the days approaching his death on 23 July 1885. Paine suppressed the identity of the Reverend John Philip Newman, altering every mention of his name to "N——." He also provided the title adopted here.

Clemens was not pleased with the text that Redpath prepared. As he explained to Henry Ward Beecher after he had called a halt to his dictation, this part of the autobiography was "pretty freely dictated, but my idea is to jack-plane it a little before I die, some day or other; I mean the rude construction & rotten grammar. It is the only dictating I ever did, & it was most troublesome & awkward work" (11 Sept 1885, CU-MARK). Clemens never did polish the texts or prepare them for publication. In fact, many years after his death his former secretary, Isabel Lyon, annotated a copy of Paine's edition, saying in part that "Mr Clemens would not have allowed" the Grant dictations "to be included in the autobiography without serious editing. . . . These Redpath notes were *notes* only, & held for drastic revision" (page 13, quoted courtesy of Kevin MacDonnell). Clemens did go on to retell the story of his involvement with Grant's memoirs in his 1906 Autobiographical Dictations (see "About General Grant's Memoirs," note at 75.28).

The Chicago G. A. R. Festival

1866.

The first time I ever saw General Grant was in the fall or winter of 1866 at one of the receptions at Washington, when he was General of the Army. I merely saw and shook hands with him along with a general crowd but had no conversation. It was there also that I first saw General Sheridan.

I next saw General Grant during his first term as President.

Senator Bill Stewart of Nevada proposed to take me in and see the President. We found him in his working costume with an old short linen duster on and it was well spattered with ink. I had acquired some trifle of notoriety through some letters which I had written in the New York Tribune during my trip round about the world in the *Quaker City* expedition. I shook hands and then there was a pause and silence. I couldn't think of anything to say. So I merely looked into the General's grim, immovable countenance a moment or two in silence and then I said: "Mr. President, I am embarrassed—are you?" He smiled a smile which would have done no discredit to a cast-iron image, and I got away under the smoke of my volley.

I did not see him again for some ten years. In the meantime I had become very thoroughly notorious.

Then, in 1879 the General had just returned from his journey through the European and Asiatic world and his progress from San Francisco eastward had been one continuous ovation and now he was to be feasted in Chicago by the veterans of the Army of the Tennessee—the first army over which he had had command. The preparations for this occasion were in keeping with the importance of it. The toast committee telegraphed me and asked me if I would be present and respond at the grand banquet to the toast to the ladies. I telegraphed back that the toast was worn out. Everything had been said about the ladies that could be said at a banquet, but there was one class of the community that had always been overlooked upon such occasions and if they would allow me I would take that class for a toast: "The Babies." They were willing—so I prepared my toast and went out to Chicago.

There was to be a prodigious procession. General Grant was to review it from a rostrum which had been built out for the purpose from the second story window of the Palmer House. The rostrum was carpeted and otherwise glorified with flags and so on.

The best place of all to see the procession was of course from this rostrum. So I sauntered upon that rostrum while as yet it was empty in the hope that I might be permitted to sit there. It was rather a conspicuous place, since upon it the public gaze was fixed, and there was a countless multitude below. Presently two gentlemen came upon that platform from the window of the hotel and stepped forward to the front. A prodigious shout went up from the vast multitude below, and I recognized in one of these two gentlemen General Grant.

The other was Carter Harrison, the mayor of Chicago, with whom I was acquainted. He saw me, stepped over to me and said wouldn't I like to be introduced to the General? I said, I should. So he walked over with me and said, "General, let me introduce Mr. Clemens," and we shook hands. There was the usual momentary pause and then the General said: "I am not embarrassed—are you?"

It showed that he had a good memory for trifles as well as for serious things.

That banquet was by all odds the most notable one I was ever present at. There were six hundred persons present, mainly veterans of the Army of the Tennessee, and that in itself would have made it a most notable occasion of the kind in my experience but there were other things which contributed. General Sherman and in fact nearly all of the surviving great Generals of the war sat in a body on a dais round about General Grant.

The speakers were of a rare celebrity and ability.

That night I heard for the first time a slang expression which had already come into considerable vogue but I had not myself heard it before.

When the speaking began about ten o'clock I left my place at the table and went away over to the front side of the great dining room where I could take in the whole spectacle at one glance. Among others, Colonel Vilas was to respond to a toast and also Colonel Ingersoll, the silver-tongued infidel, who had begun life in Illinois, and was exceedingly popular there. Vilas was from Wisconsin and was very famous as an orator. He had prepared himself superbly for this occasion.

He was about the first speaker on the list of fifteen toasts and Bob Ingersoll was the ninth.

I had taken a position upon the steps in front of the brass band, which lifted me up and gave me a good general view. Presently I noticed, leaning against the wall near me, a simple-looking young man wearing the uniform of a private and the badge of the Army of the Tennessee. He seemed to be nervous and ill at ease about something. Presently, while the second speaker was talking, this young man said: "Do you know Colonel Vilas?" I said I had been introduced to him. He sat silent a while and then said: "They say he is hell when he gets started!"

I said: "In what way? What do you mean?"

"Speaking! Speaking! They say he is lightning!"

"Yes," I said, "I have heard that he is a great speaker."

The young man shifted about uneasily for a while and then he said: "Do you reckon he can get away with Bob Ingersoll?"

I said: "I don't know."

Another pause. Occasionally he and I would join in the applause when a speaker was on his legs, but this young man seemed to applaud unconsciously.

Presently he said, "Here in Illinois we think there can't nobody get away with Bob Ingersoll."

I said: "Is that so?"

He said, "Yes: we don't think anybody can lay over Bob Ingersoll."

Then he added sadly, "But they do say that Vilas is pretty nearly hell."

At last Vilas rose to speak, and this young man pulled himself together and put on all his anxiety. Vilas began to warm up and the people began to applaud. He delivered himself of one especially fine passage and there was a general shout: "Get up on the table! Get up on the table! Stand up on the table! We can't see you!" So a lot of men standing there picked Vilas up and stood him on the table in full view of the whole great audience and he went on with his speech. The young man applauded with the rest, and I could hear the young fellow mutter without being able to make out what he said. But presently when Vilas thundered out something especially fine, there was a tremendous outburst from the whole house and then this young man said in a sort of despairing way:

"It ain't no use: Bob can't climb up to that!"

During the next hour he held his position against the wall in a sort of dazed abstraction, apparently unconscious of place or of anything else, and at last when Ingersoll mounted the supper table his worshipper merely straightened up to an attitude of attention but without manifesting any hope.

Ingersoll with his fair and fresh complexion, handsome figure and graceful carriage was beautiful to look at.

He was to respond to the toast of "The Volunteers," and his first sentence or two showed his quality. As his third sentence fell from his lips the house let go with a crash, and my private looked pleased and for the first time hopeful but he had been too much frightened to join in the applause. Presently, when Ingersoll came to the passage in which he said that these volunteers had shed their blood and perilled their lives in order that a mother might own her own child, the language was so fine, whatever it was, for I have forgotten, and the delivery was so superb that the vast multitude rose as one man and stood on their feet, shouting, stamping, and filling all the place with such a waving of napkins that it was like a snow storm. This prodigious outburst continued for a minute or two, Ingersoll standing and waiting. And now I happened to notice my private. He was stamping, clapping, shouting, gesticulating like a man who had gone truly mad. At last when quiet was restored once more, he glanced up to me with the tears in his eyes and said:

"Egod! He *didn't* get left!"

———————

My own speech was granted the perilous distinction of the place of honor. It was the last speech on the list, an honor which no person, probably, has ever sought. It was not reached until two o'clock in the morning. But when I got on my feet I knew that there was at any rate one point in my favor: the text was bound to have the sympathy of nine-tenths of the men present and of every woman, married or single, of the crowds of the sex who stood huddled in the various doorways.

I expected the speech to go off well—and it did.

In it I had a drive at General Sheridan's comparatively new twins and various other things calculated to make it go. There was only one thing in it that I had fears about, and that one thing stood where it could not be removed in case of disaster.

It was the last sentence in the speech.

I had been picturing the America of fifty years hence, with a population of two hundred million souls, and was saying that the future President, Admirals and so forth of that great coming time were now lying in their various cradles, scattered abroad over the vast expanse of this country, and then said "And now in his cradle somewhere under the flag the future illustrious Commander-in-Chief of the American armies is so little burdened with his approaching grandeur and responsibilities as to be giving his whole strategic mind at this moment to trying to find out some way to get his big toe into his mouth—something, meaning no disrespect to the illustrious guest of this evening, which he turned his entire attention to some fifty-six years ago"—

And here, as I had expected, the laughter ceased and a sort of shuddering silence took its place—for this was apparently carrying the matter too far.

I waited a moment or two to let this silence sink well home.

Then, turning toward the General I added:

"And if the child is but the father of the man there are mighty few who will doubt that he succeeded."

Which relieved the house: for when they saw the General break up in good-sized pieces they followed suit with great enthusiasm.

[A Call with W. D. Howells on General Grant]

Howells

1881.

Howells wrote me that his old father, who is well along in the seventies, was in great distress about his poor little consulate, up in Quebec. Somebody not being satisfied with the degree of poverty already conferred upon him by a thoughtful and beneficent Providence, was anxious to add to it by acquiring the Quebec consulate. So Howells thought that if we could get General Grant to say a word to President Arthur it might have the effect of stopping this effort to oust old Mr. Howells from his position. Therefore, at my suggestion Howells came down and we went to New York to lay the matter before the General. We found him at number 2, Wall street, in the principal office of Grant and Ward, brokers.

I stated the case and asked him if he wouldn't write a word on a card which Howells could carry to Washington and hand to the President.

But, as usual, General Grant was his natural self—that is to say, ready and also determined to do a great deal more for you than you could possibly have the effrontery to ask him to do. Apparently he never meets anybody half way: he comes nine-tenths of the way himself voluntarily. "No" he said,—he would do better than that and cheerfully: he was going to Washington in a couple of days to dine with the President and he would speak to him himself and make it a personal matter. Now as General Grant not only never forgets a promise but never even the shadow of a promise, he did as he said he would do, and within a week came a letter from the Secretary of State, Mr. Frelinghuysen, to say that in no case would old Mr. Howells be disturbed. [And he wasn't. He resigned, a couple of years later.]

Grant and Derby

1881.

But to go back to the interview with General Grant, he was in a humor to talk—in fact he was always in a humor to talk when no strangers were present—and he resisted all our efforts to leave him.

He forced us to stay and take luncheon in a private room and continued to talk all the time. [It was bacon and beans. Nevertheless, "How he sits and towers"—Howells, quoting from Dante.]

He remembered "Squibob" Derby at West Point very well. He said that Derby was forever drawing caricatures of the professors and playing jokes of all kinds on everybody. He also told of one thing, which I had heard before, but which I have never seen in print. At West Point, the professor was instructing and questioning a class concerning certain particulars of a possible siege and he said this, as nearly as I can remember: I cannot quote General Grant's words:

Given: That a thousand men are besieging a fortress whose equipment of men, provisions, etc., are so and so—it is a military axiom that at the end of forty-five days the fort will surrender. Now, young men, if any of you were in command of such a fortress, how would you proceed?

Derby held up his hand in token that he had an answer for that question. He said: "I would march out, let the enemy in, and at the end of forty-five days I would change places with him."

Grant's Memoirs

1881.

I tried very hard to get General Grant to write his personal memoirs for publication but he would not listen to the suggestion. His inborn diffidence made him shrink from voluntarily coming forward before the public and placing himself under criticism as an author. He had no confidence in his ability to write well, whereas I and everybody else in the world excepting himself are aware that he possesses an admirable literary gift and style. He was also sure that the book would have no sale and of course that would be a humiliation, too. He instanced the fact that General Badeau's military history of General Grant had had but a trifling sale, and that John Russell Young's account of General Grant's trip around the globe had hardly any sale at all. But I said that these were not instances in point; that what another man might tell about General Grant was nothing, while what General Grant should tell about himself with his own pen was a totally different thing. I said that the book would have an enormous sale: that it should be in two volumes sold in cash at $3 50 apiece, and that the sale in two volumes would certainly reach half a million sets. I said that from my experience I could save him from making unwise contracts with publishers and could also suggest the best plan of publication— the subscription plan—and find for him the best men in that line of business.

I had in my mind at that time the American Publishing Company of Hartford, and while I suspected that they had been swindling me for ten years I was well aware that I could arrange the contract in such a way that they could not swindle General Grant. But the General said that he had no necessity for any addition to his income. I knew that he meant by that that his investments through the firm in which his sons were partners were paying him all the money he needed. So I was not able to persuade him to write a book. He said that some day he would make very full notes and leave them behind him and then if his children chose to make them into a book that would answer.

Grant and the Chinese

1884.

Early in this year or late in 1883, if my memory serves me, I called on General Grant with Yung Wing, late Chinese Minister at Washington, to introduce Wing and let him lay before General Grant a proposition. Li-Hung-Chang, one of the greatest and most progressive men in China since the death of Prince Kung, had been trying to persuade the Imperial government to build a system of military railroads in China, and had so far succeeded in his persuasions that a majority of the government were willing to consider the matter—provided that money could be obtained for that purpose, outside of China—this money to be raised upon the customs of the country and by bonding the railway or some such way. Yung Wing believed that if General Grant would take charge of the matter here and create the syndicate the money would be easily forthcoming. He also knew that General Grant was better and more favorably known in China than any other foreigner in the world and was aware that if his name were associated with the enterprise—the syndicate—it would inspire the Chinese government and people and give them the greatest possible sense of security. We found the General cooped up in his room with a severe rheumatism resulting from a fall on the ice, which he had got some months before. He would not undertake a syndicate, because times were so hard here that people would be loath to invest money so far away. Of course Yung Wing's proposal included a liberal compensation for General Grant for his trouble, but that was a thing that the General would not listen to for a moment. He said that easier times would come by and bye, and that the money could then be raised, no doubt, and that he would enter into it cheerfully and with zeal and carry it through to the very best of his ability, but he must do it without compensation. In no case would he consent to take any money for it. Here again he manifested the very strongest interest in China, an interest which I had seen him evince on previous occasions. He said he had urged a system of railways on Li-Hung-Chang when he was in China and he now felt so sure that such a system would be a great salvation for the country and also the beginning of the country's liberation from the Tartar rule and thraldom that he would be quite willing at a favorable time to do everything he could toward carrying out that project without other compensation than the pleasure he would derive from being useful to China.

This reminds me of one other circumstance.

About 1879 or 1880, the Chinese pupils in Hartford and other New England towns had been ordered home by the Chinese government. There were two parties in the Chinese government: one headed by Li-Hung-Chang, the progressive party, which was striving to introduce Western arts and education into China, and the other was opposed to all progressive measures. Li-Hung-Chang and the progressive party kept the upper hand for some time and during this period the government had sent one hundred or more of the country's choicest youth over here to be educated. But now the other party had got the upper hand and had ordered these young people home. At this time an old Chinaman named Wong, non-progressionist, was the chief China Minister at Washington and Yung Wing was his assistant. The order disbanding the schools was a great blow to Yung Wing, who had spent many years in working for their establishment. This order came upon him with the suddenness of a thunder clap. He did not know which way to turn.

First, he got a petition signed by the Presidents of various American colleges setting forth the great progress that the Chinese pupils had made and offering arguments to show why the pupils should be allowed to remain to finish their education. This paper was to be conveyed to the Chinese government through the Minister at Pekin. But Yung Wing felt the need of a more powerful voice in the matter and General Grant occurred to him. He thought that if he could get General Grant's great name added to that petition that that alone would outweigh the signatures of a thousand college professors. So the Rev. Mr. Twichell and I went down to New York to see the General. I introduced Mr. Twichell, who had come with a careful speech for the occasion in which he intended to load the General with information concerning the Chinese pupils and the Chinese question generally. But he never got the chance to deliver it. The General took the word out of his mouth and talked straight ahead and easily revealed to Twichell the fact that the General was master of the whole matter and needed no information from anybody and also the fact that he was brimful of interest in the matter. Now as always the General was not only ready to do what we asked of him but a hundred times more. He said yes, he would sign that paper if desired, but he would do better than that: he would write a personal letter to Li-Hung-Chang and do it immediately. So Twichell and I went down stairs into the lobby of the Fifth Avenue Hotel, a crowd of waiting and anxious visitors sitting in the anteroom, and in the course of half an hour he sent for us again and put into our hands his letter to Li-Hung-Chang to be sent directly and without the intervention of the American Minister or any one else. It was a clear, compact and admirably written statement of the case of the Chinese pupils with some equally clear arguments to show that the breaking up of the schools would be a mistake. We shipped the letter and prepared to wait a couple of months to see what the result would be.

But we had not to wait so long. The moment the General's letter reached China a telegram came back from the Chinese government which was almost a copy in detail of General Grant's letter and the cablegram ended with the peremptory command to old Minister Wong to continue the Chinese schools.

It was a marvelous exhibition of the influence of a private citizen of one country over the counsels of an empire situated on the other side of the globe. Such an influence could have been wielded by no other citizen in the world outside of that empire—in fact the policy of the Imperial government had been reversed from room 45, Fifth Avenue Hotel, New York, by a private citizen of the United States.

Gerhardt

1884. (September: at the farm at Elmira.)

Gerhardt arrived home from Paris,—leaving his wife and his little boy behind him. He had found living much more expensive at Paris than it had been in J. Q. A. Ward's day. Consequently Ward's estimate of $3,000 for five years had fallen woefully short. Gerhardt's expenses for three years and a half had already amounted to $6,000. There was nothing for him to do—so he made a bust of me in the hope that it might bring him work. The times were very hard and he was not able to get anything to do.

(October.)

About this time Gerhardt heard that a competition was about ready to begin for a statue of Nathan Hale, the Revolutionary spy and patriot caught and hanged by the British. This statue had been voted by the Connecticut Legislature and the munificent price to be paid for it was $5,000. The speech which ex-Governor Hubbard had made in advocacy of the proposition was worth four times the sum.

The committee in whose hands the Legislature had placed the matter consisted of Mr. Coit, a railroad man, of New London, a modest, sensible, honorable, worthy gentleman, who while wholly unacquainted with art and confessing it, was willing and anxious to do his duty in the matter. Another committeeman was an innocent ass by the name of Barnard, who knew nothing about art and in fact about nothing else, and if he had a mind was not able to make it up on any question. As for any sense of duty, that feature was totally lacking in him—he had no notion of it whatever. The third and last committeeman was the reigning Governor of the state, Waller, a smooth-tongued liar and moral coward.

Gerhardt designed and made a clay Nathan Hale and offered it for competition.

A salaried artist of Mr. Batterson, a stone cutter, designed a figure and placed it in competition, and so also did Mr. Woods, an elderly man who was sexton of Mrs. Colt's private church.

Woods had some talent but no genius and no instruction in art. The stone cutter's man had the experience and the practice that comes from continually repeating the same forms on hideous tombstones—robust prize-fighting angels, mainly.

The figure and pedestal made by Gerhardt were worthy of a less stingy price than the Legislature had offered, decenter companionship in the competition and a cleaner and less stupid committee.

In the opinion of William C. Prime and Charles D. Warner, Gerhardt's was a very fine work of art and these men would not have hesitated to award the contract to him. The Governor looked at the three models and said that as far as he could see Gerhardt's was altogether the preferable design. Mr. Coit said the same. But it was found impossible to get the aged Barnard to come to look at Gerhardt's model. He offered among other excuses that he didn't like to give a statue to a man who still had his reputation to make—that the statue ought to be made by an artist of established reputation. When asked what artist of established reputation would make a statue for $5,000 he was not able to reply. It was difficult for some time to find out what the real reason was for this old man's delay, but it finally came out that Mrs. Colt's money and influence were at the bottom of it. Mrs. Colt was anxious to throw that statue into the hands of her sexton in some way or other. She wrote a letter to the Governor, in which she argued the claims of her sexton, and it presently became quite manifest that the Governor found himself in an uncomfortable position, for the reason that he had characterized the sexton's attempt as exceedingly poor and crude, and had also stated quite distinctly that of the three models he much preferred Gerhardt's and was ready to vote in that way.

This incredible puppy actually described Gerhardt's design to the sexton and advised him to make a new design for competition—which he did; and he used Gerhardt's design in it! The Governor had no more sense than to tell Gerhardt that he had done this thing. Taking the whole thing round it has been the most comical competition for a statue the country has ever seen. It was so ludicrous and so paltry—in every way contemptible—that I tried to get Gerhardt to retire from the competition and make a group for me to be called the Statue Committee to present portraits of these cattle and mousers over a clay image. I said I would write a history of the Nathan Hale committee to go with the statue and I believed he could put it in terra cotta and make some money out of it. But he did not wish to degrade his art in gratifying his personal spite and he declined to do it.

It is customary everywhere else, I believe, for such a committee to specify what is the latest date for the offering of designs and also a date when a judgment on them shall be rendered, but this committee made no limit—at least in writing. Their policy evidently was to give Mrs. Colt's sexton time enough to get up a satisfactory image—no matter how long that might take—and then give him the contract.

Waller failed to be reelected Governor, but was appointed Consul-General to London and sailed on the 10th of May with the Nathan Hale statue still undecided, although, as he had a personal favor to ask of a friend of Gerhardt's, just before sailing he said "Grant me the favor and I will pledge my word that the Nathan Hale business shall be settled before I sail."

Gerhardt kept his clay image wet and waiting three or four months and then he let it crumble to pieces because the prospects of the design seemed to be as far away as ever.

About General Grant's Memoirs

1885. (Spring.)

I want to set down somewhat of a history of General Grant's memoirs.

By way of preface I will make a remark or two indirectly connected therewith.

During the Garfield campaign General Grant threw the whole weight of his influence and endeavor toward the triumph of the Republican Party. He made a progress through many of the states, chiefly the doubtful ones, and this progress was a daily and nightly ovation as long as it lasted. He was received everywhere by prodigious multitudes of enthusiastic people and to strain the facts a little one might almost tell what part of the country the General was in for the moment by the red reflections on the sky caused by the torch processions and fireworks.

He was to visit Hartford from Boston and I was one of the committee sent to Boston to bring him down here. I was also appointed to introduce him to the Hartford people when the population and the soldiers should pass in review before him. On our way from Boston in the palace car I fell to talking with Grant's eldest son, Colonel Fred Grant, whom I knew very well, and it gradually came out that the General, so far from being a rich man, as was commonly supposed, had not even income enough to enable him to live as respectably as a third-rate physician.

Colonel Grant told me that the General left the White House at the end of his second term a poor man, and I think he said he was in debt but I am not positively sure. (Said he was in debt $45,000, at the end of *one* of his terms.) Friends had given the General a couple of dwelling houses but he was not able to keep them or live in either of them. This was all so shameful and such a reproach to Congress that I proposed to take the General's straitened circumstances as my text in introducing him to the people of Hartford.

I knew that if this nation, which was rising up daily to do its chief citizen unparalleled honor, had it in its power by its vote to decide the matter, that it would turn his poverty into immeasurable wealth, in an instant. Therefore, the reproach lay not with the people but with their political representatives in Congress and my speech could be no insult to the people.

I clove to my plan, and, in introducing the General, I referred to the dignities and emoluments lavished upon the Duke of Wellington by England and contrasted with that conduct our far finer and higher method toward the savior of our country: to wit—the simple carrying him in our hearts without burdening him with anything to live on.

In his reply, the General, of course, said that this country had more than sufficiently rewarded him and that he was well satisfied.

He could not have said anything else, necessarily.

A few months later I could not have made such a speech, for by that time certain wealthy citizens had privately made up a purse of a quarter of a million dollars for the General, and had invested it in such a way that he could not be deprived of it either by his own want of wisdom or the rascality of other people.

Later still, the firm of Grant and Ward, brokers and stock-dealers, was established at number 2, Wall street, New York City.

This firm consisted of General Grant's sons and a brisk young man by the name of Ferdinand Ward. The General was also in some way a partner, but did not take any active part in the business of the house.

In a little time the business had grown to such proportions that it was apparently not only profitable but it was prodigiously so.

The truth was, however, that Ward was robbing all the Grants and everybody else that he could get his hands on and the firm was not making a penny.

The General was unsuspicious, and supposed that he was making a vast deal of money, whereas indeed he was simply losing such as he had, for Ward was getting it.

About the 5th of May, I think it was, 1884, the crash came and the several Grant families found themselves absolutely penniless.

Ward had even captured the interest due on the quarter of a million dollars of the Grant fund, which interest had fallen due only a day or two before the failure.

General Grant told me that that month, for the *first time in his life,* he had paid his domestic bills with *checks.* They came back upon his hands dishonored. He told me that Ward had spared no one connected with the Grant name however remote—that he had taken all that the General could scrape together and $45,000 that the General had borrowed on his wife's dwelling house in New York; that he had taken $65,000—the sum for which Mrs. Grant had sold, recently, one of the houses which had been presented to the General; that he had taken $7,000, which some poverty-stricken nieces of his in the West had recently received by bequest, and which was all the money they had in the world—that, in a word, Ward had utterly stripped everybody connected with the Grant family.

It was necessary that something be immediately done toward getting bread.

The bill to restore to General Grant the title and emoluments of a full General in the army, on the retired list, had been lagging for a long time in Congress—in the characteristic, contemptible and stingy congressional fashion. No relief was to be looked for from that source, mainly because Congress chose to avenge on General Grant the veto of the Fitz-John Porter Bill by President Arthur.

The editors of the Century Magazine some months before conceived the excellent idea of getting the surviving heroes of the late Civil War, on both sides, to write out their personal reminiscences of the war and publish them now in the magazine. But the happy project had come to grief, for the reason that some of these heroes were quite willing to write out these things only under one condition that they insisted on as essential. They refused to write a line unless the leading actor of the war should also write.* All persuasions and arguments failed on General Grant. He would *not* write; so, the scheme fell through.

Now, however, the complexion of things had changed and General Grant was without bread. [Not figurative, but actual.]

The Century people went to him once more and now he assented eagerly. A great series of war articles was immediately advertised by the Century publishers.

I knew nothing of all this, although I had been a number of times to the General's house to pass half an hour talking and smoking a cigar.

However, I was reading one night in Chickering Hall early in November, 1884, and as my wife and I were leaving the building we stumbled over Mr. Gilder, the editor of the Century, and went home with him to a late supper at his house. We were there an hour or two and in the course of the conversation Gilder said that General Grant had written three war articles for the Century and was going to write a fourth. I pricked up my ears. Gilder went on to describe how eagerly General Grant had entertained the proposition to write when it had last been put to him and how poor he evidently was and how eager to make some trifle of bread and butter money and how the handing him a check for $500 for the first article had manifestly gladdened his heart and lifted from it a mighty burden.

The thing which astounded me was, that, admirable man as Gilder certainly is, and with a heart which is in the right place, it had never seemed to occur to him that to offer General Grant $500 for a magazine article was not only the monumental insult of the nineteenth century, but of all centuries. He ought to have known that if he had given General Grant a check for $10,000 the sum would still have been trivial; that if he had paid him $20,000 for

*Aug. '85. They deny this now, but I go bail I got that statement from Gilder himself.   SLC

a single article the sum would still have been inadequate; that if he had paid him $30,000 for a single magazine war article it still could not be called paid for; that if he had given him $40,000 for a single magazine article he would still be in General Grant's debt. Gilder went on to say that it had been impossible, months before, to get General Grant to write a single line, but that now that he had once got started it was going to be as impossible to stop him again; that, in fact, General Grant had set out deliberately to write his memoirs in full and to publish them in book form.

I went straight to General Grant's house next morning and told him what I had heard. He said it was all true.

I said I had foreseen a fortune in such a book when I had tried in 1881 to get him to write it; that the fortune was just as sure to fall now. I asked him who was to publish the book, and he said doubtless the Century Company.

I asked him if the contract had been drawn and signed?

He said it had been drawn in the rough but not signed yet.

I said I had had a long and painful experience in book making and publishing and that if there would be no impropriety in his showing me the rough contract I believed I might be useful to him.

He said there was no objection whatever to my seeing the contract, since it had proceeded no further than a mere consideration of its details without promises given or received on either side. He added that he supposed that the Century offer was fair and right and that he had been expecting to accept it and conclude the bargain or contract.

He read the rough draft aloud and I didn't know whether to cry or laugh.

Whenever a publisher in the trade thinks enough of the chances of an unknown author's book to print it and put it on the market, he is willing to risk paying the man 10 per cent royalty and that is what he does pay him. He can well venture that much of a royalty but he cannot well venture any more. If that book shall sell 3,000 or 4,000 copies there is no loss on any ordinary book, and both parties have made something; but whenever the sale shall reach 10,000 copies the publisher is getting the lion's share of the profits and would continue to get the lion's share as long thereafter as the book should continue to sell.

When such a book is sure to sell 35,000 copies an author ought to get 15 per cent: that is to say, one-half of the net profit. When a book is sure to sell 80,000 or more, he ought to get 20 per cent royalty: that is, two-thirds of the total profits.

Now, here was a book that was morally bound to sell several hundred thousand copies in the first year of its publication and yet the Century people had had the hardihood to offer General Grant the very same 10 per cent royalty which they would have offered to any unknown Comanche Indian whose book they had reason to believe might sell 3,000 or 4,000 or 5,000 copies.

If I had not been acquainted with the Century people I should have said that this was a deliberate attempt to take advantage of a man's ignorance and trusting nature, to rob him; but I do know the Century people and therefore I know that they had no such base intentions as these but were simply making their offer out of their boundless resources of ignorance and stupidity. They were anxious to do book publishing as well as magazine publishing, and had tried one book already, but owing to their inexperience had made a failure of it. So, I suppose they were anxious, and had made an offer which in the General's instance commended itself as reasonable and safe, showing that they were lamentably ignorant and that they utterly failed to rise to the size of the occasion. This was sufficiently shown in the remark of the head of that firm to me a few months later: a remark which I shall refer to and quote in its proper place.

I told General Grant that the Century offer was simply absurd and should not be considered for an instant.

I forgot to mention that the rough draft made two propositions—one at 10 per cent royalty and the other the offer of *half the profits on the book* after subtracting *every sort of expense connected with it,* including OFFICE RENT, CLERK HIRE, ADVERTISING and EVERYTHING ELSE, a most complicated arrangement and one which no business-like author would accept in preference to a 10 per cent royalty. They manifestly regarded 10 per cent and half profits as the same thing—which shows that these innocent geese expected the book to sell only 12,000 or 15,000 copies.

I told the General that I could tell him exactly what he ought to receive: that, if he accepted a royalty, it ought to be 20 per cent on the retail price of the book, or if he preferred the partnership policy then he ought to have 70 per cent of the profits on each volume over and above *the mere cost of making* that volume. I said that if he would place these terms before the Century people they would accept them; but, if they were afraid to accept them, he would simply need to offer them to any great publishing house in the country and not one would decline them. If any should decline them let *me* have the book. I was publishing my own book, under the business name of Charles L. Webster & Co., I being the company, (and Webster being my business man, on a salary, with a one-tenth interest,) and I had what I believed to be much the best-equipped subscription establishment in the country.

I wanted the General's book and I wanted it very much, but I had very little expectation of getting it. I supposed that he would lay these new propositions before the Century people, that they would accept immediately, and that there the matter would end, for the General evidently felt under great obligations to the Century people for saving him from the grip of poverty by paying him $1,500 for three magazine articles which were well worth $100,000; and he seemed wholly unable to free himself from this sense of obligation, whereas to my mind he ought rather to have considered the Century people under very high obligations to him, not only for making them a present of $100,000, but for procuring for them a great and desirable series of war articles from the other heroes of the war which they could never have got their hands on if he had declined to write. (According to Gilder.)

I now went away on a long western tour on the platform, but Webster continued to call at the General's house and watch the progress of events.

Colonel Fred Grant was strongly opposed to letting the Century people have the book and was at the same time as strongly in favor of my having it.

The General's first magazine article had immediately added 50,000 names to their list of subscribers and thereby established the fact that the Century people would still have been the gainers if they had paid General Grant $50,000 for the articles—for the reason that they could expect to keep the most of these subscribers for several years and consequently get a profit out of them in the end of $100,000 at least.

Besides this increased circulation, the number of the Century's advertising pages at once doubled—a huge addition to the magazine's cash income in itself. (An addition of $25,000 a *month* as I estimate it from what I have paid them for one-fifth of a page for six months [$1,800].)

The Century people had eventually added to the original check of $1,500 a check for $1,000 after perceiving that they were going to make a fortune out of the first of the three articles.

This seemed a fine liberality to General Grant, who is the most simple-hearted of all men; but to me it seemed merely another exhibition of incomparable nonsense, as the added check ought to have been for $30,000 instead of $1,000. Colonel Fred Grant looked upon the matter just as I did, and had determined to keep the book out of the Century people's hands if possible. This action merely confirmed and hardened him in his purpose.

While I was in the West, propositions from publishers came to General Grant daily, and these propositions had a common form—to wit: "Only tell us what your best offer is and we stand ready to make a better one."

The Century people were willing to accept the terms which I had proposed to the General but they offered nothing better. The American Publishing Company of Hartford offered the General 70 per cent of the profits but would make it more if required.

These things began to have their effect. The General began to perceive from these various views that he had narrowly escaped making a very bad bargain for his book and now he began to incline toward me for the reason, no doubt, that I had been the accidental cause of stopping that bad bargain.

He called in George W. Childs of Philadelphia and laid the whole matter before him and asked his advice. Mr. Childs said to me afterwards that it was plain to be seen that the General, on the score of friendship, was so distinctly inclined toward me that the advice which would please him best would be the advice to turn the book over to me.

He advised the General to send competent people to examine into my capacity to properly publish the book and into the capacity of the other competitors for the book. (This was done at my own suggestion—Fred Grant was present.) And if they found that my house was as well equipped in all ways as the others, that he give the book to me.

The General sent persons selected by a couple of great law firms (Clarence Seward's was one,) to make examinations, and Colonel Fred Grant made similar examinations for himself personally.

The verdict in these several cases was that my establishment was as competent to make a success of the book as was that of any of the firms competing.

The result was that the contract was drawn and the book was placed in my hands.

In the course of one of my business talks with General Grant he asked me if I felt sure I could sell 25,000 copies of his book and he asked the question in such a way that I suspected that the Century people had intimated that that was about the number of the books that they thought ought to sell. [See Roswell Smith's remark, later on.]

I replied that the best way for a man to express an opinion in such a case was to put it in money—therefore, I would make this offer: if he would give me the book I would advance him the sum of $25,000 on each volume the moment the manuscript was placed in my hands, and if I never got the $50,000 back again, out of the future copyrights due, I would never ask him to return any part of the money to me.

The suggestion seemed to *distress* him. He said he could not think of taking in advance any sum of money large or small which the publisher would not be absolutely *sure* of getting back again. Some time afterwards when the contract was being drawn and the question was whether it should be 20 per cent royalty or 70 per cent of the profits, he inquired which of the two propositions would be the best *all round*. I sent Webster to tell him that the 20 per cent royalty would be the best for him, for the reason that it was the surest, the simplest, the easiest to keep track of, and, better still, would pay him a trifle more, no doubt, than with the other plan.

He thought the matter over and then said in substance that by the 20 per cent plan *he* would be sure to make, while the publisher might possibly lose: therefore, he would not have the royalty plan, but the 70-per-cent-profit plan; since if there were profits he could not then get them all but the publisher would be sure to get 30 per cent of it.

This was just like General Grant. It was absolutely impossible for him to entertain for a moment any proposition which might prosper him at the risk of any other man.

After the contract had been drawn and signed I remembered I had offered to advance the General some money and that he had said he might possibly need $10,000 before the book issued. The circumstance had been forgotten and was not in the contract but I had the luck to remember it before leaving town; so I went back and told Colonel Fred Grant to draw upon Webster for the $10,000 whenever it should be wanted.

That was the only thing forgotten in the contract and it was now rectified and everything was smooth.

And now I come to a circumstance which I have never spoken of and which cannot be known for many years to come, for this paragraph must not be published until the mention of so private a matter cannot offend any living person.

The contract was drawn by the great law firm of Alexander & Green on my part and Clarence Seward, son of Mr. Lincoln's Secretary of State, on the part of General Grant.

Appended to the contract was a transfer of the book to General Grant's wife, and the transfer from her to my firm for the consideration of $1,000 in hand paid.

This was to prevent the General's creditors from seizing the proceeds of the book.

Webster had said yes when the sum named was $1,000 and after he had signed the contract and was leaving the law office he mentioned incidentally that the $1,000 was of course a mere formality in such a paper and means nothing. But Mr. Seward took him privately aside and said "No, it means just what it says—*for the General's family have not a penny in the house and they are waiting at this moment with lively anxiety for that small sum of money.*"

Webster was astonished. He drew a check at once and Mr. Seward gave it to a messenger boy, and told him to take it swiftly—by the speediest route—to General Grant's house, and not let the grass grow under his feet.

It was a shameful thing that the man who had saved this country and its government from destruction should still be in a position where so small a sum—so trivial an amount—as $1,000, could be looked upon as a godsend. Everybody knew that the General was in reduced circumstances, but what a storm would have gone up all over the land if the people could have known that his poverty had reached such a point as this.

The newspapers all over the land had been lauding the princely generosity of the Century people in paying General Grant the goodly sum of $1,500 for three magazine articles, whereas if they had paid him the amount which was his just due for them he would still have been able to keep his carriage and not have been worrying about $1,000. Neither the newspapers nor the public were probably aware that fifty-five years earlier the publishers of an annual in London had offered little Tom Moore twice $1,500 for *two* articles and had told him to make them long or short and to write about whatever he pleased. The difference between the financial value of any article written by Tom Moore in his best day and a *war* article written by General Grant in these days was about as one to fifty.

To go back a while. After being a month or two in the West, during the winter of 1884–5, I returned to the East, reaching New York about the 20th of February.

No agreement had at that time been reached as to the contract, but I called at General Grant's house simply to inquire after his health, for I had seen reports in the newspapers that he had been sick and confined to his house for some time.

The last time I had been at his house he told me that he had stopped smoking because of the trouble in his throat, which the physicians had said would be quickest cured in that way. But while I was in the West the newspapers had reported that this throat affection was believed to be in the nature of a cancer. However, on the morning of my arrival in New York the newspapers had reported that the physicians had said that the General was a great deal better than he had been and was getting along very comfortably. So, when I called, at the house, I went up to the General's room and shook hands and said I was very glad he was so much better and so well along on the road to perfect health again.

He smiled and said "If it were only true."

Of course I was both surprised and discomfited and asked his physician, Dr. Douglas, if the General were in truth not progressing as well as I had supposed. He intimated that the reports were rather rose-colored and that this affection was no doubt a cancer.

I am an excessive smoker and I said to the General that some of the rest of us must take warning by his case, but Dr. Douglas spoke up and said that this result must not be attributed altogether to smoking. He said it was probable that it had its *origin* in excessive smoking, but that that was not the certain reason of its manifesting itself at this time: that more than likely the real reason was the General's distress of mind and year-long depression of spirit, arising from the failure of the Grant and Ward firm.

This remark started the General at once to talking and I found then and afterwards that when he did not care to talk about any other subject, he was always ready and willing to talk about that one.

He told what I have before related about the robberies perpetrated upon him and upon all the Grant connection by this man Ward, whom he had so thoroughly trusted, *but he never uttered a phrase concerning Ward which an outraged adult might not have uttered concerning an offending child.* He spoke as a man speaks who has been deeply wronged and humiliated and betrayed; but he never used a venomous expression or one of a vengeful nature.

As for myself I was inwardly boiling all the time: I was scalping Ward, flaying him alive, breaking him on the wheel, pounding him to jelly, and cursing him with all the profanity known to the one language that I am acquainted with, and helping it out in times of difficulty and distress with odds and ends of profanity drawn from the two other languages of which I have a limited knowledge.

He told his story with deep feeling in his voice, but with no betrayal upon his countenance of what was going on in his heart. He could depend upon that countenance of his in all emergencies. It always stood by him. It never betrayed him.

July 1st or 2d, 1885, (at Mt. McGregor,) about three weeks before the General's death, Buck Grant and I sat talking an hour to each other across the General's lap—just to keep him company—he had only to listen. The news had just come that that Marine Bank man (Ward's pal—what *was* that scoundrel's name?) had been sent up for ten years. Buck Grant said the bitterest things about him he could frame his tongue to; I was about as bitter myself. The General listened for some time, then reached for his pad and pencil and wrote *"He was not as bad as the other"*—meaning Ward. It was his only comment. Even his *writing* looked gentle.

While he was talking, Colonel Grant said:

"Father is letting you see that the Grant family are a pack of fools, Mr. Clemens!"

The General combatted that statement. He said in substance that facts could be produced which would show that when Ward laid siege to a man that man would turn out to be a fool too—as much of a fool as any Grant: that all men were fools if the being successfully beguiled by Ward was proof by itself that the man was a fool. He began to present instances. He said, (in effect,) that nobody would call the President of the Erie Railroad a fool, yet Ward beguiled him to the extent of $800,000: robbed him of every cent of it. He mentioned another man who could not be called a fool, yet Ward had beguiled that man out of more than half a million dollars and had given him nothing in return for it. He instanced a man with a name something like Fisher, though that was not the name, whom he said nobody could call a fool: on the contrary, a man who had made himself very rich by being sharper and smarter than other people and who always prided himself upon his smartness and upon the fact that he could not be fooled, *he* could not be deceived by anybody; but what did Ward do in his case? He fooled him into buying a portion of a mine belonging to ex-Senator Chaffee—a property which was not for sale, which Ward could produce no authority for selling—yet he got out of *that* man $300,000 in cash, without the passage of a single piece of paper or a line of writing, to show that the sale had been made. This man came to the office of Grant and Ward every day for a good while and talked with Ward about the prospects of that rich mine, and it *was* very rich, and these two would pass directly by Mr. Chaffee and go into the next room and talk. You would think that a man of his reputation for shrewdness would at some time or other have concluded to ask Mr. Chaffee a question or two; but, no: Ward had told this man that Chaffee did not want to be known in the transaction at all, that he must seem to be at Grant and Ward's office on other business, and that he must not venture to speak to Chaffee or the whole business would be spoiled.

There was a man who prided himself on being a smart business man and yet Ward robbed him of $300,000 without giving him a scrap of anything to show that the transaction had taken place and to-day that man is not among the prosecutors of Ward at all for the reason perhaps that he would rather lose all of that money than have the fact get out that he was deceived in so childish a way.

General Grant mentioned another man who was very wealthy, whom no one would venture to call a fool, either business-wise or otherwise, yet this man came into the office one day and said "Ward, here is my check for $50,000, I have no use for it at present, I am going to make a flying trip to Europe; turn it over for me, see what you can do with it." Some time afterwards I was in the office when this gentleman returned from his trip and presented himself. He asked Ward if he had accomplished anything with that money? Ward said "Just wait a moment," went to his books, turned over a page, mumbled to himself a few moments, drew a check for $250,000, handed it to this man with the air of a person who had really accomplished nothing worth talking of! The man stared at the check a moment, handed it back to Ward, and said "That is plenty good enough for me, set that hen again," and he went out of the place. It was the last he ever saw of any of that money.

I had been discovering fools all along when the General was talking, but this instance brought me to my senses. I put myself in this fellow's place and confessed that if I had been in that fellow's clothes it was a hundred to one that I would have done the very thing that he had done, and I was thoroughly well aware that, at any rate, there was not a preacher nor a widow in Christendom who would not have done it: for these people are always seeking investments that pay illegitimately large sums; and they never, or seldom, stop to inquire into the nature of the business.

When I was ready to go, Colonel Fred Grant went down stairs with me, and stunned me by telling me confidentially that the physicians were trying to keep his father's real condition from him, but that in fact they considered him to be under sentence of death and that he would not be likely to live more than a fortnight or three weeks longer.

This was about the 21st of February, 1885.

After the 21st of February General Grant busied himself daily as much as his strength would allow in revising the manuscript of his book. It was read to him by Colonel Grant very carefully and he made the corrections as he went along. He was losing valuable time because only one-half or two-thirds of the second and last volume was as yet written. However, he was more anxious that what was written should be *absolutely correct* than that the book should be finished in an incorrect form and then find himself unable to correct it. His memory was superb and nearly any other man with such a memory would have been satisfied to trust it. Not so the General. No matter how sure he was of the fact or the date, he would never let it go until he had verified it with the official records. This constant and painstaking searching of the records cost a great deal of time, but it was not wasted. Everything stated as a fact in General Grant's book may be accepted with entire confidence as being thoroughly trustworthy.

Speaking of his memory, what a wonderful machine it was! He told me one day that he never made a report of the battles of the Wilderness until they were all over, and he was back in Washington. Then he sat down and made a full report from memory and when it was finished, examined the reports of his subordinates and found that he had made hardly an error. To be exact, he said he had made two errors.

This is his statement as I remember it, though my memory is not absolutely trustworthy and I may be overstating it.

(These and other statements of mine to be laid before Colonel Fred Grant for verification.)

The General lost some more time in one other way. Three Century articles had been written and paid for, but he had during the summer before promised to write a fourth one. He had written it in a rough draft but it had remained unfinished.

The Century people had advertised these articles and were now fearful that the General would never be able to complete them. By this time the General's condition had got abroad and the newspapers were full of reports about his perilous condition. The Century people called several times to get the fourth article and this hurt and offended Colonel Fred Grant because he knew that they were aware, as was all the world, that his father was considered to be in a dying condition. Colonel Grant thought that they ought to show more consideration—more humanity. By fits and starts the General worked at that article whenever his failing strength would permit him and was determined to finish it if possible *because his promise had been given and he would in no way depart from it while any slight possibility remained of fulfilling it.* I asked if there was no contract or no understanding as to what was to be paid by the Century people for the article. He said there was not. Then, I said, "Charge them $20,000 for it. It is well worth it—worth double the money. Charge them this sum for it in its unfinished condition and let them have it and tell them that it will be worth still more in case the General shall be able to complete it. This may modify their ardor somewhat and bring you a rest." He was not willing to put so large a price upon it but thought that if he gave it to them he might require them to pay $5,000. It was plain that the modesty of the family in money matters was indestructible.

Just about this time I was talking to General Badeau there one day when I saw a pile of type-writer manuscript on the table and picked up the first page and began to read it. I saw that it was an account of the siege of Vicksburg. I counted a page and there were about three hundred words on the page: 18,000 or 20,000 words altogether.

General Badeau said it was one of the three articles written by General Grant for the Century.

I said, "Then they have no sort of right to require the fourth article, for there is matter enough in this one to make two or three ordinary magazine articles." The copy of this and the other two articles were at this moment in the Century's safe; the fourth article agreement was therefore most amply fulfilled already without an additional article: yet the Century people considered that the contract would not be fulfilled without the fourth article and so insisted upon having it. At the ordinary price paid me for Century articles, this Vicksburg article, if I had written it, would have been worth about $700. Therefore, the Century people had paid General Grant no more than they would have paid me, and this *including* the $1,000 gratuity which they had given him.

It is impossible to overestimate the enormity of this gouge. If the Century people knew anything at all; if they were not steeped to the marrow in ignorance and stupidity, they knew that a single page of General Grant's manuscript was worth more than a hundred of mine. But they *were* steeped to such a degree in ignorance and stupidity. They were honest, honorable and good-hearted people according to their lights, and if anybody could have made them see that it was shameful to take such an advantage of a dying soldier, they would have rectified the wrong. But all the eloquence that I was able to pour out upon them went for nothing, utterly for nothing. They still thought that they had been quite generous to the General and were not able to see the matter in any other light.

Afterwards, at Mount McGregor they consented to give up half of the Vicksburg article; and they did; they gave up *more* than half of it—cut it from twenty-two galleys down to nine, and only the nine will appear in the magazine. And they added $2,500 to the $2,500 already paid. Those people could learn to be as fair and liberal as anybody, if they had the right schooling.

I will make a diversion here, and get back upon my track again later.

While I was away with G. W. Cable, giving public readings in the theatres, lecture halls, skating rinks, jails and churches of the country, the travel was necessarily fatiguing and therefore I ceased from writing letters excepting to my wife and children. This foretaste of heaven, this relief from the fret of letter-answering, was delightful, but it finally left me in the dark concerning things which I ought to have been acquainted with at the moment.

Among these the affairs of Karl Gerhardt, the young artist, should be mentioned.

I had started out on this reading pilgrimage the day after the Presidential election: that is to say, I had started on the 5th of November and had visited my home only once between that time and the 2d of March following.

During all these four months Gerhardt had been waiting for the verdict of that dilatory committee, and had taken it out in waiting: that is to say, he had sat still and done nothing to earn his bread. He had been tirelessly diligent in asking for work in the line of his art, and had used all possible means in that direction: he had written letters to every man he could hear of who was likely to need a mortuary monument for himself, or his friends, or acquaintances, and had also applied for the chance of a competition for a soldiers' monument—for all things of this sort—but always without success; the natural result, as his name was not known. He had no reputation.

When I closed my reading campaign at Washington, the last day of February, I came home and found the state of things which I have just spoken of. Gerhardt had waited four long months on that committee which would have needed four centuries in which to make up its mind, and I was thoroughly provoked. I told him that he ought to have had more pride than to permit me to support him and his family during all that time with no assistance from his idle hands. He said that he had wanted to work and had felt the humiliation of the state of things as much as any one could, but that he had been afraid of the effect which it might have if it became known that this artist who was applying for statues and monuments was not to be found in a studio but in some one's workshop. I said I thought the argument had not a leg to stand on, that he ought to have made it his business to find something to do: that he ought to have been shoveling snow, sawing wood, all these four months, and that the revelation that he had been so engaged would have been a credit to him in anybody's eyes whose respect was worth anything. It was hard to have to talk to him so plainly, but it was manifest that mere hints were valueless when leveled at him: I had tried them before. He said he would find some work to do immediately.

He came back the next day and said he had got work at Pratt & Whitney's shop and could go on corresponding with people about statues without interfering with that work.

It seemed to me that Gerhardt compactly filled James Redpath's definition of an artist: "A man who has a sense of beauty and no sense of duty."

Once, J. Q. A. Ward, in speaking of his early struggles to get a status as a sculptor, had told me that he had made his beginning by hanging around the studios of sculptors of repute and picking up odd jobs of journey work in them, for the sake of the bread he could gain in that way. I had turned this suggestion over to Gerhardt, but his reply from Paris had been an almost indignant scouting of the idea, as being a thing which no true artist could bring himself to do; and I saw by that that Gerhardt was a true artist because he was manifestly determined not to do it.

I may as well say here and be done with it that my connection with Gerhardt had very little sentiment in it, from my side of the house, and no romance. I took hold of his case, in the first place, solely because I had become convinced that he had it in him to become a very capable sculptor. I was not adopting a child, I was not adding a member to the family, I was merely taking upon myself a common duty—the duty of helping a man who was not able to help himself. I never expected him to be grateful, I never expected him to be thankful—my experience of men had long ago taught me that one of the surest ways of begetting an enemy was to do some stranger an act of kindness which should lay upon him the irritating sense of an obligation. Therefore my connection with Gerhardt had nothing sentimental or romantic about it. I told him in the first place that if the time should ever come when he could pay back to me the money expended upon him and pay it without inconvenience to himself, I should expect it at his hands, and that when it *was* paid I should consider the account entirely requited— sentiment and all: that that act would leave him free from any obligation to me. It was well all round that things had taken that shape in the beginning and had kept it, for, if the foundation had been sentiment, that sentiment would have grown sour when I saw that he did not want to work for a living in outside ways when art had no living to offer. It had saved me from applying in his case a maxim of mine that whenever a man preferred being fed by any other man to starving in independence he ought to be shot.

One evening Gerhardt appeared in the library and I hoped he had come to say he was getting along very well at the machine shop and was contented; so I was disappointed when he said he had come to show me a small bust he had been making, in clay, of General Grant, from a photograph. I was the more irritated for the reason that I had never seen a portrait of General Grant—in oil, water-colors, crayon, steel, wood, photograph, plaster, marble or any other material,—that was to me at all satisfactory; and, therefore, I could not expect that a person who had never even seen the General could accomplish anything worth considering in the way of a likeness of him.

However, when he uncovered the bust my prejudices vanished at once. The thing was not correct in its details, yet it seemed to me to be a closer approach to a good likeness of General Grant than any one which I had ever seen before. Before uncovering it Gerhardt had said he had brought it in the hope that I would show it to some member of the General's family, and get that member to point out its chief defects for correction; but I had replied that I could not venture to do that, for there was a plenty of people to pester these folks without me adding myself to the number. But a glance at the bust had changed all that in an instant. I said I would go to New York in the morning and ask the family to look at the bust and that he must come along to be within call in case they took enough interest in the matter to point out the defects.

We reached the General's house at one o'clock the next afternoon, and I left Gerhardt and the bust below and went up stairs to see the family.

And now, for the first time, the thought came into my mind, that perhaps I was doing a foolish thing, that the family must of necessity have been pestered with such matters as this so many times that the very mention of such a thing must be nauseating to them. However, I had started and so I might as well finish. Therefore I said I had a young artist down stairs who had been making a small bust of the General from a photograph and I wished they would look at it, if they were willing to do me that kindness.

Jesse Grant's wife spoke up with eagerness and said "Is it the artist who made the bust of you that is in Huckleberry Finn?" I said, yes. She said with great animation, "How good it was of you, Mr. Clemens, to think of that!" She expressed this lively gratitude to me in various ways until I began to feel somehow a great sense of merit in having originated this noble idea of having a bust of General Grant made by so excellent an artist. I will not do my sagacity the discredit of saying that I did anything to remove or modify this impression that I had originated the idea and carried it out to its present state through my own ingenuity and diligence.

Mrs. Jesse Grant added, "How strange it is; only two nights ago I dreamed that I was looking at your bust in Huckleberry Finn and thinking how nearly perfect it was, and then I thought that I conceived the idea of going to you and asking you if you could not hunt up that artist and get him to make a bust of father!"

Things were going on very handsomely!

The persons present were Colonel Fred Grant, Mrs. Jesse Grant, and Dr. Douglas.

I went down for Gerhardt and he brought up the bust and uncovered it. All of the family present exclaimed over the excellence of the likeness, and Mrs. Jesse Grant expended some more unearned gratitude upon me.

The family began to discuss the details and then checked themselves and begged Gerhardt's pardon for criticising. Of course he said that their criticisms were exactly what he wanted and begged them to go on. The General's wife said that in that case they would be glad to point out what seemed to them inaccuracies, but that he must not take their speeches as being criticisms upon his art at all. They found two inaccuracies: in the shape of the nose and the shape of the forehead. All were agreed that the forehead was wrong, but there was a lively dispute about the nose. Some of those present contended that the nose was nearly right—the others contended that it was distinctly wrong. The General's wife knelt on the ottoman to get a clearer view of the bust and the others stood about her—all talking at once. Finally the General's wife said, hesitatingly, with the mien of one who is afraid he is taking a liberty and asking too much—"If Mr. Gerhardt could see the General's nose and forehead himself, that would dispose of this dispute at once"; finally, "The General is in the next room—would Mr. Gerhardt mind going in there and making the correction himself?"

Things were indeed progressing handsomely!

Of course, Mr. Gerhardt lost no time in expressing his willingness.

While the controversy was going on concerning the nose and the forehead, Mrs. Fred Grant joined the group, and then presently each of the three ladies in turn disappeared for a few minutes and came back with a handful of photographs and hand-painted miniatures of the General.

These pictures had been made in every quarter of the world. One of them had been painted in Japan. But, good as many of these pictures were they were worthless as evidence for the reason that they contradicted each other in every detail.

The photograph apparatus had lied as distinctly and as persistently as had the hands of the miniature-artists. No two noses were alike and no two foreheads were alike.

We stepped into the General's room—all but General Badeau and Dr. Douglas.

The General was stretched out in a reclining chair with his feet supported upon an ordinary chair. He was muffled up in dressing gowns and afghans with his black woolen skull-cap on his head.

The ladies took the skull-cap off and began to discuss his nose and his forehead and they made him turn this way and that way and the other way to get different views and profiles of his features. He took it all patiently and made no complaint. He allowed them to pull and haul him about in their own affectionate fashion without a murmur. Mrs. Fred Grant, who is very beautiful and of the most gentle and loving character, was very active in this service and very deft with her graceful hands in arranging and re-arranging the General's head for inspection and repeatedly called attention to the handsome shape of his head—a thing which reminds me that Gerhardt had picked up an old plug hat of the General's down stairs and had remarked upon the perfect oval shape of the inside of it, this oval being so uniform that the wearer of the hat could never be able to know by the feel of it whether he had it right-end in front or wrong-end in front, whereas the average man's head is broad at one end and narrow at the other.

The General's wife placed him in various positions, none of which satisfied her, and finally she went to him and said—"Ulyss! Ulyss! Can't you put your feet to the floor?" He did so at once and straightened himself up.

During all this time, the General's face wore a pleasant, contented and, I should say, benignant aspect, but he never opened his lips once. As had often been the case before, so now, his silence gave ample room to guess at what was passing in his mind—and to take it out in guessing. I will remark, in passing, that the General's hands were very thin, and they showed, far more than did his face, how his long siege of confinement and illness and insufficient food had wasted him. He was at this time suffering great and increasing pain from the cancer at the root of his tongue, but there was nothing ever discoverable in the expression of his face to betray this fact as long as he was awake. When asleep his face would take advantage of him and make revelations.

At the end of fifteen minutes Gerhardt said he believed he could correct the defects now. So, we went back to the other room.

Gerhardt went to work on the clay image, everybody standing round, observing and discussing with the greatest interest.

Presently, the General astonished us by appearing there, clad in his wraps, and supporting himself in a somewhat unsure way upon a cane. He sat down on the sofa and said he could sit there if it would be for the advantage of the artist.

But his wife would not allow that. She said that he might catch cold. She was for hurrying him back at once to his invalid chair. He succumbed, and started back, but at the door he turned and said:

"Then can't Mr. Gerhardt bring the clay in here and work?"

This was several hundred times better fortune than Gerhardt could have dreamed of. He removed his work to the General's room at once. The General stretched himself out in his chair, but said that if that position would not do, he would sit up. Gerhardt said it would do very well, indeed; especially if it were more comfortable to the sitter than any other would be.

The General watched Gerhardt's swift and noiseless fingers for some time with manifest interest in his face, and no doubt this novelty was a valuable thing to one who had spent so many weeks that were tedious with sameness and unemphasized with change or diversion. By and bye, one eyelid began to droop occasionally; then everybody stepped out of the room excepting Gerhardt and myself and I moved to the rear where I would be out of sight and not be a disturbing element.

Harrison, the General's old colored body-servant, came in presently and remained a while watching Gerhardt, and then broke out with great zeal and decision:

"That's the General! Yes, sir! That's the General! Mind! I tell you! That's the General!"

Then he went away, and the place became absolutely silent.

Within a few minutes afterwards the General was sleeping, and for two hours he continued to sleep tranquilly, the serenity of his face disturbed only at intervals by a passing wave of pain. It was the first sleep he had had for several weeks uninduced by narcotics.

To my mind this bust, completed at this sitting, has in it more of General Grant than can be found in any other likeness of him that has ever been made since he was a famous man. I think it may rightly be called the best portrait of General Grant that is in existence. It has also a feature which must always be a remembrancer to this nation of what the General was passing through during the long weeks of that spring. For, into the clay image went the pain which he was enduring but which did not appear in his face when he was awake. Consequently, the bust has about it a suggestion of patient and brave and manly suffering which is infinitely touching.

At the end of two hours General Badeau entered abruptly and spoke to the General and this woke him up. But for this animal's interruption he might have slept as much longer possibly.

Gerhardt worked on as long as it was light enough to work and then he went away. He was to come again, and did come the following day; but, at the last moment, Colonel Fred Grant would not permit another sitting. He said that the face was so nearly perfect that he was afraid to allow it to be touched again, lest some of the excellence might be refined out of it, instead of adding more excellence to it. He called attention to an oil painting on the wall down stairs and asked if we knew that man. We couldn't name him—had never seen his face before. "Well," said Colonel Grant, "that was a perfect portrait of my father once: it was given up by all the family to be the best that had ever been made of him. We were entirely satisfied with it, but the artist, unhappily, was not: he wanted to do a stroke or two to make it absolutely perfect and he insisted on taking it back with him. After he had made those finishing touches it didn't resemble my father or any one else. We took it, and have always kept it as a curiosity. But with that lesson behind us we will save this bust from a similar fate."

He allowed Gerhardt to work at the hair, however: he said he might expend as much of his talent on that as he pleased but must stop there.

Gerhardt finished the hair to his satisfaction but never touched the face again. Colonel Grant required Gerhardt to promise that he would take every pains with the clay bust and then return it to him to keep as soon as he had taken a mould from it. This was done.

Gerhardt prepared the clay as well as he could for permanent preservation and gave it to Colonel Grant.

Up to the present day, May 22, 1885, no later likeness of General Grant of any kind has been made from life and if this shall chance to remain the last ever made of him from life, coming generations can properly be grateful that one so nearly perfect of him was made after the world learned his name.

Grant's Memoirs

1885. (Spring.)

Some time after the contract for General Grant's book was completed, I found that nothing but a verbal understanding existed between General Grant and the Century Company giving General Grant permission to use his Century articles in his book. There is a law of custom which gives an author the privilege of using his magazine article in any way he pleases after it shall have appeared in the magazine, and this law of custom is so well established that an author never expects to have any difficulty about getting a magazine copyright transferred to him whenever he shall ask for it with the purpose in view of putting it in a book. But in the present case I was afraid that the Century Company might fall back upon their legal rights and ignore the law of custom, in which case we should be debarred from using General Grant's Century articles in his book—an awkward state of things, because he was now too sick a man to re-write them. It was necessary that something should be done in this matter, and done at once.

Mr. Seward, General Grant's lawyer, was a good deal disturbed when he found that there was no writing. But I was not. I believed that the Century people could be relied upon to carry out any verbal agreement which they had made. The only thing I feared was that their idea of the verbal agreement and General Grant's idea of it might not coincide. So I went back to the General's house and got Colonel Fred Grant to write down what he understood the verbal agreement to be and this piece of writing he read to General Grant, who said it was correct and then signed it with his own hand: a feeble and trembling signature, but recognizable as his.

Then I sent for Webster, and our lawyer, and we three went to the Century office, where we found Roswell Smith, (the head man of the company,) and several of the editors. I stated my case plainly and simply and found that their understanding and General Grant's were identical; so, the difficulty was at an end at once, and we proceeded to draw a writing to cover the thing.

When the business was finished, or, perhaps, in the course of it, I made another interesting discovery.

I was already aware that the Century people were going to bring out all their war articles in book form eventually, General Grant's among the number; but as I knew what a small price had been paid to the General for his articles I had a vague general notion that he would receive a further payment for the use of them in their book, a remuneration which an author customarily receives in our day by another unwritten law of custom. But when I spoke of this, to my astonishment they told me that they had bought and paid for every one of these war articles with the distinct understanding that that first payment was the last. In confirmation of this amazing circumstance, they brought out a receipt which General Grant had signed, and therein it distinctly appeared that each $500 not only paid for the use of the article printed in the magazine *but also in the subsequent book!*

One thing was quite clear to me: if we consider the value of those articles to that book, we must grant that the General was paid very much less than nothing at all for their issue in the magazine.

This was altogether the sharpest trade I have ever heard of, in any line of business, horse trading included.

The Century people didn't blush and therefore it is plain that they considered the transaction fair and legitimate; and I believe myself that they had no idea that they were doing an unfair thing. It was easily demonstrable that they were buying ten-dollar gold pieces from General Grant at twenty-five cents apiece, and I think it was as easily demonstrable that they did not know that there was anything unfair about it.

During our talk Roswell Smith said to me, with the glad air of a man who has stuck a nail in his foot, "I'm glad you've got the General's book, Mr. Clemens, and glad there was somebody with courage enough to take it, under the circumstances. What do you think the General wanted to require of me?" "What?" *"He wanted me to insure a sale of 25,000 sets of his book. I wouldn't risk such a guarantee on any book that ever was published."* This is the remark I have already several times referred to. I've got Smith's exact language; (from my note-book); it proves that they thought 10 per cent royalty would actually represent half profits on General Grant's book! Imagine it.

I did not say anything, but I thought a good deal. This was one more evidence that the Century people had no more just idea of the value of the book than as many children might be expected to have. At this present writing (May 25, 1885) we have not advertised General Grant's book in any way: we have not spent a dollar in advertising of any kind; we have not even given notice by circulars or otherwise that we are ready to receive applications from book agents, and yet to-day we have *bona fide* orders for 100,000 sets of the book—that is to say, 200,000 single volumes, and these orders are from men who have bonded themselves to take and pay for them, and who have also laid before us the most trustworthy evidence that they are financially able to carry out their contracts. The territory which these men have taken is only about one-fourth of the area of the Northern states. We have also under consideration applications for 50,000 sets more and although we have confidence in the energy and ability of the men who have made these applications, we have not closed with them because as yet we are not sufficiently satisfied as to their financial strength. [Sept. 10; 250,000 sets (500,000 single copies,) have been sold, to date—and only half the ground canvassed.]

When it became known that the General's book had fallen into my hands, the New York World and a Boston paper, (I think the Herald) came out at once with the news; and, in both instances, the position was taken that, by some sort of superior under-handed smartness, I had taken an unfair advantage of the confiding simplicity of the Century people, and got the book away from them—a book which they had the right to consider their property, inasmuch as the terms of its publication had been mutually agreed upon, and the contract covering it was on the point of being signed by General Grant when I put in my meddling appearance.

None of the statements of these two papers was correct, but the Boston paper's account was considered to be necessarily correct, for the reason that it was furnished by the sister of Mr. Gilder, editor of the Century. So, there was considerable newspaper talk about my improper methods, but nobody seemed to have wit enough to discover that if one gouger *had* captured the General's book, here was evidence that he had only prevented another gouger from getting it, since the Century's terms were distinctly mentioned in the Boston paper's account as being *10 per cent royalty*. No party observed that, and nobody commented upon it. It was taken for granted all round that General Grant would have signed that 10 per cent contract without being grossly cheated.

It is my settled policy to allow newspapers to make as many misstatements about me or my affairs as they like; therefore I had no mind to contradict either of these newspapers or explain my side of the case in any way. But a reporter came to our house at Hartford from one of the editors of the Courant to ask me for my side of the matter for use in the Associated Press dispatches. I dictated a short paragraph in which I said that the statement made in the World that there was a coolness between the Century Company and General Grant, and that in consequence of it the Century would not publish any more articles by General Grant, notwithstanding the fact that they had advertised them far and wide, was not true. I said there was no coolness and no ground for coolness; that the contract for the book had been open for all competitors; that I had put in my application and had asked the General to state its terms to the other applicants in order that he might thereby be enabled to get the best terms possible; that I had got the book eventually, but by no underhand or unfair method. The statement I made was concise and brief and contained nothing offensive. It was sent over the wires to the Associated Press headquarters in New York, but it was not *issued* by that concern. It did not appear in print. I inquired why, and was told that although it was a piece of news of quite universal interest, it was also more or less of an advertisement for the book—a thing I had not thought of before. I was also told that if I had had a friend round about the Associated Press office, I could have had that thing published all over the country for a reasonable bribe. I wondered if that were true. I wondered if so great and important a concern dealt in that sort of thing.

I presently got something in the way of a confirmation in New York. A few days afterwards, I found that our lawyers, Alexander & Green, and also Mr. Webster, had been disturbed by the World's statement of this matter and had thought a correction ought to be made through the press of the country. They had imagined that the Associated Press, having for its sole business the collection of valuable news for newspapers, would be very glad to have a statement of the facts in this case. Therefore, they called on an employee of that concern and put into his hands a brief statement of the affair. He read it over, hesitated, said it was certainly a matter of great public interest but that he couldn't see any way to make the statement without its being also a pretty good advertisement for General Grant's book, and for my publishing firm; but he said if we would pay $500 he would send it over the wires to every newspaper in the country connected with that institution.

This pleasant offer was declined. But the proposition seemed to explain to me a thing which had often puzzled me. That was the frequent appearance among the Associated Press dispatches of prodigious puffs of speculative schemes. One, in particular, was a new electric light company of Boston. During a number of weeks there had been almost daily a wildly extravagant puff of this company's prosperous condition in the Associated Press dispatches of the Hartford papers. The prosperity or the unprosperity of that company was a matter of not the slightest interest to the generality of newspaper readers, and I had always wondered before why the Associated Press people should take such an apparent interest in the matter. It seemed quite satisfactorily explained now. The Associated Press had sent the World's misstatements over the wires to all parts of the country free of charge for the reason, no doubt, that that statement slandered General Grant, lied about his son, dealt the Century Company a disastrous blow, and was thoroughly well calculated to sharply injure me in both character and pocket. Therefore it was apparent that the Associated Press were willing to destroy a man for nothing, but required cash for rehabilitating him again. That was Associated Press morals. It was newspaper morals, too. Speaking in general terms it was always easy to get any print to say any injurious thing about a citizen in a newspaper, but it was next to impossible to get that paper or any other to right an injured man. We have a law of libel, but it is inoperative and merely cumbers the statute books. For several reasons: *First*—The case must take its routine place in the calendar of the court and that ensures that some months must elapse before the courts get down to it, so that whatever injury the libel might do has been already done. *Second*—A jury is afraid of the newspapers and always lets a newspaper off at the cheapest and easiest rate. As the result libel suits are very uncommon and whenever one is tried it simply serves as a reminder to later comers that the best way is to let libel suits alone and take what the newspapers choose to give you in the way of abuse.

GEN GRANT, MARK TWAIN AND THE CENTURY.—The story of Gen Grant's last days includes yet another disagreeable episode, according to the New York correspondent of the Boston Herald. It has been generally understood that Grant's papers on the war in the Century magazine have been chapters from the autobiography which he is preparing, and that they were to be followed by other chapters; and it now seems that it was all but concluded that the Century company should publish the book. Arrangements, says this correspondent, were made for the printing of the volumes and the making of the pictures, and terms nearly settled, on the basis of a royalty, when in stepped Mark Twain and spoiled it all. It is stated by this writer that Mr Clemens is the principal partner in the subscription book firm of Charles L. Webster & Co, which publishes his own books, and that Webster & Co made a proposition to Gen Grant to take his son Jesse into the enterprise of publishing and circulating the autobiography, showing the general that he could get a clean profit treble the royalty offered by the Century company. The consequence is represented to be that no more of Gen Grant's work will appear in the magazine, and it is intimated that Mark Twain cannot have any more of his "Huckleberry Finn" literature published hereafter in those offended pages. The readers of the magazine may well hope the last item of this news is true. "Brunswick," the Boston Saturday Gazette correspondent from New York, who is Miss Jeannette L. Gilder, sister of the editor of the Century, and, therefore, ought to know—gives a somewhat different account, saying:—

> The terms offered Gen Grant, by Mr Webster, are the same, I believe, as those offered by the Century company—10 per cent on the retail price. But Mr Webster's contract includes one of the young Grants, which makes it more attractive to the general. The Century company would probably have published the Grant autobiography if it had not been for the "son" clause; but that put a new aspect on the thing, and while it was perfectly natural for Gen Grant to want to see his son fixed in business, it was not so natural for the Century company to want to be forced into a bargain of this sort. The relations between Gen Grant and the Century people are still perfectly friendly, and it may be that, after all, they will publish the book.

Springfield Republican
March 9, 1885

GRANT AND HIS MEMOIRS.

———

WHY AN ADVERTISED ARTICLE
DID NOT APPEAR IN THE "CENTURY."

———

**A Brilliant Business Scheme by Which Mark Twain Takes Jesse Grant
for a Partner and Becomes the Publisher of the Forthcoming Work.**

The March number of the *Century* appeared without the promised and much-advertised article from the pen of Gen. Grant on one of the great battles of the civil war. The fact caused much comment in literary circles, and in some quarters it was thought that the absence of the article was due to the General's serious illness. Better informed people, however, have known that nearly all, if not all, the papers of the series had been prepared before the first appeared.

It has just leaked out that Gen. Grant and the *Century* Company have had a "falling out" and it is not likely that any further papers from the General will appear in the *Century*. Gen. Grant is preparing an autobiography and it was all but concluded that the book would be published by the *Century* Company. He was paid $1,000 for the article on "Shiloh," which appeared in the February number. The managers expected that chapters from the autobiography would first appear in their magazine and that the volumes would bear their imprint. Negotiations were in progress in regard to the illustrations and the printing of the volumes, and terms between Gen. Grant and the company had almost been concluded on the basis of a royalty. The contract, however, had not yet been signed when Mark Twain appeared upon the scene with more advantageous terms than the *Century* Company offered. Mark Twain, besides being a rollicking humorist, is a smart business man, and it is said that in recent years he has not shared the profits of his fun with any one. He has mastered the art of selling books by subscription, and, moreover, is the principal in the firm of Charles L. Webster & Co. Mr. Webster is a relative, and his duties are mainly to look after the regiments of agents who go about the country soliciting customers for any literary novelties that the firm may have to offer.

The story goes that Mr. Webster, acting for Mark Twain, proposed to Gen. Grant to take his son Jesse, who travelled with him during a part of his famous trip around the world, into the firm as partner. This proposition was regarded favorably, and then it was suggested that the firm would publish and circulate the General's autobiography. Mr. Webster told the General that the mechanical cost of producing each $2 volume would not exceed 30 cents, and that if large editions were sold, as was sure to be the case, the profits would be three times larger than the royalty offered by the *Century* Company. Gen. Grant accepted the offer not only because his profits would be larger but because also it would make a business for his son, who was almost "cleaned out" by the failure of Grant & Ward.

A representative of the *Century* Company when questioned about the matter said that a contract had not been completed for the publication of Gen. Grant's reminiscences, but it had been considered almost settled that the book would be issued by the company. The General visited the office almost daily, when able to go about, to consult about the material and make-up of the book and the advice given was generally followed.

"We have no grievance," continued the *Century*'s representative. "Gen. Grant had the right to go elsewhere, his main object being to create a place for his son. We were not prepared to do that."

It is said, however, that the *Century* people feel exceedingly "sore" about the matter, and it is doubtful if any more of Gen. Grant's papers will appear in the magazine. It is not likely that any passages from the forthcoming book will appear in it in advance, either.

N. Y. World

THE GENERAL'S LITERARY WORK.

FOUR ARTICLES FOR "THE CENTURY"— HIS MEMOIRS TO FILL TWO SUBSCRIPTION VOLUMES.

Many curious and anxious eyes ran over the columns of *The Century* for March expecting to find therein another paper from the pen of General Grant. The impression had gone forth that the article on Shiloh which appeared in the February number was the first of a series that were to be published regularly every month and when the March number was issued without containing the expected paper speculation was rife as to its cause. Some attributed the omission to the General's ill health; others to the fact that he was more anxious that his more important memoirs should be first completed; but it was left for *The World* to discover the fact that there had been a "falling out" between the publishers of *The Century* and General Grant and that it was not likely that any more of his papers would be published in the magazine. The cause of the falling-out was said to be that General Grant had taken the publication of his memoirs away from *The Century* and had entered into a contract for their publication by Charles L. Webster & Co., because *The Century* could not find a place for Jesse Grant in any of its departments.

The facts are that General Grant stipulated some time ago to write for *The Century* four papers on the War, and the following subjects were selected: Shiloh, Vicksburg, Chattanooga, and the Wilderness Campaign. As soon as the terms were agreed upon the General entered upon his literary work with characteristic energy, working frequently from eight to ten hours a day: and though he was hampered by the insidious disease that is now sapping his vitality, only a comparatively short interval elapsed from the time he began his labors when the papers on Shiloh, Vicksburg and Chattanooga were completed and handed over to *The Century*. They were paid for in accordance with the agreement, and are now in the possession of *The Century*. The manuscript for "The Wilderness Campaign" is completed and is now being revised by the General as rapidly as his health and other duties will permit.

There has been no falling-out between General Grant and *The Century,* and their relations are in every way cordial and pleasant. *The Century* Publishing Company entered into competition for the publication of General Grant's books and its failure to obtain the contract was simply a business incident, the General being better satisfied with the arrangements made with Webster & Co. In the negotiation for the publication of the book the question of giving his son a position was not a matter of consideration.

The contract between Webster & Co. and General Grant was signed on February 28, and it is denied at the publishers' office that taking Jesse Grant into partnership, as *The World* alleged, had anything to do with awarding them the contract, for the reason that such an arrangement has not been made. Samuel L. Clemens (Mark Twain) is a silent partner in the firm of Webster & Co., but entrusts the management of the business to his nephew, Charles L. Webster, who conducted all the negotiations with General Grant. The book is to be complete in two volumes. The manuscript for the first is completed and will be delivered to Mr. Webster, the latter part of this week. The General is working as much as possible on the materials for the second volume, which is also nearly finished, the principal labor now being that of revision. The book will be sold by subscription, and the price will probably be $3 50 a volume. It is expected that the two volumes will be ready for delivery in October or November.

N. Y. Tribune

GEN. GRANT AND HIS BOOK.

Over 100,000 Orders for the Set Received by His Publishers.

Gen. Grant has done much towards completing his book during his period of convalescence and expects to finish it within the next few days. The first volume is written and revised. Only about one hundred pages are needed to complete the second, though only a portion of it has been revised. The story of Lee's surrender was finished on Monday and revised yesterday. The General's connection with Lincoln's assassination has been related. It is his intention to begin work to-day on a description of the grand review of the Federal armies in Washington at the close of the war. He writes little himself, but dictates to a stenographer. Not only is his mind clear, but the story as he dictates it is lucid and requires but little revision. His daily average is about thirty pages and the work apparently fatigues him little, if any.

The title of the book is "The Personal Memoirs of U. S. Grant." It tells the story of his life from childhood down to the grand review. It is replete with interesting sketches and anecdote of Lincoln and other great men, with whom Gen. Grant came in contact in civil and military life. Each volume will contain about 500 pages with numerous illustrations and maps. Charles L. Webster & Co., of this city, are the publishers. The work will be published simultaneously by them in the United States, England, France, Germany and Canada. Mr. Webster will go abroad in July to arrange for translating and publishing it in foreign countries. The first volume will be issued Dec. 1, and the second about March 1, 1886. Already orders for over 100,000 sets of the "Memoirs" have been received without solicitation or advertising. At least 50,000 additional orders have come in which have not yet been accepted. It is expected that the sales will be unprecedentedly large. If nothing unforeseen happens the publishers expect to have all the manuscript in hand inside of a month. It will require but a few days to finish the second volume, after which it will be leisurely revised. Nearly all of volume II. has been written since the General was confined to the house by his present illness.

Gen. Grant yesterday sent the following letter to his publishers:

NEW YORK, May 2, 1885.

To Charles L. Webster & Co.

DEAR SIRS: My attention has been called to a paragraph in a letter published in THE WORLD newspaper of this city of Wednesday, April 29, of which the following is a part:

"The work upon his new book, about which so much has been said, is the work of Gen. Adam Badeau. Gen. Grant, I have no doubt, has furnished all of the material and all of the ideas in the memoirs as far as they have been prepared, but Badeau has done the work of composition. The most that Gen. Grant has done upon this book has been to prepare the rough notes and memoranda for its various chapters."

I will divide this into four parts and answer each of them.

First—"The work upon his new book, about which so much has been said, is the work of Gen. Adam Badeau." This is false. The composition is entirely my own.

Second—"Gen. Grant, I have no doubt, has furnished all of the material and all of the ideas in the memoirs as far as they have been prepared." This is true.

Third—"But Badeau has done the work of composition." The composition is entirely my own.

Fourth—"The most that Gen. Grant has done upon this book has been to prepare the rough notes and memoranda for its various chapters." This is false. I have not only prepared myself whatever rough notes were made, but, as above stated, have done the entire work of composition and preparing notes, and no one but myself has ever used one of such notes in any composition.

You may take such measures as you see fit to correct this report, which places me in the attitude of claiming the authorship of a book which I did not write, and is also injurious to you who are publishing and advertising such book as my work.

Yours truly,
U. S. GRANT.

N. Y. World

[The Rev. Dr. Newman]

1885.

Extract from my note book:

> April 4, 1885. General Grant is still living, this morning. Many a person between the two oceans lay hours awake, last night, listening for the booming of the fire-bells that should speak to the nation in simultaneous voice and tell it its calamity. The bell-strokes are to be thirty seconds apart and there will be sixty-three—the General's age. They will be striking in every town in the United States at the same moment—the first time in the world's history that the bells of a nation have tolled in unison, beginning at the same moment and ending at the same moment.

More than once during two weeks, the nation stood watching with bated breath expecting the news of General Grant's death.

The family in their distress desired spiritual help and one Rev. Dr. Newman was sent for to furnish it. Newman had lately gone to California where he had got a ten-thousand-dollar job to preach a funeral sermon over the son of ex-Governor Stanford, the millionaire, and a most remarkable sermon it was—and worth the money. If Newman got the facts right, neither he nor anybody else—any ordinary human being—was worthy to preach that youth's funeral sermon and it was manifest that one of the disciples ought to have been imported into California for the occasion. Newman came on from California at once, and began his ministration at the General's bedside; and if one might trust his daily reports the General had conceived a new and perfect interest in spiritual things. It is fair to presume that the most of Newman's daily reports originated in his own imagination.

Colonel Fred Grant told me that his father was, in this matter, what he was in all matters and at all times—that is to say, perfectly willing to have family prayers going on, or anything else that could be satisfactory to anybody, or increase anybody's comfort in any way; but he also said that while his father was a good man, and indeed as good as any man, Christian or otherwise, he was *not* a praying man.

Some of the speeches put into General Grant's mouth were to the last degree incredible to people who knew the General, since they were such gaudy and flowery misrepresentations of that plain-spoken man's utterances.

About the 14th or 15th of April, Rev. Mr. Newman reported that upon visiting the General in his sick chamber, the General pressed his hand and delivered himself of this astounding remark:

"Thrice have I been in the shadow of the valley of death and thrice have I come out again."

General Grant never used flowers of speech, and dead or alive he never could have uttered anything like that, either as a quotation or otherwise.

About that time I came across a gentleman in the railway train who had been connected with our embassy in China during the past sixteen years and was now at home on leave of absence, and he told me something about Newman. He said that once, when General Grant was President, Newman wanted to travel about the world a little and he was given the post of Inspector of Consulates. It was a salaried position and the salary was paid out of an appropriation set apart for that purpose. Whenever an inspector's time expired, whatever might be left unexpended of that appropriation had to be turned in to the Treasury.

This Secretary of Legation tried to make me understand how there was some crookedness about Newman's expenditures, but I am not able to call to mind in what the crookedness consisted, so I will not make the attempt. The Secretary was mainly interested in showing not that Newman was a knave but that he was simply an ass. He said he came out to China and proceeded to investigate the legation, and hauled it vigorously over the coals, and was getting along very satisfactorily with his work when the American Minister spoiled it all by calling his attention to the fact that the legation was not a consulate and did not come within the jurisdiction of his powers.

There was a social club there, composed of American ladies and gentlemen, who met occasionally to discuss things, and Newman showed a good deal of anxiety to get an invitation to address it and to furnish an essay for one of their discussions. His hints were not favorably received. So he compacted them into a clear form: in fact he invited himself. In introducing him the chairman almost apologized to the company and said in substance that Rev. Mr. Newman had asked permission to address the club.

This chilly introduction didn't distress the essayist a bit apparently. He opened his remarks with a graceful reference to the urgency which had been brought to bear upon him to address the club and which he could not politely decline.

The Secretary of Legation may have exaggerated the case, but from what I can gather Dr. Newman is really about that kind of a man.

Clemens's unsparing account of his own beguilement into financially supporting James W. Paige's development of an automatic typesetter is so manifestly autobiographical that it is judged to be among the chapters Clemens drafted for the autobiography, although he did not explicitly identify it that way. The manuscript, now in the Mark Twain Papers, was written in two separately paginated stages. The first part (twenty manuscript pages) was written in December 1890, almost ten years after Clemens began investing in the typesetter and at a point when his total investment had reached or exceeded $170,000, despite Paige's failure to produce a successful prototype. The second part (nine manuscript pages) starts with "End of 1885" and was written in late 1893 or early 1894, when Clemens had left his family in Europe and traveled to New York to participate in negotiations concerning the typesetter. He must have written it before 1 February 1894, when he reached a new agreement with Paige that he believed would make him wealthy (Notebook 33, TS pp. 47, 51, CU-MARK).

Paine quoted from the manuscript in his biography (*MTB*, 2:903–5, 913), and in his edition of the autobiography he published most of the first part (with the usual silent omissions), but only four paragraphs of the second part (*MTA*, 1:70–78). Neider did not include any part of this text in his edition. Clemens continued to excoriate Paige in the Autobiographical Dictation of 2 June 1906.

The Machine Episode

[Written in the closing days of 1890.]

This episode has now spread itself over more than one-fifth of my life—a considerable stretch of time, as I am now fifty-five years old.

Ten or eleven years ago, Dwight Buell, a jeweler, called at our house and was shown up to the billiard room—which was my study; and the game got more study than the other sciences. He wanted me to take some stock in a type-setting machine. He said it was at the Colt Arms factory, and was about finished. I took $2,000 of the stock. I was always taking little chances like that; and almost always losing by it, too—a thing which I did not greatly mind, because I was always careful to risk only such amounts as I could easily afford to lose. Some time afterward I was invited to go down to the factory and see the machine. I went, promising myself nothing; for I knew all about type-setting by practical experience, and held the settled and solidified opinion that a successful type-setting machine was an impossibility, for the reason that a machine cannot be made to *think,* and the thing that sets movable type *must* think or retire defeated. So, the performance I witnessed did most thoroughly amaze me. Here was a machine that was really setting type; and doing it with swiftness and accuracy, too. Moreover, it was distributing its case *at the same time.* The distribution was automatic: the machine fed itself from a galley of dead matter, and without human help or suggestion; for it began its work of its own accord when the type channels needed filling, and stopped of its own accord when they were full enough. The machine was almost a complete compositor; it lacked but one feature—it did not "justify" the lines; this was done by the operator's assistant.

I saw the operator set at the rate of 3,000 ems an hour, which, counting distribution, was but little short of four case-men's work.

William Hamersley was there. I had known him long, I thought I knew him well. I had great respect for him, and full confidence in him. He said he was already a considerable owner, and was now going to take as much more of the stock as he could afford. Wherefore I set down my name for an additional $3,000. It is here that the music begins.

Footnote. Hamersley now says we never had any such agreement. He will revise that remark presently.

Before very long Hamersley called on me and asked me what I would charge to raise a capital of $500,000 for the manufacture of the machines. I said I would undertake it for $100,000. He said, raise $600,000, then, and take $100,000. I agreed. I sent for my partner, Webster; he came up from New York and went back with the project. There was some correspondence. Hamersley wrote Webster a letter which will be inserted later on.

I will remark, here, that James W. Paige, the little bright-eyed, alert, smartly dressed inventor of the machine, is a most extraordinary compound of business thrift and commercial insanity; of cold calculation and jejune sentimentality; of veracity and falsehood; of fidelity and treachery; of nobility and baseness; of pluck and cowardice; of wasteful liberality and pitiful stinginess; of solid sense and weltering moonshine; of towering genius and trivial ambitions; of merciful bowels and a petrified heart; of colossal vanity and— But there the opposites stop. His vanity stands alone, sky-piercing, as sharp of outline as an Egyptian monolith. It is the only unpleasant feature in him that is not modified, softened, compensated by some converse characteristic. There is another point or two worth mentioning: he can persuade anybody; he can convince nobody. He has a crystal-clear mind, as regards the grasping and concreting of an idea which has been lost and smothered under a chaos of baffling legal language; and yet it can always be depended upon to take the simplest half dozen facts and draw from them a conclusion that will astonish the idiots in the asylum. It is because he is a dreamer, a visionary. His imagination runs utterly away with him. He is a poet; a most great and genuine poet, whose sublime creations are written in steel. He is the Shakespeare of mechanical invention. In all the ages he has no peer. Indeed, there is none that even approaches him. Whoever is qualified to fully comprehend his marvelous machine will grant that its place is upon the loftiest summit of human invention, with no kindred between it and the far foothills below.

But I must explain these strange contradictions above listed, or the man will be misunderstood and wronged. His business thrift is remarkable, and it is also of a peculiar cut. He has worked at his expensive machine for more than twenty years, but always at somebody else's cost. He spent hundreds and thousands of other folk's money, yet always kept his machine and its possible patents in his own possession, unencumbered by an embarrassing lien of any kind— except once, which will be referred to by and by. He could never be beguiled into putting a penny of his own into his work. Once he had a brilliant idea in the way of a wonderfully valuable application of electricity. To test it, he said, would cost but $25. I was paying him a salary of nearly $600 a month and was spending $1,200 on the machine besides; yet he asked me to risk the $25 and take half of the result. I declined, and he dropped the matter. Another time he was sure he was on the track of a splendid thing in electricity. It would cost only a trifle— possibly $200—to try some experiments; I was asked to furnish the money and take half of the result. I furnished money until the sum had grown to about $1,000, and everything was pronounced ready for the grand exposition. The electric current was turned on—the thing declined to go. Two years later the same thing was successfully worked out and patented by a man in the State of New York and was at once sold for a huge sum of money and a royalty-reserve besides. The drawings in the electrical journal showing the stages by which that inventor had approached the consummation of his idea, proving his way step by step as he went, were almost the twins of Paige's drawings of two years before. It was almost as if the same hand had drawn both sets. Paige said we had *had* it, and we should have *known* it if we had only tried an alternating current after failing with the direct current; said he had felt sure, at the time, that at cost of $100 he could apply the alternating test and come out triumphant. Then he added, in tones absolutely sodden with self-sacrifice, and just barely touched with reproach,

"But you had already spent so much money on the thing that I hadn't the heart to ask you to spend any more."

If I had asked him why he didn't draw on his own pocket, he would not have understood me. He could not have grasped so strange an idea as that. He would have thought there was something the matter with my mind. I am speaking honestly; he could not have understood it. A cancer of old habit and long experience could as easily understand the suggestion that it board itself a while.

In drawing contracts he is always able to take care of himself; and in every instance he will work into the contracts injuries to the other party and advantages to himself which were never considered or mentioned in the preceding verbal agreement. In one contract he got me to assign to him several hundred thousand dollars' worth of property for a certain valuable consideration—said valuable consideration being the *re-giving to me of another piece of property which was not his to give but already belonged to me!* See assignment, Aug. 12, 1890. I quite understand that I am confessing myself a fool; but that is no matter, the reader would find it out anyway, as I go along. Hamersley was our joint lawyer, and I had every confidence in his wisdom and cleanliness.

Once when I was lending money to Paige during a few months, I presently found that he was giving *receipts* to my representative instead of notes! But that man never lived who could catch Paige so nearly asleep as to palm off on *him* a piece of paper which apparently satisfied a debt when it ought to acknowledge a loan.

I must throw in a parenthesis here, or I shall do Hamersley an injustice. Here and there I have seemed to cast little reflections upon him. Pay no attention to them. I have no feeling about him, I have no harsh words to say about him. He is a great fat good-natured, kind-hearted, chicken-livered slave; with no more pride than a tramp, no more sand than a rabbit, no more moral sense than a wax figure, and no more sex than a tape-worm. He sincerely thinks he is honest, he sincerely thinks he is honorable. It is my daily prayer to God that he be permitted to live and die in those superstitions. I gave him a twentieth of my American holding, at Paige's request; I gave him a twentieth of my foreign holding at his own supplication; I advanced near $40,000 in five years to keep these interests sound and valid for him. In return, he drafted every contract which I made with Paige in all that time—clear up to September, 1890—and pronounced it good and fair; and then I signed. These unique contracts will be found in the Appendix. May they be instructive to the struggling student of law.

Yes, it is as I have said: Paige is an extraordinary compound of business thrift and commercial insanity. Instances of his commercial insanity are simply innumerable. Here are some examples. When I took hold of the machine Feb. 6, 1886, its faults had been corrected and a setter and a justifier could turn out about 3,500 ems an hour on it; possibly 4,000. There was no machine that could pretend rivalry to it. Business sanity would have said, put it on the market as it was, secure the field, and add improvements later. Paige's business insanity said, add the improvements first, and risk losing the field. And that is what he set out to do. To add a justifying mechanism to that machine would take a few months and cost $9,000 by his estimate, or $12,000 by Pratt & Whitney's. I agreed to add said justifier to *that* machine. There could be no sense in building a new machine. Yet in total violation of the agreement, Paige went immediately to work to build a new machine, although aware, by recent experience, that the cost could not fall below $150,000, and that the time consumed would be years instead of months. Well, when four years had been spent and the new machine was able to exhibit a marvelous capacity, we appointed the 12th of January for Senator Jones of Nevada to come and make an inspection. He was not promised a perfect machine, but a machine which could be perfected. He had agreed to invest one or two hundred thousand dollars in its fortunes; and had also said that if the exhibition was particularly favorable, he might take entire charge of the elephant. At the last moment Paige concluded to add an air-blast, (afterwards found to be unnecessary); wherefore, Jones had to be turned back from New York to wait a couple of months and lose his interest in the thing. A year ago, Paige made what he regarded as a vast and magnanimous concession: Hamersley and I might sell the English patent for $10,000,000! A little later a man came along who thought he could bring some Englishmen who would buy that patent, and he was sent off to fetch them. He was gone so long that Paige's confidence began to diminish, and with it his price. He finally got down to what he said was his very last and bottom price for that patent—$50,000! This was the only time in five years that I ever saw Paige in his right mind. I could furnish other examples of Paige's business insanity—enough of them to fill six or eight volumes, perhaps, but I am not writing his history, I am merely sketching his portrait.

Greatest of all mistakes that things warn't arranged so as to have four persons in the Trinity. But even then Paige wouldn't stir a peg unless he could have the boss-ship.

End of 1885.

Paige arrives at my house unheralded. [I was a small stockholder in the Farnham Co., but had seen little or nothing of Paige for a year or two.] He said "What'll you complete the machine for?"

"What will it cost?"

"$20,000—certainly not over $30,000."

"What will you give?"

"I'll give you half."

"I'll do it—but the *limit* must be $30,000."

"Hamersley's a good fellow and will be invaluable to us—we can't get along without him as our lawyer. Shan't we give him a slice?"

"Yes. How much?"

"Shall we say a tenth?"

"All right—yes."

———

The contract, (signed Feb. 6, 1886) was drawn by Hamersley. It is an excruciatingly absurd piece of paper. It bound me to requirements which had not been talked about, but they looked easy and I accepted them. But it was not till months afterward that upon trying to sell a part of my interest to raise money for the machine I found I hadn't any ownership of any kind. My 9/20 interest had become a purely *conditional* one. Failing the conditions, I would have nothing back but my $30,000 and 6 per cent interest.

Hamersley was my trusted old friend, and as *I* thought, my lawyer also. I was spending $30,000 to build his tenth of the machine. Yet he drew that contract and was present at the signing of it, and found nothing unrighteous about it.

II

The $30,000 lasted about a year, I should say. My contract was fulfilled, but Paige had fallen far short of finishing the machine—though *he* said he could finish it for $4,000; and could finish it and give it a big exhibition in New York for $10,000. After an interval, during which I did not see him, he applied for a loan of this money and offered to pay back double some day.

I sent word that I would furnish the $4,000, but would take nothing but 6 per cent. (Witness, F. G. Whitmore.)

When the $4,000 was gone, he said a little more would do. I furnished a little more and a little more, taking 6 per cent notes until at last the machine *was* finished but not absolutely perfected. It could not have stood a lengthy test-exhibition. The notes then aggregated (with interest) about $53,000 or $55,000. I was out of pocket more than $80,000, with nothing to show for it but the original idiotic contract.

I then struck the idea of asking for royalties to raise money on. I asked for five hundred. Paige said—

"You can have as many as you want. I'll give you a thousand."

I said no, I would take only five hundred.

The royalty deed was made and signed. We were all feeling fine. Paige asked me to give him back his notes. I made Whitmore do it, though he strenuously objected.

———————

I went on finishing the machine at the rate of $4,000 and upwards a month. I had no fears or doubts. [But I found royalties not very salable, and stopped trying to sell them.]

Hamersley was in a sweat to get a new contract out of Paige allowing a company to organize in the ordinary way and manufacture the machine. Presently Paige consented—and contract No. 2 was the result. It recognized my share. A rough one on me, but anything seemed better than the old contract—which was a mistake.

A few months later contract No. 3 (the May contract?) was made. It recognized my share.

These were not promising contracts for a company to take hold of.

Then came the "June" contract—a good and rational one. All this time these various contracts merely recognized my American rights. My foreign 9/20 were conditioned upon my paying the patent-expenses as they accrued (which I did) and the ultimate expenses of starting work in the foreign countries—a condition which has not yet arrived. Now none of the previous contracts actually gave me an ownership, but this June one gave me the machine and everything, bag and baggage.

However, John P. Jones thought the foreign rights should be put into this contract, and I wrote to Paige to *interline* this addition. He sent for my copy of the June contract and Whitmore brought it and left it with him—which was a mistake.

We couldn't get it from him any more. He said it wasn't a real contract, because it had a blank in it (for his salary.)

I came down from Onteora to see what the trouble was, and Whitmore urged me to stand out for the restoration of that stolen contract; but Paige insisted that a new one which he had been drawing up was much better. I signed it, and also assigned my foreign rights back to Paige, who now owned the entire thing (Hamersley's shares, too) if this contract failed to materialize. It had but six months to run.

After signing it I spoke doubtfully of my chances, and Paige shed a few tears, as usual, and was deeply hurt at being doubted; asked me if he hadn't always taken care of me? and had he ever failed of his word with me? hadn't he always said that no matter *what* happened (meaning a falling-out—which I had suggested) I should have my 9/20 of every dollar he ever got out of the machine, domestic and foreign; that if he died (as I had suggested) his family would see to it that I got my 9/20. Then—

"Here, Charley Davis, take a pen and write what I say."

He dictated and Davis wrote.

"There, now," said Paige, "are you satisfied *now?*"

I went on footing the bills, and got the machine really perfected at last, at a full cost of about $150,000, instead of the original $30,000.

Ward tells me that Paige tried his best to cheat me out of my royalties when making a contract with the Connecticut Co.

Also that he tried to cheat out of all share Mr. North (inventor of the justifying mechanism;) but that North frightened him with a lawsuit-threat, and is to get a royalty until the aggregate is $2,000,000.

Paige and I always meet on effusively affectionate terms; and yet he knows perfectly well that if I had his nuts in a steel-trap I would shut out all human succor and watch that trap till he died.

This manuscript—which has not been published before—was left to a degree unfinished, judging from Clemens's penciled (tentative) revision of its title to "Travel-Scraps from Autobiog." Now in the Mark Twain Papers, it is thought to be a draft chapter written for the autobiography on that evidence, and also because, in 1900 during a later stay in London, Clemens wrote a sequel about the city entitled "Travel-Scraps II," which he ultimately inserted in the Autobiographical Dictation of 27 February 1907. The subtitle "London, Summer, 1896," refers to the events in the piece, not the time of writing, which was clearly soon after the Clemenses arrived in Vienna in late September 1897. The "village" Clemens referred to was the area around Tedworth Square, where they lived from October 1896 until they moved to Weggis, Switzerland, in July 1897 (Notebook 39, TS p. 6, CU-MARK).

Travel-Scraps I

London, Summer, 1896

All over the world there seems to be a prejudice against the cab driver. But that is too sweeping; it must be modified. I think I may say that there is a prejudice against him in many American cities, but not in Washington, Baltimore, Philadelphia and Boston; that in Europe, as a rule, there is a prejudice against him, but not in Munich and Berlin; that there is a prejudice against him in Calcutta but not in Bombay. I think I may say that the prejudice against him is strong in London, stronger in Paris, and strongest in New York. There are courteous and reasonable cabmen in Paris, but they seem to be rare. I think that in London four out of every six cabmen are pleasant and rational beings, and are satisfied with twenty-five per cent above legal fare; and that the other two are always ready and anxious for a dispute, and burning to conduct it in a loud and frantic key.* The citizen must pay from two to three prices, when he makes his bargain beforehand, and more when he doesn't. When he makes his bargain beforehand he expects to be overcharged, and is not discontented unless the over-tax is extravagant, because he knows that the legal rate is too low, and that the hack-industry cannot live upon it. The heavy over-charge has kept the traffic down and made it meagre. The legal charge might not be too low if the traffic were as heavy as it ought to be for a city like New York, but it is not likely to expand while hackmen may continue to charge any price they please. And now that the hacks have driven all the business into the hands of the steam and electric companies, the periodical attempts to inaugurate a cheap hack-system in New York will presently begin again, I suppose. Hacks are but little needed in American cities for any but strangers who cannot find their way by tram-lines. The citizen should be thankful for the high hack-rates which have given him the trams; for by consequence he has the cheapest and swiftest city-transportation that exists in the world. London travels by omnibus—pleasant, but as deadly slow as a European

*If you call a policeman to settle the dispute you can depend on one thing—he will decide it against you every time. And so will the New York policeman. In London, if you carry your case into court, the man that is entitled to win it will win it. In New York—but no one carries a cab case into court there. It is my impression that it is now more than thirty years since any one has carried a cab case into court there. The foreigner is charged the wildest of prices, but the hotel keeper advises him to pay and keep quiet, and assures him that the court will of a certainty side with the hackman.

"lift;" and by underground railway, which is an invention of Satan himself. It goes no direct course, but always away around. When the train arrives you must jump, rush, fly, and swarm with the crowd into the first cigar box that is handy, lest you get left. You have hardly time to mash yourself into a portion of a seat before the train is off again. It goes blustering and sputtering along, puking smoke and cinders in at the window, which some one has opened in pursuance of his right to make the whole cigar box uncomfortable if his comfort requires it; the fog of black smoke smothers the lamp and dims its light, and the double row of jammed people sit there and bark at each other, and the righteous and the unrighteous pray each after his own fashion. The train stops every few minutes, and there is a new rush and scramble each time. And every quarter of an hour you change cars, and fly thirty yards to a stairway, and up the stairway and fifty yards along a corridor, and down another stairway, and plunge headlong into a train just as it moves off; and of course it is the wrong one, and you must get out at the next station and come back. But it is no matter. If you had stopped to ask the official on duty, it would have been the right train and you would have lost it by stopping to ask; and so none but idiots stop to ask. The next time that you ought to change cars you are not aware of it, and you go on. You keep on going on and on and on, wondering what has become of St. John's Wood, and if you are ever likely to get to that brick-and-mortar forest; and by and by you pull your courage together and ask a passenger if he can tell you whereabouts you are, and he says "We are just arriving at Sloane Square." You thank him, and look gratified, look as gratified as you can on the spur of the moment and without sufficient preparation, and step out, saying "It is my station." And so it is. That is where you started from. It is an hour or an hour and a half ago, and is getting toward bedtime, now. You have been plowing through tunnels all that time, and have been all around under London amongst its entrails, and been in first, second and third-class cars on a third-class ticket, and associated with all sorts of company, from Dukes and Bishops down to rank and mangy tramps and blatherskites who sat with their drunken trunnions in their laps and caressed and kissed them unembarrassed. You have missed the dinner you were aimed for, but you are alive yet, and that is something; and you have learned better than to go by tunnel any more, and that is also a gain. You cannot telephone your friend to go to bed and not keep the dinner waiting. There is not a telephone within a mile of you, and there is not a telephone within a mile of him. Years ago there was a telephone system in England, but in the country parts it is about dead, now, and what is left of it in London has no value. So you send a telegram to your friend, stating that you have met with an accident, and begging him not to wait dinner for you. You are aware that all the offices in his neighborhood close at eight in the evening and it is ten now; it is also Saturday night, and England keeps Sunday; but the telegram will reach his house Monday morning, and when he gets back from business at five in the evening he will get it, and will know then that you did not come Saturday evening, and why.

One little wee bunch of houses in London, one little wee spot, is the centre of the globe, the heart of the globe, and the machinery that moves the world is located there. It is called the City, and it, with a patch of its borderland, *is* a city. But the rest of London is not a city. It is fifty villages massed solidly together over a vast stretch of territory. Each village has its own name and its own government. Its ways are village ways, and the great body of its inhabitants are just villagers, and have the simple, honest, untraveled, unworldly look of villagers. Its shops are village shops; little cramped places where you can buy an anvil or a paper of pins, or anything between; but you can't buy two anvils, nor five papers of pins, nor seven white cravats, nor two hats of the same breed, because they do not keep such gross masses in stock. The shopman will not offer to get the things and send them to you, but will tell you where he thinks you may possibly find them. And he is not brusque and fussy and unpleasant, like a city person, but takes the simple and kindly interest of a villager in the matter, and will discuss it as long as you please. They have no hateful city ways, and indeed no ways that suggest that they have ever lived in a city.

In my village there are a lot of little postoffices and one big one—in Sloane Square. One Saturday toward dusk I visited three of the little ones and asked if there was a Sunday mail for Paris; and if so, at how late an hour could I mail my letter and catch it? Nobody knew whether there was such a mail or not, but it was believed that there was. They could not refer to a table of mails, for they had none. Could they telephone the General Postoffice and find out for me? No, they had no telephone. The big office in Sloane Square might know. I went there. There were two or three girls and a woman or two on duty. Yes, there was a Paris mail, they said; they did not know at what hour it left, but they believed it did. Were my questions unusual ones in their experience? They could not remember that any one had asked them before. And those people looked *so* friendly, and innocent, and childlike, and ignorant, and happy, and content.

I lived nine months in that village. I got my predecessor's mail along with my own, every day. He had left his new address at the postoffice, but that did little or no good. The letters came to me. I reinstructed the carriers now and then; then, for as much as a week afterward I would get my own mail only; after that, I would get the double mail again, as before.

But that was a pleasant village to live in. The spirit of accommodation was everywhere, just as it is in Germany, and just as it isn't, in a good many parts of the earth. I went to my nearest postoffice one day to send a telegram. The office was in a little shop that had thirty dollars' worth of miscellaneous merchandise in it, and a young woman was on duty. I was in a hurry. I wrote the telegram, and the young woman examined it and said she was afraid it would not reach its destination. A flaw in the address, perhaps—I do not remember what the trouble was. She wanted to call her husband and advise about the matter. I explained that I was following orders, and that if the man at the other end did not get the telegram he would have only himself to blame. But she was not satisfied with that. She reminded me that it would be a pure waste of money, and I the loser. She would rather call her husband and see about it. She had to have her way; I could not help myself; her kindly interest disarmed me, and I could not break out and say, "Oh, send it just as it is, and let me go." She brought her husband, and the two reasoned the matter out at considerable length, and finally got it arranged to their satisfaction. But I was not to get away yet. There was a new difficulty. There were apparently more words than necessary, and if I could strike out a word or two the telegram would cost only sixpence. I came near saying I would rather pay four cents extra than lose another three shillings' worth of time, but it would have been a shame to act like that when they were trying their best to do me a kindness, so I did not say it, but held in and let the ruinous expense of time run on. Amongst us, in the course of time, we managed to gut the telegram of a few of its most necessary words,

DIAGRAM OF LONDON.

					North St. Pancras	North Islington	East Islington	North Hackney				
				Hampstead	West St. Pancras	East St. Pancras	West Islington	Central Hackney	South Hackney			
Fulham	Hamm'r smith		North Paddington	East Marylebone	South St. Pancras	Central Finsbury	South Islington	Haggerston	North-East Bethnal-Green			
	South Kensington	North Kensington	South Paddington	West Marylebone	Holborn	East Finsbury	Hoxton	South-West Bethnal-gn.	Stepney			
Chelsea			Bow	Westminstr	Strand	City.	Whitechpl.	St. George-in-the-East.	Limehouse.	Mile-end.		
			Wandsw'th.	Battersea.	North Lambeth.	West Southwark.	Bermondsey	Rotherhithe.	Greenwich.		Poplar.	Bromley.
				Clapham.	Kennington	West Newington.	Walworth.	Deptford.				
					Brixton.	North Camb'rwell	Peckham.	Woolwich.				
					Norwood.	Dulwich.	Lewisham.					

and then I was free, and paid my sixpence and got back to my work; and I would be glad to repeat that pleasant experience, even at cost of half the time and twice the money. That was a London episode. I am trying to imagine such a thing happening in a New York telegraph office, but there seems to be something the matter with my imagination to-day.

The London 'bus driver does not seem like a city person, but like a blessed angel out of the country. He is often nattily dressed and nicely shaved, and often just the other way; but in either case the man is a choice man, and satisfactory. He hasn't a hard city face, nor crusty and repellent city ways, nor indeed anything about him which can be called "citified"—that epithet which suggests the absence of all spirituality, and the presence of all kinds of paltry material-isms, and mean ideals, and mean vanities, and silly cynicisms. He is a pleasant and courteous and companionable person, he is kindly and conversational, he has a placid and dignified bearing which becomes him well, and he rides serene above the crush and turmoil of London as undisturbed by it and as unconcerned about it as if he were not aware that anything of the kind was going on. The choice part of the 'bus is its roof; and the choicest places on the roof are the two seats back of the driver's elbows. The occupants of those seats talk to him all the time. That shows that he is a polite man, and interesting. And it shows that in his heart he is a villager, and has the simplicities and sincerities and spirit of comradeship which belong to a man whose city contacts have been of an undamaging infrequency. The 'bus driver not only likes to talk to his passengers, but likes to have a choice kind of passengers to talk to. I base this opinion upon some remarks made to a friend of mine by a driver toward the end of last February. My friend opened the conversation, along in the King's Road somewhere:

"I suppose you are glad the winter is about over?"

"No, I don't mind the cold weather, but I don't like the road."

"What is the matter with the road?"

"Well, I don't like the society. Just villagers, you know, that's about what they are. Good-hearted, and all that, but no style. No conversational powers. Chelsea—Walham Green—Battersea—that kind, you know. No intellectual horizon. Dull, honest, sincerely pious, and all that; but interested in the triflingest little commonplace things. I am degenerating, I know it. A man can't live on that kind of mental diet and drive a 'bus."

"Where were you before? Were you better off before?"

"Well, I should think! Hammersmith—Earl's Court—Knightsbridge. *There's* society! And brains. Yes, sir, and fashion. Top of the 'bus looks like a Queen's Drawing-Room. And the talk—well, the talk is up high—away up towards the snow-line. Away up, where, as you may say, your intellectual water boils at a hundred and forty-five. That is the ticket. I'm tired boiling mine at two hundred and twelve."

Part of the 'bus driver's serenity in the midst of the London turmoil springs no doubt from his consciousness of the fact that he and his 'bus have nothing to fear from collisions, part from his confidence in the steadiness and biddability of his horses, and the rest from the fact that he knows how to steer. Drivers of cabs and carriages know that a collision with a 'bus is not a desir-able thing, and they take pains to avoid it. The 'bus is English. When that is said, all is said. As a rule, any English thing is nineteen times as strong and twenty-three times as heavy as it needs to be. The 'bus fills these requirements. It is a lumbering big ark, it weighs no one knows how much and it minds collision with an ordinary vehicle no more than a planet would. It is a pity they did not keep the first English bicycle; it must have weighed upwards of three tons. And if it ever collided with an express train, the remains of the train must have been a spectacle.

It is an inspiring thing to see the 'bus driver steer his ark. He weaves in and out among a writhing swarm of vehicles, just barely missing them—missing them by the thickness of a shingle sometimes, sometimes by the thickness of a brick—and while you are doing the gasping and shrinking he is chatting over his shoulder, and his hands seem to be mainly idle and himself not interested in anything but his talk. It is wonderful steering, and yet it seems to do itself, it has such an effortless look.

Two horses draw the ark, only two; but they are capable. They are strong and sleek and handsome, well kept and well cared for, and on long routes they make but one trip a day. They are brought from America; they cost about two hundred and fifty dollars apiece; at the end of three years they are sold—often for more than they cost originally—and fresh importations take their place.

Here in Vienna the cab driver ranks as he ranks in all other cities of Europe—as the wittiest person in town, the ablest chaffer, the quickest and brightest at repartee. We always believe that, wherever we go; but we have to take it on trust, because the instances never chance to fall under our own personal notice. In London the cabman is noted for his smart sayings, but I did not have the luck to hear them. Many years ago, in Liverpool—however, that time it was not wit, it was humor. I was there with the late James R. Osgood, and we had several hours to spare, and much talking to do. It seemed a good idea to do the talking in a cab, and have the fresh air. The cabman asked where we wished to go. Mr. Osgood said—

"Oh, just drive around an hour or so—anywhere—we are not particular."

The man sat still, and waited. Osgood presently asked what he was waiting for, and he said—

"I want to know where I am to go."

"Why, I told you to go anywhere you pleased."

The man looked troubled, puzzled, worried. But he sat still. Presently Osgood said—

"Why don't you start?"

"Dear me, I want to start; I want to start as bad as anybody, but how can I, when you won't tell me where you want to go? I've drove for fourteen years, and I never heard of such a thing."

"Oh, do move along. I don't care where you go. Go to Balmoral."

We were very busy talking, all through these interruptions. We probably started, now. After a long time we woke up out of the talk, and Osgood looked at his watch and said it was getting toward train time. Liverpool was nowhere in sight. We were troubled, and Osgood said—

"Driver, what have you been doing? Where are you going?"

"Balmoral, sir."

"Balmoral? What are you going to Balmoral for?"

"Because you told me, sir."

"Because I told you! Did you suppose I was in earnest? How far is it?"

"Four hundred miles, sir."

"Well, well, well. This *is* a joke—what there is of it. Get along back, as fast as you can."

"Just as you say, sir."

The man had a pleasant voice and pleasant ways and manners, and a good face; a very good face indeed, but a preternaturally grave one; not melancholy, but just grave; grave and patient. He had probably never smiled in his life. He was not dull; but he was not animated, not excitable; he had the look of one who was given to much thinking, and little speaking. By his accent he was Scotch.

On our way back Osgood amused himself a good deal over this matter. That we had lost our train did not disturb him; nothing ever disturbed that comfortable soul, that rare and beautiful spirit. He chuckled over this thing in his happy and contented and almost youthful way all the way back to Liverpool, and said we could add to it and trim it up and embroider it, and get the little Kinsmen Club together in London over a supper, and tell it, and have a good time over it. And while I mourned for the lost train he invented addition after addition for the story, and richer and ever richer embroideries, and got so much wholesome pleasure out of his work that it was a comfort to see him. At the hotel we climbed out of the cab and stretched our cramped legs, and Osgood put his hand in his pocket and asked the driver—

"How much?"

"Twelve pounds, sir."

"Twelve *pounds?*"

"Yes, sir."

"Why, man, you don't mean pounds, you mean shillings."

"No, sir, it is pounds."

"By your face you are in earnest; but how do you make it out?"

"You see, sir, it wasn't I that interrupted the job, it was you. I took the job, and I never made any objections, you will allow that yourself, sir. I could have done it in eight days; call it eighty hours. I am allowed three shillings an hour outside of the city. Eighty times three shillings is—"

"Oh—you propose to charge us from here to Balmoral; is that it?"

"You remember it was my orders, sir; and the law—"

"There, don't say any more. I saw, myself, that this was a good joke on some one; I saw it early; but on account of not waiting till the details were all in, I made an error in locating it. We can't afford to stay here and examine the case in a court, and so—come, we have had you five hours; let us see if we can't arrange a compromise."

The man was willing, and proposed five pounds. Osgood gave him six. Everybody was satisfied, and there was no ill blood at the parting. We did not gather the Kinsmen together in London. Osgood said that a story which you could not add anything to by your fancy and invention wasn't worth while, and there did not seem to be any way to add anything to this one; it seemed to be born full grown.

If the cabman had been a German it could be believable that he did not know that the situation was a humorous one. But he was a Scotchman. There have been Scotchmen who have passed themselves off as being destitute of the sense of humor, but it was no credit to them that they succeeded. They could not have succeeded with intelligent people.

I believe that London is the pleasantest and most satisfying village in the world. The stranger soon grows fond of it, and the native lives and dies worshiping it. It is a most singular and interesting place, and the engaging simplicities of its fifty village populations are an unending marvel and delight to the wandering alien. For instance, he sees three or four brisk young men come along—idiots, apparently—with great loud-colored splotches painted on their faces, and wearing fantastic and bright-hued circus-costumes, and he will wonder how they can expose themselves like that and not perish with shame; and why they are not jeered at, and made fun of, and driven to concealment or suicide. But they are not thinking of being ashamed; they are gay and proud, and they hold their heads up, and smirk and grimace and gambol along, utterly complacent and happy; and they are not jeered at, but admired. They stop in the middle of the village street and begin to perform—for these sorry animals are comedians. The villagers come to the windows to see and enjoy; the maid-servants flock up the area-steps and their neat white caps with their flowing white streamers show above the level of the sidewalk; all kinds of humble folk gather and sit on the curbstones on both sides of the street and look glad and expectant. While one comedian brays a comic song, another shuffles off a pathetically rudimentary and ignorant dance to the rattle and thump of a tambourine, a third stands on his head, walks on his hands, throws summersaults and handsprings, and does other innocent little juvenile gymnastics, and the principal ass of the party—the grotesquely-dressed clown—awkwardly repeats these marvels after him, and pretends to get falls and to hurt himself, and then limps about, rubbing his stomach and ruefully shaking his head, and is so unspeakably and self-consciously, and premeditatively and ostentatiously funny that the villagers do nearly expire with laughter over it, instead of lassoing the man and lynching him.

Then the comedians play a play of unimaginable simplicity and incoherency and irrelevancy and juvenility—a play that lasts nearly ten minutes, sometimes—and the exhibition is over. All the spectators look pleased and happy, and greatly freshened-up. The whole performance has lasted twenty or thirty minutes, perhaps, and one comedian or another has passed the hat several times in the meantime. Not to the pit—the curbstone—for it is usually too poor to pay—but to the windows and the area. The solicitor holds up his cap and waltzes about with his beseeching eyes on the windows, and when a penny falls he jumps and catches it and returns a bow worth two thousand dollars. If there are as many as four comedians, and if their costumes are new and smart, the contributions are liberal; sometimes they foot up twenty-five or thirty cents for a single performance; but I have seen a troop consisting of two comedians, clothed in old and shabby finery, play seventeen minutes and collect only four cents.

Still, it was enough. It was profitable. It was more than twenty cents an hour; say two dollars for the day's work. Those young fellows would probably have found it difficult to earn that much at any ordinary work.

Next, the stranger will see three or four "nigger minstrels" going along, with banjo, bones and tambourine. They are a sorrier lot than the comedians. They are "niggers" in nothing—not even in the black paint; for it is too black, or isn't the right kind; at any rate it does not counterfeit any complexion known to our Southern States, and it is our negro that is ostensibly represented. The costumes are incredible. They counterfeit no clothes that were ever worn in this planet, or indeed anywhere in the solar system. These poor fellows furnish a "comic" performance which is so humble, and poor and pitiful, and childish, and asinine, and inadequate that it makes a person ashamed of the human race. Ah, their timorous dances—and their timorous antics—and their shamefaced attempts at funny grimacing—and their cockney-nigger songs and jokes—

they touch you, they pain you, they fill you with pity, they make you cry. I suppose that in any village but London these poor minstrels and the comedians would be mercifully taken out and drowned; but in London, no; London loves them; London has a warm big heart, and there is room and a welcome in it for all the misappreciated refuse of creation.

In all the villages of prodigious London the villagers love music. They love it with a breadth and looseness of taste not known elsewhere but in heaven. If they were up there they would not shut their ears Sundays when the congregational singing was coming up from below. To them, anything that is a noise is music. And they enjoy it, not in an insipid way, but with a rapt and whole-hearted joy. Particularly if it is doleful. And there are no people anywhere who are so generous with their money if the music is doleful enough. In London poor old ragged men and women go up and down the middle of the empty streets, Sunday afternoons, singing the most heart-breakingly desolate hymns and sorrowful ditties in weak and raspy and wheezy voices—voices that are hardly strong enough to carry across the street—and the villagers listen and are grateful, and fling pennies out of the windows, and in the deep stillness of the Sabbath afternoon you can hear the money strike upon the stones a block away. The song drones along as monotonously and as tunelessly as a morning-service snore in a back-country church in the summer time, and I think that nothing could well be more dreary and saddening. But it brings pennies—pennies instead of bricks; and you note that circumstance with surprise and disappointment; or perhaps not exactly disappointment, but something between that and regret.

Still, your respect is compelled: partly for the catholic width of taste that can find room for music like that, and partly for the spirit of benevolence that is in the breast of him who throws the penny. The spirit of benevolence is there, there can be no question about that. There is nothing that is quite so marvelous to the stranger as the free way in which England pours out money upon charities. About half or two-thirds of the time, the objects are unworthy, apparently, but that is no matter, that is nothing to the point. It is the spirit that in many instances is back of the gifts that makes the act fine. Not in all the instances, possibly not even in the majority of them; but after you have put aside the reluctant and unvoluntary contributions, there are enough of the other sort left to make you wonder and admire and take off your hat.

The first flush of enthusiasm over the Queen's approaching Jubilee sent every Englishman's hand into his pocket after money to commemorate with, and he brought it out full, and gladly contributed it. The mass of those voluntary contributions was prodigious; it was monumental for vastness. But one is perhaps justified in believing that it was by no means as imposing as the mass of the unvoluntary contributions which followed it. I was living in London in those interesting months. The journals furnished appetising reading for the disconnected stranger. Every day, and the day after, and the day following that, and so-on and so-on and so-on, week in and week out the appeals for money filed through their columns in steady and compact procession, and gave one the feeling that all England was marching by and holding out its hat—its hat and an axe; the hat in one hand and an axe to grind in the other; a stretch of hats from horizon to horizon on one side along the mighty line of march, and of axes on the other. Everybody seemed to have an axe to grind, and to recognise that now was his chance; now that his prey could not escape; now that excuses which could save his prey ordinarily would injure him at this time, make him seem unpatriotic, and shame him before his neighbors. The opportunity was the supremest that had presented itself in history; and by all the signs it was being worked with remorseless and devastating industry. Obscure people who wanted to get into notice, invented commemorative projects, and set them forth in the papers, and passed the hat. These projects were uncountable for number, and indescribable for variety. They seemed to include every possible contrivance, wise and otherwise, which by any pretext or excuse could be made commemorative of the Record Reign—and advertise the promoter. Prominent and wise people, also, came forward with projects; projects which were good and worthy, and not tainted with sordidness and self-seeking. They included statues, drinking fountains, public parks, art galleries, libraries, asylums for the insane, the inebriate, the blind, the dumb, the crippled, the poor, the aged, the orphan, the outcast; free institutions for the dissemination of all kinds of elevating culture; institutions for instruction in professional nursing; and hospitals of every conceivable kind, and practically without number. On Jubilee Day the hospitals and hospital-annexes subscribed for had multiplied to such a degree that the list of their mere names covered several fine-print octavo pages! The money involved was a dizzy figure. And on top of all that, and independent of it, the Prince of Wales's powerful name and popularity gathered in a Hospital Fund of vast dimensions to reinforce the endowments of the already existent hospitals of London.

It is believable that England furnished the money for these great things with little or no reluctance; possibly with even the same spontaneity with which she answered the famine-call from India, when she promptly handed out two and a half million dollars, although the call fell at a time when all the landscape visible to her from any point by naked eye or telescope consisted of a monotonous plain of hats held out for commemoration-assessments.

Judging by the clerical appeals in the papers, in those days, there were not more than a hundred churches in England that had not been in a damaged condition for a generation and needed commemoration repairs; and no church at all that did not need something or other which could be made to do commemorative duty. The diligence of the Church seemed to leave all other diligences far behind in the race for commemoration-money. The Church gave England a harrying such as she had never had before, and will not have again until next Record Reign. It assessed its public for all the serious and ostensibly serious things it could think of, and when that source was exhausted it turned to humor for assistance. A country clergyman ninety-two years old and proportionately obscure fell dead; whereupon there was a prompt proposition that a fund be raised for a monument—to commemorate him? No—to commemorate the Record Reign!

It is not to be disputed that in matters of charity the English are by a long way the most prodigal nation in the world. Speaking of this, we now and then, at long intervals, hear incidental mention of George Müller and his orphanages; then they pass out of our minds and memories, and we think that they have passed out of the earth. But it is not so. They go on. They have been going on for sixty years, and are as much alive to-day as ever they were. George Müller is more than ninety years old, now, but he is still at his work. He was poor when he projected his first orphanage for the sustenance of half a dozen waifs; since then he has collected and spent six or seven millions of dollars in his kindly work, and is as poor to-day as he was when he started. He has built five great orphanages; in them he clothes and teaches and feeds two thousand children at a cost of a hundred thousand dollars a year, and England furnishes the money—not through solicitation, nor advertising, nor any kind of prodding, but by distinctly *voluntary* contributions. When money runs short Müller prays—not publicly but privately—and his treasury is replenished. In sixty years his orphans have not gone to bed unfed a single day; and yet many a time they have come within fifteen minutes of it. The names of the contributors are not revealed; no lists are published; no glory is to be gained by contributing; yet every day in the year the day's necessary requirement of three or four hundred dollars arrives in the till. These splendid facts strain belief; but they are true.

Mark Twain

FOUR SKETCHES ABOUT VIENNA

These four manuscripts, now in the Mark Twain Papers, were all written in Vienna in the first half of 1898, near the start of a period during which Clemens seems to have worked more intensively on the auto-biography than at any time since 1885. All the manuscripts are specifically dated (February 3, May 6, June 4, and June 26), almost as if they were entries in a diary. They are untitled, and with one exception ("A Group of Servants"), the titles adopted here were first supplied by Paine.

- "Beauties of the German Language" is about something Clemens had decided *not* to read as part of a lecture he gave on 1 February "for a public charity" (Notebook 40, TS p. 8, CU-MARK). The text he declined to read was handed to him as a clipping as he began his lecture, and he pinned it to the last page of this manuscript as an example of his point about the German habit of compounding words. It is actually a traditional, or at least typical, German tongue twister of the kind Hank Morgan invoked in chapter 23 of *A Connecticut Yankee in King Arthur's Court* (SLC 1889).

- "Comment on Tautology and Grammar" briefly airs one of Clemens's acknowledged "foibles," his prefer-ence for "the exact word, and clarity of statement."

- "A Group of Servants," which is probably unfinished, records Clemens's secret enjoyment of his wife Olivia's attempts to control the ebullience of one of the servants hired for the house in Kaltenleutgeben (just outside Vienna), where they stayed from late May to mid-October 1898. The servant is dubbed "Wuthering Heights (which is not her name)" and proves herself a legitimate member of Mark Twain's literary family of incessant talkers, from Simon Wheeler onward.

- "A Viennese Procession," which highlights Clemens's genuine delight in public ceremony and showy costume, describes a parade in honor of the fiftieth year of the reign of Emperor Franz Joseph I of Austria (1830–1916), which was also celebrated with an extensive exhibition of "industry, commerce, agriculture, and science" (Horowitz 1898).

Paine published three of these pieces, omitting "A Group of Servants," which was first published in 2009 (*MTA*, 1:164–74; *Who Is Mark Twain?* [SLC 2009], 61–69). Neider included none in his edition.

[Beauties of the German Language]

February 3, Vienna. Lectured for the benefit of a charity last night, in the Bösendorfersaal. Just as I was going on the platform a messenger delivered to me an envelop with my name on it, and this written under it: "Please read one of these tonight." Enclosed were a couple of newspaper clippings—two versions of an anecdote, one German, the other English. I was minded to try the German one on those people, just to see what would happen, but my courage weakened when I noticed the formidable look of the closing word, and I gave it up. A pity, too, for it ought to read well on the platform, and get an encore. That or a brickbat, there is never any telling what a new audience will do; their tastes are capricious. The point of this anecdote is a justifiable gibe at the German long word, and is not as much of an exaggeration as one might think. The German long word is not a legitimate construction, but an ignoble artificial-ity, a sham. It has no recognition by the dictionary, and is not found there. It is made by jumbling a lot of words into one, in a quite unnecessary way, it is a lazy device of the vulgar and a crime against the language. Nothing can be gained, no valuable amount of space saved, by jumbling the following words together on a visiting card: "Mrs. Smith, widow of the late Commander-in-Chief of the Police Department," yet a German widow can persuade herself to do it, without much trouble: "Mrslatecommanderinchiefofthepolicedepartment'swidow Smith." This is the English version of the anecdote:

> A Dresden paper, the *Weidmann,* which thinks that there are kangaroos (Beutel-ratte) in South Africa, says the Hottentots (Hottentoten) put them in cages (kotter) provided with covers (lattengitter) to protect them from the rain. The cages are therefore called lattengitterwetterkotter, and the imprisoned kangaroo Lattengitterwetterkot-terbeutelratte. One day an assassin (attentäter) was arrested who had killed a Hottentot woman (Hottentotenmutter), the mother of two stupid and stuttering children in Strättertrotel. This woman, in the German language is entitled Hottentotenstrotter-trottelmutter, and her assassin takes the name Hottentotenstrottermutterattentäter. The murderer was confined in a kangaroo's cage—Beutelrattenlattengitterwetterkotter—whence a few days later he escaped, but fortunately he was recaptured by a Hottentot, who presented himself at the mayor's office with beaming face. "I have captured the Beutelratte," said he. "Which one?" said the mayor; "we have several." "The Attentäter-lattengitterwetterkotterbeutelratte." "Which attentäter are you talking about?" "About the Hottentotenstrottertrottelmutterattentäter." "Then why don't you say at once the Hottentotenstrottelmutterattentäterlattengitterwetterkotterbeutelratte?"

[Comment on Tautology and Grammar]

May 6. * * * I do not find that the repetition of an important word a few times—say three or four times—in a paragraph, troubles my ear if clearness of meaning is best secured thereby. But tautological repetition which has no justifying object, but merely exposes the fact that the writer's balance at the vocabulary bank has run short and that he is too lazy to replenish it from the thesaurus—that is another matter. It makes me feel like calling the writer to account. It makes me want to remind him that he is not treating himself and his calling with right re-spect; and—incidentally—that he is not treating me with proper reverence. At breakfast, this morning, a member of the family read aloud an interesting review of a new book about Mr. Gladstone in which the reviewer used the strong adjective "delightful" thirteen times. Thirteen times in a short review, not a long one. In five of the cases the word was distinctly the right one, the exact one, the best one our language can furnish, therefore it made no discord; but in the remaining cases it was out of tune. It sharped or flatted, one or the other, every time, and was as unpleasantly noticeable as is a false note in music. I looked in the thesaurus, and under a single head I found four words which would replace with true notes the false ones uttered by four of the misused "delightfuls;" and of course if I had hunted under related heads for an hour and made an exhaustive search I should have found right words, to a shade, wherewith to replace the remaining delinquents.

I suppose we all have our foibles. I like the exact word, and clarity of statement, and here and there a touch of good grammar for picturesqueness; but that reviewer cares for only the last-mentioned of these things. His grammar is foolishly correct, offensively precise. It flaunts itself in the reader's face all along, and struts and smirks and shows off, and is in a dozen ways irritating and disagreeable. To be serious, I write good grammar myself, but not in that spirit, I am thankful to say. That is to say, my grammar is of a high order, though not at the top. Nobody's is. Perfect grammar—persistent, continuous, sustained—is the fourth dimension, so to speak: many have sought it, but none has found it. Even this reviewer, this purist, with all his godless airs, has made two or three slips. At least I think he has. I am almost sure, by witness of my ear, but cannot be positive, for I know grammar by ear only, not by note, not by the rules. A generation ago I knew the rules—knew them by heart, word for word, though not their meanings—and I still know one of them: the one which says—which says—but never mind, it will come back to me presently. This reviewer even seems to know (or seems even to know, or seems to know even) how to put the word "even" in the right place; and the word "only," too. I do not like that kind of persons. I never knew one of them that came to any good. A person who is as self-righteous as that, will do other things. I know this, because I have noticed it many a time. I would never hesitate to injure that kind of a man if I could. When a man works up his grammar to that altitude, it is a sign. It shows what he will do, if he gets a chance; it shows the kind of disposition he has; I have noticed it often. I knew one once that did a lot of things. They stop at nothing.

But anyway, this grammatical coxcomb's review is interesting, as I said before. And there is one sentence in it which tastes good in the mouth, so perfectly do the last five of its words report a something which we have all felt after sitting long over an absorbing book. The matter referred to is Mr. Gladstone's boswellised conversations, and his felicitous handling of his subjects.

> One facet of the brilliant talker's mind flashes out on us after another till we tire with interest.

That is clearly stated. We recognise that feeling. In the morning paper I find a sentence of another breed.

> There had been no death before the case of Cornelius Lean which had arisen and terminated in death since the special rules had been drawn up.

By the context I know what it means, but you are without that light and will be sure to get out of it a meaning which the writer of it was not intending to convey.

[A Group of Servants]

* * * *June 4, Kaltenleutgeben.* In this family we are four. When a family has been used to a group of servants whose several terms of service with it cover these periods, to wit: 10 years, 12 years, 13 years, 17 years, 19 years, and 22 years, it is not able to understand the new ways of a new group straight off. That would be the case at home; abroad it is the case emphasized. We have been housekeeping a fortnight, now—long enough to have learned how to pronounce the servants' names, but not to spell them. We shan't ever learn to spell them; they were invented in Hungary and Poland, and on paper they look like the alphabet out on a drunk. There are four: two maids, a cook, and a middle-aged woman who comes once or twice a day to help around generally. They are good-natured and friendly, and capable and willing. Their ways are not the ways which we have been so long used to with the home tribe in America but they are agreeable, and no fault is to be found with them except in one or two particulars. The cook is a love, but she talks at a gait and with a joyous interest and energy which make everything buzz. She is always excited; gets excited over big and little things alike, for she has no sense of proportion. Whether the project in hand is a barbecued bull or a hand-made cutlet it is no matter, she loses her mind; she unlimbers her tongue, and while her breath holds out you can't tell her from a field day in the Austrian Parliament. But what of it, as long as she can cook? And she can do that. She has that mysterious art which is so rare in the world—the art of making everything taste good which comes under the enchantment of her hand. She is the kind of cook that establishes confidence with the first meal; establishes it so thoroughly that after that you do not care to know the materials of the dishes nor their names: that her hall-mark is upon them is sufficient.

The youngest of the two maids, Charlotte, is about twenty; strong, handsome, capable, intelligent, self-contained, quiet—in fact, rather reserved. She has character, and dignity.

The other maid, Wuthering Heights (which is not her name), is about forty and looks considerably younger. She is quick, smart, active, energetic, breezy, good-natured, has a high-keyed voice and a loud one, talks thirteen to the dozen, talks all the time, talks in her sleep, will talk when she is dead; is here, there, and everywhere all at the same time, and is consumingly interested in every devilish thing that is going on. Particularly if it is not her affair. And she is not merely passively interested, but takes a hand; and not only takes a hand but the principal one; in fact will play the whole game, fight the whole battle herself, if you don't find some way to turn her flank. But as she does it in the family's interest, not her own, I find myself diffident about finding fault. Not so the family. It gravels the family. I like that. Not maliciously, but because it spices the monotony to see the family graveled. Sometimes they are driven to a point where they are sure they cannot endure her any longer, and they rise in revolt; but I stand between her and harm, for I adore Wuthering Heights. She is not a trouble to me, she freshens up my life, she keeps me interested all the time. She is not monotonous, she does not stale, she is fruitful of surprises, she is always breaking out in a new place. The family are always training her, always caulking her, but it does not make me uneasy any more, now, for I know that as fast as they stop one leak she will spring another. Her talk is my circus, my menagerie, my fireworks, my spiritual refreshment. When she is at it I would rather be there than at a fire. She talks but little to me, for I understand only about half that she says, and I have had the sagacity not to betray that I understand that half. But I open my door when she is talking to the Executive at the other end of the house, and then I hear everything, and the enjoyment is without alloy, for it is like being at a show on a free ticket. She makes the Executive's head ache. I am sorry for that, of course; still it is a thing which cannot be helped. We must take things as we find them in this world.

The Executive's efforts to reconstruct Wuthering Heights are marked by wisdom, patience and gentle and persuasive speech. They will succeed, yet, and it is a pity. This morning at half past eight I was lying in my bed counterfeiting sleep; the Executive was lying in hers, reasoning with Wuthering Heights, who had just brought the hot water and was buzzing around here and there and yonder preparing the baths and putting all manner of things to rights with her lightning touch, and accompanying herself with a torrent of talk, cramped down to a low-voiced flutter to keep from waking me up.

"You talk too much, Wuthering Heights, as I have told you so often before. It is your next worst fault, and you ought to try your best to break yourself of it. I—"

"Ah, indeed yes, gnädige Frau, it is the very truth you are speaking, none knows it better than I nor is sorrier. Jessus! but it is a verdammtes defect, as in your goodness you have said, yourself, these fifty times, and—"

"*Don't!* I never use such language—and I don't like to hear it. It is dreadful. I know that it means nothing with you, and that it is common custom and came to you with your mother's milk; but it distresses me to hear it, and besides you are always putting it into *my* mouth, which—"

"Oh, bless your kind heart, gnädige Frau, you won't mind it in the least, after a little; it's only because it is strange and new to you now, that it isn't pleasant; but that will wear off in a little while, and then—oh, it's just one of those little trifling things that don't amount to a straw, you know—why, we all swear, the priest and everybody, and it's nothing, really nothing at all; but I will break myself of it, I will indeed, and this very moment will I begin, for I have lived here and there in my time, and seen things, and learned wisdom, and I know, better than a many another, that there is only one right time to begin a thing, and that is on the spot. Ah yes, by Gott, as your grace was saying only yesterday—"

"There—do be still! It is as much as a person's life is worth to make even the triflingest remark to you, it brings such a flood. And any moment your chatter may wake my husband, and he"— after a little pause, to gather courage for a deliberate mis-statement—"he can't abide it."

"I will be as the grave! I will, indeed, for sleep is to the tired, sleep is the medicine that heals the weary spirit. Heilige Mutter Gottes! before I—"

"Be *still!*"

"Zu befehl. If—"

"*Still!*"

After a little pause the Executive began a tactful and low-temperature lecture which had all the ear-marks of preparation about it. I know that easy, impromptu style, and how it is manufactured, for I have worked at that trade myself. I have forgotten to mention that Wuthering Heights has not always served in a subordinate position; she has been housekeeper in a rich family in Vienna for the past ten years; consequently the habit of bossing is still strong upon her, naturally enough.

"The cook and Charlotte complain that you interfere in their affairs. It is not right. It is not your place to do that."

"Oh, Joseph and Mary, Deuteronomy and all the saints! Think of that! Why, of course when the mistress is not in the house it is necessary that somebody—"

"No, it is not necessary at all. The cook says that the reason the coffee was cold yesterday morning was, that you removed it from the stove, and that when she put it back you removed it again."

"Ah, but what *would* one do, gnädige Frau? It was all boiling away."

"No matter, it was not your affair. And yesterday morning you would not let Madame Blank into the house, and told her no one was at home. My husband was at home. It was too bad— and she had come all the way from Vienna. Why did you do that?"

"Let her in?—I ask you would I let her in? and he hard at his work and not wishing to be disturbed, sunk in his labors up to his eyes and grinding out God knows what, for it is beyond me, though it has my sympathy, and none feels for him more than I do when he is in his lyings-in, that way—now *would* I let her in to break up his work in that idle way and she with no rational thing in the world to pester him about? now *could* I?"

"How do you know what she wanted?"

The shot struck in an unprotected place, and made silence for several seconds, for W. H. was not prepared for it and could not think of an answer right away. Then she recovered herself and said—

"Well—well, it was like this. Well, she—of course she could have had something proper and rational on her mind, but then I knew that if that was the case she would write, not come all the way out here from Vienna to—"

"Did you know she came from Vienna?"

I knew by the silence that another unfortified place had been hit. Then—

"Well, I—that is—well, she had that kind of a look which you have noticed upon a person when—when—"

"When what?"

"She—well, she *had* that kind of a look, anyway; for—"

"How did you know my husband did not want to be disturbed?"

"Know it? Oh, indeed, and well I knew it; for he was that busy that the sweat was leaking through the floor, and I said to the cook, said I—"

"He didn't do a stroke of work the whole day, but sat in the balcony smoking and reading." [In a private tone, touched with shame: "reading his own books—he is always doing it."] "You should have told him; he would have been very glad to see Madame Blank, and was disappointed when he found out what had happened. He said so, himself."

"Oh, indeed, yes, dear gnädige Frau, he would *say* it, that he would, but give your heart peace, he is always saying things which—why, I was saying to the butcher's wife no longer ago than day before yesterday—"

"*Ruhig!* and let me go on. You do twice as much of the talking as you allow me to do, and I can't have it. If—"

"It's Viennese, gnädige Frau. Custom, you see; that's just it. We all do it; it's Viennese."

"But I'm not Viennese. And I can't get reconciled to it. And your interruptions—why, it makes no difference: if I am planning with the cook, or commissioning a dienstman, or asking the postman about the trains, no matter, you break right in, uninvited, and take charge of the whole matter, and—"

"Ah, Jessus! it's just as I was saying, and how true was the word! It's Viennese—all over, Viennese. Custom, you see—all custom. Sorel Blgwrxczlzbzockowicz—she's the Princess Tzwzfzhopowic's maid—she says she always does so, and the Princess likes it, and—"

"But I am not the Princess, and I want things *my* way; can't you understand a simple thing like that? And there's another thing. Between the time that the three of us went to Vienna yesterday morning, and ten at night when we returned, you seem to have had your hands over-full. When the cook's old grandfather came to see her, what did you meddle, for?"

[A Viennese Procession]

June 26, Sunday; Kaltenleutgeben. I went in the eight o'clock train to Vienna, to see the procession. It was a stroke of luck, for at the last moment I was feeling lazy and was minded not to go. But when I reached the station, five minutes late, the train was still there, a couple of friends were there also, and so I went. At Liesing, half an hour out, we changed to a very long train, and left for Vienna with every seat occupied. That was no sign that this was a great day, for these people are not critical about shows, they turn out for anything that comes along. Half an hour later we were driving into the city; no particular bustle anywhere—indeed less than is usual on an Austrian Sunday; bunting flying, and a decoration here and there—a quite frequent thing in this Jubilee year; but as we passed the American Embassy I saw a couple of our flags out and the Minister and his menservants arranging to have another one added. This woke me up—it seemed to indicate that something really beyond the common was to the fore.

As we neared the bridge which connects the First Bezirk with the Third, a pronounced and growing life and stir were noticeable; and when we entered the wide square where the Schwarzenberg palace is, there was something resembling a jam. As far as we could see down the broad avenue of the Park Ring both sides of it were packed with people in their holiday clothes. Our cab worked its way across the square, and then flew down empty streets, all the way, to Liebenberggasse No. 7—the dwelling we were aiming for. It stands on the corner of that street and the Park Ring, and its balconies command a mile-stretch of the latter avenue. By a trifle after nine we were in the shade of the awnings of the first-floor balcony, with a dozen other guests, and ready for the procession. Ready, but it would not start for an hour, yet, and would not reach us for half an hour afterward. As to numbers it would be a large matter; for by report it would march 25,000 strong. But it isn't numbers that make the interest of a procession; I have seen a vast number of long processions which didn't pay. It is clothes that make a procession; where you have those of the right pattern you can do without length. Two or three months ago I saw one with the Emperor and an Archbishop in it; and the Archbishop was being carried along under a canopied arrangement and had his skull-cap on, and the venerable Emperor was following him on foot and bareheaded. Even if that had been the entire procession, it would have paid. I am old, now, and may never be an Emperor at all; at least in this world. I have been disappointed so many times that I am growing more and more doubtful and resigned every year; but if it ever should happen, the procession will have a fresh interest for the Archbishop, for he will walk.

The wait on the balcony was not dull. There was the spacious avenue stretching into the distance, right and left, to look at, with its double wall of massed humanity, an eager and excited lot, broiling in the sun, and a comforting spectacle to contemplate from the shade. That is, on our side of the street they were in the sun, but not on the other side, where the Park is—there was dense shade there. They were good-natured people, but they gave the policemen plenty of trouble, for they were constantly surging into the roadway and being hustled back again. They were in fine spirits, yet it was said that the most of them had been waiting there in the jam three or four hours—and two-thirds of them were women and girls.

At last a mounted policeman came galloping down the road in solitary state—first sign that pretty soon the show would open. After five minutes he was followed by a man on a decorated bicycle. Next, a marshal's assistant sped by on a polished and shiny black horse. Five minutes later—distant strains of music. Five more, and far up the street the head of the procession twinkles into view.

That *was* a procession! I wouldn't have missed it for anything. According to my understanding, it was to be composed of shooting-match clubs from all over the Austrian Empire, with a club or two from France and Germany as guests. What I had in my imagination was 25,000 men in sober dress, drifting monotonously by, with rifles slung to their backs—a New York target-excursion on a large scale. In my fancy I could see the colored brothers toting the ice-pails and targets, and swabbing off perspiration.

But this was a different matter. One of the most engaging spectacles in the world is a Wagner opera-force marching onto the stage, with its music braying and its banners flying. This was that spectacle infinitely magnified, and with the glories of the sun upon it and a countless multitude of excited witnesses to wave the handkerchiefs and do the hurrahing. It was grand, and beautiful, and sumptuous; and no tinsel, no shams; no tin armor, no cotton velvet, no make-believe silk, no Birmingham oriental rugs; everything was what it professed to be. It is the clothes that make a procession; and for these costumes all the centuries were drawn upon, even from times which were already ancient when Kaiser Rudolph himself was alive.

There were bodies of spearmen with plain steel casques of a date a thousand years ago; other bodies in more ornamental casques of a century or two later, and with breastplates added; other bodies with chain-mail elaborations—some armed with crossbows, some with the earliest crop of matchlocks; still other bodies clothed in the stunningly picturesque plate-armor and plumed great helmets of the middle of the sixteenth century. And then there were bodies of men-at-arms in the darling velvets of the Middle Ages, and nobles on horseback in the same—doublets with huge puffed sleeves, wide brigand hats with great plumes; and the rich and effective colors—old gold, black, and scarlet; deep yellow, black, and scarlet; brown, black, and scarlet. A portly figure clothed like that, with a two-handed sword as long as a billiard cue, and mounted on a big draft-horse finely caparisoned, with the sun flooding the splendid colors—a figure like that, with fifty duplicates marching in his rear, is procession enough, all by itself.

Yet that was merely a detail. All the centuries were passing by; passing by in glories of color and multiplicities of strange and quaint and curious and beautiful costumes not to be seen in this world now outside the opera and the picture-books. And now and then, in the midst of this flowing tide of splendors appeared a sharply contrasting note—a mounted committee in evening dress—swallow-tails, white kids and shiny new plug hats; and right in their rear, perhaps, a hundred capering clowns in thunder-and-lightning dress, or a band of silken pages out of ancient times, plumed and capped and daggered, dainty as rainbows, and mincing along in flesh-colored tights; and as handy at it, too, as if they had been born and brought up to it.

At intervals there was a great platform car, bethroned and grandly canopied, upholstered in silks, carpeted with oriental rugs, and freighted with girls clothed in gala costumes. There were several military companies dressed in uniforms of various bygone periods—among others, one dating back a century and a half, and another of Andreas Hofer's time and region; following this latter was a large company of men and women and girls dressed in the society fashions of a period stretching from the Directory down to about 1840—a thing worth seeing. Among the prettiest and liveliest and most picturesque costumes in the pageant were those worn by regiments and regiments of peasants, from the Tyrol, and Bohemia, and everywhere in the Empire. They are of ancient origin, but are still worn to-day.

I have seen no procession which evoked more enthusiasm than this one brought out. It would have made any country deliver its emotions, for it was a most stirring sight to see. At the end of this year I shall be sixty-three—if alive—and about the same if dead. I have been looking at processions for sixty years; and curiously enough, all my really wonderful ones have come in the last three years: one in India in '96, the Queen's Record procession in London last year, and now this one. As an appeal to the imagination—an object-lesson synopsizing the might and majesty and spread of the greatest empire the world has seen—the Queen's procession stands first; as a picture for the eye, this one beats it; and in this regard it even falls no very great way short, perhaps, of that Jeypore pageant—and that was a dream of enchantment.

In August 1898, after several months of intensive work on his autobiography, Clemens decided to write up how he came to publish what he called his first magazine article, about the burning at sea of the clipper ship *Hornet*. At the end of August he told Henry Harper, "I want to write a magazine article of a reminiscent sort. The first magazine article I ever published appeared in Harper's Monthly 31 years ago under the name of (by typographical error) *MacSwain*. Can you send it to me?" (30 Aug 1898, InU-Li). Harper must have sent him tear sheets of "Forty-Three Days in an Open Boat," which had been published in the December 1866 issue of *Harper's* several months before Clemens published his first book, *The Celebrated Jumping Frog of Calaveras County, and Other Sketches.* "Forty-Three Days" was not, of course, Mark Twain's "first magazine article," since he had already published dozens of articles in *The Californian* and in several East Coast journals. But it was the first nonfictional work he had published in so eminent a journal as *Harper's,* and even though it was by no means humorous, it obviously followed upon his decision the previous year, in October 1865, to seriously pursue a literary career (19 and 20 Oct 1865 to OC and MEC, *L1,* 322–25).

The lengthy manuscript that Clemens wrote in October 1898 is now in the Beinecke Rare Book and Manuscript Library at Yale. His Vienna typist, Marion von Kendler, made a typescript of it (now lost), which Clemens revised and eventually published in the November 1899 issue of the *Century Magazine* (SLC 1899). The *Century* publication made no mention of the autobiography, but the original manuscript shows that Clemens initially regarded the article as part of that work: "This is Chapter XIV of my unfinished Autobiography and the way it is getting along it promises to remain an unfinished one." Before the manuscript was typed he revised "unfinished" to "unpublished" and deleted the words following "Autobiography." In February 1899, when he submitted the revised typescript to *Century* editor Richard Watson Gilder, he claimed he had "abandoned my Autobiography, & am not going to finish it; but I took a reminiscent chapter out of it & had it type-written, thinking it would make a readable magazine article" (25 Feb 1899, CtY-BR). The article, which Clemens subsequently revised again at the request of one of the *Hornet* passengers, was collected in *The Man That Corrupted Hadleyburg and Other Stories and Essays* (1900) and *My Début as a Literary Person with Other Essays and Stories* (1903). The text that follows here is a critical reconstruction, based on the manuscript and revised as Clemens published it in the *Century,* not as it was reprinted in 1900 and 1903.

In 1906 Clemens considered including the piece in his Autobiographical Dictation of 20 February, noting in pencil on the typescript, "Insert, here my account of the 'Hornet' disaster, published in the 'Century' about 1898 as being a chapter from my Autobiography." For several reasons, that instruction cannot be carried out. But it shows that the piece was among those Clemens considered including in the final form of his autobiography, and it is therefore included in this section of preliminary drafts. Neither Paine nor Neider published this text.

My Debut as a Literary Person*

By Mark Twain (formerly "Mike Swain.")

October 1, 1898. In those early days I had already published one little thing ("The Jumping Frog,") in an eastern paper, but I did not consider that that counted. In my view, a person who   *1866*

---

*This is Chapter XIV of my unpublished Autobiography.

published things in a mere newspaper could not properly claim recognition as a Literary Person; he must rise away above that; he must appear in a Magazine. He would then be a Literary Person; also he would be famous—right away. These two ambitions were strong upon me. This was in 1866. I prepared my contribution, and then looked around for the best magazine to go up to glory in. I selected Harper's Monthly. The contribution was accepted. I signed it "MARK TWAIN," for that name had some currency on the Pacific Coast, and it was my idea to spread it all over the world, now, at this one jump. The article appeared in the December number, and I sat up a month waiting for the January number—for that one would contain the year's list of contributors, my name would be in it, and I should be famous and could give the banquet I was meditating.

I did not give the banquet. I had not written the "Mark Twain" distinctly; it was a fresh name to Harper's printers, and they put it *Mike Swain* or *MacSwain,* I do not remember which. At any rate I was not celebrated, and I did not give the banquet. I was a Literary Person, but that was all—a buried one; buried alive.

My article was about the burning of the clipper ship *Hornet* on the line, May 3d, 1866. There were thirty-one men on board at the time, and I was in Honolulu when the fifteen lean and ghostly survivors arrived there after a voyage of forty-three days in an open boat through the blazing tropics on *ten days' rations* of food. A very remarkable trip; but it was conducted by a captain who was a remarkable man, otherwise there would have been no survivors. He was a New Englander of the best sea-going stock of the old capable times—Captain Josiah Mitchell.

I was in the Islands to write letters for the weekly edition of the Sacramento *Union,* a rich and influential daily journal which hadn't any use for them, but could afford to spend twenty dollars a week for nothing. The proprietors were lovable and well-beloved men; long ago dead, no doubt, but in me there is at least one person who still holds them in grateful remembrance; for I dearly wanted to see the Islands, and they listened to me and gave me the opportunity when there was but slender likelihood that it could profit them in any way.

I had been in the Islands several months when the survivors arrived. I was laid up in my room at the time, and unable to walk. Here was a great occasion to serve my journal, and I not able to take advantage of it. Necessarily I was in deep trouble. But by good luck his Excellency Anson Burlingame was there at the time, on his way to take up his post in China where he did such good work for the United States. He came and put me on a stretcher and had me carried to the hospital where the shipwrecked men were, and I never needed to ask a question. He attended to all of that himself, and I had nothing to do but make the notes. It was like him to take that trouble. He was a great man, and a great American; and it was in his fine nature to come down from his high office and do a friendly turn whenever he could.

We got through with this work at six in the evening. I took no dinner, for there was no time to spare if I would beat the other correspondents. I spent four hours arranging the notes in their proper order, then wrote all night and beyond it; with this result: that I had a very long and detailed account of the *Hornet* episode ready at nine in the morning, while the correspondents of the San Francisco journals had nothing but a brief outline report—for they didn't sit up. The now-and-then schooner was to sail for San Francisco about nine; when I reached the dock she was free forward and was just casting off her stern-line. My fat envelop was thrown by a strong hand, and fell on board all right, and my victory was a safe thing. All in due time the ship reached San Francisco, but it was my complete report which made the stir and was telegraphed to the New York papers. By Mr. Cash; he was in charge of the Pacific bureau of the New York *Herald* at the time.

When I returned to California by and by, I went up to Sacramento and presented a bill for general correspondence, at twenty dollars a week. It was paid. Then I presented a bill for "special" service on the *Hornet* matter for three columns of solid nonpareil at *a hundred dollars a column*. The cashier didn't faint, but he came rather near it. He sent for the proprietors, and they came and never uttered a protest. They only laughed, in their jolly fashion, and said it was robbery, but no matter, it was a grand "scoop" (the bill or my *Hornet* report I didn't know which); "pay it; it's all right." The best men that ever owned a newspaper.

The *Hornet* survivors reached the Sandwich Islands the 15th of June. They were mere skinny skeletons; their clothes hung limp about them and fitted them no better than a flag fits the flagstaff in a calm. But they were well nursed in the hospital; the people of Honolulu kept them supplied with all the dainties they could need; they gathered strength fast, and were presently nearly as good as new. Within a fortnight the most of them took ship for San Francisco. That is, if my dates have not gone astray in my memory. I went in the same ship, a sailing vessel. Captain Mitchell of the *Hornet* was along; also the only passengers the *Hornet* had carried. These were two young gentlemen from Stamford, Connecticut—brothers: Samuel Ferguson, aged twenty-eight, a graduate of Trinity College, Hartford, and Henry Ferguson, aged eighteen, a student of the same college, and now at this present writing a professor there, a post which he has held for many years. He is fifty years old, this year—1898. Samuel had been wasting away with consumption for some years, and the long voyage around the Horn had been advised as offering a last hope for him. The *Hornet* was a clipper of the first class and a fast sailer; the young men's quarters were roomy and comfortable, and were well stocked with books, and also with canned meats and fruits to help out the ship fare with; and when the ship cleared from New York harbor in the first week of January there was promise that she would make quick and pleasant work of the fourteen or fifteen thousand miles in front of her. As soon as the cold latitudes were left behind and the vessel entered summer weather, the voyage became a holiday picnic. The ship flew southward under a cloud of sail which needed no attention, no modifying or change of any kind for days together; the young men read, strolled the ample deck, rested and drowsed in the shade of the canvas, took their meals with the captain; and when the day was done they played dummy whist with him till bedtime. After the snow and ice and tempests of the Horn the ship bowled northward into summer weather again and the trip was a picnic once more.

Until the early morning of the 3d of May. Computed position of the ship, 112° 10' west longitude; latitude, two degrees above the equator; no wind, no sea—dead calm; temperature of the atmosphere, tropical, blistering, unimaginable by one who has not been roasted in it. There was a cry of fire. An unfaithful sailor had disobeyed the rules and gone into the booby-hatch with an open light, to draw some varnish from a cask. The proper result followed, and the vessel's hours were numbered.

There was not much time to spare, but the captain made the most of it. The three boats were launched—long-boat and two quarter-boats. That the time was very short and the hurry and excitement considerable is indicated by the fact that in launching the boats a hole was stove in the side of one of them by some sort of a collision, and an oar driven through the side of another. The captain's first care was to have four sick sailors brought up and placed on deck out of harm's way—among them a "Portyghee." This man had not done a day's work on the voyage, but had lain in his hammock four months nursing an abscess. When we were taking notes in the Honolulu hospital and a sailor told this to Mr. Burlingame, the third mate, who was lying near, raised his head with an effort, and in a weak voice made this correction—with solemnity and feeling—

"*Raising* abscesses; he had a family of them. He done it to keep from standing his watch."

Any provisions that lay handy were gathered up by the men and the two passengers and brought and dumped on the deck where the "Portyghee" lay, then they ran for more. The sailor who was telling this to Mr. Burlingame, added—

"We pulled together thirty-two days' rations for the thirty-one men that way."

The third mate lifted his head again and made another correction—with bitterness:

"The Portyghee et twenty-two of them while he was soldiering there and nobody noticing. A damned hound."

The fire spread with great rapidity. The smoke and flame drove the men back, and they had to stop their incomplete work of fetching provisions, and take to the boats, with only ten days' rations secured.

Each boat had a compass, a quadrant, a copy of Bowditch's Navigator, and a Nautical Almanac, and the captain's and chief mate's boats had chronometers. There were thirty-one men, all told. The captain took an account of stock, with the following result: four hams, nearly thirty pounds of salt pork, half-box of raisins, one hundred pounds of bread, twelve two-pound cans of oysters, clams, and assorted meats, a keg containing four pounds of butter, twelve gallons of water in a forty-gallon "scuttle-butt," four one-gallon demijohns full of water, three bottles of brandy (the property of passengers), some pipes, matches, and a hundred pounds of tobacco. No medicines. Of course the whole party had to go on short rations at once.

The captain and the two passengers kept diaries; on our voyage to San Francisco we ran into a calm in the middle of the Pacific and did not move a rod during fourteen days; this gave me a chance to copy the diaries. Samuel Ferguson's is the fullest; I will draw upon it, now. When the following paragraph was written the ship was about one hundred and twenty days out from port, and all hands were putting in the lazy time about as usual, and no one was forecasting disaster:

> *May 2.* Latitude 1° 28' N.; longitude 111° 38' W. Another hot and sluggish day; at one time, however, the clouds promised wind, and there came a slight breeze—just enough to keep us going. The only thing to chronicle to-day is the quantities of fish about: nine bonitas were caught this forenoon, and some large albicores seen. After dinner the first mate hooked a fellow which he could not hold, so he let the line go to the captain, who was on the bow. He, holding on, brought the fish to with a jerk, and snap went the line, hook and all. We also saw astern, swimming lazily after us, an enormous shark, which must have been nine or ten feet long. We tried him with all sorts of lines and a piece of

pork, but he declined to take hold. I suppose he had appeased his appetite on the heads and other remains of the bonitas we had thrown overboard.

Next day's entry records the disaster. The three boats got away, retired to a short distance, and stopped. The two injured ones were leaking badly; some of the men were kept busy bailing, others patched the holes as well as they could. The captain, the two passengers and eleven men were in the long-boat, with a share of the provisions and water, and with no room to spare, for the boat was only twenty-one feet long, six wide and three deep. The chief mate and eight men were in one of the smaller boats, the second mate and seven men in the other. The passengers had saved no clothing but what they had on, excepting their overcoats. The ship, clothed in flame and sending up a vast column of black smoke into the sky, made a grand picture in the solitudes of the sea, and hour after hour the outcasts sat and watched it. Meantime the captain ciphered on the immensity of the distance that stretched between him and the nearest available land, and then scaled the rations down to meet the emergency: half a biscuit for breakfast; one biscuit and some canned meat for dinner; half a biscuit for tea; a few swallows of water for each meal. And so hunger began to gnaw while the ship was still burning.

> *May 4.* The ship burned all night very brightly; and hopes are that some ship has seen the light, and is bearing down upon us. None seen, however, this forenoon; so we have determined to go together north and a little west to some islands in 18° to 19° N. latitude, and 114° to 115° W. longitude, hoping in the meantime to be picked up by some ship. The ship sank suddenly at about 5 A.M. We find the sun very hot and scorching; but all try to keep out of it as much as we can.

They did a quite natural thing, now; waited several hours for that possible ship that might have seen the light to work her slow way to them through the nearly dead calm. Then they gave it up and set about their plans. If you will look at the map you will say that their course could be easily decided. Albemarle island (Galapagos group) lies straight eastward, nearly a thousand miles; the islands referred to in the diary indefinitely as "some islands" (Revillagigedo islands,) lie, as they think, in some widely uncertain region northward about one thousand miles and westward one hundred or one hundred and fifty miles; Acapulco on the Mexican coast lies about northeast something short of one thousand miles. You will say, random rocks in the ocean are not what is wanted; let them strike for Acapulco and the solid continent. That does look like the rational course, but one presently guesses from the diaries that the thing would have been wholly irrational—indeed, suicidal. If the boats struck for Albemarle, they would be in the "doldrums" all the way—and that means a watery perdition, with winds which are wholly crazy, and blow from all points of the compass at once and also perpendicularly. If the boats tried for Acapulco they would get out of the "doldrums" when half way there—in case they ever got half way—and then they would be in lamentable case, for there they would meet the northeast trades coming down in their teeth; and these boats were so rigged that they could not sail within eight points of the wind. So they wisely started northward, with a slight slant to the west. They had but ten days' short allowance of food; the long-boat was towing the others; they could not depend on making any sort of definite progress in the doldrums, and they had four or five hundred miles of doldrums in front of them, yet. *They* are the real equator, a tossing, roaring, rainy belt ten or twelve hundred miles broad which girdles the globe.

It rained hard the first night and all got drenched, but they filled up their water-butt. The brothers were in the stern with the captain, who steered. The quarters were cramped; no one got much sleep. "Kept on our course till squalls headed us off."

Stormy and squally the next morning, with drenching rains. A heavy and dangerous "cobbling" sea. One marvels how such boats could live in it. It is called a feat of desperate daring when one man and a dog cross the Atlantic in a boat the size of a long-boat, and indeed it is; but this long-boat was overloaded with men and other plunder, and was only three feet deep. "We naturally thought often of all at home, and were glad to remember that it was Sacrament Sunday, and that prayers would go up from our friends for us, although they know not our peril."

The captain got not even a cat-nap during the first three days and nights, but he got a few winks of sleep the fourth night. "The worst sea yet." About ten at night the captain changed his course and headed east-northeast, hoping to make "Clipperton Rock." If he failed, no matter, he would be in a better position to make those other islands. I will mention, here, that he did not find that Rock.

On the 8th of May no wind all day—sun blistering hot. They take to the oars. Plenty of dolphins, but they couldn't catch any. "I think we are all beginning to realize more and more the awful situation we are in." "It often takes a ship a week to get through the doldrums—how much longer, then, such a craft as ours." "We are so crowded that we cannot stretch ourselves out for a good sleep, but have to take it any way we can get it."

Of course this feature will grow more and more trying, but it will be human nature to cease to set it down; there will be five weeks of it, yet—we must try to remember that for the diarist, it will make our beds the softer.

The 9th of May the sun gives him a warning: "looking with both eyes, the horizon crossed thus X." "Henry keeps well, but broods over our troubles more than I wish he did." They caught two dolphins—they tasted well. "The captain believed the compass out of the way, but the long-invisible North Star came out—a welcome sight—and indorsed the compass."

May 10, latitude 7° 0′ 3″ N.; longitude 111° 32′ W. So they have made about three hundred miles of northing in the six days since they left the region of the lost ship. "Drifting in calms all day." And baking hot, of course; I have been down there, and I remember that detail. "Even as the captain says, all romance has long since vanished, and I think the most of us are beginning to look the fact of our awful situation full in the face." "We are making but little headway on our course." Bad news from the rearmost boat; the men are improvident; "they have eaten up all of the canned meats brought from the ship, and are now growing discontented." Not so with the chief mate's people—they are evidently under the eye of a *man*.

Under date of May 11: "Standing still! or worse; we lost more last night than we made yesterday." In fact, they have lost three miles of the three hundred of northing they had so laboriously made. "The cock that was rescued and pitched into the boat while the ship was on fire still lives, and crows with the breaking of dawn, cheering us a good deal." What has he been living on for a week? Did the starving men feed him from their dire poverty? "The second mate's boat out of water again, showing that they overdrink their allowance. The captain spoke pretty sharply to them." It is true; I have the remark in my old note-book; I got it of the third mate, in the hospital at Honolulu. But there is not room for it here, and it is too combustible, anyway. Besides, the third mate admired it, and what he admired he was likely to enhance.

They were still watching hopefully for ships. The captain was a thoughtful man, and probably did not disclose to them that that was substantially a waste of time. "In this latitude the horizon is filled with little upright clouds that look very much like ships." Mr. Ferguson saved three bottles of brandy from his private stores when he left the ship, and the liquor came good in these days. "The captain serves out two tablespoonsful of brandy and water—half and half—to our crew." He means the watch that is on duty; they stood regular watches—four hours on and four off. The chief mate was an excellent officer,—a self-possessed, resolute, fine all-around man. The diarist makes the following note—there is character in it: "I offered one bottle of the brandy to the chief mate, but he declined, saying he could keep the after-boat quiet, and we had not enough for all."

> *Henry Ferguson's diary to date, given in full:—May 4, 5, 6.* Doldrums. *May 7, 8, 9.* Doldrums. *May 10, 11, 12.* Doldrums:—Tells it all. Never saw, never felt, never heard, never experienced such heat, such darkness, such lightning and thunder, and wind and rain, in my life before.

That boy's diary is of the economical sort that a person might properly be expected to keep in such circumstances—and be forgiven for the economy, too. His brother, perishing of consumption, hunger, thirst, blazing heat, drowning rains, loss of sleep, lack of exercise, was persistently faithful and circumstantial with his diary from the first day to the last—an instance of noteworthy fidelity and resolution. In spite of the tossing and plunging boat he wrote it close and fine in a hand as easy to read as print.

They can't seem to get north of 7° N. They are still there the next day:

> *May 12.* A good rain last night and we caught a good deal, though not enough to fill up our tank, pails, etc. Our object is to get out of these doldrums, but it seems as if we cannot do it. To-day we have had it very variable, and hope we are on the northern edge, though we are not much above 7°. This morning we all thought we had made out a sail; but it was one of those deceiving clouds. Rained a good deal to-day, making all hands wet and uncomfortable; we filled up pretty nearly all our water-pots, however. I hope we may have a fine night, for the captain certainly wants rest, and while there is any danger of squalls, or danger of any kind, he is always on hand. I never would have believed that open boats such as ours, with their loads, could live in some of the seas we have had.

During the night, 12–13th, "the cry of *A ship!* brought us to our feet." It seemed to be the glimmer of a vessel's signal lantern rising out of the curve of the sea. There was a season of breathless hope while they stood watching, with their hands shading their eyes, and their hearts in their throats—then the promise failed; the light was a rising star. It is a long time ago—thirty-two years—and it doesn't matter now, yet one is sorry for their disappointment. "Thought often of those at home to-day, and of the disappointment they will feel next Sunday at not hearing from us by telegraph from San Francisco." It will be many weeks, yet, before the telegram is received, and it will come as a thunder-clap of joy then, and with the seeming of a miracle, for it will raise from the grave men mourned as dead. "To-day our rations were reduced to a quarter of a biscuit a meal, with about half a pint of water." This is on the 13th of May, with more than a month of voyaging in front of them yet! However, as they do not know that, "we are all feeling pretty cheerful."

In the afternoon of the 14th there was a thunder-storm "which toward night seemed to close in around us on every side, making it very dark and squally." "Our situation is becoming more and more desperate," for they were making very little northing, "and every day diminishes our small stock of provisions." They realize that the boats must soon separate, and each fight for its own life. Towing the quarter-boats is a hindering business.

That night and next day, light and baffling winds and but little progress. Hard to bear—that persistent standing still, and the food wasting away. "Everything in a perfect sop; and all so cramped, and no change of clothes." Soon the sun comes out and roasts them. "Joe caught another dolphin to-day; in his maw we found a flying-fish and two skipjacks." There is an event, now, which rouses an enthusiasm of hope: a land-bird arrives! It rests on the yard for a while, and they can look at it all they like, and envy it, and thank it for its message. As a subject for talk it is beyond price—a fresh new topic for tongues tired to death of talking upon a single theme: shall we ever see the land again; and when? Is the bird from Clipperton Rock? They hope so; and they take heart of grace to believe so. As it turned out, the bird had no message; it merely came to mock.

May 16th, "the cock still lives, and daily carols forth His praise." It will be a rainy night, "but I do not care, if we can fill up our water-butts."

On the 17th one of those majestic spectres of the deep, a water-spout, stalked by them, and they trembled for their lives. Young Henry set it down in his scanty journal, with the judicious comment that "it might have been a fine sight from a ship."

From Captain Mitchell's log for this day: *Only half a bushel of bread-crumbs left.* (And a month to wander the seas yet.)

It rained all night and all day; everybody uncomfortable. Now came a sword-fish chasing a bonita, and the poor thing, seeking help and friends, took refuge under the rudder. The big sword-fish kept hovering around, scaring everybody badly. The men's mouths watered for him, for he would have made a whole banquet; but no one dared to touch him, of course, for he would sink a boat promptly if molested. Providence protected the poor bonita from the cruel sword-fish. This was just and right. Providence next befriended the shipwrecked sailors: they got the bonita. This was also just and right. But in the distribution of mercies the sword-fish himself got overlooked. He now went away; to muse over these subtleties, probably. "The men in all the boats seem pretty well; the feeblest of the sick ones (not able for a long time to stand his watch on board the ship) is wonderfully recovered." This is the third mate's detested "Portyghee" that raised the family of abscesses.

Passed a most awful night. Rained hard nearly all the time, and blew in squalls, accompanied by terrific thunder and lightning, from all points of the compass.—*Henry's Log.*

Most awful night I ever witnessed.—*Captain's Log.*

Latitude, May 18, 11° 11'. So they have averaged but forty miles of northing a day during the fortnight. Further talk of separating. "Too bad, but it must be done for the safety of the whole." "At first I never dreamed; but now hardly shut my eyes for a cat-nap without conjuring up something or other—to be accounted for by weakness, I suppose." But for their disaster they think they would be arriving in San Francisco about this time. "I should have liked to send B— the telegram for her birthday." This was a young sister.

On the 19th the captain called up the quarter-boats and said one would have to go off on its own hook. The long-boat could no longer tow both of them. The second mate refused to go, but the chief mate was ready; in fact he was always ready when there was a man's work to the fore. He took the second mate's boat; six of its crew elected to remain, and two of his own crew came with him, (nine in the boat, now, including himself.) He sailed away, and toward sunset passed out of sight. The diarist was sorry to see him go. It was natural; one could have better spared the Portyghee. After thirty-two years I find my prejudice against this Portyghee reviving. His very looks have long ago passed out of my memory; but no matter, I am coming to hate him as religiously as ever. "Water will now be a scarce article; for as we get out of the doldrums we shall get showers only now and then in the trades. This life is telling severely on my strength. Henry holds out first-rate." Henry did not start well, but under hardships he improved straight along.

Latitude, Sunday, May 20, 12° 0' 9". They ought to be well out of the doldrums, now, but they are not. No breeze—the longed-for trades still missing. They are still anxiously watching for a sail, but they have only "visions of ships that come to naught—the shadow without the substance." The second mate catches a booby this afternoon, a bird which consists mainly of feathers; but "as they have no other meat it will go well."

May 21, they strike the trades at last! The second mate catches three more boobies, and gives the long-boat one. Dinner, "half a can of mince-meat divided up and served around, which strengthened us somewhat." They have to keep a man bailing all the time; the hole knocked in the boat when she was launched from the burning ship was never efficiently mended. "Heading about northwest, now." They hope they have easting enough to make some of those indefinite isles. Failing that, they think they will be in a better position to be picked up. It was an infinitely slender chance, but the captain probably refrained from mentioning that.

The next day is to be an eventful one.

> *May 22.* Last night wind headed us off, so that part of the time we had to steer east-southeast, and then west-northwest, and so on. This morning we were all startled by a cry of *"Sail ho!"* Sure enough, we could see it! And for a time we cut adrift from the second mate's boat, and steered so as to attract its attention. This was about half past 5 A.M. After sailing in a state of high excitement for almost twenty minutes we made it out to be the chief mate's boat. Of course we were glad to see them and have them report all well; but still it was a bitter disappointment to us all. Now that we are in the trades it seems impossible to make northing enough to strike the isles. We have determined to do the best we

can, and get in the route of vessels. Such being the determination it became necessary to cast off the other boat, which, after a good deal of unpleasantness, was done, we again dividing water and stores, and taking Cox into our boat. This makes our number fifteen. The second mate's crew wanted to all get in with us and cast the other boat adrift. It was a very painful separation.

So those isles that they have struggled for so long and so hopefully, have to be given up. What with lying birds that come to mock, and isles that are but a dream, and "visions of ships that come to naught," it is a pathetic time they are having, with much heartbreak in it. It was odd that the vanished boat, three days lost to sight in that vast solitude, should appear again. But it brought Cox—we can't be certain why. But if it hadn't, the diarist would never have seen the land again.

> *May 23.* Our chances as we go west increase in regard to being picked up, but each day our scanty fare is so much reduced. Without the fish, turtle, and birds sent us, I do not know how we should have got along. The other day I offered to read prayers morning and evening for the captain, and last night commenced. The men, although of various nationalities and religions, are very attentive, and always uncovered. May God grant my weak endeavor its issue!

Latitude, May 24, 14° 18' N. Five oysters apiece for dinner and three spoonsful of juice, a gill of water and a piece of biscuit the size of a silver dollar. "We are plainly getting weaker— God have mercy upon us all!" That night heavy seas break over the weather side and make everybody wet and uncomfortable, besides requiring constant bailing.

Next day, "nothing particular happened." Perhaps some of us would have regarded it differently. "Passed a spar, but not near enough to see what it was." They saw some whales blow; there were flying-fish skimming the seas, but none came aboard. Misty weather, with fine rain, very penetrating.

Latitude, May 26, 15° 50'. They caught a flying-fish and a booby, but had to eat them raw. "The men grow weaker, and, I think, despondent; they say very little, though." And so, to all the other imaginable and unimaginable horrors, silence is added! The muteness and brooding of coming despair. "It seems our best chance to get in the track of ships, with the hope that some one will run near enough our speck to see it." He hopes the other boats stood west and have been picked up. [They will never be heard of again in this world.]

> *Sunday, May 27.* Latitude 16° 0' 5"; longitude, by chronometer, 117° 22'. Our fourth Sunday! When we left the ship we reckoned on having about ten days' supplies, and now we hope to be able, by rigid economy, to make them last another week if possible.* Last night the sea was comparatively quiet, but the wind headed us off to about west-northwest, which has been about our course all day to-day. Another flying-fish came aboard last night, and one more to-day—both small ones. No birds. A booby is a great catch, and a good large one makes a small dinner for the fifteen of us—that is of course, as dinners go in the

---

*There are nineteen days of voyaging ahead yet.—M. T.

Hornet's long-boat. Tried this morning to read the full service to myself with the communion, but found it too much; am too weak, and get sleepy, and cannot give strict attention; so I put off half till this afternoon. I trust God will hear the prayers gone up for us at home to-day, and graciously answer them by sending us succor and help in this our season of deep distress.

The next day was "a good day for seeing a ship." But none was seen. The diarist "still feels pretty well" though very weak; his brother Henry "bears up and keeps his strength the best of any on board." "I do not feel despondent at all, for I fully trust that the Almighty will hear our and the home prayers, and He who suffers not a sparrow to fall sees and cares for us, His creatures."

Considering the situation and the circumstances, the record for next day—May 29—is one which has a surprise in it for those dull people who think that nothing but medicines and doctors can cure the sick. A little starvation can really do more for the average sick man than can the best medicines and the best doctors. I do not mean a restricted diet, I mean *total abstention from food for one or two days*. I speak from experience; starvation has been my cold and fever doctor for fifteen years, and has accomplished a cure in all instances. The third mate told me in Honolulu that the "Portyghee" had lain in his hammock for months, raising his family of abscesses and feeding like a cannibal. We have seen that in spite of dreadful weather, deprivation of sleep, scorching, drenching, and all manner of miseries, thirteen days of starvation "wonderfully recovered" him. There were four sailors down sick when the ship was burned. Twenty-five days of pitiless starvation have followed, and now we have this curious record: *"All the men are hearty and strong; even the ones that were down sick are well;* except poor Peter." When I wrote an article some months ago urging temporary abstention from food as a remedy for an inactive appetite, and for disease, I was accused of jesting, but I was in earnest. *"We are all wonderfully well and strong, comparatively speaking."* On this day the starvation-regime drew its belt a couple of buckle-holes tighter: the bread-ration was reduced from the usual piece of cracker the size of a silver dollar *to the half of that, and one meal was abolished from the daily three.* This will weaken the men physically, but if there are any diseases of an ordinary sort left in them they will disappear.

> Two quarts bread-crumbs left, one-third of a ham, three small cans of oysters, and twenty gallons of water.—*Captain's Log.*

The hopeful tone of the diaries is persistent. It is remarkable. Look at the map and see where the boat is: latitude 16° 44′, longitude 119° 20′. It is more than two hundred miles west of the Revillagigedo islands—so they are quite out of the question against the trades, rigged as this boat is. The nearest land available for such a boat is the "American Group," *six hundred and fifty miles away,* westward—still, there is no note of surrender, none even of discouragement! Yet—May 30—"we have now left: *one can of oysters; three pounds of raisins; one can of soup; one-third of a ham; three pints of biscuit-crumbs.*" And fifteen starved men to live on it while they creep and crawl six hundred and fifty miles. "Somehow I feel much encouraged by this change of course (west by north) which we have made to-day." Six hundred and fifty miles on a hatful of provisions. Let us be thankful, even after thirty-two years, that they are mercifully ignorant of the fact that it isn't six hundred and fifty that they must creep on the hatful, but *twenty-two hundred!*

Isn't the situation romantic enough, just as it stands? No. Providence added a startling detail: pulling an oar in that boat, for common-seaman's wages, was *a banished duke*—Danish. We hear no more of him; just that mention; that is all, with the simple remark added that "he is one of our best men"—a high enough compliment for a duke or any other man in those manhood-testing circumstances. With that little glimpse of him at his oar, and that fine word of praise, he vanishes out of our knowledge for all time. For all time, unless he should chance upon this note and reveal himself.

The last day of May is come. And now there is a disaster to report: think of it, reflect upon it, and try to understand how much it means, when you sit down with your family and pass your eye over your breakfast table. Yesterday there were three pints of bread-crumbs; this morning the little bag is found open and *some of the crumbs missing.* "We dislike to suspect any one of such a rascally act, but there is no question that this grave crime has been committed. Two days will certainly finish the remaining morsels. God grant us strength to reach the American Group!" The third mate told me in Honolulu that in these days the men remembered with bitterness that the "Portyghee" had devoured twenty-two days' rations while he lay waiting to be transferred from the burning ship, and that now they cursed him and swore an oath that if it came to cannibalism he should be the first to suffer for the rest.

> The captain has lost his glasses, and therefore he cannot read our pocket-prayerbooks as much as I think he would like, though he is not familiar with them.

Further of the captain: "He is a good man, and has been most kind to us—almost fatherly. He says that if he had been offered the command of the ship sooner he should have brought his two daughters with him." It makes one shudder yet, to think how narrow an escape it was.

> The two meals (rations) a day are as follows: fourteen raisins and a piece of cracker the size of a cent, for tea; a gill of water, and a piece of ham and a piece of bread, each the size of a cent, for breakfast.—*Captain's Log.*

He means a cent in *thickness* as well as in circumference. Samuel Ferguson's diary says the ham was shaved "about as thin as it could be cut."

> *June 1.* Last night and to-day sea very high and cobbling, breaking over and making us all wet and cold. Weather squally, and there is no doubt that only careful management—with God's protecting care—preserved us through both the night and the day; and really it is most marvelous how every morsel that passes our lips is blessed to us. It makes me think daily of the miracle of the loaves and fishes. Henry keeps up wonderfully, which is a great consolation to me. I somehow have great confidence, and hope that our afflictions will soon be ended, though we are running rapidly across the track of both outward and inward bound vessels, and away from them; our chief hope is a whaler, man-of-war, or some Australian ship. The isles we are steering for are put down in Bowditch, but on my map are said to be doubtful. God grant they may be there!

Hardest day yet.—*Captain's Log.*

Doubtful. It was worse than that. A week later *they sailed straight over them.*

June 2. Latitude 18° 9'. Squally, cloudy, a heavy sea. * * * I cannot help thinking of the cheerful and comfortable time we had aboard the *Hornet.*

Two days' scanty supplies left—ten rations of water apiece and a little morsel of bread. *But the sun shines, and God is merciful.*—*Captain's Log.*

Sunday, June 3. Latitude 17° 54'. Heavy sea all night, and from 4 A.M. very wet, the sea breaking over us in frequent sluices, and soaking everything aft, particularly. All day the sea has been very high, and it is a wonder that we are not swamped. Heaven grant that it may go down this evening! Our suspense and condition are getting terrible. I managed this morning to crawl, more than step, to the forward end of the boat, and was surprised to find I was so weak, especially in the legs and knees. The sun has been out again, and I have dried some things, and hope for a better night.

June 4. Latitude 17° 6'; longitude 131° 30'. Shipped hardly any seas last night, and to-day the sea has gone down somewhat, although it is still too high for comfort, as we have an occasional reminder that water is wet. The sun has been out all day, and so we have had a good drying. I have been trying for the past ten or twelve days to get a pair of drawers dry enough to put on, and to-day at last succeeded. I mention this to show the state in which we have lived. If our chronometer is anywhere near right, we ought to see the American Isles to-morrow or next day. If they are not there, we have only the chance, for a few days, of a stray ship, for we cannot eke out the provisions more than five or six days longer, and our strength is failing very fast. I was much surprised to-day to note how my legs have wasted away above my knees; they are hardly thicker than my upper arm used to be. Still I trust in God's infinite mercy, and feel sure He will do what is best for us. To survive, as we have done, thirty-two days in an open boat, with only about ten days' fair provisions for thirty-one men in the first place, and these twice divided subsequently, is more than mere unassisted *human* art and strength could have accomplished or endured.

Bread and raisins all gone.—*Captain's Log.*

Men growing dreadfully discontented, and awful grumbling and unpleasant talk is arising. God save us from all strife of men; and if we must die now, take us himself and not embitter our bitter death still more.—*Henry's Log.*

June 5. Quiet night and pretty comfortable day, though our sail and block show signs of failing, and need taking down—which latter is something of a job, as it requires the climbing of the mast. We also had bad news from forward, there being discontent and some threatening complaints of unfair allowances, etc., all as unreasonable as foolish; still these things bid us be on our guard. I am getting miserably weak, but try to keep up the best I can. If we cannot find those isles we can only try to make northwest and get in the track of Sandwich Island bound vessels, living as best we can in the meantime. To-day we changed to *one* meal, and that at about noon, with a small ration of water at 8 or 9 A.M., another at 12 M., and a third at 5 or 6 P.M.

Nothing left but a little piece of ham and a gill of water, all round.—*Captain's Log.*

They are down to one meal a day, now—such as it is—and *fifteen hundred miles to crawl yet!* And now the horrors deepen. There is talk of murder. And not only that, but worse than that—cannibalism. Now we seem to see why that curious accident happened, so long ago: I mean, Cox's return, after he had been far away and out of sight several days in the chief mate's boat. If he had not come back the captain and the two young passengers would have been slain, now, by these sailors who have become maniacs through their sufferings.

Note secretly passed by Henry to his brother:
"Cox told me last night there is getting to be a good deal of ugly talk among the men against the captain and us aft. Harry, Jack, and Fred especially. They say that the captain is the cause of all—that he did not try to save the ship at all, nor to get provisions, and even would not let the men put in some they had, and that partiality is shown us in apportioning our rations aft. Jack asked Cox the other day if he would starve first or eat human flesh. Cox answered he would starve. Jack then told him it would be only killing himself. If we do not find these islands we would do well to prepare for anything. Harry is the loudest of all."

Reply.—"We can depend on Charley, I think, and Thomas, and Cox, can we not?"

Second Note.—"I guess so, and very likely on Peter—but there is no telling. Charley and Cox are certain. There is nothing definite said or hinted as yet, as I understand Cox; but starving men are the same as maniacs. It would be well to keep a watch on your pistol, so as to have it and the cartridges safe from theft."

Henry's Log, June 5. "Dreadful forebodings. God spare us from all such horrors! Some of the men getting to talk a good deal. Nothing to write down. Heart very sad."

Henry's Log, June 6. "Passed some sea-weed, and something that looked like the trunk of an old tree, but no birds; beginning to be afraid islands not there. To-day it was said to the captain, in the hearing of all, that some of the men would not shrink, when a man was dead, from using the flesh, though they would not kill. Horrible! God give us all full use of our reason, and spare us from such things! 'From plague, pestilence, and famine, from battle and murder—and from sudden death: Good Lord deliver us!'"

June 6. Latitude 16° 30'; longitude (chron.) 134°. Dry night, and wind steady enough to require no change in sail; but this A.M. an attempt to lower it proved abortive. First, the third mate tried and got up to the block, and fastened a temporary arrangement to reeve the halyards through, but had to come down, weak and almost fainting, before finishing; then Joe tried, and after twice ascending, fixed it and brought down the block; but it was very exhausting work, and afterward he was good for nothing all day. The clew-iron which we are trying to make serve for the broken block works, however, very indifferently, and will, I am afraid, soon cut the rope. It is very necessary to get everything connected with the sail in good, easy running order before we get too weak to do anything with it.

Only three meals left.—*Captain's Log.*

June 7. Latitude 16° 35' N.; longitude 136° 30' W. Night wet and uncomfortable. To-day shows us pretty conclusively that the American Isles are not here, though we have had some signs that looked like them. At noon we decided to abandon looking any further for them, and to-night haul a little more northerly, so as to get in the way of Sandwich Island vessels, which, fortunately, come down pretty well this way—say to latitude 19° to

20° to get the benefit of the trade-winds. Of course all the westing we have made is gain, and I hope the chronometer is wrong in our favor, for I do not see how any such delicate instrument can keep good time with the constant jarring and thumping we get from the sea. With the strong trade we have, I hope that a week from Sunday will put us in sight of the Sandwich Islands, if we are not saved before that time by being picked up.

It is twelve hundred miles to the Sandwich Islands; the provisions are virtually exhausted, but not the perishing diarist's pluck.

June 8. My cough troubled me a good deal last night, and therefore I got hardly any sleep at all. Still I make out pretty well, and should not complain. Yesterday the third mate mended the block, and this P.M. the sail, after some difficulty, was got down, and Harry got to the top of the mast and rove the halyards through after some hardship, so that it now works easy and well. This getting up the mast is no easy matter at any time with the sea we have, and is very exhausting in our present state. We could only reward Harry by an extra ration of water. We have made good time and course to-day. Heading her up, however, makes the boat ship seas, and keeps us all wet; however, it cannot be helped. Writing is a rather precarious thing these times. Our meal to-day for the fifteen consists of half a can of "soup-and-bouillé"—the other half is reserved for to-morrow. Henry still keeps up grandly, and is a great favorite. God grant he may be spared!

A better feeling prevails among the men.—*Captain's Log.*

June 9. Latitude 17° 53'. Finished to-day, I may say, our whole stock of provisions.* We have only left a lower end of a ham-bone, with some of the outer rind and skin on. In regard to the water, however, I think we have got ten days' supply at our present rate of allowance. This, with what nourishment we can get from boot-legs and such chewable matter, we hope will enable us to weather it out till we get to the Sandwich Islands, or, sailing in the meantime in the track of vessels thither bound, be picked up. My hope is in the latter—for in all human probability I cannot stand the other. Still we have been marvelously protected, and God, I hope, will preserve us all in His own good time and way. The men are getting weaker, but are still quiet and orderly.

Sunday, June 10. Latitude 18° 40'; longitude 142° 34'. A pretty good night last night, with some wettings, and again another beautiful Sunday. I cannot but think how we should all enjoy it at home, and what a contrast is here! How terrible their suspense must begin to be! God grant it may be relieved before very long, and He certainly seems to be with us in everything we do, and has preserved this boat miraculously; for since we left the ship we have sailed considerably over three thousand miles, which, taking into consideration our meagre stock of provisions, is almost unprecedented. As yet I do not feel the stint of food so much as I do that of water. Even Henry, who is naturally a great water-drinker, can save half of his allowance from time to time, when I cannot. My diseased throat may have something to do with that, however.

Nothing is now left which by any flattery can be called food. But they must manage somehow for five days more, for at noon they have still eight hundred miles to go. It is a race for life, now.

*Six days to sail yet, nevertheless.—M. T.

This is no time for comments, or other interruptions from me—every moment is valuable. I will take up the boy-brother's diary, and clear the seas before it and let it fly.

HENRY FERGUSON'S LOG.

Sunday, June 10. Our ham-bone has given us a taste of food to-day, and we have got left a little meat and the remainder of the bone for to-morrow. Certainly never was there such a sweet knuckle-bone, or one which was so thoroughly appreciated. * * * I do not know that I feel any worse than I did last Sunday, notwithstanding the reduction of diet; and I trust that we may all have strength given us to sustain the sufferings and hardships of the coming week. We estimate that we are within seven hundred miles of the Sandwich Islands, and that our average, daily, is somewhat over a hundred miles, so that our hopes have some foundation in reason. Heaven send we may all live to see land!

June 11. Ate the meat and rind of our ham-bone, and have the bone and the greasy cloth from around the ham left to eat to-morrow. God send us birds or fish, and let us not perish of hunger, or be brought to the dreadful alternative of feeding on human flesh! As I feel now, I do not think anything could persuade me; but you cannot tell what you will do when you are reduced by hunger and your mind wandering. I hope and pray we can make out to reach the Islands before we get to this strait; but we have one or two desperate men aboard, though they are quiet enough now. *It is my firm trust and belief that we are going to be saved.*

All food gone.—*Captain's Log.**

June 12. Stiff breeze, and we are fairly flying—dead ahead of it—and toward the Islands. Good hopes, but the prospects of hunger are awful. Ate ham-bone to-day. It is the captain's birthday—he is fifty-four years old.

June 13. The ham-rags are not quite all gone yet, and the boot-legs, we find, are very palatable after we get the salt out of them. A little smoke, I think, does some little good; but I don't know.

June 14. Hunger does not pain us much, but we are dreadfully weak. Our water is getting frightfully low. God grant we may see land soon! *Nothing to eat*—but feel better than I did yesterday. Toward evening saw a magnificent rainbow—*the first we had seen.* Captain said, "Cheer up, boys, it's a prophecy!—*it's the bow of promise!*"

June 15. God be forever praised for His infinite mercy! *Land in sight!* Rapidly neared it and soon were *sure* of it. . . . . Two noble Kanakas swam out and took the boat ashore. We were joyfully received by two white men—Mr. Jones and his steward Charley—and a crowd of native men, women and children. They treated us splendidly—aided us, and carried us up the bank, and brought us water, poi, bananas and green cocoanuts; but the white men took care of us and prevented those who would have eaten too much from doing so. Everybody overjoyed to see us, and all sympathy expressed in faces, deeds and words. We were then helped up to the house; and help we needed. Mr. Jones and Charley are the only white men here. Treated us splendidly. Gave us first about a teaspoonful of spirits in water, and then to each a cup of warm tea with a little bread. Takes *every* care of us. Gave us later another cup of tea—and bread the same—and then let us go to rest. *It is the happiest day of my life.* . . . . God in His mercy has heard our prayer. . . . . Everybody is so kind. Words cannot tell—

*It was at this time discovered that the crazed sailors had gotten the delusion that the captain had *a million dollars* in gold concealed aft, and they were conspiring to kill him and the two passengers and seize it.—M. T.

June 16. Mr. Jones gave us a delightful bed, and we surely had a good night's rest—but not sleep—we were too happy to sleep; would keep the reality and not let it turn to a delusion—dreaded that we might wake up and find ourselves in the boat again. . . . .

———————

It is an amazing adventure. There is nothing of its sort in history that surpasses it in impossibilities made possible. In one extraordinary detail—the survival of *every person* in the boat—it probably stands alone in the history of adventures of its kind. Usually merely a part of a boat's company survive—officers, mainly, and other educated and tenderly reared men, unused to hardship and heavy labor—the untrained, roughly-reared hard workers succumb. But in this case even the rudest and roughest stood the privations and miseries of the voyage almost as well as did the college-bred young brothers and the captain. I mean, physically. The minds of most of the sailors broke down in the fourth week and went to temporary ruin, but physically the endurance exhibited was astonishing. Those men did not survive by any merit of their own, of course, but by merit of the character and intelligence of the captain—they lived by the mastery of his spirit. Without him they would have been children without a nurse; they would have exhausted their provisions in a week, and their pluck would not have lasted even as long as the provisions.

The boat came near to being wrecked, at the last. As it approached the shore the sail was let go, and came down with a run; then the captain saw that he was drifting swiftly toward an ugly reef, and an effort was made to hoist the sail again, but it could not be done, the men's strength was wholly exhausted; they could not even pull an oar. They were helpless, and death imminent. It was then that they were discovered by the two Kanakas who achieved the rescue. They swam out and manned the boat and piloted her through a narrow and hardly noticeable break in the reef—the only break in it in a stretch of thirty-five miles! The spot where the landing was made was the only one in that stretch where footing could have been found on the shore—everywhere else precipices came sheer down into forty fathoms of water. Also, in all that stretch this was the only spot where anybody lived.

Within ten days after the landing all the men but one were up and creeping about. Properly, they ought to have killed themselves with the "food" of the last few days—some of them, at any rate—men who had freighted their stomachs with strips of leather from old boots and with chips from the butter-cask, a freightage which they did not get rid of by digestion, but by other means. The captain and the two passengers did not eat strips and chips as the sailors did, but *scraped* the boot-leather and the wood and made a pulp of the scrapings by moistening them with water. The third mate told me that the boots were old, and full of holes; then added, thoughtfully, "but the holes digested the best." Speaking of digestion, here is a remarkable thing, and worth noting: during this strange voyage, and for a while afterward on shore, the bowels of some of the men virtually ceased from their functions; in some cases there was no action for twenty and thirty days, and in one case for forty-four! Sleeping, also, came to be rare. Yet the men did very well without it. During many days the captain did not sleep at all—twenty-one, I think, on one stretch.

When the landing was made, all the men were successfully protected from overeating except the "Portyghee;" he escaped the watch and ate an incredible number of bananas; a hundred and fifty-two, the third mate said, but this was undoubtedly an exaggeration; I think it was a hundred and fifty-one. He was already nearly full of leather—it was hanging out of his ears. (I do not state this on the third mate's authority, for we have seen what sort of a person he was; I state it on my own.) The Portyghee ought to have died, of course, and even now it seems a pity that he didn't; but he got well, and as early as any of them; and all full of leather, too, the way he was, and butter-timber and handkerchiefs and bananas. Some of the men did eat handkerchiefs, in those last days, also socks; and he was one of them.

It is to the credit of the men that they did not kill the rooster that crowed so gallantly, mornings. He lived eighteen days, and then stood up and stretched his neck and made a brave weak effort to do his duty once more, and died in the act. It is a picturesque detail; and so is that rainbow, too—the only one seen in the forty-three days—raising its triumphal arch in the skies for the sturdy fighters to sail under to victory and rescue.

With ten days' provisions Captain Josiah Mitchell performed this memorable voyage of forty-three days and eight hours in an open boat, sailing four thousand miles in reality and thirty-three hundred and sixty by direct courses, and brought every man safe to land. A bright, simple-hearted, unassuming, plucky, and most companionable man. I walked the deck with him twenty-eight days—when I was not copying diaries—and I remember him with reverent honor. If he is alive he is eighty-six years old, now.

If I remember rightly, Samuel Ferguson died soon after we reached San Francisco. I do not think he lived to see his home again; his disease had doubtless doomed him when he left it.

For a time it was hoped that the two quarter-boats would presently be heard of, but this hope suffered disappointment. They went down with all on board, no doubt. Not even that knightly chief mate spared.

The authors of the diaries wanted to smooth them up a little before allowing me to copy them, but there was no occasion for that, and I persuaded them out of it. These diaries are finely modest and unaffected; and with unconscious and unintentional art they rise toward the climax with graduated and gathering force and swing and dramatic intensity, they sweep you along with a cumulative rush, and when the cry rings out at last, "Land in sight!" your heart is in your mouth and for a moment you think it is yourself that have been saved. The last two paragraphs are not improvable by anybody's art; they are literary gold; and their very pauses and uncompleted sentences have in them an eloquence not reachable by any words.

The interest of this story is unquenchable; it is of the sort that time cannot decay. I have not looked at the diaries for thirty-two years, but I find that they have lost nothing in that time. Lost?—they have gained; for by some subtle law all tragic human experiences gain in pathos by the perspective of time. We realize this when in Naples we stand musing over the poor Pompeian mother, lost in the historic storm of volcanic ashes eighteen centuries ago, who lies with her child gripped close to her breast, trying to save it, and whose despair and grief have been preserved for us by the fiery envelop which took her life but eternalized her form and features. She moves us, she haunts us, she stays in our thoughts for many days, we do not know why, for she is nothing to us, she has been nothing to any one for eighteen centuries; whereas of the like case to-day we should say "poor thing, it is pitiful," and forget it in an hour.

Vienna, October, 1898.   Mark Twain

The manuscripts for these next three pieces ("Horace Greeley," "Lecture-Times," and "Ralph Keeler") are all in the Mark Twain Papers. Clemens wrote all three in Vienna at about the same time, either in late 1898 or (more likely) in early 1899. He had apparently abandoned (at least briefly) the autobiography as he had originally conceived it in favor of a "portrait gallery of contemporaries," as he told one interviewer in May 1899: "A man cannot tell the whole truth about himself, even if convinced that what he wrote would never be seen by others. . . . For that reason I confine myself to drawing the portraits of others" ("Mark Twain's Bequest," datelined "Vienna, May 22," London *Times,* 23 May 1899, 4, in Scharnhorst 2006, 333–34).

Although Clemens here placed the encounter with Greeley in 1871, it almost certainly occurred slightly earlier, sometime between 12 and 17 December 1870, while Clemens was on a week-long trip to New York (*RI 1993,* 825 n. 78). He told a nearly identical version of the story in 1905 (3 Oct 1905 to the Editor of *Harper's Weekly,* RPB-JH, published in SLC 1905e). Paine did not include this anecdote in his edition of the autobiography, but a brief typescript of it prepared for him suggests that he very likely considered doing so. He had already quoted still another version of the story in his 1912 biography (*MTB,* 1:472). Neider likewise omitted it, but Bernard DeVoto published it in the "Miscellany" section of *Mark Twain in Eruption,* which he said was "composed of fragments lifted from contexts that did not seem to me interesting enough to be run in their entirety" (*MTE,* xii–xiii, 347–48).

Horace Greeley

I met Mr. Greeley only once and then by accident. It was in 1871, in the (old) *Tribune* office. I climbed one or two flights of stairs and went to the wrong room. I was seeking Colonel John Hay and I really knew my way and only lost it by my carelessness. I rapped lightly on the door, pushed it open and stepped in. There sat Mr. Greeley, busy writing, with his back to me. I think his coat was off. But I knew who it was, anyway. It was not a pleasant situation, for he had the reputation of being pretty plain with strangers who interrupted his train of thought. The interview was brief. Before I could pull myself together and back out, he whirled around and glared at me through his great spectacles and said—

"Well, what in hell do *you* want!"

"I was looking for a gentlem—"

"Don't keep them in stock—clear out!"

I could have made a very neat retort but didn't, for I was flurried and didn't think of it till I was down stairs.

This manuscript, begun in Vienna in late 1898 or early 1899, was left incomplete, ending in mid-sentence at a moment of unresolved suspense. Like "Horace Greeley" and "Ralph Keeler," it seems to have been intended as part of a series of biographical portraits of friends and acquaintances which Clemens had temporarily adopted as a substitute for the autobiography as first conceived. The names of Nasby, De Cordova, and Hayes printed in the margins are comparable to the marginal dates Clemens later used to guide the reader in his nonchronological Autobiographical Dictations.

Clemens had long had an interest in writing up his experiences on the lecture circuit. As early as July 1869, having completed his first lecture tour of the eastern states, he used his correspondence with the San Francisco *Alta California* to describe his friend and fellow lecturer David Ross Locke (Petroleum V. Nasby): "Well, Nasby is a good fellow, and companionable, and we sat up till daylight reading Bret Harte's Condensed Novels and talking over Western lecturing experiences. But lecturing experiences, deliciously toothsome and interesting as they are, must be recounted only in secret session, with closed doors. Otherwise, what a telling magazine article one could make out of them" (SLC 1869b). Despite that caveat, his interest in writing about those experiences remained alive. In a letter to Olivia written in January 1872, he mentioned a manuscript (later published as "Sociable Jimmy") which he had sent home as something he hoped to include in his "volume of 'Lecturing Experiences'" (10 and 11 Jan 1872 to OLC, *L5*, 18, 20 n. 6; SLC 1874d). But "Lecture-Times" and the sketch following it here, "Ralph Keeler," are as close as he ever came to fulfilling that plan.

Paine included part of "Lecture-Times" under his own title, "Old Lecture Days in Boston. *Nasby, and others of Redpath's Lecture Bureau*," omitting the last four unconcluded paragraphs devoted to Isaac I. Hayes (*MTA*, 1:147–53). Neider took his text directly from Paine—duplicating his errors—and he reversed sections of the text, which he then interlarded with material extracted from "Ralph Keeler" and the Autobiographical Dictations of 11 and 12 October 1906 (*AMT*, 161–69). The present text is therefore the first time this manuscript has been published in full, as written.

Lecture-Times

I remember Petroleum Vesuvius Nasby (Locke) very well. When the Civil War began he was on the staff of the Toledo *Blade,* an old and prosperous and popular weekly newspaper. *Nasby* He let fly a Nasby letter and it made a fine strike. He was famous at once. He followed up his new lead, and gave the copperheads and the Democratic party a most admirable hammering every week, and his letters were copied everywhere, from the Atlantic to the Pacific, and read and laughed over by everybody,—at least everybody except particularly dull and prejudiced Democrats and copperheads. For suddenness, Nasby's fame was an explosion; for universality it was atmospheric. He was soon offered a company; he accepted, and was straightway ready to leave for the front; but the Governor of the State was a wiser man than were the political masters of Körner and Petöfi; for he refused to sign Nasby's commission, and ordered him to stay at home. He said that in the field Nasby would be only one soldier, handling one sword, but at home with his pen he was an army—with artillery! Nasby obeyed, and went on writing his electric letters.

I saw him first when I was on a visit to Hartford; I think it was three or four years after the war. The Opera House was packed and jammed with people to hear him deliver his lecture on "Cussed be Canaan." He had been on the platform with that same lecture—and no other—

during two or three years, and it had passed his lips several hundred times, yet even now he could not deliver any sentence of it without his manuscript—except the opening one. His appearance on the stage was welcomed with a prodigious burst of applause, but he did not stop to bow or in any other way acknowledge the greeting, but strode straight to the reading-desk, spread his portfolio open upon it and immediately petrified himself into an attitude which he never changed during the hour and a half occupied by his performance except to turn his leaves: his body bent over the desk, rigidly supported by his left arm, as by a stake, the right arm lying across his back. About once in two minutes his right arm swung forward, turned a leaf, then swung to its resting-place on his back again—just the action of a machine, and suggestive of one; regular, recurrent, prompt, exact—you might imagine you heard it *clash*. He was a great burly figure, uncouthly and provincially clothed, and he looked like a simple old farmer.

I was all curiosity to hear him begin. He did not keep me waiting. The moment he had crutched himself upon his left arm, lodged his right upon his back and bent himself over his manuscript he raised his face slightly, flashed a glance upon the audience and bellowed this remark in a thundering bull-voice—

"We are all descended from grandfathers!"

Then he went roaring right on to the end, tearing his ruthless way through the continuous applause and laughter and taking no sort of account of it. His lecture was a volleying and sustained discharge of bull's-eye hits, with the slave-power and its Northern apologists for target, and his success was due to his matter, not his manner; for his delivery was destitute of art, unless a tremendous and inspiring earnestness and energy may be called by that name. The moment he had finished his piece he turned his back and marched off the stage with the seeming of being not personally concerned with the applause that was booming behind him.

He had the constitution of an ox and the strength and endurance of a prize-fighter. Express trains were not very plenty in those days. He missed a connection, and in order to meet this Hartford engagement he had traveled two-thirds of a night and a whole day *in a cattle-car*—it was mid-winter—he went from the cattle-car to his reading-desk without dining; yet on the platform his voice was powerful and he showed no signs of drowsiness or fatigue. He sat up talking and supping with me until after midnight, and then it was I that had to give up, not he. He told me that in his first season he read his "Cussed be Canaan" twenty-five nights a month for nine successive months. No other lecturer ever matched that record, I imagine.

He said that as one result of repeating his lecture two hundred and twenty-five nights straight along, he was able to say its opening sentence without glancing at his manuscript; and sometimes even *did* it, when in a daring mood. And there was another result: he reached home the day after his long campaign, and was sitting by the fire in the evening, musing, when the clock broke into his reverie by striking eight. Habit is habit; and before he realized where he was he had thundered out, *"We are all descended from grandfathers!"*

I began as a lecturer in 1866, in California and Nevada; in 1867 lectured in New York once and in the Mississippi valley a few times; in 1868 made the whole western circuit; and in the two or three following seasons added the eastern circuit to my route. We had to bring out a new lecture every season, now, (Nasby with the rest,) and expose it in the "Star Course," Boston, for a first verdict, before an audience of twenty-five hundred in the old Music Hall; for it was by that verdict that all the lyceums in the country determined the lecture's commercial value. The campaign did not really *begin* in Boston, but in the towns around; we did not appear in Boston until we had rehearsed about a month in those towns and made all the necessary corrections and revisings.

This system gathered the whole tribe together in the city early in October, and we had a lazy and sociable time there for several weeks. We lived at Young's hotel; we spent the days in Redpath's bureau smoking and talking shop; and early in the evenings we scattered out amongst the towns and made them indicate the good and poor things in the new lectures. The country audience is the difficult audience; a passage which it will approve with a ripple will bring a crash in the city. A fair success in the country means a triumph in the city. And so, when we finally stepped onto the great stage at Music Hall we already had the verdict in our pocket.

But sometimes lecturers who were new to the business did not know the value of "trying it on a dog," and these were apt to come to Music Hall with an untried product. There was one case of this kind which made some of us very anxious when we saw the advertisement. De *De Cordova* Cordova—humorist—he was the man we were troubled about. I think he had another name, but I have forgotten what it was. He had been printing some dismally humorous things in the magazines; they had met with a deal of favor and given him a pretty wide name; and now he suddenly came poaching upon our preserve, and took us by surprise. Several of us felt pretty unwell; too unwell to lecture. We got outlying engagements postponed, and remained in town. We took front seats in one of the great galleries—Nasby, Billings and I—and waited. The house was full. When De Cordova came on, he was received with what we regarded as a quite overdone and almost indecent volume of welcome. I think we were not jealous, nor even envious, but it made us sick, anyway. When I found he was going to read a humorous *story*—from manuscript—I felt better, and hopeful, but still anxious. He had a Dickens arrangement of tall gallows-frame adorned with upholsteries, and he stood behind it under its overhead-row of hidden lights. The whole thing had a quite stylish look, and was rather impressive. The audience were so sure that he was going to be funny that they took a dozen of his first utterances on trust and laughed cordially; so cordially, indeed, that it was very hard for us to bear, and we felt very much disheartened. Still I tried to believe he would fail, for I saw that he didn't know how to read. Presently the laughter began to relax; then it began to shrink in area; and next to lose spontaneity; and next to show gaps between; the gaps widened; they widened more; more yet; still more. It was getting to be almost all gaps and silences, with that untrained and unlively voice droning through them. Then the house sat dead and emotionless for a whole ten minutes. We drew a deep sigh; it ought to have been a sigh of pity for a defeated fellow craftsman, but it was not—for we were mean and selfish, like all the human race, and it was a sigh of satisfaction to see our unoffending brother fail.

He was laboring, now, and distressed; he constantly mopped his face with his handkerchief, and his voice and his manner became a humble appeal for compassion, for help, for charity, and it was a pathetic thing to see. But the house remained cold and still, and gazed at him curiously and wonderingly.

There was a great clock on the wall, high up; presently the general gaze forsook the reader and fixed itself upon the clock-face. We knew by dismal experience what that meant; we knew what was going to happen, but it was plain that the reader had not been warned, and was ignorant. It was approaching nine, now—half the house watching the clock, the reader laboring on. At five minutes to nine, twelve hundred people rose, with one impulse, and swept like a wave down the aisles toward the doors! The reader was like a person stricken with a paralysis; he stood choking and gasping for a few moments, gazing in a white horror at that retreat, then he turned drearily away and wandered from the stage with the groping and uncertain step of one who walks in his sleep.

The management were to blame. They should have told him that the last suburban cars left at nine, and that half the house would rise and go then, no matter who might be speaking from the platform. I think De Cordova did not appear again in public.

There was another case where a lecturer brought his piece to Music Hall without first "trying it on a dog." Everybody was anxious to get a glimpse of Dr. Hayes when he was fresh from the Arctic regions and at the noon of his celebrity. He wrote out his lecture painstakingly, and it was his purpose to read all of it from the manuscript except the opening passage. This passage was of the flowery eloquent sort, and he got it by heart, with the idea of getting out of it the moving effect of an offhand burst. It was not an original idea; novices had been bitten by it before. Not twice, of course, but once.

Dr. I. I. Hayes

The vast audience received him with inspiring enthusiasm as he came down the big stage, and he looked the pleasure he felt. He laid his manuscript on the desk, and stood bowing and smiling and smiling and bowing for a stretch of minutes. At last the noise died down, and a deep hush of expectancy followed. He stepped away from the desk and stood looking out over the sea of faces a while, then slowly stretched forth his hand and began in measured tones and most impressively, somewhat in this fashion:

"When one stands, a lost waif, in the midst of the mighty solitudes of the frozen seas stretching cold and white and forbidding, mile on mile, league on league, toward the remote and dim horizons, a solemn desert out of whose bosom rise here and there and yonder stupendous ice-forms quaintly mimicking the triumphs of man, the architect and builder—frowning fortresses, stately castles, majestic temples, their bases veiled in mysterious twilight, their pinnacles and towers glowing soft and rich in the rose-flush flung from the dying fires of the midnight sun—"

A figure sped across the stage, touched the lecturer on the shoulder, then bent forward toward the audience, made a trumpet of its hands and shouted—

This manuscript, like the previous two, belongs to the series of biographies Clemens was writing in 1898–99 instead of continuing to work in the more traditional format for an autobiography. It is obviously related in other ways to Clemens's reminiscences in "Lecture-Times," but it starts somewhat earlier, when he was a newspaper reporter in San Francisco, and extends to his 1871–72 lecture tour, during which he relied on Ralph Keeler for companionship in "lecture-flights" made out to the suburbs around Boston. Paine printed this text with his usual errors and omissions (*MTA*, 1:154–64). Neider reprinted only part of it, inserting excerpts from "Lecture-Times" and the Autobiographical Dictations of 11 and 12 October 1906 (*AMT*, 161–66).

Ralph Keeler

He was a Californian. I probably knew him in San Francisco in the early days—about 1865—when I was a newspaper reporter and Bret Harte, Ambrose Bierce, Charles Warren Stoddard and Prentice Mulford were doing young literary work for Mr. Joe Lawrence's weekly periodical *The Golden Era*. At any rate I knew him in Boston a few years later, where he comraded with Howells, Aldrich, Boyle O'Reilly, and James T. Fields, and was greatly liked by them. I say he comraded with them, and that is the proper term, though he would not have given the relationship so familiar a name himself, for he was the modestest young fellow that ever was, and looked humbly up to those distinguished men from his lowly obscurity and was boyishly grateful for the friendly notice they took of him, and frankly grateful for it; and when he got a smile and a nod from Mr. Emerson and Mr. Whittier and Holmes and Lowell and Longfellow, his happiness was the prettiest thing in the world to see. He was not more than twenty-four at this time; the native sweetness of his disposition had not been marred by cares and disappointments; he was buoyant and hopeful, simple-hearted, and full of the most engaging and unexacting little literary ambitions, and whomsoever he met became his friend and—by some natural and unexplained impulse—took him under protection.

He probably never had a home nor a boyhood. He had wandered to California as a little chap from somewhere or other, and had cheerfully achieved his bread in various humble callings, educating himself as he went along, and having a good and satisfactory time. Among his various industries was clog-dancing in a "nigger" show. When he was about twenty years old he scraped together $85—in greenbacks, worth about half that sum in gold—and on this capital he made the tour of Europe and published an account of his travels in the *Atlantic Monthly*. When he was about twenty-two he wrote a novel called "Gloverson and His Silent Partners;" and not only that, but found a publisher for it. But that was not really a surprising thing, in his case, for not even a publisher is hard-hearted enough to be able to say no to some people—and Ralph was one of those people. His gratitude for a favor granted him was so simple and sincere and so eloquent and touching that a publisher would recognize that if there was no money in the book there was still a profit to be had out of it beyond the value of money and above money's reach. There *was* no money in that book; not a single penny; but Ralph Keeler always spoke of his publisher as other people speak of divinities. The publisher lost $200 or $300 on the book, of course, and knew he would lose it when he made the venture, but he got much more than the worth of it back in the author's adoring admiration of him.

Ralph had little or nothing to do, and he often went out with me to the small lecture-towns in the neighborhood of Boston. These lay within an hour of town, and we usually started at six or thereabouts, and returned to the city in the morning. It took about a month to do these Boston annexes, and that was the easiest and pleasantest month of the four or five which constituted the "lecture season." The "lyceum system" was in full flower in those days, and James Redpath's Bureau in School street, Boston, had the management of it throughout the Northern States and Canada. Redpath farmed out the lecturers in groups of six or eight to the lyceums all over the country at an average of about $100 a night for each lecturer. His commission was ten per cent; each lecturer appeared about one hundred and ten nights in the season. There were a number of good drawing names in his list: Henry Ward Beecher; Anna Dickinson; John B. Gough; Horace Greeley; Wendell Phillips; Petroleum V. Nasby; Josh Billings; Hayes, the Arctic explorer; Vincent;   the English astronomer; Parsons, Irish orator; Agassiz. He had in his list twenty or thirty men and women of light consequence and limited reputation who wrought for fees ranging from $25 to $50. Their names have perished long ago. Nothing but art could find them a chance on the platform. Redpath furnished that art. All the lyceums wanted the big guns, and wanted them yearningly, longingly, strenuously. Redpath granted their prayers—on this condition: for each house-filler allotted them they must hire several of his house-emptiers. This arrangement permitted the lyceums to get through alive for a few years, but in the end it killed them all and abolished the lecture business.

Beecher, Gough, Nasby and Anna Dickinson were the only lecturers who knew their own value and exacted it. In towns their fee was $200 and $250; in cities $400. The lyceum always got a profit out of these four (weather permitting), but generally lost it again on the house-emptiers.

There were two women who should have been house-emptiers—Olive Logan and Kate Field—but during a season or two they were not. They charged $100, and were recognized house-fillers for certainly two years. After that they were capable emptiers and were presently shelved. Kate Field had made a wide spasmodic notoriety in 1867 by some letters which she sent from Boston—by telegraph—to the *Tribune* about Dickens's readings there in the beginning of his triumphant American tour. The letters were a frenzy of praise—praise which approached idolatry—and this was the right and welcome key to strike, for the country was itself in a frenzy of enthusiasm about Dickens. Then the idea of *telegraphing* a newspaper letter was new and astonishing, and the wonder of it was in everyone's mouth. Kate Field became a celebrity at once. By and by she went on the platform; but two or three years had elapsed and her subject—Dickens—had now lost its freshness and its interest. For a while people went to see *her,* because of her name; but her lecture was poor and her delivery repellently artificial; consequently when the country's desire to look at her had been appeased, the platform forsook her.

She was a good creature, and the acquisition of a perishable and fleeting notoriety was the disaster of her life. To her it was infinitely precious, and she tried hard, in various ways, during more than a quarter of a century, to keep a semblance of life in it, but her efforts were but moderately successful. She died in the Sandwich Islands, regretted by her friends and forgotten of the world.

Olive Logan's notoriety grew out of—only the initiated knew what. Apparently it was a manufactured notoriety, not an earned one. She *did* write and publish little things in newspapers and obscure periodicals, but there was no talent in them, and nothing resembling it. In a century they would not have made her known. Her name was really built up out of newspaper paragraphs set afloat by her husband, who was a small-salaried minor journalist. During a year or two this kind of paragraphing was persistent; one could seldom pick up a newspaper without encountering it.

"It is said that Olive Logan has taken a cottage at Nahant, and will spend the summer there."

"Olive Logan has set her face decidedly against the adoption of the short skirt for afternoon wear."

"The report that Olive Logan will spend the coming winter in Paris is premature. She has not yet made up her mind."

"Olive Logan was present at Wallack's on Saturday evening, and was outspoken in her approval of the new piece."

"Olive Logan has so far recovered from her alarming illness that if she continues to improve her physicians will cease from issuing bulletins tomorrow."

The result of this daily advertising was very curious. Olive Logan's name was as familiar to a simple public as was that of any celebrity of the time, and people talked with interest about her doings and movements, and gravely discussed her opinions. Now and then an ignorant person from the backwoods would proceed to inform himself, and then there were surprises in store for all concerned:

"Who *is* Olive Logan?"

The listeners were astonished to find that they couldn't answer the question. It had never occurred to them to inquire into the matter.

"What has she *done?*"

The listeners were dumb again. They didn't know. They hadn't inquired.

"Well, then, how does she come to be celebrated?"

"Oh, it's about *something,* I don't know what. I never inquired, but I supposed everybody knew."

For entertainment I often asked these questions myself, of people who were glibly talking about that celebrity and her doings and sayings. The questioned were surprised to find that they had been taking this fame wholly on trust, and had no idea who Olive Logan was or what she had done—if anything.

On the strength of this oddly created notoriety Olive Logan went on the platform, and for at least two seasons the United States flocked to the lecture halls to look at her. She was merely a name and some rich and costly clothes, and neither of these properties had any lasting quality, though for a while they were able to command a fee of $100 a night. She dropped out of the memories of men a quarter of a century ago.

Ralph Keeler was pleasant company on my lecture-flights out of Boston, and we had plenty of good talks and smokes in our rooms after the committee had escorted us to the inn and made their good-night. There was always a committee, and they wore a silk badge of office; they received us at the station and drove us to the lecture hall; they sat in a row of chairs behind me on the stage, minstrel-fashion, and in the earliest days their chief used to introduce me to the audience; but these introductions were so grossly flattering that they made me ashamed, and so I began my talk at a heavy disadvantage. It was a stupid custom; there was no occasion for the introduction; the introducer was almost always an ass, and his prepared speech a jumble of vulgar compliments and dreary efforts to be funny; therefore after the first season I always introduced myself—using, of course, a burlesque of the time-worn introduction. This change was not popular with committee-chairmen. To stand up grandly before a great audience of his townsmen and make his little devilish speech was the joy of his life, and to have that joy taken from him was almost more than he could bear.

My introduction of myself was a most efficient "starter" for a while, then it failed. It had to be carefully and painstakingly worded, and very earnestly spoken, in order that all strangers present might be deceived into the supposition that I was only the introducer and not the lecturer; also that the flow of overdone compliments might sicken those strangers; then, when the end was reached and the remark casually dropped that I was the lecturer and had been talking about myself, the effect was very satisfactory. But it was a good card for only a little while, as I have said; for the newspapers printed it, and after that I could not make it go, since the house knew what was coming and retained its emotions.

Next I tried an introduction taken from my Californian experiences. It was gravely made by a slouching and awkward big miner in the village of Red Dog. The house, very much against his will, forced him to ascend the platform and introduce me. He stood thinking a moment, then said:

"I don't know anything about this man. At least I know only two things; one is, he hasn't been in the penitentiary, and the other is (after a pause, and almost sadly), *I don't know why.*"

That worked well for a while, then the newspapers printed it and took the juice out of it, and after that I gave up introductions altogether.

Now and then Keeler and I had a mild little adventure, but none which couldn't be forgotten without much of a strain. Once we arrived late at a town and found no committee in waiting, and no sleighs on the stand. We struck up a street, in the gay moonlight, found a tide of people flowing along, judged it was on its way to the lecture hall—a correct guess—and joined it. At the hall I tried to press in but was stopped by the ticket-taker—

"Ticket, please."

I bent over and whispered—

"It's all right—I am the lecturer."

He closed one eye impressively and said, loud enough for all the crowd to hear—

"No you don't. Three of you have got in, up to now, but the next lecturer that goes in here to-night *pays.*"

Of course we paid; it was the least embarrassing way out of the trouble. The very next morning Keeler had an adventure. About eleven o'clock I was sitting in my room reading the paper when he burst into the place all a-tremble with excitement and said—

"Come with me—quick!"

"What is it? what's happened?"

"Don't wait to talk—come with me."

We tramped briskly up the main street three or four blocks, neither of us speaking, both of us excited, I in a sort of panic of apprehension and horrid curiosity, then we plunged into a building and down through the middle of it to the further end. Keeler stopped, put out his hand, and said—

"Look."

I looked, but saw nothing except a row of books.

"What is it, Keeler?"

He said, in a kind of joyous ecstasy—

"Keep on looking—to the right; further—further to the right. There—see it? 'Gloverson and His Silent Partners!'"

And there it was, sure enough.

"This is a library! Understand? Public library. And they've got it!"

His eyes, his face, his attitude, his gestures, his whole being spoke his delight, his pride, his happiness. It never occurred to me to laugh; a supreme joy like that moves one the other way; I was stirred almost to the crying point to see so perfect a happiness.

He knew all about the book, for he had been cross-examining the librarian. It had been in the library two years, and the records showed that it had been taken out three times.

"And read, too!" said Keeler. "See—the leaves are all cut."

Moreover, the book had been "*bought,* not given—it's on the record." I think "Gloverson" was published in San Francisco. Other copies had been sold, no doubt, but this present sale was the only one Keeler was certain of. It seems unbelievable that the sale of an edition of one book could give an author this immeasurable peace and contentment, but I was there and I saw it.

Afterward Keeler went out to Ohio and hunted out one of Ossawatomie Brown's brothers on his farm and took down in long-hand his narrative of his adventures in escaping from Virginia after the tragedy of 1859—the most admirable piece of reporting, I make no doubt, that was ever done by a man destitute of a knowledge of short-hand writing. It was published in the *Atlantic Monthly,* and I made three attempts to read it but was frightened off each time before I could finish. The tale was so vivid and so real that I seemed to be living those adventures myself and sharing their intolerable perils, and the torture of it all was so sharp that I was never able to follow the story to the end.

By and by the *Tribune* commissioned Keeler to go to Cuba and report the facts of an outrage or an insult of some sort which the Spanish authorities had been perpetrating upon us according to their well-worn habit and custom. He sailed from New York in the steamer and was last seen alive the night before the vessel reached Havana. It was said that he had not made a secret of his mission, but had talked about it freely, in his frank and innocent way. There were some Spanish military men on board. It may be that he was not flung into the sea; still, the belief was general that that was what had happened.

Clemens wrote the manuscript of "Scraps from My Autobiography. From Chapter IX" (now in the Mark Twain Papers) in London in 1900. He later asked his daughter Jean to type it, probably in 1902, and then lightly revised her typescript. By early August 1906, when George Harvey was induced to read the autobiography in typescript and instantly suggested selections for publication in the *North American Review,* Clemens had already decided not to include this long reminiscence of childhood in his plan for the autobiography. Harvey read Jean's typescript and chose the first part for the *Review,* and Josephine Hobby retyped it to make printer's copy for the 21 September 1906 issue, which Clemens then revised once more (NAR 2). Clemens later decided to publish the second part in the *Review* as well, making further changes to the text before it appeared in the 3 May 1907 issue (NAR 17). Despite these several layers of revision and the inclusion of almost all of the manuscript in the serial publication, the text was never incorporated into the final form of the autobiography.

Paine misdated the manuscript 1898 and published it as "Playing 'Bear'—Herrings—Jim Wolf and the Cats," censoring it in his usual manner (*MTA,* 1:125–43). For instance, Clemens's reference to his companion as the "little black slave boy" became just "little black boy," and his exuberant "*Dey eats 'em guts and all!*" (twice) became "*Dey* eats 'em innards and all!"—both softenings that Clemens himself did not make for the *Review.* Although Neider had access to the original manuscript, he instead copied Paine's text, inserting a section from the Autobiographical Dictation of 13 February 1906 (*AMT,* 37–43, 44–47).

Scraps from My Autobiography

From Chapter IX

This was in 1849. I was fourteen years old, then. We were still living in Hannibal, Missouri, on the banks of the Mississippi, in the new "frame" house built by my father five years before. That is, some of us lived in the new part, the rest in the old part back of it—the "L." In the autumn my sister gave a party, and invited all the marriageable young people of the village. I was too young for this society, and was too bashful to mingle with young ladies anyway, therefore I was not invited—at least not for the whole evening. Ten minutes of it was to be my whole share. I was to do the part of a bear in a small fairy-play. I was to be disguised all over in a close-fitting brown hairy stuff proper for a bear. About half past ten I was told to go to my room and put on this disguise, and be ready in half an hour. I started, but changed my mind; for I wanted to practice a little, and that room was very small. I crossed over to the large unoccupied house on the corner of Main and Hill streets,* unaware that a dozen of the young people were also going there to dress for their parts. I took the little black slave boy, Sandy, with me, and we selected a roomy and empty chamber on the second floor. We entered it talking, and this gave a couple of half-dressed young ladies an opportunity to take refuge behind a screen undiscovered. Their gowns and things were hanging on hooks behind the door, but I did not see them; it was Sandy that shut the door, but all his heart was in the theatricals, and he was as unlikely to notice them as I was myself.

*That house still stands.

1849

That was a rickety screen, with many holes in it, but as I did not know there were girls behind it, I was not disturbed by that detail. If I had known, I could not have undressed in the flood of cruel moonlight that was pouring in at the curtainless windows; I should have died of shame. Untroubled by apprehensions, I stripped to the skin and began my practice. I was full of ambition; I was determined to make a hit, I was burning to establish a reputation as a bear and get further engagements; so I threw myself into my work with an abandon that promised great things. I capered back and forth from one end of the room to the other on all fours, Sandy applauding with enthusiasm; I walked upright and growled and snapped and snarled; I stood on my head, I flung handsprings, I danced a lubberly dance with my paws bent and my imaginary snout sniffing from side to side; I did everything a bear could do, and many things which no bear could ever do and no bear with any dignity would want to do, anyway; and of course I never suspected that I was making a spectacle of myself to any one but Sandy. At last, standing on my head, I paused in that attitude to take a minute's rest. There was a moment's silence, then Sandy spoke up with excited interest and said—

"Marse Sam, has you ever seen a dried herring?"

"No. What is that?"

"It's a fish."

"Well, what of it? Anything peculiar about it?"

"Yes, suh, you bet you dey is. *Dey eats 'em guts and all!*"

There was a smothered burst of feminine snickers from behind the screen! All the strength went out of me and I toppled forward like an undermined tower and brought the screen down with my weight, burying the young ladies under it. In their fright they discharged a couple of piercing screams—and possibly others, but I did not wait to count. I snatched my clothes and fled to the dark hall below, Sandy following. I was dressed in half a minute, and out the back way. I swore Sandy to eternal silence, then we went away and hid until the party was over. The ambition was all out of me. I could not have faced that giddy company after my adventure, for there would be two performers there who knew my secret, and would be privately laughing at me all the time. I was searched for but not found, and the bear had to be played by a young gentleman in his civilized clothes. The house was still and everybody asleep when I finally ventured home. I was very heavy-hearted, and full of a bitter sense of disgrace. Pinned to my pillow I found a slip of paper which bore a line which did not lighten my heart, but only made my face burn. It was written in a laboriously disguised hand, and these were its mocking terms:

"You probably couldn't have played *bear,* but you played *bare* very well—oh, very *very* well!"

We think boys are rude unsensitive animals, but it is not so in all cases. Each boy has one or two sensitive spots, and if you can find out where they are located you have only to touch them and you can scorch him as with fire. I suffered miserably over that episode. I expected that the facts would be all over the village in the morning, but it was not so. The secret remained confined to the two girls and Sandy and me. That was some appeasement of my pain, but it was far from sufficient—the main trouble remained: I was under four mocking eyes, and it might as well have been a thousand, for I suspected all girls' eyes of being the ones I so dreaded. During several weeks I could not look any young lady in the face; I dropped my eyes in confusion when any one of them smiled upon me and gave me greeting; and I said to myself, *"That is one of them,"* and got quickly away. Of course I was meeting the right girls everywhere, but if they ever let slip any betraying sign I was not bright enough to catch it. When I left Hannibal four years later, the secret was still a secret; I had never guessed those girls out, and was no longer expecting to do it. Nor wanting to, either.

One of the dearest and prettiest girls in the village at the time of my mishap was one whom I will call Mary Wilson, because that was not her name. She was twenty years old; she was dainty and sweet, peach-bloomy and exquisite, gracious and lovely in character, and I stood in awe of her, for she seemed to me to be made out of angel-clay and rightfully unapproachable by an unholy ordinary kind of boy like me. I probably never suspected *her*. But—

The scene changes. To Calcutta—forty-seven years later. It was in 1896. I arrived there on my lecturing trip. As I entered the hotel a divine vision passed out of it, clothed in the glory of the Indian sunshine—the Mary Wilson of my long-vanished boyhood! It was a startling thing. Before I could recover from the bewildering shock and speak to her she was gone. I thought maybe I had seen an apparition, but it was not so, she was flesh. She was the grand-daughter of the other Mary, the original Mary. That Mary, now a widow, was up stairs, and presently sent for me. She was old and gray-haired, but she looked young and was very hand-some. We sat down and talked. We steeped our thirsty souls in the reviving wine of the past, the pathetic past, the beautiful past, the dear and lamented past; we uttered the names that had been silent upon our lips for fifty years, and it was as if they were made of music; with reverent hands we unburied our dead, the mates of our youth, and caressed them with our speech; we searched the dusty chambers of our memories and dragged forth incident after incident, episode after episode, folly after folly, and laughed such good laughs over them, with the tears running down; and finally Mary said suddenly, and without any leading-up—

"Tell me! What is the special peculiarity of dried herrings?"

It seemed a strange question at such a hallowed time as this. And so inconsequential, too. I was a little shocked. And yet I was aware of a stir of some kind away back in the deeps of my memory somewhere. It set me to musing—thinking—searching. Dried herrings. Dried her-rings. The peculiarity of dr . . . . I glanced up. Her face was grave, but there was a dim and shadowy twinkle in her eye which— All of a sudden I knew! and far away down in the hoary past I heard a remembered voice murmur, "Dey eats 'em guts and all!"

"At—last! I've found one of you, anyway! Who was the other girl?"

But she drew the line there. She wouldn't tell me.

But a boy's life is not all comedy; much of the tragic enters into it. The drunken tramp— mentioned in "Tom Sawyer" or "Huck Finn"—who was burned up in the village jail, lay upon my conscience a hundred nights afterward and filled them with hideous dreams—dreams in which I saw his appealing face as I had seen it in the pathetic reality, pressed against the window-bars, with the red hell glowing behind him—a face which seemed to say to me, "If you had not given me the matches, this would not have happened; you are responsible for my death." I was *not* responsible for it, for I had meant him no harm, but only good, when I let

1849

him have the matches; but no matter, mine was a trained Presbyterian conscience, and knew but the one duty—to hunt and harry its slave upon all pretexts and on all occasions; particularly when there was no sense nor reason in it. The tramp—who was to blame—suffered ten minutes; I, who was not to blame, suffered three months.

The shooting down of poor old Smarr in the main street* at noonday supplied me with some more dreams; and in them I always saw again the grotesque closing picture—the great family Bible spread open on the profane old man's breast by some thoughtful idiot, and rising and sinking to the labored breathings, and adding the torture of its leaden weight to the dying struggles. We are curiously made. In all the throng of gaping and sympathetic onlookers there was not one with common sense enough to perceive that an anvil would have been in better taste there than the Bible, less open to sarcastic criticism, and swifter in its atrocious work. In my nightmares I gasped and struggled for breath under the crush of that vast book for many a night.

All within the space of a couple of years we had two or three other tragedies, and I had the ill luck to be too near-by on each occasion. There was the slave man who was struck down with a chunk of slag for some small offence; I saw him die. And the young Californian emigrant who was stabbed with a bowie knife by a drunken comrade: I saw the red life gush from his breast. And the case of the rowdy young Hyde brothers and their harmless old uncle: one of them held the old man down with his knees on his breast while the other one tried repeatedly to kill him with an Allen revolver which wouldn't go off. I happened along just then, of course.

Then there was the case of the young Californian emigrant who got drunk and proposed to raid the "Welshman's house" all alone one dark and threatening night.† This house stood half way up Holliday's Hill ("Cardiff" Hill), and its sole occupants were a poor but quite respectable widow and her blameless daughter. The invading ruffian woke the whole village with his ribald yells and coarse challenges and obscenities. I went up there with a comrade—John Briggs, I think—to look and listen. The figure of the man was dimly visible; the women were on their porch, but not visible in the deep shadow of its roof, but we heard the elder woman's voice. She had loaded an old musket with slugs, and she warned the man that if he stayed where he was while she counted ten it would cost him his life. She began to count, slowly; he began to laugh. He stopped laughing at "six;" then through the deep stillness, in a steady voice, followed the rest of the tale: "seven . . . . eight . . . . nine"—a long pause, we holding our breath— "ten!" A red spout of flame gushed out into the night, and the man dropped, with his breast riddled to rags. Then the rain and the thunder burst loose and the waiting town swarmed up the hill in the glare of the lightning like an invasion of ants. Those people saw the rest; I had had my share and was satisfied. I went home to dream, and was not disappointed.

My teaching and training enabled me to see deeper into these tragedies than an ignorant person could have done. I knew what they were for. I tried to disguise it from myself, but down

*See "Adventures of Huckleberry Finn."
†Used in—"Huck Finn," I think.

in the secret deeps of my troubled heart I knew—and I *knew* I knew. They were inventions of Providence to beguile me to a better life. It sounds curiously innocent and conceited, now, but to me there was nothing strange about it; it was quite in accordance with the thoughtful and judicious ways of Providence as I understood them. It would not have surprised me, nor even over-flattered me if Providence had killed off that whole community in trying to save an asset like me. Educated as I had been, it would have seemed just the thing, and well worth the expense. *Why* Providence should take such an anxious interest in such a property—that idea never entered my head, and there was no one in that simple hamlet who would have dreamed of putting it there. For one thing, no one was equipped with it.

It is quite true: I took all the tragedies to myself; and tallied them off in turn as they happened, saying to myself in each case, with a sigh, "Another one gone—and on my account; this ought to bring me to repentance; His patience will not always endure." And yet privately I believed it would. That is, I believed it in the daytime; but not in the night. With the going down of the sun my faith failed, and the clammy fears gathered about my heart. It was then that I repented. Those were awful nights, nights of despair, nights charged with the bitterness of death. After each tragedy I recognised the warning and repented; repented and begged; begged like a coward, begged like a dog; and not in the interest of those poor people who had been extinguished for my sake, but only in my own interest. It seems selfish, when I look back on it now.

My repentances were very real, very earnest; and after each tragedy they happened every night for a long time. But as a rule they could not stand the daylight. They faded out and shredded away and disappeared in the glad splendor of the sun. They were the creatures of fear and darkness, and they could not live out of their own place. The day gave me cheer and peace, and at night I repented again. In all my boyhood life I am not sure that I ever tried to lead a better life in the daytime—or wanted to. In my age I should never think of wishing to do such a thing. But in my age, as in my youth, night brings me many a deep remorse. I realise that from the cradle up I have been like the rest of the race—never quite sane in the night. When "Injun Joe" died*. . . . But never mind: in an earlier chapter I have already described what a raging hell of repentance I passed through then. I believe that for months I was as pure as the driven snow. After dark.

It was back in those far-distant days—1848 or '9—that Jim Wolf came to us. He was from   *1849* Shelbyville, a hamlet thirty or forty miles back in the country, and he brought all his native sweetnesses and gentlenesses and simplicities with him. He was approaching seventeen, a grave and slender lad, trustful, honest, honorable, a creature to love and cling to. And he was incredibly bashful. He was with us a good while, but he could never conquer that peculiarity; he could not be at ease in the presence of any woman, not even in my good and gentle mother's; and as to speaking to any girl, it was wholly impossible. He sat perfectly still, one day—there were ladies chatting in the room—while a wasp up his leg stabbed him cruelly a dozen times; and all the sign he gave was a slight wince for each stab, and the tear of torture in his eye. He was too bashful to move.

*Used in "Tom Sawyer."

It is to this kind that untoward things happen. My sister gave a "candy-pull" on a winter's night. I was too young to be of the company, and Jim was too diffident. I was sent up to bed early, and Jim followed of his own motion. His room was in the new part of the house, and his window looked out on the roof of the L annex. That roof was six inches deep in snow, and the snow had an ice-crust upon it which was as slick as glass. Out of the comb of the roof projected a short chimney, a common resort for sentimental cats on moonlight nights—and this was a moonlight night. Down at the eaves, below the chimney, a canopy of dead vines spread away to some posts, making a cosy shelter, and after an hour or two the rollicking crowd of young ladies and gentlemen grouped themselves in its shade, with their saucers of liquid and piping-hot candy disposed about them on the frozen ground to cool. There was joyous chaffing and joking and laughter—peal upon peal of it.

About this time a couple of old disreputable tom-cats got up on the chimney and started a heated argument about something; also about this time I gave up trying to get to sleep, and went visiting to Jim's room. He was awake and fuming about the cats and their intolerable yowling. I asked him, mockingly, why he didn't climb out and drive them away. He was nettled, and said over-boldly that for two cents he *would*.

It was a rash remark, and was probably repented of before it was fairly out of his mouth. But it was too late—he was committed. I knew him; and I knew he would rather break his neck than back down, if I egged him on judiciously.

"Oh, of course you would! Who's doubting it?"

It galled him, and he burst out, with sharp irritation—

"Maybe *you* doubt it!"

"I? Oh, no, I shouldn't think of such a thing. You are always doing wonderful things. With your mouth."

He was in a passion, now. He snatched on his yarn socks and began to raise the window, saying in a voice unsteady with anger—

"*You* think I dasn't—*you* do! Think what you blame please—*I* don't care what you think. I'll show you!"

The window made him rage; it wouldn't stay up. I said—

"Never mind, I'll hold it."

Indeed, I would have done anything to help. I was only a boy, and was already in a radiant heaven of anticipation. He climbed carefully out, clung to the window-sill until his feet were safely placed, then began to pick his perilous way on all fours along the glassy comb, a foot and a hand on each side of it. I believe I enjoy it now as much as I did then; yet it is near fifty years ago. The frosty breeze flapped his short shirt about his lean legs; the crystal roof shone like polished marble in the intense glory of the moon; the unconscious cats sat erect upon the chimney, alertly watching each other, lashing their tails and pouring out their hollow grievances; and slowly and cautiously Jim crept on, flapping as he went, the gay and frolicsome young creatures under the vine-canopy unaware, and outraging these solemnities with their misplaced laughter. Every time Jim slipped I had a hope; but always on he crept and disappointed it. At last he was within reaching distance. He paused, raised himself carefully up, measured his distance deliberately, then made a frantic grab at the nearest cat—and missed. Of course he lost his balance. His heels flew up, he struck on his back, and like a rocket he darted down the roof feet first, crashed through the dead vines and landed in a sitting posture in fourteen saucers of red-hot candy, in the midst of all that party—and dressed as *he* was: this lad who could not look a girl in the face with his clothes on. There was a wild scramble and a storm of shrieks, and Jim fled up the stairs, dripping broken crockery all the way.

The incident was ended. But I was not done with it yet, though I supposed I was. Eighteen or twenty years later I arrived in New York from California, and by that time I had failed in all my other undertakings and had stumbled into literature without intending it. This was early in 1867. I was offered a large sum to write something for the *Sunday Mercury,* and I answered with the tale of "Jim Wolf and the Cats." I also collected the money for it—twenty-five dollars. It seemed over-pay, but I did not say anything about that, for I was not so scrupulous then as I am now.

A year or two later "Jim Wolf and the Cats" appeared in a Tennessee paper in a new dress—as to spelling; it was masquerading in a Southern dialect. The appropriator of the tale had a wide reputation in the West, and was exceedingly popular. Deservedly so, I think. He wrote some of the breeziest and funniest things I have ever read, and did his work with distinguished ease and fluency. His name has passed out of my memory.

A couple of years went by; then the original story—my own version—cropped up again and went floating around in the original spelling, and with my name to it. Soon first one paper and then another fell upon me vigorously for "stealing" Jim Wolf and the Cats from the Tennessee man. I got a merciless basting, but I did not mind it. It's all in the game. Besides, I had learned, a good while before that, that it is not wise to keep the fire going under a slander unless you can get some large advantage out of keeping it alive. Few slanders can stand the wear of silence.

But I was not done with Jim and the Cats yet. In 1873 I was lecturing in London in the Queen's Concert Rooms, Hanover Square, and living at the Langham hotel, Portland Place. I had no domestic household on that side of the water, and no official household except George Dolby, lecture-agent, and Charles Warren Stoddard, the Californian poet, now (1900) Professor of English literature in the Roman Catholic University, Washington. Ostensibly Stoddard was my private secretary; in reality he was merely my comrade—I hired him in order to have his company. As secretary there was nothing for him to do except to scrap-book the daily reports of the great trial of the Tichborne Claimant for perjury. But he made a sufficient job out of that, for the reports filled six columns a day and he usually postponed the scrap-booking until Sunday; then he had forty-two columns to cut out and paste in—a proper labor for Hercules. He did his work well, but if he had been older and feebler it would have killed him once a week. Without doubt he does his literary lectures well, but also without doubt he prepares them fifteen minutes before he is due on his platform and thus gets into them a freshness and sparkle which they might lack if they underwent the staling process of over-study.

He was good company when he was awake. He was refined, sensitive, charming, gentle, generous, honest himself and unsuspicious of other people's honesty, and I think he was the purest male I have known, in mind and speech. George Dolby was something of a contrast to him, but the two were very friendly and sociable together, nevertheless. Dolby was large and ruddy, full of life and strength and spirits, a tireless and energetic talker, and always overflowing with good-nature and bursting with jollity. It was a choice and satisfactory menagerie, this pensive poet and this gladsome gorilla. An indelicate story was a sharp distress to Stoddard; Dolby told him twenty-five a day. Dolby always came home with us after the lecture, and entertained Stoddard till midnight. Me too. After he left, I walked the floor and talked, and Stoddard went to sleep on the sofa. I hired him for company.

Dolby had been agent for concerts, and theatres, and Charles Dickens and all sorts of shows and "attractions" for many years; he had known the human being in many aspects, and he didn't much believe in him. But the poet did. The waifs and estrays found a friend in Stoddard; Dolby tried to persuade him that he was dispensing his charities unworthily, but he was never able to succeed. One night a young American got access to Stoddard at the Concert Rooms and told him a moving tale. He said he was living on the Surrey side, and for some strange reason his remittances had failed to arrive from home; he had no money, he was out of employment, and friendless; his girl-wife and his new baby were actually suffering for food; for the love of heaven could he lend him a sovereign until his remittances should resume? Stoddard was deeply touched, and gave him a sovereign on my account. Dolby scoffed, but Stoddard stood his ground. Each told me his story later in the evening, and I backed Stoddard's judgment. Dolby said we were women in disguise, and not a sane kind of women, either.

The next week the young man came again. His wife was ill with the pleurisy, the baby had the botts, or something, I am not sure of the name of the disease; the doctor and the drugs had eaten up the money, the poor little family were starving. If Stoddard, "in the kindness of his heart could only spare him another sovereign," etc., etc. Stoddard was much moved, and spared him a sovereign for me. Dolby was outraged. He spoke up and said to the customer—

"Now young man, you are going to the hotel with us and state your case to the other member of the family. If you don't make him believe in you I shan't honor this poet's drafts in your interest any longer, for I don't believe in you myself."

The young man was quite willing. I found no fault in him. On the contrary I believed in him at once, and was solicitous to heal the wounds inflicted by Dolby's too frank incredulity; therefore I did everything I could think of to cheer him up and entertain him and make him feel at home and comfortable. I spun many yarns; among others the tale of Jim Wolf and the Cats. Learning that he had done something in a small way in literature, I offered to try to find a market for him in that line. His face lighted joyfully at that, and he said that if I could only sell a small manuscript to Tom Hood's Annual for him it would be the happiest event of his sad life and he would hold me in grateful remembrance always. That was a most pleasant night for three of us, but Dolby was disgusted and sarcastic.

Next week the baby died. Meantime I had spoken to Tom Hood and gained his sympathy. The young man had sent his manuscript to him, and the very day the child died the money for the manuscript came—three guineas. The young man came with a poor little strip of crape around his arm and thanked me, and said that nothing could have been more timely than that money, and that his poor little wife was grateful beyond words for the service I had rendered. He wept, and in fact Stoddard and I wept with him, which was but natural. Also Dolby wept. At least he wiped his eyes and wrung out his handkerchief, and sobbed stertorously and made other exaggerated shows of grief. Stoddard and I were ashamed of Dolby, and tried to make the young man understand that he meant no harm, it was only his way. The young man said sadly that he was not minding it, his grief was too deep for other hurts; that he was only thinking of the funeral, and the heavy expenses which—

We cut that short and told him not to trouble about it, leave it all to us; send the bills to Mr. Dolby and—

"Yes," said Dolby, with a mock tremor in his voice, "send them to me, and I will pay them. What, are you going? You must not go alone in your worn and broken condition; Mr. Stoddard and I will go with you. Come, Stoddard. We will comfort the bereaved mamma and get a lock of the baby's hair."

It was shocking. We were ashamed of him again, and said so. But he was not disturbed. He said—

"Oh, I know this kind, the woods are full of them. I'll make this offer: if he will show me his family I will give him twenty pounds. Come!"

The young man said he would not remain to be insulted; and he said good-night and took his hat. But Dolby said he would go with him, and stay by him until he found the family. Stoddard went along to soothe the young man and modify Dolby. They drove across the river and all over Southwark, but did not find the family. At last the young man confessed that there wasn't any.

The thing he sold to Tom Hood's Annual for three guineas was "Jim Wolf and the Cats." And he did not put my name to it.

So that small tale was sold three times. I am selling it again, now. It is one of the best properties I have come across.

"Scraps from My Autobiography. Private History of a Manuscript That Came to Grief" consists of a manuscript of thirty-six leaves, along with a typewritten section, extensively annotated by Clemens, of some forty pages. It survives in the Mark Twain Papers and previously has been published only in part. In it Clemens vented his very considerable irritation in a sarcastic letter (never sent) to one T. Douglas Murray, an acquaintance who had invited him in October 1899 to write an introduction to an English translation of the trial records for Joan of Arc. When Clemens sent him his introduction, Murray had the temerity to "edit" it, far exceeding the sort of tinkering Clemens would tolerate from any editor. Paine included only the first and last sections (*MTA*, 1:175–89). He omitted the middle section, which was Clemens's recreation of the "'Edited' Introduction," a typed copy of the typescript he received back from Murray onto which he copied, in great detail, Murray's proposed revisions. That section is published here for the first time.

Scraps from My Autobiography

Private History of a Manuscript That Came to Grief

It happened in London; not recently, and yet not very many years ago. An acquaintance had proposed to himself a certain labor of love, and when he told me about it I was interested. His idea was, to have a fine translation made of the evidence given in the Joan of Arc Trials and Rehabilitation, and placed before the English-speaking world. A translation had been made and published a great many years before, but had achieved no currency, and in fact was not entitled to any, for it was a piece of mere shoemaker-work. But we should have the proper thing, now; for this acquaintance of mine was manifestly a Joan-enthusiast, and as he had plenty of money and nothing to do but spend it, I took at par his remark that he had employed the most competent person in Great Britain to open this long-neglected mine and confer its riches upon the public. When he asked me to write an Introduction for the book, my pleasure was complete, my vanity satisfied.

At this moment, by good fortune, there chanced to fall into my hands a biographical sketch of me of so just and laudatory a character—particularly as concerned one detail—that it gave my spirit great contentment; and also set my head to swelling—I will not deny it. For it contained praises of the very thing which I most loved to hear praised—*the good quality of my English;* moreover, they were uttered by four English and American literary experts of high authority.

I am as fond of compliments as another, and as hard to satisfy as the average; but these satisfied me. I was as pleased as you would have been if they had been paid to you.

It was under the inspiration of that great several-voiced verdict that I set about that Introduction for Mr. X's book; and I said to myself that I would put a quality of English into it which would establish the righteousness of that judgment. I said I would treat the subject with the reverence and dignity due it; and would use plain, simple English words, and a phrasing undefiled by meretricious artificialities and affectations.

I did the work on those lines; and when it was finished I said to myself very privately, ...

But never mind. I delivered the manuscript to Mr. X, and went home to wait for the praises. On the way, I met a friend. Being in a happy glow over this pleasant matter, I could not keep my secret: I wanted to tell somebody, and I told him. For a moment he stood curiously measuring me up and down with his eye, without saying anything; then he burst into a rude, coarse laugh, which hurt me very much. He followed this up by saying—

"*He* is going to edit the Translation of the Trials when it is finished? *He?*"

"He said he would."

"Why, what does he know about editing?"

"I don't know; but that is what he said. Do you think he isn't competent?"

"Competent? He is innocent, vain, ignorant, good-hearted, red-headed, and all that—there isn't a better-meaning man; but he doesn't know anything about literature and has had no literary training or experience: *he* can't edit anything."

"Well, all I know is, he is going to try."

"Indeed he will. He is quite unconscious of his incapacities; he would undertake to edit Shakspeare, if invited—and improve him, too. The world cannot furnish his match for guileless self-complacency; yet I give you my word he doesn't know enough to come in when it rains."

This gentleman's ability to judge was not to be questioned. Therefore, by the time I reached home I had concluded to ask Mr. X not to edit the Translation, but to turn that work over to some expert whose name on the title page would be valuable.

Three days later Mr. X brought my Introduction to me, neatly type-copied. He was in a state of considerable enthusiasm, and said:

"Really I find it quite good—quite, I assure you."

There was an airy and patronizing complacency about this damp compliment which affected my head, and healthfully checked the swelling which was going on there.

I said, with cold dignity, that I was glad the work had earned his approval.

"Oh it has, I assure you," he answered with large cheerfulness, "I assure you it quite has. I have gone over it very thoroughly, yesterday and last night and today, and I find it quite creditable—quite. I have made a few corrections—that is, suggestions, and—"

"Do you mean to say that you have been ed—"

"Oh, nothing of consequence, nothing of consequence, I assure you," he said, patting me on the shoulder and genially smiling; "only a few little things that needed just a mere polishing touch—nothing of consequence, I assure you. Let me have it back as soon as you can, so that I can pass it on to the printers and let them get to work on it while I am editing the Translation."

I sat idle and alone, a time, thinking grieved thoughts, with the edited Introduction unopened in my hand. I could not look at it yet awhile—I had no heart for it, for my pride was deeply wounded. It was the only time I had been edited in thirty-two years; except by Mr. Howells, and he did not intrude his help but furnished it at my request. "And now here is a half-stranger, obscure, destitute of literary training, destitute of literary experience, destitute of—"

But I checked myself there; for that way lay madness. I must seek calm; for my self-respect's sake I must not descend to unrefined personalities. I must keep in mind that this person was innocent of injurious intent, and was honorably trying to do me a service. To feel harshly toward him, speak harshly of him—this was not the right Christian spirit. These just thoughts tranquilised me and restored to me my better self, and I opened the Introduction at the middle.

I will not deny it, my feelings rose to 104 in the shade:

"The idea! That this long-eared animal—this literary kangaroo—this bastard of the Muses—this illiterate hostler, with his skull full of axle-grease—this . . . . "

But I stopped there, for this was not the right Christian spirit.

I subjected myself to an hour of calming meditation, then carried the raped Introduction to that friend whom I have mentioned above, and showed it to him. He fluttered the leaves over, then broke into another of those ill-bred laughs which are such a mar to him.

"I knew he would!" he said—as if gratified. "Didn't I tell you he would edit Shakspeare?"

"Yes, I know; but I did not suppose he would edit *me*."

"Oh, you didn't. Well now you see that he is even equal to *that*. I tell you there are simply no bounds to that man's irreverence."

"I realize it, now," I said.

"Well, what are you going to do? Let him put it in his book—either edited or *un*edited?"

"Of course not."

"That is well. You are becoming rational again. But what are your plans? You are not going to stop where you are, are you? You will write him a letter, and give him Hark from the Tomb?"

"No. I shall write him a letter, but not in that spirit, I trust."

"*Why* shan't you?"

"Because he has meant me a kindness, and I hope I am not the man to reward him for it in that way."

The friend looked me over, a while, pensively, then said—

"Mark, I am ashamed of you. This is mere school-girl sentimentality. You ought to baste him—you know it yourself."

I said I had no such feeling in my heart, and should put nothing of the kind in my letter.

"I shall point out his errors to him in gentleness, and in the unwounding language of persuasion. Many a literary beginner has been disheartened and defeated by the uncharitable word, wantonly uttered: this one shall get none such from me. It is more Christian-like to do a good turn than an ill one; and you ought to encourage me in my attitude, not scoff at it. This man shall not be my enemy; I will make him my lasting and grateful friend."

I felt that I was in the right; and I went home and began the letter, and found pleasure and contentment in the labor, for I had the encouragement and support of an approving conscience.

The letter will be found in its proper place in this chapter of my Autobiography.

The "Edited" Introduction

~~JOAN OF~~ ‸Jeanne d'‸ *ARC.*

I.

1. The evidence furnished ~~at the~~ ‸in her‸ Trial*s* and Rehabilitation has given us ~~Joan of~~ ‸Jeanne d'‸ Arc's history in clear and minute detail. Among‸st‸ ~~all~~ the multitude of biographies that freight the shelves of the world's libraries, this is the only one ~~whose~~ ‸the‸ validity ‸of which‸ is confirmed to us by oath. It gives ~~us~~ a vivid picture of a career and ‸of‸ a personality of so extraordinary a character that we are helped to accept them ‸both‸ as actualities by the very fact that ~~both~~ ‸they‸ are ‸quite‸ beyond the inventive reach of fiction. ~~The public part of the~~ ‸Her public‸ career occupied ~~only~~ a mere breath of time—~~it covered but~~ ‸only‸ two years; but what a career it was! The personality which made it possible is one to be reverently studied, loved, and marvelled at, but not to be wholly understood and accounted for by even the most searching analysis.

2. ~~In Joan of~~ ‸Jeanne d'‸Arc at the age of sixteen ~~there was~~ ‸gave‸ no promise of a romance. She lived in a dull little village on the frontiers of civilization; she had been nowhere and had seen nothing; she knew none but simple shepherd folk; she had never seen a person of note; she hardly knew what a soldier looked like; she had never ridden a horse, nor had a warlike weapon in her hand; she could neither read nor write.~~;~~ ‸s‸She could spin and sew, she knew her catechism‸,‸ ~~and~~ her prayers and ~~the~~ ‸some‸ fabulous histories of the Saints, ~~and~~ this was all her learning. ~~That was Joan~~ at sixteen. What did she know of law? of evidence? of courts? of the Attorney's trade? of legal procedure? Nothing. Less than nothing. Thus exhaustively equipped with ignorance she went before the court at Toul to contest a false charge of breach of promise of marriage; she conducted her cause herself, without any one's help or advice or ‸without‸ any ~~one's~~ friendly sympathy, and won it. She called no witnesses of her own, but vanquished the prosecution by using with deadly effectiveness its own testimony. The astonished judge threw the case out of court, and spoke of her as "this marvellous child."

She went now to the veteran Commandant of Vaucouleurs and demanded an escort of soldiers, saying she must march to the help of the King of France, since she was commissioned of God to win back his lost Kingdom for him and ‸to‸ set the crown upon his head. The Commandant said~~/~~‸:‸ "What, you?—you are only a child." ~~And he~~ ‸He‸ advised that she ‸should‸ be taken back to her village‸,‸ and have her ears boxed. ~~But she said s~~She must obey God, ‸she said,‸ and would come again~~/~~ and again~~/~~ and yet again, and finally she would get the soldiers. She said truly. In time he yielded, after months of delay and refusal, and gave her ~~the soldiers; and~~ ‸an escort; he‸ took off his ‸own‸ sword and gave ‸it to‸ her ~~that;~~ and said "Go—and let come what may." She made her long journey, ~~and~~ spoke with the King and convinced him. ~~Then s~~She was ‸then‸ summoned before the University of Poitiers to prove that she *was* commissioned of God and not Satan, and daily during three weeks she sat before that learned congress unafraid, ~~and~~ capably ~~answered~~ ‸answering‸ their deep questions out of her ignorant but ~~able~~ ‸clear‸ head‸,‸ ~~and~~ her simple and honest heart.~~, and a~~‸A‸gain she ~~won~~ ‸gained‸ her case, ~~and~~ ‸together‸ with ~~it~~ the wondering admiration of all that august company.

3. And now, aged seventeen, she was made Commander-in-Chief, with a royal prince and the veteran generals of France ~~for~~ ,as, subordinates.~~; and a~~A~~t~~ the head of the first army she had ever seen, she marched ~~to~~ ,against, Orleans, carried the commanding fortresses of the enemy by storm in three desperate assaults, and in ten days raised a siege which had defied the might of France for seven months.

4. After a tedious and insane delay caused by the King's instability of character and the treacherous counsels of his ministers, she got permission to take the field again. She took Jargeau by storm; then Meung; she forced Beaugency to surrender; then—in the open field— she won the memorable victory of Patay against Talbot the English lion, ~~and broke~~ ,so breaking, the back of the Hundred Years' War. It was a campaign ~~which~~ ,that, cost but seven weeks of ~~time~~ ,effort,; yet the political results would have been cheap if the time expended had been fifty years. Patay, that unsung and long-forgotten battle, ~~was the Moscow~~ ,led directly to the downfall, of the English power in France; from the blow struck that day it was destined never to recover. It was the beginning of the end of an alien ~~dominion~~ ,domination, which had ridden France intermittently for three hundred years.

Rather unkind to French feelings— referring to Moscow.

5. Then followed the great campaign of the Loire, the capture of Troyes by assault, ,the surrendering of towns and fortresses, and the triumphal march/ past, ~~surrendering towns and fortresses,~~ to Rheims, where, ~~Joan~~ ,in the Cathedral, Jeanne, put the crown upon ~~her King's head in the Cathedral,~~ ,the head of her King, amid wild public rejoicings, and with her old peasant father ,and brother, there to see these things and believe ~~his~~ ,their, eyes if ~~he~~ ,they, could. She had restored the crown and the lost sovereignty: the King was grateful for once in his shabby ~~poor~~ life, and asked her to name her ,own, reward and ~~have~~ ,take, it. She asked ~~for~~ nothing for herself, but begged that the taxes of her native village might be remitted forever~~;~~: ~~T~~the prayer was granted, and the promise kept for three hundred and sixty years. ~~Then it~~ ,It, was ,then, broken, and ,it, remains broken to-day. France was very poor ~~then~~ ,at that time,, she is very rich now; but she has been collecting those taxes for more than a hundred years.

6. ~~Joan~~ ,Jeanne, asked one other favour: ~~that now that~~ ,Now, her mission ~~was~~ ,being, fulfilled she ~~might~~ ,begged to, be allowed to ~~go back~~ ,return, to her village and take up her humble life again with her mother and the friends of her childhood; for she had no pleasure in the cruelties of war, ~~and~~ ,whereas, the sight of blood and suffering wrung her heart. Sometimes in battle she did not draw her sword, lest in the splendid madness of the onset she might forget herself and take an enemy's life. ~~with it.~~ In the Rouen Trials, one of her quaintest speeches, —coming from the gentle and girlish source it did, —was her naive remark that she had "never killed any one." Her prayer for leave to ~~go back~~ ,return, to the rest and peace of her village home was,, however,, not granted.

7. Then she ~~wanted~~ ,wished, to march at once upon Paris, ,to, take it, and ,to, drive the English out of France. She was hampered in ~~all the~~ ,every, way/ that treachery and the King's vacillation could devise, but she forced her way to Paris at last, and ,there, fell badly wounded in a successful assault upon one of the gates. Of course her men lost heart at once—she was the only heart they had~~;~~ ~~T~~they fell back. She begged ~~to be allowed~~ ,permission, to remain at the front, saying victory was sure: "I will take Paris now or die!" she ~~said~~ ,cried,. But she was removed from the field by force, the King ordered a retreat, and actually disbanded his

army. In accordance with a beautiful old military custom ~~Joan~~ ˄Jeanne˄ devoted her silver armour and hung it up in the Cathedral of St. Denis. ~~Its~~ ˄Her˄ great days were over.

8. Then, by command, she followed the King and his frivolous Court˄ ~~and endured~~ ˄enduring˄ a gilded captivity for a time, as well as her free spirit could; and whenever inaction became unbearable she gathered some men together and rode away ~~and~~ ˄to˄ assaulted ˄and capture˄ a stronghold˄ ~~and captured it.~~ At last in a sortie against the enemy, from Compiègne on the 24th of May, (when she was ~~turned~~ ˄now˄ eighteen), she ~~was herself~~ ˄herself was˄ captured/ after a gallant ~~fight.~~ ˄struggle.˄ It was her last ~~battle~~ ˄fight˄. She was to follow the drums no more.

9. Thus ended the briefest epoch-making military career ˄known˄ in history. It lasted only a year and a month, but it ~~found~~ ˄restored to˄ France an English province, and furnishes the reason that France is France to-day and ~~not an English~~ ˄no longer a˄ province ~~yet.~~ ˄of her rival.˄ Thirteen months! It was indeed a short career; but in the ˄ensuing˄ centuries ~~that have since elapsed~~ five hundred millions of Frenchmen have lived and died ~~blest by~~ ˄under˄ the benefactions it conferred˄ ~~; and so~~ ˄So˄ long as France shall endure, the mighty debt must grow. And France is ~~grateful; we often hear her say it. Also~~ ˄not ungrateful. She, however, is˄ thrifty: she ˄still continues to˄ collect/ the Domremy taxes.

II.

IN CAPTIVITY.

1. ~~Joan~~ ˄Jeanne˄ was fated to spend the ~~rest~~ ˄remainder˄ of her life behind bolts and bars. She was a prisoner of war, not a criminal, therefore hers was recognized as an honourable captivity. By the rules of war she ~~must be~~ ˄should have been˄ held to ransom, and a fair price could not ~~be refused, if~~ ˄have been refused, had it been˄ offered. ~~John~~ ˄Jean˄ of Luxemburg paid her the just compliment of ~~requiring~~ ˄demanding˄ a prince's ransom for her; ~~I~~ ˄I˄n ~~that~~ ˄those˄ days that phrase represented a definite sum—61,125 francs. It was of course supposable that either the King or grateful France or both would fly with the money ~~and~~ ˄to˄ set their fair young ~~benefactor~~ ˄benefactress˄ free. But this did not happen. ~~In~~ ˄During˄ five ~~and a half~~ months ˄and more˄ neither King nor country stirred a hand nor offered a ~~penny~~ ˄sou˄. Twice ~~Joan~~ ˄Jeanne˄ tried to escape. Once by a trick she succeeded for a moment, and locked her jailor in behind her; but she was discovered and caught˄ ~~; in~~ ˄In˄ the other case she let herself down from a tower sixty feet high;/ but her rope was too short and she ~~got~~ ˄sustained˄ a fall that ˄wholly˄ disabled her˄ and ~~she could not get away.~~ ˄so prevented her escape.˄

2. Finally Cauchon, Bishop of Beauvais, paid the ˄blood-˄money and bought Joan˄ —ostensibly for the Church˄ —to be tried for wearing male attire and for other impieties, but ~~really~~ ˄in reality˄ for the English, the enemy into whose hands the poor girl was so piteously anxious ~~not~~ ˄never˄ to fall. She was now shut up in the dungeons of the Castle of Rouen and kept in an iron cage, with her hands˄ ~~and~~ feet and neck ˄both˄ chained to a ˄wooden block and˄ pillar˄ ~~; and f~~ ˄F˄rom that time forth during all the months of her imprisonment ~~till~~ ˄until˄ the end, several rough English soldiers stood guard over her night and day˄ —~~and~~ not outside her room but in it. It was a dreary and hideous captivity, but it did not conquer her: nothing

could break that invincible spirit. ~~From first to last s~~She was a prisoner a ˄for the whole˄ year; ~~and she spent~~ the last three months of ~~it~~ ˄which she passed˄ on trial for her life, before a formidable array of ecclesiastical judges, ~~and~~ disputing the ground with them foot by foot and inch by inch with brilliant ~~generalship~~ ˄fence˄ and dauntless pluck. The spectacle of that solitary girl~~, forlorn~~ ˄stands alone in its pathos and ˄in˄ its sublimity. Forlorn˄ and friendless, without advocate or adviser, ~~and~~ without ˄even˄ the help and guidance of ~~any~~ a copy of the charges brought against her or rescript of the complex and voluminous ~~daily~~ proceedings of the court ~~to modify~~ ˄by which to relieve˄ the crushing strain upon her ~~astonishing~~ ˄astounding˄ memory, fighting ~~that~~ a long battle ~~serene and~~ undismayed against ~~these~~ colossal odds.~~, stands alone in its pathos and its sublimity; it~~ ˄It˄ has nowhere its ~~mate,~~ ˄match,˄ neither in the annals of fact nor in the ~~creations of fable.~~ ˄realms of fiction.˄

3. ~~And how~~ ˄How˄ fine and great were the ~~things she daily said, how fresh and crisp—and she so worn in body,~~ ˄words she spoke day by day, her ready answers, her bright demeanour, and crisp criticisms, and she so worn in body,˄ so starved, ~~and~~ ˄so˄ tired, ~~and~~ ˄so˄ harried!~~/~~ ~~They~~ ˄Her utterances˄ run through the whole gamut of feeling and expression, ~~+~~ from scorn and defiance, ~~uttered~~ ˄spoken˄ with soldierly fire and frankness, ~~all down the scale~~ to wounded dignity clothed in words of noble pathos.~~; as, w~~When her patience was exhausted by the pestering attempts of her persecutors to ~~find out~~ ˄discover˄ what ~~kind of~~ devil's-witchcraft she had employed to rouse the war-spirit in her soldiers she ~~burst~~ ˄cried˄ out: ~~with~~ "What I said was, 'Ride these English down'—and I did it myself!" ~~and as, w~~When insultingly asked why it was that *her* standard had place at the crowning of the King in the Cathedral of Rheims rather than ~~the standards~~ ˄those˄ of ~~the~~ other captains, she uttered that touching speech, "It had borne the burden, it had earned the honour,"~~+~~ a phrase which fell from her lips without ~~preparation, but whose~~ ˄premeditation, the˄ moving beauty and simple grace ~~it~~ ˄of which˄ would bankrupt the art~~s~~ of language to surpass.

4. Although ~~she was~~ on trial for her life, she was the only witness called on either side; the only witness summoned to testify before a packed jury commissioned with a definite task—to find her guilty, whether she ~~was~~ ˄were˄ guilty or not. She must be convicted out of her own mouth, there being no other way to accomplish it. Every advantage that learning has over ignorance, age over youth, experience over inexperience, chicane over artlessness;~~/~~ every trick and trap ~~and gin~~ devisable by malice and the cunning of sharp intellects practised in ˄the˄ setting ˄of˄ snares for the unwary,~~+~~ all these were employed against her without shame; and when these arts were one by one defeated by the marvellous intuitions of her alert and penetrating mind, Bishop Cauchon stooped to a final baseness which it degrades human speech to describe.~~: a~~A priest who pretended to come from the region of her own home and to be a pitying friend,~~and~~ anxious to help her in her sore need, was smuggled into her cell; he misused his sacred office to steal her confidence~~; and~~ ˄so that˄ she confided to him ~~the things~~ ˄facts˄ sealed from revealment by her Voices which her prosecutors had tried so long in vain to trick her into betraying. A concealed confederate set it all down and delivered it to Cauchon, who used ~~Joan's~~ ˄Jeanne's˄ secrets, thus obtained, for her ruin.

Throughout the Trial~~,~~ ~~whatever the~~ ˄the testimony of the˄ foredoomed witness ~~said~~ was twisted from its true meaning, when possible, and made to tell against her; ~~and~~ whenever an answer of hers was beyond the reach of ~~twisting~~ ‚garbling,‚ it was not allowed to go upon the record. ~~It was upon~~ ‚On‚ one of these latter occasions ~~that~~ she uttered that pathetic reproach+ to Cauchon: "~~Ah,~~ "you set down everything that is against me, but ~~you will not set down what is for me."~~ ‚nothing that is in my favour."‚

5. That ~~this~~ ‚her‚ untrained ~~young creature's~~ genius for war was ~~wonderful~~ ‚marvelous,‚ ~~and~~ that her generalship ~~suggested an old and educated~~ ‚was that of a tried and trained‚ military experience, we have the sworn testimony of two of her veteran subordinates,‚+ one the Duc d'Alençon, ‚brother to the King of France;‚ the other the greatest of the French generals of the time, Dunois, Bastard of Orleans.‚;t That her ~~genius was as great—possibly even greater—~~ ‚power was equally great ~~if not greater‚~~ in the subtle ~~warfare~~ ‚strife‚ of the forum, we have for witness the records of the Rouen Trial, that protracted exhibition of intellectual fence maintained with credit against the masterminds of France.‚;t That her moral greatness was peer to her intellect we call the Rouen Trial again to witness, with ~~their~~ ‚its‚ testimony to a fortitude which patiently and steadfastly endured during twelve weeks the wasting forces of captivity, chains, loneliness, sickness, darkness, hunger, thirst, cold, shame, insult, abuse, broken sleep, treachery, ingratitude, exhausting sieges of cross-examination, ‚and‚ the threat of torture/ with the rack ~~before~~ ‚facing‚ her and the executioner standing ready: yet never surrendering, never asking quarter, the frail wreck of her as unconquerable the last day as was her invincible spirit the first.

6. Great as she was in so many ways, she was perhaps ~~even~~ greatest of all in the lofty things just named, +her patient endurance, her steadfastness, her granite fortitude. We may ~~not~~ ‚never‚ hope ~~to~~ easily ‚to‚ find her ~~mate and twin~~ ‚equal‚ in these majestic qualities.‚;w Where we lift our eyes highest we find only a strange and curious contrast—there in the captive eagle beating his broken wings ~~on~~ ‚upon‚ the Rock of St. Helena.

7. The Trial ended with her condemnation. ~~But as~~ ‚As‚ she had conceded nothing, confessed nothing, this was victory for her, defeat for Cauchon. But his evil resources were not yet exhausted. She was persuaded to ~~agree to~~ sign a paper of slight import, then by treachery ~~a paper~~ ‚another‚ was substituted which contained a recantation ~~and~~ ‚together with‚ a detailed confession of everything ~~which~~ ‚that‚ had been charged against her during the Trial and denied and repudiated by her persistently ~~during the three months; and this~~ ‚throughout‚. This‚ false paper she ignorantly signed;‚ ~~This~~ ‚it‚ was victory for Cauchon. He followed it eagerly and pitilessly up by at once setting a trap for her ~~which~~ ‚that‚ she could not escape. When she realised this she gave up the long ‚fruitless‚ struggle, denounced the treason which ‚that‚ had been practised against her, repudiated the false confession, reasserted the truth of the testimony ~~which~~ she had given ~~in~~ ‚at‚ the Trial, and went to her martyrdom with the peace of God in her tired heart, and on her lips endearing words and loving prayers for the cur she had crowned and the nation of ingrates she had saved.

8. When the ~~fires rose about her and~~ ‚flames leapt up and enveloped her frail form‚ and she begged for a cross for her ~~dying~~ ‚parched‚ lips to kiss, it was not a friend but an enemy, not a Frenchman but an alien, not a comrade in arms but an English soldier that answered ~~that~~ ‚her‚ pathetic prayer. He broke a stick across his knee, bound the pieces together in the form of the symbol she so loved, and gave it ‚to‚ her.‚ ~~and his~~ ‚This‚ gentle deed is not forgotten, nor ‚ever‚ will be.

(easier translation)

THE REHABILITATION.

Twenty-five years ~~afterwards~~ ˄later˄ the Process of Rehabilitation was instituted, ~~there being~~ ˄in consequence of˄ a growing doubt as to the validity of a sovereignty that had been rescued and set upon its feet by ~~a person~~ ˄one˄ who had been ~~proven~~ ˄declared˄ by the Church ~~to be~~ a witch and a familiar of evil spirits. ~~Joan's~~ ˄Jeanne's˄ old generals,/ her secretary,/ several aged relations and other villagers of Domremy,/ surviving judges and secretaries of the Rouen and Poitiers Processes—a cloud of witnesses, some of whom had been her enemies and persecutors,˄ ⸌came and made oath and testified,~~; and what they said was written down.~~ ˄Their statements were taken down as evidence.˄ In that sworn testimony the moving and beautiful history of ~~Joan of~~ ˄Jeanne d'˄Arc is laid bare/ from her childhood to her martyrdom. From the verdict she rises stainlessly pure, in mind and heart, in speech,˄ ~~and~~ deed and spirit;/ and will so endure to the end of time.

IV.

~~THE RIDDLE OF ALL TIME.~~ ˄An Eternal Enigma.˄

"Riddle"—
Anglice?

1. She is the Wonder of the Ages. ~~And w~~When we consider her origin, her early ~~circumstances,~~ ˄environment,˄ her sex, and that she did all ~~the things~~ upon which her renown rests while ~~she was~~ still a young girl, we recognize that,˄ ~~while~~ ˄so long as˄ our race ~~continues she will be also the Riddle of the Ages. When we set about~~ ˄endures, the circumstances of her career will remain an insoluble problem. When we try to˄ account~~ing~~ for a Napoleon,˄ ~~or a~~ Shakspeare or a Raphael, ~~or~~ a Wagner or an Edison or ˄for˄ other extraordinary persons, we understand that the measure of ~~his~~ ˄individual˄ talent will not explain the whole result, nor even the ~~largest~~ ˄greater˄ part of it.~~; no, it is~~ ˄The explanation must be sought in˄ the atmosphere ~~in~~ ˄amid˄ which the talent was cradled.˄ ~~that explains; it is~~ ˄When we know˄ the training ~~which~~ it received while ~~it grew,~~ ˄young,˄ the nurture it ~~got~~ ˄derived˄ from reading, study/ ˄and˄ example, the encouragement it gathered from self-recognition and ~~recognition from the outside~~ ˄approval from its environment,˄ at each stage of ~~its~~ development: when we know all these ~~details, then we know why the man was ready when his opportunity came.~~ ˄details, we can understand how the genius was ˄created and˄ evolved ~~and thus was ready to seize his~~ by steady and congenial growth.˄ We should expect Edison's ~~surroundings~~ ˄environment˄ and atmosphere to have the largest share in discovering him to himself and to the world; ~~and~~ we should expect him to live and die undiscovered in a land where an inventor could find no comradeship, no sympathy, no ~~ambition-rousing atmosphere of~~ recognition ~~and~~ ˄or˄ applause.˄ ~~—Dahomey, for instance.~~ Dahomey,˄ for instance,˄ could not ~~find~~ ˄produce˄ an Edison.˄ ~~out; in Dahomey an Edison could not find himself out. Broadly speaking, g~~Genius is ~~not~~ born with ˄out˄ sight.~~;~~ ~~but blind; and it is not itself that opens its eyes, but the subtle~~ ˄Its eyes are opened by the subtle˄ influences of a myriad of stimulating exterior circumstances.

2. We all know this to be ~~not a guess, but~~ a mere commonplace fact, a truism. Lorraine was ~~Joan of~~ ˄Jeanne d'˄Arc's Dahomey. ~~And there~~ ˄Here˄ the ~~Riddle~~ ˄problem˄ confronts us. We

can understand ~~how she could~~ ˏthat she mightˏ be born with ˏintuitiveˏ military genius,ʃ with leonine courage,ʃ with incomparable fortitude,ʃ with a mind ~~which~~ ˏthatˏ was in several particulars a prodigy,—ˏa mind which included among its special~~ities~~ ˏmanifestationsˏ the lawyer's gift of detecting traps laid by the adversary in cunning and treacherous arrangements of seemingly innocent words,ʃ the orator's gift of eloquence,ʃ the advocate's gift of presenting a case in clear and ~~compact~~ ˏconciseˏ form,ʃ the judge's gift of sorting and weighing evidence,ʃ and,ˏ finally, something recognisable as more than a mere trace of the statesman's gift of ~~understanding~~ ˏgraspingˏ a political situation and how to make profitable use of such opportunities as it offers.ˏ;wWe can comprehend ~~how she could be born with~~ ˏthat,ˏ these great qualities; ~~but we cannot comprehend~~ ˏmight exist in Jeanne d'Arc at her birth, but,ˏ how they became ~~immediately usable~~ ˏinstantly available,ˏ and effective without the developing forces of a

2 *"comprehends."*

sympathetic ~~atmosphere~~ ˏenvironmentˏ and the training which comes of teaching, study, practice—years of practice—~~and~~ ˏno less than by,ˏ the crowning help of a thousand mistakes ˏis beyond our understanding.ˏ We ~~can understand how~~ ˏknow,ˏ the possibilities of the future perfect peach ~~are~~ ˏto be,ˏ all lying ~~hid~~ ˏdormant,ˏ in the humble bitter-almond;—~~but~~ we cannot conceive of the peach springing direct~~ly~~ from the almond without the intervening long seasons of patient cultivation and development. Out of a cattle-pasturing peasant village lost in the remotenesses of an unvisited wilderness and atrophied with ages of stupefaction and ignorance we ~~cannot~~ ˏfail to,ˏ see a ~~Joan of~~ ˏJeanne d'ˏArc ~~issue~~ ˏissuing,ˏ equipped to the last detail for her amazing career,ˏ ~~and hope to be able~~ ˏnor can we hope,ˏ to explain the riddle of it, labour at it as we may.

3. It is beyond us. All ~~the~~ ˏourˏ rules fail in this girl's case. In the world's history she stands alone—~~quite~~ ˏabsolutely,ˏ alone. Others have ~~been great~~ ˏshone,ˏ in their first ˏgreat,ˏ public exhibitions of generalship, valour, legal talent, diplomacy, fortitude, but ~~always~~ their previous years and associations had ˏinvariably,ˏ been in a ~~larger or smaller~~ ˏgreater or less,ˏ degree a preparation for ~~these~~ ˏsuch,ˏ things. There have been no exceptions to the rule:—~~But Joan~~ ˏYet Jeanne,ˏ was competent in a law case at sixteen without ever having seen a law book,ʃ or a court house before; she ~~had~~ had no training in soldiership and no associations with it, yet she was a competent general ~~in~~ ˏon,ˏ her first campaign; she was brave in her first battle, yet her courage had ~~had~~ ˏreceived,ˏ no education—not even the education which a boy's courage ~~gets from~~ ˏobtains through,ˏ never-ceasing reminders that it is not permissible in a boy to be a coward.;~~but only in a girl; friendless, a~~Alone, ~~ignorant~~ ˏunaided,ˏ, in the ~~blossom~~ ˏbloom,ˏ of her youth she sat week after week, a prisoner in chains, before ~~her~~ ˏan,ˏ assemblage of judges,ʃ—enemies hunting her to her death, the ablest minds in France,ʃ—~~and answered~~ ˏanswering,ˏ them out of an untaught wisdom ~~which~~ ˏthat,ˏ overmatched their learning, baffled their tricks and treacheries with a native sagacity ~~which~~ ˏthat,ˏ compelled their wonder, and scored ~~every~~ ˏeach,ˏ day a victory against ~~these~~ incredible odds.ˏ ~~and camped unchallenged on the field.~~ In the history of the human intellect, untrained, inexperienced, and using only its birthright equipment of untried capacities, there is nothing which approaches this. ~~Joan of~~ ˏJeanne d',ˏArc stands alone, and must continue to stand alone, by reason of the ~~unfellowed~~ ˏunique,ˏ fact that in the things wherein she was great she was so without shade or suggestion of help from preparatory teaching, practice, environment, or experience. There is no one ˏwith whom,ˏ to compare her,ˏ

~~with,~~ none ˏby whom, to measure her; ~~by;~~ for all others among the illustrious *grew* toward their high place in an atmosphere and surroundings ~~which~~ ˏthat, discovered their gift to them, ~~and~~ ˏthat, nourished ~~it~~ and promoted it, intentionally or unconsciously. There have been other ~~young~~ ˏborn, generals, but they were not girls; young generals, but they had been soldiers before they ~~were generals~~ ˏearned the baton,˸ ~~she~~ ˏJeanne, *began* as a general; she commanded the first army she ever saw, she led it from victory to victory, and never lost a battle, ~~with it;~~ ˏtˏThere have been young commanders-in-chief, but none so young as she: she is the only soldier in history who has held the supreme command of a nation's armies at the age of seventeen.

V.

AS PROPHET.

Her history has still another feature which sets her apart and leaves her without fellow or competitor: there have been many uninspired prophets, but she was the only one who ever ventured the daring detail of naming, ~~along~~ ˏin connection, with a foretold event, the ~~event's~~ precise nature/ ˏof that event, the special time-limit ˏand place, within which it would occur, ~~and the place—and scored~~ ˏand in every case realized the complete, *fulfilment*. At Vaucouleurs she said she must ~~go to~~ ˏsee, the King and be made ~~his~~ general~~, and~~ ˏof his forces in order to, break the English power, and crown her sovereign—"at Rheims." ~~It all happened.~~ It was all to happen "next year"—and it did. She foretold her first wound, ~~and~~ its character and date a month ~~in advance, and the~~ ˏbeforehand; this, prophecy was recorded in a public record-book three weeks in advance. She repeated it the morning of the ~~named~~ date/ ˏnamed, and it was fulfilled before night. At Tours she foretold the limit of her military career, ╋ saying it would end in one year from the time of ~~this~~ ˏher, utterance, ╋ and she was right. She foretold her martyrdom, ╋ using *that word*/— and naming a time three months ~~away~~ ˏdistant,—and again she was right. At a ~~time~~ ˏperiod, when France seemed hopelessly and permanently in the hands of the English she twice asserted in her prison before her judges that within seven years,' time, the English would meet with a mightier disaster than had been the fall of Orleans: it happened within five, ~~—the fall of Paris.~~ ˏwhen Paris fell, Other prophecies of hers came true, both as to the event named and the time-limit prescribed.

VI.

HER CHARACTER.

She was deeply religious, and believed that she had daily speech with angels; that she saw them face to face, ~~and~~ that they counselled her, ~~advised~~ ˏcomforted, her, and brought commands to her direct from God. She had a childlike faith in the heavenly origin of her apparitions and her Voices, and not ~~any~~ threat ~~of any form~~ of death ~~was able to~~ ˏin any form could, frighten it out of her loyal heart. She ~~was~~ ˏhad, a beautiful, ~~and~~ simple and lovable character. In the records of the Trial/ this comes out in clear and shining detail. She was gentle, ~~and~~ winning and affectionate; she loved her home, her friends and her village life; she was miserable in the presence of pain and suffering; she was full of compassion: on the field of her most splendid victory she forgot her triumphs to hold in her lap the head of a dying enemy and ˄to˄ comfort his passing spirit with pitying words; in an age when it was common to slaughter prisoners, she stood dauntless between hers and harm, and saved them alive; she was forgiving, generous, unselfish, magnanimous, she was pure from all spot or stain of baseness. And always she was a *girl,* ~~and~~ dear and worshipful, as is meet ~~for~~ ˄in˄ that estate.~~:~~ ˄w˄When she fell wounded, the first time, she was frightened~~/~~ and cried when she saw ~~her~~ ˄the˄ blood gushing from her breast; but she˄,˄ ~~was Joan of~~ ˄Jeanne d'˄Arc, ~~and~~ when presently she found that her generals were sounding the retreat, ~~she~~ staggered to her feet and led the assault again and took that place by storm. There ~~is~~ ˄was˄ no blemish in ~~that~~ ˄the˄ rounded and beautiful character~~/~~ ˄of Jeanne, the Maid.˄ ~~There was no self-conceit in it, no vanity. Only once in her life did she forget whom she was, and use the language of brag and boast. In those exhausting Trials she sat in her chains five and six dreary hours every day in her dungeon, answering her judges; and many times the questions were wearisomely silly and she lost interest, and no doubt her mind went dreaming back to the free days in the field and the fierce joys of battle. One day, at such a time, a tormentor broke the monotony with a fresh new theme, asking, "Did you learn any trade at home?" Then her head went up and her eyes kindled; and the stormer of bastiles, tamer of Talbot the English lion, thunder-breathing deliverer of a cowed nation and a hunted king, answered "Yes! to sew and to spin; and when it comes to that, I am not afraid to be matched against any woman in Rouen!" It was the only time she ever bragged: let us be charitable and forget it.~~

VII.

HER FACE AND FORM.

How strange it is!—that almost invariably the artist remembers only one detail—one minor and meaningless detail of the personality of ~~Joan of~~ ˄Jeanne d'˄Arc,~~/~~ that she was a peasant girl~~+~~ and forgets all the rest!~~; and s~~˄S˄o he paints her as a strapping middle-aged fish˄wife,˄ ~~erwoman,~~ with costume and face to match. He is ˄a˄ slave to his one ˄prevailing˄ idea, and ~~forgets~~ ˄omits˄ to observe that ~~the~~ supremely great souls are never lodged in ~~big~~ ˄gross˄ bodies. No ~~brawn,~~ ˄tissue,˄ no muscle, could endure the ~~work that their bodies must do~~ ˄strain of their physical efforts˄; they ~~do~~ ˄perform˄ their miracles ~~by~~ ˄through˄ the spirit, which has fifty times the strength and staying-power of brawn and muscle. The Napoleons are little, not big; ~~and~~ they work twenty hours ~~in~~ ˄out of˄ the twenty-four, and come up fresh while ˄the˄ big soldiers with little hearts faint around them with fatigue. We know what ~~Joan of Arc~~ ˄Jeanne˄ was like, without ~~asking—~~ ˄inquiring,˄ merely by what she did. The artist should paint her *spirit*—then he could not fail to paint her body right. She would rise before us, ~~then,~~ ˄in such wise,˄ a vision to win us, not ˄to˄ repel: a lithe˄,˄ slender˄ young ~~slender~~ figure, instinct with "the unbought grace of youth," ~~dear and bonny and~~ ˄wholly˄ lovable, the face beautiful, ~~and~~ transfigured with the light of ~~that lustrous~~ ˄her luminous˄ intellect and the fires of ~~that~~ ˄her˄ unquenchable spirit. ˄"It was a miraculous thing," said Guy de Laval, writing from Selles, "to see her and hear her."˄

    2. Taking into account, as I have suggested before, all the circumstances,˄+ her origin,

Insert this remark.

youth, sex, illiteracy, early environment, ~~and~~ ,together with, the obstructing conditions under which she ~~exploited~~ ,demonstrated, her high gifts and made her conquests in the field ~~and~~ ,no less than, before the courts that tried her for her life, ⊬ she is by far the most extraordinary person the human race has ~~ever~~ ,yet, produced/,, nor does there exist in any language so remarkable a history as the official record of Jeanne d'Arc's trial and rehabilitation.

3. I have studied the career of Jeanne d'Arc for years past; I have, moreover, written and published a story of her life: but I am ever ready, as now, to break another lance in honour of the Maid.,

The Letter.

Dear Mr. X:

I find on my desk the first two pages of Miss Z's Translation, with your emendations marked in them. Thank you for sending them.

I have examined the first page of my amended Introduction, and will begin, now, and jot down some notes upon your corrections. If I find any changes which shall not seem to me to be improvements, I will point out my reasons for thinking so. In this way I may chance to be helpful to you, and thus profit you, perhaps, as much as you have desired to profit me.

NOTES.

SECTION I. *First Paragraph.*

"Jeanne d'Arc." This is rather cheaply pedantic, and is not in very good taste. Joan is not known by that name among plain people of our race and tongue. I notice that the name of the Deity occurs several times in the brief instalment of the Trials which you have favored me with; to be consistent, it will be necessary that you strike out "God" and put in "Dieu." Do not neglect this.

First line. What is the trouble with *"at the"*? And why *"Trial"*? Has some uninstructed person deceived you into the notion that there was but one, instead of half a dozen?

Amongst. Wasn't *"among"* good enough?

Next half-dozen Corrections. Have you failed to perceive that by taking the word *"both"* out of its proper place you have made foolishness of the sentence? And don't you see that your smug *"of which"* has turned *that* sentence into reporter's English? *"Quite."* Why do you intrude that shop-worn favorite of yours where there is nothing useful for it to do? Can't you rest easy in your literary grave without it?

Next Sentence. You have made no improvement in it; did you change it merely to *be* changing something?

Second Paragraph. Now you have begun on my punctuation. Don't you realize that you ought not to intrude your help in a delicate art like that, with your limitations? And do you think you have added just the right smear of polish to the closing clause of the sentence?

Second Paragraph. How do you know it was his "own" sword? It could have been a borrowed one. I am cautious in matters of history, and you should not put statements in my mouth for which you cannot produce vouchers. Your other corrections are rubbish.

Third Paragraph. Ditto.

Fourth Paragraph. Your word "directly" is misleading; it could be construed to mean "at once." Plain clarity is better than ornate obscurity. I note your sensitive marginal remark: *"Rather unkind to French feelings—referring to Moscow."* Indeed I have not been concerning myself about French feelings, but only about stating the facts. I have said several uncourteous things about the French—calling them a "nation of ingrates," in one place,—but you have been so busy editing commas and semicolons that you overlooked them and failed to get scared at them. The next paragraph ends with a slur at the French, but I have reasons for thinking you mistook it for a compliment. It is discouraging to try to penetrate a mind like yours. You ought to get it out and dance on it. That would take some of the rigidity out of it. And you ought to use it sometimes; that would help. If you had done this every now and then along through life, it would not have petrified.

Fifth Paragraph. Thus far, I regard this as your masterpiece! You are really perfect in the great art of reducing simple and dignified speech to clumsy and vapid commonplace.

Sixth Paragraph. You have a singularly fine and aristocratic disrespect for homely and unpretending English. Every time I use "go back" you get out your polisher and slick it up to "return." "Return" is suited only to the drawing-room—it is ducal, and says itself with a simper and a smirk.

Seventh Paragraph. "Permission" is ducal. Ducal and affected. *"Her"* great days were *not* "over;" they were only half over. Didn't you know that? Haven't you read anything at all about Joan of Arc? The truth is, you do not pay any attention; I told you on my very first page that the public part of her career lasted two years, and you have forgotten it already. You really must get your mind out and have it repaired; you see, yourself, that it is all caked together.

Eighth Paragraph. She "rode away *to* assault and capture a stronghold." Very well; but you do not tell us whether she succeeded or not. You should not worry the reader with uncertainties like that. I will remind you once more that clarity is a good thing in literature. An apprentice cannot do better than keep this useful rule in mind. *Closing Sentences.* Corrections which are not corrections.

Ninth Paragraph. "Known" history. That word is a polish which is too delicate for me; there doesn't seem to be any sense in it. This would have surprised me, last week.

Second Sentence. It cost me an hour's study before I found out what it meant. I see, now, that it is intended to mean what it meant before. It really does accomplish its intent, I think, though in a most intricate and slovenly fashion. What was your idea in re-framing it? Merely in order that you might add this to your other editorial contributions and be able to say to people that the most of the Introduction was your work? I am afraid that that was really your sly and unparliamentary scheme. Certainly we do seem to live in a very wicked world.

Closing Sentence. There is your empty *"however"* again. I cannot think what makes you so flatulent.

II. In Captivity. "Remainder." It is curious and interesting to notice what an attraction a fussy, mincing, nickel-plated artificial word has for you. This is not well.

Third Sentence. But she *was* held to ransom; it wasn't a case of "should have been." And it wasn't a case of "*if* it had been offered;" it *was* offered, and also accepted, as the second paragraph shows. You ought never to edit except when awake.

Fourth Sentence. Why do you wish to change that? It was more than "demanded," it was *required.* Have you no sense of shades of meaning, in words?

Fifth Sentence. Changing it to "benefactress" takes the dignity out of it. If I had called her a braggart, I suppose you would have polished her into a braggartess, with your curious and random notions about the English tongue.

Closing Sentence. "Sustained" is sufficiently nickel-plated to meet the requirements of your disease, I trust. "Wholly" adds nothing; the sentence means just what it meant before. In the rest of the sentence you sacrifice simplicity to airy fussiness.

Second Paragraph. It was *not* blood-money, O unteachable ass, any more than is the money that buys a house or a horse; it was an ordinary business-transaction of the time, and was not dishonorable. "With her hands, feet and neck *both* chained," etc. The restricted word "both" cannot be applied to three things, but only to two. *"Fence:"* You "lifted" that word from further along—and with what valuable result? The next sentence—after your doctoring of it—has no meaning. The one succeeding it—after your doctoring of it—refers to nothing, wanders around in space, has no meaning and no reason for existing, and is by a shade or two more demented and twaddlesome than anything hitherto ground out of your strange and interesting editorial-mill.

Closing Sentence. "Neither" for "either." Have you now debauched the grammar to your taste?

Third Paragraph. It was sound English before you decayed it. Sell it to the museum.

Fourth Paragraph. I note the compliment you pay yourself, margined opposite the closing sentence: *"Easier translation."* But it has two defects. In the first place it is a *mis*translation, and in the second place it translates half of the grace out of Joan's remark.

Fifth Paragraph. Why are you so prejudiced against fact, and so indecently fond of fiction? Her generalship was *not* "that of a tried and trained military experience," for she hadn't had any, and no one swore that she had had any. I had stated the facts, you should have reserved your fictions. *Note:* To be intelligible, that whole paragraph must consist of a single sentence; in breaking it up into several, you have knocked the sense all out of it.

Eighth Paragraph. "When the flames leapt up and enveloped her frail form" is handsome, very handsome, even elegant, but it isn't yours; you hooked it out of "The Costermonger's Bride; or The Fire-Fiend's Foe," price 3 farthings; boards 2d. To take other people's things is not right, and God will punish you. *"Parched"* lips? How do you know they were? Why do you make statements which you cannot verify, when you have no motive for it but to work in a word which you think is nobby?

III. THE REHABILITATION. "Their statements were taken down *as evidence.*" Wonderful! If you had failed to mention that particular, many persons might have thought they were taken down as entertainment.

IV. THE RIDDLE OF ALL TIME. I note your marginal remark: *"Riddle—Anglice?"* Look in your spelling-book. "We can understand how the genius was created," etc., "by steady and congenial growth." We can't understand anything of the kind; genius is not "created" by any farming process—it is *born*. You are thinking of potatoes. *Note:* Whenever I say "circumstances" you change it to "environment;" and you persistently change my thats into whiches and my whiches into thats. This is merely silly, you know.

Second Paragraph. I note your marginal remark, "2 *comprehends*." I suppose some one has told you that repetition is tautology, and then has left you to believe that repetition is always tautology. But let it go; with your limitations one would not be able to teach you how to distinguish between the repetition which isn't tautology and the repetition which is.

Closing Sentence. Your tipsy emendation, when straightened up on its legs and examined, is found to say this: We fail to see her issue thus equipped, and we cannot understand why. That is to say, she did *not* issue so equipped, and you cannot make out why she didn't. *That* is the riddle that defeats you, labor at it as you may? Why, if that had happened, it wouldn't be a riddle at all—except to you—but a thing likely to happen to nearly anybody, and not matter for astonishment to any intelligent person standing by at the time—or later. There *is* a riddle, but you have mistaken the nature of it. I cannot tell how, labor at it as I may; and I will try to point it out to you so that you can see some of it. We do *not* fail to see her issue so equipped, we *do* see her. That is the whole marvel, mystery, riddle. That she, an ignorant country girl, sprang upon the world equipped with amazing natural gifts is not the riddle—it could have happened to you if you had been some one else; but the fact that those talents were instantly and effectively usable *without previous training* is the mystery which we cannot master, the riddle which we cannot solve. Do you get it?

Third Paragraph. Drunk.

V. As Prophet. "And in *every case* realized the complete fulfilment." How do you know she did that? There is no testimony to back up that wild assertion. I was particular not to claim that all her prophecies came true; for that would have been to claim that we have her whole list, whereas it is likely that she made some that failed and did not get upon the record. People do not record prophecies that failed. Such is not the custom.

VI. Her Character. "Comforted" is a good change, and quite sane. But you are not playing fair; you are getting some sane person to help you. *Note:* When I wrote "counseled her, advised her," *that* was tautology; the "2 comprehends" was a case of repetition which was *not* tautological. But I am sure you will never be able to learn the difference. *Note:* "But she, Jeanne d'Arc, when presently she found," etc. That is the funniest yet, and the commonplacest. But it isn't original, you got it out of "How to Write Literary Without Any Apprenticeship," sixpence to the trade; retail, sevenpence farthing. *Erased Passage:* I note with admiration your marginal remark explaining your objection to it: *"Is it warrantable to assert that she bragged? Is it in good taste? It was assuredly foreign to her character."* I will admit that my small effort at playfulness was not much of a pearl; but such as it was, I realize that I threw it into the wrong trough.

VII. Her Face and Form. You have misunderstood me again. I did not mean that the artist had several ideas and one prevailing one, I meant that he had only *one* idea. In that same sentence, "omits" and "forgets" have just the same meaning; have you any clear idea, then, why you made the change? Is it your notion that "gross" is an improvement on "big," "perform" an improvement on "do," "inquiring" an improvement on "asking," and "in such wise" an improvement on "then," or have you merely been seduced by the fine large sound of those words? Are you incurably hostile to simplicity of speech? And finally, do you not see that you have edited all the dignity out of the paragraph and substituted simpering commonplace for it, and that your addition at the end is a deliciously flat and funny anti-climax? Still, I note your command in the margin, *"Insert this remark,"* and I dutifully obey.

Second Paragraph. "Exploited" was worth a shilling, there; you have traded it for a word not worth tuppence-ha'penny, and got cheated, and serves you right. Read "rightly," if it shocks you. *Close of Paragraph:* You have exploited another anti-climax—and in the form, too, of an impudent advertisement of your book. It seems to me that for a person of your elegance of language you are curiously lacking in certain other delicacies.

Third Paragraph. I must reserve my thanks. "Moreover" is a parenthesis, when interjected in that fashion; a parenthesis is evidence that the man who uses it does not know how to write English or is too indolent to take the trouble to do it; a parenthesis usually throws the emphasis upon the wrong word, and has done it in this instance; a man who will wantonly use a parenthesis will steal. For these reasons I am unfriendly to the parenthesis. When a man puts one into my mouth his life is no longer safe. "Breaking a lance" is a knightly and sumptuous phrase, and I honor it for its hoary age and for the faithful service it has done in the prize-composition of the school-girl, but I have ceased from employing it since I got my puberty, and must solemnly object to fathering it here. And besides, it makes me hint that I have broken one of those things before, in honor of the Maid, an intimation not justified by the facts. I did not break any lances or other furniture, I only wrote a book about her.

Truly Yours
Mark Twain

———————

It cost me something to restrain myself and say these smooth and half-flattering things to this immeasurable idiot, but I did it, and have never regretted it. For it is higher and nobler to be kind to even a shad like him than just. If we should deal out justice only, in this world, who would escape? No, it is better to be generous; and in the end more profitable, for it gains gratitude for us, and love, and it is far better to have the love of a literary strumpet like this than the reproaches of his wounded spirit. Therefore I am glad I said no harsh things to him, but spared him, the same as I would a tape-worm. It is reward enough for me to know that my children will be proud of their father for this, when I am gone. I could have said hundreds of unpleasant things about this tadpole, but I did not even feel them.

This untitled manuscript of twenty-two leaves in the Mark Twain Papers, here assigned the title "Reflections on a Letter and Book," was probably written in late April or early May 1903. Clemens designated it *"Auto."* on the first page, which transcribes a letter to him from one Hilary Trent (pseudonym of R.M. Manley), author of *Mr. Claghorn's Daughter*. Manley asked Clemens to read his book, obviously hoping that he would comment on it. Clemens used the occasion to ridicule the selfishness of the entire human race, himself included: "We do no benevolences whose *first* benefit is not for ourselves." On 26 April 1903 he wrote Manley that he had read the book "with a strong interest, because I am in sympathy with its sermon" and because he approved of "the grace & vigor of your style & because of the attractions of the story as a story" (transcript in CU-MARK; Clemens allowed a condensed version of this "puff" to be used in advertisements for the book). Manley's "sermon" was in fact an attack on Presbyterian doctrine in general and the Westminster Confession of Faith in particular. Near the end of his manuscript Clemens inserted clippings of three articles about recent events that he thought were relevant to his argument, but he made no attempt to actually integrate them into his text. In the four concluding pages, however, he did devote one paragraph to the Westminster Catechism, which the first article had reported as being under revision.

All of the physical evidence (ink, paper, pagination) establishes that these pages make up a single work, but the connection between the first seventeen and the last four seemed so tentative to Paine that he actually turned them (by virtue of penciled titles) into separate works. He published the first section in "Unpublished Chapters from the Autobiography of Mark Twain" in the August 1922 issue of *Harper's Monthly* (SLC 1922c, 312–15), supplying the title "A Young Author Sends Mark Twain a Book," but he did not reprint it in his edition of the autobiography. He did not publish the second section, on which he penciled what seemed to him an appropriate title, "Moral and Intellectual Man." Neider declined to include even the first part, and the present text is therefore the first time the manuscript has been published in full.

[Reflections on a Letter and a Book]

Another of those peculiarly depressing letters—a letter cast in artificially humorous form, whilst no art could make the subject humorous: to me.

> Dear Sir:—I have written a book—naturally, which fact, however, since I am not your enemy need give you no occasion to rejoice. Nor need you grieve, though I am sending you a copy. If I knew of any way of compelling you to read it I would do so, but unless the first few pages have that effect, I can do nothing. Try the first few pages. I have done a great deal more than that with your books, so perhaps you owe me something—say ten pages. If after that attempt you put it aside, I shall be sorry—for you!
>
> I am afraid that the above looks flippant—but think of the twitterings of the soul of him who brings in his hand an unbidden book, written by himself. To such a one much is due in the way of indulgence. Will you remember that? Have you forgotten early twitterings of your own?

The coat-of-arms of the human race ought to consist of a man with an axe on his shoulder proceeding toward a grindstone. Or, it ought to represent the several members of the human race holding out the hat to each other. For we are all beggars. Each in his own way. One beggar is too proud to beg for pennies, but will beg a loan of dollars, knowing he can't repay;

another will not beg a loan, but will beg for a postmastership; another will not do that but will beg for an introduction to "society;" one, being rich, will not beg a hod of coal of the railway company, but will beg a pass; his neighbor will not beg coal, nor pass, but in social converse with a lawyer will place before him a supposititious case in the hope of getting an opinion out of him for nothing; one who would disdain to beg for any of these things will beg frankly for the Presidency. None of the lot is ashamed of himself, but he despises the rest of the mendicants. Each admires his own dignity, and carefully guards it, but in his opinion the others haven't any.

Mendicancy is a matter of taste and temperament, no doubt, but certainly no human being is without a form of it. I know my own form, you know yours; let us curtain it from view and abuse the others. To every man cometh, at intervals, a man with an axe to grind. To you, reader, among the rest. By and by that axe's aspect becomes familiar to you—when you are the proprietor of the grindstone—and the moment you catch sight of it you perceive that it is the same old axe; then you withdraw within yourself, and stick out your spines. If you are the Governor, you know that this stranger wants a position. The first six times the axe came, you were deceived—after that, humiliated. The bearer of it poured out such noble praises of you and of your political record that your lips trembled, the moisture dimmed your eyes, there was a lump in your throat, and you were thankful that you had lived to have this happiness; then the stranger disclosed his axe and his real motive in coming and in applauding, and you were ashamed of yourself and of your race, recognizing that you had been coarsely affronted by this person whom you had treated hospitably. Six repetitions are sure to cure you. After that, (if you are not a candidate for re-election), you interrupt the compliments and say—

"Yes-yes, that is all right, never mind about that; come down to business—what is it you want?"

No matter how big or how little your place in life may be, you have a grindstone, and people will bring axes to you. None escapes.

Also, you are in the business yourself. You privately rage at the man who brings his axe to you, but every now and then you carry yours to somebody and ask a whet. I don't carry mine to strangers, I draw the line there; perhaps that is your way. This is bound to set us up on a high and holy pinnacle and make us look down in cold rebuke upon persons who carry their axes to strangers.

Now, then, since we all carry axes, and must, and cannot break ourselves of it, why has not a best way to do it been invented by some wise and thoughtful person? There can be no reason but one: from the beginning of time each member of the human race, while recognizing with shame and angry disapproval that everybody else is an axe-bearer and beggar, has all the while deceived himself with the superstition that he is free of the taint. And so it would never occur to him to plan out for the help and benefit of the race a scheme which could not advantage himself. For that is human nature.

But—let us recognize it and confess it—we *are* all concerned to plan out a best way to approach a person's grindstone, for we are all beggars; a best way, a way which shall as nearly as possible avoid offensiveness, a way which shall best promise to secure a grinding for the axe. How would this plan answer, for instance:

Never convey the axe yourself; send it by another stranger; or by your friend; or by the grindstone-man's friend; or by a person who is friend to both of you.

Of course this last is best-best, but the others are good. You see, when you dispatch the axe yourself, (along with your new book, for instance,) you are making one thing absolutely certain: the grindstone-man will be all ready with a prejudice against it and an aversion, before he has even looked at it. Because—why, merely because you have tied his hands, you have not left him independent, he feels himself cornered, and he frets at this, he chafes, he resents as an impertinence your taking this unfair advantage of him—and he is right. He knows you meant to take a mean advantage of him—with all your clumsy arts you have not deceived him. He knows you framed your letter with deliberation, to a distinct end: to compel an answer. You have paid him homage: by all the laws of courtesy, he has got to pay for it. And he cannot choose the way: he has to pay for it in thanks and return-compliments. Your ingenuities resemble those of the European professional beggar: to head you off from pretending you did not receive his letter, he *registers* it—and he's *got* you!

I respect my own forms of passing the hat, but not other people's. I realize that this is natural. Among my forms is not that of sending my books to strangers. To do that is to beg for a puff—it has that object, whether the object is confessed in words or not. Since that is not my form of soliciting alms, I look down upon it with a polar disdain. It seems to me that this also is natural. The first time a stranger ever sent me his book, I was as pleased as a child, and I took all the compliments at par; I supposed the letter was written just to get in those compliments. I didn't read between the lines, I didn't know there was anything between the lines. However, as the years dragged along and brought experience I became an expert on invisibles, and could find more meat between the lines than anywhere else. After that, those letters gave me no pleasure; they inarticulately, but strenuously, demanded pay for the compliments, and they made me ashamed of the offerer; and also of myself, for being a person who, by the offerer's estimate, was on a low enough grade to value compliments on those terms.

Although I am finding so much fault with this matter I am not ignorant of the fact that compliments are not often given away. A return is expected. And one gets it, too—though not always when the compliments are sent by letter. When an audience applauds, it isn't aware that it is requiring pay for that compliment. But it is; and if the applause is not in some way thankfully acknowledged by the recipient of it,—by bow and smile, for instance—the audience will discover that it *was* expecting an equivalent. Also, it will withdraw its trade, there and then; it is not going to give something for nothing, not if it knows itself. When a beautiful girl catches a compliment in our eye, she pays spot cash for it with a dear little blush. We did not know we were expecting pay, but if she should flash offended dignity at us, instead of that little blush, we should then know better. She would get no more of our trade on those terms. But in truth, compliments are sometimes actually *given* away, and no bill presented. I know it can occur as much as once in a century, for it has happened once to me, and I am not a century old, yet. It was twenty-nine years ago. I was lecturing in London at the time. I received a most lovely letter, sparkling and glowing with cordial and felicitous praises—and there was *no name signed, and no address!*

It was all mine—all free—all gratis—no bill enclosed, nothing to pay, no possible *way* to pay—an absolutely free gift! It is the only gratis compliment I have ever received, it is the only gratis compliment I have ever even heard of. Whenever a stranger tags his compliment with his name and address, it stands for C.O.D. He may not consciously and deliberately intend it so, but that is because he has not the habit of searching his motives to the bottom. People avoid that. And that is wise in its way, for the most of one's motives are best concealed from oneself. I know this by long experience and close examination of my own.

It is not right for a stranger to send me his book himself. It is an embarrassment for him, it is an embarrassment for me. I have not earned this treatment, I have not done him any harm. Why not send it through B, and instruct B to say to me, "Take no notice of this unless you are really moved to do it, for A is modest and sensitive, and he would be offended if he knew what I am doing."

The absence of the club over me would make me feel so grateful that I should find merits in that book that had no existence there nor anywhere else. But no, the author always sends it himself. He knows he is doing an unfair thing; he is ashamed of it, and playfully tries to pretend he isn't, but his letter always gives him away. He is aware that he is begging. And not for a candid opinion of his book, but for a puff. He is aware that you will want to say that to him, but he is also aware that your self-love will not let you do it. One of two things he always puts in: 1, he admires you; 2, you probably asked and received help and encouragement yourself when you were a struggling beginner. It is a curious absence of tact. He wants a gratuity of you, and prepares the way by putting the thing at you as an obligation—it's your *duty* to grant it. It may be true, but we resent it, just the same; we don't want strangers to dictate our duties to us. Sometimes the stranger does this ungracious thing facetiously, sometimes he does it in very plain English; but he is in serious earnest in both cases, and you do not like it any better in the one case than in the other.

I am built just as other people are built, so far as I can discover, and therefore I do prize a good hearty compliment above rubies; and am grateful for it, and as glad as you are yourself when I can in sincerity return the mate to it. But when a man goes beyond compliment, it does not give me pleasure, it makes me ashamed. It makes *me* ashamed; I am not thinking about him, I am thinking about myself; he may humiliate himself if he likes, it is his privilege, but *I* do not want to be humiliated. Adulation. Adulation—spoken or hinted. And never earned; never due, to any human being. What a king must suffer! For he knows, deep down in his heart, that he is a poor, cheap, wormy thing like the rest of us, a sarcasm, the Creator's prime miscarriage in inventions, the moral inferior of all the animals, the inferior of each one of them in one superb physical specialty or another, the superior of them all in one gift only, and that one not up to *his* estimation of it—intellect.

I do not know how to answer that stranger's letter. I wish he had spared me. Never mind about him—I am thinking about myself; I wish he had spared *me*. The book has not arrived, yet; but no matter, I am prejudiced against it.

I suppose the reader—if he is an old and experienced person—already knows what it was that I did. I followed custom. I did what one always does after searching for new spirit-quieting methods and finding none: I fell back upon the old, old, over-worked and over-fatigued dodge, trick, subterfuge, polite lie, and wrote him thanking him for his book and promising myself— "at an early date"—the pleasure of reading it.

That set me free: I was not obliged to read the book, now, unless I chose. Being free, my prejudice was gone. My prejudice being gone, a very natural curiosity took its place. Since I could examine the book without putting myself under an obligation of any sort, I opened it and began, as soon as it came. It was a costly adventure for me. I had work to do and no time to spare, but I was not able to put the book down until I had finished it. It embarrassed me a little to write the author and confess this fact, right on the heels of that courteously-discourteous letter which had preceded it, but I did it. I did it because I could get more peace for my spirit out of doing it than out of leaving it undone. Were you thinking I did it to give that author pleasure? I did—at *second hand*. We do no benevolences whose *first* benefit is not for ourselves.

PRESBYTERIAN DOCTRINE.

Two-thirds of the Presbyteries in Favor of Revising Confession of Faith.

PHILADELPHIA, April 27.—The Rev. Dr. W. H. Roberts, Stated Clerk of the Presbyterian General Assembly, announced to-day that two-thirds of the presbyteries had voted in favor of revising the Confession of Faith and of the declaratory statement elucidating chapters 3 and 10 of the Confession. The subject will be finally disposed of by the General Assembly, which will meet in Los Angeles, Cal., next month. It is expected that the overtures from the presbyteries will be enacted by the General Assembly.

RUSSIAN MASSACRE OF JEWS.

Dispatch to a Local Jewish Paper Telling of the Slaughter at Kishinev—120 Reported Killed.

The *Jewish Daily News* will print this afternoon the following cable dispatch in reference to the anti-Jewish riot in Kishinev, Russia:

"St. Petersburg, April 25th.—(Taken across the border line for transmission in order to escape the Censor.)—The anti-Jewish riots in Kishinev, Bessarabia, are worse than the Censor will permit to publish. There was a well laid plan for the general massacre of Jews on the day following the Russian Easter. The mob was led by priests and the general cry: "Kill the Jews!" was taken up all over the city. The Jews were taken totally unaware, and were slaughtered like sheep. The dead number 120, and the injured about 500.

"The scenes of horror attending this massacre are beyond description. Babes were literally torn to pieces by the frenzied and blood-thirsty mob. The local police made no attempt to check the reign of terror. At sunset the streets were piled with corpses and wounded. Those who could make their escape fled in terror and the city is now practically deserted of Jews.

"Just as in the riots of 1880–1881, there is a popular belief among the Russian peasants that the Czar decreed the slaughtering of Jews. The immediate cause of the riot, however, is the ritual murder accusation against the Jews in Dubosary, government of Kherson. Immediate relief is wanted."

After waiting a year to make up his mind as to whether the story of Adam and Eve was a myth, Gilbert A. Lovell, of Plainfield, N.J., a young churchman who was denied by the Presbytery of Elizabeth a license to preach the Gospel because he expressed his disbelief in that part of the book of Genesis, was to-day licensed by the Presbytery at its spring session held in Perth Amboy.

Lovell and Harrison K. Wright, of Plainfield, applied last spring to the Presbytery for license, but as both held the same opinion as to Adam and Eve being mythical, they were each rejected by a large majority. Afterward a special session of the Presbytery was held to give them an opportunity to recant. Mr. Wright appeared before it and declared his views had changed on the disputed subject, and he was willing to acknowledge his mistake. His explanation and other answers proved satisfactory. He got his license, and later was ordained by the Presbytery.

Lovell, however, sent word he would wait a year before making another try for a license. Meanwhile he evidently experienced a change of heart, as his examination to-day on all theological points gave entire satisfaction to the Presbytery, which will set a date for his ordination.

We have no respectworthy evidence that the human being has morals. He is himself the only witness. Persons who do not know him value his testimony. They think he is not shallow and vain because he so despises the peacock for possessing these qualities. They are deceived into not regarding him as a beast and a brute, because he uses these terms to disapprovingly describe qualities which he possesses, yet which are not possessed by any creature but himself. On his verbal testimony they take him for every creditable thing which he particularly isn't, and (intentionally?) refrain from examining the testimony of his acts. It is the safest way, but man did not invent it, it was the polecat. From the beginning of time the polecats have quite honestly and naively regarded themselves as representing in the animal kingdom what the rose represents in the vegetable kingdom. This is because they do not examine.

Man thinks he is not a fiend. It is because he has not examined the Westminster Catechism which he invented. He and the polecat— But it is not fair to class them together, the polecat has not invented a Westminster Catechism.

However, moralless man, bloody and atrocious man, is high above the other animals in his one great and shining gift—intellectuality. It took him ages and ages to demonstrate the full magnitude and majesty of his gift, but he has accomplished it at last. For ages it was a mean animal indeed that was not vastly his superior in certain splendid faculties. In the beginning he had nothing but the puny strength of his unweaponed hands to protect his life with, and he was as helpless as a rabbit when the lion, the tiger, the elephant, the mastodon and the other mighty beasts came against him; in endurance he was far inferior to the other creatures; in fleetness on the land there was hardly an animal in the whole list that couldn't shame him; in fleetness in the water every fish could excel him; his eyesight was a sarcasm: for seeing minute things it was blindness as compared to the eyesight of the insects, and the condor could see a sheep further than he could see a hotel. But by the ingenuities of his intellect he has equipped himself with all these gifts artificially and has made them unapproachably effective. His locomotive can outstrip all birds and beasts in speed and beat them all in endurance; there are no eyes in the animal world that can compete with his microscope and his telescope; the strength of the tiger and the elephant is weakness, compared with the force which he carries in his mile-range terrible gun. In the beginning he was given "dominion" over the animal creation—a very handsome present, but it was mere words and represented a non-existent sovereignty. But he has turned it into an existent sovereignty, himself, and is master, of late. In physical talents he was a pauper when he started; by grace of his intellect he is incomparably the richest of all the animals now. But he is still a pauper in morals—incomparably the poorest of the creatures in that respect. The gods value morals alone; they have paid no compliments to intellect, nor offered it a single reward. If intellect is welcome anywhere in the other world, it is in hell, not heaven.

This 1903 text survives in an untitled, previously unpublished manuscript now in the Mark Twain Papers. Clemens identified it as "*Autobiog.*" in the upper left corner of the first page, adding (and later canceling) "*Hannibal, 1842,*" the place and year of the first anecdote about his experience with castor oil. Clemens was always skeptical of doctors and had long since concluded that they were of little or no assistance to their patients. "I am not afraid of doctors in ordinary or trifling ailments, but in a serious case I should not allow any one to persuade me to call one," he wrote Henry H. Rogers on 8 January 1900 (Salm, in *HHR*, 425). In the present rather desultory essay, however, he remained more or less focused on what he considered the unfairness of the way contemporary doctors charged for their services. For an indispensable overview of Clemens's attitude toward doctors and medical practice in general, see *Mark Twain and Medicine: "Any Mummery Will Cure"* (Ober 2003).

Paine planned to publish this manuscript in his edition of the autobiography, using the title adopted here and placing it after "Scraps from My Autobiography. Private History of a Manuscript That Came to Grief" (*MTA*, 1:175–89). He suppressed the names of several physicians when he prepared his typescript for the printer. For reasons unknown, however, he decided not to include it, even after it had been set in type.

[Something about Doctors]

I was seven years old when I came so near going to Heaven that time. I do not know why I did not go; I was prepared. This was habit. I had been sick a considerable part of those seven years, and had naturally formed the custom of being prepared. Religion was made up almost exclusively of fire and brimstone in those days, and this furnished a motive for preparation which none but the very thoughtless neglected. To be honest, I will acknowledge that I sometimes neglected it myself; but it was only when I was well. I do not remember what malady it was that came so near to removing me from this life, that time, but I remember what it was that defeated it. It was half a teacupful of castor oil—straight. That is, without molasses, or other ameliorations. Many took molasses with their oil, but I was not of that class. Perhaps I knew that nothing could make oil palatable, for I had had a large experience; I had drunk barrels of castor oil in my time. No, not barrels, kegs; let us postpone exaggerations to a properer time and subject.

The castor oil saved me. I had begun to die, the family were grouped for the function; they were familiar with it, so was I. I had performed the star part so many times that I knew just what to do at each stage without a rehearsal, although so young; and they—they had played the minor rôles so often that they could do it asleep. They often went to sleep when I was dying. At first it used to hurt me, but later I did not mind it, but got some one to joggle them, then went on with my rendition. I can see us at it, to this day.

Dr. Meredith was our family physician in those days; he probably removed from the hamlet of Florida to the village of Hannibal about the same time that we did, in order to keep my custom. No, that could not have been the reason; I have already said that in that early geological period the doctor was paid by the year and furnished the drugs himself; therefore he would not really value my custom, if sane. He often tried to kill me, I suppose; it would be but natural, for he had a family to support, and was a man of good judgment and right intentions, but he never succeeded in a single instance. It was the irony of fate that his own son Charles should pull me out of Bear creek at last when another half minute would have ended my life. He never smiled again.

Consider the wisdom and righteousness of that old-time custom—the paying of the physician by the year. Consider what a safeguard it was, for both the physician's livelihood and self-respect, and the family's health. The physician had a regular and assured income, and that was an advantage to him; the family were safe from his invasions when nothing was the matter, and goodness knows that was an advantage to the family.

Look at the difference in our day. What is the common, the universal, custom of the physician with a limited practice? It is this: to keep on coming and coming, long after the patient has ceased to need him—and charging for every visit. Almost as a rule—I might fairly leave that "almost" out—you are driven to the unpleasant compulsion of discharging him, in order to get rid of him. As a consequence you dread to call him again; and you put it off just as long as you can without peril.

I make this charge deliberately. I draw it from four sources: from my own experience, from the experience of friends, from the statements (hotly worded) of distinguished New York and London physicians, and from editorial statements in the medical journals. Your physician knows you are afraid to discharge him, lest it turn out that you did it too early; he takes a discreditable advantage of this fear.

The hard-driven physician comes no oftener than he is obliged to. As soon as it is safe to say it, he says, "I shall not come again unless you send for me."

In Hartford our old family physician, Dr. Taft, made us familiar with that remark, but we never got it out of his neglected successor. Eight years ago (in 1895) I arrived from Europe and went straight to Elmira, N.Y. In the bath-tub, that evening, (May 26), I found a round, flat pink spot on the outside of my port thigh, the size of a dime. The next morning we moved up on the East Hill, and called up a doctor (Theron Wales), from below and he said it was an incipient carbuncle. He began to treat it. And also began to talk. To let him tell it, the carbuncle had always been the master of the human race until by God's mercy he became a member of it. Then he sang the long list of his victories, carbuncle by carbuncle, naming the proprietor in each case and the place on him where the carbuncle roosted, and the illustrious methods whereby he had conducted those carbuncles to a happy and spectacular finish. This was a very dull man, by nature and acquirement, but he was an old friend of the kinship, and I had to endure him, though I give you my word that as between his society and the carbuncle's, I would have selected the carbuncle's every time. He had the special characteristic of every limited-practice physician whom I have ever known: he was tedious, witless, commonplace, a stayer, loved to hear himself talk, and was a spirit-rotting bore.

With all his boasted experience he knew nothing about carbuncles that was not known by our old ex-slave cook, Aunty Cord, and he did nothing with mine which she could not have done as well or better. He applied that ancient persuader, a slice of raw salt pork, and came daily while it was doing its work. Came to watch it, I suppose; the cat could have done it as effectively, and certainly the cook could—and gratis. Then he lanced it, and came daily for thirty days more; sometimes to dress the wound—which the cook could have done as well as he—but most of the time for no conceivable reason, unless to exhaust me with his two-hour visits and his colorless conversation. So many of these visits were professionally objectless that I took them for social visits, or I would have retired him.

He not only charged me for every one of those odious visitations, but charged me a third more than he would have charged a resident. I did not find out this latter detail—this robbery,—until six months ago.

That burglar still keeps up that custom—of paying what people take for social calls, after his professional services are no longer needed, and then charging for them after the family, growing suspicious, have given him a large hint and gotten rid of him.

He did not cure my carbuncle. He watched over it forty-five days like a tender and ignorant carbuncle-angel, then I started across the country with my family. I lectured every night for twenty-three nights, the nightly dressing of the cavern left by the carbuncle going on every night, and at last the place was healed and I walked aboard the ship at Vancouver unassisted.

Carbuncles have families, when they are treated by bunglers. Mine's first son was born at sea and was lanced in Sydney. The second son was born in Melbourne, but there was a real doctor there—Fitz Gerald—a doctor with an immense practice, and he said he would cure it in twenty-four hours. He kept his word; also, he taught us his art, and we squelched the rest of the family, one by one, as they arrived. Only one of them lasted two days. The carbuncle-expert of Elmira charged me $135 for half-curing one carbuncle. If I had not been obliged to leave on the lecture-tour he would be propagating that one's posterity to this day.

That Elmira leech knew that I had fallen heir to a heavy debt, and was starting on a year's journey around the globe to lecture it off and set myself free, but that did not move him to spare me when he had a chance to afflict me with social calls and charge pirate-rates for them. I resolved that I would never again sit in the Sunday school that he superintended, and I have kept my word to this day. However, I was never in it anyway.

It is a bad business to get the *habit* of getting sick. You will find it hard to break. From my seventh year to my fifty-sixth I had had the habit of being well—I had hardly known what sickness was, in all that time. Then the change came. We were living in Berlin. On a very cold winter's night I lectured for the benefit of an English or American church-charity in a hall that was as hot as the Hereafter. On my way home, I froze. I spent thirty-four days in bed, with congestion of the wind'ard lung. That was the beginning. That lung has remained in a damaged condition ever since. Whenever I catch a cold in the head it descends at once to the bronchial tubes, and I have to send for the medical plumber. That is, I used to do that, but when I found out at last that to relieve it, modify it, shorten its stay or cure it were all beyond his art, I ceased from calling him and allowed the cough to bark itself out at its leisure and perish of fatigue. Its term is six weeks, under these conditions. Before giving up, I experimented with ten physicians in different parts of the world.

In the beginning of '96 I caught a cold in Ceylon, and by the time we reached Bombay, a few days later, my tubes were in bad shape and I sent for the plumber. He bore the great name of Sidney Smith. I took his dreadful medicine seven days, with no improvement, then I discharged him. He charged me double price per visitation because I was not a resident. It was the custom, I was told. I thought it would have been as rational to charge me double because I was a Presbyterian. I paid half the bill.

I barked at audiences all about India for six weeks, then the cough expired by statute of limitation. I had attacks in London, later. The first doctor (Parsons), soon confessed that he was making no progress with the case, and retired from the struggle with honor; the other one (Ogilvie), probably concluded before long, that the case was beyond his science, for he stopped bothering with it, but came every day and told ancient anecdotes for an hour and enjoyed them—I could see it. I was deceived again; I took these wearisome afflictions for social calls, and forebore to protect myself. But at last I saw that in my weak state the burden of his society was a positive danger, so I pulled the remains of my resolution together and discharged him. He charged full rates for all those visits, whereas he knew quite well that to collect on a full half of them was plain dishonesty.

This text survives in an untitled 1906 typescript made by Josephine Hobby, now in the Mark Twain Papers. Hobby copied an earlier typescript, now lost, created by Jean Clemens from Isabel Lyon's notes of Clemens's original dictation in April 1904, and Clemens briefly revised and corrected Hobby's copy. It is the only one of the six known Florentine dictations that Clemens did not include in his final text for the autobiography (see the Introduction, note 55).

Clemens's friendship with multimillionaire Henry Huttleston Rogers (1840–1909), vice-president of Standard Oil, began in the fall of 1893, when Clemens's publishing firm, Charles L. Webster and Company, was close to financial collapse. Rogers became Clemens's financial adviser and provided the funds needed to keep the company afloat, at least temporarily. The firm nevertheless declared bankruptcy in April 1894, but not before Rogers arranged for the transfer of all Clemens's assets, including the copyright on his books, to Olivia Clemens, on the grounds that she was owed more than $60,000 by the bankrupt firm.

Clemens created the dictation at a time when Olivia was quite ill and Rogers had just recently been very publicly sued for several million dollars by the Bay State Gas Company. After Rogers's death Clemens wrote, "I am grateful to his memory for many a kindness and many a good service he did me, but gratefulest of all for the saving of my copyrights; a service which saved me and my family from want, and assured us permanent comfort and prosperity" (SLC 1909b; see also AD, 26 May 1906; *HHR*, 10–26, 42–43; "Mark Twain's Company in Trouble," New York *Times,* 19 Apr 1894, 9).

Paine published the dictation under the title he gave it, "Henry H. Rogers," but without the article from the Boston *Sunday Post* that Clemens instructed be reproduced at the end, and he also joined it with the later manuscript about Rogers (SLC 1909b; *MTA,* 1:250–56). Neider declined to include any part of this text.

[Henry H. Rogers]

1893–1904

Florence. Spring of 1904. (April.)

Mr. Rogers has been visiting the witness stand periodically in Boston for more than a year now. For eleven years he has been my closest and most valuable friend. His wisdom and steadfastness saved my copyrights from being swallowed up in the wreck and ruin of Charles L. Webster and Co., and his commercial wisdom has protected my pocket ever since in those lucid intervals wherein I have been willing to listen to his counsels and abide by his advice—a thing which I do half the time and half the time I don't.

He is four years my junior; he is young in spirit, and in looks, complexion and bearing, easy and graceful in his movements, kind-hearted, attractive, winning, a natural gentleman, the best bred gentleman I have met on either side of the ocean in any rank of life from the Kaiser of Germany down to the boot-black. He is affectionate, endowed with a fine quality of humor, and with his intimates he is a charming comrade. I am his principal intimate and that is my idea of him. His mind is a bewildering spectacle to me when I see it dealing with vast business complexities like the affairs of the prodigious Standard Oil Trust, the United States Steel and the rest of the huge financial combinations of our time—for he and his millions are in them all, and his brain is a very large part of the machinery which keeps them alive and going. Many a time in the past eleven years my small and troublesome affairs have forced me to spend days and weeks of waiting-time down in the city of New York, and my waiting-refuge has been his private office in the Standard Oil Building, stretched out on a sofa behind his chair, observing his processes, smoking, reading, listening to his reasonings with the captains of industry and intruding advice where it was not invited, not desired and in no instance adopted so far as I remember. A patient man, I can say that for him.

This private office was a spacious high-ceiled chamber on the eleventh floor of the Standard Oil Building, with large windows which looked out upon the moving life of the river with the Colossus of Liberty enlightening the world holding up her torch in the distance. When I was not there it was a solitude, since in those intervals no one occupied the place except Mr. Rogers and his brilliant private secretary, Miss Katharine I. Harrison, who he once called in on an emergency thirteen or fourteen years ago from among the seven hundred and fifty clerks laboring for the Standard Oil in the building. She was nineteen or twenty years old then and did stenographic work and typewriting at the wage of that day which was fifteen or twenty dollars a week. He has a sharp eye for capacity and after trying Miss Harrison for a week he promoted her to the post of chief of his private secretaries and raised her wages. She has held the post ever since; she has seen the building double its size and increase its clerical servants to fifteen hundred and her own salary climb to ten thousand dollars a year. She is the only private secretary who sits in the sanctum, the others are in the next room and come at the bell call. Miss Harrison is alert, refined, well read in the good literature of the day, is fond of paintings and buys them, she is a cyclopedia in whose head is written down the multitudinous details of Mr. Rogers's business, order and system are a native gift with her, Mr. Rogers refers to her as he would to a book and she responds with the desired information with a book's confidence and accuracy. Several times I have heard Mr. Rogers say that she is quite able to conduct his affairs, substantially, without his help.

Necessarily Mr. Rogers's pecuniary aid was sought by his full share of men and women without capital who had ideas for sale—ideas worth millions if their exploitation could be put in charge of the right man. Mr. Rogers's share of these opportunities was so large that if he had received and conversed with all his applicants of that order he might have made many millions per hour it is true but he would not have had half an hour left in the day for his own business. He could not see all of these people, therefore he saw none of them, for he was a fair and just man. For his protection, his office was a kind of fortress with outworks, these outworks being several communicating rooms into which no one could get access without first passing through an outwork where several young colored men stood guard and carried in the cards and requests and brought back the regrets. Three of the communicating rooms were for consultations, and they were seldom unoccupied. Men sat in them waiting—men who were there by appointment—appointments not loosely specified but specified by the minute hand of the clock. These rooms had ground glass doors, and their privacy was in other ways protected and secured. Mr. Rogers consulted with a good many men in those rooms in the course of his day's work of six hours; and whether the matter in hand was small and simple or great and complicated it was discussed and despatched with marvelous celerity. Every day these consultations supplied a plenty of vexations and exasperations for Mr. Rogers—I know this quite well—but if ever they found revealment in his face or manner it could have been for only a moment or two for the signs were gone when he re-entered his private office and he was always his brisk and cheerful self again and ready to be chaffed and joked, and reply in kind. His spirit was often heavily burdened, necessarily, but it cast no shadow, and those about him sat always in the sunshine.

Sometimes the value of his securities went down by the million day after day, sometimes they went up as fast, but no matter which it was the face and bearing exhibited by him were only proper to a rising market. Several times every day Miss Harrison had to act in a diplomatic capacity. Men called whose position in the world was such that they could not be dismissed with the formula "engaged" along with Mr. Rogers's regrets, and to these Miss Harrison went out and explained, pleasantly and tactfully, and sent them away comfortable. Mr. Rogers transacted a vast amount of business during his six hours daily, but there always seemed time enough in the six hours for it.

That Boston Gas lawsuit came on at a bad time for Mr. Rogers, for his health was poor and remained so during several months. Every now and then he had to stay in his country house at Fairhaven, Mass., a week or two at a time, leaving his business in Miss Harrison's hands and conferring with her once or twice daily by long distance telephone. To prepare himself for the witness stand was not an easy thing, but the materials for it were to be had, for Mr. Rogers never destroyed a piece of paper that had writing on it and as he was a methodical man he had ways of tracing out any paper he needed no matter how old it might be. The papers needed in the gas suit, wherein Mr. Rogers was sued for several millions of dollars, went back in date a good many years and were numberable by the hundreds; but Miss Harrison ferreted them all out from the stacks and bales of documents in the Standard Oil vaults and caused them to be listed and annotated by the other secretaries. This work cost weeks of constant labor, but it left Mr. Rogers in shape to establish for himself an unsurpassable reputation as a witness.

I wish to make a momentary digression here and call up an illustration of what I have been saying about Mr. Rogers's habits in the matter of order and system. When he was a young man of twenty-four out in the oil regions of Pennsylvania and straitened in means he had some business relations with another young man; time went on, they separated and lost sight of each other. After a lapse of twenty years this man's card came in one day, and Mr. Rogers had him brought into the private office. The man showed age, his clothes showed that he was not prosperous, and his speech and manner indicated that hard luck had soured him toward the world and the Fates. He brought a bill against Mr. Rogers, oral in form, for fifteen hundred dollars—a bill thirty years old. Mr. Rogers drew the check and gave it to him, saying he could not allow him to lose it though he almost deserved to lose it for risking the claim thirty years without presenting it. When he was gone Mr. Rogers said,

"My memory is better than his; I paid the money at the time; knowing this, I know I took a receipt although I do not remember that detail. To satisfy myself that I have not been careless, I will have that receipt searched out."

It took a day or two, but it was found, and I saw it, then it was sent back to its place again amongst the archives.

Here follows that Boston sketch.

PEN PICTURES OF THE BIG STANDARD OIL MILLIONAIRE, H. H. ROGERS, AS HE APPEARED DURING THE PRESENT GAS HEARING

———

Boston has had the unique experience of having on the witness stand in court one of the wealthiest and brainiest men in this country, a man in the charmed inner circle of the very inner circle of the little ring of financial giants that make up the most powerful aggregation of wealth in this country. It has seen him for four days probed with an incessant volley of questions by one of the ablest lawyers in the Commonwealth and it saw him step off the witness stand at the end as calm and serene and unruffled, and fresh and vigorous, as though he were two score of years younger than he is, and as though he had just finished a pleasure trip on his yacht, instead of having passed through what to most men would be an extremely trying ordeal.

And for verbal fencing, Henry H. Rogers showed that he, by replies that were as quick as a flash and as impenetrable as adamant, is entitled to wear a crown of superiority over any witness examined in Massachusetts for many a day.

When he had finished the court had gleaned precious little about the case beyond what it had already learned from Mr. Winsor, except for Mr. Rogers' version of the famous telephone conversation with Mr. Lawson, and that certainly is interesting, in view of the fact that Mr. Lawson's understanding seems to have been quite different from Mr. Rogers', this difference apparently throwing a sidelight upon the present relations between the two men that is interesting, to say the least.

It is reported that Mr. Whipple, keen as he is, unrelenting in his pursuit of a fact, acknowledges that Mr. Rogers was the best fencer he ever met in his legal career. That he was enough for Mr. Whipple, sometimes a little too much, was the general opinion of those who saw the two cross swords.

Mr. Rogers was ill soon after he came to Boston. Our east wind, or the smell of escaping gas with the lid partially off, or something else, was too much for him, and he took to his humble bed in Boston's Waldorf-Astoria, or the nearest thing to it that the Hub possesses. There were some people who thought that meant that he was going to dodge, that he would be too ill to testify and leave Boston in the lurch, just as a famous operatic star or an actress sometimes does. But the people who knew him said: "No, Mr. Rogers is no dodger; he is a fighter in the heavyweight championship class, and he will see it through." And he did.

One afternoon Mr. Winsor, after some 10 trying days on the witness stand, answered his last question, smiled his last smile to the court and spectators and stepped down.

The next morning a few "supes" and players of minor parts came on and did their little turn. Then a tall, distinguished-looking gentleman, one bearing the mark of a leader among men, took the centre of the stage, the witness box. For the first time the crowd in the court room got a good look at the man of many millions as Mr. Rogers faced the questioning counsel.

The court gave permission to the witness to sit while he gave his evidence, in consideration of his recent illness.

Mr. Rogers is all that his pictures represent him to be, and much, very much, more. The first thing that almost anyone would notice is his head, a literal "dome of thought," large, finely shaped, extraordinarily high above the line of the eyes, rounded and fully developed in the back, the head of a man with tremendous capacity for thought, a strong, forceful head, that of a man capable of planning and of executing his plans, distinctly the head of a man of affairs, of tremendous affairs.

The head might attract more attention than the face, although the latter is clearly that of a man of high standing among men, clear cut, almost ascetic in some of its lines, aggressive as to the chin, firm as to the mouth, keen as to the eyes.

The gray, well-trimmed mustache, the alert, vigorous, trim, well kept, well groomed, well set up figure, impart a military air that fits perfectly upon this man of power.

Mr. Whipple is ready to begin his bombardment of questions. Mr. Rogers sits at ease, his legs crossed, his arms upon the rails at the side of the witness box, his head thrown up and back, his eyes inscrutable, his whole demeanor that of waiting on the defence. He doesn't pose at all, apparently. Many men do in similar positions. Their whole attitude is one of consciousness of being looked at and of trying to look as impressive as possible. But Mr. Rogers isn't one of that sort. His attitudes fit him as well as the clothes he wears, and that is to perfection.

Mr. Whipple asks the customary questions as to name, residence, etc. Then as to occupation and as to this Mr. Rogers gives some inkling as to his baffling course as a witness. He admitted that he had been in the petroleum business for 40 years, and said: "I am trying to think if I have been in the gas business." Everybody laughs. Evidently Mr. Rogers is going to be a very amusing witness, at times. Even Mr. Whipple, who can take a joke, even if it is on himself, smiles.

And this smile of Mr. Rogers is worth seeing. It isn't any little, skimpy, cold, selfish, calculating smile, but the real, genuine, simon-pure article. It makes one think that Mr. Rogers, to those who have the privilege of knowing him well, might be a very pleasant, even a jolly, companion. Shakspere says one may smile and smile and be a villain, but it's hard to believe it if he smiles just as Mr. Rogers does. It isn't any smile that won't come off, however, for the next instant it has vanished and the keen, alert, waiting look has taken its place.

During the first day Mr. Rogers smiled quite often as he deftly parried his opponent's thrusts, but towards the end of that day, Mr. Whipple, who smiles the hardest when he is about to do his worst, got in a pretty good blow and Mr. Rogers put on a serious and a rather annoyed look. Mr. Whipple wanted Mr. Rogers to produce a certain private correspondence book, and Mr. Rogers objected to doing this. Just as matters began to wax rather warm the judge poured oil on the troubled waters by adjourning court.

The next morning Mr. Rogers, urbane and pleasant, produced the book. That was Friday, and court adjourned to Monday to give Mr. Whipple time to look over the book so as to use its contents to the best advantage.

Monday morning the siege of Mr. Rogers' citadel of knowledge of gas affairs was renewed by Mr. Whipple and a full day was put in at questions and answers. Whether the court was enlightened much by the day's developments is not to be stated, but it is pretty certain that the public wasn't. The way Mr. Rogers parried questions that he didn't want to answer was well worth listening to. Here is a sample of it.

Q. Were your relations with Mr. Addicks unfriendly in 1901? A. I cannot answer as to that.

Q. Well, as to 1902? A. Oh, we had our differences.

Tuesday was an unusually fruitful day as to interesting topics, at least.

Time and again when Mr. Whipple asked questions as to points on which Mr. Rogers' recollection was a bit hazy, the witness would refer counsel to his books and papers and memoranda, saying that if anything could be found in them bearing upon the matter at hand, he would be willing and even glad to have it produced.

There were several smiles by the witness, the audience and even the court, during this day. At one time Mr. Rogers smiled at some inward recollection aroused by the reading of a personal note to him from Mr. Winsor, following a trip the latter had had as Mr. Rogers' guest on the millionaire's yacht. This seemed to annoy Mr. Whipple. He walked up close to the witness and fired the question at short range, with briar points in his tone: "Why do you smile, Mr. Rogers?" "I smile because it is natural for me to smile," said Mr. Rogers, in his very pleasantest, most affable way. Talk about a soft answer turning away wrath! Mr. Rogers is a past master of that little trick all right.

Tuesday was the day Mr. Rogers told of the telephone conversation with Mr. Lawson, and, in view of Mr. Lawson's version Friday last of the same conversation, Mr. Rogers' statement is well worth repeating:

"I called up Mr. Lawson on the telephone and asked him how he felt about this reorganization of the New England Gas and Coke Company. He said he felt very unpleasantly. I asked him how, and he recited some private grievances."

Mr. Whipple—State what they were.

Mr. Rogers—He said, "You know how I feel towards Mr. Whitney and those other people down there, who interfered with me in reference to the New York Yacht Club matter. If I were able I'd rather lose $1,000,000 than make any compromise with them." I told him if he felt in that frame of mind and preferred it to business it was one thing. He asked me my judgment, and I told him that I thought it would be a wise thing for him to participate in the reorganization.

He said: "Well, that's the way I feel about it, but I am willing to be influenced by you, and take your advice in the matter." I said, "It is not for me to advise, it is for you to determine."

He made some few remarks which I cannot recall, and finally said, "Well, what can I get?" I said: "I don't know. What do you want?" He said: "I think I ought to have 15 or 20 per cent out of the profits of the reorganization." I said: "That's pretty steep, considering that you are not to do much."

He said: "Well, do the best you can. I am willing to leave it to you."

I went back and reported to Mr. Winsor that I thought Mr. Lawson would be glad to have an interest in the reorganization.

Mr. Winsor asked: "What interest does he want?" I said I thought he would like to have 15 or 20 per cent. Mr. Winsor said: "I think that is pretty steep for not doing very much." "Well," I said, "maybe it is a little too much," and it was finally settled that Mr. Lawson was to have 10 per cent for the reorganization and any profits that came from his own securities. Mr. Winsor said it was all right, and we took a piece of paper out of my desk and he wrote the memorandum and I initialed it, giving the substance of the conversation with Mr. Lawson.

Next morning I told Mr. Lawson over the telephone of the arrangement, and he said it was all right.

Another time that Mr. Rogers smiled, and caused everybody within hearing to smile, too, was when he was telling on Thursday, his last day on the stand, and near the close of his evidence, of his "scolding" Mr. Addicks.

"Perhaps my words were somewhat emphatic," Mr. Rogers confessed to Mr. Whipple in a burst of confidence.

Q. Let us see what you do say when you get emphatic with J. Edward Addicks and take him to task? A. Well, in the interest of courtesy, and having a little modesty yet, I do not think I want to go into it further.

Q. Did you use words to Mr. Addicks that you do not care to repeat here? A. I must confess that at the time I was very positive. (Laughter.) In substance I said that his letters or that of his man (Senator Allee) were outrageous, and I wanted to know what he meant by having "his man" send them to me. He said he knew nothing about them, and I think that is all there was about the case.

Q. Did you threaten Mr. Addicks? A. Oh, no; I never threaten anybody. (Laughter.)

Q. But you scolded him? A. We just had a little talk. It seems that sometimes I am not half as furious as I think I am. (Laughter.)

Then Mr. Rogers smiled, not a grim smile, either, but a sort of a happy, reminiscent smile, like that of a 10-year-old boy who remembers an extra piece of mince pie.

Soon after that Mr. Rogers stepped off the stand for good, bowed pleasantly to the newspaper men to whom he hardly ever failed to speak as he passed them, and left the courtroom.

He certainly made one of the most entertaining witnesses Boston has heard in a long time. We shall be pleased to see you in a similar capacity again, Mr. Rogers.

HEATH.

The following text is preserved in an untitled manuscript in the Mark Twain Papers. Clemens labeled it "Autobiog." at the top of the first page, but he did not integrate it with the final text of the autobiography. Paine penciled a title on the first page of the manuscript: "Anecdote of Jean. Her love of Animals." The disaster portrayed in Jean's picture book occurred on 1 November 1755, when a powerful series of earthquakes, followed by fires and a tsunami, destroyed much of Lisbon and killed an estimated 60,000 people and an unknown number of animals. The event became a focal point for debates on the nature of divine providence, and was frequently depicted in works of art.

Paine omitted this text from the autobiography, but in his biography of Clemens he retold the story, partly by paraphrasing this manuscript (*MTB*, 3:1530). The full text is printed here for the first time.

[Anecdote of Jean]

Feb. 20 '05.

Jean's deep love and tenderness for animals continues; and of course will always continue, since it is a part of her temperament. Temperaments are born, not made, and they cannot be changed, by time, nor training, nor by any other force. Katy has been recalling a beautiful incident, apropos of this. When Jean was a little child, Katy was one day amusing her with a picture-book. One picture represented the Lisbon earthquake: the earth was gaping open and the people were tumbling into the chasm. Jean was not interested. Katy turned to the next picture: the same earthquake, but this time it was the *animals* that were being swallowed up. Jean's eyes filled at once and she said "poor things!" Katy said—

"Why, you didn't care for the *people*."

Jean said—

"Oh, *they* could *speak*."

An Early Attempt,

AUTOBIOGRAPHY OF
MARK TWAIN

The chapters which immedia
ow consti moment
(after I was) by man
pts to put my life on a per
first part

It starts out

suffers the fate others
ently abandoned for some othe
wer interest. This is not to b
dered at, for its plan is the ol
old unflexible & difficult on
lan that starts you at the cra
es you straight for the grave
no side-excursions permit
e way. Whereas the side-excurs
the life of the life-voyage, & sho
lso, of its history.

An Early Attempt

The chapters which immediately follow constitute a fragment of one of my many attempts (after I was in my forties) to put my life on paper.

It starts out with good confidence, but suffers the fate of its brethren—is presently abandoned for some other and newer interest. This is not to be wondered at, for its plan is the old, old, old unflexible and difficult one—the plan that starts you at the cradle and drives you straight for the grave, with no side-excursions permitted on the way. Whereas the side-excursions are the life of our life-voyage, and should be, also, of its history.

My Autobiography [Random Extracts from It]

* * * * So much for the earlier days, and the New England branch of the Clemenses. The other brother settled in the South, and is remotely responsible for me. He has collected his reward generations ago, whatever it was. He went South with his particular friend Fairfax, and settled in Maryland with him, but afterward went further and made his home in Virginia. This is the Fairfax whose descendants were to enjoy a curious distinction—that of being American-born English earls. The founder of the house was Lord General Fairfax of the Parliamentary army, in Cromwell's time. The earldom, which is of recent date, came to the American Fairfaxes through the failure of male heirs in England. Old residents of San Francisco will remember "Charley," the American earl of the mid-'60s—tenth Lord Fairfax according to Burke's Peerage, and holder of a modest public office of some sort or other in the new mining town of Virginia City, Nevada. He was never out of America. I knew him, but not intimately. He had a golden character, and that was all his fortune. He laid his title aside, and gave it a holiday until his circumstances should improve to a degree consonant with its dignity; but that time never came, I think. He was a manly man, and had fine generosities in his make-up. A prominent and pestilent creature named Ferguson, who was always picking quarrels with better men than himself, picked one with him, one day, and Fairfax knocked him down. Ferguson gathered himself up and went off mumbling threats. Fairfax carried no arms, and refused to carry any now, though his friends warned him that Ferguson was of a treacherous disposition and would be sure to take revenge by base means sooner or later. Nothing happened for several days; then Ferguson took the earl by surprise and snapped a revolver at his breast. Fairfax wrenched the pistol from him and was going to shoot him, but the man fell on his knees and begged, and said "*Don't* kill me—I have a wife and children." Fairfax was in a towering passion, but the appeal reached his heart, and he said, "*They* have done me no harm," and he let the rascal go.

Back of the Virginian Clemenses is a dim procession of ancestors stretching back to Noah's time. According to tradition, some of them were pirates and slavers in Elizabeth's time. But this is no discredit to them, for so were Drake and Hawkins and the others. It was a respectable trade, then, and monarchs were partners in it. In my time I have had desires to be a pirate myself. The reader—if he will look deep down in his secret heart, will find—but never mind what he will find there: I am not writing his Autobiography, but mine. Later, according to tradition, one of the procession was Ambassador to Spain in the time of James I, or of Charles I, and married there and sent down a strain of Spanish blood to warm us up. Also, according to tradition, this one or another—Geoffrey Clement, by name—helped to sentence Charles to death. I have not examined into these traditions myself, partly because I was indolent, and partly because I was so busy polishing up this end of the line and trying to make it showy; but the other Clemenses claim that they have made the examination and that it stood the test. Therefore I have always taken for granted that I did help Charles out of his troubles, by ancestral proxy. My instincts have persuaded me, too. Whenever we have a strong and persistent and ineradicable instinct, we may be sure that it is not original with us, but inherited—inherited from away back, and hardened and perfected by the petrifying influence of time. Now I have been always and unchangingly bitter against Charles, and I am quite certain that this feeling trickled down to me through the veins of my forebears from the heart of that judge; for it is not my disposition to be bitter against people on my own personal account. I am not bitter against Jeffreys. I ought to be, but I am not. It indicates that my ancestors of James II's time were indifferent to him; I do not know why; I never could make it out; but that is what it indicates. And I have always felt friendly toward Satan. Of course that is ancestral; it must be in the blood, for I could not have originated it.

. . . And so, by the testimony of instinct, backed by the assertions of Clemenses who said they had examined the records, I have always been obliged to believe that Geoffrey Clement the martyr-maker was an ancestor of mine, and to regard him with favor, and in fact pride. This has not had a good effect upon me, for it has made me vain, and that is a fault. It has made me set myself above people who were less fortunate in their ancestry than I, and has moved me to take them down a peg, upon occasion, and say things to them which hurt them before company.

A case of the kind happened in Berlin several years ago. William Walter Phelps was our Minister at the Emperor's Court, then, and one evening he had me to dinner to meet Count S., a cabinet minister. This nobleman was of long and illustrious descent. Of course I wanted to let out the fact that I had some ancestors, too; but I did not want to pull them out of their graves by the ears, and I never could seem to get a chance to work them in in a way that would look sufficiently casual. I suppose Phelps was in the same difficulty. In fact he looked distraught, now and then—just as a person looks who wants to uncover an ancestor purely by accident, and cannot think of a way that will seem accidental enough. But at last, after dinner, he made a try. He took us about his drawing-room, showing us the pictures, and finally stopped before a rude and ancient engraving. It was a picture of the court that tried Charles I. There was a pyramid of judges in Puritan slouch hats, and below them three bare-headed secretaries seated at a table. Mr. Phelps put his finger upon one of the three, and said with exulting indifference—

"An ancestor of mine."

I put my finger on a judge, and retorted with scathing languidness—

"Ancestor of mine. But it is a small matter. I have others."

It was not noble in me to do it. I have always regretted it since. But it landed him. I wonder how he felt? However, it made no difference in our friendship; which shows that he was fine

Jane Lampton Clemens, Keokuk, Iowa, 1888.
Photograph by George Hassall.

Pamela Clemens Moffett, early 1860s. Courtesy of
Mrs. Kate Gilmore and the Mark Twain Boyhood
Home and Museum, Hannibal.

Orion Clemens, early 1860s. Nevada
Historical Society.

Henry Clemens, ca. 1858. Mark Twain Boyhood
Home and Museum, Hannibal.

Samuel L. Clemens and Olivia L. Langdon. The porcelaintypes in purple velvet cases they exchanged during their engagement in 1869. His photograph was taken by Edwin P. Kellogg, Hartford.

Clara Spaulding with Susy Clemens in her lap, Olivia and Samuel Clemens, and John Brown, Edinburgh, August 1873. Photograph by John Moffat. Mark Twain House and Museum, Hartford.

Karl Gerhardt's bust of Grant, 1885. Mark Twain House and Museum, Hartford.

Karl Gerhardt, 1880s. Courtesy of Kevin MacDonnell.

The Paige typesetter. Photograph by Albert Bigelow Paine.

Clara, Jean, and Susy Clemens with their dog Hash, Hartford, 1884. Photograph by Horace L. Bundy.

Margaret (Daisy) Warner as the Pauper and Susy Clemens as the Prince in their costumes for the *Prince and the Pauper* play, Hartford, March 1886. Mark Twain House and Museum, Hartford.

Cast of *A Love-Chase:* Clara Clemens as Art, Daisy Warner as Literature, Jean Clemens as Cupid, Susy Clemens as Music, and Fanny Freese as a shepherd boy, Hartford, 1889. Mark Twain House and Museum, Hartford.

Olivia, Samuel, and Clara Clemens with James B. Pond (Clemens's lecture agent) and his wife, Martha, aboard the SS *Warrimoo,* 23 August 1895, before the Clemenses departed from Victoria, B.C., on the world tour of 1895–96. Courtesy of Kevin Mac Donnell.

Clemens in front of his boyhood home in Hannibal, Missouri, while preparations were made for his formal photograph, 31 May 1902. Photograph by Anna Schnizlein. Mark Twain Boyhood Home and Museum, Hannibal.

The formal photograph, Hannibal, 31 May 1902, by Herbert Tomlinson.

Recipients of honorary degrees at the University of Missouri, 4 June 1902: Clemens with Ethan Allen Hitchcock, Secretary of the Interior; Robert S. Brookings, millionaire founder of the Brookings Institute; James Wilson, Secretary of Agriculture; and botanist Beverly T. Galloway. Used by permission of The State Historical Society of Missouri.

Two views *(above right and below)* of Clemens in his study at Quarry Farm, Elmira, New York, 1903. Mark Twain House and Museum, Hartford.

Villa di Quarto, Florence, Italy, 1903–4.

Clemens in the garden of the Villa di Quarto, 1904. Photograph by Isabel Lyon.

Staff at the Villa di Quarto, 1904: Carlo Cosi, the chef; Adelasia Curradi, the upstairs maid; Gigia Brunori, the kitchen maid; Katy Leary; Celestino Bruschi, the footman; Theresa Bini; Ugo Piemontini, the butler (possibly the Countess Massiglia's "handsome chief manservant"); and Emilio Talorici (?), the coachman. Photograph by Jean Clemens.

Clara Clemens in the garden of the Villa di Quarto, 1904. Photograph by Jean Clemens.

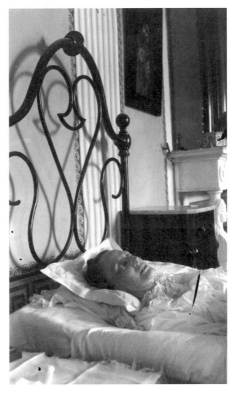

Olivia Clemens on her deathbed, Villa di Quarto, June 1904. Photograph by Jean Clemens.

Jean Clemens on her horse outside the Villa di Quarto, 1904. Photograph by Isabel Lyon.

Clara and Samuel Clemens with cats on shipboard after Olivia's death, "July 1904, on the way home from Naples, bringing Mrs. Clemens." Photograph and note by Isabel Lyon.

Samuel and Jean Clemens at the Copley Greene house ("Lone Tree Hill"), Dublin, New Hampshire, 1905. Photograph by Isabel Lyon.

Patrick McAleer holding a rabbit, Dublin, New Hampshire, 1905. Photograph by Isabel Lyon.

Isabel Lyon on Mount Monadnock, Dublin, New Hampshire, 1906. Photograph by Albert Bigelow Paine.

Upton House, Dublin, New Hampshire, 1906. Photograph by Isabel Lyon.

Albert Bigelow Paine, Dublin, New Hampshire, summer of 1906.

Albert Bigelow Paine with his wife, Dora, and their youngest daughter, Joy, Dublin, New Hampshire, summer of 1906.

Clemens in Henry H. Rogers's car with Ernest Keeler, Rogers's driver, 1906. Photograph by Albert Bigelow Paine.

Clemens at his seventieth birthday dinner at Delmonico's, 5 December 1905, with Kate Douglas Riggs, Joseph H. Twichell, Bliss Carman, Ruth McEnery Stuart, Mary E. Wilkins Freeman, Henry Mills Alden, and Henry H. Rogers. Photograph by Joseph Byron, New York.

Booker T. Washington speaking on behalf of the Tuskegee Institute at its "silver jubilee" celebration, with Clemens sitting behind him on stage at Carnegie Hall, 22 January 1906. Photograph by Underwood and Underwood.

Helen Keller and Clemens, 1895. The inscription is in Clemens's hand.

Clemens and Henry H. Rogers outside the Princess Hotel, Bermuda, 1908. Photograph by Isabel Lyon.

Joseph H. Twichell and Clemens, February 1905. Photograph by Jean Clemens.

William Dean Howells and Clemens, Lakewood, New Jersey, 28 December 1907.

Dorothy and George Harvey with Clemens, ca. 1903. The identifications are in Clemens's hand.

Richard Watson Gilder, October 1904. Photograph by Jean Clemens.

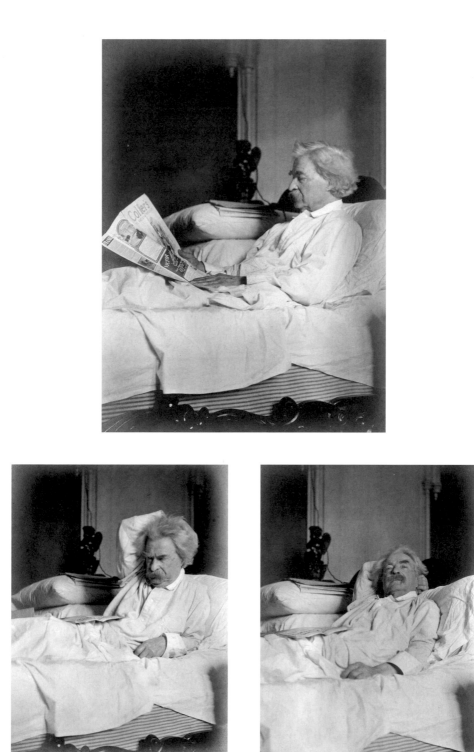

Three views of Clemens in his bed at 21 Fifth Avenue, New York, from a series of photographs taken by Albert Bigelow Paine in late February or early March 1906. In the top photograph, Clemens is reading the 24 February 1906 issue of *Collier's Weekly* with the morning newspapers piled on the pillow next to him.

Samuel Clemens, Boston, Massachusetts, 1869. Photograph by James Wallace Black. Courtesy of Kevin Mac Donnell.

and high, notwithstanding the humbleness of his origin. And it was also creditable in me, too, that I could overlook it. I made no change in my bearing toward him, but always treated him as an equal.

But it was a hard night for me in one way. Mr. Phelps thought I was the guest of honor, and so did Count S.; but I didn't, for there was nothing in my invitation to indicate it. It was just a friendly off-hand note, on a card. By the time dinner was announced Phelps was himself in a state of doubt. Something had to be done; and it was not a handy time for explanations. He tried to get me to go out with him, but I held back; then he tried S., and he also declined. There was another guest, but there was no trouble about him. We finally went out in a pile. There was a decorous plunge for seats, and I got the one at Mr. Phelps's left, the Count captured the one facing Phelps, and the other guest had to take the place of honor, since he could not help himself. We returned to the drawing-room in the original disorder. I had new shoes on, and they were tight. At eleven I was privately crying; I couldn't help it; the pain was so cruel. Conversation had been dead for an hour. S. had been due at the bedside of a dying official ever since half past nine. At last we all rose by one blessed impulse and went down to the street door without explanations—in a pile, and no precedence; and so, parted.

The evening had its defects; still, I got my ancestor in, and was satisfied.

Among the Virginian Clemenses were Jere. (already mentioned), and Sherrard. Jere. Clemens had a wide reputation as a good pistol-shot, and once it enabled him to get on the friendly side of some drummers when they would not have paid any attention to mere smooth words and arguments. He was out stumping the State at the time. The drummers were grouped in front of the stand, and had been hired by the opposition to drum while he made his speech. When he was ready to begin, he got out his revolver and laid it before him, and said in his soft, silky way—

"I do not wish to hurt anybody, and shall try not to; but I have got just a bullet apiece for those six drums, and if you should want to play on them, don't stand behind them."

Sherrard Clemens was a Republican Congressman from West Virginia in the war days, and then went out to St. Louis, where the James Clemens branch lived, and still lives, and there he became a warm rebel. This was after the war. At the time that he was a Republican I was a rebel; but by the time he had become a rebel I was become (temporarily) a Republican. The Clemenses have always done the best they could to keep the political balances level, no matter how much it might inconvenience them. I did not know what had become of Sherrard Clemens; but once I introduced Senator Hawley to a Republican mass meeting in New England, and then I got a bitter letter from Sherrard from St. Louis. He said that the Republicans of the North—no, the "mudsills of the North"—had swept away the old aristocracy of the South with fire and sword, and it ill became me, an aristocrat by blood, to train with that kind of swine. Did I forget that I was a Lambton?

That was a reference to my mother's side of the house. As I have already said, she was a Lambton—Lambton with a *p,* for some of the American Lamptons could not spell very well in early times, and so the name suffered at their hands. She was a native of Kentucky, and married my father in Lexington in 1823, when she was twenty years old and he twenty-four. Neither of them had an overplus of property. She brought him two or three negroes, but nothing else, I think. They removed to the remote and secluded village of Jamestown, in the mountain solitudes of east Tennessee. There their first crop of children was born, but as I was of a later vintage I do not remember anything about it. I was postponed—postponed to Missouri. Missouri was an unknown new State and needed attractions.

I think that my eldest brother, Orion, my sisters Pamela and Margaret, and my brother Benjamin were born in Jamestown. There may have been others, but as to that I am not sure. It was a great lift for that little village to have my parents come there. It was hoped that they would stay, so that it would become a city. It was supposed that they would stay. And so there was a boom; but by and by they went away, and prices went down, and it was many years before Jamestown got another start. I have written about Jamestown in the "Gilded Age," a book of mine, but it was from hearsay, not from personal knowledge. My father left a fine estate behind him in the region round about Jamestown—75,000 acres.* When he died in 1847 he had owned it about twenty years. The taxes were almost nothing (five dollars a year for the whole), and he had always paid them regularly and kept his title perfect. He had always said that the land would not become valuable in his time, but that it would be a commodious provision for his children some day. It contained coal, copper, iron and timber, and he said that in the course of time railways would pierce to that region, and then the property would be property in fact as well as in name. It also produced a wild grape of a promising sort. He had sent some samples to Nicholas Longworth, of Cincinnati, to get his judgment upon them, and Mr. Longworth had said that they would make as good wine as his Catawbas. The land contained all these riches; and also oil, but my father did not know that, and of course in those early days he would have cared nothing about it if he had known it. The oil was not discovered until about 1895. I wish I owned a couple of acres of the land now. In which case I would not be writing Autobiographies for a living. My father's dying charge was, "Cling to the land and wait; let nothing beguile it away from you." My mother's favorite cousin, James Lampton, who figures in the "Gilded Age" as "Colonel Sellers," always said of that land—and said it with blazing enthusiasm, too,—"There's millions in it—millions!" It is true that he always said that about everything—and was always mistaken, too; but this time he was right; which shows that a man who goes around with a prophecy-gun ought never to get discouraged: if he will keep up his heart and fire at everything he sees, he is bound to hit something by and by.

Many persons regarded "Colonel Sellers" as a fiction, an invention, an extravagant impossibility, and did me the honor to call him a "creation;" but they were mistaken. I merely put him on paper as he was; he was not a person who could be exaggerated. The incidents which looked most extravagant, both in the book and on the stage, were not inventions of mine but were facts of his life; and I was present when they were developed. John T. Raymond's audiences used to come near to dying with laughter over the turnip-eating scene; but, extravagant as the scene was, it was faithful to the facts, in all its absurd details. The thing happened in Lampton's own house, and I was present. In fact I was myself the guest who ate the turnips. In the hands of a great actor that piteous scene would have dimmed any manly spectator's eyes with tears, and racked his ribs apart with laughter at the same time. But Raymond was

*Correction (1906)—it was above 100,000 it appears.

great in humorous portrayal only. In that he was superb, he was wonderful—in a word, great; in all things else he was a pigmy of the pigmies. The real Colonel Sellers, as I knew him in James Lampton, was a pathetic and beautiful spirit, a manly man, a straight and honorable man, a man with a big, foolish, unselfish heart in his bosom, a man born to be loved; and he was loved by all his friends, and by his family worshiped. It is the right word. To them he was but little less than a god. The real Colonel Sellers was never on the stage. Only half of him was there. Raymond could not play the other half of him; it was above his level. That half was made up of qualities of which Raymond was wholly destitute. For Raymond was not a manly man, he was not an honorable man nor an honest one, he was empty and selfish and vulgar and ignorant and silly, and there was a vacancy in him where his heart should have been. There was only one man who could have played the whole of Colonel Sellers, and that was Frank Mayo.*

It is a world of surprises. They fall, too, where one is least expecting them. When I introduced Sellers into the book, Charles Dudley Warner, who was writing the story with me, proposed a change of Sellers's Christian name. Ten years before, in a remote corner of the West, he had come across a man named Eschol Sellers, and he thought that Eschol was just the right and fitting name for our Sellers, since it was odd, and quaint, and all that. I liked the idea, but I said that that man might turn up and object. But Warner said it couldn't happen; that he was doubtless dead by this time, a man with a name like that couldn't live long; and be he dead or alive we must have the name, it was exactly the right one and we couldn't do without it. So the change was made. Warner's man was a farmer in a cheap and humble way. When the book had been out a week, a college-bred gentleman of courtly manners and ducal upholstery arrived in Hartford in a sultry state of mind and with a libel suit in his eye, and *his* name was Eschol Sellers! He had never heard of the other one, and had never been within a thousand miles of him. This damaged aristocrat's program was quite definite and business-like: the American Publishing Company must suppress the edition as far as printed, and change the name in the plates, or stand a suit for $10,000. He carried away the Company's promise and many apologies, and we changed the name back to Colonel Mulberry Sellers, in the plates. Apparently there is nothing that cannot happen. Even the existence of two unrelated men wearing the impossible name of Eschol Sellers is a possible thing.

James Lampton floated, all his days, in a tinted mist of magnificent dreams, and died at last without seeing one of them realized. I saw him last in 1884, when it had been twenty-six years since I ate the basin of raw turnips and washed them down with a bucket of water in his house. He was become old and white-headed, but he entered to me in the same old breezy way of his earlier life, and he was all there, yet—not a detail wanting: the happy light in his eye, the abounding hope in his heart, the persuasive tongue, the miracle-breeding imagination— they were all there; and before I could turn around he was polishing up his Aladdin's lamp and flashing the secret riches of the world before me. I said to myself, "I did not overdraw him by a shade, I set him down as he was; and he is the same man to-day: Cable will recognize him."

*Raymond was playing "Colonel Sellers" in about 1876 and along there. About twenty years later Mayo dramatized "Pudd'nhead Wilson" and played the title rôle very delightfully.

I asked him to excuse me a moment, and ran into the next room, which was Cable's; Cable and I were stumping the Union on a reading-tour. I said—

"I am going to leave your door open, so that you can listen. There is a man in there who is interesting."

I went back and asked Lampton what he was doing, now. He began to tell me of a "small venture" he had begun in New Mexico through his son; "only a little thing—a mere trifle—partly to amuse my leisure, partly to keep my capital from lying idle, but mainly to develop the boy—develop the boy; fortune's wheel is ever revolving, he may have to work for his living some day—as strange things have happened in this world. But it's only a little thing—a mere trifle, as I said."

And so it was—as he began it. But under his deft hands it grew, and blossomed, and spread—oh, beyond imagination. At the end of half an hour he finished; finished with this remark, uttered in an adorably languid manner:

"Yes, it is but a trifle, as things go nowadays—a bagatelle—but amusing. It passes the time. The boy thinks great things of it, but he is young, you know, and imaginative; lacks the experience which comes of handling large affairs, and which tempers the fancy and perfects the judgment. I suppose there's a couple of millions in it, possibly three, but not more, I think; still, for a boy, you know, just starting in life, it is not bad. I should not want him to make a fortune—let that come later. It could turn his head, at his time of life, and in many ways be a damage to him."

Then he said something about his having left his pocket-book lying on the table in the main drawing-room at home, and about its being after banking hours, now, and—

I stopped him, there, and begged him to honor Cable and me by being our guest at the lecture—with as many friends as might be willing to do us the like honor. He accepted. And he thanked me as a prince might who had granted us a grace. The reason I stopped his speech about the tickets was because I saw that he was going to ask me to furnish them to him and let him pay next day; and I knew that if he made the debt he would pay it if he had to pawn his clothes. After a little further chat he shook hands heartily and affectionately, and took his leave. Cable put his head in at the door, and said—

"That was Colonel Sellers."

Chapter

1847 As I have said, that vast plot of Tennessee land* was held by my father twenty years—intact. When he died in 1847, we began to manage it ourselves. Forty years afterward, we had managed it all away except 10,000 acres, and gotten nothing to remember the sales by. About 1887—possibly it was earlier—the 10,000 went. My brother found a chance to trade it for a house and lot in the town of Corry, in the oil regions of Pennsylvania. About 1894 he sold this property for $250. That ended the Tennessee Land.

*100,000 acres.

If any penny of cash ever came out of my father's wise investment but that, I have no recollection of it. No, I am overlooking a detail. It furnished me a field for Sellers and a book. Out of my half of the book I got $15,000 or $20,000; out of the play I got $75,000 or $80,000—just about a dollar an acre. It is curious: I was not alive when my father made the investment, therefore he was not intending any partiality; yet I was the only member of the family that ever profited by it. I shall have occasion to mention this land again, now and then, as I go along, for it influenced our life in one way or another during more than a generation. Whenever things grew dark it rose and put out its hopeful Sellers hand and cheered us up, and said "Do not be afraid—trust in me—wait." It kept us hoping and hoping, during forty years, and forsook us at last. It put our energies to sleep and made visionaries of us—dreamers, and indolent. We were always going to be rich next year—no occasion to work. It is good to begin life poor; it is good to begin life rich—these are wholesome; but to begin it *prospectively* rich! The man who has not experienced it cannot imagine the curse of it.

My parents removed to Missouri in the early thirties; I do not remember just when, for I was not born then, and cared nothing for such things. It was a long journey in those days, and must have been a rough and tiresome one. The home was made in the wee village of Florida, in Monroe County, and I was born there in 1835. The village contained a hundred people and I increased the population by 1 per cent. It is more than the best man in history ever did for any other town. It may not be modest in me to refer to this, but it is true. There is no record of a person doing as much—not even Shakspeare. But I did it for Florida, and it shows that I could have done it for any place—even London, I suppose.

Recently some one in Missouri has sent me a picture of the house I was born in. Heretofore I have always stated that it was a palace, but I shall be more guarded, now.

I remember only one circumstance connected with my life in it. I remember it very well, though I was but two and a half years old at the time. The family packed up everything and started in wagons for Hannibal, on the Mississippi, thirty miles away. Toward night, when they camped and counted up the children, one was missing. I was the one. I had been left behind. Parents ought always to count the children before they start. I was having a good enough time playing by myself until I found that the doors were fastened and that there was a grisly deep silence brooding over the place. I knew, then, that the family were gone, and that they had forgotten me. I was well frightened, and I made all the noise I could, but no one was near and it did no good. I spent the afternoon in captivity and was not rescued till the gloaming had fallen and the place was alive with ghosts.

My brother Henry was six months old at that time. I used to remember his walking into a fire outdoors when he was a week old. It was remarkable in me to remember a thing like that, which occurred when I was so young. And it was still more remarkable that I should cling to the delusion, for thirty years, that I *did* remember it—for of course it never happened; he would not have been able to walk at that age. If I had stopped to reflect, I should not have burdened my memory with that impossible rubbish so long. It is believed by many people that an impression deposited in a child's memory within the first two years of its life cannot remain there five years, but that is an error. The incident of Benvenuto Cellini and the salamander must be accepted as authentic and trustworthy; and then that remarkable and indisputable instance in the experience of Helen Keller—however, I will speak of that at another time. For many years I believed that I remembered helping my grandfather drink his whisky toddy when I was six weeks old, but I do not tell about that any more, now; I am grown old, and my memory is not as active as it used to be. When I was younger I could remember anything, whether it had happened or not; but my faculties are decaying, now, and soon I shall be so I cannot remember any but the latter. It is sad to go to pieces like this, but we all have to do it.

My uncle, John A. Quarles, was a farmer, and his place was in the country four miles from Florida. He had eight children, and fifteen or twenty negroes, and was also fortunate in other ways. Particularly in his character. I have not come across a better man than he was. I was his guest for two or three months every year, from the fourth year after we removed to Hannibal till I was eleven or twelve years old. I have never consciously used him or his wife in a book, but his farm has come very handy to me in literature, once or twice. In "Huck Finn" and in "Tom Sawyer Detective" I moved it down to Arkansas. It was all of six hundred miles, but it was no trouble, it was not a very large farm; five hundred acres, perhaps, but I could have done it if it had been twice as large. And as for the morality of it, I cared nothing for that; I would move a State if the exigencies of literature required it.

It was a heavenly place for a boy, that farm of my uncle John's. The house was a double log one, with a spacious floor (roofed in) connecting it with the kitchen. In the summer the table was set in the middle of that shady and breezy floor, and the sumptuous meals—well, it makes me cry to think of them. Fried chicken; roast pig; wild and tame turkeys, ducks, and geese; venison just killed; squirrels, rabbits, pheasants, partridges, prairie chickens; home-made bacon and ham; hot biscuits, hot batter-cakes, hot buckwheat cakes, hot "wheatbread," hot rolls, hot corn pone; fresh corn boiled on the ear, succotash, butter-beans, string beans, tomatoes, peas, Irish potatoes, sweet potatoes; buttermilk, sweet milk, "clabber;" watermelons, musk melons, canteloups—all fresh from the garden—apple pie, peach pie, pumpkin pie, apple dumplings, peach cobbler—I can't remember the rest. The way that the things were cooked was perhaps the main splendor—particularly a certain few of the dishes. For instance, the corn bread, the hot biscuits and wheatbread, and the fried chicken. These things have never been properly cooked in the North—in fact, no one there is able to learn the art, so far as my experience goes. The North thinks it knows how to make corn bread, but this is gross superstition. Perhaps no bread in the world is quite as good as Southern corn bread, and perhaps no bread in the world is quite so bad as the Northern imitation of it. The North seldom tries to fry chicken, and this is well; the art cannot be learned north of the line of Mason and Dixon, nor anywhere in Europe. This is not hearsay; it is experience that is speaking. In Europe it is imagined that the custom of serving various kinds of bread blazing hot is "American," but that is too broad a spread: it is custom in the South, but is much less than that in the North. In the North and in Europe hot bread is considered unhealthy. This is probably another fussy superstition, like the European superstition that ice-water is unhealthy. Europe does not need ice-water, and does not drink it; and yet, notwithstanding this, its word for it is better than ours, because it describes it, whereas ours doesn't. Europe calls it "iced" water. Our word describes water made from melted ice—a drink which has a characterless taste, and which we have but little acquaintance with.

It seems a pity that the world should throw away so many good things merely because they are unwholesome. I doubt if God has given us any refreshment which, taken in moderation, is unwholesome, except microbes. Yet there are people who strictly deprive themselves of each and every eatable, drinkable and smokable which has in any way acquired a shady reputation. They pay this price for health. And health is all they get for it. How strange it is; it is like paying out your whole fortune for a cow that has gone dry.

The farm-house stood in the middle of a very large yard, and the yard was fenced on three sides with rails and on the rear side with high palings; against these stood the smoke-house; beyond the palings was the orchard, beyond the orchard were the negro quarter and the tobacco fields. The front yard was entered over a stile, made of sawed-off logs of graduated heights; I do not remember any gate. In a corner of the front yard were a dozen lofty hickory trees and a dozen black walnuts, and in the nutting season riches were to be gathered there.

Down a piece, abreast the house, stood a little log cabin against the rail fence; and there the woody hill fell sharply away, past the barns, the corn-crib, the stables and the tobacco-curing house, to a limpid brook which sang along over its gravelly bed and curved and frisked in and out and here and there and yonder in the deep shade of overhanging foliage and vines—a divine place for wading, and it had swimming-pools, too, which were forbidden to us and therefore much frequented by us. For we were little Christian children, and had early been taught the value of forbidden fruit.

In the little log cabin lived a bedridden white-headed slave woman whom we visited daily, and looked upon with awe, for we believed she was upwards of a thousand years old and had talked with Moses. The younger negroes credited these statistics, and had furnished them to us in good faith. We accommodated all the details which came to us about her; and so we believed that she had lost her health in the long desert-trip coming out of Egypt, and had never been able to get it back again. She had a round bald place on the crown of her head, and we used to creep around and gaze at it in reverent silence, and reflect that it was caused by fright through seeing Pharaoh drowned. We called her "Aunt" Hannah, Southern fashion. She was superstitious like the other negroes; also, like them, she was deeply religious. Like them, she had great faith in prayer, and employed it in all ordinary exigencies, but not in cases where a dead certainty of result was urgent. Whenever witches were around she tied up the remnant of her wool in little tufts, with white thread, and this promptly made the witches impotent.

All the negroes were friends of ours, and with those of our own age we were in effect comrades. I say in effect, using the phrase as a modification. We were comrades, and yet not comrades; color and condition interposed a subtle line which both parties were conscious of, and which rendered complete fusion impossible. We had a faithful and affectionate good friend, ally and adviser in "Uncle Dan'l," a middle-aged slave whose head was the best one in the negro-quarter, whose sympathies were wide and warm, and whose heart was honest and simple and knew no guile. He has served me well, these many, many years. I have not seen him for more than half a century, and yet spiritually I have had his welcome company a good part of that time, and have staged him in books under his own name and as "Jim," and carted him all around—to Hannibal, down the Mississippi on a raft, and even across the Desert of Sahara in a balloon—and he has endured it all with the patience and friendliness and loyalty which were his birthright. It was on the farm that I got my strong liking for his race and my appreciation of certain of its fine qualities. This feeling and this estimate have stood the test of sixty years and more and have suffered no impairment. The black face is as welcome to me now as it was then.

In my schoolboy days I had no aversion to slavery. I was not aware that there was anything wrong about it. No one arraigned it in my hearing; the local papers said nothing against it; the local pulpit taught us that God approved it, that it was a holy thing, and that the doubter need only look in the Bible if he wished to settle his mind—and then the texts were read aloud to us to make the matter sure; if the slaves themselves had an aversion to slavery they were wise and said nothing. In Hannibal we seldom saw a slave misused; on the farm, never.

There was, however, one small incident of my boyhood days which touched this matter, and it must have meant a good deal to me or it would not have stayed in my memory, clear and sharp, vivid and shadowless, all these slow-drifting years. We had a little slave boy whom we had hired from some one, there in Hannibal. He was from the Eastern Shore of Maryland, and had been brought away from his family and his friends, half way across the American continent, and sold. He was a cheery spirit, innocent and gentle, and the noisiest creature that ever was, perhaps. All day long he was singing, whistling, yelling, whooping, laughing—it was maddening, devastating, unendurable. At last, one day, I lost all my temper, and went raging to my mother, and said Sandy had been singing for an hour without a single break, and I couldn't stand it, and *wouldn't* she please shut him up. The tears came into her eyes, and her lip trembled, and she said something like this—

"Poor thing, when he sings, it shows that he is not remembering, and that comforts me; but when he is still, I am afraid he is thinking, and I cannot bear it. He will never see his mother again; if he can sing, I must not hinder it, but be thankful for it. If you were older, you would understand me; then that friendless child's noise would make you glad."

It was a simple speech, and made up of small words, but it went home, and Sandy's noise was not a trouble to me any more. She never used large words, but she had a natural gift for making small ones do effective work. She lived to reach the neighborhood of ninety years, and was capable with her tongue to the last—especially when a meanness or an injustice roused her spirit. She has come handy to me several times in my books, where she figures as Tom Sawyer's "Aunt Polly." I fitted her out with a dialect, and tried to think up other improvements for her, but did not find any. I used Sandy once, also; it was in "Tom Sawyer;" I tried to get him to whitewash the fence, but it did not work. I do not remember what name I called him by in the book.

I can see the farm yet, with perfect clearness. I can see all its belongings, all its details: the family room of the house, with a "trundle" bed in one corner and a spinning-wheel in another—a wheel whose rising and falling wail, heard from a distance, was the mournfulest of all sounds to me, and made me homesick and low-spirited, and filled my atmosphere with the wandering spirits of the dead; the vast fireplace, piled high, on winter nights, with flaming hickory logs from whose ends a sugary sap bubbled out but did not go to waste, for we scraped it off and ate it; the lazy cat spread out on the rough hearthstones, the drowsy dogs braced against the jambs and blinking; my aunt in one chimney corner knitting, my uncle in the other smoking his corn-cob pipe; the slick and carpetless oak floor faintly mirroring the dancing flame-tongues and freckled with black indentations where fire-coals had popped out and died a leisurely death; half a dozen children romping in the background twilight; "split"-bottomed chairs here and there, some with rockers; a cradle—out of service, but waiting, with confidence; in the early cold mornings a snuggle of children, in shirts and chemises, occupying the hearthstone and procrastinating—they could not bear to leave that comfortable place and go out on the wind-swept floor-space between house and kitchen where the general tin basin stood, and wash.

Along outside of the front fence ran the country road; dusty in the summertime, and a good place for snakes—they liked to lie in it and sun themselves; when they were rattlesnakes or puff adders, we killed them; when they were black snakes, or racers, or belonged to the fabled "hoop" breed, we fled, without shame; when they were "house-snakes" or "garters" we carried them home and put them in Aunt Patsy's work-basket for a surprise; for she was prejudiced against snakes, and always when she took the basket in her lap and they began to climb out of it it disordered her mind. She never could seem to get used to them; her opportunities went for nothing. And she was always cold toward bats, too, and could not bear them; and yet I think a bat is as friendly a bird as there is. My mother was Aunt Patsy's sister, and had the same wild superstitions. A bat is beautifully soft and silky; I do not know any creature that is pleasanter to the touch, or is more grateful for caressings, if offered in the right spirit. I know all about these coleoptera, because our great cave, three miles below Hannibal, was multitudinously stocked with them, and often I brought them home to amuse my mother with. It was easy to manage if it was a school day, because then I had ostensibly been to school and hadn't any bats. She was not a suspicious person, but full of trust and confidence; and when I said "There's something in my coat-pocket for you," she would put her hand in. But she always took it out again, herself; I didn't have to tell her. It was remarkable, the way she couldn't learn to like private bats. The more experience she had, the more she could not change her views.

I think she was never in the cave in her life; but everybody else went there. Many excursion-parties came from considerable distances up and down the river to visit the cave. It was miles in extent, and was a tangled wilderness of narrow and lofty clefts and passages. It was an easy place to get lost in; anybody could do it—including the bats. I got lost in it myself, along with a lady, and our last candle burned down to almost nothing before we glimpsed the search-party's lights winding about in the distance.

"Injun Joe" the half-breed got lost in there once, and would have starved to death if the bats had run short. But there was no chance of that; there were myriads of them. He told me all his story. In the book called "Tom Sawyer" I starved him entirely to death in the cave, but that was in the interest of art; it never happened. "General" Gaines, who was our first town-drunkard before Jimmy Finn got the place, was lost in there for the space of a week, and finally pushed his handkerchief out of a hole in a hilltop near Saverton, several miles down the river from the cave's mouth, and somebody saw it and dug him out. There is nothing the matter with his statistics except the handkerchief. I knew him for years, and he hadn't any. But it could have been his nose. That would attract attention.

The cave was an uncanny place, for it contained a corpse—the corpse of a young girl of fourteen. It was in a glass cylinder enclosed in a copper one which was suspended from a rail which bridged a narrow passage. The body was preserved in alcohol, and it was said that loafers and rowdies used to drag it up by the hair and look at the dead face. The girl was the daughter of a St. Louis surgeon of extraordinary ability and wide celebrity. He was an eccentric man, and did many strange things. He put the poor thing in that forlorn place himself.

He was a physician as well as a surgeon; and sometimes in cases where medicines failed to save, he developed other resources. He fell out, once, with a family whose physician he was, and after that they ceased to employ him. But a time came when he was once more called. The lady of the house was very ill, and had been given up by her doctors. He came into the room and stopped, and stood still, and looked around upon the scene; he had his great slouch hat on, and a quarter of an acre of gingerbread under his arm, and while he looked meditatively about, he broke hunks from his cake, munched them, and let the crumbs dribble down his breast to the floor. The lady lay pale and still, with her eyes closed; about the bed, in the solemn hush, were grouped the family softly sobbing, some standing, some kneeling. Presently the doctor began to take up the medicine bottles and sniff at them contemptuously and throw them out of the open window. When they were all gone he ranged up to the bed, laid his slab of gingerbread on the dying woman's breast, and said roughly—

"What are you idiots sniveling about?—there's nothing the matter with this humbug. Put out your tongue!"

The sobbings stopped and the angry mourners changed their attitudes and began to upbraid the doctor for his cruel behavior in this chamber of death; but he interrupted them with an explosion of profane abuse, and said—

"A pack of snuffling fat-wits, do you think you can teach me my business? I tell you there is nothing the matter with the woman—nothing the matter but laziness. What she wants is a beefsteak and a washtub. With her damned society training, she—"

Then the dying woman rose up in bed, and the light of battle was in her eye. She poured out upon the doctor her whole insulted mind—just a volcanic irruption, accompanied by thunder and lightning, whirlwinds and earthquakes, pumice stone and ashes. It brought the reaction which he was after, and she got well. This was the lamented Dr. McDowell, whose name was so great and so honored in the Mississippi Valley a decade before the Civil War.

Chapter

Beyond the road where the snakes sunned themselves was a dense young thicket, and through it a dim-lighted path led a quarter of a mile; then out of the dimness one emerged abruptly upon a level great prairie which was covered with wild strawberry plants, vividly starred with prairie pinks, and walled in on all sides by forests. The strawberries were fragrant and fine, and in the season we were generally there in the crisp freshness of the early morning, while the dew-beads still sparkled upon the grass and the woods were ringing with the first songs of the birds.

Down the forest-slopes to the left were the swings. They were made of bark stripped from hickory saplings. When they became dry they were dangerous. They usually broke when a child was forty feet in the air, and this was why so many bones had to be mended every year. I had no ill luck myself, but none of my cousins escaped. There were eight of them, and at one time and another they broke fourteen arms among them. But it cost next to nothing, for the doctor worked by the year—$25 for the whole family. I remember two of the Florida doctors, Chowning and Meredith. They not only tended an entire family for $25 a year, but furnished the medicines themselves. Good measure, too. Only the largest persons could hold a whole dose. Castor oil was the principal beverage. The dose was half a dipperful, with half a dipperful of New Orleans molasses added to help it down and make it taste good, which it never did. The next stand-by was calomel; the next, rhubarb; and the next, jalap. Then they bled the patient, and put mustard plasters on him. It was a dreadful system, and yet the death-rate was not heavy. The calomel was nearly sure to salivate the patient and cost him some of his teeth. There were no dentists. When teeth became touched with decay or were otherwise ailing, the doctor knew of but one thing to do: he fetched his tongs and dragged them out. If the jaw remained, it was not his fault.

Doctors were not called, in cases of ordinary illness; the family's grandmother attended to those. Every old woman was a doctor, and gathered her own medicines in the woods, and knew how to compound doses that would stir the vitals of a cast-iron dog. And then there was the "Indian doctor;" a grave savage, remnant of his tribe, deeply read in the mysteries of nature and the secret properties of herbs; and most backwoodsmen had high faith in his powers and could tell of wonderful cures achieved by him. In Mauritius, away off yonder in the solitudes of the Indian ocean, there is a person who answers to our Indian doctor of the old times. He is a negro, and has had no teaching as a doctor, yet there is one disease which he is master of and can cure, and the doctors can't. They send for him when they have a case. It is a child's disease of a strange and deadly sort, and the negro cures it with a herb-medicine which he makes, himself, from a prescription which has come down to him from his father and grand-father. He will not let any one see it. He keeps the secret of its components to himself, and it is feared that he will die without divulging it; then there will be consternation in Mauritius. I was told these things by the people there, in 1896.

We had the "faith-doctor," too, in those early days—a woman. Her specialty was tooth-ache. She was a farmer's old wife, and lived five miles from Hannibal. She would lay her hand on the patient's jaw and say "Believe!" and the cure was prompt. Mrs. Utterback. I remember her very well. Twice I rode out there behind my mother, horseback, and saw the cure performed. My mother was the patient.

Dr. Meredith removed to Hannibal, by and by, and was our family physician there, and saved my life several times. Still, he was a good man and meant well. Let it go.

I was always told that I was a sickly and precarious and tiresome and uncertain child, and lived mainly on allopathic medicines during the first seven years of my life. I asked my mother about this, in her old age—she was in her eighty-eighth year—and said:

"I suppose that during all that time you were uneasy about me?"

"Yes, the whole time."

"Afraid I wouldn't live?"

After a reflective pause—ostensibly to think out the facts—

"No—afraid you would."

It sounds like a plagiarism, but it probably wasn't.

The country schoolhouse was three miles from my uncle's farm. It stood in a clearing in the woods, and would hold about twenty-five boys and girls. We attended the school with more or less regularity once or twice a week, in summer, walking to it in the cool of the morning by the forest paths, and back in the gloaming at the end of the day. All the pupils brought their dinners in baskets—corn dodger, buttermilk and other good things—and sat in the shade of the trees at noon and ate them. It is the part of my education which I look back upon with the most satisfaction. My first visit to the school was when I was seven. A strapping girl of fifteen, in the customary sunbonnet and calico dress, asked me if I "used tobacco"—meaning did I chew it. I said, no. It roused her scorn. She reported me to all the crowd, and said—

"Here is a boy seven years old who can't chaw tobacco."

By the looks and comments which this produced, I realized that I was a degraded object; I was cruelly ashamed of myself. I determined to reform. But I only made myself sick; I was not able to learn to chew tobacco. I learned to smoke fairly well, but that did not conciliate anybody, and I remained a poor thing, and characterless. I longed to be respected, but I never was able to rise. Children have but little charity for each other's defects.

As I have said, I spent some part of every year at the farm until I was twelve or thirteen years old. The life which I led there with my cousins was full of charm, and so is the memory of it yet. I can call back the solemn twilight and mystery of the deep woods, the earthy smells, the faint odors of the wild flowers, the sheen of rain-washed foliage, the rattling clatter of drops when the wind shook the trees, the far-off hammering of wood-peckers and the muffled drumming of wood-pheasants in the remotenesses of the forest, the snap-shot glimpses of disturbed wild creatures skurrying through the grass,—I can call it all back and make it as real as it ever was, and as blessed. I can call back the prairie, and its loneliness and peace, and a vast hawk hanging motionless in the sky, with his wings spread wide and the blue of the vault showing through the fringe of their end-feathers. I can see the woods in their autumn dress, the oaks purple, the hickories washed with gold, the maples and the sumachs luminous with crimson fires, and I can hear the rustle made by the fallen leaves as we plowed through them. I can see the blue clusters of wild grapes hanging amongst the foliage of the saplings, and I remember the taste of them and the smell. I know how the wild blackberries looked, and how they tasted; and the same with the pawpaws, the hazelnuts and the persimmons; and I can feel the thumping rain, upon my head, of hickory nuts and walnuts when we were out in the frosty dawns to scramble for them with the pigs, and the gusts of wind loosed them and sent them down. I know the stain of blackberries, and how pretty it is; and I know the stain of walnut hulls, and how little it minds soap and water; also what grudged experience it had of either of them. I know the taste of maple sap, and when to gather it, and how to arrange the troughs and the delivery-tubes, and how to boil down the juice, and how to hook the sugar after it is made; also how much better hooked sugar tastes than any that is honestly come by, let bigots say what they will. I know how a prize watermelon looks when it is sunning its fat rotundity among pumpkin vines and "simblins;" I know how to tell when it is ripe without "plugging" it; I know how inviting it looks when it is cooling itself in a tub of water under the bed, waiting; I know how it looks when it lies on the table in the sheltered great floor-space between house and kitchen, and the children gathered for the sacrifice and their mouths watering; I know the crackling sound it makes when the carving knife enters its end, and I can see the split fly along in front of the blade as the knife cleaves its way to the other end; I can see its halves fall apart and display the rich red meat and the black seeds, and the heart standing up, a luxury fit for the elect; I know how a boy looks, behind a yard-long slice of that melon, and I know how he feels; for I have been there. I know the taste of the watermelon which has been honestly come by, and I know the taste of the watermelon which has been acquired by art. Both taste good, but the experienced know which tastes best. I know the look of green apples and peaches and pears on the trees, and I know how entertaining they are when they are inside of a person. I know how ripe ones look when they are piled in pyramids under the trees, and how pretty they are and how vivid their colors. I know how a frozen apple looks, in a barrel down cellar in the winter time, and how hard it is to bite, and how the frost makes the teeth ache, and yet how good it is, notwithstanding. I know the disposition of elderly people to select the specked apples for the children, and I once knew ways to beat the game. I know the look of an apple that is roasting and sizzling on a hearth on a winter's evening, and I know the comfort that comes of eating it hot, along with some sugar and a drench of cream. I know the delicate art and mystery of so cracking hickory nuts and walnuts on a flatiron with a hammer that the kernels will be delivered whole, and I know how the nuts, taken in conjunction with winter apples, cider and doughnuts, make old people's old tales and old jokes sound fresh and crisp and enchanting, and juggle an evening away before you know what went with the time. I know the look of Uncle Dan'l's kitchen as it was on privileged nights when I was a child, and I can see the white and black children grouped on the hearth, with the firelight playing on their faces and the shadows flickering upon the walls, clear back toward the cavernous gloom of the rear, and I can hear Uncle Dan'l telling the immortal tales which Uncle Remus Harris was to gather into his book and charm the world with, by and by; and I can feel again the creepy joy which quivered through me when the time for the ghost story of the "Golden Arm" was reached—and the sense of regret, too, which came over me, for it was always the last story of the evening, and there was nothing between it and the unwelcome bed.

I can remember the bare wooden stairway in my uncle's house, and the turn to the left above the landing, and the rafters and the slanting roof over my bed, and the squares of moonlight on the floor, and the white cold world of snow outside, seen through the curtainless window. I can remember the howling of the wind and the quaking of the house on stormy nights, and how snug and cosy one felt, under the blankets, listening; and how the powdery snow used to sift in, around the sashes, and lie in little ridges on the floor, and make the place look chilly in the morning, and curb the wild desire to get up—in case there was any. I can remember how very dark that room was, in the dark of the moon, and how packed it was with ghostly stillness when one woke up by accident away in the night, and forgotten sins came flocking out of the secret chambers of the memory and wanted a hearing; and how ill chosen the time seemed for this kind of business; and how dismal was the hoo-hooing of the owl and the wailing of the wolf, sent mourning by on the night wind.

I remember the raging of the rain on that roof, summer nights, and how pleasant it was to lie and listen to it, and enjoy the white splendor of the lightning and the majestic booming and crashing of the thunder. It was a very satisfactory room; and there was a lightning rod which was reachable from the window, an adorable and skittish thing to climb up and down, summer nights, when there were duties on hand of a sort to make privacy desirable.

I remember the 'coon and 'possum-hunts, nights, with the negroes, and the long marches through the black gloom of the woods, and the excitement which fired everybody when the distant bay of an experienced dog announced that the game was treed; then the wild scramblings and stumblings through briars and bushes and over roots to get to the spot; then the lighting of a fire and the felling of the tree, the joyful frenzy of the dogs and the negroes, and the weird picture it all made in the red glare—I remember it all well, and the delight that every one got out of it, except the 'coon.

I remember the pigeon seasons, when the birds would come in millions, and cover the trees, and by their weight break down the branches. They were clubbed to death with sticks; guns were not necessary, and were not used. I remember the squirrel-hunts, and prairie-chicken hunts, and wild turkey hunts, and all that; and how we turned out, mornings, while it was still dark, to go on these expeditions, and how chilly and dismal it was, and how often I regretted that I was well enough to go. A toot on a tin horn brought twice as many dogs as were needed, and in their happiness they raced and scampered about, and knocked small people down, and made no end of unnecessary noise. At the word, they vanished away toward the woods, and we drifted silently after them in the melancholy gloom. But presently the gray dawn stole over the world, the birds piped up, then the sun rose and poured light and comfort all around, everything was fresh and dewy and fragrant, and life was a boon again. After three hours of tramping we arrived back wholesomely tired, overladen with game, very hungry, and just in time for breakfast.

Chapter

My uncle and his big boys hunted with the rifle, the youngest boy and I with a shot-gun—a small single-barrelled shot-gun which was properly suited to our size and strength; it was not much heavier than a broom. We carried it turn-about, half an hour at a time. I was not able to hit anything with it, but I liked to try. Fred and I hunted feathered small game, the others hunted deer, squirrels, wild turkeys, and such things. Jim and his father were the best shots. They killed hawks and wild geese and such-like on the wing; and they didn't wound or kill squirrels, they *stunned* them. When the dogs treed a squirrel, the squirrel would scamper aloft and run out on a limb and flatten himself along it hoping to make himself invisible in that way—and not quite succeeding. You could see his wee little ears sticking up. You couldn't see his nose, but you knew where it was. Then the hunter, despising a "rest" for his rifle, stood up and took off-hand aim at the limb and sent a bullet into it immediately under the squirrel's nose, and down tumbled the animal, unwounded but unconscious; the dogs gave him a shake and he was dead. Sometimes when the distance was great and the wind not accurately allowed for, the bullet would hit the squirrel's head; the dogs could do as they pleased with that one— the hunter's pride was hurt, and he wouldn't allow it to go into the game-bag.

In the first faint gray of the dawn the stately wild turkeys would be stalking around in great flocks, and ready to be sociable and answer invitations to come and converse with other excursionists of their kind. The hunter concealed himself and imitated the turkey-call by sucking the air through the leg-bone of a turkey which had previously answered a call like that and lived only just long enough to regret it. There is nothing that furnishes a perfect turkey-call except that bone. Another of Nature's treacheries, you see; she is full of them; half the time she doesn't know which she likes best—to betray her child or protect it. In the case of the turkey she is badly mixed: she gives it a bone to be used in getting it into trouble, and she also furnishes it with a trick for getting itself out of the trouble again. When a mamma-turkey answers an invitation and finds she has made a mistake in accepting it, she does as the mamma-partridge does—remembers a previous engagement and goes limping and scrambling away, pretending to be very lame; and at the same time she is saying to her not-visible children, "Lie low, keep still, don't expose yourselves; I shall be back as soon as I have beguiled this shabby swindler out of the county."

When a person is ignorant and confiding, this immoral device can have tiresome results. I followed an ostensibly lame turkey over a considerable part of the United States one morning, because I believed in her and could not think she would deceive a mere boy, and one who was trusting her and considering her honest. I had the single-barrelled shot-gun, but my idea was to catch her alive. I often got within rushing distance of her, and then made my rush; but always, just as I made my final plunge and put my hand down where her back had been, it wasn't there; it was only two or three inches from there and I brushed the tail feathers as I landed on my stomach—a very close call, but still not quite close enough; that is, not close enough for success, but just close enough to convince me that I could do it next time. She always waited for me, a little piece away, and let on to be resting and greatly fatigued; which was a lie, but I believed it, for I still thought her honest long after I ought to have begun to doubt her, long after I ought to have been suspecting that this was no way for a high-minded bird to be acting. I followed, and followed and followed, making my periodical rushes, and getting up and brushing the dust off, and resuming the voyage with patient confidence; indeed with a confidence which grew, for I could see by the change of climate and vegetation that we were getting up into the high latitudes, and as she always looked a little tireder and a little more discouraged after each rush, I judged that I was safe to win, in the end, the competition being purely a matter of staying power and the advantage lying with me from the start because she was lame.

Along in the afternoon I began to feel fatigued myself. Neither of us had had any rest since we first started on the excursion, which was upwards of ten hours before, though latterly we had paused a while after rushes, I letting on to be thinking about something, and she letting on to be thinking about something else; but neither of us sincere, and both of us waiting for the other to call game but in no real hurry about it, for indeed those little evanescent snatches of rest were very grateful to the feelings of us both, it would naturally be so, skirmishing along like that ever since dawn and not a bite in the meantime; at least for me, though sometimes as she lay on her side fanning herself with a wing and praying for strength to get out of this difficulty a grasshopper happened along whose time had come, and that was well for her, and fortunate, but I had nothing—nothing the whole day.

More than once, after I was very tired, I gave up taking her alive, and was going to shoot her, but I never did it, although it was my right, for I did not believe I could hit her; and besides, she always stopped and posed, when I raised the gun, and this made me suspicious that she knew about me and my marksmanship, and so I did not care to expose myself to remarks.

I did not get her, at all. When she got tired of the game at last, she rose from almost under my hand and flew aloft with the rush and whir of a shell and lit on the highest limb of a great tree and sat down and crossed her legs and smiled down at me, and seemed gratified to see me so astonished.

I was ashamed, and also lost; and it was while wandering the woods hunting for myself that I found a deserted log cabin and had one of the best meals there that in my life-days I have eaten. The weed-grown garden was full of ripe tomatoes, and I ate them ravenously though I had never liked them before. Not more than two or three times since have I tasted anything that was so delicious as those tomatoes. I surfeited myself with them, and did not taste another one until I was in middle life. I can eat them now, but I do not like the look of them. I suppose we have all experienced a surfeit at one time or another. Once, in stress of circumstances, I ate part of a barrel of sardines, there being nothing else at hand, but since then I have always been able to get along without sardines.

The Latest Attempt

Finally, in Florence in 1904, I hit upon the right way to do an Autobiography: start it at no particular time of your life; wander at your free will all over your life; talk only about the thing which interests you for the moment; drop it the moment its interest threatens to pale, and turn your talk upon the new and more interesting thing that has intruded itself into your mind meantime.

Also, make the narrative a combined Diary *and* Autobiography. In this way you have the vivid things of the present to make a contrast with memories of like things in the past, and these contrasts have a charm which is all their own. No talent is required to make a combined Diary and Autobiography interesting.

And so, I have found the right plan. It makes my labor amusement—mere amusement, play, pastime, and wholly effortless. It is the first time in history that the right plan has been hit upon.

The Final (and Right) Plan

I will construct a text—to precede the Autobiography; also a Preface, to follow said Text.

What a wee little part of a person's life are his acts and his words! His real life is led in his head, and is known to none but himself. All day long, and every day, the mill of his brain is grinding, and his *thoughts,* (which are but the mute articulation of his *feelings,*) not those other things, are his history. His *acts* and his *words* are merely the visible thin crust of his world, with its scattered snow summits and its vacant wastes of water—and they are so trifling a part of his bulk! a mere skin enveloping it. The mass of him is hidden—it and its volcanic fires that toss and boil, and never rest, night nor day. *These are his life,* and they are not written, and cannot be written. Every day would make a whole book of eighty thousand words—three hundred and sixty-five books a year. Biographies are but the clothes and buttons of the man—the biography of the man himself cannot be written.

Preface. As from the Grave

I.

In this Autobiography I shall keep in mind the fact that I am speaking from the grave. I am literally speaking from the grave, because I shall be dead when the book issues from the press. At any rate—to be precise—nineteen-twentieths of the book will not see print until after my death.

I speak from the grave rather than with my living tongue, for a good reason: I can speak thence freely. When a man is writing a book dealing with the privacies of his life—a book which is to be read while he is still alive—he shrinks from speaking his whole frank mind; all his attempts to do it fail, he recognizes that he is trying to do a thing which is wholly impossible to a human being. The frankest and freëst and privatest product of the human mind and heart is a love letter; the writer gets his limitless freedom of statement and expression from his sense that no stranger is going to see what he is writing. Sometimes there is a breach of promise case by and by; and when he sees his letter in print it makes him cruelly uncomfortable, and he perceives that he never would have unbosomed himself to that large and honest degree if he had known that he was writing for the public. He cannot find anything in the letter that was not true, honest, and respect-worthy; but no matter, he would have been very much more reserved if he had known he was writing for print.

It has seemed to me that I could be as frank and free and unembarrassed as a love letter if I knew that what I was writing would be exposed to no eye until I was dead, and unaware, and indifferent.

II.

My editors, heirs and assigns are hereby instructed to leave out of the first edition all characterizations of friends and enemies that might wound the feelings of either the persons characterized or their families and kinship. This book is not a revenge-record. When I build a fire under a person in it, I do not do it merely because of the enjoyment I get out of seeing him fry, but because he is worth the trouble. It is then a compliment, a distinction; let him give thanks and keep quiet. I do not fry the small, the commonplace, the unworthy.

From the first, second, third and fourth editions all sound and sane expressions of opinion must be left out. There may be a market for that kind of wares a century from now. There is no hurry. Wait and see.

III.

The editions should be issued twenty-five years apart. Many things that must be left out of the first will be proper for the second; many things that must be left out of both will be proper for the third; into the fourth—or at least the fifth—the whole Autobiography can go, unexpurgated.

Mark Twain

Here begin the Florentine Dictations.

[John Hay]

Florence, Italy. 31st January 1904.

A quarter of a century ago I was visiting John Hay, now Secretary of State, at Whitelaw Reid's house in New York, which Hay was occupying for a few months while Reid was absent on a holiday in Europe. Temporarily also, Hay was editing Reid's paper, the New York *Tribune*. I remember two incidents of that Sunday visit particularly well, and I think I shall use them presently to illustrate something which I intend to say. One of the incidents is immaterial, and I hardly know why it is that it has stayed with me so many years. I must introduce it with a word or two. I had known John Hay a good many years, I had known him when he was an obscure young editorial writer on the *Tribune* in Horace Greeley's time, earning three or four times the salary he got, considering the high character of the work which came from his pen. In those earlier days he was a picture to look at, for beauty of feature, perfection of form and grace of carriage and movement. He had a charm about him of a sort quite unusual to my western ignorance and inexperience—a charm of manner, intonation, apparently native and unstudied elocution, and all that—the groundwork of it native, the ease of it, the polish of it, the winning naturalness of it, acquired in Europe where he had been Chargé d'Affaires some time at the Court of Vienna. He was joyous and cordial, a most pleasant comrade.

Now I am coming to it. John Hay was not afraid of Horace Greeley.

I will leave that remark in a paragraph by itself; it cannot be made too conspicuous. John Hay was the only man who ever served Horace Greeley on the *Tribune* of whom that can be said. In the past few years, since Hay has been occupying the post of Secretary of State with a succession of foreign difficulties on his hands such as have not fallen to the share of any previous occupant of that chair, perhaps, when we consider the magnitude of the matters involved, we have seen that that courage of his youth is his possession still, and that he is not any more scarable by kings and emperors and their fleets and armies than he was by Horace Greeley.

I arrive at the application now. That Sunday morning, twenty-five years ago, Hay and I had been chatting and laughing and carrying-on almost like our earlier selves of '67, when the door opened and Mrs. Hay, gravely clad, gloved, bonneted, and just from church, and fragrant with the odors of Presbyterian sanctity, stood in it. We rose to our feet at once, of course,—rose through a swiftly falling temperature—a temperature which at the beginning was soft and summerlike, but which was turning our breath and all other damp things to frost crystals by the time we were erect—but we got no opportunity to say the pretty and polite thing and offer the homage due: the comely young matron forestalled us. She came forward smileless, with disapproval written all over her face, said most coldly, "Good morning Mr. Clemens," and passed on and out.

There was an embarrassed pause—I may say a very embarrassed pause. If Hay was waiting for me to speak, it was a mistake; I couldn't think of a word. It was soon plain to me that the bottom had fallen out of his vocabulary, too. When I was able to walk I started toward the door, and Hay, grown gray in a single night, so to speak, limped feebly at my side, making no moan, saying no word. At the door his ancient courtesy rose and bravely flickered for a moment, then went out. That is to say, he tried to ask me to call again, but at that point his ancient sincerity rose against the fiction and squelched it. Then he tried another remark, and that one he got through with. He said pathetically, and apologetically,

"She is very strict about Sunday."

More than once in these past few years I have heard admiring and grateful people say, and have said it myself—

"He is not afraid of this whole nation of eighty millions when his duty requires him to do an unpopular thing."

Twenty-five years have gone by since then, and through manifold experiences I have learned that no one's courage is absolutely perfect; that there is always some one who is able to modify his pluck.

The other incident of that visit was this: in trading remarks concerning our ages I confessed to forty-two and Hay to forty. Then he asked if I had begun to write my autobiography, and I said I hadn't. He said that I ought to begin at once, and that I had already lost two years. Then he said in substance this:

"At forty a man reaches the top of the hill of life and starts down on the sunset side. The ordinary man, the average man, not to particularize too closely and say the commonplace man, has at that age succeeded or failed; in either case he has lived all of his life that is likely to be worth recording; also in either case the life lived is worth setting down, and cannot fail to be interesting if he comes as near to telling the truth about himself as he can. And he *will* tell the truth in spite of himself, for his facts and his fictions will work loyally together for the protection of the reader; each fact and each fiction will be a dab of paint, each will fall in its right place, and together they will paint his portrait; not the portrait *he* thinks they are painting, but his real portrait, the inside of him, the soul of him, his character. Without intending to lie he will lie all the time; not bluntly, consciously, not dully unconsciously, but half-consciously—consciousness in twilight; a soft and gentle and merciful twilight which makes his general form comely, with his virtuous prominences and projections discernible and his ungracious ones in shadow. His truths will be recognizable as truths, his modifications of facts which would tell against him will go for nothing, the reader will see the fact through the film and know his man. There is a subtle devilish something or other about autobiographical composition that defeats all the writer's attempts to paint his portrait *his* way."

Hay meant that he and I were ordinary average commonplace people, and I did not resent my share of the verdict, but nursed my wound in silence. His idea that we had finished our work in life, passed the summit and were westward bound down hill, with me two years ahead of him and neither of us with anything further to do as benefactors to mankind, was all a mistake. I had written four books then, possibly five. I have been drowning the world in literary wisdom ever since, volume after volume; since that day's sun went down he has been the historian of Mr. Lincoln, and his book will never perish; he has been Ambassador, brilliant orator, competent and admirable Secretary of State, and would be President next year if we were a properly honest and grateful nation instead of an ungrateful one, a nation which has usually not been willing to have a chief magistrate of gold when it could get one of tin.

I had lost two years, but I resolved to make up that loss. I resolved to begin my autobiography at once. I did begin it, but the resolve melted away and disappeared in a week and I threw my beginning away. Since then, about every three or four years I have made other beginnings and thrown them away. Once I tried the experiment of a diary, intending to inflate that into an autobiography when its accumulation should furnish enough material, but that experiment lasted only a week; it took me half of every night to set down the history of the day, and at the week's end I did not like the result.

Within the last eight or ten years I have made several attempts to do the autobiography in one way or another with a pen, but the result was not satisfactory, it was too literary. With the pen in one's hand, narrative is a difficult art; narrative should flow as flows the brook down through the hills and the leafy woodlands, its course changed by every boulder it comes across and by every grass-clad gravelly spur that projects into its path; its surface broken but its course not stayed by rocks and gravel on the bottom in the shoal places; a brook that never goes straight for a minute, but *goes,* and goes briskly, sometimes ungrammatically, and sometimes fetching a horseshoe three-quarters of a mile around and at the end of the circuit flowing within a yard of the path it traversed an hour before; but always *going,* and always following at least one law, always loyal to that law, the law of *narrative,* which *has no law.* Nothing to do but make the trip; the how of it is not important so that the trip is made.

With a pen in the hand the narrative stream is a canal; it moves slowly, smoothly, decorously, sleepily, it has no blemish except that it is all blemish. It is too literary, too prim, too nice; the gait and style and movement are not suited to narrative. That canal stream is always reflecting; it is its nature, it can't help it. Its slick shiny surface is interested in everything it passes along the banks, cows, foliage, flowers, everything. And so it wastes a lot of time in reflections.

Notes on "Innocents Abroad"

Dictated in Florence, Italy, April, 1904.

I will begin with a note upon the dedication. I wrote the book in the months of March and April 1868, in San Francisco. It was published in August 1869. Three years afterward Mr. Goodman, of Virginia City, Nevada, on whose newspaper I had served ten years before, came East, and we were walking down Broadway one day when he said— *1868*

"How did you come to steal Oliver Wendell Holmes's dedication and put it in your book?"

I made a careless and inconsequential answer, for I supposed he was joking. But he assured me that he was in earnest. He said—

"I'm not discussing the question of whether you stole it or didn't—for that is a question that can be settled in the first bookstore we come to—I am only asking you *how* you came to steal it, for that is where my curiosity is focalized."

I couldn't accommodate him with this information, as I hadn't it in stock. I could have made oath that I had not stolen anything, therefore my vanity was not hurt nor my spirit troubled. At bottom I supposed that he had mistaken another book for mine, and was now getting himself into an untenable place and preparing sorrow for himself and triumph for me. We entered a bookstore and he asked for "The Innocents Abroad" and for the dainty little blue and gold edition of Dr. Oliver Wendell Holmes's poems. He opened the books, exposed their dedications and said—

"Read them. It is plain that the author of the second one stole the first one, isn't it?"

I was very much ashamed, and unspeakably astonished. We continued our walk, but I was not able to throw any gleam of light upon that original question of his. I could not remember ever having seen Dr. Holmes's dedication. I knew the poems, but the dedication was new to me.

I did not get hold of the key to that secret until months afterward, then it came in a curious way, and yet it was a natural way; for the natural way provided by nature and the construction of the human mind for the discovery of a forgotten event is to employ another forgotten event for its resurrection.

I received a letter from the Rev. Dr. Rising, who had been rector of the Episcopal church in Virginia City in my time, in which letter Dr. Rising made reference to certain things which had happened to us in the Sandwich Islands six years before; among other things he made *1866* casual mention of the Honolulu Hotel's poverty in the matter of literature. At first I did not see the bearing of the remark, it called nothing to my mind. But presently it did—with a flash! There was but one book in Mr. Kirchhof's hotel, and that was the first volume of Dr. Holmes's blue and gold series. I had had a fortnight's chance to get well acquainted with its contents, for I had ridden around the big island (Hawaii) on horseback and had brought back so many saddle boils that if there had been a duty on them it would have bankrupted me to pay it. They kept me in my room, unclothed, and in persistent pain for two weeks, with no company but cigars and the little volume of poems. Of course I read them almost constantly; I read them from beginning to end, then read them backwards, then began in the middle and read them both ways, then read them wrong end first and upside down. In a word, I read the book to rags, and was infinitely grateful to the hand that wrote it.

Here we have an exhibition of what repetition can do, when persisted in daily and hourly over a considerable stretch of time, where one is merely reading for entertainment, without thought or intention of preserving in the memory that which is read. It is a process which in the course of years dries all the juice out of a familiar verse of Scripture, leaving nothing but a sapless husk behind. In that case you at least know the origin of the husk, but in the case in point I apparently preserved the husk but presently forgot whence it came. It lay lost in some dim corner of my memory a year or two, then came forward when I needed a dedication, and was promptly mistaken by me as a child of my own happy fancy.

I was new, I was ignorant, the mysteries of the human mind were a sealed book to me as yet, and I stupidly looked upon myself as a tough and unforgivable criminal. I wrote to Dr. Holmes and told him the whole disgraceful affair, implored him in impassioned language to believe that I had never intended to commit this crime, and was unaware that I had committed it until I was confronted with the awful evidence. I have lost his answer; I could better have afforded to lose an uncle. Of these I had a surplus, many of them of no real value to me, but that letter was beyond price, beyond uncledom, and unsparable. In it Dr. Holmes laughed the kindest and healingest laugh over the whole matter, and at considerable length and in happy phrase assured me that there was no crime in unconscious plagiarism; that I committed it every day, that he committed it every day, that every man alive on the earth who writes or speaks commits it every day and not merely once or twice but every time he opens his mouth; that all our phrasings are spiritualized shadows cast multitudinously from our readings; that no happy phrase of ours is ever quite original with us, there is nothing of our own in it except some slight change born of our temperament, character, environment, teachings and associations; that this slight change differentiates it from another man's manner of saying it, stamps it with our special style, and makes it our own for the time being; all the rest of it being old, mouldy, antique, and smelling of the breath of a thousand generations of them that have passed it over their teeth before!

In the thirty-odd years which have come and gone since then, I have satisfied myself that what Dr. Holmes said was true.

I wish to make a note upon the preface of the "Innocents." In the last paragraph of that brief preface, I speak of the proprietors of the *Daily Alta California* having "waived their rights" in certain letters which I wrote for that journal while absent on the *Quaker City* trip. I was young then, I am white-headed now, but the insult of that word rankles yet, now that I am reading that paragraph for the first time in many years, reading it for the first time since it was written, perhaps. There were rights, it is true—such rights as the strong are able to acquire over the weak and the absent. Early in '66 George Barnes invited me to resign my reportership on his paper, the San Francisco *Morning Call,* and for some months thereafter I was without money or work; then I had a pleasant turn of fortune. The proprietors of the Sacramento *Union,* a great and influential daily journal, sent me to the Sandwich Islands to write four letters a month at twenty dollars apiece. I was there four or five months, and returned to find myself about the best known honest man on the Pacific coast. Thomas Maguire, proprietor of several theatres, said that now was the time to make my fortune—strike while the iron was hot!—

break into the lecture field! I did it. I announced a lecture on the Sandwich Islands, closing the advertisement with the remark "Admission one dollar; doors open at half past 7, the trouble begins at 8." A true prophecy. The trouble certainly did begin at 8, when I found myself in front of the only audience I had ever faced, for the fright which pervaded me from head to foot was paralysing. It lasted two minutes and was as bitter as death, the memory of it is indestructible, but it had its compensations, for it made me immune from timidity before audiences for all time to come. I lectured in all the principal Californian towns and in Nevada, then lectured once or twice more in San Francisco, then retired from the field rich—for me—and laid out a plan to sail westward from San Francisco and go around the world. The proprietors of the *Alta* engaged me to write an account of the trip for that paper—fifty letters of a column and a half each, which would be about two thousand words per letter, and the pay to be twenty dollars per letter.

I went East to St. Louis to say good-bye to my mother, and then I was bitten by the prospectus of Captain Duncan of the *Quaker City* Excursion, and I ended by joining it. During the trip I wrote and sent the fifty letters; six of them miscarried, and I wrote six new ones to complete my contract. Then I put together a lecture on the trip and delivered it in San Francisco at great and satisfactory pecuniary profit, then I branched out into the country and was aghast at the result: I had been entirely forgotten, I never had people enough in my houses to sit as a jury of inquest on my lost reputation! I inquired into this curious condition of things and found that the thrifty owners of that prodigiously rich *Alta* newspaper had *copyrighted* all those poor little twenty-dollar letters, and had threatened with prosecution any journal which should venture to copy a paragraph from them!

And there I was! I had contracted to furnish a large book, concerning the excursion, to the American Publishing Company of Hartford, and I supposed I should need all those letters to fill it out with. I was in an uncomfortable situation—that is, if the proprietors of this stealthily acquired copyright should refuse to let me use the letters. That is just what they did; Mr. Mac— something—I have forgotten the rest of his name*—said his firm were going to make a book out of the letters in order to get back the thousand dollars which they had paid for them. I said that if they had acted fairly and honorably, and had allowed the country press to use the letters or portions of them, my lecture-skirmish on the coast would have paid me ten thousand dollars, whereas the *Alta* had lost me that amount. Then he offered a compromise: he would publish the book and allow me 10 per cent royalty on it. The compromise did not appeal to me, and I said so. I was now quite unknown outside of San Francisco, the book's sale would be confined to that city, and my royalty would not pay me enough to board me three months; whereas my eastern contract, if carried out, could be profitable to me, for I had a sort of reputation on the Atlantic seaboard acquired through the publication of six excursion-letters in the New York *Tribune* and one or two in the *Herald*.

In the end Mr. MacCrellish agreed to suppress his book, on certain conditions: in my preface I must thank the *Alta* for waiving its "rights" and granting me permission. I objected

*May 20, 1906. I recall it now—MacCrellish.   M. T.

to the thanks. I could not with any large degree of sincerity thank the *Alta* for bankrupting my lecture-raid. After considerable debate my point was conceded and the thanks left out.

Noah Brooks was editor of the *Alta* at the time, a man of sterling character and equipped with a right heart, also a good historian where facts were not essential. In biographical sketches

1902 of me written many years afterward (1902), he was quite eloquent in praises of the generosity of the *Alta* people in giving to me without compensation a book which, as history had afterward shown, was worth a fortune. After all the fuss, I did not levy heavily upon the *Alta* letters. I found that they were newspaper matter, not book matter. They had been written here and there and yonder, as opportunity had given me a chance working-moment or two during our feverish flight around about Europe or in the furnace-heat of my stateroom on board the *Quaker City,* therefore they were loosely constructed, and needed to have some of the wind and water squeezed out of them. I used several of them—ten or twelve, perhaps. I wrote the rest of "The Innocents Abroad" in sixty days, and I could have added a fortnight's labor with the pen and gotten along without the letters altogether. I was very young in those days, exceedingly young, marvelously young, younger than I am now, younger than I shall ever be again, by hundreds of years. I worked every night from eleven or twelve until broad day in the morning, and as I did two hundred thousand words in the sixty days, the average was more than three thousand words a day—nothing for Sir Walter Scott, nothing for Louis Stevenson,

1897 nothing for plenty of other people, but quite handsome for me. In 1897, when we were living in Tedworth Square, London, and I was writing the book called "Following the Equator" my

1904 average was eighteen hundred words a day; here in Florence, (1904), my average seems to be fourteen hundred words per sitting of four or five hours.*

I was deducing from the above that I have been slowing down steadily in these thirty-six years, but I perceive that my statistics have a defect: three thousand words in the spring of 1868 when I was working seven or eight or nine hours at a sitting has little or no advantage over the sitting of to-day, covering half the time and producing half the output. Figures often beguile me, particularly when I have the arranging of them myself; in which case the remark attributed to Disraeli would often apply with justice and force:

"There are three kinds of lies: lies, damned lies, and statistics."

[Robert Louis Stevenson and Thomas Bailey Aldrich]

But it was on a bench in Washington Square that I saw the most of Louis Stevenson. It was an outing that lasted an hour or more and was very pleasant and sociable. I had come with him from his house, where I had been paying my respects to his family. His business in the Square was to absorb the sunshine. He was most scantily furnished with flesh, his clothes seemed to fall into hollows as if there might be nothing inside but the frame for a sculptor's statue. His long face and lank hair and dark complexion and musing and melancholy expression seemed

---

*With the pen, I mean. This Autobiography is dictated, not written.

to fit these details justly and harmoniously, and the altogether of it seemed especially planned to gather the rays of your observation and focalize them upon Stevenson's special distinction and commanding feature, his splendid eyes. They burned with a smouldering rich fire under the pent-house of his brows, and they made him beautiful.

*   *   *   *   *   *   *   *   *   *   *

I said I thought he was right about the others, but mistaken as to Bret Harte; in substance I said that Harte was good company and a thin but pleasant talker; that he was always bright, but never brilliant; that in this matter he must not be classed with Thomas Bailey Aldrich, nor must any other man, ancient or modern; that Aldrich was always witty, always brilliant, if there was anybody present capable of striking his flint at the right angle; that Aldrich was as sure and prompt and unfailing as the red hot iron on the blacksmith's anvil—you had only to hit it competently to make it deliver an explosion of sparks. I added—

"Aldrich has never had his peer for prompt and pithy and witty and humorous sayings. None has equaled him, certainly none has surpassed him, in the felicity of phrasing with which he clothed these children of his fancy. Aldrich was always brilliant, he couldn't help it, he is a fire-opal set round with rose diamonds; when he is not speaking, you know that his dainty fancies are twinkling and glimmering around in him; when he speaks the diamonds flash. Yes, he was always brilliant, he will always be brilliant; he will be brilliant in hell—you will see."

Stevenson, smiling a chuckly smile, "I hope not."

"Well, you will, and he will dim even those ruddy fires and look like a transfigured Adonis backed against a pink sunset."

*   *   *   *   *   *   *   *   *   *   *

There on that bench we struck out a new phrase—one or the other of us, I don't remember which—"submerged renown." Variations were discussed: "submerged fame," "submerged reputation," and so on, and a choice was made; "submerged renown" was elected, I believe. This important matter rose out of an incident which had been happening to Stevenson in Albany. While in a book shop or book stall there he had noticed a long rank of small books cheaply but neatly gotten up, and bearing such titles as "Davis's Selected Speeches," "Davis's Selected Poetry," Davis's this and Davis's that and Davis's the other thing; compilations, every one of them, each with a brief, compact, intelligent and useful introductory chapter by this same Davis, whose first name I have forgotten. Stevenson had begun the matter with this question:

"Can you name the American author whose fame and acceptance stretch widest in the States?"

I thought I could, but it did not seem to me that it would be modest to speak out, in the circumstances. So I diffidently said nothing. Stevenson noticed, and said—

"Save your delicacy for another time—you are not the one. For a shilling you can't name the American author of widest note and popularity in the States. But I can."

Then he went on and told about that Albany incident. He had inquired of the shopman—

"Who is this Davis?"

The answer was—

"An author whose books have to have freight trains to carry them, not baskets. Apparently you have not heard of him?"

Stevenson said no, this was the first time. The man said—

"Nobody has heard of Davis; you may ask all around and you will see. You never see his name mentioned in print, not even in advertisements; these things are of no use to Davis, not any more than they are to the wind and the sea. You never see one of Davis's books floating on top of the United States, but put on your diving armor and get yourself lowered away down and down and down till you strike the dense region, the sunless region of eternal drudgery and starvation wages—there you'll find them by the million. The man that gets that market, his fortune is made, his bread and butter are safe, for those people will never go back on him. An author may have a reputation which is confined to the surface, and lose it and become pitied, then despised, then forgotten, entirely forgotten—the frequent steps in a surface reputation. A surface reputation, however great, is always mortal, and always killable if you go at it right—with pins and needles, and quiet slow poison, not with the club and the tomahawk. But it is a different matter with the submerged reputation—down in the deep water; once a favorite there, always a favorite; once beloved, always beloved; once respected, always respected, honored, and believed in. For, what the reviewer says never finds its way down into those placid deeps; nor the newspaper sneers, nor any breath of the winds of slander blowing above. Down there they never hear of these things. Their idol may be painted clay, up there at the surface, and fade and waste and crumble and blow away, there being much weather there; but down below he is gold and adamant and indestructible."

[Villa di Quarto]

January. 1904.

This villa is situated three or four miles from Florence, and has several names. Some call it the Villa Reale di Quarto, some call it the Villa Principessa, some call it the Villa Granduchessa; this multiplicity of names was an inconvenience to me for the first two or three weeks, for as I had heard the place called by only one name, when letters came for the servants directed to the care of one or the other of the other names, I supposed a mistake had been made and remailed them. It has been explained to me that there is reason for these several names. Its name Quarto it gets from the district which it is in, it being in the four-mile radius from the centre of Florence. It is called Reale because the King of Würtemberg occupied it at one time; Principessa and Granduchessa because a Russian daughter of the imperial house occupied it at another. There is a history of the house somewhere, and some time or other I shall get it and see if there are any details in it which could be of use in this chapter. I should like to see that book, for as an evolutionist I should like to know the beginning of this dwelling and the several stages of its evolution. Baedeker says it was built by Cosimo I, by [   ], architect. I have learned this within the past three minutes, and it wrecks my development scheme. I was surmising that the house began in a small and humble way, and was the production of a poor farmer whose idea of home and comfort it was; that following him a generation or two later came a successor of better rank and larger means who built an addition; that successor after successor added more bricks and more bulk as time dragged on, each in his turn leaving a detail behind him of paint or wall-paper to distinguish his reign from the others; that finally in the last century came the three that precede me, and added their specialties. The King of Würtemberg broke out room enough in the centre of the building—about a hundred feet from each end of it,—to put in the great staircase, a cheap and showy affair, almost the only wooden thing in the whole edifice, and as comfortable and sane and satisfactory as it is out of character with the rest of the asylum. The Russian Princess, who came with native superstitions about cold weather, added the hot-air furnaces in the cellar and the vast green majolica stove in the great hall where the King's staircase is—a stove which I thought might possibly be a church—a nursery church for children, so imposing is it for size and so richly adorned with basso relievos of an ultra pious sort. It is loaded and fired from a secret place behind the partition against which it is backed. Last of all came Satan also, the Countess Massiglia, present owner of the house, an American product, and male in everything but sex. She added a cheap and stingy arrangement of electric bells, inadequate acetylene-gas plant, obsolete water closets, perhaps a dozen pieces of machine-made boarding-house furniture, and some fire-auction carpets which blaspheme the standards of color and art all day long, and never quiet down until the darkness comes and pacifies them.

However, if the house was built for Cosimo four hundred years ago and with an architect on deck, I suppose I must dismiss those notions about the gradual growth of the house in bulk. Cosimo would want a large house, he would want to build it himself so that he could have it just the way he wanted it. I think he had his will. In the architecture of this barrack there has been no development. There was no architecture in the first place and none has been added, except the King's meretricious staircase, the Princess's ecclesiastical stove, and the Countess's obsolete water closets. I am speaking of art-architecture; there is none.

There is no more architecture of that breed discoverable in this long stretch of ugly and ornamentless three-storied house-front than there is about a rope walk or a bowling alley. The shape and proportions of the house suggest those things, it being two hundred feet long by sixty wide. There is no art-architecture inside the house, there is none outside.

We arrive now at practical architecture—the useful, the indispensable, which plans the inside of a house and by wisely placing and distributing the rooms, or by stupidly and ineffectually distributing them, makes the house a convenient and comfortable and satisfactory abiding place or the reverse. The inside of the house is evidence that Cosimo's architect was not in his right mind. And it seems to me that it is not fair and not kind in Baedeker to keep on exposing his name and his crime down to this late date. I am nobler than Baedeker, and more humane, and I suppress it. I don't remember what it was, anyway.

I shall go into the details of this house, not because I imagine it differs much from any other old-time palace or new-time palace on the continent of Europe, but because every one of its crazy details interests me, and therefore may be expected to interest others of the human race, particularly women. When they read novels they usually skip the weather, but I have noticed that they read with avidity all that a writer says about the furnishings, decorations, conveniences, and general style of a home.

The interior of this barrack is so chopped up and systemless that one cannot deal in exact numbers when trying to put its choppings-up into statistics.

In the basement or cellar there are as follows:

Stalls and boxes for many horses—right under the principal bed-chamber. The horses noisily dance to the solicitations of the multitudinous flies all night.

Feed-stores.

Carriage-house.

Acetylene-gas plant.

A vast kitchen. Put out of use years ago.

Another kitchen.

Coal-rooms.

Coke-rooms.

Peat-rooms.

Wood-rooms.

Three furnaces.

Wine-rooms.

Various store-rooms for all sorts of domestic supplies.

Lot of vacant and unclassified rooms.

Labyrinth of corridors and passages, affording the stranger an absolute certainty of getting lost.

A vast cesspool! It is cleaned out every thirty years.

Couple of dark stairways leading up to the ground floor.

About twenty divisions as I count them.

This cellar seems to be of the full dimension of the house's foundations—say two hundred feet by sixty.

The ground floor, where I am dictating—is cut up into twenty-three rooms, halls, corridors, and so forth. The next floor above contains eighteen divisions of the like sort, one of which is the billiard room and another the great drawing-room.

The top story consists of twenty bedrooms and a furnace. Large rooms they necessarily are, for they are arranged ten on a side, and they occupy that whole space of two hundred feet long by sixty wide, except that there is a liberal passage or hallway between them. There are good fireplaces up there, and they would make charming bed-chambers if handsomely and comfortably furnished and decorated. But there would need to be a lift—not a European lift, with its mere stand-up space, and its imperceptible movement, but a roomy and swift American one.

These rooms are reached now by the same process by which they were reached in Cosimo's time—by leg power. Their brick floors are bare and unpainted, their walls are bare, and painted the favorite European color, which is now and always has been an odious stomach-turning yellow. It is said that these rooms were intended for servants only and that they were meant to accommodate two or three servants apiece. It seems certain that they have not been occupied by any but servants in the last fifty or a hundred years, otherwise they would exhibit some remains of decoration.

If then they have always been for the use of servants only, where did Cosimo and his family sleep? Where did the King of Würtemberg bestow his dear ones? For below that floor there are not any more than three good bed-chambers and five devilish ones. With eighty cut-ups in the house and with but four persons in my family, this large fact is provable: that we can't invite a friend to come and stay a few days with us, because there is not a bedroom unoccupied by ourselves that we could offer him without apologies. In fact we have no friend whom we love so little and respect so moderately as to be willing to stuff him into one of those vacant cells.

Yes—where did the vanished aristocracy sleep? I mean the real aristocracy, not the American Countess, for she required no room to speak of. When we arrived her husband was far away in the Orient serving his country in a diplomatic capacity, the Countess's mother had gone home to America and the Countess was keeping solitary and unvisited state in this big mansion with her head servant, the steward of the estate, as society and protector. To go on with my details: this little room where I am dictating these informations on this 8th day of January 1904, is on the east side of the house. It is level with the ground and one may step from its nine- or ten-foot-high vast door into the terrace garden, which is a great square level space surrounded by an ornamental iron railing with vases of flowers distributed here and there along its top. It is a pretty terrace with abundant green grass, with handsome trees, with a great fountain in the middle, and with roses of various tints nodding in the balmy air, and flashing back the rays of the January sun. Beyond the railing to the eastward stretches the private park, and through its trees curves the road to the far-off iron gate on the public road, where there is neither porter nor porter's lodge nor any way to communicate with the mansion. Yet from time immemorial the Italian villa has been a fortress hermetically sealed up in high walls of masonry and with entrance guarded by locked iron gates. The gates of Italy have always been locked at nightfall and kept locked the night through. No Italian trusted his contadini neighbors in the old times, and his successor does not trust them now. There are bells and porters for the convenience of outsiders desiring to get in at other villas, but it is not the case with this one, and apparently never has been. Surely it must have happened now and then that these Kings and nobilities got caught out after the gates were locked. Then how did they get in? We shall never know. The question cannot be answered. It must take its place with the other unsolved mystery of where the aristocracy slept during those centuries when they occupied this fortress.

To return to that glass door. Outside it are exceedingly heavy and coarse Venetian shutters, a fairly good defence against a catapult.

These, like the leaves of the glass door, swing open in the French fashion, and I will remark in passing that to my mind the French window is as rational and convenient as the English-American window is the reverse of this. Inside the glass door (three or four inches inside of it) are solid doors made of boards, good and strong and ugly. The shutters, the glass door and these wooden-door defences against intrusion of light and thieves are all armed with strong and heavy bolts which are shot up and down by the turning of a handle. The house-walls being very thick, these doors and shutters and things do not crowd each other, there is plenty of space between them, and there is room for more in case we should get to feeling afraid. This shuttered glass door, this convenient exit to the terrace and garden, is not the only one on this side of the house from which one can as handily step upon the terrace. There is a procession of them stretching along, door after door, along the east or rear front of the house, from its southern end to its northern end—eleven in the procession. Beginning at the south end they afford exit from a parlor; a large bedroom, (mine); this little twelve by twenty reception room where I am now at work; and a ten by twelve ditto, which is in effect the beginning of a corridor forty feet long by twelve wide with three sets of triple glass doors for exit to the terrace. The corridor empties into a dining room, and the dining room into two large rooms beyond, all with glass-door exits to the terrace. When the doors which connect these seven rooms and the corridor are thrown open the two-hundred-foot stretch of variegated carpeting with its warring and shouting and blaspheming tumult of color makes a fine and almost contenting receding and diminishing perspective, and one realizes that if some sane person could have the privilege and the opportunity of burning the existing carpets and instituting harmonies of color in their place the reformed perspective would be very beautiful. Above each of the eleven glass doors is a duplicate on the next floor. Ten feet by six, of glass. And above each of these on the topmost floor is a smaller window—thirty-three good openings for light on this eastern front, the same on the western front, and nine of ampler size on each end of the house. Fifty-six of these eighty-four windows contain double enough glass to equip the average window of an American dwelling, yet the house is by no means correspondingly light. I do not know why, perhaps it is because of the dismal upholstering of the walls.

Villa di Quarto is a palace; Cosimo built it for that, his architect intended it for that, it has always been regarded as a palace, and an old resident of Florence told me the other day that it was a good average sample of the Italian palace of the great nobility, and that its grotesqueness and barbarities, incongruities and destitution of conveniences are to be found in the rest. I am able to believe this because I have seen some of the others.

I think there is not a room in this huge confusion of rooms and halls and corridors and cells and waste spaces which does not contain some memento of each of its illustrious occupants, or at least two or three of them.

We will examine the parlor at the head of that long perspective which I have been describing. The arched ceiling is beautiful both in shape and decoration. It is finely and elaborately frescoed. The ceiling is a memento of Cosimo. The doors are draped with heavy pale blue silk, faintly figured, that is the King of Würtemberg's relic. The gleaming white brass-banded porcelain pagoda which contains an open fireplace for wood is a relic of the Russian Princess and a remembrancer of her native experiences of cold weather. The light gray wall-paper figured with gold flowers is anybody's—we care not to guess its pedigree. The rest of the room is manifestly a result of the Countess Massiglia's occupation. Its shouting inharmonies and disorders manifestly had their origin in her chaotic mind. The floor is covered with a felt-like filling of strenuous red, one can almost see Pharaoh's host floundering in it. There are four rugs scattered about like islands, violent rugs whose colors swear at each other and at the Red Sea. There is a sofa upholstered in a coarse material, a frenzy of green and blue and blood, a cheap and undeceptive imitation of Florentine embroidery. There is a sofa and two chairs upholstered in pale green silk, figured, the wood is of three different breeds of American walnut, flimsy, cheap, machine-made. There is a French-walnut sofa upholstered in figured silk of a fiendish crushed-strawberry tint of a faded aspect, and there is an arm-chair which is a mate to it. There is a plain and naked black walnut table without a cover to modify its nudity; under it is a large round ottoman covered with the palest of pale green silk, a sort of glorified mushroom which curses with all its might at the Red Sea and the furious rugs and the crushed-strawberry relics. Against the wall stands a tall glass-fronted bookcase, machine-made—the material, American butternut. It stands near enough to the King of Würtemberg's heavy silken door-drapery to powerfully accent its cheapness and ugliness by contrast. Upon the walls hang three good water-colors, six or eight very bad ones, a pious-looking portrait of the Countess in bridal veil and low neck, and a number of photographs of members of her tribe. One of them is a picture of the Count, who has a manly and intelligent face and looks like a gentleman. What possessed him to become proprietor of the Countess he probably could not explain at this late day himself.

The whole literature of this vast house is contained in that fire-auction American bookcase. There are four shelves. The top one is made up of indiscriminate literature of good quality; the next shelf is made up of cloth-covered books devoted to Christian Science and spiritualism—forty thin books; the two remaining shelves contain fifty-four bound volumes of Blackwood, in date running backward from about 1870. This bookcase and its contents were probably imported from America by the Countess's mother, who tore herself away some months ago and returned to Philadelphia. One cannot attribute the Blackwoods to the Countess, they contain nothing that could interest her. It is most unlikely that the religious shelf could enlist her sympathies, her moral constitution being made up of envy, hate, malice and treachery. She is easily the most fiendish character I have ever encountered in any walk of life.

The room just described must be dignified with that imposing title, library, on account of the presence in it of that butternut bookcase and its indigent contents. It does duty, now, as a private parlor for Mrs. Clemens during those brief and widely separated occasions when she is permitted to leave for an hour the bed to which she has been so long condemned. We are in the extreme south end of the house, if there is any such thing as a south end to a house, where orientation cannot be determined by me, because I am incompetent in all cases where an object does not point directly north or south. This one slants across between, and is therefore a confusion to me. This little private parlor is in one of the two corners of what I call the south end of the house. The sun rises in such a way that all the morning it is pouring its light in through the thirty-three glass doors or windows which pierce the side of the house which looks upon the terrace and garden, as already described; the rest of the day the light floods this south end of the house, as I call it; at noon the sun is directly above Florence yonder in the distance in the plain—directly above those architectural features which have been so familiar to the world in pictures for some centuries: the Duomo, the Campanile, the Tomb of the Medici and the beautiful tower of the Palazzo Vecchio; above Florence, but not very high above it, for it never climbs quite half way to the zenith in these winter days; in this position it begins to reveal the secrets of the delicious blue mountains that circle around into the west, for its light discovers, uncovers, and exposes a white snow-storm of villas and cities that you cannot train yourself to have confidence in, they appear and disappear so mysteriously and so as if they might be not villas and cities at all but the ghosts of perished ones of the remote and dim Etruscan times; and late in the afternoon the sun sinks down behind those mountains somewhere, at no particular time and at no particular place, so far as I can see.

This "library," or boudoir, or private parlor opens into Mrs. Clemens's bedroom, and it and the bedroom together stretch all the way across the south end of the house. The bedroom gets the sun before noon, and is prodigally drenched and deluged with it the rest of the day. One of its windows is particularly well calculated to let in a liberal supply of sunshine, for it contains twelve great panes, each of them more than two feet square. The bedroom is thirty-one feet long by twenty-four wide, and there has been a time when it and the "library" had no partition between, but occupied the whole breadth of the south end of the house in an unbroken stretch. It must have been a ball-room or banqueting room at that time. I suggest this merely because perhaps not even Cosimo would need so much bedroom, whereas it would do very well indeed as a banqueting room because of its proximity to the cooking arrangements, which were not more than two or three hundred yards away, down cellar, a very eligible condition of things indeed in the old times. Monarchs cannot have the conveniences which we plebeians are privileged to luxuriate in—they can't, even to-day. If I were invited to spend a week in Windsor Castle it would gladden me and make me feel proud; but if there was any hint about regular boarders I should let on that I didn't hear. As a palace Windsor Castle is great; great for show, spaciousness, display, grandeur, and all that; but the bedrooms are small, uninviting and inconvenient, and the arrangements for delivering food from the kitchen to the table are so clumsy, and waste so much time that a meal there probably suggests recent cold storage. This is only conjecture; I did not eat there. In Windsor Castle the courses are brought up by dumb waiter from the profound depth where the vast kitchen is, they are then transferred by rail on a narrow little tramway to the territory where the dinner is to have place. This trolley was still being worked by hand when I was there four years ago; still it was without doubt a great advance upon Windsor Castle transportation of any age before Queen Victoria's. It is startling to reflect that what we call conveniences in a dwelling-house, and which we regard as necessities, were born so recently that hardly one of them existed in the world when Queen Victoria was born. The valuable part—to *my* thinking the valuable part—of what we call civilization had no existence when she emerged upon the planet. She sat in her chair in that venerable fortress and saw it grow from its mustard seed to the stupendous tree which it had become before she died. She saw the whole of the new creation, she saw everything that was made, and without her witness was not anything made that was made. A very creditable creation indeed, taking all things into account; since man, quite unassisted, did it all out of his own head. I jump to this conclusion because I think that if Providence had been minded to help him, it would have occurred to Providence to do this some hundred thousand centuries earlier. We are accustomed to seeing the hand of Providence in everything. Accustomed because if we missed it, or thought we missed it, we had discretion enough not to let on. We are a tactful race. We have been prompt to give Providence the credit of this fine and showy new civilization and we have been quite intemperate in our praises of this great benefaction; we have not been able to keep still over this splendid five-minute attention, we can only keep still about the ages of neglect which preceded it and which it makes so conspicuous. When Providence washes one of his worms into the sea in a tempest, then starves him and freezes him on a plank for thirty-four days, and finally wrecks him again on an uninhabited island, where he lives on shrimps and grasshoppers and other shell-fish for three months, and is at last rescued by some old whisky-soaked profane and blasphemous infidel of a tramp captain, and carried home gratis to his friends, the worm forgets that it was Providence that washed him overboard, and only remembers that Providence rescued him. He finds no fault, he has no sarcasms for Providence's crude and slow and labored ingenuities of invention in the matter of life-saving, he sees nothing in these delays and ineffectivenesses but food for admiration, to him they seem a marvel, a miracle; and the longer they take and the more ineffective they are, the greater the miracle; meantime he never allows himself to break out in any good hearty unhandicapped thanks for the tough old shipmaster who really saved him, he damns him with faint praise as "the instrument," his rescuer "under Providence."

To get to that corner room with its bookcase freighted with twenty dollars' worth of ancient Blackwood and modern spiritualistic literature, I have passed through—undescribed—a room that is my bedroom. Its size is good, its shape is good—thirty feet by twenty-two. Originally it was fifty feet long, stretching from one side of the house to the other, in the true Italian fashion which makes everybody's bedroom a passageway into the next room—Kings, nobles, serfs and all; but this American Countess, the present owner, cut off twenty feet of the room and reattached ten feet of it to the room as a bath-room, and devoted the rest to a hallway. This bedroom is lighted by one of those tall glass doors, already described, which gives upon the terrace. It is divided across the middle by some polished white pillars as big as my body, with Doric capitals, supporting a small arch at each end and a long one in the middle; this is indeed grandeur, and is quite imposing. The fireplace is of a good size, is of white marble, and the carvings upon it are of the dainty and graceful sort proper to its age, which is probably four hundred years. The fireplace and the stately columns are aristocratic, they recognize their kinship, and they smile at each other. That is, when they are not swearing at the rest of the room's belongings. The front half of the room is aglare with a paper loud of pattern, atrocious in color, and cheap beyond the dreams of avarice. The rear half is painted from floor to ceiling a dull, dead and repulsive yellow. It seems strange that yellow should be the favorite in Europe whereby to undecorate a wall; I have never seen the yellow wall which did not depress me and make me unhappy. The floor of the room is covered with a superannuated nightmare of a carpet whose figures are vast and riotous, and whose indignant reds and blacks and yellows quarrel day and night and refuse to be reconciled. There is a door opening into the bath-room, and at that same end of the room is a door opening into a small box of a hall which leads to another convenience. Those two doors strictly follow the law of European dwellings, whether built for the prince or for the pauper. That is to say they are rude, thin, cheap planks, flimsy; the sort of door which in the South the negro attaches to his chicken coop. These doors, like all such doors on the Continent, have a gimlet handle in place of a door-knob. It wrenches from the socket a bolt which has no springs and which will not return to that socket except upon compulsion. You can't slam a door like that, it would simply rebound. That gimlet handle catches on any garment that tries to get by; if tearable it tears it; if not tearable it stops the wearer with a suddenness and a violence and an unexpectedness which breaks down all his religious reserves, no matter who he may be.

The bedroom has a door on each side of the front end, so that anybody may tramp through that wants to at any time of the day or night, this being the only way to get to the room beyond, where the precious library is bookcased. Furniture: a salmon-colored silk sofa, a salmon-colored silk chair, a pair of ordinary wooden chairs, and a stuffed chair whose upholstery is of a species unknown to me but devilish; in the corner, an ordinary thin-legged kitchen table; against one wall a wardrobe and a dressing bureau; on the opposite side a rickety chest of drawers made of white pine painted black, and ornamented with imitation brass handles; brass double bedstead. One will concede that this room is not over-embarrassed with furniture. The two clapboard doors already spoken of are mercifully concealed by parti-colored hangings of unknown country and origin; the three other doors already mentioned are hooded with long curtains that descend to the floor and are caught apart in the middle to permit the passage of people and light. These curtains have a proud and ostentatious look which deceives no one, it being based upon a hybrid silk with cotton for its chief ingredient. The color is a solid yellow, and deeper than the yellow of the rearward half of the walls; and now here is a curious thing: one may look from one of these colors to the other fifty times and each time he will think that the one he is looking at is the ugliest. It is a most curious and interesting effect. I think that if one could get himself toned down to where he could look upon these curtains without passion he would then perceive that it takes both of them together to be the ugliest color known to art.

We have considered these two yellows, but they do not exhaust the matter, there is still another one in the room. This is a lofty and sumptuous canopy over the brass bedstead, and is made of brilliant and shiny and shouting lemon-colored satin—genuine satin, almost the only genuine thing in the whole room. It is of the nobility, it is of the aristocracy, it belongs with the majestic white pillars and the dainty old marble fireplace; all the rest of the room's belongings are profoundly plebeian, they are exiles, they are sorrowful outcasts from their rightful home, which is the poor house.

On the wall of the front end, in large frames, hang photographs of the pair who are responsible for the Countess's presence in this world. It would be in better taste if they looked less gratified about it. On the end wall of the yellow half of the room hang a couple of framed engravings, female angels engaged in their customary traffic of transporting departed persons to heaven over a distant prospect of city and plain and mountain.

The discords of this room, in colors, in humble poverty and showy and self-complacent pretentiousness, are repeated everywhere one goes in the huge house.

I am weary of particulars. One may travel two hundred feet down either side of the house, through an aimless jumble of useless little reception rooms and showy corridors, finding nothing sane or homelike till he reaches the dining room at the end.

On the next floor, over the Blackwood library, there is a good bedroom well furnished, and with a fine stone balcony and the majestic view, just mentioned, enlarged and improved. Thence northward two hundred feet cut up in much the same disarray as is that ground floor. But in the midst is a great drawing-room about forty feet square and perhaps as many high, handsomely and tastefully hung with brocaded silk, and with a very beautifully frescoed ceiling. But the place has a most angry look; for, scattered all about it are divans and sofas and chairs and lofty window-hangings of that same fierce lemon-colored satin heretofore noted as forming the canopy of the brass bedstead down stairs. When one steps suddenly into that great place on a splendid Florentine day it is like entering hell on a Sunday morning when the brightest and yellowest brimstone fires are going.

I think I have said that the top floor has twenty rooms. They are not furnished, they are spacious, and from all of them one has a wide and charming view. Properly furnished they would be pleasant, homelike, and in every way satisfactory.

End of March. Now that we have lived in this house four and one-half months my prejudices have fallen away one by one, and the place has become very homelike to me. Under certain conditions I should like to go on living in it indefinitely. Indeed I could reduce the conditions to two and be quite satisfied. I should want that stable over which the Countess lives, since it is not pleasant to have the horses stabled under Mrs. Clemens's bed-chamber. Also I should wish the Countess to move out of Italy; out of Europe; out of the planet. I should want her bonded to retire to her place in the next world and inform me which of the two it was, so that I could arrange for my own hereafter.

The friends who secured this house for me while I was still in America were as well acquainted with the Countess's pestiferous character as was gossipy Florence, but they allowed her to beguile them into the belief that she was going to Paris to live as soon as her expensive house was off her hands. It was a mistake. She never meant to go. She could not endure life without the daily and hourly society of her handsome chief manservant, and she was not rich enough to take him along.

There being nothing in the lease requiring the Countess to go to Paris or to some other heaven suited to her style, I soon realized that there was no way of abolishing her; and so after two and a half months of her odorous presence in the neighborhood, her stable dwelling being within the grounds of the estate, I gave it up and have been house hunting ever since. House hunting in any country is difficult and depressing, in the regions skirting Florence it leads to despair, and if persisted in will end in suicide. Professor Willard Fiske, the scholar, who bought the Walter Savage Landor villa fourteen or fifteen years ago, tells me that he examined three hundred villas before he found one that would suit him; yet he was a widower without child or dependent, and merely needed a villa for his lone self. I was in it twelve years ago and it seemed to me that he had not bought a villa but only a privilege—the privilege of building it over again and making it humanly habitable. During the first three weeks of February I climbed around, over and prowled through an average of six large villas a week but found none that would answer, in the circumstances. One of the circumstances and the most important of all being that we are in Italy by the command of physicians in the hope that in this mild climate Mrs. Clemens will get her health back. She suddenly lost it nineteen months ago, being smitten helpless by nervous prostration complicated with an affection of the heart of several years' standing, and the times since this collapse that she has been able to stand on her feet five minutes at a time have been exceedingly rare. I have examined two villas that were about as large as this one, but the interior architecture was so ill contrived that there was not comfortable room in them for my family of four persons. As a rule the bed-chambers served as common hallways, which means that for centuries Tom, Dick and Harry of both sexes and all ages have moved in procession to and fro through those ostensibly private rooms.

Every villa I examined had a number of the details which I was ordered to find, four possessed almost every one of them. In the case of the four the altitudes were not satisfactory to the doctors; two of them were too high, the other pair too low. These fifteen or twenty villas were all furnished. The reader of these notes will find that word in the dictionary, and it will be defined there; but that definition can have no value to a person who is desiring to know what the word means over here when it is attached to an advertisement proposing to let a dwelling-house. Here it means a meagre and scattering array of cheap and rickety chairs, tables, sofas etc., upholstered in worn and damaged fragments of sombre and melancholy hue that suggest the grave and compel the desire to retire to it. The average villa is properly a hospital for ailing and superannuated furniture. In its best days this furniture was never good nor comely nor attractive nor comfortable. When that best day was, was too long ago for any one to be able to date it now.

Each time that I have returned from one of these quests I have been obliged to concede that the insurrection of color in this Villa di Quarto is a rest to the eye after what I had been sighing and sorrowing over in those others, and that this is the only villa in the market so far as I know that has furniture enough in it for the needs of the occupants.

Also I will concede that I was wrong in thinking this villa poverty-stricken in the matter of conveniences; for by contrast with those others this house is rich in conveniences.

Some time ago a lady told me that she had just returned from a visit to the country palace of a Princess, a huge building standing in the midst of a great and beautiful and carefully kept flower garden, the garden in its turn being situated in a great and beautiful private park. She was received by a splendid apparition of the footman species who ushered her into a lofty and spacious hall richly garnished with statuary, pictures and other ornaments, fine and costly, and thence down an immensely long corridor which shone with a similar garniture, superb and showy to the last degree; and at the end of this enchanting journey she was delivered into the Princess's bed-chamber and received by the Princess, who was ailing slightly, and in bed. The room was very small, it was without bric-à-brac or prettinesses for the comfort of the eye and spirit, the bedstead was iron, there were two wooden chairs and a small table, and in the corner stood an iron tripod which supported a common white wash-bowl. The costly glories of the house were all for show, no money had been wasted on its mistress's comfort. I had my doubts about this story when I first acquired it, I am more credulous now.

A word or two more concerning the furnishings of the Villa di Quarto. The rooms contain an average of four pictures each, say two photographs or engravings and two oil or water-color paintings of chromo degree. A number of these paintings are from the Countess's hand, and several of them exhibit talent of a moderate sort. One of her works is a portrait, apparently from a photograph, of the Philadelphia man whose intimacies with her enabled her first husband to relieve himself of her society by divorce. This divorced lady was flourishing under her maiden name of Paxton when she was married to the Count in Philadelphia. In America she is a married woman, in Italy she is not.

She has studied art. Twenty-five or thirty drawings upholster the walls of a north room of this house—which must have been her studio. These nude men and women are of the detailed and uncompromising nakedness which is the special product of class instruction in the art schools. If I read the Countess aright, it cost her a pang not to hang them in the drawing-room.

High up on the walls of the great entrance hall hang several of those little shiny white cherubs which one associates with the name of Della Robbia. The walls of this hall are further decorated, or at least relieved, by the usual great frameless oval oil portraits of long-departed aristocrats which one customarily finds thus displayed in all Florentine villas. In the present case the portraits were painted by artists of chromo rank, with the exception of one. As I have had no teaching in art I cannot decide what is a good picture and what isn't, according to the established standards; I am obliged to depend on my own crude standards. According to these the picture which I am now considering sets forth a most noble, grave, and beautiful face, faultless in all details, and with beautiful and faultless hands; and if it belonged to me I would never take a lesson in art lest the picture lose for me its finished, complete, and satisfying perfection.

The Countess is two or three years past forty, and by the generous supply of portraits and photographs of her distributed over the house one perceives that she has once been comely and at intervals pretty. She now paints her face and dyes her hair, and in other ways tries to preserve the tradition of those lost days; but she carries that within her which defeats the dearest efforts of art and spoils their attempts to keep her exterior aspects in satisfactory shape. That interior something is her spirit, her disposition. She is excitable, malicious, malignant, vengeful, unforgiving, selfish, stingy, avaricious, coarse, vulgar, profane, obscene, a furious blusterer on the outside and at heart a coward. Her lips are as familiar with lies, deceptions, swindles and treacheries as are her nostrils with breath. She has not a single friend in Florence, she is not received in any house. I think she is the best hated person I have ever known, and the most liberally despised. She is an oppressor by nature, and a taker of mean advantages. She is hated by every peasant and every person on the estate and in the neighborhood of it, with the single exception of her paramour, the steward. She told me that when she bought the estate the first thing she did was to drive from it every peasant family but one. She did not make this as a confession, the whole tone of it was that of a boast, and nowhere in it was there any accent of pity. She knew that those people and their fathers had held those small homes for generations, and had by authority of the kindly customs of the country regarded them as being secure to them so long as their conduct should remain good. She knew that to turn them out upon the world was to them a terrible calamity; that it was almost the equivalent to sweeping Islanders into the sea. She knew that these people were bound to their homes by their heart-strings. One of the peasants whom she evicted lived six weeks and died with nothing the matter with him. That is, nothing the matter with him that a physician's drugs could reach, nothing that is named in the medical man's books, nothing for which his science has provided either diagnosis or remedy. The man's friends had no doubts as to the nature of his malady. They said his heart was where anybody's heart would be—in his home; and that when that was taken from him his heart went with it, and thereby his life was spoiled, and no longer livable with profit. The Countess boasted to me that nothing American is still left in her, and that she is wholly Italian now. She plainly regarded this as a humiliation for America, and she as plainly believed she was gracing Italy with a compliment of a high and precious order. America still stands. Italy may survive the benefaction of the Countess's approval, we cannot tell.

There is something pathetically comical about this forlorn exile's dream and its failure. She imagined that a title was all that was needed to frank her into the heaven of the privileged orders of Europe, whereas she finds she is not even able to penetrate the outer fringe of it. She overlooked an all important detail—money. If she had had that her destitution of character would not have counted. Lacking that, her soiled name, her execrable nature, and her residence in a stable with her manservant and the other cattle, all count against her. She brought no money, and had none to bring. If she had a credit of ten millions at the bank not many doors would be closed against her; being lean of purse, none is open to her. She has assailed, she has furiously assailed ladies in the street for not returning her visits and for pretending to be out when she called. This is regarded as not good form. Hers is a curious situation. It is good to be a real noble, it is good to be a real American, it is a calamity to be neither the one thing nor the other, a politico-social bastard on both counts.

The trivial maliciousness that this soured outcast can invent! My agent here, a solicitor, paid twenty-five hundred francs—the rent of the first quarter—before we sailed from America, and this secured possession for the first day of November. On that date he tried to put our servants in the house, and the Countess drove him and them away, and he stood it like a little man! She said no one would be allowed to enter until the inventory had been made out and signed. She put that detail off a week, and this gave her an opportunity to rob the house. She removed from it all the furniture she could stow and use in her apartment of twelve rooms over the stable and cattle stalls. We arrived on the 7th, stayed in town two days, to rest my invalid wife from the racking railway journey from Genoa; the Countess's head servant and the solicitor reported the house in good order, and we made the long drive on the 9th and entered into occupation, to find that no fires had been lighted in the furnaces or elsewhere and that the place was in condition for no office but the preservation of products requiring cold storage.

Jean and our old Katy had preceded us by half an hour to make sure that everything was in right shape. They found the Countess on hand and lording it over the house which had been taken and paid for; no bed had been prepared for the invalid, the Countess refused to give up the keys to the bedding closets, and said she would not allow a bed to be made for any one until the inventory should have been gone over and signed. She wouldn't tell where in the vast building our trunks were concealed; otherwise bedding could have been taken from these. When we arrived we soon found out where our trunks were and we set the servants to work to prepare a bed. We selected for Mrs. Clemens the sacred room with the silken tapestry; the Countess forbade the presence in that room of any sick person and appealed to the lease and to my lawyer, who was present, in support of this prohibition. She was correct in her position. The lease showed that this reptile with the filthy soul had protected her house and her body against physical contamination by inserting in the lease a clause prohibiting the lessee from introducing into that particular bedroom any person suffering from an illness of any kind whether contagious or otherwise, and whether the illness might be "large or small" to use the words of the translation of the lease; and to these rigors she had added a clause breaking the lease in case I should bring a contagious disease into the house. All these sillinesses my salaried ass had conceded.

During the fifteen months that Mrs. Clemens had been a helpless invalid she had constantly received the gentle courtesies and kindly attentions which human beings of whatsoever rank or nationality always and everywhere accord to helplessness. This American Countess was the first of the race to deny these graces and to inflict physical pain and damage instead.

Considering the known character of the woman the lease was not a curiosity, for it left many loopholes for the gratification of her whims and caprices and malices, but left no holes for our escape or defence. Her rights were set forth in detail in writing, in every instance, whereas some of our most important ones had no protection other than her oral promises. These promises were ignored and repudiated from the start, and quite frankly. By oral promise we could occupy as much of the stable as we pleased, but the written lease confined us to the stable under Mrs. Clemens's room. By oral agreement she was to leave the estate as soon as we moved in—a most important detail, and by all means should have been in writing, for no one acquainted with the Countess would endure the stench of her presence within a mile of his dwelling if it could be helped. By oral promise we were to have command of the reservoir which furnished water to the house—which was another exceedingly important detail; but as it was not in writing she was able to keep that command herself and she continues to keep it, and now and then to use it against our convenience and our health. The lease gave us not a single privilege outside the building except exit and entrance through the grounds; we were not consulted as to what hours the great gates should be open, it pleased her to close them for the night at six o'clock wherefore we were not only prisoners from that time until the next morning, but we were disastrously unaware of it because she gave us no notice. I say disastrously for the reason that upon one occasion our expensive Florentine specialist, Professor Grocco, with his assistant physician arrived at the outer gate four hundred yards from the villa at six o'clock in the evening and found the gate locked. There being no bell there was no way to give us notice. The assistant, Dr. Nesti, went scouting and found a gate open which led into the podere; through this they drove unimpeded to the villa. The pretext for closing the great gates out at the main road and those contiguous to our house was to protect the podere from thieves, whereas that podere gate was often left open all night.

The Countess invented various other ways to inconvenience us, and I supposed that the motive was merely and solely malice, but it turns out that that was not the whole of it. She was trying to force us to throw pecuniary advantages in the way of her temporary husband, her chief manservant. She had expected that we would buy all supplies through him and thus extend to him the same opportunities to rob us which he was enjoying in robbing her. She was curiously communicative in this matter. She told me I had made a mistake in not buying the winter's fuel through that man; and in not buying the winter supply of wine and oil through him; and in not furnishing a cart and horse to our cook wherewith to drive into Florence daily for the perishable foods for the table; and in not getting *him* to have our washing done for us; and in not making it worth his while to be friendly with us as regards the water; since he could shut it off whenever he pleased, and could also waste it and make it necessary for us to buy water outside and have it hauled to us—a thing which he did once for a week or two.

The lease forbade me to add an improvement or a convenience anywhere about the house without first getting her consent in writing. Our physicians were three or four miles away in Florence; several times Mrs. Clemens had desperate need of them, and each time it cost us more than an hour and a half of precious time to send in and get them. A telephone was necessary, and I asked the Countess to allow me to put one in. She said I might, but that she must be sent for when the telephone people should arrive to put in the instrument, so that she might determine for herself whereabouts in the house she would allow it to be located. It did not occur to me to ask her to put the permission in writing, for I was not yet able to realize that I was not dealing with a human being but with a reptile. Through Mr. Cecchi, the manager of the bank, the contract was at once made with the Telephone Company; there were twenty-seven orders ahead of me, but by courtesy of the Company and in consideration of the desperate need I had of the telephone, I was placed at the head of the list; my instrument was promptly put in, and in the last days of January it began its work in perfect order. It maintained this perfect order an hour and then died. During a whole month thereafter Mr. Cecchi did his best to find out what the trouble was. The Company furnished all sorts of excuses except rational ones, and still the telephone remained dumb. Close upon the end of January I heard from a trustworthy source that the Countess had said to a friend of hers, the only one she has in Italy apparently, that if I had put the telephone matter into the hands of her paramour there would never have been any trouble about it. I went to town and Mr. Cecchi telephoned the Company and asked them to state once for all when they proposed to blow the breath of life into my telephone. They answered that the Countess was threatening them with a suit for eighteen francs damage which they had caused by erecting a telephone pole in her podere, the actual damage being, if anything, not above five francs. Also that they had just received an order from the Countess, accompanied by a threat from her lawyer, requiring them to take my telephone out on or before the fourth day of February at noon. I asked Mr. Cecchi to say to the Company that if I found myself unable to communicate with my house by telephone before sunset I should bring suit for twenty-five thousand francs damages for failure to fulfill their contract with me. Communication with my house was perfected within the hour, and has never since been interrupted. The Countess's excuse for forbidding a telephone whose special and particular office was to speedily call physicians to save a neighbor's threatened life, was that I had no permission from her in writing and had not notified her to come and say where the instrument might be placed. I was losing my belief in hell until I got acquainted with the Countess Massiglia.

We have lived in a Florentine villa before. This was twelve years ago. This was the Villa Viviani, and was pleasantly and commandingly situated on a hill in the suburb of Settignano, overlooking Florence and the great valley. It was secured for us and put in comfortable order by a good friend, Mrs. Ross, whose stately castle was a twelve minutes' walk away. She still lives there, and has been a help to us more than once since we got into the fangs of the titled animal who owns the Villa di Quarto. The year spent in the Villa Viviani was something of a contrast to the five months which we have now spent in this ducal barrack. Among my old manuscripts and random and spasmodic diaries I find some account of that pleasantly remembered year, and will make some extracts from the same and introduce them here.

When we were passing through Florence in the spring of '92 on our way to Germany, the diseased world's bath-house, we began negotiations for a villa, and friends of ours completed them after we were gone. When we got back three or four months later, everything was ready, even to the servants and the dinner. It takes but a sentence to state that, but it makes an indolent person tired to think of the planning and work and trouble that lie concealed in it. For it is less trouble and more satisfaction to bury two families than to select and equip a home for one.

The situation of the villa was perfect. It was three miles from Florence, on the side of a hill. The flowery terrace on which it stood looked down upon sloping olive groves and vineyards;

to the right, beyond some hill-spurs, was Fiesole, perched upon its steep terraces; in the immediate foreground was the imposing mass of the Ross castle, its walls and turrets rich with the mellow weather-stains of forgotten centuries; in the distant plain lay Florence, pink and gray and brown, with the rusty huge dome of the cathedral dominating its centre like a captive balloon, and flanked on the right by the smaller bulb of the Medici chapel and on the left by the airy tower of the Palazzo Vecchio; all around the horizon was a billowy rim of lofty blue hills, snowed white with innumerable villas. After nine months of familiarity with this panorama, I still think, as I thought in the beginning, that this is the fairest picture on our planet, the most enchanting to look upon, the most satisfying to the eye and the spirit. To see the sun sink down, drowned in his pink and purple and golden floods, and overwhelm Florence with tides of color that make all the sharp lines dim and faint and turn the solid city to a city of dreams, is a sight to stir the coldest nature and make a sympathetic one drunk with ecstasy.

Sept. 26. '92. Arrived in Florence. Got my head shaved. This was a mistake. Moved to the villa in the afternoon. Some of the trunks brought up in the evening by the contadino—if that is his title. He is the man who lives on the farm and takes care of it for the owner, the Marquis. The contadino is middle-aged and like the rest of the peasants—that is to say, brown, handsome, good-natured, courteous, and entirely independent without making any offensive show of it. He charged too much for the trunks, I was told. My informant explained that this was customary.

Sept. 27. The rest of the trunks brought up this morning. He charged too much again, but I was told that this also was customary. It is all right, then. I do not wish to violate the customs. Hired landau, horses and coachman. Terms, four hundred and eighty francs a month and a pourboire to the coachman, I to furnish lodging for the man and the horses, but nothing else. The landau has seen better days and weighs thirty tons. The horses are feeble, and object to the landau; they stop and turn around every now and then and examine it with surprise and suspicion. This causes delay. But it entertains the people along the road. They came out and stood around with their hands in their pockets and discussed the matter with each other. I was told they said that a forty-ton landau was not the thing for horses like those—what they needed was a wheelbarrow.

I will insert in this place some notes made in October concerning the villa:

This is a two-story house. It is not an old house—from an Italian standpoint, I mean. No doubt there has always been a nice dwelling on this eligible spot since a thousand years B.C.; but this present one is said to be only two hundred years old. Outside, it is a plain square building like a box, and is painted a light yellow and has green window-shutters. It stands in a commanding position on an artificial terrace of liberal dimensions which is walled around with strong masonry. From the walls the vineyards and olive orchards of the estate slant away toward the valley; the garden about the house is stocked with flowers and a convention of lemon bushes in great crockery tubs; there are several tall trees—stately stone pines—also fig trees and trees of breeds not familiar to me; roses overflow the retaining-walls and the battered and mossy stone urns on the gate-posts in pink and yellow cataracts, exactly as they do on the drop-curtains of theatres; there are gravel walks shut in by tall laurel hedges. A back corner of the terrace is occupied by a dense grove of old ilex trees. There is a stone table in there, with stone benches around it. No shaft of sunlight can penetrate that grove. It is always deep twilight in there, even when all outside is flooded with the intense sun-glare common to this region. The carriage road leads from the inner gate eight hundred feet to the public road, through the vineyard, and there one may take the horse-car for the city, and will find it a swifter and handier convenience than a sixty-ton landau. On the east (or maybe it is the south) front of the house is the Viviani coat of arms in plaster, and near it a sun dial which keeps very good time.

The house is a very fortress for strength. The main walls—of brick covered with plaster—are about three feet thick; the partitions of the rooms, also of brick, are nearly the same thickness. The ceilings of the rooms on the ground floor are more than twenty feet high, those of the upper floors are also higher than necessary. I have several times tried to count the rooms in the house, but the irregularities baffle me. There seem to be twenty-eight.

The ceilings are frescoed, the walls are papered. All the floors are of red brick covered with a coating of polished and shining cement which is as hard as stone and looks like it; for the surfaces have been painted in patterns, first in solid colors and then snowed over with varicolored freckles of paint to imitate granite and other stones. Sometimes the body of the floor is an imitation of gray granite with a huge star or other ornamental pattern of imitation fancy marbles in the centre; with a two-foot band of imitation red granite all around the room whose outer edge is bordered with a six-inch stripe of imitation lapis-lazuli; sometimes the body of the floor is red granite, then the gray is used as a bordering stripe. There are plenty of windows, and worlds of sun and light; these floors are slick and shiny and full of reflections, for each is a mirror in its way, softly imaging all objects after the subdued fashion of forest lakes.

There is a tiny family chapel on the main floor, with benches for ten or twelve persons, and over the little altar is an ancient oil painting which seems to me to be as beautiful and as rich in tone as any of those Old-Master performances down yonder in the galleries of the Pitti and the Uffizi. Botticelli, for instance; I wish I had time to make a few remarks about Botticelli—whose real name was probably Smith.

The curious feature of the house is the salon. This is a spacious and lofty vacuum which occupies the centre of the house; all the rest of the house is built around it; it extends up through both stories and its roof projects some feet above the rest of the building. That vacuum is very impressive. The sense of its vastness strikes you the moment you step into it and cast your eyes around it and aloft. I tried many names for it: the Skating Rink, the Mammoth Cave, the Great Sahara, and so on, but none exactly answered. There are five divans distributed along its walls; they make little or no show, though their aggregate length is fifty-seven feet. A piano in it is a lost object. We have tried to reduce the sense of desert space and emptiness with tables and things, but they have a defeated look and do not do any good. Whatever stands or moves under that soaring painted vault is belittled.

Over the six doors are huge plaster medallions which are supported by great naked and handsome plaster boys, and in these medallions are plaster portraits in high relief of some grave and beautiful men in stately official costumes of a long past day—Florentine senators and judges, ancient dwellers here and owners of this estate. The date of one of them is 1305—middle-aged, then, and a judge—he could have known, as a youth, the very creators of Italian art, and he could have walked and talked with Dante, and probably did. The date of another is 1343—he could have known Boccaccio and spent his afternoons yonder in Fiesole gazing down on plague-reeking Florence and listening to that man's improper tales, and he probably did. The date of another is 1463—he could have met Columbus, and he knew the Magnificent Lorenzo, of course. These are all Cerretanis—or Cerretani-Twains, as I may say, for I have adopted myself into their family on account of its antiquity, my origin having been heretofore too recent to suit me.

But I am forgetting to state what it is about that Rink that is so curious—which is, that it is not really vast, but only seems so. It is an odd deception, and unaccountable; but a deception it is. Measured by the eye it is sixty feet square and sixty high; but I have been applying the tape-line, and find it to be but forty feet square and forty high. These are the correct figures; and what is interestingly strange is, that the place continues to look as big now as it did before I measured it.

This is a good house, but it cost very little, and is simplicity itself, and pretty primitive in most of its features. The water is pumped to the ground floor from a well by hand labor, and then carried up stairs by hand. There is no drainage; the cesspools are right under the windows. This is the case with everybody's villa.

The doors in this house are like the doors of the majority of the houses and hotels of Italy—plain, thin, unpaneled boards painted white. This makes the flimsiest and most unattractive door known to history. The knob is not a knob, but a thing like the handle of a gimlet—you can get hold of it only with your thumb and forefinger. Still, even that is less foolish than our American door-knob, which is always getting loose and turning futilely round and round in your hand, accomplishing nothing.

The windows are all of the rational continental breed; they open apart, like doors; and when they are bolted for the night they don't rattle, and a person can go to sleep.

There are cunning little fireplaces in the bedrooms and sitting-rooms, and lately a big aggressive looking German stove has been set up on the south frontier of the Great Sahara.

The stairs are made of granite blocks, the hallways of the second floor are of red brick. It is a safe house. Earthquakes cannot shake it down, fire cannot burn it. There is absolutely nothing burnable but the furniture, the curtains and the doors. There is not much furniture, it is merely summer furniture—or summer bareness, if you like. When a candle set fire to the curtains in a room over my head the other night where samples of the family slept, I was wakened out of my sleep by shouts and screams, and was greatly terrified until an answer from the window told me what the matter was: that the window curtains and hangings were on fire. In America I should have been more frightened than ever, then, but this was not the case here. I advised the samples to let the fire alone, and go to bed; which they did, and by the time they got to sleep there was nothing of the attacked fabrics left. We boast a good deal in America of our fire departments, the most efficient and wonderful in the world, but they have something better than that to boast of in Europe—a rational system of building which makes human life safe from fire and renders fire departments needless. We boast of a thing which we ought to be ashamed to require.

This villa has a roomy look, a spacious look; and when the sunshine is pouring in and lighting up the bright colors of the shiny floors and walls and ceilings there is a large and friendly suggestion of welcome about the aspects, but I do not know that I have ever seen a continental dwelling which quite met the American standard of a home in all the details. There is a trick about an American house that is like the deep-lying untranslatable idioms of a foreign language—a trick uncatchable by the stranger, a trick incommunicable and undescribable; and that elusive trick, that intangible something, whatever it is, is just the something that gives the home look and the home feeling to an American house and makes it the most satisfying refuge yet invented by men—and women, mainly women. The American house is opulent in soft and varied colors that please and rest the eye, and in surfaces that are smooth and pleasant to the touch, in forms that are shapely and graceful, in objects without number which compel interest and cover nakedness; and the night has even a higher charm than the day, there, for the artificial lights do really give light instead of merely trying and failing; and under their veiled and tinted glow all the snug cosiness and comfort and charm of the place is at its best and loveliest. But when night shuts down on the continental home there is no gas or electricity to fight it, but only dreary lamps of exaggerated ugliness and of incomparable poverty in the matter of effectiveness.

Sept. 29. '92. I seem able to forget everything except that I have had my head shaved. No matter how closely I shut myself away from drafts it seems to be always breezy up there. But the main difficulty is the flies. They like it up there better than anywhere else; on account of the view, I suppose. It seems to me that I have never seen any flies before that were shod like these. These appear to have talons. Wherever they put their foot down they grab. They walk over my head all the time, and cause me infinite torture. It is their park, their club, their summer resort. They have garden parties there, and conventions, and all sorts of dissipation. And they fear nothing. All flies are daring, but these are more daring than those of other nationalities. These cannot be scared away by any device. They are more diligent, too, than the other kinds: they come before daylight and stay till after dark. But there are compensations. The mosquitoes are not a trouble. There are very few of them, they are not noisy, and not much interested in their calling. A single unkind word will send them away, if said in English, which impresses them because they do not understand it, then they come no more that night. We often see them weep when they are spoken to harshly. I have got some of the eggs to take home. If this breed can be raised in our climate they will be a great advantage. There seem to be no fleas here. This is the first time we have struck this kind of an interregnum in fifteen months. Everywhere else the supply exceeds the demand.

Oct. 1. Finding that the coachman was taking his meals in the kitchen, I reorganized the contract to include his board, at thirty francs a month. That is what it would cost him up above us in the village, and I think I can feed him for two hundred and save thirty out of it. Saving thirty is better than not saving anything.

That passage from the diary reminds me that I did an injudicious thing along about that time which bore fruit later. As I was to give the coachman, Vittorio, a monthly pourboire, of course I wanted to know the amount. So I asked the coachman's *padrone* (master), instead of asking somebody else—anybody else. He said thirty francs a month would be about right. I was afterwards informed that this was an overcharge, but that it was customary, there being no customary charges except overcharges. However, at the end of that month the coachman demanded an extra pourboire of fifteen francs. When I asked why, he said his padrone had taken his other pourboire away from him. The padrone denied this in Vittorio's presence, and Vittorio seemed to retract. The padrone *said* he did, and he certainly had that aspect, but I had to take the padrone's word for it as interpreter of the coachman's Italian. When the padrone was gone the coachman resumed the charge, and as we liked him—and also believed him—we made his aggregate pourboire forty-five francs a month after that, and never doubted that the padrone took two-thirds of it. We were told by citizens that it was customary for the padrone to seize a considerable share of his dependents' pourboire, and also the custom for the padrone to deny it. That padrone is an accommodating man, and a most capable and agreeable talker, speaking English like an archangel, and making it next to impossible for a body to be dissatisfied with him; yet his seventy-ton landau has kept us supplied with lame horses for nine months, whereas we were entitled to a light carriage suited to hill-climbing, and fastidious people would have made him furnish it.

The Cerretani family, of old and high distinction in the great days of the Republic, lived on this place during many centuries. Along in October we began to notice a pungent and suspicious odor which we were not acquainted with and which gave us some little apprehension, but I laid it on the dog, and explained to the family that that kind of a dog always smelt that way when he was up to windward of the subject, but privately I knew it was not the dog at all. I believed it was our adopted ancestors, the Cerretanis. I believed they were preserved under the house somewhere, and that it would be a good scheme to get them out and air them. But I was mistaken. I made a secret search and had to acquit the ancestors. It turned out that the odor was a harmless one. It came from the wine-crop, which was stored in a part of the cellars to which we had no access. This discovery gave our imaginations a rest; and it turned a disagreeable smell into a pleasant one. But not until we had so long and so lavishly flooded the house with odious disinfectants that the dog left and the family had to camp in the yard most of the time. It took two months to disinfect the disinfectants and persuade our wealth of atrocious stenches to emigrate. When they were finally all gone and the wine-fragrance resumed business at the old stand, we welcomed it with effusion and have had no fault to find with it since.

Oct. 6. I find myself at a disadvantage here. Four persons in the house speak Italian and nothing else, one person speaks German and nothing else, the rest of the talk is in the French, English and profane languages. I am equipped with but the merest smattering in these tongues, if I except one or two. Angelo speaks French—a French which he could get a patent on, because he invented it himself; a French which no one can understand, a French which resembles no other confusion of sounds heard since Babel, a French which curdles the milk. He prefers it to his native Italian. He loves to talk it; loves to listen to himself; to him it is music; he will not let it alone. The family would like to get their little Italian savings into circulation, but he will not give change. It makes no difference what language he is addressed in, his reply is in French—his peculiar French, his grating uncanny French, which sounds like shoveling anthracite down a coal-chute. I know a few Italian words and several phrases, and along at first I used to keep them bright and fresh by whetting them on Angelo; but he partly couldn't understand them and partly didn't want to, so I have been obliged to withdraw them from the market for the present. But this is only temporary. I am practising, I am preparing. Some day I shall be ready for him, and not in ineffectual French, but in his native tongue. I will seethe this kid in its mother's milk.

Oct. 27. The first month is finished. We are wonted, now. It is agreed that life at a Florentine villa is an ideal existence. The weather is divine, the outside aspects lovely, the days and the nights tranquil and reposeful, the seclusion from the world and its worries as satisfactory as a dream. There is no housekeeping to do, no plans to make, no marketing to superintend—all these things do themselves, apparently. One is vaguely aware that somebody is attending to them, just as one is aware that the world is being turned over and the constellations worked and the sun shoved around according to the schedule, but that is all; one does not feel personally concerned, or in any way responsible. Yet there is no head, no chief executive; each servant minds his or her own department, requiring no supervision and having none. They hand in elaborately itemized bills once a week, then the machinery goes silently on again, just as before. There is no noise, or fussing, or quarreling or confusion—up stairs. I don't know what goes on below. Late in the afternoons friends come out from the city and drink tea in the open air, and tell what is happening in the world; and when the great sun sinks down upon Florence and the daily miracle begins, they hold their breath and look. It is not a time for talk.

Now comes the New York dictation, beginning January 9, 1906.

Note for the Instruction of Future Editors and Publishers of This Autobiography

I shall scatter through this Autobiography newspaper clippings without end. When I do not copy them into the text it means that I do not make them a part of the autobiography—at least not of the earlier editions. I put them in on the theory that if they are not interesting in the earlier editions, a time will come when it may be well enough to insert them for the reason that age is quite likely to make them interesting although in their youth they may lack that quality.

January 9, 1906

The more I think of this, the more nearly impossible the project seems. The difficulties of it grow upon me all the time. For instance, the idea of blocking out a consecutive series of events which have happened to me, or which I imagine have happened to me—I can see that that is impossible for me. The only thing possible for me is to talk about the thing that something suggests at the moment—something in the middle of my life, perhaps, or something that happened only a few months ago.

The only way is for me to write an autobiography—and then, in your case, if you are going to collect from that mass of incidents a brief biography, why you would have to read the thing through and select certain matter—arrange your notes and then write a biography. That biography would have to be measured by the mass of the autobiography. You would publish this during my life—that is your idea? (Meaning Mr. Paine's book.)

Mr. Paine said: The time of publication could be determined later.

Mr. Clemens. Yes, that is so, and what is your idea as to length?

Mr. Paine. The autobiography ought not to exceed 100,000 words? If it grew, and was very interesting, then it could run out to 120,000?

Mr. Clemens. I should make it in a general way 80,000 words, with 20,000 privilege.

It is my purpose to extend these autobiographical notes to 600,000 words, and possibly more. But that is going to take a long time—a long time.

Mr. Paine. These notes that we are making here will be of the greatest assistance to you in writing the autobiography.

Mr. Clemens. My idea is this: that I write an autobiography. When that autobiography is finished—or before it is finished, but no doubt after it is finished—then you take the manuscript and we can agree on how much of a *biography* to make, 80 or 100,000 words, and in that way we can manage it. But this is no holiday excursion—it is a journey. So my idea is that I do the autobiography, that I own the manuscript, and that I pay for it, and that finally, at the proper time, why then you begin to gather from this manuscript your biography.

Mr. Paine. You have a good deal of this early material in readiness. Suppose while you are doing this autobiography you place portions of that, from time to time, in my hands, so that I can begin to prepare my notes and material for the other book.

Mr. Clemens. That can be arranged. Supposing that we should talk here for one or two hours five days in the week—or several days in the week, as it should happen—how many thousand years is it going to take to put together as much as 600,000 words? Let us proceed on this idea, then, and start it, and see, after a few days, if it is going to work.

Now then, let us arrive at the cost of this—say it is to be so many thousand words. You charge in that way, don't you? (One dollar an hour for dictation, and five cents a hundred words for writing out notes.) We will try this—see whether it is dull or interesting, or whether it will bore us and we will want to commit suicide. I hate to get at it. I hate to begin, but I imagine that if you are here to make suggestions from time to time, we can make it go along, instead of having it drag.

January 9, 1906.

Now let me see, there was something I wanted to talk about—and I supposed it would stay in my head. I know what it is—about the big Bonanza in Nevada. I want to read from the commercial columns of the New York *Times,* of a day or two ago, what practically was the beginning of the great Bonanza in Nevada, and these details seem to me to be correct—that in Nevada, during 1871, John Mackay and Fair got control of the "Consolidated Virginia Mine" for $26,000; that in 1873, two years later, its 108,000 shares sold at $45 per share; and that it was at that time that Fair made the famous silver ore find of the great Bonanza. Also, according to these statistics, in November '74 the stock went to 115, and in the following month suddenly jumped up to 610, and in the next month—January '75—it reached 700. The shares of the companion mine, the "California," rose in four months from 37 to 780—a total property which in 1869 was valued on the Mining Exchange at $40,000, was quoted six years later at $160,000,000. I think those dates are correct. That great Bonanza occupies a rather prominent place in my mind for the reason that I knew persons connected with it. For instance, I knew John Mackay very well—that would be in 1862, '63 and '64, I should say. I don't remember what he was doing when I came to Virginia in 1862 from starving to death down in the so-called mines of Esmeralda, which consisted in that day merely of silver-bearing quartz— plenty of bearing, and didn't have much load to carry in the way of silver—and it was a happy thing for me when I was summoned to come up to Virginia City to be local editor of the Virginia City *Enterprise* during three months, while Mr. William H. Wright should go East, to Iowa, and visit his family whom he hadn't seen for some years. I took the position of local editor with joy, because there was a salary of forty dollars a week attached to it and I judged that that was all of thirty-nine dollars more than I was worth, and I had always wanted a position which paid in the opposite proportion of value to amount of work. I took that position with pleasure, not with confidence—but I had a difficult job. I was to furnish one column of leaded nonpareil every day, and as much more as I could get on paper before the paper should go to press at two o'clock in the morning. By and by, in the course of a few months I met John Mackay, with whom I had already been well acquainted for some time. He had established a broker's office on C street, in a new frame house, and it was rather sumptuous for that day and place, for it had part of a carpet on the floor and two chairs instead of a candle-box. I was envious of Mackay, who had not been in such very smooth circumstances as this before, and I offered to trade places with him—take his business and let him have mine—and he asked me how much mine was worth. I said forty dollars a week. He said "I never swindled anybody in my life, and I don't want to begin with you. This business of mine is not worth forty dollars a week. You stay where you are and I will try to get a living out of this."

I left Nevada in 1864 to avoid a term in the penitentiary (in another chapter I shall have to explain that) so that it was all of ten years, apparently, before John Mackay developed suddenly into the first of the hundred-millionaires. Apparently his prosperity began in '71—that discovery was made in '71. I know how it was made. I remember those details, for they came across the country to me in Hartford. There was a tunnel 1,700 feet long which struck in from 'way down on the slope of the mountain and passed under some portion of Virginia City, at a great depth. It was striking for a lode which it did not find, and I think the search had been long abandoned. Now in groping around in that abandoned tunnel Mr. Fair (afterwards U.S. Senator and multimillionaire,) came across a body of rich ore—so the story ran—and he came and reported his find to John Mackay. They examined this treasure and found that there was a very great deposit of it. They prospected it in the usual way and proved its magnitude, and that it was extremely rich. They thought it was a "chimney"—belonging probably to the "California," away up on the mountain-side, which had an abandoned shaft—or possibly the "Virginia" mine which was not worked then—nobody caring anything about the "Virginia," an empty mine. These men determined that this body of ore properly belonged to the "California" mine and by some trick of nature had been shaken down the mountain-side. They got O'Brien—who was a silver expert in San Francisco—to come in as capitalist, and they bought up a controlling interest in the abandoned claims, and no doubt got it at that figure—$26,000,—six years later to be worth $160,000,000.

As I say, I was not there. I had been here in the East, six, seven, or eight years—but friends of mine were interested. John P. Jones, who has lately resigned as U.S. Senator after an uninterrupted term of perhaps thirty years, was living in San Francisco. He had a great affection for a couple of old friends of mine—Joseph T. Goodman and Denis McCarthy. They had been proprietors of that paper that I served—the Virginia City *Enterprise*—and they had enjoyed great prosperity in that position. They were young journeymen printers, type-setting in San Francisco in 1858, and they went over the Sierras when they heard of the discovery of silver in that unknown region of Nevada, to push their fortunes. When they arrived at that miserable little camp, Virginia City, they had no money to push their fortunes with. They had only youth, energy, hope. They found Williams there, ("Stud" Williams was his society name,) who had started a weekly newspaper, and he had one journeyman, who set up the paper, and printed it on a hand press with Williams's help and the help of a Chinaman. They all slept in one room—cooked and slept and worked, and disseminated intelligence in this paper of theirs. Well, Williams was in debt fourteen dollars. He didn't see any way to get out of it with his newspaper, and so he sold the paper to Denis McCarthy and Goodman for two hundred dollars, they to assume the debt of fourteen dollars and also pay the two hundred dollars, in this world or the next—there was no definite arrangement about that. But as Virginia City developed new mines were discovered, new people began to flock in, and there was talk of a faro bank and a church and all those things that go to make a frontier Christian city. There was vast prosperity, and Goodman and Denis reaped the advantage of it. Their own prosperity was so great that they built a three-story brick building, which was a wonderful thing for that town, and their business increased so mightily that they would often plant out eleven columns of new ads per day on a standing galley and leave them there to sleep and rest and breed income. When any man objected, after searching the paper in the hope of seeing his advertisement, they would say "We are doing the best we can." Now and then the advertisements would appear, but the standing galley was doing its money-coining work all the time. But after a while Nevada Territory was turned into a State, in order to furnish office for some people who needed office, and by and by the paper, from paying those boys twenty to forty thousand dollars a year, ceased to pay anything. I suppose they were glad to get rid of it—and probably on the old terms—to some journeyman who was willing to take the old fourteen dollars' indebtedness and pay it when he could.

These boys went down to San Francisco, setting type again. They were delightful fellows, always ready for a good time, and that meant that everybody got their money except themselves. And when the Bonanza was about to be discovered, Joe Goodman arrived here from somewhere that he'd been—I suppose trying to make business, or a livelihood, or something—and he came to see me to borrow three hundred dollars to take him out to San Francisco. And if I remember rightly he had no prospect in front of him at all, but thought he would be more likely to find it out there among the old friends, and he went to San Francisco. He arrived there just in time to meet Jones (afterwards U.S. Senator,) who was a delightful man. Jones met him and said privately "There has been a great discovery made in Nevada, and I am on the inside." Denis was setting type in one of the offices there. He was married, and was building a wooden house, to cost $1,800, and he had paid a part and was building it on instalments out of his wages. And Jones said "I am going to put you and Denis in privately on the big Bonanza. I am on the inside, I will watch it and we will put this money up on a margin. Therefore when I say it is time to sell, it will be very necessary to sell." So he put up 20 per cent margins for those two boys—and that is the time when this great spurt must have happened which sent that stock up to the stars in one flight—because, as the history was told to me by Joe Goodman, when that thing happened Jones said to Goodman and Denis "Now then, sell. You can come out $600,000 ahead, each of you, and that is enough. Sell."

"No," Joe objected, "It will go higher."

Jones said, "I am on the inside, you are not. Sell."

Joe's wife implored him to sell, he wouldn't do it. Denis's family implored him to sell. Denis wouldn't sell. And so it went on during two weeks. Each time the stock made a flight Jones tried to get the boys to sell. They wouldn't do it. They said, "It is going higher." When he said "Sell at $900,000," they said "No, it will go to a million."

Then the stock began to go down very rapidly. After a little, Joe sold, and he got out with

$600,000 cash. Denis waited for the million, but he never got a cent. His holding was sold for the "mud"—so that he came out without anything and had to begin again setting type.

That is the story, as it was told to me many years ago—I imagine by Joe Goodman, I don't remember now. Denis, by and by, died poor,—never got a start again.

Joe Goodman immediately went into the broker business. $600,000 was just good capital. He wasn't in a position to retire yet. And he sent me the three hundred dollars, and said that now he had started in the broking business and that he was making an abundance of money. I didn't hear any more then for a long time; then I learned that he had not been content with mere broking but had speculated on his own account and lost everything he had. And when that happened, John Mackay, who was always a good friend of the unfortunate, lent him $4,000 to buy a grape ranch with in Fresno County, and Joe went up there. He didn't know anything about the grape culture, but he and his wife learned it in a very little while. He learned it a little better than anybody else, and got a good living out of it until 1886 or '87; then he sold it for several times what he paid for it originally.

He was here a year ago and I saw him. He lives in the garden of California—in Alameda. Before this eastern visit he had been putting in twelve years of his time in the most unpromising and difficult and stubborn study that anybody has undertaken since Champollion's time; for he undertook to find out what those sculptures mean that they find down there in the forests of Central America. And he did find out; and published a great book, the result of his twelve years of study. In this book he furnishes the meanings of those hieroglyphs—and his position as a successful expert in that complex study is recognized by the scientists in that line in London and Berlin, and elsewhere. But *he* is no better known than he was before—he is known only to those people. His book was published in about 1901.

This account in the New York *Times* says that in consequence of that strike in the great Bonanza a tempest of speculation ensued, and that the group of mines right around that centre reached a value in the stock market of close upon $400,000,000; and six months after that, that value had been reduced by three-quarters; and by 1880, five years later, the stock of the "Consolidated Virginia" was under $2 a share, and the stock in the "California" was only $1.75—for the Bonanza was now confessedly exhausted.

January 10, 1906

I have to make several speeches within the next two or three months, and I have been obliged to make a few speeches during the last two months—and all of a sudden it is borne in upon me that people who go out that way to make speeches at gatherings of one kind or another, and at social banquets particularly, put themselves to an unnecessary amount of trouble, often, in the way of preparation. As a rule, your speech at a social banquet is not an important part of your equipment for that occasion, for the reason that as a rule the banquet is merely given to celebrate some event of merely momentary interest, or to do honor to some guest of distinction,—and so there is nothing of large consequence—nothing, I mean, that one should feel bound to concentrate himself upon in talking upon such an occasion, whereas the really important matter, perhaps, is that the speaker make himself reasonably interesting while he is on his feet, and avoid wearying and exasperating the people who are not privileged to make speeches, and also not privileged to get out of the way when other people begin. So, common charity for those people should require that the speaker make some kind of preparation, instead of going to the place absolutely empty.

The person who makes frequent speeches can't afford much time for their preparation, and he probably goes to that place empty, (just as I am in the habit of doing), purposing to gather texts from other unprepared people who are going to speak before he speaks. Now it is perfectly true that if you can get yourself located along about number 3, and from that lower down on the program, it can be depended on with certainty that one or another of those previous speakers will furnish all the texts needed. In fact you are likely to have more texts than you do need, and so they can become an embarrassment. You would like to talk to all of those texts, and of course that is a dangerous thing. You should choose one of them and talk to that one—and it is a hundred to one that before you have been on your feet two minutes you will wish you had taken the other one. You will get away from the one you have chosen, because you will perceive that there was another one that was better.

I am reminded of this old, old fact in my experience by what happened the other night at The Players, where twenty-two of my friends of ancient days in the Players Club gave me a dinner in testimony of their satisfaction in having me back again after an absence of three years, occasioned by the stupidity of the Board of Management of that Club—a Board which had been in office ever since the founding of the Club; and if it were not the same old Board that they had in the beginning it amounted to the same, because they must have been chosen, from time to time, from the same asylum that had furnished the original Board.

On this occasion Brander Matthews was chairman, and he opened the proceedings with an easy and comfortable and felicitous speech. Brander is always prepared and competent when he is going to make a speech. Then he called up Gilder, who came empty, and probably supposed he was going to be able to fill from Brander's tank, whereas he struck a disappointment. He labored through and sat down not entirely defeated, but a good deal crippled. Frank Millet (painter) was next called up. He struggled along through his remarks, exhibiting two things— one, that he had prepared, and couldn't remember the details of his preparation, and the other that his text was a poor text. In his talk the main sign of preparation was that he tried to recite two considerable batches of poetry—good poetry—but he lost confidence and turned it into bad poetry by bad recitation. Sculpture was to have been represented, and Saint-Gaudens had accepted and had promised a speech, but at the last moment he was not able to come, and a man who was thoroughly unprepared had to get up and make a speech in Saint-Gaudens's place. He did not hit upon anything original or disturbing in his remarks, and, in fact, they were so tottering and hesitating and altogether commonplace that really he seemed to have hit upon something new and fresh when he finished by saying that he had not been expecting to be called upon to make a speech! I could have finished his speech for him, I had heard it so many times.

Those people were unfortunate because they were *thinking*—that is Millet and Gilder were—all the time that Matthews was speaking—they were trying to keep in mind the little preparations which they had made, and this prevented them from getting something new and fresh in the way of a text out of what Brander was saying. In the same way Millet was still thinking about his preparation while Gilder was talking, and so he overlooked possible texts furnished by Gilder. But as I had asked Matthews to put me last on the list of speakers, I had all the advantages possible to the occasion. For I came without a text, and these boys furnished plenty of texts for me, because my mind was not absorbed in trying to remember my preparations—they didn't exist. I spoiled, in a degree, Brander's speech, because his speech had been prepared with direct reference to introducing me, the guest of the occasion—and he had to turn that all around and get out of it, which he did very gracefully, explaining that his speech was a little lop-sided and wrong end first because I had asked to be placed last in the list of speakers. I had a plenty good enough time, because Gilder had furnished me a text; Brander had furnished me a text; Millet had furnished me a text. These texts were fresh, hot from the bat, and they produced the same eager disposition to take hold of them and talk that they would have produced in ordinary conversation around a table in a beer mill.

Now then, I know how banquet-speeches should be projected, because I have been thinking over this matter. This is my plan. Where it is merely a social banquet for a good time—such as the one which I am to attend in Washington on the 27th, where the company will consist of the membership of the Gridiron Club, (newspaper correspondents exclusively, I think) with as guests the President and Vice-President of the United States and two others—certainly that is an occasion where a person will be privileged to talk about any subject except politics and theology, and even if he is asked to talk to a toast he needn't pay any attention to the toast, but talk about anything. Now then, the idea is this—to take the newspaper of that day, or the newspaper of that evening, and glance over the headings in the telegraphic page—a perfect bonanza of texts, you see! I think a person could pull that day's newspaper out of his pocket and talk that company to death before he would run out of material. If it were to-day, you have the Morris incident. And that reminds me how unexciting the Morris incident will be two or three years from now—maybe six months from now—and yet what an irritating thing it is to-day, and has been for the past few days. It brings home to one this large fact: that the events of life are mainly small events—they only seem large when we are close to them. By and by they settle down and we see that one doesn't show above another. They are all about one general low altitude, and inconsequential. If you should set down every day, by shorthand, as we are doing now, the happenings of the previous day, with the intention of making out of the massed result an autobiography, it would take from one to two hours—and from that to four hours—to set down the autobiographical matter of that one day, and the result would be a consumption of from five to forty thousand words. It would be a volume. Now one must not imagine that because it has taken all day Tuesday to write up the autobiographical matter of Monday, there will be nothing to write on Wednesday. No, there will be just as much to write on Wednesday as Monday had furnished for Tuesday. And that is because life does not consist mainly—or even largely—of facts and happenings. It consists mainly of the storm of thoughts that is forever blowing through one's head. Could you set them down stenographically? No. Could you set down any considerable fraction of them stenographically? No. Fifteen stenographers hard at work couldn't keep up. Therefore a full autobiography has never been written, and it never will be. It would consist of three hundred and sixty-five double-size volumes per year—and so if I had been doing my whole autobiographical duty ever since my youth all the library buildings on the earth could not contain the result.

I wonder what the Morris incident will look like in history fifty years from now. Consider these circumstances: that here at our own doors the mighty insurance upheaval has not settled down to a level yet. Even yesterday, and day before, the discredited millionaire insurance magnates had not all been flung out and buried from sight under the maledictions of the nation, but some of the McCurdies, McCalls, Depews, Hydes, and Alexanders were still lingering in positions of trust, such as directorships in banks. Also we have to-day the whole nation's attention centred upon the Standard Oil Corporation, the most prodigious commercial force existing upon the planet. All the American world are standing breathless and wondering if the Standard Oil is going to come out of its Missourian battle crippled, and if crippled, how much crippled. Also we have Congress threatening to overhaul the Panama Canal Commission to see what it has done with the fifty-nine millions, and to find out what it proposes to do with the recently added eleven millions. Also there are three or four other matters of colossal public interest on the board to-day. And on the other side of the ocean we have Church and State separated in France; we have a threat of war between France and Germany upon the Morocco question; we have a crushed revolution in Russia, with the Czar and his family of thieves—the grand dukes—recovering from their long fright and beginning to butcher the remnants of the revolutionaries in the old confident way that was the Russian way in former days for three centuries; we have China furnishing a solemn and awful mystery. Nobody knows what it is, but we are sending three regiments in a hurry from the Philippines to China, under the generalship of Funston, the man who captured Aguinaldo by methods which would disgrace the lowest blatherskite that is doing time in any penitentiary. Nobody seems to know what the Chinese mystery is, but everybody seems to think that a giant convulsion is impending there.

That is the menu as it stands to-day. These are the things which offer themselves to the world's attention to-day. Apparently they are large enough to leave no space for smaller matters, yet *the Morris incident comes up and blots the whole thing out.* The Morris incident is making a flurry in Congress, and for several days now it has been rioting through the imagination of the American nation and setting every tongue afire with excited talk. This autobiography will not see the light of print until after my death. I do not know when that is going to happen, and do not feel a large interest in the matter anyway. It may be some years yet, but if it does not occur within the next three months I am confident that by that time the nation, encountering the Morris incident in my autobiography, would be trying to remember what the incident was, and not succeeding. That incident, which is so large to-day, will be so small three or four months from now it will then have taken its place with the abortive Russian revolution and these other large matters, and nobody will be able to tell one from the other by difference of size.

This is the Morris incident. A Mrs. Morris, a lady of culture, refinement, and position, called at the White House and asked for a moment's conversation with President Roosevelt. Mr. Barnes, one of the private secretaries, declined to send in her card, and said that she couldn't see the President, that he was busy. She said she would wait. Barnes wanted to know what her errand was, and she said that some time ago her husband had been dismissed from the public service and she wanted to get the President to look into his case. Barnes, finding that it was a military case, suggested that she go to the Secretary of War. She said she had been to the War Office but could not get admission to the Secretary—she had tried every means she could think of, but had failed. Now she had been advised by the wife of a member of the Cabinet to ask for a moment's interview with the President.

Well, without going into a multiplicity of details, the general result was that Barnes still persisted in saying that she could not see the President, and he also persisted in inviting her, in the circumstances, to go away. She was quiet, but she still insisted on remaining until she could see the President. Then the "Morris incident" happened. At a sign from Barnes a couple of policemen on guard there rushed forward and seized this lady, and began to drag her out of the place. She was frightened, and she screamed. Barnes says she screamed repeatedly, and in a way which "aroused the whole White House"—though nobody came to see what was happening. This might give the impression that this was something that was happening six or seven times a day, since it didn't cause any excitement. But this was not so. Barnes has been a private secretary long enough to work his imagination, probably, and that accounts for most of the screaming—though the lady did *some* of it herself, as she concedes. The woman was dragged out of the White House. She says that in the course of dragging her along the roadway her clothes were soiled with mud and some of them stripped in rags from her back. A negro gathered up her ancles, and so relieved her from contact with the ground. He supporting her by the ancles, and the two policemen carrying her at the other end, they conveyed her to a place—apparently a police station of some kind, a couple of blocks away—and she was dripping portemonnaies and keys, and one thing or another, along the road, and honest people were picking them up and fetching them along. Barnes entered a charge against her of insanity. Apparently the police inspector regarded that as rather a serious charge, and as he probably had not had one like it before and did not quite know how it ought to be handled, he would not allow her to be delivered to her friends until she had deposited five dollars in his till. No doubt this was to keep her from disappearing from the United States—and he might want to take up this serious charge presently and thresh it out.

That lady still lies in her bed at the principal hotel in Washington, disabled by the shock, and naturally very indignant at the treatment which she has received—but her calm and mild, unexcited and well worded account of her adventure is convincing evidence that she was not insane, even to the moderate extent of five dollars' worth.

There you have the facts. It is as I have said—for a number of days they have occupied almost the entire attention of the American nation; they have swept the Russian revolution out of sight, the China mystery, and all the rest of it. It is this sort of thing which makes the right material of an autobiography. You set the incident down which for the moment is to you the most interesting. If you leave it alone three or four weeks you wonder why you ever thought of setting such a thing down—it has no value, no importance. The champagne that made you drunk with delight or exasperation at the time has all passed away; it is stale. But that is what human life consists of—little incidents and big incidents, and they are all of the same size if we let them alone. An autobiography that leaves out the little things and enumerates only the big ones is no proper picture of the man's life at all; his life consists of his feelings and his interests, with here and there an incident apparently big or little to hang the feelings on.

That Morris incident will presently have no importance whatever, and yet the biographer of President Roosevelt will find it immensely valuable if he will consider it—examine it—and be sagacious enough to perceive that it throws a great deal of light upon the President's character. Certainly a biography's chiefest feature is the exhibition of the *character* of the man whose biography is being set forth. Roosevelt's biographer will light up the President's career step by step, mile after mile, through his life's course, with illuminating episodes and incidents. He should set one of the lamps by the Morris incident, for it indicates character. It is a thing which probably could not have happened in the White House under any other President who has ever occupied those premises. Washington wouldn't call the police and throw a lady out over the fence! I don't mean that Roosevelt would. I mean that Washington wouldn't have any Barneses in his official family. It is the Roosevelts that have the Barneses around. That private secretary was perfectly right in refusing access to the President—the President can't see everybody on everybody's private affairs, and it is quite proper, then, that he should refuse to see anybody on a private affair—treat all the nation alike. That is a thing which has been done, of course, from the beginning until now—people have always been refused admission to the President on private matters, every day, from Washington's time to ours. The secretaries have always carried their point; Mr. Barnes carried his. But, according to the president in office at the time, the methods have varied—one president's secretary has managed it in one way, another president's secretary has managed it in another way—but it never would have occurred to any previous secretary to manage it by throwing the lady over the fence.

Theodore Roosevelt is one of the most impulsive men in existence. That is the reason why he has impulsive secretaries. President Roosevelt probably never thinks of the right way to do anything. That is why he has private secretaries who are not able to think of the right way to do anything. We naturally gather about us people whose ways and dispositions agree with our own. Mr. Roosevelt is one of the most likable men that I am acquainted with. I have known him, and have occasionally met him, dined in his company, lunched in his company, for certainly twenty years. I always enjoy his society, he is so hearty, so straightforward, outspoken, and so absolutely sincere. These qualities endear him to me when he is acting in his capacity of private citizen—they endear him to all his friends. But when he is acting under their impulse as President, they make of him a sufficiently queer president. He flies from one thing to another with incredible dispatch—throws a somersault and is straightway back again where he was last week. He will then throw some more somersaults and nobody can foretell where he is finally going to land after the series. Each act of his, and each opinion expressed, is likely to abolish or controvert some previous act or expressed opinion. This is what is happening to him all the time as President. But every opinion that he expresses is certainly his sincere opinion at that moment, and it is as certainly not the opinion which he was carrying around in his system three or four weeks earlier, and which was just as sincere and honest as the latest one. No, he can't be accused of insincerity—that is not the trouble. His trouble is that his newest interest is the one that absorbs him; absorbs the whole of him from his head to his feet, and for the time being it annihilates all previous opinions and feelings and convictions. He is the most popular human being that has ever existed in the United States, and that popularity springs from just these enthusiasms of his—these joyous ebullitions of excited sincerity. It makes him so much like the rest of the people. They see themselves reflected in him. They also see that his impulses are not often mean. They are almost always large, fine, generous. He can't stick to one of them long enough to find out what kind of a chick it would hatch if it had a chance, but everybody recognizes the generosity of the intention and they admire it and love him for it.

January 11, 1906

I received the following letter some days ago, from Mrs. Laura K. Hudson:

> 287 Quincy St.
> Jan 3d 06.

Mr. Samuel L. Clemens.
My Dear Sir.

Some twenty years ago we were in the first years of our married life; the first two small instalments of a growing family kept us severely domestic and my husband and I used to spend our happy evenings together he reading aloud from magazine or book and I meanwhile sewing and listening. One evening he read from one of the New York papers the report of some function—I have a hazy idea it was a Press Club dinner or other jamboree—during which "Mark Twain" read aloud a paper which to me seemed the best and funniest thing our great favorite had ever written. And now that the growing family has gotten its growth and has grown very fond of "Mark Twain" I have searched high and low in every collection of his works for this delightful bit of fun but always in vain. May I therefore apply to Mr. Clemens for some help?

It was about a miner in his mountain-hut; to whom come three men for food and a night's shelter. They give their names as Longfellow, Holmes and Whittier and the way they are described—the last-mentioned with "double-chins way down to his stomach"—by the miner who tells the story and the highflown quotations from their own writings which they give in answer to the miner's *very* gruff and to-the-point questions are fun of the funniest kind. The miner stands it until in answer to some self-satisfied remark of his in reference to his comfortable cabin the Pseudo-Holmes retorts:

"Build thee more stately mansions, oh my soul!" and so on through the entire stanza. Then he rises in his wrath and puts the three poets out.

Any light you can throw on the name and possible whereabouts of this delightful child of your muse will be most gratefully received by my husband, my three sons and their "Mark-Twain"-loving Mother; who begs leave to call herself

> Yours Most Cordially
> Laura K. Hudson.

This morning I dictated an answer to my secretary, Miss Lyon, as follows:

Dear Mrs. Hudson:

I am forever your debtor for reminding me of that curious passage in my life. During the first year or two after it happened, I could not bear to think of it. My pain and shame were so intense, and my sense of having been an imbecile so settled, established and confirmed, that I drove the episode entirely from my mind—and so all these twenty-eight or twenty-nine years I have lived in the conviction that my performance of that time was coarse, vulgar and destitute of humor. But your suggestion that you and your family found humor in it twenty-eight years ago moved me to look into the matter. So I commissioned a Boston typewriter to delve among the Boston papers of that bygone time, and send me a copy of it.

It came this morning, and if there is any vulgarity about it I am not able to discover it. If it isn't innocently and ridiculously funny, I am no judge. I will see to it that you get a copy.

Address of Samuel L. Clemens ("Mark Twain") From a report of the dinner given by the Publishers of the Atlantic Monthly in honor of the Seventieth Anniversary of the Birth of John Greenleaf Whittier, at the Hotel Brunswick, Boston, December 17, 1877, as published in the BOSTON EVENING TRANSCRIPT, December 18, 1877

———

Mr. Chairman—This is an occasion peculiarly meet for the digging up of pleasant reminiscences concerning literary folk; therefore I will drop lightly into history myself. Standing here on the shore of the Atlantic and contemplating certain of its largest literary billows, I am reminded of a thing which happened to me thirteen years ago, when I had just succeeded in stirring up a little Nevadian literary puddle myself, whose spume-flakes were beginning to blow thinly Californiawards. I started an inspection tramp through the southern mines of California. I was callow and conceited, and I resolved to try the virtue of my nom de guerre. I very soon had an opportunity. I knocked at a miner's lonely log cabin in the foot hills of the Sierras just at night-fall. It was snowing at the time. A jaded, melancholy man of fifty, barefooted, opened to me. When he heard my nom de guerre, he looked more dejected than before. He let me in—pretty reluctantly, I thought—and after the customary bacon and beans, black coffee and a hot whiskey, I took a pipe. This sorrowful man had not said three words up to this time. Now he spoke up and said in the voice of one who is secretly suffering, "You're the fourth—I'm a-going to move." "The fourth what?" said I. "The fourth littery man that's been here in twenty-four hours—I'm a-going to move." "You don't tell me!" said I; "who were the others?" "Mr. Longfellow, Mr. Emerson, and Mr. Oliver Wendell Holmes—consound the lot!"

You can easily believe I was interested. I supplicated—three hot whiskeys did the rest—and finally the melancholy miner began. Said he—

"They came here just at dark yesterday evening, and I let them in of course. Said they were going to Yosemite. They were a rough lot, but that's nothing; everybody looks rough that travels afoot. Mr. Emerson was a seedy little bit of a chap, red-headed. Mr. Holmes was as fat as a balloon; he weighed as much as three hundred, and had double chins all the way down to his stomach. Mr. Longfellow was built like a prize fighter. His head was cropped and bristly, like as if he had a wig made of hair-brushes. His nose lay straight down his face, like a finger with the end joint tilted up. They had been drinking; I could see that. And what queer talk they used! Mr. Holmes inspected this cabin, then he took me by the buttonhole, and says he—

> "'Through the deep caves of thought
> I hear a voice that sings;
> Build thee more stately mansions,
> O my soul!'

"Says I, 'I can't afford it, Mr. Holmes, and moreover I don't want to.' Blamed if I liked it pretty well, either, coming from a stranger, that way. However, I started to get out my bacon and beans, when Mr. Emerson came and looked on a while, and then *he* takes me aside by the buttonhole and says—

> "'Give me agates for my meat;
> Give me cantharids to eat;
> From air and ocean bring me foods,
> From all zones and altitudes.'

"Says I, 'Mr. Emerson, if you'll excuse me, this ain't no hotel.' You see it sort of riled me—I warn't used to the ways of littery swells. But I went on a-sweating over my work, and next comes Mr. Longfellow and buttonholes me, and interrupts me. Says he,

> "'Honor be to Mudjekeewis!
> You shall hear how Pau-Puk-Keewis—'

"But I broke in, and says I, 'Begging your pardon, Mr. Longfellow, if you'll be so kind as to hold your yawp for about five minutes and let me get this grub ready, you'll do me proud.' Well, sir, after they'd filled up I set out the jug. Mr. Holmes looks at it and then he fires up all of a sudden and yells—

> "'Flash out a stream of blood-red wine!
> For I would drink to other days.'

"By George, I was getting kind of worked up. I don't deny it, I was getting kind of worked up. I turns to Mr. Holmes, and says I, 'Looky here, my fat friend, I'm a-running this shanty, and if the court knows herself, you'll take whiskey-straight or you'll go dry.' Them's the very words I said to him. Now I didn't want to sass such famous littery people, but you see they kind of forced me. There ain't nothing onreasonable 'bout me; I don't mind a passel of guests a-tread'n on my tail three or four times, but when it comes to *standing* on it it's different, 'and if the court knows herself,' I says, 'you'll take whiskey-straight or you'll go dry.' Well, between drinks they'd swell around the cabin and strike attitudes and spout. Says Mr. Longfellow—

> "'This is the forest primeval.'

"Says Mr. Emerson—

> "'Here once the embattled farmers stood,
> And fired the shot heard round the world.'

"Says I, 'O, blackguard the premises as much as you want to—it don't cost a cent.' Well, they went on drinking, and pretty soon they got out a greasy old deck and went to playing euchre at ten cents a corner—on trust. I begun to notice some pretty suspicious things. Mr. Emerson dealt, looked at his hand, shook his head, says—

> "'I am the doubter and the doubt—'

and ca'mly bunched the hands and went to shuffling for a new lay out. Says he—

"'They reckon ill who leave me out;
    They know not well the subtle ways
    I keep. I pass, and deal *again!*'

"Hang'd if he didn't go ahead and do it, too! O, he was a cool one! Well, in about a minute, things were running pretty tight, but all of a sudden I see by Mr. Emerson's eye that he judged he had 'em. He had already corralled two tricks and each of the others one. So now he kind of lifts a little in his chair and says—

"'I tire of globes and aces!—
    Too long the game is played!'

—and down he fetched a right bower. Mr. Longfellow smiles as sweet as pie and says—

"'Thanks, thanks to thee, my worthy friend,
    For the lesson thou hast taught';

—and blamed if he didn't down with *another* right bower! Well, sir, up jumps Holmes, a-war-whooping as usual, and says—

"'God help them if the tempest swings
    The pine against the palm!'

—and I wish I may go to grass if he didn't swoop down with *another* right bower! Emerson claps his hand on his bowie, Longfellow claps his on his revolver, and I went under a bunk. There was going to be trouble; but that monstrous Holmes rose up, wobbling his double chins, and says he, 'Order, gentlemen; the first man that draws, I'll lay down on him and smother him!' All quiet on the Potomac, you bet!

"They were pretty how-come-you-so, by now, and they begun to blow. Emerson says, 'The nobbiest thing I ever wrote was Barbara Frietchie.' Says Longfellow, 'It don't begin with my Biglow Papers.' Says Holmes, 'My Thanatopsis lays over 'em both.' They mighty near ended in a fight. Then they wished they had some more company—and Mr. Emerson pointed at me and says—

"'Is yonder squalid peasant all
    That this proud nursery could breed?'

"He was a-whetting his bowie on his boot—so I let it pass. Well, sir, next they took it into their heads that they would like some music; so they made me stand up and sing 'When Johnny Comes Marching Home' till I dropped—at thirteen minutes past four this morning. That's what *I*'ve been through, my friend. When I woke at seven, they were leaving, thank goodness, and Mr. Longfellow had my only boots on, and his'n under his arm. Says I, 'Hold on, there, Evangeline, what are you going to do with *them?*' He says, 'Going to make tracks with 'em; because—

"'Lives of great men all remind us
        We can make our lives sublime;
    And, departing, leave behind us
        Footprints on the sands of Time.'

"As I said, Mr. Twain, you are the fourth in twenty-four hours—and I'm a-going to move; I ain't suited to a littery atmosphere."

I said to the miner, "Why, my dear sir, *these* were not the gracious singers to whom we and the world pay loving reverence and homage; these were impostors."

The miner investigated me with a calm eye for a while; then said he, "Ah! impostors, were they? are *you?*"

I did not pursue the subject, and since then I haven't travelled on my nom de guerre enough to hurt. Such was the reminiscence I was moved to contribute, Mr. Chairman. In my enthusiasm I may have exaggerated the details a little, but you will easily forgive me that fault, since I believe it is the first time I have ever deflected from perpendicular fact on an occasion like this.

What I have said to Mrs. Hudson is true. I did suffer during a year or two from the deep humiliations of that episode. But at last, in 1878, in Venice, my wife and I came across Mr. and Mrs. A. P. Chamberlaine, of Concord, Massachusetts, and a friendship began then of the sort which nothing but death terminates. The Chamberlaines were very bright people and in every way charming and companionable. We were together a month or two in Venice and several months in Rome, afterwards, and one day that lamented break of mine was mentioned. And when I was on the point of lathering those people for bringing it to my mind when I had gotten the memory of it almost squelched, I perceived with joy that the Chamberlaines were indignant about the way that my performance had been received in Boston. They poured out their opinions most freely and frankly about the frosty attitude of the people who were present at that performance, and about the Boston newspapers for the position they had taken in regard to the matter. That position was that I had been irreverent beyond belief, beyond imagination. Very well, I had accepted that as a fact for a year or two, and had been thoroughly miserable about it whenever I thought of it—which was not frequently, if I could help it. Whenever I thought of it I wondered how I ever could have been inspired to do so unholy a thing. Well, the Chamberlaines comforted me, but they did not persuade me to continue to think about the unhappy episode. I resisted that. I tried to get it out of my mind, and let it die, and I succeeded. Until Mrs. Hudson's letter came the other day, it had been a good twenty-five years since I had thought of that matter; and when she said that the thing was funny I wondered if possibly she might be right. At any rate, my curiosity was aroused, and I wrote to Boston and got the whole thing copied, as above set forth.

I vaguely remember some of the details of that gathering—dimly I can see a hundred people—no, perhaps fifty—shadowy figures sitting at tables feeding, ghosts now to me, and nameless forever more. I don't know who they were, but I can very distinctly see seated at the grand table and facing the rest of us, Mr. Emerson, supernaturally grave, unsmiling; Mr. Whittier, grave, lovely, his beautiful spirit shining out of his face—a Quaker, but smiley and sweet; Mr. Longfellow, with his silken white hair and his benignant face; Dr. Oliver Wendell Holmes, flashing smiles and affection and all good-fellowship everywhere like a rose-diamond whose facets are being turned toward the light first one way and then another—a charming man, and always fascinating, whether he was talking or whether he was sitting still (what *he* would call still, but what would be more or less motion to other people). I can see those figures with entire distinctness across this abyss of time.

One other feature is clear—Willie Winter (for these past thousand years dramatic editor of the New York *Tribune,* and still occupying that high post in his old age) was there. He was much younger then than he is now, and he showed it. It was always a pleasure to me to see

Willie Winter at a banquet. During a matter of twenty years I was seldom at a banquet where Willie Winter was not also present, and where he did not read a charming poem written for the occasion. He did it this time, and it was up to standard. There was never any vigor in his poetry, but it was always smooth, wavy, and dainty, happy, choicely phrased, and as good to listen to as music—and he did love to recite those occasional poems, with a love that is beyond understanding. There was no doubt of his joy in the performance. His delight in it was absolutely innocent; his unoffending admiration of his poems; his perfect manner of reading them—it was all beautiful to see. He recited from memory, sometimes, a very long speech, exquisitely phrased, faultlessly modeled, yet sounding exactly as if it was pouring unprepared out of heart and brain. He was a perfect reciter of both his poetry and his prose, and in both instances they were music. But if he was well down in the list of performers, then his performance was worth two or three times as much as it was when he was appointed to enter the field earlier, because if he was down a little way in the list it gave him a chance to drink a thimbleful of champagne, and that was all that was necessary for Willie Winter. I can see him so clearly: his small figure bent persuasively forward, his face glowing with inspiration—part of it from his poetry, the rest from his thimbleful of champagne. He would throw out a dainty line or two and then glance up this way, that way, the other way, collecting appreciation; and in the meantime he would be, not spitting—that is vulgar—but doing what any man properly charged with champagne does when he feels that he has got his mouth full of raw cotton and must rid himself of it. He did that all the way through, while he was reciting, and he was the happiest man in the world. And on this particular occasion that I am speaking of he was charming. It was a beautiful thing to see, and I wished he was drunker. He got such effects out of that thimbleful of champagne I wondered what would happen if he had had a tubfull.

Now at that point ends all that was pleasurable about that notable celebration of Mr. Whittier's seventieth birthday—because *I* got up at that point and followed Winter, with what I have no doubt I supposed would be the gem of the evening—the gay oration above quoted from the Boston paper. I had written it all out the day before, and had perfectly memorized it, and I stood up there at my genial and happy and self-satisfied ease, and began to deliver it. Those majestic guests, that row of venerable and still active volcanoes, listened, as did everybody else in the house, with attentive interest. Well, I delivered myself of—we'll say the first two hundred words of my speech. I was expecting no returns from that part of the speech, but this was not the case as regarded the rest of it. I arrived now at the dialogue: "The old miner said 'You are the fourth, I'm going to move.' 'The fourth what?' said I. He answered, 'The fourth littery man that has been here in twenty-four hours. I am going to move.' 'Why, you don't tell me,' said I. 'Who were the others?' 'Mr. Longfellow, Mr. Emerson, Mr. Oliver Wendell Holmes, consound the lot'"—

Now then the house's *attention* continued, but the expression of interest in the faces turned to a sort of black frost. I wondered what the trouble was. I didn't know. I went on, but with difficulty—I struggled along, and entered upon that miner's fearful description of the bogus Emerson, the bogus Holmes, the bogus Longfellow, always hoping—but with a gradually perishing hope—that somebody would laugh, or that somebody would at least smile, but nobody did. I didn't know enough to give it up and sit down, I was too new to public speaking, and so I went on with this awful performance, and carried it clear through to the end, in front of a body of people who seemed turned to stone with horror. It was the sort of expression their faces would have worn if I had been making these remarks about the Deity and the rest of the Trinity; there is no milder way in which to describe the petrified condition and the ghastly expression of those people.

When I sat down it was with a heart which had long ceased to beat. I shall never be as dead again as I was then. I shall never be as miserable again as I was then. I speak now as one who doesn't know what the condition of things may be in the next world, but in this one I shall never be as wretched again as I was then. Howells, who was near me, tried to say a comforting word, but couldn't get beyond a gasp. There was no use—he understood the whole size of the disaster. He had good intentions, but the words froze before they could get out. It was an atmosphere that would freeze anything. If Benvenuto Cellini's salamander had been in that place he would not have survived to be put into Cellini's autobiography. There was a frightful pause. There was an awful silence, a desolating silence. Then the next man on the list had to get up—there was no help for it. That was Bishop—Bishop, now forgotten, had just burst handsomely upon the world with a most acceptable novel, which had appeared in the *Atlantic Monthly,* a place which would make any novel respectable and any author noteworthy. In this case the novel itself was recognized as being, without extraneous help, respectable. Bishop was away up in the public favor, and he was an object of high interest, consequently there was a sort of national expectancy in the air; we may say our American millions were standing, from Maine to Texas and from Alaska to Florida, holding their breath, their lips parted, their hands ready to applaud when Bishop should get up on that occasion, and for the first time in his life speak in public. It was under these damaging conditions that he got up to "make good," as the vulgar say. I had spoken several times before, and that is the reason why I was able to go on without dying in my tracks, as I ought to have done—but Bishop had had no experience. He was up facing those awful deities—facing those other people, those strangers—facing human beings for the first time in his life, with a speech to utter. No doubt it was well packed away in his memory, no doubt it was fresh and usable, until I had been heard from. I suppose that after that, and under the smothering pall of that dreary silence, it began to waste away and disappear out of his head like the rags breaking from the edge of a fog, and presently there wasn't any fog left. He didn't go on—he didn't last long. It was not many sentences after his first, before he began to hesitate, and break, and lose his grip, and totter, and wobble, and at last he slumped down in a limp and mushy pile.

Well, the program for the occasion was probably not more than one-third finished, but it ended there. Nobody rose. The next man hadn't strength enough to get up, and everybody looked so dazed, so stupefied, paralysed, it was impossible for anybody to do anything, or even try. Nothing could go on in that strange atmosphere. Howells mournfully, and without words, hitched himself to Bishop and me and supported us out of the room. It was very kind—he was most generous. He towed us tottering away into some room in that building, and we sat down there. I don't know what my remark was now, but I know the nature of it. It was the kind of remark you make when you know that nothing in the world can help your case. But Howells was honest—he *had* to say the heart-breaking things he did say: that there was no help for this calamity, this shipwreck, this cataclysm; that this was the most disastrous thing that had ever happened in anybody's history—and then he added, "That is, for *you*—and consider what you have done for Bishop. It is bad enough in your case, you deserve to suffer. You have committed this crime, and you deserve to have all you are going to get. But here is an innocent man. Bishop had never done you any harm, and see what you have done to him. He can never hold his head up again. The world can never look upon Bishop as being a live person. He is a corpse."

That is the history of that episode of twenty-eight years ago, which pretty nearly killed me with shame during that first year or two whenever it forced its way into my mind.

Now then, I take that speech up and examine it. As I said, it arrived this morning, from Boston. I have read it twice, and unless I am an idiot, it hasn't a single defect in it from the first word to the last. It is just as good as good can be. It is smart; it is saturated with humor. There isn't a suggestion of coarseness or vulgarity in it anywhere. What could have been the matter with that house? It is amazing, it is incredible, that they didn't shout with laughter, and those deities the loudest of them all. Could the fault have been with me? Did I lose courage when I saw those great men up there whom I was going to describe in such a strange fashion? If that happened, if I showed doubt, that can account for it, for you can't be successfully funny if you show that you are afraid of it. Well, I can't account for it, but if I had those beloved and revered old literary immortals back here now on the platform at Carnegie Hall I would take that same old speech, deliver it, word for word, and melt them till they'd run all over that stage. Oh, the fault must have been with *me*, it is not in the speech at all.

All Boston shuddered for several days. All gaieties ceased, all festivities; even the funerals were without animation. There has never been so awful a time in Boston. Even the Massacre did not produce a like effect, nor the Anthony Burns episode, nor any other solemnity in Boston's history. But I am glad that that lady mentioned this speech, which I should never have thought of again I suppose, for now I am going to apply the test, and I am going to find out whether it was Boston or whether it was myself that was in fault at that sad time of Mr. Bishop's obsequies; for next summer I will drop down from the New Hampshire hills with that typewritten ancient speech in my hand, and I will go before the massed intellect of Boston—the Twentieth Century Club—and without revealing what it is that I am asking permission to talk about, I will lay those ancient facts before that unprejudiced jury and read that speech to them and see what the result will be. If they do not laugh and admire I shall commit suicide there. I would just as soon do it there as any place; and one time is as good as another to me.

January 12, 1906

This talk about Mr. Whittier's seventieth birthday reminds me that my own seventieth arrived recently—that is to say, it arrived on the 30th of November, but Colonel Harvey was not able to celebrate it on that date because that date had been preempted by the President to be used as Thanksgiving Day, a function which originated in New England two or three centuries ago when those people recognized that they really had something to be thankful for—annually, not oftener—if they had succeeded in exterminating their neighbors, the Indians, during the previous twelve months instead of getting exterminated by their neighbors the Indians. Thanksgiving Day became a habit, for the reason that in the course of time, as the years drifted on, it was perceived that the exterminating had ceased to be mutual and was all on the white man's side, consequently on the Lord's side, consequently it was proper to thank the Lord for it and extend the usual annual compliments. The original reason for a Thanksgiving Day has long ago ceased to exist—the Indians have long ago been comprehensively and satisfactorily exterminated and the account closed with Heaven, with the thanks due. But, from old habit, Thanksgiving Day has remained with us, and every year the President of the United States and the Governors of all the several States and the territories set themselves the task, every November, to advertise for something to be thankful for, and then they put those thanks into a few crisp and reverent phrases, in the form of a Proclamation, and this is read from all the pulpits in the land, the national conscience is wiped clean with one swipe, and sin is resumed at the old stand.

The President and the Governors had to have my birthday—the 30th—for Thanksgiving Day, and this was a great inconvenience to Colonel Harvey, who had made much preparation for a banquet to be given to me on that day in celebration of the fact that it marked my seventieth escape from the gallows, according to *his* idea—a fact which he regarded with favor and contemplated with pleasure, because he is my publisher and commercially interested. He went to Washington to try to get the President to select another day for the national Thanksgiving, and I furnished him with arguments to use which I thought persuasive and convincing, arguments which ought to persuade him even to put off Thanksgiving Day a whole year—on the ground that nothing had happened during the previous twelvemonth except several vicious and inexcusable wars, and King Leopold of Belgium's usual annual slaughters and robberies in the Congo State, together with the Insurance revelations in New York, which seemed to establish the fact that if there was an honest man left in the United States, there was *only* one, and we wanted to celebrate his seventieth birthday. But the Colonel came back unsuccessful, and put my birthday celebration off to the 5th of December.

I had twice as good a time at this seventieth, as I had had at Mr. Whittier's seventieth, twenty-eight years earlier. In the speech which I made were concealed many facts. I expected everybody to discount those facts 95 per cent and that is probably what happened. That does not trouble me, I am used to having my statements discounted. My mother had begun it before I was seven years old. Yet all through my life my facts have had a substratum of truth, and therefore they were not without preciousness. Any person who is familiar with me knows how to strike my average, and therefore knows how to get at the jewel of any fact of mine and dig it out of its blue-clay matrix. My mother knew that art. When I was seven or eight, or ten, or twelve years old—along there—a neighbor said to her, "Do you ever believe anything that that boy says?" My mother said "He is the wellspring of truth, but you can't bring up the whole well with one bucket"—and she added, "I know his average, therefore he never deceives me. I discount him 30 per cent for embroidery, and what is left is perfect and priceless truth, without a flaw in it anywhere."

Now to make a jump of forty years, without breaking the connection: that word "embroidery" was used again in my presence and concerning me, when I was fifty years old, one night at Reverend Frank Goodwin's house in Hartford, at a meeting of the Monday Evening Club. The Monday Evening Club still exists. It was founded about forty-five years ago by that theological giant, Rev. Dr. Bushnell, and some comrades of his, men of large intellectual calibre and more or less distinction, local or national. I was admitted to membership in it in the fall of 1871 and was an active member thenceforth until I left Hartford in the summer of 1891. The membership was restricted, in those days, to eighteen—possibly twenty. The meetings began about the 1st of October and were held in the private houses of the members every fortnight thereafter throughout the cold months until the 1st of May. Usually there were a dozen members present—sometimes as many as fifteen. There was an essay and a discussion. The essayists followed each other in alphabetical order through the season. The essayist could choose his own subject and talk twenty minutes on it, from manuscript or orally, according to his preference. Then the discussion followed, and each member present was allowed ten minutes in which to express his views. The wives of these people were always present. It was their privilege. It was also their privilege to keep still; they were not allowed to throw any light upon the discussion. After the discussion there was a supper, and talk, and cigars. This supper began at ten o'clock promptly, and the company broke up and went away at midnight. At least they did except upon one occasion. In my recent Birthday speech I remarked upon the fact that I have always bought cheap cigars, and that is true. I have never bought costly ones, and whenever I go to a rich man's house to dinner I conceal cheap cigars about my person, as a protection against his costly ones. There are enough costly Havana cigars in my house to start a considerable cigar shop with, but I did not buy one of them—I doubt if I have ever smoked one of them. They are Christmas presents from wealthy and ignorant friends, extending back for a long series of years. Among the lot, I found, the other day, a double-handful of J. Pierpont Morgan's cigars, which were given to me three years ago by his particular friend, the late William E. Dodge, one night when I was at dinner in Mr. Dodge's house. Mr. Dodge did not smoke, and so he supposed that those were super-excellent cigars, because they were made for Mr. Morgan in Havana out of special tobacco and cost $1.66 apiece. Now whenever I buy a cigar that costs six cents I am suspicious of it. When it costs four and a quarter or five cents I smoke it with confidence. I carried those sumptuous cigars home, after smoking one of them at Mr. Dodge's house to show that I had no animosity, and here they lie ever since. They cannot beguile me. I am waiting for somebody to come along whose lack of education will enable him to smoke them and enjoy them.

Well, that night at the Club—as I was saying—George, our colored butler, came to me when the supper was nearly over, and I noticed that he was pale. Normally his complexion was a clear black, and very handsome, but now it had modified to old amber. He said,

"Mr. Clemens, what are we going to do? There is not a cigar in the house but those old Wheeling long nines. Can't nobody smoke them but you. They kill at thirty yards. It is too late to telephone—we couldn't get any cigars out from town—what can we do? Ain't it best to say nothing, and let on that we didn't think?"

"No" I said, "that would not be honest. Fetch out the long nines"—which he did.

I had just come across those "long nines" a few days or a week before. I hadn't seen a long nine for years. When I was a cub pilot on the Mississippi in the late '50s, I had had a great affection for them, because they were not only—to my mind—perfect, but you could get a basketful of them for a cent—or a dime, they didn't use cents out there in those days. So when I saw them advertised in Hartford I sent for a thousand at once. They were sent out to me in badly battered and disreputable-looking old square pasteboard boxes, two hundred in a box. George brought the box, which was caved in on all sides, looking the worst it could, and began to pass them around. The conversation had been brilliantly animated up to that moment—but now a frost fell upon the company. That is to say, not all of a sudden, but the frost fell upon each man as he took up a cigar and held it poised in the air—and there, in the middle, his sentence broke off. That kind of thing went on all around the table, until when George had completed his crime the whole place was full of a thick solemnity and silence.

Those men began to light the cigars. Rev. Dr. Parker was the first man to light. He took three or four heroic whiffs—then gave it up. He got up with the remark that he had to go to the bedside of a dying parishioner, which I knew was a lie, because if that had been the truth he would have gone earlier. He started out. Rev. Dr. Burton was the next man. He took only one whiff, and followed Parker. He furnished a pretext, and you could see by the sound of his voice that he didn't think much of the pretext, and was vexed with Parker for getting in ahead with a dying client. Rev. Mr. Twichell followed, with a good hearty pretext—nothing in it, and he didn't expect anybody to find anything in it, but Twichell is always more or less honest, to this day, and it cost him nothing to say that he had to go now because he must take the midnight train for Boston. Boston was the first place that occurred to him—he would have said Jerusalem if he had thought of it.

It was only a quarter to eleven when they began to distribute pretexts. At ten minutes to eleven all those people were out of the house, and praying, no doubt, that the pretext might be overlooked, in consideration of the circumstances. When nobody was left but George and me I was cheerful—I had no compunctions of conscience, no griefs of any kind. But George was beyond speech, because he held the honor and credit of the family above his own, and he was ashamed that this smirch had been put upon it. I told him to go to bed and try to sleep it off. I went to bed myself. At breakfast in the morning when George was taking a cup of coffee from Mrs. Clemens's hand, I saw it tremble in his hand. I knew by that sign that there was something on his mind. He brought the cup to me and asked impressively,

"Mr. Clemens, how far is it from the front door to the upper gate?"

I said "It is a hundred and twenty-five steps."

He said "Mr. Clemens, you can start at the front door and you can go plumb to the upper gate and tread on one of them cigars every time."

Now by this roundabout and gradual excursion I have arrived at that meeting of the Club at Reverend Frank Goodwin's house which I spoke of a while back, and where that same word was used in my presence, and to me, which I mentioned as having been used by my mother as much as forty years before. The subject under discussion was Dreams. The talk passed from mouth to mouth in the usual serene way. The late Charles Dudley Warner delivered his views in the smooth and pleasantly flowing fashion which he had learned in his early manhood when he was an apprentice to the legal profession. He always spoke pleasingly, always smoothly, always choicely, never excitedly, never aggressively, always kindly, gently, and always with a lambent and playful and inconspicuous thread of humor appearing and disappearing along through his talk, like the tinted lights in an opal. To my thinking, there was never much body to what he said, never much juice in it; never anything very substantial to carry away and think about, yet it was always a pleasure to listen to him. Always his art was graceful and charming. Then came the late Colonel Greene, who had been a distinguished soldier in the Civil War, and who at the time that I speak of was high up in the Connecticut Mutual and on his way to become its President presently, and in time to die in that harness and leave behind him a blemishless reputation, at a time when the chiefs of the New York insurance companies were approaching the eternal doom of their reputations. Colonel Greene discussed the Dream question in his usual way—that is to say, he began a sentence and went on and on, dropping a comma in here and there at intervals of eighteen inches, never hesitating for a word, drifting straight along like a river at half bank with no reefs in it; the surface of his talk as smooth as a mirror; his construction perfect, and fit for print without correction, as he went along. And when the hammer fell, at the end of his ten minutes, he dumped in a period right where he was and stopped—and it was just as good there as it would have been anywhere else in that ten minutes' sentence. You could look back over that speech and you'd find it dimly milestoned along with those commas which he had put in and which could have been left out just as well, because they merely staked out the march, and nothing more. They could not call attention to the scenery, because there wasn't any. His speech was always like that—perfectly smooth, perfectly constructed; and when he had finished, no listener could go into court and tell what it was he had said. It was a curious style. It was impressive—you always thought, from one comma to another, that he was going to strike something presently, but he never did. But this time that I speak of, the burly and magnificent Rev. Dr. Burton sat with his eyes fixed upon Greene from the beginning of the sentence until the end of it. He looked as the lookout on a whaleship might look who was watching where a whale had gone down and was waiting and watching for it to reappear; and no doubt that was the figure that was in Burton's mind, because when at last Greene finished, Burton threw up his hands and shouted "There she blows!"

The elder Hamersley took his appointed ten minutes, easily, comfortably, with good phrasing, and most entertainingly—and this was always to be expected of the elder Hamersley.

Then his son, Will Hamersley, a young lawyer, now this many years a Judge of the Connecticut Supreme Court, took his chance in the Dream question. And I can't imagine anything more distressing than a talk from Will Hamersley—a talk from the Will Hamersley *of those days*. You *always* knew that before he got through he would certainly say something—something that you could carry away, something that you could consider, something that you couldn't easily put out of your mind. But you also knew that you would suffer many a torture before he got that thing out. He would hesitate and hesitate, get to the middle of a sentence and search around and around and around for a word, get the wrong word, search again, get another wrong one, search again and again—and so he would go on in that way till everybody was in misery on his account, hoping that he would arrive in the course of time, and yet sinking deeper and deeper toward despair, with the conviction that this time he was not going to arrive. He would seem to get so far away from any possible goal that you would feel convinced that he could not cover the intervening space and get there before his ten minutes would come to an end and leave him suspended between heaven and earth. But, sure as a gun, before that ten minutes ended Will Hamersley would arrive at his point and fetch it out with such a round and complete and handsome and satisfying unostentatious crash that you would be lifted out of your chair with admiration and gratitude.

Joe Twichell sometimes took his turn. If he talked, it was easily perceptible that it was because he had something to say, and he was always able to say it well. But almost as a rule, he said nothing, and gave his ten minutes to the next man—and whenever he gave it to Charles E. Perkins he ran the risk of getting lynched on his way home by the rest of the membership. Charles E. Perkins was the dullest white man in Connecticut—and he probably remains that to this day; I have not heard of any real competitor. Perkins would moon along, and moon along, and moon along, using the most commonplace, the most dreary, the most degraded English, with never an idea in it by any chance. But *he* never gave his ten minutes to anybody. He always used it up to the last second. Then there was always a little gap—had to be for the crowd to recover before the next man could begin. Perkins, when he would get entirely lost in his talk and didn't know where he was in his idiotic philosophizings, would grasp at narrative, as the drowning man grasps at a straw. If a drowning man ever does that—which I doubt. Then he would tell something in his experiences, thinking perhaps it had something to do with the question in hand. It generally hadn't—and this time he told about a long and arduous and fatiguing chase which he had had in the Maine woods on a hot summer's day, after some kind of a wild animal that he wanted to kill, and how at last, chasing eagerly after this creature across a wide stream, he slipped and fell on the ice, and injured his leg—whereupon a silence and confusion. Perkins noticed that something was wrong, and then it occurred to him that there was a kind of discrepancy in hunting animals on the ice in summertime, so he switched off to theology. He always did that. He was a rabid Christian, and member of Joe Twichell's church. Joe Twichell could get together the most impossible Christians that ever assembled in anybody's congregation; and as a usual thing he couldn't run his church systematically on account of new deacons who didn't understand the business—the recent deacons having joined their predecessors in the Penitentiary down there at Wethersfield. Perkins would wind up with some very pious remarks—and in fact they all did that. Take the whole crowd—the crowd that was almost always present—and this remark applies to them. There was J. Hammond Trumbull, the most learned man in the United States. He knew everything—everything in detail that had ever happened in this world, and a lot that was going to happen, and a lot that couldn't ever possibly happen. He was thoroughly posted, and yet if there was a prize offered for the man that could put up the most uninteresting ten minutes' talk, you wouldn't know whether to bet on him or on Perkins—*he* would close with some piety. Henry C. Robinson—Governor Henry C. Robinson—a brilliant man, a most polished and effective and eloquent speaker, an easy speaker, a speaker who had no difficulties to encounter in delivering himself—always closed with some piety. A. C. Dunham, a man really great in his line—that is to say the commercial line—a great manufacturer, an enterprising man, a capitalist, a most competent and fascinating talker, a man who never opened his mouth without a stream of practical pearls flowing from it—*he* always closed with some piety—

January 13, 1906

The piety-ending was used also by Franklin and Johnson, and possibly by the rest of the Club—most likely by the rest of the Club. But I recall that that ending was a custom with Franklin and with Johnson. Franklin was a bluff old soldier. He was a West Pointer and, I think, had served in the Mexican war. He commanded one of McClellan's armies in the Civil War at the time that McClellan was commander-in-chief. He was an ideal soldier, simple-hearted, good, kind, affectionate; set in his opinions, his partialities and his prejudices, believing everything which he had been taught to believe about politics, religion, and military matters; thoroughly well educated in the military science—in fact I have already said that, because I have said he was a West Pointer. He knew all that was worth knowing in that specialty, and was able to reason well upon his knowledge, but his reasoning faculty did not shine when he was discussing other things. Johnson was a member of Trinity, and was easily the most brilliant member of the Club. But his fine light shone not in public, but in the privacy of the Club, and his qualities were not known outside of Hartford.

I had long been suffering from these intolerable and inexcusable exudations of misplaced piety, and for years had wanted to enter a protest against them, but had struggled against the impulse and had always been able to conquer it, until now. But this time Perkins was too much for me. He was the feather that broke the camel's back. The substance of his wandering twaddle—if by chance it had substance—was that there is nothing in dreams. Dreams merely proceed from indigestion—there is no quality of intelligence in them—they are thoroughly fantastic and without beginning, logical sequence, or definite end. Nobody, in our day, but the stupid or the ignorant attaches any significance to them. And then he went on blandly and pleasantly to say that dreams had *once* had a mighty importance, that they had had the illustrious honor of being used by the Almighty as a means of conveying desires, warnings, commands, to people whom He loved or hated—that these dreams are set down in Holy Writ; that no sane man challenges their authenticity, their significance, their verity.

I followed Perkins, and I remember with satisfaction that I said not one harsh thing, vexed as I was, but merely remarked, without warmth, that these tiresome damned prayer-meetings might better be adjourned to the garret of some church, where they belonged. It is *centuries* ago that I did that thing. It was away back, back, back, so many, many years ago—and yet I have always regretted it, because from that time forth, to the last meeting which I attended (which would be at the beginning of the spring of 1891) the piety-ending was never used again. No, perhaps I am going too far; maybe I am putting too much emphasis upon my regret. Possibly when I said that about regret, I was doing what people so often unconsciously do, trying to place myself in a favorable light after having made a confession that makes such a thing more or less difficult. No, I think it quite likely that I never regretted it at all.

Anybody could see that the piety-ending had no importance, for the reason that it was manifestly perfunctory. The Club was *founded* by a great clergyman; it always had more clergymen in it than good people. Clergymen are not able to sink the shop without falling under suspicion. It was quite natural that the original members should introduce that kind of ending to their speeches. It was also quite natural that the rest of the membership, being church members, should take up the custom, turn it into a habit, and continue it without ever happening to notice that it was merely a mouth function, had no heart in it, and therefore utterly valueless to themselves and to everybody else.

I do not now remember what form my views concerning dreams took at that time. I don't remember now what my notion about dreams was then, but I do remember telling a dream by way of illustrating some detail of my speech, and I also remember that when I had finished it Rev. Dr. Burton made that doubting remark which contained that word I have already spoken of sixteen or seventeen times as having been uttered by my mother, in some such connection, forty or fifty years before. I was probably engaged in trying to make those people believe that now and then, by some accident, or otherwise, a dream which was prophetic turned up in the dreamer's mind. The date of my memorable dream was about the beginning of May, 1858. It was a remarkable dream, and I had been telling it several times every year for more than fifteen years—and now I was telling it again, here in the Club.

In 1858 I was a steersman on board the swift and popular New Orleans and St. Louis packet, *Pennsylvania,* Captain Klinefelter. I had been lent to Mr. Brown, one of the pilots of the *Pennsylvania,* by my owner, Mr. Horace E. Bixby, and I had been steering for Brown about eighteen months, I think. Then in the early days of May, 1858, came a tragic trip—the last trip of that fleet and famous steamboat. I have told all about it in one of my books called "Old Times on the Mississippi." But it is not likely that I told the dream in that book. I will ask Miss Lyon to see—but I will go on and dictate the dream now, and it can go into the waste-basket if it shall turn out that I have already published it. It is impossible that I can ever have published it, I think, because I never wanted my mother to know about that dream, and she lived several years after I published that volume.

I had found a place on the *Pennsylvania* for my brother Henry, who was two years my junior. It was not a place of profit, it was only a place of promise. He was "mud" clerk. Mud clerks received no salary, but they were in the line of promotion. They could become, presently, third clerk and second clerk, then chief clerk—that is to say, purser. The dream begins when Henry had been mud clerk about three months. We were lying in port at St. Louis. Pilots and steersmen had nothing to do during the three days that the boat lay in port in St. Louis and New Orleans, but the mud clerk had to begin his labors at dawn and continue them into the night, by the light of pine-knot torches. Henry and I, moneyless and unsalaried, had billeted ourselves upon our brother-in-law, Mr. Moffett, as night lodgers while in port. We took our meals on board the boat. No, I mean *I* lodged at the house, not Henry. He spent the *evenings* at the house, from nine until eleven, then went to the boat to be ready for his early duties. On the night of the dream he started away at eleven, shaking hands with the family, and said good-bye according to custom. I may mention that hand-shaking as a good-bye was not merely the custom of that family, but the custom of the region—the custom of Missouri, I may say. In all my life, up to that time, I had never seen one member of the Clemens family kiss another one—except once. When my father lay dying in our home in Hannibal—the 24th of March 1847—he put his arm around my sister's neck and drew her down and kissed her, saying "Let me die." I remember that, and I remember the death rattle which swiftly followed those words, which were his last. These good-byes of Henry's were always executed in the family sitting-room on the second floor, and Henry went from that room and down stairs without further ceremony. But this time my mother went with him to the head of the stairs and said good-bye *again*. As I remember it she was moved to this by something in Henry's manner, and she remained at the head of the stairs while he descended. When he reached the door he hesitated, and climbed the stairs and shook hands good-bye once more.

In the morning, when I awoke I had been dreaming, and the dream was so vivid, so like reality, that it deceived me, and I thought it *was* real. In the dream I had seen Henry a corpse. He lay in a metallic burial case. He was dressed in a suit of my clothing, and on his breast lay a great bouquet of flowers, mainly white roses, with a red rose in the centre. The casket stood upon a couple of chairs. I dressed, and moved toward that door, thinking I would go in there and look at it, but I changed my mind. I thought I could not yet bear to meet my mother. I thought I would wait a while and make some preparation for that ordeal. The house was in Locust street, a little above 13th, and I walked to 14th, and to the middle of the block beyond, before it suddenly flashed upon me that there was nothing real about this—it was only a dream. I can still feel something of the grateful upheaval of joy of that moment, and I can also still feel the remnant of doubt, the suspicion that maybe it *was* real, after all. I returned to the house almost on a run, flew up the stairs two or three steps at a jump, and rushed into that sitting-room—and was made glad again, for there was no casket there.

We made the usual eventless trip to New Orleans—no, it was not eventless, for it was on the way down that I had the fight with Mr. Brown* which resulted in his requiring that I be left ashore at New Orleans. In New Orleans I always had a job. It was my privilege to watch the freight-piles from seven in the evening until seven in the morning, and get three dollars for it. It was a three-night job and occurred every thirty-five days. Henry always joined my watch about nine in the evening, when his own duties were ended, and we often walked my rounds and chatted together until midnight. This time we were to part, and so the night before the boat sailed I gave Henry some advice. I said "In case of disaster to the boat, don't lose your head—leave that unwisdom to the passengers—they are competent—they'll attend to it. But you rush for the hurricane-deck, and astern to one of the life-boats lashed aft the wheel-house, and obey the mate's orders—thus you will be useful. When the boat is launched, give such help as you can in getting the women and children into it, and be sure you don't try to get into it yourself. It is summer weather, the river is only a mile wide, as a rule, and you can swim that without any trouble." Two or three days afterward the boat's boilers exploded at Ship Island, below Memphis, early one morning—and what happened afterward I have already told in "Old Times on the Mississippi." As related there, I followed the *Pennsylvania* about a day later, on another boat, and we began to get news of the disaster at every port we touched at, and so by the time we reached Memphis we knew all about it.

I found Henry stretched upon a mattress on the floor of a great building, along with thirty or forty other scalded and wounded persons, and was promptly informed, by some indiscreet person, that he had inhaled steam; that his body was badly scalded, and that he would live but a little while; also, I was told that the physicians and nurses were giving their whole attention

*See "Old Times on the Mississippi."

to persons who had a chance of being saved. They were short-handed in the matter of physicians and nurses; and Henry and such others as were considered to be fatally hurt were receiving only such attention as could be spared, from time to time, from the more urgent cases. But Dr. Peyton, a fine and large-hearted old physician of great reputation in the community, gave me his sympathy and took vigorous hold of the case, and in about a week he had brought Henry around. Dr. Peyton never committed himself with prognostications which might not materialize, but at eleven o'clock one night he told me that Henry was out of danger, and would get well. Then he said "At midnight these poor fellows lying here and there all over this place will begin to mourn and mutter and lament and make outcries, and if this commotion should disturb Henry it will be bad for him; therefore ask the physicians on watch to give him an eighth of a grain of morphine, but this is not to be done unless Henry shall show signs that he is being disturbed."

Oh well, never mind the rest of it. The physicians on watch were young fellows hardly out of the medical college, and they made a mistake—they had no way of measuring the eighth of a grain of morphine, so they guessed at it and gave him a vast quantity heaped on the end of a knife-blade, and the fatal effects were soon apparent. I think he died about dawn, I don't remember as to that. He was carried to the dead-room and I went away for a while to a citizen's house and slept off some of my accumulated fatigue—and meantime something was happening. The coffins provided for the dead were of unpainted white pine, but in this instance some of the ladies of Memphis had made up a fund of sixty dollars and bought a metallic case, and when I came back and entered the dead-room Henry lay in that open case, and he was dressed in a suit of my clothing. He had borrowed it without my knowledge during our last sojourn in St. Louis; and I recognized instantly that my dream of several weeks before was here exactly reproduced, so far as these details went—and I think I missed one detail; but that one was immediately supplied, for just then an elderly lady entered the place with a large bouquet consisting mainly of white roses, and in the centre of it was a red rose, and she laid it on his breast.

I told the dream there in the Club that night just as I have told it here.

January 15, 1906

Rev. Dr. Burton swung his leonine head around, focussed me with his eye, and said:
"When was it that this happened?"
"In June, '58."
"It is a good many years ago. Have you told it several times since?"
"Yes, I have, a good many times."
"How many?"
"Why, I don't know how many."
"Well, strike an average. How many times a year do you think you have told it?"
"Well I have told it as many as six times a year, possibly oftener."
"Very well, then you've told it, we'll say, seventy or eighty times since it happened?"

"Yes," I said, "that's a conservative estimate."

"Now then, Mark, a very extraordinary thing happened to me a great many years ago, and I used to tell it a number of times—a good many times—every year, for it was so wonderful that it always astonished the hearer, and that astonishment gave me a distinct pleasure every time. I never suspected that that tale was acquiring any auxiliary advantages through repetition until one day after I had been telling it ten or fifteen years it struck me that either I was getting old, and slow in delivery, or that the tale was longer than it was when it was born. Mark, I diligently and prayerfully examined that tale with this result: that I found that its proportions were now, as nearly as I could make out, one part fact, straight fact, fact pure and undiluted, golden fact, and twenty-four parts embroidery. I never told that tale afterwards—I was never able to tell it again, for I had lost confidence in it, and so the pleasure of telling it was gone, and gone permanently. How much of this tale of yours is embroidery?"

"Well," I said "I don't know. I don't think any of it is embroidery. I think it is all just as I have stated it, detail by detail."

"Very well," he said, "then it is all right, but I wouldn't tell it any more; because if you keep on, it will begin to collect embroidery sure. The safest thing is to stop now."

That was a great many years ago. And to-day is the first time that I have told that dream since Dr. Burton scared me into fatal doubts about it. No, I don't believe I can say that. I don't believe that I ever really had any doubts whatever concerning the salient points of the dream, for those points are of such a nature that they are *pictures,* and pictures can be remembered, when they are vivid, much better than one can remember remarks and unconcreted facts. Although it has been so many years since I have told that dream, I can see those pictures now just as clearly defined as if they were before me in this room. I have not told the entire dream. There was a good deal more of it. I mean I have not told all that happened in the dream's fulfillment. After the incident in the death room I may mention one detail, and that is this. When I arrived in St. Louis with the casket it was about eight o'clock in the morning, and I ran to my brother-in-law's place of business, hoping to find him there, but I missed him, for while I was on the way to his office he was on his way from the house to the boat. When I got back to the boat the casket was gone. He had conveyed it out to his house. I hastened thither, and when I arrived the men were just removing the casket from the vehicle to carry it up stairs. I stopped that procedure, for I did not want my mother to see the dead face, because one side of it was drawn and distorted by the effects of the opium. When I went up stairs, there stood the two chairs—placed to receive the coffin—just as I had seen them in my dream; and if I had arrived two or three minutes later, the casket would have been resting upon them, precisely as in my dream of several weeks before.

Now then, Twichell—but never mind about Twichell. There is a telephone message from his daughter, Mrs. Wood, to say he is in town and will come here to dinner and stay all night.

I think it was at that same dream meeting that a very curious thing happened. It didn't happen then—it happened in the night, afterward. No, it didn't happen there at all. It happened at the house of James Goodwin, father of Reverend Francis Goodwin, and also father of the great Connecticut Mutual Insurance Company. Mr. James Goodwin was an old man at the time that I speak of, but in his young days, when he used to drive stage between Hartford and Springfield, he conceived the idea of starting a Mutual Insurance Company, and he collected a little capital in the way of subscriptions—enough to start the business in a modest way—and he gave away the rest of the stock where he could find people willing to accept it—(though they were rather scarce) and now he had lived to see that stock worth two hundred and fifty and nobody willing to sell at that price, or any other. He had long ago forgotten how to drive stage—but it was no matter. He was worth seven millions, and didn't need to work for a living any longer. Reverend Frank Goodwin, his son, an Episcopal clergyman, was a man of many accomplishments; and among others, he was an architect. He planned and built a huge granite mansion for his father, and I think it was in that mansion that that curious thing happened that night. However I don't know about that. No, it didn't happen there. It happened in Francis Goodwin's own house in the neighborhood. I don't mind excursioning around in an autobiography—there is plenty of room. I don't mind it so long as I get the things right at last, when they are important. It happened in this way. Frank Goodwin had a burglar alarm in his house. The annunciator was right at his ear, on the port side of his bed. He would put the whole house on the alarm—every window and every door—at bedtime, then, at five o'clock in the morning the cook would descend from her bedroom and open the kitchen door and that would set the alarm to buzzing in Goodwin's ear. Now as that happened every morning straight along, week in and week out, Goodwin soon became so habituated to it that it didn't disturb him. It aroused him, partly, from his sleep sometimes—sometimes it probably did not affect his sleep at all, but from old habit he would automatically put out his left hand and shut off that alarm. By that act he shut off the alarm from the entire house, leaving not a window or a door on it from five o'clock in the morning thenceforth until he should set the alarm the next night at bedtime.

The night that I speak of was one of those dismal New England November nights, close upon the end of the month, when the pestiferous New England climate furnishes those regions a shake-down just in the way of experiment and to get its hand in for business when the proper time comes, which is December. Well, the wind howled, and the snow blew along in clouds when we left that house about midnight. It was a wild night. It was like a storm at sea, for boom and crash and roar and furious snow-drive. It was no kind of a night for burglars to be out in, and yet they *were* out. Goodwin was in bed, with his house on the alarm by half past twelve. Not very long afterward the burglars arrived. Evidently they knew all about the burglar alarm, because instead of breaking into the kitchen they sawed their way in—that is to say, they sawed a great panel out of the kitchen door and stepped in without alarming the alarm. They went all over the house at their leisure; they collected all sorts of trinkets and trumpery; and all of the silverware. They carried these things to the kitchen, put them in bags, and then they gathered together a sumptuous supper, with champagne and Burgundy, and so on, and ate that supper at their leisure. Then when they were ready to leave—say at three o'clock in the morning—the champagne and the Burgundy had had an influence, and they became careless for a moment, but one moment was enough. In that careless moment a burglar unlocked and opened the kitchen door, and of course the alarm went off. Rev. Mr. Goodwin put out his left hand and shut it off and went on sleeping peacefully, but the burglars bounded out of the place and left all their swag behind them. A burglar alarm is a valuable thing if you know how to utilize it.

When Rev. Mr. Goodwin was finishing his father's mansion, I was passing by one day. I thought I would go in and see how the house was coming along, and in the first room I entered I found Mr. Goodwin and a paperhanger. Then Mr. Goodwin told me this curious story. He said,

"This room has been waiting a good while. This is Morris paper, and it didn't hold out. You will see there is one space there, from the ceiling half way to the floor, which is blank. I sent to New York and ordered some more of the paper—it couldn't be furnished. I applied in Philadelphia and in Boston, with the same result. There was not a bolt of that paper left in America, so far as any of these people knew. I wrote to London. The answer came back in those same monotonous terms—that paper was out of print—not a yard of it to be found. Then I told the paperhanger to strip the paper off and we would replace it with some other pattern, and I was very sorry, because I preferred that pattern to any other. Just then a farmer-looking man halted in front of the house, started to walk that single-plank approach, that you have just walked, and come in; but he saw that sign up there—'No admittance'—a sign which did not obstruct your excursion into this place—but it halted *him*. I said 'Come in, come in.' He came in, and this being the first room on the route, he naturally glanced in. He saw the paper on the wall and remarked casually 'I am acquainted with that pattern. I've got a bolt of it at home down on my farm in Glastonbury.' It didn't take long to strike up a trade with him for that bolt, which had been lying in his farm-house for he didn't know how long, and he hadn't any use for it—and now we are finishing up that lacking patch there."

It was only a coincidence, but I think it was a very curious and interesting one.

MRS. MORRIS'S ILLNESS TAKES A SERIOUS TURN

Cabinet Officers Urge President to Disavow Violence to Her.

A DISCUSSION IN THE HOUSE

Mr. Sheppard Criticises the President and Republican Leaders Try to Stop Him.

Special to The New York Times.

WASHINGTON, Jan. 10.—Mrs. Minor Morris, who on Thursday was dragged from the White House, is to-night in a critical condition.

She seemed to be on the road to recovery on Saturday, and her physicians held out hopes that she would be able to be out by Monday. At the beginning of this week her condition took an unfavorable turn, and she has been growing steadily worse. She had a congestive chill to-day and has continued to grow worse. It is evident to-night that her nervous system has suffered something approaching a collapse.

The bruises inflicted upon her by the policemen have not disappeared, a striking evidence of their severity. Her arms, shoulders, and neck still bear testimony to the nature of her treatment. Mentally and physically she is suffering severely.

It was learned to-day that two Cabinet officers, one of whom is Secretary Taft, have been laboring with the President for two days to get him to issue a statement disavowing the action of Assistant Secretary Barnes, who ordered Mrs. Morris expelled, and expressing his regret for the way she was treated. They have also urged him to promise to take action which will make impossible the repetition of such an occurrence.

The President has held out stoutly against the advice of these two Cabinet officers. He authorized Mr. Barnes to make the statement that he gave out, in which the treatment of Mrs. Morris was justified, and it is not easy to take the other tack now. On high authority, however, it is learned that the two Cabinet officers have not ceased their labors. They both look on the matter not as "a mere incident," but as a serious affair.

The Morris incident was brought up in the House to-day just before adjournment by Mr. Sheppard of Texas. He was recognized for fifteen minutes, in the ordinary course of the debate on the Philippine Tariff bill, and began at once to discuss the resolution he introduced Monday calling for an investigation of the expulsion. He excused himself for speaking on the resolution at this time, saying that as it was not privileged he could not obtain its consideration without the consent of the Committee on Rules.

He went on to describe the incident at the White House. He had proceeded only a minute or two when he was interrupted by Gen. Grosvenor, who rose to the point of order that the remarks were not germane to the Philippine Tariff bill.

"I will show the gentleman that it is germane," cried Mr. Sheppard. "It is just as proper for this country to have a Chinese wall around the White House as it is to have such a wall around the United States."

"Well, if he thinks it is proper to thus arraign the President and his household," said Mr. Grosvenor, "let him go on."

"If the President had heard the howl of a wolf or the growl of a bear from the adjacent offices," retorted Mr. Sheppard, "the response would have been immediate, but the wail of an American woman fell upon unresponsive ears."

There had been several cries of protest when Gen. Grosvenor interrupted Mr. Sheppard, many of whose Democratic friends gathered about him and urged him to proceed. They applauded his reply to Mr. Grosvenor, and the Ohioan did not press his point.

"These unwarrantable and unnecessary brutalities," continued Mr. Sheppard, "demand an investigation. Unless Congress takes some action we shall soon witness in a free republic a condition where citizens cannot approach the President they have created without fear of bodily harm from arbitrary subordinates."

Mr. Sheppard had nearly reached the close of his remarks when Mr. Payne, the titular floor leader of the Republicans, renewed the Grosvenor point of order. Mr. Olmstead of Pennsylvania, in the chair, however, ruled that with the House sitting in Committee of the Whole on the state of the Union, remarks need not be germane.

Mr. Payne interrupted again, to ask a question.

"If a gentleman has the facts upon which to found his attack," he said, "does he not think the police court is the better place to air them?"

"The suggestion is a reflection upon the gentleman himself, although he is a friend of mine," replied Sheppard.

When the speech was finished Grosvenor got the floor and said he had been aware of the rules when he did not press his point.

"But I made the point," he continued, "merely to call the attention of the young gentleman from Texas in a mild and fatherly manner, to my protest against his remarks. I hoped he would refrain from further denunciation of the President. He has introduced a resolution which is now pending before the proper committee. That resolution asks for facts and I supposed that the gentleman would wait for the facts until that resolution is brought into the House.

"I know no difference in proper conduct between the President's office and household and the humblest home in this Nation, but I don't believe a condition has arisen such that the husband of this woman cannot take care of the situation."

A high Government official to-night added to the accounts of the expulsion an incident, which he said was related to him by an eyewitness. While the policemen and their negro assistant were dragging Mrs. Morris through the grounds the scene was witnessed by the women servants, some of whom called out, "Shame!" One of the policemen pressed his hand down on Mrs. Morris's mouth to stifle her cries for help, and at that sight a man servant, a negro, rushed forward and shouted:

"Take your hand off that white woman's face! Don't treat a white woman that way!"

The policeman paid no attention to the man, and continued his efforts to stifle Mrs. Morris's cries.

The reason I want to insert that account of the Morris case, which is making such a lively stir all over the United States, and possibly the entire world, in these days, is this. Some day, no doubt these autobiographical notes will be published. It will be after my death. It may be five years from now, it may be ten, it may be fifty—but whenever the time shall come, even if it should be a century hence—I claim that the reader of that day will find the same strong interest in that narrative that the world has in it to-day, for the reason that the account speaks of the thing in the language we naturally use when we are talking about something that has just happened. That form of narrative is able to carry along with it for ages and ages the very same interest which we find in it to-day. Whereas if this had happened fifty years ago, or a hundred, and the historian had dug it up and was putting it in *his* language, and furnishing you a long-distance view of it, the reader's interest in it would be pale. You see, it would not be *news* to him, it would be history; merely history; and history can carry on no successful competition with *news,* in the matter of sharp interest. When an eye-witness sets down in narrative form some extraordinary occurrence which he has witnessed, that is *news*—that is the news form, and its interest is absolutely indestructible; time can have no deteriorating effect upon that episode. I am placing that account there largely as an experiment. If any stray copy of this book shall, by any chance, escape the paper-mill for a century or so, and then be discovered and read, I am betting that that remote reader will find that it is still *news,* and that it is just as interesting as any news he will find in the newspapers of his day and morning—if newspapers shall still be in existence then—though let us hope they won't.

These notions were born to me in the fall of 1867, in Washington. That is to say, thirty-nine years ago. I had come back from the *Quaker City* Excursion. I had gone to Washington to write "The Innocents Abroad," but before beginning that book it was necessary to earn some money to live on meantime, or borrow it—which would be difficult, or take it where it reposed unwatched—which would be unlikely. So I started the first Newspaper Correspondence Syndicate that an unhappy world ever saw. I started it in conjunction with William Swinton, a brother of the Admirable John Swinton. William Swinton was a brilliant creature, highly educated, accomplished. He was such a contrast to me that I did not know which of us most to admire, because both ends of a contrast are equally delightful to me. A thoroughly beautiful woman and a thoroughly homely woman are creations which I love to gaze upon, and which I cannot tire of gazing upon, for each is perfect in her own line, and it is *perfection,* I think, in many things, and perhaps most things, which is the quality that fascinates us. A splendid literature charms us; but it doesn't charm *me* any more than its opposite does—"hog-wash" literature. At another time I will explain that word, "hog-wash," and offer an example of it which lies here on the bed—a book which was lately sent to me from England, or Ireland.

Swinton kept a jug. It was sometimes full, but seldom as full as himself—and it was when he was fullest that he was most competent with his pen. We wrote a letter apiece once a week and copied them and sent them to twelve newspapers, charging each of the newspapers a dollar apiece. And although we didn't get rich, it kept the jug going and partly fed the two of us. We earned the rest of our living with magazine articles. My trade in that line was better than his, because I had written six letters for the New York *Tribune* while I was out on the *Quaker City* Excursion, and one pretty breezy one for the New York *Herald* after I got back, and so I had a good deal of a reputation to trade on. Every now and then I was able to get twenty-five dollars for a magazine article. Riley and I were supporting the cheap boarding-houses at that time. It took two of us to do it, and even then the boarding-houses perished. I have always believed, since, that cheap boarding-houses that do business on credit make a mistake—but let Riley go for the present. I will speak of him another time.

I had a chance to write a magazine article about an ancient and moss-grown claim which was disturbing Congress that session, a claim which had been disturbing Congress ever since the War of 1812, and was always getting paid, but never satisfied. The claim was for Indian corn and for provender consumed by the American troops in Maryland or somewhere around there, in the War of 1812. I wrote the article, and it is in one of my books, and is there called "Concerning the Great Beef Contract." It was necessary to find out the price of Indian corn in 1812, and I found that detail a little difficult. Finally I went to A. R. Spofford, who was the Librarian of Congress then—Spofford the man with the prodigious memory,—and I put my case before him. He knew every volume in the Library and what it contained, and where it was located. He said promptly, "I know of only two sources which promise to afford this information: 'Tooke on Prices'" (he brought me the book) "and the New York *Evening Post.* In those days newspapers did not publish market reports, but about 1809 the New York *Evening Post* began to print market reports on sheets of paper about note-paper size, and fold these in the journal." He brought me a file of the *Evening Post* for 1812. I examined "Tooke" and then began to examine the *Post*—and I was in a great hurry. I had less than an hour at my disposal. But in the *Post* I found a personal narrative which chained my attention at once. It was a letter from a gentleman who had witnessed the arrival of the British and the burning of the Capitol. The matter was bristling with interest for him and he delivered his words hot from the bat. That letter must have been read with fiery and absorbing interest three days later in New York, but not with any more absorbing interest than the interest which was making my blood leap fifty-nine years later. When I finished that account I found I had used up all the time that was at my disposal, and more.

January 15th, continued.

That incident made a strong impression upon me. I believed I had made a discovery—the discovery already indicated—the discovery of the wide difference in interest between "news" and "history;" that news is history in its first and best form, its vivid and fascinating form; and that history is the pale and tranquil reflection of it.

This reminds me that in this daily dictation of autobiographical notes, I am mixing these two forms together all the time. I am hoping by this method of procedure to secure the values of both. I am sure I have found the right way to spin an autobiography at last, after my many experiments. Years ago I used to make skeleton notes to use as texts in writing autobiographical chapters, but really those notes were worth next to nothing. If I expanded them upon the page at once, while their interest was fresh in my mind, they were useful, but if I left them unused for several weeks, or several months, their power to suggest and excite had usually passed away. They were faded flowers, their fragrance was gone. But I believe in this present plan. When you arrive with your stenographic plant at eleven, every morning, you find me placid and comfortable in bed, smoking, untroubled by the fact that I must presently get to work and begin to dictate this history of mine. And if I were depending upon faded notes for inspiration, I should have trouble, and my work would soon become distasteful. But by my present system I do not need any notes. *The thing uppermost in a person's mind* is the thing to talk about or write about. The thing of new and immediate interest is the pleasantest text he can have—and you can't come here at eleven o'clock, or any other hour, and catch me without a new interest—a perfectly fresh interest—because I have either been reading the infernal newspapers and got it there, or I have been talking with somebody; and in either case the new interest is present—the interest which I most wish to dictate about. So you see the result is that this narrative of mine is sure to begin every morning in diary form, because it is sure to begin with something which I have just read, or something which I have just been talking about. That text, when I am done with it—if I ever get done with it, and I don't seem to get done with any text—but it doesn't matter, I am not interested in getting done with anything. I am only interested in talking along and wandering around as much as I want to, regardless of results to the future reader. By consequence, here we have diary and history combined; because as soon as I wander from the present text—the thought of to-day—that digression takes me far and wide over an uncharted sea of recollection, and the result of that is *history*. Consequently my autobiography is diary and history combined. The privilege of beginning every day in the diary form is a valuable one. I may even use a larger word, and say it is a precious one, for it brings together widely separated things that are in a manner related to each other and consequently pleasant surprises and contrasts are pretty sure to result every now and then.

Did I dictate something about John Malone, three or four days ago? Very well, then, if I didn't I must have been talking with somebody about John Malone. I remember now, it was with Mr. Volney Streamer. He is Librarian of the Players Club. He called here to bring me a book which he has published, and, in a general way, to make my acquaintance. I was a foundation member of the Players Club, but ceased to be a member three years ago, through an absurdity committed by the Management of that Club, a Management which has always been idiotic; a Management which from the beginning has been selected from, not the nearest asylum in the city, but the most competent one. (And some time I wish to talk about that.) Several times, during this lapse of three years, old friends of mine and comrades in the Club— David Munro, that charming Scot, editor of the *North American Review;* Robert Reid, the artist; Saint-Gaudens, the sculptor; John Malone, the ex-actor, and others, have been resenting the conduct of that Management—the conduct, I mean, which resulted in my segregation from the Club,—and they have always been trying to find a way of restoring me to the fold without damaging my pride. At last they found a way. They made me an honorary member. This handsome honor afforded me unlimited gratification, and I was glad to get back under such flattering conditions. (I don't like that word, but let it go, I can't think of the right one at the moment.) Then David Munro and the others put up the fatted calf for the lost sheep in the way of a dinner to me. Midway of the dinner I got a glimpse, through a half-open pantry door, of that pathetic figure, John Malone. There he was, left out, of course. Sixty-five years old; and his history may be summarized—his history for fifty years—in those two words, those eloquent words—"left out." He has been left out, and left out, and left out, as the years drifted by for nearly two generations. He was always expecting to be counted in. He was always pathetically hoping to be counted in; and that hope never deserted him through all those years, and yet was never in any instance realized. During all those years that I used to drop in at The Players for a game of billiards and a chat with the boys, John Malone was always there until midnight, and after. He had a cheap lodging in the Square—somewhere on Gramercy Park, but the Club was his real home. He told me his history once. His version of it was this:

He was an apprentice in a weekly little newspaper office in Willamette, Oregon, and by and by Edwin Booth made a one-night stand there with his troupe, and John got stage-struck and joined the troupe, and traveled with it around about the Pacific coast in various useful histrionic capacities—capacities suited to a beginner; sometimes assisting by appearing on the stage to say "My lord, the carriage waits," later appearing armored in shining tin, as a Roman soldier, and so on, gradually rising to higher and higher eminences, and by and by he stood shoulder to shoulder with John McCullough, and the two stood next in rank after Edwin Booth himself on the tragic stage. It was a question which of the two would succeed Booth when Booth should retire, or die. According to Malone, his celebrity quite equalled McCullough's in those days, and the chances were evenly balanced. A time came when there was a great opportunity—a great part to be played in Philadelphia. Malone was chosen for the part. He missed his train. John McCullough was put into that great place and achieved a success which *made* him for life. Malone was sure that if he had not missed the train he would have achieved that success himself; he would have secured the enduring fame which fell to John McCullough's lot; he would have moved on through life serene, comfortable, fortunate, courted, admired, applauded, as was John McCullough's case from that day until the day of his death. Malone believed with all his heart that fame and fortune were right there within his reach at that time, and that he lost them merely through missing his train. He dated his decline from that day. He declined, and declined, and declined, little by little, and little by little, and year after year, until there came a time when he was no longer wanted on the stage; when even minor part after minor part slipped from his grasp, and at last engagements ceased altogether—engagements of any kind. Yet he was always believing, and always expecting, that a turn of fortune would come; that he would get a chance on the stage in some great part; and that *one* chance, he said, was all he wanted. He was convinced that the world would not question that he was the rightful successor of Edwin Booth, and from that day forth he would be a famous and happy and fortunate man. He never gave up that hope. Three or four years ago, I remember his jubilation over the fact that he had been chosen by some private theatrical people to play Othello in one of the big theatres of New York. And I remember his grief and deep depression when those private theatrical people gave up the enterprise, at the last moment, and canceled Malone's engagement, snatching from him the greatness which had once more been just within his reach.

As I was saying, at mid-dinner that night I saw him through the half-open door. There he remained through the rest of the dinner, "left out," always left out. But at the end of the speeches, when a number of us were standing up in groups and chatting, he crept meekly in and found his way to the vacant chair at my side, and sat down. I sat down at once, and began to talk with him. I was always fond of him—I think everybody was. And presently the President of the New York City College came and bent over John and asked me something about my last summer, and how I had liked it up in the New Hampshire hills, at Dublin. Then, in order to include John in the conversation, he asked him if he was acquainted with that region, and if he had ever been in Dublin. Malone said dreamily, and with the air of a man who was trying to think up long-gone things, "How does it lie as regards Manchester?" President Finley told him, and then John said "I have never been to Dublin, but I have a sort of recollection of Manchester. I am pretty sure I was there once—but it was only a one-night stand, you know."

It filled my soul with a gentle delight, a gracious satisfaction, the way he said that—"Only a one-night stand." It seemed to reveal that in his half-century of day-dreaming he had been an Edwin Booth, and unconscious that he was only John Malone—that he was an Edwin Booth, with a long and great and successful career behind him, in which "one-night stands" sank into insignificance and the memory unused to treasuring such little things could not keep tally of them. He said it with the splendid indifference and serenity of a Napoleon who was making an indolent effort to remember a skirmish in which a couple of soldiers had been killed, but was not finding it really worth while to dig deep after such a fact.

Yesterday I spoke to Volney Streamer about John Malone. I had a purpose in this, though I did not tell Streamer what it was. David Munro was not able to be at that dinner, and so, to get satisfaction, he is providing another, for the 6th of February. David told me the guests he was inviting, and said that if there was anybody that I would like to invite, think it over and send him the name. I did think it over, and I have written down here on this pad the name of the man I selected—John Malone—hoping that he would not have to be left out this time, and knowing he wouldn't be left out unless David should desire it, and I didn't think David would desire it. However, I took the opportunity to throw out a feeler or two in talking with Volney Streamer, merely asking him how John Malone stood with the membership of The

Players now—and that question was quickly and easily answered—that everybody liked John Malone, and everybody pitied him.

Then he told me John Malone's history. It differed in some points from the history which Malone had given me, but not in essentials, I should say. One fact came out which I had not known about—that John was not a bachelor, but had a married daughter living here somewhere in New York. Then as Streamer went on, came this surprise: that *he* was a member of Edwin Booth's Company when John Malone joined it a thousand years ago, and that he had been a comrade of John's in the Company all over the Pacific coast and the rest of the States for years and years. There, you see, an entire stranger drops in here in the most casual way, and the first thing I know he is an ancient and moss-grown and mildewed comrade of the man who is for the moment uppermost in my mind. That is the way things happen when you are doing a diary and a history combined, and you can't catch these things in any other way but just that. If you try to remember them, with the intention of writing them down in the form of history a month or a year hence, why, when you get to them the juice is all out of them—you can't bring to mind the details. And moreover, they have lost their quality of surprise and joy, anyway. That has all wasted and passed away.

Very well——Yesterday Reverend Joe Twichell arrived from Hartford to take dinner and stay all night and swap some lies, and he sat here by the bed the rest of the afternoon, and we talked, and I told him all about John Malone. Twichell came in after breakfast this morning (the 16th) to chat again, and he brought me this, which he had cut out of the morning paper:

VETERAN ACTOR DEAD.

———

John Malone Was Historian of The Players' Club.

John Malone, the historian of the Players' Club and one of the oldest actors in the country, was stricken with apoplexy yesterday afternoon in front of Bishop Greer's residence, 7 Gramercy Park, a few doors from the club. Bishop Greer saw him fall, and, with the assistance of his servants carried Mr. Malone into his house. He was unconscious, and the Bishop telephoned to Police Headquarters.

An ambulance was sent from Bellevue Hospital, and Mr. Malone was taken to the institution by Dr. Hawkes. Later the Players had him removed to the Post-Graduate Hospital, where he died last night.

Mr. Malone was 65 years old, and had supported all the notable actors of a past generation. For a long time he was associated with Booth and Barrett. He had appeared on the stage but infrequently of late years, devoting the greater part of his time to magazine work. He lived with a married daughter in West 147th Street, but visited the Players' Club nearly every day. He was on his way to the club when stricken.

So there is another surprise, you see. While Twichell and I were talking about John Malone he was passing from this life. His disappointments are ended. At last he is not "left out." It was a long wait, but the best of all fortunes is his at last.

I started to say, a while ago, that when I had seemingly made that discovery of the difference between "news" and "history" thirty-nine years ago, I conceived the idea of a magazine to be called *The Back Number,* and to contain nothing but ancient news; narratives culled from mouldy old newspapers and mouldy old books; narratives set down by eye-witnesses at the time that the episodes treated of happened.

Wednesday, January 17, 1906

January 16th, continued. About General Sickles.

With considerable frequency, since then, I have tried to get publishers to make the experiment of such a magazine, but I was never successful. I was never able to convince a publisher that *The Back Number* would interest the public. Not one of them was able to conceive of the idea of a sane human being finding interest in stale things. I made my latest effort three years ago. Again I failed to convince. But I, myself, am not convinced. I am quite sure that *The Back Number* would succeed and become a favorite. I am also sure of another thing—that *The Back Number* would have this advantage over any other magazine that was ever issued, to wit: that the man who read the first paragraph in it would go on and read the magazine entirely through, skipping nothing—whereas there is no magazine in existence which ever contains three articles which can be depended upon to interest the reader. It is necessary to put a *dozen* articles into a magazine of the day in order to hit six or eight tastes. One man buys the magazine for one of its articles, another is attracted by another, another by a third; but no man buys the magazine because of the whole of its contents. I contend that *The Back Number* would be bought for the whole of its contents, and that each reader would read the whole.

"Mr. Paine, you and I will start that magazine, and try the experiment, if you are willing to select the ancient news from old books and newspapers, and do the rest of the editorial work. Are you willing?"

Mr. Paine. "I should be very willing, when we get so that we can undertake it."

"Very well, then we will, by and by, make that experiment."

Twichell and I stepped across the street, that night, in the rain, and spent an hour with General Sickles. Sickles is eighty-one years old, now. I had met him only once or twice before, although there has been only the width of 9th street between us for a year. He is too old to make visits, and I am too lazy. I remember when he killed Philip Barton Key, son of the author of "The Star-Spangled Banner," and I remember the prodigious excitement it made in the country. I think it cannot be far from fifty years ago. My vague recollection of it is that it happened in Washington, and that I was there at the time.

I have felt well acquainted with General Sickles for thirty-eight or thirty-nine years, because I have known Twichell that long. Twichell was a chaplain in Sickles's brigade in the Civil War, and he was always fond of talking about the General. Twichell was under Sickles all through the war. Whenever he comes down from Hartford he makes it his duty to go and pay his respects to the General. Sickles is a genial old fellow; a handsome and stately military figure; talks smoothly, in well-constructed English—I may say perfectly constructed English. His talk is full of interest and bristling with points, but as there are no emphases scattered through it anywhere, and as there is no animation in it, it soon becomes oppressive by its monotony, and it makes the listener drowsy. Twichell had to step on my foot once or twice. The late Bill Nye once said "I have been told that Wagner's music is better than it sounds." That felicitous description of a something which so many people have tried to describe, and couldn't, does seem to fit the General's manner of speech exactly. His talk is much better than it is. No, that is not the idea—there seems to be a lack there somewhere. Maybe it is another case of the sort just quoted. Maybe Nye would say that "it is better than it sounds." I think that is it. His talk does *not* sound entertaining, but it *is* distinctly entertaining.

Sickles lost a leg at Gettysburg, and I remember Twichell's account of that circumstance. He talked about it on one of our long walks, a great many years ago, and although the details have passed out of my memory, I still carry the picture in my mind as presented by Twichell. The leg was carried off by a cannon ball. Twichell, and others, carried the General out of the battle, and they placed him on a bed made of boughs, under a tree. There was no surgeon present, and Twichell and Rev. Father O'Hagan, a Catholic priest, made a make-shift tourniquet and stopped the gush of blood—*checked* it, perhaps is the right term. A newspaper correspondent appeared first. General Sickles considered himself a dying man, and (if Twichell is as truthful a person as the character of his cloth requires him to be) General Sickles put aside everything connected with a future world in order to go out of this one in becoming style. And so he dictated his "last words" to that newspaper correspondent. That was Twichell's idea—I remember it well—that the General, no doubt influenced by the fact that several people's last words have been so badly chosen—whether by accident or intention—that they have outlived all the rest of the man's fame, was moved to do his last words in a form calculated to petrify and preserve them for the future generations. Twichell quoted that speech. I have forgotten what it was, now, but it was well chosen for its purpose.

Now when we sat there in the General's presence listening to his monotonous talk—it was about himself, and is always about himself, and always seems modest and unexasperating, inoffensive,—it seemed to me that he was just the kind of man who would risk his salvation in order to do some "last words" in an attractive way. He murmured and warbled, and warbled, and it was all just as simple and pretty as it could be. And also I will say this: that he never made an ungenerous remark about anybody. He spoke severely of this and that and the other person— officers in the war—but he spoke with dignity and with courtesy. There was no malignity in what he said. He merely pronounced what he evidently regarded as just criticisms upon them.

I noticed then, what I had noticed once before, four or five months ago, that the General valued his lost leg away above the one that is left. I am perfectly sure that if he had to part with either of them he would part with the one that he has got. I have noticed this same thing in several other Generals who had lost a portion of themselves in the Civil War. There was General Fairchild, of Wisconsin. He lost an arm in one of the great battles. When he was Consul General in Paris and we Clemenses were sojourning there some time or other, and grew to be well acquainted with him and with his family, I know that whenever a proper occasion—an occasion which gave General Fairchild an opportunity to elevate the stump of the lost arm and wag it with effect—occurred, that is what he did. It was easy to forgive him for it, and I did it.

General Noyes was our Minister to France at the time. He had lost a leg in the war. He was a pretty vain man, I will say that for him, and anybody could see—certainly I saw—that whenever there was a proper gathering around, Noyes presently seemed to disappear. There wasn't anything left of him but the leg which he didn't have.

Well, General Sickles sat there on the sofa and talked. It was a curious place. Two rooms of considerable size—parlors opening together with folding-doors—and the floors, the walls, the ceilings, cluttered up and overlaid with lion skins, tiger skins, leopard skins, elephant skins; photographs of the General at various times of life—photographs *en civil;* photographs in uniform; gushing sprays of swords fastened in trophy form against the wall; flags of various kinds stuck here and there and yonder; more animals; more skins; here and there and everywhere more and more skins; skins of wild creatures, always, I believe;—beautiful skins. You couldn't walk across that floor anywhere without stumbling over the hard heads of lions and things. You couldn't put out a hand anywhere without laying it upon a velvety, exquisite tiger skin or leopard skin, and so on—oh, well, all the kinds of skins were there; it was as if a menagerie had undressed in the place. Then there was a most decided and rather unpleasant odor, which proceeded from disinfectants and preservatives and things such as you have to sprinkle on skins in order to discourage the moths—so it was not altogether a pleasant place, on that account. It was a kind of museum; and yet it was not the sort of museum which seemed dignified enough to be the museum of a great soldier—and so famous a soldier. It was the sort of museum which should delight and entertain little boys and girls. I suppose that that museum reveals a part of the General's character and make. He is sweetly and winningly childlike.

Once, in Hartford, twenty or twenty-five years ago, just as Twichell was coming out of his gate Sunday morning to walk to his church and preach, a telegram was put into his hand. He read it immediately, and then, in a manner, collapsed. It said "General Sickles died last night at midnight."

Well, you can see, now, that it wasn't so. But no matter—it was so to Joe at the time. He walked along—walked to the church—but his mind was far away. All his affection and homage and worship of his General had come to the fore. His heart was full of these emotions. He hardly knew where he was. In his pulpit, he stood up and began the service, but with a voice over which he had almost no command. The congregation had never seen him thus moved, before, in his pulpit. They sat there and gazed at him and wondered what was the matter; because he was now reading, in this broken voice and with occasional tears trickling down his face, what to them seemed a quite unemotional chapter—that one about Moses begat Aaron, and Aaron begat Deuteronomy, and Deuteronomy begat St. Peter, and St. Peter begat Cain, and Cain begat Abel—and he was going along with this, and half crying—his voice continually breaking. The congregation left the church that morning without being able to account for this most extraordinary thing—as it seemed to them. That a man who had been a soldier for more than four years, and who had preached in that pulpit so many, many times on really

1880

moving subjects, without even the quiver of a lip, should break all down over the Begats, was a thing which they couldn't understand. But there it is—any one can see how such a mystery as that would arouse the curiosity of those people to the boiling-point.

Twichell has had many adventures. He has more adventures in a year than anybody else has in five. One Saturday night he noticed a bottle on his wife's dressing-bureau. He thought the label said "Hair Restorer," and he took it in his room and gave his head a good drenching and sousing with it and carried it back and thought no more about it. Next morning when he got up his head was a bright green! He sent around everywhere and couldn't get a substitute-preacher, so he had to go to his church himself and preach—and he did it. He hadn't a sermon in his barrel—as it happened—of any lightsome character, so he had to preach a very grave one—a very serious one—and it made the matter worse. The gravity of the sermon did not harmonize with the gaiety of his head, and the people sat all through it with handkerchiefs stuffed in their mouths to try to keep down their joy. And Twichell told me that he was sure he never had seen his congregation—the whole body of his congregation—the *entire* body of his congregation—absorbed in interest in his sermon, from beginning to end, before. Always there had been an aspect of indifference, here and there, or wandering, somewhere; but this time there was nothing of the kind. Those people sat there as if they thought, "Good for this day and train only: we must have all there is of this show, not waste any of it." And he said that when he came down out of the pulpit more people waited to shake him by the hand and tell him what a good sermon it was, than ever before. And it seemed a pity that these people should do these fictions in such a place—right in the church—when it was quite plain they were not interested in the sermon at all; they only wanted to get a near view of his head.

Well, Twichell said—no, Twichell didn't say, *I* say, that as the days went on and Sunday followed Sunday, the interest in Twichell's hair grew and grew; because it didn't stay merely and monotonously green, it took on deeper and deeper shades of green; and then it would change and become reddish, and would go from that to some other color—purplish, yellowish, bluish, and so on—but it was never a solid color. It was always mottled. And each Sunday it was a little more interesting than it was the Sunday before—and Twichell's head became famous, and people came from New York and Boston, and South Carolina, and Japan, and so on, to look. There wasn't seating capacity for all the people that came while his head was undergoing these various and fascinating mottlings. And it was a good thing in several ways, because the business had been languishing a little, and now a lot of people joined the church so that they could have the show, and it was the beginning of a prosperity for that church which has never diminished in all these years. Nothing so fortunate ever happened to Joe as that.

Well, he was telling—oh no, it was years ago, that he was telling about the sutler. In the Sickles brigade was a sutler, a Yankee, who was a wonderful person in the way of competency. All other sutlers got out of things on the eve of battle, during battle, after battle; not so with this sutler. He never got out of anything, and so he was very greatly respected and admired.

There were times when he would get drunk. These were periodical drunks. You couldn't tell when he was going to have an experience of that kind, therefore you did not know how to provide for it. It was very necessary to provide for it, because when he was drunk he had no respect for anybody's feelings or desires. If he wanted to do so and so he would do it; nothing could coax him to do some other way. If he didn't want to do a thing nobody could persuade him to do it. On one of these occasions of sutlerian eclipse General Sickles had invited some other Generals to dine with him in his headquarters-tent; his cook or his orderly, or somebody—the proper person—came to him aghast, and said "The sutler is drunk. We can't have any dinner. There isn't anything to cook and the sutler won't sell us anything."

"Did you tell him it was *General Sickles* who wanted these things?"

"Yes, sir. It didn't make any difference with the sutler."

"Well, can't you get him to—"

"No, sir, we can't get him to do anything. We have got some beans, and that is all we have got. We have tried to get him to sell us just a pound of pork for the General, and he says he won't."

General Sickles said "Send for the chaplain. Let Chaplain Twichell go there. He is popular with that sutler; that sutler has great respect and reverence for Chaplain Twichell. Let him go there and see if he can't prevail on the sutler to sell him a pound of salt pork for General Sickles."

Twichell went on the errand—stated his errand.

The sutler propped himself unsteadily against some kind of a support, collected his thoughts, and the suitable words, and said,

"Sell you a pound of pork for General Sickles? *Naw.* Go back and tell him I wouldn't sell you a pound of pork for God."

That was Twichell's story of the episode.

But I have wandered from that tree where General Sickles lay bleeding, and arranging his last words. It was three-quarters of an hour before a surgeon could be found, for that was a tremendous battle and surgeons were needed everywhere. When the surgeon arrived it was after nightfall. It was a still and windless July night, and there was a candle burning—I think somebody sat near the General's head and held this candle in his hand. It threw just light enough to make the General's face distinct, and there were several dim figures waiting around about. Into this group, out of the darkness, bursts an aide; springs lightly from his horse, approaches this white-faced expiring General, straightens himself up soldier-fashion, salutes, and reports in the most soldierly and matter-of-fact way that he has carried out an order given him by the General, and that the movement of the regiments to the supporting point designated has been accomplished.

The General thanked him courteously. I am sure Sickles must have been always polite. It takes *training* to enable a person to be properly courteous when he is dying. Many have tried it. I suppose very few have succeeded.

Thursday, January 18, 1906

Senator Tillman speaks of Morris case—Funeral of John Malone
contrasted with funeral of Empress of Austria—Leads up to dueling.

Senator Tillman, of South Carolina, has been making a speech—day before yesterday—of frank and intimate criticism of the President,—the President of the United States, as he calls him; whereas so far as my knowledge goes, there has been no such functionary as President of the United States for forty years, perhaps, if we except Cleveland. I do not call to mind any other President of the United States—there may have been one or two—*perhaps* one or two, who were not always and persistently presidents of the Republican party, but were now and then for a brief interval really Presidents of the United States. Tillman introduces into this speech the matter of the expulsion of Mrs. Morris from the White House, and I think his arraignment of the President was a good and capable piece of work. At any rate, his handling of it suited me very well, and tasted very good in my mouth. I was glad that there was somebody to take this matter up, whether from a generous motive or from an ungenerous one, and give it an airing. It was needed. The whole nation, and the entire press, have been sitting by in meek and slavish silence, everybody privately wishing—just as was my own case—that some person with some sense of the proprieties would rise up and denounce this outrage as it ought to be denounced. Tillman makes a point which charms me. I wanted to use it myself, days ago, but I was already arranging a scheme in another matter of public concern which may invite a brick or two in my direction, and one entertainment of this sort at a time is plenty for me. That point was this: that the President is always prodigal of letters and telegrams to Tom, Dick and Harry, about everything and nothing. He seems never to lack time from his *real* duties to attend to duties that do not exist. So, at the very time when he should have been throwing off one or two little lines to say to Mrs. Morris and her friends that, being a gentleman, he was hastening to say he was sorry that his idiot assistant secretary had been turning the nation's official mansion into a sailor boarding-house, and that he would admonish Mr. Barnes, and the rest of the reception-room garrison to deal more gently with the erring in future, and to abstain from any conduct in the White House which would rank as disgraceful in any other respectable dwelling in the land,—

I don't like Tillman. His second cousin killed an editor, three years ago, without giving that editor a chance to defend himself. I recognize that it is almost always wise, and is often in a manner *necessary,* to kill an editor, but I think that when a man is a United States Senator he ought to require his second cousin to refrain as long as he can, and then do it in a handsome way, running some personal risk himself. I have not known Tillman to do many things that were greatly to his credit during his political life, but I am glad of the position which he has taken this time. The President has persistently refused to listen to such friends of his as are not insane—men who have tried to persuade him to disavow Mr. Barnes's conduct and express regret for that occurrence. And now Mr. Tillman uses that point which I spoke of a minute ago, and uses it with telling effect. He reminds the Senate that at the very time that the President's dignity would not allow him to send to Mrs. Morris or her friends a kindly and regretful line, he had time enough to send a note of compliment and admiration to a prize-fighter in the Far West. If the President had been an unpopular person, that point would have been seized upon early, and much and disastrous notice taken of it. But, as I have suggested before, the nation and the newspapers have maintained a loyal and humiliated silence about it, and have waited prayerfully and hopefully for some reckless person to say the things which were in their hearts, and which they could not bear to utter. Mrs. Morris embarrasses the situation, and extends and keeps alive the discomfort of eighty millions of people, by lingering along near to death, yet neither rallying nor dying; to do either would relieve the tension. For the present, the discomfort must continue. Mr. Tillman certainly has not chloroformed it.

(That Birthday speech of mine was the text which I meant to use along here. I don't want to get too far away from it at any one time and I ought to get back to that.)

We buried good old John Malone the actor, this morning. His old friends of the Players Club attended in a body. It was the second time in my life that I had been present at a Catholic funeral. And as I sat in the church, my mind went back, by natural process, to that other one, and the contrast strongly interested me. That first one was the funeral of the Empress of Austria, who was assassinated six or eight years ago. There was a great concourse of the ancient nobility of the Austrian Empire; and as that patchwork of old kingdoms and principalities consists of nineteen states and eleven nationalities, and as these nobles came clothed in the costumes which their ancestors were accustomed to wear on state occasions three or four or five centuries ago, the variety and magnificence of the costumes made a picture which cast far into the shade all the notions of splendor and magnificence which in the course of my life I had accumulated from the opera, the theatre, the picture-galleries, and from books. Gold, silver, jewels, silks, satins, velvets; they were all there in brilliant and beautiful confusion, and in that sort of perfect harmony which Nature herself observes and is master of, when she paints and groups her flowers and her forests and floods them with sunshine. The military and civic milliners of the Middle Ages knew their trade. Infinite as was the variety of the costumes displayed, there was not an ugly one, nor one that was a discordant note in the harmony, or an offence to the eye. When those massed costumes were still, they were softly, richly, sensuously beautiful; when the mass stirred, the slightest movement set the jewels and metals and bright colors afire, and swept it with flashing lights which sent a sort of ecstasy of delight through me.

But it was different this morning. This morning the clothes were all alike. They were simple, and devoid of color. The Players were clothed as they are always clothed, except that they wore the high silk hat of ceremony. Yet, in its way, John Malone's funeral was as impressive as had been that of the Empress. There was no inequality between John Malone and the Empress except the artificial inequalities which have been invented and established by man's childish vanity. The Empress and John were just equals in the essentials of goodness of heart and a blameless life. Both passed by the onlooker, in their coffins, respected, esteemed, honored; both traveled the same road from the church, bound for the same resting-place—according to Catholic doctrine, Purgatory—to be removed thence to a better land or to remain in Purgatory accordingly as the contributions of their friends, in cash or prayer, shall determine. The priest told us, in an admirably framed speech, about John's destination, and the terms upon which he might continue his journey or must remain in Purgatory. John was poor; his friends are poor. The Empress was rich; her friends are rich. John Malone's prospects are not good, and I lament it.

Perhaps I am in error in saying I have been present at only two Catholic funerals. I think I was present at one in Virginia City, Nevada, in the neighborhood of forty years ago—or perhaps it was down in Esmeralda, on the borders of California—but if it happened, the memory of it can hardly be said to exist, it is so indistinct. I *did* attend one or two funerals— maybe a dozen—out there; funerals of desperadoes who had tried to purify society by exterminating other desperadoes—and *did* accomplish the purification, though not according to the program which they had laid out for this office.

Also, I attended some funerals of persons who had fallen in duels—and maybe it was a duelist whom I helped to ship. But would a duelist be buried by the Church? In inviting his own death, wouldn't he be committing suicide, substantially? Wouldn't that rule him out? Well, I don't remember how it was, now, but I think it was a duelist.

Friday, January 19, 1906

About Dueling.

In those early days dueling suddenly became a fashion in the new Territory of Nevada, and
1864   by 1864 everybody was anxious to have a chance in the new sport, mainly for the reason that he was not able to thoroughly respect himself so long as he had not killed or crippled somebody in a duel or been killed or crippled in one himself.

At that time I had been serving as city editor on Mr. Goodman's Virginia City *Enterprise* for a matter of two years. I was twenty-nine years old. I was ambitious in several ways, but I had entirely escaped the seductions of that particular craze. I had had no desire to fight a duel; I had no intention of provoking one. I did not feel respectable, but I got a certain amount of satisfaction out of feeling safe. I was ashamed of myself; the rest of the staff were ashamed of me—but I got along well enough. I had always been accustomed to feeling ashamed of myself, for one thing or another, so there was no novelty for me in the situation. I bore it very well. Plunkett was on the staff; R. M. Daggett was on the staff. These had tried to get into duels, but for the present had failed, and were waiting. Goodman was the only one of us who had done anything to shed credit upon the paper. The rival paper was the Virginia *Union*. Its editor for a little while was Tom Fitch, called the "silver-tongued orator of Wisconsin"—that was where he came from. He tuned up his oratory in the editorial columns of the *Union,* and Mr. Goodman invited him out and modified him with a bullet. I remember the joy of the staff when Goodman's challenge was accepted by Fitch. We ran late that night, and made much of Joe Goodman. He was only twenty-four years old; he lacked the wisdom which a person has at twenty-nine, and he was as glad of being *it* as I was that I wasn't. He chose Major Graves for his second (that name is not right, but it's close enough, I don't remember the Major's name). Graves came over to instruct Joe in the dueling art. He had been a major under Walker, the "gray-eyed man of destiny," and had fought all through that remarkable man's filibustering campaign in Central America. That fact gauges the Major. To say that a man was a major under Walker, and came out of that struggle ennobled by Walker's praise, is to say that the Major was not merely a brave man but that he was brave to the very utmost limit of that word. All of Walker's men were like that. I knew the Gillis family intimately. The father made the campaign under Walker, and with him one son. They were in the memorable Plaza fight, and stood it out to the last against overwhelming odds, as did also all of the Walker men. The son was killed at the father's side. The father received a bullet through the eye. The old man—for he was an old man at the time—wore spectacles, and the bullet and one of the glasses went into his skull and remained there—but often, in after years, when I boarded in the old man's home in San Francisco, whenever he became emotional I used to see him shed tears and *glass,* in a way that was infinitely moving. It is wonderful how glass breeds when it has a fair chance. This glass was all broken up and ruined, so it had no market value; but in the course of time he exuded enough to set up a spectacle shop with. There were some other sons: Steve, George, and Jim, very young chaps—the merest lads—who wanted to be in the Walker expedition, for they had their father's dauntless spirit. But Walker wouldn't have them; he said it was a serious expedition, and no place for children.

The Major was a majestic creature, with a most stately and dignified and impressive military bearing, and he was by nature and training courteous, polite, graceful, winning; and he had that quality which I think I have encountered in only one other man—Bob Howland—a mysterious quality which resides in the eye; and when that eye is turned upon an individual or a squad, in warning, that is enough. The man that has that eye doesn't need to go armed; he can move upon an armed desperado and quell him and take him prisoner without saying a single word. I saw Bob Howland do that, once—a slender, good-natured, amiable, gentle, kindly little skeleton of a man, with a sweet blue eye that would win your heart when it smiled upon you, or turn cold and freeze it, according to the nature of the occasion.

The Major stood Joe up straight; stood Steve Gillis up fifteen paces away; made Joe turn his right side towards Steve, cock his navy six-shooter—that prodigious weapon—and hold it straight down against his leg; told him that *that* was the correct position for the gun—that the position ordinarily in use at Virginia City (that is to say, the gun straight up in the air, then brought slowly down to your man) was all wrong. At the word *"One,"* you must raise the gun slowly and steadily to the place on the other man's body that you desire to convince. Then, after a pause, *"two, three—fire—Stop!"* At the word "stop," you may fire—but not earlier. You may give yourself as much time as you please *after* that word. Then, when you fire, you may advance and go on firing at your leisure and pleasure, if you can get any pleasure out of it. And, in the meantime, the other man, if he has been properly instructed and is alive to his privileges, is advancing on *you,* and firing—and it is always likely that more or less trouble will result.

Naturally, when Joe's revolver had risen to a level it was pointing at Steve's breast, but the Major said "No, that is not wise. Take all the risks of getting murdered yourself, but don't run any risk of murdering the other man. If you survive a duel you want to survive it in such a way that the memory of it will not linger along with you through the rest of your life and interfere with your sleep. Aim at your man's leg; not at the knee, not above the knee; for those are dangerous spots. Aim below the knee; cripple him, but leave the rest of him to his mother."

By grace of these truly wise and excellent instructions, Joe tumbled his man down with a bullet through his lower leg, which furnished him a permanent limp. And Joe lost nothing but a lock of hair, which he could spare better then than he could now. For when I saw him here in New York a year ago, his crop was gone; he had nothing much left but a fringe, with a dome rising above.

1864 About a year later I got *my* chance. But I was not hunting for it. Goodman went off to San Francisco for a week's holiday, and left me to be chief editor. I had supposed that that was an easy berth, there being nothing to do but write one editorial per day; but I was disappointed in that superstition. I couldn't find anything to write an article about, the first day. Then it occurred to me that inasmuch as it was the 22d of April, 1864, the next morning would be the three-hundredth anniversary of Shakspeare's birthday—and what better theme could I want than that? I got the Cyclopedia and examined it, and found out who Shakspeare was and what he had done, and I borrowed all that and laid it before a community that couldn't have been better prepared for instruction about Shakspeare than if they had been prepared by art. There wasn't enough of what Shakspeare had done to make an editorial of the necessary length, but I filled it out with what he hadn't done—which in many respects was more important and striking and readable than the handsomest things he had really accomplished. But next day I was in trouble again. There were no more Shakspeares to work up. There was nothing in past history, or in the world's future possibilities, to make an editorial out of, suitable to that community; so there was but one theme left. That theme was Mr. Laird, proprietor of the Virginia *Union*. *His* editor had gone off to San Francisco too, and Laird was trying his hand at editing. I woke up Mr. Laird with some courtesies of the kind that were fashionable among newspaper editors in that region, and he came back at me the next day in a most vitriolic way. He was hurt by something I had said about him—some little thing—I don't remember what it was now—probably called him a horse-thief, or one of those little phrases customarily used to describe another editor. They were no doubt just, and accurate, but Laird was a very sensitive creature, and he didn't like it. So we expected a challenge from Mr. Laird, because according to the rules—according to the etiquette of dueling as reconstructed and reorganized and improved by the duelists of that region—whenever you said a thing about another person that he didn't like, it wasn't sufficient for him to talk back in the same offensive spirit: etiquette required him to send a challenge; so we waited for a challenge—waited all day. It didn't come. And as the day wore along, hour after hour, and no challenge came, the boys grew depressed. They lost heart. But I was cheerful; I felt better and better all the time. They couldn't understand it, but I could understand it. It was my *make* that enabled me to be cheerful when other people were despondent. So then it became necessary for us to waive etiquette and challenge Mr. Laird. When we reached that decision, they began to cheer up, but *I* began to lose some of my animation. However, in enterprises of this kind you are in the hands of your friends; there is nothing for you to do but to abide by what they consider to be the best course. Daggett wrote a challenge for me, for Daggett had the language—the right language—the convincing language—and I lacked it. Daggett poured out a stream of unsavory epithets upon Mr. Laird, charged with a vigor and venom of a strength calculated to persuade him; and Steve Gillis, my second, carried the challenge and came back to wait for the return. It didn't come. The boys were exasperated, but I kept my temper. Steve carried another challenge, hotter than the other, and we waited again. Nothing came of it. I began to feel quite comfortable. I began to take an interest in the challenges myself. I had not felt any before; but it seemed to me that I was accumulating a great and valuable reputation at no expense, and my delight in this grew and grew, as challenge after challenge was declined, until by midnight I was beginning to think that there was nothing in the world so much to be desired as a chance to fight a duel. So I hurried Daggett up; made him keep on sending challenge after challenge. Oh, well, I overdid it: Laird accepted. I might have known that that would happen—Laird was a man you couldn't depend on.

The boys were jubilant beyond expression. They helped me make my will, which was another discomfort—and I already had enough. Then they took me home. I didn't sleep any—didn't want to sleep. I had plenty of things to think about, and less than four hours to do it in—because five o'clock was the hour appointed for the tragedy, and I should have to use up one hour—beginning at four—in practising with the revolver and finding out which end of it to level at the adversary. At four we went down into a little gorge, about a mile from town, and borrowed a barn door for a mark—borrowed it of a man who was over in California on a visit—and we set the barn door up and stood a fence-rail up against the middle of it, to represent Mr. Laird. But the rail was no proper representative of him, for he was longer than a rail and thinner. Nothing would ever fetch him but a line shot, and then as like as not he would split the bullet—the worst material for dueling purposes that could be imagined. I began on the rail. I couldn't hit the rail; then I tried the barn door; but I couldn't hit the barn door. There was nobody in danger except stragglers around on the flanks of that mark. I was thoroughly discouraged, and I didn't cheer up any when we presently heard pistol-shots over in the next little ravine. I knew what that was—that was Laird's gang out practising him. They would hear my shots, and of course they would come up over the ridge to see what kind of a record I was making—see what their chances were against me. Well, I hadn't any record; and I knew that if Laird came over that ridge and saw my barn door without a scratch on it, he would be as anxious to fight as I was—or as I had been at midnight, before that disastrous acceptance came.

Now just at this moment, a little bird, no bigger than a sparrow, flew along by and lit on a sage-bush about thirty yards away. Steve whipped out his revolver and shot its head off. Oh, he was a marksman—much better than I was. We ran down there to pick up the bird, and just then, sure enough, Mr. Laird and his people came over the ridge, and they joined us. And when Laird's second saw that bird, with its head shot off, he lost color, he faded, and you could see that he was interested. He said,

"Who did that?"

Before I could answer, Steve spoke up and said quite calmly, and in a matter-of-fact way, "Clemens did it."

The second said, "Why, that is wonderful. How far off was that bird?"

Steve said, "Oh, not far—about thirty yards."

The second said, "Well, that is astonishing shooting. How often can he do that?"

Steve said languidly, "Oh, about four times out of five?"

I knew the little rascal was lying, but I didn't say anything. The second said, "Why that is *amazing* shooting; I supposed he couldn't hit a church."

He was supposing very sagaciously, but I didn't say anything. Well, they said good morning. The second took Mr. Laird home, a little tottery on his legs, and Laird sent back a note in his own hand declining to fight a duel with me on any terms whatever.

Well, my life was saved—saved by that accident. I don't know what the bird thought about that interposition of Providence, but I felt very, very comfortable over it—satisfied and content. Now, we found out, later, that Laird had hit *his* mark four times out of six, right along. If the duel had come off, he would have so filled my skin with bullet-holes that it wouldn't have held my principles.

By breakfast-time the news was all over town that I had sent a challenge and Steve Gillis had carried it. Now that would entitle us to two years apiece in the penitentiary, according to the brand-new law. Judge North sent us no message as coming from himself, but a message *came* from a close friend of his. He said it would be a good idea for us to leave the Territory by the first stage-coach. This would sail next morning, at four o'clock—and in the meantime we would be searched for, but not with avidity; and if we were in the Territory after that stage-coach left, we would be the first victims of the new law. Judge North was anxious to have some object-lessons for that law, and he would absolutely keep us in the prison the full two years. He wouldn't pardon us out to please anybody.

Well, it seemed to me that our society was no longer desirable in Nevada; so we stayed in our quarters and observed proper caution all day—except that once Steve went over to the hotel to attend to another customer of mine. That was a Mr. Cutler. You see Laird was not the only person whom I had tried to reform during my occupancy of the editorial chair. I had looked around and selected several other people, and delivered a new zest of life into them through warm criticism and disapproval—so that when I laid down my editorial pen I had four horse-whippings and two duels owing to me. We didn't care for the horse-whippings; there was no glory in them; they were not worth the trouble of collecting. But honor required that some notice should be taken of that other duel. Mr. Cutler had come up from Carson City, and had sent a man over with a challenge from the hotel. Steve went over to pacify him. Steve weighed only ninety-five pounds, but it was well known throughout the Territory that with his fists he could whip anybody that walked on two legs, let his weight and science be what they might. Steve was a Gillis, and when a Gillis confronted a man and had a proposition to make the proposition always contained business. When Cutler found that Steve was my second he cooled down; he became calm and rational, and was ready to listen. Steve gave him fifteen minutes to get out of the hotel, and half an hour to get out of town or there would be results. So *that* duel went off successfully, because Mr. Cutler immediately left for Carson a convinced and reformed man.

I have never had anything to do with duels since. I thoroughly disapprove of duels. I consider them unwise, and I know they are dangerous. Also, sinful. If a man should challenge me now, I would go to that man and take him kindly and forgivingly by the hand and lead him to a quiet retired spot, and *kill* him. Still, I have always taken a great interest in other people's duels. One always feels an abiding interest in any heroic thing which has entered into his own experience.

In 1878, fourteen years after my unmaterialized duel, Messieurs Fourtou and Gambetta fought a duel which made heroes of both of them in France, but made them rather ridiculous throughout the rest of the world. I was living in Munich that fall and winter, and I was so interested in that funny tragedy that I wrote a long account of it, and it is in one of my books, somewhere—an account which had some inaccuracies in it, but as an exhibition of the *spirit* of that duel, I think it was correct and trustworthy. And when I was living in Vienna, thirty-four years after my ineffectual duel, my interest in that kind of incident was still strong; and I find here among my Autobiographical manuscripts of that day a chapter which I began concerning it, but did not finish. I wanted to finish it but held it open in the hope that the Italian Ambassador, M. Nigra, would find time to furnish me the *full* history of Signor Cavallotti's adventures in that line. But he was a busy man; there was always an interruption before he could get well started; so my hope was never fulfilled. The following is the unfinished chapter.

As concerns dueling. This pastime is as common in Austria to-day as it is in France. But with this difference, that here in the Austrian States the duel is dangerous, while in France it is not. Here it is tragedy, in France it is comedy; here it is a solemnity, there it is monkey-shines; here the duelist risks his life, there he does not even risk his shirt. Here he fights with pistol or sabre, in France with a hair-pin—a blunt one. Here the desperately wounded man tries to walk to the hospital; there they paint the scratch so that they can find it again, lay the sufferer on a stretcher, and conduct him off the field with a band of music.

At the end of a French duel the pair hug and kiss and cry, and praise each other's valor; then the surgeons make an examination and pick out the scratched one, and the other one helps him onto the litter and pays his fare; and in return the scratched one treats to champagne and oysters in the evening, and then "the incident is closed," as the French say. It is all polite, and gracious, and pretty and impressive. At the end of an Austrian duel the antagonist that is alive gravely offers his hand to the other man, utters some phrases of courteous regret, then bids him good-bye and goes his way, and that incident also is closed. The French duelist is painstakingly protected from danger, by the rules of the game. His antagonist's weapon cannot reach so far as his body; if he get a scratch it will not be above his elbow. But in Austria the rules of the game do not provide against danger, they carefully provide *for* it, usually. Commonly the combat must be kept up until one of the men is disabled; a non-disabling slash or stab does not retire him.

For a matter of three months I watched the Viennese journals, and whenever a duel was reported in their telegraphic columns I scrap-booked it. By this record I find that dueling in Austria is not confined to journalists and old maids, as in France, but is indulged in by military men, journalists, students, physicians, lawyers, members of the legislature, and even the Cabinet, the Bench and the police. Dueling is forbidden by law; and so it seems odd to see the makers and administrators of the laws dancing on their work in this way. Some months ago Count Badeni, at that time chief of the Government, fought a pistol-duel here in the capital city of the Empire with representative Wolf, and both of those distinguished Christians came near getting turned out of the Church—for the Church as well as the State forbids dueling.

In one case, lately, in Hungary, the police interfered and stopped a duel after the first innings. This was a sabre-duel between the chief of police and the city attorney. Unkind things were said about it by the newspapers. They said the police remembered their duty uncommonly well when their own officials were the parties concerned in duels. But I think the underlings showed good bread-and-butter judgment. If their superiors had carved each other well, the public would have asked Where were the police? and their places would have been endangered; but custom does not require them to be around where mere unofficial citizens are explaining a thing with sabres.

There was another duel—a double duel—going on in the immediate neighborhood at the time, and in this case the police obeyed custom and did not disturb it. Their bread and butter was not at stake there. In this duel a physician fought a couple of surgeons, and wounded both—one of them lightly, the other seriously. An undertaker wanted to keep people from interfering, but that was quite natural again.

Selecting at random from my record, I next find a duel at Tarnopol between military men. An officer of the Tenth Dragoons charged an officer of the Ninth Dragoons with an offence against the laws of the card-table. There was a defect or a doubt somewhere in the matter, and this had to be examined and passed upon by a Court of Honor. So the case was sent up to Lemberg for this purpose. One would like to know what the defect was, but the newspaper does not say. A man here who has fought many duels and has a graveyard, says that probably the matter in question was as to whether the accusation was true or not; that if the charge was a very grave one—cheating, for instance—proof of its truth would rule the guilty officer out of the field of honor; the Court would not allow a gentleman to fight with such a person. You see what a solemn thing it is; you see how particular they are; any little careless act can lose you your privilege of getting yourself shot, here. The Court seems to have gone into the matter in a searching and careful fashion, for several months elapsed before it reached a decision. It then sanctioned a duel and the accused killed his accuser.

Next I find a duel between a prince and a major; first with pistols—no result satisfactory to either party; then with sabres, and the major badly hurt.

Next, a sabre-duel between journalists—the one a strong man, the other feeble and in poor health. It was brief; the strong one drove his sword through the weak one, and death was immediate.

Next, a duel between a lieutenant and a student of medicine. According to the newspaper report these are the details. The student was in a restaurant one evening; passing along, he halted at a table to speak with some friends; near-by sat a dozen military men; the student conceived that one of these was "staring" at him; he asked the officer to step outside and explain. This officer and another one gathered up their caps and sabres and went out with the student. Outside—this is the student's account—the student introduced himself to the offending officer and said "You seemed to stare at me;" for answer, the officer struck at the student with his fist; the student parried the blow; both officers drew their sabres and attacked the young fellow, and one of them gave him a wound on the left arm; then they withdrew. This was Saturday night. The duel followed on Monday, in the military riding-school—the customary dueling-ground all over Austria, apparently. The weapons were pistols. The dueling-terms were somewhat beyond custom in the matter of severity, if I may gather that from the statement that the combat was fought "unter sehr schweren Bedingungen"—to wit, "Distance, fifteen steps—with three steps advance." There was but one exchange of shots. The student was hit. "He put his hand on his breast, his body began to bend slowly forward, then collapsed in death and sank to the ground."

It is pathetic. There are other duels in my list, but I find in each and all of them one and the same ever-recurring defect—the *principals* are never present, but only their sham representatives. The *real* principals in any duel are not the duelists themselves, but their families. They do the mourning, the suffering, theirs is the loss and theirs the misery. They stake all that, the duelist stakes nothing but his life, and that is a trivial thing compared with what his death must cost those whom he leaves behind him. Challenges should not mention the duelist; he has nothing much at stake, and the real vengeance cannot reach him. The challenge should summon the offender's old gray mother, and his young wife and his little children,—these, or any to whom he is a dear and worshiped possession—and should say, "You have done me no harm, but I am the meek slave of a custom which requires me to crush the happiness out of your hearts and condemn you to years of pain and grief, in order that I may wash clean with your tears a stain which has been put upon me by another person."

The logic of it is admirable: a person has robbed me of a penny; I must beggar ten innocent persons to make good my loss. Surely nobody's "honor" is worth all that.

Since the duelist's family are the real principals in a duel, the State ought to compel them to be present at it. Custom, also, ought to be so amended as to require it; and without it no duel ought to be allowed to go on. If that student's unoffending mother had been present and watching the officer through her tears as he raised his pistol, he—why, he would have fired in the air. We know that. For we know how we are all made. Laws ought to be based upon the ascertained facts of our nature. It would be a simple thing to make a dueling-law which would stop dueling.

As things are now, the mother is never invited. She submits to this; and without outward complaint, for she, too, is the vassal of custom, and custom requires her to conceal her pain when she learns the disastrous news that her son must go to the dueling field, and by the powerful force that is lodged in habit and custom she is enabled to obey this trying requirement—a requirement which exacts a miracle of her, and gets it. Last January a neighbor of ours who has a young son in the army was wakened by this youth at three o'clock one morning, and she sat up in bed and listened to his message:

"I have come to tell you something, mother, which will distress you, but you must be good and brave, and bear it. I have been affronted by a fellow-officer, and we fight at three this afternoon. Lie down and sleep, now, and think no more about it."

She kissed him good night and lay down paralysed with grief and fear, but said nothing. But she did not sleep; she prayed and mourned till the first streak of dawn, then fled to the nearest church and implored the Virgin for help; and from that church she went to another and another and another; church after church, and still church after church, and so spent all the day until three o'clock on her knees in agony and tears; then dragged herself home and sat down, comfortless and desolate, to count the minutes, and wait, with an outward show of calm, for what had been ordained for her—happiness, or endless misery. Presently she heard the clank of a sabre—she had not known before what music was in that sound—and her son put his head in and said:

"X was in the wrong, and he apologized."

So that incident was closed; and for the rest of her life the mother will always find something pleasant about the clank of a sabre, no doubt.

In one of my listed duels—however, let it go, there is nothing particularly striking about it except that the seconds interfered. And prematurely, too, for neither man was dead. This was certainly irregular. Neither of the men liked it. It was a duel with cavalry sabres, between an editor and a lieutenant. The editor walked to the hospital, the lieutenant was carried. In this country an editor who can write well is valuable, but he is not likely to remain so unless he can handle a sabre with charm.

The following very recent telegram shows that also in France duels are humanely stopped as soon as they approach the (French) danger-point:

(Reuter's Telegram.)

PARIS, March 5.

The duel between Colonels Henry and Picquart took place this morning in the Riding School of the Ecole Militaire, the doors of which were strictly guarded in order to prevent intrusion. The combatants, who fought with swords, were in position at ten o'clock.

At the first re-engagement Lieut.-Colonel Henry was slightly scratched in the forearm, and just at the same moment his own blade appeared to touch his adversary's neck. Senator Ranc, who was Colonel Picquart's second, stopped the fight, but as it was found that his principal had not been touched, the combat continued. A very sharp encounter ensued, in which Colonel Henry was wounded in the elbow, and the duel then terminated.

After which, the stretcher and the band. In lurid contrast with this delicate flirtation, we have this fatal duel of day before yesterday in Italy, where the earnest Austrian duel is in vogue. I knew Cavallotti slightly, and this gives me a sort of personal interest in his duel. I first saw him in Rome several years ago. He was sitting on a block of stone in the Forum, and was writing something in his note-book—a poem or a challenge, or something like that—and the friend who pointed him out to me said, "That is Cavallotti—he has fought thirty duels; do not disturb him." I did not disturb him.

May 13, 1907. It is a long time ago. Cavallotti—poet, orator, satirist, statesman, patriot—was a great man, and his death was deeply lamented by his countrymen—many monuments to his memory testify to this. In his duels he killed several of his antagonists and disabled the rest. By nature he was a little irascible. Once when the officials of the library of Bologna threw out his books the gentle poet went up there and challenged the whole fifteen! His parliamentary duties were exacting, but he proposed to keep coming up and fighting duels between trains until all those officials had been retired from the activities of life. Although he always chose the sword to fight with, he had never had a lesson with that weapon. When game was called he waited for nothing, but always plunged at his opponent and rained such a storm of wild and original thrusts and whacks upon him that the man was dead or crippled before he could bring his science to bear. But his latest antagonist discarded science, and won. He held his sword straight forward like a lance when Cavallotti made his plunge—with the result that he impaled himself upon it. It entered his mouth and passed out at the back of his neck. Death was instantaneous.

Tuesday, January 23, 1906

About the meeting at Carnegie Hall, in interest of Booker Washington's Tuskegee Institute—Leads up to unpleasant political incident which happened to Mr. Twichell.

There was a great mass meeting at Carnegie Hall last night, in the interest of Booker Washington's Tuskegee Educational Institute in the South, and the interest which New York people feel in that Institute was quite manifest, in the fact that although it was not pleasant weather there were three thousand people inside the hall and two thousand outside, who were trying to get in when the performances were ready to begin at eight o'clock. Mr. Choate presided, and was received with a grand welcome when he marched in upon the stage. He is fresh from his long stay in England, as our Ambassador, where he won the English people by the gifts of his heart, and won the royalties and the Government by his able diplomatic service, and captured the whole nation with his fine and finished oratory. For thirty-five years Choate has been the handsomest man in America. Last night he seemed to me to be just as handsome as he was thirty-five years ago, when I first knew him. And when I used to see him in England, five or six years ago, I thought him the handsomest man in that country.

It was at a Fourth of July reception in Mr. Choate's house in London that I first met Booker Washington. I have met him a number of times since, and he always impresses me pleasantly. Last night he was a mulatto. I didn't notice it until he turned, while he was speaking, and said something to me. It was a great surprise to me to see that he was a mulatto, and had blue eyes. How unobservant a dull person can be. Always, before, he was black, to me, and I had never noticed whether he had eyes at all, or not. He has accomplished a wonderful work in this quarter of a century. When he finished his education at the Hampton Colored School twenty-five years ago, he was unknown, and hadn't a penny, nor a friend outside his immediate acquaintanceship. But by the persuasions of his carriage and address and the sincerity and honesty that look out of his eyes, he has been enabled to gather money by the hatful here in the North, and with it he has built up and firmly established his great school for the colored people of the two sexes in the South. In that school the students are not merely furnished a book education, but are taught thirty-seven useful trades. Booker Washington has scraped together many hundreds of thousands of dollars, in the twenty-five years, and with this money he has taught and sent forth into Southern fields among the colored people, six thousand trained colored men and women; and his student roll now numbers fifteen hundred names. The Institute's property is worth a million and a half, and the establishment is in a flourishing condition. A most remarkable man is Booker Washington. And he is a fervent and effective speaker, on the platform.

CHOATE AND TWAIN PLEAD FOR TUSKEGEE

Brilliant Audience Cheers Them and Booker Washington.

HUMORIST RAPS TAX DODGERS

Says Everybody Swears, Especially Off—
Friends of Negro Institution Trying to Raise $1,800,000

To give Booker T. Washington a good start toward collecting the $1,800,000 which he wants to carry back from the North to Tuskegee Institute, Mark Twain, Joseph H. Choate, Robert C. Ogden, and Dr. Washington himself spoke in Carnegie Hall last night. Incidentally, it was a "silver jubilee" celebration, since Tuskegee Institute was founded in 1881.

The big house was crowded to its utmost capacity, and there were as many more outside who would have gone in had there been room. The spectacle reminded one of the campaign days last November, when District Attorney Jerome and his attendant spellbinders were packing Carnegie Hall.

But last night it was by no means a gathering of the "populace" alone. Women in brilliant gowns, resplendent with jewels, and men in evening dress filled the boxes. Despite the avowed object of the meeting—to get money from the audience and others—there was an atmosphere of good humor and light-heartedness. Mark Twain's "teachings" were met with such volleys of laughter that the man who never grows old could hardly find intervals in which to deliver his precepts. That part of Mr. Clemens's address which referred to wealthy men who swear off tax assessments was applauded with especial fervor.

The occupants of the boxes included Mrs. John D. Rockefeller, Mrs. Henry H. Rogers, Mrs. Clarence H. Mackay, Mrs. Morris K. Jesup, J. G. Phelps Stokes, Isaac N. Seligman, George Foster Peabody, John Crosby Brown, Carl Schurz, Mrs. W. H. Schieffelin, Mrs. William Jay Schieffelin, Mrs. Joseph H. Choate, Mrs. Henry Villard, Nicholas Murray Butler, Mrs. Robert C. Ogden, Mrs. Cleveland H. Dodge, Mrs. Alfred Shaw, Mrs. Felix M. Warburg, Mrs. R. Fulton Cutting, Mrs. Collis P. Huntington, Mrs. Robert B. Minturn, Mrs. Jacob H. Schiff, Mrs. Paul M. Warburg, and Mrs. Arthur Curtis James.

A negro octet sang between the speeches. Their songs were old-fashioned melodies and revival songs, and their deep, full voices filled the whole house.

William Jay Schieffelin opened the meeting by telling its object and urging that all the help possible be given to Dr. Washington. He announced that in April a special train would leave New York for Tuskegee and that the round-trip ticket would cost $50, covering all expenses. On this occasion the twenty-fifth anniversary of the founding of Tuskegee will be celebrated at the school itself by speeches by Secretary of War Taft, President Eliot of Harvard, Bishop Galloway, and Andrew Carnegie.

Choate Praises Washington.

"We assemble to-night," said Mr. Choate, when Mr. Schieffelin presented him, "to celebrate the 'silver jubilee' of Tuskegee Institute, twenty-five years old to-day, the success of which as a nucleus and centre of negro education in the South is the triumph and glory of Dr. Booker T. Washington. I believe he does not claim to be the originator of it. It began in 1881 in a shanty and with thirty pupils. Now what do we behold? A great educational establishment with 2,300 acres and more than eight buildings, peculiarly fitted for the tasks they are supposed to assist.

"It has sent forth more than 6,000 pupils as examples to and teachers of the negro race. It has now an enrollment of 1,500 pupils and an endowment fund of more than $1,000,000. Like all the other great educational institutions of to-day, the more it has and the more it wants the more it gets and the more it can use.

"I read that in a recent speech Dr. Washington declared that he was proud of his race. I am sure his race is proud of him. And I know I can say that the great mass of the American people, both North and South, are also proud of him. And there are few Americans on whom European nations look with such peculiar interest and sympathy as Dr. Washington. It was my pleasure to see him in my own hired house [laughter] in London, surrounded by English men and English women, who were delighted to make his acquaintance and listen to his words.

Negro Problem a Wide One.

"This tremendous negro problem, which was left when slavery was abolished and will last much longer than slavery lasted, no more rests on the white people of the South than on the negroes or on the white people of the North. It was forced upon the South by the irresistible force of the whole Nation. In the South they, white and negro, have done their part well. I read in a book, which I hope everybody has read, by Mr. Murphy, Secretary of the Southern Education Board, that the illiteracy of the negroes in the South has been wiped away more than one half since the war. How has it been accomplished? Out of the means of the Southern States. They have done nobly. By taxation $109,000,000 was raised between 1870 and 1900 for the education of negroes. How many people in the South—like some people we have had here in New York—stood between the appropriations and the recipients, I do not know, but it was a great achievement.

"None of the Tuskegee graduates is in an asylum. It is not the educated negroes who make themselves enemies to the South; it is uneducated negroes. The desire for these Tuskegee graduates is greater than Tuskegee can satisfy.

Integrity of the Races.

"The maintenance of the integrity of the races, which, with the approval of both races, has formed the basis of Southern civilization, has given opportunity to negro lawyers, negro doctors, and ministers in every profession and industry, and the negroes are making the most of it." Then Mr. Choate turned toward Mark Twain:

"If I were to present the next speaker as Samuel L. Clemens," he said, "some would ask, 'Who is he?' but when I present him as Mark Twain—"

He could get no further. The applause which broke out lasted a full three minutes.

"I heard him speak at the dinner on his seventieth birthday," continued Mr. Choate, "and the gist of his speech was that he had never done any work in his life. He said he had never worked at anything he didn't like, and so it wasn't work at all. He said that when he had an interesting job before him he lay in bed all day. And to-day, I understand, he has been in bed all day."

When Mark Twain could be heard he said:

MARK TWAIN'S ADDRESS.

"These habits, of which Mr. Choate has told you, are the very habits which have kept me young until I am 70 years old. I have lain in bed all day to-day, expect to lie in bed all day to-morrow, and will continue to lie in bed all day throughout the year. There is nothing so refreshing, nothing is so comfortable, and nothing fits one so well for the kind of work which he calls pleasure. Mr. Choate has been careful not to pay me any compliments. It wasn't because he didn't want to—he just couldn't think of any.

"I came here in the responsible capacity of policeman—to watch Mr. Choate. This is an occasion of grave and serious importance, and it seemed necessary for me to be present so that if he tried to work off any statements that required correction, reduction, refutation or exposure there would be a tried friend of the public here to protect the house. But I can say in all frankness and gratitude that nothing of the kind has happened. He has not made one statement whose veracity fails to tally exactly with my own standard. I have never seen a person improve so.

"This does not make me jealous. It only makes me thankful. Thankful and proud; proud of a country that can produce such men—two such men. And all in the same century. We can't be with you always; we are passing away—passing away; soon we shall be gone, and then—well, everything will have to stop, I reckon. It is a sad thought. But in spirit I shall still be with you. Choate, too—if he can.

Nothing to Refute.

"There being nothing to explain, nothing to refute, nothing to excuse, there is nothing left for me to do now but resume my natural trade—which is teaching. At Tuskegee they thoroughly ground the student in the Christian code of morals; they instill into him the indisputable truth that this is the highest and best of all systems of morals; that the Nation's greatness, its strength, and its repute among the other nations is the product of that system; that it is the foundation upon which rests the American character; that whatever is commendable, whatever is valuable in the individual American's character is the flower and fruit of that seed.

"They teach him that this is true in every case, whether the man be a professing Christian or an unbeliever; for we have none but the Christian code of morals, and every individual is under its character-building powerful influence and dominion from the cradle to the grave; he breathes it in with his breath, it is in his blood and bone, it is the web and woof and fibre of his mental and spiritual heredities and ineradicable. And so every born American among the eighty millions, let his creed or destitution of creed be what it may, is indisputably a Christian to this degree—that his moral constitution is Christian.

Two Codes of Morals.

"All this is true, and no student will leave Tuskegee ignorant of it. Then what will he lack under this head? What is there for me to teach him under this head that he may possibly not acquire there, or may acquire in a not sufficiently emphasized form? Why this large fact, this important fact—that there are two separate and distinct kinds of Christian morals, so separate, so distinct, so unrelated that they are no more kin to each other than are archangels and politicians. The one kind is Christian private morals, the other is Christian public morals.

"The loyal observance of Christian private morals has made this Nation what it is—a clean and upright people in its private domestic life, an honest and honorable people in its private commercial life; no alien nation can claim superiority over it in these regards, no critic, foreign or domestic, can challenge the validity of this truth. During 363 days in the year the American citizen is true to his Christian private morals, and keeps undefiled the Nation's character at its best and highest; then in the other two days of the year he leaves his Christian private morals at home, and carries his Christian public morals to the tax office and the polls and does the best he can to damage and undo his whole year's faithful and righteous worth.

Political Morality.

"Without a blush he will vote for an unclean boss if that boss is his party's Moses, without compunction he will vote against the best man in the whole land if he is on the other ticket. Every year, in a number of cities and States, he helps to put corrupt men in office, every year he helps to extend the corruption wider and wider; year after year he goes on gradually rotting the country's political life, whereas if he would but throw away his Christian public morals and carry his Christian private morals to the polls he could promptly purify the public service and make the possession of office a high and honorable distinction and one to be coveted by the very best men the country could furnish. But now—well, now he contemplates his unpatriotic work and sighs and grieves and blames every man but the right one—which is himself.

As to Tax Dodgers.

"Once a year he lays aside his Christian private morals and hires a ferryboat and piles up his bonds in a warehouse in New Jersey for three days, and gets out his Christian public morals and goes to the Tax Office and holds up his hand and swears he wishes he may never—never if he's got a cent in the world, so help him! The next day the list appears in the papers—a column and a quarter of names in fine print, and every man in the list a billionaire and a member of a couple of churches.

"I know all those people. I have friendly, social, and criminal intercourse with the whole of them. They never miss a sermon when they are so as to be around, and they never miss swearing-off day, whether they are so as to be around or not. The innocent cannot remain innocent in the disintegrating atmosphere of this thing. I used to be an honest man. I am crumbling. No—I have crumbled. When they assessed me at $75,000 a fortnight ago I went out and tried to borrow the money, and couldn't; then when I found they were letting a whole crop of millionaires live in New York at a third of the price they were charging me I was hurt. I was indignant, and said: 'This is the last feather! I am not going to run this town all by myself.' In that moment—in that memorable moment—I began to crumble.

Mark Twain Disintegrates.

"In fifteen minutes the disintegration was complete. In fifteen minutes I was become just a mere moral sandpile, and I lifted up my hand along with those seasoned and experienced deacons and swore off every rag of personal property I've got in the world, clear down to cork leg, glass eye, and what is left of my wig.

"Those tax officers were moved, they were profoundly moved; they had long been accustomed to seeing hardened old grafters act like that, and they could endure the spectacle; but they were expecting better things of me, a chartered professional moralist, and they were saddened. I fell visibly in their respect and esteem, and I should have fallen in my own, except that I had already struck bottom and there wasn't any place to fall to.

Does a Gentleman Swear Off?

"At Tuskegee they will jump to misleading conclusions from insufficient evidence, along with Dr. Parkhurst, and they will deceive the student with the superstition that no gentleman ever swears. Look at those good millionaires; aren't they gentlemen? Well, they swear. Only once a year, maybe, but there's enough bulk to it to make up for the lost time. And do they lose anything by it? No, they don't; they save enough in three minutes to support the family seven years. When they swear do we shudder? No—unless they say damn. Then we do. It shrivels us all up.

"Yet we ought not to feel so about it, because we all swear—everybody. Including the ladies. Including Dr. Parkhurst, that strong and brave and excellent citizen, but superficially educated. For it is not the word that is the sin, it is the spirit back of the word. When an irritated lady says 'Oh!' the spirit back of it is 'damn,' and that is the way it is going to be recorded against her. It always makes me so sorry when I hear a lady swear like that. But if she says 'damn,' and says it in an amiable, nice way, it isn't going to be recorded at all.

"The idea that no gentleman ever swears is all wrong; he can swear and still be a gentleman if he does it in a nice and benevolent and affectionate way. The historian John Fiske, whom I knew well and loved, was a spotless and most noble and upright Christian gentleman, and yet he swore once. Not exactly that, maybe; still he—but I will tell you about it.

"One day when he was deeply immersed in his work his wife came in much moved and profoundly distressed, and said, 'I am sorry to disturb you, John, but I must, for this is a serious matter, and needs to be attended to at once.' Then, lamenting, she brought a grave accusation against their little son. She said: 'He has been saying his Aunt Mary is a fool and his Aunt Martha is a damned fool.' Mr. Fiske reflected upon the matter a minute, then said: 'Oh, well, it's about the distinction I should make between them myself.'

"Mr. Washington, I beg you to convey these teachings to your great and prosperous and most beneficent educational institution, and add them to the prodigal mental and moral riches wherewith you equip your fortunate protégés for the struggle of life."

Robert C. Ogden, after his introduction by Mr. Choate, said that before he began his formal address, which was "Financial Rousement" of the occasion, he wanted to answer Mark Twain's remarks on profanity.

"I want to say," said Mr. Ogden, "that my friend's allusions to the ethics of profanity are not at all original. I knew all about them years ago, and he would not have known as much as he does had he never lived in Hartford. I remember hearing a distinguished Puritan say once there, banging his fist on the desk in front of him during a debate, that he'd be damned if he would allow such a proposition to go through. In answer to this Henry Clay Trumbull said that it was fine to see a man who could say damn with such profound reverence."

Mr. Ogden then went on to tell the needs of Tuskegee. He said that the best intelligence of the country, North and South, admitted the peculiar educational duty that was owing to the negroes that had become a part of the population of the Nation.

Applause for Washington.

Mr. Ogden said that there were three distinct appeals. An added income of $90,000 a year was needed, an added endowment of $1,800,000 was essential, and a heating plant, to cost $34,000, was necessary.

Just before Booker T. Washington entered the hall a messenger boy handed him a note from Thomas Dixon, Jr., in which the writer said he would contribute $10,000 to Tuskegee if Mr. Washington would state at the meeting that he did not desire social equality for the negro, and that Tuskegee was opposed to the amalgamation of the races. When asked what he had to say on the subject Mr. Washington said:

"I will make no answer whatever. I have nothing to say."

Mr. Washington got a fine reception when he came forward to speak, and there was great applause when he said in the course of his address:

"One point we might consider as settled. We are through experimenting and speculating as to where the ten millions of black people are to live. We have reached the unalterable determination that we are going to remain here in America, and the greater part of us are going to remain for all time in the Southern States. In this connection I do not hesitate to say that from my point of view the great body of our people find a more encouraging opportunity in the South than elsewhere.

"Since we are to forever constitute a part of the citizenship of this country, there is but one question to be answered: Shall we be among the best citizens or among the worst?

"Every race of people should be judged by its best type, not by its lowest," said Mr. Washington. "One has no right to pass judgment upon a people until he has taken the pains to see something of their progress, after they have had a reasonable chance.

"Wherever we have been able to reach the people through education they have improved morally at a rapid pace, and crime has decreased. After making diligent inquiry we cannot find a single man or woman who holds a diploma from the Hampton Institute in Virginia or the Tuskegee Institute in Alabama in the walls of a penitentiary.

"No two groups of people can live side by side where one is in ignorance and poverty without its condition affecting the other. The black man must be lifted or the white man will be injured in his moral and spiritual life. The degradation of the one will mean the degradation of the other.

"I do not overlook the seriousness of the problem that is before us, nor do I set any limits upon the growth of my race. In my opinion, it is the most important and far-reaching problem that the Nation has had before it; but you cannot make equally good citizens where in one part of the country a child has $1.50 expended for his education and in another part of the country another child has $20 spent for his enlightenment.

"The negro in many ways has proved his worth and loyalty to this country. What he now asks is that through such institutions as Hampton, Fisk, and Tuskegee he shall be given the chance to render high and intelligent service to our country in the future. I have faith that such an opportunity will be given him."

When the affair was over, and the people began to climb up on the stage and pass along and shake hands, the usual thing happened. It always happens. I shake hands with people who used to know my mother intimately in Arkansas, in New Jersey, in California, in Jericho—and I have to seem so glad and so happy to meet these persons who knew in this intimate way one who was so near and dear to me. And this is the kind of thing that gradually turns a person into a polite liar and deceiver, for my mother was never in any of those places.

One pretty creature was glad to see me again, and remembered being at my house in Hartford—I don't know when, a great many years ago, it was. Now she was mistaking me for somebody else. It *couldn't* have happened to her. But I was very cordial, because she *was* very pretty. And I said "I have been longing to meet you these many, many years, for you have been celebrated throughout all the ages. You are the 'unborn child.' From the beginning of time, you have been used as a symbol. When people want to be emphatic—when they want to reach the utmost limit of lack of knowledge—they say 'He is as innocent as the unborn child; he is as ignorant as the unborn child.' You were not there, at the time you think of, except in spirit. You hadn't arrived in the flesh." She was very nice. We might have had a good long chat except for the others that I had to talk with and work up reminiscences that belonged in somebody else's experiences, not my own.

There was one young fellow, brisk, but not bright, overpoweringly pleasant and cordial, in his way. He said his mother used to teach school in Elmira, New York, where he was born and bred and where the family continued to reside, and that she would be very glad to know that he had met me, and shaken hands, for he said "She is always talking about you. She holds you in high esteem, although, as she says, she has to confess that of all the boys that ever she had in her school, you were the most troublesome."

"Well," I said, "those were my last school days, and through long practice in being troublesome, I had reached the summit by that time, because I was more than thirty-three years old."

It didn't affect him in the least. I don't think he even heard what I said he was so eager to tell me all about it, and I said to him once more, so as to spare him, and me, that I was never in a schoolhouse in Elmira, New York, even on a visit, and that his mother must be mistaking *me* for some of the Langdons, the family into which I married. No matter, he didn't hear it— kept on his talk with animation and delight, and has gone to tell his mother, I don't know what. He didn't get anything out of me to tell her, for he never heard anything I said.

These episodes used to vex me, years and years ago. But they don't vex me now. I am older. If a person thinks that he has known me at some time or other, all I require of him is that he shall consider it a distinction to have known me; and then, as a rule, I am perfectly willing to remember all about it and add some things that he has forgotten.

Twichell came down from Hartford to be present at that meeting, and we chatted and smoked after we got back home. And reference was made again to that disastrous Boston speech which I made at Whittier's seventieth birthday dinner; and Joe asked me if I was still minded to submit that speech to that Club in Washington, day after to-morrow, where Colonel Harvey and I are to be a couple of the four guests. And I said "No," I had given that up—which was true. Because I have examined that speech a couple of times since, and have changed my notion about it—changed it entirely. I find it gross, coarse,—well, I needn't go on with particulars. I didn't like any part of it, from the beginning to the end. I found it always offensive and detestable. How do I account for this change of view? I don't know. I can't account for it. I am the person concerned. If I could put myself outside of myself and examine it from the point of view of a person not personally concerned in it, then no doubt I could analyze it and explain to my satisfaction the change which has taken place. As it is, I am merely moved by instinct. My instinct said, formerly, that it was an innocent speech, and funny. The same instinct, sitting cold and judicial, as a court of last resort, has reversed that verdict. I expect this latest verdict to remain.* I don't remove the speech from the autobiography, because I think that this change of mind about it is interesting, whether the speech is or not, and therefore let it stay.

Twichell had a letter with him which interested me, and, by request, he left it with me, to be returned to him after I shall have used it. This letter is from the Reverend Charles Stowe, a son of Harriet Beecher Stowe. The letter is now about two months old—but in that time Joe

*May 25. It did remain—until day before yesterday; then I gave it a final and vigorous reading—*aloud*—and dropped straight back to my former admiration of it. M.T.

has pretty nearly worn it out, reading it to people. That is, reading a certain passage in it to people. He read that passage to me, to wit:

> I was reading in the volume of Rev. Dr. Burton's "Remains," as the old folks used to say, your remarks at his funeral. I think for beauty of diction, richness of thought and delicacy and strength of psychological analysis, it is up to any of the masters of our tongue. The passage I admire most of all is the one beginning "Men marked the sunshine in him," etc. I think the whole thing a gem, but this passage is a masterpiece of beautiful and dignified English. It is a shame that men like Dr. Parker and Dr. Burton are in the battle of life, in a way—no, that men like *you* and Dr. Burton are in a way like the 130-gun ships of the Spanish fleet at Trafalgar, outclassed by pigmies.

And Joe said "Mark, what do you think of that?"

I said "Well, Joe, I don't want to commit myself. Send me the passage, and then I will furnish my opinion."

Joe said "You know the charm of this whole thing lies in the fact that it wasn't *I* that did that wonderful gem—it was Parker."

But Twichell is getting a lot of satisfaction out of it. Some time ago, his daughters gathered together a large company of their young friends of the two sexes, and while they were in the midst of their banquet Joe came in and greeted them, and was welcomed. But, necessarily, with his gray head, he was in a considerable degree an embarrassment, and the hilarity without perhaps entirely breaking off, was diminished to the proper degree of reverence for Joe's cloth and age. That being just the right atmosphere—just the right conditions, for an impressive reading of that passage in this letter, Joe read it with apparent pride, and almost juvenile vanity—while those young people dropped their eyes in pity for an old man who could display his vanities in such a way and take such a childish delight in them. Joe's daughters turned crimson; glanced at each other, and were ready to cry over this humiliating exhibition. Then of course Twichell finished his performance by informing them that these praises were all deserved, but not by him—for Mr. Stowe had made a mistake. If he had gone and taken another look at that passage which he so highly praised, he would have noticed that it was the work of Rev. Dr. Parker, and not of himself.

At one of the Monday morning meetings of the clergy Twichell did the same thing. And with such excellent effect that in the midst of his reading Parker himself spoke out and said "Now Joe, this is too much. We know you can do fine things; we know you can do wonderful things; but you never did anything as wonderful as this that Charley Stowe is talking about. He is no competent critic, that is quite manifest. There isn't anything in English Literature worthy of such an intemperate encomium as this that Charley Stowe is passing on your Burton speech."

Then Joe explained that Parker was only damaging himself, because it was Parker's speech he was reading about.

Parker is still in the harness. He has been shepherd of the same congregation—its children, and its grandchildren, and its great-grandchildren—for forty-six years. Joe says he is just as marvelous an artist in English phrasing, and just as fine and deep in thought as ever he was. To my knowledge, this is saying a great deal. For Parker was one of our remarkable men when

I knew him in the old Hartford days, and we had eight or ten men in that town who were 'way above the average.

Twichell's congregation—the only congregation he has ever had since he entered the ministry—celebrated the fortieth anniversary of his accession to that pulpit, a couple of weeks ago. Joe entered the army as chaplain in the very beginning of the Civil War. He was a young chap, and had just been graduated from Yale, and the Yale Theological Seminary. He made all the campaigns of the Army of the Potomac. When he was mustered out, that congregation I am speaking of called him, and he has served them ever since, and always to their satisfaction—except once.

I have found among my old manuscripts one which I perceive to be about twenty-two years old. It has a heading, and looks as if I had meant it to serve as a magazine article. I can clearly see, now, why I didn't print it. It is full of indications that its inspiration was what happened to Twichell about that time, and which produced a situation for him which he will not forget until he is dead, if he even forgets it then. I think I can see, all through this artful article, that I was trying to hint at Twichell, and the episode of that preacher whom I met on the street, and hint at various things that were exasperating me. And now that I read that old article, I perceive that I probably saw that my art was not ingenious enough—that I hadn't covered Twichell up, and hadn't covered up the episode that I was hinting at—that anybody in Hartford could read everything between the lines that I was trying to conceal.

I will insert this venerable article in this place, and then take up that episode in Joe's history and tell about it.

The Character of Man

Concerning Man—he is too large a subject to be treated as a whole; so I will merely discuss a detail or two of him at this time. I desire to contemplate him from this point of view—this premiss: that he was not made for any useful purpose, for the reason that he hasn't served any; that he was most likely not even made *intentionally;* and that his working himself up out of the oyster bed to his present position was probably matter of surprise and regret to the Creator. * * * * For his history, in all climes, all ages and all circumstances, furnishes oceans and continents of proof that of all the creatures that were made he is the most detestable. Of the entire brood he is the only one—the solitary one—that possesses malice. That is the basest of all instincts, passions, vices—the most hateful. That one thing puts him below the rats, the grubs, the trichinæ. He is the only creature that inflicts pain for sport, knowing it to *be* pain. But if the cat knows she is inflicting pain when she plays with the frightened mouse, then we must make an exception here; we must grant that in one detail man is the moral peer of the cat. *All* creatures kill—there seems to be no exception; but of the whole list, man is the only one that kills for fun; he is the only one that kills in malice, the only one that kills for revenge. Also—in all the list he is the only creature that has a nasty mind.

Shall he be extolled for his noble qualities, for his gentleness, his sweetness, his amiability, his lovingness, his courage, his devotion, his patience, his fortitude, his prudence, the various charms and graces of his spirit? The other animals share *all* these with him, yet are free from the blacknesses and rottennesses of his character.

* * * * There are certain sweet-smelling sugar-coated lies current in the world which all politic men have apparently tacitly conspired together to support and perpetuate. One of these is, that there is such a thing in the world as independence: independence of thought, independence of opinion, independence of action. Another is, that the world loves to *see* independence—admires it, applauds it. Another is, that there is such a thing in the world as toleration—in religion, in politics, and such matters; and with it trains that already mentioned auxiliary lie that toleration is admired, and applauded. Out of these trunk-lies spring many branch ones: to wit, the lie that not all men are slaves; the lie that men are glad when other men succeed; glad when they prosper; glad to see them reach lofty heights; sorry to see them fall again. And yet other branch-lies: to wit, that there is heroism in man; that he is not mainly made up of malice and treachery; that he is sometimes not a coward; that there is something about him that ought to be perpetuated—in heaven, or hell, or somewhere. And these other branch-lies, to wit: that conscience, man's moral medicine chest, is not only created by the Creator, but is put into man ready-charged with the right and only true and authentic correctives of conduct—and the duplicate chest, with the self-same correctives, unchanged, unmodified, distributed to all nations and all epochs. And yet one other branch-lie, to wit, that I am I, and you are you; that we are units, individuals, and have natures of our own, instead of being the tail-end of a tape-worm eternity of ancestors extending in linked procession back—and back—and back—to our source in the monkeys, with this so-called individuality of ours a decayed and rancid mush of inherited instincts and teachings derived, atom by atom, stench by stench, from the entire line of that sorry column, and not so much new and original matter in it as you could balance on a needle point and examine under a microscope. This makes well nigh fantastic the suggestion that there can be such a thing as a personal, original and responsible nature in a man, separable from that in him which is not original, and findable in such quantity as to enable the observer to say, This is a man, not a procession.

* * * * Consider that first mentioned lie: that there is such a thing in the world as independence; that it exists in individuals, that it exists in bodies of men. Surely if anything *is* proven, by whole oceans and continents of evidence, it is that the quality of independence was almost wholly left out of the human race. The scattering exceptions to the rule only emphasize it, light it up, make it glare. The whole population of New England meekly took their turns, for years, in standing up in the railway trains, without so much as a complaint above their breath, till at last these uncounted millions were able to produce exactly one single independent man, who stood to his rights and made the railroad give him a seat. Statistics and the law of probabilities warrant the assumption that it will take New England forty years to breed his fellow. There is a law, with a penalty attached, forbidding trains to occupy the Asylum street crossing more than five minutes at a time. For years people and carriages used to wait there nightly as much as twenty minutes on a stretch while New England trains monopolized that crossing. I used to hear men use vigorous language about that insolent wrong—but they waited, just the same.

We are discreet sheep; we wait to see how the drove is going, and then go with the drove. We have two opinions: one private, which we are afraid to express; and another one—the one we use—which we force ourselves to wear to please Mrs. Grundy, until habit makes us comfortable in it, and the custom of defending it presently makes us love it, adore it, and forget how pitifully we came by it. Look at it in politics. Look at the candidates whom we loathe, one year, and are afraid to vote against the next; whom we cover with unimaginable filth, one year, and fall down on the public platform and worship, the next—and keep on doing it until the habitual shutting of our eyes to last year's evidences brings us presently to a sincere and stupid belief in this year's.* Look at the tyranny of party—at what is called party allegiance, party loyalty—a snare invented by designing men for selfish purposes—and which turns voters into chattels, slaves, rabbits; and all the while, their masters, and they themselves are shouting rubbish about liberty, independence, freedom of opinion, freedom of speech, honestly unconscious of the fantastic contradiction; and forgetting or ignoring that their fathers and the churches shouted the same blasphemies a generation earlier when they were closing their doors against the hunted slave, beating his handful of humane defenders with Bible-texts and billies, and pocketing the insults and licking the shoes of his Southern master.

If we would learn what the human race really *is,* at bottom, we need only observe it in election times. A Hartford clergyman met me in the street, and spoke of a new nominee—denounced the nomination, in strong, earnest words—words that were refreshing for their independence, their manliness.† He said, "I ought to be proud, perhaps, for this nominee is a relative of mine; on the contrary I am humiliated and disgusted; for I know him intimately—familiarly—and I know that he is an unscrupulous scoundrel, and always has been." You should have seen this clergyman preside at a political meeting forty days later; and urge, and plead, and gush—and you should have heard him paint the character of this same nominee. You would have supposed he was describing the Cid, and Great-heart, and Sir Galahad, and Bayard the Spotless all rolled into one. Was he sincere? Yes—by that time; and therein lies the pathos of it all, the hopelessness of it all. It shows at what trivial cost of effort a man can teach himself a lie, and learn to believe it, when he perceives, by the general drift, that that is the popular thing to do. Does he believe his lie *yet?* Oh, probably not; he has no further use for it. It was but a passing incident; he spared to it the moment that was its due, then hastened back to the serious business of his life.

And what a paltry poor lie is that one which teaches that independence of action and opinion is prized in men, admired, honored, rewarded. When a man leaves a political party, he is treated as if the party owned him—as if he were its bond slave, as most party men plainly are—and had stolen himself, gone off with what was not his own. And he is traduced, derided, despised, held up to public obloquy and loathing. His character is remorselessly assassinated; no means, however vile, are spared to injure his property and his business.

The preacher who casts a vote for conscience' sake, runs the risk of starving. And is rightly served; for he has been teaching a falsity—that men respect and honor independence of thought and action.

Mr. Beecher may be charged with a *crime,* and his whole following will rise as one man,

* *Jan. 11, '06.* It is long ago, but it plainly means Blaine.   M. T.

† *Jan. 11, '06.* I can't remember his name. It began with K, I think. He was one of the American revisers of the New Testament, and was nearly as great a scholar as Hammond Trumbull.

and stand by him to the bitter end; but who so poor to be his friend when he is charged with casting a vote for conscience' sake? Take the editor so charged—take—take anybody.

All the talk about tolerance, in anything or anywhere, is plainly a gentle lie. It does not exist. It is in no man's heart; but it unconsciously and by moss-grown inherited habit, drivels and slobbers from all men's lips. Intolerance is everything for one's self, and nothing for the other person. The main-spring of man's nature is just that—selfishness.

Let us skip the other lies, for brevity's sake. To consider them would prove nothing, except that man is what he is—loving, toward his own, lovable, to his own,—his family, his friends— and otherwise the buzzing, busy, trivial, enemy of his race—who tarries his little day, does his little dirt, commends himself to God, and then goes out into the darkness, to return no more, and send no messages back—selfish even in death.

Wednesday, January 24, 1906

Tells of the defeat of Mr. Blaine for the Presidency, and how Mr. Clemens's, Mr. Twichell's, and Mr. Goodwin's votes were cast for Cleveland.

It is plain, I think, that this old article was written about twenty-two years ago, and that it followed by about three or four months the defeat of James G. Blaine for the Presidency and the election of Grover Cleveland, the Democratic candidate—a temporary relief from a Republican-party domination which had lasted a generation. I had been accustomed to vote for Republicans more frequently than for Democrats, but I was never a Republican and never a Democrat. In the community, I was regarded as a Republican, but I had never so regarded myself. As early as 1865 or '66 I had had this curious experience: that whereas up to that time I had considered myself a Republican, I was converted to a no-party independence by the wisdom of a rabid Republican. This was a man who was afterward a United States Senator, and upon whose character rests no blemish that *I* know of, except that he was the father of the William R. Hearst of to-day, and therefore grandfather of Yellow Journalism—that calamity of calamities.

1865 or '66

Hearst was a Missourian; I was a Missourian. He was a long, lean, practical, common-sense, uneducated man of fifty, or thereabouts. I was shorter and better informed—at least I thought so. One day, in the Lick House in San Francisco, he said:

"I am a Republican; I expect to remain a Republican always. It is my purpose, and I am not a changeable person. But look at the condition of things. The Republican party goes right along, from year to year, scoring triumph after triumph, until it has come to think that the political power of the United States is its property, and that it is a sort of insolence for any other party to aspire to any part of that power. Nothing can be worse for a country than this. To lodge all power in one party and keep it there, is to insure bad government, and *the sure and gradual deterioration of the public morals.* The parties ought to be so nearly equal in strength as to make it necessary for the leaders on both sides to choose the very best men they can find. Democratic fathers ought to divide up their sons between the two parties if they can, and do their best in this way to equalize the powers. I have only one son. He is a little boy, but I am already instructing him, persuading him, preparing him, to vote against me when he comes of age, let me be on whichever side I may. He is already a good Democrat, and I want him to remain a good Democrat—until I become a Democrat myself. Then I shall shift him to the other party, if I can."

It seemed to me that this unlettered man was at least a wise one. And I have never voted a straight ticket from that day to this. I have never belonged to any party from that day to this. I have never belonged to any church from that day to this. I have remained absolutely free in those matters. And in this independence I have found a spiritual comfort and a peace of mind quite above price.

When Blaine came to be talked of by the Republican leaders as their probable candidate for the Presidency, the Republicans of Hartford were very sorry, and they thought they foresaw his defeat, in case he should be nominated. But they stood in no great fear of his nomination. The Convention met in Chicago, and the balloting began. In my house we were playing billiards. Sam Dunham was present; also F. G. Whitmore, Henry C. Robinson, Charles E. Perkins and Edward M. Bunce. We took turns in the game, and, meanwhile, discussed the political situation. George, the colored butler, was down in the kitchen on guard at the telephone. As fast as a ballot was received at the political headquarters down town, it was telephoned out to the house, and George reported it to us through the speaking-tube. Nobody present was seriously expecting the nomination of Mr. Blaine. All these men were Republicans, but they had no affection for Blaine. For two years, the Hartford *Courant* had been holding Blaine up to scorn and contumely. It had been denouncing him daily. It had been mercilessly criticising his political conduct and backing up the criticisms with the deadly facts. Up to that time the *Courant* had been a paper which could be depended on to speak its sincere mind about the prominent men of both parties, and its judgments could be depended upon as being well and candidly considered, and sound. It had been my custom to pin my faith to the *Courant,* and accept its verdicts at par.

The billiard game and the discussion went on and on, and by and by, about mid-afternoon, George furnished us a paralysing surprise through the speaking-tube. Mr. Blaine was the nominee! The butts of the billiard cues came down on the floor with a bump, and for a while the players were dumb. They could think of nothing to say. Then Henry Robinson broke the silence. He said, sorrowfully, that it was hard luck to have to vote for that man. I said:

"But we *don't* have to vote for him."

Robinson said "Do you mean to say that you are not going to vote for him?"

"Yes," I said, "that is what I mean to say. I am not going to vote for him."

The others began to find their voices. They sang the same note. They said that when a party's representatives choose a man, that ends it. If they choose unwisely it is a misfortune, but no loyal member of the party has any right to withhold his vote. He has a plain duty before him and he can't shirk it. He must vote for that nominee.

I said that no party held the privilege of dictating to me how I should vote. That if party loyalty was a form of patriotism, I was no patriot, and that I didn't think I was much of a patriot anyway, for oftener than otherwise what the general body of Americans regarded as the patriotic course was not in accordance with my views; that if there was any valuable difference between being an American and a monarchist it lay in the theory that the American could decide for himself what is patriotic and what isn't; whereas the king could dictate the monarchist's patriotism for him—a decision which was final and must be accepted by the victim; that in my belief I was the only person in the sixty millions—with Congress and the Administration back of the sixty millions—who was privileged to construct my patriotism for me.

They said "Suppose the country is entering upon a war—where do you stand then? Do you arrogate to yourself the privilege of going your own way in the matter, in the face of the nation?"

"Yes," I said, "that is my position. If I thought it an unrighteous war I would say so. If I were invited to shoulder a musket in that cause and march under that flag, I would decline. I would not voluntarily march under this country's flag, nor any other, when it was my private judgment that the country was in the wrong. If the country *obliged* me to shoulder the musket I could not help myself, but I would never volunteer. To volunteer would be the act of a traitor to myself, and consequently traitor to my country. If I refused to volunteer, I should be *called* a traitor, I am well aware of that—but that would not make me a traitor. The unanimous vote of the sixty millions could not make me a traitor. I should still be a patriot, and, in my opinion, the only one in the whole country."

There was a good deal of talk, but I made no converts. They were all candid enough to say that they did not want to vote for Mr. Blaine, but they all said they would *do* it nevertheless. Then Henry Robinson said:

"It is a good while yet before election. There is time for you to come around; and you will come around. The influences about you will be too strong for you. On election day you will vote for Blaine."

I said I should not go to the polls at all.

The *Courant* had an uncomfortable time thence until midnight. General Hawley, the editor-in-chief (and he was also commander-in-chief of the paper), was at his post in Congress, and the telegraphing to and fro between the *Courant* and him went on diligently until midnight. For two years the *Courant* had been making a "tar baby" of Mr. Blaine, and adding tar every day—and now it was called upon to praise him, hurrah for him, and urge its well instructed clientele to elevate the "tar baby" to the chief magistracy of the nation. It was a difficult position, and it took the *Courant* people and General Hawley nine hours to swallow the bitter pill. But at last General Hawley reached a decision, and at midnight the pill was swallowed. Within a fortnight the *Courant* had acquired some facility in praising where it had so long censured; within another month the change in its character was become complete—and to this day it has never recovered its virtue entirely, though under Charles Hopkins Clark's editorship it has gotten back 90 per cent of it, by my estimate.

Charles Dudley Warner was the active editor at the time. He could not stomach the new conditions. He found himself unable to turn his pen in the other direction and make it proceed backwards, therefore he decided to retire his pen altogether. He withdrew from the editorship, resigned his salary, lived thenceforth upon his income as a part proprietor of the paper, and upon the proceeds of magazine work and lecturing, and kept his vote in his pocket on election day.

The conversation with the learned American member of the Board of scholars which revised the New Testament did occur as I have outlined it in that old article. He was vehement in his denunciation of Blaine, his relative, and said he should never vote for him. But he was so used to revising New Testaments that it took him only a few days to revise this one. I had hardly finished with *him* when I came across James G. Batterson. Batterson was President of the great Travelers Insurance Company. He was a fine man; a strong man; and a valuable citizen. He was fully as vehement as that clergyman had been in his denunciations of Blaine—but inside of two weeks he was presiding at a great Republican ratification meeting; and to hear him talk about Blaine and his perfections, a stranger would have supposed that the Republican party had had the good fortune to secure an archangel as its nominee.

Time went on. Election day was close at hand. Late one frosty night, Twichell, the Reverend Francis Goodwin and I were tramping homeward through the deserted streets in the face of a wintry gale, after a séance of our Monday Evening Club, and after a supper-table debate over the political situation, in which the fact had come out—to the astonishment and indignation of everybody, the ladies included—that three traitors were present. That Goodwin, Twichell and I were going to keep our votes in our pockets instead of casting them for the archangel. Along in that homeward tramp, somewhere, Goodwin had a happy idea, and brought it out. He said,

"Why are we keeping back these three votes from Blaine? Plainly the answer is, to do what we can to defeat Blaine. Very well then, these are three votes against Blaine. The common-sense procedure would be to cast six votes against him by turning in our three votes for Cleveland."

Even Twichell and I could see that there was sense in that, and we said,

"That is a very good thing to do and we'll do it."

On election day we went to the polls and consummated our hellish design. At that time the voting was public. Any spectator could see how a man was voting—and straightway this crime was known to the whole community. This double crime,—in the eyes of the community. To withhold a vote from Blaine was bad enough, but to add to that iniquity by actually voting for the Democratic candidate was criminal to a degree for which there was no adequate language discoverable in the dictionary.

From that day forth, for a good while to come, Twichell's life was a good deal of a burden to him. To use a common expression, his congregation "soured" on him, and he found small pleasure in the exercise of his clerical office—unless perhaps he got some healing for his hurts, now and then, through the privilege of burying some of those people of his. It would have been a benevolence to bury the whole of them, I think, and a profit to the community. But if that was Twichell's feeling about it, he was too charitable in his nature and too kindly to expose it. He never said it to me, and I think that if he would have said it to any one, I should have been the one.

Twichell had most seriously damaged himself with his congregation. He had a young family to support. It was a large family already, and it was growing. It was becoming a heavier and heavier burden every year—but his salary remained always the same. It became less and less competent to keep up with the domestic drain upon it, and if there had ever been any prospect of increasing this salary, that prospect was gone now. It was not much of a salary. It was four thousand dollars. He had not asked for more, and it had not occurred to the congregation to offer it. Therefore his vote for Cleveland was a distinct disaster to him. That exercise of his ostensible great American privilege of being free and independent in his political opinions and actions, proved a heavy calamity. But the Reverend Francis Goodwin continued to be respected as before—that is publicly; privately he was damned. But publicly he had suffered no harm. Perhaps it was because the public approval was not a necessity in his case. His father was worth seven millions, and was old. The Reverend Francis was in the line of promotion, and would soon inherit.

As far as I was myself concerned, I did not need to worry. I did not draw my living from Hartford. It was quite sufficient for my needs. Hartford's opinion of me could not affect it; and besides it had long been known among my friends that I had never voted a straight ticket, and was therefore so accustomed to crime that it was unlikely that disapproval of my conduct could reform me—and maybe I wasn't worth the trouble anyway.

By and by, about a couple of months later, New Year's Eve arrived, and with it the annual meeting of Joe's congregation and the annual sale of the pews.

Thursday, February 1, 1906

Subject of January 24th continued—Mr. Twichell's unpopular vote.

Joe was not quite present. It was not etiquette for him to be within hearing of the business-talks concerning the church's affairs. He remained in the seclusion of the church parlor, ready to be consulted if that should be necessary. The congregation was present in full force; every seat was occupied. The moment the house was called to order, a member sprang to his feet and moved that the connection between Twichell and the church be dissolved. The motion was promptly seconded. Here, and there, and yonder, all over the house, there were calls of "Question! Question!" But Mr. Hubbard, a middle-aged man, a wise and calm and collected man, business manager and part owner of the *Courant,* rose in his place and proposed to discuss the motion before rushing it to a vote. The substance of his remarks was this,—(which I must put in my own language, of course, as I was not there).

"Mr. Twichell was the first pastor you have ever had. You have never wanted another until two months ago. You have had no fault to find with his ministrations as your pastor, but he has suddenly become unfit to continue them because he is unorthodox in his politics, according to your views. Very well, he *was* fit; he has become unfit. He *was* valuable; his value has passed away, apparently—but only apparently. His highest value remains—if I know this congregation. When he assumed this pastorate this region was an outlying district, thinly inhabited, its real estate worth next to nothing. Mr. Twichell's personality was a magnet which immediately began to draw population in this direction. It has continued to draw it from that day to this. As a result, your real estate, almost valueless in the beginning, ranges now at very high prices. Reflect, before you vote upon this resolution. The church in West Hartford is waiting upon this vote with deep solicitude. That congregation's real estate stands at a low figure. What they are anxious to have now above everything else, under God, is a price-raiser. Dismiss Mr.

Twichell to-night, and they will hire him to-morrow. Prices there will go up; prices here will go down. That is all. I move the vote."

Twichell was not dismissed. That was twenty-two years ago. It was Twichell's first pulpit after his consecration to his vocation. He occupies it yet, and has never had another. The fortieth anniversary of his accession to it was celebrated by that congregation and its descendants a couple of weeks ago, and there was great enthusiasm. Twichell has never made any political mistakes since. His persistency in voting right has been an exasperation to me these many years, and has been the cause and inspiration of more than one vicious letter from me to him. But the viciousness was all a pretense. I have never found any real fault with him for voting his infernal Republican ticket, for the reason that situated as he was, with a large family to support, his first duty was not to his political conscience but to his family conscience. A sacrifice had to be made; a duty had to be performed. His very first duty was to his family, not to his political conscience. He sacrificed his political independence, and saved his family by it. In the circumstances, this was the highest loyalty, and the best. If he had been a Henry Ward Beecher it would not have been his privilege to sacrifice his political conscience, because in case of dismissal a thousand pulpits would have been open to him, and his family's bread secure. In Twichell's case, there would have been some risk—in fact, a good deal of risk. That he, or any other expert, could have raised the prices of real estate in West Hartford is, to my mind, exceedingly doubtful. I think Mr. Hubbard worked his imagination to the straining point when he got up that scare that night. I believe it was safest for Twichell to remain where he was if he could. He saved his family, and that was his first duty, in my opinion.

In this country there are perhaps eighty thousand preachers. Not more than twenty of them are politically independent—the rest cannot be politically independent. They must vote the ticket of their congregations. They do it, and are justified. They themselves are mainly the reason why they have no political independence, for they do not preach political independence from their pulpits. They have their large share in the fact that the people of this nation have no political independence.

February 1, 1906.

To-morrow will be the thirty-sixth anniversary of our marriage. My wife passed from this life one year and eight months ago, in Florence, Italy, after an unbroken illness of twenty-two months' duration.

1867   I saw her first in the form of an ivory miniature in her brother Charley's stateroom in the steamer *Quaker City* in the Bay of Smyrna, in the summer of 1867, when she was in her twenty-second year. I saw her in the flesh for the first time in New York in the following December. She was slender and beautiful and girlish—and she was both girl and woman. She remained both girl and woman to the last day of her life. Under a grave and gentle exterior burned inextinguishable fires of sympathy, energy, devotion, enthusiasm, and absolutely limitless affection. She was *always* frail in body, and she lived upon her spirit, whose hopefulness and courage were indestructible. Perfect truth, perfect honesty, perfect candor, were qualities of her character which were born with her. Her judgments of people and things were sure and accurate. Her intuitions almost never deceived her. In her judgments of the characters and acts of both friends and strangers, there was always room for charity, and this charity never failed. I have compared and contrasted her with hundreds of persons, and my conviction remains that hers was the most perfect character I have ever met. And I may add that she was the most winningly dignified person I have ever known. Her character and disposition were of the sort that not only invite worship but command it. No servant ever left her service who deserved to remain in it. And as she could choose with a glance of her eye, the servants she selected did in almost all cases deserve to remain, and they *did* remain. She was always cheerful; and she was always able to communicate her cheerfulness to others. During the nine years that we spent in poverty and debt, she was always able to reason me out of my despairs and find a bright side to the clouds and make me see it. In all that time I never knew her to utter a word of regret concerning our altered circumstances, nor did I ever know her children to do the like. For she had taught them, and they drew their fortitude from her. The love which she bestowed upon those whom she loved took the form of worship, and in that form it was returned—returned by relatives, friends, and the servants of her household. It was a strange combination which wrought into one individual, so to speak, by marriage—her disposition and character and mine. She poured out her prodigal affection in kisses and caresses, and in a vocabulary of endearments whose profusion was always an astonishment to me. I was born *reserved* as to endearments of speech, and caresses, and hers broke upon me as the summer waves break upon Gibraltar. I was reared in that atmosphere of reserve. As I have already said in an earlier chapter, I never knew a member of my father's family to kiss another member of it except once, and that at a death-bed. And our village was not a kissing community. The kissing and caressing ended with courtship—along with the deadly piano-playing of that day.

She had the heart-free laugh of a girl. It came seldom, but when it broke upon the ear it was as inspiring as music. I heard it for the last time when she had been occupying her sick-bed for more than a year, and I made a written note of it at the time—a note not to be repeated.

To-morrow will be the thirty-sixth anniversary. We were married in her father's house in Elmira, New York, and went next day, by special train, to Buffalo, along with the whole Langdon family, and with the Beechers and the Twichells, who had solemnized the marriage. We were to live in Buffalo, where I was to be one of the editors of the Buffalo *Express,* and a part owner of the paper. I knew nothing about Buffalo, but I had made my household arrangements there through a friend, by letter. I had instructed him to find a boarding-house of as respectable a character as my light salary as editor would command. We were received at about nine o'clock at the station in Buffalo and were put into several sleighs and driven all over America, as it seemed to me—for apparently we turned all the corners in the town and followed all the streets there were—I scolding freely and characterizing that friend of mine in very uncomplimentary words for securing a boarding-house that apparently had no definite locality. But there was a conspiracy—and my bride knew of it, but I was in ignorance. Her father, Jervis Langdon, had bought and furnished a new house for us in the fashionable street, Delaware Avenue, and had laid in a cook and housemaids, and a brisk and electric young coachman, an Irishman, Patrick McAleer—and we were being driven all over that city in order that one sleighful of those people could have time to go to the house and see that the gas was lighted all over it, and a hot supper prepared for the crowd. We arrived at last, and when I entered that fairy place my indignation reached high-water mark, and without any reserve I delivered my opinion to that friend of mine for being so stupid as to put us into a boarding-house whose terms would be far out of my reach. Then Mr. Langdon brought forward a very pretty box and opened it and took from it a deed of the house. So the comedy ended very pleasantly, and we sat down to supper.

The company departed about midnight, and left us alone in our new quarters. Then Ellen, the cook, came in to get orders for the morning's marketing—and neither of us knew whether beefsteak was sold by the barrel or by the yard. We exposed our ignorance, and Ellen was full of Irish delight over it. Patrick McAleer, that brisk young Irishman, came in to get his orders for next day—and that was our first glimpse of him.

Thirty-six years have gone by. And this letter from Twichell comes this morning, from Hartford.

> Hartford.
> Jan 31.
>
> Dear Mark:
>
> I am sorry to say that the news about Patrick is very bad. I saw him Monday. He *looked* pretty well and was in cheerful spirits. He told me that he was fast recovering from an operation performed on him last week Wednesday, and would soon be out again. But a nurse who followed me from the room when I left told me that the poor fellow was deceived. The operation had simply disclosed the fact that nothing could be done for him.
>
> Yesterday I asked the Surgeon (Johnson, living opposite us) if that were so. He said 'Yes'; that the trouble was cancer of the liver and that there was no help for it in surgery; the case was quite hopeless; the end was not many weeks off. A pitiful case, indeed! Poor Patrick! His face brightened when he saw me. He told me, the first thing, that he had just heard from Jean. His wife and son were with him. Whether they suspect the truth I don't know. I doubt if the wife does: but the son looked very sober. May be he only has been told.
>
> Yrs aff.
> Joe

Jean had kept watch of Patrick's case by correspondence with Patrick's daughter Nancy, and so we already knew that it was hopeless. In fact, the end seems to be nearer than Twichell suspects. Last night I sent Twichell word that I *knew* Patrick had only a day or two to live, and he must not forget to provide a memorial wreath and pin a card to it with my name and Clara's and Jean's, signed to it, worded "In loving remembrance of Patrick McAleer, faithful and valued friend of our family for thirty-six years."

I wanted to say that he had *served* us thirty-six years, but some people would not have understood that. He served us constantly for twenty-six years. Then came that break when we spent nine or ten years in Europe. But if Patrick himself could see his funeral wreath—then I should certainly say, in so many words, that he served us thirty-six years. For last summer, when we were located in the New Hampshire hills, at Dublin, we had Patrick with us. Jean had gone to Hartford the 1st of May and secured his services for the summer. Necessarily, a part of our household was Katy Leary, who has been on our roster for twenty-six years; and one day Jean overheard Katy and Patrick disputing about this length of service. Katy said she had served the family longer than Patrick had. Patrick said it was nothing of the kind; that he had already served the family ten years when Katy came, and that he had now served it thirty-six years.

He was just as brisk there in the New Hampshire hills as he was thirty-six years ago. He was sixty-four years old, but was just as slender, and trim, and handsome, and just as alert and springy on his feet as he was in those long-vanished days of his youth. He was the most perfect man in his office that I have ever known, for this reason: that he never neglected any detail, howsoever slight, of his duties, and there was never any occasion to give him an order about anything. He conducted his affairs without anybody's help. There was always plenty of feed for the horses; the horses were always shod when they needed to be shod; the carriages and sleighs were always attended to; he kept everything in perfect order. It was a great satisfaction to have such a man around. I was not capable of telling anybody what to do about anything. He was my particular servant, and I didn't need to tell him anything at all. He was just the same in the New Hampshire hills. I never gave him an order while he was there, the whole five months; and there was never anything lacking that belonged in his jurisdiction.

When we had been married a year or two Patrick took a wife, and they lived in a house which we built and added to the stable. They reared eight children. They lost one, two or three years ago—a thriving young man, assistant editor of a Hartford daily paper, I think. The children were all educated in the public schools and in the High School. They are all men and women now, of course.

Our first child, Langdon Clemens, was born the 7th of November, 1870, and lived twenty-two months. Susy was born the 19th of March, 1872, and passed from life in the Hartford home, the 18th of August, 1896. With her, when the end came, were Jean, and Katy Leary, and John and Ellen (the gardener and his wife). Clara and her mother and I arrived in England from around the world on the 31st of July, and took a house in Guildford. A week later, when Susy, Katy and Jean should have been arriving from America, we got a letter instead.

1870
1872
1896

Friday, February 2, 1906

**Subject of February 1st continued—The death of Susy Clemens—
Ends with mention of Dr. John Brown.**

It explained that Susy was slightly ill—nothing of consequence. But we were disquieted, and began to cable for later news. This was Friday. All day no answer—and the ship to leave Southampton next day, at noon. Clara and her mother began packing, to be ready in case the news should be bad. Finally came a cablegram saying "Wait for cablegram in the morning." This was not satisfactory—not reassuring. I cabled again, asking that the answer be sent to Southampton, for the day was now closing. I waited in the postoffice that night till the doors were closed, toward midnight, in the hope that good news might still come, but there was no message. We sat silent at home till one in the morning, waiting—waiting for we knew not what. Then we took the earliest morning train, and when we reached Southampton the message was there. It said the recovery would be long, but certain. This was a great relief to me, but not to my wife. She was frightened. She and Clara went aboard the steamer at once and sailed for America, to nurse Susy. I remained behind to search for another and larger house in Guildford.

That was the 15th of August, 1896. Three days later, when my wife and Clara were about half way across the ocean, I was standing in our dining room thinking of nothing in particular, when a cablegram was put into my hand. It said "Susy was peacefully released to-day."

It is one of the mysteries of our nature that a man, all unprepared, can receive a thunder-stroke like that and live. There is but one reasonable explanation of it. The intellect is stunned by the shock and but gropingly gathers the meaning of the words. The power to realize their full import is mercifully wanting. The mind has a dumb sense of vast loss—that is all. It will take mind and memory months, and possibly years, to gather together the details and thus learn and know the whole extent of the loss. A man's house burns down. The smoking wreckage represents only a ruined home that was dear through years of use and pleasant associations. By and by, as the days and weeks go on, first he misses this, then that, then the other thing. And when he casts about for it he finds that it was in that house. Always it is an *essential*—there was but one of its kind. It cannot be replaced. It was in that house. It is irrevocably lost. He did not realize that it was an essential when he had it; he only discovers it now when he finds himself balked, hampered, by its absence. It will be years before the tale of lost essentials is complete, and not till then can he truly know the magnitude of his disaster.

The 18th of August brought me the awful tidings. The mother and the sister were out there in mid-Atlantic, ignorant of what was happening; flying to meet this incredible calamity. All that could be done to protect them from the full force of the shock was done by relatives and good friends. They went down the Bay and met the ship at night, but did not show themselves until morning, and then only to Clara. When she returned to the stateroom she did not speak, and did not need to. Her mother looked at her and said,

"Susy is dead."

At half past ten o'clock that night, Clara and her mother completed their circuit of the globe, and drew up at Elmira by the same train and in the same car which had borne them and me westward from it one year, one month, and one week before. And again Susy was there—not waving her welcome in the glare of the lights as she had waved her farewell to us thirteen months before, but lying white and fair in her coffin, in the house where she was born.

The last thirteen days of Susy's life were spent in our own house in Hartford, the home of her childhood and always the dearest place in the earth to her. About her she had faithful old friends—her pastor, Mr. Twichell, who had known her from the cradle, and who had come a long journey to be with her; her uncle and aunt, Mr. and Mrs. Theodore Crane; Patrick, the coachman; Katy, who had begun to serve us when Susy was a child of eight years; John and Ellen, who had been with us many years. Also Jean was there.

At the hour when my wife and Clara set sail for America, Susy was in no danger. Three hours later there came a sudden change for the worse. Meningitis set in, and it was immediately apparent that she was death-struck. That was Saturday, the 15th of August.

"That evening she took food for the last time." (Jean's letter to me.) The next morning the brain-fever was raging. She walked the floor a little in her pain and delirium, then succumbed to weakness and returned to her bed. Previously she had found hanging in a closet a gown which she had seen her mother wear. She thought it was her mother, dead, and she kissed it, and cried. About noon she became blind (an effect of the disease) and bewailed it to her uncle.

From Jean's letter I take this sentence, which needs no comment:

"About one in the afternoon Susy spoke for the last time."

It was only one word that she said when she spoke that last time, and it told of her longing. She groped with her hands and found Katy, and caressed her face and said "mamma."

How gracious it was that in that forlorn hour of wreck and ruin, with the night of death closing around her, she should have been granted that beautiful illusion—that the latest vision which rested upon the clouded mirror of her mind should have been the vision of her mother, and the latest emotion she should know in life the joy and peace of that dear imagined presence.

About two o'clock she composed herself as if for sleep, and never moved again. She fell into unconsciousness and so remained two days and five hours, until Tuesday evening at seven minutes past seven, when the release came. She was twenty-four years and five months old.

On the 23d her mother and her sisters saw her laid to rest—she that had been our wonder and our worship.

In one of her own books I find some verses which I will copy here. Apparently she always put borrowed matter in quotation marks. These verses lack those marks, and therefore I take them to be her own.

> Love came at dawn, when all the world was fair,
> When crimson glories, bloom, and song were rife;
> Love came at dawn when hope's wings fanned the air,
> And murmured "I am life."
>
> Love came at even, when the day was done,
> When heart and brain were tired, and slumber pressed;
> Love came at eve, shut out the sinking sun,
> And whispered "I am rest."

The summer seasons of Susy's childhood were spent at Quarry Farm on the hills east of Elmira, New York, the other seasons of the year at the home in Hartford. Like other children, she was blithe and happy, fond of play; *un*like the average of children she was at times much given to retiring within herself and trying to search out the hidden meanings of the deep things that make the puzzle and pathos of human existence, and in all the ages have baffled the inquirer and mocked him. As a little child aged seven, she was oppressed and perplexed by the maddening repetition of the stock incidents of our race's fleeting sojourn here, just as the same thing has oppressed and perplexed maturer minds from the beginning of time. A myriad of men are born; they labor and sweat and struggle for bread; they squabble and scold and fight; they scramble for little mean advantages over each other; age creeps upon them; infirmities follow; shames and humiliations bring down their prides and their vanities; those they love are taken from them, and the joy of life is turned to aching grief. The burden of pain, care, misery, grows heavier year by year; at length ambition is dead; pride is dead; vanity is dead; longing for release is in their place. It comes at last—the only unpoisoned gift earth ever had for them—and they vanish from a world where they were of no consequence; where they achieved nothing; where they were a mistake and a failure and a foolishness; where they have left no sign that they have existed—a world which will lament them a day and forget them forever. Then another myriad takes their place, and copies all they did, and goes along the same profitless road, and vanishes as they vanished—to make room for another and another and a million other myriads to follow the same arid path through the same desert and accomplish what the first myriad, and all the myriads that came after it accomplished—nothing!

"Mamma, what is it all for?" asked Susy, preliminarily stating the above details in her own halting language, after long brooding over them alone in the privacy of the nursery.

A year later, she was groping her way alone through another sunless bog, but this time she reached a rest for her feet. For a week, her mother had not been able to go to the nursery, evenings, at the child's prayer hour. She spoke of it—was sorry for it, and said she would come to-night, and hoped she could continue to come every night and hear Susy pray, as before. Noticing that the child wished to respond, but was evidently troubled as to how to word her answer, she asked what the difficulty was. Susy explained that Miss Foote (the governess) had been teaching her about the Indians and their religious beliefs, whereby it appeared that they had not only a God, but several. This had set Susy to thinking. As a result of this thinking, she had stopped praying. She qualified this statement—that is she modified it—saying she did not now pray "in the same way" as she had formerly done. Her mother said,

"Tell me about it, dear."

"Well, mamma, the Indians believed they knew, but now we know they were wrong. By and by it can turn out that we are wrong. So now I only pray that there may be a God and a heaven—or something better."

I wrote down this pathetic prayer in its precise wording, at the time, in a record which we kept of the children's sayings, and my reverence for it has grown with the years that have passed over my head since then. Its untaught grace and simplicity are a child's, but the wisdom and the pathos of it are of all the ages that have come and gone since the race of man has lived, and longed, and hoped, and feared, and doubted.

To go back a year—Susy aged seven. Several times her mother said to her,

"There, there, Susy, you mustn't cry over little things."

This furnished Susy a text for thought. She had been breaking her heart over what had seemed vast disasters—a broken toy; a picnic canceled by thunder and lightning and rain; the mouse that was growing tame and friendly in the nursery caught and killed by the cat—and now came this strange revelation. For some unaccountable reason, these were not vast calamities. Why? How is the size of calamities measured? What is the rule? There must be some way to tell the great ones from the small ones; what is the law of these proportions? She examined the problem earnestly and long. She gave it her best thought, from time to time, for two or three days—but it baffled her—defeated her. And at last she gave up and went to her mother for help.

"Mamma, what is '*little* things'?"

It seemed a simple question—at first. And yet before the answer could be put into words, unsuspected and unforeseen difficulties began to appear. They increased; they multiplied; they brought about another defeat. The effort to explain came to a standstill. Then Susy tried to help her mother out—with an instance, an example, an illustration. The mother was getting ready to go down town, and one of her errands was to buy a long-promised toy watch for Susy.

"If you forgot the watch, mamma, would that be a little thing?"

She was not concerned about the watch, for she knew it would not be forgotten. What she was hoping for was that the answer would unriddle the riddle and bring rest and peace to her perplexed little mind.

The hope was disappointed, of course—for the reason that the size of a misfortune is not determinable by an outsider's measurement of it, but only by the measurements applied to it by the person specially affected by it. The king's lost crown is a vast matter to the king, but of no consequence to the child. The lost toy is a great matter to the child, but in the king's eyes it is not a thing to break the heart about. A verdict was reached, but it was based upon the above model, and Susy was granted leave to measure her disasters thereafter with her own tape-line.

I will throw in a note or two here touching the time when Susy was seventeen. She had written a play modeled upon Greek lines, and she and Clara and Margaret Warner, and other young comrades had played it to a charmed housefull of friends in our house in Hartford. Charles Dudley Warner and his brother, George, were present. They were near neighbors and warm friends of ours. They were full of praises of the workmanship of the play, and George Warner came over the next morning and had a long talk with Susy. The result of it was this verdict:

"She is the most interesting person I have ever known, of either sex."

Remark of a lady—Mrs. Cheney, I think, author of the biography of her father, Rev. Dr. Bushnell:

"I made this note after one of my talks with Susy: 'She knows all there is of life and its meanings. She could not know it better if she had lived it out to its limit. Her intuitions and ponderings and analyzings seem to have taught her all that my sixty years have taught me.'"

Remark of another lady; she is speaking of Susy's last days:

"In those last days she walked as if on air, and her walk answered to the buoyancy of her spirits and the passion of intellectual energy and activity that possessed her."

I return now to the point where I made this diversion. From her earliest days, as I have already indicated, Susy was given to examining things and thinking them out by herself. She was not trained to this; it was the make of her mind. In matters involving questions of fair or unfair dealing, she reviewed the details patiently, and surely arrived at a right and logical conclusion. In Munich, when she was six years old, she was harassed by a recurrent dream, in which a ferocious bear figured. She came out of the dream each time sorely frightened, and crying. She set herself the task of analyzing this dream. The reasons of it? The purpose of it? The origin of it? No—the moral aspect of it. Her verdict, arrived at after candid and searching investigation, exposed it to the charge of being one-sided and unfair in its construction: for (as she worded it), *she* was "never the one that ate, but always the one that was eaten."

Susy backed her good judgment in matters of morals with conduct to match—even upon occasions when it caused her sacrifice to do it. When she was six and her sister Clara four, the pair were troublesomely quarrelsome. Punishments were tried as a means of breaking up this custom—these failed. Then rewards were tried. A day without a quarrel brought candy. The children were their own witnesses—each for or against her own self. Once Susy took the candy, hesitated, then returned it with a suggestion that she was not fairly entitled to it. Clara kept hers,—so, here was a conflict of evidence; one witness *for* a quarrel, and one against it. But the better witness of the two was on the affirmative side, and the quarrel stood proved, and no candy due to either side. There seemed to be no defence for Clara—yet there was, and Susy furnished it; and Clara went free. Susy said "I don't know whether she felt wrong in her heart, but I didn't feel right in my heart."

It was a fair and honorable view of the case, and a specially acute analysis of it for a child of six to make. There was no way to convict Clara now, except to put her on the stand again and review her evidence. There was a doubt as to the fairness of this procedure, since her former evidence had been accepted, and not challenged at the time. The doubt was examined, and canvassed—then she was given the benefit of it and acquitted; which was just as well, for in the meantime she had eaten the candy, anyway.

Whenever I think of Susy I think of Marjorie Fleming. There was but one Marjorie Fleming. There can never be another. No doubt I think of Marjorie when I think of Susy mainly because Dr. John Brown, that noble and beautiful soul—rescuer of marvelous Marjorie from oblivion—was Susy's great friend in her babyhood—her worshipper and willing slave.

1873 In 1873, when Susy was fourteen months old, we arrived in Edinburgh from London, fleeing thither for rest and refuge, after experiencing what had been to us an entirely new kind of life—six weeks of daily lunches, teas, and dinners away from home. We carried no letters of introduction; we hid ourselves away in Veitch's family hotel in George street, and prepared to have a comfortable season all to ourselves. But by good fortune this did not happen. Straightway Mrs. Clemens needed a physician, and I stepped around to 23 Rutland street to see if the author of "Rab and His Friends" was still a practising physician. He was. He came, and for six weeks thereafter we were together every day, either in his house or in our hotel.

Monday, February 5, 1906

Dr. John Brown, continued—Incidents connected with Susy Clemens's childhood—Bad spelling, etc.

His was a sweet and winning face—as beautiful a face as I have ever known. Reposeful, gentle, benignant—the face of a saint at peace with all the world and placidly beaming upon it the sunshine of love that filled his heart. Doctor John was beloved by everybody in Scotland; and I think that on its downward sweep southward it found no frontier. I think so because when, a few years later, infirmities compelled Doctor John to give up his practice, and Mr. Douglas, the publisher, and other friends, set themselves the task of raising a fund of a few thousand dollars whose income was to be devoted to the support of himself and his maiden sister (who was in age) the fund was not only promptly made up, but so *very* promptly that the books were closed before friends a hundred miles south of the line had had an opportunity to contribute. No public appeal was made. The matter was never mentioned in print. Mr. Douglas and the other friends applied for contributions by private letter only. Many complaints came from London, and everywhere between, from people who had not been allowed an opportunity to contribute. This sort of complaint is so new to the world—so strikingly unusual, that I think it worth while to mention it.

Doctor John was very fond of animals, and particularly of dogs. No one needs to be told this who has read that pathetic and beautiful masterpiece, "Rab and His Friends." After his death, his son, Jock, published a little memorial of him which he distributed privately among the friends; and in it occurs a little episode which illustrates the relationship that existed between Doctor John and the other animals. It is furnished by an Edinburgh lady whom Doctor John used to pick up and carry to school or back in his carriage frequently at a time when she was twelve years old. She said that they were chatting together tranquilly one day, when he suddenly broke off in the midst of a sentence and thrust his head out of the carriage window eagerly—then resumed his place with a disappointed look on his face. The girl said "Who is it? Some one you know?" He said "No, a dog I *don't* know."

He had two names for Susy—"Wee wifie" and "Megalopis." This formidable Greek title was conferred in honor of her big big brown eyes. Susy and the Doctor had a good deal of romping together. Daily he unbent his dignity and played "bear" with the child. I do not now remember which of them was the bear, but I think it was the child. There was a sofa across a corner of the parlor with a door behind it opening into Susy's quarters, and she used to lie in wait for the Doctor behind the sofa—not lie in wait, but stand in wait; for you could only get just a glimpse of the top of her yellow head when she stood upright. According to the rules of the game, she was invisible, and this glimpse did not count. I think she must have been the bear, for I can remember two or three occasions when she sprang out from behind the sofa and surprised the Doctor into frenzies of fright, which were not in the least modified by the fact that he knew that the "bear" was there, and was coming.

It seems incredible that Doctor John should ever have wanted to tell a grotesque and rollicking anecdote. Such a thing seems so out of character with that gentle and tranquil nature that——but no matter. I tried to teach him the anecdote, and he tried his best for two or three days to perfect himself in it—and he never succeeded. It was the most impressive exhibition that ever was. There was no human being, nor dog, of his acquaintance in all Edinburgh that would not have been paralysed with astonishment to step in there and see Doctor John trying to do that anecdote. It was one which I have told some hundreds of times on the platform, and which I was always very fond of, because it worked the audience so hard. It was a stammering man's account of how he got cured of his infirmity—which was accomplished by introducing a whistle into the midst of every word which he found himself unable to finish on account of the obstruction of the stammering. And so his whole account was an absurd mixture of stammering and whistling—which was irresistible to an audience properly keyed up for laughter. Doctor John learned to do the mechanical details of the anecdote, but he was never able to inform these details with expression. He was preternaturally grave and earnest all through, and so when he fetched up with the climaxing triumphant sentence at the end—but I must quote that sentence, or the reader will not understand. It was this:

"The doctor told me that whenever I wanted to sta- (whistle) sta- (whistle) sta- (whistle) *ammer,* I must whistle; and I did, and it k- (whistle) k- (whistle) k- (whistle) k—ured me *entirely!*"

The Doctor could not master that triumphant note. He always gravely stammered and whistled and whistled and stammered it through, and it came out at the end with the solemnity and the gravity of the Judge delivering sentence to a man with the black cap on.

He was the loveliest creature in the world—except his aged sister, who was just like him. We made the round of his professional visits with him in his carriage every day for six weeks. He always brought a basket of grapes, and we brought books. The scheme which we began with on the first round of visits was the one which was maintained until the end—and was based upon this remark, which he made when he was disembarking from the carriage at his first stopping place, to visit a patient: "Entertain yourselves while I go in here and reduce the population."

As a child, Susy had a passionate temper; and it cost her much remorse and many tears before she learned to govern it, but after that it was a wholesome salt, and her character was the stronger and healthier for its presence. It enabled her to be good with dignity; it preserved her not only from being good for vanity's sake, but from even the appearance of it. In looking back over the long-vanished years it seems but natural and excusable that I should dwell with longing affection and preference upon incidents of her young life which made it beautiful to us, and that I should let its few and small offences go unsummoned and unreproached.

In the summer of 1880, when Susy was just eight years of age, the family were at Quarry Farm, on top of a high hill three miles from Elmira, New York, where we always spent our summers, in those days. Hay-cutting time was approaching, and Susy and Clara were counting the hours, for the time was big with a great event for them; they had been promised that they might mount the wagon and ride home from the fields on the summit of the hay mountain. This perilous privilege, so dear to their age and species, had never been granted them before. Their excitement had no bounds. They could talk of nothing but this epoch-making adventure, now. But misfortune overtook Susy on the very morning of the important day. In a sudden outbreak of passion she corrected Clara—with a shovel, or a stick, or something of the sort. At any rate, the offence committed was of a gravity clearly beyond the limit allowed in the nursery. In accordance with the rule and custom of the house, Susy went to her mother to confess and to help decide upon the size and character of the punishment due. It was quite understood that as a punishment could have but one rational object and function—to act as a reminder and warn the transgressor against transgressing in the same way again—the children would know about as well as any how to choose a penalty which would be rememberable and effective. Susy and her mother discussed various punishments, but none of them seemed adequate. This fault was an unusually serious one, and required the setting up of a danger-signal in the memory that would not blow out nor burn out, but remain a fixture there and furnish its saving warning indefinitely. Among the punishments mentioned was deprivation of the hay-wagon ride. It was noticeable that this one hit Susy hard. Finally, in the summing up, the mother named over the list and asked,

"Which one do you think it ought to be, Susy?"

Susy studied, shrank from her duty, and asked,

"Which do you think, mamma?"

"Well, Susy, I would rather leave it to you. *You* make the choice, yourself."

It cost Susy a struggle, and much and deep thinking and weighing—but she came out where any one who knew her could have foretold she would—

"Well, mamma, I'll make it the hay-wagon, because you know the other things might not make me remember not to do it again, but if I don't get to ride on the hay-wagon I can remember it easily."

In this world the real penalty, the sharp one, the lasting one, never falls otherwise than on the wrong person. It was not *I* that corrected Clara, but the remembrance of poor Susy's lost hay ride still brings *me* a pang—after twenty-six years.

Apparently Susy was born with humane feelings for the animals, and compassion for their troubles. This enabled her to see a new point in an old story, once, when she was only six years old—a point which had been overlooked by older, and perhaps duller, people for many ages. Her mother told her the moving story of the sale of Joseph by his brethren, the staining of his coat with the blood of the slaughtered kid, and the rest of it. She dwelt upon the inhumanity of the brothers; their cruelty toward their helpless young brother; and the unbrotherly treachery which they practised upon him; for she hoped to teach the child a lesson in gentle pity and mercifulness which she would remember. Apparently her desire was accomplished, for the tears came into Susy's eyes and she was deeply moved. Then she said,

"Poor little kid."

A child's frank envy of the privileges and distinctions of its elders is often a delicately flattering attention and the reverse of unwelcome, but sometimes the envy is not placed where the beneficiary is expecting it to be placed. Once when Susy was seven, she sat breathlessly absorbed in watching a guest of ours adorn herself for a ball. The lady was charmed by this homage; this mute and gentle admiration; and was happy in it. And when her pretty labors were finished, and she stood at last perfect, unimprovable, clothed like Solomon in his glory, she paused, confident and expectant, to receive from Susy's tongue the tribute that was burning in her eyes. Susy drew an envious little sigh and said,

"I wish *I* could have crooked teeth and spectacles!"

Once, when Susy was six months along in her eighth year, she did something one day, in the presence of company, which subjected her to criticism and reproof. Afterward, when she was alone with her mother, as was her custom she reflected a little while over the matter. Then she set up what I think—and what the shade of Burns would think—was a quite good philosophical defence:

"Well, mamma, you know I didn't see myself, and so I couldn't know how it looked."

In homes where the near friends and visitors are mainly literary people—lawyers, judges, authors, professors and clergymen—the children's ears become early familiarized with wide vocabularies. It is natural for them to pick up any words that fall in their way; it is natural for them to pick up big and little ones indiscriminately; it is natural for them to use without fear any word that comes to their net, no matter how formidable it may be as to size. As a result, their talk is a curious and funny musketry-clatter of little words, interrupted at intervals by the heavy-artillery crash of a word of such imposing sound and size that it seems to shake the ground and rattle the windows. Sometimes the child gets a wrong idea of a word which it has picked up by chance, and attaches to it a meaning which impairs its usefulness—but this does not happen as often as one might expect it would. Indeed it happens with an infrequency which may be regarded as remarkable. As a child, Susy had good fortune with her large words, and she employed many of them. She made no more than her fair share of mistakes. Once when she thought something very funny was going to happen (but it didn't) she was racked and torn with laughter, by anticipation. But apparently she still felt sure of her position, for she said,

"If it had happened, I should have been transformed (transported) with glee."

And earlier, when she was a little maid of five years, she informed a visitor that she had been in a church only once, and that was the time when Clara was "crucified" (Christened).

In Heidelberg, when she was six, she noticed that the Schloss gardens——

Dear me, how remote things do come together! I break off that sentence to remark that at a luncheon up town, yesterday, I reminded the hostess that she had not made me acquainted with all the guests. She said yes, she was aware of that—that by request of one of the ladies she had left me to guess that lady out for myself; that I had known that lady for a day, more than a quarter of a century ago, and that the lady was desirous of finding out how long it would take me to dig her up out of my memory. The rest of the company were in the game, and were anxious to see whether I would succeed or fail. It seemed to me, as the time drifted along, that I was never going to be able to locate that woman; but at last, when the luncheon was nearly finished, a discussion broke out as to where the most comfortable hotel in the world was to be found. Various hotels on the several sides of the ocean were mentioned, and at last somebody reminded her that she had not put forward a preference yet, and she was asked to name the hotel that she thought was, from her point of view, the most satisfactory and comfortable hotel on the planet, and she said promptly "The 'Slosh,' at Heidelberg."

I said at once, "I am sincerely glad to meet you again, Mrs. Jones, after this long stretch of years—but you were Miss Smith in those days. Have I located you?"

"Yes," she said, "you have."

I *knew* I had. During that day at Heidelberg, so many ages ago, many charitable people tried furtively to get that young Miss Smith to adopt the prevailing pronunciation of Schloss, by *saying* Schloss softly and casually every time she said "Slosh," but nobody succeeded in converting her. And I knew perfectly well that this was that same old Smith girl, because there could not be two persons on this planet at one and the same time who could preserve and stick to a mispronunciation like that for nearly a generation.

As I was saying, when I interrupted myself—in Heidelberg when Susy was six, she noticed that the Schloss gardens were populous with snails creeping all about everywhere. One day she found a new dish on her table and inquired concerning it, and learned that it was made of snails. She was awed and impressed, and said,

"Wild ones, mamma?"

She was thoughtful and considerate of others—an acquired quality, no doubt. No one seems to be born with it. One hot day, at home in Hartford, when she was a little child, her mother borrowed her fan several times (a Japanese one, value five cents), refreshed herself with it a moment or two, then handed it back with a word of thanks. Susy knew her mother would use the fan all the time if she could do it without putting a deprivation upon its owner. She also knew that her mother could not be persuaded to do that. A relief must be devised somehow;

Susy devised it. She got five cents out of her money-box and carried it to Patrick and asked him to take it down town (a mile and a half) and buy a Japanese fan and bring it home. He did it—and thus thoughtfully and delicately was the exigency met and the mother's comfort secured. It is to the child's credit that she did not save herself expense by bringing down another and more costly kind of fan from up stairs, but was content to act upon the impression that her mother desired the Japanese kind—content to accomplish the desire and stop with that, without troubling about the wisdom or unwisdom of it.

Sometimes while she was still a child, her speech fell into quaint and strikingly expressive forms. Once—aged nine or ten—she came to her mother's room when her sister Jean was a baby and said Jean was crying in the nursery, and asked if she might ring for the nurse. Her mother asked,

"Is she crying hard?"—meaning cross, ugly.

"Well, no, mamma. It is a weary, lonesome cry."

It is a pleasure to me to recall various incidents which reveal the delicacies of feeling which were so considerable a part of her budding character. Such a revelation came once in a way which, while creditable to her heart, was defective in another direction. She was in her eleventh year, then. Her mother had been making the Christmas purchases, and she allowed Susy to see the presents which were for Patrick's children. Among these was a handsome sled for Jimmy, on which a stag was painted; also, in gilt capitals the word "DEER." Susy was excited and joyous over everything until she came to this sled. Then she became sober and silent—yet the sled was the choicest of all the gifts. Her mother was surprised, and also disappointed, and said,

"Why Susy, doesn't it please you? Isn't it fine?"

Susy hesitated, and it was plain that she did not want to say the thing that was in her mind. However, being urged, she brought it haltingly out:

"Well, mamma, it *is* fine, and of course it *did* cost a good deal—but—but—why should that be mentioned?"

Seeing that she was not understood, she reluctantly pointed to that word "DEER." It was her orthography that was at fault, not her heart. She had inherited both from her mother.

The ability to spell is a natural gift. The person not born with it can never become perfect in it. I was always able to spell correctly. My wife, and her sister, Mrs. Crane, were always bad spellers. Once when Clara was a little chap, her mother was away from home for a few days, and Clara wrote her a small letter every day. When her mother returned, she praised Clara's letters. Then she said, "But in one of them, Clara, you spelled a word wrong."

Clara said, with quite unconscious brutality, "Why mamma, how did *you* know?"

More than a quarter of a century has elapsed, and Mrs. Crane is under our roof here in New York, for a few days. Her head is white now, but she is as pretty and winning and sweet as she was in those ancient times at her Quarry Farm, where she was an idol and the rest of us were the worshippers. Her gift of imperfect orthography remains unimpaired. She writes a great many letters. This was always a passion of hers. She was never able to live happily unless she could see that incomparable orthography flowing from her pen. Yesterday she asked me how to spell New Jersey, and I knew by her look, after she got the information, that she was regretting she hadn't asked somebody years ago. The miracles which she and her sister, Mrs. Clemens, were able to perform without help of dictionary or spelling book, are incredible. During the year of my engagement—1869—while I was out on the lecture platform, the daily letter that came for me generally brought me news from the front—by which expression I refer to the internecine war that was always going on in a friendly way between these two orthographists about the spelling of words. One of these words was scissors. They never seemed to consult a dictionary; they always wanted something or somebody that was more reliable. Between them, they had spelled scissors in seven different ways, a feat which I am certain no person now living, educated or uneducated, can match. I have forgotten how I was required to say which of the seven ways was the right one. I couldn't do it. If there had been fourteen ways, none of them would have been right. I remember only one of the instances offered—the other six have passed from my memory. That one was "sicisiors." That way of spelling it looked so reasonable—so plausible, to the discoverer of it, that I was hardly believed when I decided against it. Mrs. Crane keeps by her, to this day, a little book of about thirty pages of note-paper, on which she has written, in a large hand, words which she needs to use in her letters every day—words which the cat could spell without prompting or tuition, and yet are words which Mrs. Crane never allows herself to risk upon paper without looking at that vocabulary of hers, each time, to make certain.

During my engagement year, thirty-seven years ago, a considerable company of young people amused themselves in the Langdon homestead one night with the game of "Verbarium," which was brand-new at the time and very popular. A text-word was chosen and each person wrote that word in large letters across the top of a sheet of paper, then sat with pencil in hand and ready to begin as soon as game was called. The player could begin with the first letter of that text-word and build words out of the text-word during two minutes by the watch. But he must not use a letter that was not *in* the text-word and he must not use any letter in the text-word twice, unless the letter occurred twice in the text-word. I remember the first bout that we had at that game. The text-word was *California*. When game was called everybody began to set down words as fast as he could make his pencil move—"corn," "car," "cone," and so on, digging out the shortest words first because they could be set down more quickly than the longer ones. When the two minutes were up, the scores were examined, and the prize went to the person who had achieved the largest number of words. The good scores ranged along between thirty and fifty or sixty words. But Mrs. Crane would not allow her score to be examined. She was plainly doubtful about getting that prize. But when persuasion failed to avail we chased her about the place, captured her and took her score away from her by force. She had achieved only one word, and that was *calf*—which she had spelled "caff." And she never would have gotten even that one word honestly—she had to introduce a letter that didn't belong in the text-word in order to get it.

Tuesday, February 6, 1906

Playing "The Prince and the Pauper"—Acting charades, etc.

When Susy was twelve and a half years old, I took to the platform again, after a long absence from it, and raked the country for four months in company with George W. Cable. Early in

November we gave a reading one night in Chickering Hall, in New York, and when I was walking home in a dull gloom of fog and rain I heard one invisible man say to another invisible man, this, in substance: "General Grant has actually concluded to write his autobiography." That remark gave me joy, at the time, but if I had been struck by lightning in place of it, it would have been better for me and mine. However, that is a long story, and this is not the place for it.

To Susy, as to all Americans, General Grant was the supremest of heroes, and she longed for a sight of him. I took her to see him one day——however let that go. It belongs elsewhere. I will return to it by and by.

In the midst of our reading-campaign, I returned to Hartford from the Far West, reaching home one evening just at dinner time. I was expecting to have a happy and restful season by a hickory fire in the library with the family, but was required to go at once to George Warner's house, a hundred and fifty yards away, across the grounds. This was a heavy disappointment, and I tried to beg off but did not succeed. I couldn't even find out why I must waste this precious evening in a visit to a friend's house when our own house offered so many and superior advantages. There was a mystery somewhere, but I was not able to get to the bottom of it. So we tramped across in the snow, and I found the Warner drawing-room crowded with seated people. There was a vacancy in the front row, for me—in front of a curtain. At once the curtain was drawn, and before me, properly costumed, was the little maid, Margaret Warner, clothed in Tom Canty's rags, and beyond an intercepting railing was Susy Clemens, arrayed in the silks and satins of the prince. Then followed with good action and spirit the rest of that first meeting between the prince and the pauper. It was a charming surprise, and to me a moving one. Other episodes of the tale followed, and I have seldom in my life enjoyed an evening so much as I enjoyed that one. This lovely surprise was my wife's work. She had patched the scenes together from the book, and had trained the six or eight young actors in their parts, and had also designed and furnished the costumes.

Afterward, I added a part for myself (Miles Hendon), also a part for Katy and a part for George. I think I have not mentioned George before. He was a colored man—the children's darling, and a remarkable person. He had been a member of the family a number of years at that time. He had been born a slave, in Maryland, and was set free by the Proclamation when he was just entering young-manhood. He was body-servant to General Devens all through the war, and then had come North and for eight or ten years had been earning his living by odd jobs. He came out to our house once, an entire stranger, to clean some windows—and remained eighteen years. Mrs. Clemens could always tell enough about a servant by the look of him—more, in fact, than she, or anybody else, could tell about him by his recommendations.

We played "The Prince and the Pauper" a number of times in our house to seated audiences of eighty-four persons, which was the limit of our space, and we got great entertainment out of it. As *we* played the piece it had several superiorities over the play as presented on the public stage in England and America, for we always had both the prince and the pauper on deck, whereas these parts were always doubled on the public stage—an economical but unwise departure from the book, because it necessitated the excision of the strongest and most telling of the episodes. We made a stirring and handsome thing out of the coronation scene. This could not be accomplished otherwise than by having both the prince and the pauper present at the same time. Clara was the little Lady Jane Grey, and she performed the part with electrifying spirit. Twichell's littlest cub, now a grave and reverend clergyman, was a page. He was so small that people on the back seats could not see him without an opera-glass, but he held up Lady Jane's train very well. Jean was only something past three years old, therefore was too young to have a part, but she produced the whole piece every day independently, and played all the parts herself. For a one-actor piece it was not bad. In fact, it was very good—very entertaining. For she was in very deep earnest, and besides she used an English which none but herself could handle with effect.

Our children and the neighbors' children played well; easily, comfortably, naturally, and with high spirit. How was it that they were able to do this? It was because they had been in training all the time from their infancy. They grew up in our house, so to speak, playing charades. We never made any preparation. We selected a word, whispered the parts of it to the little actors; then we retired to the hall where all sorts of costumery had been laid out ready for the evening. We dressed the parts in three minutes and each detachment marched into the library and performed its syllable, then retired, leaving the fathers and mothers to guess that syllable if they could. Sometimes they could.

Will Gillette, now world famous actor and dramatist, learned a part of his trade by acting in our charades. Those little chaps, Susy and Clara, invented charades themselves in their earliest years, and played them for the entertainment of their mother and me. They had one high merit—none but a high grade intellect could guess them. Obscurity is a great thing in a charade. These babies invented one once which was a masterpiece in this regard. They came in and played the first syllable, which was a conversation in which the word *red* occurred with suggestive frequency. Then they retired—came again continuing an angry dispute which they had begun outside, and in which several words like *just, fair, unfair, unjust,* and so on, kept occurring; but we noticed that the word *just* was in the majority—so we set that down along with the word *red,* and discussed the probabilities while the children went out to re-costume themselves. We had thus "red," "just." They soon appeared and began to do a very fashionable morning call, in which the one made many inquiries of the other concerning some lady whose name was persistently suppressed, and who was always referred to as "her," even when the grammar did not permit that form of the pronoun. The children retired. We took an account of stock and, so far as we could see, we had three syllables, "red," "just," "her." But that was all. The combination did not seem to throw any real glare on the future completed word. The children arrived again, and stooped down and began to chat and quarrel and carry on, and fumble and fuss at the *register!*—(red-just-her). With the exception of myself, this family was never strong on spelling.

In "The Prince and the Pauper" days, and earlier and later—especially later, Susy and her nearest neighbor, Margaret Warner, often devised tragedies and played them in the schoolroom, with little Jean's help—with closed doors—no admission to anybody. The chief characters were always a couple of queens, with a quarrel in stock—historical when possible, but a quarrel anyway, even if it had to be a work of the imagination. Jean always had one function—only one. She sat at a little table about a foot high and drafted death-warrants for these queens to sign. In the course of time, they completely wore out Elizabeth and Mary Queen of Scots—also all of Mrs. Clemens's gowns that they could get hold of—for nothing charmed these monarchs like having four or five feet of gown dragging on the floor behind. Mrs. Clemens and I spied upon them more than once, which was treacherous conduct—but I don't think we very seriously minded that. It was grand to see the queens stride back and forth and reproach each other in three- or four-syllable words dripping with blood; and it was pretty to see how tranquil Jean was through it all. Familiarity with daily death and carnage had hardened her to crime and suffering in all their forms, and they were no longer able to hasten her pulse by a beat. Sometimes when there was a long interval between death-warrants she even leaned her head on her table and went to sleep. It was then a curious spectacle of innocent repose and crimson and volcanic tragedy.

Two or three weeks ago, when I sat talking with the divine Sarah—Sarah the illustrious, the unapproachable—and I was trading English for her French, and neither of us making wages at it, she could have detected a strong, but far away, interest in my eyes if she had examined closely, for while I was seeing her I was also seeing another Sarah Bernhardt of long years ago—Susy Clemens. Susy had seen the Bernhardt play once. And always after that she was fond of doing impassioned imitations of her great heroine's tragic parts. She did them strikingly well, too.

Wednesday, February 7, 1906

Susy Clemens's Biography of her father—Mr. Clemens's opinion of critics, etc.

When Susy was thirteen, and was a slender little maid with plaited tails of copper-tinged brown hair down her back, and was perhaps the busiest bee in the household hive, by reason of the manifold studies, health exercises and recreations she had to attend to, she secretly, and of her own motion, and out of love, added another task to her labors—the writing of a biography of me. She did this work in her bedroom at night, and kept her record hidden. After a little, the mother discovered it and filched it, and let me see it; then told Susy what she had done, and how pleased I was, and how proud. I remember that time with a deep pleasure. I had had compliments before, but none that touched me like this; none that could approach it for value in my eyes. It has kept that place always since. I have had no compliment, no praise, no tribute from any source, that was so precious to me as this one was and still is. As I read it *now,* after all these many years, it is still a king's message to me, and brings me the same dear surprise it brought me then—with the pathos added, of the thought that the eager and hasty hand that sketched it and scrawled it will not touch mine again—and I feel as the humble and unexpectant must feel when their eyes fall upon the edict that raises them to the ranks of the noble.

Yesterday while I was rummaging in a pile of ancient note-books of mine which I had not seen for years, I came across a reference to that biography. It is quite evident that several times, at breakfast and dinner, in those long past days, I was posing for the biography. In fact, I clearly remember that I *was* doing that—and I also remember that Susy detected it. I remember saying a very smart thing, with a good deal of an air, at the breakfast table one morning, and that Susy observed to her mother privately, a little later, that papa was doing that for the biography.

I cannot bring myself to change any line or word in Susy's sketch of me, but will introduce passages from it now and then just as they came in their quaint simplicity out of her honest heart, which was the beautiful heart of a child. What comes from that source has a charm and grace of its own which may transgress all the recognized laws of literature, if it choose, and yet be literature still, and worthy of hospitality. I shall print the whole of this little biography, before I am done with it—every word, every sentence.

The spelling is frequently desperate, but it was Susy's, and it shall stand. I love it, and cannot profane it. To me, it is gold. To correct it would alloy it, not refine it. It would spoil it. It would take from it its freedom and flexibility and make it stiff and formal. Even when it is most extravagant I am not shocked. It is Susy's spelling, and she was doing the best she could—and nothing could better it for me.

She learned languages easily; she learned history easily; she learned music easily; she learned all things easily, quickly, and thoroughly—except spelling. She even learned that, after a while. But it would have grieved me but little if she had failed in it—for although good spelling was my one accomplishment I was never able to greatly respect it. When I was a schoolboy, sixty years ago, we had two prizes in our school. One was for good spelling, the other for amiability. These things were thin, smooth, silver disks, about the size of a dollar. Upon the one was engraved in flowing Italian script the words "Good Spelling," on the other was engraved the word "Amiability." The holders of these prizes hung them about the neck with a string—and those holders were the envy of the whole school. There wasn't a pupil that wouldn't have given a leg for the privilege of wearing one of them a week, but no pupil ever got a chance except John Robards and me. John Robards was eternally and indestructibly amiable. I may even say devilishly amiable; fiendishly amiable; exasperatingly amiable. That was the sort of feeling that we had about that quality of his. So he always wore the amiability medal. I always wore the other medal. That word "always" is a trifle too strong. We lost the medals several times. It was because they became so monotonous. We needed a change—therefore several times we traded medals. It was a satisfaction to John Robards to *seem* to be a good speller—which he wasn't. And it was a satisfaction to me to seem to be amiable, for a change. But of course these changes could not long endure—for some schoolmate or other would presently notice what had been happening, and that schoolmate would not have been human if he had lost any time in reporting this treason. The teacher took the medals away from us at once, of course—and we always had them back again before Friday night. If we lost the medals Monday morning, John's amiability was at the top of the list Friday afternoon when the teacher came to square up the week's account. The Friday afternoon session always closed with "spelling down." Being in disgrace, I necessarily started at the foot of my division of spellers, but I always slaughtered both divisions and stood alone with the medal around my neck when the campaign was finished. I *did* miss on a word once, just at the end of one of these conflicts, and so lost the medal. I left the first *r* out of February—but that was to accommodate a sweetheart. My passion was so strong just at that time that I would have left out the whole alphabet if the word had contained it.

As I have said before, I never had any large respect for good spelling. That is my feeling yet. Before the spelling book came with its arbitrary forms, men unconsciously revealed shades of their characters, and also added enlightening shades of expression to what they wrote by their spelling, and so it is possible that the spelling book has been a doubtful benevolence to us.

Susy began the biography in 1885, when I was in the fiftieth year of my age. She begins in this way:

1885

> We are a very happy family. We consist of Papa, Mamma, Jean, Clara and me. It is papa
> I am writing about, and I shall have no trouble in not knowing what to say about him, as
> he is a *very* striking character.

But wait a minute—I will return to Susy presently.

In the matter of slavish imitation, man is the monkey's superior all the time. The average man is destitute of independence of opinion. He is not interested in contriving an opinion of his own, by study and reflection, but is only anxious to find out what his neighbor's opinion is and slavishly adopt it. A generation ago, I found out that the latest review of a book was pretty sure to be just a reflection of the *earliest* review of it; that whatever the first reviewer found to praise or censure in the book would be repeated in the latest reviewer's report, with nothing fresh added. Therefore more than once I took the precaution of sending my book, in manuscript, to Mr. Howells, when he was editor of the *Atlantic Monthly,* so that he could prepare a review of it at leisure. I knew he would say the truth about the book—I also knew that he would find more merit than demerit in it, because I already knew that that was the condition of the book. I allowed no copy of it to go out to the press until after Mr. Howells's notice of it had appeared. That book was always safe. There wasn't a man behind a pen in all America that had the courage to find anything in the book which Mr. Howells had not found— there wasn't a man behind a pen in America that had spirit enough to say a brave and original thing about the book on his own responsibility.

I believe that the trade of critic, in literature, music, and the drama, is the most degraded of all trades, and that it has no real value—certainly no large value. When Charles Dudley Warner and I were about to bring out "The Gilded Age," the editor of the *Daily Graphic* persuaded me to let him have an advance copy, he giving me his word of honor that no notice of it would appear in his paper until after the *Atlantic Monthly* notice should have appeared. This reptile published a review of the book within three days afterward. I could not really complain, because he had only given me his word of honor as security; I ought to have required of him something substantial. I believe his notice did not deal mainly with the merit of the book, or the lack of it, but with my moral attitude toward the public. It was charged that I had used my reputation to play a swindle upon the public; that Mr. Warner had written as much as half of the book, and that I had used my name to float it and give it currency; a currency—so the critic averred—which it could not have acquired without my name, and that this conduct of mine was a grave fraud upon the people. The *Graphic* was not an authority upon any subject whatever. It had a sort of distinction, in that it was the first and only illustrated daily newspaper that the world had seen; but it was without character; it was poorly and cheaply edited; its opinion of a book or of any other work of art was of no consequence. Everybody knew this, yet all the critics in America, one after the other, copied the *Graphic*'s criticism, merely changing the phraseology, and left me under that charge of dishonest conduct. Even the great Chicago *Tribune,* the most important journal in the Middle West, was not able to invent anything fresh, but adopted the view of the humble *Daily Graphic,* dishonesty-charge and all.

However, let it go. It is the will of God that we must have critics, and missionaries, and Congressmen, and humorists, and we must bear the burden. Meantime, I seem to have been drifting into criticism myself. But that is nothing. At the worst, criticism is nothing more than a crime, and I am not unused to that.

What I have been traveling toward all this time is this: the first critic that ever had occasion to describe my personal appearance littered his description with foolish and inexcusable errors whose aggregate furnished the result that I was distinctly and distressingly unhandsome. That description floated around the country in the papers, and was in constant use and wear for a quarter of a century. It seems strange to me that apparently no critic in the country could be found who could look at me and have the courage to take up his pen and destroy that lie. That lie began its course on the Pacific coast, in 1864, and it likened me in personal appearance to Petroleum V. Nasby, who had been out there lecturing. For twenty-five years afterward, no critic could furnish a description of me without fetching in Nasby to help out my portrait. I knew Nasby well, and he was a good fellow, but in my life I have not felt malignant enough about any more than three persons to charge those persons with resembling Nasby. It hurts me to the heart, these things. To this day, it hurts me to the heart. I was always handsome. Anybody but a critic could have seen it. And it had long been a distress to my family—including Susy—that the critics should go on making this wearisome mistake, year after year, when there was no foundation for it. Even when a critic wanted to be particularly friendly and complimentary to me, he didn't dare to go beyond my clothes. He never ventured beyond that old safe frontier. When he had finished with my clothes he had said all the kind things, the pleasant things, the complimentary things he could risk. Then he dropped back on Nasby.

1864

Yesterday I found this clipping in the pocket of one of those ancient memorandum-books of mine. It is of the date of thirty-nine years ago, and both the paper and the ink are yellow with the bitterness that I felt in that old day when I clipped it out to preserve it and brood over it, and grieve about it. I will copy it here, to wit:

> A correspondent of the Philadelphia *Press,* writing of one of Schuyler Colfax's receptions, says of our Washington correspondent: "Mark Twain, the delicate humorist, was present; quite a lion, as he deserves to be. Mark is a bachelor, faultless in taste, whose snowy vest is suggestive of endless quarrels with Washington washerwomen; but the heroism of Mark is settled for all time, for such purity and smoothness were never seen before. His lavender gloves might have been stolen from some Turkish harem, so delicate were they in size; but more likely—anything else were more likely than that. In form and feature he bears some resemblance to the immortal Nasby; but whilst Petroleum is brunette to the core, Twain is golden, amber-hued, melting, blonde."

Let us return to Susy's Biography now, and get the opinion of one who is unbiassed.

Papa's appearance has been described many times, but very incorrectly. He has beautiful gray hair, not any too thick or any too long, but just right; a Roman nose, which greatly improves the beauty of his features; kind blue eyes and a small mustache. He has a wonderfully shaped head and profile. He has a very good figure—in short, he is an extrodinarily fine looking man. All his features are perfect, exept that he hasn't extrodinary teeth. His complexion is very fair, and he doesn't ware a beard. He is a very good man and a very funny one. He *has* got a temper, but we all of us have in this family. He is the loveliest man I ever saw or ever hope to see—and oh, so absent-minded. He does tell perfectly delightful stories. Clara and I used to sit on each arm of his chair and listen while he told us stories about the pictures on the wall.

I remember the story-telling days vividly. They were a difficult and exacting audience—those little creatures.

Thursday, February 8, 1906

Susy Clemens's Biography, continued—Romancer to the children—Incident of the spoon-shaped drive—The burglar alarm does its whole duty.

Along one side of the library, in the Hartford home, the bookshelves joined the mantelpiece—in fact there were shelves on both sides of the mantelpiece. On these shelves, and on the mantelpiece, stood various ornaments. At one end of the procession was a framed oil painting of a cat's head, at the other end was a head of a beautiful young girl, life-size—called Emmeline, because she looked just about like that—an impressionist water-color. Between the one picture and the other there were twelve or fifteen of the bric-à-brac things already mentioned, also an oil painting by Elihu Vedder, "The Young Medusa." Every now and then the children required me to construct a romance—always impromptu—not a moment's preparation permitted—and into that romance I had to get all that bric-à-brac and the three pictures. I had to start always with the cat and finish with Emmeline. I was never allowed the refreshment of a change, end-for-end. It was not permissible to introduce a bric-à-brac ornament into the story out of its place in the procession.

These bric-à-bracs were never allowed a peaceful day, a reposeful day, a restful Sabbath. In their lives there was no Sabbath, in their lives there was no peace; they knew no existence but a monotonous career of violence and bloodshed. In the course of time, the bric-à-brac and the pictures showed wear. It was because they had had so many and such tumultuous adventures in their romantic careers.

As romancer to the children I had a hard time, even from the beginning. If they brought me a picture, in a magazine, and required me to build a story to it, they would cover the rest of the page with their pudgy hands to keep me from stealing an idea from it. The stories had to come hot from the bat, always. They had to be absolutely original and fresh. Sometimes the children furnished me simply a character or two, or a dozen, and required me to start out at once on that slim basis and deliver those characters up to a vigorous and entertaining life of crime. If they heard of a new trade, or an unfamiliar animal, or anything like that, I was pretty sure to have to deal with those things in the next romance. Once Clara required me to build a sudden tale out of a plumber and a "bawgunstrictor," and I had to do it. She didn't know what a boa-constrictor was, until he developed in the tale—then she was better satisfied with it than ever.

From Susy's Biography.

Papa's favorite game is billiards, and when he is tired and wishes to rest himself he stays up all night and plays billiards, it seems to rest his head. He smokes a great deal almost incessantly. He has the mind of an author exactly, some of the simplest things he cant understand. Our burglar alarm is often out of order, and papa had been obliged to take the mahogany-room off from the alarm altogether for a time, because the burglar alarm had been in the habit of ringing even when the mahogany-room window was closed. At length he thought that perhaps the burglar alarm might be in order, and he decided to try and see; accordingly he put it on and then went down and opened the window; conse-quently the alarm bell rang, it would even if the alarm had been in order. Papa went de-spairingly upstairs and said to mamma, "Livy the mahogany-room won't go on. I have just opened the window to see."

"Why, Youth," mamma replied "if you've opened the window, why of coarse the alarm will ring!"

"That's what I've opened it for, why I just went down to see if it would ring!"

Mamma tried to explain to papa that when he wanted to go and see whether the alarm would ring while the window was closed he *mustn't* go and open the window—but in vain, papa couldn't understand, and got very impatient with mamma for trying to make him believe an impossible thing true.

This is a frank biographer, and an honest one; she uses no sandpaper on me. I have, to this day, the same dull head in the matter of conundrums and perplexities which Susy had discov-ered in those long-gone days. Complexities annoy me; they irritate me; then this progressive feeling presently warms into anger. I cannot get far in the reading of the commonest and simplest contract—with its "parties of the first part," and "parties of the second part," and "parties of the third part,"—before my temper is all gone. Ashcroft comes up here every day and pathetically tries to make me understand the points of the lawsuit which we are conducting against Henry Butters, Harold Wheeler, and the rest of those Plasmon thieves, but daily he has to give it up. It is pitiful to see, when he bends his earnest and appealing eyes upon me and says, after one of his efforts, "Now you *do* understand *that,* don't you?"

I am always obliged to say "I *don't,* Ashcroft. I wish I could understand it, but I don't. Send for the cat."

In the days which Susy is talking about, a perplexity fell to my lot one day. F. G. Whitmore was my business agent, and he brought me out from town in his buggy. We drove by the porte-cochère and toward the stable. Now this was a *single* road, and was like a spoon whose handle stretched from the gate to a great round flower-bed in the neighborhood of the stable. At the approach to the flower-bed the road divided and circumnavigated it, making a loop, which I have likened to the bowl of the spoon. As we neared the loop, I saw that Whitmore was laying his course to port, (I was sitting on the starboard side—the side the house was on), and was going to start around that spoon-bowl on that left-hand side. I said,

"Don't do that, Whitmore; take the right-hand side. Then I shall be next to the house when we get to the door."

He said, "*That* will not happen in *any* case, it doesn't make any difference which way I go around this flower-bed."

I explained to him that he was an ass, but he stuck to his proposition, and I said,

"Go on and try it, and see."

He went on and tried it, and sure enough he fetched me up at the door on the very side that he had said I would be. I was not able to believe it then, and I don't believe it yet.

I said, "Whitmore, that is merely an accident. You can't do it again."

He said he could—and he drove down into the street, fetched around, came back, and actually did it again. I was stupefied, paralysed, petrified, with these strange results, but they did not convince me. I didn't believe he could do it another time, but he did. He said he could do it all day, and fetch up the same way every time. By that time my temper was gone, and I asked him to go home and apply to the asylum and I would pay the expenses; I didn't want to see him any more for a week.

I went up stairs in a rage and started to tell Livy about it, expecting to get her sympathy for me and to breed aversion in her for Whitmore; but she merely burst into peal after peal of laughter, as the tale of my adventure went on, for her head was like Susy's: riddles and complexities had no terrors for it. Her mind and Susy's were analytical; I have tried to make it appear that mine was different. Many and many a time I have told that buggy experiment, hoping against hope that I would some time or other find somebody who would be on my side, but it has never happened. And I am never able to go glibly forward and state the circumstances of that buggy's progress without having to halt and consider, and call up in my mind the spoon-handle, the bowl of the spoon, the buggy and the horse, and my position in the buggy: and the minute I have got that far and try to turn it to the left it goes to ruin; I can't see how it is ever going to fetch me out right when we get to the door. Susy is right in her estimate. I can't understand things.

That burglar alarm which Susy mentions led a gay and careless life, and had no principles. It was generally out of order at one point or another; and there was plenty of opportunity, because all the windows and doors in the house, from the cellar up to the top floor, were connected with it. However, in its seasons of being out of order it could trouble us for only a very little while: we quickly found out that it was fooling us, and that it was buzzing its blood-curdling alarm merely for its own amusement. Then we would shut it off, and send to New York for the electrician—there not being one in all Hartford in those days. When the repairs were finished we would set the alarm again and re-establish our confidence in it. It never did any real business except upon one single occasion. All the rest of its expensive career was frivolous and without purpose. Just that one time it performed its duty, and its whole duty—gravely, seriously, admirably. It let fly about two o'clock one black and dreary March morning, and I turned out promptly, because I knew that it was not fooling, this time. The bath-room door was on my side of the bed. I stepped in there, turned up the gas, looked at the annunciator, and turned off the alarm—so far as the door indicated was concerned—thus stopping the racket. Then I came back to bed. Mrs. Clemens opened the debate:

"What was it?"

"It was the cellar door."

"Was it a burglar, do you think?"

"Yes," I said, "of course it was. Did you suppose it was a Sunday-school superintendent?"

"No. What do you suppose he wants?"

"I suppose he wants jewelry, but he is not acquainted with the house and he thinks it is in the cellar. I don't like to disappoint a burglar whom I am not acquainted with, and who has done me no harm, but if he had had common sagacity enough to inquire, I could have told him we kept nothing down there but coal and vegetables. Still it may be that he *is* acquainted with this place, and that what he really wants is coal and vegetables. On the whole, I think it is vegetables he is after."

"Are you going down to see?"

"No; I could not be of any assistance. Let him select for himself; I don't know where the things are."

Then she said, "But suppose he comes up to the ground floor!"

"That's all right. We shall know it the minute he opens a door on that floor. It will set off the alarm."

Just then the terrific buzzing broke out again. I said,

"He has arrived. I told you he would. I know all about burglars and their ways. They are systematic people."

I went into the bath-room to see if I was right, and I was. I shut off the dining room and stopped the buzzing, and came back to bed. My wife said,

"What do you suppose he is after now?"

I said, "I think he has got all the vegetables he wants and is coming up for napkin-rings and odds and ends for the wife and children. They all have families—burglars have—and they are always thoughtful of them, always take a few necessaries of life for themselves, and fill out with tokens of remembrance for the family. In taking them they do not forget us: those very things represent tokens of his remembrance of us, and also of our remembrance of him. We never get them again; the memory of the attention remains embalmed in our hearts."

"Are you going down to see what it is he wants now?"

"No," I said, "I am no more interested than I was before. They are experienced people,— burglars; *they* know what they want; I should be no help to him. I *think* he is after ceramics and bric-à-brac and such things. If he knows the house he knows that that is all that he can find on the dining room floor."

She said, with a strong interest perceptible in her tone, "Suppose he comes up here!"

I said, "It is all right. He will give us notice."

"What shall we do then?"

"Climb out of the window."

She said, a little restively, "Well, what is the use of a burglar alarm for us?"

"You have seen, dear heart, that it has been useful up to the present moment, and I have explained to you how it will be continuously useful after he gets up here."

That was the end of it. He didn't ring any more alarms. Presently I said,

"He is disappointed, I think. He has gone off with the vegetables and the bric-à-brac, and I think he is dissatisfied."

We went to sleep, and at a quarter before eight in the morning I was out, and hurrying, for I was to take the 8.29 train for New York. I found the gas burning brightly—full head—all over the first floor. My new overcoat was gone; my old umbrella was gone; my new patent-leather shoes, which I had never worn, were gone. The large window which opened into the ombra at the rear of the house was standing wide. I passed out through it and tracked the burglar down the hill through the trees; tracked him without difficulty, because he had blazed his progress with imitation silver napkin-rings, and my umbrella, and various other things which he had disapproved of; and I went back in triumph and proved to my wife that he *was* a disappointed burglar. I had suspected he would be, from the start, and from his not coming up to our floor to get human beings.

Things happened to me that day in New York. I will tell about them another time.

From Susy's Biography.

Papa has a peculiar gait we like, it seems just to sute him, but most people do not; he always walks up and down the room while thinking and between each coarse at meals.

A lady distantly related to us came to visit us once in those days. She came to stay a week, but all our efforts to make her happy failed, we could not imagine why, and she got up her anchor and sailed the next morning. We did much guessing, but could not solve the mystery. Later we found out what the trouble was. It was my tramping up and down between the courses. She conceived the idea that I could not stand her society.

That word "Youth," as the reader has perhaps already guessed, was my wife's pet name for me. It was gently satirical, but also affectionate. I had certain mental and material peculiarities and customs proper to a much younger person than I was.

From Susy's Biography.

Papa is very fond of animals particularly of cats, we had a dear little gray kitten once that he named "Lazy" (papa always wears gray to match his hair and eyes) and he would carry him around on his shoulder, it was a mighty pretty sight! the gray cat sound asleep against papa's gray coat and hair. The names that he has given our different cats, are realy remarkably funny, they are namely Stray Kit, Abner, Motley, Fraeulein, Lazy, Bufalo Bill, Soapy Sall, Cleveland, Sour Mash, and Pestilence and Famine.

At one time when the children were small, we had a very black mother-cat named Satan, and Satan had a small black offspring named Sin. Pronouns were a difficulty for the children. Little Clara came in one day, her black eyes snapping with indignation, and said,

"Papa, Satan ought to be punished. She is out there at the greenhouse and there she stays and stays, and his kitten is down stairs crying."

Papa uses very strong language, but I have an idea not nearly so strong as when he first maried mamma. A lady acquaintance of his is rather apt to interupt what one is saying, and papa told mamma that he thought he should say to the lady's husband "I am glad Susy Warner wasn't present when the Deity said 'Let there be light.'"

It is as I have said before. This is a frank historian. She doesn't cover up one's deficiencies, but gives them an equal showing with one's handsomer qualities. Of course I made the remark which she has quoted—and even at this distant day I am still as much as half persuaded that if Susy Warner had been present when the Creator said "Let there be light" she would have interrupted Him and we shouldn't ever have got it.

From Susy's Biography.

Papa said the other day, "I am a mugwump and a mugwump is pure from the marrow out." (Papa knows that I am writing this biography of him, and he said this for it.) He doesn't like to go to church at all, why I never understood, until just now, he told us the other day that he couldn't bear to hear any one talk but himself, but that he could listen to himself talk for hours without getting tired, of course he said this in joke, but I've no dought it was founded on truth.

Friday, February 9, 1906

The "strong language" episode in the bath-room—Susy's reference to "The Prince and the Pauper"—The mother and the children help edit the books—Reference to ancestors.

Susy's remark about my strong language troubles me, and I must go back to it. All through the first ten years of my married life I kept a constant and discreet watch upon my tongue while in the house, and went outside and to a distance when circumstances were too much for me and I was obliged to seek relief. I prized my wife's respect and approval above all the rest of the human race's respect and approval. I dreaded the day when she should discover that I was but a whited sepulcher partly freighted with suppressed language. I was so careful, during ten years, that I had not a doubt that my suppressions had been successful. Therefore I was quite as happy in my guilt as I could have been if I had been innocent.

But at last an accident exposed me. I went into the bath-room one morning to make my toilet, and carelessly left the door two or three inches ajar. It was the first time that I had ever failed to take the precaution of closing it tightly. I knew the necessity of being particular about this, because shaving was always a trying ordeal for me, and I could seldom carry it through to a finish without verbal helps. Now this time I was unprotected, but did not suspect it. I had no extraordinary trouble with my razor on this occasion, and was able to worry through with mere mutterings and growlings of an improper sort, but with nothing noisy or emphatic about them—no snapping and barking. Then I put on a shirt. My shirts are an invention of my own.

They open in the back, and are buttoned there—when there are buttons. This time the button was missing. My temper jumped up several degrees in a moment, and my remarks rose accordingly, both in loudness and vigor of expression. But I was not troubled, for the bath-room door was a solid one and I supposed it was firmly closed. I flung up the window and threw the shirt out. It fell upon the shrubbery where the people on their way to church could admire it if they wanted to; there was merely fifty feet of grass between the shirt and the passer-by. Still rumbling and thundering distantly, I put on another shirt. Again the button was absent. I augmented my language to meet the emergency, and threw that shirt out of the window. I was too angry—too insane—to examine the third shirt, but put it furiously on. Again the button was absent, and that shirt followed its comrades out of the window. Then I straightened up, gathered my reserves, and let myself go like a cavalry charge. In the midst of that great assault, my eye fell upon that gaping door, and I was paralysed.

It took me a good while to finish my toilet. I extended the time unnecessarily in trying to make up my mind as to what I would best do in the circumstances. I tried to hope that Mrs. Clemens was asleep, but I knew better. I could not escape by the window. It was narrow, and suited only to shirts. At last I made up my mind to boldly loaf through the bedroom with the air of a person who had not been doing anything. I made half the journey successfully. I did not turn my eyes in her direction, because that would not be safe. It is very difficult to look as if you have not been doing anything when the facts are the other way, and my confidence in my performance oozed steadily out of me as I went along. I was aiming for the left-hand door because it was furthest from my wife. It had never been opened from the day that the house was built, but it seemed a blessed refuge for me now. The bed was this one, wherein I am lying now, and dictating these histories morning after morning with so much serenity. It was this same old elaborately carved black Venetian bedstead—the most comfortable bedstead that ever was, with space enough in it for a family, and carved angels enough surmounting its twisted columns and its headboard and footboard to bring peace to the sleepers, and pleasant dreams. I had to stop in the middle of the room. I hadn't the strength to go on. I believed that I was under accusing eyes—that even the carved angels were inspecting me with an unfriendly gaze. You know how it is when you are convinced that somebody behind you is looking steadily at you. You *have* to turn your face—you can't help it. I turned mine. The bed was placed as it is now, with the foot where the head ought to be. If it had been placed as it should have been, the high headboard would have sheltered me. But the footboard was no sufficient protection, for I could be seen over it. I was exposed. I was wholly without protection. I turned, because I couldn't help it—and my memory of what I saw is still vivid, after all these years.

Against the white pillows I saw the black head—I saw that young and beautiful face; and I saw the gracious eyes with a something in them which I had never seen there before. They were snapping and flashing with indignation. I felt myself crumbling; I felt myself shrinking away to nothing under that accusing gaze. I stood silent under that desolating fire for as much as a minute, I should say—it seemed a very, very long time. Then my wife's lips parted, and from them issued—*my latest bath-room remark*. The language perfect, but the expression velvety, unpractical, apprentice-like, ignorant, inexperienced, comically inadequate, absurdly weak and unsuited to the great language. In my lifetime I had never heard anything so out of tune, so inharmonious, so incongruous, so ill-suited to each other as were those mighty words set to that feeble music. I tried to keep from laughing, for I was a guilty person in deep need of charity and mercy. I tried to keep from bursting, and I succeeded—until she gravely said "There, now you know how it sounds."

Then I exploded; the air was filled with my fragments, and you could hear them whiz. I said "Oh Livy, if it sounds like *that* God forgive me, I will never do it again!"

Then she had to laugh herself. Both of us broke into convulsions, and went on laughing until we were physically exhausted and spiritually reconciled.

The children were present at breakfast—Clara aged six and Susy eight—and the mother made a guarded remark about strong language; guarded because she did not wish the children to suspect anything—a guarded remark which censured strong language. Both children broke out in one voice with this comment, "Why mamma, papa uses it."

I was astonished. I had supposed that that secret was safe in my own breast, and that its presence had never been suspected. I asked,

"How did you know, you little rascals?"

"Oh," they said, "we often listen over the ballusters when you are in the hall explaining things to George."

From Susy's Biography.

One of papa's latest books is "The Prince and the Pauper" and it is unquestionably the best book he has ever written, some people want him to keep to his old style, some gentleman wrote him, "I enjoyed Huckleberry Finn immensely and am glad to see that you have returned to your old style." That enoyed me that enoyed me greatly, because it trobles me (Susy was troubled by that word, and uncertain; she wrote a *u* above it in the proper place, but reconsidered the matter and struck it out) to have so few people know papa, I mean realy know him, they think of Mark Twain as a humorist joking at everything; "And with a mop of reddish brown hair which sorely needs the barbars brush a roman nose, short stubby mustache, a sad care-worn face, with maney crow's feet" etc. That is the way people picture papa, I have wanted papa to write a book that would reveal something of his kind sympathetic nature, and "The Prince and the Pauper" partly does it. The book is full of lovely charming ideas, and oh the language! It is *perfect*. I think that one of the most touching scenes in it, is where the pauper is riding on horseback with his nobles in the "recognition procession" and he sees his mother oh and then what followed! How she runs to his side, when she sees him throw up his hand palm outward, and is rudely pushed off by one of the King's officers, and then how the little pauper's consceince troubles him when he remembers the shameful words that were falling from his lips, when she was turned from his side "I know you not woman" and how his grandeurs were stricken value-less, and his pride consumed to ashes. It is a wonderfully beautiful and touching little scene, and papa has described it so wonderfully. I never saw a man with so much variety of feeling as papa has; now the "Prince and the Pauper" is full of touching places, but there is most always a streak of humor in them somewhere. Now in the coronation—in the stirring coronation, just after the little king has got his crown back again papa brings that in about the Seal, where the pauper says he used the Seal "to crack nuts with." Oh it is so funny and nice! Papa very seldom writes a passage without some humor in it somewhere, and I don't think he ever will.

The children always helped their mother to edit my books in manuscript. She would sit on the porch at the farm and read aloud, with her pencil in her hand, and the children would keep an alert and suspicious eye upon her right along, for the belief was well grounded in them that whenever she came across a particularly satisfactory passage she would strike it out. Their suspicions were well founded. The passages which were so satisfactory to them always had an element of strength in them which sorely needed modification or expurgation, and was always sure to get it at their mother's hand. For my own entertainment, and to enjoy the protests of the children, I often abused my editor's innocent confidence. I often interlarded remarks of a studied and felicitously atrocious character purposely to achieve the children's brief delight, and then see the remorseless pencil do its fatal work. I often joined my supplications to the children's, for mercy, and strung the argument out and pretended to be in earnest. They were deceived, and so was their mother. It was three against one, and most unfair. But it was very delightful, and I could not resist the temptation. Now and then we gained the victory and there was much rejoicing. Then I privately struck the passage out myself. It had served its purpose. It had furnished three of us with good entertainment, and in being removed from the book by me it was only suffering the fate originally intended for it.

From Susy's Biography.

Papa was born in Missouri. His mother is Grandma Clemens (Jane Lampton Clemens) of Kentucky. Grandpa Clemens was of the F.F.V's of Virginia.

Without doubt it was I that gave Susy that impression. I cannot imagine why, because I was never in my life much impressed by grandeurs which proceed from the accident of birth. I did not get this indifference from my mother. She was always strongly interested in the ancestry of the house. She traced her own line back to the Lambtons of Durham, England—a family which had been occupying broad lands there since Saxon times. I am not sure, but I think that those Lambtons got along without titles of nobility for eight or nine hundred years, then produced a great man, three-quarters of a century ago, and broke into the peerage. My mother knew all about the Clemenses of Virginia, and loved to aggrandize them to me, but she has long been dead. There has been no one to keep those details fresh in my memory, and they have grown dim.

There was a Jere. Clemens who was a United States Senator, and in his day enjoyed the usual senatorial fame—a fame which perishes whether it spring from four years' service or forty. After Jere. Clemens's fame as a Senator passed away, he was still remembered for many years on account of another service which he performed. He shot old John Brown's Governor Wise in the hind leg in a duel. However, I am not very clear about this. It may be that Governor Wise shot *him* in the hind leg. However, I don't think it is important. I think that the only thing that is really important is that one of them got shot in the hind leg. It would have been better and nobler and more historical and satisfactory if both of them had got shot in the hind leg—but it is of no use for me to try to recollect history, I never had a historical mind. Let it go. Whichever way it happened I am glad of it, and that is as much enthusiasm as I can get up for a person bearing my name. But I am forgetting the *first* Clemens—the one that stands furthest back toward the really original *first* Clemens, which was Adam.

Monday, February 12, 1906

**Susy's Biography continued—Some of the tricks played in "Tom Sawyer"—
The broken sugar-bowl—Skating on the Mississippi with Tom Nash, etc.**

From Susy's Biography.

> Clara and I are sure that papa played the trick on Grandma, about the whipping, that
> is related in "The Adventures of Tom Sayer:" "Hand me that switch." The switch hovered
> in the air, the peril was desperate—"My, look behind you Aunt!" The old lady whirled
> around and snatched her skirts out of danger. The lad fled on the instant, scrambling up
> the high board fence and dissapeared over it.

Susy and Clara were quite right about that.
Then Susy says:

> And we know papa played "Hookey" all the time. And how readily would papa pretend
> to be dying so as not to have to go to school!

These revelations and exposures are searching, but they are just. If I am as transparent to
other people as I was to Susy, I have wasted much effort in this life.

> Grandma couldn't make papa go to school, so she let him go into a printing-office to
> learn the trade. He did so, and gradually picked up enough education to enable him to do
> about as well as those who were more studious in early life.

It is noticeable that Susy does not get overheated when she is complimenting me, but maintains a proper judicial and biographical calm. It is noticeable, also, and it is to her credit as a
biographer, that she distributes compliment and criticism with a fair and even hand.

My mother had a good deal of trouble with me, but I think she enjoyed it. She had none at
all with my brother Henry, who was two years younger than I, and I think that the unbroken
monotony of his goodness and truthfulness and obedience would have been a burden to her
but for the relief and variety which I furnished in the other direction. I was a tonic. I was valuable to her. I never thought of it before, but now I see it. I never knew Henry to do a vicious
thing toward me, or toward any one else—but he frequently did righteous ones that cost me
as heavily. It was his duty to report me, when I needed reporting and neglected to do it myself,
and he was very faithful in discharging that duty. He is "Sid" in "Tom Sawyer." But Sid was
not Henry. Henry was a very much finer and better boy than ever Sid was.

It was Henry who called my mother's attention to the fact that the thread with which she
had sewed my collar together to keep me from going in swimming, had changed color. My
mother would not have discovered it but for that, and she was manifestly piqued when she
recognized that that prominent bit of circumstantial evidence had escaped her sharp eye. That
detail probably added a detail to my punishment. It is human. We generally visit our shortcom-
ings on somebody else when there is a possible excuse for it—but no matter, I took it out of
Henry. There is always compensation for such as are unjustly used. I often took it out of him—

sometimes as an advance payment for something which I hadn't yet done. These were occasions when the opportunity was too strong a temptation, and I had to draw on the future. I did not need to copy this idea from my mother, and probably didn't. It is most likely that I invented it for myself. Still she wrought upon that principle upon occasion.

If the incident of the broken sugar-bowl is in "Tom Sawyer"—I don't remember whether it is or not—that is an example of it. Henry never stole sugar. He took it openly from the bowl. His mother knew he wouldn't take sugar when she wasn't looking, but she had her doubts about me. Not exactly doubts, either. She knew very well I *would*. One day when she was not present, Henry took sugar from her prized and precious old-English sugar-bowl, which was an heirloom in the family—and he managed to break the bowl. It was the first time I had ever had a chance to tell anything on him, and I was inexpressibly glad. I told him I was going to tell on him, but he was not disturbed. When my mother came in and saw the bowl lying on the floor in fragments, she was speechless for a minute. I allowed that silence to work; I judged it would increase the effect. I was waiting for her to ask "Who did that?"—so that I could fetch out my news. But it was an error of calculation. When she got through with her silence she didn't ask anything about it—she merely gave me a crack on the skull with her thimble that I felt all the way down to my heels. Then I broke out with my injured innocence, expecting to make her very sorry that she had punished the wrong one. I expected her to do something remorseful and pathetic. I told her that I was not the one—it was Henry. But there was no upheaval. She said, without emotion, "It's all right. It isn't any matter. You deserve it for something you've done that I didn't know about; and if you haven't done it, why then you deserve it for something that you are going to do, that I shan't hear about."

There was a stairway outside the house, which led up to the rear part of the second story. One day Henry was sent on an errand, and he took a tin bucket along. I knew he would have to ascend those stairs, so I went up and locked the door on the inside, and came down into the garden, which had been newly plowed and was rich in choice firm clods of black mould. I gathered a generous equipment of these, and ambushed him. I waited till he had climbed the stairs and was near the landing and couldn't escape. Then I bombarded him with clods, which he warded off with his tin bucket the best he could, but without much success, for I was a good marksman. The clods smashing against the weatherboarding fetched my mother out to see what was the matter, and I tried to explain that I was amusing Henry. Both of them were after me in a minute, but I knew the way over that high board fence and escaped for that time. After an hour or two, when I ventured back, there was no one around and I thought the incident was closed. But it was not. Henry was ambushing me. With an unusually competent aim for him, he landed a stone on the side of my head which raised a bump there which felt like the Matterhorn. I carried it to my mother straightway for sympathy, but she was not strongly moved. It seemed to be her idea that incidents like this would eventually reform me if I harvested enough of them. So the matter was only educational. I had had a sterner view of it than that, before.

It was not right to give the cat the Pain-Killer; I realize it now. I would not repeat it in these days. But in those "Tom Sawyer" days it was a great and sincere satisfaction to me to see Peter perform under its influence—and if actions *do* speak as loud as words, he took as much interest in it as I did. It was a most detestable medicine, Perry Davis's Pain-Killer. Mr. Pavey's negro man, who was a person of good judgment and considerable curiosity, wanted to sample it, and I let him. It was his opinion that it was made of hellfire.

Those were the cholera days of '49. The people along the Mississippi were paralysed with fright. Those who could run away, did it. And many died of fright in the flight. Fright killed three persons where the cholera killed one. Those who couldn't flee kept themselves drenched with cholera preventives, and my mother chose Perry Davis's Pain-Killer for me. She was not distressed about herself. She avoided that kind of preventive. But she made me promise to take a teaspoonful of Pain-Killer every day. Originally it was my intention to keep the promise, but at that time I didn't know as much about Pain-Killer as I knew after my first experiment with it. She didn't watch Henry's bottle—she could trust Henry. But she marked my bottle with a pencil, on the label, every day, and examined it to see if the teaspoonful had been removed. The floor was not carpeted. It had cracks in it, and I fed the Pain-Killer to the cracks with very good results—no cholera occurred down below.

It was upon one of these occasions that that friendly cat came waving his tail and supplicating for Pain-Killer—which he got—and then went into those hysterics which ended with his colliding with all the furniture in the room and finally going out of the open window and carrying the flower-pots with him, just in time for my mother to arrive and look over her glasses in petrified astonishment and say "What in the world is the matter with Peter?"

I don't remember what my explanation was, but if it is recorded in that book it may not be the right one.

Whenever my conduct was of such exaggerated impropriety that my mother's extempory punishments were inadequate, she saved the matter up for Sunday, and made me go to church Sunday night—which was a penalty sometimes bearable, perhaps, but as a rule it was not, and I avoided it for the sake of my constitution. She would never believe that I had been to church until she had applied her test: she made me tell her what the text was. That was a simple matter, and caused me no trouble. I didn't have to go to church to get a text. I selected one for myself. This worked very well until one time when my text and the one furnished by a neighbor, who had been to church, didn't tally. After that my mother took other methods. I don't know what they were now.

In those days men and boys wore rather long cloaks in the winter-time. They were black, and were lined with very bright and showy Scotch plaids. One winter's night when I was starting to church to square a crime of some kind committed during the week, I hid my cloak near the gate and went off and played with the other boys until church was over. Then I returned home. But in the dark I put the cloak on wrong-side out, entered the room, threw the cloak aside, and then stood the usual examination. I got along very well until the temperature of the church was mentioned. My mother said,

"It must have been impossible to keep warm there on such a night."

I didn't see the art of that remark, and was foolish enough to explain that I wore my cloak all the time that I was in church. She asked if I kept it on from church home, too. I didn't see the bearing of that remark. I said that that was what I had done. She said,

"You wore it in church with that red Scotch plaid outside and glaring? Didn't that attract any attention?"

Of course to continue such a dialogue would have been tedious and unprofitable, and I let it go, and took the consequences.

That was about 1849. Tom Nash was a boy of my own age—the postmaster's son. The Mississippi was frozen across, and he and I went skating one night, probably without permission. I cannot see why we should go skating in the night unless without permission, for there could be no considerable amusement to be gotten out of skating at night if nobody was going to object to it. About midnight, when we were more than half a mile out toward the Illinois shore, we heard some ominous rumbling and grinding and crashing going on between us and the home side of the river, and we knew what it meant—the ice was breaking up. We started for home, pretty badly scared. We flew along at full speed whenever the moonlight sifting down between the clouds enabled us to tell which was ice and which was water. In the pauses we waited; started again whenever there was a good bridge of ice; paused again when we came to naked water and waited in distress until a floating vast cake should bridge that place. It took us an hour to make the trip—a trip which we made in a misery of apprehension all the time. But at last we arrived within a very brief distance of the shore. We waited again; there was another place that needed bridging. All about us the ice was plunging and grinding along and piling itself up in mountains on the shore, and the dangers were increasing, not diminishing. We grew very impatient to get to solid ground, so we started too early and went springing from cake to cake. Tom made a miscalculation, and fell short. He got a bitter bath, but he was so close to shore that he only had to swim a stroke or two—then his feet struck hard bottom and he crawled out. I arrived a little later, without accident. We had been in a drenching perspiration, and Tom's bath was a disaster for him. He took to his bed sick, and had a procession of diseases. The closing one was scarlet fever, and he came out of it stone deaf. Within a year or two speech departed, of course. But some years later he was taught to talk, after a fashion—one couldn't always make out what it was he was trying to say. Of course he could not modulate his voice, since he couldn't hear himself talk. When he supposed he was talking low and confidentially, you could hear him in Illinois.

Four years ago (1902) I was invited by the University of Missouri to come out there and receive the honorary degree of LL.D. I took that opportunity to spend a week in Hannibal—a city now, a village in my day. It had been fifty-three years since Tom Nash and I had had that adventure. When I was at the railway station ready to leave Hannibal, there was a crowd of citizens there. I saw Tom Nash approaching me across a vacant space, and I walked toward him, for I recognized him at once. He was old and white-headed, but the boy of fifteen was still visible in him. He came up to me, made a trumpet of his hands at my ear, nodded his head toward the citizens and said confidentially—in a yell like a fog-horn—

"Same damned fools, Sam!"

From Susy's Biography.

Papa was about twenty years old when he went on the Mississippi as a pilot. Just before he started on his tripp Grandma Clemens asked him to promise her on the Bible not to touch intoxicating liquors or swear, and he said "Yes, mother, I will," and he kept that promise seven years when Grandma released him from it.

Under the inspiring influence of that remark, what a garden of forgotten reforms rises upon my sight!

Tuesday, February 13, 1906

Susy's Biography continued—Cadet of Temperance—First meeting of Mr. Clemens and Miss Langdon—Miss Langdon an invalid—Dr. Newton.

I recall several of them without much difficulty. In Hannibal, when I was about fifteen, I was for a short time a Cadet of Temperance, an organization which probably covered the whole United States during as much as a year—possibly even longer. It consisted in a pledge to refrain, during membership, from the use of tobacco; I mean it consisted partly in that pledge and partly in a red merino sash, but the red merino sash was the main part. The boys joined in order to be privileged to wear it—the pledge part of the matter was of no consequence. It was so small in importance that contrasted with the sash it was, in effect, non-existent. The organization was weak and impermanent because there were not enough holidays to support it. We could turn out and march and show the red sashes on May-day with the Sunday-schools, and on the Fourth of July with the Sunday-schools, the independent Fire Company and the Militia Company. But you can't keep a juvenile moral institution alive on two displays of its sash per year. As a private, I could not have held out beyond one procession, but I was Illustrious Grand Worthy Secretary and Royal Inside Sentinel, and had the privilege of inventing the passwords and of wearing a rosette on my sash. Under these conditions, I was enabled to remain steadfast until I had gathered the glory of two displays—May-day and the Fourth of July. Then I resigned straightway; and straightway left the Lodge.

I had not smoked for three full months, and no words can adequately describe the smoke-appetite that was consuming me. I had been a smoker from my ninth year—a private one during the first two years, but a public one after that—that is to say, after my father's death. I was smoking, and utterly happy, before I was thirty steps from the Lodge door. I do not now know what the brand of the cigar was. It was probably not choice, or the previous smoker would not have thrown it away so soon. But I realized that it was the best cigar that was ever made. The previous smoker would have thought the same, if he had been without a smoke for three months. I smoked that stub without shame. I could not do it now without shame, because now I am more refined than I was then. But I would smoke it, just the same. I know myself, and I know the human race, well enough to know that.

In those days the native cigar was so cheap that a person who could afford anything, could afford cigars. Mr. Garth had a great tobacco factory, and there was a small shop in the village for the retail sale of his products. He had one brand of cigars which even poverty itself was able to buy. He had had these in stock a good many years, and although they looked well enough on the outside, their insides had decayed to dust and would fly out like a puff of vapor when they were broken in two. This brand was very popular on account of its extreme cheapness. Mr. Garth had other brands which were cheap, and some that were bad, but the supremacy

1850

over them enjoyed by this brand was indicated by its name. It was called "Garth's damnedest." We used to trade old newspapers (exchanges) for that brand.

There was another shop in the village where the conditions were friendly to penniless boys. It was kept by a lonely and melancholy little hunchback, and we could always get a supply of cigars by fetching a bucket of water for him from the village pump, whether he needed water or not. One day we found him asleep in his chair—a custom of his—and we waited patiently for him to wake up, which was a custom of ours. But he slept so long, this time, that at last our patience was exhausted, and we tried to wake him—but he was dead. I remember the shock of it yet.

In my early manhood, and in middle-life, I used to vex myself with reforms, every now and then. And I never had occasion to regret these divergencies, for whether the resulting depriva-tions were long or short, the rewarding pleasure which I got out of the vice when I returned to it, always paid me for all that it cost. However, I feel sure that I have written about these experiments in the book called "Following the Equator." By and by I will look and see. Mean-time, I will drop the subject and go back to Susy's sketch of me:

From Susy's Biography.

After papa had been a pilot on the Mississippi for a time, Uncle Orion Clemens, his brother, was appointed Secretary of the State of Nevada, and papa went with him out to Nevada to be his secretary. Afterwards he became interested in mining in California; then he reported for a newspaper and was on several newspapers. Then he was sent to the Sandwich Islands. After that he came back to America and his friends wanted him to lecture so he lectured. Then he went abroad on the Quaker City, and on board that ship he became equainted with Uncle Charlie (Mr. C. J. Langdon, of Elmira, New York). Papa and Uncle Charlie soon became friends, and when they returned from their journey Grandpa Langdon, Uncle Charlie's father, told Uncle Charlie to invite Mr. Clemens to dine with them at the St. Nicholas Hotel, in New York. Papa accepted the invitation and went to dine at the St. Nicholas with Grandpa and there he met mamma (Olivia Louise Langdon) first. But they did not meet again until the next August, because papa went away to California, and there wrote "The Inocense Abroad."

I will remark here that Susy is not quite correct as to that next meeting. That first meeting was on the 27th of December, 1867, and the next one was at the house of Mrs. Berry, five days later. Miss Langdon had gone there to help Mrs. Berry receive New Year guests. I went there at ten in the morning to pay a New Year call. I had thirty-four calls on my list, and this was the first one. I continued it during thirteen hours, and put the other thirty-three off till next year.

1867

From Susy's Biography.

Mamma was the daughter of Mr. Jervis Langdon, (I don't know whether Grandpa had a middle name or not) and Mrs. Olivia Lewis Langdon, of Elmira, New York. She had one brother and one sister, Uncle Charlie (Charles J. Langdon) and Aunt Susie (Susan Langdon Crane). Mamma loved Grandpa more than any one else in the world. He was her idol and she his, I think mamma's love for grandpa must have very much resembled my love for mamma. Grandpa was a great and good man and we all think of him with respect and love. Mamma was an invalid when she was young, and had to give up study a long time.

She became an invalid at sixteen, through a partial paralysis caused by falling on the ice, and she was never strong again while her life lasted. After that fall she was not able to leave her bed during two years, nor was she able to lie in any position except upon her back. All the great physicians were brought to Elmira, one after another, during that time, but there was no helpful result. In those days both worlds were well acquainted with the name of Dr. Newton, a man who was regarded in both worlds as a quack. He moved through the land in state; in magnificence, like a portent; like a circus. Notice of his coming was spread upon the dead walls in vast colored posters, along with his formidable portrait, several weeks beforehand.

One day Andrew Langdon, a relative of the Langdon family, came to the house and said: "You have tried everybody else, now try Dr. Newton, the quack. He is down town at the Rathbun House practising upon the well-to-do at war prices and upon the poor for nothing. *I saw him* wave his hands over Jake Brown's head and take his crutches away from him and send him about his business as good as new. *I saw him* do the like with some other cripples. *They* may have been 'temporaries' instituted for advertising purposes, and not genuine. But Jake is genuine. Send for Newton."

Newton came. He found the young girl upon her back. Over her was suspended a tackle from the ceiling. It had been there a long time, but unused. It was put there in the hope that by its steady motion she might be lifted to a sitting posture, at intervals, for rest. But it proved a failure. Any attempt to raise her brought nausea and exhaustion, and had to be relinquished. Newton made some passes about her head with his hands; then he put an arm behind her shoulders and said "Now we will sit up, my child."

The family were alarmed, and tried to stop him, but he was not disturbed, and raised her up. She sat several minutes, without nausea or discomfort. Then Newton said that that would do for the present, he would come again next morning; which he did. He made some passes with his hands and said, "Now we will walk a few steps, my child." He took her out of bed and supported her while she walked several steps; then he said "I have reached the limit of my art. She is not cured. It is not likely that she will *ever* be cured. She will never be able to walk far, but after a little daily practice she will be able to walk one or two hundred yards, and she can depend on being able to do *that* for the rest of her life."

His charge was fifteen hundred dollars, and it was easily worth a hundred thousand. For from the day that she was eighteen, until she was fifty-six, she was always able to walk a couple of hundred yards without stopping to rest; and more than once I saw her walk a quarter of a mile without serious fatigue.

Newton was mobbed in Dublin, in London, and in other places. He was rather frequently mobbed in Europe and in America, but never by the grateful Langdons and Clemenses. I met Newton once, in after years, and asked him what his secret was. He said he didn't know, but thought perhaps some subtle form of electricity proceeded from his body and wrought the cures.

Wednesday, February 14, 1906

About the accident which prolonged Mr. Clemens's visit at the Langdons'.

From Susy's Biography.

Soon papa came back East and papa and mamma were married.

It sounds easy and swift and unobstructed, but that was not the way of it. It did not happen in that smooth and comfortable way. There was a deal of courtship. There were three or four proposals of marriage and just as many declinations. I was roving far and wide on the lecture beat, but I managed to arrive in Elmira every now and then and renew the siege. Once I dug an invitation out of Charley Langdon to come and stay a week. It was a pleasant week, but it had to come to an end. I was not able to invent any way to get the invitation enlarged. No schemes that I could contrive seemed likely to deceive. They did not even deceive *me,* and when a person cannot deceive himself the chances are against his being able to deceive other people. But at last help and good fortune came, and from a most unexpected quarter. It was one of those cases so frequent in the past centuries, so infrequent in our day—a case where the hand of Providence is in it.

I was ready to leave for New York. A democrat wagon stood outside the main gate with my trunk in it, and Barney, the coachman, in the front seat with the reins in his hand. It was eight or nine in the evening, and dark. I bade good-bye to the grouped family on the front porch, and Charley and I went out and climbed into the wagon. We took our places back of the coachman on the remaining seat, which was aft toward the end of the wagon, and was only a temporary arrangement for our accommodation, and was not fastened in its place; a fact which—most fortunately for me, and for the unborn tribe of Clemenses—we were not aware of. Charley was smoking. Barney touched up the horse with the whip. He made a sudden spring forward. Charley and I went over the stern of the wagon backward. In the darkness the red bud of fire on the end of his cigar described a curve through the air which I can see yet. This was the only visible thing in all that gloomy scenery. I struck exactly on the top of my head and stood up that way for a moment, then crumbled down to the earth unconscious. It was a very good unconsciousness for a person who had not rehearsed the part. It was a cobblestone gutter, and they had been repairing it. My head struck in a dish formed by the conjunction of four cobblestones. That depression was half full of fresh new sand, and this made a competent cushion. My head did not touch any of those cobblestones. I got not a bruise. I was not even jolted. Nothing was the matter with me at all. Charley was considerably battered, but in his solicitude for me he was substantially unaware of it. The whole family swarmed out, Theodore Crane in the van with a flask of brandy. He poured enough of it between my lips to strangle me and make me bark, but it did not abate my unconsciousness. I was taking care of that myself. It was very pleasant to hear the pitying remarks drizzling around over me. That was one of the happiest half-dozen moments of my life. There was nothing to mar it—except that I had escaped damage. I was afraid that this would be discovered sooner or later, and would shorten my visit. I was such a dead weight that it required the combined strength of Barney and Mr. Langdon,

Theodore and Charley, to lug me into the house, but it was accomplished. I was there. I recognized that this was victory. I was there. I was safe to be an incumbrance for an indefinite length of time—but for a length of time, at any rate, and a Providence was in it. They set me up in an arm-chair in the parlor and sent for the family physician. Poor old devil, it was wrong to rout him out, but it was business, and I was too unconscious to protest. Mrs. Crane—dear soul, she was in this house three days ago, gray and beautiful, and as sympathetic as ever—Mrs. Crane brought a bottle of some kind of liquid fire whose function was to reduce contusions. But I knew that mine would deride it and scoff at it. She poured this on my head and pawed it around with her hand, stroking and massaging, the fierce stuff dribbling down my back-bone and marking its way, inch by inch, with the sensation of a forest fire. But *I* was satisfied. When she was getting worn out, her husband, Theodore, suggested that she take a rest and let Livy carry on the assuaging for a while. That was very pleasant. I should have been obliged to recover presently if it hadn't been for that. But under Livy's manipulations—if they had continued—I should probably be unconscious to this day. It was very delightful, those manipulations. So delightful, so comforting, so enchanting, that they even soothed the fire out of that fiendish successor to Perry Davis's Pain-Killer.

Then that old family doctor arrived and went at the matter in an educated and practical way—that is to say, he started a search expedition for contusions and humps and bumps, and announced that there were none. He said that if I would go to bed and forget my adventure I would be all right in the morning—which was not so. I was *not* all right in the morning. I didn't intend to be all right, and I was far from being all right. But I said I only needed rest, and I didn't need that doctor any more.

I got a good three days' extension out of that adventure, and it helped a good deal. It pushed my suit forward several steps. A subsequent visit completed the matter, and we became engaged conditionally; the condition being that the parents should consent.

In a private talk, Mr. Langdon called my attention to something I had already noticed— which was that I was an almost entirely unknown person; that no one around about knew me except Charley, and he was too young to be a reliable judge of men; that I was from the other side of the continent; and that only those people out there would be able to furnish me a character, in case I had one—so he asked me for references. I furnished them, and he said we would now suspend our industries and I could go away and wait until he could write to those people and get answers.

In due course answers came. I was sent for and we had another private conference. I had referred him to six prominent men, among them two clergymen (these were all San Franciscans) and he himself had written to a bank cashier who had in earlier years been a Sunday-school superintendent in Elmira, and well known to Mr. Langdon. The results were not promising. All those men were frank to a fault. They not only spoke in disapproval of me, but they were quite unnecessarily and exaggeratedly enthusiastic about it. One clergyman, (Stebbins,) and that ex-Sunday-school superintendent, (I wish I could recall his name), added to their black testimony the conviction that I would fill a drunkard's grave. It was just one of those usual long-distance prophecies. There being no time-limit, there is no telling how long you may have to wait. I have waited until now, and the fulfillment seems as far away as ever.

The reading of the letters being finished, there was a good deal of a pause, and it consisted largely of sadness and solemnity. I couldn't think of anything to say. Mr. Langdon was apparently in the same condition. Finally he raised his handsome head, fixed his clear and candid eye upon me and said "What kind of people are these? Haven't you a friend in the world?"

I said "Apparently not."

Then he said "I'll be your friend myself. Take the girl. I know you better than they do."

Thus dramatically and happily was my fate settled. Afterward, hearing me talking lovingly, admiringly, and fervently of Joe Goodman, he asked me where Goodman lived.

I told him out on the Pacific coast.

He said "Why he seems to be a friend of yours. Is he?"

I said "Indeed he is; the best one I ever had."

"Why then," he said, "what could you have been thinking of? Why didn't you refer me to him?"

I said "Because he would have lied just as straightforwardly on the other side. The others gave me all the vices, Goodman would have given me all the virtues. You wanted unprejudiced testimony, of course. I knew you wouldn't get it from Goodman. I did believe you would get it from those others, and possibly you did. But it was certainly less complimentary than I was expecting."

The date of our engagement was February 4th, 1869. The engagement ring was plain, and of heavy gold. That date was engraved inside of it. A year later I took it from her finger and *1869* prepared it to do service as a wedding ring by having the wedding-date added and engraved *1870* inside of it—February 2, 1870. It was never again removed from her finger for even a moment.

In Italy, a year and eight months ago, when death had restored her vanished youth to her sweet face and she lay fair and beautiful and looking as she had looked when she was girl and *1904* bride, they were going to take that ring from her finger to keep for the children. But I prevented that sacrilege. It is buried with her.

In the beginning of our engagement the proofs of my first book, "The Innocents Abroad," began to arrive, and she read them with me. She also edited them. She was my faithful, judicious and painstaking editor from that day forth until within three or four months of her death—a stretch of more than a third of a century.

Thursday, February 15, 1906

Susy's Biography continued—Death of Mr. Langdon—
Birth of Langdon Clemens—Burlesque map of Paris.

From Susy's Biography.

Papa wrote mamma a great many beautiful love letters when he was engaged to mamma, but mamma says I am too young to see them yet; I asked papa what I should do for I didn't (know) how I could write a Biography of him without his love letters, papa said that I could write mamma's opinion of them, and that would do just as well. So I'll do as papa says, and mamma says she thinks they are the loveliest love letters that ever were written, she says that Hawthorne's love letters to Mrs. Hawthorne are far inferior to these. Mamma (and papa) were going to board first in Bufalo and grandpa said he would find them a good boarding-house. But he afterwards told mamma that he had bought a pretty house for them, and had it all beautifully furnished, he had also hired a young coachman, Patrick McAleer, and had bought a horse for them, which all would be ready waiting for them, when they should arive in Bufalo; but he wanted to keep it a secret from "Youth," as grandpa called papa. What a delightful surprise it was! Grandpa went down to Bufalo with mamma and papa. And when they drove up to the house, papa said he thought the landlord of such a boarding-house must charge a great deal to those who wanted to live there. And when the secret was told papa was delighted beyond all degree. Mamma has told me the story many times, and I asked her what papa said when grandpa told him that the delightful boarding-house was his home, mamma answered that he was rather embariesed and so delighted he didn't know what to say. About six months after papa and mamma were married grandpa died; it was a terrible blow on mamma, and papa told Aunt Sue he thought Livy would never smile again, she was so broken hearted. Mamma couldn't have had a greater sorrow than that of dear grandpa's death, or any that could equal it exept the death of papa. Mamma helped take care of grandpa during his illness and she couldn't give up hope till the end had realy come.*

Surely nothing is so astonishing, so unaccountable, as a woman's endurance. Mrs. Clemens and I went down to Elmira about the 1st of June to help in the nursing of Mr. Langdon. Mrs. Clemens, her sister, (Susy Crane,) and I did all the nursing both day and night, during two months until the end. Two months of scorching, stifling heat. How much of the nursing did I do? My main watch was from midnight till four in the morning—nearly four hours. My other watch was a mid-day watch, and I think it was only three hours. The two sisters divided the remaining seventeen hours of the twenty-four between them, and each of them tried generously and persistently to swindle the other out of a part of her watch. The "on" watch could not be depended upon to call the "off" watch—excepting when I was the "on" watch.

I went to bed early every night, and tried to get sleep enough by midnight to fit me for my work, but it was always a failure. I went on watch sleepy and remained miserably sleepy and wretched straight along through the four hours. I can still see myself sitting by that bed in the melancholy stillness of the sweltering night, mechanically waving a palm-leaf fan over the drawn white face of the patient; I can still recall my noddings, my fleeting unconsciousnesses, when the fan would come to a standstill in my hand, and I would wake up with a start and a hideous shock. I can recall all the torture of my efforts to keep awake; I can recall the sense of the indolent march of time, and how the hands of the tall clock seemed not to move at all, but to stand still. Through the long vigil there was nothing to do but softly wave the fan—and the gentleness and monotony of the movement itself helped to make me sleepy. The malady was cancer of the stomach, and not curable. There were no medicines to give. It was a case of slow

*August 6, 1870—S.L.C.

and steady perishing. At long intervals, the foam of champagne was administered to the patient, but no other nourishment, so far as I can remember.

A bird of a breed not of my acquaintance used to begin a sad and wearisome and monotonous piping in the shrubbery near the window a full hour before the dawn, every morning. He had no company; he conducted this torture all alone, and added it to my stock. He never stopped for a moment. I have experienced few things that were more maddening than that bird's lamentings. During all that dreary siege I began to watch for the dawn long before it came; and I watched for it like the duplicate, I think, of the lonely castaway on an island in the sea, who watches the horizon for ships and rescue. When the first faint gray showed through the window-blinds I felt as no doubt that castaway feels when the dim threads of the looked-for ship appear against the sky.

I was well and strong, but I was a man and afflicted with a man's infirmity—lack of endurance. But neither of those young women was well nor strong; still I never found either of them sleepy or unalert when I came on watch; yet, as I have said, they divided seventeen hours of watching between them in every twenty-four. It is a marvelous thing. It filled me with wonder and admiration; also with shame, for my dull incompetency. Of course the physicians begged those daughters to permit the employment of professional nurses, but they would not consent. The mere mention of such a thing grieved them so that the matter was soon dropped, and not again referred to.

All through her life Mrs. Clemens was physically feeble, but her spirit was never weak. She lived upon it all her life, and it was as effective as bodily strength could have been. When our children were little she nursed them through long nights of sickness, as she had nursed her father. I have seen her sit up and hold a sick child upon her knees and croon to it and sway it monotonously to and fro to comfort it, a whole night long, without complaint or respite. But I could not keep awake ten minutes at a time. My whole duty was to put wood on the fire. I did it ten or twelve times during the night, but always had to be called every time, and was always asleep again before I finished the operation, or immediately afterward.

No, there is nothing comparable to the endurance of a woman. In military life she would tire out any army of men, either in camp or on the march. I still remember with admiration that woman who got into the overland stage-coach somewhere on the plains, when my brother and I crossed the continent in the summer of 1861, and who sat bolt upright and cheerful, stage after stage, and showed no wear and tear. In those days, the one event of the day in Carson City was the arrival of the overland coach. All the town was usually on hand to enjoy the event. The men would climb down out of the coach doubled up with cramps, hardly able to walk; their bodies worn, their spirits worn, their nerves raw, their tempers at a devilish point; but the women stepped out smiling and apparently unfatigued.

1861

From Susy's Biography.

After grandpapa's death mamma and papa went back to Bufalo; and three months afterward dear little Langdon was born. Mamma named him Langdon after grandpapa, he was a wonderfully beautiful little boy, but very, very delicate. He had wonderful blue eyes, but such a blue that mamma has never been able to describe them to me so that I could see them clearly in my mind's eye. His delicate health was a constant anxiety to mamma, and he was so good and sweet that that must have troubled her too, as I know it did.

He was prematurely born. We had a visitor in the house and when she was leaving she wanted Mrs. Clemens to go to the station with her. I objected. But this was a visitor whose desire Mrs. Clemens regarded as law. The visitor wasted so much precious time in taking her leave that Patrick had to drive in a gallop to get to the station in time. In those days the streets of Buffalo were not the model streets which they afterward became. They were paved with large cobblestones, and had not been repaired since Columbus's time. Therefore the journey to the station was like the Channel passage in a storm. The result to Mrs. Clemens was a premature confinement, followed by a dangerous illness. In my belief there was but one physician who could save her. That was the almost divine Mrs. Gleason, of Elmira, who died at a great age two years ago, after being the idol of that town for more than half a century. I sent for her and she came. Her ministrations were prosperous, but at the end of a week she said she was obliged to return to Elmira, because of imperative engagements. I felt *sure* that if she could stay with us three days more Livy would be out of all danger. But Mrs. Gleason's engagements were of such a nature that she could not consent to stay. This is why I placed a private policeman at the door with instructions to let no one pass out without my privity and consent. In these circumstances, poor Mrs. Gleason had no choice—therefore she stayed. She bore me no malice for this, and most sweetly said so when I saw her silken white head and her benignant and beautiful face for the last time, which was three years ago.

Before Mrs. Clemens was quite over her devastating illness, Miss Emma Nye, a former schoolmate of hers, arrived from South Carolina to pay us a visit, and was immediately taken with typhoid fever. We got nurses—professional nurses of the type of that day, and of previous centuries—but we had to watch those nurses while they watched the patient, which they did in their sleep, as a rule. I watched them in the daytime, Mrs. Clemens at night. She slept between medicine-times, but she always woke up at the medicine-times and went in and woke up the nurse that was on watch and saw the medicines administered. This constant interruption of her sleep seriously delayed Mrs. Clemens's recovery. Miss Nye's illness proved fatal. During the last two or three days of it, Mrs. Clemens seldom took her clothes off, but stood a continuous watch. Those two or three days are among the blackest, the gloomiest, the most wretched of my long life.

The resulting periodical and sudden changes of mood in me, from deep melancholy to half insane tempests and cyclones of humor, are among the curiosities of my life. During one of these spasms of humorous possession I sent down to my newspaper office for a huge wooden capital *M* and turned it upside-down and carved a crude and absurd map of Paris upon it, and published it, along with a sufficiently absurd description of it, with guarded and imaginary compliments of it bearing the signatures of General Grant and other experts. The Franco-Prussian war was in everybody's mouth at the time, and so the map would have been valuable—if it had been valuable. It wandered to Berlin, and the American students there got much satisfaction out of it. They would carry it to the big beer halls and sit over it at a beer table and discuss it with violent enthusiasm and apparent admiration, in English, until their purpose was accomplished, which was to attract the attention of any German soldiers that might be present. When that had been accomplished, they would leave the map there and go off, jawing, to a little distance and wait for results. The results were never long delayed. The soldiers would pounce upon the map and discuss it in German and lose their tempers over it and blackguard it and abuse it and revile the author of it, to the students' entire content. The soldiers were always divided in opinion about the author of it, some of them believing he was ignorant, but well-intentioned; the others believing he was merely an idiot.

Friday, February 16, 1906

Susy's Biography mentions little Langdon—The change of residence from Buffalo to Hartford—Mr. Clemens tells of the sale of his Buffalo paper to Mr. Kinney—Speaks of Jay Gould, McCall, and Rockefeller.

From Susy's Biography.

While Langdon was a little baby he used to carry a pencil in his little hand, that was his great plaything; I believe he was very seldom seen without one in his hand. When he was in Aunt Susy's arms and would want to go to mamma he would hold out his hands to her with the backs of his hands out toward her instead of with his palmes out. (About a year and five months) after Langdon was born I was born, and my chief occupation then was to cry, so I must have added greatly to mamma's care. Soon after little Langdon was born (a year) papa and mamma moved to Hartford to live. Their house in Bufalo reminded them too much of dear grandpapa, so they moved to Hartford soon after he died.

Soon after little Langdon was born a friend of mamma's came to visit her (Emma Nigh) and she was taken with the typhoid fever, while visiting mamma. At length she became so delirious, and so hard to take care of that mamma had to send to some of her friends in Elmira to come and help take care of her. Aunt Clara came, (Miss Clara L. Spaulding). She is no relation of ours but we call her Aunt Clara because she is such a great friend of mamma's. She came and helped mamma take care of Emma Nigh, but in spite of all the good care that she received, she grew worse and died.

Susy is right. Our year and a half in Buffalo had so saturated us with horrors and distress that we became restless and wanted to change, either to a place with pleasanter associations or with none at all. In accordance with the hard terms of that fearful law—the year of mourning—which deprives the mourner of the society and comradeship of his race when he most needs it, we shut ourselves up in the house and became recluses, visiting no one and receiving visits from no one. There was one exception—a single exception. David Gray— poet, and editor of the principal newspaper,—was our intimate friend, through his intimacy and mine with John Hay. David had a young wife and a young baby. The Grays and the Clemenses visited back and forth frequently, and this was all the solace the Clemenses had in their captivity.

When we could endure imprisonment no longer, Mrs. Clemens sold the house and I sold my one-third interest in the newspaper, and we went to Hartford to live. I have some little business sense now, acquired through hard experience and at great expense; but I had none in those days. I had bought Mr. Kinney's share of that newspaper (I think the name was Kinney) at his price—which was twenty-five thousand dollars. Later I found that all that I had bought of real value was the Associated Press privilege. I think we did not make a very large use of that privilege. It runs in my mind that about every night the Associated Press would offer us five thousand words at the usual rate, and that we compromised on five hundred. Still that privilege was worth fifteen thousand dollars, and was easily salable at that price. I sold my whole share in the paper—including that solitary asset—for fifteen thousand dollars. Kinney (if that was his name) was so delighted at his smartness in selling a property to me for twenty-five thousand that was not worth three-fourths of the money, that he was not able to keep his joy to himself, but talked it around pretty freely and made himself very happy over it. I could have explained to him that what he mistook for his smartness was a poor and driveling kind of thing. If there had been a triumph, if there had been a mental exhibition of a majestic sort, it was not his smartness; it was my stupidity; the credit was all due to me. He was a brisk and ambitious and self-appreciative young fellow, and he left straightway for New York and Wall Street, with his head full of sordid and splendid dreams—dreams of the "get rich quick" order; dreams to be realized through the dreamer's smartness and the other party's stupidity.

Jay Gould had just then reversed the commercial morals of the United States. He had put a blight upon them from which they have never recovered, and from which they will not recover for as much as a century to come. Jay Gould was the mightiest disaster which has ever befallen this country. The people had *desired* money before his day, but *he* taught them to fall down and worship it. They had respected men of means before his day, but along with this respect was joined the respect due to the character and industry which had accumulated it. But Jay Gould taught the entire nation to make a god of the money and the man, no matter how the money might have been acquired. In my youth there was nothing resembling a worship of money or of its possessor, in our region. And in our region no well-to-do man was ever charged with having acquired his money by shady methods.

The gospel left behind by Jay Gould is doing giant work in our days. Its message is "Get money. Get it quickly. Get it in abundance. Get it in prodigious abundance. Get it dishonestly if you can, honestly if you must."

This gospel does seem to be almost universal. Its great apostles, to-day, are the McCurdys, McCalls, Hydes, Alexanders, and the rest of that robber gang who have lately been driven out of their violated positions of trust in the colossal insurance companies of New York. President McCall was reported to be dying day before yesterday. The others have been several times reported, in the past two or three months, as engaged in dying. It has been imagined that the cause of these death-strokes was sorrow and shame for the robberies committed upon the two or three million policy holders and their families, and the widow and the orphan—but every now and then one is astonished to find that it is not the outraged conscience of these men that is at work; they are merely sick and sore because they have been exposed.

Yesterday—as I see by the morning paper—John A. McCall quite forgot about his obsequies and sat up and became impressive, and worked his morals for the benefit of the nation. He knew quite well that anything which a prodigiously rich man may say—whether in health or moribund—will be spread by the newspapers from one end of this continent to the other and be eagerly read by every creature who is able to read. McCall sits up and preaches to his son—ostensibly to his son—really to the nation. The man seems to be sincere, and I think he *is* sincere. I believe his moral sense is atrophied. I believe he really regards himself as a high and holy man. And I believe he thinks he is so regarded by the people of the United States. He has been worshiped because of his wealth, and particularly because of his shady methods of acquiring it, for twenty years. And I think he has become so accustomed to this adulation, and so beguiled and deceived by it, that he does really think himself a fine and great and noble being, and a proper model for the emulation of the rising generation of young men.

John D. Rockefeller is quite evidently a sincere man. Satan, twaddling sentimental sillinesses to a Sunday-school, could be no burlesque upon John D. Rockefeller and his performances in his Cleveland Sunday-school. When John D. is employed in that way he strikes the utmost limit of grotesqueness. He can't be burlesqued—he is himself a burlesque. I know Mr. Rockefeller pretty well, and I am convinced that he is a sincere man.

I also believe in *young* John D.'s sincerity. When he twaddles to his Bible Class every Sunday, he exposes himself just after his father's fashion. He stands up and with admirable solemnity and confidence discusses the Bible with the inspiration and the confidence of an idiot—and does it in all honesty and good faith. I know him, and I am quite sure he is sincere.

McCall has the right and true Rockefeller whang. He snivels owlishly along and is evidently as happy and as well satisfied with himself as if there wasn't a stain upon his name, nor a crime in his record. Listen—here is his little sermon:

FEBRUARY 16, 1906.

———

WORK, WORK, SAYS McCALL.

———

Tells of His Last Cigar in a Talk with His Son.

Special to The New York Times.

LAKEWOOD, Feb. 15.—John A. McCall felt so much better to-day that he had a long talk with his son, John C. McCall, and told many incidents of his career.

"John," he said to his son, "I have done many things in my life for which I am sorry, but I've never done anything of which I feel ashamed.

"My counsel to young men who would succeed is that they should take the world as they find it, and then work—work!"

Mr. McCall thought the guiding force of mankind was will power, and in illustration he said:

"Some time ago, John, your mother and I were sitting together, chatting. I was smoking a cigar. I liked a cigar, and enjoyed a good, quiet smoke. She objected to it.

"'John,' said she, 'why don't you throw that cigar away?'

"I did so.

"'John,' she added, 'I hope you'll never smoke again.'

"The cigar I threw away was my last. I determined to quit then and there, and did so. That was exactly thirty-five years ago."

Mr. McCall told his son many stories of his business life and seemed in a happier frame of mind than usual. This condition was attributed partly to the fact that he received hundreds of telegrams to-day congratulating him on his statement of yesterday reiterating his friendship for Andrew Hamilton.

"Father received a basketful of dispatches from friends in the North, South, East, and West commending him for his statement about his friend Judge Hamilton," said young Mr. McCall to-night. "The telegrams came from persons who wished him good health and recovery. It has made him very happy."

Mr. McCall had a sinking spell at 3 o'clock this morning, but it was slight, and he recovered before it was deemed necessary to send for a physician.

Milk and bouillons are now his sole form of nourishment. He eats no solids and is rapidly losing weight.

Drs. Vanderpoel and Charles L. Lindley held a conference at the McCall house at 5 o'clock this evening, and later told Mrs. McCall and Mrs. Darwin P. Kingsley, his daughter, that Mr. McCall's condition was good, and that there was no immediate danger.

John C. McCall gave out this statement to-night: "Mr. McCall has had a very favorable day and is somewhat better."

Following it comes the kind of bulletin which is given out, from day to day, when a king or other prodigious personage has had a favorable day, and is somewhat better—a fact which will interest and cheer and comfort the rest of the human race, nobody can explain why.

The sons and daughters of Jay Gould move, to-day, in what is regarded as the best society—the aristocratic society—of New York. One of his daughters married a titled Frenchman, ten or twelve years ago, a noisy and silly ruffian, gambler, and gentleman, and agreed to pay his debts, which amounted to a million or so. But she only agreed to pay the existing debts, not the future ones. The future ones have become present ones now, and are colossal. To-day she is suing for a separation from her shabby purchase, and the world's sympathy and compassion are with her, where it belongs.

Kinney went to Wall Street to become a Jay Gould and slaughter the innocents. Then he sank out of sight. I never heard of him again, nor saw him during thirty-five years. Then I encountered a very seedy and shabby tramp on Broadway—it was some months ago—and the tramp borrowed twenty-five cents of me. To buy a couple of drinks with, I suppose. He had a pretty tired look and seemed to need them. It was Kinney. His dapperness was all gone; he showed age, neglect, care, and that something which indicates that a long fight is over and that defeat has been accepted.

Mr. Langdon was a man whose character and nature were made up pretty exclusively of excellencies. I think that he had greatness in him also—executive greatness—and that it would have exhibited itself if his lines had been cast in a large field instead of in a small and obscure one. He once came within five minutes of being one of the great railway magnates of America.

Tuesday, February 20, 1906

About Rear-Admiral Wilkes—And meeting Mr. Anson Burlingame
in Honolulu.

MRS. MARY WILKES DEAD.

———

Florence, Italy, Feb. 19.—Mrs. Mary Wilkes, widow of Rear-Admiral Wilkes, U.S.N.,
is dead, aged eighty-five.

It is death-notices like this that enable me to realize in some sort how long I have lived.
They drive away the haze from my life's road and give me glimpses of the beginning of it—
glimpses of things which seem incredibly remote.

When I was a boy of ten, in that village on the Mississippi River which at that time was so
incalculably far from any place and is now so near to all places, the name of Wilkes, the explorer,
was in everybody's mouth, just as Roosevelt's is to-day. What a noise it made; and how wonderful the glory! How far away and how silent it is now. And the glory has faded to tradition.
Wilkes had discovered a new world, and was another Columbus. That world afterward turned
mainly to ice and snow. But it was not *all* ice and snow—and in our late day we are rediscovering it, and the world's interest in it has revived. Wilkes was a marvel in another way, for he had
gone wandering about the globe in his ships and had looked with his own eyes upon its furthest
corners, its dreamlands—names and places which existed rather as shadows and rumors than
as realities. But everybody visits those places now, in outings and summer excursions, and no
fame is to be gotten out of it.

One of the last visits I made in Florence—this was two years ago—was to Mrs. Wilkes. She
had sent and asked me to come, and it seemed a chapter out of the romantic and the impossible
that I should be looking upon the gentle face of the sharer in that long-forgotten glory. We
talked of the common things of the day, but my mind was not present. It was wandering among
the snow-storms and the ice floes and the fogs and mysteries of the Antarctic with this patri-
archal lady's young husband. Nothing remarkable was said; nothing remarkable happened.
Yet a visit has seldom impressed me so much as did this one.

Here is a pleasant and welcome letter, which plunges me back into the antiquities again.

Knollwood
Westfield, New Jersey.
February 17, 1906.

My dear Mr. Clemens:—

I should like to tell you how much I thank you for an article which you wrote once,
long ago, (1870 or '71) about my grandfather, Anson Burlingame.

In looking over the interesting family papers and letters, which have come into my
possession this winter, nothing has impressed me more deeply than your tribute. I have
read it again and again. I found it pasted into a scrap-book and apparently it was cut from
a newspaper. It is signed with your name.

It seems to bring before one more clearly, than anything I have been told or read, my grandfather's personality and achievements. . . . .

Family traditions grow less and less in the telling. Young children are so impatient of anecdotes, and when they grow old enough to understand their value, frequent repetitions, as well as newer interests and associations seem to have dulled, not the memory, but the spontaneity and joy of telling about the old days—so unless there is something written and preserved, how much is lost to children of the good deeds of their fathers.

Perhaps it will give you a little pleasure to know that after all these years, the words you wrote about "a good man, and a very, very great man" have fallen into the heart of one to whom his fame is very near and precious.

You say "Mr. Burlingame's short history—for he was only forty-seven—reads like a fairy-tale. Its successes, its surprises, its happy situations occur all along, and each new episode is always an improvement upon the one which went before it." That seems to have been very true and it is interesting to hear, although it has the sad ring of Destiny. But how shall I ever thank you for words like these? "He was a true man, a just man, a generous man, in all his ways and by all his instincts a noble man—a man of great brain, a broad, and deep and mighty thinker. He was a great man, a very, very great man. He was imperially endowed by nature, he was faithfully befriended by circumstances, and he wrought gallantly always in whatever station he found himself." How indeed shall I thank you for these words or tell you how deeply they have touched me, and how truly I shall endeavor to teach them to my children.

That your fame may be as sacred as this, is my earnest, grateful wish, not wholly the inevitable, imperishable fame that is laid down for you, but the sweet and precious fame, to your family and friends forever, of the fair attributes you ascribe to my grandfather, which could never have been discerned by one who was not like him in spirit.

With the hope some time of knowing you,

Yours sincerely,
Jean Burlingame Beatty.
(Mrs. Robert Chetwood Beatty.)

This carries me back forty years, to my first meeting with that wise and just and humane and charming man and great citizen and diplomat, Anson Burlingame. It was in Honolulu. He had arrived in his ship, on his way out on his great mission to China, and I had the honor and profit of his society daily and constantly during many days. He was a handsome and stately and courtly and graceful creature, in the prime of his perfect manhood, and it was a contenting pleasure to look at him. His outlook upon the world and its affairs was as wide as the horizon, and his speech was of a dignity and eloquence proper to it. It dealt in no commonplaces, for he had no commonplace thoughts. He was a kindly man, and most lovable. He was not a petty politician, but a great and magnanimous statesman. He did not serve his country alone, but China as well. He held the balances even. He wrought for justice and humanity. All his ways were clean; all his motives were high and fine.

He had beautiful eyes; deep eyes; speaking eyes; eyes that were dreamy, in repose; eyes that could beam and persuade like a lover's; eyes that could blast when his temper was up, I judge. Potter, (that is the name, I think,) the Congressional bully, found this out in his day, no doubt. Potter had bullied everybody, insulted everybody, challenged everybody, cowed everybody, and was cock of the walk in Washington. But when he challenged the new young Congressman from the West he found a prompt and ardent man at last. Burlingame chose bowie-knives at short range, and Potter apologized and retired from his bullyship with the laughter of the nation ringing in his ears.

When Mr. Burlingame arrived at Honolulu I had been confined to my room a couple of weeks—by night to my bed, by day to a deep-sunk splint-bottom chair like a basket. There was another chair but I preferred this one, because my malady was saddle-boils.

When the boat-load of skeletons arrived after forty-three days in an open boat on ten days' provisions—survivors of the clipper *Hornet* which had perished by fire several thousand miles away—it was necessary for me to interview them for the Sacramento *Union,* a journal which I had been commissioned to represent in the Sandwich Islands for a matter of five or six months. Mr. Burlingame put me on a cot and had me carried to the hospital, and during several hours he questioned the skeletons and I set down the answers in my note-book. It took me all night to write out my narrative of the *Hornet* disaster, and——but I will go no further with the subject now. I have already told the rest in some book of mine.

Mr. Burlingame gave me some advice, one day, which I have never forgotten, and which I have lived by for forty years. He said, in substance:

"Avoid inferiors. Seek your comradeships among your superiors in intellect and character; always *climb.*"

Mr. Burlingame's son—now editor of *Scribner's Monthly* this many years, and soon to reach the foothills that lie near the frontiers of age—was with him there in Honolulu; a handsome boy of nineteen, and overflowing with animation, activity, energy, and the pure joy of being alive. He attended balls and fandangos and *hula hulas* every night—anybody's, brown, half white, white—and he could dance all night and be as fresh as ever the next afternoon. One day he delighted me with a joke which I afterwards used in a lecture in San Francisco, and from there it traveled all around in the newspapers. He said "If a man compel thee to go with him a mile, go *with* him Twain."

When it was new, it seemed exceedingly happy and bright, but it has been emptied upon me upwards of several million times since—never by a witty and engaging lad like Burlingame, but always by chuckle-heads of base degree, who did it with offensive eagerness and with the conviction that they were the first in the field. And so it has finally lost its sparkle and bravery, and is become to me a seedy and repulsive tramp whose proper place is in the hospital for the decayed, the friendless and the forlorn.

Wednesday, February 21, 1906

Mr. Langdon just escapes being a railway magnate—Mr. Clemens's dealings with Bliss, the publisher.

But I am wandering far from Susy's Biography. I remember that I was about to explain a remark which I had been making about Susy's grandfather Langdon having just barely escaped once the good luck—or the bad luck—of becoming a great railway magnate. The incident has interest for me for more than one reason. Its details came to my knowledge in a chance way in a conversation which I had with my father-in-law when I was arranging a contract with my publisher for "Roughing It," my second book. I told him the publisher had arrived from Hartford, and would come to the house in the afternoon to discuss the contract and complete it with the signatures. I said I was going to require half the profits over the essential costs of manufacture. He asked if that arrangement would be perfectly fair to both parties, and said it was neither good business nor good morals to make contracts which gave to one side the advantage. I said that the terms which I was proposing were fair to both parties. Then Mr. Langdon after a musing silence said, with something like a reminiscent sorrow in his tone,

"When you and the publisher shall have gotten the contract framed to suit you both and no doubts about it are left in your minds, *sign* it—sign it to-day, don't wait till to-morrow."

It transpired that he had acquired this wisdom which he was giving me gratis, at considerable expense. He had acquired it twenty years earlier, or thereabouts, at the Astor House in New York, where he and a dozen other rising and able business men were gathered together to secure a certain railroad which promised to be a good property by and by, if properly developed and wisely managed. This was the Lehigh Valley railroad. There were a number of conflicting interests to be reconciled before the deal could be consummated. The men labored over these things the whole afternoon, in a private parlor of that hotel. They dined, then reassembled and continued their labors until after two in the morning. Then they shook hands all around in great joy and enthusiasm, for they had achieved success, and had drawn a contract in the rough which was ready for the signatures. The signing was about to begin; one of the men sat at the table with his pen poised over the fateful document, when somebody said "Oh, we are tired to death. There is no use in continuing this torture any longer. Everything's satisfactory; let's sign in the morning." All assented, and that pen was laid aside.

Mr. Langdon said "We got five or ten minutes' additional sleep that night, by that postponement, but it cost us several millions apiece, and it was a fancy price to pay. If we had paid out of our existing means, and the price had been a single million apiece, we should have had to sit up, for there wasn't a man among us who could have met the obligation completely. The contract was never signed. We had traded a Bank of England for ten minutes' extra sleep—a very small sleep, an apparently unimportant sleep, but it has kept us tired ever since. When you've got your contract right, this afternoon, sign it."

I followed that advice. It was thirty-five years ago, but it has kept me tired ever since. I was dealing with the salaried manager of the American Publishing Company of Hartford, E. Bliss, junior, a Yankee of the Yankees. I will tell about this episode in a later chapter. He was a tall, lean, skinny, yellow, toothless, bald-headed, rat-eyed professional liar and scoundrel. I told him my terms. He suggested that they were a little high. I showed him letters which I had received from various reputable firms, offering me this rate. I also showed him a letter from perhaps the best firm in America offering me three-fourths of the profits above cost of manufacture. I showed him still another letter from a far better firm than his own, offering me the whole of the profits and saying it would be content with what they could get out of the book as an advertisement. I said I did not care to consider these offers, and that I should prefer to remain where my success had been accomplished for me, but that I must insist upon half profits.

Bliss then said that on the whole perhaps my requirement was fair—sufficiently fair, at any rate, although there was argument that as his house had found me penniless and unknown, and had created me, so to speak, this service ought to be considered and compensated in the contract. It did not occur to me to remind him of a conversation which we had had nine months after the publication of "The Innocents Abroad," in which he had effusively thanked me for saving that publishing-house's life—a talk in which he had said that when my book was issued the Company's stock couldn't be given away, but at the end of nine months the stock had paid three 20 per cent dividends; cleared the Company of debt; was quoted at two hundred, and was not purchasable even at that gilded rate. I forgot to mention—for I didn't know it—that my 5 per cent royalty on that book represented only a fifth of the book's profits, and that for each dollar paid me by the Company, the Company had made four.

Bliss said he would go to the hotel and draw up the contract in accordance with the agreed terms. When he brought the contract, it had nothing in it about half profits. It was a royalty again—$7\frac{1}{2}$ per cent this time. I said that that was not what we had agreed upon. He said that in so many words it wasn't, but that in *fact* the terms were still better for *me* than half profits, because that up to a sale of one hundred thousand copies my profit on the book would be some trifle more than half, and that only on a sale of two hundred thousand copies would the Company get back that advantage.

I asked him if he was telling me the strict truth. He said he was. I asked him if he could hold up his hand and make oath that what he had said was absolutely true. He said he could. I asked him to put up his hand, which he did, and I swore him.

He published that book and the next one, at $7\frac{1}{2}$ per cent royalty. He published the next two at 10 per cent. But when I came back from Europe bringing the manuscript of still another book—"A Tramp Abroad," at the end of 1879—the doubts which had been lingering in my *1879* mind for all these years took the form of almost the conviction that this animal had been swindling me all the while, and I said that this time the words "half profits above cost of manufacture" must go into the contract or I would carry the book elsewhere—that I was tired of the royalty terms and believed it was a swindle upon me.

He accepted this proposition with effusion, and came back to my house the next day with that kind of contract. I saw that it did not mention the American Publishing Company, but only E. Bliss, junior. Apparently I was dealing solely with him. I inquired. He said "Yes," that it was a mean crowd, an ungrateful crowd; that it would have lost me long ago if it had not been for him; yet that it was in no sufficient degree grateful for this service, although it knew quite well that I was the sole source of its prosperities and even of its bread and butter. He said the Company had been threatening to reduce his salary; that he wanted to leave and set up for himself; and that he wanted nothing further to do with those skinflints.

The idea pleased me, for I detested those people myself, and was quite willing to leave them. So we signed the contract.

That rascal told me afterward that he took that contract and shook it in the face of the Board of Directors and said,

"I'll sell it to you for three-fourths of the profits above cost of manufacture. My salary must be continued at the present rate; my son's salary must be continued at the present rate, also. Those are the terms. Take them or leave them."

It could be that this was true. If it was true it was without doubt the only time during Bliss's sixty years that he opened his mouth without a lie escaping through the gaps in his teeth. I never heard him tell the truth, so far as I can remember. He was a most repulsive creature. When he was after dollars he showed the intense earnestness and eagerness of a circular-saw. In a small, mean, peanut-stand fashion, he was sharp and shrewd. But above that level he was destitute of intelligence; his brain was a loblolly, and he had the gibbering laugh of an idiot. It is my belief that Bliss never did an honest thing in his life, when he had a chance to do a dishonest one. I have had contact with several conspicuously mean men, but they were noble compared to this bastard monkey.

Bliss escaped me, and got into his grave a month or two before the first statement of account was due on "A Tramp Abroad." When the statement was presented of course it was a revelation. I saw that through those royalty deceptions, Bliss had been robbing me ever since the day that I had signed the $7\frac{1}{2}$ per cent contract for "Roughing It." I was present, as a partner in the contract, when that statement was laid before the Board of Directors in the house of Mr. Newton Case, in Hartford.

I denounced Bliss, and said that the Board must have known of these swindles, and was an accessory to them after the fact. But they denied it.

Now was my time to do a wise thing, for once in my life. But of course I did a foolish thing instead of it, old habits being hard to break. I ought to have continued with that Company and squeezed it. I ought to have made my terms five-sixths of the profits and continued the squeeze to this day. The Company would have been obliged to endure it, and I should have gotten my due. But I severed our relations, in a fine large leather-headed passion, and carried "The Prince and the Pauper" to J. R. Osgood, who was the loveliest man in the world, and the most incapable publisher. All I got out of that book was seventeen thousand dollars. But he thought he could do better next time. So I gave him "Old Times on the Mississippi," but said I should prefer that he make the book at my expense and sell it at a royalty to be paid by me to him. When he had finished making the plates and printing and binding the first edition, these industries of his had cost me fifty-six thousand dollars, and I was becoming uncomfortable through the monotony of signing checks. Osgood botched it again, dear good soul. I think my profit on that book was only thirty thousand dollars. It may have been more, but it is long ago and I can give only my impression.

I made still one more experiment outside of my proper line. I brought to New York Charles L. Webster, a young relative of mine by marriage, and with him to act as clerk and manager I published "Huckleberry Finn" myself. It was a little book; nothing much was to be expected from it pecuniarily—but at the end of three months after its publication, Webster handed me the statement of results and a check for fifty-four thousand five hundred dollars. This persuaded me that as a publisher I was not altogether a failure.

Thursday, February 22, 1906

**Susy's remarks about her grandfather Langdon—Mr. Clemens tells about
Mr. Atwater—Mr. David Gray; and about meeting David Gray, junior,
at a dinner recently.**

I have wandered far from Susy's chat about her grandfather, but that is no matter. In this autobiography it is my purpose to wander whenever I please and come back when I get ready. I have now come back, and we will set down what Susy has to say about her grandfather.

From Susy's Biography.

I mentioned that mamma and papa couldn't stay in their house in Bufalo because it reminded so much of grandpapa. Mamma received a letter from Aunt Susy in which Aunt Susy says a good deal about grandpapa, and the letter showed so clearly how much every one that knew grandpapa loved and respected him, that mamma let me take it to copy what is in it about grandpapa, and mamma thought it would fit in nicely here.

"Quarry Farm.
April 16, '85.

Livy dear, are you not reminded by to-day's report of General Grant of father? You remember how as Judge Smith and others whom father had chosen as executors were going out of the room, he said 'Gentlemen I shall live to bury you all'—smiled, and was cheerful. At that time he had far less strength than General Grant seems to have, but that same wonderful courage to battle with the foe. All along there has been much to remind me of father—of his quiet patience—in General Grant. There certainly is a marked likeness in the souls of the two men. Watching, day by day, the reports from the Nation's sick room brings to mind so vividly the days of that summer of 1870. And yet they seem so far away. I seemed as a child, compared with now, both in years and experience. The best and the hardest of life have been since then to me, and I know this is so in your life. All before seems dreamy. I sepose this was because our lives had to be all readjusted to go on without that great power in them. Father was quietly such a power in so many lives beside ours, Livy dear—not in kind or degree the same to any one but oh, a power!

The evening of the last company, I was so struck with the fact that Mr. Atwater stood quietly before father's portrait a long time and turning to me said, 'We shall never see his like again,' with a tremble and a choking in his voice—this after fifteen years, and from a business friend. And some stranger, a week ago, spoke of his habit of giving, as so remarkable, he having heard of father's generosity. . . . "

I remember Mr. Atwater very well. There was nothing citified about him or his ways. He was in middle age, and had lived in the country all his life. He had the farmer look, the farmer gait; he wore the farmer clothes, and also the farmer goatee, a decoration which had been universal when I was a boy, but was now become extinct in some of the western towns and in all of the eastern towns and cities. He was transparently a good and sincere and honest man. He was a humble helper of Mr. Langdon, and had been in his employ many years. His rôle was general utility. If Mr. Langdon's sawmills needed unscientific but plain common-sense inspection, Atwater was sent on that service. If Mr. Langdon's timber rafts got into trouble on account of a falling river or a rising one, Atwater was sent to look after the matter.

Atwater went on modest errands to Mr. Langdon's coal mines; also to examine and report upon Mr. Langdon's interests in the budding coal-oil fields of Pennsylvania. Mr. Atwater was *always* busy, always moving, always useful in humble ways, always religious, and always ungrammatical, except when he had just finished talking and had used up what he had in stock of that kind of grammar. He was effective—that is, he was effective if there was plenty of time. But he was constitutionally slow, and as he had to discuss all his matters with whomsoever came along, it sometimes happened that the occasion for his services had gone by before he got them in. Mr. Langdon never would discharge Atwater, though young Charley Langdon suggested that course now and then. Young Charley could not *abide* Atwater, because of his provoking dilatoriness and of his comfortable contentment in it. But I loved Atwater. Atwater was a treasure to me. When he would arrive from one of his inspection journeys and sit at the table, at noon, and tell the family all about the campaign in delicious detail, leaving out not a single inane, inconsequential and colorless incident of it, I heard it gratefully; I enjoyed Mr. Langdon's placid patience with it; the family's despondency and despair; and more than all these pleasures together, the vindictiveness in young Charley's eyes and the volcanic disturbances going on inside of him which I could not see, but which I knew were there.

I am dwelling upon Atwater just for love. I have nothing important to say about Atwater—in fact only one thing to say about him at all. And even that one thing I could leave unmentioned if I wanted to—but I don't want to. It has been a pleasant memory to me for a whole generation. It lets in a fleeting ray of light upon Livy's gentle and calm and equable spirit. Although she could feel strongly and utter her feelings strongly, none but a person familiar with her and with all her moods would ever be able to tell by her language that that language was violent. Young Charley had many and many a time tried to lodge a seed of unkindness against Atwater in Livy's heart, but she was as steadfast in her fidelity as was her father, and Charley's efforts always failed. Many and many a time he brought to her a charge against Atwater which he believed would bring the longed-for bitter word, and at last he scored a success—for "all things come to him who waits."

I was away at the time, but Charley could not wait for me to get back. He was too glad, too eager. He sat down at once and wrote to me while his triumph was fresh and his happiness hot and contenting. He told me how he had laid the whole exasperating matter before Livy and then had asked her "*Now* what do you say?" And she said "*Damn* Atwater."

Charley knew that there was no need to explain this to me. He knew I would perfectly understand. He knew that I would know that he was not quoting, but was *translating*. He knew that I would know that his translation was exact, was perfect, that it conveyed the precise length, breadth, weight, meaning and force of the words which Livy had really used. He knew that I would know that the phrase which she really uttered was "I disapprove of Atwater."

He was quite right. In her mouth that word "disapprove" was as blighting and withering and devastating as another person's damn.

One or two days ago I was talking about our sorrowful and pathetic brief sojourn in Buffalo, where we became hermits, and could have no human comradeship except that of young

David Gray and his young wife and their baby boy. It seems an *age* ago. Last night I was at a large dinner party at Norman Hapgood's palace up-town, and a very long and very slender gentleman was introduced to me—a gentleman with a fine, alert and intellectual face, with a becoming gold *pince-nez* on his nose and clothed in an evening costume which was perfect from the broad spread of immaculate bosom to the rosetted slippers on his feet. His gait, his bows, and his intonations were those of an English gentleman, and I took him for an earl. I said I had not understood his name, and asked him what it was. He said "David Gray." The effect was startling. His very father stood before me, as I had known him in Buffalo thirty-six years ago. This apparition called up pleasant times in the beer mills of Buffalo with David Gray and John Hay when this David Gray was in his cradle, a beloved and troublesome possession. And this contact kept me in Buffalo during the next hour, and made it difficult for me to keep up my end of the conversation at my extremity of the dinner-table. The text of my reveries was "What was he born for? What was his father born for? What was I born for? What is anybody born for?"

His father was a poet, but was doomed to grind out his living in a most uncongenial oc-cupation—the editing of a daily political newspaper. He was a singing bird in a menagerie of monkeys, macaws, and hyenas. His life was wasted. He had come from Scotland when he was five years old; he had come saturated to the bones with Presbyterianism of the bluest, the most uncompromising and most unlovely shade. At thirty-three, when I was comrading with him, his Presbyterianism was all gone and he had become a frank rationalist and pronounced un-believer. After a few years news came to me in Hartford that he had had a sunstroke. By and by the news came that his brain was affected, as a result. After another considerable interval I heard, through Ned House, who had been visiting him, that he was no longer able to compe-tently write either politics or poetry, and was living quite privately and teaching a daily Bible Class of young people, and was interested in nothing else. His unbelief had passed away; his early Presbyterianism had taken its place.

This was true. Some time after this I telegraphed and asked him to meet me at the railway station. He came, and I had a few minutes' talk with him—this for the last time. The same sweet spirit of the earlier days looked out of his deep eyes. He was the same David I had known before,—great, and fine, and blemishless in character, a creature to adore.

Not long afterward he was crushed and burned up in a railway disaster, at night—and I probably thought then, as I was thinking now, through the gay laughter-and-chatter fog of that dinner-table, "What was he born for? What was the use of it?" These tiresome and mo-notonous repetitions of the human life—where is their value? Susy asked that question when she was a little child. There was nobody then who could answer it; there is nobody yet.

When Mr. Langdon died, on the 6th of August, 1870, I found myself suddenly introduced *1870* into what was to me a quite new rôle—that of business man, temporarily.

Friday, February 23, 1906

**Mr. Clemens tells how he became a business man—
Mentions his brother Orion's autobiography.**

During the previous year or year and a half, Mr. Langdon had suffered some severe losses through a Mr. Talmage Brown, who was an annex of the family by marriage. Brown had paved Memphis, Tennessee, with the wooden pavement so popular in that day. He had done this as Mr. Langdon's agent. Well managed, the contract would have yielded a sufficient profit, but through Brown's mismanagement it had merely yielded a large loss. With Mr. Langdon alive, this loss was not a matter of consequence, and could not cripple the business. But with Mr. Langdon's brain and hand and credit and high character removed, it was another matter. He was a dealer in anthracite coal. He sold this coal over a stretch of country extending as far as Chicago, and he had important branches of his business in a number of cities. His agents were usually considerably in debt to him, and he was correspondingly in debt to the owners of the mines. His death left three young men in charge of the business—young Charley Langdon, Theodore Crane, and Mr. Slee. He had recently made them partners in the business, by gift. But they were unknown. The business world knew J. Langdon, a name that was a power, but these three young men were ciphers without a unit. Slee turned out afterward to be a very able man, and a most capable and persuasive negotiator, but at the time that I speak of his qualities were quite unknown. Mr. Langdon had trained him, and he was well equipped for his headship of the little firm. Theodore Crane was competent in his line—that of head clerk and superintendent of the subordinate clerks. No better man could have been found for that place; but his capacities were limited to that position. He was good and upright and indestructibly honest and honorable, but he had neither desire nor ambition to be anything above chief clerk. He was much too timid for larger work or larger responsibilities. Young Charley was twenty-one, and not any older than his age—that is to say, he was a boy. His mother had indulged him from the cradle up, and had stood between him and such discomforts as duties, studies, work, responsibility, and so on. He had gone to school only when he wanted to, as a rule, and he didn't want to often enough for his desire to be mistaken for a passion. He was not obliged to study at home when he had the headache, and he usually had the headache—the thing that was to be expected. He was allowed to play when his health and his predilections required it, and they required it with a good deal of frequency, because *he* was the judge in the matter. He was not required to read books, and he never read them. The results of this kind of bringing up can be imagined. But he was not to blame for them. His mother was his worst enemy, and she became this merely through her love for him, which was an intense and steadily burning passion. It was a most pathetic case. He had an unusually bright mind; a fertile mind; a mind that should have been fruitful. But because of his mother's calamitous indulgence, it got no cultivation and was a desert. Outside of business, it is a desert yet.

Charley's deadly training had made him conceited, arrogant, and overbearing. Slee and Theodore had a heavier burden to carry than had been the case with Mr. Langdon. Mr. Langdon had had nothing to do but manage the business, whereas Slee and Crane had to manage the business and Charley besides. Charley was the most difficult part of the enterprise. He was a good deal given to reorganizing and upsetting Mr. Slee's most promising arrangements and negotiations. Then the work had to be all done over again.

However, I started to tell how I became, all of a sudden, a business person—a matter which was entirely out of my line. A careful statement of Mr. Langdon's affairs showed that the assets were worth eight hundred thousand dollars, and that against them was merely the ordinary obligations of the business. Bills aggregating perhaps three hundred thousand dollars—possibly four hundred thousand—would have to be paid; half in about a month, the other half in about two months. The collections to meet these obligations would come in further along. With Mr. Langdon alive, these debts could be no embarrassment. He could go to the Bank in the town, or in New York, and borrow the money without any trouble, but these boys couldn't do that. They could get one hundred and fifty thousand dollars cash, at once, but that was all. It was Mr. Langdon's life insurance. It was paid promptly, but it could not go far—that is it could not go far enough. It did not fall short much—in fact only fifty thousand dollars, but where to get the fifty thousand dollars was a puzzle. They wrote to Mr. Henry W. Sage, of Ithaca, an old and warm friend and former business partner of Mr. Langdon, and begged him to come to Elmira and give them advice and help. He replied that he would come. Then, to my consternation, the young firm appointed *me* to do the negotiating with him. It was like asking me to calculate an eclipse. I had no idea of how to begin nor what to say. But they brought the big balance-sheet to the house and sat down with me in the library and explained, and explained, and explained, until at last I did get a fairly clear idea of what I must say to Mr. Sage.

When Mr. Sage came he and I went to the library to examine that balance-sheet, and the firm waited and trembled in some other part of the house. When I got through explaining the situation to Mr. Sage I got struck by lightning again—that is to say, he furnished me a fresh astonishment. He was a man with a straight mouth and a wonderfully firm jaw. He was the kind of man who puts his whole mind on a thing and keeps that kind of a mouth shut and locked all the way through, while the other man states the case. On this occasion I should have been grateful for some slight indication from him, during my long explanation, which might indicate that I was making at least some kind of an impression upon him, favorable or unfavorable. But he kept my heart on the strain all the way through, and I never could catch any hint of what was passing through his mind. But at the finish he spoke out with that robust decision which was a part of his character and said:

"Mr. Clemens, you've got as clear a business head on your shoulders as I have come in contact with for years. What are you an author for? You ought to be a business man."

I knew better, but it was not diplomatic to say so, and I didn't. Then he said,

"All you boys need is my note for fifty thousand dollars, at three months, handed in at the Bank, and with that support you will not need the money. If it shall be necessary to extend the note, tell Mr. Arnot it will be extended. The business is all right. Go ahead with it and have no fears. It is my opinion that this note will come back to me without your having extracted a dollar from it, at the end of the three months."

It happened just as he had said. Old Mr. Arnot, the Scotch banker, a very rich and very careful man and life-long friend of Mr. Langdon, watched the young firm and advised it out of his rich store of commercial wisdom, and at the end of the three months the firm was an established and growing concern, and the note was sent back to Mr. Sage without our having needed to extract anything from it. It was a small piece of paper, insignificant in its dimensions, insignificant in the sum which it represented, but formidable was its influence, and formidable was its power, because of the man who stood behind it.

The Sages and the Twichells were very intimate. One or two years later, Mr. Sage came to Hartford on a visit to Joe, and as soon as he had gone away Twichell rushed over to our house eager to tell me something; something which had astonished him, and which he believed would astonish me. He said,

"Why Mark, you know, Mr. Sage, one of the best business men in America, says that you have quite extraordinary business talents."

Again I didn't deny it. I would not have had that superstition dissipated for anything. It supplied a long felt want. We are always more anxious to be distinguished for a talent which we do not possess than to be praised for the fifteen which we do possess.

1870 All this was in 1870. Thirty-five years drifted by, and a year ago, in this house, Charley sat by this bed and casually remarked that if he were going to select what he considered the proudest moment of his life he should say that it was after he had explained the balance-sheet to Mr. Sage and had heard him say "Boy as you are, you carry on your shoulders one of the most remarkable business heads I have ever encountered."

Again I didn't say anything. What could be the use? That appropriation of my great achievement had without doubt been embedded in Charley's mind for a good many years, and I never could have gotten it out by argument and persuasion. Nothing but dynamite could do it.

I wonder if we are not all constructed like that. I think it likely that we all get to admiring other people's achievements and then go on telling about them and telling about them, until insensibly, and without our suspecting it, we shove the achiever out and take his place. I know of one instance of this. In the other room you will find a bulky manuscript, an autobiography of my brother Orion, who was ten years my senior in age. He wrote that autobiography at my suggestion, twenty years ago, and brought it to me in Hartford, from Keokuk, Iowa. I had urged him to put upon paper all the well remembered incidents of his life, and to not confine himself to those which he was proud of, but to put in also those which he was ashamed of. I said I did not suppose he could do it, because if anybody could do that thing it would have been done long ago. The fact that it has never been done is very good proof that it can't be done. Benvenuto tells a number of things that any *other* human being would be ashamed of, but the fact that he tells them seems to be very good evidence that he was not ashamed of them; and the same, I think, must be the case with Rousseau and his "Confessions."

I urged Orion to try to tell the truth, and tell the whole of it. I said he *couldn't* tell the truth of course—that is, he could not lie successfully about a shameful experience of his, because the truth would sneak out between the lies and he couldn't help it—that an autobiography is always two things: it is an absolute lie and it is an absolute truth. The author of it furnishes the lie, the reader of it furnishes the truth—that is, he gets at the truth by insight. In that autobiography my brother adopts and makes his own an incident which occurred in my life when I was two and a half years old. I suppose he had often heard me tell it. I suppose that by and by he got to telling it himself and told it a few times too often—told it so often that at last it became his own adventure and not mine. I think perhaps I have already mentioned this incident, but I will state it again briefly.

When our family moved by wagon from the hamlet of Florida, Missouri, thirty miles to Hannibal, on the Mississippi, they did not count the children, and I was left behind. I was two and a half years old. I was playing in the kitchen. I was all alone. I was playing with a little pyramid of meal which had sifted to the floor from the meal barrel through a hole contributed by a rat. By and by I noticed how still it was; how solemn it was; and my soul was filled with nameless terrors. I ran through the house; found it empty, still, silent—awfully silent, frightfully still and lifeless. Every living creature gone; I the one and sole living inhabitant of the globe, and the sun going down. Then an uncle of mine arrived on horseback to fetch me. The family had traveled peacefully along, I don't know how many hours, before at last some one had discovered the calamity that had befallen it.

My brother tells that incident in his autobiography gravely, tells it as an experience of his own, whereas if he had stopped to think a minute, it could properly be a striking and picturesque adventure in the life of a toddling child of two and a half, but when he makes it an experience of his own, it does not make a hero of the person it happened to, because there could be nothing heroic or blood-curdling about the leaving behind of a young man twelve and a half years old. My brother did not notice that discrepancy. It seems incredible that he could write it down as his adventure and not cipher a little on the circumstances—but evidently he didn't, and there it stands in his autobiography as the impressive adventure of a child of twelve and a half.

Monday, February 26, 1906

Susy comes to New York with her mother and father—Aunt Clara visits them at the Everett House—Aunt Clara's ill luck with horses—The omnibus incident in Germany—Aunt Clara now ill at Hoffman House, result of horseback accident thirty years ago—Mr. Clemens takes Susy to see General Grant—Mr. Clemens's account of his talk with General Grant— Mr. Clemens gives his first reading in New York—Also tells about one in Boston—Memorial to Mr. Longfellow—And one in Washington.

From Susy's Biography.

Papa made arrangements to read at Vassar College the 1st of May, and I went with him. We went by way of New York City. Mamma went with us to New York and stayed two days to do some shopping. We started Tuesday, at ½ past two o'clock in the afternoon, and reached New York about ¼ past six. Papa went right up to General Grants from the station and mamma and I went to the Everett House. Aunt Clara came to supper with us up in our room.

1885

This is the same Aunt Clara who has already been mentioned several times. She had been my wife's playmate and schoolmate from the earliest times, and she was about my wife's age, or two or three years younger—mentally, morally, spiritually, and in all ways, a superior and lovable personality.

Persons who think there is no such thing as luck—good or bad—are entitled to their opinion, although I think they ought to be shot for it. However this is merely an opinion itself; there is nothing binding about it. Clara Spaulding had the average human being's luck in all things save one; she was subject to ill luck with horses. It pursued her like a disease. Every now and then a horse threw her. Every now and then carriage horses ran away with her. At intervals omnibus horses ran away with her. Usually there was but one person hurt, and she was selected for that function. In Germany once our little family started from the Inn (in Worms, I think it was) to go to the station. The vehicle of transportation was a great long omnibus drawn by a battery of four great horses. Every seat in the 'bus was occupied, and the aggregate of us amounted to a good two dozen persons, possibly one or two more. I said playfully to Clara Spaulding "I think you ought to walk to the station. It isn't right for you to imperil the lives of such a crowd of inoffensive people as this." When we had gone a quarter of a mile and were briskly approaching a stone bridge which had no protecting railings, the battery broke and began to run. Outside we saw the long reins dragging along the ground and a young peasant racing after them and occasionally making a grab for them. Presently he achieved success, and none too soon, for the 'bus had already entered upon the bridge when he stopped the team. The two dozen lives were saved. Nobody offered to take up a collection, but I suggested to our friend and excursion-comrade—American Consul at a German city—that we get out and tip that young peasant. The Consul said, with an enthusiasm native to his character,

"Stay right where you are. Leave me to attend to that. His fine deed shall not go unrewarded."

He jumped out and arranged the matter, and we continued our journey. Afterward I asked him what he gave the peasant, so that I could pay my half. He told me, and I paid it. It is twenty-eight years ago, yet from that day to this, although I have passed through some stringent seasons, I have never seriously felt or regretted that outlay. It was twenty-three cents.

Clara Spaulding, now Mrs. John B. Stanchfield, has a son who is a senior in college, and a daughter who is in college in Germany. She is in New York at present, and I went to the Hoffman House yesterday to see her, but it was as I was expecting: she is too ill to see any but physicians and nurses. This illness has its source in a horseback accident which fell to her share thirty years ago, and which resulted in broken bones of the foot and ancle. The broken bones were badly set, and she always walked with a limp afterwards. Some months ago the foot and ancle began to pain her unendurably and it was decided that she must come to New York and have the bones rebroken and reset. I saw her in the private hospital about three weeks after that operation, and the verdict was that the operation was successful. This turned out to be a mistake. She came to New York a month or six weeks ago, and another rebreaking and resetting was accomplished. A week ago, when I called, she was able to hobble about the room by help of crutches, and she was very happy in the conviction that now she was going to have no more trouble. But it appears that this dreadful surgery-work must be done over once more. But she is not fitted for it. The pain is reducing her strength, and I was told that it has been for the past three days necessary to exclude her from contact with all but physicians and nurses.

From Susy's Biography.

We and Aunt Clara were going to the theatre right after supper, and we expected papa to take us there and to come home as early as he could. But we got through dinner and he didn't come, and didn't come, and mamma got more perplexed and worried, but at last we thought we would have to go without him. So we put on our things and started down stairs but before we'd goten half down we met papa coming up with a great bunch of roses in his hand. He explained that the reason he was so late was that his watch stopped and he didn't notice and kept thinking it an hour earlier than it really was. The roses he carried were some Col. Fred Grant sent to mamma. We went to the theatre and enjoyed "Adonis" (word illegible) acted very much. We reached home about ½ past eleven o'clock and went right to bed. Wednesday morning we got up rather late and had breakfast about ½ past nine o'clock. After breakfast mamma went out shopping and papa and I went to see papa's agent about some business matters. After papa had gotten through talking to Cousin Charlie, (Webster) papa's agent, we went to get a friend of papa's, Major Pond, to go and see a Dog Show with us. Then we went to see the dogs with Major Pond and we had a delightful time seeing so many dogs together; when we got through seeing the dogs papa thought he would go and see General Grant and I went with him—this was April 29, 1885. Papa went up into General Grant's room and he took me with him, I felt greatly honored and delighted when papa took me into General Grant's room and let me see the General and Col. Grant, for General Grant is a man I shall be glad all my life that I have seen. Papa and General Grant had a long talk together and papa has written an account of his talk and visit with General Grant for me to put into this biography.

Susy has inserted in this place that account of mine—as follows:

April 29, 1885.

I called on General Grant and took Susy with me. The General was looking and feeling far better than he had looked or felt for some months. He had ventured to work again on his book that morning—the first time he had done any work for perhaps a month. This morning's work was his first attempt at dictating, and it was a thorough success, to his great delight. He had always said that it would be impossible for him to dictate anything, but I had said that he was noted for clearness of statement, and as a narrative was simply a statement of consecutive facts, he was consequently peculiarly qualified and equipped for dictation. This turned out to be true. For he had dictated two hours that morning to a shorthand writer, had never hesitated for words, had not repeated himself, and the manuscript when finished needed no revision. The two hours' work was an account of Appomattox—and this was such an extremely important feature that his book would necessarily have been severely lame without it. Therefore I had taken a shorthand writer there before, to see if I could not get him to write at least a few lines about Appomattox.[*] But he was at that time not well enough to undertake it. I was aware that of all the hundred versions of Appomattox, not one was really correct. Therefore I was extremely anxious that he should leave behind him the truth. His throat was not distressing him, and his voice was much better and stronger than usual. He was so delighted to have gotten Appomattox accomplished once more in his life—to have gotten the matter off his mind— that he was as talkative as his old self. He received Susy very pleasantly, and then fell to

[*]I was his publisher. I was putting his "Personal Memoirs" to press at the time.   S.L.C.

talking about certain matters which he hoped to be able to dictate next day; and he said in substance that, among other things, he wanted to settle once for all a question that had been bandied about from mouth to mouth and from newspaper to newspaper. That question was "With whom originated the idea of the march to the sea? Was it Grant's, or was it Sherman's idea?" Whether I, or some one else (being anxious to get the important fact settled) asked him with whom the idea originated, I don't remember. But I remember his answer. I shall always remember his answer. General Grant said:

"Neither of us originated the idea of Sherman's march to the sea. The enemy did it."

He went on to say that the enemy, however, necessarily originated a great many of the plans that the general on the opposite side gets the credit for; at the same time that the enemy is doing that, he is laying open other moves which the opposing general sees and takes advantage of. In this case, Sherman had a plan all thought out, of course. He meant to destroy the two remaining railroads in that part of the country, and that would finish up that region. But General Hood did not play the military part that he was expected to play. On the contrary, General Hood made a dive at Chattanooga. This left the march to the sea open to Sherman, and so after sending part of his army to defend and hold what he had acquired in the Chattanooga region, he was perfectly free to proceed, with the rest of it, through Georgia. He saw the opportunity, and he would not have been fit for his place if he had not seized it.

"He wrote me" (the General is speaking) "what his plan was, and I sent him word to go ahead. My staff were opposed to the movement." (I think the General said they tried to persuade him to stop Sherman. The chief of his staff, the General said, even went so far as to go to Washington without the General's knowledge and get the ear of the authorities, and he succeeded in arousing their fears to such an extent that they telegraphed General Grant to stop Sherman.)

Then General Grant said "Out of deference to the Government, I telegraphed Sherman and stopped him twenty-four hours; and then considering that that was deference enough to the Government, I telegraphed him to go ahead again."

I have not tried to give the General's language, but only the general idea of what he said. The thing that mainly struck me was his terse remark that the enemy originated the idea of the march to the sea. It struck me because it was so suggestive of the General's epigrammatic fashion—saying a great deal in a single crisp sentence. (This is my account, and signed "Mark Twain.")

Susy Resumes.

After papa and General Grant had had their talk, we went back to the hotel where mamma was, and papa told mamma all about his interview with General Grant. Mamma and I had a nice quiet afternoon together.

That pair of devoted comrades were always shutting themselves up together when there was opportunity to have what Susy called "a cosy time." From Susy's nursery days to the end of her life, she and her mother were close friends; intimate friends, passionate adorers of each other. Susy's was a beautiful mind, and it made her an interesting comrade. And with the fine mind she had a heart like her mother's. Susy never had an interest or an occupation which she was not glad to put aside for that something which was in all cases more precious to her—a visit with her mother. Susy died at the right time, the fortunate time of life; the happy age—twenty-four years. At twenty-four, such a girl has seen the best of life—life as a happy dream. After that age the risks begin; responsibility comes, and with it the cares, the sorrows, and the inevitable tragedy. For her mother's sake I would have brought her back from the grave if I could, but I would not have done it for my own.

From Susy's Biography.

Then papa went to read in public; there were a great many authors that read, that Thursday afternoon, beside papa; I would have liked to have gone and heard papa read, but papa said he was going to read in Vassar just what he was planning to read in New York, so I stayed at home with mamma.

I think that that was the first exploitation of a new and devilish invention—the thing called an Authors' Reading. This witch's Sabbath took place in a theatre, and began at two in the afternoon. There were nine readers on the list, and I believe I was the only one who was qualified by experience to go at the matter in a sane way. I knew, by my old acquaintanceship with the multiplication table, that nine times ten are ninety, and that consequently the average of time allowed to each of these readers should be restricted to ten minutes. There would be an introducer, and he wouldn't understand his business—this disastrous fact could be counted upon as a certainty. The introducer would be ignorant, windy, eloquent, and willing to hear himself talk. With nine introductions to make, added to his own opening speech—well, I could not go on with these harrowing calculations; I foresaw that there was trouble on hand. I had asked for the sixth place in the list. When the curtain went up and I saw that our half-circle of minstrels were all on hand, I made a change in my plan. I judged that in asking for sixth place I had done all that was necessary to establish a fictitious reputation for modesty, and that there could be nothing gained by pushing this reputation to the limit; it had done its work and it was time, now, to leave well enough alone, and do better. So I asked to be moved up to third place, and my prayer was granted.

The performance began at a quarter past two, and I, number three in a list of ten (if we include the introducer) was not called to the bat until a quarter after three. My reading was ten minutes long. When I had selected it originally, it was twelve minutes long, and it had taken me a good hour to find ways of reducing it by two minutes without damaging it. I was through in ten minutes. Then I retired to my seat to enjoy the agonies of the audience. I did enjoy them for an hour or two; then all the cruelty in my nature was exhausted, and my native humanity came to the front again. By half past five a third of the house was asleep; another third were dying; and the rest were dead. I got out the back way and went home.

During several years, after that, the Authors' Readings continued. Every now and then we assembled in Boston, New York, Philadelphia, Baltimore, Washington, and scourged the people. It was found impossible to teach the persons who managed these orgies any sense. Also it was found impossible to teach the readers any sense. Once I went to Boston to help in one of these revels which had been instigated in the interest of a memorial to Mr. Longfellow. Howells was always a member of these traveling afflictions, and I was never able to teach him to rehearse his proposed reading by the help of a watch and cut it down to a proper length. He couldn't seem to learn it. He was a bright man in all other ways, but whenever he came to select a reading for one of these carousals his intellect decayed and fell to ruin. I arrived at his house in Cambridge the night before the Longfellow Memorial occasion, and I probably asked him to show me his selection. At any rate, he showed it to me—and I wish I may never attempt the truth again if it wasn't seven thousand words. I made him set his eye on his watch and keep game while I should read a paragraph of it. This experiment proved that it would take me an hour and ten minutes to read the whole of it, and I said "And mind you, this is not allowing anything for such interruptions as applause—for the reason that after the first twelve minutes there wouldn't be any."

He had a time of it to find something short enough, and he kept saying that he never would find a short enough selection that would be good enough—that is to say, he never would be able to find one that would stand exposure before an audience.

I said "It's no matter. Better that than a long one—because the audience could stand a bad short one, but couldn't stand a good long one."

We got it arranged at last. We got him down to fifteen minutes, perhaps. But he and Dr. Holmes and Aldrich and I had the only short readings that day out of the most formidable accumulation of authors that had ever thus far been placed in position before the enemy—a battery of sixteen. I think that that was the occasion when we had sixteen. If it wasn't then it was in Washington, in 1888. Yes, I think that that occasion was the time when we had that irresistible, that unconquerable force. It was in the afternoon, in the Globe Theatre, and the place was packed, and the air would have been very bad only there wasn't any. I can see that mass of people yet, opening and closing their mouths like fishes gasping for breath. It was intolerable.

That graceful and competent speaker, Professor Norton, opened the game with a very handsome speech, but it was a good twenty minutes long. And a good ten minutes of it, I think, were devoted to the introduction of Dr. Oliver Wendell Holmes, who hadn't any more need of an introduction than the Milky Way. Then Dr. Holmes recited—as only Dr. Holmes could recite it—"The Last Leaf," and the house rose as one individual and went mad with worshiping delight. And the house stormed along, and stormed along, and got another poem out of the Doctor as an encore; it stormed again and got a third one—though the storm was not so violent this time as had been the previous outbreaks. By this time Dr. Holmes had himself lost a part of his mind, and he actually went on reciting poem after poem until silence had taken the place of encores, and he had to do the last encore by himself. He was the loveliest human being in Boston, and it was a pathetic thing that he should treat himself so.

I had learned, long ago, to stipulate for third place on the program. The performance began at two o'clock. My train for Hartford would leave at four o'clock. I would need fifteen minutes for transit to the station. I needed ten minutes for my reading. I did my reading in the ten minutes; I fled at once from the theatre, and I came very near not catching that train. I was told afterward that by the time reader number eight stepped forward and trained his gun on the house, the audience were drifting out of the place in groups, shoals, blocks, and avalanches, and that about that time the siege was raised and the conflict given up, with six or seven readers still to hear from.

At the reading in Washington, in the spring of '88 there was a crowd of readers. They all came overloaded, as usual. Thomas Nelson Page read forty minutes by the watch, and he was no further down than the middle of the list. We were all due at the White House at half past nine. The President and Mrs. Cleveland were present, and at half past ten they had to go away—the President to attend to some official business which had been arranged to be considered after our White House reception, it being supposed by Mr. Cleveland, who was inexperienced in Authors' Readings, that our reception at the White House would be over by half past eleven, whereas if he had known as much about Authors' Readings as he knew about other kinds of statesmanship, he would have known that we were not likely to get through before time for early breakfast.

I think that it was upon the occasion of this visit to Washington that Livy, always thoughtful of me, prepared me for my visit to the Executive Mansion. No, it wasn't—that was earlier. She was with me, this time, and could look after me herself.

Monday, March 5, 1906

Mrs. Clemens's warning to Mr. Clemens when he attends the Cleveland reception at White House—Describes the Paris house in which they lived in 1893—Also room in Villa Viviani—Also dining room in house at Riverdale—Tells how Mr. Clemens was "dusted off" after the various dinners—and the card system of signals—Letter from Mr. Gilder regarding Mr. Cleveland's sixty-ninth birthday—Mason.

I was always heedless. I was born heedless; and therefore I was constantly, and quite unconsciously, committing breaches of the minor proprieties, which brought upon me humiliations which ought to have humiliated me but didn't, because I didn't know anything had happened. But Livy knew; and so the humiliations fell to her share, poor child, who had not earned them and did not deserve them. She always said I was the most difficult child she had. She was very sensitive about me. It distressed her to see me do heedless things which could bring me under criticism, and so she was always watchful and alert to protect me from the kind of transgressions which I have been speaking of.

When I was leaving Hartford for Washington, upon the occasion referred to, she said "I have written a small warning and put it in a pocket of your dress vest. When you are dressing to go to the Authors' Reception at the White House you will naturally put your fingers in your vest pockets, according to your custom, and you will find that little note there. Read it carefully, and do as it tells you. I cannot be with you, and so I delegate my sentry duties to this little note. If I should give you the warning by word of mouth, now, it would pass from your head and be forgotten in a few minutes."

It was President Cleveland's first term. I had never seen his wife—the young, the beautiful, the good-hearted, the sympathetic, the fascinating. Sure enough, just as I had finished dressing to go to the White House I found that little note, which I had long ago forgotten. It was a grave little note, a serious little note, like its writer, but it made me laugh. Livy's gentle gravities often produced that effect upon me, where the expert humorist's best joke would have failed, for I do not laugh easily.

When we reached the White House and I was shaking hands with the President, he started to say something but I interrupted him and said,

"If your Excellency will excuse me, I will come back in a moment; but now I have a very important matter to attend to, and it must be attended to at once."

I turned to Mrs. Cleveland, the young, the beautiful, the fascinating, and gave her my card, on the back of which I had written *"He didn't"*—and I asked her to sign her name below those words.

She said "He didn't? He didn't what?"

"Oh," I said, "never mind. We cannot stop to discuss that now. This is urgent. Won't you please sign your name?" (I handed her a fountain pen.)

"Why," she said, "I cannot commit myself in that way. Who is it that didn't?—and what is it that he didn't?"

"Oh," I said, "time is flying, flying, flying. Won't you take me out of my distress and sign your name to it? It's all right. I give you my word it's all right."

She looked nonplused; but hesitatingly and mechanically she took the pen and said,

"I will sign it. I will take the risk. But you must tell me all about it, right afterward, so that you can be arrested before you get out of the house in case there should be anything criminal about this."

Then she signed; and I handed her Mrs. Clemens's note, which was very brief, very simple, and to the point. It said *"Don't wear your arctics in the White House."* It made her shout; and at my request she summoned a messenger and we sent that card at once to the mail on its way to Mrs. Clemens in Hartford.

1893–94   During 1893 and '94 we were living in Paris, the first half of the time at the Hotel Brighton, in the rue de Rivoli, the other half in a charming mansion in the rue de l'Université, on the other side of the Seine, which, by good luck, we had gotten hold of through another man's ill luck. This was Pomeroy, the artist. Illness in his family had made it necessary for him to go to the Riviera. He was paying thirty-six hundred dollars a year for the house, but allowed us to have it at twenty-six hundred. It was a lovely house; large, quaint, indefinite, charmingly furnished and decorated; built upon no particular plan; delightfully rambling, uncertain, and full of surprises. You were always getting lost in it, and finding nooks and corners and rooms which you didn't know were there and whose presence you had not suspected before. It was built by a rich French artist; and he had also furnished it and decorated it with his own hand. The studio was cosiness itself. We used it as drawing-room, sitting-room, living-room, dancing-room—we used it for everything. We couldn't get enough of it. It is odd that it should have been so cosy, for it was forty feet long, forty feet high, and thirty feet wide, with a vast fireplace on each side in the middle, and a musicians' gallery at one end. But we had, before this, found out that under the proper conditions spaciousness and cosiness do go together most affectionately and congruously. We had found it out a year or two earlier, when we were living in the Villa Viviani three miles outside the walls of Florence. That house had a room in it which was forty feet square and forty feet high, and at first we couldn't endure it. We called it the Mammoth Cave; we called it the skating-rink; we called it the Great Sahara; we called it all sorts of names intended to convey our disrespect. We had to pass through it to get from one end of the house to the other, but we passed straight through and did not loiter—and yet before long, and without our knowing how it came about, we found ourselves infesting that vast place day and night, and preferring it to any other part of the house.

Four or five years ago, when we took a house on the banks of the Hudson, at Riverdale, we drifted from room to room on our tour of inspection, always with a growing doubt as to whether we wanted that house or not. But at last when we arrived in a dining room that was sixty feet long, thirty feet wide, and had two great fireplaces in it, that settled it.

But I have wandered. What I was proposing to talk about was quite another matter—to wit: in that pleasant Paris house Mrs. Clemens gathered little dinner companies together once or twice a week, and it goes without saying that in these circumstances my defects had a large chance for display. *Always,* always without fail, as soon as the guests were out of the house, I saw that I had been miscarrying again. Mrs. Clemens explained to me the various things which I had been doing which should have been left undone, and she was always able to say,

"I have told you over and over again, yet you do these same things every time, just as if I never had warned you."

The children always waited up to have the joy of overhearing this. Nothing charmed them, nothing delighted them, nothing satisfied their souls like seeing me under the torture. The moment we started up stairs we would hear skurrying garments, and we knew that those children had been at it again. They had a name for this performance. They called it "dusting-off papa." They were obedient young rascals as a rule, by habit, by training, by long experience; but they drew the line there. They couldn't be persuaded to obey the command to stay out of hearing when I was being dusted off.

At last I had an inspiration. It is astonishing that it had not occurred to me earlier. I said,

"Why Livy, you know that dusting me off *after* these dinners is not the wise way. You could dust me off after every dinner for a year and I should always be just as competent to do the forbidden thing at each succeeding dinner as if you had not said a word, because in the meantime I have forgotten all these instructions. I think the correct way is for you to dust me off immediately before the guests arrive, and then I can keep some of it in my head and things will go better."

She recognized that that was wisdom, and that it was a very good idea. Then we set to work to arrange a system of signals to be delivered by her to me during dinner; signals which would indicate definitely which particular crime I was now engaged in, so that I could change to another. Apparently one of the children's most precious joys had come to an end and passed out of their life. I supposed that that was so, but it wasn't. The young unteachables got a screen arranged so that they could be behind it during the dinner and listen for the signals and entertain themselves with them. The system of signals was very simple, but it was very effective. If Mrs. Clemens happened to be so busy, at any time, talking with her elbow-neighbor, that she overlooked something that I was doing, she was sure to get a low-voiced hint from behind that screen in these words:

"Blue card, mamma;" or "red card, mamma"—"green card, mamma"—so that I was under double and triple guard. What the mother didn't notice the children detected for her.

As I say, the signals were quite simple, but very effective. At a hint from behind the screen, Livy would look down the table and say, in a voice full of interest, if not of counterfeited apprehension, "What did you do with the blue card that was on the dressing-table—"

That was enough. I knew what was happening—that I was talking the lady on my right to death and never paying any attention to the one on my left. The blue card meant "Let the lady on your right have a reprieve; destroy the one on your left;" so I would at once go to talking vigorously to the lady on my left. It wouldn't be long till there would be another hint, followed by a remark from Mrs. Clemens which had in it an apparently casual reference to a red card, which meant "Oh, are you going to sit there all the evening and never say anything? Do wake up and talk." So I waked up and drowned the table with talk. We had a number of cards, of different colors, each meaning a definite thing, each calling attention to some crime or other in my common list; and that system was exceedingly useful. It was entirely successful. It was like Buck Fanshaw's riot, it broke up the riot before it got a chance to begin. It headed off crime after crime all through the dinner, and I always came out at the end successful, triumphant, with large praises owing to me, and I got them on the spot.

It is a far call back over the accumulation of years to that night in the White House when Mrs. Cleveland signed the card. Many things have happened since then. The Cleveland family have been born since then. Ruth, the first-born, whom I never knew, but with whom I corresponded when she was a baby, lived to reach a blooming and lovely young maidenhood, then passed away.

To-day comes this letter, and it brings back the Clevelands, and the past, and my lost little correspondent.

> Editorial Department
> The Century Magazine. March 3, 1906.
> Union Square, New York.
> My dear Mr. Clemens:
>   President Finley and I are collecting letters to Ex-President Cleveland from his friends, appropriate to his 69th birthday.
>   If the plan appeals to you, will you kindly send a sealed greeting under cover to me at the above address, and I will send it, and the other letters, South to him in time for him to get them, all together, on the 18th of the present month.
>   Yours sincerely,
>   R. W. Gilder.
>   G.
> Mr. Samuel L. Clemens.

1867–69   When the little Ruth was about a year or a year and a half old, Mason, an old and valued friend of mine, was Consul General at Frankfort-on-the-Main. I had known him well in 1867, '68 and '69, in America, and I and mine had spent a good deal of time with him and his family in Frankfort
1878   in '78. He was a thoroughly competent, diligent, and conscientious official. Indeed he possessed these qualities in so large a degree that among American Consuls he might fairly be said to be monumental, for at that time our consular service was largely—and I think I may say mainly—in

the hands of ignorant, vulgar, and incapable men who had been political heelers in America, and had been taken care of by transference to consulates where they could be supported at the Government's expense instead of being transferred to the poor house, which would have been cheaper and more patriotic. Mason, in '78, had been Consul General in Frankfort several years—four, I think. He had come from Marseilles with a great record. He had been Consul there during thirteen years, and one part of his record was heroic. There had been a desolating cholera epidemic, and Mason was the only representative of any foreign country who stayed at his post and saw it through. And during that time he not only represented his own country, but he represented all the other countries in Christendom and did their work, and did it well and was praised for it by them in words of no uncertain sound. This great record of Mason's had saved him from official decapitation straight along while Republican Presidents occupied the chair, but now it was occupied by a Democrat. Mr. Cleveland was not seated in it—he was not yet inaugurated—before he was deluged with applications from Democratic politicians desiring the appointment of a thousand or so politically useful Democrats to Mason's place. Mason wrote me and asked me if I couldn't do something to save him from destruction.

Tuesday, March 6, 1906

Mr. Clemens makes Baby Ruth intercede in behalf of Mr. Mason, and he is retained in his place—Mr. Clemens's letter to Ex-President Cleveland— Mr. Cleveland as sheriff, in Buffalo—As Mayor he vetoes ordinance of railway corporation—Mr. Clemens and Mr. Cable visit Governor Cleveland at Capitol, Albany—Mr. Clemens sits on the bells and summons sixteen clerks—The Lyon of St. Mark.

I was very anxious to keep him in his place, but at first I could not think of any way to help him, for I was a mugwump. We, the mugwumps, a little company made up of the unenslaved of both parties, the very best men to be found in the two great parties—that was our idea of it—voted sixty thousand strong for Mr. Cleveland in New York and elected him. Our principles were high, and very definite. We were not a party; we had no candidates; we had no axes to grind. Our vote laid upon the man we cast it for no obligation of any kind. By our rule we could not ask for office; we could not accept office. When voting, it was our duty to vote for the best man, regardless of his party name. We had no other creed. Vote for the best man—that was creed enough.

Such being my situation, I was puzzled to know how to try to help Mason, and, at the same time, save my mugwump purity undefiled. It was a delicate place. But presently, out of the ruck of confusions in my mind, rose a sane thought, clear and bright—to wit: since it was a mugwump's duty to do his best to put the best man in office, necessarily it must be a mugwump's duty to try to *keep* the best man in when he was already there. My course was easy now. It might not be quite delicate for a mugwump to approach the President directly, but I could approach him indirectly, with all delicacy, since in that case not even courtesy would require him to take notice of an application which no one could prove had ever reached him.

Yes, it was easy and simple sailing now. I could lay the matter before Ruth, in her cradle, and wait for results. I wrote the little child, and said to her all that I have just been saying about mugwump principles and the limitations which they put upon me. I explained that it would not be proper for me to apply to her father in Mr. Mason's behalf, but I detailed to her Mr. Mason's high and honorable record and suggested that she take the matter in her own hands and do a patriotic work which I felt some delicacy about venturing upon myself. I asked her to forget that her father was only President of the United States, and her subject and servant; I asked her not to put her application in the form of a command, but to modify it, and give it the fictitious and pleasanter form of a mere request—that it would be no harm to let him gratify himself with the superstition that he was independent and could do as he pleased in the matter. I begged her to put stress, and plenty of it, upon the proposition that to keep Mason in his place would be a benefaction to the nation; to enlarge upon that, and keep still about all other considerations.

In due time I received a letter from the President, written with his own hand, signed by his own hand, acknowledging Ruth's intervention and thanking me for enabling him to save to the country the services of so good and well-tried a servant as Mason, and thanking me, also, for the detailed fulness of Mason's record, which could leave no doubt in any one's mind that Mason was in his right place and ought to be kept there.

In the beginning of Mr. Cleveland's second term a very strong effort to displace Mason was made, and Mason wrote me again. He was not hoping that we would succeed this time, because the assault upon his place was well organized, determined, and exceedingly powerful, but he hoped I would try again and see what I could do. I was not disturbed. It seemed to me that he did not know Mr. Cleveland or he would not be disturbed himself. I believed I knew Mr. Cleveland, and that he was not the man to budge an inch from his duty in any circumstances, and that he was a Gibraltar against whose solid bulk a whole Atlantic of assaulting politicians would dash itself in vain.

I wrote Ruth Cleveland once more. Mason remained in his place; and I think he would have remained in it without Ruth's intercession. There have been other Presidents since, but Mason's record has protected him, and the many and powerful efforts to dislodge him have all failed. Also, he has been complimented with promotions. He was promoted from Consul General in Frankfort to Consul General at Berlin, our highest consular post in Germany. A year ago he was promoted another step—to the consul-generalship in Paris, and he holds that place yet.

Ruth, the child, remained not long in the earth to help make it beautiful and to bless the home of her parents. But, little creature as she was, she did high service for her country, as I have shown, and it is right that this should be recorded and remembered.

In accordance with the suggestion made in Gilder's letter (as copied in yesterday's talk) I have written the following note to Ex-President Cleveland.

> Honored Sir: Your patriotic virtues have won for you the homage of half the nation and the enmity of the other half. This places your character as a citizen upon a summit as high as Washington's. The verdict is unanimous and unassailable. The votes of both sides are necessary in cases like these, and the votes of the one side are quite as valuable

as are the votes of the other. Where the votes are all in a public man's favor the verdict is against him. It is sand, and history will wash it away. But the verdict for you is rock, and will stand.

S.L. Clemens

As of date March 18/06.

When Mr. Cleveland was a member of a very strong and prosperous firm of lawyers, in Buffalo, just before the seventies, he was elected to the mayoralty. Presently a formidably rich and powerful railway corporation worked an ordinance through the city government whose purpose was to take possession of a certain section of the city inhabited altogether by the poor, the helpless, and the inconsequential, and drive those people out. Mr. Cleveland vetoed the ordinance. The other members of his law firm were indignant, and also terrified. To them the thing which he had done meant disaster to their business. They waited upon him and begged him to reconsider his action. He declined to do it. They insisted. He still declined. He said that his official position imposed upon him a duty which he could not honorably avoid; therefore he should be loyal to it; that the helpless situation of these inconsequential citizens made it his duty to stand by them and be their friend, since they had no other; that he was sorry if this conduct of his must bring disaster upon the firm, but that he had no choice; his duty was plain, and he would stick to the position which he had taken. They intimated that this would lose him his place in the firm. He said he did not wish to be a damage to the co-partnership, therefore they could remove his name from it, and without any hard feeling on his part.

During the time that we were living in Buffalo in '70 and '71, Mr. Cleveland was sheriff, *1870–71* but I never happened to make his acquaintance, or even see him. In fact, I suppose I was not even aware of his existence. Fourteen years later, he was become the greatest man in the State. I was not living in the State at the time. He was Governor, and was about to step into the post of President of the United States. At that time I was on the public highway in company with another bandit, George W. Cable. We were robbing the public with readings from our works during four months—and in the course of time we went to Albany to levy tribute, and I said "We ought to go and pay our respects to the Governor."

So Cable and I went to that majestic Capitol building and stated our errand. We were shown into the Governor's private office, and I saw Mr. Cleveland for the first time. We three stood chatting together. I was born lazy, and I comforted myself by turning the corner of a table into a sort of seat. Presently the Governor said,

"Mr. Clemens, I was a fellow citizen of yours in Buffalo a good many months, a good while ago, and during those months you burst suddenly into a mighty fame, out of a previous long continued and no doubt proper obscurity—but I was a nobody, and you wouldn't notice me nor have anything to do with me. But now that I have become somebody, you have changed your style, and you come here to shake hands with me and be sociable. How do you explain this kind of conduct?"

"Oh," I said, "it is very simple, your Excellency. In Buffalo you were nothing but a sheriff. I was in society. I couldn't afford to associate with sheriffs. But you are a Governor, now, and you are on your way to the Presidency. It is a great difference, and it makes you worth while."

There appeared to be about sixteen doors to that spacious room. From each door a young man now emerged, and the sixteen lined up and moved forward and stood in front of the Governor with an aspect of respectful expectancy in their attitude. No one spoke for a moment. Then the Governor said,

"You are dismissed, gentlemen. Your services are not required. Mr. Clemens is sitting on the bells."

There was a cluster of sixteen bell-buttons on the corner of the table; my proportions at that end of me were just right to enable me to cover the whole of that nest, and that is how I came to hatch out those sixteen clerks.

While I think of it—last year when we were summering in that incomparable region, that perfection of inland grace and charm and loveliness which is not to be found elsewhere on the planet—the New Hampshire hills—our nearest neighbors were the Abbott Thayers, that family of gifted artists, old friends of mine. They lived down hill in a break in the forest, a quarter or a half-mile away; and for a few days they had as guests a couple of bright and lovely young fellows, to wit: Bynner, the young poet, a member of McClure's magazine staff, and Guy Faulkner, of the staff of another of the magazines. I had never seen them, but as their trade and mine was the same, they wanted to come and see me. They discussed the proprieties of this invasion a day or two and tried to make up their minds. They knew Miss Lyon, my secretary, very well. At last one of them said "Oh come, it'll be all right. Let's go up and see the lions." The other said "But how do we know that the old lion is there just now?" To this remark came the reply "Well, we can see the Lyon of St. Mark, anyway."

Wednesday, March 7, 1906

Susy's Biography—John Hay incident—Giving the young girl the French novel—Susy and her father escort Mrs. Clemens to train, then go over Brooklyn Bridge—On the way to Vassar they discuss German profanity— Mr. Clemens tells of the sweet and profane German nurse—The arrival at Vassar and the dreary reception—Told by Susy—The reading, etc.— Mr. Clemens's opinion of girls—He is to talk to the Barnard girls this afternoon.

From Susy's Biography.

The next day mamma planned to take the four o'clock car back to Hartford. We rose quite early that morning and went to the Vienna Bakery and took breakfast there. From there we went to a German bookstore and bought some German books for Clara's birthday.

Dear me, the power of association to snatch mouldy dead memories out of their graves and make them walk! That remark about buying foreign books throws a sudden white glare upon the distant past; and I see the long stretch of a New York street with an unearthly vividness, and John Hay walking down it, grave and remorseful. I was walking down it too, that morning, and I overtook Hay and asked him what the trouble was. He turned a lusterless eye upon me and said:

"My case is beyond cure. In the most innocent way in the world I have committed a crime which will never be forgiven by the sufferers, for they will never believe—oh, well, no, I was going to say they would never believe that I did the thing innocently. The truth is they will know that I acted innocently, because they are rational people; but what of that? I never can look them in the face again—nor they me, perhaps."

Hay was a young bachelor, and at that time was on the *Tribune* staff. He explained his trouble in these words, substantially:

1869

"When I was passing along here yesterday morning on my way down town to the office, I stepped into a bookstore where I am acquainted, and asked if they had anything new from the other side. They handed me a French novel, in the usual yellow paper cover, and I carried it away. I didn't even look at the title of it. It was for recreation-reading, and I was on my way to my work. I went mooning and dreaming along, and I think I hadn't gone more than fifty yards when I heard my name called. I stopped, and a private carriage drew up at the sidewalk and I shook hands with the inmates—mother and young daughter, excellent people. They were on their way to the steamer to sail for Paris. The mother said,

"'I saw that book in your hand and I judged by the look of it that it was a French novel. Is it?'

"I said it was.

"She said, 'Do let me have it, so that my daughter can practise her French on it on the way over.'

"Of course I handed her the book, and we parted. Ten minutes ago I was passing that bookstore again, and some devil's inspiration reminded me of yesterday and I stepped in and fetched away another copy of that book. Here it is. Read the first page of it. That is enough. You will know what the rest is like. I think it must be the foulest book in the French language— one of the foulest, anyway. I would be ashamed to offer it to a harlot—but, oh dear, I gave it to that sweet young girl without shame. Take my advice; don't give away a book until you have examined it."

From Susy's Biography.

Then mamma and I went to do some shopping and papa went to see General Grant. After we had finnished doing our shopping we went home to the hotel together. When we entered our rooms in the hotel we saw on the table a vase full of exquisett red roses. Mamma who is very fond of flowers exclaimed "Oh I wonder who could have sent them." We both looked at the card in the midst of the roses and saw that it was written on in papa's handwriting, it was written in German. "Liebes Geshchenk on die Mamma." (I am sure I didn't say "on"—that is Susy's spelling, not mine; also I am sure I didn't spell Geschenk so liberally as all that. S.L.C.) Mamma was delighted. Papa came home and gave mamma her ticket; and after visiting a while with her went to see Major Pond and mamma and I sat down to our lunch. After lunch most of our time was taken up with packing, and at about three o'clock we went to escort mamma to the train. We got on board the train with her and stayed with her about five minutes and then we said good-bye to her and the train started for Hartford. It was the first time I had ever beene away from home without mamma in my life, although I was 13 yrs. old. Papa and I drove back to the hotel and got Major Pond and then went to see the Brooklyn Bridge we went across it to

Brooklyn on the cars and then walked back across it from Brooklyn to New York. We enjoyed looking at the beautiful scenery and we could see the bridge moove under the intense heat of the sun. We had a perfectly delightful time, but weer pretty tired when we got back to the hotel.

The next morning we rose early, took our breakfast and took an early train to Pough-keepsie. We had a very pleasant journey to Poughkeepsie. The Hudson was magnificent—shrouded with beautiful mist. When we arived at Poughkeepsie it was raining quite hard; which fact greatly dissapointed me because I very much wanted to see the outside of the buildings of Vasser College and as it rained that would be impossible. It was quite a long drive from the station to Vasser College and papa and I had a nice long time to discuss and laugh over German profanity. One of the German phrases papa particularly enjoys is "O heilige maria Mutter Jesus!" Jean has a German nurse, and this was one of her phrases, there was a time when Jean exclaimed "Ach Gott!" to every trifle, but when mamma found it out she was shocked and instantly put a stop to it.

It brings that pretty little German girl vividly before me—a sweet and innocent and plump little creature with peachy cheeks; a clear-souled little maiden and without offence, notwith-standing her profanities, and she was loaded to the eyebrows with them. She was a mere child. She was not fifteen yet. She was just from Germany, and knew no English. She was always scattering her profanities around, and they were such a satisfaction to me that I never dreamed of such a thing as modifying her. For my own sake, I had no disposition to tell on her. Indeed I took pains to keep her from being found out. I told her to confine her religious exercises to the children's quarters, and urged her to remember that Mrs. Clemens was prejudiced against pieties on week days. To the children, the little maid's profanities sounded natural and proper and right, because they had been used to that kind of talk in Germany, and they attached no evil importance to it. It grieves me that I have forgotten those vigorous remarks. I long hoarded them in my memory as a treasure. But I remember one of them still, because I heard it so many times. The trial of that little creature's life was the children's hair. She would tug and strain with her comb, accompanying her work with her misplaced pieties. And when finally she was through with her triple job she always fired up and exploded her thanks toward the sky, where they belonged, in this form: "Gott sei Dank ich bin schon fertig mit'm Gott verdammtes Haar!" (I believe I am not quite brave enough to translate it.)

From Susy's Biography.

We at length reached Vassar College and she looked very finely, her buildings and her grounds being very beautiful. We went to the front doore and rang the bell. The young girl who came to the doore wished to know who we wanted to see. Evidently we were not expected. Papa told her who we wanted to see and she showed us to the parlor. We waited, no one came; and waited, no one came, still no one came. It was beginning to seem pretty awkward, "Oh well this is a pretty piece of business," papa exclaimed. At length we heard footsteps coming down the long corridor and Miss C, (the lady who had invited papa) came into the room. She greeted papa very pleasantly and they had a nice little chatt to-gether. Soon the lady principal also entered and she was very pleasant and agreable. She showed us to our rooms and said she would send for us when dinner was ready. We went into our rooms, but we had nothing to do for half an hour exept to watch the rain drops as they fell upon the window panes. At last we were called to dinner, and I went down without papa as he never eats anything in the middle of the day. I sat at the table with the lady principal and enjoyed very much seing all the young girls trooping into the dining-room. After dinner I went around the College with the young ladies and papa stayed in his room and smoked. When it was supper time papa went down and ate supper with us and we had a very delightful supper. After supper the young ladies went to their rooms to dress for the evening. Papa went to his room and I went with the lady principal. At length the guests began to arive, but papa still remained in his room until called for. Papa read in the chapell. It was the first time I had ever heard him read in my life—that is in public. When he came out on to the stage I remember the people behind me exclaimed "Oh how queer he is! Isn't he funny!" I thought papa was very funny, although I did not think him queer. He read "A Trying Situation" and "The Golden Arm," a ghost story that he heard down South when he was a little boy. "The Golden Arm" papa had told me before, but he had startled me so that I did not much wish to hear it again. But I had resolved this time to be prepared and not to let myself be startled, but still papa did, and very very much; he startled the whole roomful of people and they jumped as one man. The other story was also very funny and interesting and I enjoyed the evening inexpressibly much. After papa had finished reading we all went down to the collation in the dining-room and after that there was dancing and singing. Then the guests went away and papa and I went to bed. The next morning we rose early, took an early train for Hartford and reached Hartford at ½ past 2 o'clock. We were very glad to get back.

How charitably she treats that ghastly experience! It is a dear and lovely disposition, and a most valuable one, that can brush away indignities and discourtesies and seek and find the pleasanter features of an experience. Susy had that disposition, and it was one of the jewels of her character that had come to her straight from her mother. It is a feature that was left out of me at birth. And, at seventy, I have not yet acquired it. I did not go to Vassar College profes-sionally, but as a guest—as a guest, and gratis. Aunt Clara (now Mrs. John B. Stanchfield) was a graduate of Vassar and it was to please her that I inflicted that journey upon Susy and myself. The invitation had come to me from both the lady mentioned by Susy and the President of the College—a sour old saint who has probably been gathered to his fathers long ago; and I hope they enjoy him; I hope they value his society. I think I can get along without it, in either end of the next world.

We arrived at the College in that soaking rain, and Susy has described, with just a sugges-tion of dissatisfaction, the sort of reception we got. Susy had to sit in her damp clothes half an hour while we waited in the parlor; then she was taken to a fireless room and left to wait there again, as she has stated. I do not remember that President's name, and I am sorry. He did not put in an appearance until it was time for me to step upon the platform in front of that great garden of young and lovely blossoms. He caught up with me and advanced upon the platform with me and was going to introduce me. I said in substance:

"You have allowed me to get along without your help thus far, and if you will retire from the platform I will try to do the rest without it."

I did not see him any more, but I detest his memory. Of course my resentment did not extend to the students, and so I had an unforgetable good time talking to them. And I think they had a good time too, for they responded "as one man," to use Susy's unimprovable phrase.

Girls are charming creatures. I shall have to be twice seventy years old before I change my mind as to that. I am to talk to a crowd of them this afternoon, students of Barnard College, (the sex's annex to Columbia University,) and I think I shall have just as pleasant a time with those lassies as I had with the Vassar girls twenty-one years ago.

Thursday, March 8, 1906

The Barnard lecture—Subject Morals—Letter from brother of Captain Toncray—Mr. Clemens replied that original of "Huckleberry Finn" was Tom Blankenship—Tom's father Town Drunkard—Describes Tom's character—Death of Injun Joe—Storm which came that night—Incident of the Episcopal sextons and their reforms—Mr. Dawson's school in Hannibal—Arch Fuqua's great gift.

It turned out just so. It was an affectionate and hilarious good time. Miss Taylor, and two other charming girls, conveyed me from this house—corner of 9th street and Fifth Avenue—to the College by way of Central Park and Riverside Drive, and properly petted me and flattered me all the way, in accordance with the conditions which I had already exacted of Miss Taylor and Mrs. (Professor) Lord—these conditions being that I must be caressed and complimented all the way. Miss Russell, President of Barnard, is young and beautiful. I found in the Dean, Miss Hill, an acquaintance of many years ago, when she was a junior in Smith College. We three went on the stage together. The floor and the gallery were compactly jammed with the youth and beauty and erudition of Barnard—a satisfying spectacle to look at.

I put my watch on the table and kept game myself, allowing myself an hour. I lectured upon Morals; and earnestly, imploringly, and even pathetically, inculcated them and urged them upon those masses of girls—along with illustrations—more illustrations than morals—and I never knew so grave a subject to create so much noise before.

A reception followed. I had the privilege of shaking hands with all of them, and was flattered to my content, and told them so. They all said that my lessons had gone home to them and that from now on they should lead a better life.

For thirty years, I have received an average of a dozen letters a year from strangers who remember me, or whose fathers remember me as boy and young man. But these letters are almost always disappointing. I have not known these strangers nor their fathers. I have not heard of the names they mention; the reminiscences to which they call my attention have had no part in my experience; all of which means that these strangers have been mistaking me for somebody else. But at last I have the refreshment, this morning, of a letter from a man who deals in names that were familiar to me in my boyhood. The writer encloses a newspaper clipping which has been wandering through the press for four or five weeks, and he wants to know if his brother, Captain Toncray, was really the original of "Huckleberry Finn."

"HUCKLEBERRY FINN" DEAD.

Original of Mark Twain's Famous Character
Had Led Quiet Life in Idaho.

[BY DIRECT WIRE TO THE TIMES.]
WALLACE (Idaho) Feb. 2.—[Exclusive Dispatch.] Capt. A. O. Toncray, commonly known as "Huckleberry Finn," said to be the original of Mark Twain's famous character, was found dead in his room at Murray this morning from heart failure.

Capt. Toncray, a native of Hannibal, Mo., was 65 years old. In early life, he ran on steamboats on the Mississippi and the Missouri rivers, in frequent contact with Samuel L. Clemens, and tradition has it "Mark Twain" later used Toncray as his model for "Huckleberry Finn." He came to Murray in 1884 and had been living a quiet life since. *1884*

I have replied that "Huckleberry Finn" was Tom Blankenship. As this inquirer evidently knew the Hannibal of the forties, he will easily recall Tom Blankenship. Tom's father was at one time Town Drunkard, an exceedingly well defined and unofficial office of those days. He succeeded "General" Gaines, and for a time he was sole and only incumbent of the office; but afterward Jimmy Finn proved competency and disputed the place with him, so we had two town-drunkards at one time—and it made as much trouble in that village as Christendom experienced in the fourteenth century when there were two Popes at the same time.

In "Huckleberry Finn" I have drawn Tom Blankenship exactly as he was. He was ignorant, unwashed, insufficiently fed; but he had as good a heart as ever any boy had. His liberties were totally unrestricted. He was the only really independent person—boy or man—in the community, and by consequence he was tranquilly and continuously happy, and was envied by all the rest of us. We liked him; we enjoyed his society. And as his society was forbidden us by our parents, the prohibition trebled and quadrupled its value, and therefore we sought and got more of his society than of any other boy's. I heard, four years ago, that he was Justice of the Peace in a remote village in Montana, and was a good citizen and greatly respected.

During Jimmy Finn's term he (Jimmy) was not exclusive; he was not finical; he was not hypercritical; he was largely and handsomely democratic—and slept in the deserted tan-yard with the hogs. My father tried to reform him once, but did not succeed. My father was not a professional reformer. In him the spirit of reform was spasmodic. It only broke out now and then, with considerable intervals between. Once he tried to reform Injun Joe. That also was a failure. It was a failure, and we boys were glad. For Injun Joe, drunk, was interesting and a benefaction to us, but Injun Joe, sober, was a dreary spectacle. We watched my father's experiments upon him with a good deal of anxiety, but it came out all right and we were satisfied. Injun Joe got drunk oftener than before, and became intolerably interesting.

I think that in "Tom Sawyer" I starved Injun Joe to death in the cave. But that may have been to meet the exigencies of romantic literature. I can't remember now whether he died in the cave or out of it, but I do remember that the news of his death reached me at a most unhappy time—that is to say, just at bedtime on a summer night when a prodigious storm of thunder and lightning accompanied by a deluging rain that turned the streets and lanes into rivers, caused me to repent and resolve to lead a better life. I can remember those awful thunder-bursts and the white glare of the lightning yet, and the wild lashing of the rain against the window-panes. By my teachings I perfectly well knew what all the wild riot was for—Satan had come to get Injun Joe. I had no shadow of doubt about it. It was the proper thing when a person like Injun Joe was required in the underworld, and I should have thought it strange and unaccountable if Satan had come for him in a less impressive way. With every glare of lightning I shriveled and shrunk together in mortal terror, and in the interval of black darkness that followed I poured out my lamentings over my lost condition, and my supplications for just one more chance, with an energy and feeling and sincerity quite foreign to my nature.

But in the morning I saw that it was a false alarm and concluded to resume business at the old stand and wait for another reminder.

The axiom says "History repeats itself." A week or two ago my nephew, by marriage, Edward Loomis, dined with us, along with his wife, my niece (née Julie Langdon). He is Vice-President of the Delaware and Lackawanna Railway system. The duties of his office used to carry him frequently to Elmira, New York; the exigencies of his courtship carried him there still oftener, and so in the course of time he came to know a good many of the citizens of that place. At dinner he mentioned a circumstance which flashed me back over about sixty years and landed me in that little bedroom on that tempestuous night, and brought to my mind how creditable to me was my conduct through that whole night, and how barren it was of moral spot or fleck during that entire period: he said Mr. Buckly was sexton, or something, of the Episcopal church in Elmira, and had been for many years the competent superintendent of all the church's worldly affairs, and was regarded by the whole congregation as a stay, a blessing, a priceless treasure. But he had a couple of defects—not large defects, but they seemed large when flung against the background of his profoundly religious character: he drank a good deal, and he could outswear a brakeman. A movement arose to persuade him to lay aside these vices, and after consulting with his pal, who occupied the same position as himself in the other Episcopal church, and whose defects were duplicates of his own and had inspired regret in the congregation he was serving, they concluded to try for reform—not wholesale, but half at a time. They took the liquor pledge and waited for results. During nine days the results were entirely satisfactory, and they were recipients of many compliments and much congratulation. Then on New Year's Eve they had business a mile and a half out of town, just beyond the New York State line. Everything went well with them that evening in the bar-room of the inn—but at last the celebration of the occasion by those villagers came to be of a burdensome nature. It was a bitter cold night and the multitudinous hot toddies that were circulating began by and by to exert a powerful influence upon the new prohibitionists. At last Buckly's friend remarked,

"Buckly, does it occur to you that we are *outside the diocese?*"

That ended reform No. 1. Then they took a chance in reform No. 2. For a while that one prospered, and they got much applause. I now reach the incident which sent me back a matter of sixty years, as I have remarked a while ago.

One morning this step-nephew of mine, Loomis, met Buckly on the street and said,

"You have made a gallant struggle against those defects of yours. I am aware that you failed on No. 1, but I am also aware that you are having better luck with No. 2."

"Yes," Buckly said, "No. 2 is all right and sound up to date, and we are full of hope."

Loomis said, "Buckly, of course you have your troubles like other people, but they never show on the outside. I have never seen you when you were not cheerful. Are you always cheerful? Really always cheerful?"

"Well, no" he said, "no, I can't say that I am always cheerful, but— well, you know that kind of a night that comes: *say*—you wake up 'way in the night and the whole world is sunk in gloom and there are storms and earthquakes and all sorts of disasters in the air threatening, and you get cold and clammy; and when that happens to me I recognize how sinful I am and it all goes clear to my heart and wrings it and I have such terrors and terrors!—oh they are indescribable, those terrors that assail and thrill me, and I slip out of bed and get on my knees and pray and pray and pray and promise that I *will* be good, if I can only have another chance. And then, you know, in the morning the sun shines out *so* lovely, and the birds sing and the whole world is so beautiful, and—*b' God I rally!*"

Now I will quote a brief paragraph from this letter which I have received from Mr. Toncray. He says:

> You no doubt are at a loss to know who I am. I will tell you. In my younger days I was a resident of Hannibal, Mo., and you and I were schoolmates attending Mr. Dawson's school along with Sam and Will Bowen and Andy Fuqua and others whose names I have forgotten. I was then about the smallest boy in school, for my age, and they called me little Aleck Toncray for short.

I don't remember Aleck Toncray, but I knew those other people as well as I knew the town-drunkards. I remember Dawson's schoolhouse perfectly. If I wanted to describe it I could save myself the trouble by conveying the description of it to these pages from "Tom Sawyer." I can remember the drowsy and inviting summer sounds that used to float in through the open windows from that distant boy-paradise, Cardiff Hill, (Holliday's Hill,) and mingle with the murmurs of the studying pupils and make them the more dreary by the contrast. I remember Andy Fuqua, the oldest pupil—a man of twenty-five. I remember the youngest pupil, Nannie Owsley, a child of seven. I remember George Robards, eighteen or twenty years old, the only pupil who studied Latin. I remember—in some cases vividly, in others vaguely—the rest of the twenty-five boys and girls. I remember Mr. Dawson very well. I remember his boy, Theodore, who was as good as he could be. In fact he was inordinately good, extravagantly good, offensively good, detestably good—and he had pop-eyes—and I would have drowned him if I had had a chance. In that school we were all about on an equality, and, so far as I remember, the passion of envy had no place in our hearts, except in the case of Arch Fuqua—the other one's brother. Of course we all went barefoot in the summertime. Arch Fuqua was about my own age—ten or eleven. In the winter we could stand him, because he wore shoes then, and his great gift was hidden from our sight and we were enabled to forget it. But in the summertime he was a bitterness to us. He was our envy, for he could double back his big toe and let it fly and you could hear it snap thirty yards. There was not another boy in the school that could approach this feat. He had not a rival as regards a physical distinction—except in Theodore Eddy, who could work his ears like a horse. But he was no real rival, because you couldn't hear him work his ears; so all the advantage lay with Arch Fuqua.

I am not done with Dawson's school; I will return to it in a later chapter.

Friday, March 9, 1906

Mr. Clemens tells of several of his schoolmates in Mr. Dawson's Hannibal school—George Robards and Mary Moss—John Robards, who traveled far—John Garth and Helen Kercheval—Mr. Kercheval's slave woman and his apprentice save Mr. Clemens from drowning in Bear Creek—Meredith, who became a guerrilla chief in Civil War—Will and Sam Bowen, Mississippi pilots—Died of yellow fever.

1845   I am talking of a time sixty years ago, and upwards. I remember the names of some of those schoolmates, and, by fitful glimpses, even their faces rise dimly before me for a moment—only just long enough to be recognized; then they vanish. I catch glimpses of George Robards, the Latin pupil—slender, pale, studious, bending over his book and absorbed in it, his long straight black hair hanging down below his jaws like a pair of curtains on the sides of his face. I can see him give his head a toss and flirt one of the curtains back around his head—to get it out of his way, apparently; really to show off. In that day it was a great thing among the boys to have hair of so flexible a sort that it could be flung back in that way, with a flirt of the head. George Robards was the envy of us all. For there was no hair among us that was so competent for this exhibition as his—except, perhaps, the yellow locks of Will Bowen and John Robards. My hair was a dense ruck of short curls, and so was my brother Henry's. We tried all kinds of devices to get these crooks straightened out so that they would flirt, but we never succeeded. Sometimes, by soaking our heads and then combing and brushing our hair down tight and flat to our skulls, we could get it straight, temporarily, and this gave us a comforting moment of joy; but the first time we gave it a flirt it all shriveled into curls again and our happiness was gone.

George was a fine young fellow in all ways. He and Mary Moss were sweethearts and pledged to eternal constancy, from a time when they were merely children. But Mr. Lakenan arrived now and became a resident. He took an important position in the little town at once, and maintained it. He brought with him a distinguished reputation as a lawyer. He was educated, cultured; he was grave even to austerity; he was dignified in his conversation and deportment. He was a rather oldish bachelor—as bachelor oldishness was estimated in that day. He was a rising man. He was contemplated with considerable awe by the community, and as a catch he stood at the top of the market. That blooming and beautiful thing, Mary Moss, attracted his favor. He laid siege to her and won. Everybody said she accepted him to please her parents, not herself. They were married. And everybody again, testifying, said he continued her schooling all by himself, proposing to educate her up to standard and make her a meet companion for him. These things may be true. They may not be true. But they were interesting. That is the main requirement in a village like that. George went away, presently, to some far-off region and there he died—of a broken heart, everybody said. That could be true, for he had good cause. He would go far before he would find another Mary Moss.

How long ago that little tragedy happened! None but the white heads know about it now. Lakenan is dead these many years, but Mary still lives, and is still beautiful, although she has grandchildren. I saw her and one of her married daughters when I went out to Missouri four years ago to receive an honorary LL.D. from Missouri University.

John Robards was the little brother of George; he was a wee chap with silky golden curtains to his face which dangled to his shoulders and below, and could be flung back ravishingly. When he was twelve years old he crossed the plains with his father amidst the rush of the gold seekers of '49; and I remember the departure of the cavalcade when it spurred westward. We *1849* were all there to see and to envy. And I can still see that proud little chap sailing by on a great horse, with his long locks streaming out behind. We were all on hand to gaze and envy when he returned, two years later, in unimaginable glory—*for he had traveled!* None of us had ever been forty miles from home. But he had crossed the continent. He had been in the gold-mines, that fairyland of our imagination. And he had done a still more wonderful thing. He had been in ships—in ships on the actual ocean; in ships on three actual oceans. For he had sailed down the Pacific and around the Horn among icebergs and through snow-storms and wild wintry gales, and had sailed on and turned the corner and flown northward in the trades and up through the blistering equatorial waters—and there in his brown face were the proofs of what he had been through. We would have sold our souls to Satan for the privilege of trading places with him.

I saw him when I was out on that Missouri trip four years ago. He was old then—though not quite so old as I—and the burden of life was upon him. He said his granddaughter, twelve years old, had read my books and would like to see me. It was a pathetic time, for she was a prisoner in her room and marked for death. And John knew that she was passing swiftly away. Twelve years old—just her grandfather's age when he rode away on that great journey with his yellow hair flapping behind him. In her I seemed to see that boy again. It was as if he had come back out of that remote past and was present before me in his golden youth. Her malady was heart disease, and her brief life came to a close a few days later.

Another of those schoolboys was John Garth. And one of the prettiest of the schoolgirls was Helen Kercheval. They grew up and married. He became a prosperous banker and a prominent and valued citizen; and a few years ago he died, rich and honored. *He died.* It is what I have to say about so many of those boys and girls. The widow still lives, and there are grandchildren. In her pantalette days and my barefoot days she was a schoolmate of mine. I saw John's tomb when I made that Missouri visit.

Her father, Mr. Kercheval, had an apprentice in the early days when I was nine years old, and he had also a slave woman who had many merits. But I can't feel very kindly or forgivingly toward either that good apprentice boy or that good slave woman, for they saved my life. One day when I was playing on a loose log which I supposed was attached to a raft—but it wasn't—it tilted me into Bear Creek. And when I had been under water twice and was coming up to make the third and fatal descent my fingers appeared above the water and that slave woman seized them and pulled me out. Within a week I was in again, and that apprentice had to come along just at the wrong time, and he plunged in and dived, pawed around on the bottom and found me, and dragged me out and emptied the water out of me, and I was saved again. I was drowned seven times after that before I learned to swim—once in Bear Creek and six times in the Mississippi. I do not now know who the people were who interfered with the intentions of a Providence wiser than themselves, but I hold a grudge against them yet. When I told the tale of these remarkable happenings to Rev. Dr. Burton of Hartford, he said he did not believe it. *He slipped on the ice the very next year and sprained his ancle.*

Another schoolmate was John Meredith, a boy of a quite uncommonly sweet and gentle disposition. He grew up, and when the Civil War broke out he became a sort of guerrilla chief on the Confederate side, and I was told that in his raids upon Union families in the country parts of Monroe County—in earlier times the friends and familiars of his father— he was remorseless in his devastations and sheddings of blood. It seems almost incredible that this could have been that gentle comrade of my school days; yet it can be true, for Robespierre when he was young was like that. John has been in his grave many and many a year.

Will Bowen was another schoolmate, and so was his brother, Sam, who was his junior by a couple of years. Before the Civil War broke out both became St. Louis and New Orleans pilots. While Sam was still very young he had a curious adventure. He fell in love with a girl of sixteen, only child of a very wealthy German brewer. He wanted to marry her, but he and she both thought that the papa would not only not consent, but would shut his door against Sam. The old man was not so disposed, but they were not aware of that. He had his eye upon them, and it was not a hostile eye. That indiscreet young couple got to living together sur- reptitiously. Before long the old man died. When the will was examined it was found that he had left the whole of his wealth to Mrs. Samuel A. Bowen. Then the poor things made another mistake. They rushed down to the German suburb, Carondelet, and got a German magistrate to marry them and date the marriage back a few months. The old brewer had some nieces and nephews and cousins, and different kinds of assets of that sort, and they traced out the fraud and proved it and got the property. This left Sam with a girl wife on his hands and the necessity of earning a living for her at the pilot wheel. After a few years Sam and another pilot were bringing a boat up from New Orleans when the yellow fever broke out among the few passengers and the crew. Both pilots were stricken with it and there was nobody to take their place at the wheel. The boat was landed at the head of Island 82 to wait for succor. Death came swiftly to both pilots—and there they lie buried, unless the river has cut the graves away and washed the bones into the stream, a thing which has probably hap- pened long ago.

Monday, March 12, 1906

Mr. Clemens comments on the killing of six hundred Moros—Men, women and children—In a crater bowl near Jolo in the Philippines—Our troops commanded by General Wood—Contrasts this "battle" with various other details of our military history—The newspapers' attitude toward the announcements—The President's message of congratulation.

We will stop talking about my schoolmates of sixty years ago, for the present, and return to them later. They strongly interest me, and I am not going to leave them alone permanently. Strong as that interest is, it is for the moment pushed out of the way by an incident of to-day, which is still stronger. This incident burst upon the world last Friday in an official cablegram from the commander of our forces in the Philippines to our Government at Washington. The substance of it was as follows:

A tribe of Moros, dark skinned savages, had fortified themselves in the bowl of an extinct crater not many miles from Jolo; and as they were hostiles, and bitter against us because we have been trying for eight years to take their liberties away from them, their presence in that position was a menace. Our commander, General Leonard Wood, ordered a reconnaissance. It was found that the Moros numbered six hundred, counting women and children; that their crater bowl was in the summit of a peak or mountain twenty-two hundred feet above sea level, and very difficult of access for Christian troops and artillery. Then General Wood ordered a surprise, and went along himself to see the order carried out. Our troops climbed the heights by devious and difficult trails, and even took some artillery with them. The kind of artillery is not specified, but in one place it was hoisted up a sharp acclivity by tackle a distance of some three hundred feet. Arrived at the rim of the crater, the battle began. Our soldiers numbered five hundred and forty. They were assisted by auxiliaries consisting of a detachment of native constabulary in our pay—their numbers not given—and by a naval detachment, whose numbers are not stated. But apparently the contending parties were about equal as to number—six hundred men on our side, on the edge of the bowl; six hundred men, women and children in the bottom of the bowl. Depth of the bowl, fifty feet.

General Wood's order was "Kill or capture the six hundred."

The battle began—it is officially called by that name—our forces firing down into the crater with their artillery and their deadly small arms of precision; the savages furiously returning the fire, probably with brickbats—though this is merely a surmise of mine, as the weapons used by the savages are not nominated in the cablegram. Heretofore the Moros have used knives and clubs mainly; also ineffectual trade-muskets when they had any.

The official report stated that the battle was fought with prodigious energy on both sides during a day and a half, and that it ended with a complete victory for the American arms. The completeness of the victory is established by this fact: that of the six hundred Moros not one was left alive. The brilliancy of the victory is established by this other fact, to wit: that of our six hundred heroes only fifteen lost their lives.

General Wood was present and looking on. His order had been "Kill *or* capture those savages." Apparently our little army considered that the "or" left them authorized to kill *or* capture according to taste, and that their taste had remained what it has been for eight years, in our army out there—the taste of Christian butchers.

The official report quite properly extolled and magnified the "heroism" and "gallantry" of our troops; lamented the loss of the fifteen who perished, and elaborated the wounds of thirty-two of our men who suffered injury, and even minutely and faithfully described the nature of the wounds, in the interest of future historians of the United States. It mentioned that a private had one of his elbows scraped by a missile, and the private's name was mentioned. Another private had the end of his nose scraped by a missile. His name was also mentioned—by cable, at one dollar and fifty cents a word.

Next day's news confirmed the previous day's report and named our fifteen killed and thirty-two wounded *again,* and once more described the wounds and gilded them with the right adjectives.

Let us now consider two or three details of our military history. In one of the great battles of the Civil War 10 per cent of the forces engaged on the two sides were killed and wounded. At Waterloo, where four hundred thousand men were present on the two sides, fifty thousand fell, killed and wounded, in five hours, leaving three hundred and fifty thousand sound and all right for further adventures. Eight years ago, when the pathetic comedy called the Cuban war was played, we summoned two hundred and fifty thousand men. We fought a number of showy battles, and when the war was over we had lost two hundred and sixty-eight men out of our two hundred and fifty thousand, in killed and wounded in the field, and just *fourteen times as many* by the gallantry of the army doctors in the hospitals and camps. We did not exterminate the Spaniards—far from it. In each engagement we left an average of *2 per cent* of the enemy killed or crippled on the field.

Contrast these things with the great statistics which have arrived from that Moro crater! There, with six hundred engaged on each side, we lost fifteen men killed outright, and we had thirty-two wounded—counting that nose and that elbow. The enemy numbered six hundred—including women and children—and we abolished them utterly, leaving not even a baby alive to cry for its dead mother. *This is incomparably the greatest victory that was ever achieved by the Christian soldiers of the United States.*

Now then, how has it been received? The splendid news appeared with splendid display-heads in every newspaper in this city of four million and thirteen thousand inhabitants, on Friday morning. But there was not a single reference to it in the editorial columns of any one of those newspapers. The news appeared again in all the evening papers of Friday, and again those papers were editorially silent upon our vast achievement. Next day's additional statistics and particulars appeared in all the morning papers, and still without a line of editorial rejoicing or a mention of the matter in any way. These additions appeared in the evening papers of that same day (Saturday) and again without a word of comment. In the columns devoted to correspondence, in the morning and evening papers of Friday and Saturday, nobody said a word about the "battle." Ordinarily those columns are teeming with the passions of the citizen; he lets no incident go by, whether it be large or small, without pouring out his praise or blame, his joy or his indignation about the matter in the correspondence column. But, as I have said, during those two days he was as silent as the editors themselves. So far as I can find out, there was only one person among our eighty millions who allowed himself the privilege of a public remark on this great occasion—that was the President of the United States. All day Friday he was as studiously silent as the rest. But on Saturday he recognized that his duty required him to say something, and he took his pen and performed that duty. If I know President Roosevelt—and I am sure I do—this utterance cost him more pain and shame than any other that ever issued from his pen or his mouth. I am far from blaming him. If I had been in his place my official duty would have compelled me to say what he said. It was a convention, an old tradition, and he had to be loyal to it. There was no help for it. This is what he said:

Washington, March 10.

Wood, Manila:—
I congratulate you and the officers and men of your command upon the brilliant feat of arms wherein you and they so well upheld the honor of the American flag.
(Signed) Theodore Roosevelt.

His whole utterance is merely a convention. Not a word of what he said came out of his heart. He knew perfectly well that to pen six hundred helpless and weaponless savages in a hole like rats in a trap and massacre them in detail during a stretch of a day and a half, from a safe position on the heights above, was no brilliant feat of arms—and would not have been a brilliant feat of arms even if Christian America, represented by its salaried soldiers, had shot them down with Bibles and the Golden Rule instead of bullets. He knew perfectly well that our uniformed assassins had *not* upheld the honor of the American flag, but had done as they have been doing continuously for eight years in the Philippines—that is to say, they had dishonored it.

The next day, Sunday,—which was yesterday—the cable brought us additional news—still more splendid news—still more honor for the flag. The first display-head shouts this information at us in stentorian capitals: "WOMEN SLAIN IN MORO SLAUGHTER."

"Slaughter" is a good word. Certainly there is not a better one in the Unabridged Dictionary for this occasion.

The next display line says:

"With Children They Mixed in Mob in Crater, and All Died Together."

They were mere naked savages, and yet there is a sort of pathos about it when that word *children* falls under your eye, for it always brings before us our perfectest symbol of innocence and helplessness; and by help of its deathless eloquence color, creed and nationality vanish away and we see only that they are children—merely children. And if they are frightened and crying and in trouble, our pity goes out to them by natural impulse. We see a picture. We see the small forms. We see the terrified faces. We see the tears. We see the small hands clinging in supplication to the mother; but we do not see those children that we are speaking about. We see in their places the little creatures whom we know and love.

The next heading blazes with American and Christian glory like to the sun in the zenith: *"Death List is Now 900."*

I was never so enthusiastically proud of the flag till now!

The next heading explains how safely our daring soldiers were located. It says:

"Impossible to Tell Sexes Apart in Fierce Battle on Top of Mount Dajo."

The naked savages were so far away, down in the bottom of that trap, that our soldiers could not tell the breasts of a woman from the rudimentary paps of a man—so far away that they couldn't tell a toddling little child from a black six-footer. *This was by all odds the least dangerous battle that Christian soldiers of any nationality were ever engaged in.*

The next heading says:

"Fighting for Four Days."

So our men were at it four days instead of a day and a half. It was a long and happy picnic with nothing to do but sit in comfort and fire the Golden Rule into those people down there and imagine letters to write home to the admiring families, and pile glory upon glory. Those savages fighting for their liberties had the four days too, but it must have been a sorrowful time for them. Every day they saw two hundred and twenty-five of their number slain, and this provided them grief and mourning for the night—and doubtless without even the relief and consolation of knowing that in the meantime they had slain four of their enemies and wounded some more on the elbow and the nose.

The closing heading says:

"Lieutenant Johnson Blown from Parapet by Exploding Artillery Gallantly Leading Charge."

Lieutenant Johnson has pervaded the cablegrams from the first. He and his wound have sparkled around through them like the serpentine thread of fire that goes excursioning through the black crisp fabric of a fragment of burnt paper. It reminds one of Gillette's comedy farce of a few years ago, "Too Much Johnson." Apparently Johnson was the only wounded man on our side whose wound was worth anything as an advertisement. It has made a great deal more noise in the world than has any similarly colossal event since "Humpty Dumpty" fell off the wall and got injured. The official dispatches do not know which to admire most, Johnson's adorable wound or the nine hundred murders. The ecstasies flowing from Army Headquarters on the other side of the globe to the White House, at a dollar and a half a word, have set fire to similar ecstasies in the President's breast. It appears that the immortally wounded was a Rough Rider under Lieutenant Colonel Roosevelt at San Juan Hill—that extinguisher of Waterloo—when the Colonel of the regiment, the present Major General Dr. Leonard Wood, went to the rear to bring up the pills and missed the fight. The President has a warm place in his heart for anybody who was present at that bloody collision of military solar systems, and so he lost no time in cabling to the wounded hero "How are you?" And got a cable answer, "Fine, thanks." This is historical. This will go down to posterity.

Johnson was wounded in the shoulder with a slug. The slug was in a shell—for the account says the damage was caused by an exploding shell which blew Johnson off the rim. The people down in the hole had no artillery; therefore it was our artillery that blew Johnson off the rim.

And so it is now a matter of historical record that the only officer of ours who acquired a wound of advertising dimensions got it at our hands, not the enemy's. It seems more than probable that if we had placed our soldiers out of the way of our own weapons, we should have come out of the most extraordinary battle in all history without a scratch.

Wednesday, March 14, 1906

Moro slaughter continued—Luncheon for George Harvey—Opinions of the guests as to Moro fight—Cable from General Wood explaining and apologizing—What became of the wounded?—President Roosevelt's joy over the splendid achievement—Manner in which he made Wood Major General—McKinley's joy over capture of Aguinaldo.

The ominous paralysis continues. There has been a slight sprinkle—an exceedingly slight sprinkle—in the correspondence columns, of angry rebukes of the President for calling this cowardly massacre a "brilliant feat of arms," and for praising our butchers for "holding up the honor of the flag" in that singular way; but there is hardly a ghost of a whisper about the feat of arms in the editorial columns of the papers.

I hope that this silence will continue. It is about as eloquent and as damaging and effective as the most indignant words could be, I think. When a man is sleeping in a noise, his sleep goes placidly on; but if the noise stops, the stillness wakes him. This silence has continued five days now. Surely it must be waking the drowsy nation. Surely the nation must be wondering what it means. A five-day silence following a world-astonishing event has not happened on this planet since the daily newspaper was invented.

At a luncheon party of men convened yesterday to God-speed George Harvey, who is leaving to-day for a vacation in Europe, all the talk was about the brilliant feat of arms; and no one had anything to say about it that either the President or Major General Dr. Wood, or the damaged Johnson, would regard as complimentary, or as proper comment to put into our histories. Harvey said he believed that the shock and shame of this episode would eat down deeper and deeper into the hearts of the nation and fester there and produce results. He believed it would destroy the Republican party and President Roosevelt. I cannot believe that the prediction will come true, for the reason that prophecies which promise valuable things, desirable things, good things, worthy things, never come true. Prophecies of this kind are like wars fought in a good cause—they are so rare that they don't count.

Day before yesterday the cable-note from the happy General Dr. Wood was still all glorious. There was still proud mention and elaboration of what was called the "desperate hand-to-hand fight," Dr. Wood not seeming to suspect that he was giving himself away, as the phrase goes— since if there was any very desperate hand-to-hand fighting it would necessarily happen that nine hundred hand-to-hand fighters, if really desperate, would surely be able to kill more than fifteen of our men before their last man and woman and child perished.

Very well, there was a new note in the dispatches yesterday afternoon—just a faint sugges-tion that Dr. Wood was getting ready to lower his tone and begin to apologize and explain. He announces that he assumes full responsibility for the fight. It indicates that he is aware that there is a lurking disposition here amidst all this silence to blame somebody. He says there was "no wanton destruction of women and children in the fight, though many of them were killed by force of necessity because the Moros used them as shields in the hand-to-hand fighting."

This explanation is better than none; indeed it is considerably better than none. Yet if there was so much hand-to-hand fighting there must have arrived a time, toward the end of the four days' butchery, when only one native was left alive. We had six hundred men present; we had lost only fifteen; why did the six hundred kill that remaining man—or woman, or child?

Dr. Wood will find that explaining things is not in his line. He will find that where a man has the proper spirit in him and the proper force at his command, it is easier to massacre nine hundred unarmed animals than it is to explain why he made it so remorselessly complete. Next he furnishes us this sudden burst of unconscious humor, which shows that he ought to edit his reports before he cables them:

"Many of the Moros feigned death and butchered the American hospital men who were relieving the wounded."

We have the curious spectacle of hospital men going around trying to relieve the wounded savages—for what reason? The savages were all massacred. The plain intention was to massacre them all and leave none alive. Then where was the use in furnishing mere temporary relief to a person who was presently to be exterminated? The dispatches call this battue a "battle." In what way was it a battle? It has no resemblance to a battle. In a battle there are always as many as five wounded men to one killed outright. When this so-called battle was over, there were certainly not fewer than two hundred wounded savages lying on the field. What became of them? Since not one savage was left alive!

The inference seems plain. We cleaned up our four days' work and made it complete by butchering those helpless people.

1901   The President's joy over the splendid achievement of his fragrant pet, General Wood, brings to mind an earlier Presidential ecstasy. When the news came, in 1901, that Colonel Funston had penetrated to the refuge of the patriot, Aguinaldo, in the mountains, and had captured him by the use of these arts, to wit: by forgery, by lies, by disguising his military marauders in the uniform of the enemy, by pretending to be friends of Aguinaldo's and by disarming suspi-cion by cordially shaking hands with Aguinaldo's officers and in that moment shooting them down—when the cablegram announcing this "brilliant feat of arms" reached the White House, the newspapers said that that meekest and mildest and gentlest and least masculine of men, President McKinley, could not control his joy and gratitude, but was obliged to express it in motions resembling a dance. Also President McKinley expressed his admiration in another way. He instantly shot that militia Colonel aloft over the heads of a hundred clean and honor-able veteran officers of the army and made him a Brigadier General in the regular service, and clothed him in the honorable uniform of that rank, thus disgracing the uniform, the flag, the nation, and himself.

Wood was an army surgeon, during several years, out West among the Indian hostiles. Roosevelt got acquainted with him and fell in love with him. When Roosevelt was offered the colonelcy of a regiment in the iniquitous Cuban-Spanish war, he took the place of Lieutenant Colonel and used his influence to get the higher place for Wood. After the war Wood became our Governor General in Cuba and proceeded to make a mephitic record for himself. Under President Roosevelt, this doctor has been pushed and crowded along higher and higher in the military service—always over the heads of a number of better men—and at last when Roosevelt wanted to make him a Major General in the regular army (with only five other Major Generals between him and the supreme command) and knew, or believed, that the Senate would not confirm Wood's nomination to that great place, he accomplished Wood's appointment by a very unworthy device. He could appoint Wood himself, and make the appointment good, between sessions of Congress. There was no such opportunity, but he invented one. A special session was closing at noon. When the gavel fell extinguishing the special session, a regular session began instantly. Roosevelt claimed that there was an interval there determinable as the twentieth of a second by a stop-watch, and that during that interval no Congress was in session. By this subterfuge he foisted this discredited doctor upon the army and the nation, and the Senate hadn't spirit enough to repudiate it.

March 15, 1906

Monday, March 5, 1906. Mr. Clemens talks to the West Side Young Men's Christian Association in the Majestic Theatre—Miss Lyon meets one of the Christian young men at the door—Patrick's funeral—Luncheon next day at the Hartford Club—Mr. Clemens meets eleven of his old friends—They tell many stories: Rev. Dr. McKnight and the Jersey funeral—Mr. Twichell's story on board the *Kanawha*, about Richard Croker's father—The Mary Ann story—Decoration Day and the fiery Major and Mr. Twichell's interrupted prayer.

POLICE HUSTLE CROWD AWAITING MARK TWAIN

———

Bungle at the Majestic Theatre Angers Y.M.C.A. Men.

———

WOULDN'T OPEN THE DOORS

———

Mr. Clemens Gives Some Advice About the Treatment of Corporations and Talks About Gentlemen.

Members of the West Side Branch of the Young Men's Christian Association found that entering the Majestic Theatre yesterday afternoon to hear an address by Mark Twain had a close resemblance to a football match. No one was injured, but for a few minutes the police were hustling the crowd backward and forward by sheer force, a mounted man was sent to push his way through the thickest of the press and the jam was perilous.

The doors of the theatre should have been opened at 3 o'clock, and about three hundred persons were there at that time. It was an orderly crowd of young men with a sprinkling of elderly ones, but Capt. Daly of the West Forty-seventh Street Station would not allow them to be admitted until he had summoned the reserves. It took twenty minutes for these to arrive and every moment the crush grew greater. Still there was no disorder and the police as they formed into line had to face nothing more dangerous than a little good-humored chaff.

The crowd was ranged in a rough column facing the main doors of the lobby. The Young Men's Christian Association authorities came out several times and asked the Captain to allow the doors to be opened.

"If you do it, I'll take away my men and there'll be a lot of people hurt or killed," he replied. "I know how to handle crowds."

Then he proceeded to handle the crowds. He tried to swing the long solid line up against the southwestern side of Columbus Circle and force them in by the side entrance of the lobby, instead of the one they faced. First he sent a mounted man right through the column. The patrolmen followed and in a moment the orderly gathering was hustled and thrust in all directions.

Capt. Daly's next manoeuvre was to open the side door. The crowd surged up, but he had them pushed back, and closed the door again. The crowd was utterly bewildered. Then the Young Men's Christian Association authorities opened one-half of the door on their own responsibility. Through this narrow passage the crowd squeezed. The plate glass in the half that was closed was shattered to atoms, and the men surged forward. A few coats were torn, but in spite of the way in which they had been handled everybody kept his temper. If there had been any disorderly element present nothing could have avoided serious accidents. In the end all but 500 gained admission.

Hold Police Responsible.

At the opening of the meeting, the Rev. Dr. Charles P. Fagnani, the Chairman, said: "The management desires to disclaim all responsibility for what has happened. [Cheers.] The matter was taken out of their hands by the police. [Hisses.] We wanted to open the doors earlier, but our lords and masters, the police, took the matter into their own hands and settled it in their own way. [Hisses.] You have been accustomed long enough to being brutally treated by the police, and I do not see why you should mind it. [A voice: "You're right."] Some day you will take matters into your own hands and will decide that the police shall be the servants of the citizens."

At the end of the meeting, Charles F. Powlison, Secretary of the West Side Branch, stated he had been asked to submit a resolution condemning the action of the police, but it has been decided it was better not to do so.

Mark Twain was introduced as a man "well worth being clubbed to hear." He was greeted with a storm of applause that lasted over a minute.

"I thank you for this signal recognition of merit," he said. "I have been listening to what has been said about citizenship. You complain of the police. You created the police. You are responsible for the police. They must reflect you, their masters. Consider that before you blame them.

"Citizenship is of the first importance in a land where a body of citizens can change the whole atmosphere of politics, as has been done in Philadelphia. There is less graft there than there used to be. I was going to move to Philadelphia, but it is no place for enterprise now.

"Dr. Russell spoke of organization. I was an organization once myself for twelve hours, and accomplished things I could never have done otherwise. When they say 'Step lively,' remember it is not an insult from a conductor to you personally, but from the President of the road to you, an embodiment of American citizenship. When the insult is flung at your old mother and father, it shows the meanness of the omnipotent President, who could stop it if he would.

Mark Twain Got the Stateroom.

"I was an organization once. I was traveling from Chicago with my publisher and stenographer—I always travel with a bodyguard—and engaged a stateroom on a certain train. For above all its other conveniences the stateroom gives the privilege of smoking. When we arrived at the station the conductor told us he was sorry the car with our stateroom was left off. I said: 'You are under contract to furnish a stateroom on this train. I am in no hurry. I can stay here a week at the road's expense. It'll have to pay my expenses and a little over.'

"Then the conductor called a grandee, and, after some argument, he went and bundled some meek people out of the stateroom, told them something not strictly true, and gave it me. About 11 o'clock the conductor looked in on me, and was very kind and winning. He told me he knew my father-in-law—it was much more respectable to know my father-in-law than me in those days. Then he developed his game. He was very sorry the car was only going to Harrisburg. They had telegraphed to Harrisburg, Pittsburg, San Francisco, and couldn't get another car. He threw himself on my mercy. But to him I only replied:

"'Then you had better buy the car.'

"I had forgotten all about this, when some time after Mr. Thomson of the Pennsylvania heard I was going to Chicago again, and wired:

"'I am sending my private car. Clemens cannot ride on an ordinary car. He costs too much.'"

Yesterday, in the afternoon, I talked to the West Side Young Men's Christian Association in the Majestic Theatre. The audience was to have been restricted to the membership, or at least to the membership's sex, but I had asked for a couple of stage boxes and had invited friends of mine of both sexes to occupy them. There was trouble out at the doors, and I became afraid that these friends would not get in. Miss Lyon volunteered to go out and see if she could find them and rescue them from the crowd. She was a pretty small person for such a service, but maybe her lack of dimensions was in her favor, rather than against it. She plowed her way through the incoming masculine wave and arrived outside, where she captured the friends, and also had an adventure. Just as the police were closing the doors of the theatre and announcing to the crowd that the place was full and no more could be admitted, a flushed and excited man crowded his way to the door and got as much as his nose in, but there the officer closed the door and the man was outside. He and Miss Lyon were for the moment the centre of attention—she because of her solitariness in that sea of masculinity, and he because he had been defeated before folks, a thing which we all enjoy, even when we are West Side Young Christians and ought to let on that we don't. The man looked down at Miss Lyon—anybody can do that without standing on a chair—and he began pathetically—I say *began* pathetically; the pathos of his manner and his words was confined to his beginning. He began on Miss Lyon, then shifted to the crowd for a finish. He said "I have been a member of this West Side Young Men's Christian Association in good standing for seven years, and have always done the best I could, yet never once got any reward." He paused half an instant, shot a bitter glance at the closed door, and added with deep feeling "It's just my God damned luck."

I think it damaged my speech for Miss Lyon. The speech was well enough—certainly better than the report of it in the papers—but in spite of her compliments, I knew there was nothing in it as good as what she had heard outside; and by the delight which she exhibited in that outsider's eloquence I knew that she knew it.

I will insert here a passage from the newspaper report, because it refers to Patrick.

Definition of a Gentleman.

Mark Twain went on to speak of the man who left $10,000 to disseminate his definition of a gentleman. He denied that he had ever defined one, but said if he did he would include the mercifulness, fidelity, and justice the Scripture read at the meeting spoke of. He produced a letter from William Dean Howells, and said:

"He writes he is just 69, but I have known him longer than that. 'I was born to be afraid of dying, not of getting old,' he says. Well, I'm the other way. It's terrible getting old. You gradually lose your faculties and fascinations and become troublesome. People try to make you think you are not. But I know I'm troublesome.

"Then he says no part of life is so enjoyable as the eighth decade. That's true. I've just turned it, and I enjoy it very much. 'If old men were not so ridiculous'—why didn't he speak for himself? 'But,' he goes on, 'they are ridiculous, and they are ugly.' I never saw a letter with so many errors in it. Ugly! I was never ugly in my life! Forty years ago I was not so good-looking. A looking glass then lasted me three months. Now I can wear it out in two days.

"'You've been up in Hartford burying poor old Patrick. I suppose he was old, too,' says Mr. Howells. No, he was not old. Patrick came to us thirty-six years ago—a brisk, lithe young Irishman. He was as beautiful in his graces as he was in his spirit, and he was as honest a man as ever lived. For twenty-five years he was our coachman, and if I were going to describe a gentleman in detail I would describe Patrick.

"At my own request I was his pall-bearer with our old gardener. He drove me and my bride so long ago. As the little children came along he drove them, too. He was all the world to them, and for all in my house he had the same feelings of honor, honesty, and affection.

"He was 60 years old, ten years younger than I. Howells suggests he was old. He was not so old. He had the same gracious and winning ways to the end. Patrick was a gentleman, and to him I would apply the lines:

So may I be courteous to men, faithful to friends,
True to my God, a fragrance in the path I trod."

At the funeral I saw Patrick's family. I had seen no member of it for a good many years. The children were men and women. When I had seen them last they were little creatures. So far as I could remember I had not seen them since as little chaps they joined with ours, and with the children of the neighbors, in celebrating Christmas Eve around a Christmas tree in our house, on which occasion Patrick came down the chimney (apparently) disguised as St. Nicholas, and performed the part to the admiration of the little and the big alike.

John, our old gardener, was a fellow pall-bearer with me. The rest were Irish coachmen and laborers—old friends of Patrick. The Cathedral was half filled with people.

I spent the night at Twichell's house, that night, and at noon next day at the Hartford Club I met, at a luncheon, eleven of my oldest friends—Charley Clark, editor of the *Courant;* Judge Hamersley, of the Supreme Court; Colonel Cheney, Sam Dunham, Twichell, Rev. Dr. Parker, Charles E. Perkins, Archie Welch. A deal of pretty jolly reminiscing was done, interspersed with mournings over beloved members of the old comradeship whose names have long ago been carved upon their gravestones.

The Rev. Dr. McKnight was one of these. He was a most delightful man. And in his day he was almost a rival of Twichell in the matter of having adventures. Once when he was serving professionally in New York, a new widower came and begged him to come over to a Jersey town and conduct the funeral of his wife. McKnight consented, but said he should be very uneasy if there should be any delay, because he must be back in New York at a certain hour to officiate at a funeral in his own church. He went over to that Jersey town and when the family and friends were all gathered together in the parlor he rose behind the coffin, put up his hands in the solemn silence and said,

"Let us pray."

There was a twitch at his coat-tail and he bent down to get the message. The widower whispered and said,

"Not yet, not yet—wait a little."

McKnight waited a while. Then remembering that time was passing and he must not miss his train and the other funeral, he rose again, put up his hands and said,

"Let us pray."

There was another twitch at his coat-tail. He bent down and got the same message. "Not yet, not yet—wait a little."

He waited; became uneasier than ever; got up the third time, put up his hands and got another twitch. This time when he bent down the man explained. He whispered:

"Wait a little. She's not all here. Stomach's at the apothecary's."

Several things were told on Twichell illustrative of his wide catholicity of feeling and conduct, and I was able to furnish something in this line myself. Three or four years ago, when Sir Thomas Lipton came over here to race for the America cup, I was invited to go with Mr. Rogers and half a dozen other worldlings in Mr. Rogers's yacht, the *Kanawha,* to see the race. Mr. Rogers is fond of Twichell and wanted to invite him to go also, but was afraid to do it because he thought Twichell would be uncomfortable among those worldlings. I said I didn't think that would be the case. I said Twichell was chaplain in a fighting brigade all through the Civil War, and was necessarily familiar with about all the different kinds of worldlings that could be started; so Mr. Rogers told me—though with many misgivings—to invite him, and that he would do his best to see that the worldlings should modify their worldliness and pay proper respect and deference to Twichell's cloth.

When Twichell and I arrived at the pier at eight in the morning, the launch was waiting for us. All the others were on board. The yacht was anchored out there ready to sail. Twichell and I went aboard and ascended to the little drawing-room on the upper deck. The door stood open, and as we approached we heard hilarious laughter and talk proceeding from that place, and I recognized that the worldlings were having a worldly good time. But as Twichell appeared in the door all that hilarity ceased as suddenly as if it had been shut off with an electric button, and the gay faces of the worldlings at once put on a most proper and impressive solemnity. The last word we had heard from these people was the name of Richard Croker, the celebrated Tammany leader, all-round blatherskite and chief pillager of the municipal till. Twichell shook hands all around and broke out with,

"I heard you mention Richard Croker. I knew his father very well indeed. He was head teamster in our brigade in the Civil War—the Sickles brigade—a fine man; as fine a man as a person would want to know. He was always splashed over with mud, of course, but that didn't matter. The man inside the muddy clothes was a whole man; and he was educated; he was highly educated. He was a man who had read a great deal. And he was a Greek scholar; not a mere surface scholar, but a real one; used to read aloud from his Greek Testament, and when he hadn't it handy he could recite from it from memory, and he did it well, and with spirit. Presently I was delighted to see that every now and then he would come over of a Sunday morning and sit under the trees in our camp with our boys and listen to my ministrations. I couldn't refrain from introducing myself to him—that is I couldn't refrain from speaking to him about this, and I said,

"Mr. Croker, I want to tell you what a pleasure it is to see you come and sit with my boys and listen to me. For I know what it must cost you to do this, and I want to express my admiration for a man who can put aside his religious prejudices and manifest the breadth and tolerance that you have manifested." He flushed, and said with eloquent emphasis—

"Mr. Twichell, do you take me for a God damned papist?"

Mr. Rogers said to me, aside, "This relieves me from my burden of uneasiness."

Twichell, with his big heart, his wide sympathies, and his limitless benignities and charities and generosities, is the kind of person that people of all ages and both sexes fly to for consolation and help in time of trouble. He is always being levied upon by this kind of persons. Years ago—many years ago—a soft-headed young donkey who had been reared under Mr. Twichell's spiritual ministrations sought a private interview—a very private interview—with him, and said,

"Mr. Twichell, I wish you would give me some advice. It is a very important matter with me. It lies near my heart, and I want to proceed wisely. Now it is like this: I have been down to the Bermudas on the first vacation I have ever had in my life, and there I met a most charming young lady, native of that place, and I fell in love with her, Mr. Twichell. I fell in love with her, oh so deeply! Well, I can't describe it, Mr. Twichell. I can't describe it. I have never had such feelings before, and they just consume me; they burn me up. When I got back here I found I couldn't think of anybody but that girl. I wanted to write to her, but I was afraid. I was afraid. It seemed too bold. I ought to have taken advice, perhaps—but really I was not myself. I *had* to write—I couldn't help it. So I wrote to her. I wrote to her as guardedly as my feelings would allow—but I had the sense all the time that I was too bold—I was too bold—she wouldn't like it. I—well, sometimes I would almost think maybe she would answer; but then there would come a colder wave and I would say—'No, I shall never hear from her—she will be offended.' But at last, Mr. Twichell, a letter *has* come. I don't know how to contain myself. I want to write again, but I may spoil it—I may spoil it—and I want your advice. Tell me if I had better venture. Now here she has written—here is her letter, Mr. Twichell. She says this: she says—she says— 'You say in your letter you wish it could be your privilege to see me half your time. How would you like it to see me *all* the time?' What do you think of that, Mr. Twichell? How does that strike you? Do you think she is not offended? Do you think that that indicates a sort of a shadowy leaning toward me? Do you think it, Mr. Twichell? Could you say that?"

"Well," Twichell said, "I would not like to be too sanguine. I would not like to commit myself too far. I would not like to put hopes into your mind which could fail of fruition, but, on the whole—on the whole—daring is a good thing in these cases. Sometimes daring—a bold front—will accomplish things that timidity would fail to accomplish. I think I would write her—guardedly of course—but write her."

"Oh Mr. Twichell, oh you don't know how happy you do make me. I'll write her right away. But I'll be guarded. I'll be careful—careful."

Twichell read the rest of the letter—saw that this girl was just simply throwing herself at this young fellow's head and was going to capture him by fair means or foul, but capture him. But he sent the young fellow away to write the guarded letter.

In due time he came with the girl's second letter and said,

"Mr. Twichell, will you read that? Now read that. How does that strike you? Is she kind of leaning my way? I wish you could say so, Mr. Twichell. You see there, what she says. She says— 'You offer to send me a present of a ring—' I did it, Mr. Twichell! I declare it was a bold thing— but—but—I couldn't help it—I did that intrepid thing—and that is what she says: 'You offer to send me a ring. But my father is going to take a little vacation excursion in the New England States and he is going to let me go with him. If you should send the ring here it might get lost. We shall be in Hartford a day or two; won't it be safer to wait till then and you put it on my finger yourself?'

"What do you think of that, Mr. Twichell? How does it strike you? Is she leaning? Is she leaning?"

"Well," Twichell said, "I don't know about that. I must not be intemperate. I must not say things too strongly, for I might be making a mistake. But I think—I think—on the whole I think she is leaning—I do—I think she is leaning—"

"Oh Mr. Twichell, it does my heart so much good to hear you say that! Mr. Twichell, if there was anything I could do to show my gratitude for those words—well, you see the condition I am in—and to have you say that—"

Twichell said "Now wait a minute—now let's not make any mistake here. Don't you know that this is a most serious position? It can have the most serious results upon two lives. You know there is such a thing as a mere passing fancy that sets a person's soul on fire for the moment. That person thinks it is love, and that it is permanent love—that it is real love. Then he finds out, by and by, that it was but a momentary insane passion—and then perhaps he has committed himself for life, and he wishes he was out of that predicament. Now let us make sure of this thing. I believe that if you try, and conduct yourself wisely and cautiously—I don't feel sure, but I believe that if you conduct yourself wisely and cautiously you can beguile that girl into marrying you."

"Oh Mr. Twichell, I can't express—"

"Well never mind expressing anything. What I am coming at is this: let us make sure of our position. If this is *real* love, go ahead! If it is nothing but a passing fancy, drop it right here, for both your sakes. Now tell me, is it real love? If it is real love how do you arrive at that conclusion? Have you some way of proving to your entire satisfaction that this *is* real, genuine, lasting, permanent love?"

"Mr. Twichell, I can tell you this. You can just judge for yourself. From the time that I was a baby in the cradle, up, Mr. Twichell, I have had to sleep close to my mother, with a door open between, because I have always been subject to the most horrible nightmares, and when they break out my mother has to come running from her bed and appease me and comfort me and pacify me. Now then, Mr. Twichell, from the cradle up, whenever I got hit with those nightmare convulsions I have always sung out Mamma, Mamma, Mamma. Now I sing out Mary Ann, Mary Ann, Mary Ann."

So they were married. They moved to the West and we know nothing more about the romance.

Fifteen or twenty years ago, Decoration Day happened to be more like the Fourth of July for temperature than like the 30th of May. Twichell was orator of the day. He pelted his great crowd of old Civil War soldiers for an hour in the biggest church in Hartford, while they mourned and sweltered. Then they marched forth and joined the procession of other wilted old soldiers that were oozing from other churches, and tramped through clouds of dust to the cemetery and began to distribute the flags and the flowers—a tiny flag and a small basket of flowers to each military grave. This industry went on and on and on, everybody breathing dust—for there was nothing else to breathe; everybody streaming with perspiration; everybody tired and wishing it was over. At last there was but one basket of flowers left, only one grave still undecorated. A fiery little Major whose patience was all gone, was shouting,

"Corporal Henry Jones, Company C, Fourteenth Connecticut Infantry—"

No response. Nobody seemed to know where that corporal was buried.

The Major raised his note a degree or two higher.

"Corporal Henry *Jones,* Company C, Fourteenth Connecticut Infantry!—doesn't anybody know where that man is buried?"

No response. Once, twice, three times, he shrieked again, with his temper ever rising higher and higher,—

"Corporal Henry JONES! Company C! Fourteenth Connecticut Infantry!—doesn't ANYBODY know where that man is buried?"

No response. Then he slammed the basket of flowers on the ground and said to Twichell,

"Proceed with the finish."

The crowd massed themselves together around Twichell with uncovered heads, the silence and solemnity interrupted only by subdued sneezings, for these people were buried in the dim cloud of dust. After a pause Twichell began an impressive prayer, making it brief to meet the exigencies of the occasion. In the middle of it he made a pause. The drummer thought he was through, and let fly a rub-a-dub-dub—and the little Major stormed out "*Stop* that drum!" Twichell tried again. He got almost to the last word safely, when somebody trod on a dog and the dog let out a howl of anguish that could be heard beyond the frontier. The Major said,

"God damn that dog!"—and Twichell said,

"Amen."

That is, he said it as a finish to his own prayer, but it fell so exactly at the right moment that it seemed to include the Major's, too, and so he felt greatly honored, and thanked him.

Friday, March 16, 1906

Schoolmates of sixty years ago—Mary Miller, one of Mr. Clemens's first sweethearts—Artimisia Briggs, another—Mary Lacy, another— Jimmy McDaniel, to whom Mr. Clemens told his first humorous story— Mr. Richmond, Sunday-school teacher, afterwards owner of Tom Sawyer's cave, which is now being ground into cement—Hickman, the showy young captain—Reuel Gridley and the sack of flour incident—The Levin Jew boys called Twenty-two—George Butler, nephew of Ben Butler—The incident of getting into bed with Will Bowen to catch the measles, and the successful and nearly fatal case which resulted.

We will return to those school children of sixty years ago. I recall Mary Miller. She was not my first sweetheart, but I think she was the first one that furnished me a broken heart. I fell in love with her when she was eighteen and I was nine, but she scorned me, and I recognized that this was a cold world. I had not noticed that temperature before. I believe I was as miserable as even a grown man could be. But I think that this sorrow did not remain with me long. As I remember it, I soon transferred my worship to Artimisia Briggs, who was a year older than Mary Miller. When I revealed my passion to her she did not scoff at it. She did not make fun of it. She was very kind and gentle about it. But she was also firm, and said she did not want to be pestered by children.

And there was Mary Lacy. She was a schoolmate. But she also was out of my class because of her advanced age. She was pretty wild and determined and independent. She was ungovernable, and was considered incorrigible. But that was all a mistake. She married, and at once settled down and became in all ways a model matron and was as highly respected as any matron in the town. Four years ago she was still living, and had been married fifty years.

Jimmy McDaniel was another schoolmate. His age and mine about tallied. His father kept the candy shop and he was the most envied little chap in the town—after Tom Blankenship ("Huck Finn")—for although we never saw him eating candy, we supposed that it was, nevertheless, his ordinary diet. He pretended that he never ate it, and didn't care for it because there was nothing forbidden about it—there was plenty of it and he could have as much of it as he wanted. Still there was circumstantial evidence that suggested that he only scorned candy in

1845

public to show off, for he had the worst teeth in town. He was the first human being to whom I ever told a humorous story, so far as I can remember. This was about Jim Wolf and the cats; and I gave him that tale the morning after that memorable episode. I thought he would laugh his remaining teeth out. I had never been so proud and happy before, and I have seldom been so proud and happy since. I saw him four years ago when I was out there. He was working in a cigar-making shop. He wore an apron that came down to his knees and a beard that came nearly half as far, and yet it was not difficult for me to recognize him. He had been married fifty-four years. He had many children and grandchildren and great-grandchildren, and also even posterity, they all said—thousands—yet the boy to whom I had told the cat story when we were callow juveniles was still present in that cheerful little old man.

Artimisia Briggs got married not long after refusing me. She married Richmond, the stone mason, who was my Methodist Sunday-school teacher in the earliest days, and he had one distinction which I envied him: at some time or other he had hit his thumb with his hammer and the result was a thumb-nail which remained permanently twisted and distorted and curved and pointed, like a parrot's beak. I should not consider it an ornament now, I suppose, but it had a fascination for me then, and a vast value, because it was the only one in the town. He was a very kindly and considerate Sunday-school teacher, and patient and compassionate, so he was the favorite teacher with us little chaps. In that school they had slender oblong paste-board blue tickets, each with a verse from the Testament printed on it, and you could get a blue ticket by reciting two verses. By reciting five verses you could get three blue tickets, and you could trade these at the bookcase and borrow a book for a week. I was under Mr. Richmond's spiritual care every now and then for two or three years, and he was never hard upon me. I always recited the same five verses every Sunday. He was always satisfied with the performance. He never seemed to notice that these were the same five foolish virgins that he had been hearing about every Sunday for months. I always got my tickets and exchanged them for a book. They were pretty dreary books, for there was not a bad boy in the entire bookcase. They were *all* good boys and good girls and drearily uninteresting, but they were better society than none, and I was glad to have their company and disapprove of it.

Twenty years ago Mr. Richmond had become possessed of Tom Sawyer's cave in the hills three miles from town, and had made a tourist-resort of it. But that cave is a thing of the past now. In 1849 when the gold seekers were streaming through our little town of Hannibal, many of our grown men got the gold fever, and I think that all the boys had it. On the Saturday holidays in summertime we used to borrow skiffs whose owners were not present and go down the river three miles to the cave hollow, (Missourian for "valley"), and there we staked out claims and pretended to dig gold, panning out half a dollar a day at first; two or three times as much, later, and by and by whole fortunes, as our imaginations became inured to the work. Stupid and unprophetic lads! We were doing this in play and never suspecting. Why, that cave hollow and all the adjacent hills were made of gold! But we did not know it. We took it for dirt. We left its rich secret in its own peaceful possession and grew up in poverty and went wandering about the world struggling for bread—and this because we had not the gift of prophecy. That region was all dirt and rocks to us, yet all it needed was to be ground up and scientifically handled and it was gold. That is to say, the whole region was a cement mine—and they make the finest kind of Portland cement there now, five thousand barrels a day, with a plant that cost two million dollars.

Several months ago a telegram came to me from there saying that Tom Sawyer's cave was now being ground into cement—would I like to say anything about it in public? But I had nothing to say. I was sorry we lost our cement mine but it was not worth while to talk about it at this late day, and, take it all around, it was a painful subject anyway. There are seven miles of Tom Sawyer's cave—that is to say the lofty ridge which conceals that cave stretches down the bank of the Mississippi seven miles to the town of Saverton.

For a little while Reuel Gridley attended that school of ours. He was an elderly pupil; he was perhaps twenty-two or twenty-three years old. Then came the Mexican war and he volunteered. A company of infantry was raised in our town and Mr. Hickman, a tall, straight, handsome athlete of twenty-five, was made captain of it and had a sword by his side and a broad yellow stripe down the leg of his gray pants. And when that company marched back and forth through the streets in its smart uniform—which it did several times a day for drill—its evolutions were attended by all the boys whenever the school hours permitted. I can see that marching company yet, and I can almost feel again the consuming desire that I had to join it. But they had no use for boys of twelve and thirteen, and before I had a chance in another war the desire to kill people to whom I had not been introduced had passed away.

I saw the splendid Hickman in his old age. He seemed about the oldest man I had ever seen—an amazing and melancholy contrast with the showy young captain I had seen preparing his warriors for carnage so many, many years before. Hickman is dead—it is the old story. As Susy said, "What is it all for?"

Reuel Gridley went away to the wars and we heard of him no more for fifteen or sixteen years. Then one day in Carson City while I was having a difficulty with an editor on the sidewalk—an editor better built for war than I was—I heard a voice say "Give him the best you've got, Sam, I'm at your back." It was Reuel Gridley. He said he had not recognized me by my face but by my drawling style of speech.

He went down to the Reese River mines about that time and presently he lost an election bet in his mining camp, and by the terms of it he was obliged to buy a fifty-pound sack of self-rising flour and carry it through the town, preceded by music, and deliver it to the winner of the bet. Of course the whole camp was present and full of fluid and enthusiasm. The winner of the bet put up the sack at auction for the benefit of the United States Sanitary Fund, and sold it. The purchaser put it up for the Fund and sold it. The excitement grew and grew. The sack was sold over and over again for the benefit of the Fund. The news of it came to Virginia City by telegraph. It produced great enthusiasm, and Reuel Gridley was begged by telegraph to bring the sack and have an auction in Virginia City. He brought it. An open barouche was provided, also a brass band. The sack was sold over and over again at Gold Hill, then was brought up to Virginia City toward night and sold—and sold again, and again, and still again, netting twenty or thirty thousand dollars for the Sanitary Fund. Gridley carried it across California and sold it at various towns. He sold it for large sums in Sacramento and in San Francisco. He brought it East, sold it in New York and in various other cities, then carried it out to a great Fair at St. Louis, and went on selling it; and finally made it up into small cakes and sold those at a dollar apiece. First and last, the sack of flour which had originally cost ten dollars, perhaps, netted more than two hundred thousand dollars for the Sanitary Fund. Reuel Gridley has been dead these many, many years—it is the old story.

In that school were the first Jews I had ever seen. It took me a good while to get over the awe of it. To my fancy they were clothed invisibly in the damp and cobwebby mould of antiquity. They carried me back to Egypt, and in imagination I moved among the Pharaohs and all the shadowy celebrities of that remote age. The name of the boys was Levin. We had a collective name for them which was the only really large and handsome witticism that was ever born in that Congressional district. We called them "Twenty-two"—and even when the joke was old and had been worn threadbare we always followed it with the explanation, to make sure that it would be understood, "Twice Levin—twenty-two."

There were other boys whose names remain with me. Irving Ayres—but no matter, he is dead. Then there was George Butler, whom I remember as a child of seven wearing a blue leather belt with a brass buckle, and hated and envied by all the boys on account of it. He was a nephew of General Ben Butler and fought gallantly at Ball's Bluff and in several other actions of the Civil War. He is dead, long and long ago.

Will Bowen (dead long ago), Ed Stevens (dead long ago), and John Briggs were special mates of mine. John is still living.

1845   In 1845, when I was ten years old, there was an epidemic of measles in the town and it made a most alarming slaughter among the little people. There was a funeral almost daily, and the mothers of the town were nearly demented with fright. My mother was greatly troubled. She worried over Pamela and Henry and me, and took constant and extraordinary pains to keep us from coming into contact with the contagion. But upon reflection I believed that her judgment was at fault. It seemed to me that I could improve upon it if left to my own devices. I cannot remember now whether I was frightened about the measles or not, but I clearly remember that I grew very tired of the suspense I suffered on account of being continually under the threat of death. I remember that I got so weary of it and so anxious to have the matter settled one way or the other, and promptly, that this anxiety spoiled my days and my nights. I had no pleasure in them. I made up my mind to end this suspense and be done with it. Will Bowen was dangerously ill with the measles and I thought I would go down there and catch them. I entered the house by the front way and slipped along through rooms and halls, keeping sharp watch against discovery, and at last I reached Will's bed-chamber in the rear of the house on the second floor and got into it uncaptured. But that was as far as my victory reached. His mother caught me there a moment later and snatched me out of the house and gave me a most competent scolding and drove me away. She was so scared that she could hardly get her words out, and her face was white. I saw that I must manage better next time, and I did. I hung about the lane at the rear of the house and watched through cracks in the fence until I was convinced that the conditions were favorable; then I slipped through the back yard and up the back way and got into the room and into the bed with Will Bowen without being observed. I don't know how long I was in the bed. I only remember that Will Bowen, as society, had no value for me, for he was too sick to even notice that I was there. When I heard his mother coming I covered up my head, but that device was a failure. It was dead summertime—the cover was nothing more than a limp blanket or sheet, and anybody could see that there were two of us under it. It didn't remain two very long. Mrs. Bowen snatched me out of the bed and conducted me home herself, with a grip on my collar which she never loosened until she delivered me into my mother's hands along with her opinion of that kind of a boy.

It was a good case of measles that resulted. It brought me within a shade of death's door. It brought me to where I no longer took any interest in anything, but, on the contrary, felt a total absence of interest—which was most placid and tranquil and sweet and delightful and enchanting. I have never enjoyed anything in my life any more than I enjoyed dying that time. I *was,* in effect, dying. The word had been passed and the family notified to assemble around the bed and see me off. I knew them all. There was no doubtfulness in my vision. They were all crying, but that did not affect me. I took but the vaguest interest in it, and that merely because I was the centre of all this emotional attention and was gratified by it and vain of it.

When Dr. Cunningham had made up his mind that nothing more could be done for me he put bags of hot ashes all over me. He put them on my breast, on my wrists, on my ancles; and so, very much to his astonishment—and doubtless to my regret—he dragged me back into this world and set me going again.

Tuesday, March 20, 1906

About young John D. Rockefeller's Sunday-school talks—Mr. Clemens is asked, as honorary member, to talk to the Bible Class—His letter of refusal—He accepts invitation from General Fred Grant to speak at Carnegie Hall April 10th, for benefit of Robert Fulton Memorial Association—His letter of acceptance.

One of the standing delights of the American nation in these days is John D. Rockefeller, junior's, Bible Class adventures in theology. Every Sunday young Rockefeller explains the Bible to his class. The next day the newspapers and the Associated Press distribute his explanations all over the continent and everybody laughs. The entire nation laughs, yet in its innocent dulness never suspects that it is laughing at itself. But that is what it is doing.

Young Rockefeller, who is perhaps thirty-five years old, is a plain, simple, earnest, sincere, honest, well-meaning, commonplace person, destitute of originality or any suggestion of it. And if he were traveling upon his mental merit instead of upon his father's money, his explanations of the Bible would fall silent and not be heard of by the public. But his father ranks as the richest man in the world, and this makes his son's theological gymnastics interesting and important. The world believes that the elder Rockefeller is worth a billion dollars. He pays taxes on two million and a half. He is an earnest uneducated Christian, and for years and years has been Admiral of a Sunday-school in Cleveland, Ohio. For years and years he has discoursed about himself to his Sunday-school and explained how he got his dollars; and during all these years his Sunday-school has listened in rapture and has divided its worship between him and his Creator—unequally. His Sunday-school talks are telegraphed about the country and are as eagerly read by the nation as are his son's.

As I have said, the nation laughs at young Rockefeller's analyzations of the Scriptures. Yet the nation must know that these analyzations are exactly like those which it hears every Sunday from its pulpits, and which its forebears have been listening to for centuries without a change of an idea—in case an idea has ever occurred in one of these discourses. Young John's methods are the ordinary pulpit methods. His deductions of golden fancy from sordid fact are exactly the same which the pulpit has traded in for centuries. Every argument he uses was already worn threadbare by the theologians of all the ages before it came in its rags to him. All his reasonings are like all the reasonings of all the pulpit's stale borrowings from the dull pulpits of the centuries. Young John has never studied a doctrine for himself; he has never examined a doctrine upon its real merits; he has never examined a doctrine for any purpose but to make it fit the notions which he got at second-hand from his teachers. His talks are quite as original and quite as valuable as any that proceed from any other theologian's lips, from the Pope of Rome down to himself. The nation laughs at young John's profound and clumsy examinations of Joseph's character and conduct, yet the nation has always heard Joseph's character and conduct examined in the same clumsy and stupid way by its pulpits, and the nation should reflect that when they laugh at young John they are laughing at themselves. They should reflect that young John is using no new whitewash upon Joseph. He is using the same old brush and the same old whitewash that have made Joseph grotesque in all the centuries.

I have known and liked young John for many years, and I have long felt that his right place was in the pulpit. I am sure that the foxfire of his mind would make a proper glow there—but I suppose he must do as destiny has decreed and succeed his father as master of the colossal Standard Oil Corporation. One of his most delightful theological deliverances was his exposition, three years ago, of the meaning—the real meaning, the bottom meaning—of Christ's admonition to the young man who was overburdened with wealth yet wanted to save himself if a convenient way could be found: "Sell all thou hast and give to the poor." Young John reasoned it out to this effect:

"Whatever thing stands between you and salvation, remove that obstruction at any cost. If it is money, give it away, to the poor; if it is property, sell the whole of it and give the proceeds to the poor; if it is military ambition, retire from the service; if it is an absorbing infatuation for any person or thing or pursuit, fling it far from you and proceed with a single mind to achieve your salvation."

The inference was plain. Young John's father's millions and his own were a mere incident in their lives and not in any way an obstruction in their pursuit of salvation. Therefore Christ's admonition could have no application to them. One of the newspapers sent interviewers to six or seven New York clergymen to get their views upon this matter, with this result: that all of them except one agreed with young Rockefeller. I do not know what we should do without the pulpit. We could better spare the sun—the moon, anyway.

Three years ago I went with young John to his Bible Class and talked to it—not theologically, that would not have been in good taste, and I prefer good taste to righteousness. Now whoever—on the outside—goes there and talks to that Bible Class is by that act entitled to honorary membership in it. Therefore I am an honorary member. Some days ago a Bible Class official sent me word that there would be a quinquennial meeting of these honoraries in their church day after to-morrow evening, and it was desired that I should come there and help do the talking. If I could not come, would I send a letter which could be read to those people?

I was already overburdened with engagements, so I sent my regrets and the following letter:

March 14, 1906.

Mr. Edward M. Foote, Chairman.

Dear Friend and Fellow-Member:

Indeed I should like to attend the reunion of the fellowship of honorary members of Mr. Rockefeller's Bible Class, (of whom I am one, by grace of service rendered,) but I must be discreet and not venture. This is on account of Joseph. He might come up as an issue, and then I could get into trouble, for Mr. Rockefeller and I do not agree as to Joseph. Eight years ago I quite painstakingly and exhaustively explained Joseph, by the light of the 47th chapter of Genesis, in a *North American Review* article which has since been transferred to volume XXII of my Collected Works; then I turned my attention to other subjects, under the impression that I had settled Joseph for good and all and left nothing further for anybody to say about him. Judge, then, of my surprise and sorrow, when by the newspapers I lately saw that Mr. Rockefeller had taken hold of Joseph—quite manifestly unaware that I had already settled Joseph—and was trying to settle him again.

In every sentence uttered by Mr. Rockefeller there was evidence that he was not acquainted with Joseph. Therefore it was plain to me that he had never read my article. He has certainly not read it, because his published estimate of Joseph differs from mine. This could not be, if he had read the article. He thinks Joseph was Mary's little lamb; this is an error. He was—he—but you look at the article, then you will see what he was.

For ages Joseph has been a most delicate and difficult problem. That is, for everybody but me. It is because I examine him on the facts as they stand recorded, the other theologians don't. Overborne by a sense of duty, they paint the facts. They paint some of them clear out. Paint them out, and paint some better ones in, which they get out of their own imaginations. They make up a Joseph-statement on the plan of the statement which a shaky bank gets up for the beguilement of the bank-inspector. They spirit away light-throwing liabilities, and insert fanciful assets in their places. Am I saying the thing that isn't true? Sunday before last the very learned and able Dr. Silverman was thus reported in the *Times:*

> But the farmers, the agriculturists, and the shepherds, who depended for their living on the product of the land, suffered most during a famine. To prevent utter starvation Joseph had the people from the country removed to the cities, from one end of the borders of Egypt even to the other end thereof, (Genesis, xlvii, 21,) and there he supported them. As long as they had money he gave them food for money, but when this was exhausted he took their cattle, their horses, their herds and asses, and even their land, when necessary, as a pledge for food. The Government then fed the cattle, horses, &c., which otherwise would have died.
>
> Later the land [the ownership?] was returned to the former owners; they were given seed to sow the land; they received as many of their cattle, horses, herds, &c., as they needed, and in payment were only required to give the Government one-fifth part of all their increase in animals or produce.
>
> The whole plan of Joseph was statesmanlike, as well as humanitarian. It appealed at once to Pharaoh and his counselors, and it is no wonder that Joseph was appointed Viceroy of All Egypt. Joseph successfully combated all the human sharks and speculators who had for years despoiled the poor in the season of famine and reduced them to starvation and beggary. He held the land and animals of the needy

as pledge, and then returned them their patrimony. [The ownership?] He charged them only a fair market price for the food they received. Without the wise institutions of public storehouses which Joseph had erected the people would have lost all their possessions, the whole country would have been reduced to misery, and thousands upon thousands would have died, as had been the case in previous seasons of famine.

That is Dr. Silverman's bank-statement—all painted and gilded and ready for the inspector. This is the Bible's statement. The italics are mine:

And there was no bread in all the land; for the famine was very sore, so that the land of Egypt and all the land of Canaan fainted by reason of the famine.

And Joseph gathered up *all* of the money that was found in the land of Egypt, and in the land of Canaan, for the corn which they bought; and Joseph brought the money into Pharaoh's house.

And when money failed in the land of Egypt, and in the land of Canaan, *all* the Egyptians came unto Joseph, and said, Give us bread: for why should we die in thy presence? for the money faileth.

And Joseph said, Give your cattle; and I will give you for your cattle, if money fail.

And they brought their cattle unto Joseph: and Joseph gave them bread in exchange for horses, and for the flocks, and for the cattle of the herds, and for the asses: and he fed them with bread *for all their cattle* that year.

When that year was ended, they came unto him the second year, and said unto him, We will not hide it from my lord, how that our money is spent; my lord also hath our herds of cattle; there is *not aught left* in the sight of my lord, but *our bodies, and our lands:*

Wherefore shall we die before thine eyes, both we and our land? buy *us* and *our land* for bread, and we and our land will be servants unto Pharaoh: and give us seed that we may live, and not die, that the land be not desolate.

And Joseph *bought* all the land of Egypt for Pharaoh; for the Egyptians *sold* every man his field, because the famine prevailed over them: so *the land became Pharaoh's.*

And as for the people, he removed them to cities from one end of the borders of Egypt even to the other end thereof.

Only the land of the priests bought he not; for the priests had a portion assigned them of Pharaoh, and did eat their portion which Pharaoh gave them: wherefore they sold not their lands.

Then Joseph said unto the people, Behold I have *bought you* this day *and your land* for Pharaoh: lo, here is seed for you, and ye shall sow the land.

And it shall come to pass in the increase, that ye shall give the fifth part unto Pharaoh, and four parts shall be your own, for seed of the field, and for your own food, and for them of your households, and for food for your little ones.

And they said, Thou hast saved our lives: let us find grace in the sight of my lord, and we will be Pharaoh's servants.

And Joseph made it a law over the land of Egypt unto this day, that Pharaoh should have the fifth part; except the land of the priests only, which became not Pharaoh's.

I do not find anything there about a "pledge." It looks to me like a brand-new asset—for Joseph. And a most handsome and ameliorating one, too—if a body could find some kind of authority for it. But I can't find it; I do not find that Joseph made loans to those distressed peasants and secured the loans by mortgage on their lands and animals, I seem to find that he took the land itself—to the last acre, and the animals too, to the last hoof. And I do not get the impression that Joseph charged those starving unfortunates "only a fair market price for the food they received." No, I get the impression that he skinned them of every last penny they had; of every last acre they had; of every last animal they had; then bought the whole nation's *bodies* and *liberties* on a "fair market" valuation for bread and the chains of slavery. Is it conceivable that there can be a "fair market price," or any price whatever, estimable in gold, or diamonds, or bank notes, or government bonds, for a man's supremest possession—that one possession without which his life is totally worthless—his liberty?

Joseph acted handsome by the clergy; it is the most I can say for him. Politic, too. They haven't forgotten it yet.

No, I thank you cordially and in all sincerity, but I am afraid to come, I must not venture to come, for I am sensitive, I am humane, I am tender in my feelings, and I could not bear it if young Mr. Rockefeller, whom I think a great deal of, should get up and go to whitewashing Joseph again. But you have my very best wishes.

Mark Twain,
Honorary Member of the Bible Class.

I sent that letter privately to young John himself, and asked him to make himself perfectly free with it, and please suppress it if it seemed to him improper matter to be read in a church. He suppressed it—which shows that he has a level Standard Oil head notwithstanding his theology. Then he asked me to go to the meeting of honoraries and talk and said I might choose my own subject and talk freely. He suggested a subject which he had been experimenting with himself before his Bible Class, a couple of months ago—lying. The subject suited me very well. I had read the newspaper reports of his discourse and had perceived that he was like all the other pulpits. He knew nothing valuable about lying; that, like all other pulpits, he imagines that there has been somebody upon this planet, at some time or other, who was not a liar; that he imagines like all other pulpits——however I have treated this matter in one of my books, and it is not necessary to treat it again in this place.

It was agreed that young John is to call at the house day after to-morrow evening and take me to his church, I to be free to talk about lying, if I like, or talk upon some freshly interesting subject instead, in case there should be a person there capable of starting a fresh subject in such an atmosphere.

But, after all, I can't go. I am fighting off my annual bronchitis, and the doctor has forbidden it. I am sorry, for I am sure I know more about lying than anybody who has lived on this planet before me. I believe I am the only person alive who is sane upon this subject. I have been familiar with it for seventy years. The first utterance I ever made was a lie, for I pretended that a pin was sticking me, whereas it was not so. I have been interested in this great art ever since. I have practised it ever since; sometimes for pleasure, usually for profit. And to this day I do not always know when to believe myself, and when to take the matter under consideration.

I shall be unspeakably sorry if the bronchitis catches me, for that will mean six weeks in bed—my annual tribute to it for the last sixteen years. I shall be sorry because I want to be in condition to appear at Carnegie Hall on the night of April 10th and take my permanent leave of the platform. I never intend to lecture for pay again, and I think I shall never lecture again where the audience has paid to get in. I shall go on talking, but it will be for fun, not money. I can get lots of it to do.

My first appearance before an audience was forty years ago, in San Francisco. If I live to take my farewell in Carnegie Hall on the night of the 10th, I shall see, and see constantly, what no one else in that house will see. I shall see two vast audiences—the San Francisco audience of forty years ago and the one which will be before me at that time. I shall see that early audience with as absolute distinctness in every detail as I see it at this moment, and as I shall see it while looking at the Carnegie audience. I am promising myself a great, a consuming pleasure, on that Carnegie night, and I hope that the bronchitis will leave me alone and let me enjoy it.

I was vaguely meditating a farewell stunt when General Fred Grant sent a gentleman over here a week ago to offer me a thousand dollars to deliver a talk for the benefit of the Robert Fulton Memorial Association of which he is the President and I Vice-President. This was the very thing, and I accepted at once, and said I would without delay write some telegrams and letters from Fred Grant to myself and sign his name to them, and I would answer those telegrams and letters and sign my name to them, and in this way we could make a good advertisement and I could thus get the fact before the public that I was now delivering my last and final platform talk for money. I wrote the correspondence at once. General Grant approved it, and I here insert it.

PRIVATE AND CONFIDENTIAL.

[Correspondence.]

Telegram.

Headquarters Department of the East,
Governors Island, New York.

Mark Twain, New York.
    Would you consider a proposal to talk at Carnegie Hall for the benefit of the Robert Fulton Memorial Association, of which you are a Vice-President, for a fee of a thousand dollars?

F. D. Grant,
President
Fulton Memorial Association.

Telegraphic Answer.

Major General F. D. Grant,
Headquarters Department of the East,
Governors Island, New York.
    I shall be glad to do it, but I must stipulate that you keep the thousand dollars and add it to the Memorial Fund as my contribution.

Clemens.

Letters.

Dear Mr. Clemens: You have the thanks of the Association, and the terms shall be as you say. But why give all of it? Why not reserve a portion—why should you do this work wholly without compensation?

Truly Yours
Fred D. Grant.

Major General Grant,
Headquarters Department of the East.
Dear General: Because I stopped talking for pay a good many years ago, and I could not resume the habit now without a great deal of personal discomfort. I love to hear myself talk, because I get so much instruction and moral upheaval out of it, but I lose the bulk of this joy when I charge for it. Let the terms stand.

General, if I have your approval, I wish to use this good occasion to retire permanently from the platform.

Truly Yours
S. L. Clemens.

Dear Mr. Clemens:
Certainly. But as an old friend, permit me to say, Don't do that. Why should you?—you are not old yet.

Yours truly
Fred D. Grant.

Dear General:
I mean the *pay*-platform; I shan't retire from the gratis-platform until after I am dead and courtesy requires me to keep still and not disturb the others.

What shall I talk about? My idea is this: to instruct the audience about Robert Fulton, and . . . . Tell me—was that his real name, or was it his nom de plume? However, never mind, it is not important—I can skip it, and the house will think I knew all about it, but forgot. Could you find out for me if he was one of the Signers of the Declaration, and which one? But if it is any trouble, let it alone, I can skip it. Was he out with Paul Jones? Will you ask Horace Porter? And ask him if he brought both of them home. These will be very interesting facts, if they can be established. But never mind, don't trouble Porter, I can establish them anyway. The way I look at it, they are historical gems—gems of the very first water.

Well, that is my idea, as I have said: first, excite the audience with a spoonful of information about Fulton, then quiet them down with a barrel of illustration drawn by memory from my books—and if you don't say anything the house will think they never heard of it before, because people don't really read your books, they only say they do, to keep you from feeling bad. Next, excite the house with another spoonful of Fultonian fact. Then tranquillize them again with another barrel of illustration. And so on and so on, all through the evening; and if you are discreet and don't tell them the illustrations don't illustrate anything, they won't notice it and I will send them home as well informed about Robert Fulton as I am myself. Don't you be afraid; I know all about audiences, they believe everything you say, except when you are telling the truth.

Truly Yours
S. L. Clemens.

P. S. Mark all the advertisements *"Private and Confidential,"* otherwise the people will not read them.   M. T.

Dear Mr. Clemens:

How long shall you talk? I ask in order that we may be able to say when carriages may be called.

> Very Truly Yours
> Hugh Gordon Miller.
> Secretary.

Dear Mr. Miller:

I cannot say for sure. It is my custom to keep on talking till I get the audience cowed. Sometimes it takes an hour and fifteen minutes, sometimes I can do it in an hour.

> Sincerely Yours
> S. L. Clemens.

Mem. My charge is *two boxes free.* Not the choicest—*sell* the choicest, and give me any six-seat boxes you please.

> SLC

I want Fred Grant (in uniform) on the stage; also the rest of the officials of the Association; also other distinguished people—all the attractions we can get. Also, a seat for Mr. Albert Bigelow Paine, who may be useful to me if he is near me and on the front.

> SLC

Private and Confidential.

At Carnegie Hall
(put in the date)
MR. MARK TWAIN
will take
PERMANENT LEAVE (very large)
of the platform (very small type)

═══════

Proceeds to go to the Robert Fulton
Memorial Fund.

═══════

Tickets $ . . . . obtainable
at . . . . and at . . . .

═══════

BOXES WILL BE SOLD BY AUCTION
at . . . . on (date)

INSTRUMENTAL MUSIC
preceding the talk.

═══════

At 8.40 INTERMISSION
of 10 minutes

Wednesday, March 21, 1906

Mental telegraphy—Letter from Mr. Jock Brown—Search for Dr. John Brown's letters a failure—Mr. Twichell and his wife, Harmony, have an adventure in Scotland—Mr. Twichell's picture of a military execution—Letter relating to foundation of the Players Club—The mismanagement which caused Mr. Clemens to be expelled from the Club—He is now an honorary member.

Certainly mental telegraphy is an industry which is always silently at work—oftener than otherwise, perhaps, when we are not suspecting that it is affecting our thought. A few weeks ago when I was dictating something about Dr. John Brown of Edinburgh and our pleasant relations with him during six weeks there, and his pleasant relations with our little child, Susy, he had not been in my mind for a good while—a year, perhaps—but he has often been in my mind since, and his name has been frequently upon my lips and as frequently falling from the point of my pen. About a fortnight ago I began to plan an article about him and about Marjorie Fleming, whose first biographer he was, and yesterday I began the article. To-day comes a letter from his son Jock, from whom I had not previously heard for a good many years. He has been engaged in collecting his father's letters for publication. This labor would naturally bring me into his mind with some frequency, and I judge that his mind telegraphed his thoughts to me across the Atlantic. I imagine that we get most of our thoughts out of somebody else's head, by mental telegraphy—and not always out of heads of acquaintances but, in the majority of cases, out of the heads of strangers; strangers far removed—Chinamen, Hindoos, and all manner of remote foreigners whose language we should not be able to understand, but whose thoughts we can read without difficulty.

7 Greenhill Place
Edinburgh

8th March, 1906.

Dear Mr Clemens,

I hope you remember me, Jock, son of Dr John Brown. At my father's death I handed to Dr J. T. Brown all the letters I had to my father, as he intended to write his life, being his cousin and life long friend. He did write a memoir, published after his death in 1901, but he made no use of the letters and it was little more than a critique of his writings. If you care to see it I shall send it. Among the letters which I got back in 1902 were some from you and Mrs Clemens. I have now got a large number of letters written by my father between 1830 and 1882 and intend publishing a selection in order to give the public an idea of the man he was. This I think they will do. Miss E. T. MacLaren is to add the necessary notes. I now write to ask you if you have letters from him and if you will let me see them and use them. I enclose letters from yourself and Mrs Clemens which I should like to use, 15 sheets typewritten. Though I did not write as I should to you on the death of Mrs Clemens, I was very sorry to hear of it through the papers, and as I now read these letters, she rises before me, gentle and loveable as I knew her. I do hope you will let me use her letter, it is most beautiful. I also hope you will let me use yours. . . .

I am
Yours very sincerely
John Brown

We have searched for Doctor John's letters but without success. I do not understand this. There ought to be a good many, and none should be missing, for Mrs. Clemens held Doctor John in such love and reverence that his letters were sacred things in her eyes and she preserved them and took watchful care of them. During our ten years' absence in Europe many letters and like memorials became scattered and lost, but I think it unlikely that Doctor John's have suffered this fate. I think we shall find them yet.

These thoughts about Jock bring back to me the Edinburgh of thirty-three years ago, and the thought of Edinburgh brings to my mind one of Reverend Joe Twichell's adventures. A quarter of a century ago, Twichell and Harmony, his wife, visited Europe for the first time, and made a stay of a day or two in Edinburgh. They were devotees of Scott, and they devoted that day or two to ransacking Edinburgh for things and places made sacred by contact with the Magician of the North. Toward midnight, on the second night, they were returning to their lodgings on foot; a dismal and steady rain was falling, and by consequence they had George street all to themselves. Presently the rainfall became so heavy that they took refuge from it in a deep doorway, and there in the black darkness they discussed with satisfaction all the achievements of the day. Then Joe said:

"It has been hard work, and a heavy strain on the strength, but we have our reward. There isn't a thing connected with Scott in Edinburgh that we haven't seen or touched—not one. I mean the things a stranger *could* have access to. There is *one* we haven't seen, but it's not accessible—a private collection of relics and memorials of Scott of great interest, but I do not know where it is. I can't get on the track of it. I wish we could, but we can't. We've got to give the idea up. It would be a grand thing to have a sight of that collection, Harmony."

A voice out of the darkness said "Come up stairs and I will show it to you!"

And the voice was as good as its word. The voice belonged to the gentleman who owned the collection. He took Joe and Harmony up stairs, fed them and refreshed them; and while they examined the collection he chatted and explained. When they left at two in the morning they realized that they had had the star time of their trip.

Joe has always been on hand when anything was going to happen—except once. He got delayed in some unaccountable way, or he would have been blown up at Petersburg when the mined defences of that place were flung heavenward in the Civil War.

When I was in Hartford the other day he told me about another of his long string of providential opportunities. I think he thinks Providence is always looking out for him when interesting things are going to happen. This was the execution of some deserters during the Civil War. When we read about such things in history we always have one and the same picture—blindfolded men kneeling with their heads bowed; a file of stern and alert soldiers fronting them with their muskets ready; an austere officer in uniform standing apart who gives sharp terse orders, "Make ready. Take aim. Fire!" There is a belch of flame and smoke, the victims fall forward expiring, the file shoulders arms, wheels, marches erect and stiff-legged off the field, and the incident is closed.

Joe's picture is different. And I suspect that it is the true one—the common one. In this picture the deserters requested that they might be allowed to stand, not kneel; that they might not be blindfolded, but permitted to look the firing file in the eye. Their request was granted.

They stood erect and soldierly; they kept their color, they did not blench; their eyes were steady. *But these things could not be said of any other person present.* A General of Brigade sat upon his horse white-faced—white as a corpse. The officer commanding the squad was white-faced—white as a corpse. The firing file were white-faced, and their forms wobbled so that the wobble was transmitted to their muskets when they took aim. The officer of the squad could not command his voice, and his tone was weak and poor, not brisk and stern. When the file had done its deadly work it did not march away martially erect and stiff-legged. It wobbled.

This picture commends itself to me as being the truest one that any one has yet furnished of a military execution.

In searching for Dr. Brown's letters—a failure—we have made a find which we were not expecting. Evidently it marks the foundation of the Players Club, and so it has value for me.

Daly's Theatre

UNDER THE MANAGEMENT OF AUGUSTIN DALY. MANAGERS OFFICE.

New York, Jan 2d 1888.

Mr Augustin Daly will be very much pleased to have Mr S. L. Clemens meet Mr Booth, Mr Barrett and Mr Palmer and a few friends at Lunch on Friday next January 6th (at one oclock in Delmonico's) to discuss the formation of a new club which it is thought will claim your interest.

R.S.V.P.

All the founders, I think, were present at that luncheon—among them Booth, Barrett, Palmer, General Sherman, Bispham, Aldrich, and the rest. I do not recall the other names. I think Laurence Hutton states in one of his books that the Club's name—The Players—had been already selected and accepted before this luncheon took place, but I take that to be a mistake. I remember that several names were proposed, discussed, and abandoned at the luncheon; that finally Thomas Bailey Aldrich suggested that compact and simple name, The Players; and that even that happy title was not immediately accepted. However the discussion was very brief. The objections to it were easily routed and driven from the field, and the vote in its favor was unanimous.

I lost my interest in the Club three years ago—for cause—but it has lately returned to me, to my great satisfaction. Mr. Booth's bequest was a great and generous one—but he left two. The other one was not much of a benefaction. It was Magonigle, a foolish old relative of his who needed a support. As Secretary he governed the Club and its Board of Managers like an autocrat from the beginning until three or four months ago, when he retired from his position superannuated. From the beginning, I left my dues and costs to be paid by my business agent in Hartford—Mr. Whitmore. He attended to all business of mine. I interested myself in none of it. When we went to Europe in '91 I left a written order in the Secretary's office continuing Whitmore in his function of paymaster of my club dues. Nothing happened until a year had gone by. Then a bill for dues reached me in Europe. I returned it to Magonigle and reminded him of my order, which had not been changed. Then for a couple of years the bills went to Whitmore, after which a bill came to me in Europe. I returned it with the previous remarks repeated. But about every two years the sending of bills to me would be resumed. I sent them back with the usual remarks. Twice the bills were accompanied by offensive letters from the

Secretary. These I answered profanely. At last we came home, in 1901. No bills came to me for a year. Then we took a residence at Riverdale-on-the-Hudson, and straightway came a Players bill for dues. I was aweary, aweary, and I put it in the waste-basket. Ten days later the bill came again, and with it a shadowy threat. I waste-basketed it. After another ten days the bill came once more, and this time the threat was in a concreted condition. It said very peremptorily that if the bill were not paid within a week I would be expelled from the Club and posted as a delinquent. This went the way of its predecessors into the waste-basket. On the named day I was expelled and posted—and I was much gratified, for I was tired of being Magonigled every little while.

Robert Reid, David Munro, and other special friends in the Club were astonished and put themselves in communication with me to find out what this strange thing meant. I explained to them. They wanted me to state the case to the Management and require a reconsideration of the decree of expulsion, but I had to decline that proposition. And therefore things remained as they were until a few months ago when the Magonigle retired from the autocracy. The boys thought that my return to the Club would be plain and simple sailing now, but I thought differently. I was no longer a member. I could not become a member without consenting to be voted for like any other candidate, and I would not do that. The Management had expelled me upon the mere statement of a clerk that I was a delinquent. Neither they nor the clerk could know whether I ever received those bills and threats or not, since they had been transmitted by the mail. They had not asked me to testify in my defence. Their books would show that I had never failed to pay, and pay promptly. They might properly argue from that that I had not all of a sudden become a rascal, and that I might be able to explain the situation if asked. The Board's whole proceeding had been like *all* the Board's proceedings from the beginning— arbitrary, insolent, stupid. That Board's proper place, from the beginning, was the idiot asylum. I could not allow myself to be voted for again, because from my view of the matter I had never lawfully and legitimately ceased to be a member. However, when Providence disposed of Magonigle, a way fair and honorable to all concerned was easily found to bridge the separating crack. I was made an honorary member, and I have been glad to resume business at the old stand.

Thursday, March 22, 1906

Susy's Biography—Langdon's illness and death—Susy tells of interesting
men whom her father met in England and Scotland—Dr. John Brown,
Mr. Charles Kingsley, Mr. Henry M. Stanley, Sir Thomas Hardy, Mr. Henry
Irving, Robert Browning, Sir Charles Dilke, Charles Reade, William
Black, Lord Houghton, Frank Buckland, Tom Hughes, Anthony Trollope,
Tom Hood, Dr. MacDonald, and Harrison Ainsworth—Mr. Clemens tells
of meeting Lewis Carroll—Of luncheon at Lord Houghton's—Letters
from Mr. and Mrs. Clemens to Dr. Brown—Mr. Clemens's regret that
he did not take Mrs. Clemens for last visit to Dr. Brown.

I stopped in the middle of mamma's early history to tell about our tripp to Vassar because I was afraid I would forget about it, now I will go on where I left off. Some time after Miss Emma Nigh died papa took mamma and little Langdon to Elmira for the summer. When in Elmira Langdon began to fail but I think mamma did not know just what was the matter with him.

I was the cause of the child's illness. His mother trusted him to my care and I took him a long drive in an open barouche for an airing. It was a raw, cold morning, but he was well wrapped about with furs and, in the hands of a careful person, no harm would have come to him. But I soon dropped into a reverie and forgot all about my charge. The furs fell away and exposed his bare legs. By and by the coachman noticed this, and I arranged the wraps again, but it was too late. The child was almost frozen. I hurried home with him. I was aghast at what I had done, and I feared the consequences. I have always felt shame for that treacherous morning's work and have not allowed myself to think of it when I could help it. I doubt if I had the courage to make confession at that time. I think it most likely that I have never confessed until now.

From Susy's Biography.

At last it was time for papa to return to Hartford, and Langdon was real sick at that time, but still mamma decided to go with him, thinking the journey might do him good. But after they reached Hartford he became very sick, and his trouble prooved to be diptheeria. He died about a week after mamma and papa reached Hartford. He was burried by the side of grandpa at Elmira, New York. (Susy rests there with them. S.L.C.) After that, mamma became very very ill, so ill that there seemed great danger of death, but with a great deal of good care she recovered. Some months afterward mamma and papa (and Susy, who was perhaps fourteen or fifteen months old at the time—S.L.C.) went to Europe and stayed for a time in Scotland and England. In Scotland mamma and papa became very well equanted with Dr. John Brown, the author of "Rab and His Friends," and he met, but was not so well equanted with, Mr. Charles Kingsley, Mr. Henry M. Stanley, Sir Thomas Hardy grandson of the Captain Hardy to whom Nellson said "Kiss me Hardy," when dying on shipboard, Mr. Henry Irving, Robert Browning, Sir Charles Dilke, Mr. Charles Reade, Mr. William Black, Lord Houghton, Frank Buckland, Mr. Tom Hughes, Anthony Trollope, Tom Hood, son of the poet—and mamma and papa were quite well equanted with Dr. Macdonald and family, and papa met Harison Ainsworth.

I remember all these men very well indeed, except the last one. I do not recall Ainsworth. By my count, Susy mentions fourteen men. They are all dead except Sir Charles Dilke and Mr. Tom Hughes.

We met a great many other interesting people, among them Lewis Carroll, author of the immortal "Alice"—but he was only interesting to look at, for he was the stillest and shyest full-grown man I have ever met except "Uncle Remus." Dr. MacDonald and several other lively talkers were present, and the talk went briskly on for a couple of hours, but Carroll sat still all the while except that now and then he answered a question. His answers were brief. I do not remember that he elaborated any of them.

At a dinner at Smalley's we met Herbert Spencer. At a large luncheon party at Lord Hough-ton's we met Sir Arthur Helps, who was a celebrity of world-wide fame at the time, but is quite forgotten now. Lord Elcho, a large vigorous man, sat at some distance down the table. He was talking earnestly about Godalming. It was a deep and flowing and unarticulated rumble, but I got the Godalming pretty clearly every time it broke free of the rumble, and as all the strength was on the first end of the word it startled me every time, because it sounded so like swearing. In the middle of the luncheon Lady Houghton rose, remarked to the guests on her right and on her left in a matter-of-fact way, "Excuse me, I have an engagement," and without further ceremony she went off to meet it. This would have been doubtful etiquette in America. Lord Houghton told a number of delightful stories. He told them in French, and I lost nothing of them but the nubs.

I will insert here one or two of the letters referred to by Jock Brown in the letter which I received from him a day or two ago, and which we copied into yesterday's record.

June 22, 1876.

Dear Doctor Brown,

Indeed I was a happy woman to see the familiar handwriting. I do hope that we shall not have to go so long again without a word from you. I wish you could come over to us for a season; it seems as if it would do you good, you and yours would be so very welcome.

We are now where we were two years ago when Clara (our baby) was born, on the farm on the top of a high hill where my sister spends her summers. The children are grown fat and hearty, feeding chickens and ducks twice a day, and are keenly alive to all the farm interests. Mr. J. T. Fields was with us with his wife a short time ago, and you may be sure we talked most affectionately of you. We do so earnestly desire that you may continue to improve in health; do let us know of your welfare as often as possible. Love to your sister. Kind regards to your son please.

As ever affectionately your friend,

Livy L. Clemens.

(1875)

Dear Doctor Brown,

We had grown so very anxious about you that it was a great pleasure to see the dear, familiar handwriting again, but the contents of the letter did make us *inexpressibly sad*. We have talked so much since about your coming to see us. Would not the change do you good? Could you not trust yourself with us? We would do everything to make you comfortable and happy that we could, and you have so many admirers in America that would be so happy and proud to welcome you. Is it not possible for you to come? Could not your son bring you? Perhaps the entire change would give you a new and healthier lease of life.

Our children are both well and happy; I wish that you could see them. Susy is very motherly to the little one. Mr. Clemens is hard at work on a new book now. He has a new book of sketches recently out, which he is going to send you in a few days; most of the sketches are old, but some few are new.

Oh Doctor Brown how can you speak of your life as a wasted one? What you have written has alone done an *immense* amount of good, and I know for I speak from experi-ence that one must get good every time they meet and chat with you. I receive good every time I even *think* of you. Can a life that produces such an effect on others be a wasted life?

I feel that while you live the world is sweeter and better. You ask if Clara is "queer and wistful and commanding," like your Susy. We think she is more queer, (more quaint) perhaps more commanding, but not nearly so wistful in her ways as "your Susy." The nurse that we had with us in Edinburgh had to leave me to take care of a sister ill with consumption. We have had ever since a quiet lady-like German girl. I must leave a place for Mr. C. Do think about coming to us. Give my love to your sister and your son.

Affectionately,
Livy L. Clemens.

Dear Doctor, if you and your son Jock only *would* run over here! What a welcome we would give you! and besides, you would forget cares and the troubles that come of them. To forget pain is to be painless; to forget care is to be rid of it; to go abroad is to accomplish both. Do try the prescription!

Always with love,
Saml. L. Clemens.

P.S. Livy, you haven't *signed* your letter. Don't forget *that*. S.L.C.
P.P.S. I hope you will excuse Mr. Clemens's P.S. to me; it is characteristic for him to put it right on the letter. *Livy* L.C.

Hartford, June 1, 1882.

My dear Mr. Brown,

I was three thousand miles from home, at breakfast in New Orleans, when the damp morning paper revealed the sorrowful news among the cable dispatches. There was no place in America, however remote, or however rich or poor or high or humble, where words of mourning for your honored father were not uttered that morning, for his works had made him known and loved all over the land. To Mrs. Clemens and me, the loss is a personal one, and our grief the grief which one feels for one who was peculiarly near and dear. Mrs. Clemens has never ceased to express regret that we came away from England the last time without going to see him, and often we have since projected a voyage across the Atlantic for the sole purpose of taking him by the hand and looking into his kind eyes once more before he should be called to his rest.

We both thank you greatly for the Edinburgh papers which you sent. My wife and I join in affectionate remembrances and greetings to yourself and your aunt, and in the sincere tender of our sympathies.

Faithfully yours,
S.L. Clemens.

P.S. Our Susy is still "Megalopis." He gave her that name.

Can you spare us a photograph of your father? We have none but the one taken in group with ourselves.

It was my fault that she never saw Doctor John in life again. How many crimes I committed against that gentle and patient and forgiving spirit! I always told her that if she died first, the rest of my life would be made up of self-reproaches for the tears I had made her shed. And she always replied that if I should pass from life first, she would never have to reproach herself without having loved me the less devotedly or the less constantly because of those tears. We had this conversation again, and for the thousandth time, when the night of death was closing about her—though we did not suspect that.

In the letter last quoted above, I say "Mrs. Clemens has never ceased to express regret that we came away from England the last time without going to see him." I think that that was intended to convey the impression that *she* was a party concerned in our leaving England without going to see him. It is not so. She urged me, she begged me, she implored me to take her to Edinburgh to see Doctor John—but I was in one of my devil moods, and I would not do it. I would not do it because I should have been obliged to continue the courier in service until we got back to Liverpool. It seemed to me that I had endured him as long as I could. I wanted to get aboard ship and be done with him. How childish it all seems now! And how brutal—that I could not be moved to confer upon my wife a precious and lasting joy because it would cause me a small inconvenience. I have known few meaner men than I am. By good fortune this feature of my nature does not often get to the surface, and so I doubt if any member of my family except my wife ever suspected how much of that feature there was in me. I suppose it never failed to arrive at the surface when there was opportunity, but it was as I have said—the opportunities have been so infrequent that this worst detail of my character has never been known to any but two persons—Mrs. Clemens, who suffered from it, and I, who suffer from the remembrance of the tears it caused her.

Friday, March 23, 1906

Some curious letter superscriptions which have come to Mr. Clemens—Our inefficient postal system under Postmaster-General Key—Reminiscences of Mrs. Harriet Beecher Stowe—Story of Reverend Charley Stowe's little boy.

A good many years ago Mrs. Clemens used to keep as curiosities some of the odd and strange superscriptions that decorated letters that came to me from strangers in out-of-the-way corners of the earth. One of these superscriptions was the work of Dr. John Brown, and the letter must have been the first one he wrote me after we came home from Europe in August or September, *1874* '74. Evidently the Doctor was guessing at our address from memory, for he made an amusing mess of it. The superscription was as follows:

> Mr. S. L. Clemens.
> (Mark Twain),
> Hartford, N.Y.
> Near Boston, U.S.A.

Now then comes a fact which is almost incredible, to wit: the New York postoffice which did not contain a single salaried idiot who could not have stated promptly who the letter was for and to what town it should go, actually sent that letter to a wee little hamlet hidden away in the remotenesses of the vast State of New York—for what reason? Because that lost and never previously heard-of hamlet was named Hartford. The letter was returned to the New York postoffice from that hamlet. It was returned innocent of the suggestion "Try Hartford Connecticut," although the hamlet's postmaster knew quite well that that was the Hartford the writer of the letter was seeking. Then the New York postoffice opened the envelope, got Doctor John's address out of it, then enclosed it in a fresh envelope and sent it back to Edinburgh. Doctor John then got my address from Menzies, the publisher, and sent the letter to me again. He also enclosed the former envelope—the one that had had the adventures—and his anger at our postal system was like the fury of an angel. He came the nearest to being bitter and offensive that ever he came in his life, I suppose. He said that in Great Britain it was the Postal Department's boast that by no ingenuity could a man so disguise and conceal a Smith or a Jones or a Robinson in a letter address that the department couldn't find that man, whereas—then he let fly at our system, which was apparently designed to defeat a letter's attempts to get to its destination when humanly possible.

Doctor John was right about our department—at that time. But that time did not last long. I think Postmaster-General Key was in office then. He was a new broom, and he did some astonishing sweeping for a while. He made some cast-iron rules which worked great havoc with the nation's correspondence. It did not occur to him—rational things seldom occurred to him—that there were several millions of people among us who seldom wrote letters; who were utterly ignorant of postal rules, and who were quite sure to make blunders in writing letter addresses whenever blunders were possible, and that it was the Government's business to do the very best it could by the letters of these innocents and help them get to their destinations, instead of inventing ways to block the road. Key suddenly issued some boiler-iron rules—one of them was that a letter must go to the place named on the envelope, and the effort to find its man must stop there. He must not be searched for. If he wasn't at the place indicated the letter must be returned to the sender. In the case of Doctor John's letter the postoffice had a wide discretion—not so very wide either. It must go to a Hartford. That Hartford must be near Boston; it must also be in the State of New York. It went to the Hartford that was furthest from Boston, but it filled the requirement of being in the State of New York—and it got defeated.

Another rule instituted by Key was that letter superscriptions could not end with "Philadelphia"—or "Chicago," or "San Francisco," or "Boston," or "New York," but, in every case, must add the *State,* or go to the Dead Letter Office. Also, you could not say "New York, N.Y.," you must add the word *City* to the first "New York" or the letter must go to the Dead Letter Office.

During the first thirty days of the dominion of this singular rule sixteen hundred thousand tons of letters went to the Dead Letter Office from the New York postoffice alone. The Dead Letter Office could not contain them and they had to be stacked up outside the building. There was not room outside the building inside the city, so they were formed into a rampart around the city; and if they had had it there during the Civil War we should not have had so much trouble and uneasiness about an invasion of Washington by the Confederate armies. They could neither have climbed over nor under that breastwork nor bored nor blasted through it. Mr. Key was soon brought to a more rational frame of mind.

Then a letter arrived for me enclosed in a fresh envelope. It was from a village priest in Bohemia or Galicia, and was boldly addressed:

Mark Twain,
Somewhere.

It had traveled over several European countries; it had met with hospitality and with every possible assistance during its wide journey; it was ringed all over, on both sides, with a chain-mail mesh of postmarks—there were nineteen of them altogether. And one of them was a New York postmark. The postal hospitalities had ceased at New York—within three hours and a half of my home. There the letter had been opened, the priest's address ascertained, and the letter had then been returned to him, as in the case of Dr. John Brown.

Among Mrs. Clemens's collection of odd addresses was one on a letter from Australia, worded thus:

Mark Twain,
God knows where.

That superscription was noted by newspapers, here and there and yonder while it was on its travels, and doubtless suggested another odd superscription invented by some stranger in a far-off land—and this was the wording of it:

Mark Twain.
Somewhere,
(Try Satan).

That stranger's trust was not misplaced. Satan courteously sent it along.

This morning's mail brings another of these novelties. It comes from France—from a young English girl—and is addressed:

Mark Twain
———

c/o President Roosevelt.
The White House
Washington
America
———

U.S.A.

It was not delayed, but came straight along bearing the Washington postmark of yesterday.

In a diary which Mrs. Clemens kept for a little while, a great many years ago, I find various mentions of Mrs. Harriet Beecher Stowe, who was a near neighbor of ours in Hartford, with no fences between. And in those days she made as much use of our grounds as of her own, in pleasant weather. Her mind had decayed, and she was a pathetic figure. She wandered about all the day long in the care of a muscular Irish woman. Among the colonists of our neighborhood the doors always stood open in pleasant weather. Mrs. Stowe entered them at her own free will, and as she was always softly slippered and generally full of animal spirits, she was able to deal in surprises, and she liked to do it. She would slip up behind a person who was deep in dreams and musings and fetch a war whoop that would jump that person out of his clothes. And she had other moods. Sometimes we would hear gentle music in the drawing-room and would find her there at the piano singing ancient and melancholy songs with infinitely touching effect.

Her husband, old Professor Stowe, was a picturesque figure. He wore a broad slouch hat. He was a large man, and solemn. His beard was white and thick and hung far down on his breast. His nose was enlarged and broken up by a disease which made it look like a cauliflower. The first time our little Susy ever saw him she encountered him on the street near our house and came flying wide-eyed to her mother and said "Santa Claus has got loose!"

Which reminds me of Reverend Charley Stowe's little boy—a little boy of seven years. I met Reverend Charley crossing his mother's grounds one morning and he told me this little tale. He had been out to Chicago to attend a Convention of Congregational clergymen, and had taken his little boy with him. During the trip he reminded the little chap, every now and then, that he must be on his very best behavior there in Chicago. He said "We shall be the guests of a clergyman, there will be other guests—clergymen and their wives—and you must be careful to let those people see by your walk and conversation that you are of a godly household. Be very careful about this." The admonition bore fruit. At the first breakfast which they ate in the Chicago clergyman's house he heard his little son say in the meekest and most reverent way to the lady opposite him,

"Please, won't you, for Christ's sake, pass the butter?"

Monday, March 26, 1906

John D.'s Bible Class again—Mr. Clemens comments on several newspaper clippings—Tells Mr. Howells the scheme of this autobiography—Tells the newspaper account of girl who tried to commit suicide—Newspapers in remote villages and in great cities contrasted—Remarks about Captain E. L. Marsh and Dick Higham—Higbie's letter, and *Herald* letter to Higbie.

ROCKEFELLER, JR., ON WEALTH

—

Not to be Put Before God, but All Right as a Goal for the Ambitious.

John D. Rockefeller, Jr., apologized yesterday to the members of his Bible class for having monopolized all the time of the Sunday hour heretofore, and promised never to do so again, unless his subject should be such that discussion of it would not be practical.

"It is better," he said, "that we have a general discussion, and as many of us as possible express our views."

Then Mr. Rockefeller raised a question calculated to give the members opportunity for discussion. He took up the Ten Commandments, and after dividing them into the first five as relating to man's obligations to God and the second five as relating to man's obligation to his neighbor, he said:

"We are so in the habit of following and obeying most of the Commandments that it is useless to take them up. Let us take the First and Fourth Commandments. Let us now consider the First Commandment, and see if we worship only one God. Many of us give our first thought to our pleasures, and it is very frequently the case to-day that our first thought is for worldly possessions. A stranger coming here would say that the God of New York was the God of Wealth. When we think of pleasure or of wealth before we think of God, then we violate the First Commandment.

"I do not mean to say that we should not be moved by ambition or be given to innocent pleasure, but I mean to say that when we put God second to these aims, we are then not worshipping Him as we should.

"When the rich young man was told to go and give all his possessions to the poor, it was because Christ realized that the rich young man was thinking first of his wealth and then of God, and violating the First Commandment.

"In the consideration of the Fourth Commandment, let us try to discover what is the proper way to observe the Sabbath. How far are we justified in violating the restrictions put down in that commandment?"

Several discussed Sabbath observance. Then Mr. Rockefeller said:

"The subject is one that should give rise to general and helpful discussion. Is it right for me to play golf, to ride a bicycle, or go to the country on Sunday? That is what we want to know. We are here seeking truth. Let us think it over during the week and next Sunday be prepared with our views. Then we may reach a just conclusion."

Young John D., you see, has been dripping theology again, yesterday. I missed his reunion of the honorary membership of his Bible Class last Thursday night, through illness, and I was very sincerely sorry. I had to telephone him not to come for me. However, perhaps it was of profit to me to be obliged to stay away, for I was going to say some things about lying which would have been too nakedly true for Bible Class consumption. That Bible Class is so uninured to anything resembling either truth or sense that I think a clean straight truth falling in its midst would make as much havoc as a bombshell.

BABY ADVICE IN A CAR.

Old Man Got It, 5-Year-Old Gave It, Mother Said, "Shut Up."

A benevolent-looking old man clung to a strap in a crowded Broadway car bound up-town Saturday afternoon. In a corner seat in front of him huddled a weak-looking little woman who clasped a baby to her breast. Beside her sat another child, a girl perhaps 5 years old, who seemed to be attracted by the old man's kindly face, for she gazed at him and the baby with her bright, intelligent eyes opened wide. He smiled at her interest and said to her:

"My! What a nice baby! Just such a one as I was looking for. I am going to take it."

"You can't," declared the little girl, quickly. "She's my sister."

"What! Won't you give her to me?"

"No, I won't."

"But," he insisted, and there was real wistfulness in his tones, "I haven't a baby in my home."

"Then write to God. He'll send you one," said the child, confidently.

The old man laughed. So did the other passengers. But the mother evidently scented blasphemy.

"Tillie," said she, "shut up and behave yourself!"

That is a scrap which I have cut from this morning's *Times*. It is very prettily done, charmingly done; done with admirable ease and grace—with the ease and grace that are born of feeling and sympathy, as well as of practice with the pen. Every now and then a newspaper reporter astonishes me with felicities like this. I was a newspaper reporter myself forty-four years ago, and during three subsequent years—but as I remember it I and my comrades never had time to cast our things in a fine literary mould. That scrap will be just as touching and just as beautiful three hundred years hence as it is now.

I intend that this autobiography shall become a model for all future autobiographies when it is published, after my death, and I also intend that it shall be read and admired a good many centuries because of its form and method—a form and method whereby the past and the present are constantly brought face to face, resulting in contrasts which newly fire up the interest all along like contact of flint with steel. Moreover, this autobiography of mine does not select from my life its showy episodes, but deals merely in the common experiences which go to make up the life of the average human being, and the narrative must interest the average human being because these episodes are of a sort which he is familiar with in his own life, and in which he sees his own life reflected and set down in print. The usual, conventional autobiographer seems to particularly hunt out those occasions in his career when he came into contact with celebrated persons, whereas his contacts with the uncelebrated were just as interesting to him, and would be to his reader, and were vastly more numerous than his collisions with the famous.

Howells was here yesterday afternoon, and I told him the whole scheme of this autobiography and its apparently systemless system—only apparently systemless, for it is not that. It is a deliberate system, and the law of the system is that I shall talk about the matter which for the moment interests me, and cast it aside and talk about something else the moment its interest for me is exhausted. It is a system which follows no charted course and is not going to follow any such course. It is a system which is a complete and purposed jumble—a course which begins nowhere, follows no specified route, and can never reach an end while I am alive, for the reason that if I should talk to the stenographer two hours a day for a hundred years, I should still never be able to set down a tenth part of the things which have interested me in my lifetime. I told Howells that this autobiography of mine would live a couple of thousand years without any effort and would then take a fresh start and live the rest of the time.

He said he believed it would, and asked me if I meant to make a library of it.

I said that that was my design, but that if I should live long enough the set of volumes could not be contained merely in a city, it would require a State, and that there would not be any Rockefeller alive, perhaps, at any time during its existence who would be able to buy a full set, except on the instalment plan.

Howells applauded, and was full of praises and endorsement, which was wise in him and judicious. If he had manifested a different spirit I would have thrown him out of the window. I like criticism, but it must be my way.

Day before yesterday there was another of those happy literary efforts of the reporters, and I meant to cut it out and insert it to be read with a sad pleasure in future centuries, but I forgot and threw the paper away. It was a brief narrative, but well stated. A poor little starved girl of sixteen, clothed in a single garment, in mid-winter, (albeit properly speaking this is spring) was brought in her pendent rags before a magistrate by a policeman, and the charge against her was that she had been found trying to commit suicide. The Judge asked her why she was moved to that crime, and she told him, in a low voice broken by sobs, that her life had become a burden which she could no longer bear; that she worked sixteen hours a day in a sweat-shop; that the meagre wage she earned had to go toward the family support; that her parents were never able to give her any clothes or enough to eat; that she had worn this same ruined garment as long back as she could remember; that her poor companions were her envy because often they had a penny to spend for some pretty trifle for themselves; that she could not remember when she had had a penny for such a purpose. The court, the policemen, and the other specta-tors cried with her—a sufficient proof that she told her pitiful tale convincingly and well. And the fact that I also was moved by it, at second-hand, is proof that that reporter delivered it from his heart through his pen, and did his work well.

In the remote parts of the country the weekly village newspaper remains the same curious production it was when I was a boy, sixty years ago, on the banks of the Mississippi. The met-ropolitan daily of the great city tells us every day about the movements of Lieutenant General so and so and Rear-Admiral so and so, and what the Vanderbilts are doing, and what hedge beyond the frontiers of New York John D. Rockefeller is hiding behind to keep from being dragged into court and made to testify about alleged Standard Oil iniquities. These great dailies keep us informed of Mr. Carnegie's movements and sayings; they tell us what President Roose-velt said yesterday and what he is going to do to-day. They tell us what the children of his family have been saying, just as the princelings of Europe are daily quoted—and we notice that the remarks of the Roosevelt children are distinctly princely in that the things they say are rather notably inane and not worth while. The great dailies kept us overwhelmed, for a matter of two months, with a daily and hourly and most minute and faithful account of everything Miss Alice and her fiancé were saying and doing and what they were going to say and what they were going to do, until at last, through God's mercy they got married and went under cover and got quiet.

Now the court-circular of the remote village newspaper has always dealt, during these sixty years, with the comings and goings and sayings of *its* local princelings. They have told us during all those years, and they still tell us, what the principal grocery man is doing and how he has bought a new stock; they tell us that relatives are visiting the ice-cream man, that Miss Smith has arrived to spend a week with the Joneses, and so on, and so on. And all that record is just as intensely interesting to the villagers as is the record I have just been speaking of, of the do-ings and sayings of the colossally conspicuous personages of the United States. This shows that human nature is all alike; it shows that we like to know what the big people are doing, so that we can envy them. It shows that the big personage of a village bears the same proportion to the little people of the village that the President of the United States bears to the nation. It shows that *conspicuousness* is the only thing necessary in a person to command our interest and, in a larger or smaller sense, our worship. We recognize that there are *no* trivial occurrences in life if we get the right focus on them. In a village they are just as prodigious as they are when the subject is a personage of national importance.

The Swangos.

From The Hazel Green (Ky.) Herald.

Dr. Bill Swango is able to be in the saddle again.

Aunt Rhod Swango visited Joseph Catron and wife Sunday.

Mrs. Shiloh Swango attended the auction at Maytown Saturday.

W. W. Swango has a nice bunch of cattle ready for the Mount Sterling market.

James Murphy bought ten head of cattle from W. W. Swango last week.

Mrs. John Swango of Montgomery County visited Shiloh Swango and family last week.

Mrs. Sarah Ellen Swango, wife of Wash, the noted turkey trader of Valeria, was the guest of Mrs. Ben Murphy Saturday and Sunday.

Now that is a very genuine and sincere and honest account of what the Swangos have been doing lately in the interior of Kentucky. We see at a glance what a large place that Swango tribe hold in the admiration and worship of the villagers of Hazel Green, Kentucky. In this account, change Swango to *Vanderbilt;* then change it to *Carnegie;* next time change it to *Rockefeller;* next time change it to the *President;* next time to the *Mayor of New York;* next time to Alice's new husband. Last change of all, change *Mrs. Shiloh Swango* to *Mrs. Alice Roosevelt Longworth.* Then it's a court-circular, all complete and dignified.

CAPT. E. L. MARSH.

—

Former Elmiran Who Died at Des Moines, Iowa, Recently.

Captain E. L. Marsh, aged sixty-four years, died at Des Moines, Iowa, a week ago Friday—February 23—after a long illness. The deceased was born in Enfield, Tompkins county, N. Y., in 1842, later came to Elmira to live with his parents and in 1857 left Elmira to locate in Iowa, where he has lived the greater part of the time since, the only exception being brief times of residence in the south and east. He enlisted in Company D, of the Second Iowa at Des Moines, and was elected a captain in that regiment. He served throughout the war with marked courage and efficiency. After the war Captain Marsh went to New Orleans, where he remained during most of the reconstruction period and then went to New York, where he engaged in paving business for several years. He went back to Des Moines in 1877 and resided there during the almost thirty years since. He engaged in the real estate business there with great success. He was married in 1873 and is survived by his wife and two children. Captain Marsh was a member of the Loyal legion, Commandery of Iowa, and was senior vice commander of the order for Iowa. He was a member of the G.A.R. also, and a member of the Congregational church. Captain Marsh was the son of Mr. and Mrs. Sheppard Marsh, and Mrs. Marsh was twin sister of the late Mrs. Jervis Langdon of this city. Captain Marsh was a very dear and close friend of his cousin, General Charles J. Langdon, of Elmira.

This clipping from a Des Moines, Iowa, newspaper, arrives this morning. Ed Marsh was a cousin of my wife, and I remember him very well. He was present at our wedding thirty-six years ago, and was a handsome young bachelor. Aside from my interest in him as a cousin of my young bride, he had another interest for me in the fact that in his Company of the Second Iowa Infantry was Dick Higham. Five years before the war Dick, a good-natured, simple-minded, winning lad of seventeen, was an apprentice in my brother's small printing-office in Keokuk, Iowa. He had an old musket and he used to parade up and down with it in the office, and he said he would rather be a soldier than anything else. The rest of us laughed at him and said he was nothing but a disguised girl, and that if he were confronted by the enemy he would drop his gun and run.

But we were not good prophets. By and by when President Lincoln called for volunteers Dick joined the Second Iowa Infantry, about the time that I was thrown out of my employment as Mississippi River pilot and was preparing to become an imitation soldier on the Confederate side in Ralls County, Missouri. The Second Iowa was moved down to the neighborhood of St. Louis and went into camp there. In some way or other it disgraced itself—and if I remember rightly the punishment decreed was that it should never unfurl its flag again until it won the privilege by gallantry in battle. When General Grant, by and by—February '62—was ordering the charge upon Fort Donelson the Second Iowa begged for the privilege of leading the assault, and got it. Ed Marsh's Company, with Dick in it serving as a private soldier, moved up the hill and through and over the felled trees and other obstructions in the forefront of the charge, and Dick fell with a bullet through the centre of his forehead—thus manfully wiping from the slate the chaffing prophecy of five or six years before. Also, what was left of the Second Iowa finished that charge victorious, with its colors flying, and never more to be furled in disgrace.

Ed Marsh's sister also was at our wedding. She and her brother bore for each other an almost idolatrous love, and this endured until about a year ago. About the time of our marriage, that sister married a blatherskite by the name of Talmage Brown. He was a smart man, but unscrupulous and intemperately religious. Through his smartness he acquired a large fortune, and in his will, made shortly before his death, he appointed Ed Marsh as one of the executors. The estate was worth a million dollars or more, but its affairs were in a very confused condition. Ed Marsh and the other one or two executors performed their duty faithfully, and without remuneration. It took them years to straighten out the estate's affairs, but they accomplished it. During the succeeding years all went pleasantly. But at last, about a year ago, some relatives of the late Talmage Brown persuaded the widow to bring suit against Ed Marsh and his fellow executors for a large sum of money which it was pretended they had either stolen or had wasted by mismanagement. That severed the devoted relationship which had existed between the brother and sister throughout their lives. The mere bringing of the suit broke Ed Marsh's heart, for he was a thoroughly honorable man and could not bear even the breath of suspicion. He took to his bed and the case went to court. He had no word of blame for his sister, and said that no one was to blame but the Browns. They had poisoned her mind. The case was heard in court. Then the Judge threw it out with many indignant comments. The Browns rose to leave the court room but he commanded them to wait and hear what else he had to say. Then in dignified language he skinned them alive, pronounced them frauds and swindlers and let them go. But the news of the rehabilitation reached Marsh too late to save him. He did not rally. He has been losing ground gradually for the past two months, and now at last the end has come.

This morning arrives a letter from my ancient silver-mining comrade, Calvin H. Higbie, a man whom I have not seen nor had communication with for forty-four years. Higbie figures in a chapter of mine in "Roughing It," where the tale is told of how we discovered a rich blind lead in the "Wide West Mine" in Aurora—or, as we called that region then, Esmeralda—and how instead of making our ownership of that exceedingly rich property permanent by doing ten days' work on it, as required by the mining laws, he went off on a wild goose chase to hunt for the mysterious cement mine; and how I went off nine miles to Walker River to nurse Captain John Nye through a violent case of spasmodic rheumatism or blind staggers, or some malady of the kind; and how Cal and I came wandering back into Esmeralda one night just in time to be too late to save our fortune from the jumpers.

I will insert here this letter, and as it will not see the light until Higbie and I are in our graves, I shall allow myself the privilege of copying his punctuation and his spelling, for to me they are a part of the man. He is as honest as the day is long. He is utterly simple-minded and straightforward, and his spelling and his punctuation are as simple and honest as he is himself. He makes no apology for them, and no apology is needed. They plainly state that he is not educated, and they as plainly state that he makes no pretense to being educated.

Greenville, Plumas co. California
March 15—1906

Saml. L. Clemens.
New York city, N.Y.
My Dear Sir—

Two or three parties have ben after me to write up my recolections of Our associations in Nevada, in the early 60s and have come to the conclusion to do so, and have ben jocting down incidents that came to mind, for several years. What I am in dout is, the date you came to Aurora, Nevada—allso, the first trip you made over thee Sieras to California, after coming to Nev. allso as near as passable date, you tended sick man, on, or near Walker River, when our mine was jumped, dont think for a moment that I intend to steal any of your Thunder, but onely to mention some istnstances that you failed to mention, in any of your articles, Books &c. that I ever saw. I intend to submit the articles to you so that you can see if anything is objectionabl, if so to erase, same, and add anything in its place you saw fit—

I was burned out a few years since, and all old data, went up in smoke, is the reason I ask for above dates. have ben sick more or less for 2 or 3 years, unable to earn anything to speak of, and the finances are getting pretty low, and I will admit that it is mainly for the purpose of Earning a little money, that my first attempt at writing will be made—and I should be so pleased to have your candid opinion, of its merits, and what in your wisdom in such matters, would be its value for publication. I enclose a coppy of Herald in answer to enquiry I made, if such an article was desired.

Hoping to hear from you as soon as convenient, I remain with great respect,

Yours &c
C. H. Higbie.

[Copy.]

New York, Mar. 6—/06

C. H. Higbie,
Greenville—Cal.
Dr Sir

I should be glad indeed to receive your account of your experiences with Mark Twain, if they are as interesting as I should imagine they would be the Herald would be quite willing to pay you verry well for them, of course, it would be impassible for me to set a price on the matter until I had an opertunity of examining it. if you will kindly send it on, with the privilege of our authenticating it through Mr Clemens, I shall be more than pleased, to give you a Quick decision and make you an offer as it seems worth to us. however, if you have any particular sum in mind which you think should be the price I would suggest that you communicate with me to that effect.

Yours truly
New York Herald,
By Geo. R. Miner,
Sunday Editor

I have written Higbie and asked him to let me do his literary trading for him. He can shovel sand better than I can—as will appear in the next chapter—but I can beat him all to pieces in the art of fleecing a publisher.

Tuesday, March 27, 1906

Higbie's spelling—Mr. Clemens's scheme for getting Higbie a job at the Pioneer—In 1863 Mr. Clemens goes to Virginia City to be sole reporter on *Territorial Enterprise*—Mr. Clemens tries his scheme for finding employment for the unemployed on a young St. Louis reporter with great success—Also worked the scheme for his nephew, Mr. Samuel E. Moffett.

I have allowed Higbie to assist the *Herald* man's spelling and make it harmonize with his own. He has done it well and liberally, and without prejudice. To my mind he has improved it, for I have had an aversion to good spelling for sixty years and more, merely for the reason that when I was a boy there was not a thing I could do creditably except spell according to the book. It was a poor and mean distinction, and I early learned to disenjoy it. I suppose that this is because the ability to spell correctly is a talent, not an acquirement. There is some dignity about an acquirement, because it is a product of your own labor. It is wages earned, whereas to be able to do a thing merely by the grace of God, and not by your own effort, transfers the distinction to our heavenly home—where possibly it is a matter of pride and satisfaction, but it leaves you naked and bankrupt.

Higbie was the first person to profit by my great and infallible scheme for finding work for the unemployed. I have tried that scheme, now and then, for forty-four years. So far as I am aware it has always succeeded, and it is one of my high prides that I invented it, and that in basing it upon what I conceived to be a fact of human nature I estimated that fact of human nature accurately.

Higbie and I were living in a cotton-domestic lean-to at the base of a mountain. It was very cramped quarters, with barely room for us and the stove—wretched quarters indeed, for every now and then, between eight in the morning and eight in the evening, the thermometer would make an excursion of fifty degrees. We had a silver-mining claim under the edge of a hill half a mile away, in partnership with Bob Howland and Horatio Phillips, and we used to go there every morning carrying with us our luncheon, and remain all day picking and blasting in our shaft, hoping, despairing, hoping again, and gradually but surely running out of funds. At last, when we were clear out and still had struck nothing, we saw that we must find some other way of earning a living. I secured a place in a near-by quartz mill to screen sand with a long-handled shovel. I hate a long-handled shovel. I never could learn to swing it properly. As often as any other way the sand didn't reach the screen at all, but went over my head and down my back, inside of my clothes. It was the most detestable work I have ever engaged in, but it paid ten dollars a week and board—and the board was worth while, because it consisted not only of bacon, beans, coffee, bread and molasses, but we had stewed dried apples every day in the week just the same as if it were Sunday. But this palatial life, this gross and luxurious life, had to come to an end, and there were two sufficient reasons for it. On my side, I could not endure the heavy labor; and on the Company's side, they did not feel justified in paying me to shovel sand down my back; so I was discharged just at the moment that I was going to resign.

If Higbie had taken that job all would have been well and everybody satisfied, for his great frame would have been competent. He was muscled like a giant. He could handle a long-handled shovel like an emperor, and he could work patiently and contentedly twelve hours on a stretch without ever hastening his pulse or his breath. Meantime, he had found nothing to do, and was somewhat discouraged. He said, with an outburst of pathetic longing, "If I could only get a job at the Pioneer!"

I said "What kind of a job do you want at the Pioneer?"

He said "Why, laborer. They get five dollars a day."

I said "If that's all you want I can arrange it for you."

Higbie was astonished. He said "Do you mean to say that you know the foreman there and could get me a job and yet have never said anything about it?"

"No" I said, "I don't know the foreman."

"Well" he said, "who is it you know? How is it you can get me the job?"

"Why," I said, "that's perfectly simple. If you will do as I tell you to do, and don't try to improve on my instructions, you shall have the job before night."

He said eagerly "I'll obey the instructions, I don't care what they are."

"Well," I said, "go there and say that you want work as a laborer; that you are tired of being idle; that you are not used to being idle, and can't stand it; that you just merely want the refreshment of work, and require nothing in return."

He said "Nothing?"

I said, "That's it—nothing."

"No wages at all?"

"No, no wages at all."

"Not even board?"

"No, not even board. You are to work for nothing. Make them understand that—that you are perfectly willing to work for nothing. When they look at that figure of yours that foreman will understand that he has drawn a prize. You'll get the job."

Higbie said indignantly, "Yes, a hell of a job."

I said, "You said you were going to do it, and now you are already criticising. You have said you would obey my instructions. You are always as good as your word. Clear out, now, and get the job."

He said he would.

I was pretty anxious to know what was going to happen—more anxious than I would have wanted him to find out. I preferred to seem entirely confident of the strength of my scheme, and I made good show of that confidence. But really I was very anxious. Yet I believed that I knew enough of human nature to know that a man like Higbie would not be flung out of that place without reflection when he was offering those muscles of his for nothing. The hours dragged along and he didn't return. I began to feel better and better. I began to accumulate confidence. At sundown he did at last arrive and I had the joy of knowing that my invention had been a fine inspiration and was successful.

He said the foreman was so astonished at first that he didn't know how to take hold of the proposition, but that he soon recovered and was evidently very glad that he was able to accommodate Higbie and furnish him the refreshment he was pining for.

Higbie said "How long is this to go on?"

I said "The terms are that you are to stay right there; do your work just as if you were getting the going wages for it. You are never to make any complaint; you are never to indicate that you would like to have wages or board. This will go on one, two, three, four, five, six days, according to the make of that foreman. Some foremen would break down under the strain in a couple of days. There are others who would last a week. It would be difficult to find one who could stand out a whole fortnight without getting ashamed of himself and offering you wages. Now let's suppose that this is a fortnight-foreman. In that case you will not be there a fortnight. Because the men will spread it around that the very ablest laborer in this camp is so fond of work that he is willing and glad to do it without pay. You will be regarded as the latest curiosity. Men will come from the other mills to have a look at you. You could charge admission and get it, but you mustn't do that. Stick to your colors. When the foremen of the other mills cast their eyes upon this bulk of yours and perceive that you are worth two ordinary men they'll offer you half a man's wages. You are not to accept until you report to your foreman. Give him an opportunity to offer you the same. If he doesn't do it then you are free to take up with that other man's offer. Higbie, you'll be foreman of a mine or a mill inside of three weeks, and at the best wages going."

It turned out just so—and after that I led an easy life, with nothing to do, for it did not occur to me to take my own medicine. I didn't want a job as long as Higbie had one. One was enough for so small a family—and so during many succeeding weeks I was a gentleman of leisure, with books and newspapers to read and stewed dried apples every day for dinner the same as Sunday, and I wanted no better career than this in this life. Higbie supported me handsomely, never once complained of it, never once suggested that I go out and try for a job at no wages and keep myself.

That would be in 1862. I parted from Higbie about the end of '62—or possibly it could have been the beginning of '63—and went to Virginia City, for I had been invited to come there and take William H. Wright's place as sole reporter on the *Territorial Enterprise* and do Wright's work for three months while he crossed the plains to Iowa to visit his family. However I have told all about this in "Roughing It." *1862*

I have never seen Higbie since, in all these forty-four years.

Shortly after my marriage, in 1870, I received a letter from a young man in St. Louis who was possibly a distant relative of mine—I don't remember now about that—but his letter said that he was anxious and ambitious to become a journalist—and would I send him a letter of introduction to some St. Louis newspaper and make an effort to get him a place as a reporter? It was the first time I had had an opportunity to make a new trial of my great scheme. I wrote him and said I would get him a place on any newspaper in St. Louis; he could choose the one he preferred, but he must promise me to faithfully follow out the instructions which I should give him. He replied that he would follow out those instructions to the letter and with enthusiasm. His letter was overflowing with gratitude—premature gratitude. He asked for the instructions. I sent them. I said he must not use a letter of introduction from me or from any one else. He must go to the newspaper of his choice and say that he was idle, and weary of being idle, and wanted work—that he was pining for work, longing for work—that he didn't care for wages, didn't want wages, but would support himself—he wanted work, nothing but work, and not work of a particular kind, but any kind of work they would give him to do. He would sweep out the editorial rooms; he would keep the ink-stands full, and the mucilage bottles, he would run errands, he would make himself useful in every way he could. *1870*

I suspected that my scheme would not work with everybody—that some people would scorn to labor for nothing, and would think it matter for self-contempt; also that many persons would think me a fool to suggest such a project; also that many persons would not have character enough to go into the scheme in a determined way and test it. I was interested to know what kind of a candidate this one was, but of course I had to wait some time to find out. I had told him he must never ask for wages; he must never be beguiled into making that mistake; that sooner or later an offer of wages would come from somewhere, and in that case he must go straight to his employer and give him the opportunity to offer him the like wages, in which case he must stay where he was—that as long as he was in anybody's employ he must never ask for an advance of wages; that would always come from somewhere else if he proved his worthiness.

The scheme worked again. That young fellow chose his paper, and during the first few days he did the sweeping out and other humble work; and kept his mouth shut. After that the staff began to take notice of him. They saw that they could employ him in lots of ways that saved time and effort for them at no expense. They found that he was alert and willing. They began presently to widen his usefulness. Then he ventured to risk another detail of my instructions; I had told him not to be in a hurry about it, but to make his popularity secure first. He took up that detail now. When he was on his road between office and home, and when he was out on errands, he kept his eyes open and whenever he saw anything that could be useful in the local columns he wrote it out, then went over it and abolished adjectives, went over it again and extinguished other surplusages, and finally when he got it boiled down to the plain facts with the ruffles and other embroideries all gone, he laid it on the city editor's desk. He scored several successes, and saw his stuff go into the paper unpruned. Presently the city editor when short of help sent him out on an assignment. He did his best with it, and with good results. This happened with more and more frequency. It brought him into contact with all the reporters of all the newspapers. He made friends with them and presently one of them told him of a berth that was vacant, and that he could get it and the wages too. He said he must see his own employers first about it. In strict accordance with my instructions he carried the offer to his own employers, and the thing happened which was to be expected. They said they could pay that wage as well as any other newspaper—stay where he was.

This young man wrote me two or three times a year and he always had something freshly encouraging to report about my scheme. Now and then he would be offered a raise by another newspaper. He carried the news to his own paper; his own paper stood the raise every time and he remained there. Finally he got an offer which his employers could not meet and then they parted. This offer was a salary of three thousand a year, to be managing editor on a daily in a Southern city of considerable importance, and it was a large wage for that day and region. He held that post three years. After that I never heard of him any more.

About 1886 my nephew, Samuel E. Moffett, a youth in the twenties, lost his inherited property and found himself obliged to hunt for something to do by way of making a living. He was an extraordinary young fellow in several ways. A nervous malady had early unfitted him for attending school in any regular way, and he had come up without a school education—but this was no great harm for him, for he had a prodigious memory and a powerful thirst for knowledge. At twelve years he had picked up, through reading and listening, a large and varied treasury of knowledge, and I remember one exhibition of it which was very offensive to me. He was visiting in our house and I was trying to build a game out of historical facts drawn from all the ages. I had put in a good deal of labor on this game, and it was hard labor, for the facts were not in my head. I had to dig them painfully out of the books. The boy looked over my work, found that my facts were not accurate and the game, as it stood, not usable. Then he sat down and built the whole game out of his memory. To me it was a wonderful performance, and I was deeply offended.

As I have said, he wrote me from San Francisco in his early twenties, and said he wanted to become a journalist, and would I send him some letters of introduction to the newspaper editors of that city? I wrote back and put him strictly under those same old instructions. I sent him no letter of introduction and forbade him to use one furnished by anybody else. He followed the instructions strictly. He went to work in the *Examiner,* a property of William R. Hearst. He cleaned out the editorial rooms and carried on the customary drudgeries required by my scheme. In a little while he was on the editorial staff at a good salary. After two or three years the salary was raised to a very good figure indeed. After another year or two he handed in his resignation—for in the meantime he had married and was living in Oakland, or one of those suburbs, and did not like the travel to and fro between the newspaper and his home in the late hours of the night and the morning. Then he was told to stay in Oakland, write his editorials there and send them over, and the large salary was continued. By and by he was brought to New York to serve on Mr. Hearst's New York paper, and when he finally resigned from that employment he had been in Mr. Hearst's employ sixteen years without a break. Then he became an editorial writer on the New York *World* with the privilege of living out of town and sending his matter in. His wage was eight thousand dollars a year. A couple of years ago *Collier's Weekly* offered him an easy berth and one which was particularly desirable in his case, since it would deal mainly with historical matters, past and present—and that was an industry which he liked. The salary was to be ten thousand dollars. He came to me for advice, and I told him to accept, which he did. When Mr. Pulitzer found that he was gone from the *World* he was not pleased with his managing editor for letting him go, but his managing editor was not to blame. He didn't know that Moffett was going until he received his resignation. Pulitzer offered Moffett a billet for twenty years, this term to be secured in such a way that it could not be endangered by Pulitzer's death, and to this offer was added the extraordinary proposition that Moffett could name his own salary. But of course Moffett remains with Collier, his agreement with *Collier's* having been already arrived at satisfactorily to both parties.

Wednesday, March 28, 1906

Orion Clemens's personality—His adventure at the house of
Dr. Meredith—His three o'clock a.m. call on young lady—Death of
Mr. Clemens's father, just after having been made County Judge—
Mr. Clemens's small income after having become bankrupt through
maladministration of Charles L. Webster.

My brother's experience was another conspicuous example of my scheme's efficiency. I will talk about that by and by. But for the moment my interest suddenly centres itself upon his personality, moved thereto by this passing mention of him—and so I will drop other matters and sketch that personality. It is a very curious one. In all my seventy years I have not met the twin of it.

Orion Clemens was born in Jamestown, Fentress County, Tennessee, in 1825. He was the *1825* family's first-born, and antedated me ten years. Between him and me came a sister, Margaret, who died, aged ten, in 1837 in that village of Florida, Missouri, where I was born; and Pamela, *1837* mother of Samuel E. Moffett, who was an invalid all her life and died in the neighborhood of New York a year ago, aged about seventy-five, after experimenting with every malady known to the human race and with every medicine and method of healing known to that race, and enjoying each malady in its turn and each medicine and each healing method, with an enthusiasm known only to persons with a passion for novelties. Her character was without blemish, and she was of a most kindly and gentle disposition. Also there was a brother, Benjamin, who *1843* died in 1843 aged ten or twelve.

Orion's boyhood was spent in that wee little log hamlet of Jamestown up there among the "knobs"—so called—of east Tennessee, among a very sparse population of primitives who were as ignorant of the outside world and as unconscious of it as were the other wild animals that inhabited the forest around. The family migrated to Florida, Missouri, then moved to Hannibal, Missouri, when Orion was twelve and a half years old. When he was fifteen or sixteen he was sent to St. Louis and there he learned the printer's trade. One of his characteristics was eagerness. He woke with an eagerness about some matter or other every morning; it consumed him all day; it perished in the night and he was on fire with a fresh new interest next morning before he could get his clothes on. He exploited in this way three hundred and sixty-five red hot new eagernesses every year of his life—until he died sitting at a table with a pen in his hand, in the early morning, jotting down the conflagration for that day and preparing to enjoy the fire and smoke of it until night should extinguish it. He was then seventy-two years old. But I am forgetting another characteristic, a very pronounced one. That was his deep glooms, his despondencies, his despairs; these had their place in each and every day along with the eagernesses. Thus his day was divided—no, not divided, mottled—from sunrise to midnight with alternating brilliant sunshine and black cloud. Every day he was the most joyous and hopeful man that ever was, I think, and also every day he was the most miserable man that ever was.

While he was in his apprenticeship in St. Louis, he got well acquainted with Edward Bates, who was afterwards in Mr. Lincoln's first cabinet. Bates was a very fine man, an honorable and upright man, and a distinguished lawyer. He patiently allowed Orion to bring to him each new project; he discussed it with him and extinguished it by argument and irresistible logic—at first. But after a few weeks he found that this labor was not necessary; that he could leave the new project alone and it would extinguish itself the same night. Orion thought he would like to become a lawyer. Mr. Bates encouraged him, and he studied law nearly a week, then of course laid it aside to try something new. He wanted to become an orator. Mr. Bates gave him lessons. Mr. Bates walked the floor reading from an English book aloud and rapidly turning the English into French, and he recommended this exercise to Orion. But as Orion knew no French, he took up that study and wrought at it like a volcano for two or three days; then gave it up. During his apprenticeship in St. Louis he joined a number of churches, one after another, and taught in their Sunday-schools—changing his Sunday-school every time he changed his religion. He was correspondingly erratic in his politics—Whig to-day, Democrat next week, and anything fresh that he could find in the political market the week after. I may remark here that throughout his long life he was always trading religions and enjoying the change of scenery. I will also remark that his sincerity was never doubted; his truthfulness was never doubted; and in matters of business and money his honesty was never questioned. Notwithstanding his forever-recurring caprices and changes, his principles were high, always high, and absolutely unshakable. He was the strangest compound that ever got mixed in a human mould. Such a person as that is given to acting upon impulse and without reflection; that was Orion's way. Everything he did he did with conviction and enthusiasm and with a vainglorious pride in the thing he was doing—and no matter what that thing was, whether good, bad, or indifferent, he repented of it every time in sackcloth and ashes before twenty-four hours had sped. Pessimists are born, not made. Optimists are born, not made. But I think he was the only person I have ever known in whom pessimism and optimism were lodged in exactly equal proportions.

Except in the matter of grounded principle, he was as unstable as water. You could dash his spirits with a single word; you could raise them into the sky again with another one. You could break his heart with a word of disapproval; you could make him as happy as an angel with a word of approval. And there was no occasion to put any sense or any vestige of mentality of any kind into these miracles; anything you might say would answer.

He had another conspicuous characteristic, and it was the father of those which I have just spoken of. This was an intense lust for approval. He was so eager to be approved, so girlishly anxious to be approved by anybody and everybody, without discrimination, that he was commonly ready to forsake his notions, opinions and convictions at a moment's notice in order to get the approval of any person who disagreed with them. I wish to be understood as reserving his fundamental principles all the time. He never forsook those to please anybody. Born and reared among slaves and slave-holders, he was yet an abolitionist from his boyhood to his death. He was always truthful; he was always sincere; he was always honest and honorable. But in light matters—matters of small consequence, like religion and politics and such things—he never acquired a conviction that could survive a disapproving remark from a cat.

He was always dreaming; he was a dreamer from birth, and this characteristic got him into trouble now and then. Once when he was twenty-three or twenty-four years old, and was become a journeyman, he conceived the romantic idea of coming to Hannibal without giving us notice, in order that he might furnish to the family a pleasant surprise. If he had given notice, he would have been informed that we had changed our residence and that that gruff old bass-voiced sailor-man, Dr. Meredith, our family physician, was living in the house which we had formerly occupied and that Orion's former room in that house was now occupied by Dr. Meredith's two ripe old-maid sisters. Orion arrived at Hannibal per steamboat in the middle of the night, and started with his customary eagerness on his excursion, his mind all on fire with his romantic project and building and enjoying his surprise in advance. He was always enjoying things in advance; it was the make of him. He never could wait for the event, but must build it out of dream-stuff and enjoy it beforehand—consequently sometimes when the event happened he saw that it was not as good as the one he had invented in his imagination, and so he had lost profit by not keeping the imaginary one and letting the reality go.

When he arrived at the house he went around to the back door and slipped off his boots and crept up stairs and arrived at the room of those old maids without having wakened any sleepers. He undressed in the dark and got into bed and snuggled up against somebody. He was a little surprised, but not much—for he thought it was our brother Ben. It was winter, and the bed was comfortable, and the supposed Ben added to the comfort—and so he was dropping off to sleep very well satisfied with his progress so far and full of happy dreams of what was going to happen in the morning. But something else was going to happen sooner than that, and it happened now. The old maid that was being crowded squirmed and struggled and presently came to a half waking condition and protested against the crowding. That voice paralysed Orion. He couldn't move a limb; he couldn't get his breath; and the crowded one began to paw around, found Orion's new whiskers and screamed "Why it's a man!" This removed the paralysis, and Orion was out of the bed and clawing around in the dark for his clothes in a fraction of a second. Both maids began to scream, then, so Orion did not wait to get his whole wardrobe.

He started with such parts of it as he could grab. He flew to the head of the stairs and started down, and was paralysed again at that point, because he saw the faint yellow flame of a candle soaring up the stairs from below and he judged that Dr. Meredith was behind it, and he was. He had no clothes on to speak of, but no matter, he was well enough fixed for an occasion like this, because he had a butcher-knife in his hand. Orion shouted to him, and this saved his life, for the Doctor recognized his voice. Then in those deep-sea-going bass tones of his that I used to admire so much when I was a little boy, he explained to Orion the change that had been made, told him where to find the Clemens family, and closed with some quite unnecessary advice about posting himself before he undertook another adventure like that—advice which Orion probably never needed again as long as he lived.

One bitter December night, Orion sat up reading until three o'clock in the morning and then, without looking at a clock, sallied forth to call on a young lady. He hammered and hammered at the door; couldn't get any response; didn't understand it. Anybody else would have regarded that as an indication of some kind or other and would have drawn inferences and gone home. But Orion didn't draw inferences, he merely hammered and hammered, and finally the father of the girl appeared at the door in a dressing-gown. He had a candle in his hand and the dressing-gown was all the clothing he had on—except an expression of unwelcome which was so thick and so large that it extended all down his front to his instep and nearly obliterated the dressing-gown. But Orion didn't notice that this was an unpleasant expression. He merely walked in. The old gentleman took him into the parlor, set the candle on a table, and stood. Orion made the usual remarks about the weather, and sat down—sat down and talked and talked and went on talking—that old man looking at him vindictively and waiting for his chance—waiting treacherously and malignantly for his chance. Orion had not asked for the young lady. It was not customary. It was understood that a young fellow came to see the girl of the house, not the founder of it. At last Orion got up and made some remark to the effect that probably the young lady was busy and he would go now and call again. That was the old man's chance, and he said with fervency "Why good God, aren't you going to stop to breakfast?"

1847   When my father died, in 1847, the disaster happened—as is the customary way with such things—just at the very moment when our fortunes had changed and we were about to be comfortable once more, after several years of grinding poverty and privation which had been inflicted upon us by the dishonest act of one Ira Stout, to whom my father had lent several thousand dollars—a fortune in those days and in that region. My father had just been elected County Judge. This modest prosperity was not only quite sufficient for us and for our ambitions, but he was so esteemed—held in such high regard and honor throughout the county— that his occupancy of that dignified office would, in the opinion of everybody, be his possession as long as he might live. He went to Palmyra, the county-seat, to be sworn in, about the end of February. In returning home, horseback, twelve miles, a storm of sleet and rain assailed him and he arrived at the house in a half frozen condition. Pleurisy followed and he died on the 24th of March.

Thus our splendid new fortune was snatched from us and we were in the depths of poverty again. It is the way such things are accustomed to happen.

When I became a bankrupt through the ignorance and maladministration of Charles L. Webster, after having been robbed of a hundred and seventy thousand dollars by James W. Paige* during the seven immediately preceding years, we went to Europe in order to be able to live on what was left of our income, and it was sufficiently slender. During the succeeding ten or twelve years it was often as low as twelve thousand a year, and at no time did it reach above twenty thousand a year, I think. I am sure it did not reach above twelve thousand until two years before we returned from Europe, in October 1900. Then it improved considerably, but it was too late to be of much service to Mrs. Clemens. She had endured the economies of that long stretch of years without a single murmur, and now when fortune turned in our favor it was too late. She was stricken down, and after twenty-two months of suffering she died. In Florence, Italy, June 5, 1904.

As I have said, the Clemens family was penniless. Orion came to the rescue.

Thursday, March 29, 1906

Mr. Clemens as apprentice to Mr. Ament—Wilhelm II's dinner, and potato incident—The printing of Reverend Alexander Campbell's sermon— Incident of dropping watermelon on Henry's head—Orion buys Hannibal *Journal* which is a failure—Then he goes to Muscatine, Iowa, and marries— Mr. Clemens starts out alone to see the world—Visits St. Louis, New York, Philadelphia, Washington—Then goes to Muscatine and works in Orion's office—Finds fifty-dollar bill—Thinks of going to explore the Amazon and collect coca—Gets Horace Bixby to train him as pilot—Starts with Orion for Nevada when Orion is made Secretary to Territory of Nevada.

But I am in error. Orion did not come to Hannibal until two or three years after my father's death. He remained in St. Louis. Meantime he was a journeyman printer and earning wages. Out of his wage he supported my mother and my brother Henry, who was two years younger than I. My sister Pamela helped in this support by taking piano pupils. Thus we got along, but it was pretty hard sledding. I was not one of the burdens, because I was taken from school at once, upon my father's death, and placed in the office of the Hannibal *Courier,* as printer's apprentice, and Mr. Ament, the editor and proprietor of the paper, allowed me the usual emolument of the office of apprentice—that is to say board and clothes, but no money. The clothes consisted of two suits a year, but one of the suits always failed to materialize and the other suit was not purchased so long as Mr. Ament's old clothes held out. I was only about half as big as Ament, consequently his shirts gave me the uncomfortable sense of living in a circus-tent, and I had to turn up his pants to my ears to make them short enough.

There were two other apprentices. One was Wales McCormick, seventeen or eighteen years old and a giant. When he was in Ament's clothes they fitted him as the candle-mould fits the

---

*Inventor of a type-setting machine of a most ingenious and marvelous character. There is but one; it is in Cornell University: preserved as a curiosity. It is all of that.

candle—thus he was generally in a suffocated condition, particularly in the summertime. He was a reckless, hilarious, admirable creature; he had no principles, and was delightful company. At first we three apprentices had to feed in the kitchen with the old slave cook and her very handsome and bright and well-behaved young mulatto daughter. For his own amusement—for he was not generally laboring for other people's amusement—Wales was constantly and persistently and loudly and elaborately making love to that mulatto girl and distressing the life out of her and worrying the old mother to death. She would say "Now Marse Wales, Marse Wales, can't you behave yourself?" With encouragement like that, Wales would naturally renew his attentions and emphasize them. It was killingly funny to Ralph and me. And, to speak truly, the old mother's distress about it was merely a pretense. She quite well understood that by the customs of slave-holding communities it was Wales's right to make love to that girl if he wanted to. But the girl's distress was very real. She had a refined nature, and she took all Wales's extravagant love-making in resentful earnest.

We got but little variety in the way of food at that kitchen table, and there wasn't enough of it anyway. So we apprentices used to keep alive by arts of our own—that is to say, we crept into the cellar nearly every night, by a private entrance which we had discovered, and we robbed the cellar of potatoes and onions and such things, and carried them down town to the printing-office, where we slept on pallets on the floor, and cooked them at the stove and had very good times. Wales had a secret of cooking a potato which was noble and wonderful and all his own. Since his day I have seen a potato cooked in that way only once. It was when Wilhelm II, Emperor of Germany, commanded my presence at a private feed toward the end of the year

1901 1901. And when that potato appeared on the table it surprised me out of my discretion and made me commit the unforgivable sin, before I could get a grip on my discretion again—that is to say, I made a joyful exclamation of welcome over the potato, addressing my remark to the Emperor at my side without waiting for him to take the first innings. I think he honestly tried to pretend that he was not shocked and outraged, but he plainly was; and so were the other half-dozen grandees who were present. They were all petrified, and nobody could have said a word if he had tried. The ghastly silence endured for as much as half a minute, and would have lasted until now, of course, if the Emperor hadn't broken it himself, for no one else there would have ventured that. It was at half past six in the evening, and the frost did not get out of the atmosphere entirely until close upon midnight, when it did finally melt away—or wash away—under generous floods of beer.

As I have indicated, Mr. Ament's economies were of a pretty close and rigid kind. By and by, when we apprentices were promoted from the basement to the ground floor and allowed to sit at the family table, along with the one journeyman, Pet McMurry, the economies continued. Mrs. Ament was a bride. She had attained to that distinction very recently, after waiting a good part of a lifetime for it, and she was the right woman in the right place, according to the Amentian idea, for she did not trust the sugar-bowl to us, but sweetened our coffee herself. That is she went through the motions. She didn't really sweeten it. She seemed to put one heaping teaspoonful of brown sugar into each cup, but, according to Wales, that was a deceit. He said she dipped the spoon in the coffee first to make the sugar stick, and then scooped the sugar out of the bowl with the spoon upside-down, so that the effect to the eye was a heaped-up spoon, whereas the sugar on it was nothing but a layer. This all seems perfectly true to me, and yet that thing would be so difficult to perform that I suppose it really didn't happen, but was one of Wales's lies.

I have said that Wales was reckless, and he was. It was the recklessness of ever-bubbling and indestructible good spirits flowing from the joy of youth. I think there wasn't anything that that vast boy wouldn't have done to procure five minutes' entertainment for himself. One never knew where he would break out next. Among his shining characteristics was the most limitless and adorable irreverence. There didn't seem to be anything serious in life for him; there didn't seem to be anything that he revered.

Once the celebrated founder of the at that time new and wide-spread sect called Campbellites, arrived in our village from Kentucky, and it made a prodigious excitement. The farmers and their families drove or tramped into the village from miles around to get a sight of the illustrious Alexander Campbell and to have a chance to hear him preach. When he preached in a church many had to be disappointed, for there was no church that would begin to hold all the applicants; so in order to accommodate all, he preached in the open air in the public square, and that was the first time in my life that I had realized what a mighty population this planet contains when you get them all together.

He preached a sermon on one of these occasions which he had written especially for that occasion. All the Campbellites wanted it printed, so that they could save it and read it over and over again, and get it by heart. So they drummed up sixteen dollars, which was a large sum then, and for this great sum Mr. Ament contracted to print five hundred copies of that sermon and put them in yellow paper covers. It was a sixteen-page duodecimo pamphlet, and it was a great event in our office. As we regarded it, it was a book, and it promoted us to the dignity of book printers. Moreover, no such mass of actual money as sixteen dollars, in one bunch, had ever entered that office on any previous occasion. People didn't pay for their paper and for their advertising in money, they paid in dry-goods, sugar, coffee, hickory wood, oak wood, turnips, pumpkins, onions, watermelons—and it was very seldom indeed that a man paid in money, and when that happened we thought there was something the matter with him.

We set up the great book in pages—eight pages to a form—and by help of a printer's manual we managed to get the pages in their apparently crazy but really sane places on the imposing-stone. We printed that form on a Thursday. Then we set up the remaining eight pages, locked them into a form and struck a proof. Wales read the proof, and presently was aghast, for he had struck a snag. And it was a bad time to strike a snag, because it was Saturday; it was approaching noon; Saturday afternoon was our holiday, and we wanted to get away and go fishing. At such a time as this, Wales struck that snag and showed us what had happened. He had left out a couple of words in a thin-spaced page of solid matter and there wasn't another break-line for two or three pages ahead. What in the world was to be done? Overrun all those pages in order to get in the two missing words? Apparently there was no other way. It would take an hour to do it. Then a revise must be sent to the great minister; we must wait for him to read the revise; if he encountered any errors we must correct them. It looked as if we might lose half the afternoon before we could get away. Then Wales had one of his brilliant ideas. In the line in which the "out" had been made occurred the name Jesus Christ. Wales reduced that to J. C.

It made room for the missing words, but it took 99 per cent of the solemnity out of a particularly solemn sentence. We sent off the revise and waited. We were not intending to wait long. In the circumstances we meant to get out and go fishing before that revise should get back, but we were not speedy enough. Presently that great Alexander Campbell appeared at the far end of that sixty-foot room, and his countenance cast a gloom over the whole place. He strode down to our end and what he said was brief but it was very stern, and it was to the point. He read Wales a lecture. He said "So long as you live, don't you ever diminish the Savior's name again. Put it *all* in." He repeated this admonition a couple of times to emphasize it, then he went away.

In that day the common swearers of the region had a way of their own of *emphasizing* the Savior's name when they were using it profanely, and this fact intruded itself into Wales's incorrigible mind. It offered him an opportunity for a momentary entertainment which seemed to him to be more precious and more valuable than even fishing and swimming could afford. So he imposed upon himself the long and weary and dreary task of overrunning all those three pages in order to improve upon his former work and incidentally and thoughtfully improve upon the great preacher's admonition. He enlarged the offending J. C. into Jesus H. Christ. Wales knew that that would make prodigious trouble, and it did. But it was not in him to resist it. He had to succumb to the law of his make. I don't remember what his punishment was, but he was not the person to care for that. He had already collected his dividend.

It was during my first year's apprenticeship in the *Courier* office that I did a thing which I have been trying to regret for fifty-five years. It was a summer afternoon and just the kind of weather that a boy prizes for river excursions and other frolics, but I was a prisoner. The others were all gone holidaying. I was alone and sad. I had committed a crime of some sort and this was the punishment. I must lose my holiday, and spend the afternoon in solitude besides. I had the printing-office all to myself, there in the third story. I had one comfort, and it was a generous one while it lasted. It was the half of a long and broad watermelon, fresh and red and ripe. I gouged it out with a knife, and I found accommodation for the whole of it in my person—though it did crowd me until the juice ran out of my ears. There remained then the shell, the hollow shell. It was big enough to do duty as a cradle. I didn't want to waste it, and I couldn't think of anything to do with it which could afford entertainment. I was sitting at the open window which looked out upon the sidewalk of the main street three stories below, when it occurred to me to drop it on somebody's head. I doubted the judiciousness of this, and I had some compunctions about it too, because so much of the resulting entertainment would fall to my share and so little to the other person. But I thought I would chance it. I watched out of the window for the right person to come along—the safe person—but he didn't come. Every time there was a candidate he or she turned out to be an unsafe one, and I had to restrain myself. But at last I saw the right one coming. It was my brother Henry. He was the best boy in the whole region. He never did harm to anybody, he never offended anybody. He was exasperatingly good. He had an overflowing abundance of goodness—but not enough to save him this time. I watched his approach with eager interest. He came strolling along, dreaming his pleasant summer dream and not doubting but that Providence had him in his care. If he had known where I was he would have had less confidence in that superstition. As he approached his form became more and more foreshortened. When he was almost under me he was so foreshortened that nothing of him was visible from my high place except the end of his nose and his alternately approaching feet. Then I poised the watermelon, calculated my distance and let it go, hollow side down. The accuracy of that gunnery was beyond admiration. He had about six steps to make when I let that canoe go, and it was lovely to see those two bodies gradually closing in on each other. If he had had seven steps to make, or five steps to make, my gunnery would have been a failure. But he had exactly the right number to make, and that shell smashed down right on the top of his head and drove him into the earth up to the chin. The chunks of that broken melon flew in every direction like a spray, and they broke third story windows all around. They had to get a jack such as they hoist buildings with to pull him out. I wanted to go down there and condole with him, but it would not have been safe. He would have suspected me at once. I expected him to suspect me anyway, but as he said nothing about this adventure for two or three days—I was watching him in the meantime in order to keep out of danger—I was deceived into believing that this time he didn't suspect me. It was a mistake. He was only waiting for a sure opportunity. Then he landed a cobblestone on the side of my head which raised a bump there so large that I had to wear two hats for a time. I carried this crime to my mother, for I was always anxious to get Henry into trouble with her and could never succeed. I thought that I had a sure case this time when she should come to see that murderous bump. I showed it to her but she said it was no matter. She didn't need to inquire into the circumstances. She knew I had deserved it, and the best way would be for me to accept it as a valuable lesson, and thereby get profit out of it.

About 1849 or 1850 Orion severed his connection with the printing-house in St. Louis and came up to Hannibal and bought a weekly paper called the Hannibal *Journal,* together with its plant and its good-will, for the sum of five hundred dollars cash. He borrowed the cash at 10 per cent interest, from an old farmer named Johnson who lived five miles out of town. Then he reduced the subscription price of the paper from two dollars to one dollar. He reduced the rates for advertising in about the same proportion, and thus he created one absolute and unassailable certainty—to wit: that the business would never pay him a single cent of profit. He took me out of the *Courier* office and engaged my services in his own at three dollars and a half a week, which was an extravagant wage, but Orion was always generous, always liberal with everybody except himself. It cost him nothing in my case, for he never was able to pay me a penny as long as I was with him. By the end of the first year he found he must make some economies. The office rent was cheap, but it was not cheap enough. He could not afford to pay rent of any kind, so he moved the whole plant into the house we lived in, and it cramped the dwelling-place cruelly. He kept that paper alive during four years, but I have at this time no idea how he accomplished it. Toward the end of each year he had to turn out and scrape and scratch for the fifty dollars of interest due Mr. Johnson, and that fifty dollars was about the only cash he ever received or paid out, I suppose, while he was proprietor of that newspaper, except for ink and printing-paper. The paper was a dead failure. It had to be that from the start. Finally he handed it over to Mr. Johnson, and went up to Muscatine, Iowa, and acquired a small interest in a weekly newspaper there. It was not a sort of property to marry on—but no matter. He came across a winning and pretty girl who lived in Quincy, Illinois, a few miles below Keokuk, and they became engaged. He was always falling in love with girls, but by some accident or other he had never gone so far as engagement before. And now he achieved nothing but misfortune by it, because he straightway fell in love with a Keokuk girl—at least he imagined that he was in love with her, whereas I think she did the imagining for him. The first thing he knew he was engaged to her, and he was in a great quandary. He didn't know whether to marry the Keokuk one or the Quincy one, or whether to try to marry both of them and suit every one concerned. But the Keokuk girl soon settled that for him. She was a master spirit and she ordered him to write the Quincy girl and break off that match, which he did. Then he married the Keokuk girl and they began a struggle for life which turned out to be a difficult enterprise, and very unpromising.

To gain a living in Muscatine was plainly impossible, so Orion and his new wife went to Keokuk to live, for she wanted to be near her relatives. He bought a little bit of a job printing-plant—on credit, of course—and at once put prices down to where not even the apprentices could get a living out of it, and this sort of thing went on.

I had not joined the Muscatine migration. Just before that happened (which I think was *1853* in 1853) I disappeared one night and fled to St. Louis. There I worked in the composing-room of the *Evening News* for a time, and then started on my travels to see the world. The world was New York City, and there was a little World's Fair there. It had just been opened where the great reservoir afterward was, and where the sumptuous public library is now being built— Fifth Avenue and 42d street. I arrived in New York with two or three dollars in pocket change and a ten-dollar bank-bill concealed in the lining of my coat. I got work at villainous wages in the establishment of John A. Gray and Green in Cliff street, and I found board in a sufficiently villainous mechanics' boarding-house in Duane street. The firm paid my wages in wildcat money at its face value, and my week's wage merely sufficed to pay board and lodging. By and by I went to Philadelphia and worked there some months as a "sub" on the *Inquirer* and the *1854* *Public Ledger.* Finally I made a flying trip to Washington to see the sights there, and in 1854 I went back to the Mississippi Valley, sitting upright in the smoking-car two or three days and nights. When I reached St. Louis I was exhausted. I went to bed on board a steamboat that was bound for Muscatine. I fell asleep at once, with my clothes on, and didn't wake again for thirty-six hours.

I worked in that little job office in Keokuk as much as two years, I should say, without ever collecting a cent of wages, for Orion was never able to pay anything—but Dick Higham and I had good times. I don't know what Dick got, but it was probably only uncashable promises.

1856 or 1857   One day in the mid-winter of 1856 or 1857—I think it was 1856—I was coming along the main street of Keokuk in the middle of the forenoon. It was bitter weather—so bitter that that street was deserted, almost. A light dry snow was blowing here and there on the ground and on the pavement, swirling this way and that way and making all sorts of beautiful figures, but very chilly to look at. The wind blew a piece of paper past me and it lodged against a wall of a house. Something about the look of it attracted my attention and I gathered it in. It was a fifty-dollar bill, the only one I had ever seen, and the largest assemblage of money I had ever encountered in one spot. I advertised it in the papers and suffered more than a thousand dollars' worth of solicitude and fear and distress during the next few days lest the owner should see the advertisement and come and take my fortune away. As many as four days went by without an applicant; then I could endure this kind of misery no longer. I felt sure that another four could not go by in this safe and secure way. I felt that I must take that money out of danger. So I bought a ticket for Cincinnati and went to that city. I worked there several months in the printing-office of Wrightson and Company. I had been reading Lieutenant Herndon's account of his explorations of the Amazon and had been mightily attracted by what he said of coca. I made up my mind that I would go to the head-waters of the Amazon and collect coca and trade in it and make a fortune. I left for New Orleans in the steamer *Paul Jones* with this great idea filling my mind. One of the pilots of that boat was Horace Bixby. Little by little I got acquainted with him, and pretty soon I was doing a lot of steering for him in his daylight watches. When I got to New Orleans I inquired about ships leaving for Pará and discovered that there weren't any, and learned that there probably wouldn't be any during that century. It had not occurred to me to inquire about these particulars before leaving Cincinnati, so there I was. I couldn't get to the Amazon. I had no friends in New Orleans and no money to speak of. I went to Horace Bixby and asked him to make a pilot out of me. He said he would do it for a hundred dollars cash in advance. So I steered for him up to St. Louis, borrowed the money from my brother-in-law and closed the bargain. I had acquired this brother-in-law several years before. This was Mr. William A. Moffett, a merchant, a Virginian—a fine man in every way. He had married my sister Pamela, and the Samuel E. Moffett of whom I have been speaking was their son. Within eighteen months I became a competent pilot, and I served that office until the Mississippi River traffic was brought to a standstill by the breaking out of the Civil War.

Meantime Orion had been sweating along with his little job-printing office in Keokuk, and he and his wife were living with his wife's family—ostensibly as boarders, but it is not likely that Orion was ever able to pay the board. On account of charging next to nothing for the work done in his job office, he had almost nothing to do there. He was never able to get it through his head that work done on a profitless basis deteriorates and is presently not worth anything, and that customers are then obliged to go where they can get better work, even if they must pay better prices for it. He had plenty of time, and he took up Blackstone again. He also put up a sign which offered his services to the public as a lawyer. He never got a case, in those days, nor even an applicant, although he was quite willing to transact law business for nothing and furnish the stationery himself. He was always liberal that way.

Presently he moved to a wee little hamlet called Alexandria, two or three miles down the river, and he put up that sign there. He got no bites. He was by this time very hard aground. But by this time I was beginning to earn a wage of two hundred and fifty dollars a month as pilot, and so I supported him thenceforth until 1861, when his ancient friend, Edward Bates, then a member of Mr. Lincoln's first cabinet, got him the place of Secretary of the new Territory of Nevada, and Orion and I cleared for that country in the overland stage-coach, I paying the fares, which were pretty heavy, and carrying with me what money I had been able to save— this was eight hundred dollars, I should say—and it was all in silver coin and a good deal of a nuisance because of its weight. And we had another nuisance, which was an Unabridged Dictionary. It weighed about a thousand pounds, and was a ruinous expense, because the

1861

stage-coach Company charged for extra baggage by the ounce. We could have kept a family for a time on what that dictionary cost in the way of extra freight—and it wasn't a good dictionary anyway—didn't have any modern words in it—only had obsolete ones that they used to use when Noah Webster was a child.

Friday, March 30, 1906

Mr. Clemens's interview with Tchaykoffsky, and Mr. Clemens's views regarding the Russian revolution—Mr. Clemens presides at meeting of the Association formed in interest of the adult blind—His first meeting with Helen Keller—Helen Keller's letter, which Mr. Clemens read at this meeting.

I will drop Orion for the present and return and pick him up by and by. For the moment I am more interested in the matters of to-day than I am in Orion's adventures and mine of forty-five years ago.

Three days ago a neighbor brought the celebrated Russian revolutionist, Tchaykoffsky, to call upon me. He is grizzled, and shows age—as to exteriors—but he has a Vesuvius, inside, which is a strong and active volcano yet. He is so full of belief in the ultimate and almost immediate triumph of the revolution and the destruction of the fiendish autocracy, that he almost made me believe and hope with him. He has come over here expecting to arouse a conflagration of noble sympathy in our vast nation of eighty millions of happy and enthusiastic freemen. But honesty obliged me to pour some cold water down his crater. I told him what I believed to be true—that the McKinleys and the Roosevelts and the multimillionaire disciples of Jay Gould—that man who in his brief life rotted the commercial morals of this nation and left them stinking when he died—have quite completely transformed our people from a nation with pretty high and respectable ideals to just the opposite of that; that our people have no ideals now that are worthy of consideration; that our Christianity which we have always been so proud of—not to say so vain of—is now nothing but a shell, a sham, a hypocrisy; that we have lost our ancient sympathy with oppressed peoples struggling for life and liberty; that when we are not coldly indifferent to such things we sneer at them, and that the sneer is about the only expression the newspapers and the nation deal in with regard to such things; that his mass meetings would not be attended by people entitled to call themselves representative Americans, even if they may call themselves Americans at all; that his audiences will be composed of foreigners who have suffered so recently that they have not yet had time to become Americanized and their hearts turned to stone in their breasts; that these audiences will be drawn from the ranks of the poor, not those of the rich; that they will give, and give freely, but they will give from their poverty and the money result will not be large. I said that when our windy and flamboyant President conceived the idea, a year ago, of advertising himself to the world as the new Angel of Peace, and set himself the task of bringing about the peace between Russia and Japan and had the misfortune to accomplish his misbegotten purpose, no one in all this nation except Dr. Seaman and myself uttered a public protest against this folly of follies. That at that time I believed that that fatal peace had postponed the Russian nation's imminent liberation from its age-long chains indefinitely—probably for centuries; that I believed at that time that Roosevelt had given the Russian revolution its death-blow, and that I am of that opinion yet.

I will mention here, in parenthesis, that I came across Dr. Seaman last night for the first time in my life, and found that his opinion also remains to-day as he expressed it at the time that that infamous peace was consummated.

Tchaykoffsky said that my talk depressed him profoundly, and that he hoped I was wrong. I said I hoped the same.

He said "Why, from this very nation of yours came a mighty contribution only two or three months ago, and it made us all glad in Russia. You raised two millions of dollars in a breath—in a moment, as it were—and sent that contribution, that most noble and generous contribution, to suffering Russia. Does not that modify your opinion?"

"No," I said, "it doesn't. That money came not from Americans, it came from Jews; much of it from rich Jews, but the most of it from Russian and Polish Jews on the East Side—that is to say, it came from the very poor. The Jew has always been benevolent. Suffering can always move a Jew's heart and tax his pocket to the limit. He will be at your mass meetings. But if you find any Americans there put them in a glass case and exhibit them. It will be worth fifty cents a head to go and look at that show and try to believe in it."

He asked me to come to last night's meeting and speak, but I had another engagement, and could not do it. Then he asked me to write a line or two which could be read at the meeting, and I did that cheerfully.

New York *Times*.

ARMS TO FREE RUSSIA, TCHAYKOFFSKY'S APPEAL

———

Revolutionist Speaks to Cheering Audience of 3,000.

———

SAYS THE BATTLE IS NEAR

———

Mark Twain Writes That He Hopes Czars and Grand Dukes Will Soon Become Scarce.

———

"Tovarishzy!"

When Nicholas Tchaykoffsky, hailed by his countrymen here as the father of the revolutionary movement in Russia, spoke this word last night in Grand Central Palace 3,000 men and women rose to their feet, waved their hats, and cheered madly for three minutes. The word means "Comrades!" It is the watchword of the revolutionists. The spirit of revolution possessed the mass meeting called to greet the Russian patriot now visiting New York.

Fight is what he wants, and arms to fight with. He told the audience so last night and, by their cheers, they promised to do their part in supplying the sinews of war.

Mark Twain could not attend because he had already accepted an invitation to another meeting, but he sent this letter:

Dear Mr. Tchaykoffsky: I thank you for the honor of the invitation, but I am not able to accept it because Thursday evening I shall be presiding at a meeting whose object is to find remunerative work for certain classes of our blind who would gladly support themselves if they had the opportunity.

My sympathies are with the Russian revolution, of course. It goes without saying. I hope it will succeed, and now that I have talked with you I take heart to believe it will. Government by falsified promises, by lies, by treachery, and by the butcher knife, for the aggrandizement of a single family of drones and its idle and vicious kin has been borne quite long enough in Russia, I should think. And it is to be hoped that the roused nation, now rising in its strength, will presently put an end to it and set up the republic in its place. Some of us, even the whiteheaded, may live to see the blessed day when Czars and Grand Dukes will be as scarce there as I trust they are in heaven. Most sincerely yours,

MARK TWAIN.

Mr. Tchaykoffsky made an impassioned appeal for help to inaugurate a real revolution and overturn the Czar and all his allies.

The prior engagement which I spoke of to Tchaykoffsky was an engagement to act as Chairman at the first meeting of the Association which was formed five months ago in the interest of the adult blind. Joseph H. Choate and I had a very good time there, and I came away with the conviction that that excellent enterprise is going to flourish, and will bear abundant fruit. It will do for the adult blind what Congress and the several legislatures do so faithfully and with such enthusiasm for our lawless railway corporations, our rotten beef trusts, our vast robber dens of insurance magnates; in a word, for each and all of our multimillionaires and their industries—protect them, take watchful care of them, preserve them from harm like a Providence, and secure their prosperity, and increase it. The State of New York contains six thousand listed blind persons and also a thousand or so who have not been searched out and listed. There are between three and four hundred blind children. The State confines its benevolence to these. It confers upon them a book education. It teaches them to read and write. It feeds them and shelters them. And of course it pauperizes them, because it furnishes them no way of earning a living for themselves. The State's conduct toward the adult blind—and this conduct is imitated by the legislatures of most of the other States—is purely infamous. Outside of the Blind Asylums the adult blind person has a hard time. He lives merely by the charity of the compassionate, when he has no relatives able to support him—and now and then, as a benevolence, the State stretches out its charitable hand and lifts him over to Blackwell's Island and submerges him among that multitudinous population of thieves and prostitutes.

But in Massachusetts, in Pennsylvania, and in two or three other States, Associations like this new one we have formed have been at work for some years, supported entirely by private subscriptions, and the benefits conferred and the work accomplished are so fine and great that their official reports read like a fairy-tale. It seems almost proven that there are not so very many things accomplishable by persons gifted with sight which a blind person cannot learn to do and do as well as that other person.

Helen Keller was to have been present last night but she is ill in bed, and has been ill in bed during several weeks, through overwork in the interest of the blind, the deaf, and the dumb. I need not go into any particulars about Helen Keller. She is fellow to Caesar, Alexander, Napoleon, Homer, Shakspeare, and the rest of the immortals. She will be as famous a thousand years from now as she is to-day.

I remember the first time I ever had the privilege of seeing her. She was fourteen years old then. She was to be at Laurence Hutton's house on a Sunday afternoon, and twelve or fifteen men and women had been invited to come and see her. Henry Rogers and I went together. The company had all assembled and had been waiting a while. The wonderful child arrived now, with her about equally wonderful teacher, Miss Sullivan. The girl began to deliver happy ejaculations, in her broken speech. Without touching anything, and without seeing anything, of course, and without hearing anything, she seemed to quite well recognize the character of her surroundings. She said "Oh the books, the books, so many, many books. How lovely!"

The guests were brought one after another and introduced to her. As she shook hands with each she took her hand away and laid her fingers lightly against Miss Sullivan's lips, who spoke against them the person's name. When a name was difficult, Miss Sullivan not only spoke it against Helen's fingers but spelled it upon Helen's hand with her own fingers—stenographically, apparently, for the swiftness of the operation was suggestive of that.

Mr. Howells seated himself by Helen on the sofa and she put her fingers against his lips and he told her a story of considerable length, and you could see each detail of it pass into her mind and strike fire there and throw the flash of it into her face. Then I told her a long story, which she interrupted all along and in the right places, with cackles, chuckles, and care-free bursts of laughter. Then Miss Sullivan put one of Helen's hands against her lips and spoke against it the question "What is Mr. Clemens distinguished for?" Helen answered, in her crippled speech, "For his humor." I spoke up modestly and said "And for his wisdom." Helen said the same words instantly—"And for his wisdom." I suppose it was a case of mental telegraphy, since there was no way for her to know what it was I had said.

After a couple of hours spent very pleasantly, some one asked if Helen would remember the feel of the hands of the company after this considerable interval of time, and be able to discriminate the hands and name the possessors of them. Miss Sullivan said "Oh she will have no difficulty about that." So the company filed past, shook hands in turn, and with each handshake Helen greeted the owner of the hand pleasantly and spoke the name that belonged to it without hesitation, until she encountered Mr. Rogers, toward the end of the procession. She shook hands with him, then paused, and a reflecting expression came into her face. Then she said "I am glad to meet you now, I have not met you before." Miss Sullivan told her she was mistaken, this gentleman was introduced to her when she first arrived in the room. But Helen was not affected by that. She said no, she never had met this gentleman before. Then Mr. Rogers said that perhaps the confusion might be explained by the fact that he had his glove on when he was introduced to Helen. Of course that explained the matter.

This was not in the afternoon, as I have mis-stated. It was in the forenoon, and by and by the assemblage proceeded to the dining room and sat down to the luncheon. I had to go away before it was over, and as I passed by Helen I patted her lightly on the head and passed on. Miss Sullivan called to me and said "Stop, Mr. Clemens, Helen is distressed because she did not recognize your hand. Won't you come back and do that again?" I went back and patted her lightly on the head, and she said at once "Oh, it's Mr. Clemens."

Perhaps some one can explain this miracle, but I have never been able to do it. Could she feel the wrinkles in my hand through her hair? Some one else must answer this. I am not competent.

As I have said, Helen was not able to leave her sick-bed, but she wrote a letter, two or three days ago, to be read at the meeting, and Miss Holt, the secretary, sent it to me by a messenger at mid-afternoon yesterday. It was lucky for me that she didn't reserve it and send it to me on the platform last night, for in that case I could not have gotten through with it. I read it to the house without a break in my voice, and also without even a tremor in it that could be noticed, I think. But it was because I had read it aloud to Miss Lyon at mid-afternoon, and I knew the dangerous places and how to be prepared for them. I told the house in the beginning that I had this letter and that I would read it at the end of the evening's activities. By and by when the end had arrived and Mr. Choate had spoken, I introduced the letter with a few words. I said that if I knew anything about literature, here was a fine and great and noble sample of it; that this letter was simple, direct, unadorned, unaffected, unpretentious, and was moving and beautiful and eloquent; that no fellow to it had ever issued from any girl's lips since Joan of Arc, that immortal child of seventeen, stood alone and friendless in her chains, five centuries ago, and confronted her judges—the concentrated learning and intellect of France—and fenced with them week by week and day by day, answering them out of her great heart and her untaught but marvelous mind, and always defeating them, always camping on the field and master of it as each day's sun went down. I said I believed that this letter, written by a young woman who has been stone deaf, dumb, and blind ever since she was eighteen months old, and who is one of the most widely and thoroughly educated women in the world, would pass into our literature as a classic and remain so. I will insert the letter here.

Wrentham, Mass., March 27, 1906.

My dear Mr. Clemens:

It is a great disappointment to me not to be with you and the other friends who have joined their strength to uplift the blind. The meeting in New York will be the greatest occasion in the movement which has so long engaged my heart: and I regret keenly not to be present and feel the inspiration of living contact with such an assembly of wit, wisdom and philanthropy. I should be happy if I could have spelled into my hand the words as they fall from your lips, and receive, even as it is uttered, the eloquence of our newest Ambassador to the blind. We have not had such advocates before. My disappointment is softened by the thought that never at any meeting was the right word so sure to be spoken. But, superfluous as all other appeal must seem after you and Mr. Choate have spoken, nevertheless, as I am a woman, I cannot be silent, and I ask you to read this letter, knowing that it will be lifted to eloquence by your kindly voice.

To know what the blind man needs, you who can see must imagine what it would be not to see, and you can imagine it more vividly if you remember that before your journey's end you may have to go the dark way yourself. Try to realize what blindness means to those whose joyous activity is stricken to inaction.

It is to live long, long days, and life is made up of days. It is to live immured, baffled, impotent, all God's world shut out. It is to sit helpless, defrauded, while your spirit strains and tugs at its fetters, and your shoulders ache for the burden they are denied, the rightful burden of labor.

The seeing man goes about his business confident and self-dependent. He does his share of the work of the world in mine, in quarry, in factory, in counting-room, asking of others no boon, save the opportunity to do a man's part and to receive the laborer's guerdon. In an instant accident blinds him. The day is blotted out. Night envelopes all the visible world. The feet which once bore him to his task with firm and confident stride stumble and halt and fear the forward step. He is forced to a new habit of idleness, which like a canker consumes the mind and destroys its beautiful faculties. Memory confronts him with his lighted past. Amid the tangible ruins of his life as it promised to be he gropes his pitiful way. You have met him on your busy thoroughfares with faltering feet and outstretched hands, patiently "dredging" the universal dark, holding out for sale his petty wares, or his cap for your pennies; and this was a Man with ambitions and capabilities.

It is because we know that these ambitions and capabilities can be fulfilled, that we are working to improve the condition of the adult blind. You cannot bring back the light to the vacant eyes; but you can give a helping hand to the sightless along their dark pilgrimage. You can teach them new skill. For work they once did with the aid of their eyes you can substitute work that they can do with their hands. They ask only opportunity, and opportunity is a torch in darkness. They crave no charity, no pension, but the satisfaction that comes from lucrative toil, and this satisfaction is the right of every human being.

At your meeting New York will speak its word for the blind, and when New York speaks, the world listens. The true message of New York is not the commercial ticking of busy telegraphs, but the mightier utterances of such gatherings as yours. Of late our periodicals have been filled with depressing revelations of great social evils. Querulous critics have pointed to every flaw in our civic structure. We have listened long enough to the pessimists. You once told me you were a pessimist, Mr. Clemens; but great men are usually mistaken about themselves. You are an optimist. If you were not, you would not preside at the meeting. For it is an answer to pessimism. It proclaims that the heart and the wisdom of a great city are devoted to the good of mankind, that in this the busiest city in the world no cry of distress goes up, but receives a compassionate and generous answer. Rejoice that the cause of the blind has been heard in New York; for the day after, it shall be heard round the world.

Yours sincerely,
Helen Keller

EXPLANATORY NOTES

These notes are intended to clarify and supplement the autobiographical writings and dictations in this volume by identifying people, places, and incidents, and by explaining topical references and literary allusions. In addition, they attempt to point out which of Clemens's statements are contradicted by historical evidence, providing a way to understand more fully how his memories of long-past events and experiences were affected by his imagination and the passage of time. Although some of the notes contain cross-references to texts or notes elsewhere in the volume, the Index is an indispensable tool for finding information about a previously identified person or event.

All references in the notes are keyed to this volume by page and line: for example, 1.1 means page 1, line 1 of the text. All of Clemens's text is included in the line count (except for the main titles of pieces); excluded are the editorial headnotes in the first section, "Preliminary Manuscripts and Dictations." Most of the source works are cited by an author's name and a date, a short title, or an abbreviation. Works by members of the Clemens family may be found under the writer's initials: SLC, OLC (Olivia), OSC (Susy), and CC (Clara). All abbreviations, authors, and short titles used in citations are fully defined in References. Most citations include a page number ("*L1,* 263," or "Angel 1881, 345"), but citations to works available in numerous editions may instead supply a chapter number or its equivalent, such as a book or act number. All quotations from holograph documents are transcribed verbatim from the originals (or photocopies thereof), even when a published form—a more readily available source—is also cited for the reader's convenience. The location of every unique document or manuscript is identified by the standard Library of Congress abbreviation, or the last name of the owner, all of which are defined in References.

PRELIMINARY MANUSCRIPTS AND DICTATIONS, 1870–1905

[The Tennessee Land] (*Source:* MS in CU-MARK, written in 1870)

61.1–3   monster tract of land ... was purchased by my father ... seventy-five thousand acres at one purchase] Although John Marshall Clemens may have acquired a tract as large as forty thousand acres in a single transaction, he also bought numerous smaller parcels, beginning as early as 1826 and continuing until at least 1841. In 1857, ten years after his death, the family had ownership records for twenty-four tracts of unknown acreage. After surveying the land in 1858, Orion concluded that he could establish title to some 30,000 acres, less than half of the 75,000 acres that Clemens estimates here.

61.1   my father] See the Appendix "Family Biographies" (pp. 654–57) for information about Clemens's immediate family.

62.28–29   the great financial crash of '34, and in that storm my father's fortunes were wrecked] President Andrew Jackson's attack on the second Bank of the United States precipitated a money crisis in 1834. Many state banks were unable to meet the demand for loans, which caused numerous businesses to fail. John Clemens, who belonged to the Whig party (formed in opposition to the Jacksonian Democrats), may well have felt the effects of this economic downturn (Wecter 1952, 36–37).

62.38–39   candidate for county judge, with a certainty of election] Shortly before his death Clemens did declare his candidacy for office, but it was for the position of clerk of the circuit court, not for "county judge" (*Inds,* 309–11; see also AD, 28 Mar 1906, where Clemens mistakenly recalled that his father had "just been elected").

62.41–63.1   "going security" for Ira —— . . . took the benefit of the new bankrupt law] In his manuscript, Clemens first wrote Ira Stout's full name, then—in the same ink— substituted dashes for his surname. John Marshall Clemens had dealings with Ira Stout, a land speculator, in late 1839. He purchased Hannibal property from Stout, at an inflated value, which he had to sell at a loss in 1843 to pay his creditors. The transaction by which John Clemens became responsible for Stout's debts has not been identified. Clemens also mentioned Stout's perfidy in 1897 in "Villagers of 1840–3," and again in his Autobiographical Dictation of 28 March 1906 (*Inds,* 104, 310, 349–50). The federal "bankrupt law" of 1841 enabled debtors, for the first time, to escape payment of their debts, while providing for little or no compensation of creditors. It was repealed two years later.

63.10–11   After my father's death . . . on a temporary basis] When John Marshall Clemens died in March of 1847, the Clemenses were living with Dr. Orville Grant's family in a house at Hill and Main. They remained there for several months before moving to the "temporary" quarters, which have not been identified. Eventually they returned to the house that their father had built in late 1843 or early 1844—the "Boyhood Home" that still stands at 206 Hill Street (Wecter 1952, 102, 113, 121; AD, 2 Dec 1906).

63.11–12   My brother . . . bought a worthless weekly newspaper] Orion began the weekly Hannibal *Western Union* in mid-1850, and within a year bought the Hannibal *Journal,* publishing the first issue of the *Journal and Western Union* in September 1851. He edited the combined paper, employing Clemens as his assistant for much of the time, until September 1853, when he sold it and moved to Muscatine, Iowa (link note preceding 24 Aug 1853 to JLC, *L1,* 1–2; *Inds,* 311).

63.14–16   but we were disappointed in a sale . . . decided to sell all or none] Nothing is known about this potential deal. In 1850 Arnold Buffum of the Tennessee Land Office, a land agency in New York, suggested the land be offered for ten cents an acre, but no sale took place (Buffum's letter does not survive, but is described in *MTBus,* 17). Clemens claimed that on two later occasions he negotiated sales of the land which Orion rejected. In 1865 a buyer agreed to pay $200,000 for an unspecified number of acres, intending to settle European immigrants on it to grow grapes and produce wine; Orion's "temperance virtue" quashed that deal (AD, 5 Apr 1906; 13 Dec 1865 to OC and MEC, *L1,* 326–27). Then in 1869, Jervis Langdon offered $30,000 in cash and stock, but Orion again demurred, citing his fear that Clemens would "unconsciously cheat" his future father-in-law (9 Nov 1869 to PAM, *L3,* 388–89 n. 2). Exasperated by Orion's scruples, Clemens renounced his own share, and by 1870 wanted nothing more to do with "that hated property" (9 Sept 1870 to OC, *L4,* 193). Orion henceforth assumed all responsibility for it. Over many years, Orion disposed of the land, either through his own efforts or through hired agents, both in large parcels (ten thousand acres) and in small ones (fewer than three hundred acres). Some of it was sold for cash—of unknown amounts—and some was traded for other property. At least one unscrupulous buyer failed to pay at all. Ultimately, the proceeds may have barely covered the cost of the property taxes. Orion regretfully acknowledged his failure in an 1878 letter to his sister and mother: "I am so sorry to hear you are cramped for means," he wrote, "it gave me another twinge of conscience that I fooled away the Tennessee land, and some of your money with it" (OC to PAM and JLC, 2 Nov 1878, CU-MARK; OC to SLC, 4 Nov 1880, CU-MARK; Wecter 1952, 31–32, 278 n. 9; also the following documents provided courtesy of Barbara Schmidt: *Fentress County Deeds* 1820–48, Vol. A:161, 236, 244, 288, 293, 335; *Fentress County Land Grants,* Book T:46; "Declaration" with "Exhibits 1–6," filed 15 May 1907, U.S. National Archives and Records Administration 1907–9).

[Early Years in Florida, Missouri] (*Source:* MS in NNAL, written in 1877)

64.20   My uncle, John A. Quarles] John Adams Quarles (1802–76) was married to Martha Ann Lampton, with whom he had ten children. She was the younger sister of Clemens's mother. He settled in Florida, Missouri, in the mid-1830s, where he became a prosperous merchant and farmer. After the Clemens family moved to Hannibal in 1839, Clemens spent his summers at the Quarles farm, from about age seven until he was eleven or twelve (*Inds,* 342). For a longer reminiscence of life on the farm see "My Autobiography [Random Extracts from It]."

64.21   "bit" calicoes] Presumably calicoes were sold at the rate of one "bit" (one-eighth of a dollar) per yard (Ramsay and Emberson 1963, 21).

65.18   my father owned slaves] In about 1833 John Marshall Clemens bought "one negro man" from Rawley Chapman (b. 1793) in Tennessee—his only documented slave purchase. The family also owned a woman named "Jenny," who had been given to Clemens's parents in about 1825. Clemens recalled that she was the "only slave we ever owned in my time" (*Inds,* 327; record of bill of sale, *Fentress County Deeds,* Vol. A:233). See "Jane Lampton Clemens" (*Inds,* 82–92) for a fuller discussion of the family's attitude toward slavery.

65.20   "stogy" shoes] A rough heavy kind of shoe; the name is supposedly derived from "Conestoga," a town in Pennsylvania.

THE GRANT DICTATIONS (*Source:* TS in CU-MARK, dictated in 1885)

The Chicago G.A.R. Festival

67 title   The Chicago G.A.R. Festival] More properly, the "Thirteenth Annual Reunion of the Society of the Army of the Tennessee." The G.A.R. (Grand Army of the Republic) was a fraternal organization of all Union veterans, and one of the sponsors of this nearly week-long event in Chicago, which, as Clemens explains, was a celebration of the returning Grant "by the veterans of the Army of the Tennessee—the first army over which he had had command" (67.19–20).

67.2–3   first time I ever saw General Grant was in the fall or winter of 1866 at one of the receptions at Washington] Clemens misremembered the year of the reception: see the note at 67.6–13. Ulysses S. Grant (1822–85) graduated from West Point and served with distinction in the Mexican War, demonstrating remarkable courage and leadership qualities. He resigned his commission in 1854 and made a meager living as a farmer and merchant. At the outbreak of the Civil War, he reenlisted in the army, eventually emerging as the leading Union general. After Grant's important victories at Vicksburg and Chattanooga, President Lincoln appointed him general-in-chief of all the Union armies, and in 1866 he received the title of General of the Army—a unique rank equivalent to a four-star general, previously awarded only to George Washington. As president of the United States for two terms, from 1869 to 1877, he failed to curb the widespread corruption in his administration but was not directly implicated in it. In the dictations that follow, Clemens describes Grant's later years: his unsuccessful bid in 1880 for a third presidential term, his financial reverses, the writing and publication of his memoirs, and his final illness.

67.5   General Sheridan] Philip H. Sheridan (1831–88), a brilliant military strategist and one of the most respected Union generals, was, like Grant, a West Point graduate. After the Civil War he served in New Orleans, defeating a small French army stationed in Mexico, and then led campaigns against the Plains Indians. In 1888 he was made General of the Army, but died shortly thereafter. Later that year Clemens's firm, Charles L. Webster and Company, published Sheridan's *Personal Memoirs.*

67.6–13   I next saw General Grant . . . I am embarrassed—are you?"] Clemens served, briefly, as secretary for Republican Senator William M. Stewart of Nevada (1827–1909) in Washington during the winter of 1867–68, shortly after returning from the *Quaker City* expedition. His fifty letters about the trip written to the San Francisco *Alta California,* half a dozen to the New York *Tribune,* and one to the New York *Herald,* supplied more than half the content of *The Innocents Abroad,* his first major book, published in 1869 (*L2:* 7 June 1867 and 9 Aug 1867 to JLC and family, 59 n. 5, 78–79; 22 Nov 1867 and 24 Nov 1867 to Young, 109 n. 2, 113–14; 2 Dec 1867 and 23 June 1868 to Bliss, 119–20, 232 n. 1). Clemens could not have met Grant in 1866, since he did not arrive in the East from San Francisco until early 1867. In a December 1867 notebook entry Clemens wrote, "Acquainted with Gen Grant—said I was glad to see him—he said I had the advantage of him" (*N&J1,* 491). The note probably alluded not to an actual meeting, but to an imaginary one, similar to the one in the manuscript that Clemens wrote on 6 December and left unpublished entitled "Interview with Gen. Grant" (SLC 1867t). It is likely that here Clemens alludes to a reception he attended in Washington in mid-January 1868; in a letter to the San Francisco *Alta California* he mentioned shaking hands with Grant and noted that "General Sheridan was there" (SLC 1868a). He wrote his family just days later that he had "called at Gen. Grant's house last night. He was out at a dinner party, but Mrs. Grant said she would keep him at home on Sunday evening. I *must* see him, because he is good for *one* letter for the Alta, & part of a lecture for San F" (20 Jan 1868 to SLC and PAM, Paine's transcript in CU-MARK). That *Alta* interview probably never took place, but his calling "at Gen. Grant's house" implies that they had been formally introduced at the reception. Their second meeting at which Clemens claimed to be "embarrassed" actually occurred in mid-1870, during a brief trip to Washington where he met up with Senator Stewart. Clemens described his encounter with Grant, then serving his first term as president, on the day it occurred, in a letter of 8 July to his wife (6 July 1870 and 8 July 1870 to OLC, *L4*, 164–67). Clemens misplaced the year of his first meeting as 1866 rather than 1868, and may therefore have misplaced the year of the second by almost the same increment, making it early 1869 rather than mid-1870. By 1870 the *Quaker City* voyage was no longer news and *The Innocents Abroad* had given Mark Twain more than "some trifle of notoriety."

67.17–19   Then, in 1879 . . . Army of the Tennessee] In 1877–79 Grant undertook a tour through Europe and Asia, accompanied by his wife, son Jesse, Adam Badeau, and John Russell Young, during which he was graciously received by numerous foreign dignitaries and heads of state. The banquet held in Chicago on 13 November 1879 was the culmination of four days of celebration (for a full account of the tour see Jean Edward Smith 2001, 606–13).

68.1   Carter Harrison, the mayor of Chicago] Carter Henry Harrison, Sr. (1825–93), served as mayor of Chicago from 1879 to 1887, and again briefly in 1893, until his assassination in October. His friendship with Clemens has not been otherwise documented.

68.4–5   "I am not embarrassed—are you?"] See the Autobiographical Dictation of 27 August 1906 for another account of the meetings with Grant.

68.10   General Sherman] William Tecumseh Sherman (1820–91) entered the army after graduating from West Point in 1840 and served in the Mexican War. In 1853 he resigned his commission and took a position as a banker. At the outbreak of the Civil War he was commissioned colonel; he attained the rank of brigadier general after the capture of Vicksburg in 1863. His famous March to the Sea through Georgia divided the Confederacy and hastened the end of the war. He succeeded Grant as General of the Army in 1869, and engaged in the Indian Wars until his retirement in 1884. His *Memoirs,* published in 1875, were highly acclaimed.

68.17   Colonel Vilas was to respond to a toast] William F. Vilas (1840–1908) of Madison, Wisconsin, was admitted to the bar in 1860. He attained the rank of lieutenant colonel during the Civil War, and later became postmaster general of the United States (1885–88), secretary of the interior (1888–89), and a U.S. senator from Wisconsin (1891–97). He responded to the toast "Our First Commander, Gen. U.S. Grant" ("Banquet of the Army of the Tennessee," New York *Times,* 15 Nov 1879, 1).

69.15–17   Ingersoll . . . was to respond to the toast of "The Volunteers,"] Robert G. Ingersoll (1833–99) was trained as a lawyer. He raised and commanded the Eleventh Illinois Cavalry Regiment during the Civil War, fought at the battles of Shiloh and Corinth, and was captured by the Confederates in 1863. After the war he served as attorney general of Illinois. Known for his radical views on religion and slavery, he was a gifted and popular orator who advocated humanism and agnosticism, making him the target of frequent criticism. At the banquet he responded to the toast "The Volunteer Soldiers of the Union Army" ("Banquet of the Army of the Tennessee," New York *Times*, 15 Nov 1879, 1). Afterwards Clemens wrote in a letter to his wife, Olivia:

> I heard four speeches which I can never forget. One by Emory Storrs, one by Gen. Vilas (O, wasn't it wonderful!) one by Gen. Logan (mighty stirring), one by somebody whose name escapes me, & one by that splendid old soul, Col. Bob Ingersoll,—oh, it was just the supremest combination of English words that was ever put together since the world began. My soul, how handsome he looked, as he stood on that table, in the midst of those 500 shouting men, & poured the molten silver from his lips! Lord, what an organ is human speech when it is played by a master! All these speeches may look dull in print, but how the lightnings glared around them when they were uttered, & how the crowd roared in response! (14 Nov 1879 to OLC, *Letters 1876–1880*)

And to William Dean Howells he wrote:

> Bob Ingersoll's speech was sadly crippled by the proof-readers, but its music will sing through my memory always as the divinest that ever enchanted my ears. And I shall always see him as he stood that night on a dinner table, under the flash of lights & banners, in the midst of seven hundred frantic shouters, the most beautiful human creature that ever lived. "They fought that a mother might own her child"—the words look like any other [in] print, but Lord bless me, he borrowed the very accent of the angel of Mercy to say them in, & you should have seen that vast house rise to its feet. (17 Nov 1879 to Howells, *Letters 1876–1880*)

When he returned to Hartford, Clemens wrote Ingersoll asking for a copy of his speech (9 Dec 1879 to Ingersoll, *Letters 1876–1880*). The printed copy sent by Ingersoll is in the Mark Twain Papers, so identified by Clemens. The sentence he quoted in part to Howells reads as follows:

> Grander than the Greek, nobler than the Roman, the soldiers of the Republic, with patriotism as shoreless as the air, battled for the rights of others, for the nobility of labor, fought that mothers might own their babies, that arrogant idleness should not scar the back of patient toil, and that our country should not be a many-headed monster made of warring states, but a nation, sovereign, great, and free. ("The Grand Banquet at the Palmer House, Chicago, Thursday, Nov. 13th, 1879," CU-MARK)

69.29   "Egod! He *didn't* get left!"] This was evidently the "slang expression" that was new to Clemens (68.13). While it originally referred to missing a boat or train connection, in the late 1870s it came to mean "lose out" in general. Clemens recorded this exact remark about

Ingersoll in his 1882 notebook (*N&J2,* 373, 507; see, for example, "How a Lawyer Got Left," *Puck* 3 [24 Apr 1878]: 4).

70.13   the child is but the father of the man] A slight misquotation from "The Rainbow," by William Wordsworth.

70.15–16   for when they saw the General break up in good-sized pieces they followed suit with great enthusiasm] Clemens described this occasion in his letter to Howells:

> Gen. Grant sat at the banquet like a statue of iron & listened without the faintest sugges-
> tion of emotion to fourteen speeches which tore other people all to shreds, but when I lit
> in with the fifteenth & last, his time was come! I shook him up like dynamite & he sat
> there fifteen minutes & laughed & cried like the mortalest of mortals. But bless you I had
> measured this unconquerable conqueror, & went at my work with the confidence of
> conviction, for I knew I could lick him. He told me he had shaken hands with 15,000
> people that day & come out of it without an ache or pain, but that my truths had racked
> all the bones of his body apart. (17 Nov 1879 to Howells, *Letters 1876–1880*)

For the full text of "The Babies," see Budd 1992a, 727–29.

[A Call with W. D. Howells on General Grant]

70.18   1881] The year should be 1882: see the note at 70.19–37.

70.19   Howells] William Dean Howells (1837–1920) was born at Martin's Ferry, Ohio, into a large family with radical political and religious tendencies. He was apprenticed to his father, a printer, and became a journalist. With, as he was to say, "an almost entire want of schooling," he read widely in his father's library, teaching himself Spanish, German, French, and Italian (Howells to John S. Hart, 2 July 1871, in Howells 1979, 375). In recognition of his support of Lincoln's 1860 presidential campaign, Howells was rewarded with a consulship in Venice (1861). Returning to America in 1865, he rose as a journalist, moving to Cambridge, Massachusetts, to be assistant editor (1866–71) and then editor (1871–81) of the *Atlantic Monthly.* In 1881 he retired to concentrate on writing. Among his personal friends were Henry Adams, William and Henry James, and jurist Oliver Wendell Holmes, Jr. (son of the poet). His friendship with Clemens dates from his review of *The Innocents Abroad* in 1869 (Howells 1869). Howells used his position at the epicenter of American letters to help assure Mark Twain's literary success; he also served his friend as editor, proofreader, and sounding-board. In literature, Howells championed and practiced realism. His best novels, out of a vast output, are usually considered to be *The Rise of Silas Lapham* (1885) and *A Hazard of New Fortunes* (1890); he memorialized Clemens in *My Mark Twain* (1910).

70.19–37   his old father . . . resigned, a couple of years later] Howells's father, William Cooper Howells (1807–94), was appointed U.S. consul at Toronto in 1878, after serving for four years as the consul at Quebec. Howells learned in late January 1882 that his father might lose his position, and on 2 March wrote him that he planned "to spend Sunday with Mark Twain who is a great friend of Grant's, and can possibly get me access to him" (Howells to

William C. Howells, 2 Mar 1882, in Howells 1980, 10–11). Clemens and Howells called on Grant in New York on 10 March. In *My Mark Twain,* Howells reported that Grant was "very simple and very cordial, and I was instantly the more at home with him, because his voice was the soft, rounded, Ohio River accent to which my years [*i.e.,* ears] were earliest used from my steamboating uncles, my earliest heroes. When I stated my business he merely said, Oh no; that must not be; he would write to Mr. Arthur" (Howells 1910, 71). Grant acted so promptly that Secretary of State Frederick T. Frelinghuysen (1817–85) responded the following day, "You may inform Mr. Clemens that it is not our purpose to make a change in the Consulate at Toronto" (Frelinghuysen to Grant, 11 Mar 1882, CU-MARK). Grant forwarded the letter to Clemens, and he in turn wrote Howells, on 14 March, "This settles the matter—at least for some time to come—& permanently, I imagine. You see the General is a pretty prompt man" (MH-H, in *MTHL,* 1:394). The elder Howells resigned his post in June 1883 (21 June 1874 to Howells, *L6,* 166 n. 2; Howells 1979, 61, 196; Howells 1980, 10–11, 14, 58–59).

71.7–8   "How he sits and towers"...Dante] Howells quoted this phrase in a letter to Clemens from Bethlehem, New Hampshire, of 9 August 1885: "We had a funeral service for Grant, here, yesterday, and all the time while they were pumping song and praise over his great memory, I kept thinking of the day when we lunched on pork and beans with him in New York, and longing to make them feel and see how far above their hymns he was even in such an association. How he 'sits and towers' as Dante says" (CU-MARK, in *MTHL,* 2:536). Less than a month later, on 10 September, Clemens added this quotation to his dictated typescript, inserting in brackets the words "It was bacon and beans" and Howells's presumed quote from Dante. The phrase is not, however, from Dante, but from a sonnet by Italian dramatist and poet Vittorio Alfieri (1749–1803): "Siena, dal colle ove torreggia e siede" ("Siena, from the hill where she towers and sits"). Howells's source was E. A. Brigidi's *La Nuova Guida di Siena* (a work he drew on for his *Tuscan Cities*), where it appeared without citation (Brigidi 1885, 11; Howells 1886, 126, 139). Many years later Howells recalled that the "baked beans and coffee were of about the railroad-refreshment quality; but eating them with Grant was like sitting down to baked beans and coffee with Julius Caesar, or Alexander, or some other great Plutarchan captain" (Howells 1910, 72).

71.9–18   "Squibob" Derby at West Point...would change places with him] Howells later recalled:

> Grant seemed to like finding himself in company with two literary men, one of whom at least he could make sure of, and unlike that silent man he was reputed, he talked constantly, and so far as he might he talked literature. At least he talked of John Phoenix, that delightfulest of the early Pacific Slope humorists, whom he had known under his real name of George H. Derby, when they were fellow-cadets at West Point. (Howells 1910, 72)

George Horatio Derby (1823–61), a captain in the U.S. Army Corps of Topographical Engineers, was known primarily for the humorous sketches he wrote under his pseudonym while stationed on the Pacific Coast. These were collected in *Phoenixiana; or, Sketches and Burlesques* (1856) and, posthumously, *The Squibob Papers* (1865) (15 Dec 1866 to JLC and family, *L1,* 374 n. 2).

71.27–29 General Badeau's military history . . . John Russell Young's account . . . had hardly any sale at all] Adam Badeau (1831–95) became Grant's military secretary in 1864, and by the time he retired from the army in 1869 (with the brevet rank of brigadier general) the two men had become close friends. President Grant appointed Badeau U.S. consul in London, where he served from 1870 to 1881, except for a leave from his post to travel with Grant for the first five months of his 1877–79 world tour. Between 1868 and 1881 Badeau published his three-volume *Military History of Ulysses S. Grant* (Badeau 1868–81; *N&J3,* 107 n. 137; 15 June 1873 to Badeau, *L5,* 382 n. 1). John Russell Young (1840–99) had a distinguished career as a journalist with several newspapers before becoming managing editor of the New York *Tribune* from 1866 to 1869. In 1872 he accepted a position as foreign correspondent for the New York *Herald.* He accompanied Grant on his tour, which he chronicled in *Around the World with General Grant* (1879). Appointed by President Chester A. Arthur as U.S. minister to China in 1882 (through Grant's influence), Young mediated a number of disputes involving the United States, China, and France before returning to the *Herald* in 1885 (14 May 1869 to OLL, *L3,* 230 n. 6; 17 or 18 June 1873 to Young, *L5,* 383 n. 1).

71.34–35 best plan of publication—the subscription plan] Subscription publishers sold books in advance of publication through agents who went door to door, largely in rural areas, and persuaded people to place orders by showing them a bound "prospectus" with sample pages and illustrations. Subscription books typically cost more than those sold in bookstores, and were the best way to ensure high profits—a lesson that Clemens had learned from his own experience, beginning in 1869 with the American Publishing Company.

71.36–37 American Publishing Company . . . swindling me for ten years] In early 1872, shortly after the publication of *Roughing It,* Clemens began to suspect that his publisher, Elisha P. Bliss, Jr., of the American Publishing Company, was cheating him by overstating his production expenses. He was reassured by Bliss's explanation, however, and stayed with the firm through the publication of *A Tramp Abroad* in 1880 (see *RI 1993,* 877–80; AD, 21 Feb 1906, note at 370.32–33). Although after Bliss's death in 1880 Clemens considered suing the company, he decided that Francis Bliss, who had succeeded his father, had treated him fairly (26 Oct 1881 to Webster, NPV, in *MTBus,* 173–74; 28 Dec 1881 to Osgood and Company and 31 Dec 1881 to Osgood, MH-H, in *MTLP,* 147–49; 3? Oct 1882 to Elliott, CU-MARK; 6 Oct 1882 to Webster, NPV, in *MTBus,* 203–4). By mid-1883 he was willing to recommend the firm to fellow author George Washington Cable:

> If I were going to advise you to issue through a Hartford house, I would say, every time, go to my former publishers, the American Publishing Company, 284 Asylum st. They swindled me out of huge sums of money in the old days, but they do know how to push a book; and besides, I think they are honest people now. I think there was only one thief in the concern, and he is shoveling brimstone now. (4 June 1883 to Cable, LNT)

Grant and the Chinese

72.6 Yung Wing, late Chinese Minister at Washington] Yung Wing (1828–1912) was raised in a peasant family in southern China and learned to read and write English at a missionary school. He came to the United States with his teacher in 1847 and graduated from Yale College in 1854. In 1876 he was appointed minister to Washington jointly with Chin Lan Pin, a position he declined, agreeing instead to serve as Chin's assistant minister (1878–81). Clemens became acquainted with Yung through their mutual friend the Reverend Joseph Twichell (Yung 1909, 1, 3, 7, 13, 19–21, 27, 41, 173, 180–90, 197–200; New York *Times:* "The Chinese Ambassadors," 29 Sept 1878, 1; "China's Backward Step," 2 Sept 1881, 5; 21 Feb 1875 to Sprague and others, *L6,* 393 n. 3).

72.7–9   Li-Hung-Chang . . . military railroads in China] Li Hung Chang (1823–1901), viceroy of the Chinese capital province of Zhili from 1870 to 1896, was, as Clemens claimed, a progressive politician who promoted modernization of the army and the building of railroads. Clemens first approached Grant about the railroad project in early 1881. Twichell described the circumstances in a journal entry for 25–28 March of that year:

> Yung Wing arrives from Washington full of business. The Chinese Gov. (so he is advised) is soon to embark in a great Rail Road enterprize, and he wants the United States to get in ahead of England and all the world in furnishing the men and the capital involved in carrying out the project. . . . Accordingly M. T. is called on for counsel and aid. He writes to Gen. G. at once. Answer comes promptly that he is on the point of setting out for Mexico, but will be sure to seize an opportunity to write en route to Li Hung Chang making recommendations in the line of Y. W.'s ideas. (Twichell 1874–1916)

Neither Clemens's letter nor Grant's reply is known to survive. On 1 April Grant wrote to Clemens while en route to Mexico, enclosing the promised letter to Li:

> If you will show this letter to Yung Wing, and he approves of it, and then forward it to Li Hung Chang, I will be much obliged to you.
> I regret much not reading your letter when it was received. Had I done so I would have arranged for a meeting with you and friends no matter what I had to do. (CU-MARK)

In a second letter of the same day he added, "On my return to New York I will be very glad to meet you with Yung Wing, and any others you, or he, choose to bring, to talk on this subject" (CU-MARK). Clemens wrote to thank Grant on 22 April: "Your letter to the viceroy has gone at a fortunate time, for it will strengthen his hands at a needed season" (quoted in Dawson 1902). Clemens's recollection that he and Yung called on Grant three years later to discuss the project, in early 1884, is confirmed by his remark below about Grant's "fall on the ice," an accident that occurred in December 1883 (Badeau 1887, 416).

72.8   Prince Kung] Prince Gong (1833–98), as he is now more commonly known, was head of China's Grand Council. As the most prominent statesman in China during the 1860s and 1870s, he pursued an agenda of modernization and cooperation with Western countries. Clemens had evidently read a false newspaper report that the prince had committed suicide after the emperor deposed him, but he had only retired from public life ("Prince Kung," Chicago *Tribune,* 2 May 1884, 5).

72.33–34   About 1879 or 1880, the Chinese pupils . . . had been ordered home by the

Chinese government] Yung's life work was to promote the education of Chinese students in the United States. As a result of his efforts, in 1872 the Chinese government established the Chinese Educational Commission, which brought more than a hundred boys to Hartford for a program of studies intended to prepare them for government service in their native country. Yung was appointed co-commissioner with Chin Lan Pin. Both Chin and Woo Tsze Tun, who became co-commissioner in 1876, were conservatives who feared that the mission was a threat to traditional Chinese culture. According to Yung, Woo's "malicious misrepresentations and other falsehoods" ultimately persuaded the Chinese government, with the consent of Viceroy Li, to take steps to abolish the program in late 1880 (Yung 1909, 200–210).

73.2–3   Wong, non-progressionist, was the chief China Minister] Although Clemens did not correctly recall Minister Chin's name, he did accurately describe his role in bringing about the end of the Chinese Mission (Yung 1909, 203).

73.13   Rev. Mr. Twichell] Joseph H. Twichell (1838–1918), the son of a tanner, was born in Connecticut. He graduated from Yale in 1859, but his studies at Union Seminary were interrupted by Civil War service as chaplain of the Seventy-first New York Volunteers. In 1865 he completed his divinity studies at Andover Seminary and accepted the pastorate of Asylum Hill Congregational Church (Hartford, Connecticut), where he would remain for the rest of his career. The same year, he married Julia Harmony Cushman (1843–1910); they had nine children. He struck up a friendship with Clemens in 1868, which deepened when the Clemenses moved to the Hartford neighborhood of Nook Farm, where the Twichells also lived. Twichell preached a "muscular Christianity" more concerned with social progress than with doctrine, and was broad-minded enough to be Clemens's confidant and adviser. He accompanied Clemens to Bermuda in 1877 and to Europe in 1878; in *A Tramp Abroad* he is the model for the character of Harris. He was one of Clemens's closest friends, presiding at both his wedding and his funeral.

73.13–22   went down to New York to see the General . . . do it immediately] Twichell, who had befriended Yung and strongly endorsed his work, asked Clemens to enlist Grant's support. The two men called on Grant in New York on 21 December 1880. Clemens wrote Howells, "Grant took in the whole situation in a jiffy, & before Joe had more than fairly got started, the old man said: '*I'll write the Viceroy a letter*—a separate letter—& bring strong reasons to bear upon him'" (24 Dec 1880 to Howells, *Letters 1876–1880*).

73.31–33   General Grant's letter . . . peremptory command to old Minister Wong to continue the Chinese schools] In March 1881 Clemens wrote to thank Grant for his intervention, announcing that the "Mission in Hartford is saved. The order to take the students home to China was revoked by the Viceroy three days ago—by cable. This cablegram mentions the receipt of your letter" (15 Mar 1881 to Grant, OKeU).

73.36–37   policy of the Imperial government had been reversed] Ultimately, the efforts of Grant and others to continue the mission were futile. By July 1881 it had been abolished and the students recalled to China (New York *Times:* "China's Educational Mission," 16 July 1881, 5; "China's Backward Step," 2 Sept 1881, 5).

Gerhardt

74.1   at the farm at Elmira] From 1871 until 1889, the Clemens family spent their summers at Quarry Farm, the Elmira, New York, residence of Olivia's sister and brother-in-law, Susan and Theodore Crane. Susy, Clara, and Jean were all born there. The property had been purchased in 1869 by Jervis Langdon, who bequeathed it to his daughter Susan. Named after an old slate quarry on the site, it was situated outside the city, on a hill overlooking the Chemung River. In 1874 Susan built an octagonal study on the hill above the house for Clemens to use as a writer's retreat. There he worked on *The Adventures of Tom Sawyer* (1876), *A Tramp Abroad* (1880), *The Prince and the Pauper* (1881), *Life on the Mississippi* (1883), *Adventures of Huckleberry Finn* (1885), and *A Connecticut Yankee in King Arthur's Court* (1889) (17 Mar 1871 to Bliss, *L4,* 366–67 n. 3; Cotton 1985, 59).

74.2–7   Gerhardt . . . not able to get anything to do] Clemens befriended Karl Gerhardt (1853–1940), a young self-taught sculptor and chief mechanic for a tool manufacturer in Hartford, in February 1881. His wife, Josephine (called "Hattie"), initiated the relationship by calling on Clemens and persuading him to visit her husband's studio. Clemens, impressed by Gerhardt's talent, sought the opinions of several artists, who endorsed his judgment: painter James Wells Champney (1843–1903), sculptor John Quincy Adams Ward (1830–1910), and sculptor Augustus Saint-Gaudens (see AD, 16 Jan 1906, note at 284.7–8). Clemens offered to loan Gerhardt $3,000 to study at the École des Beaux-Arts in Paris, an amount that Ward and others assumed would easily support the artist and his wife for five years. Gerhardt exhausted his stipend (and supplements) in less than four years and returned to the United States in the summer of 1884, leaving his wife in Paris with their infant daughter, Olivia (named in honor of Olivia Clemens; his "little boy," Lawrence, was not yet born). Having failed to secure any work, he sculpted a clay bust of Clemens, and a plaster casting of it was photographed to provide a second frontispiece for *Huckleberry Finn.* In the late 1880s Gerhardt won a number of important commissions for memorial statues, but by the end of the decade work became scarce. In the mid-1890s he was briefly in partnership with architect Walter Sanford and was employed by a bicycle manufacturer. Sometime after Hattie died in 1897, he moved to New Orleans and lived in obscurity, doing some sculpting but chiefly tending bar and doing other odd jobs until his own death in 1940 (21 Feb 1881 to Howells [1st], NN-BGC, and 7 Aug 1884 to Howells, MH-H, in *MTHL,* 1:350–55, 2:497–98; "Art Notes," New York *Times,* 6 Mar 1881, 8; letters to the Gerhardts: 30 Sept and 1 Oct 1882, MB; 26 Mar 1883, CLjC; 14–25 June 1883, CU-MARK; 1 Aug 1883, CtHMTH; *HF 2003,* xxvii, 374; AskART 2008e; see Schmidt 2009c).

74.12–13   The speech . . . was worth four times the sum] Richard D. Hubbard (1818–84) was a Yale graduate and lawyer who served as governor of Connecticut from 1877 to 1879. On 28 March 1883 he addressed the state legislature in Hartford proposing that a statue of Nathan Hale be commissioned for the exterior of the capitol building. A brief sample will explain Clemens's sarcasm:

> Nathan Hale perished more than a century ago, a bloody sacrifice on a bloody altar. . . .
> In the lonely watches of that prison night whose early dawn was to end his days—yes, in

that night's thickest gloom and still more in that morning's horror of great darkness that was to deliver his body from the power of hell, it pleased God—this also I dare affirm—it pleased God to come nigh unto his waiting servant; to uncurtain the future for a space of time, and to let down to his watching eyes a prophetic vision of his country's coming independence. ("Connecticut's Martyr Spy," Hartford *Courant*, 29 Mar 1883, 1)

74.14–21 The committee...Mr. Coit...Barnard...Waller] Robert Coit (1830–1904), president of the New London Northern Railroad Company since 1881, served as a Connecticut state senator from 1880 to 1883 ("Robert Coit Dead," Hartford *Courant*, 20 June 1904, 1; *Biographical Review* 1898, 276–77). Henry Barnard (1811–1900) was an educator and editor who devoted his career to the improvement of public schools and held a number of government positions. He acquired a reputation, however, as an inept administrator who failed to complete his obligations. He was appointed to the committee to replace Hubbard, who died in February 1884. Thomas M. Waller (1840–1924) practiced law and entered politics in 1867, serving as a state legislator, secretary of state, mayor of New London, and governor from 1883 to 1885.

74.23–24 A salaried artist...Mrs. Colt's private church] The "salaried artist" has not been identified. James G. Batterson (1823–1901), a prominent Hartford businessman and founder of the Travelers Insurance Company, was the president of the New England Granite Works, which specialized in producing "artistic memorials" in granite, marble, and bronze. Enoch S. Woods, a sculptor with a studio in Hartford, was the sexton of the Church of the Good Shepherd. This Episcopal church had been built in 1866 by Elizabeth Jarvis Colt (1826–1905), the widow of Samuel Colt (the founder of Colt's Patent Fire-Arms Manufacturing Company), as a memorial to her late husband and the three children she had lost in infancy (Geer 1886, 42, 207, 245, 297, 521). Woods created a model of Hale "as he had prepared himself for the hangman's rope, standing bare-headed and with his hands pinioned" ("A Sculptor's Model of Nathan Hale," Hartford *Courant*, 12 July 1883, 2).

74.31 William C. Prime] Clemens had satirized *Tent Life in the Holy Land* (1857), an idealized travel narrative by journalist and author William C. Prime (1825–1905), in chapters 46 and 48 of *The Innocents Abroad*—calling him "Grimes"—and in 1908 still considered him a "gushing pietist" (AD, 31 Oct 1908). In late 1885 and early 1886, however, Clemens was negotiating with Prime for the right to publish *McClellan's Own Story*, a work that Prime edited on behalf of General George B. McClellan's widow. The book was issued in 1887 by Webster and Company (31 Jan 1886 to Prime, DLC; *N&J3*, 218).

74.31 Charles D. Warner] Charles Dudley Warner (1829–1900), an essayist, travel writer, and editor of the Hartford *Courant*, was a central figure in the Hartford Nook Farm community. With Clemens he coauthored *The Gilded Age* (1873–74), a satirical novel that lent its name to the materialism and political corruption in American society after the Civil War. Warner had met Gerhardt at the same time as Clemens and continued to take an interest in his career (link note following 20–22 Dec 1872 to Twichell, *L5*, 259–60; 21 Feb 1881 to Howells [1st], NN-BGC, in *MTHL*, 1:350–55; 5 Apr 1884 to the Gerhardts, CtHMTH).

75.26 the prospects...seemed to be as far away as ever] In December the committee—

which by then consisted of Coit, Barnard, and Governor Henry B. Harrison (Waller's successor)—at last awarded the contract to Gerhardt. Olin L. Warner, a sculptor who had studied with the same Paris mentor as Gerhardt (François Jouffroy), persuaded the committee that his sketch was superior to the full-sized model that Woods submitted. A year later Gerhardt's clay model, a figure of "heroic size . . . standing with his arms partly outstretched," was approved, and was cast in bronze. Both Clemens and Gerhardt attended the unveiling ceremony in June 1887; the Reverend Joseph Twichell gave the invocation, and Charles Dudley Warner (a new committee member) made the presentation address (Hartford *Courant:* "The Nathan Hale Statue," 22 Dec 1885, 2; 22 Dec 1886, 1; "The Hale Statue Unveiled," 15 June 1887, 5; "The Hale Statue," 15 June 1887, 1).

About General Grant's Memoirs

75.28   a history of General Grant's memoirs] See the Autobiographical Dictations of 6 February, 28 May, 29 May, 31 May, 1 June, and 2 June 1906 for Clemens's later recollections of the events he describes below. See also *N&J3,* 122–25, for an overview of the circumstances surrounding the publication of Grant's *Personal Memoirs* (1885–86).

75.30–31   During the Garfield campaign . . . Republican Party] Grant himself had been a potential candidate for a third term as president at the June 1880 Republican convention. Although he did not actively campaign for the nomination, he indicated his willingness to run if drafted. Although many of his supporters backed him through thirty-six ballots, the nomination finally went to James A. Garfield. Grant pledged his support, and at Garfield's invitation, joined his campaign (Jean Edward Smith 2001, 614–17). Garfield defeated Democrat Winfield Hancock, but was in office only six months before his assassination, in July 1881. He was succeeded by his vice-president, Chester A. Arthur.

76.1   Grant's eldest son, Colonel Fred Grant] Ulysses S. Grant married Julia Dent (1826–1902), the daughter of a Missouri farmer, in 1848. Frederick Dent (1850–1912) was their first child, followed by Ulysses S., Jr. (1852–1929), Ellen Wrenshall (1855–1922), and Jesse Root, Jr. (1858–1934). As a youth Frederick spent much of the Civil War at his father's side, serving with distinction. After graduating from West Point in 1871, he joined a cavalry regiment, and later served on the staffs of several generals, attaining the rank of lieutenant colonel. In 1877–79 he joined his father and mother on their world tour. He resumed his military career during the Spanish-American War, reaching the rank of major general. Ulysses S. Grant, Jr. (called "Buck"), a graduate of Harvard and Columbia Law School, became a stockbroker. After the failure of his firm, he recovered with the help of his father-in-law, Jerome B. Chaffee, a former state senator (see the note at 83.30). Jesse Grant studied at Cornell, but left to accompany his parents on the early part of their world tour. He attended Columbia Law School for only a year (McFeely 1981, 22, 489–90, 521).

76.5–8   the General left the White House . . . live in either of them] No evidence has been found that Grant was in debt after either term as president. After leaving the White House in March 1877, he spent $85,000 of his own money (earned from investments) on his world tour.

After their return the Grants still had $100,000 invested, which provided an annual income of less than $6,000. This amount was not sufficient to maintain their standard of living (it barely covered the cost of their rooms at the Fifth Avenue Hotel). The Grants also owned a house in Philadelphia, given to them in 1865, and "four or five little houses" they had purchased in Washington (Julia Dent Grant 1975, 161, 322). Grant had resigned from the army in 1869—giving up his unique title of General of the Army, awarded by an act of Congress in July 1866—and was therefore ineligible to be placed on the retired list; nor did he qualify for a pension by virtue of his political office: former presidents received no government support until 1958 (Badeau 1887, 316, 418; Jean Edward Smith 2001, 419–20, 607–8; Stephanie Smith 2006).

76.15–20   in introducing the General, I referred to the dignities and emoluments . . . he was well satisfied] Clemens accompanied the Grant party from Boston to Hartford on the morning of 16 October 1880, and introduced the general at a gathering in Bushnell Park that afternoon. His speech included the following remarks:

> When Wellington won Waterloo—a battle about on a level with some dozen of your victories—sordid England tried to *pay* him for that service—with wealth and grandeurs! She made him a duke, and gave him $4,000,000. If you had done and suffered for any other country what you have done and suffered for your own, you would have been affronted in the same sordid way. (Laughter.) But thank God this vast and rich and mighty republic is imbued to the core with a delicacy which will forever preserve her from so degrading you. (Renewed laughter.) Your country loves you, your country is proud of you, your country is grateful to you. (Applause.) Her applauses, which have been thundering in your ears all these weeks and months, will never cease while the flag you saved continues to wave. (Great applause.)
> Your country stands ready, from this day forth[,] to testify her measureless love, and pride, and gratitude towards you in every conceivable—*inexpensive* way. (Roars of laughter.) ("Grant. His Reception in Hartford," Hartford *Courant,* 18 Oct 1880, 1)

Clemens sent Howells a clipping of his speech, with the remark that "Gen. Grant came near laughing his entire head off" (19 Oct 1880 to Howells, *Letters 1876–1880*). Grant replied that what the American people had given him was "of more value than gold and silver. No amount of the latter could compensate for the respect and kind feelings of my fellow-citizens" ("Grant. His Reception in Hartford," Hartford *Courant,* 18 Oct 1880, 1).

76.22–25   certain wealthy citizens . . . rascality of other people] At the end of 1880 George Jones of the New York *Times* and other friends came to the Grants' rescue by raising a trust fund of $250,000, which was invested in railroad bonds to provide a guaranteed income of $15,000 a year (Goldhurst 1975, 12–13, 21).

76.26–30   Grant and Ward, brokers and stock-dealers . . . business of the house] The principals in the firm, established in mid-1880, were Ulysses S. Grant, Jr., and Ferdinand Ward. Ward, the son of a minister, grew up in Geneseo, New York. He went to New York in 1875, and worked as a clerk in the produce exchange. He began building his fortune by "speculating in memberships" on the exchange, and later inherited a fortune upon the death of his father-in-law, an officer of the Marine National Bank ("Wall Street Startled," New York *Times,* 7 May 1884, 5). By the early 1880s he was reputed to be worth $750,000, and was known as the "Young Napoleon" of the financial world. Grant and Ward invested $100,000 each. In November 1880 General Grant and James D. Fish, president of the Marine National Bank, each added $100,000, and became "special" partners. The Grants put in cash, while the other two men pledged securities. Frederick Grant and, to a lesser extent, Jesse Grant also invested with the firm (McFeely 1981, 489–90; Jean Edward Smith 2001, 619; New York *Times:* "The Fish-Grant Letters," 28 May 1884, 5; advertisement for "Grant & Ward, Bankers," 8 Dec 1881, 7; Goldhurst 1975, 13–14).

76.37–38   5th of May . . . penniless] The firm collapsed on 6 May 1884 and simultaneously caused the closure of the Marine National Bank. For several years, investors had made unrealistic profits, collecting annual dividends sometimes as high as 40 percent. Grant and his son had left everything in Ward's hands, and believed themselves millionaires. Ward's scheme was to induce investors to buy securities, retain them on deposit as collateral on multiple loans from the Marine Bank (with the collusion of Fish), and then pay out the borrowed funds in large dividends to other investors. The scheme collapsed when Ward finally could not repay the loans. The securities he had pledged to the bank did not cover the loss, which in turn caused the bank to fail. The estimated liabilities of the firm of Grant and Ward totaled nearly $17 million, with actual assets of about $67,000 (Goldhurst 1975, 13–19; Jean Edward Smith 2001, 619–21; McFeely 1981, 490; New York *Times:* "Wall Street Startled," 7 May 1884, 1; "Ward's Curious Methods," 13 May 1884, 1; "Debts of Grant & Ward," 8 July 1884, 8; "Ferdinand Ward Arraigned," 5 June 1885, 8).

76.42–77.7   Ward had spared no one . . . connected with the Grant family] The New York house, purchased with money from a $100,000 fund raised by wealthy friends, belonged to Mrs. Grant. The Grants assumed an existing mortgage and gave the balance of the gift— $52,000—to Ward, who falsely claimed that it was invested in bonds. The $65,000 was most likely from the sale of the Philadelphia house (Badeau 1887, 420; Julia Dent Grant 1975, 161, 323–24). According to Badeau, Grant

> was ruined; one son was a partner in the wreck and the liabilities; another[,] the agent of the firm, was bankrupt for half a million; his youngest son on the 3d of May had deposited all his means, about $80,000, in the bank of his father and brother, and the bank suspended payment on the 6th; his daughter had made a little investment of $12,000 with the firm; one sister had put in $5,000, another $25,000; a nephew had invested a few thousands, the savings of a clerkship; and other personal friends had been induced by Grant's name and advice to invest still more largely. (Badeau 1887, 421)

In one sense it cannot be claimed that Grant lost his initial investment, because he and his son had each been drawing as much as $3,000 a month from the firm for living expenses. So between late 1880 and early 1884, they probably received an amount equal to their original investment, plus a reasonable return. What Grant had lost, however, was a putative fortune: he believed that his withdrawals did not affect his principal, which was now alleged to be about a million dollars. In addition, he was now responsible for the liabilities of the firm. (Mrs. Grant eventually paid out about $190,000 from the proceeds of Grant's *Memoirs* to settle these business debts.) And, finally, he had borrowed $150,000 from William H. Vanderbilt in a last-minute effort to avert the disaster, in the belief that Ward would return the money immediately. To repay the debt, Grant made over all his assets to Vanderbilt, including deeds to his real estate. (When Vanderbilt offered to return the property to Mrs. Grant and forgive the debt, the Grants refused.) Mrs. Grant—whose property was considered separate—still owned two houses in Washington, which she sold to raise money; loans from friends provided additional funds for living expenses (Goldhurst 1975, 3–5, 13, 22–25, 250; "Gen. Grant's Testimony," New York *Tribune,* 28 Mar 1885, 1; Badeau 1887, 419–20, 423, 432–33).

77.9–13   bill to restore to General Grant . . . Fitz-John Porter Bill by President Arthur] Major General Fitz-John Porter (1822–1901) was convicted by a court martial in January 1863 of disobeying orders at the second battle of Bull Run. Many believed he was innocent of the charges, arguing that the orders were based on false information, and would have resulted in a doomed assault. In 1879 Porter was exonerated by a board of inquiry, and in early 1880 his supporters began a long campaign to restore him to his army rank on the retired list, either by legislation or by executive action. Late in 1880 a bill authorizing the president to similarly reinstate Grant was introduced in Congress. These were the first of a series of "relief" bills for both men that were debated in Congress over the next several years. When at last a bill for Porter passed both houses, President Arthur vetoed it in July 1884, claiming that it was unconstitutional because it named a specific person, a power not granted to Congress. Meanwhile, after the failure of Grant and Ward in May 1884, a second bill to reinstate Grant had been introduced in Congress. President Arthur, who wanted to avoid contradicting his earlier position in the Porter case, asked Congress to confer a pension upon Grant without presidential action—a form of charity that Grant "indignantly declined to receive" (Badeau 1887, 432). In January 1885 a final bill was proposed, authorizing the president to place one former general on the army retired list with the corresponding "rank and full pay." The Porter bill and the Grant bill both passed the Senate, but were stalled in the House, in part because some congressmen wanted to retaliate against Arthur by forcing a veto. Finally, less than half an hour before Congress was to adjourn *sine die* at noon on 4 March, the last bill was passed. The timing was so close that at 11:45 the assistant doorkeeper "stood upon a chair and pushed the hands of the Senate clock back six minutes, while everybody laughed at the cheating of time." The bill was signed at once, and at "11:53 by the corrected time" the president proffered Grant's nomination, which was unanimously approved. Clemens, who was present when Grant heard the news, sent a telegram to his wife: "We were at General Grants at noon and a telegram arrived that the last act of the expiring congress late this morning retired him with full Generals rank and accompanying emoluments. The effect upon him was like raising the dead" ("Gen. Grant's Retirement," New York *Times,* 5 Mar 1885, 1; 4 Mar 1885 to OLC, CU-MARK). Unfortunately, the result of these efforts was essentially honorary. Grant died less than five months later, and his pay, $13,600 a year, was not continued to his widow. In December 1885, however, Congress awarded Mrs. Grant her own pension of $5,000 a year. Porter's case was not resolved until July 1886, when he was restored to his former rank by a special act of Congress and awarded an annual pension of $3,375 (New York *Times:* "Fitz John Porter Whitewashed," 29 Mar 1879, 2; "Gen. Grant's Former Salaries," 14 Dec 1880, 1; "Fitz John Porter's Case," 12 Jan 1880, 1; "In Vindication of Porter," 3 Jan 1882, 5; "Porter's Last Hope Gone," 16 Apr 1882, 1; "Still Seeking a Pardon," 1 Jan 1884, 1; "The Fitz John Porter Bill Killed," 4 July 1884, 1; "For Gen. Grant's Benefit," 8 May 1884, 1; "Mrs. Grant's Pension Approved," 27 Dec 1885, 1; "Army and Navy News," 7 July 1886, 3; *Annual Cyclopaedia 1883,* 236–48; *Annual Cyclopaedia 1884,* 207–8; *Annual Cyclopaedia 1885,* 203–4, 225–27; Badeau 1887, 340–41, 432, 443; Jean Edward Smith 2001, 624–25; Los Angeles *Times:* "The Retired List," 22 Oct 1893, 9; "Current Notes," 22 May 1885, 2; "Will Mrs. Grant Have a Pension?" Utica *Observer,* undated clipping in Scrapbook 22:59, CU-MARK).

77.27–31   I was reading . . . going to write a fourth] In the winter of 1884–85, Clemens was on a lecture tour with George Washington Cable. Olivia was present at the first of their two performances in New York at Chickering Hall, on 18 and 19 November. Grant's four war articles ("The Battle of Shiloh," "The Siege of Vicksburg," "Chattanooga," and "Preparing for the Wilderness Campaign") were published in the *Century* between February 1885 and February 1886. They were part of "Battles and Leaders of the Civil War," a series of articles by dozens of authors, including generals from both sides of the conflict, which appeared from November 1884 to October 1887 and was then collected in four volumes (Ulysses S. Grant 1885a, 1885b, 1885c, 1886; Johnson and Buel 1887–88).

77 *footnote*   *Aug. '85 . . . Gilder himself] Richard Watson Gilder (1844–1909) was a poet and the influential editor of the *Century Magazine* from its first issue in November 1881 until his death (see Johnson 1923, 88–96). This footnote is one of several comments that Clemens added in August 1885 to the text he had dictated in May.

79.21–22   Charles L. Webster & Co. . . . one-tenth interest] Charles L. Webster (1851–91), a surveyor and civil engineer from Fredonia, New York, had married Annie Moffett, the daughter of Clemens's sister, Pamela, in 1875. Clemens hired him as his general manager in 1881, giving him broad responsibility for both his business and personal affairs. In 1884, when Clemens established his own publishing company, he relied on Webster to run the business, at a salary of $2,500 a year, supplemented (starting in 1885) by one-third of the profits up to $20,000 a year, and one-tenth of earnings beyond that (contracts dated 10 Apr 1884 and 20 Mar 1885, NPV). Webster and Company published all of Clemens's books from *Huckleberry Finn* (1885) to *Tom Sawyer Abroad* (1894), as well as other works. Clemens forced Webster to retire, ostensibly because of ill health, in 1888; he returned to Fredonia, where he died at age thirty-nine. The publishing firm, which had been losing money for several years, declared bankruptcy on 18 April 1894 ("Mark Twain's Company in Trouble," New York *Times,* 19 Apr 1894, 9).

80.22   George W. Childs] Childs (1829–94) was the editor and publisher of the Philadelphia *Public Ledger* from 1864 until his death. He was a highly respected and admired businessman and philanthropist, as well as a good friend of Grant's (*N&J3,* 100 n. 111).

80.30–31   Clarence Seward's was one] Clarence A. Seward (1828–97) established the firm of Seward, Da Costa and Guthrie in 1867; it became one of the most prominent and successful law practices in New York.

80.35   the contract was drawn . . . in my hands] Clemens delegated Webster to negotiate with Grant. On 27 February 1885, Grant agreed to allow the firm to issue his book in return for 70 percent of the net profits. The amount of money ultimately paid to Mrs. Grant has not been determined, but Webster Company records show that by 1 October 1887 she had received checks totaling about $397,000 (Fred Grant to Charles L. Webster and Co., 22 July 1887, CU-MARK; "Cash Statement | Oct. 1ˢᵗ 1887 | Chas. L. Webster & Co.," CU-MARK; N&J3, 94–97, 142, 312–13, 316 n. 47). Clemens estimated that she received between $420,000 and $450,000; the Webster Company's portion was therefore at least $180,000. These amounts are equivalent—by some estimates—to $8 million and $3.4 million, respectively, in today's dollars. In 1908 Fred Grant placed the figure even higher, claiming that the "first checks received for royalties on the sale of the book amounted to $534,000" ("Gen. Frederick Dent Grant's Recollections of His Famous Father," Washington *Post,* 3 May 1908, SM4, 8). On 6 July 1885, Clemens drafted a letter to the editor of the Boston *Herald* in response to a letter from its New York correspondent, published on 20 June. Clemens protested the claim that he had made an offer to Grant

> "which no regular publisher felt like competing with." I merely offer *double as much* for General Grant's book as the Century Co had offered—that is all. I suggested to Gen. Grant that he submit my offer to the Century & other great publishing houses, & *close with the one that offered him the best terms.* He did it, & my offer was duplicated by *several* "regular publishers," the Century among the number; & two firms *exceeded* my offer. But none of them could exceed my *facilities* for publishing a subscription book—nor *equal* them, either—a fact which I proved to the satisfaction of General Grant's lawyer; & that is why I got the book. (MS draft in CU-MARK)

80.39   Roswell Smith's remark] Smith (1829–92), publisher of the *Century Magazine,* had been one of the journal's founders in 1870, when it was called *Scribner's Monthly.* The change of name took place in 1881, when the magazine severed its connection with the Scribner firm, but Smith continued as its publisher (Mott 1957, 457, 467).

82.7–8   annual in London had offered little Tom Moore] The diminutive Irish writer Thomas Moore (1779–1852) published his first poetry collection under the pen name "Thomas Little." The "annual in London" has not been identified.

82.30   Dr. Douglas] John H. Douglas was a leading New York throat specialist; in October 1884 he diagnosed Grant's affliction as cancer of the throat ("Sinking into the Grave," New York *Times,* 1 Mar 1885, 2).

83.9   Mt. McGregor] On 16 June 1885 the Grants traveled to a cottage owned by a friend, financier Joseph W. Drexel, on Mount McGregor, a summer resort near Saratoga Springs, New York. Grant stayed there, attended by his family and Dr. Douglas, until his death on 23 July (New York *Times:* "Resting at Mount McGregor," 17 June 1885, 1; "A Hero Finds Rest," 24 July 1885, 1).

83.11–12   Marine Bank man . . . sent up for ten years] James D. Fish was sentenced in June 1885 to ten years in Auburn State Prison ("On the Way to Auburn," New York *Times,* 28 June 1885, 7).

83.22   President of the Erie Railroad] Hugh J. Jewett (1817–98) served as president of the Erie Railroad from 1874 to 1884, and was credited with rescuing it from insolvency. He was one of the largest creditors of the Marine Bank when it failed ("The Marine Bank Failure," New York *Times,* 14 May 1884, 1).

83.30   ex-Senator Chaffee] Ulysses S. Grant, Jr., married Fannie Josephine Chaffee, the daughter of Jerome B. Chaffee, in 1880. Chaffee became wealthy from mining, land specula-tion, and banking in Colorado, and served as one of the state's first senators in 1876–79. Chaffee himself was another of Ward's victims: he lost about $500,000 in bonds that he had given to Ward to use as securities on loans (McFeely 1981, 489; "Senator Chaffee's Bonds," New York *Times,* 28 Dec 1884, 12).

85.24   I was talking to General Badeau there one day] Badeau recalled a conversation with "one of the greatest wits of this generation" that took place when they met on a visit to Grant as he "lay lingering in his final illness":

> The visitor was a personal friend as well as an admirer of Grant, and he and I talked of the great revulsion in popular feeling which had occurred—the sympathy and affection that had revived as soon as the hero was known to be dying. It made me think of Lincoln, reviled and maligned for years, but in one night raised to the rank of a martyr and placed by the side of Washington. "Yes," said the other, with the terrible sententiousness almost of Voltaire: "The men that want to set up a new religion ought always to get themselves cruci-fied." (Badeau 1887, 590)

86.11   I will make a diversion here, and get back upon my track again later] Albert Bigelow Paine published this "diversion" (86.11–91.18) in *Mark Twain's Autobiography* under the title "Gerhardt and the Grant Bust"; he placed it after his incomplete text of "About General Grant's Memoirs," which ends with "that sort of thing" (93.41–42; *MTA,* 1:57–68). Physical evidence in the typescript as well as several references and dates in the text itself show, however, that Clemens dictated the text as it is presented here (see the Textual Commentary, *MTPO*).

86.12   away with G. W. Cable, giving public readings] George Washington Cable (1844–1925), a New Orleans native, was known for his stories of Creole life. He and Clemens became friends in 1881, and from November 1884 through February 1885 they joined in a lecture tour. Billed as the "Twins of Genius," they spoke in more than sixty cities in the East, Midwest, and Canada. Clemens gave readings from his forthcoming *Huckleberry Finn* (which issued in February) and other works, and Cable read from several of his books and sang Creole songs (Cardwell 1953, 1–3, 12; *HF 2003,* 578).

86.18   the Presidential election] Grover Cleveland, a Democrat, defeated James G. Blaine in the 1884 election.

87.7–11   J. Q. A. Ward . . . no true artist could bring himself to do] On 5 April 1884, before Gerhardt returned from Paris, Clemens wrote to him, "I would strongly advise that you now write A. St Gaudens & J. Q. A. Ward, & ask them if they can give you employment & wages in their establishments in New York. If they can & will, *that* is a certainty; it is sure bread &

butter; & is of course better & wiser than setting up for one's self without capital" (CtHMTH). Gerhardt replied on 27 May that he strongly preferred to work independently, and pleaded, "Don't make me be a second fiddle that would kill me" (CU-MARK).

88.8–9   We reached the General's house . . . to see the family] Clemens wrote an account of this visit in his notebook on the day it took place, 20 March 1885 (*N&J3*, 106–7).

88.16   Jesse Grant's wife] Elizabeth Chapman Grant (known as "Lizzie") married Jesse in San Francisco in 1880 (McFeely 1981, 484).

89.5   Mrs. Fred Grant] Ida Honoré married Fred Grant in 1874 (Goldhurst 1975, 117).

90.20   Harrison, the General's old colored body-servant] Harrison Tyrrell had been Grant's devoted valet for many years (McFeely 1981, 519). In a letter of 11 September 1885 Clemens wrote to Henry Ward Beecher about Grant's loyalty to him:

> You remember Harrison, the colored body-servant? the whole family hated him, but that did not make any difference, the General always stood at his back, wouldn't allow him to be scolded; always excused his failures & ~~crimes~~ & deficiencies with the one unvarying formula, "We are responsible for these things in his race—it is not fair to visit our fault upon them—let him *alone;*" so they did let him alone, under compulsion. (CU-MARK, in *MTL,* 2:460–61)

90.29   best portrait of General Grant that is in existence] For an image of the bust see the photograph following page 204; see also Schmidt 2009d.

91.17–18   after the world learned his name] Here, at the end of the account of the bust of Grant, Clemens wrote "Depew's speech" in the bottom margin of the page as a prompt to himself. It wasn't until the Autobiographical Dictation of 1 June 1906, however, that he actually described the speech, which was delivered at a banquet in Grant's honor by Chauncey M. Depew (1834–1928), a prominent attorney and director of several railroads. There Clemens noted that it was "the most telling speech I ever listened to—the best speech ever made by the capable Depew, and the shortest."

92.3–4   we proceeded to draw a writing to cover the thing] Webster wrote to Clemens on 15 April 1885 that he had just signed a contract with the Century Company, which stipulated that all of Grant's "future articles" in the *Century Magazine*—that is, the second, third, and fourth—were to be copyrighted by Webster and Company "in the name of U. S. Grant." In regard to the *Memoirs,* Webster agreed "not to publish first vol before Dec. 1st next, and second vol before Mch. 1st next" (CU-MARK).

92.32   Smith's exact language] Clemens's extant notebook contains no such remark. Clemens did, however, note that

> Mr. R S . . . said to me shortly after the contract was signed, "I am glad on GG's account that there was somebody with pluck enough to give such a figure[;] I should have been chary of venturing it myself." . . .
>
> 10 p c.

~~This was a perfectly fair & honorable offer, for it was based upon a possible sale of 25,000 sets. But I was not figuring on 25,000, I was figuring on a possible 300,000. Each of us could be mistaken, but I believed I was right.~~ (*N&J3*, 182–84)

93.7–8 New York World and a Boston paper, (I think the Herald)] Clemens appended four clippings at the end of his typescript, which are included in the text; among them is the *World* article, which appeared on 9 March 1885 (see 95.24–96.27). No copy of the *Herald* has been found, but another article that Clemens appended, from the 9 March Springfield (Mass.) *Republican* (see 94.36–95.21), repeats the information reported by the New York correspondent of the *Herald*.

93.9–11 I had taken an unfair advantage . . . got the book away from them] Robert Underwood Johnson, an associate editor of the *Century Magazine,* wrote many years later that Paine's account of the Grant negotiations in *Mark Twain: A Biography* (*MTB,* 2:799–803)— which was based on this dictation—"leaves something to be desired. It places Mr. Roswell Smith in the attitude of treating the author in a somewhat niggardly manner, the fact being that the matter was wholly in the hands of General Grant, on whose terms it was to have been undertaken":

> As to the first offer of Mr. Clemens, the difference between it and ours was very slight, if any: in one case a larger royalty being computed on the net returns and in the other a smaller on the gross. Mr. Clemens made a later alternative offer of a considerable cash advance, a large percentage of the profits, and a guaranty of a certain sale. Had we known of this we should have been able to meet the situation. We were at the disadvantage that Mark Twain, who was a frequent visitor at the Sixty-sixth Street house, knew our terms and we did not know his.
>
> Nevertheless, with all respect to Roswell Smith's motives, which were above criticism, it remains that his failure to secure this work beyond peradventure within the five months from the time he was invited to Long Branch in September until the signing of the contract in February was, from a business point of view, a signal exception in the successful career of a publisher of imagination, boldness, and resourcefulness. His omission to clinch the matter did not reflect the alertness and enterprise of his associates, but he had the disadvantage of having as a rival a man of winning personality, shrewd business ability, and large horizon. The result cast a gloom over the younger members of the Century Co., who never ceased to think that in our hands this phenomenal book would have reached as phenomenal a sale as it did in Mr. Clemens's; for at that time the success of the War Series had put the Century Co. in close touch with the public in the matter of military history. We thought it hard that another should have "plowed with our heifer." (Johnson 1923, 218–19)

In late October 1884 Smith was still confident that Grant would place his book with the Century Company. In a letter of 9 September 1884 he wrote to Gilder that Grant was

> thoroughly intelligent in relation to the subscription book business, and very much disgusted with the way it is usually managed. He remarked that he did not propose to pay a scalawag canvasser $6 for selling a $12 book, not worth much more than half the money, as in some cases he quoted. His ideas agree with ours—to make a good book, manufacture

it handsomely, sell it at a reasonable price, and make it so commanding that we can secure competent agents at a fair commission. (Rosamond Gilder 1916, 123–24)

Johnson later learned from Fred Grant that "his father's decision had been influenced chiefly by the fact that Mr. Clemens had convinced him that . . . his own firm had been successful publishers of subscription books, while the Century Co. had done little in that line" (Johnson 1923, 218).

93.14–16   Boston paper's account . . . sister of Mr. Gilder] Jeannette L. Gilder (1849–1916) corresponded from New York for the Boston *Saturday Evening Gazette* (not the *Herald,* as Clemens suggests) under the pseudonym "Brunswick." Her letter to the *Gazette* is largely reprinted in the article from the Springfield (Mass.) *Republican* of 9 March 1885 that here follows Clemens's dictation (see 95.13–21). Although less well known than her brother Richard Watson Gilder, Jeannette Gilder pursued a successful literary career. In 1881 she cofounded a literary magazine, *The Critic,* with her other brother, Joseph B. Gilder, which they edited together until 1906. Her work appeared in a variety of newspapers and magazines, and she compiled several literary anthologies.

94.14–16   new electric light company of Boston . . . prosperous condition] In the spring of 1883, numerous articles in the Hartford *Courant* reported on the rapid growth of the American Electric and Illuminating Company of Boston, incorporated a year earlier. Its successful plan to establish subsidiary companies throughout New England was expected to pay shareholders "substantial dividends" (Hartford *Courant,* 20 Feb 1883, 3).

94.22   lied about his son] See the note at 95.3–4.

94.34–35   in the way of abuse] Clemens's dictation ends here. Redpath added two typed comments. The first, *"To be followed by Duncan's libel suit,"* referred to the lawsuit for libel that Charles C. Duncan—former captain of the *Quaker City* and organizer of the 1867 Holy Land excursion—brought against the New York *Times* in 1883. Duncan objected to an article published on 10 June which reported remarks of Clemens's condemning his misuse of public funds in his position as New York shipping commissioner. Clemens claimed that the *Times* reporter had misrepresented his comments. Duncan technically won his suit in March 1884, but was awarded only twelve cents in damages. No 1885 dictation about the lawsuit has been found (*N&J3,* 18 n. 34; "Mr. Mark Twain Excited," New York *Times,* 10 June 1883, 1; see also *N&J2,* 35 n. 26). Redpath's second note read: "See two pages of newspaper statements about Grant's book and the Century people and Mark Twain affixed." These "statements," which survive in four clippings preserved with the typescript, are transcribed at the end of Clemens's dictated text.

94.36–38   Gen Grant, Mark Twain and the Century . . . correspondent of the Boston Herald] The first part of this article (through "news is true," 95.10), from the Springfield (Mass.) *Republican* of 9 March 1885, reports information published in the Boston *Herald,* presumably on 7 or 8 March; no copy of the *Herald* has been located.

95.3–4   Webster & Co . . . his son Jesse] Jesse and Fred Grant were both interested in a partnership in Webster and Company, an arrangement that neither Clemens nor Webster favored. Clemens's first known mention of the idea was in a letter of 21 July 1885 to Edward H. House: "Neither of the General's sons is a partner. We all *talked* about that, but it was never seriously considered. Col. Fred talks about it yet—but if seriously it doesn't sound so" (ViU). On 20 December 1885 Clemens alluded to the scheme in a letter to Webster. At that time the partnership was "a consideration" in the firm's negotiations to secure the right to publish Grant's letters to his wife—a deal that was never concluded (NPV, in *MTBus,* 347). Although discussions of a Grant partnership continued into early spring 1886, neither of Grant's sons joined the business (8 Feb 1886 to Webster, NPV, in *MTBus,* 353–54; Webster to SLC, 10 Feb 1886 and 20 Mar 1886, CU-MARK; see *N&J3,* 218, 220, 222).

95.10–21 "Brunswick," . . . publish the book] Jeannette Gilder's column, "New York Gossip," which began with a long section on Grant's medical news, appeared in the *Saturday Evening Gazette* on 7 March 1885. The Springfield *Republican* accurately quoted her discussion of Grant's book, omitting only two brief passages about subscription books and the series of war articles in the *Century Magazine.*

96.28 N.Y. World] From the issue of 9 March 1885.

97.30 N.Y. Tribune] From the issue of 10 March 1885.

97.38 General's connection with Lincoln's assassination] Abraham Lincoln and his wife invited the Grants to accompany them to Ford's Theater on 14 April 1865, the night that John Wilkes Booth assassinated the president. The Grants did not attend because they were visiting their children at school in New Jersey. Booth's co-conspirators planned to assassinate two men who were not at the theater: Secretary of State William Seward (who was injured but survived) and Vice-President Andrew Johnson (who was not actually attacked). It is probable, but not certain, that Grant was another intended victim.

98.20–39 work of Gen. Adam Badeau . . . book which I did not write] Grant prepared most of the manuscript of his *Memoirs* himself, but occasionally dictated to his son Fred, or to a stenographer, Noble E. Dawson. Badeau provided editing services, for which he was to receive nothing if the book earned less than $20,000, $5,000 if it earned $20,000, and $5,000 more if it earned $30,000. The false accusation that Grant was not doing his own writing was based on information from "General George P. Ihrie, who had served with Grant in Mexico. Ihrie had inadvertently remarked to a Washington columnist that the General was no writer" (Goldhurst 1975, 118, 153, 193–94). Clemens was so outraged by the *World* article that he briefly considered initiating a lawsuit. He wrote to Fred Grant on 30 April 1885:

> The General's work this morning is rather damaging evidence against the World's intrepid lie. The libel suit ought to be instituted at once; damages placed at nothing less than $250,000 or $300,000; no apologies accepted from the World, & no compromise permitted for anything but a sum of money that will cripple—yes, *disable*—that paper financially. The suit ought to be brought in the General's name, & the expense of it paid out of the book's general expense account. (NPV, in *MTBus,* 319)

By 3 May he had reconsidered and wrote to Webster:

I have watched closely & have not seen a single reference to the World's lie in any newspaper. So it is possible that it fell dead & did no harm. I suppose Alexander & Green have decided that a libel suit against a paper which hasn't influence enough to get its lies copied, would be a waste of energy & money (as you give me no news of any kind about the matter.) If that is their verdict, & if the lie has *not* been copied around, it is no doubt the right & sensible verdict. I recognize the fact that for General Grant to sue the World would be an enormously valuable advertisement for that daily issue of unmedicated closet-paper. (NPV, in *MTBus,* 323)

Badeau responded to the *World* article by demanding a new financial arrangement with Grant: $1,000 a month until the book was done, and 10 percent of the profits. After a bitter exchange of letters, Badeau withdrew from the project. He and Grant never met again (Goldhurst 1975, 194–200, 251). After Grant's death, Badeau threatened Mrs. Grant with a lawsuit to claim what he was owed. The dispute was settled in 1888, when Badeau accepted $10,000 plus interest (as stipulated in the original contract), and agreed that the composition of the *Memoirs* "was entirely that of Gen. Grant, and to limit his claim to that of suggestion, revision, and verification" ("Gen. Badeau's Suit Ended," New York *Times,* 31 Oct 1888, 8).

98.44   N. Y. World] From the issue of 6 May 1885.

[The Rev. Dr. Newman]

99.2   *Extract from my note book*] This extract is a near verbatim rendering of Clemens's notebook entry (see *N&J3,* 117–18).

99.12   Rev. Dr. Newman] John Philip Newman (1826–99) was ordained as a minister in the Methodist Episcopal church in 1849. After serving as chaplain of the U.S. Senate from 1869 to 1874—during which time he became a confidant of Julia Grant's—he was appointed inspector of U.S. consuls in Asia by President Grant (Goldhurst 1975, 187–88).

99.14   ex-Governor Stanford] Leland Stanford (1824–93) was trained in the law. He went West in 1852 to join his brothers in various mercantile pursuits, and served as governor of California from 1861 to 1863. He became immensely wealthy from his partnership in the Central Pacific Railroad corporation, which completed the transcontinental railroad in 1869. His only son, Leland, Jr., died at age fifteen in March 1884 while visiting Italy. His body was brought home and held in a vault while his family built a mausoleum on their property in Palo Alto, said to be "as magnificent as an Oriental palace." At the memorial service held in Grace Church in San Francisco on 30 December, $20,000 was spent on floral decorations. Newman delivered a eulogy, the "most fulsome ever delivered in the Western Hemisphere," comparing "young Stanford to all the great of earth, and then, as if weary of the effort to find a fitting prototype for him among human beings, he boldly declared that the boy was some sort of a reproduction of Jesus Christ" ("California Astonished," Chicago *Tribune,* 2 Jan 1885, 3).

99.33–34   "Thrice have I been . . . come out again."] A similar version of Newman's remark was reported in the New York *Times* on 16 April 1885, and doubtless in other newspapers as well ("A Day of Hopefulness," 4).

The Machine Episode (*Source:* MS in CU-MARK, written in 1890 and 1893–94)

101.4–7   Ten or eleven years ago, Dwight Buell . . . was about finished] Dwight H. Buell
owned a shop on Main Street in Hartford, and was a director of the Farnham Type-Setter
Manufacturing Company. The machine he wanted Clemens to invest in was invented by James
W. Paige, who—in collaboration with the Farnham Company—was building a prototype in
a workshop at Samuel Colt's firearms factory in Hartford. Clemens first purchased stock in
the Farnham Company in the fall of 1881 (Geer 1882, 341, 455; 18 Oct 1881 and 25 Oct 1881
to Webster, NPV, in *MTBus,* 171–73).

101.21–22   rate of 3,000 ems an hour . . . four case-men's work] A compositor setting
material by hand pulled the metal types for characters and spaces one at a time from a case—a
wooden tray divided into compartments—and placed them, in reverse order, in a composing
stick. The full stick was then transferred to a galley tray, where the types were held in place to
allow a proof to be printed. The "dead matter"—types that had already been set and used for
printing—was then distributed by hand back into the case for reuse. An "em" was a measure
equal to the square of the height of one type, and therefore varied according to the size of the
font. The ems in one line were multiplied by the number of lines to determine the quantity of
typeset material (Pasko 1894, 145; Stewart 1912, 21, 61, 85). In September 1890, shortly before
writing the present account, Clemens claimed that an operator of the Paige compositor could
set 8,000 ems of type per hour, more than ten times what a hand typesetter could produce
(11 Sept 1890 and 27 Sept 1890 to Jones, CU-MARK; printed document enclosed with the
letter of 11 Sept, "Saving-Capacity of the Several Machines," annotated by Clemens, photocopy
in CU-MARK).

101.23   William Hamersley] Hamersley (1838–1920), an attorney, served from 1868 to
1888 as the state prosecutor for Hartford County. In 1886 he was elected to the lower house
of the Connecticut General Assembly, and in 1893–94 served as Superior Court Judge. As
president of the Farnham Company, he was one of the earliest investors in the typesetting
machine (Connecticut State Library 2006; *N&J3,* 141 n. 50).

102.1–2   I set down my name for an additional $3,000] In mid-1882 Clemens recorded
in his notebook that he owned two hundred shares in the Farnham Company, worth $5,000
(*N&J2,* 491).

102.9   Hamersley wrote Webster a letter which will be inserted later on] Clemens did not
insert a letter into this account, nor has any letter from Hamersley to Webster been found.

102.10   James W. Paige] In the early 1870s in Rochester, New York, Paige (1842–1917)
set about inventing a typesetting machine, which was granted a patent in 1874. This original
machine, however, lacked any mechanism for justifying or distributing type. Paige moved to
Hartford, and in 1877 joined with the Farnham Company, which was developing a distributor
for its own typesetter, a "gravity machine with converging channels" (Legros and Grant 1916,
378). Paige began to design a new machine that could both set and distribute type. By 1882,
when he produced a working model, the enterprise had cost nearly $90,000. The Farnham
Company withdrew its support, and Clemens agreed to find additional investors (Lee 1987;

"Private Circular to the Stockholders of the Farnham Type-Setter Manufacturing Company,"
26 Jan 1891, CU-MARK; *N&J3*, 36 n. 69).

102.34–35   wonderfully valuable application of electricity] Clemens may be referring to
another of Paige's inventions, a printing telegraph. Clemens tried to promote the project for
several months in 1885 (*N&J3*, 170, 181 n. 12).

102.38   splendid thing in electricity] In the summer of 1887, while perfecting a dynamo
for his typesetter, Paige had an idea for a revolutionary electromagnetic motor that might be
very lucrative. Although Clemens briefly supported his experiment, on 16 August he signed a
contract stipulating that Paige was to proceed at his own expense. Clemens received a one-half
share in the invention and agreed to reimburse Paige should it prove successful (*N&J3*, 338
n. 111; "1887. Agreement of J. W. Paige regarding Magnetic Electro Motor dated 16th August,"
CU-MARK).

103.7   he could apply the alternating test and come out triumphant] In a notebook entry
dated 1 November 1888 Clemens remarked on Nikola Tesla's recently patented alternating-
current motor:

> I have just seen the drawings and description of an electrical machine lately patented by
> a Mr. Tesla, & sold to the Westinghouse Company, which will revolutionize the whole
> electric business of the world. It is the most valuable patent since the telephone. The draw-
> ings & description show that this is the *very* machine, in every detail which Paige invented
> nearly 4 years ago.

Tesla "tried everything that we tried, as the drawings & descriptions prove; & he tried one
thing more—a thing which we had canvassed—the *alternating* current. *That* solved the difficulty & achieved success" (*N&J3*, 431).

103.20–21   *another piece of property* . . . assignment, Aug. 12, 1890] This contract stipulated that Paige would grant Clemens all "right, title and interest in his inventions . . . and in
the domestic and foreign patents obtained and that may be obtained therefor," in return for
one-quarter of the gross receipts from the eventual sales or rentals of the machine. For the
agreement to be valid, Clemens had to pay Paige $250,000 within six months. The property
that "already belonged" to Clemens was evidently the foreign royalties. He made the following
notebook entry in April 1893, when he met with Paige in Chicago:

> Paige . . . called again tonight. I asked him if his conscience troubled him any about
> the way he had treated me. He said he could almost forgive me for that word. He said
> it broke his heart when I left him and the machine to fight along the best way they could
> &c. &c. . . . When his European patent affairs are settled, he is going to put me in for a
> handsome royalty on every European machine. ~~This would be very generous except for
> the fact that his present contract with the Connecticut Co already does that for me.~~
> We parted immensely good friends. (Notebook 33, TS pp. 8–9, CU-MARK; *N&J3*,
> 576 n. 4; "Copy of Contract between S. L. Clemens & James W. Paige—Aug 12th 1890,"
> CU-MARK)

103.38–39   contracts will be found in the Appendix] No such appendix—presumably a collection of all the contracts with Paige—has been found.

104.6   Pratt & Whitney's] The Pratt and Whitney Company, a machine and tool manufacturer incorporated in Hartford in 1869, was engaged to produce the prototype (Geer 1882, 254, 459).

104.16–17   Jones . . . lose his interest in the thing] John P. Jones (1829–1912), a native of England, went to California at the start of the gold rush, settling in Nevada in 1867. He became superintendent and then part owner of the Crown Point mine in Gold Hill, which struck a rich vein of silver and made him wealthy: by 1874 his monthly income was reported to be half a million dollars (29 Mar and 4 Apr 1875 to Wright, *L6,* 439 n. 5). He represented Nevada as a U.S. senator from 1873 to 1903. Clemens's attempts to induce Jones to invest in the typesetter began in early 1887, and continued for several years. In July 1890 Jones inspected the machine during one of its operational intervals and made a token investment of $5,000. In early September Clemens had a contract drawn up whereby Jones agreed to "use his best endeavors" to raise $950,000 and "organize a corporation" which would purchase Clemens's interest and assume his obligation to pay Paige $250,000 by February 1891. Jones may never have signed this agreement; in any event, on 11 February he wrote that he had been unable to interest any investors. In fact, two of the men he had approached were "large stockholders in the 'Mergenthaler,'" the Paige machine's chief competitor (Jones to SLC, 11 Feb 1891, CU-MARK; see the note at 106.23–24). Clemens drafted a reply, which he apparently never sent: "For a whole year you have breathed the word of promise to my ear to break it to my hope at last. It is stupefying, it is unbelievable" (14–28 Feb 1891 to Jones, CU-MARK; *N&J3,* 278–79 n. 183, 565 n. 261, 572–73, 576–77 n. 6; 8 Sept 1890 [with enclosed contract] and 11 Sept 1890 to Jones, CU-MARK; 22 Feb 1891 to Goodman, NN-BGC).

104.27   End of 1885] These words mark the beginning of the second section of Clemens's account, written several years after the first part. It begins on a new sequence of pages, and was probably written in late 1893 or early 1894, when Clemens was in New York working with Henry Rogers to negotiate a new contract with Paige (see the note at 106.23–24).

105.1–6   The contract . . . $30,000 and 6 per cent interest] A contract of 6 February 1886 stipulated that Clemens would pay Paige's expenses up to $30,000, plus an annual salary of $7,000, and Hamersley would provide "professional services," while the machine was perfected. After a successful prototype was tested, Clemens and Hamersley were to raise the money to manufacture it. A corporation would then be formed, with Clemens receiving 9/20 of the stock. If they failed to obtain the "necessary capital" within three years, however, they were entitled to reimbursement of the money they had advanced, from any profit that "may at any time thereafter accrue." In the meantime, Paige retained "title of the property purchased with the money furnished . . . in pursuance of this agreement" ("Agreement," CU-MARK).

105.17   F. G. Whitmore] Franklin Gray Whitmore (1846–1926), owner of a real estate office and Clemens's Hartford business agent, supervised the building of the typesetter at the Pratt and Whitney works in 1886 (Burpee 1928, 3:952; *N&J3,* 189 n. 27).

105.27   royalty deed was made and signed] By the terms of a deed of 26 September 1889

Clemens paid Paige $100,000 (presumably with funds already advanced) in return for a royalty of $500 on every machine that would eventually be sold. Clemens then tried to sell his interest at a cost of $1,000 for each "five hundredth part of my interest in the royalty of five hundred dollars" ("Deed" in CU-MARK; *N&J3,* 518 n. 119).

105.33–38   contract No. 2 . . . contract No. 3 (the May contract?) . . . "June" contract] A contract drawn up in December 1889 ("No. 2"), which provided for the establishment of a corporation and gave Clemens 9/20 of the stock (an amount equal to his current interest in the typesetter), may never have been ratified. The "May" and "June" contracts have not been found (*N&J3,* 576 n. 5, 579 n. 23; contract of 14 Dec 1889 in CU-MARK).

106.11–13   I signed it . . . It had but six months to run] That is, the contract signed in August 1890 (see the note at 103.20–21).

106.20   Charley Davis, take a pen and write what I say] Charles E. Davis was the Pratt and Whitney engineer who supervised the manufacture of the typesetter. When Clemens visited Chicago in April 1893 to check on the progress of the machine, he received a visit from Davis, who mentioned that he "still holds the paper which Paige dictated to him one day to quiet me, in which he says that no matter what happened he and I would always share and share alike in the results of the machine" (Notebook 33, TS p. 9, CU-MARK; *N&J3,* 246 n. 71).

106.23–24   I went on footing the bills . . . instead of the original $30,000] Clemens's total investment, which he elsewhere estimated to be as much as $170,000, was equivalent to over $3 million in today's dollars (SLC 1899a; AD, 28 Mar 1906). He finally stopped financing the machine in late February 1891, having failed to raise the necessary $250,000 to buy out Paige. Clemens traded his stock for royalties on future sales, hoping to eventually recover much of his loss. The following year, Paige contracted with the Webster Manufacturing Company in Chicago (Towner K. Webster, principal) to build a new machine, and the Pratt and Whitney prototype was dismantled and moved to that city. The invention continued to attract backers, among them a group of New York brokers who formed the Connecticut Company in 1892 and bought an interest in the Webster Manufacturing Company. In 1893 Henry Huttleston Rogers (the Standard Oil executive who took charge of Clemens's financial affairs) organized the Paige Compositor Manufacturing Company—later superseded by the Regius Manufacturing Company—which negotiated with Paige, seeking to resolve the claims of the numerous investors and secure Clemens's interest. The rebuilt machine continued to show promise, and in the fall of 1894 was tested by the Chicago *Herald.* According to one account, the machine performed well despite delays for repairs, and "delivered more corrected live matter" of the highest "artistic merit" than "any one of the thirty-two Linotype machines which were in operation in the same composing department" (Legros and Grant 1916, 381). But by then the 1890 model of the Linotype machine, invented by Ottmar Mergenthaler and based on a simpler and more practical concept, had captured the market. Clemens's hopes were finally shattered. One of Paige's patent attorneys later called the machine an "intellectual miracle," the "greatest thing of the kind that has been accomplished in all of the ages"—but it was too impractical to be a commercial success: with eighteen thousand parts, it was impossible to manufacture in quantity, and too complicated to run long without repairs (Legros and Grant 1916, 381, 391).

Rogers persuaded the Linotype Company to buy Paige's patents, in order to eliminate any possible competition. Paige himself died in poverty in 1917 (25 Feb 1891 to OC, CU-MARK; *HHR,* 12–20, 25–26, 148 n. 2; Lee 1987, 59–60; *N&J3,* 546 n. 190; 11 Nov 1894 and 28 Nov 1894 to Rogers, Salm, and 2 Jan 1895 to Rogers, CU-MARK, in *HHR,* 94–95, 98–100, 115; *Scientific American* 1901).

106.25–29 Ward tells me . . . Mr. North . . . is to get a royalty until the aggregate is $2,000,000] Henry S. Ward was a New York broker who owned an interest in the typesetter through the Connecticut Company. Charles R. North was a Pratt and Whitney machinist; Paige agreed to pay him "$200 a month out of his salary & $400 to $500 per machine until he shall have received $2,000,000" (*HHR,* 12, 31–34; Notebook 33, TS p. 8, CU-MARK).

106.31 had his nuts in a steel-trap] This remark alludes to an incident that Clemens actually witnessed, in which an acquaintance "got his Nüsse caught in the steel trap" of a sitz-bath (Fischer 1983, 47–48 n. 85; *N&J3,* 132, 135–36, 234, 356).

Travel-Scraps I (*Source:* MS in CU-MARK, written in 1897)

108.26 trunnions] Clemens evidently uses "trunnions" to mean trulls, trollops. A trunnion is a pin or pivot.

110 DIAGRAM OF LONDON] The diagram illustrates Clemens's remark that London "is fifty villages massed solidly together" (108.40–41). It is reproduced from a London newspaper article that Clemens clipped out and altered in his own hand. For some unexplained reason, he relocated Bow, in East London, to the West End, placing it (absurdly) in the region of Hanover Square.

112.19 Liverpool] No period of time during which Clemens and Osgood (see the note at 112.20) were both in Liverpool has been identified. Possibly Clemens was thinking of 10 September 1872, which they spent "driving about Warwickshire in an open barouche," but the reference to the Kinsmen club suggests a later date (11 Sept 1872 to OLC, *L5,* 155; see the note at 113.10).

112.20 James R. Osgood] Clemens's sometime publisher James Ripley Osgood (1836–92) started out as a clerk with Boston publishers Ticknor and Fields in 1855, later becoming a partner. After Fields retired in 1870, the firm was reorganized as James R. Osgood and Company. Setbacks and mismanagement drove Osgood and Company out of business, but it was reorganized under the same name in 1880, publishing works by William Dean Howells, George Washington Cable, and Walt Whitman, among others. Osgood published three of Clemens's books: *The Prince and the Pauper* (1881), *The Stolen White Elephant, Etc.* (1882), and *Life on the Mississippi* (1883). The sales of these books disappointed Clemens, but his affection for the man himself was undiminished. Osgood spent his last years in London (Edgar 1986, 341–47; for details of Osgood's role as Clemens's publisher, see AD, 21 Feb 1906, note at 372.25–27).

113.10 Kinsmen Club together in London] The Kinsmen, a private social club for artists and performers, was founded in New York in April 1882. It was an informal society; a founding member, drama critic Laurence Hutton, wrote that "there were to be no dues, no fees, no club-house, no constitution, no by-laws, no officers, 'no nothing' but good fellowship and good times." At the second meeting, in March 1883, Hutton invited Clemens to join, while Osgood, though he was a businessman and no artist, ebulliently forced his way into membership. A London "chapter" was established in 1883. On both shores the Kinsmen included many of Clemens's other friends and associates, among them Howells, Warner, Twichell, Thomas Bailey Aldrich, Francis D. Millet, Brander Matthews, and Richard Watson Gilder (Hutton 1909, 325–29; Matthews 1917, 232–33).

115.29   the Queen's approaching Jubilee] On 23 September 1896 Queen Victoria noted in her journal: "To-day is the day on which I have reigned longer, by a day, than any English sovereign." She requested that celebrations be postponed until her "Diamond Jubilee," or sixtieth year on the throne, which was celebrated across the British Empire in 1897 (Harlow and Carter 1999, 392; see "A Viennese Procession," note at 126.9 [2nd of 2]).

116.15   Prince of Wales's powerful name] Albert Edward, who became King Edward VII in 1901.

116.36   George Müller and his orphanages] George Friedrich Müller (1805–98), a Prussian-born evangelical preacher, settled in Bristol in 1832 and founded the Ashley Down Orphanage. It was remarkable both for the sheer number of orphans housed and educated, and for Müller's literal interpretation of "the Lord will provide"—the orphanage never solicited donations.

FOUR SKETCHES ABOUT VIENNA (*Source:* MS in CU-MARK, written in 1898)

[Beauties of the German Language]

118.1   *February 3, Vienna.* Lectured . . . last night] Clemens lectured in Vienna on 1 February, as he recorded in his notebook: "*Tuesday, Feb. 1, '98.* Lectured in Vienna for a public charity. Several rows of seats were $4 apiece. Still, there was far from room enough in the hall for all that applied for tickets" (Notebook 40, TS p. 8, CU-MARK). The lecture was favorably reviewed the following day in the Vienna *Neue Freie Presse* ("Mark Twain als Erzähler," 2 Feb 1898, 7).

[Comment on Tautology and Grammar]

119.22   *May 6.* * * *] A series of asterisks was Clemens's typical signal that he had omitted some portion of text (see "Special Sorts" in the "Guide to Editorial Practice," *L6,* 703–4).

119.29–30   Mr. Gladstone] The English statesman William Ewart Gladstone (1809–98) served four times as prime minister of the United Kingdom.

120.29–30   no death before the case of Cornelius Lean . . . special rules] Cornelius Lean, an employee of the London firm of Bryant and May, manufacturers of matches, died in late April 1898 of necrosis of the jaw, the result of exposure to white phosphorus. As a result of investigations into the deaths of Lean and others, the firm was found to be in violation of special rules passed between 1891 and 1895 requiring that all cases of the disease be reported (Satre 1982, 8–9, 19–24).

[A Group of Servants]

120.33   *June 4, Kaltenleutgeben*] The Clemens family spent the summer of 1898, from late May to mid-October, in Kaltenleutgeben, staying in "a furnished villa at the end of a water-cure village, & Mrs. Clemens & Jean will try the treatment. It is ½ to ¾ of an hour from Vienna by train. The villa is most pleasantly situated, with a dense pine wood bordering immediately on its back-garden, & with wooded hills all about" (13 May 1898 to Rogers, Salm, in *HHR*, 345–46; Notebook 40, TS p. 48, CU-MARK).

121.21   Wuthering Heights] It is not clear why Clemens appropriated the name of Emily Brontë's classic novel (1847) for the garrulous older maid; he may have had in mind the narrator of the story, Ellen (Nelly) Dean, a household servant. According to one scholar, the maid's "actual name sounded something like" the sobriquet (Dolmetsch 1992, 220; Dolmetsch provides no evidence to support his assertion).

122.10   gnädige Frau] "Madam."

122.29   Heilige Mutter Gottes!] "Holy mother of God!"

122.31   Zu befehl] "At your command"—that is, an emphatic assent.

123.36   *Ruhig!*] "Silence!"

123.40   dienstman] Anglicized form of *dienstmann:* a man who performs miscellaneous tasks for a small fee (Hawthorne 1876, 290–93).

[A Viennese Procession]

124.17   Minister] Charlemagne Tower (1848–1923), the U.S. minister at Vienna from 1897–99, was an acquaintance of Clemens's (see AD, 22 Aug 1907).

125.27   Kaiser Rudolph] Either Rudolf I (1218–91), founder of the house of Hapsburg, who brought Austria under his rule as king of Germany; or Rudolf II of Austria (1552–1612), an educated and intelligent ruler who suffered from mental illness.

126.9   Andreas Hofer's] Hofer (1767–1810), a Tyrolean innkeeper, led a rebellion against Napoleon in 1809. Ultimately captured and executed, he was considered an Austrian martyr.

126.11   Directory] The Executive Directory, a body of five men, held power in France from 1795 to 1799. During this regime, the next-to-last period of the French Revolution, Napoleon defeated the Austrians and their allies.

126.19   India in '96] Clemens saw a religious procession in Jaipur in March 1896 and described it in chapter 60 of *Following the Equator* (1897): "For color, and picturesqueness, and novelty, and outlandishness, and sustained interest and fascination, it was the most satisfying show I had ever seen."

126.19 Queen's Record procession] Queen Victoria's Record Reign and Diamond Jubilee were celebrated in 1897 by numerous events, including a procession to St. Paul's Cathedral on 22 June. A short service of thanksgiving was held there before the queen returned to Buckingham Palace. She later noted in her journal, "No one ever, I believe, has met with such an ovation as was given me, passing through those six miles of streets." Clemens cabled three reports of the occasion to the Hearst newspapers (Hibbert 2001, 457–59; SLC 1897d, 1897e, 1897f).

My Debut as a Literary Person (*Sources:* MS in CtY-BR, written in 1898; *Century Magazine,* November 1899 [SLC 1899d])

127.2–3 I had already published one little thing ("The Jumping Frog,") in an eastern paper] "Jim Smiley and His Jumping Frog" appeared in the New York *Saturday Press* of 18 November 1865. Clemens, who was living in San Francisco at that time, soon learned that his story was being praised and widely reprinted in the eastern press. In early 1867 he included it in his first book, *The Celebrated Jumping Frog of Calaveras County, and Other Sketches,* published in May (*ET&S2,* 262–72; 20 Jan 1866 to JLC and PAM, *L1,* 327–28, 330 n. 3).

128.5 I selected Harper's Monthly] Founded in 1850, *Harper's New Monthly Magazine* had built its reputation by serializing the novels of famous British writers such as Dickens and Thackeray, later adding American contributions in fiction, travel, current events, and poetry. By 1866 it was "so very successful that we may well consider it an index to the literary culture and general character of the nation" (Mott 1938, 383–405).

128.5–12 I signed it "MARK TWAIN," . . . they put it *Mike Swain* or *MacSwain*] In Nevada Territory Clemens began signing his work "Mark Twain" in early February 1863, and his pseudonym gained wider recognition with the publication and frequent reprinting of the "Jumping Frog" tale (16 Feb 1863 to JLC and PAM, *L1,* 245–46 n. 1). "Forty-three Days in an Open Boat" appeared unsigned, however, in the December 1866 issue of *Harper's New Monthly Magazine* (SLC 1866c), as did most of the articles by other contributors. The table of contents for volume 34 (which the December issue was part of) did not appear until May 1867; it attributed Clemens's article to *"Mark Swain."*

128.15 burning of the clipper ship *Hornet* on the line, May 3d, 1866] The *Hornet* left New York, bound for San Francisco, on 15 January 1866. It burned and sank in the Pacific Ocean near the equator, about fifteen hundred miles off the coast of South America (*MTH,* 102).

128.20–21 New Englander of the best sea-going stock . . . Captain Josiah Mitchell] Josiah Angier Mitchell (1812?–76) of Freeport, Maine, was the first in his family to "make the sea his profession—as the result of a pleasant trip to Havana for his health when a boy" (*MTH,* 107–8 n. 5).

128.22–24 was in the Islands to write letters for the "weekly edition" . . . well-beloved men] The owners of the Sacramento *Union*—James Anthony, Paul Morrill, and Henry W. Larkin—engaged Clemens to write a series of letters from the Sandwich Islands. He left San Francisco on 7 March 1866 in the steamer *Ajax,* arriving in Honolulu eleven days later. Some details of Clemens's arrangement with the *Union* are unclear. He told his mother and sister he would remain in the islands "a month" and write "twenty or thirty letters" for the paper; in the event he remained four months and wrote twenty-five letters, which appeared in both the daily and weekly editions (*RI 1993,* 706–7; 5 Mar 1866 to JLC and PAM, *L1,* 333–34; *MTH,* 93, 256).

128.28–29   I was laid up in my room] Clemens was suffering from saddle boils (mentioned in "Notes on 'Innocents Abroad'").

128.30–32   his Excellency Anson Burlingame . . . good work for the United States] Anson Burlingame (1820–70) was a founder of the Republican Party and a Republican congressman from Massachusetts (1855–61). In 1861 he was appointed U.S. minister resident to China, and until the end of his term in 1867 he promoted diplomacy between China and the Western powers. In June 1866 he was en route to China after a leave of absence in the United States. When he died in 1870, Clemens praised him as a man who acted "in the broad interest of the world, instead of selfishly seeking to acquire advantages for his own country alone" (SLC 1870a; 21 June 1866 to JLC and PAM, *L1,* 345–46 n. 5; see also AD, 20 Feb 1906).

129.3–4   my complete report . . . telegraphed to the New York papers. By Mr. Cash] Clemens mentioned the *Hornet* survivors briefly in a letter to the Sacramento *Union* dated 22 June, before they had traveled to Honolulu from their landing site on the island of Hawaii. His full report, datelined 25 June, was written after he had interviewed the survivors—primarily the third mate, John S. Thomas. It was carried to San Francisco on the schooner *Milton Badger* and appeared on the front page of the Sacramento *Daily Union* on 19 July 1866, under the headline "Burning of the Clipper Ship Hornet at Sea." No information has been found about republication of the article in New York newspapers, or about "Mr. Cash" (SLC 1866b; SLC 1866c; *MTH,* 109–10; 27 June 1866 to JLC and PAM, *L1,* 348 n. 1).

129.17–18   Within a fortnight the most of them took ship . . . I went in the same ship] The *Hornet*'s longboat landed on 15 June 1866; Clemens and the survivors departed Honolulu on the clipper *Smyrniote* on 19 July, more than a month later (*MTH,* 107 n. 5; 19 July 1866 to Damon, *L1,* 349 n. 2).

129.20–22   Samuel Ferguson . . . Henry Ferguson . . . a professor there] Samuel Ferguson (1837–66) and Henry Ferguson (1848–1917) were the sons of a New York businessman and grew up in Stamford, Connecticut. Henry resumed his studies at Trinity College, Hartford, graduated in 1868, and was ordained an Episcopal priest. From 1883 to 1906 he held a professorship in history and political science at the college. Although Clemens and Henry Ferguson both lived in Hartford in the 1880s they seem not to have been in contact until Clemens published "My Debut as a Literary Person" in 1899 (Hartford *Courant:* "Death of a Trinity College Graduate," 4 Oct 1866, 8; "Prof. Ferguson Dies at His Home," 31 Mar 1917, 9). Clemens's use of the Fergusons' diaries proved somewhat troublesome. In early October 1899, shortly before the article appeared, Clemens wrote to Gilder, "Can't you send to Professor Henry Ferguson, Trinity College, Hartford, & get him to photograph a page or two of Samuel Ferguson's Diary for reproduction?" (Oct 1899 to Gilder, TxU-Hu). Ferguson declined. When the article was published Ferguson wrote to Clemens, objecting to the use of the diaries, and

Clemens offered to withdraw the piece from his forthcoming collection, *The Man That Corrupted Hadleyburg* (SLC 1900b). Ferguson, somewhat mollified, asked that future reprintings disguise the real names of the crewmen, that he himself be less "distinctly identified," and that his brother Samuel's ailment be called "lung fever" (pneumonia) instead of "consumption" (tuberculosis) (Ferguson to SLC, 10 Nov 1899, CtY-BR, and 8 Dec 1899, CU-MARK; 20 Nov 1899 to Ferguson and 21 Dec 1899 to Ferguson, CtY-BR). Clemens honored these requests; he also softened the language about mutiny, insanity, and cannibalism. His revisions were reflected in the texts published in *The Man That Corrupted Hadleyburg* and in a later reprinting, *My Début as a Literary Person with Other Essays and Stories* (SLC 1903a).

129.39   There was a cry of fire . . . the vessel's hours were numbered] The *Hornet*'s cargo was highly inflammable: it included 2,400 cases of kerosene and 6,200 boxes of candles ("Burning of the Ship Hornet," New York *Times,* 22 Aug 1866, 2).

130.5   Portyghee] "Antonio Possene" (the name recorded by Captain Mitchell) was apparently from the Cape Verde Islands, a Portuguese colony since the fifteenth century (Mitchell 1866; "Burning of the Ship Hornet," New York *Times,* 22 Aug 1866, 2).

130.16   soldiering] Malingering or shirking, more usually spelled as pronounced— "sogering" or "sodgering."

130.21–22   Bowditch's Navigator . . . Nautical Almanac] The *New American Practical Navigator,* a manual of navigation, was first published by Nathaniel Bowditch in 1802. *The American Ephemeris and Nautical Almanac* has been published by the U.S. Naval Observatory since 1852.

130.26   forty-gallon "scuttle-butt,"] Potable water on a ship was stored in a scuttled butt—that is, a cask with a hole in it. "Scuttlebutt" came to mean "gossip" because of the drinkers' conversations.

130.29–31   The captain and the two passengers kept diaries . . . chance to copy the diaries] The journals of all three men are extant, but the copies that Clemens made on board the *Smyrniote* do not survive (Mitchell 1866, Henry Ferguson 1866, Samuel Ferguson 1866). Although the diary quotations included in the 1866 *Harper's* article (which he left virtually unaltered for the 1898 piece) were nearly all rephrased, abridged, or expanded, he did not invent any fictional embellishments.

131.26   Revillagigedo islands] An uninhabited archipelago roughly three hundred miles south-southwest of the tip of Baja California.

132.6–7   cobbling] Choppy.

132.14   Clipperton Rock] Clipperton Rock surmounts a coral atoll roughly seven hundred miles southwest of Acapulco.

132.25–26   the sun gives him a warning: "looking with both eyes, the horizon crossed thus X."] Samuel Ferguson's more explicit diary entry clarifies this remark: "Sun very hot indeed and gave me a warning to keep out of it in a very peculiar doubling of the sight with both eyes while with either one it seemed right. With both eyes the horizon crossed thus X" (Samuel Ferguson 1866, entry for 9 May).

132.42–133.1   The captain spoke pretty sharply . . . remark in my old note-book] In his manuscript, Clemens began to quote the captain's speech, and then canceled it: "You ought to be ashamed of yourselves that you have no proper thankfulness for the infinite mercies of God in these disciplinary days of sanctified peril." This remark is not found in Clemens's extant notebooks, but at least one notebook from this period is unrecovered.

133.2   third mate, in the hospital at Honolulu] The third mate—Clemens's chief informant—was John S. Thomas, whom Clemens characterized in his Sacramento *Union* report as "a very intelligent and a very cool and self-possessed young man" who "kept a very accurate log of his remarkable voyage in his head" (*N&J1*, 100–102; SLC 1866c).

133.11–12   The chief mate was an excellent officer . . . fine all-around man] The chief mate—Samuel F. Hardy of Chatham, Massachusetts—was responsible for starting the *Hornet* fire. Nevertheless, Clemens praised him generously throughout this account (SLC 1866c; "Burning of the Ship Hornet," New York *Times,* 22 Aug 1866, 2; Mitchell 1866).

136.10–11   it brought Cox . . . if it hadn't, the diarist would never have seen the land again] See the note at 140.4–5.

137.22   I wrote an article . . . urging temporary abstention from food] "Starvation" diets or, more usually, *near*-starvation diets were a feature of the nineteenth-century medical landscape. Since the 1880s Clemens had confidently recommended fasting as a cure for "any ordinary ailment." The article he refers to here, "At the Appetite-Cure," was published in the *Cosmopolitan* for August 1898 (SLC 1898b, 433; Ober 2003, 207–10).

138.4   *a banished duke*—Danish] Clemens derived this information from Samuel Ferguson's diary, which he quoted in his 1866 *Harper's* article: "We have here a man who might have been a Duke had not political troubles banished him from Denmark" (SLC 1866d, 109). There was but one Dane in the longboat; he recorded his name at the end of Samuel's diary as "Carl Henrich Kaatmann, geboren Augustenborg" (Samuel Ferguson 1866, entry for 30 Dec). The claim of the Prince of Augustenborg to the Danish dukedoms of Schleswig and Holstein sparked a European conflict that was widely reported in the 1860s ("What the European War Is About," *Circular* 3 [11 June 1866]: 102).

138.38–139.2   The isles we are steering for are put down in Bowditch . . . *sailed straight over them*] Although Bowditch's *Navigator* locates a "Cluster of Islands" at 16–17° N, 133–136° W, they do not exist. The *Hornet* survivors gave up their search for them on 7 June, when they were slightly west of those coordinates (Bowditch 1854, 375).

139.5   ten rations of water apiece] Captain Mitchell's entry for 2 June actually reads "10 raisins apiece"; Clemens evidently misread it as "rations" and added "of water" to supply some kind of sense (Mitchell 1866).

140.4–5   Cox's return . . . the two young passengers would have been slain] The mention of James Cox is rendered somewhat cryptic by the omission of certain details. Here we are told that Cox's return saved the captain and the passengers, but also that the crewmen resolved that they "would not kill" (140.26). Clemens's 1866 *Harper's* article asserts that the men *were* in fact prepared to kill, and that only Cox's warning, and his vigilance, prevented them. Some of the sailors planned

> to watch until such time as the Captain might become worn out and fall asleep, and then kill him and the passengers. They were afraid of Ferguson's pistol and the Captain's hatchet, and laid many a plan for getting hold of these weapons. They told Cox . . . they would kill him if he exposed them. He refused to join the conspiracy, and they said he should die; and so, after that, day after day and night after night, he did not go to sleep, but kept watch upon them in fear for his life. The Captain and passengers remained under arms, and watched also, but talked pleasantly, and gave no sign that they knew what was in the men's minds. (SLC 1866d, 113)

Seaman Frederick Clough ("Fred," 140.9)—implicated here in the "ugly talk" of mutiny and cannibalism—recalled these events rather differently in an article published in 1900: "We had almost reached the last chance then, and by this I mean the casting of lots for the sacrifice of one of us, so that the others might live to tell the story. To this agreement of a gamble for life or death all of us consented without the least hesitation" (Irvine 1900, 575). Captain Mitchell, for his part, noted laconically on 5 June: "A conspiracy formed to Murder me" (Mitchell 1866). According to a note made by Clemens while copying the diaries, "Capt. knew for days this murderous discontent was brewing by the distraught air of some of the men & the guilty look of others—& he staid on guard—slept no more—kept his hatchet hid & close at hand" (*N&J1*, 173).

140.27–28   'From plague, pestilence, and famine, from battle and murder—and from sudden death: Good Lord deliver us!'] Henry quotes the Litany from the Book of Common Prayer.

141.17   soup-and-bouillé] Clemens explained this term in his original dispatch to the Sacramento *Union:*

> That last expression of the third mate's occurred frequently during his narrative, and bothered me so painfully with its mysterious incomprehensibility, that at length I begged him to explain to me what this dark and dreadful "soup-and-bully" might be. With the Consul's assistance he finally made me understand the French dish known as "soup bouil-lon" is put up in cans like preserved meats, and the American sailor is under the impression that its name is a sort of general title which describes any . . . edible whatever which is hermetically sealed in a tin vessel, and with that high contempt for trifling conventionali-ties which distinguishes his class, he has seen fit to modify the pronunciation into "soup-and-bully." (SLC 1866c)

144.8–10   rooster . . . effort to do his duty once more, and died in the act] This account is at variance with Clemens's 1866 report to the Sacramento *Union,* in which he wrote that the rooster "was transferred to the chief mate's boat and sailed away on the eighteenth day"; his fate was therefore unknown. Frederick Clough, who was in the longboat, recalled that when the rooster "sang for the last time and died, he was cast into the sea" (SLC 1866c; Irvine 1900, 576).

144.19   If I remember rightly, Samuel Ferguson died soon after we reached San Francisco] Samuel died in San Francisco on 1 October 1866 ("Death of a Trinity College Graduate," Hartford *Courant,* 4 Oct 1866, 8).

Horace Greeley (*Source:* MS in CU-MARK, written in 1898–99)

145.1   Mr. Greeley] Horace Greeley (1811–72) grew up in New Hampshire and Vermont. He left school at fourteen to help his father with farming and odd jobs, and at age fifteen was apprenticed to a printer. Over the succeeding years he developed his skills as a journalist, writing for numerous New York newspapers and journals. In 1841 he founded the New York *Tribune* and remained its editor until his death. Through his newspaper, which gained enormous national influence, he attacked slavery and poverty and championed the rights of African Americans, women, and the working class. He made a brief bid to enter politics, but suffered a crushing defeat by Grant in the presidential election of 1872 and died shortly thereafter.

Lecture-Times (*Source:* MS in CU-MARK, written in 1898–99)

146.1–5   I remember Petroleum Vesuvius Nasby (Locke) very well . . . a most admirable hammering every week] David Ross Locke (1833–88) left school at an early age and was apprenticed to a printer, after which he worked on a succession of newspapers. At the outbreak of the Civil War he was the owner and editor of the Bucyrus (Ohio) *Journal.* It was not until a year later that he published his first satirical piece as Petroleum V. Nasby, an ignorant, bigoted, and boorish character who promoted liberal causes by seeming to oppose them. The popularity of the Nasby letters brought Locke to the attention of the proprietor of the Toledo *Blade,* who hired him as editor in 1865. Locke later became a part owner, and the Nasby letters, which he continued to write until shortly before his death, were an important feature of the weekly edition (*L3:* 20 and 21 Jan 1869 to OLL, 56 n. 1; 10 Mar 1869 to OLL and Langdon, 160 n. 5; Austin 1965, 11–12; Marchman 1957).

146.5–7   his letters were copied everywhere . . . copperheads] According to an obituary of Locke:

> These political satires sprang at once into tremendous popularity. They were copied into newspapers everywhere, quoted in speeches, read around camp-fires of Union armies and exercised enormous influence in molding public opinion North in favor of vigorous prosecution of the war. Secretary Boutwell declared in a speech at Cooper Union, New York, at the close of the war that the success of the Union army was due to three causes— the army, the navy, and the Nasby letters. . . . These letters were a source of the greatest delight to President Lincoln, who always kept them in his table drawer for perusal at odd times. ("Death of D. R. Locke," Washington *Post,* 16 Feb 1888, 4)

George S. Boutwell (1818–1905) was secretary of the treasury, 1869–73.

146.9–12   Governor of the State was a wiser man than were the political masters of Körner and Petöfi . . . he was an army—with artillery!] Locke himself almost certainly told Clemens this anecdote, which is also reported in an obituary, and there is no reason to doubt its substance. Nasby did, however, receive a commission as a second lieutenant in the Ohio Volunteer Infantry, signed on 5 November 1861 by Governor William Dennison, which required him to recruit a company of thirty men within fifteen days. The 16 November issue of the Bucyrus *Journal* contained Locke's "valedictory," and announced that he was "recruiting a company." Ultimately Locke paid a substitute to fight in his place (Marchman 1957; John M. Harrison 1969, 64–66; "Death of D. R. Locke," Washington *Post,* 16 Feb 1888, 4). Theodor Körner (1791–1813) and Sándor Petöfi (1823–49) were nationalist poets killed in battle: Körner died fighting for Prussia in the Napoleonic wars, and Petöfi died in the unsuccessful Hungarian revolt against the Austrians.

146.14–15 I saw him first . . . three or four years after the war] Clemens heard Locke lecture in Hartford on 9 March 1869 (10 Mar 1869 to OLL and Langdon, *L3,* 158, 159–60 n. 1).

147.20–21 with the slave-power and its Northern apologists for target] For his "Cussed be Canaan" lecture Locke posed as Nasby (without the peculiar dialect he employed in print), making it clear that Nasby's views were not his own. His argument—couched in satire—was that African Americans should be granted full equality, both economically and politically (John M. Harrison 1969, 192–96). In a letter to the San Francisco *Alta California* Clemens described the lecture as "a very unvarnished narrative of the negro's career, from the flood to the present day":

> For instance, the interpolating of the word white in State Constitutions existing under a great general Constitution which declares all men to be equal, is neatly touched by a recommendation that the Scriptures be so altered, at the same time, as to make them pleasantly conform to men's notions—thus: "Suffer little white children to come unto me, and forbid them not!" (SLC 1869b)

147.39–41 I began as a lecturer in 1866 . . . added the eastern circuit to my route] Clemens delivered his first lecture, on the Sandwich Islands, in San Francisco on 2 October 1866. For his account of that experience, and the tour that followed, see "Notes on 'Innocents Abroad.'" In March and April 1867 he lectured on the same topic in St. Louis and other towns on the Mississippi, and then three times in New York and Brooklyn in May. In January 1868 he gave "The Frozen Truth" in Washington, D.C., a new lecture about his *Quaker City* voyage, before returning to the West (for the last time), where he delivered it in San Francisco on 14 and 15 April. He then performed it in several of the California and Nevada towns that he had visited on his 1866 tour, lecturing for the last time in San Francisco on 2 July. During the 1868–69 season Clemens toured from 17 November until 20 March, delivering "The American Vandal Abroad" (also about the *Quaker City* trip) throughout the Midwest and East (*L1:* link note following 25 Aug 1866 to Bowen, 361–62; 29 Oct 1866 to Howland, 362 n. 1; 2 Nov 1866 to JLC and family, 366–67 nn. 3, 4; *L2:* 19 Mar 1867 to Webb, 19 n. 2; link note following 1 May 1867 to Harte, 40–44; 8 Jan 1868 to JLC and PAM, 147 n. 7; 2–14 Apr 1868 to Fairbanks, 208; 14 Apr 1868 to Williams, 209–10 n. 2; 1 and 5 May 1868 to Fairbanks, 213 n. 4; 5 July 1868 to Bliss, 233 n. 1; *L3:* enclosure with 12 Jan 1869 to Fairbanks, 453–57; "Lecture Schedule, 1868–1870," 481–83).

148.8   Redpath's bureau] In the Autobiographical Dictation of 11 October 1906, Clemens describes James Redpath (1833–91) as a man of "honesty, sincerity, kindliness, and pluck." An abolitionist, author, journalist, and social reformer, Redpath founded the Boston Lyceum Bureau (later called the Redpath Lyceum Bureau) in 1868, in partnership with George L. Fall. This business, one of the first of its kind, managed the tours of popular lecturers, readers, and musicians, arranging bookings and negotiating fees with local committees in cities both large and small. Lecturers paid their own traveling expenses, in addition to a 10 percent commission. (See "Ralph Keeler," the next sketch, for more about the Redpath Bureau.) Redpath arranged Clemens's 1869–70 tour, with the lecture "Our Fellow Savages of the Sandwich Islands," and his 1871–72 tour, with "Roughing It" (after "Reminiscences of Some un-Commonplace Characters I Have Chanced to Meet" and "Artemus Ward, Humorist" were tried and discarded). Clemens did not tour during the 1870–71 season (Eubank 1969, 91–115, 119–20; *L3:* 20 Apr 1869 to Redpath, 199 n. 1; 10 May 1869 to Redpath, 214–16, 217–18 n. 8; 30, 31 Oct and 1 Nov 1869 to OLL, 383–84 n. 9; "Lecture Schedule, 1868–1870," 483–86; *L4:* 24 Oct 1871 to Redpath, 478; 8 Dec 1871 to Redpath and Fall, 511; "Lecture Schedule, 1871–1872," 557–63).

148.15–16   De Cordova—humorist] Raphael J. De Cordova (1822–1901) was a merchant until 1857, when an economic panic forced him to turn to writing and lecturing. He served on the staff of the New York *Evening Express* for a time, and contributed to the New York *Times,* but became best known as a humorous writer and lecturer. During the 1871–72 season he offered eight humorous talks through the Redpath Bureau, and he continued to appear on the platform until at least 1878 ("Death List of a Day," New York *Times,* 5 Apr 1901, 9; *Annual Cyclopaedia 1901,* 419; *Lyceum* 1871, 17–18).

148.21   We took front seats in one of the great galleries—Nasby, Billings and I] Josh Billings (Henry Wheeler Shaw, 1818–85) was well known for the homespun philosophy he expressed in his humorous essays and sketches. *Josh Billings' Farmer's Allminax,* his third book and the first of a series of ten comic annuals, was published in October 1869 and sold over ninety thousand copies in three months. Clemens, Billings, and Nasby were photographed together in the second week of November of that year, when all three were in Boston on tour. On 27 October Billings delivered his popular lecture "Milk and Natral Histry" at Boston's Music Hall, where Nasby appeared on 9 November, and Clemens himself the following night. De Cordova gave four readings at Tremont Temple (not Music Hall) in mid-November; the three men probably heard him on 8 or 12 November ("Lecture Course," Boston *Post,* 6 Nov 1869, 3; *L3:* 9 Nov 1869 to PAM, 386–87, 389 n. 4; 15 and 16 Nov 1869 to OLL, 397 n. 3; 24 and 25 Nov 1869 to OLL, 406, 408 n. 10).

148.25–27   Dickens arrangement of tall gallows-frame . . . overhead-row of hidden lights] Clemens heard Dickens read in New York on 31 December 1867, when he accompanied Olivia Langdon and her family (8 Jan 1868 to JLC and PAM, *L2,* 146 n. 3). He described the occasion for his *Alta California* readers:

> Mr. Dickens had a table to put his book on, and on it he had also a tumbler, a fancy decanter and a small bouquet. Behind him he had a huge red screen—a bulkhead—a sounding-

board, I took it to be—and overhead in front was suspended a long board with reflecting lights attached to it, which threw down a glory upon the gentleman, after the fashion in use in the picture-galleries for bringing out the best effects of great paintings. Style!—There is style about Dickens, and style about all his surroundings. (SLC 1868c)

148.40–41   But the house remained cold and still, and gazed at him curiously and wonderingly] The Boston correspondent of the Springfield (Mass.) *Republican* agreed with Clemens's opinion of De Cordova, but not with his assessment of the audience's reaction: "Mr De Cordova is, among the lecturers, what one of the illustrated weeklies of the poorer sort would be among newspapers, provided it were better printed and on better paper. There is no wit in him, and no humor. His audience, however, seemed pleased, and not bored by his vivacious nothingness" (William S. Robinson 1869).

149.13–14   Dr. Hayes when he was fresh from the Arctic regions] Isaac I. Hayes (1832–81), a physician and explorer, accompanied Elisha Kent Kane on an Arctic expedition in 1853–55. He later led two Arctic expeditions of his own, in 1860–61 and 1869. The Redpath Lyceum booked his popular lectures from 1869 to 1878 (9 Mar 1858 to OC and MEC, *L1*, 78 n. 6; Eubank 1969, 295–306).

Ralph Keeler (*Source:* MS in CU-MARK, written in 1898–99)

150.1–2   San Francisco in the early days—about 1865—when I was a newspaper reporter] Clemens was hired as the local reporter for the San Francisco *Morning Call* in June 1864, soon after arriving from Virginia City, Nevada Territory. (He had corresponded for the *Call* from Nevada the previous year.) The "fearful drudgery" (as he characterized it) of covering the news of the courts and theaters—plus other events of interest he could discover—ended in October, when he was "advised" to resign (see AD, 13 June 1906; *CofC,* 16–24; 18? May 1863 to JLC and PAM, *L1,* 254 n. 7).

150.2–4   Bret Harte ... *The Golden Era*] As the most important literary weekly in San Francisco in the early 1860s, the *Golden Era* provided a vehicle for the apprentice work of many western writers. Its editor from 1860 to 1866, Joseph E. Lawrence, was known for his genial nature and generosity. He aimed at pleasing both a rural and urban readership by offering serialized sensation novels, poetry, and local news and gossip, as well as higher-quality literature. Clemens contributed several articles to the *Golden Era* in late 1863 and early 1864, but later that year abandoned it in favor of a new journal, the more "high-toned" *Californian* (*L1:* link note following 19 Aug 1863 to JLC and PAM, 265–66; 25 Sept 1864 to JLC and PAM, 312, 314 n. 5). Harte (1836–1902) began setting type in 1860 for the *Golden Era,* which was soon publishing his verse and prose sketches. When the *Californian* began publication in May 1864 he became a major contributor, and, while serving as its editor in the fall, solicited Clemens's work. (Clemens discusses Harte at length in the Autobiographical Dictations of 13 June, 14 June, and 18 June 1906, and 4 February 1907.) Ambrose Bierce (1842–?1914) did not arrive in San Francisco until early 1867, by which time Clemens had left for the East Coast. The two must have met in April or July 1868, when Clemens was on his last visit to San Francisco. Bierce's first published article appeared in the *Californian* in September 1867, and his first *Golden Era* article was in the July 1868 issue. Lawrence invited Prentice Mulford (1834–91) to write for the *Golden Era* in 1866, after reading his poems and humorous stories in the Sonora *Union Democrat*. For Stoddard, see "Scraps from My Autobiography. From Chapter IX," note at 161.27–30 (1 May 1867 to Harte, *L2*, 40 n. 1; Walker 1969, 119–32, 142–45, 190–91; Bierce 1868; Joshi and Schultz 1999, 75–76; Davidson 1988, 23; *L6:* 8 Apr 1874 to Chatto and Windus, 102 n. 1; 1 Feb 1875 to Stoddard, 364, 366 n. 4; Hart 1987, 46–47, 191, 208, 337–38).

150.5   Aldrich] See "Robert Louis Stevenson and Thomas Bailey Aldrich."

150.5   Boyle O'Reilly] John Boyle O'Reilly (1844–90) was an Irish poet, editor, and nationalist. Convicted of conspiracy for his activism in the Fenian movement, he was transported to Australia in 1868 but escaped to America the following year. He edited the Boston *Pilot* for many years, in which he advocated Home Rule, and became a popular lecturer.

150.5   James T. Fields] James Thomas Fields (1817–81) became a partner in the publishing company of William D. Ticknor and Co. when only twenty-five, and then the head of Ticknor and Fields in 1854. He edited the *Atlantic Monthly,* published by his firm, from 1861 to 1871, and was also a poet and the author of several books of reminiscences (Winship 1995, 17–18).

150.10–11   Mr. Emerson . . . Longfellow] Ralph Waldo Emerson (1803–82), John Greenleaf Whittier (1807–92), Oliver Wendell Holmes (1809–94), James Russell Lowell (1819–91), and Henry Wadsworth Longfellow (1807–82) all published their works through firms with which James T. Fields was associated: Ticknor and Fields and, after 1868, Fields, Osgood and Co. (Austin 1953, 16, 38).

150.17–23   He probably never had a home . . . an account of his travels in the *Atlantic Monthly*] Ralph Olmstead Keeler (1840–73) was born in Ohio. Orphaned at age eight, he was sent to an uncle in Buffalo but ran away and began a vagabond life, working first on lake steamers and trains, and then as an entertainer in "negro" minstrel shows. After supporting himself through four years of college, he went to study in Germany, where he corresponded for several journals. He moved to San Francisco around 1863, where he lived by teaching and lecturing, as well as writing a humorous column—and a number of stories—for the *Golden Era* (1 Nov 1871 to OLC, *L4,* 485–86 n. 3; Walker 1939, 138–42). His articles for the *Atlantic Monthly*—"Three Years as a Negro Minstrel" (July 1869) and "The Tour of Europe for $181 in Currency" (July 1870)—were later collected in *Vagabond Adventures,* published by Fields, Osgood and Co. (Keeler 1869b, Keeler 1870a, Keeler 1870b).

150.23–24   "Gloverson and His Silent Partners;" . . . found a publisher for it] Keeler's novel, set in San Francisco, was a conventional and unimaginative tale with the stock ingredients of romance, adversity, pathos, and comic relief. Howells, in a fond reminiscence of Keeler, recalled reviewing his manuscript for possible publication in the *Atlantic Monthly*. When he "reported against it," Keeler published the book in 1869 "at his own cost" (Howells 1900, 276). In 1874 Clemens facetiously predicted to Howells that this "noble classic" would be "translated into all the languages of the earth" and "adored by all nations & known to all creatures" (20 Nov 1874 to Howells [1st], *L6,* 291, also in AD, 12 Sept 1908; Keeler 1869a; Walker 1969, 141–42).

151.3–7   he often went out with me ... "lecture season."] Clemens enjoyed Keeler's company in November 1871, while on a lecture tour that lasted from mid-October 1871 to late February 1872. Between 31 October and 17 November Clemens appeared twice in Boston and in several nearby towns (*L4:* 1 Nov 1871 to OLC, 484, 485–86 n. 3; "Lecture Schedule, 1871–72," 557–60).

151.7–8   James Redpath's Bureau in School street, Boston] See "Lecture-Times," note at 148.8. The bureau opened on 29 Bromfield Street, and in 1871 moved to 36 Bromfield. It was never on School Street (Eubank 1969, 105).

151.12–14   Henry Ward Beecher ... English astronomer ... Parsons, Irish orator] The following people were on one or more of Redpath's lists of available lecturers between 1869 and 1873: Henry Ward Beecher (1813–87), the famous liberal pastor of Plymouth Church in Brooklyn; Anna Dickinson (1842–1932), an eloquent promoter of women's rights; John B. Gough (1817–86), a temperance advocate; Wendell Phillips (1811–84), a social reformer; John H. Vincent (1832–1920), a religious educator; and William Parsons, an orator on literary and historical subjects. For Petroleum V. Nasby (David Ross Locke), Josh Billings (Henry Wheeler Shaw), and Isaac I. Hayes, who were also among Redpath's clients, see "Lecture-Times," notes at 146.1–5, 148.21, and 149.13–14. Horace Greeley, one of the most popular speakers on the lecture circuit, was not on Redpath's "regular" list but may have been one of the clients for whom he planned special engagements in large cities. The name of the "English astronomer" evidently escaped Clemens's memory; a space for a name remains in the manuscript. He may have been Richard A. Proctor (1837–88), a renowned author and astronomer who made his first American lecture tour in 1873–74 but did not appear on Redpath's list until many years later (*Lyceum* 1871, 29–34; Eubank 1969, 241, 295–301; Chicago *Tribune:* "'Self-Made Men,'" 21 Sept 1871, 4; "Prof. Proctor's Lectures," 26 Feb 1874; Pond 1900, 178–79, 347).

151.14   Agassiz] Swiss-born Harvard naturalist Louis Agassiz (1807–73) and his less famous son, Alexander (1835–1910), were both active on the lecture circuit. Clemens heard the younger Agassiz speak at Newport in 1875, but neither man was on Redpath's roster (link note following 29? July 1875 to Redpath, *L6,* 521–22).

151.29–152.2   Kate Field ... forgotten of the world] Field (1838–96) began her career as a journalist in 1859, writing letters from Italy to several American newspapers. Her first work for the New York *Tribune* was a series of articles on the 1866 American tour of Italian actress Adelaide Ristori, which led to an assignment to cover Charles Dickens's second (and last) American reading tour. Her reviews were expanded and collected in *Pen Photographs of Charles Dickens's Readings* (Field 1868). She made her debut as a lecturer in 1869, reading her essay "Woman in the Lyceum," and continued to appear on the platform for most of her life. After an unsuccessful attempt at acting, in 1890 she started a newspaper, *Kate Field's Washington,* and was its principal writer. In 1895 she went to Hawaii for her health, and died there of pneumonia (Scharnhorst 2004, 159–61; "Miss Kate Field on 'Woman in the Lyceum,'" New York *Times,* 4 May 1869, 5; Field 1996, xxii–xxv, xxviii, xxix–xxx; 30 Jan 1871 to Redpath, *L4,* 323–24 n. 3).

152.3–7   Olive Logan's notoriety . . . her husband, who was a small-salaried minor journalist] Olive Logan (1839–1909), the daughter of a comedian and dramatist, enjoyed some success as an actress until her retirement from the stage in 1868. She published several books, the most successful of which was *Before the Footlights and Behind the Scenes,* an account of theater life. For two seasons, from 1869 to 1871, she was engaged by the Redpath Lyceum, offering lectures such as "The Passions," "Paris, City of Luxury," and "Girls," which promoted women's rights. In December 1871, Logan (who was divorced) married her second husband, William Wirt Sikes (1836–83). He worked as a journalist for several newspapers in New York State and contributed stories to periodicals such as *Harper's Monthly* and *The Youth's Companion.* Like his wife, Sikes lectured for Redpath from 1869 to 1871, delivering "The Peculiar Perils of Great Cities" and "After Dark in New York," in which he described "dangerous haunts of vice and crime." In 1876 he was appointed U.S. consul at Cardiff, Wales, and later wrote works about the history and folklore of the region (*Lyceum* 1870, 9, 15; 8 Jan 1870 to OLL [1st], *L4,* 9 n. 3; Olive Logan 1870; see also AD, 11 Apr 1906).

153.8–9   after the first season I always introduced myself—using, of course, a burlesque of the time-worn introduction] Clemens began introducing himself during the winter of 1869–70, while on his second eastern lecture tour (the first that Redpath arranged). On 8 December, in Washington, he announced that since he "knew considerably more about himself than anybody else, he thought he was better qualified to perform that ceremony. He had studied the usual form, and he thought he had finally mastered it" ("Mark Twain's Savages," Washington [D.C.] *Morning Chronicle,* 9 Dec 1869, 4). Several days later, in Meriden, Connecticut, he opened with the speech that became his standard introduction for the rest of the season, with slight variations:

> I have the pleasure of introducing to you Mr. Samuel Clemens, otherwise Mark Twain, a gentleman whose high character and unimpeachable veracity are only surpassed by his personal comeliness and native modesty. [Applause, for the audience began to smell a rat and take him for the lecturer.] And, continued he, with the utmost *sang froid,* I am the gentleman referred to. I suppose I ought to ask pardon for breaking the usual custom on such occasions and introducing myself, but it could not be avoided, as the gentleman who was to introduce me did not know my real name, hence I relieved him of his duties. ("Mark Twain's Lecture," Meriden *Republican,* 13 Dec 1869, 2)

153.21–26   introduction taken from my Californian experiences . . . *I don't know why*] Clemens began his 1871–72 lecture tour in mid-October with the same introduction he had used in 1869–70 (see the note at 153.8–9). By 1 December, however, he had adopted the new one. He had lectured in the mining town of Red Dog, California, on 24 October 1866 ("Our Lecture Course," Oswego [N.Y.] *Commercial Advertiser and Times,* 2 Dec 1871, 4; "Mark Twain," Easton [Pa.] *Express,* 24 Nov 1871; link note following 25 Aug 1866 to Bowen, *L1,* 362; see also *MTB,* 1:295).

154.27–31   one of Ossawatomie Brown's brothers . . . tragedy of 1859 . . . *Atlantic Monthly*] Militant abolitionist John Brown earned the nickname "Ossawatomie" from his battles against proslavery forces near the Kansas town of that name. Keeler interviewed two of Brown's sons on their Ohio farm, located on Put-in-Bay Island in Lake Erie. The younger son, Owen, had been with his father at the failed attack on the U.S. armory at Harpers Ferry, Virginia (now West Virginia), in 1859. Brown was captured and executed for treason, but Owen was among those who escaped, and he told Keeler of his experiences on that night, and during the following days, in great detail. Keeler's long article in the *Atlantic Monthly* was published posthumously, in March 1874 (Keeler 1874).

154.35–41 the *Tribune* commissioned Keeler to go to Cuba . . . that was what had happened] In 1868, Cuba began a war of rebellion against Spain—known as the Ten Years' War—which was ultimately unsuccessful. Although the United States remained neutral in the conflict, there was widespread sympathy for the rebellion among Americans. In October 1873 the Spanish captured the *Virginius,* a ship transporting arms to the insurgents, and executed over fifty of the men on board, many of whom were Americans. In late November Keeler traveled to Cuba as a correspondent for the New York *Tribune,* and over the next few weeks submitted several letters about the crisis. At the start of his return trip in mid-December, he disappeared from a steamship in Cuban waters. Although his fate was never known, it was believed that he was assassinated as a result of the violent anti-American sentiment arising from the *Virginius* incident. Howells, who eulogized Keeler in the March 1874 issue of the *Atlantic Monthly,* speculated that he had been "stabbed and thrown into the sea" by a Spanish officer who discovered that he was an American journalist (Halstead 1897, 41, 49; Howells 1874a, 366).

Scraps from My Autobiography. From Chapter IX (*Sources:* MS in CU-MARK, written in 1900; 1902 TS by Jean Clemens; TS3 [partial])

155.5 my sister] Pamela, who turned twenty-two on 13 September 1849; see the Appendix "Family Biographies" (p. 655).

155.13 black slave boy, Sandy] Sandy was owned by "a master back in the country" but was hired out to work for the Clemenses ("Jane Lampton Clemens," *Inds,* 89; see also "My Autobiography [Random Extracts from It]").

157.7–8 one whom I will call Mary Wilson] The real "Mary" was Sarah H. Robards (1836–1918); she and her brothers George and John were all Hannibal schoolmates of Clemens's, and she studied piano with his sister Pamela (see AD, 8 Mar 1906, note at 399.28–29, and AD, 9 Mar 1906, note at 401.7–16). Clemens recalled her in his 1902 notebook: "Sally Robards—pret[t]y. Describe her now in her youth & again in 50 ys After when she reveals herself" (Notebook 45, TS p. 21, CU-MARK). She married riverboat pilot and captain Barton Stone Bowen, the brother of William Bowen, who was probably Clemens's closest childhood friend (*Inds,* 304–5, 345).

157.12–13 It was in 1896. I arrived there on my lecturing trip] Clemens reached Calcutta on his world lecture tour in February 1896 (see "Something about Doctors," note at 190.10–12.

157.16–17 grand-daughter of the other Mary] After the death of her first husband, Barton

Bowen, in 1868, Sarah Robards married the Reverend H. H. Haley. The granddaughter has not been identified (*Inds*, 345; *Robards Family Genealogy* 2009, part 14:65).

157.36–37   drunken tramp—mentioned in "Tom Sawyer" or "Huck Finn"—who was burned up in the village jail] This incident does not occur in either book, although there is an oblique allusion to it in chapter 23 of *Tom Sawyer*, where Tom and Huck give some matches to Muff Potter when he is in jail. Chapter 56 of *Life on the Mississippi*, however, contains a dramatic account of the tramp's death and Clemens's subsequent struggle with his conscience.

158.5   shooting down of poor old Smarr in the main street] William Perry Owsley murdered Sam Smarr (b. 1788) in 1845. Smarr, a beef farmer, was described as a generally peaceful man who became abusive when drunk. He offended Owsley by accusing him of stealing $2,000 from a friend, and by repeatedly insulting him and threatening his life. Owsley, a wealthy merchant, shot Smarr to death in a Hannibal street before many witnesses, but was acquitted of the crime. In "Villagers of 1840–3" (1897) Clemens wrote that after the trial his "party brought him huzzaing in from Palmyra at midnight. But there was a cloud upon him—a social chill—and presently he moved away" (*Inds*, 101, 339–40, 348). He recreated the incident in chapter 21 of *Huckleberry Finn*, where Colonel Sherburn shoots "old Boggs" (see *HF 2003*, 436). In a letter of 11 January 1900 Clemens recalled, "I can't ever forget Boggs, because I saw him die, with a family Bible spread open on his breast" (11 Jan 1900 to Goodrich-Freer, ViU).

158.15–16   slave man who was struck down . . . I saw him die] In "Jane Lampton Clemens" (1890), Clemens recalled:

> There were no hard-hearted people in our town—I mean there were no more than would be found in any other town of the same size in any other country; and in my experience hard-hearted people are very rare everywhere. Yet I remember that once when a white man killed a negro man for a trifling little offence everybody seemed indifferent about it—as regarded the slave—though considerable sympathy was felt for the slave's owner, who had been bereft of valuable property by a worthless person who was not able to pay for it. (*Inds*, 89)

158.16–18   young Californian emigrant who was stabbed . . . I saw the red life gush from his breast] Clemens noted in 1897 that all emigrants "went through there. One stabbed to death—saw him. . . . Saw the corpse in my father's office" (Autobiographical Fragment #160, CU-MARK). The body was carried to the office of John Marshall Clemens, the justice of the peace; Clemens saw it because he was hiding there to avoid being punished for skipping school. He recalled this traumatic experience repeatedly, in lectures and writings. See, for example, chapter 18 of *The Innocents Abroad*: "I put my hands over my eyes and counted till I could stand it no longer, and then—the pallid face of a man was there, with the corners of the mouth drawn down, and the eyes fixed and glassy in death!" (*Inds*, 101, 284).

158.18   young Hyde brothers and their harmless old uncle] Richard (Dick) Hyde (b. 1830?) and his brother Ed were ruffians whom Clemens described in "Villagers of 1840–3" as "tough and dissipated." The brothers—or perhaps Richard and another brother, Henry—were the models for the Stover brothers in "Hellfire Hotchkiss" (*Inds,* 96, 327).

158.22–25   young Californian emigrant who got drunk . . . blameless daughter] Clemens's recollection of this incident, which occurred in 1850, varies slightly from the account published in the Hannibal *Missouri Courier,* the newspaper where Clemens worked as a "printer's devil" at the time:

> Caleb W. Lindley, a stranger from Illinois, was shot in this city on Friday night last, by a woman named Weir, a widow, living in a house on Holliday's Hill. He with several others, went to the house of the woman about 11 o'clock at night and demanded admittance, with permission to stay all night. Being refused, they threatened to do violence to the house, if their demands were not gratified. The woman ordered them away, and threatened to shoot, if they did not cease to molest her. One of them, Lindley, bolder than the rest, approached, and told her to "shoot ahead." She accordingly fired, and he fell pierced with two balls and several buck shot.

The woman, a poor widow with several children, was not charged with a crime (20 May 1850, quoted in Wecter 1952, 159–60). The incident was the basis for chapters 29 and 30 of *Tom Sawyer,* in which Huck overhears Injun Joe threatening to disfigure the widow Douglas and summons help from the "Welchman" and his "brace of tall sons," who live on Cardiff Hill (the fictional name for Holliday's Hill), to thwart the attack.

158.26–27   a comrade—John Briggs, I think] See the Autobiographical Dictation of 16 March 1906, note at 420.17–18.

159.27–28   in an earlier chapter I have already described what a raging hell of repentance I passed through then] No such pre-1900 account has been found. Clemens returns to the subject of his temporary repentance in the Autobiographical Dictation of 8 March 1906.

159.30   Jim Wolf] Wolf (b. 1833?) was an apprentice printer who lodged with the Clemens family in the early 1850s when he worked with Samuel on Orion Clemens's Hannibal *Western Union* (begun in 1850). Clemens, amused by his bashfulness, humorously described his slow response to the threat of an office fire in his first published piece, "A Gallant Fireman," printed in Orion's newspaper in January 1851 (SLC 1851). Wolf was also the prototype for the bumpkin Nicodemus Dodge in chapter 23 of *A Tramp Abroad* (1880) (*Inds,* 351).

161.9–10   I was offered a large sum . . . "Jim Wolf and the Cats."] Clemens contributed his first piece to the New York *Sunday Mercury* in 1864—"Doings in Nevada," 7 February—at the urging of Artemus Ward, after the two had met in Virginia City and enjoyed a "period of continuous celebration" in December 1863. "Jim Wolf and the Tom-Cats," which appeared on 14 July 1867, was his ninth (and last) contribution to that journal (SLC 1864a, 1864b, 1867b, 1867c, 1867d, 1867f, 1867g, 1867j, 1867k).

161.13–17   "Jim Wolf and the Cats" appeared in a Tennessee paper . . . His name has passed out of my memory] The Tennessee newspaper printing has not been found. In 1885, however, A. H. Warner (otherwise unidentified) sent Clemens a handwritten transcription of a corrupt version of the text, which he had copied from an unknown source. Although Clemens's original included a sprinkling of dialect words, this derivative text carried the concept much further. For example, "Our winder looked out onto the roof" was altered to "Wal our winder looked out onter the ruff." It is likely that Clemens saw a printing of this text, or a variant of it, in the late 1860s; the popular "appropriator" has not been identified (A. H. Warner to SLC, 22 July 1885, and "Jim Wolfe and the Cats," DV 275, CU-MARK).

161.24–27   In 1873 I was lecturing in London . . . George Dolby, lecture-agent] The time referred to is December 1873. Dolby (d. 1900) was an experienced theatrical agent who in 1872 had tried and failed to persuade Clemens to lecture during his first visit to England. Clemens returned to London a year later, this time with his wife and infant daughter, Susy, and Dolby succeeded in booking him for five October days in London and one in Liverpool. At that point Olivia became desperately homesick, and Clemens accompanied his family home but immediately returned without them for a second round of lectures arranged by Dolby, from 1 to 20 December 1873 in London, and 8 to 10 January 1874 in Leicester and Liverpool (*L5:* 15 Sept 1872 to OLC, 159–60; link note following 29 Sept 1873 to MacDonald, 446–47; 19 Sept 1873 to Stoddard, 456–58; 22 Nov 1873 to Lee, 481; 30 Dec 1873 to Fitzgibbon, 539, 541 n. 4).

161.27–30   Charles Warren Stoddard . . . to have his company] Stoddard (1843–1909) began contributing poems anonymously to the San Francisco *Golden Era* in 1861. He had been friends with Clemens in San Francisco since at least 1865. In 1867, with help from Bret Harte, Stoddard published *Poems,* his first book. Clemens wrote him in April from New York: "I want to endorse your book, because I know all about poetry & I know you can write the genuine article. Your book will be a success—your book *shall* be a success—& I will destroy any man that says the contrary" (23 Apr 1867 to Stoddard, *L2,* 30–31 n. 1). Highly praised by some critics, *Poems* failed to win general acclaim. Stoddard had been raised as a Presbyterian, but converted that same year to Catholicism, an experience he wrote about in *A Troubled Heart and How It Was Comforted at Last* (1885). His most successful works were travel essays, a collection of which, *South-Sea Idyls,* was published in 1873. He traveled to England in mid-October 1873 as a roving reporter for the San Francisco *Chronicle,* and Clemens hired him as a secretary and companion in December. Over the following decade Stoddard traveled extensively in Europe, the Middle East, and Hawaii, writing travel columns for the *Chronicle* and various journals. He taught literature in 1885–86 at the University of Notre Dame, and then from 1889 to 1902 at the Catholic University of America in Washington (link note following 14 Nov 1873 to OLC, *L5,* 476–78; *L6:* 9 Jan 1874 to Moore, 16 n. 1; 12 Jan 1874 to Finlay, 19–20 n. 1; James 1911; Austen 1991, 4, 58, 65–69, 82, 88, 100, 103–14).

161.31   great trial of the Tichborne Claimant for perjury] In 1866 an Australian butcher claimed to be Roger Charles Tichborne (b. 1829), the heir to the Tichborne baronetcy and estates who it was thought had been lost at sea in 1854. The claimant was acknowledged by Tichborne's mother (and several other people), but after her death he lost an ejection suit against the present baronet and was then charged with perjury. His trial, which lasted from April 1873 to February 1874 and included testimony about forged documents, multiple aliases, murder, seduction, and insanity, fascinated the public. The jury determined that he was Arthur Orton, of Wapping. He was convicted and sentenced to fourteen years in prison, of which he served ten. The identity of the claimant remains unresolved: at least one modern historian, Douglas Woodruff, has supported his claim. Clemens, who was personally interested in claimants, asked Stoddard to "scrap-book these trial reports," intending to "boil the thing down into a more or less readable sketch some day." In 1897 he devoted two pages to the case in chapter 15 of *Following the Equator,* but made no other literary use of the scrapbooks, which survive in the Mark Twain Papers (19 Oct 1873 to Stoddard, *L5,* 456–57; Scrapbooks 13–18, CU-MARK).

162.6   Dolby had been agent for . . . Charles Dickens] Dolby escorted Dickens on his reading tours in Great Britain and America between 1866 and 1869. Dickens found him to be an amiable companion and efficient manager, and they became friends (15 Sept 1872 to OLC, *L5,* 160 n. 1; see also Dolby 1885).

162.18–19   baby had the botts] "Botts" (more commonly "bots") is a condition in many animals caused by an infestation of botfly larvae. The only species of botfly to attack humans is *Dermatobia hominis,* which deposits its eggs under the skin.

162.32   Tom Hood's Annual] Clemens had met humorist and illustrator Tom Hood (1835–74), the editor of the London magazine *Fun,* on his first trip to England, in 1872. Hood heard Clemens tell a story and encouraged him to write it down for inclusion in *Tom Hood's Comic Annual for 1873,* where it appeared as "How I Escaped Being Killed in a Duel" (SLC 1872a; 11 Sept 1872 to OLC, *L5,* 155, 157 n. 10).

163.19–20   thing he sold to Tom Hood's Annual . . . he did not put my name to it] The stolen Jim Wolf sketch, retitled "A Yankee Story" and attributed to "G. R. Wadleigh," was published in *Tom Hood's Comic Annual for 1874* (SLC 1876j; Hood 1873, 78–79). George R. Wadleigh (b. 1845) was born in Boston, and listed himself in the 1881 census as a journalist (*British Census* 1881, f. 129, p. 23; see also *N&J2,* 147). He probably found the text in *Practical Jokes with Artemus Ward, Including the Story of the Man Who Fought Cats,* by "Mark Twain and Other Humorists," an unauthorized collection of stories issued in 1872 in London by John Camden Hotten. Stoddard also wrote an account of the incident:

> There was an American who besieged us at the Langham as well as at the lecture-hall. His story was pitiful. Snatched from a foreign office by a change in the administration, a lovely young wife at the point of death, he penniless in a strange land, a born gentleman, delicately reared, unacquainted with toil,—would Mark be good enough to loan him a few pounds until he could hear from his estates at home? Mark did; how could he avoid it, when the unfortunate man assured him that they had been friends for years and that they had played many a (forgotten) game of billiards in days gone by? Well, a week later, when the person in question had disappeared, one of Mark's early sketches was discovered in a copy of *London Fun,* bearing the name of the unfortunate; and there were two or three others on file, which, however, were detected in season to save them from the same fate. Coöperative authorship is not always agreeable, and this fellow proved he was one of the biggest frauds on record. (Charles Warren Stoddard 1903, 72–73)

Scraps from My Autobiography. Private History of a Manuscript That Came to Grief (*Sources:* MS and TS [of the "'Edited' Introduction" only], written in 1900, CU-MARK)

164.2–10   An acquaintance had proposed . . . the most competent person in Great Britain] The official records of Joan of Arc's trials for heresy—the original one, which resulted in her execution in 1431, and the retrial, more than twenty years later, which annulled her condemnation—were first transcribed and published in five volumes by French archaeologist and historian Jules Quicherat in the 1840s. His work comprised selections, translated into modern French, of the original medieval French and Latin documents (Quicherat 1841–49). Clemens's "acquaintance" was T. Douglas Murray, a wealthy barrister and amateur historian. In 1899 he asked Clemens to write an introduction to an English translation, the first ever published. Clemens was mistaken in his reference here to a translation published "a great many years before." In the present case there were evidently two translators, one for each language (see the note at 164.11–12). Clemens was an obvious choice for this task. In 1896 he had published *Personal Recollections of Joan of Arc,* a historical novel for which he did extensive research. The work was an affectionate homage to his favorite historical figure, and he sometimes said it was his best work, a judgment shared chiefly with his family. Murray published his book (without Clemens's participation) in 1902, with his own preface, introduction, and notes. He did not identify the "competent" translators (*MTB,* 3:1033–34; Murray 1902; Sayre 1932).

164.11–12   When he asked me to write an Introduction for the book, my pleasure was complete, my vanity satisfied] On 3 September 1899 Clemens wrote to Henry H. Rogers about the assignment: "The Official Records of the Joan of Arc Trials (in Rouen & the Rehabilitation) have at last been translated *in full* into English, & I was asked to write an Introduction, & have just finished it after a long & painstaking siege of work. I am to help edit it, & my name will go on the title page with those of the two translators. I expect it to be ever so readable & interesting a book" (Salm, in *HHR,* 409–10).

165.20–32   Introduction . . . Let me have it back as soon as you can] Clemens initially invited Murray's editing. In September 1899 he wrote, "When I send the Introduction, I must get you to do two things for me—knock the lies out of it & purify the grammar (which I think stinks, in one place.)" (3 Sept 1899 to Murray, CU-MARK; see the text shown as deleted at 175.10–11: "forget whom she was"). By January 1900 Clemens had reviewed a typed version, on which Murray had made suggestions, returning it with the note, "I have retained several of the emendations made, & have added some others" (31 Jan 1900 to Murray, CU-MARK). Murray, however, continued to edit this first typescript, making numerous additional changes before having a clean copy made; he then revised this second typescript still further. By the time Clemens withdrew from the project, he had received a third typescript, incorporating Murray's editing on the second one (all three typescripts are in CU-MARK).

166.21–22   Hark from the Tomb] Serious or earnest reproof, as in Isaac Watts's hymn "A Funeral Thought": "Hark! from the tombs a doleful sound; / My ears, attend the cry— / Ye living men, come, view the ground / Where you must shortly lie.'"

166.23   I shall write him a letter, but not in that spirit, I trust] Clemens wrote three letters to Murray expressing dismay at his editing. One, which clearly he never intended to send, comprises the last section of this sketch, and is undated. He drafted two other letters on 27 August 1900, only one of which he actually posted. The first contained passages like the following:

> I will hold no grudge against you for thinking you could improve my English for me, for I believe you innocently meant well, & did not know any better. Your lack of literary training, literary perception, literary judgment, literary talent, along with a deficient knowledge of grammar & of the meanings of words—these are to blame, not you. (CU-MARK)

He was more restrained in the second letter, which he did send:

> I am afraid you did not quite clearly understand me. The time-honored etiquette of the situation—new to you by reason of inexperience—is this: an author's MS. is not open to any editor's uninvited emendations. It must be accepted as it stands, or it must be declined; there is no middle course. Any alteration of it—even to a word—closes the incident, & that author & that editor can have no further literary dealings with each other. It was your right to say that the Introduction was not satisfactory to you, but it was not within your rights to contribute your pencil's assistance toward making it satisfactory.
>
> Therefore, even if you now wished to use my MS. in its original form, untouched, I could not permit it. Nor in any form, of course.
>
> I shall be glad to have the original when convenient, but there is no hurry. When you return will answer quite well. If you have any copies of it—either amended or unamended—please destroy them, lest they fall into careless hands & get into print. Indeed I would not have that happen for anything in the world.
>
> I am speaking in this very definite way because I perceive from your letter (notwithstanding what I said to you) that you still contemplate inserting in the book the Introduction, in some form or other. Whereas no line of it must be inserted in any form, amended or original. (CU-MARK)

Murray replied immediately, on 30 August, promising to return "all existing copies, including the original; and you may be sure that not a word of your MS shall be produced" (CU-MARK).

167.1   The "Edited" Introduction] At this point in his manuscript Clemens wrote, "Here insert the 'edited' Introduction." To represent the introduction as revised by Murray, Clemens began with a clean typescript of his original introduction and copied onto it, by hand, about three-quarters of the markings that Murray had made on two different stages of the text. For the most part Clemens represented Murray's revisions accurately, although he occasionally altered them, perhaps inadvertently. The revisions are shown here with diagonal slashes for deletions of single characters, horizontal rules for deletions of more than one character, and carets for inserted characters (for a full explanation of this transcription system, called "plain text," see "Guide to Editorial Practice," *L6*, 709–14).

179.34–36   your marginal remark . . . *foreign to her character*] This remark of Murray's does not appear on any of the surviving typescripts of Clemens's introduction. It may have been written on a now-lost carbon copy, or it could have been erased from an existing typescript: many of Murray's penciled revisions were inexplicably erased, but are still faintly visible.

[**Reflections on a Letter and a Book**] (*Source:* MS in CU-MARK, written in 1903)

181.3   Dear Sir:—I have written a book] The author of this letter signed his name, "Hilary Trent," and added a postscript notifying Clemens that his book, *Mr. Claghorn's Daughter,* would "be sent you by the J. S. Ogilvie Publishing Co." Clemens omitted the signature and postscript when inserting the letter here. Trent's 1903 novel blends domestic melodrama with an attack on the Westminster Confession of Faith, the creed of the American Presbyterian church—specifically what was controversially called its doctrine of "infant damnation" (see the note at 185.15–16). The publisher's advertising claimed that Hilary Trent was "a well-known writer who conceals his identity under a nom-de-plume" ("Mr. Claghorn's Daughter," New York *Sun,* 23 May 1903, 7), but documentary and internal evidence indicates that he was R. M. Manley, a decidedly little-known writer who harbored strong feelings about the Westminster Confession (Manley 1903; Manley 1897; Manley to SLC, 29 Apr 1903 and 4 May 1903, CU-MARK).

185.15–16   revising the Confession of Faith . . . chapters 3 and 10 of the Confession] The connection between Clemens's screed on self-interest and the newspaper clippings that follow it is Presbyterian doctrine, the subject of Trent's book (see the note at 181.3). In the late nineteenth century, American Presbyterians began to consider revisions to the Westminster Confession of Faith. Debate centered on chapter 3, which states that some souls have been predestined "unto everlasting life and others foreordained to everlasting death" (section 3); and chapter 10, which asserts that "elect infants" are saved, while infants (as well as adults) who are "not elected" cannot be saved (sections 3–4). Historically, this latter chapter has been interpreted as damning not only many Christian infants, but also all non-Christians (a fact which may bear upon Clemens's inclusion of the clipping that follows, about the massacre of Russian Jews). In 1902, the year before the writing of the present essay, the Presbyterian church had adopted a statement endorsing a liberal construction of the disputed chapters; it was appended to the Confession in 1903 (Macpherson 1881, 48, 85–86; Briggs 1890, 21–22, 98–130; "Presbyterian Creed Revision Adopted," New York *Times,* 23 May 1902, 5).

186.27   Westminster Catechism] The catechism based on the Westminster Confession would have been familiar to Clemens from his early religious training (see Fulton 2006, 140–55).

[**Something about Doctors**] (*Source:* MS in CU-MARK, written in 1903)

188.19–20   Dr. Meredith . . . village of Hannibal] Dr. Hugh Meredith (1806–64), born in Pennsylvania, was a personal friend and business associate of Clemens's father in Florida, Missouri, and then in Hannibal. The two men collaborated in planning improvements in both towns. Dr. Meredith joined the 1849 Gold Rush, but returned in early 1851. For several weeks in the winter of 1851–52 he edited Orion Clemens's Hannibal *Journal* while Orion attended to the family's property in Tennessee (*Inds,* 335; Wecter 1952, 55; see AD, 28 Mar 1906).

188.21–22   I have already said . . . furnished the drugs himself] See "My Autobiography [Random Extracts from It]," written in 1897–98 (215.3–6).

189.1   his own son Charles] Charles (b. 1833?) was the oldest of Dr. Meredith's five children. He accompanied his father to the California gold fields, and later made a second trip west (*Inds,* 335).

189.21–22   our old family physician, Dr. Taft . . . neglected successor] Cincinnatus A. Taft (1822–84) began practicing homeopathic medicine in Hartford in 1846, and became the Clemenses' physician after they moved there in 1871. He was well loved by his patients; after his death Clemens praised him as a man "full of courteous grace and dignity" whose "heart was firm and strong . . . and freighted with human sympathies" (18 July 1884 to the Editor of the Hartford *Courant,* CtHMTH; 17 Feb 1871 to JLC and family, *L4,* 333 n. 3). Taft's "successor" has not been identified; the family did not find another satisfactory physician for several years (19 Apr 1888 to Langdon, CtHMTH).

189.25   Theron Wales] Theron A. Wales (b. 1842) received his medical degree in 1873 from the University of Pennsylvania, and immediately established a practice in Elmira. According to *A History of the Valley and County of Chemung,* his "superior literary attainments" earned him a "reputation as a writer upon various topics" (Towner 1892, "Personal References," 133; *L4:* SLC and OLC to the Langdons, 9 Feb 1870, 68 n. 6; 22 Feb 1871 to OC, 335 n. 2).

189.37   our old ex-slave cook, Aunty Cord] Mary Ann ("Auntie") Cord (1798–1888) was the cook at Quarry Farm, the Cranes' property near Elmira. Thirteen years after she had been separated from her family by the slave market, she was miraculously reunited with her youngest son, who had escaped to Elmira and become a Union soldier. Clemens wrote a moving account of her history, "A True Story, Repeated Word for Word as I Heard It," which appeared in the *Atlantic Monthly* in November 1874 (SLC 1874b; 2 Sept 1874 to Howells, *L6,* 219 n. 2).

190.10–12   I lectured every night for twenty-three nights . . . ship at Vancouver] To recover financially from the failure of the Paige typesetting-machine venture, and the collapse of Charles L. Webster and Company in 1894, Clemens undertook a year-long world lecture tour in July 1895, accompanied by his wife and their daughter Clara. He opened in Cleveland, and made more than twenty appearances in the United States and Canada before embarking from Vancouver for Australia, New Zealand, Ceylon, India, Mauritius, and South Africa. In July 1896 they returned to England, where Clemens wrote *Following the Equator,* based on the trip.

190.27–30   We were living in Berlin . . . congestion of the wind'ard lung] The Clemenses sojourned in Berlin in the winter of 1891–92. Clemens lectured there on 13 January (the occasion has not been further identified), and wrote in his notebook, "Went to our cousin's (Frau Generalin von Versen) ball, after the lecture; we all came home at 2 am., & I have been in bed ever since—three weeks—with congestion of lungs and influenza" (Notebook 31, TS p. 21, CU-MARK; see AD, 29 Mar 1906, note at 456.25–26).

190.39–42   Sidney Smith . . . I paid half the bill] Clemens wrote to Dr. Smith on 1 February 1896, complaining about his fee:

> Twenty-five rupees per visit seems unaccountably large, & I have waited, in order to make some inquiries. I find from conversation with some of your well-to-do patients in Bombay that you charge them Rs. 10 per visit.
>
>   There may be some mistake somewhere & it may be that you can explain it. . . . Meantime I enclose cheque for Rs. 40 & will await an explanation of the seemingly extra charge. (CU-MARK)

[Henry H. Rogers] (*Source:* TS in CU-MARK, made in 1906 from a 1904 typescript [now lost] of Clemens's dictation)

192.15–17   Standard Oil Trust . . . keeps them alive and going] From a small beginning as an oil investor, Rogers had advanced to a position of immense power and wealth. In 1890 he became a vice-president and a director of the Standard Oil Company, and his financial interests extended to natural gas, copper, steel, banking, and railroads. Although generous and amiable with his friends, he earned the sobriquet "hell hound" for his ruthless (and, by more rigorous standards, unethical) business practices (*HHR,* 2–7).

194.21   gas suit, wherein Mr. Rogers was sued for several millions of dollars] The lawsuit stemmed from a war for control of gas distribution in Boston that began in 1894. The principal combatants were Rogers, of Standard Oil, and J. Edward Addicks, of the Bay State Gas Company of Delaware (see the note at 196.40). In 1896 the Standard Oil interest won control over all the Boston gas companies, and Addicks abandoned the competition. In the ensuing years, however, a number of disputes developed over control of the various companies and the price of stocks traded in the consolidation transactions. The plaintiff in the lawsuit, filed in 1903, was the Bay State Gas Company. Among the defendants were the Massachusetts Gas Companies, a trust formed in 1902 that now controlled the industry in Boston; Kidder, Peabody and Company, the investment banking firm that handled the stock sales; and Henry H. Rogers. The plaintiff alleged that in 1902 some of the stocks were sold at artificially low prices, defrauding the Delaware Company and forcing it into a "fictitious default" ("Industrial Affairs," *Wall Street Journal,* 17 June 1903, 5). One of the disputed transactions—the 1896 sale of his Brookline Gas Company—earned Rogers a $3 million profit, money that should have gone to investors. The case was not resolved until 1907, when Rogers agreed to return half of the $3 million (*HHR,* 76 n. 1, 306 n. 3; New York *Times:* "Standard Oil in Control," 1 Nov 1896, 6; "Bay State Gas War Ended," 21 Jan 1898, 1; "Decision on Gas Merger," 13 Dec 1903, 17; "Rogers a Defendant in Boston Gas Suit," 3 Apr 1904, FS2; Chicago *Tribune:* "Gas Suit for $3,000,000," 16 Apr 1904, 6; "Rogers to Share Gas Deal Profits," 1 Feb 1907, 2).

194.42   Here follows that Boston sketch] The article that follows, a "pen picture" of Rogers as a witness in the gas lawsuit, appeared in the Boston *Sunday Post* of 27 March 1904. Katharine Harrison, Rogers's secretary, forwarded Clemens a clipping of the sketch, which he acknowledged in a letter to Rogers of 12 April 1904:

The Boston sketch has just arrived & I thank that ten-thousand-dollar secretary of yours for sending it: the one I have read so much about, recently as being as unpumpable as the Sphynx, & the only secretary of her sex that either earns that salary or gets it. That sketch is fine, superfine, gilt-edged; you will live *one* while before you see it bettered. It is a portrait to the life—in it I see you & I hear you, the same as if I were present; & by help of its vivid suggestiveness my fancy can fill in a lot of things the writer had to leave out for lack of room. (Salm, in *HHR,* 562)

195.18   Mr. Winsor] Robert Winsor (1858–1930), a prominent financier, was a partner in the investment banking firm of Kidder, Peabody and Company ("Robert Winsor Dies," New York *Times,* 8 Jan 1930, 25).

195.18–19   famous telephone conversation with Mr. Lawson] Wealthy businessman and stockbroker Thomas W. Lawson (1857–1925) had become an active player in the gas company maneuvers in 1895. In the late 1890s he was the chief promoter and stockbroker in the consolidation of mining properties to form the Amalgamated Copper Company, which made millions for himself, Rogers, and William Rockefeller, but brought financial ruin to many investors. In 1902 he was involved in the transactions that led to the gas lawsuit. He testified that Rogers had offered him $1 million to withdraw his opposition to the reorganization of the New England Gas and Coke Company, a supplier whose indebtedness had forced it into receivership (see the note at 197.14). Rogers denied the charge, offering a different version of a telephone conversation that took place on 8 March 1902. Rogers's "foul act of perjury," as Lawson called it, ended their association, and in July 1904 Lawson began a series of articles in *Everybody's Magazine,* exposing the rapacious and unethical business machinations of the financial world in general, and Addicks, Standard Oil, and Rogers in particular. In 1905 the articles were collected in a book: *Frenzied Finance: The Crime of Amalgamated* (Lawson 1905, 2–4, 23–31, 117, 123, 343–45; Adams 1903, 270–71; "Massachusetts Gas Trial," *Wall Street Journal,* 26 Mar 1904, 5; New York *Times:* "Rogers Denies He Got Lawson Million," 5 Apr 1904, 1; "Calls Rogers Bad Trustee," 14 Apr 1904, 5).

195.23   Mr. Whipple] Sherman L. Whipple (1862–1930), the attorney for the plaintiff, was a graduate of Yale Law School and well known for his skill at examining witnesses ("Bay State Gas Hearing," Washington *Post,* 3 Oct 1903, 1).

196.22   Shakspere says one may smile and smile and be a villain] "My tables! Meet it is I set it down / That one may smile, and smile, and be a villain" (*Hamlet,* act 1, scene 5).

196.40   Mr. Addicks] J. Edward Addicks (1841–1919) was an aggressive financier who established the Bay State Gas Company in 1884. After accumulating a fortune from his gas investments, he turned to speculation in copper mining, participating with Lawson and Rogers in promoting the Amalgamated Copper Company (see the note at 195.18–19). Beginning in 1889 he spent seventeen years trying to win a seat in the U.S. Senate, but failed despite spending an estimated $3 million ("J. E. Addicks of Boston Finance Fame Dies at 78," Chicago *Tribune,* 8 Aug 1919, 16).

197.14   Mr. Whitney] Henry M. Whitney (1839–1923), a Boston "captain of industry," was largely responsible for the development of the electric streetcar system in the Boston area. In early 1896 he entered the gas business as a new supplier of cheap gas, in competition with the Standard Oil and Addicks interests. His company, the New England Gas and Coke Company, ran into debt in 1902 and was forced to reorganize. Its assets passed to a new trust, the Massachusetts Gas Companies. This trust's purchase of the stock of the Bay State Company in 1903, allegedly at artificially low prices, was the basis of the current lawsuit (Adams 1903, 259, 266–67, 270–72; Lawson 1905, 134).

197.14–16   those other people . . . Yacht Club matter] In 1901, a boat that Lawson had built expressly to enter the New York Yacht Club Race was disqualified on the grounds that only members of the club were eligible to compete. A club member was quoted as saying Lawson had previously applied for membership and been blackballed; Lawson denied ever having made an application ("A Club of Snobs," Washington *Post,* 9 Mar 1901, 6; "Mr. Lawson Will Challenge Any Yacht," New York *Times,* 10 Mar 1901, 1).

197.49   Senator Allee] James Frank Allee (1857–1938) served as a Republican senator from Delaware from 1903 to 1907.

[**Anecdote of Jean**] (*Source:* MS in CU-MARK)

199 *title*   Jean] Jean's life is briefly outlined in the Appendix "Family Biographies" (p. 657).

AUTOBIOGRAPHY OF MARK TWAIN

Sources: Unless otherwise noted, the texts of *Autobiography of Mark Twain* are based on one or more typescripts in the Mark Twain Papers: TS1, TS2, TS3, or TS4. These are described in References and, in more detail, in the Introduction and Note on the Text.

An Early Attempt

203.1–2   The chapters which immediately follow . . . to put my life on paper] Clemens wrote the title page and "Early Attempt" preface for *Autobiography of Mark Twain* in June 1906, when he conceived his final plan for the work; his manuscript survives in the Mark Twain Papers. See the Introduction for a discussion of this plan and a facsimile of the manuscript (figures 2–3).

My Autobiography [Random Extracts from It]

203 *title*   My Autobiography [Random Extracts from It]] Clemens wrote this long reminiscence, with several internal chapter breaks, in Vienna over the winter of 1897–98; his manuscript survives in the Mark Twain Papers. A forty-four-page typescript that was made from the manuscript is now lost. Clemens revised the typescript, almost certainly in 1906, shortly before he asked Josephine Hobby to transcribe it (see AD, 9 Jan 1906, note at 250.19–21). Clemens identified this manuscript as "From Chapter II" of his autobiography (see p. 14 for a facsimile of its first page). The manuscript begins with two stanzas from Edward Fitzgerald's translation of *The Rubáiyát of Omar Khayyám:*

> We are no other than a moving row
> Of Magic Shadow-shapes that come and go
>   Round with the Sun-illumined Lantern held
> In Midnight by the Master of the Show;
>
> But helpless Pieces of the Game He plays
> Upon this Chequer-board of Nights and Days;
>   Hither and thither moves, and checks, and slays,
> And one by one back in the Closet lays.

Collation establishes that Clemens deleted both the chapter designation and the poem on the missing stage, and they are therefore omitted from the text here (see the Textual Commentary, *MTPO*). He had known and loved Fitzgerald's *Rubáiyát* since 22 December 1875, when he saw it excerpted on the front page of the Hartford *Courant.* He recalled in 1907, "No poem had ever given me so much pleasure before, and none has given me so much pleasure since; it is the only poem I have ever carried about with me; it has not been from under my hand for twenty-eight years" (AD, 7 Oct 1907).

203.8   * * * * So much for the . . . New England branch of the Clemenses] No earlier section about the "New England branch" survives, and it remains unclear whether any previous text was ever written. In his draft of the preface entitled "An Early Attempt," Clemens first wrote "The chapters which immediately follow constitute a fragment of one of my many attempts (after I was in my forties) to put my life on paper. The first part of it is lost." He then deleted the second sentence. Clemens's ancestor Robert Clements (1595–1658) emigrated from England in 1642 and settled in Massachusetts, where he helped establish the town of Haverhill. Robert's great-grandson Ezekiel (1696–1778)—presumably the "other brother who settled in the South"—first went to Virginia (not Maryland, as Clemens claimed) in about 1743, but did not settle there permanently until about 1765. Clemens descended from Ezekiel through his son Jeremiah (1732–1811) (Lampton 1990, 78–79; Bell 1984, 4–8, 13, 24–25).

203.10–18   He went South with his particular friend Fairfax . . . American earl . . . Virginia City, Nevada] Clemens was slightly mistaken about the Fairfax family. The title of baron (not earl) was granted to the Fairfax family in 1627, and was not of "recent date." It was Thomas Fairfax, the third baron (1612–71), grandson of the first baron, who served as general-in-chief of the parliamentary armies and won several crucial battles against the forces of Charles I. He resigned his command to Cromwell in 1650, and had no role in the king's execution. Nine years later he helped to restore the monarchy. In describing the "particular friend" of the "other brother" Clemens probably meant William Fairfax, who emigrated to New England, and later settled in Virginia to manage the family estates. Clemens's friend was Charles Snowden Fairfax (1829–69), the tenth baron, who was William's great-great-grandson. Clemens probably met Charles in San Francisco in the early 1860s. He served in the California legislature in 1853 and 1854, and in 1856 was appointed clerk of the state supreme court. The town of Fairfax, in Marin County, where he owned a large estate, was named after him (Burke 1904, 587–88; Ellis 1939, 48–49; Gudde 1962, 100).

203.21–30   A prominent and pestilent creature . . . let the rascal go] This altercation took place in Sacramento, California, in 1859. Fairfax, the clerk of the state supreme court, quarreled with Harvey Lee (not "Ferguson") over Lee's recent appointment as the official reporter of court decisions. Fairfax slapped Lee, who drew a sword from his cane and wounded him in the lung. Fairfax thereupon threatened Lee with a pistol, but refrained from shooting him out of pity for his family (Ellis 1939, 49).

203.32–33   some of them were pirates . . . so were Drake and Hawkins] Sir Francis Drake (1540–96) and his cousin Sir John Hawkins (1532–95) raided Spanish ships under the patronage of Queen Elizabeth I.

204.1–4   one of the procession . . . Clement, by name—helped to sentence Charles to death] The ancestor who went to Spain has not been identified. The other putative ancestor, Gregory (not Geoffrey) Clements (1594–1660), was a London merchant and member of Parliament. In January 1649 he was a member of the high court of justice that tried Charles I and signed the king's death warrant. In 1660, when the monarchy was restored under Charles II, Clements went into hiding, but was found and executed that October. Extensive genealogical research has not revealed any family connection to Gregory; Clemens's earliest known ancestor was Richard Clements of Leicester (1506–71) (Lampton 1990, 78; Bell 1984, 4–7).

204.13–14   I am not bitter against Jeffreys] George Jeffreys (1645–89), lord chief justice of England and later lord chancellor, is known as "hanging Judge Jeffreys" for the punishments he handed out at the "bloody assizes" of 1685, when he tried the followers of the duke of Monmouth after their rebellion against James II. In 1688, when the king fled the country, Jeffreys was placed in the Tower of London, where he died the following year.

204.25–26 William Walter Phelps was our Minister at the Emperor's Court] Phelps (1839–94), a graduate of Yale University and Columbia Law School, served several terms as a congressman from New Jersey, and briefly as minister to Austria-Hungary (in 1881–82), before being appointed minister to the court of Wilhelm II, the emperor of Germany, in June 1889. Phelps's amiability and lavish hospitality made him very popular in Berlin society. This dinner no doubt took place in the winter of 1891, during the Clemenses' sojourn in that city. Clemens already knew Phelps, but the two families became better acquainted during that time (*MTB*, 3:933).

204.26–27 Count S., a cabinet minister . . . of long and illustrious descent] In a passage that Clemens deleted from his manuscript, "Count S." was identified as "the Empress Frederick's Hofmeister, Count Seckendorff." The Empress Frederick (1840–1901), the oldest daughter of Queen Victoria, was the widow of Frederick III and the mother of the current emperor. Her "master of the household" and close confidant was Count Goetz von Seckendorff (1841–1910), a lover of literature and the arts (Washington *Post*: "Von Seckendorff Dead," 3 Mar 1910, 9; "Revives Court Gossip," 4 Mar 1910, 1; Victoria 1913, 300–301). In the deleted manuscript passage Clemens further explained, "This nobleman was descended from the Seckendorff whom Wilhelmina, Margravine of Bayreuth, has made immortal in her Memoirs." This earlier Seckendorff was a minister to King Frederick William I of Prussia. Clemens owned two copies of the *Memoirs* of the king's daughter, Princess Wilhelmine (1709–58), published in 1877 and 1887. In 1897 he composed one chapter of a historical fiction about her before abandoning the project (*N&J3*, 295; Gribben 1980, 2:771–73; SLC 1897c; see Wilhelmine 1877).

205.18 Among the Virginian Clemenses were Jere. (already mentioned) and Sherrard] Jeremiah Clemens (1814–65) descended from Ezekiel Clemens of Virginia (see the note at 203.8), and was therefore a distant cousin. A lawyer, army officer, newspaper editor, and author, he was a member of the Alabama legislature, and later represented that state as a Democratic U.S. senator (1849–53). At the start of the Civil War he supported the Confederacy, but in 1864 changed allegiance to the Union. Sherrard Clemens (1820–80), another of Ezekiel's descendants, was trained as a lawyer. He represented Virginia as a Democratic U.S. congressman in 1852–53, and again in 1857–61. The "James Clemens branch" of the family descended from Ezekiel through his son James (1734–95). Clemens was acquainted with James's grandson, James Clemens, Jr. (1791–1878), a well-to-do doctor in St. Louis (Lampton 1990, 80; 21 June 1866 to JLC and PAM, *L1*, 346 n. 6; "Sherrard Clemens," New York *Times*, 3 June 1880, 5; *N&J1*, 36 n. 40; Bell 1984, 31–36; see also AD, 9 Feb 1906).

205.29–36 I was a rebel . . . with that kind of swine] Clemens alludes to his brief stint, at the beginning of the Civil War, in the Marion Rangers, a company in the Missouri State Guard. Although the guard was officially loyal to the Union (see Dempsey 2003, 256–72), the volunteers themselves believed they were fighting for the South: in "The Private History of a Campaign That Failed," Clemens's account of the experience, he claimed that he "became a rebel" (SLC 1885b; see the link note following 26 Apr 1861 to OC, *L1,* 121). By 1868 he had become a Republican, although his allegiance wavered in 1884, when—with the other so-called "mug-wumps"—he backed Grover Cleveland against James G. Blaine. In the 1876 election Clemens supported Republican Rutherford B. Hayes, who defeated Samuel J. Tilden, a Democrat. At a large Republican rally in Hartford on 30 September 1876, Clemens made a speech in support of Hayes, concluding with an introduction for Connecticut Senator Joseph R. Hawley ("Just Before the Battle," Hartford *Evening Post,* 2 Oct 1876, 2, in Scrapbook 8:25–27, CU-MARK; 13 and 14 Feb 1869 to OLL, *L3,* 97 n. 5; for Hawley see AD, 24 Jan 1906, note at 317.23–24). The only surviving letter from Sherrard Clemens to Clemens was written several weeks before this event, on 2 September, but it suggests that the description here was not exaggerated. Sherrard, evidently reacting to a newspaper notice, wrote:

> I regret, very deeply, to see, that you have announced your adhesion, to that inflated bladder, from the bowels of Sarah Burchard, Rutherford Burchard Hayes. You come, with myself, from Gregory Clemens, the regicide, who voted for the death of Charles and who was beheaded, disembolled, and drawn in a hurdle. It is good, for us, to have an ancestor, who escaped, the ignominy of being hung. But, I would rather have, such an ancestor, than adhere, to such a pitiful ninnyhammer, as Hayes, who is the mere, representative, of wall street brokers, three ball men, Lombardy Jews, European Sioux, class legislation, special priviledges to the few, and denial of equality of taxation, to the many—the mere convenient pimp, of the bondholders and office holders, about 150 thousand people, against over 40.000.000. If you, have, any more opinions for *newspaper scalpers,* it might be well, for your *literary* reputation, if you, should *keep them to yourself,* unless you desire to be considered a *"Political Innocent Abroad."* (Sherrard Clemens to SLC, 2 Sept 1876, CU-MARK)

205.41   married my father in Lexington in 1823, when she was twenty years old and he twenty-four] In autobiographical notes written in 1899 for Samuel Moffett, his nephew, to use as a basis for a biographical essay, Clemens asserted that his parents "began their young married life in Lexington, Ky., with a small property in land & six inherited slaves. They presently removed to Jamestown, Tennessee" (SLC 1899a, 2). Upon reading her son's essay, which repeated these facts, Pamela Moffett objected: "There are plenty of people who know that your grandma did not belong to the bluegrass region of Kentucky. She was born and brought up in Columbia Adair Co. in the southern part of the state, quite outside of the bluegrass region. She never lived in Lexington, and I doubt if she ever saw the place" (PAM to Moffett, 15 Oct 1899, CU-MARK; Moffett 1899, 523–24). "Lexington" was altered to "Columbia" when the essay was reprinted in book form the following year (SLC 1900a, 314–33). See the Appendix "Family Biographies" (pp. 654–55).

206.2–6   their first crop of children . . . may have been others] Clemens had six siblings, three of whom died in childhood. Five were born in Tennessee: Orion, Pamela Ann, Pleasant Hannibal (b. 1828 or 1829, died at three months), Margaret (1830–39), and Benjamin (1832–42). Henry (1838–58) was born in Missouri (*MTB,* 1:5–12; Wecter 1952, 33–36; see "Genealogy of the Clemens Family," *L1,* 382–83, and *Inds,* 311–15).

206.10–11   "Gilded Age," a book of mine] In this novel, written by Mark Twain with

Charles Dudley Warner (SLC 1873–74), the fictional Tennessee village of Obedstown is based on Clemens's knowledge of Jamestown.

206.11–12   My father left a fine estate behind him in the region round about Jamestown—75,000 acres] See the note at 208.37.

206.19–20   Nicholas Longworth, of Cincinnati . . . as good wine as his Catawbas] Longworth (1782–1863), known as the "father of American grape culture," was trained as a lawyer, but his primary interest was in horticulture. His cultivation of the Catawba grape made viticulture feasible in Ohio and resulted in a viable wine-making industry in the Cincinnati area.

206.25–26   James Lampton, who figures in the "Gilded Age" as "Colonel Sellers,"] Colonel Sellers, the irrepressible speculator and visionary in *The Gilded Age*, was based on James J. Lampton (1817–87), one of Jane Clemens's first cousins. He was trained in both law and medicine, but later in life had his own business as a cotton and tobacco agent. In the late 1850s he lived in St. Louis, where Clemens often visited when he was a Mississippi River pilot (*Inds,* 329).

206.35–36   John T. Raymond's audiences . . . dying with laughter over the turnip-eating scene] Comic actor John T. Raymond (1836–87), born John O'Brien, achieved his most notable success as Colonel Mulberry Sellers in *Colonel Sellers,* a theatrical adaptation of *The Gilded Age.* He opened in the play in New York City on 16 September 1874, and continued to perform the popular role intermittently for the rest of his life. The "turnip-eating scene" is in chapter 11 of the novel (*L6:* 22? July 1874 to Howells, 195 n. 4; 11 Jan 1875 to Raymond, 346 n. 1; 24 or 25 Aug? 1875 to Raymond, 528 n. 2; "Notes of the Stage," New York *Times,* 7 Feb 1887, 4).

207.12   Frank Mayo] Clemens met Mayo (1839–96) on the West Coast, probably between 1863 and 1865 in San Francisco, when Mayo was the leading actor at Maguire's Opera House. By the mid-1860s he was appearing in classical roles and character parts on the Boston and New York stages. He was best known for his title role in *Davy Crockett,* which he enacted more than two thousand times. In 1894 Clemens granted him permission to dramatize *Pudd'nhead Wilson,* and he appeared as the title character for the first time in April 1895. He died the following year while taking the play on a western tour. Clemens told Mayo's wife, in his letter of condolence, "We were friends—Frank Mayo and I—for more than thirty years; & my original love for him suffered no decay, no impairment in all that time. All his old friends can say the same; & it is a noble testimony to the sweetness of his spirit & the graces of his character" (16 July 1896 to Mayo, CU-MARK; 9–22 Mar 1872 to Mayo, *L5,* 61–62 n. 2).

207.23–28   *his* name was Eschol Sellers! . . . we changed the name back to Colonel Mulberry Sellers, in the plates] Early impressions of the first edition read "Eschol Sellers"; the American Publishing Company changed the name to "Beriah Sellers" in the plates for later printings. The name became "Mulberry Sellers" in the *Gilded Age* play and remained so for *The American Claimant* in 1892 (SLC 1874a, 1892; 8? Nov 1874 to Watterson, *L5,* 274 n. 2).

208.1–2   Cable and I were stumping the Union on a reading-tour] See "About General Grant's Memoirs," note at 86.12.

208.6   his son] Lampton had one son, Lewis (b. 1855) (Lampton 1990, 141).

208.31   Chapter] This is the first of three unnumbered "Chapter" headings within the piece (the others are at 214.31 and 218.24). Although Clemens never supplied the numbers for these headings, he did not delete them, and they have therefore been retained in the present text.

208.37   That ended the Tennessee Land] See "The Tennessee Land." Orion's trade has not been documented. In an 1881 letter, however, Pamela wrote to Orion and his wife, Mollie, "I have some good news to tell you: Charley [Webster] has sold the very last acre of Tennessee land. Is not that something to rejoice over? He traded it for a lot in St. Paul Minn. which was assessed last year at $800. or $850. and this year at $1,050" (20 May 1881, CU-MARK).

209.24–33   I remember it very well . . . place was alive with ghosts] Clemens's recollection cannot be entirely accurate: he was nearly four when his family moved to Hannibal in November 1839. Paine asserted that the incident occurred on a summer visit to the Quarles farm in Florida, and Dixon Wecter noted that Clemens was seven or eight at the time (*MTB*, 1:24–25, 30; Wecter 1952, 52–53; see also AD, 23 Feb 1906). A cousin and childhood playmate of Clemens's, Tabitha Quarles Greening, related a version of the story that closely resembles his. According to her, the family rode off "leaving little Sam making mud pies on the opposite side of the house":

> A half hour later my grandfather, Wharton Lampton . . . came riding along and found Sam busily engaged in his culinary work. He appreciated the situation, and, lifting the boy up in front of him, rode after the movers, and when he had traveled seven or eight miles caught up with them. So busy were they contemplating what was then considered a long journey and making plans for their future that the absence of the to-be "Mark Twain" had not been noticed. The matter was taken as a huge joke by all concerned, Sam included, and the journey resumed.
>
> To those who didn't know the Clemens family this may seem a little overdrawn, but it is absolutely true. ("Mark Twain's Boyhood," New York *Times,* 11 Nov 1899, 5)

209.34–38   My brother Henry . . . at that age] Henry did in fact burn his feet sometime before he was fifteen months old, when the family left Florida. Jane Clemens recalled in 1880:

> Henrys nurse was a negro boy they were playing in the yard. Henry was high enough to hold the top of the kettle and peep over. This time there was hot embers he ran into the hot embers bare footed. I set on one chair with a wash bowl on another & held Henry in my armes & his feet in the cold water or he would have gone in to spasems before your father got there from the store with the Dr. Mrs Penn came every day for some time & made egg oil to put on his feet. (JLC to OC, 25 Apr 80, CU-MARK)

209.41   incident of Benvenuto Cellini and the salamander] Traditional lore asserted that the salamander lived in fire. In his autobiography, the Italian artist Benvenuto Cellini (1500–71) recalled that when he was five, his father saw a salamander "sporting" in the flames of the fireplace. He boxed his son's ears to make him "remember that that lizard which you see in the fire is a salamander, a creature which has never been seen before by any one of whom we have credible information" (Cellini 1896, 7–8; it is not known which edition of this work Clemens owned: see Gribben 1980, 1:134).

209.42–210.1   that remarkable and indisputable instance in the experience of Helen Keller] Keller (1880–1968) became blind and deaf after an illness at nineteen months. Taught by Anne Sullivan to communicate with sign language and Braille, she graduated from Radcliffe College in 1904 with honors. Keller was world famous as a writer and social activist, working especially as a tireless advocate for the blind. Clemens had felt great admiration and affection for her since meeting her in March 1894, praising her as "this wonder of all the ages" in chapter 61 of *Following the Equator*. In *Midstream: My Later Life* she wrote a moving account of her 1909 visit with Clemens at Stormfield. In a speech later that year he called her "the most marvelous person of her sex that has existed on this earth since Joan of Arc" (Fatout 1976, 642). The "indisputable instance" was presumably the recollection of her early illness, especially the tender care of her mother, which she recorded in her autobiography (see AD, 30 Mar 1906, and AD, 20 Nov 1906; Keller 2003, 16; Keller 1929, 47–69).

210.12–13   In "Huck Finn" and in "Tom Sawyer Detective" I moved it down to Arkansas] The Quarles farm was the prototype for the Phelps farm in *Huckleberry Finn* and "Tom Sawyer, Detective" (SLC 1896c; *Inds,* 342).

211.36–42   "Uncle Dan'l," a middle-aged slave . . . and even across the Desert of Sahara in a balloon] Quarles freed his "old and faithful servant Dann" in 1855. Daniel appears as Uncle Dan'l in *The Gilded Age,* and as Jim in *Huckleberry Finn, Tom Sawyer Abroad* (SLC 1894a), and the stories "Huck Finn and Tom Sawyer among the Indians" (SLC 1884) and "Tom Sawyer's Conspiracy" (SLC 1897–?1902) (*Inds,* 316–17).

212.32–34   I used Sandy once, also; it was in "Tom Sawyer;" . . . I do not remember what name I called him by in the book] Sandy appears in chapters 1 and 2 of *Tom Sawyer* as Jim, "the small colored boy" (*Inds,* 346).

213.20   coleoptera] Bats belong to the order Chiroptera, not Coleoptera (beetles).

213.33–36   "Injun Joe" the half-breed . . . I starved him entirely to death in the cave, but that was in the interest of art; it never happened] Injun Joe is found dead in chapter 33 of *Tom Sawyer*. His prototype has not been identified. Several Hannibal residents thought that he was based on a half-Cherokee man named Joe Douglas, but Douglas himself claimed that he did not arrive in Hannibal until 1862, nine years after Clemens had left. In 1902 Clemens noted, "If this man you speak of is Injun Jo . . . he must be about 95 years old. The half-breed Indian who gave me the idea of the character was about 35 years old 60 years ago" ("Tom Sawyer Characters in Hannibal," St. Louis *Post Dispatch,* 2 June 1902, 5; "Recalling Days of Old," St. Louis *Globe-Democrat,* 1 June 1902, 4; "Mark Twain's Reunion," New York *Herald,* 15 June 1902, section V:9; Wecter 1952, 151, 299 n. 30; Edgar White 1924, 53).

213.36–37   "General" Gaines, who was our first town-drunkard before Jimmy Finn got the place] Gaines was one of the sources for the character of Huck's father in *Huckleberry Finn,* and Clemens used his expression "Whoop! Bow your neck and spread!" in the speech of a raftsman in chapter 3 of *Life on the Mississippi*. Gaines also appears in chapter 1 of "Huck and Tom among the Indians" and in the working notes for "Tom Sawyer's Conspiracy" (20 Feb 1870 to Bowen, *L4,* 50; *HF 2003,* 110, 407–11; *Inds,* 33–81, 134–213, 319–20; *HH&T,* 383). James Finn (d. 1845) was the primary model for Huck's father. In chapter 56 of *Life on the Mississippi,* Clemens wrote that he died "a natural death in a tan vat, of a combination of delirium tremens and spontaneous combustion." He also mentioned Finn in a letter to the San Francisco *Alta California* published on 26 May 1867 (SLC 1867h), and in chapter 23 of *A Tramp Abroad* (*Inds,* 318–19; see also AD, 8 Mar 1906).

214.3–4   The girl was the daughter of a St. Louis surgeon of extraordinary ability and wide celebrity] Joseph Nash McDowell (1805–68), originally from Kentucky, was a brilliant anatomist and teacher who was notorious for his eccentric behavior. (For example, after an armed mob attacked him for robbing a grave, he claimed that the light from a halo worn by his mother's ghost had helped him to escape.) In 1840 he founded McDowell College in St. Louis, the first medical school west of the Mississippi, where for twenty years he had a thriving surgical practice. During the Civil War he served as a surgeon for the Confederacy. In the 1840s he bought a large cave near Hannibal (the model for "McDougal's cave" in chapters 29–33 of *Tom Sawyer*), locked it, and stored his daughter's corpse there to see if the limestone in the cavern would "petrify" it. In chapter 55 of *Life on the Mississippi,* Clemens wrote that McDowell turned the cave into a "mausoleum for his daughter" (Ober 2003, 81–93; see AD, 16 Mar 1906, 418.29–419.8 and notes).

215.4–5   Florida doctors, Chowning and Meredith] For Meredith, see "Something about Doctors," note at 188.19–20. Dr. Meredith's Florida medical partner was Dr. Thomas Jefferson Chowning (b. 1809), who delivered the premature infant Samuel Clemens (Wecter 1952, 43).

215.20–28   In Mauritius . . . told these things by the people there, in 1896] Clemens visited Mauritius in April 1896 while on his world lecture tour. He wrote about this healer in Notebook 37 (TS p. 54, CU-MARK), but omitted the passage from *Following the Equator,* where he described his Mauritius visit in chapters 62 and 63.

215.31   Mrs. Utterback] The "faith-doctor" was Polly Rouse Utterback (1792?–1870). She is said to have treated Jane Clemens for neuralgia as well as toothache. She was the prototype for "Mother Utterback" in "Captain Montgomery," where Clemens quoted a sample of her "quaint conversation" (SLC 1866a). He also recalled Mrs. Utterback, though not by name, in "Christian Science and the Book of Mrs. Eddy" (SLC 1899c; *Portrait* 1895, 447; *Ralls Census* 1850, 156; Ellsberry 1965b, 1:35; Varble 1964, 180–81).

216.41   simblins] A type of squash with a scalloped ridge (Ramsay and Emberson 1963, 207).

217.25–27   immortal tales which Uncle Remus Harris . . . ghost story of the "Golden Arm"] Joel Chandler Harris (1848–1908), a native of Georgia, pursued a successful career as a journalist, but achieved literary fame as the author of *Uncle Remus: His Songs and His Sayings* (1880), a collection of animal folktales told in the voice of an elderly slave. Clemens became acquainted with Harris after writing him, probably in July 1881, to praise the book but did not meet him until April 1882, when he traveled down the Mississippi River in preparation for writing *Life on the Mississippi* (Julia Collier Harris 1918, 167; *N&J2,* 362 n. 21, 434, 468 n. 127, 551 n. 55; see also Gribben 1980, 1:295–96). Clemens wrote Harris again on 10 August 1881, "Uncle Remus is most deftly drawn, & is a lovable & delightful creation; he, & the little boy, & their relations with each other, are high & fine literature" (GEU). Clemens was fond of telling "The Golden Arm," and sent his own version to Harris, enclosed with this letter:

> Of course I *tell* it in the negro dialect—that is necessary; but I have not written it so, for I can't spell it in your matchless way. It is marvelous the way you & Cable spell the negro & creole dialects.
>
> Two grand features are lost in print: the wierd wailing, the rising & falling cadences of the wind, so easily mimicked with one's mouth; & the impressive pauses & eloquent silences, & subdued utterances, toward the end of the yarn (which chain the attention of the children hand & foot, & they sit with parted lips & breathless, to be wrenched limb from limb with the sudden & appalling "YOU got it!") I have so gradually & impressively worked up the last act, with a "grown" audience, as to create a rapt & intense stillness; & then made them jump clear out of their skins, almost, with the final shout. It's a lovely story to tell.
>
> Old Uncle Dan'l, a slave of my uncle's aged 60, used to tell us children yarns every night by the kitchen fire (no other light); & the last yarn demanded, every night, was this one. By this time there was but a ghostly blaze or two flickering about the back-log. We would huddle close about the old man, & begin to shudder with the first familiar words; & under the spell of his impressive delivery we always fell a prey to that climax at the end when the rigid black shape in the twilight sprang at us with a shout.
>
> When you come to glance at the tale you will recollect it—it is as common & familiar as the Tar Baby. Work up the atmosphere with your customary skill & it will "go" in print.

218.25   My uncle and his big boys . . . the youngest boy and I] John Quarles had two "big boys": Benjamin L. (1826–1902) and James A. (1827–66). "Fred" was a younger son, William Frederick (1833–98), who was about two years older than Clemens (Selby 1973, 23).

220.16   sardines] The manuscript contains the incomplete text of an anecdote that Clemens evidently deleted on the missing typescript. It begins, "An appetite for almost any delicacy can be permanently destroyed by a single surfeit of it. It is so with salt pork. One of my oldest friends has had proof of this. He ate too much salt pork in the Adirondacks one summer, twenty years ago, and has not liked it since." Clemens gives a full account of this incident in the Autobiographical Dictation of 10 October 1906, where he identifies his friend as Joseph Twichell (see also *N&J2,* 379 n. 67).

The Latest Attempt; The Final (and Right) Plan; Preface. As from the Grave

220 *title*–221 *title*   The Latest Attempt . . . As from the Grave] This three-part preface, like the "Early Attempt" preface, was written in mid-1906. With the exception of the middle section, it survives in manuscript. The text "I will construct a text . . . cannot be written" is a 1906 typescript with Clemens's insertions and revisions on it. The pages are all reproduced in facsimile in the Introduction (figures 5–12).

THE FLORENTINE DICTATIONS

[John Hay]

222.9   I was visiting John Hay, now Secretary of State] John Milton Hay (1838–1905) and Clemens probably first met in 1867 through a mutual friend, David Gray of the Buffalo *Courier*. Hay, like Clemens, grew up in a small town on the Mississippi River—Warsaw, Illinois, which is less than sixty miles from Hannibal, Missouri—and this common background fostered their friendship. Hay graduated from Brown University and was admitted to the Illinois bar in 1861. But he soon gave up the law to work as assistant private secretary to Abraham Lincoln (1861–65), living in the White House and becoming his intimate companion. At the end of the war Hay was appointed secretary to the U.S. legation in Paris, then chargé d'affaires at Vienna (1867–68), and secretary of legation at Madrid (1869–70). In 1870 he accepted an editorial position on the New York *Tribune* under Horace Greeley, and then, after Greeley's death in 1872, assisted the new editor, Whitelaw Reid. He gave up his *Tribune* position in 1875 and pursued a literary career as a poet, novelist, and biographer of Lincoln (see the note at 224.14–15). He achieved his chief fame, however, as a diplomat and statesman, serving as assistant secretary of state (1878–81), ambassador to Great Britain (1897–98), and secretary of state (1898–1905) (31 Dec 1870 to Reid, *L4,* 292–93, n. 3; 26 Jan 1872 to Redpath, *L5,* 35 n. 2; Thayer 1915, 1:83, 330–35).

222.9–11   Whitelaw Reid's house in New York . . . editing Reid's paper, the New York *Tribune*] Whitelaw Reid (1837–1912), a native of Ohio, joined the staff of the New York *Tribune* in 1868. After the death of Horace Greeley, its founder and editor, he became the owner as well as the editor-in-chief, and soon solicited contributions from Clemens. Reid was married in April 1881 and for six months, while he traveled in Europe with his bride, Hay replaced him as editor and lived in his New York house. Reid later served as minister to France (1889–92) and ambassador to Great Britain (1905–12) (link note following 20–22 Dec 1872 to Twichell, *L5,* 263; Thayer 1915, 1:405, 451–55).

222.27–28   a succession of foreign difficulties on his hands] In 1898 Hay inherited from his predecessor a dispute with Canada over Alaska's boundaries, which was not finally resolved until 1903. He helped to negotiate the Treaty of Paris (1898), ending the Spanish-American War. During the Boxer Rebellion (1900) he took action to rescue the Peking hostages, while successfully promoting the "Open Door Policy" toward China. Most recently, he had been responsible for several treaties (1900–1903) that allowed the United States to build the Panama Canal and secure its control over the Canal Zone (Thayer 1915, 2:202–49).

222.30–31   not any more scarable by kings and emperors and their fleets and armies] Clemens alludes to the conflict in 1901–3 with the German kaiser and his allies, who sent a fleet of warships to blockade Venezuelan ports and threatened to invade the country, in violation of the Monroe Doctrine (Thayer 1915, 2:284–90).

223.3   Mrs. Hay] Hay was married on 4 February 1874 to Clara L. Stone (1849–1915), whose father, Amasa Stone, was a wealthy contractor, railroad magnate, and philanthropist in Cleveland, Ohio. The couple had four children, and by Hay's own account, their marriage was a happy one. In 1905, shortly before his death, he recorded in his diary, "I have lived to be old, something I never expected in my youth. I have had many blessings, domestic happiness being the greatest of all" (Thayer 1915, 1:351, 2:408).

223.27–28 I confessed to forty-two and Hay to forty] At the time of his residence in Reid's New York house, Hay was forty-two and Clemens was forty-five. It is likely that Clemens's recollection here conflated more than one discussion with Hay, and that their conversation about autobiography took place several years earlier, in 1877 or 1878.

224.14–15 the historian of Mr. Lincoln] Hay and a collaborator, John G. Nicolay (1832–1901), published several works about Lincoln. Their association began in 1860, when Nicolay was appointed Lincoln's private secretary and recruited Hay to be his assistant. During their tenure in the White House they began to select materials for a biography of Lincoln, and in 1874 began to solicit additional material from Lincoln's son, Robert. In 1885 they signed a contract with the Century Company, receiving an unprecedented fifty thousand dollars for the serialization rights. Their biography was published in the *Century Magazine* from 1886 to 1890, and in the latter year was issued in ten volumes as *Abraham Lincoln: A History*. In a review of the work William Dean Howells wrote, "We can be glad of the greatest biography of Lincoln not only as the most important work yet accomplished in American history, but as one of the noblest achievements of literary art" (Howells 1891, 479). Four years later, in 1894, Hay and Nicolay published *Abraham Lincoln: Complete Works* (Thayer 1915, 2:16–18, 49).

Notes on "Innocents Abroad"

225.3–5 Mr. Goodman, of Virginia City, Nevada, on whose newspaper I had served ten years before, . . . walking down Broadway] After Clemens joined the staff of the Virginia City *Territorial Enterprise* in the fall of 1862, Joseph T. Goodman was quick to recognize his talent, and the two became lifelong friends (see AD, 9 Jan 1906, note at 252.32–253.1). The meeting described here took place in late December 1869 or early January 1870, when Goodman stopped in New York City en route to Europe (*L1:* 9 Sept 1862 to Clagett, 241 n. 5; 21 Oct 1862 to OC and MEC, 242 n. 2; 18 and 19 Dec 1869 to OLL, *L3,* 432 n. 2). In his original dictation, after the word "before," Clemens added, "and of whom I have had much to say in the book called 'Roughing It'—I seem to be overloading the sentence and I apologize—." He deleted the remark when revising the typescript for publication in the *North American Review* (NAR 12). It is also omitted here, because he did not make the revision as a "softening" to accommodate a contemporary readership.

225.17–19 dainty little blue and gold edition of Dr. Oliver Wendell Holmes's poems . . . exposed their dedications] Starting in 1856, the Boston firm of Ticknor and Fields published a series of handy volumes containing the best contemporary and classic literature, distinctively bound in blue cloth with gilt spine and edges. *Poems,* by physician and author Oliver Wendell Holmes, was first printed in this "Blue and Gold" series in 1862. The dedication Clemens refers to was that of the section entitled "Songs in Many Keys": "TO | THE MOST INDULGENT OF READERS, | THE KINDEST OF CRITICS, | MY BELOVED

MOTHER, | ALL THAT IS LEAST UNWORTHY OF HER | IN THIS VOLUME | Is Dedicated | BY HER AFFECTIONATE SON" (Holmes 1862). Clemens's dedication in *The Innocents Abroad* read: "To | My Most Patient Reader | and | Most Charitable Critic, | MY AGED MOTHER, | This Volume is Affectionately | Inscribed" (SLC 1869a, iii; Winship 1995, 122–23).

225.29–31   letter from the Rev. Dr. Rising . . . Sandwich Islands six years before] The Reverend Franklin S. Rising (1833?–68) arrived in Virginia City in April 1862 to become the rector of St. Paul's Episcopal Church. Suffering from poor health, he sailed for the Sandwich Islands in February 1866 to convalesce. Clemens was in the islands from March to July 1866, writing travel letters for the Sacramento *Union,* which he later used as the basis for chapters 63–74 of *Roughing It* (see "My Debut as a Literary Person," note at 128.22–24). Rising appears in chapter 47 of *Roughing It* as the naive minister baffled by the slang of Scotty Briggs. Since Rising died in a steamboat accident in December 1868, Clemens must have misremembered the year of his letter, which is not known to survive (30 July, 6, 7, 10, and 24 Aug 1866 to JLC and PAM, *L1,* 352, 354 n. 3; 19 and 20 Dec 1868 to OLL, *L2,* 333, 337 n. 2; *RI 1993,* 669).

226.12–13   I wrote to Dr. Holmes and told him the whole disgraceful affair] No such letter has been found, although in 1869 Clemens sent a copy of *The Innocents Abroad* to Holmes, who replied with a warm letter of appreciation (30 Sept 1869 to Holmes, *L3,* 364–65, 365–66 n. 1).

226.31–32   the proprietors of the *Daily Alta California* having "waived their rights" in certain letters] The preface concluded: "In this volume I have used portions of letters which I wrote for the *Daily Alta California,* of San Francisco, the proprietors of that journal having waived their rights and given me the necessary permission" (SLC 1869a). Clemens's dispute over his right to reuse his travel letters—which he describes in more detail below—took place in February and late April or early May 1868 (*L2:* 22? Feb 1868 to MEC, 198–99; 5 May 1868 to Bliss, 215–16; 27 and 28 Feb 1869 to Fairbanks, *L3,* 125 n. 3).

226.36–37   Early in '66 George Barnes . . . San Francisco *Morning Call*] Clemens worked as the local reporter for the *Morning Call* from June to October 1864 (not 1866). His boss, George Eustace Barnes (d. 1897), was a Canadian who moved to New York City as a boy and began his career there as a printer for the *Tribune.* Although he recognized Clemens's "peculiar genius," he soon discovered that his new employee was not suited for his tedious but demanding assignment to provide news about theaters, law courts, and other items of local interest. In chapter 58 of *Roughing It* Clemens noted, "I neglected my duties and became about worthless, as a reporter for a brisk newspaper. And at last one of the proprietors took me aside, with a charity I still remember with considerable respect, and gave me an opportunity to resign my berth and so save myself the disgrace of a dismissal" (*RI 1993,* 404; *CofC,* 11–25; see also AD, 13 June 1906).

226.41–227.1   Thomas Maguire, proprietor of several theatres . . . a lecture on the Sandwich Islands] Maguire (1820–96), originally from Ireland, was San Francisco's best-known theatrical manager for several decades. He arrived in California in 1849 and in 1850 opened his first theater. In the 1860s he owned the Opera House, on Washington Street near Montgomery, as well as Maguire's Academy of Music, a more splendid theater on Pine Street near Montgomery, where Clemens made his lecture debut on 2 October 1866. The lecture, which he later repeatedly revised, held a place in his platform repertoire for nearly a decade. For his own earlier account of the experience see chapter 78 of *Roughing It* (*RI 1993*, 532–36, 741–43; Lloyd 1876, 153–54).

227.2–3 "Admission one dollar; doors open at half past 7, the trouble begins at 8."] The advertisement in the San Francisco *Alta California* offered "Dress Circle" seats at one dollar, and "Family Circle" seats at fifty cents: "Doors open at 7 o'clock. The trouble to begin at 8 o'clock" ("Maguire's Academy of Music," 2 Oct 1866, 4). The phrase soon became proverbial. Less than a year later Clemens found it scrawled on the cell wall of a New York City jail (SLC 1867i).

227.7–9 I lectured in all the principal Californian towns and in Nevada . . . retired from the field rich . . . go around the world] Clemens toured the towns of northern California and western Nevada Territory, accompanied by his friend and agent Denis E. McCarthy, from 11 October to 10 November 1866. He lectured again in San Francisco on 16 November, and then in several other Bay Area towns, before making a final appearance in San Francisco on 10 December. According to Paine, Clemens earned about four hundred dollars from his first San Francisco lecture, after paying his expenses, but his profit from the ensuing tour is not known. His intention to visit the Orient and then circumnavigate the world grew out of an invitation from Anson Burlingame, the U.S. minister to China, who befriended him in the Sandwich Islands in June 1866 and urged him to visit Peking in early 1867 (see chapter 79 of *Roughing It; RI 1993*, 537–42, 743–45; *MTB*, 1:294; 27 June 1866 to JLC and PAM, *L1*, 347–48; see also AD, 20 Feb 1906).

227.9–12 proprietors of the *Alta* . . . twenty dollars per letter] For an analysis of how much Clemens was paid see 15 Apr 1867 to JLC and family, *L2*, 23–24 n. 1.

227.13–14 prospectus of Captain Duncan of the *Quaker City* Excursion] Charles C. Duncan (1821–98) of Bath, Maine, went to sea as a boy and took command of a ship while still a young man. In 1853 he became a New York shipping and commission merchant, but his business went bankrupt in 1865. Hoping to recover from this loss, in 1867 he arranged an excursion to Europe and the Holy Land sponsored by the parishioners of Henry Ward Beecher's Plymouth Church in Brooklyn. Duncan leased the *Quaker City* and had the ship completely refitted to provide the passengers with comfortable accommodations. The prospectus described the planned itinerary for the voyage (which was to last from early June to late October), the available shipboard amenities, the guidelines for side trips ashore, the cost of passage ($1,250 in currency), and estimated personal expenses ($5 per day in gold). All passengers were required to obtain the approval of a "committee on applications" (for details of the excursion see *L2:* 15 Apr 1867 to JLC and family, 23–26 nn. 1–4; "Prospectus of the *Quaker City* Excursion," 382–84).

227.15–16 I wrote and sent the fifty letters . . . complete my contract] For Clemens's list of the letters he thought he had written, and the number actually published, see 1–2 Sept 1867 to JLC and family, *L2*, 89–90 n. 1.

227 *footnote* MacCrellish] Frederick MacCrellish (1828–82) went to California from Pennsylvania in 1852 and worked on two San Francisco newspapers, the *Herald* and the *Ledger.* In 1854 he became the commercial editor of the *Alta California,* and a part owner two years later (2? Mar 1867 to the Proprietors of the San Francisco *Alta California, L2,* 17 n. 1).

228.3–6 Noah Brooks . . . praises of the generosity of the *Alta* people] Brooks (1830–1903) began his journalism career in Boston, and during the Civil War corresponded from Washington for the Sacramento *Union.* Clemens met Brooks in 1865 or 1866, when he was the managing editor of the *Alta California.* After returning East in 1871, Brooks worked for both the New York *Tribune* and the *Times,* and throughout his life wrote books on travel and history, as well as personal memoirs (7 Mar 1873 to Reid, *L5,* 313 n. 2). He is known to have written only one biographical sketch of Clemens: "Mark Twain in California," published in the *Century Magazine* in 1898. His account of the dispute, however, defends Clemens, not the "*Alta* people":

> During the summer of that year, while Clemens was in the Eastern States, there came to us a statement, through the medium of the Associated Press, that he was preparing for publication his letters which had been printed in the "Alta California." The proprietors of that newspaper were wroth. They regarded the letters as their private property. Had they not bought and paid for them? Could they have been written if they had not furnished the money to pay the expenses of the writer? And although up to that moment there had been no thought of making in San Francisco a book of Mark Twain's letters from abroad, the proprietors of the "Alta California" began at once their preparations to get out a cheap paper-covered edition of those contributions. An advance notice in the press despatches sent from California was regarded as a sort of answer to the alleged challenge of Mark Twain and his publishers. This sent the perplexed author hurrying back to San Francisco in quest of an ascertainment of his real rights in his own letters. Amicable counsels prevailed. The cheap San Francisco edition of the book was abandoned, and Mark Twain was allowed to take possession of his undoubted copyright, and his book of letters, entitled "The Innocents Abroad," was published in the latter part of that year—1868. (Brooks 1898, 99)

228.27–29 remark attributed to Disraeli . . . statistics."] This remark was first attributed to British statesman and author Benjamin Disraeli (1804–81) in the London *Times* on 27 July 1895. Although the quip appeared in print as early as 1892, it has not been traced with certainty to Disraeli. For a full discussion, see Shapiro 2006, 208.

[Robert Louis Stevenson and Thomas Bailey Aldrich]

228.30 Louis Stevenson] Clemens met Stevenson (1850–94) in April 1888. Ill with lung disease, Stevenson had spent the winter with his wife and stepson at a well-known health resort at Saranac Lake in the Adirondacks. He wrote to Clemens on 13 April, proposing that they meet in New York City, where he planned to stay from 19 to 26 April. Clemens, an admirer of *Treasure Island* and *Kidnapped,* was pleased when Stevenson wrote him that he had read *Huckleberry Finn* "four times, and am quite ready to begin again tomorrow" (13? Apr 1888,

CU-MARK). Later in the year Stevenson left on a Pacific cruise, spending the rest of his life on various islands in the South Seas (15 and 17 Apr 1888 to Stevenson, CLjC; Baetzhold 1970, 203–6).

229.6   I said that I thought he was right about the others] The "others" were presumably mentioned in the portion of the text that Clemens omitted, signaled by the line of asterisks. Another omission occurs below (at 229.22). The two gaps may have been part of the original 1904 typescript (now lost), but it is more likely that they were the result of Clemens's revisions before it was retyped in 1906.

229.7   Harte was good company and a thin but pleasant talker] See "Ralph Keeler," note at 150.2–4. Clemens's friendship with Harte had ended acrimoniously in 1877 with the failure of *Ah Sin,* the play on which they collaborated. In a later dictation Clemens explained that Harte's character spoiled his "sharp wit," which "consisted solely of sneers and sarcasms; when there was nothing to sneer at, Harte did not flash and sparkle" (AD, 4 Feb 1907; *N&J3,* 2).

229.8   Thomas Bailey Aldrich] Aldrich (1836–1907), an immensely popular poet and novelist and a pillar of the New England literary establishment, grew up in Portsmouth, New Hampshire, which served as the setting for many of his literary works. In 1852, lacking the funds to attend Harvard, he moved to New York City to work as a clerk in his uncle's business. He soon began to publish poems, and joined the editorial staffs of several journals. During 1861–62 he was a Civil War correspondent for the New York *Tribune.* He married Lilian Woodman in 1865 and moved to Boston, where in 1866 he became editor of the literary magazine *Every Saturday,* a post he held through 1874. He succeeded William Dean Howells as editor of the *Atlantic Monthly* in 1881, a position he retained until 1890. Clemens first met Aldrich, after some months' correspondence, in November 1871, and the two enjoyed a lifelong friendship. Among Clemens's tributes to Aldrich as a conversationalist is a remark recorded by Paine: "When Aldrich speaks it seems to me he is the bright face of the moon, and I feel like the other side" (*MTB,* 2:642 n. 1; 15 Jan 1871 to the Editor of *Every Saturday, L4,* 304 n. 1).

229.28–31   "Davis's Selected Speeches," . . . I have forgotten] No such series of books by "Davis" has been found. Possibly Stevenson (or Clemens) misremembered the name of William Brisbane Dick (1826–1901), coproprietor of Dick and Fitzgerald, a publishing firm founded in 1858. Compilations of prose and poetry, as well as books for entertainment or self-improvement, bulked large in their catalog, which included *Dick's Recitations and Readings, American Card Player, Dick's Comic Dialogues, Dick's Irish Dialect Recitations, Dick's Art of Wrestling,* and *Dick's Society Letter-Writer for Ladies,* all issued between 1866 and 1887. In 1867 Clemens himself had considered offering the publishers a collection of his Sacramento *Union* letters from the Sandwich Islands (Cox 2000, 85–86; *N&J1,* 176–77 n. 166).

[Villa di Quarto]

230.22   January] The first part of this dictation, through "under Providence" (237.8), survives in a typescript made by Jean Clemens in 1904 and revised by Clemens, now in the Mark Twain Papers. It is the only one of Jean's Florentine typescripts known to survive.

230.24   Villa Reale di Quarto] Olivia's doctors having advised a milder climate, Clemens removed his family to this Tuscan villa in the autumn of 1903. The family party consisted of Samuel, Olivia, Clara, and Jean, together with Katy Leary, their longtime servant, and Margaret Sherry, a trained nurse. They left New York in the steamer *Princess Irene* on 24 October, arriving at Genoa on 6 November. They made their way by train to Florence and were installed in the Villa di Quarto by 9 November. Later that month they were joined by Isabel V. Lyon, who had been hired in 1902 as Olivia's secretary, but had since assumed more general duties; Lyon's mother accompanied her (*MTB*, 3:1209; Notebook 46, TS p. 28, CU-MARK; Hartford *Courant*: "Clemens Family at Genoa," 7 Nov 1903, 15; "Mr. Clemens in Florence," 9 Nov 1903, 1; before 1 Nov 1903 to Unidentified, CU-MARK).

230.30   King of Würtemberg] After the collapse of the Napoleonic Empire in 1814, the Villa di Quarto was the home of Jérôme Bonaparte (1784–1860), Napoleon's youngest brother and the former king of Westphalia. He was not the king of Württemberg, but his wife, Princess Catherine, was a daughter of Frederick I, the first king of Württemberg (1754–1816).

230.31   a Russian daughter of the imperial house] The Grand Duchess Maria Nicolaievna (1819–76), a daughter of Tsar Nicholas I, purchased the villa in 1865 ("The Home of an American Countess in Italy," *Town and Country,* Sept 1907, 10–13).

230.35   Baedeker says it was built by Cosimo I, by [   ], architect] The typescript leaves a blank space for the name, and Clemens added the brackets, fulfilling his promise, further on in the text, to "suppress" the name of the architect (231.35–36). Clemens's likely source of information, the 1903 Baedeker guide to northern Italy, stated that the Villa di Quarto was built by Niccolò Tribolo (1500–1550) for Cosimo I de' Medici (1519–74), grand duke of Tuscany. Other sources indicate that the building dates from the preceding century (Baedeker 1903, 525; "The Home of an American Countess in Italy," *Town and Country,* Sept 1907, 10–13).

231.13   Countess Massiglia] The Countess Massiglia (1861–1953), whom Clemens called "the American bitch who owns this Villa," was born Frances Paxton, in Philadelphia (25–26 Feb 1904 to Rogers, Salm, in *HHR,* 557; U.S. National Archives and Records Administration 1950–54). She had been married and divorced before meeting Count Annibale Raybaudi-Massiglia, an Italian diplomat whom she married in about 1891. In addition to his remarks here, Clemens wrote about the countess in an unpublished sketch entitled "The Countess Massiglia" (SLC 1904a), and in his letters and notebooks. His only published mention of her during his lifetime was a glancing blow in a 1905 article, "Concerning Copyright" (Hartford *Courant*: "Mr. Clemens in Florence," 9 Nov 1903, 1; "Twain and Countess at Law," 22 Aug 1904, 7; "The Home of an American Countess in Italy," *Town and Country,* Sept 1907, 10; SLC 1905b, 2). By a strange coincidence, Isabel Lyon had known the countess slightly

in Philadelphia about 15 years ago. I came in contact with her because M^r. John Lockwood boarded with her mother at 20th & Cherry Streets. The mother was vicious; & the daughter who was then M^rs. Barney Campau, behaved abominably with M^r. Fred. Lockwood, ruining the happiness of that family. . . . When I saw her as I did the evening of the day that we arrived here—she of course said she had never seen me. I soon made it quite plain to her that she had— But enough— Here she remains, although she said she was going to spend the winter in Paris. She has furnished an apartment over the stables for herself & the big Roman steward of the place—& they two live there together to the annoyance of society. . . . Here she remains, a menace to the peace of the Clemens household, with her painted hair, her great coarse voice—her slitlike vicious eyes—her dirty clothes—& her terrible manners. (Lyon 1903–6, 36–38)

233.23   contadini] Peasants, farmers.

235.14   Blackwood] *Blackwood's Edinburgh Magazine,* a British literary monthly.

236.29–30   without her witness was not anything made that was made] Compare John 1:3, "and without him was not any thing made that was made."

238.34   majestic view, just mentioned] Clemens deleted the passage mentioning the view, which originally ended the previous paragraph. It described a "charming room" from which "one has a far stretching prospect of mountain and valley with Florence low-lying and bunched together far away in the middle distance."

239.23–24   Professor Willard Fiske . . . Walter Savage Landor villa] Fiske (1831–1904) was a scholar of Northern European languages whom the Clemenses had met through their mutual friend Charles Dudley Warner. A seasoned traveler, Fiske twice helped the Clemenses with their arrangements to lease Florentine villas, in 1892 and 1903. Having inherited a vast fortune, in 1892 he purchased a villa that had once belonged to English poet and essayist Walter Savage Landor (1775–1864) (Horatio S. White 1925, 3, 393–95; "Like a Romance," Hartford *Courant,* 27 May 1890, 3; see also AD, 10 Apr 1906).

240.42–241.1   little shiny white cherubs which one associates with the name of Della Robbia] The Florentine sculptor Luca della Robbia (1400?–1482) was the principal member of a family of artists who specialized in the use of glazed terra cotta to decorate walls and ceilings.

241.9   lesson in art lest the picture . . . perfection] At this point in the text Clemens dictated the following instruction to himself, "Here Insert Rhone Voyage." He clearly referred to a manuscript entitled "The Innocents Adrift," a highly fictionalized account of his ten-day boat trip down the Rhône River in September 1891. Clemens never finished it, but he continued to revise it and consider mining it for extracts; a brief one appears in chapter 55 of *Following the Equator.* In 1923, Paine published an abridged and rewritten version as "Down the Rhône." Clemens probably did not intend to interpolate it in its entirety. He may have meant to use the section of it wherein his fictive fellow voyagers debate the proper qualifications for the appreciation of high art. But clearly he did not follow through on his intention (SLC 1891a; SLC 1923, 129–68; Arthur L. Scott 1963).

242.22   our old Katy] Household servant Katy Leary had sailed with the Clemenses from New York in October 1903. At the time of this dictation she had been in their service for twenty-three years and had long been "regarded," as Clemens wrote, "as a part of the family" (Notebook 39, TS p. 51, CU-MARK; see also AD, 1 Feb 1906).

243.21   podere] Property, estate.

244.29   a good friend, Mrs. Ross, whose stately castle was a twelve minutes' walk away] Janet Duff Gordon Ross (1842–1927), the daughter of a baronet, lived at Poggio Gherardo, a villa that she and her husband had purchased in 1888. She enjoyed a wide social circle of writers and artists, and published several books of her own—a family biography, sketches of Tuscan life, and collections of autobiographical essays. She described her 1892 meeting with Clemens:

> In May our friend Professor Fiske, who lived near Fiesole, brought a delightful man to see us, Mr. Clemens, better known as Mark Twain. We at once made friends. The more we saw of him the more we liked the kindly, shrewd, amusing, and quaint man. He asked whether there was any villa to be had near by, and from our terrace we showed him Villa Viviani, between us and Settignano. I promised to get him servants and have all ready for the autumn. (Ross 1912, 318–19)

244.31   year spent in the Villa Viviani] The Clemenses stayed at the villa from late September 1892 to late March 1893.

244.35   When we were passing through Florence] The source of the text from here to the end is Clemens's manuscript, now in the Mark Twain Papers.

246.46   the Magnificent Lorenzo] Lorenzo de' Medici, known as "the Magnificent" (1449–92), was the effectual ruler of Florence from 1469 to his death.

Autobiographical Dictation, 9 January 1906

250.19–21   you are going to collect from that mass of incidents . . . and then write a biography] Clemens was speaking to Albert Bigelow Paine (1861–1937), who planned to write his biography. Paine grew up in Iowa and Illinois, leaving school at fifteen. At twenty he went to St. Louis, where he worked as a photographer; several years later he operated a photographic supply business in Kansas. After one of his stories was accepted by *Harper's Weekly,* he moved to New York in 1895, where he wrote for periodicals and published books for both children and adults. In 1899 he became an editor of *St. Nicholas,* a magazine for young people, and in 1904 published *Th. Nast: His Period and His Pictures,* the first of his many biographies. His *Mark Twain: A Biography* appeared in 1912, and was followed by editions of the *Letters* (1917), *Autobiography* (1924), and *Notebook* (1935). Paine explained in his edition of the autobiography:

> It was in January, 1906, that the present writer became associated with Mark Twain as his biographer. Elsewhere I have told of that arrangement and may omit most of the story here. It had been agreed that I should bring a stenographer, to whom he would dictate notes for my use, but a subsequent inspiration prompted him to suggest that he might in this way continue his autobiography, from which I would be at liberty to draw material for my own undertaking. We began with this understanding, and during two hours of the forenoon, on several days of each week, he talked pretty steadily to a select audience of two, wandering up and down the years as inclination led him, relating in his inimitable way incidents, episodes, conclusions, whatever the moment presented to his fancy. (*MTA,* 1:ix–x)

Paine devoted a chapter of his biography to an account of his conversation with Clemens at The Players club dinner on 3 January 1906, and the "arrangement" they agreed on three days later (see *MTB,* 4:1257–66; AD, 10 Jan 1906). Clemens's secretary, Isabel V. Lyon, made a note of their discussion in her diary on 6 January 1906:

> Albert Bigelow Paine came this morning to talk over the matter of writing M^r. Clemens's Biography—M^r. Clemens has consented to have some shorthander come & take down the chat that is to flow from M^r. Clemens's lips—I hope it may prove inspirational—The commercial machine (Columbia Graphophonic) that M^r. Clemens was looking upon as a boon—hasn't proved so—He dictated his birthday speech into it—and a few letters—but that is all—There is something infinitely sad in the voice as it is reproduced from the cylenders—and how strickening it would be to hear the voice of one gone— (Lyon 1906, 6)

The "shorthander," one of the "select audience of two" for the Autobiographical Dictations, was stenographer and typist Josephine S. Hobby (1862–1950), formerly a secretary to Mary Mapes Dodge, the editor of *St. Nicholas* magazine from 1872 until her death in 1905 (for the "birthday speech" see AD, 12 Jan 1906; Lyon 1906, 47, 71–72; "Aide to Mark Twain Dies," New York *Times,* 31 Jan 1950, 21; see also the Introduction, pp. 25–27).

251.19–29   I want to read . . . quoted six years later at $160,000,000] The article Clemens "read" from has not been found in the New York *Times.* His account is substantially confirmed by independent sources, however, including the astonishing rise in the 1874–75 stock prices (see Lord 1883, 309, 314–15). John W. Mackay (1831–1902) was born in Ireland and came to America as a boy. From 1851 until 1859 he was a miner in California and then moved to Nevada. In January 1872, in partnership with James G. Fair (1831–94), also originally from Ireland, and two others (see the note at 252.25), Mackay took control of the Consolidated Virginia mine, whose stock in the previous year had fallen below $2 per share. The "Big Bonanza" silver strike in the Consolidated Virginia and the adjacent California mine, made in October 1874, was ultimately valued as high as $1.5 billion (*L6:* 24 Mar 1875 to Bliss, 425 n. 2; 29 Mar and 4 Apr 1875 to Wright, 439 nn. 5, 9).

251.32–38   when I came to Virginia in 1862 . . . forty dollars a week attached to it] Clemens arrived in Aurora, in the rich Esmeralda mining district claimed by both Nevada Territory and California, in April 1862. There, living hand to mouth, he immediately set about wielding pick and shovel while energetically speculating in mining "feet," or shares, to the extent his limited funds allowed. That April he also began contributing letters, under the pen name "Josh," to the Virginia City *Territorial Enterprise.* Before the end of July, partly on the strength of the "Josh" letters, none of which survive, he was offered the post of local reporter, as a temporary substitute for the paper's local editor, William Wright (1829–98), best known under his pen name, "Dan De Quille." By late September 1862, having failed to strike it rich in Aurora, Clemens had relocated to Virginia City and was reporting for the *Enterprise.* His earliest extant articles appeared in the paper on 1 October 1862 (see *ET&S1,* 389–91). He remained on the *Enterprise* staff until he left Virginia City for San Francisco in late May 1864. For his vivid accounts of his experiences in Aurora and Virginia City see his letters of the period (10? Apr 1862 to OC through 28 May 1864 to Cutler, *L1,* 184–301) and chapters 35–37, 40–49, 51–52, and 54–55 of *Roughing It.*

251.41–42   one column of leaded nonpareil every day] Nonpareil was a small (six point) type, commonly used in newspapers.

252.1–9   I met John Mackay . . . I will try to get a living out of this] It is not known when Mackay and Clemens first became acquainted. According to the *Second Directory of Nevada Territory,* by sometime in 1863 Mackay was living on C Street and was working as the superintendent of the Milton Silver Mining Company (Kelly 1863, 254). Clemens gave a similar account of their Virginia City encounter in an 1897 interview (Budd 1977, 78).

252.10–11   I left Nevada in 1864 to avoid a term . . . have to explain that] See the Autobiographical Dictation of 19 January 1906.

252.21   chimney] A "chimney," or "ore-shoot," was "a body of ore, usually of elongated form, extending downward within a vein" (Raymond 1881, 19, 20).

252.25   O'Brien—who was a silver expert in San Francisco] William Shoney O'Brien (1826–78), like Mackay and Fair a native of Ireland, had come to San Francisco in 1849 where he had a succession of businesses—including a tobacco shop, a newspaper agency, a ship chandlery, and a saloon—before becoming a dealer in silver stocks. He and his San Francisco partner, James Clair Flood (1826–89), along with Mackay and Fair, came to be known as the "Bonanza Firm" and together controlled the Comstock Lode (Oscar Lewis 1947, 222–23; Hart 1987, 358–59).

252.30–31   John P. Jones . . . thirty years] See "The Machine Episode," note at 104.16–17.

252.32–253.1   Joseph T. Goodman . . . Williams . . . sold the paper to Denis McCarthy and Goodman] Goodman (1838–1917) emigrated from New York to California in 1854 and worked as a compositor and writer on San Francisco newspapers. He and McCarthy (1840–85) were fellow typesetters on two journals there, the *Mirror* and the *Golden Era,* before buying into the Virginia City *Territorial Enterprise,* then owned by Jonathan Williams (d. 1876), in March 1861. By 1865 Goodman was the sole proprietor; he sold out at a considerable profit in February 1874, not to "some journeyman" but to the Enterprise Publishing Company (21 Oct 1862 to OC and MEC, *L1,* 242 n. 2; Angel 1881, 317).

253.20–22   And when the Bonanza . . . to San Francisco] Following his February 1874 sale of the *Enterprise,* Goodman had at least two opportunities to see Clemens that year. In April, after moving to San Francisco, he and his first wife, Ellen (1837?–93), stopped in the East on their way to Europe; they returned in October, the same month the "Big Bonanza" silver discovery was made. Although Goodman could have met with Clemens in April, it is more likely that he would have needed a loan at the trip's conclusion if he found himself temporarily short of ready cash for the return to San Francisco (*L6:* 23 Apr 1874 to Finlay, 115–16 n. 5; 29 Mar and 4 Apr 1875 to Wright, 439 n. 8).

253.27–254.4   Denis . . . never got a start again] After selling his interest in the *Enterprise* in 1865, McCarthy went to San Francisco, where he invested unsuccessfully in the stock market and soon lost his considerable profit. He was working as the managing editor of the San Francisco *Chronicle* when the "Big Bonanza" was discovered in 1874, and through successful speculation earned another fortune. He returned to Virginia City and bought the *Evening*

Chronicle, which became, within a year, the most widely circulated newspaper in Nevada history. Goodman told Clemens in 1881 that McCarthy's strong "appetite for liquor" had made him seriously ill, and his death four years later was apparently the result of "dissipation" (Goodman to SLC, 11 Dec 1881, CU-MARK; Angel 1881, 326–27; "Death of D. E. McCarthy," Virginia City *Evening Chronicle,* 17 Dec 1885, 2).

254.5–14 Joe Goodman . . . several times what he paid for it originally] Goodman was a member of the San Francisco Stock and Exchange Board from 1877 to 1880 and then became a raisin farmer in Fresno, southeast of the city. He had informed Clemens of the change in occupations in a letter of 9 March 1881:

> I got busted in San Francisco—dead broke. Mackay (who owns half of the *Enterprise*) offered to buy the other half and give it to me; but I saw no profit in it,—Virginia City will soon be as desolate a place as Baalbec,—and, besides, my health was too poor to undertake literary work; so I borrowed $4,000 from Mackay and have started in to vine-growing in this region. I don't know how it will turn out—and don't care much. We are about 200 miles from San Francisco, in the San Joaquin Valley. Four or five years ago it was all a desert, but they have brought in irrigating ditches and the land is being rapidly settled—some places already being marvelously fine. I have only 130 acres, but it is quite as much as I shall be able to get under cultivation. At present it is the merest and most desolate speck in the desert you can imagine. Mrs. Goodman gets so homesick she almost cries her eyes out. But, if I live, I will make it a paradise—on a small scale. If you and Mrs. Clemens should ever come to California you will want to see this wonderful southern country, and I extend you a hearty invitation to come and visit us. Should you chance to come soon there would be only the original desert prospect, so far as my ranch is concerned, but there shall be a fountain of welcome for you, and an oasis of hospitality, and—to make the picture complete—I will import a bird for the occasion to sing in the solitude. (CU-MARK)

Goodman remained in Fresno until 1891, when he moved to Alameda, California (Goodman to Alfred B. Nye, 6 Nov 1905, CU-BANC; Joseph L. King 1910, 59, 339, 344).

254.16–23 Before this eastern visit . . . published in about 1901] In a letter of 24 May 1902, Goodman informed Clemens:

> Eighteen years ago my attention was called to the inscriptions on the ruins of Central America and Yucatan, and I inconsiderately said I could decipher them. I worked seven years without accomplishing a thing, but then I succeeded in breaking an opening into the mystery. In 1895 they sent for me to come to London and publish the results of my studies up to then. I telegraphed you from Chicago to try to meet me in New York, but as I heard nothing from you I supposed you didn't get the message in time. Since then I've kept on working at the glyphs until I have the whole thing pretty well thrashed out, and am now putting it into book form. So far as concerns me and mine, the pursuit has been a sheer waste of time, money and nerve force. There is no hope of profit in it. Not a thousand persons care anything about the study. The only compensation is that I found out what nobody else could, and that my name will always be associated with the unraveling of the Maya glyphs, as Champollion's is with the Egyptian. But that is poor pay for what will be twenty years' hard work. I will send you a copy of the London volume—not that I think

it will interest you at all, but as a curiosity. I have since discovered that I made a few mistakes in it, but the bulk of it will stand the test of all time. (CU-MARK)

At the urging of prominent archaeologist Alfred P. Maudslay (1850–1931), Goodman traveled to London in 1895. There in 1897 he published his findings as *The Archaic Maya Inscriptions,* a book-length work that Maudslay later made the appendix to his own multivolume *Archaeology.* In 1898 Goodman published a monograph, *The Maya Graphic System: Reasons for Believing It to Be Nothing but a Cipher Code,* and in 1905 he published an article, "Maya Dates" (Tozzer 1931, 403, 407–8; Goodman 1897; Goodman 1898; Goodman 1905; Maudslay and Goodman 1889–1902). Modern scholarship has validated Goodman's confidence in his discoveries. Michael D. Coe, in *Breaking the Maya Code,* noted that Goodman "made some truly lasting contributions," among them "calendrical tables . . . still in use among scholars working out Maya dates" and his "amazing achievement" in proposing "a correlation between the Maya Long Count calendar and our own" (Coe 1999, 112, 114). Jean François Champollion (1790–1832), considered the father of Egyptology, was the first to decipher Egyptian hieroglyphics.

254.24 account in the New York *Times*] The article referred to at 251.20, which has not been found.

254.24–29 strike in the great Bonanza . . . now confessedly exhausted] The total value of the Consolidated Virginia, the California, and the other mines of the Comstock Lode declined from more than $393 million in 1875 to just under $7 million in 1880 (Angel 1881, 619–20).

Autobiographical Dictation, 10 January 1906

254.30–31 I have to make several speeches . . . last two months] Between 10 November 1905 and 11 April 1906, Clemens spoke on at least twenty-five occasions. The events included a Washington, D.C., dinner attended by members of the Roosevelt administration (25 November); his own seventieth birthday dinner (5 December); a benefit for Russian Jews (18 December); a dinner for him at The Players (3 January); a Tuskegee Institute fundraiser at Carnegie Hall (22 January); a meeting of the Gridiron Club in Washington, attended by Theodore Roosevelt (27 January); remarks on copyright to the House of Representatives (29 January); a New York Press Club dinner in memory of Charles Dickens (8 February); a Barnard College reception (7 March); a meeting of the New York State Association for Promoting the Interests of the Blind (29 March); a Vassar College Students' Aid Society benefit (2 April); and a dinner for Russian author Maxim Gorky (11 April) (see Schmidt 2008a for a full list; texts of several of the speeches can be found in Fatout 1976; New York *Times*: "Choate and Twain Plead for Tuskegee," 23 Jan 1906, 1; "President in 'Panama' Has a Jolly Time," 28 Jan 1906, 4; "Twain on Rockefeller, Jr.," 8 Feb 1906, 9; "Three New Plays at Vassar Aid Benefit," 3 Apr 1906, 9; "Gorky and Mark Twain Plead for Revolution," 12 Apr 1906, 4).

255.18–19 my friends of ancient days in the Players Club gave me a dinner] The dinner for Clemens was held on 3 January 1906 at a house at 16 Gramercy Park in New York, which actor Edwin Booth (1833–93) had given to the club for its headquarters. Booth had conceived of the club as a place where actors could "associate on intimate and equal terms with the fore-most authors, painters, sculptors, architects, musicians, editors, publishers, and patrons of the arts" (Lanier 1938, 47). Clemens was a charter member and had attended the organizational luncheon convened by Booth at Delmonico's restaurant on 6 January 1888. Walter Oettel, Edwin Booth's former valet and the longtime majordomo of The Players club, recalled that at the 3 January 1906 dinner "the table decorations and favors were stuffed frogs, à propos of his tale, 'The Jumping Frog.'" Oettel reported that the dinner was hosted by some two dozen club members, among them Brander Matthews (see the note at 255.24), who presided; John H. Finley (1863–1940), author, former *Harper's Weekly* editor, and president of City College of New York; Daniel Frohman (see the note at 255.19–22); poet and *Century Magazine* editor Richard Watson Gilder (see "About General Grant's Memoirs," note at 77 *footnote*); poet and *Century Magazine* associate editor Robert Underwood Johnson (1853–1937); Francis D. Millet (see the note at 255.28–29); David A. Munro, who was unable to attend (see AD, 16 Jan 1906, and note at 284.7); Albert Bigelow Paine; and Robert Reid (see AD, 16 Jan 1906, note at 284.7–8; Oettel 1943, 53–54, 94; *N&J3*, 429 n. 73; Lanier 1938, passim; "Players Dine Mark Twain," New York *Times,* 4 Jan 1906, 2).

255.19–22   an absence of three years, occasioned by the stupidity of the Board . . . it amounted to the same] The original board members were Booth; actor Lawrence Barrett (1838–91); merchant William Bispham (d. 1909); brothers Augustin (1838–99) and Joseph F. Daly (1840–1916), the former an eminent playwright, producer, and theater owner, the latter a lawyer and judge; actor Henry Edwards (d. 1891); dramatic critic, biographer, and *Harper's Magazine* literary editor Laurence Hutton (1843–1904); actor Joseph Jefferson (1829–1905); and theatrical manager Albert M. Palmer (1838–1905). Bispham, Joseph F. Daly, Jefferson, and Palmer were still on the board in 1903 when Clemens withdrew from the club (see AD, 21 Mar 1906, for Clemens's further account of his "expulsion"). The other board members then were author Charles E. Carryl (1841–1920); actor John Drew (1853–1927); theatrical manager and producer Daniel Frohman (1851–1940); actor and theatrical manager Frank W. Sanger (1849–1904); and actor Francis Wilson (1854–1935). Carryl had sent Clemens a form letter, dated 12 January 1903, expelling him for "non-payment of dues." In the top margin of the letter Clemens wrote: "Expelled! (by the mistake of an idiot Secretary)" (CU-MARK). The invitation to return, sent on 10 November 1904, slightly misquoted Carolina Oliphant's popular lyric, addressed to Bonnie Prince Charlie: "Will ye no com back again? / Better lo'ed ye canna be" (Reid et al. to SLC, NNWH). On 11 November Clemens replied, on mourning stationery, "Surely those lovely verses went to Prince Charlie's heart, if he had one, & certainly they have gone to mine. I shall be glad & proud to come back again. . . . It will be many months before I can foregather with you, for this black border is not perfunctory, not a convention; it symbolizes the loss of one whose memory is the only thing I worship" (11 Nov 1904 to Reid and The Players, NNWH). In her 1906 diary, Lyon noted Clemens's triumphant return from the dinner:

> Mr Clemens has just come home at midnight, from a dinner at "The Players" where he was made an honorary member. It was a great night for all the rest of them, because he had stayed away so long.

At midnight he stood at the foot of my flight of stairs in happy mood, with a Japanese paper frog hanging by a hind leg from his coat lapel, & this he handed to me as I went down the stairs to greet him. He knew I would be up & waiting to register his safe return. (Lyon 1906, unnumbered leaf inserted after p. 2)

255.24   Brander Matthews] Matthews (1852–1929), a prominent writer and critic, was a professor of literature and drama at Columbia University (1892–1924). He and Clemens first met in March 1883 when Clemens joined the Kinsmen club, of which Matthews was a founding member (see "Travel-Scraps I," note at 113.10). In 1887 and 1888 the two men had disagreed in print about international copyright, which placed a temporary strain on their friendship. In 1922 Matthews recalled that episode and other details of their acquaintance in "Memories of Mark Twain" (Matthews 1922; see also Matthews 1917, 231, and *N&J3,* 345–46, 348, 362–68, 373).

255.28–29   Frank Millet (painter)] Francis D. Millet (1846–1912) was born in Massachusetts. He earned a degree in literature from Harvard University, but decided to study art in Antwerp, Venice, and Rome. He later served as an artist-correspondent during the Russo-Turkish War (1877–78). Many of his portraits and murals depicted historical subjects. He died on the *Titanic.*

255.33–36   Sculpture . . . make a speech in Saint-Gaudens's place] Sculptor Augustus Saint-Gaudens (see AD, 16 Jan 1906, note at 284.7–8) was one of three Players who were unable to attend and sent telegrams of regret; the others were David Munro and author Thomas Bailey Aldrich (see "Robert Louis Stevenson and Thomas Bailey Aldrich"). It is not known who spoke extemporaneously "in Saint-Gaudens's place" ("Players Welcome Mark Twain," New York *Tribune,* 4 Jan 1906, 7).

256.5–6   For I came without a text, and these boys furnished plenty of texts for me] The texts of the other speeches have not been found. Clemens "told the amusing story of English Mary," which is reprinted in his "Speech at The Players, 3 January 1906" (Oettel 1943, 54–57; see the Appendix, pp. 662–63). Clemens had first told this story in three letters of 17 July 1877 to his wife in Elmira, as the actual events were unfolding in their Hartford household. In 1897 or 1898 he fictionalized the episode in a tale he called "Wapping Alice," which he did not succeed in publishing in his lifetime. Then he reworked it again in his Autobiographical Dictation of 10 April 1907 (for the early versions see SLC 1981, 7–24, 39–67). Appropriately, he read the "Jumping Frog" story (SLC 1865) as an encore.

256.17–19   one which I am to attend in Washington on the 27th . . . President and Vice-President of the United States] At the 27 January annual dinner of the Gridiron Club, a prestigious and convivial journalistic society organized in 1885, "Mr. Samuel L. Clemens was in his happiest vein, and spoke for nearly twenty minutes. He was introduced by an alleged roustabout on a Mississippi steamboat who heaved the lead and shouted 'mark twain' as he reported the depth of the water" ("A Night in Panama," Washington *Post,* 28 Jan 1906, 1, 6). The Gridiron Club forbade reporting of speeches, and no text of Clemens's remarks is known to survive. President Theodore Roosevelt also spoke, as did other members of his administration, and numerous congressmen and other luminaries attended, but Vice-President Charles W. Fairbanks (1852–1918) was not among them.

256.26   Morris incident] See Clemens's account below and the note at 258.34.

257.6–9   Even yesterday . . . in banks] On 6 September 1905, a New York State legislative committee had begun an investigation of longtime and widespread abuses in the life insurance industry, including extravagant executive salaries; illegal political contributions, both to finance electoral campaigns (especially to Republican presidential candidates) and to influence legislation; illicit dealing in stocks and bonds; and entangling alliances with banks. The investigation—reported exhaustively in the New York press—focused primarily on the Mutual Reserve Life Insurance Company, the New York Life Insurance Company, and the Equitable Life Assurance Society. On 22 February 1906 the committee issued its report to the New York State legislature, along with twenty-five proposed reform bills, all of which were signed into law by 27 April 1906. The executives who came under fire were Richard A. McCurdy and his son Robert H. McCurdy, president and foreign manager, respectively, of Mutual Life (these two, and the senior McCurdy's son-in-law, collected $4,643,926 in salaries and commissions between 1885 and 1905); John A. McCall and his son John C. McCall, president and secretary, respectively, of New York Life; Chauncey M. Depew, Republican senator from New York and for years the highly paid special counsel of Equitable Life and a member of its executive committee; and James W. Alexander and James H. Hyde, president and first vice-president of Equitable Life, respectively. The influence of these men extended far beyond the three insurance companies. In October 1905, for example, Hyde was reported to be a director of forty-five corporations and Depew a director of seventy-four. As a result of the investigation at least some of those connections were severed. By 10 January 1906 the McCurdys, Depew, the elder McCall, Alexander, and Hyde had all resigned from—or failed to be reelected to—bank directorships (New York *Times,* numerous articles, 15 Aug 1905–28 Apr 1906). Clemens returns to the subject in his Autobiographical Dictation of 16 February 1906.

257.9–13   we have to-day . . . Standard Oil Corporation . . . how much crippled] The Standard Oil Company and its subsidiaries were being sued in the New York Supreme Court by Missouri Attorney General Herbert S. Hadley, in support of his ongoing suits in Missouri courts for Standard's violation of that state's antitrust laws. On 10 January 1906, the New York *Times* reported at length on the previous day's New York proceedings, highlighting the evasive testimony and arrogant demeanor of the vice-president of Standard Oil, Clemens's good friend Henry H. Rogers (New York *Times:* "H. H. Rogers Summoned to the Supreme Court," 10 Jan 1906, 1; "Herbert S. Hadley—the Man from Missouri," 14 Jan 1906, SM4; see also "Henry H. Rogers").

257.13–15   we have Congress threatening to overhaul the Panama Canal Commission . . . recently added eleven millions] In mid-December 1905 Congress had "added" $11 million to the $59 million already expended since 1904 on preparatory work and to acquire the rights and assets of the failed French Panama Canal company. Nevertheless, the New York *Times* observed on 21 December, the commission had "not yet decided what kind of canal it will build. Neither the engineers nor the Commissioners know whether we are to spend $150,000,000 more, or $200,000,000 more. Nobody knows how much the canal will cost." On 9 January 1906, the Senate voted to investigate "all matters relating to the Panama Canal." Actual construction began later in 1906. The canal opened in 1914, at a total cost of about $375 million (New York *Times:* "Money for the Canal," 12 Dec 1905, 8; "Taft Agrees to Accept $11,000,000 for Canal," 13 Dec 1905, 4; "A Rooseveltian Episode," 21 Dec 1905, 8; "Panama Investigation Voted by the Senate," 10 Jan 1906, 4; "The President's Responsibility," 22 Jan 1906, 6; Panama Canal Authority 2008).

257.16–17   Church and State separated in France] A bill providing for the separation had become effective on 7 December 1905. It marked "the culmination of the strained relations which have long existed between the French Government and the Vatican" and ended a system dating "from 1801, when the Concordat was signed by Pius VII. and Napoleon. Under the Concordat the churches were Government property, and the clergy was paid by the State." The change was not universally welcomed: there was rioting and other protest "encouraged and indirectly fomented by leaders of the anti-Republican Party, and probably to some extent by the priests of the Roman Church" (New York *Times:* "End of State Church Declared in France," 7 Dec 1905, 8; "The Religious Troubles in France," 4 Feb 1906, 6).

257.17–18   we have a threat . . . Morocco question] Since late 1905 France and Germany had been moving toward war over political control of (and commercial access to) Morocco. Germany had not joined a 1904 agreement in which Great Britain, Spain, and Italy had accepted French domination, and now objected to France's "special privileges"—especially in policing the country (New York *Times:* "The Conference of Algeciras," 6 Jan 1906, 8; "Clash in Moroccan Conference Expected," 7 Jan 1906, 3). The conflict was resolved diplomatically on 31 March 1906 with a new agreement, largely brokered by the United States, that addressed the commercial issues and provided for shared police responsibility without undermining French hegemony ("Morocco Conference Ends with Agreement," New York *Times,* 1 Apr 1906, 4).

257.18–21   we have a crushed revolution in Russia . . . three centuries] The Russian Revolution of 1905 began in January, on "Bloody Sunday," when troops fired on a peaceful protest march in St. Petersburg, killing more than a thousand participants. Rebellion against the tyranny of Tsar Nicholas II (1868–1918) then spread, culminating in September and October of that year in a general strike that paralyzed the entire country. Nicholas was forced to issue his October Manifesto, providing for a parliament and freedom of speech, the press, and assembly. He soon reneged on these reforms, however, and by December 1905 the revolt was over, with its leaders under arrest.

257.21–26   we have China furnishing a solemn and awful mystery . . . convulsion is impending there] In January 1906 a "curious unrest in parts of China" seemed "a puzzle" to the Western world: "There are two elements clearly enough present in this feeling. One is distrust and dislike of foreigners from the Occident; the other is discontent with the Imperial Government. But it is by no means certain that each of these sentiments is felt by all who feel the other" ("The Outlook in China," New York *Times,* 8 Jan 1906, 8). It was feared that there might even be "a general uprising of the people against the entire political system of the empire."

Consequently, two U.S. infantry regiments and two batteries of field artillery were dispatched to the Philippines (which the United States had controlled since the end of the Spanish-American War in 1898), to be ready in the event that troops had to be "landed in China for the protection of American lives and property" ("America Preparing for Crash in China," New York *Times*, 7 Jan 1906, 1). One of the infantry brigades was under the command of General Frederick Funston, who captured Emilio Aguinaldo, the leader of the Filipino insurgents (see AD, 14 Mar 1906, 408.30–42 and note). Although China remained newsworthy well into 1906, the anticipated explosion did not come and no U.S. brigades were sent.

258.34 There you have the facts] Clemens's account is consistent in its details with the report in the New York *Times* of 5 January 1906 ("Drag Hull's Sister from White House," 1). On 4 January Mrs. Minor Morris had gone to the White House, hoping to convince President Theodore Roosevelt to intervene to have her physician husband restored to his post at the Army Medical Bureau, from which he had been abruptly dismissed. She alleged that the dismissal had been instigated by her brother, Republican Congressman John A. T. Hull of Iowa, with whom Mrs. Morris was bitterly disputing the settlement of their father's estate. After she was carried and dragged from the White House at the order of Benjamin F. Barnes, an assistant presidential secretary, she was imprisoned on a charge of disorderly conduct. To prevent her immediate release on bail, a charge of insanity also was brought against her. After two examining physicians pronounced her sane, however, she was released after several hours and allowed to return to her room at the Willard Hotel, where she was soon under medical care for bruising, shock, and nervous prostration. Her own "calm and mild, unexcited and well worded account" of the incident appeared in the New York *Times* on 6 January ("Mrs. Morris Tells of White House Expulsion," 1). The Morris incident remained a national *cause célèbre* for more than six months, with attempts at congressional inquiries, all deflected, and with repeated calls for the president to accept responsibility, disavow Barnes's actions, and apologize, all rejected. In April Roosevelt confirmed his faith in Barnes by appointing him Washington postmaster. And in May, during Barnes's Senate confirmation hearings, the White House was charged with using false testimony, from a physician who never actually treated Mrs. Morris, to impugn her reputation and question her sanity (New York *Times*: numerous articles, Jan–June 1906).

259.3–6 Morris incident ... the President's character] In the margin of the typescript alongside this passage, Paine wrote, "Not to be used for 50 years from 1920—." Nevertheless, he included the passage in his 1924 edition of *Mark Twain's Autobiography* (*MTA*, 1:288).

259.13 It is the Roosevelts that have the Barneses around] Clemens was not alone in seeing Roosevelt's imperiousness behind Barnes's behavior. The Hartford *Times,* for example, condemned the "new spirit of high mightiness in the White House, which differs widely from anything which has been seen there heretofore" ("From the Hartford Times," New York *Times,* 12 Jan 1906, 8).

259.32–36 He flies from one thing to another ... opinion] On 7 January 1906, Lyon recorded in her diary another of Clemens's vivid descriptions of Roosevelt: "This morning Mr. Clemens was speaking of Roosevelt & his great blustering—& he said that 'he is magnificent when his ears are pricked up & his tail is in the air & he attacks a lightning express, only to be lost in the dust the express creates'" (Lyon 1906, 7).

260.2   these joyous ebullitions of excited sincerity] Clemens was not always so tolerant of Roosevelt's "opinions and feelings and convictions." In 1907, in his copy of a volume of Roosevelt's "ideas expressed on many occasions," Clemens altered the title page from *A Square Deal* to "BANALITIES," and the title of the publisher's introductory remarks from "Foreword" to "A PUKE BY A DISINTERESTED PUBLISHER" (Roosevelt 1906, volume in CU-MARK). He was always careful, however, to avoid any public criticism, as he explained in a letter to his daughter Clara in February 1910:

> Roosevelt closed my mouth years ago with a deeply valued, gratefully received, unasked favor; & with all my bitter detestation of him I have never been able to say a venomous thing about him in print since—that benignant deed always steps in the way & lays its consecrated hand upon my lips. I ought not to allow it to do this; & I am ashamed of allowing it, but I cannot help it, since I am made in that way, & did not make myself. (21, 22, and 23 Feb 1906 to CC, photocopy in CU-MARK)

Autobiographical Dictation, 11 January 1906

260 *title*   January 11, 1906] The first page of this dictation is reproduced in facsimile in the Introduction (figure 14).

261.11–16   Address of Samuel L. Clemens . . . as published in the BOSTON EVENING TRANSCRIPT, December 18, 1877] This heading was not in the Boston *Evening Transcript*'s lengthy account of the dinner and speeches ("The Atlantic Dinner," 1, 3). It must have been supplied by the unidentified "Boston typewriter" (*i.e.,* typist) who transcribed the speech from the newspaper. The *Transcript* text was based (probably indirectly) on Clemens's own manuscript. On 19 December, the Boston *Globe* reported, "At the Atlantic dinner, Monday night, a reporter sent a note to Mr. Samuel L. Clemens asking him for the manuscript of his speech. In reply 'Mark' wrote: 'Yes, if you will put in the applause in the right places, especially if there isn't any'" ("Table Gossip," 4). Several newspapers printed the text on the morning after the speech, any one of which could have been the source of the *Transcript*'s version in the evening edition (see the Textual Commentary, *MTPO*).

261.18   Mr. Chairman—] Henry O. Houghton (1823–95), publisher of the *Atlantic Monthly* and the "chief host" of the dinner, gave the opening address. He introduced William Dean Howells, editor of the magazine and Clemens's close friend, as the man who would "take charge of the proceedings" (see "A Call with W. D. Howells on General Grant," note at 70.19). Howells spoke and then introduced each of the other speakers ("The Atlantic Dinner," Boston *Evening Transcript,* 18 Dec 1877, 1, 3).

261.21–24   I am reminded of a thing which happened . . . California] In May of 1864, having achieved fame and notoriety during twenty months as local reporter and editor for the Virginia City *Territorial Enterprise,* Clemens left Nevada for San Francisco, where he worked as local reporter for the San Francisco *Morning Call* and also contributed to the *Californian,* a literary weekly. In early December 1864 ("thirteen years ago," in 1877) Clemens accepted an invitation from his friend Steve Gillis to leave San Francisco and join his brother James Gillis and Dick Stoker at their cabin at Jackass Hill, Tuolumne County. Steve had recently been jailed for fighting, and Clemens signed a $500 bond for his bail; when Steve decided to return to Virginia City rather than face trial, Clemens became liable for the whole amount. Clemens, out of work save for a few articles in the *Californian,* was short of funds himself, having lost or cashed in his valuable shares of the Hale and Norcross Silver Mining Company. It was this trip to Jackass Hill and nearby Angels Camp (in Calaveras County) that he refers to here as an "inspection tramp of the southern mines." The visit turned into a twelve-week retreat during which he stayed with Gillis and Stoker, helped them "pocket-mine," and listened to tales like the "Jumping Frog" and the blue-jay yarn. Clemens returned to San Francisco in late February 1865. The notebook he kept during the trip is in the Mark Twain Papers (*L1:* link note following 28 May 1864 to Cutler, 302–3; 18 Oct 1864 to OC, 317; link note following 11 Nov 1864 to OC, 320–21; *N&J1,* 63–82).

262.1–4 "'Through . . . soul!'] From Holmes's "The Chambered Nautilus" (1858).

262.9–12 "'Give me . . . altitudes.'] From Emerson's "Mithridates" (1847).

262.16–17 "'Honor . . . Pau-Puk-Keewis—'] From Longfellow's "The Song of Hiawatha" (1855). The verses are not consecutive: the first is the opening line of book 2; the second is the opening line of book 16.

262.22–23 "'Flash . . . days.'] From Holmes's "Mare Rubrum" (1858).

262.33 "'This . . . primeval.'] The opening line of Longfellow's "Evangeline: A Tale of Acadie" (1847).

262.35–36 "'Here . . . world.'] From Emerson's "Concord Hymn" (1837).

262.41–263.3 "'I am . . . *again!*'] Rearranged and adapted lines from Emerson's "Brahma" (1857).

263.8–9 "'I tire . . . played!'] Adapted from Emerson's "Song of Nature" (1859), where the first line actually reads "I tire of globes and races."

263.11–12 "'Thanks . . . taught'] From Longfellow's "The Village Blacksmith" (1841).

263.13 and blamed if he didn't down with *another* right bower] A "right bower" was the jack of trumps, the highest card in the game of euchre, and therefore unique in each deck of cards.

263.15–16 "'God help . . . palm!'] From Holmes's "A Voice of the Loyal North" (1861).

263.21 All quiet on the Potomac] The famous Civil War song "All Quiet Along the Potomac Tonight" was from a poem by Ethel Lynn Beers (1827–79) entitled "The Picket-Guard," which had first appeared in *Harper's Weekly* in 1861. In 1863 it was set to music by John Hill Hewitt (1801–90).

263.22 how-come-you-so] Drunk.

263.23–24 Barbara Frietchie . . . Biglow Papers . . . Thanatopsis] "Barbara Frietchie" (1863) was actually by John Greenleaf Whittier. "The Biglow Papers" (1846–67) were by James Russell Lowell. "Thanatopsis" (1817, revised 1821) was by William Cullen Bryant. Neither Lowell nor Bryant attended the dinner.

263.27–28   "'Is yonder . . . breed?'] From Emerson's "Monadnoc" (1847).

263.31   'When Johnny Comes Marching Home'] This popular Civil War song was by bandmaster and composer Patrick Sarsfield Gilmore (1829–92), who published it in 1863 under the pseudonym "Louis Lambert" (Library of Congress 2008).

263.36–39   "'Lives . . . Time.'] From Longfellow's "Psalm of Life" (1838).

264.9–19   Mr. and Mrs. A. P. Chamberlaine . . . I had been irreverent beyond belief, beyond imagination] The Clemenses had met Augustus P. Chamberlaine and his wife in Venice in October 1878. The Chamberlaines' acquaintance with Emerson permitted them to assure Clemens then that his Whittier dinner speech had not given offense to the venerable poets (see *N&J2,* 220–21). There had in fact been some negative comments in the press in the days following the dinner. The Boston *Transcript,* for example, noted that the speech "was in bad taste and entirely out of place" (19 Dec 1877, 4); and the Worcester *Gazette* opined that "Mark's sense of propriety needs development, and it is not his first offense" (reprinted in the Boston *Evening Traveller,* 26 Dec 1877, 1). Several other newspapers, however, gave Clemens positive reviews. The Boston *Advertiser* noted that "the amusement was intense, while the subjects of the wit, Longfellow, Emerson and Holmes, enjoyed it as much as any" ("Whittier's Birthday," 18 Dec 1877, 1). The Boston *Globe* reported that the speech "produced the most violent bursts of hilarity" and that "Mr. Emerson seemed a little puzzled about it, but Mr. Longfellow laughed and shook, and Mr. Whittier seemed to enjoy it keenly" ("The Whittier Dinner," 18 Dec 1877, 8). The Boston *Journal* observed that Clemens's speech "soon aroused uproarious merriment" ("Whittier's Birthday," 18 Dec 1877, unknown page), and the *Evening Traveller* noted that Clemens "served up a characteristic series of parodies on Longfellow, Emerson, and Holmes, 'setting the table in a roar' as is his wont" ("A Bard's Birthday Banquet," 18 Dec 1877, 1). Nevertheless, on 27 December 1877, in the depths of his remorse, and with Howells's encouragement, he wrote letters of apology addressed to Holmes, Emerson, and Longfellow. On 29 December Holmes replied that "it grieves me to see that you are seriously troubled about what seems to me a trifling matter. It never occurred to me for a moment to take offence, or to feel wounded by your playful use of my name" (CU-MARK). On 31 December Ellen Emerson replied for her father—not to Clemens himself, but to Olivia—saying that although the family was "disappointed" in Clemens's speech, "no shadow of indignation has ever been in any of our minds. The night of the dinner, my Father says, he did not hear Mr Clemens's speech he was so far off, and my Mother says that when she read it to him the next day it amused him" (CU-MARK). And on 6 January 1878 Longfellow wrote Clemens that the incident was "a matter of such slight importance. The newspapers have made all the mischief. A bit of humor at a dinner table is one thing; a report of it in the morning papers is another" (CU-MARK). By 5 February 1878 Clemens had rebounded sufficiently from his initial embarrassment to write his *Quaker City* mentor, Mary Mason Fairbanks:

> I am pretty dull in some things, & very likely the Atlantic speech was in ill taste; but that is the worst that can be said of it. I am sincerely sorry if it in any wise hurt those great poets' feelings—I never wanted to do that. But nobody has ever convinced me

that that speech was not a good one——for me; above my average, considerably. (*Letters 1876–1880*)

(For an extended discussion of the Whittier dinner speech and its aftermath, including texts of Clemens's letter of apology and the responses to it, see Smith 1955; see also AD, 23 Jan 1906, for additional comments on the speech.)

264.38–39 I can see those figures with entire distinctness across this abyss of time] There were sixty *Atlantic* contributors and associates at the dinner. Whittier, Emerson, Holmes, Longfellow, Houghton, and Howells were at the head of the table. Clemens's good friend James R. Osgood was seated on one side of him, and on the other was their mutual friend Charles Fairchild, a Boston paper manufacturer. Elsewhere were seated Charles Dudley Warner and James Hammond Trumbull (see AD, 12 Jan 1906, note at 272.31–32). Other more casual acquaintances of Clemens's were present, including agriculturist and sanitary engineer George E. Waring (1833–98), Unitarian minister Thomas W. Higginson (1823–1911), and poet and fiction writer John T. Trowbridge (1827–1916). Many of the guests, including Clemens, had also attended the *Atlantic*'s 15 December 1874 dinner for its contributors (see the link note following 14 Dec 1874 to Howells, *L6,* 317–20).

264.40–265.5 Willie Winter . . . did love to recite those occasional poems] William Winter (1836–1917) was dramatic critic of the New York *Tribune* from 1865 to 1909 and also the author of several biographies of actors. He did not attend the Whittier birthday dinner. The occasion Clemens recalled was the 3 December 1879 *Atlantic Monthly* breakfast for Oliver Wendell Holmes. In a well-received speech intended to redeem his 1877 performance, Clemens described how he had committed "unconscious plagiarism" by echoing Holmes's dedication to "Songs in Many Keys" in *The Innocents Abroad* (see "Notes on 'Innocents Abroad,'" note at 225.17–19). Winter appeared later in the roster of speakers and read his thirteen-stanza tribute, "Hearts and Holmes" ("The Holmes Breakfast," Boston *Advertiser,* 4 Dec 1879, 1), which concluded:

> True bard, true soul, true man, true friend!
>   Ah, lightly on that reverend head
> Ye snows of wintry age descend,
>   Ye shades of mortal night be shed!
> Peace guide and guard him to the end,
>   And God defend!

266.9–10 Howells, who was near me . . . couldn't get beyond a gasp] Howells was seated at the head table, not close to Clemens. Nevertheless, given that newspaper reports do not confirm that Clemens's speech was generally perceived to be a "disaster," it is likely that it was chiefly Howells's reaction that persuaded Clemens that it was.

266.12–13 If Benvenuto Cellini's salamander . . . autobiography] See "My Autobiography [Random Extracts from It]," note at 209.41.

266.15–17 Bishop . . . a most acceptable novel . . . in the *Atlantic Monthly*] William Henry

Bishop (1847–1928) was the author of *Detmold: A Romance*, serialized in the *Atlantic Monthly* from December 1877 through June 1878 and published in book form in 1879 (Bishop 1877–78; Bishop 1879).

266.32–33   at last he slumped down in a limp and mushy pile] Bishop's speech did not follow Clemens's. According to press reports, several speakers intervened, including poet Richard H. Stoddard and Charles Dudley Warner. Bishop spoke "last on the regular list," well past midnight, and after Whittier, Emerson, Holmes, and Longfellow had all left ("Whittier's Birthday," Boston *Advertiser,* 18 Dec 1877, 1; Boston *Evening Transcript,* "The Atlantic Dinner," 18 Dec 1877, 3). No account of Bishop's speech is known to survive, other than the Boston *Journal*'s observation that he was one of those who talked "briefly and suitably" ("Whittier's Birthday," 18 Dec 1877, unknown page) and the Boston *Evening Traveller*'s remark that he "closed very gracefully the list of regular speakers" ("A Bard's Birthday Banquet," 18 Dec 1877, 1).

266.34–35   the program . . . ended there] The program did not conclude prematurely, as Clemens implied. By most newspaper accounts, following Bishop's satisfactory delivery of the last "regular" speech, there was just one additional speaker before the festivities ended around 1 A.M. on 18 December.

267.22–23   Even the Massacre did not produce a like effect, nor the Anthony Burns episode] The Boston Massacre occurred on 5 March 1770, when British troops opened fire on a rioting crowd and killed five colonists. Anthony Burns (1834–62) was a slave who fled from Richmond, Virginia, to Boston in 1854. That same year he was arrested and convicted under the Fugitive Slave Act of 1850, occasioning mass protests on a scale unknown since the days of the Revolution. After his forced return to Virginia, Boston supporters purchased his freedom and paid for his education at Oberlin College; he later became a Baptist minister.

267.27   the New Hampshire hills] Clemens spent the summer of 1906 at Upton Farm, near Dublin, New Hampshire, dictating his autobiography.

267.28–29   I will go before . . . Twentieth Century Club] The Twentieth Century Club (since 1934 the Twentieth Century Association for the Promotion of a Finer Public Spirit and a Better Social Order) was begun in Boston in January 1894. Membership was open to

> men and women over the age of 21 who had "rendered some service in the fields of science, art, religion, government, education or social service; and those who in their business, home life, or civic relations have made some contribution to the life of the community, state or nation, worthy of recognition. . . ." Club activities centered around Saturday Luncheons. Begun as men-only affairs, they were opened to women by 1895. . . . Speakers were told to expect vigorous questioning. . . . Speakers included: newspaper editors, reformers, missionaries, socialists, educators, authors, labor leaders, economists and others. (Massachusetts Historical Society 2008)

Clemens had appeared before the club on 4 November 1905, speaking satirically on peace, missionaries, and statesmanship (SLC 1905f). He is not known to have resurrected the Whittier dinner speech before the club. For his additional remarks on that speech, see the Autobiographical Dictation of 23 January 1906.

Autobiographical Dictation, 12 January 1906

267 *title*   January 12, 1906] The first page of this dictation is reproduced in facsimile in the Introduction (figure 15).

267.35   Colonel Harvey] George Brinton McClellan Harvey (1864–1928) worked as a reporter for the Springfield (Mass.) *Republican* and the Chicago *News* before he became managing editor of Pulitzer's New York *World* while still in his twenties. He made a very large fortune building electric railways, and in 1899 he purchased the venerable *North American Review* and became its editor. The following year he became president of the financially troubled Harper and Brothers, and in 1901 he also became editor of *Harper's Weekly*. It was he who negotiated with Clemens and Rogers to secure the 1903 contract that gave Harper essentially exclusive rights to everything Clemens wrote or had written. In an interview published on 3 March 1907 by the Washington *Post* Harvey identified Clemens as the best-paid writer in the United States, thanks to this contract, which guaranteed payment for "everything he wrote, whether it was printed or thrown away" ("Mark Twain's Exclusive Publisher Tells What the Humorist Is Paid," A12). His title of "Colonel" was civilian rather than military, and was the rank he held from 1885 to 1892 as an aide-de-camp on New Jersey gubernatorial staffs (*HHR,* 513 n. 2).

268.15–16   President and the Governors had to have my birthday—the 30th—for Thanksgiving Day] In 1789 George Washington created the first nationally designated Thanksgiving Day, held on 26 November that year. Subsequently, the holiday was appointed by presidential and gubernatorial proclamation, but irregularly and not on a uniform date. In 1863, Abraham Lincoln proclaimed that a national Thanksgiving Day henceforth would be celebrated on the last Thursday in November, which in 1905 was the fifth Thursday, and also Clemens's birthday. In 1939 Franklin D. Roosevelt changed the date to the third Thursday of November, and in 1941 Congress passed legislation definitively establishing Thanksgiving as the fourth Thursday in November.

268.23–24   several vicious and inexcusable wars] In addition to the Russian Revolution (see AD, 10 Jan 1906, note at 257.18–21), Clemens doubtless alludes to the Russo-Japanese War and possibly to uprisings in Yemen, Crete, the French Congo, and German East Africa (Tanzania), all in 1904–5.

268.24–25   King Leopold . . . slaughters and robberies in the Congo State] Leopold II (1835–1909) had been king of Belgium since 1865. Between 1878 and 1884, with the help of explorer Henry M. Stanley, he had personally acquired treaty rights to a vast section of central Africa (now the Democratic Republic of the Congo), which he organized into the Congo Free State and then, over the next decade, brought under his ruthless control. He ruled it as his private commercial empire, enriching himself while exploiting and brutalizing the Africans compelled to work for the mining and rubber companies that were his concessionaires. Clemens's scathing satire, *King Leopold's Soliloquy,* written in 1905, helped bring these cruelties under scrutiny (SLC 1905a). In 1908 Leopold was forced to relinquish control of the Congo Free State to the Belgian government.

268.25   Insurance revelations in New York] See the Autobiographical Dictation of 10 January 1906.

268.28   birthday celebration . . . 5th of December] The lavish banquet to commemorate Clemens's birthday was held at Delmonico's restaurant in New York. Following this paragraph he dictated the instruction "(Here paste in the proceedings of the Birthday Banquet)." This was not done in any of the later typescripts, however, where the instruction was merely retranscribed. The "proceedings," including photographs of the guests as well as texts of the speeches and other tributes, filled thirty-two pages in the 23 December 1905 "Mark Twain's Birthday Souvenir Number" of *Harper's Weekly* (SLC 1905g). In his Autobiographical Dictation of 16 December 1908, Clemens again noted, "I think I will insert here (if I have not inserted it in some earlier chapter of this autobiography) the grand account of the banquet." A facsimile of the publication is available at *MTPO*.

268.30   In the speech which I made were concealed many facts] Clemens's speech is reprinted in the Appendix, pp. 657–61.

269.1–6   when I was fifty . . . 1891] The Hartford Monday Evening Club held its first meeting on 18 January 1869. Horace Bushnell (1802–76), the minister of Hartford's North Church of Christ (later Park Congregational Church) from 1833 to 1859 and the author of numerous important theological works, was the prime mover in the club's creation. The constitution adopted in February 1869 set the membership at twenty. Despite Clemens's recollection, the essayists did not regularly follow each other in alphabetical order. Clemens became a member in 1873 and continued on the membership roll until his death in 1910, although he ceased to attend meetings after the family left Hartford in June 1891. The Reverend Francis Goodwin (1839–1923), a prominent Protestant Episcopal clergyman who served several Hartford churches, and was also an architect, became a member in 1877. The topic of the evening at Goodwin's house that Clemens recalled here, "Dreams," indicates that the meeting took place on 21 January 1884, when he was forty-eight. Most of the men present were founding members; five joined later, as noted below. Like Clemens, they all remained on the membership list until their deaths (Howell Cheney 1954, passim; "Francis Goodwin" in "Hartford Residents" 1974).

269.14–16   The wives . . . were not allowed to throw any light upon the discussion] "It was the early rule that the wife of the host invited two or three of her intimates to sit with her. . . . At rare times the hostess engaged in the conversation. . . . The predominance of the feeling of members is that the Club should be limited in its audience to men" (Howell Cheney 1954, 6).

269.24–26   J. Pierpont Morgan's cigars . . . at dinner in Mr. Dodge's house] John Pierpont Morgan (1837–1913) was the preeminent American banker, financier, and art collector of his day. William E. Dodge (1832–1903) had succeeded his father of the same name (1805–83) as a partner in Phelps, Dodge and Company, leading wholesalers of copper and other metals, and also continued his father's numerous charitable, religious, and philanthropic activities.

269.34   George, our colored butler] George Griffin. See the Autobiographical Dictation of 6 February 1906.

269.38   Wheeling long nines] Wheeling, West Virginia, had been a center for the manufacture of cigars, particularly cheap cigars, since the 1820s. "Long nine" as a generic term for a cheap cigar was in use at least by 1830 (Ohio County Public Library 2008; Mathews 1951, 2:1000).

270.1   When I was . . . late '50s] Clemens first boarded the *Paul Jones,* piloted by Horace Bixby, in Cincinnati bound for New Orleans on 16 February 1857. He returned to St. Louis working informally as Bixby's apprentice, or steersman, on 15 March aboard the *Colonel Crossman.* He received his license on 9 April 1859, and continued as a pilot until mid-May 1861, when the Civil War put an end to commercial traffic on the river. He recounted his experiences on the river in *Life on the Mississippi,* especially chapters 4–21 (see also the link note following 5 Aug 1856 to HC through 26 Apr 1861 to OC, *L1,* 69–121; Branch 1992, 2–3).

270.12   Rev. Dr. Parker] Edwin Pond Parker (1836–1920), a Congregational clergyman, was pastor of Hartford's Second Church of Christ from 1860 until 1912, when he became pastor emeritus.

270.15   Rev. Dr. Burton] Nathaniel J. Burton (1824–87) was pastor of Hartford's Fourth Congregational Church (1857–70) and Park Congregational Church (1870–87).

270.18   Rev. Mr. Twichell] Joseph H. Twichell, pastor of Hartford's Asylum Hill Congregational Church from 1865 to 1912, was one of Clemens's closest friends (see "Grant and the Chinese," note at 73.13).

270.34–35   you can start at the front door and . . . tread on one of them cigars every time] Clemens had included many of the details of this story of the long nines in "Conversations with Satan," written in 1897–98 (see SLC 2009, 42–44).

271.6–8   the late Colonel Greene . . . President presently] Jacob L. Greene (1837–1905) was breveted lieutenant colonel for distinguished gallantry and faithful and meritorious service during the Civil War. A lawyer, he was secretary of the Connecticut Mutual Life Insurance Company from 1871 until 1878 and in the latter year became its president. He joined the Monday Evening Club in 1883 (Heitman 1903, 1:475).

271.29–32   elder Hamersley . . . his son, Will Hamersley . . . Supreme Court] William James Hamersley (1808–77) was a journalist, book publisher, and former Hartford mayor (1853–54, 1862–64). For William Hamersley, see "The Machine Episode," note at 101.23 (Trumbull 1886, 1:117–18, 385, 612, 620, 624; "Death of the Hon. William James Hamersley," Hartford *Courant,* 16 May 1877, 2).

272.8–9   Charles E. Perkins] For about ten years (until 1882), Perkins (1832–1917) was Clemens's Hartford attorney. He became a club member in 1871 (12 Aug 1869 to Bliss, *L3,* 294 n. 4; 8 May 1872 to Perkins, *L5,* 84 n. 1).

272.29   Penitentiary down there at Wethersfield] The Wethersfield (Connecticut) State Prison opened in 1827 and remained in operation until 1963 (Connecticut State Library 2008b).

272.31–32   J. Hammond Trumbull, the most learned man in the United States] Hartford historian James Hammond Trumbull (1821–97) provided the multilingual chapter headings for *The Gilded Age*.

272.36–37   Governor Henry C. Robinson] Robinson (1832–1900), an attorney and business executive, was mayor of Hartford from 1872 to 1874. Although twice nominated by the Republican Party for governor of Connecticut (in 1876 and 1878), he never held that office (Burpee 1928, 3:41; Connecticut State Library 2008a).

272.39–40   A. C. Dunham . . . capitalist] Austin Cornelius Dunham (1833–1917), a wool merchant, inventor, and founder and since 1882 president of the Hartford Electric Light Company, joined the Monday Evening Club in 1870 (3 Oct 1874 to Howells, *L6*, 248 n. 3; Connecticut Light and Power 2008).

Autobiographical Dictation, 13 January 1906

273.3–5   Franklin was a . . . West Pointer . . . Mexican war . . . Civil War at the time that McClellan was commander-in-chief] General William Buel Franklin (1823–1903) graduated first in the West Point class of 1843, then served capably with the army's Topographical Engineers, and in the Mexican War (1846–48). His Civil War service, in part under General George B. McClellan, was checkered, however. Despite successes, he was blamed, evidently unfairly, for the Union loss at Fredericksburg (1862) and served the rest of his army career in relative obscurity. After his resignation from the army in 1866 he became vice-president of Colt's Patent Fire-Arms Manufacturing Company in Hartford, a post he held until 1888. He joined the Hartford Monday Evening Club in 1871 ("Franklin Dead," Hartford *Courant*, 9 Mar 1903, 13).

273.11–12   Johnson was a member of Trinity . . . most brilliant member of the Club] Charles Frederick Johnson (1836–1931), a literary historian, critic, and poet, was a professor of mathematics at the U.S. Naval Academy from 1865 to 1870 and then a professor of English literature, active and emeritus, at Trinity College in Hartford from 1883 until his death. He became a member of the Monday Evening Club in 1886 ("Prof. Charles F. Johnson," New York *Times*, 10 Jan 1931, 11).

273.38   not able to sink the shop] Not able to refrain from "talking shop."

274.14–22   In 1858 I was a steersman . . . never wanted my mother to know about that dream] Clemens recounted his and his nineteen-year-old brother Henry's employment aboard the steamer *Pennsylvania* in chapters 18–20 of *Life on the Mississippi*. He began his temporary service under Captain William Brown in November 1857. On 13 June 1858 three or four of the *Pennsylvania*'s boilers exploded and the boat sank, causing the deaths of between fifty and a hundred and fifty passengers and crew, including Henry and Captain Brown (see also the note at 275.20–21). Mentioned in this passage are Captain John S. Klinefelter (1810–85) and Horace E. Bixby (1826–1912), who supervised Clemens's piloting apprenticeship (for Clemens's on-the-spot account of the *Pennsylvania* disaster and Henry's death, see 15 June 1858 to Moffett through 21 June 1858 to Moffett, *L1*, 80–86; see also Branch 1985). At the time of this dictation, Clemens had not described his prophetic dream of Henry in that book or elsewhere; he later published this account in the *North American Review,* as part of the series of "Chapters from My Autobiography," in April 1907 (NAR 16). Clemens's niece, Annie Moffett, said in recollections published by her son in 1946 that Jane Clemens did know of the dream, and

> often talked about it. He had told them about it before he went away, but the family were not impressed; indeed they were amused that he took it so seriously.
>
> The story as the family used to tell it was not quite like Uncle Sam's version. They said his dream occurred in the daytime. The family including Henry were in my mother's room and Sam was asleep in the next room. He came in and told them what he had dreamed. My grandmother said he went back and dreamed the same dream a second and third time, but I think that was her embellishment. (*MTBus,* 37)

274.32   our brother-in-law, Mr. Moffett] William A. Moffett, a St. Louis commission merchant, married Clemens's older sister, Pamela Ann, in 1851 (link note preceding 24 Aug 1853 to JLC, *L1,* 2; see the Appendix "Family Biographies" (p. 655).

275.20–21   I had the fight . . . I be left ashore at New Orleans] In chapter 19 of *Life on the Mississippi* Clemens recalled his fight with Brown. In order to prevent him from assaulting Henry with "a ten-pound lump of coal," he had used "a heavy stool" to hit "Brown a good honest blow which stretched him out." The incident evidently occurred on 3 June 1858. Although Captain Klinefelter was sympathetic to Clemens, his inability to replace Brown, and Brown's refusal to continue supervising Clemens, led to his being left in New Orleans (*L1:* link note following 1 June 1857 to Taylor, 75; 18 June 1858 to MEC, 82 n. 2).

275.28   hurricane-deck . . . wheel-house] The hurricane deck usually was the third deck. "The name was derived from the ever-present breeze that made it a favorite viewing place on warm evenings. It was the location of the boat's large signal bell." Wheelhouses covered the paddlewheels ("Glossary of Steamboat Terms" 2008; for diagrams of a typical Mississippi River steamboat, see *HF 2003,* 405).

275.33–34   I have already told in "Old Times on the Mississippi."] In chapter 20 of *Life on the Mississippi,* Clemens wrote that after Henry was thrown into the river by the explosion, he returned to the burning boat to help others before he was overcome by his own injuries. But in an article written in late June or early July 1858, in which he precisely reconstructed the effect of the explosion on Henry, Clemens made no mention of this heroism (reproduced in facsimile in Branch 1985, 36). Here, as elsewhere, Clemens refers to *Life on the Mississippi* as "Old Times on the Mississippi," the series of *Atlantic Monthly* articles that were reprinted in chapters 4–17 and form the core of the book (SLC 1875a; see 18 June 1858 to MEC, *L1,* 84 n. 7).

276.3–4   Dr. Peyton . . . fatal effects were soon apparent. I think he died about dawn] Clemens recalled Thomas F. Peyton in an 1876 letter: "What a magnificent man he was! What healing it was just to look at him & hear his voice!" (25 Oct 1876 to Unidentified, *Letters 1876–1880*). Henry died on 21 June 1858; Clemens's identification of the immediate cause of death as an inadvertent overdose of morphine has not been confirmed.

Autobiographical Dictation, 15 January 1906

277.37   his daughter, Mrs. Wood] Julia Curtis Twichell (b. 1869) had been married to New York lawyer Howard Ogden Wood (1866–1940) since 1892 ("Twichell," in "Hartford Residents" 1974; New York *Times:* "Wood–Twichell," 27 Apr 1892, 5; "Howard Ogden Wood, a Philanthropist, 74," 17 June 1940, 15).

277.41–278.11   house of James Goodwin . . . granite mansion for his father] James Goodwin (1803–78) had owned a mail stage line and afterward was a director of the Hartford and New Haven Railroad and an incorporator and president of the Connecticut Mutual Life Insurance Company, the largest of Hartford's insurance firms and one of the largest in the United States, with assets of over $40 million by 1875. The house his son designed and built for him on Woodland Street in Hartford was "one of the most extensive private houses in the city, and one of marked architectural importance" (see 3 July 1874 to OLC, *L6,* 176–77 n. 4).

279.7   Morris paper] Wallpaper designed by English author and artist William Morris (1834–96) and produced by his firm.

279.24   MRS. MORRIS'S ILLNESS TAKES A SERIOUS TURN] Clemens's allusion to William Morris, in the previous paragraph, evidently triggered his recall of the completely unrelated Mrs. Minor Morris, and prompted him to have this article from the 11 January 1906 New York *Times* pasted into the typescript of this dictation. He had discussed Mrs. Morris's experience in the White House of President Theodore Roosevelt at length in his dictation of 10 January. The article mentions William Howard Taft (1857–1930), at this time secretary of war; John Morris Sheppard (1875–1941), Democratic congressman from Texas; Charles Henry Grosvenor (1833–1917), Union veteran and Republican congressman from Ohio; Sereno Elisha Payne (1843–1914), chairman of the House Ways and Means Committee, one of the most powerful Republican congressmen; and Marlin Edgar Olmsted (1847–1913), Republican congressman from Pennsylvania, an authority on parliamentary procedure.

280.13   Philippine Tariff bill] The bill, sponsored by Congressman Sereno E. Payne, proposed to permit Philippine sugar to enter the United States for three years at one-fourth of current duties, and subsequently to establish free trade between the islands and the United States. Vigorously opposed by the domestic sugar industry, the bill nevertheless passed by a wide margin in the House of Representatives on 16 January 1906, only to be buried in committee in the Senate on 2 March. Attempts to revive it later in 1906 and in 1907 failed (New York *Times:* numerous articles, 3 Jan 1906–27 Dec 1907).

281.36–37   *Quaker City* Excursion . . . "The Innocents Abroad,"] See "The Chicago G. A. R. Festival," note at 67.6–13.

281.39–41   So I started . . . John Swinton] William Swinton (1833–92), brother of journalist and social reformer John Swinton (1829–1901), was a controversial Civil War correspondent for the New York *Times.* He later was a professor of English at the University of California at Berkeley (1869–74), and the author of military histories as well as textbooks on geography, grammar, and literature. Clemens roomed for a time with Swinton in Washington in the winter of 1867–68, while he worked for Senator William Stewart of Nevada and contributed letters to the New York *Tribune* and *Herald,* the San Francisco *Alta California,* the Virginia City *Territorial Enterprise,* and the Chicago *Republican.* Although it is possible that they collaborated on a "Newspaper Correspondence Syndicate," no firm evidence of it has been found (4 Dec 1867 to Young, *L2,* 125–26 n. 1).

282.12–13   six letters for the New York *Tribune* . . . got back] Clemens's six *Quaker City* letters to the *Tribune* were: "The Mediterranean Excursion," published on 30 July 1867; "The Mediterranean Excursion," published on 6 September; "Americans on a Visit to the Emperor of Russia," published on 19 September; "A Yankee in the Orient," published on 25 October; "The American Colony in Palestine," published on 2 November; and "The Holy Land. First Day in Palestine," published on 9 November. The "pretty breezy one for the New York *Herald*" was "The Cruise of the Quaker City," which poked bitter fun at the "pilgrims" and their activities and was published on the morning of 20 November 1867, the day after the excursion ended and just hours after Clemens wrote it (SLC 1867l, 1867m, 1867n, 1867o, 1867p, 1867r, 1867s; *L2:* 20 Nov 1867 to JLC and family [1st], 104; enclosure with 20 Nov 1867 to JLC and family, 399–406).

282.14–15   Every now and then I was able to get twenty-five dollars for a magazine article] Only one such article published in the winter of 1868 has been identified: "General Washington's Negro Body-Servant. A Biographical Sketch," which appeared in the February 1868 *Galaxy* magazine (SLC 1868b). How much the *Galaxy* paid for it is not known.

282.15–18   Riley and I . . . I will speak of him another time] John Henry Riley (1830?–72) was a newspaper reporter in San Francisco in the early 1860s when Clemens met him. In late 1865 he moved to Washington, where he was the regular correspondent for the San Francisco *Alta California,* also contributed to other papers, and served as clerk to the House Committee on Mines and Mining. In 1870 Clemens concocted a plan for Riley to visit the recently discovered diamond fields of South Africa to gather material for a book that Clemens would write. Subsidized by Clemens, Riley undertook the trip, and submitted travel notes to Clemens, but Clemens postponed work on the book, and then abandoned it entirely when Riley died of cancer in September 1872 (for further details, see *L4,* especially 2 Dec 1870 to Bliss and 2 Dec 1870 to Riley, 256–66, and *L5*). Clemens depicted Riley in "Riley—Newspaper Correspondent" in the November 1870 *Galaxy* magazine and modeled the "mendicant Blucher," in chapter 59 of *Roughing It,* on him (SLC 1870e; *RI 1993,* 702). He did not, however, speak of him again in the Autobiographical Dictations.

282.19–24   I had a chance . . . "Concerning the Great Beef Contract."] The article described here was "The Facts in the Case of George Fisher, Deceased," published in the January 1871 issue of *Galaxy* magazine. Clemens confused it with "The Facts in the Case of the Great Beef Contract," about an unpaid 1861 military supply obligation, published in the May 1870 *Galaxy.* He included both sketches in his 1875 collection, *Mark Twain's Sketches, New and Old* (SLC 1871b, 1870b, 1875c).

282.25–26   A. R. Spofford . . . Librarian of Congress then] Ainsworth Rand Spofford (1825–1908), former associate editor of the Cincinnati *Commercial,* became chief assistant to the librarian of Congress in 1861 and then became librarian himself in 1864. He remained in the post until 1897, when he became chief assistant once again, for the remainder of his life. Clemens probably first met him in Washington in the winter of 1867–68. He corresponded with Spofford about copyright on more than one occasion (see *L4, L5,* and *L6*).

282.29   Tooke on Prices] Thomas Tooke's *A History of Prices, and of the State of the Circulation, from 1793 to 1837; Preceded by a Brief Sketch of the State of the Corn Trade in the Last Two Centuries* (Tooke 1838–57).

Autobiographical Dictation, 16 January 1906

283.13–14   When you arrive . . . at eleven] Clemens was addressing his stenographer, Josephine Hobby.

283.36–284.1   Did I dictate something about John Malone . . . my acquaintance] For Malone, see the note at 286.38–39. Volney Streamer (1850–1915), librarian of The Players club since December 1905, had been an actor in Edwin Booth's company, was a literary adviser at Brentano's (the famed New York booksellers), and compiled several collections of literary excerpts, including *Voices of Doubt and Trust* (Streamer 1897), copies of which Clemens acquired in February 1902 and December 1905. Both were gifts; the second might well have been presented personally by Streamer. Clemens also owned *In Friendship's Name* (Streamer 1904), possibly another 1905 gift from the author (see Gribben 1980, 2:673–74; "Volney Streamer," New York *Times,* 15 Apr 1915, 13).

284.5   And some time . . . about that] He already had; see the Autobiographical Dictation of 10 January 1906, especially the note at 255.19–22.

284.7   David Munro . . . editor of the *North American Review*] Munro (1844–1910) was born in Scotland and attended Edinburgh University. After emigrating to the United States as a young man, he worked in the literary department of Harper and Brothers. He became the manager of the *North American Review* in 1889, and seven years later became an editor as well. Since George Harvey's purchase of the journal in 1899, Munro had served as his assistant editor. In addition, he was a Greek scholar who contributed to a comparative Greek-English New Testament and other publications ("David A. Munro Dead," New York *Times,* 10 Mar 1910, 9).

284.7–8   Robert Reid, the artist; Saint-Gaudens, the sculptor] Reid (1862–1929), an American Impressionist painter and muralist, was born in Massachusetts and attended the School of the Museum of Fine Arts in Boston, completing his studies in New York and Paris. Augustus Saint-Gaudens (1848–1907) was born in Dublin but grew up in New York City. He took art classes there at the Cooper Union, and then studied in Paris under François Jouffroy at the École des Beaux-Arts and later in Rome. He was known primarily for his public sculptures of famous people.

284.31   John McCullough] McCullough (1832–85) emigrated from Ireland at the age of fourteen. He settled in Philadelphia, where he taught himself to read and write, studied drama, and at twenty-four made his stage debut. In 1861 he joined the touring company of actor and playwright Edwin Forrest (1806–72). Later he was for a time a theatrical manager as well as an actor in San Francisco, then performed extensively throughout the United States, becoming one of the most eminent and popular actors of the day.

285.18–19 President of the New York City College] John H. Finley (see AD, 10 Jan 1906, note at 255.18–19).

285.36 he is providing another, for the 6th of February] No information about this dinner has been discovered.

286.27 Bishop Greer] David Hummell Greer (1844–1919), Episcopal clergyman and rector at St. Bartholomew's Church in New York (1888–1903), became bishop coadjutor of New York in 1904.

286.31 Dr. Hawkes] Forbes Robert Hawkes (1865–1940), a prominent surgeon, was a professor of clinical surgery at the Post-Graduate Hospital in New York from 1901 to 1905.

286.38–39 John Malone . . . passing from this life] Like Clemens, Malone had been an incorporator and charter member of The Players club. Isabel Lyon wrote in her diary on 16 January, "John Malone is dead—Mʳ. Clemens had me telephone to Volney Streamer at the Players that if they are short of pall bearers, he will be one—Yesterday Mʳ Clemens was talking with Mʳ Twichell about John Malone: & now he is dead" (Lyon 1906, 16). Twichell had cut Malone's obituary from the New York *Times* of 16 January. When inserting it into this dictation, Clemens corrected the *Times*'s "Mr. Malone was 78 years old," but how accurately is unknown. The New York *Tribune*'s obituary noted that Malone "was fifty-six years old, though many supposed him older" ("Apoplexy Kills Actor," 16 Jan 1906, 7). Clemens was in fact one of the pallbearers at Malone's funeral, on 18 January, at the Church of St. Francis Xavier, on West Sixteenth Street ("Funeral of Actor John Malone," New York *Times,* 19 Jan 1906, 11; Lanier 1938, 358).

287.1–5 I started to say . . . happened] About 1893 Clemens drafted a prospectus for *The Back Number.* He noted there that the idea had come to him "when I was a newspaper correspondent in Washington," that is, in the winter of 1867–68 (SLC 1893, 1; see also AD, 17 Jan 1906).

Autobiographical Dictation, 17 January 1906

287.7–11 I have tried to get publishers . . . latest effort three years ago] Clemens's first attempt to make *The Back Number* a reality evidently came in November 1893, shortly after he prepared a prospectus for it (SLC 1893). He tried, unsuccessfully, to enlist the support of John Brisben Walker, editor of *Cosmopolitan* magazine. Clemens thought that Samuel E. Moffett, his nephew, could edit the magazine. Nothing is known of his 1903 effort to interest a publisher (Notebook 33, TS pp. 37, 38, 39a, CU-MARK).

287.26–32 Twichell and I stepped across the street . . . I was there at the time] Clemens and Twichell visited Daniel Edgar Sickles (1823–1914) at his home at 23 Fifth Avenue (Clemens lived at 21 Fifth Avenue on the corner of 9th Street) on the evening of 15 January 1906. Sickles was a former lawyer, Democratic congressman from New York (1857–61, 1893–95), and a controversial diplomat and Civil War general. On 27 February 1859 he fatally shot Francis Scott Key's son on Pennsylvania Avenue, near the White House, because the younger Key had had an affair with his wife. Sickles was acquitted on the grounds of temporary insanity by a jury that shared the widespread public opinion that he had acted justifiably. This was the first time that the temporary-insanity defense was used. On the day of the shooting Clemens had arrived in St. Louis on the *Aleck Scott,* serving as a cub pilot under Bixby ("Steamboat Calendar," *L1,* 388; Twichell 1874–1916, 2:117–18; New York *Times:* "Dreadful Tragedy," 28 Feb 1859, 1; "The Sickles Tragedy," 27 Apr 1859, 1; "The Acquittal of Mr. Sickles," 28 Apr 1859, 4; "Gen. Sickles Dies; His Wife at Bedside," 4 May 1914, 1).

287.34 Twichell was a chaplain in Sickles's brigade in the Civil War] The regiment in which Twichell served as chaplain from 1861 to 1864 was part of the Excelsior Brigade commanded by Sickles, which saw action in several important battles (Twichell 2006, 1, 4).

288.5–6 The late Bill Nye . . . Wagner's music is better than it sounds] Edgar Wilson (Bill) Nye (1850–96) was a journalist and then a popular humorist and lecturer. Clemens himself is often mistakenly credited with this remark.

288.12–26 Sickles lost a leg at Gettysburg . . . Twichell quoted that speech] The bloody Union victory at Gettysburg consumed the first three days of July 1863. Twichell described the battle in a letter of 5 July to his sister, Sarah Jane, in which he gave an account of Sickles that must have been very like the one he later gave to Clemens during one of their regular walks in the Hartford woods:

> At a little before sunset the sad intelligence spread that Gen. Sickles was wounded. He had been the master-spirit of the day and by his courage, coolness and skill had averted a threatened defeat. All felt that his loss was a calamity. I met the ambulance in which he had been placed, accompanied it, helped lift him out, and administered the chloroform at the amputation. His right leg was torn to shreds, just below the knee—so low that it was impossible to save the knee. His bearing and words were of the noblest character. "If I die," said he, "let me die on the field," "God bless our noble cause," "In a war like this, one man isn't much," "My trust is in God," were some of the things he said. I loved him then, as I never did before. He has been removed, but we are informed that he is doing well. (Twichell 2006, 2, 249)

Joseph O'Hagan (1826–78), a Jesuit, was Twichell's Catholic counterpart with Sickles's Excelsior Brigade. He and Twichell remained close after the war (see 1 Feb 1875 to Stoddard, *L6,* 367 n. 6).

288.39–42 There was General Fairchild . . . grew to be well acquainted with him and his family] Lucius Fairchild (1831–96) lost his left arm at Gettysburg on 1 July 1863. A few months later he was mustered out of the Union army with the rank of brigadier general. He subsequently served three terms as governor of Wisconsin (1866–72) and then entered the diplomatic service. One of his postings, from 1878 to 1880, was as the U.S. consul general in Paris. The Clemenses became friendly with him and his wife while living there, sometime between late February and early July 1879, during the European excursion that became the basis of *A Tramp Abroad* (*N&J2,* 48, 287, 315–16).

289.4   General Noyes . . . lost a leg in the war] Edward Follansbee Noyes (1832–90) interrupted his law career in 1861 to join the Union army, rising to the rank of brigadier general. His left leg was amputated as a result of a wound he suffered in battle on 4 July 1864. After the war he served as a judge, as governor of Ohio (1871–73), and then as U.S. minister to France (1878–81).

Autobiographical Dictation, 18 January 1906

292.3–4   Senator Tillman . . . frank and intimate criticism of the President] Democratic Senator Benjamin Ryan Tillman (1847–1918) delivered his furious attack on Theodore Roosevelt in a packed Senate chamber on 17 January 1906 ("Tillman Fiercely Attacks Roosevelt," New York *Times,* 18 Jan 1906, 1).

292.10   matter of the expulsion of Mrs. Morris from the White House] For details of the Morris expulsion and Roosevelt's indifference to it, see the Autobiographical Dictations of 10 and 15 January 1906. According to the New York *Times* report of Tillman's speech, which Clemens probably saw, women in the Senate galleries "wept as Tillman told of the treatment accorded to Mrs. Morris. At times Tillman himself shed tears and in a broken voice appealed for the cause of honor and truth. Not a sound of applause was heard. The Senate and the spectators were simply breathless as one intense furious blast after another came from the Senator" ("Tillman Fiercely Attacks Roosevelt," 18 Jan 1906, 1).

292.18   I was already arranging a scheme in another matter of public concern] The "scheme" has not been identified.

292.29   His second cousin killed an editor] On 15 January 1903, Benjamin Tillman's nephew (not his second cousin), James H. Tillman (1869–1911), the lame duck lieutenant governor of South Carolina, shot Narciso Gener Gonzales (b. 1858), editor of the Columbia *State,* on Main Street in Columbia. Gonzales died four days later. He had been a bitter political opponent of James Tillman's and in 1902, during Tillman's unsuccessful campaign for governor, used the *State* to denounce him repeatedly, and truthfully, as a debauched liar and drunkard. Although Benjamin Tillman was not on good terms with his nephew at the time and regarded him as a political opponent, he made a show of supporting him. On 15 October 1903 a jury acquitted James Tillman, who had justified his premeditated attack on Gonzales with a bogus claim of self-defense (New York *Times:* numerous articles, 16 Jan–30 Oct 1903; Monk 2003).

292.38–293.2   He reminds the Senate . . . a note of compliment and admiration to a prize-fighter in the Far West] Tillman noted that Roosevelt had written "a letter of sympathy to Fitzsimmons, the prize fighter . . . made public about the time Mrs. Morris was treated so brutally" ("Tillman Fiercely Attacks Roosevelt," New York *Times,* 18 Jan 1906, 1). The letter to Robert Fitzsimmons was in the news in late December 1905, several days before the Morris incident. Reportedly it was "simply to extend the season's greetings" and was not in sympathy for Fitzsimmons's loss of his world light-heavyweight championship in San Francisco on 20 December (New York *Times:* "O'Brien Wins Fight in Thirteenth Round," 21 Dec 1905, 7; "Roosevelt to Fitzsimmons," 31 Dec 1905, 5).

293.12   We buried good old John Malone the actor, this morning] See the Autobiographical Dictation of 16 January 1906.

293.15–30   funeral of the Empress of Austria . . . ecstasy of delight through me] On 10 September 1898, while Clemens and his family were living in Austria, Elisabeth Amalie Eugenie (b. 1837), the empress of Austria, was assassinated in Geneva by Luigi Luccheni, "a demented Italian anarchist without nationalistic motives." The state funeral, on 17 September 1898, "furnished one of the most extravagant displays of funereal pomp ever seen in the history of European royalty" (Dolmetsch 1992, 81). Clemens wrote about it in "The Memorable Assassination," first published in 1917 (SLC 1917, 167–81).

294.6–7   in Virginia City . . . borders of California] See the Autobiographical Dictation of 9 January 1906, note at 251.32–38.

Autobiographical Dictation, 19 January 1906

294.21–22   serving as city editor . . . for a matter of two years] See the Autobiographical Dictation of 9 January 1906.

294.28   Plunkett . . . R. M. Daggett was on the staff] J. R. (Joe) Plunkett was a native of New York who had migrated to California in 1852 and to Nevada Territory in 1860, settling in Virginia City, where he was a miner and an editorial writer for the *Territorial Enterprise*. Rollin M. Daggett (1831–1901), also from New York, had been a journalist in San Francisco, founding the weekly *Golden Era* (1852) and the daily *Evening Mirror* (1860). Moving to Virginia City in 1862, he became a partner in a mining stock brokerage and also a part-time reporter for the *Enterprise*. In 1864 he joined the paper's editorial staff and in 1874 succeeded Goodman as editor-in-chief. Later he served as a Republican congressman from Nevada (1879–81) and U.S. minister resident to Hawaii (1882–85) (Marsh, Clemens, and Bowman 1972, 467 n. 27; Wright 1893; 17 Sept 1864 to Wright, *L1*, 310–11 n. 3).

294.29–33   Goodman was the only one . . . Tom Fitch . . . modified him with a bullet] Thomas Fitch (1838–1923), born and raised in New York City, had been a Milwaukee newspaper editor and a California newspaper editor, lawyer, and assemblyman before relocating to Virginia City in 1863. That year he became the editor of the Virginia City *Union*. The details of his dispute with Goodman are not known. On 1 August 1863 Virginia City police foiled their first attempt at a duel, an incident Clemens reported for the *Enterprise* of 2 August and for the San Francisco *Morning Call* of 2 August and 6 August. On 28 September 1863 the two editors succeeded in dueling, in California, so as to avoid prosecution under Nevada territorial law (see the note at 298.12–13). Fitch was wounded in the right leg below the knee, but survived to employ his famed powers of oratory as Washoe County, Nevada, district attorney (1865–66) and as a Republican congressman from Nevada (1869–71). Clemens may have written the 29 September 1863 *Enterprise* report of the duel (see *ET&S1*, 262–66; *L1*: 26 May 1864 to OC, 300 n. 3; 11 Nov 1864 to OC, 319 n. 4).

294.38–295.2   He had been a major under Walker . . . campaign in Central America] In 1855 William Walker (1824–60), a physician, lawyer, and journalist, led a small volunteer military force on an expedition to assist a revolutionary faction in Nicaragua. In 1856 the government he established was recognized by the United States, and Walker had himself inaugurated as president. In 1857, however, after less than a year in office, he was defeated by an alliance of Central American countries and forced to leave Nicaragua. He made an abortive attempt to return that same year, and another in 1860 that ended with his death by firing squad in Honduras.

295.5–15   I knew the Gillis family . . . Steve, George, and Jim, very young chaps] Stephen E. Gillis (1838–1918) was one of Clemens's closest Nevada friends. A typesetter by training, he was the foreman of the *Territorial Enterprise* when Clemens joined the paper in 1862. Gillis remained principally in Virginia City, working as a news editor on the *Enterprise* and then on the Virginia City *Chronicle,* until 1894. He then moved to Jackass Hill, California, where he lived with his brothers James (1830–1907) and William (1840–1929), both of them miners and friends of Clemens's. Clemens was visiting Jim and Billy Gillis on Jackass Hill and in Angels Camp when, in February 1865, he first heard a version of the "Jumping Frog" tale that he made, and that made him, famous (see AD, 11 Jan 1906, note at 261.21–24). Late in 1864 and again in 1865 he lived with Steve and Billy Gillis and their father, Angus (1800–1870), in San Francisco. The brother who died campaigning with William Walker was Philip H. Gillis (1834–56). According to the family genealogy assembled by Billy Gillis in 1924, there was no brother named George (*L1:* 21 May 1864 to Laird, 291–92 n. 3; 25 Sept 1864 to JLC and PAM, 313–14 n. 3; 28 Sept 1864 to OC and MEC, 316 n. 3; link note following 11 Nov 1864 to OC, 320–22; 26 Jan 1870 to Gillis, *L4,* 35–39; *N&J1,* 63–90; William R. Gillis to H. A. Williams, 31 May 1924, photocopy in CU-MARK courtesy of Peter A. Evans; for more on Jim Gillis, see AD, 26 May 1907).

295.20   Bob Howland] Clemens met Robert Muir Howland (1838–90), a native of New York State, in Carson City, Nevada Territory, in 1861. Howland was a mine superintendent and a mine and foundry owner in Aurora who also served as the town marshal. In 1864 he was appointed warden of the territorial prison at Carson City, and in 1883 became a U.S. deputy marshal for California. In chapter 21 of *Roughing It* he appears briefly, but dramatically, as Bob H——, who, during a windstorm, springs "up out of a sound sleep," knocks over his fellow boarders' live spider collection, and shouts, "Turn out, boys—the tarantulas is loose!" Clemens and Howland remained friendly, corresponding regularly, until Howland's death (*RI 1993,* 145; 29 Oct 1861 to Phillips, *L1,* 142 n. 2).

296.7–18   Goodman went off to San Francisco . . . things he had really accomplished] On 18 March 1864, writing from Virginia City, Clemens informed his sister that he was filling in as editor of the *Enterprise* because "Joe Goodman is gone to the Sandwich Islands" (18 Mar 1864 to PAM, *L1,* 275). In chapter 55 of *Roughing It* he gave an account of his stint as Goodman's replacement that did not explicitly mention an editorial on Shakespeare:

> Mr. Goodman went away for a week and left me the post of chief editor. It destroyed me. The first day, I wrote my "leader" in the forenoon. The second day, I had no subject and put it off till the afternoon. The third day I put it off till evening, and then copied an elaborate editorial out of the "American Cyclopedia," that steadfast friend of the editor,

all over this land. The fourth day I "fooled around" till midnight, and then fell back on the Cyclopedia again. The fifth day I cudgeled my brain till midnight, and then kept the press waiting while I penned some bitter personalities on six different people. The sixth day I labored in anguish till far into the night and brought forth—nothing. The paper went to press without an editorial. The seventh day I resigned. On the eighth, Mr. Goodman returned and found six duels on his hands—my personalities had borne fruit. (*RI 1993*, 377–78)

Goodman actually returned to Virginia City on 8 April 1864, well before Shakespeare's birthday. There is no evidence that there were any challenges awaiting him (18 Mar 1864 to PAM, *L1*, 280 n. 15).

296.21–297.9   That theme was Mr. Laird . . . Laird accepted] The dispute between James L. Laird and Clemens occurred in May 1864, not in March–April while Clemens was the substitute editor of the *Territorial Enterprise*. It had at its heart an exchange of inflammatory columns in the Virginia City *Union* and the *Enterprise,* the latter written by Clemens, about funds raised in Nevada Territory for the U.S. Sanitary Commission, which aided sick and wounded Union soldiers (for full details, including Clemens's challenge to Laird and the response, see 20 May 1864 to MEC through 28 May 1864 to Cutler, *L1*, 287–301).

298.12–13   two years apiece in the penitentiary . . . brand-new law] This law was not "brand-new" in May of 1864. It was section 35 of "An Act concerning Crimes and Punishments," which had been passed on 26 November 1861. It established a penalty of from two to ten years' imprisonment for both the sending and delivering of a challenge (26 May 1864 to OC, *L1*, 300 n. 2).

298.13   Judge North] John W. North (1815–90) was an associate justice of the territorial supreme court from 1862 to 1864 (*L1:* 29, 30, and 31 Jan 1862 to MEC, 145–46 n. 2; 13 Apr 1862 to OC, 189 n. 12).

298.22–36   That was a Mr. Cutler . . . immediately left for Carson] William K. Cutler, whose wife, Ellen, was president of the Carson City committee that had raised funds for the U.S. Sanitary Commission, had been offended by some of Clemens's remarks in the *Territorial Enterprise* and had written to him in protest. Clemens responded defiantly on 28 May 1864, inviting Cutler to challenge him to a duel. It is not known whether Cutler obliged or, if he did, how much of the present account is accurate. What is known is that Clemens himself abruptly departed Nevada Territory on 29 May 1864 (see *L1:* 23 May 1864 to Cutler, 296–97; 25 May 1864 to OC and MEC, 297–99; 26 May 1864 to OC, 299–301; 28 May 1864 to Cutler and the link note that follows, 301–3).

299.1–6   In 1878 . . . I think it was correct and trustworthy] On 21 November 1878, two French politicians, the Republican Léon Gambetta (1838–82) and the Bonapartist Marie François Oscar Bardy de Fourtou (1836–97), fought a duel in which shots were exchanged but no one was injured. In 1880 Clemens ridiculed the encounter in "The Great French Duel," chapter 8 of *A Tramp Abroad*. One of his "inaccuracies" was his claim that his "long personal friendship with M. Gambetta" resulted in his acting as Gambetta's second "under a French name," which accounted "for the fact that in all the newspaper reports M. Gambetta's second was apparently a Frenchman" (New York *Times:* "The Latest Foreign News," 22 Nov 1878, 1; "General Foreign News," 23 Nov 1878, 1; "Belligerents of the Day," 7 Dec 1878, 1; Child 1887, 521–24).

299.9–11   Italian Ambassador, M. Nigra . . . Signor Cavallotti's adventures in that line] Constantino Nigra (1828–1907) was the Italian ambassador to Vienna from 1885 to 1904, one of several diplomatic posts he held. Felice Carlo Emmanuele Cavallotti (1842–98) was an Italian politician, author, and journalist known for fighting duels (see the notes at 302.14 and 302.30–33).

299.12–13   the unfinished chapter] The sixteen-page manuscript of his "unfinished chapter" was pasted onto the pages of the typescript. Entitled "Dueling," it was written in Vienna on 8 March 1898; Paine published it in 1923 in *Europe and Elsewhere* (SLC 1898a).

299.39–42   Some months ago Count Badeni . . . the State forbids dueling] On 25 September 1897, Kasimir Felix Badeni (1846–1909), the Galician-born Austrian premier, fought a duel with Karl Hermann Wolf (1862–1941), a German Nationalist leader who had called him a "Polish pig." Badeni suffered a superficial wound to his right wrist. Although dueling was illegal and considered a mortal sin by the church, neither man was prosecuted or excommunicated (New York *Times:* "Premier Badeni Wounded," 26 Sept 1897, 5; "The Badeni-Wolff Duel," 27 Sept 1897, 5; "Count Badeni Not to Be Punished," 28 Sept 1897, 7; Dolmetsch 1992, 67).

300.41–42   unter sehr schweren Bedingungen] Under very severe conditions.

302.3–12   duel between Colonels Henry and Picquart . . . the duel then terminated] French army colonels Georges Picquart (1854–1914) and Hubert-Joseph Henry (1846–98) were among the principal figures in the Dreyfus Affair, a long controversy that began with the 1894 rigged conviction of Captain Alfred Dreyfus (1859–1935), a Jew victimized by anti-Semitic elements in the army and the press, for passing secret information to Germany. Picquart discovered that Dreyfus was not responsible for the treason and came to his defense, despite official warnings to conceal the discovery. In February 1898 Picquart and Henry testified for and against Émile Zola, respectively, in Zola's trial for libel for his writings in support of Dreyfus. During testimony Henry called Picquart a liar, which resulted in their 5 March 1898 duel. Henry subsequently confessed to forging much of the evidence against Dreyfus and then, on 31 August 1898, committed suicide. Picquart, whose defense of Dreyfus had led to his dismissal from the army, was reinstated when Dreyfus was finally exonerated in 1906. Arthur Ranc (1831–1908) was a French politician, novelist, and writer on history and politics ("Col. Picquart Wins a Duel," New York *Times,* 6 Mar 1898, 7).

302.14   fatal duel of day before yesterday in Italy] Clemens alludes to the 6 March 1898 duel in Rome in which Felice Cavallotti was killed by a political and journalistic adversary. Sources differ as to whether it was his thirty-second or thirty-third duel ("Roman Duel Ends Fatally," New York *Times,* 7 Mar 1898, 1).

302.19   I did not disturb him] Clemens's "Dueling" manuscript ends here; there was no additional text in the first typed version of this dictation. But the presence of pinholes on the last leaf indicates that there was originally a newspaper clipping appended: below these words on the second, revised typescript, the following instruction is typed: "Here insert—and translate—the German article about Caval[l]otti's duels." When Clemens later read this second typescript he canceled the instruction and below it wrote the paragraph that follows, dated 13 May 1907. It is possible that the added paragraph includes his own paraphrase of the unidentified "German article."

302.30–33   He held his sword . . . Death was instantaneous] According to the New York *Times,* when the duel began, Cavallotti "attacked his opponent vigorously":

> The first two engagements were without result, but in the third Signor Cavallotti received a thrust in the throat that severed his jugular. At first it was thought he was injured only slightly, but the gravity of the wound was perceived on his putting his hand to his mouth. He withdrew it covered with blood, and thereafter he could not utter a word. . . . Signor Cavallotti expired in ten minutes without speaking again. ("Roman Duel Ends Fatally," 7 Mar 1898, 1)

Autobiographical Dictation, 23 January 1906

302.37–38   Booker Washington's Tuskegee Educational Institute] Washington (1856–1915), born into slavery in Virginia, taught himself to read. He attended Hampton Institute and became a teacher there. Chosen to head the Tuskegee Normal and Industrial Institute in Alabama in 1881, he was a prominent advocate for the education and advancement of African Americans. Espousing a policy of "separate but equal" facilities for the races, he secured white as well as black support for the institute and his larger goals, while clandestinely supporting more militant efforts to achieve full civil rights for African Americans.

303.2–10   Mr. Choate presided . . . Fourth of July reception in Mr. Choate's house in London] Renowned lawyer, diplomat, and wit Joseph H. Choate (1832–1917) was U.S. ambassador to Britain from 1899 to 1905. Clemens had been acquainted with him since at least 1876, and they had shared the platform on several occasions. Clemens first met Washington at Choate's reception on Independence Day 1899—where there were over fifteen hundred guests. The day before, Choate had introduced Washington's lecture on the "condition and prospects of the coloured race in America" at Essex Hall, London ("The Coloured Race in America," London *Times,* 4 July 1899, 13; New York *Times:* "Forefathers' Day," 23 Dec 1876, 1; "Independence Day Abroad," 5 July 1899, 7).

303.29   CHOATE AND TWAIN PLEAD FOR TUSKEGEE] Clemens dictated the instruction "Here insert the newspaper account of the meeting at Carnegie (of Jan. 22nd). The future editor of this biography can use what he chooses of it, or leave it out." Hobby transcribed the entire article, which is also reproduced here. In the Autobiographical Dictation of 3 April 1906 he again wrote "[Insert Carnegie Hall speech here.]" on the typescript.

303.40   Robert C. Ogden] Ogden (1836–1913), a businessman and philanthropist, was a trustee of Tuskegee Institute and the Hampton Institute as well.

304.3–4   last November, when District Attorney Jerome . . . packing Carnegie Hall]
William Travers Jerome (1859–1934), the district attorney of New York County, opposed the
corrupt Tammany Hall "bosses." He held rallies at Carnegie Hall on 18 October and 1 No-
vember 1905; at the latter he was introduced by "attendant spellbinder" Joseph H. Choate
(New York *Times:* "Jerome Forces Expect a Big Crowd To-Night," 18 Oct 1905, 5; "Whip the
Bosses, Choate's Bugle Call," 2 Nov 1905, 1).

304.11   wealthy men who swear off tax assessments] Under New York City tax laws of
the time, "a person assessed for personal property may 'swear off' the assessment by making
oath that he does not own so much" (Hoxie 1910, 59).

304.22   William Jay Schieffelin] Schieffelin (1866–1955), a prominent businessman and
civic reformer, was a trustee of Tuskegee Institute ("W. J. Schieffelin of Drug Firm Dies," New
York *Times,* 1 May 1955, 88).

304.26–27   Secretary of War Taft, President Eliot of Harvard, Bishop Galloway, and
Andrew Carnegie] William Howard Taft, secretary of war since 1904 and later president
(1909–13); Charles William Eliot (1834–1926), president of Harvard University (1869–1909),
which granted Washington an honorary degree in 1896; Bishop Charles B. Galloway (1849–
1909) of the Methodist Episcopal Church South in Mississippi; and Scottish-born industrialist
and philanthropist Andrew Carnegie (1835–1919) ("Bishop Galloway Dead," New York
Times, 13 May 1909, 7).

305.6–8   I read in a book . . . by Mr. Murphy, Secretary of the Southern Education
Board . . . wiped away more than one half] Edgar Gardner Murphy (1869–1913), an Episcopal
clergyman and amateur astronomer, was the board's executive secretary from 1903 to 1908.
Choate referred to *Problems of the Present South,* in which Murphy claimed that "the illiteracy
of the negro males of voting age has been reduced in the Southern States from 88 per cent in
1870 to 52 per cent in 1900" (Murphy 1904, 165; Bailey 2009).

307.37   Dr. Parkhurst] In 1892, New York Presbyterian clergyman Charles Henry
Parkhurst (1842–1933) preached a sermon attacking the Tammany government's complicity
in crime and vice. A grand jury decided that his charges were made without sufficient evidence;
but Parkhurst rose to the empirical challenge, researching New York's underworld in person
and through detectives, obtaining enough data to instigate the Lexow Investigation and Tammany's defeat (1894).

308.8–9   historian John Fiske, whom I knew well and loved] The historian John Fiske
(1842–1901) published many works on evolutionary theory, and was a popular lyceum circuit
lecturer. He lived in Cambridge, Massachusetts; Clemens knew him through Howells
(*MTHL,* 1:36–37, 181 n. 5).

308.12–15   his wife . . . little son] Fiske married Abby M. Brooks (1840–1925) in 1864
and they had six children ("Obituary Notes," New York *Times,* 13 Jan 1925, 19).

308.29   Henry Clay Trumbull] James Hammond Trumbull's brother was a Hartford
Congregational minister and author (1830–1903).

308.39   Thomas Dixon, Jr.] Dixon (1864–1946), born in North Carolina but a resident of New York City, was an actor, lawyer, politician, and Baptist minister before becoming an immensely popular and controversial author. At the time of this Tuskegee benefit, his latest novel was *The Clansman* (1905), in which the Ku Klux Klan free the South from "negro rule"; the book was ultimately the basis of D. W. Griffith's *The Birth of a Nation* (1915).

310.12   Langdons, the family into which I married] See the Autobiographical Dictation of 1 February 1906, note at 321.25–27.

310.20–22   reference was made . . . in Washington, day after to-morrow] Clemens spoke at the meeting of the Gridiron Club on 27 January 1906. Its tradition of inviting the president and other officials for an annual satirical "roast" continues to this day. In 1906 the target of fun was the Panama Canal; President Roosevelt, Secretary of War Taft, and Colonel Harvey were among the invited guests. Evidently Clemens considered reviving his Whittier dinner speech for this occasion; earlier he had spoken of delivering it at Boston's Twentieth Century Club ("A Night in Panama," Washington *Post,* 28 Jan 1906, 1, 6).

310.37–38   Reverend Charles Stowe, a son of Harriet Beecher Stowe] Charles Edward Stowe (1850–1934), a Congregationalist minister, was the youngest of the seven children of fellow Nook Farm residents Harriet Beecher Stowe (1811–96), the author of *Uncle Tom's Cabin* (1852) and other works, and her husband, Calvin Ellis Stowe (1802–86), a retired professor of theology (10 and 11 Jan 1872 to OLC, *L5,* 20 n. 4; "Rites Set for Rev. C. E. Stowe, Son of Author," Los Angeles *Times,* 26 July 1934, 6; "Nook Farm Genealogy" 1974, 5, 28–29).

310 *footnote*   *May 25 . . . I gave it a final and vigorous reading . . . my former admiration of it.   M. T.] On his copy of the Whittier dinner seating plan, Clemens later wrote: "*Note, 1907.* This is Mr. Whittier's 70th birthday dinner—that disastrous cataclysm! ~~See account of it in my Autobiography. SLC~~" (CU-MARK). Given his praises of the speech in the present dictation and in the dictation of 11 January 1906, it is likely that "disastrous cataclysm" was ironic hyperbole.

311.3–4   Rev. Dr. Burton's "Remains," . . . your remarks at his funeral] See the Autobiographical Dictation of 12 January 1906. By "Burton's 'Remains'" is meant the posthumous collection of his lectures, which was prefaced with the funeral orations by both Twichell and Parker (Burton 1888, 27).

312.21   The Character of Man] Clemens dictated the instruction, "Put old MS. here." He wrote this essay in 1884 or 1885, and revised the manuscript in January 1906 before Hobby transcribed it. The essay was first published in Paine's edition of the autobiography (*MTA,* 2:7–13; see also *WIM,* 60–64, 586).

312.26–27   Creator. * * * *] Here, and below at 313.1 and 313.26, Clemens canceled passages in his manuscript and substituted asterisks to indicate the omissions. The canceled passages are transcribed in the Textual Commentary, *MTPO.*

313.32–35   one single independent man . . . to breed his fellow] In his manuscript Clemens interlined "H. L. Goodwin" in pencil above "fellow" and then canceled the interlineation in ink. Henry Leavitt Goodwin (1821–99) was a longtime resident of East Hartford, a member of the Connecticut general assembly in the early 1870s, and always much involved in public affairs. Over the course of years he "protested irregularities in the Hartford transit system and the New York, New Haven, and Hartford Railroad Company" (*WIM,* 537; "Henry L. Goodwin Dead," Hartford *Courant,* 17 Mar 1899, 1). It has not been determined when this "one single independent man" took his stand for seating.

313.35–36   Asylum street crossing] In Hartford.

313.42   Mrs. Grundy] An imaginary personage, proverbially standing for the threat of society's disapproval; derived originally from Thomas Morton's play *Speed the Plough* (1798).

314.15–18   Hartford clergyman . . . relative of mine] Clemens probably refers to Matthew Brown Riddle (1836–1916), professor at Hartford Theological Seminary from 1871 to 1887. Well known locally as one of the principal American contributors to the Revised Version of the New Testament (1881), he seems also to have been related to James G. Blaine (*WIM,* 537; "Dr. M. B. Riddle Dead, Aged 80," Hartford *Courant,* 2 Sept 1916, 18).

314.22–23   the Cid, and Great-heart, and Sir Galahad, and Bayard the Spotless] These paragons of virtue are drawn variously from legend, literature, and history. The Cid, Rodrigo Diaz de Bivar (ca. 1030–99), is Spain's great hero of medieval romance; Great-heart is from Part Two of Bunyan's *The Pilgrim's Progress* (1678); Sir Galahad, in Arthurian legend, is the knight whose purity enables him to attain the Holy Grail; Bayard the Spotless is French knight Pierre du Terrail (1475–1524).

314.35   The preacher who casts a vote for conscience' sake, runs the risk of starving] Clemens expands on this comment in the Autobiographical Dictations of 24 January and 1 February 1906.

314.38–315.1   Mr. Beecher may be charged with a *crime* . . . stand by him to the bitter end] In 1872 Henry Ward Beecher, the world-famous preacher of Plymouth Church in Brooklyn, was accused of committing adultery with Elizabeth Tilton, one of his parishioners. In August 1874 Beecher was officially exonerated by a church council, whose verdict was strongly approved by the parishioners. That same month, Theodore Tilton sued Beecher for alienation of affections; the trial ended in a hung jury in 1875 (29? July 1874 to Twichell, n. 2, *L6,* 202–3; Applegate 2006, 440–42).

314 *footnote*   Blaine] James G. Blaine (1830–93), the Republican presidential candidate in 1884, was accused by many, including some in his own party, of graft during his terms as congressman. Clemens joined with the faction of Republicans (the "mugwumps") who repudiated Blaine and pledged to vote for Grover Cleveland, or another candidate, in protest. Their objections to Blaine are set forth in the public letter "To the Republican Voters of Connecticut," which was signed by some one hundred Connecticut Republicans, including Clemens and Twichell ("Connecticut Independents," New York *Times,* 13 Oct 1884, 1; *N&J3,* 77–78 n. 39; see AD, 24 Jan 1906).

314 *footnote*   Hammond Trumbull] See the Autobiographical Dictation of 12 January 1906, note at 272.31–32.

315.1–2   but who so poor to be his friend . . . a vote for conscience' sake] In 1884 Beecher, formerly a staunch Republican, declared he could not vote for Blaine, and campaigned for

Cleveland, despite the revelation that Cleveland had fathered an illegitimate child. Beecher's support of Cleveland—and the suspicion it engendered that he felt for Cleveland as a fellow adulterer—earned him public mockery and private threats (Chicago *Tribune:* "Campaign Chronicles," 30 Sept 1884, 2; "Beecher's Support of Cleveland," 20 Oct 1884, 7; Beecher and Scoville 1888, 576–81; Applegate 2006, 462–64).

315.2   Take the editor so charged] Clemens apparently alludes to Charles Dudley Warner, who was editor and part owner of the Hartford *Courant* (see AD, 24 Jan 1906, and note at 317.35–40).

Autobiographical Dictation, 24 January 1906

315.14   this old article] That is, "The Character of Man" (AD, 23 Jan 1906).

315.23–24   father of the William R. Hearst of to-day, and therefore grandfather of Yellow Journalism] George Hearst (1820–91) was born into a family of farmers in Franklin County, Missouri. He migrated West with the Gold Rush and by the 1860s owned several silver and copper mines, which he would develop into a colossal mining empire. In 1886 he was appointed to the seat vacated by the death of California Senator John Miller, and was subsequently elected for a full term. In 1880 he acquired the San Francisco *Examiner,* chiefly for the propagation of his political opinions and ambitions; his son William Randolph Hearst (1863–1951) made it the cornerstone of a newspaper empire whose publications were frequently criticized as sensationalist and irresponsible. On Clemens's attitude toward "yellow journalism," see Budd 1981.

316.13–14   Sam Dunham . . . Edward M. Bunce] Samuel G. Dunham (b. 1849), brother of Austin Dunham, was a Hartford wool merchant at the time of Blaine's nomination, and later vice-president of the Hartford Electric Light Company and a director of the Aetna Life Insurance Company (Dunham 1907, 38–39; Geer 1882, 65). Like Ned Bunce, he played billiards regularly at Clemens's house. Bunce (1841–98), also of a prominent Hartford family, was for many years a cashier at the Phoenix National Bank and a director of the Connecticut Mutual Life Insurance Company (*N&J2,* 382 n. 76, 426 n. 229; "Edward M. Bunce," Hartford *Courant,* 22 Nov 1898, 5). He was a close friend of the Clemens family; after his early death, Clemens wrote, "Ned was nearer & dearer to the children than was any other person not of the blood" (2 Dec 1898 to Bunce, CtHMTH).

316.17   George] George Griffin.

317.23–24   General Hawley, the editor-in-chief . . . of the paper . . . his post in Congress] In addition to being editor and part owner of the Hartford *Courant,* Joseph Roswell Hawley (1826–1905) was a lawyer, antislavery crusader, founder of the Connecticut Republican party, Civil War veteran (retired as a brevet major-general), and, briefly, governor of Connecticut (1866). At the time of Blaine's nomination he was a U.S. senator (13 and 14 Feb 1869 to OLL, *L3,* 97 n. 5).

317.33   Charles Hopkins Clark's editorship] Clark (1848–1926) became editor-in-chief in 1900; he had been on the editorial staff since 1871, the year he graduated from Yale (29 Apr 1875 to Holland, *L6,* 471 n. 2).

317.35–40   Charles Dudley Warner . . . election day] Clemens was in error: Warner neither refused to toe the *Courant*'s party line nor resigned as editor. In an 1884 letter Clemens chastised Warner, along with others, for concealing his private reservations: "Even *I* do not loathe Blaine more than they do; yet Hawley is howling for Blaine, Warner & Clark are eating their daily crow in the paper for him" (31 Aug 1884 to Howells, NN-BGC, in *MTHL,* 2:500–503; Kenneth R. Andrews 1950, 115).

317.41   conversation with the learned American member] Probably Matthew Riddle (see AD, 23 Jan 1906, 314.15–18 and note).

318.3–4   James G. Batterson . . . Travelers Insurance Company] Batterson (1823–1901) was also president of the New England Granite Works and an amateur Egyptologist ("James G. Batterson," New York *Times,* 19 Sept 1901, 7).

318.23–24   At that time the voting was public] Only in the 1890s did the secret ballot begin to be used in the United States. In Connecticut in 1884, the voter was observed; he was permitted to fold the ballot so that it could not easily be read, but social and political pressures guaranteed that this option was seldom exercised (Lynde Harrison 1890).

318.37–319.1   Twichell had most seriously damaged himself . . . his vote for Cleveland] Clemens's extended account of Twichell's vote and its aftermath is distorted. In the first place, Twichell is represented as having voted for Cleveland; in fact, he could not bring himself to support the Democrats in any cause, and cast his vote for the Prohibition Party candidate. Furthermore, although Twichell's vote did cause "displeasure," as he put it, "among my friends and parishioners," there is no evidence that he was ever asked to resign his pastorate (Kenneth R. Andrews 1950, 115–16; Strong 1966, 87–88; Courtney 2008, 216–20).

Autobiographical Dictation, 1 February 1906

319.22–23   Mr. Hubbard . . . business manager and part owner of the *Courant*] Stephen A. Hubbard (1827–90) had been part owner and managing editor of the Hartford *Courant* since 1867 (McNulty 1964, 91; "Obituary," Hartford *Courant,* 13 Jan 1890, 1).

320.4–6   fortieth anniversary . . . weeks ago] Twichell's fortieth year as pastor of Asylum Hill Congregational Church was celebrated on 13 December 1905 ("Rev. Mr. Twichell 40 Years Pastor," Hartford *Courant,* 14 Dec 1905, 12).

320.32–34   I saw her first in the form of an ivory miniature . . . the following December] Olivia's brother, Charles Langdon, was a youth of seventeen when his parents sent him on the *Quaker City* excursion as a safe alternative to a traditional grand tour. He struck up a friendship with Clemens near the end of the voyage, and showed him the miniature of Olivia on 5 or 6 September 1867, when the ship was in the Bay of Smyrna (link note following 8 June 1867 to McComb, *L2,* 63–64). Clemens's Autobiographical Dictations leave some room for doubt about the dates of his first meetings with Olivia. The dictation of 13 February 1906 states that they were introduced on 27 December 1867 and met again five days later; this ignores a known meeting on 31 December, when Clemens went with the Langdons to hear Dickens read at Steinway Hall (see AD, 12 Oct 1907). It is possible that this, and not the twenty-seventh, was the day he met Olivia (*L2:* 8 Jan 1868 to JLC and PAM, 145–46 n. 3; "Itinerary of the *Quaker City* Excursion," 394–95; "Mr. Dickens' Readings," New York *Times,* 31 Dec 1867, 4; for the excursion see "Notes on 'Innocents Abroad,'" note at 227.13–14).

321.7–8   nine years that we spent in poverty and debt] Clemens paid his debts in full in 1898, with the proceeds from his 1895–96 world lecture tour and the book based on it, *Following the Equator* (see "Something about Doctors," note at 190.10–12).

321.18   As I have already said in an earlier chapter] See the Autobiographical Dictation of 13 January 1906.

321.25–27   her father's house in Elmira, New York . . . with the whole Langdon family] Jervis Langdon (1809–70), a native of New York State, married Olivia Lewis in 1832, and the pair settled in Elmira in 1845. He became prosperous in the lumber business and then wealthy in the coal trade, which he entered in 1855. His extensive operations included mines in Pennsylvania and Nova Scotia, and a huge rail and shipping network supplying coal to western New York State, Chicago, and the Far West. An ardent abolitionist, Jervis Langdon served as a "conductor" on the Underground Railroad, and counted Frederick Douglass, whom he had helped to escape from slavery, among his friends. He died in 1870 of stomach cancer, leaving bequests totaling a million dollars. Olivia's inheritance was to remain central in the life of the Clemens family. Charles Jervis Langdon (1849–1916), Olivia's brother, succeeded his father in the management of the family's coal business; he also exercised considerable responsibility for his sister's inherited investments. In 1880 he served on Governor Alonzo B. Cornell's staff as commissary general, and was for many years one of Elmira's police commissioners (24 and 25 Aug 1868 to JLC and family, *L2,* 244 n. 3; "In Memoriam," Elmira *Saturday Evening Review,* 13 Aug 1870, 5; Towner 1892, 615).

321.28–29   I was to be one of the editors of the Buffalo *Express,* and a part owner of the paper] With the financial assistance of Jervis Langdon, Clemens purchased a one-third interest in the Buffalo *Express* in August 1869, becoming at the same time "associate editor" (*MTB,* 1:385–89; see 14 Aug 1869 to Bliss, *L3,* 296 n. 2).

321.30   a friend] John D. F. Slee, chief officer of Langdon's coal firm, played a part in the "conspiracy" described by Clemens. In December 1869 Slee wrote to Clemens that "boarding *anyhow* is miserable business" but that he had arranged rooms in a respectable boardinghouse and would appreciate advance notice of the couple's arrival, that he might "meet and accompany you to your 'Quarters'" (Slee to SLC, 27 Dec 1869, CU-MARK; 27 Feb 1869 to OLL, 24 and 25 Nov 1869 to OLL, *L3,* 119 n. 4, 406 n. 1).

321.37–38   Delaware Avenue, and had laid in a cook] The Clemenses' new house in Buffalo was at 472 Delaware Avenue. The cook and housekeeper, Ellen White, was a former Langdon family servant (6 Feb 1870 to Bowen, *L4,* 54–55 n. 5).

322.3   So the comedy ended very pleasantly] For other accounts of the Clemenses' wedding and the surprise in Buffalo, see the link note following 28–31 Jan 1870 to Twichell, *L4,* 42–49.

322.27 Patrick's daughter Nancy] Anne (Nancy) McAleer, born in 1883, was a near contemporary of Jean's (*Hartford Census* 1900, 8B; *Hartford Census* 1910, 7B).

322.31–42 Patrick McAleer, faithful and valued friend of our family . . . served it thirty-six years] McAleer (1844?–1906) was born in County Tyrone, Ireland, and emigrated to America at age sixteen. He married Mary Reagan of Elmira, New York; they had nine children, one of whom evidently died in infancy ("Coachman Many Years for Mark Twain," Hartford *Courant,* 26 Feb 1906, 6; *Hartford Census* 1910, 7B). McAleer moved with the Clemenses from Buffalo to Hartford, working for them, almost without interruption, until 1891. He returned briefly to the Clemens household in Dublin, New Hampshire, in 1905; in a letter of 20 May 1905 to his daughter Clara, Clemens described his delight in seeing him again:

> And Patrick! He is a vision out of a time when your mother was a girl & I a lad! And what a pleasure he is to my eye, & how the view of him fits in with the rest of the scenery! The same, same Patrick—trim, shapely, alert, competent for all things, taking two steps to any other man's one, not a gray hair nor any other sign of age about him, & his voice that same old pleasant sound! He served us twenty-two years & is a youth yet. (MoHM)

323.13–14 They lost one . . . assistant editor of a Hartford daily paper] One of McAleer's sons, Edward McAleer, a plumber, died in January 1905 at age thirty; nothing is known of a son who worked for a newspaper ("Killed by a Fall," Hartford *Courant,* 30 Jan 1905, 5).

Autobiographical Dictation, 2 February 1906

324.32 her uncle and aunt, Mr. and Mrs. Theodore Crane] Susan Langdon Crane (1836–1924) was born Susan Dean, but was orphaned at the age of four and adopted by the Langdon family. Although she was nearly ten years older than Olivia, her foster sister, they remained close throughout their lives. In 1858 she married Theodore Crane (1831–89), who later became a partner in the Langdon family coal business. The Cranes lived at Quarry Farm, outside Elmira. The uncle present during Susy's final illness was Charles Langdon, not Crane, who had died some years earlier (19 Aug 1896 to OLC [1st], CU-MARK, in *LLMT,* 321–22; Notebook 39, TS p. 55, CU-MARK).

325.15–25 In one of her own books I find some verses . . . whispered "I am rest."] As Clemens later discovered (see AD, 22 Jan 1907), this poem was not written by Susy but by Canadian poet William Wilfred Campbell (1860?–1918). Entitled "Love," it was first published in the October 1891 issue of the *Century Magazine,* where Susy most likely saw it (Campbell 1891).

326.13–21 Miss Foote (the governess) had been teaching her . . . God and a heaven—or something better] Since about 1880 Susy and Clara's Hartford governess had been Lilly Gillette Foote (1860–1932), a "recent graduate of Cambridge University's Newnham College, . . . worldly, well-travelled, and socially progressive," and also "the niece of Harriet Foote Hawley, one of the five Hartford women who in October 1880 founded the Connecticut Indian Association, a female native rights advocacy organization" (Salsbury 1965, 426; Driscoll 2005, 8). Clemens was not above learning something from his daughter and her governess. In 1884 he extensively annotated Richard Irving Dodge's *Our Wild Indians: Thirty-Three Years' Personal Experience among the Red Men of the Great West* (Dodge 1883), saying at one point that "The Indian's bad God is the twin of our only God; his good God is better than any heretofore devised by man." Also: "Our illogical God is all-powerful in name, but impotent in fact; the Great Spirit is not all-powerful, but does the very best he can for his injun and does it free of charge." And: "We have to keep our God placated with prayers, and even then we are never sure of him—how much higher and finer is the Indian's God" (*HH&T,* 90; quoted in Driscoll 2005, 5).

326.22–23   I wrote down this pathetic prayer . . . children's sayings] In 1881 Clemens did indeed record this exchange in "A Record of the Small Foolishnesses of Susie & 'Bay' Clemens (Infants)":

> Susie (9 yrs old,) had been sounding the deeps of life, & pondering the result. Meantime the governess had been instructing her about the American Indians. One day Mamma, with a smitten conscience, said—
> "Susie, I have been so busy that I haven't been in at night lately to hear you say your prayers. Maybe I can come in tonight. Shall I?"
> Susie hesitated, waited for her thought to formulate itself, then brought it out:
> "Mamma, I don't pray as much as I used to—& I don't pray in the same way. Maybe you would not approve of the way I pray now."
> "Tell me about it, Susie."
> "Well, mamma, I don't know that I can make you understand; but you know, the Indians thought they knew: & they had a great many gods. We know, now, that they were wrong. By & by, maybe it will be found out that *we* are wrong, too. So, now, I only pray *that there may be a God—& a heaven—*OR SOMETHING BETTER."
> It was a philosophy that a sexagenarian need not have been ashamed of having evolved. (SLC 1876–85, 89–90)

327.11–13   She had written a play . . . friends in our house in Hartford] Susy's play, entitled *A Love-Chase,* was performed in the drawing room of the Hartford house on Thanksgiving night 1889, and repeated twice on later occasions. The cast included Susy, Clara, Jean, and Margaret (Daisy) Warner (1872–1931), the daughter of George and Lilly Warner (3 Dec 1889 to Baxter, NN-BGC). Clemens gave a fuller version in "Memorial to Susy":

> When Susy was nearly seventeen she wrote a play herself—a lovely little fancy, formed upon Greek lines. There were songs in it, & music, & several dances. There were only five characters: Music, Art, Literature, Cupid, & a shepherd lad. Susie was Music, Margaret Warner was Literature, Clara was Art, Fanny Frees was the shepherd lad, & our Jean— what there was of her—was Cupid. She was very little. Susy was a vision. I can see her yet as she parted the curtains & stood there, young, fresh, aglow with excitement, & clothed in a tumbling cataract of pink roses. (SLC 1896–1906, 42–43)

327.14   George] George H. Warner (1833–1919) worked for the American Emigrant Company, which helped foreign settlers. His wife, Lilly (1835–1915), was the former Elisabeth Gillette (link note following 7 Mar 1872 to OC, *L5,* 56).

327.19 Mrs. Cheney, I think, author of the biography of her father] Mary Bushnell Cheney published *Life and Letters of Horace Bushnell* in 1880.

327.31 In Munich] The Clemens family—Samuel, Olivia, Susy, and Clara, with family friend Clara Spaulding and the children's nurse Rosina Hay—toured Europe in 1878–79, visiting Germany, Switzerland, Italy, France, Belgium, Holland, and England. They were in Munich from November 1878 through February 1879. This European tour furnished Clemens with material for his travel book *A Tramp Abroad* (*N&J2*, 3, 41–43, 48).

327.36 *she* was "never the one that ate, but always the one that was eaten."] Clemens recorded Susy's comment in his manuscript "A Record of the Small Foolishnesses of Susie & 'Bay' Clemens (Infants)," where it is given in Susy's "exact language": "But mamma, the trouble is, that I am never the *bear* but always the PERSON" (SLC 1876–85, 31).

327.38 When she was six and her sister Clara four] In "Small Foolishnesses" Clemens dated this incident 7 December 1880, at which time Susy was eight, and Clara six (SLC 1876–85, 86).

328.12 Marjorie Fleming] Marjorie (properly Marjory) Fleming, born in Kirkcaldy (Fife, Scotland) in 1803, died of spinal meningitis at the age of eight, leaving behind her a small but precocious body of writing: letters, journals, and poems. In 1858, H. B. Farnie published selections from her works in *Pet Marjorie: A Story of Child Life Fifty Years Ago*. Dr. John Brown (1810–82), an Edinburgh physician and man of letters best known for his dog story "Rab and His Friends" (1858), published an elaborate essay inspired by Farnie's book in 1863, developing a sentimental and undocumented friendship between Marjory and Sir Walter Scott. Brown's essay was frequently reprinted in book form. When the Clemenses befriended Dr. Brown in 1873, he gave Olivia a copy. Clemens's enthusiasm for this literary child heroine found belated expression in his magazine article "Marjorie Fleming, the Wonder Child" (SLC 1909d). Susy might have reminded Clemens of Marjory for reasons beyond their connection with Dr. Brown: both were precocious literary talents, both died of meningitis, and Clemens was now engaged in publishing Susy's juvenilia (Fleming 1935, xiii–xxii; Farnie 1858; OLC and SLC to Langdon, 2 and 6 Aug 1873, *L5*, 428–29 n. 2; John Brown 1863a, 1863b; Gribben 1980, 1:87).

328.16 In 1873 . . . we arrived in Edinburgh] The Clemens family—with Clara Spaulding, Clemens's secretary (Samuel C. Thompson), and Susy's nursemaid (Nellie)—arrived in London in May 1873 expecting to stay in England until October. Clemens was greatly lionized, and his social schedule left the family little time for sightseeing, leisure, and the collection of materials for a book. Clemens wrote to Mary Mason Fairbanks on 6 July: "We seem to see nothing but English social life; we seem to find no opportunity to see London sights. . . . nothing, in fact, to make a book of"; and to Warner he complained, "We only dine. We do nothing else." For relief, they decided to "'do' Scotland," and went to Edinburgh (*L5:* 12 May 1873 to Redpath, 364; OLC and SLC to Langdon, 17 May 1873, 366–67; 6 July 1873 to Fairbanks, 402; 10? July 1873 to Warner, 411).

Autobiographical Dictation, 5 February 1906

328.30–33 Mr. Douglas, the publisher . . . the support of himself and his maiden sister]
Brown suffered from depression. On 28 February 1876 George Barclay wrote to Clemens that
Brown's health had "so completely given way under the strain of professional practice, as to
make in the opinion of his friends more than doubtful whether Dr Brown will ever be able
safely to attempt *regular* practice as a physician again" (CU-MARK). The friends who took it
upon themselves to raise the fund were headed by Barclay and Edinburgh publisher David
Douglas. For his part, Clemens gave a public reading with the proceeds going (confidentially)
to Brown. In a letter of 5 May, Barclay acknowledged receipt of £40 from Clemens, adding
that almost £7,000 had been raised and that Brown had announced his retirement. That same
year Brown was awarded a royal pension "for distinguished literary eminence" (CU-MARK).
Brown's sister, Isabella Cranston Brown (1812–88), had managed his household since the
marriage of his daughter in 1866 (17 Mar 1876 to Redpath, n. 2, *Letters 1876–1880;* OLC
and SLC to Langdon, 2 and 6 Aug 1873, *L5,* 427, 429 n. 3).

329.11–12 "Who is it? Some one you know?" He said "No, a dog I *don't* know."] This
anecdote comes from Elizabeth T. McLaren's memoir, *Dr. John Brown and His Sister Isabella:
Outlines.* This little book was published in 1889 by Brown's half-brother, Alex. Olivia's copy,
signed and dated 1890, is in the Mark Twain Papers (McLaren 1889, 14).

329.14 her big big brown eyes] In the first typescript of this dictation, Susy's eyes are
"blue"; Clemens apparently revised that to "brown," the reading in the second typescript (his
actual inscription is now illegible). He complained that he was almost never able to recall the
eye color of others, even those closest to him. On one occasion—which he recalled took place
in 1886—it was discovered that he did not know the eye color of any of his three daughters
(see AD, 8 Nov 1906).

329.30 that anecdote . . . told some hundreds of times on the platform] Clemens frequently told the "whistling story" in his 1871–74 lectures, and on other occasions as well; he
had Colonel Sellers tell it in act four of the *Gilded Age* play. He usually attributed the story to
Artemus Ward (SLC 1874a; link note following 10 Nov 1875 to Seaver, *L6,* 590–91).

331.12 sale of Joseph by his brethren] Genesis 37.

331.21–27 Once when Susy . . . crooked teeth and spectacles!] The version of this anecdote
set down at the time in Clemens's "Record of Small Foolishnesses" reveals that the "guest" was
actually Olivia, and gives Susy's exclamation as "I wish *I* could have crooked teeth & spectacles,
like mamma!" (SLC 1876–85, 37).

331.31 what the shade of Burns would think] See Robert Burns, "To a Louse, On Seeing
One on a Lady's Bonnet at Church" (Burns 1969, 157):

> O wad some Pow'r the giftie gie us
> *To see oursels as others see us!*
> It wad frae monie a blunder free us
>   An' foolish notion . . .

332.9–22　Schloss gardens . . . "The 'Slosh,' at Heidelberg."] The Schloss (castle) overlooking the town of Heidelberg has been a picturesque ruin since the eighteenth century. Adjoining it are the extensive Schloss Gardens, a place of public recreation, where Susy saw the "wild" snails. The first-class Schloss-Hotel—the subject of the interpolated anecdote—was on a hill above the castle, and was directly connected to the Schloss Gardens; the Clemenses stayed there from May through late July 1878. Clemens wrote about these places in chapters 2 and 4 and appendix B of *A Tramp Abroad* (Baedeker 1880, 226–29; *N&J2*, 79 n. 74).

334.11　sicisiors] Clemens reacted to Olivia's spelling of this word in his letter of 17 January 1869: "'Sicisiors' don't spell *scissors*, you funny little orthographist" (*L3*, 45). Olivia's own letter is not extant. Some of Clemens's remarks here about spelling, and about Susan Crane's spelling in particular, recast material he had used long before at a spelling bee in 1875 ("Clemens's 'Spelling Match' Speech," *L6*, 659–63).

Autobiographical Dictation, 6 February 1906

334.36–37　I took to the platform again . . . in company with George W. Cable] From 1874 to 1884 Clemens made no lecture tours, giving only isolated readings (Fatout 1976, 651–56). His tour with George Washington Cable extended from November 1884 through February 1885.

335.3　General Grant has actually concluded to write his autobiography] See "About General Grant's Memoirs."

335.8–9　took her to see him . . . I will return to it by and by] See the Autobiographical Dictation of 26 February 1906.

335.18–21　At once the curtain was drawn . . . Susy Clemens, arrayed in the silks and satins of the prince] The first performance of the family's *Prince and the Pauper* play took place on 14 March 1885, after the Clemens-Cable lecture tour had ended. For Susy's own account of the play and its preparation, see the Autobiographical Dictation of 8 August 1906 (14 Mar 1885 to Pond, NN-BGC).

335.28–32　George . . . had been born a slave, in Maryland . . . body-servant to General Devens all through the war] George Griffin (1849?–97) was the Clemens family's butler from at least 1875 until their removal to Europe in 1891. He was born in Virginia, not Maryland; during the Civil War he served General Charles Devens (1820–91). After leaving the Clemens family he moved to New York City, where, according to Clemens, he became a waiter at the Union League Club and did business as a private banker (4 Nov 1875 to Howells, *L6*, 583 n. 5; Grace King 1932, 86; SLC 1906a, 21–23).

336.3　Twichell's littlest cub, now a grave and reverend clergyman] Joseph Hooker Twichell (1883–1961), Joseph and Harmony Twichell's eighth child and youngest son, graduated from Yale in 1906 and four years later earned a Bachelor of Divinity degree from the Hartford Theological Seminary (Hartford Seminary Record 1910, 222; Courtney 2008, 224, 261–62). He was the only Twichell child to become a clergyman; presumably Clemens was making a joke about his youth.

336.18 Will Gillette, now world famous actor and dramatist] William Hooker Gillette (1853–1937) was Lilly Warner's younger brother. After graduating from Hartford Public High School in 1873, he studied acting in St. Louis and New Orleans, playing minor roles with a stock company. In 1875, assisted by Clemens's personal recommendation and financial support, he secured a role in the touring production of the *Gilded Age* play, and went on to a long and successful career as an actor and dramatist. He became particularly associated with the role of Sherlock Holmes (OLC and SLC to Langdon, 14 Mar 1875, *L6,* 413–14 n. 8).

337.12 the divine Sarah] Sarah Bernhardt (stage name of Rosine Bernard, 1844–1923) was the most famous actress of her time. Susy saw her perform at least twice in Florence in 1893, in two of her most famous vehicles, *Adrienne Lecouvreur* and *La Tosca.* At the time of this dictation, Clemens had recently spoken at a Bernhardt performance benefiting the Jews of Russia (OSC to CC, 24 Jan 1893, TS in CU-MARK; "Mark Twain Speaks After Bernhardt Acts," New York *Times,* 19 Dec 1905, 9).

Autobiographical Dictation, 7 February 1906

337.20–24 When Susy was thirteen . . . writing of a biography of me] Clemens wrote in his notebook in early April 1885, "Susie, aged 13, (1885), has begun to write my biography— solely of her own motion—a thing about which I feel proud & gratified" (*N&J3,* 112; quoted more fully in the Introduction, p. 9). She worked on the biography until July 1886.

338.8 I shall print the whole of this little biography] Clemens ultimately used most, but by no means all, of Susy's text.

338.10 The spelling is frequently desperate, but it was Susy's, and it shall stand] Collation of Susy's manuscript with Hobby's typescript demonstrates that the text was transmitted orally to Hobby—that is, Clemens evidently read Susy's text aloud and directed Hobby to spell many of the words incorrectly, as in the original (see the Textual Commentary for AD, 2 Feb 1906, *MTPO*). Occasionally Susy spelled something properly that was rendered erroneously in the typescript, and vice versa. Clemens also sometimes adapted her prose to the surrounding dictation.

338.30 John Robards] See the Autobiographical Dictation of 9 March 1906, note at 401.7–16.

339.17–18 I took the precaution of sending my book, in manuscript, to Mr. Howells, when he was editor of the *Atlantic Monthly*] William Dean Howells was assistant editor (to 1871) and then editor (1871–81) of the *Atlantic Monthly.* During that time he reviewed in its pages *The Innocents Abroad* (1869), *Roughing It* (1872), *Sketches New and Old* (1875), *Tom Sawyer* (1876), and *A Tramp Abroad* (1880). Of these, the only ones he read "in manuscript" were *Tom Sawyer* and *A Tramp Abroad;* he did, however, continue to read many of Clemens's books in manuscript and review them in other journals (Budd 1999, 71–73, 105–6, 151–52, 157–58, 186–88, 215, 292–95, 407).

339.28–340.5 "The Gilded Age," . . . Chicago *Tribune* . . . adopted the view of the humble

Daily Graphic, dishonesty-charge and all] Clemens is incorrect in asserting that the New York *Daily Graphic* "scooped" the *Atlantic Monthly* in reviewing *The Gilded Age.* The *Atlantic* did not review *The Gilded Age* at all: since Howells felt he could not recommend it, he merely noted it as "received" (Howells 1874b, 374; Howells 1979, 46). As for the *Daily Graphic,* almost a year earlier its editor, David G. Croly, had given Clemens space to advertise the forthcoming novel. Clemens's letter, reproduced by the *Graphic* in facsimile, read in part:

> I consider it one of the most astonishing novels that ever was written. Night after night I sit up reading it over & over again & crying. It will be published early in the fall, with plenty of pictures. Do you consider this an advertisement?—& if so, do you charge for such things, when a man is your friend & is an orphan? (17 Apr 1873 to Croly, *L5,* 341–44; see "Photographs and Manuscript Facsimiles, 1872–73," *L5,* 668–71)

The *Graphic* reviewed *The Gilded Age* rather roughly, calling it an "incoherent series of sketches" and "a rather dreary failure." But it seems to have been the Chicago *Tribune* that originated the charges of "fraud," "deliberate deceit," and "abus[ing] the people's trust." The imputed offense was the authors' sale of substandard goods, not the use of Mark Twain's name to sell Warner's work ("Literary Notes," New York *Daily Graphic,* 23 Dec 1873, 351; "The Twain-Warner Novel," Chicago *Tribune,* 1 Feb 1874, 9).

340.28–31   I found this clipping . . . of the date of thirty-nine years ago . . . I will copy it here] The clipping itself does not survive, but the "correspondent of the Philadelphia *Press*" has been identified as Emily Edson Briggs (1830–1910), who wrote under the pen name "Olivia." The passage, drawn from her column datelined 2 March 1868 (in Briggs 1906, 45–47), was reprinted in one of the newspapers for which Clemens corresponded from Washington in early 1868—the Chicago *Republican,* the San Francisco *Alta California,* or the Virginia City *Territorial Enterprise.*

Autobiographical Dictation, 8 February 1906

341.19–20   Emmeline . . . an impressionist water-color] This painting was by Italian society portraitist Daniele Ranzoni (1843–89). Clemens bought it in Milan as a birthday present for Olivia in 1878. Its nickname of "Emmeline" may be related to the fictional picture made by Emmeline Grangerford described in chapter 17 of *Huckleberry Finn (N&J2,* 187 n. 50).

341.22   oil painting by Elihu Vedder, "The Young Medusa."] American painter Elihu Vedder (1836–1923) had been resident in Rome since 1867. Clemens bought "The Young Medusa" after a visit to Vedder's studio on 9 November 1878. If the painting was anything like the drawing by Vedder on the same theme, it depicted "the calm face of a woman with flowing locks. Tiny serpents are just springing from her forehead" (Soria 1964, 603–4; *N&J2,* 244–45 and n. 60).

342.11   Our burglar alarm] By 1877 the Clemenses' Hartford house had been outfitted with what one newspaper referred to as "Jerome's famous burglar alarm." By 1880 the house had an electrically operated system, installed (and repeatedly serviced) by the New York firm of A. G. Newman. Doors and windows were fitted with magnetic contacts linked to an electrical circuit; when the system was armed, opening a door or window closed the circuit and sounded the alarm. A central device called the "annunciator" indicated which door or window had been opened; the annunciator also had switches for disconnecting all or part of the house from the alarm, and a clock for automatic regulation. Clemens's struggles with the alarm form the basis of his 1882 story "The McWilliamses and the Burglar Alarm" (17 July 1877 to OLC [1st], *Letters 1876–1880;* "Burglar Alarms," Hartford *Courant,* 12 Mar 1878, 2; Newman to SLC, 18 May 1880, CU-MARK; 22 Feb 1883 to Webster, NPV; Houston 1898, 11, 22; SLC 1882b).

342.31 Ashcroft] Ralph W. Ashcroft (1875–1947), born in Cheshire, England, was secretary and treasurer of the Plasmon Company of America in 1905 when Clemens considered legal action against it for mismanagement of his investments. Impressed with Ashcroft, Clemens took him to England in June 1907, and began to rely on him as his business adviser. At Ashcroft's suggestion, the name "Mark Twain" was registered as a trademark, a step in the formation of The Mark Twain Company (1908). In 1909 Ashcroft married Isabel Lyon, Clemens's secretary. For a time Ashcroft and Lyon managed Clemens's business affairs, but in April 1909 he dismissed them. His lengthy and accusatory "Ashcroft-Lyon Manuscript" (SLC 1909b) describes their mismanagement as he saw it. Ashcroft subsequently worked as an advertising director for various Canadian business firms; he and Lyon divorced in 1926 (*HHR,* 735–36; Ashcroft 1904; Ashcroft to Lyon, 1 Mar 1906, CU-MARK; "Memorandum for Mr. Rogers re. Clemens' Matter," CU-MARK; "Business Leader, Friend and Aide of Mark Twain," Toronto *Globe and Mail,* 9 Jan 1947, 7; Lystra 2004, 265).

342.33 Henry Butters, Harold Wheeler, and the rest of those Plasmon thieves] Plasmon, a powdered milk extract, was first marketed in Vienna while Clemens was living there in 1897–99. He came to see the product as a remedy for everything from Olivia's illness to world famine. In his 1909 "Ashcroft-Lyon Manuscript," he recounted his Plasmon entanglements, which began with an investment in the British branch of the firm:

> By May, 1900, we had the enterprise on its feet & doing a promising business. Then some Americans wanted the rights for America.... The American company was presently started in New York. Henry A. Butters of California was one of the promoters & directors. He swindled me out of $12,500 & helped Wright, a subordinate, to swindle me out of $7,000 more.
>
> Two of the directors—Butters and another—proceeded to gouge the company out of its cash capital. By about 1905 they had sucked it dry, & the company went bankrupt. (SLC 1909b, 8–9)

Clemens's grievance was set forth in more detail by his lawyer, John B. Stanchfield:

> Mr. Clemens contributed to the enterprise $25,000 ... and believed that he was purchasing stock in the corporation, and that for every share that he bought, he was entitled to another share as a bonus. This was the arrangement Butters had told him had been made....
>
> It seems that Butters, who was the directing agent of the American corporation at the time, had the avails of Mr. Clemens' moneys credited to his personal account, and transferred his own shares to the extent of 250 to Mr. Clemens. (Enclosure with Stanchfield to SLC, 4 Mar 1905, CU-MARK)

Henry A. Butters (1830–1908) was a San Francisco capitalist; his associates Howard E. Wright and Harold Wheeler successively managed the American Plasmon Company. Clemens began threatening Butters with a suit for grand larceny early in 1905. He returned to the subject of the Plasmon fiasco in the Autobiographical Dictations of 30 August 1907 and 31 October 1908 (8–9 Apr 1900 to Rogers, Salm, in *HHR*, 438–42; Ober 2003, 169–72; "Death Claims Railroad Man," Los Angeles *Times*, 27 Oct 1908, 15; Ashcroft 1904; 11 and 14 Mar 1909 to CC, MS draft in CU-MARK).

343.28–29   I can't see how it is ever going to fetch me out right when we get to the door] Clemens's perplexity in this matter of the spoon-shaped drive of the house in Hartford can be better understood with the aid of a diagram he sketched in an 1892 notebook, reproduced here. No matter which way the buggy rounds the loop, a passenger seated to the right of the driver will end up on the side away from the house (Notebook 31, TS p. 37, CU-MARK).

345.9   ombra] The term that the Clemenses used for the veranda that surrounded the house; it means "shade" in Italian.

346.9   Susy Warner] Charles Dudley Warner's wife (1838?–1921) was a talented pianist and a close friend of Olivia's. Susy Clemens's manuscript biography left a blank for Susan Warner's name. Clemens supplied it in his dictation, but when he prepared the text for publication in the *North American Review*, he toyed with a pseudonym ("Tabitha Wilson") before settling on "your wife" for the text he published there (24 and 25 Nov 1869 to OLL, *L5*, 407 n. 3; NAR 4).

Autobiographical Dictation, 9 February 1906

349.18–23   His mother is Grandma Clemens . . . F.F.V's of Virginia . . . always strongly interested in the ancestry of the house] In Clemens's lifetime the phrase "First Families of Virginia" was used informally to designate those who claimed descent from the earliest settlers of the state. The present-day Order of First Families of Virginia was founded in 1912. Susy apparently read an interview with her grandmother published in the Chicago *Inter-Ocean* sometime in March or April 1885 which was widely reprinted. The last paragraph read:

> Mrs. Clemens was Miss Jane Lampton before her marriage and was a native of Kentucky. Mr. Clemens was of the F. F. V.'s of Virginia. They did not accumulate property and the father left the family at his death nothing but, in Mark's own words, "a sumptuous stock of pride and a good old name," which, it will be allowed, has proved in this case at least a sufficient inheritance. ("Mark Twain's Boyhood. An Interview with the Mother of the Famous Humorist," New York *World*, 12 Apr 1885, 19, reprinting the Chicago *Inter-Ocean*)

349.23–26   Lambtons of Durham . . . broke into the peerage] The Lambton family's residence in County Durham, England, can be traced nearly to the time of the Norman Conquest (1066). John George Lambton (1792–1840) was created first earl of Durham in 1833; his grandson, also John George Lambton (1855–1928), became the third earl in 1879. Jane Clemens's paternal grandfather, William Lampton (1724–90), who evidently belonged to a collateral branch of the family, emigrated to Virginia about 1740 (Burke 1904, 528–29; Debrett 1980, P409; Selby 1973, 112; Keith 1914, 3–4, 7).

349.29–33   Jere. Clemens . . . shot old John Brown's Governor Wise in the hind leg in a duel] Clemens mistook the identities of both combatants. It was not Jeremiah Clemens but Sherrard Clemens who fought O. Jennings Wise—a *son* of Henry Alexander Wise, the governor of Virginia from 1856 to 1860, when abolitionist John Brown was active. Sherrard Clemens was severely wounded in the right thigh; Wise was uninjured (see "My Autobiography [Random Extracts from It]," note at 205.18; 21 June 1866 to JLC and PAM, *L1,* 346 n. 6; "The Wise and Clemens Duel," New York *Times,* 24 Sept 1858, 2).

Autobiographical Dictation, 12 February 1906

350.4   trick on Grandma, about the whipping] This incident occurs in chapter 1 of *Tom Sawyer.*

350.15–17   Grandma couldn't make papa go to school . . . those who were more studious in early life] Susy found this information in the April 1885 interview with Jane Clemens. She quoted nearly verbatim the last sentence in the following paragraph:

> When Sam's father died, which occurred when Sam was eleven years of age, I thought then, if ever, was the proper time to make a lasting impression on the boy and work a change in him, so I took him by the hand and went with him into the room where the coffin was and in which the father lay, and with it between Sam and me I said to him that here in this presence I had some serious requests to make of him, and that I knew his word, once given, was never broken. For Sam never told a falsehood. He turned his streaming eyes upon me and cried out: "Oh mother, I will do anything, anything you ask of me, except to go to school; I can't do that!" That was the very request I was going to make. Well, we afterwards had a sober talk, and I concluded to let him go into a printing office to learn the trade, as I couldn't have him running wild. He did so, and has gradually picked up enough education to enable him to do about as well as those who were more studious in early life. ("Mark Twain's Boyhood. An Interview with the Mother of the Famous Humorist," New York *World,* 12 Apr 1885, 19, reprinting the Chicago *Inter-Ocean*)

350.30–31   It was Henry . . . the thread . . . had changed color] See *Tom Sawyer,* chapter 1.

351.5   If the incident of the broken sugar-bowl is in "Tom Sawyer"] It is in chapter 3.

351.39   to give the cat the Pain-Killer] See *Tom Sawyer,* chapter 12. Perry Davis's Pain-Killer was invented in 1840 and enjoyed widespread success. The label indicated that it could be taken internally "for Chills, Cramps, Colic" or applied externally for "Sore Throat, Sprains, Bruises, Chilblains." Its main ingredient was alcohol, with added camphor and cayenne pepper (Ober 2003, 54–60).

351.42–352.1   Mr. Pavey's negro man] Jesse H. Pavey was the proprietor of a Hannibal tavern until 1850, when he moved his family to St. Louis (*Inds,* 340).

352.3–6 cholera days of '49 . . . chose Perry Davis's Pain-Killer for me] Cholera visited the Mississippi valley perennially throughout Clemens's youth. After its appearance in New Orleans in February 1849 it soon spread northward along the Mississippi River. Numerous deaths in Hannibal caused fear of a major epidemic like the one that was ravaging St. Louis, and the Pain-Killer was used as a preventive (Holcombe 1884, 297–98; Wecter 1952, 213–14; Ober 2003, 45–54).

352.19–20 I don't remember what my explanation was . . . may not be the right one] Tom's "explanation" was as follows:

> "Now, sir, what did you want to treat that poor dumb beast so, for?"
> "I done it out of pity for him—because he hadn't any aunt."
> "Hadn't any aunt!—you numscull. What has that got to do with it?"
> "Heaps. Because if he'd a had one she'd a burnt him out herself! She'd a roasted his bowels out of him 'thout any more feeling than if he was a human!" (SLC 1982, 96)

353.3 Tom Nash was a boy of my own age—the postmaster's son] Clemens's schoolmate Thomas S. Nash was the son of Abner O. Nash (1804?–59) and his second wife. In "Villagers of 1840–3" (1897) Clemens noted that he became a house painter. Abner Nash was a former storekeeper and president of Hannibal's Board of Trustees; although his "mother was Irish, had family jewels, and claimed to be aristocracy," he had been forced to declare bankruptcy in 1844 and accept a low-paying postmastership in 1849 (*Inds,* 96, 337–38).

353.23 closing one was scarlet fever, and he came out of it stone deaf] In the working notes for the "St. Petersburg Fragment," the second extant version of "The Mysterious Stranger," Clemens wrote that "Tom Nash's mother took in a deserted child; it gave scarlet-fever death to 3 of her children & deaf[ness] to 2" (*MSM,* 416; see also *Inds,* 96).

353.28–29 Four years ago . . . receive the honorary degree of LL.D.] Clemens traveled to Missouri in late May–early June 1902, to receive an honorary LL.D. from the University of Missouri at Columbia (4 June). He also spent a few days in both St. Louis and Hannibal, his final visit to the scenes of his childhood and youth (New York *Times:* "Degree for Mark Twain," 5 June 1902, 2; "Mark Twain among Scenes of His Early Life," 8 June 1902, 28; Notebook 45, TS pp. 14–17, CU-MARK).

353.38–40 Papa was about twenty years old . . . he said "Yes, mother, I will,"] Of course this too came from the interview with Jane Clemens:

> He was about twenty years old when he went on the Mississippi as a pilot. I gave him up then, for I always thought steamboating was a wicked business, and was sure he would meet bad associates. I asked him if he would promise me on the Bible not to touch intoxicating liquors nor swear, and he said: "Yes, mother, I will." He repeated the words after me, with my hand and his clasped on the holy book, and I believe he always kept that promise. ("Mark Twain's Boyhood. An Interview with the Mother of the Famous Humorist," New York *World,* 12 Apr 1885, 19, reprinting the Chicago *Inter-Ocean*)

Autobiographical Dictation, 13 February 1906

354.5–6   I was for a short time a Cadet of Temperance] Started in 1846 in Germantown, Pennsylvania, the Cadets of Temperance was a youth auxiliary of the Sons of Temperance. Initiates pledged to abstain from alcohol and tobacco. The Hannibal "Section" was founded in 1850, and Clemens was among the earliest members; his signature is the first on its manuscript "Constitution." His friend Tom Nash and his brother Henry were also members. By his own report Clemens resigned in early July 1850. His name figures in a manuscript list of cadets dated "Nov. 25 1850," possibly recording members delinquent in paying dues. His experience as a cadet is transferred to Tom in *Tom Sawyer,* chapter 22, and these ritualized temperance meetings are burlesqued in "The Autobiography of a Damned Fool," chapter 4 (SLC 1877b; Eddy 1887, 340; SLC 1867h; Wecter 1952, 152–54; Cadets of Temperance [1850]; *S&B,* 149–53).

354.32   Mr. Garth] See the Autobiographical Dictation of 9 March 1906, note at 401.30–34.

355.2   We used to trade old newspapers (exchanges)] The post office allowed a newspaper publisher to send a single "exchange copy" to an unlimited number of papers, free of postage. This arrangement functioned as a primitive wire service, with news items being picked up and circulated nationwide. Having perused and clipped articles from the "exchanges," a newspaper office would throw them away (Kielbowicz 1989, 141–61).

355.13–14   However, I feel sure that I have written . . . "Following the Equator."] See *Following the Equator,* chapter 1.

355.17–22   papa had been a pilot . . . out to Nevada to be his secretary . . . Quaker City] See the Autobiographical Dictations of 12 January 1906 (note at 270.1) and 29 March 1906, as well as "Notes on 'Innocents Abroad.'"

355.30–32   That first meeting . . . five days later] See the Autobiographical Dictation of 1 February 1906, note at 320.32–34.

356.3–4   She became an invalid . . . and she was never strong again while her life lasted] The nature of Olivia's ailment has been much debated. She became ill earlier, and recovered later, than Clemens allowed for in this dictation. Already "in very delicate health" at the age of fourteen (1860), she was treated by doctors and spent time at the Elmira Water Cure. Showing little improvement, she was sent to a sanatorium in Washington, D.C., and then to the Institute of Swedish Movement Cure in New York City, which prescribed kinesipathy (curative muscle movements). She spent more than two years there before returning home to Elmira. The visit from "Dr." Newton (see the note at 356.7–8) occurred on 30 November 1864. Olivia's case was recalled by Newton's private secretary, writing about the cures wrought during that period:

> One of these was at Elmira, N.Y., where Dr. N. went to treat Miss Libbie Langdon, whom he cured, and she has since married the author known as "Mark Twain." Dr. N. found her suffering with spinal disease; could not be raised to a sitting posture in her bed for over four years. She was almost like death itself. With one characteristic treatment he made her to cross the room with assistance, and in a few days the cure was complete. (Newton 1879, 294)

Langdon family letters and papers, however, show that despite Newton's visits Olivia's health was still seriously impaired. She had a second visit from Newton on 3 June 1865, and was still unable to walk almost a year after that. A second stay at the Movement Institute in 1866 recovered her considerably; she regained her mobility but, as Clemens says, her health remained fragile (Skandera-Trombley 1994, 83–85, 90, 92–94).

356.7–8 Dr. Newton, a man who was regarded in both worlds as a quack] James Rogers Newton (1810–83), a businessman from Newport, Rhode Island, performed massively attended public "healings" in both America and England. He was not well regarded by either the scientific or the religious community. He seems to have had no medical training, and attributed his powers variously to "magnetic force," "controlling spirits," and "the Father that dwelleth in me." His usual practice was "the laying on of hands," but some remedies were less conventional: one patient suffering from tuberculosis was told "Go, take a male chicken, cut off the head, split it in the back, and place it, warm, on your breast" (Newton 1879, 206–71, 112–13, 38; "Rev. Dr. Buckley and Newton the Healer" 1883, 519; Ober 2003, 129–34). There is no independent documentation of Clemens's own meeting with Newton (356.37–40).

356.11 Andrew Langdon] Langdon (1835–1919) was Olivia's first cousin.

356.22–27 Newton made some passes . . . "Now we will walk a few steps, my child."] Paine revised this passage on the typescript as follows, presumably in order to lend the whole transaction a more conventional, Christian cast:

> Newton ~~made some passes about her head with his hands;~~ ˌopened the windows—long darkened—and delivered a short, fervent prayer;ˌ then he put an arm behind her shoulders and said "Now we will sit up, my child."
> The family were alarmed, and tried to stop him, but he was not disturbed, and raised her up. She sat several minutes, without nausea or discomfort. Then Newton said, ~~that that would do for the present, he would come again next morning; which he did. He made some passes with his hands and said,~~ "Now we will walk a few steps, my child."

Paine partly explained himself in the margin, saying "He came but once ABP" (TS1, 309–10). The historical record shows that Paine was mistaken.

Autobiographical Dictation, 14 February 1906

357.5–8 There were three or four proposals of marriage . . . stay a week] Clemens's courtship of Olivia was accomplished between his lecturing engagements in the fall of 1868. In early September she turned down his offer of marriage, but by the end of November, after two more refusals, she accepted. Clemens slightly exaggerated when he said his planned visit was extended by three days (357.8, 358.23): Olivia wrote on the day of his departure, 29 September, that he had planned to stay one day, and stayed one more because of his accident (*L2:* 7 and 8 Sept 1868 to OLL, 247–49; 28 Nov 1868 to Twichell, 293–94; OLL to Hooker, 29 Sept 1868, CtHSD).

357.15 democrat wagon] "A light wagon without a top, containing several seats, and usually drawn by two horses" (Whitney and Smith 1889–91, 2:1526–27).

358.33–38 I had referred him to six prominent men . . . (Stebbins,)] Only two of the men to whom Clemens referred Langdon in late November 1868 are known, both clergymen. The Reverend Horatio Stebbins (1821–1902), pastor of the First Unitarian Church, replied (in Clemens's paraphrase): "'Clemens is a humbug—shallow & superficial—a man who has talent, no doubt, but will make a trivial & possibly a worse use of it—a man whose life promised little & has accomplished less—a humbug, Sir, a humbug.' That was the *spirit* of the remarks—I have forgotten the precise language" (25 Aug 1869 to Stoddard, *MTPO* [a fuller text than published in *L3*]). The other clergyman was the Reverend Charles Wadsworth (1814–82), pastor of Howard Presbyterian Church. Langdon himself wrote to James S. Hutchinson, a former employee then working as a bank cashier in San Francisco, asking him to investigate Clemens's reputation. Hutchinson interviewed James B. Roberts, one of Wadsworth's deacons, and reported his assessment: "I would rather bury a daughter of mine than have her marry such a fellow" (Hutchinson 1910). On 29 December, even before these troubling estimates could have reached Elmira, Clemens provided the Langdons with ten additional references (*L2:* 17 June 1868 to Fairbanks, 229 n. 2; 29 Dec 1868 to Langdon, 358–59, 360–61 n. 2).

359.8–13 Joe Goodman . . . Why didn't you refer me to him?] Clemens had in fact referred Langdon to Goodman and other known friends—but only after he realized what the likely result of the first six names would be, one month after giving them to Langdon (29 Dec 1868 to Langdon, *L2, 358*).

Autobiographical Dictation, 15 February 1906

360.3 Hawthorne's love letters . . . are far inferior] Julian Hawthorne included the love letters in his biography of his parents, issued around the time that Susy was writing. All of Clemens's extant letters are published in *Mark Twain's Letters, Volume 3* (Hawthorne 1885; see "Calendar of Courtship Letters," *L3,* 473–80).

362.3–10 He was prematurely born . . . followed by a dangerous illness] The "visitor whose desire Mrs. Clemens regarded as law" was apparently Mary Mason Fairbanks; her visit, and the dash for the station with which it ended, occurred in late October 1870. Langdon was born one month prematurely, on 7 November 1870. Three months later, in early February 1871, Olivia began to show symptoms of typhoid (*L4:* 5 Nov 1870 to OC, 222 n. 5; 17 Feb 1871 to JLC and family, 332 n. 1; for Langdon's death see AD, 22 Mar 1906).

362.11 Mrs. Gleason, of Elmira] The Clemenses sent for Dr. Rachel Brooks Gleason (1820–1905), a physician and cofounder of the Elmira Water Cure, a health resort at which Langdon family members had often been treated (22 Feb 1871 to OC, *L4,* 335 n. 2).

362.21–28 Before Mrs. Clemens was quite over her devastating illness, Miss Emma Nye . . . illness proved fatal] Clemens reversed the actual sequence of events. Emma Nye (1846–70) was staying with the Clemenses on her way from Aiken, South Carolina, to Detroit; she lay ill with typhoid fever in the Clemenses' own bed for almost a month, dying there on

29 September 1870. Olivia's illness followed Nye's death (*L4:* 31 Aug 1870 to PAM, 186 n. 3; SLC and OLC to Fairbanks, 2 Sept 1870, 189 n. 2; 7 Sept 1870 to Wolcott, 191; 9 Oct 1870 to Redpath, 206 n. 1).

362.35–36 a crude and absurd map of Paris upon it, and published it] In the fall of 1870, newspapers closely followed the reports of the Franco-Prussian War. The German army began advancing on Paris in early September, and many American newspapers published maps showing the city's fortifications. Mark Twain's burlesque (reproduced below) was printed in the Buffalo *Express* on 17 September 1870 (SLC 1870d). Clemens's inscription on it reads: "Mr. Spofford, could I get you to preserve this work of art among the geographical treasures of the Congressional Library?" (see 10? Oct 1870 to Spofford, *L4,* 207).

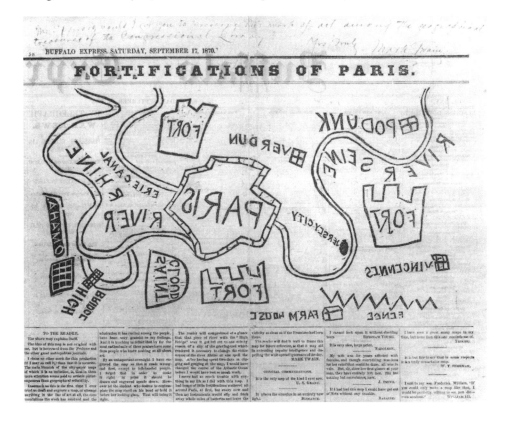

Autobiographical Dictation, 16 February 1906

363.14 Aunt Susy's] Susan Crane's.

363.19 dear grandpapa] Jervis Langdon.

363.20–21 (Emma Nigh) . . . typhoid fever] See the Autobiographical Dictation of 15 February 1906, 362.21–28 and note.

363.23–25 (Miss Clara L. Spaulding) . . . great friend of mamma's] Spaulding (1849–1935) was the daughter of a prosperous Elmira, New York, lumber merchant; in 1886 she married lawyer John Barry Stanchfield (9 and 31 Mar 1869 to Crane, *L3,* 182 n. 6). She is further discussed in the Autobiographical Dictation of 26 February 1906.

363.32–33   David Gray . . . editor of the principal newspaper] Gray (1836–88) was born in Edinburgh and came to the United States in 1849. Settling in Buffalo in 1856, he worked as a secretary, librarian, and bookkeeper before becoming a journalist. When Clemens moved to Buffalo in 1869, Gray had just married Martha Guthrie and was managing editor of the *Courier,* a rival paper to Clemens's Buffalo *Express.* Gray rose to be editor-in-chief of the *Courier,* but in 1882 ill health forced him to retire; in 1888 he was fatally injured in a railway accident (SLC and OLC to the Langdons, 27 Mar 1870, *L4,* 102 n. 9). Clemens talks of him further in the Autobiographical Dictation of 22 February 1906.

364.2–9   bought Mr. Kinney's share of that newspaper . . . I sold . . . for fifteen thousand dollars] Clemens bought his share of the Buffalo *Express* not from "Mr. Kinney" but from Thomas A. Kennett (1843–1911) in August 1869, and sold it again in March 1871 (for details of the purchase and sale see 12 Aug 1869 to Bliss, *L3,* 294 n. 2, and 3 Mar 1871 to Riley, *L4,* 338–39, n. 3). Clemens returned to Kennett (still calling him Kinney) later in this dictation: see the note at 366.29–32.

364.19   Jay Gould had just then reversed the commercial morals of the United States] Gould (1836–92) was an unscrupulous financier and railroad speculator whose name became a byword for ruthless greed. As a director of the Erie Railroad, with James Fisk (1834–72), he looted the company; his attempt to corner the gold market in 1869 triggered the panic of "Black Friday," ruining many investors. For part or all of the next two decades he controlled several major railways and the Western Union Telegraph Company, and owned the New York *World* from 1879 to 1883. At his death his estate was valued at $72 million. Clemens's attitude toward Gould was not unusual: Gould was denounced early and often as the poisoner of the American republic. And when Daniel Beard pictured the slave driver in *A Connecticut Yankee,* he used Gould as a model—with Clemens's enthusiastic endorsement ("Jay Gould's Will Filed," New York *Times,* 13 Dec 1892, 10; see Budd 1962, 44, 84, 114, 204; *CY,* 17, 405, 567).

364.32–34   McCurdys, McCalls . . . insurance companies of New York] See the Autobiographical Dictation of 10 January 1906, note at 257.6–9.

364.34–36   President McCall was reported to be dying . . . The others . . . engaged in dying] Clemens presumably refers to reports such as the following, all from the New York *Times:* "M'Call, on Deathbed, Defends Hamilton," 15 Feb 1906, 1; "President M'Curdy out of the Mutual," 30 Nov 1905, 1; "John A. McCall Quits N. Y. Life Presidency," 1 Jan 1906, 1 (where James W. Alexander is said to be "a physical wreck").

365.11–17   John D. Rockefeller . . . after his father's fashion] See the Autobiographical Dictation of 20 March 1906, where Clemens discusses the Rockefellers and their Sunday school classes at length.

366.29–32   Kinney went to Wall Street . . . borrowed twenty-five cents of me] Kennett worked briefly as a Wall Street broker, then returned to journalism, editing various trade publications. He died in a Bronx clinic for destitute consumptives (12 Aug 1869 to Bliss, *L3,*

294 n. 2; New York *Times:* "Editor Kennett Dead," 30 June 1911, 9; "Praise for St. Joseph's Hospital," 26 May 1895, 17).

Autobiographical Dictation, 20 February 1906

367.11–12   name of Wilkes, the explorer, was in everybody's mouth] Charles Wilkes (1798–1877) was captain of the United States Exploring Expedition of 1838–42, the first international maritime expedition that the country had sponsored. Its mission was to explore the Pacific Ocean, the Antarctic regions, and the West Coast of North America. Wilkes commanded a squadron of six vessels, two of which, early in 1840, surveyed a long stretch of Antarctic coastline. The existence of a land mass within the Antarctic circle had been suspected for centuries. British and French explorers had sighted land in the area before the U.S. expedition, but nationalist sentiment made Wilkes, for Clemens as for many other Americans, the "discoverer" of Antarctica. Wilkes retired from the navy with the rank of rear admiral ("Antarctic Discoveries" 1840, 210, 214–19).

367.15–16   in our late day we are rediscovering it, and the world's interest in it has revived] After a lull of many decades, the "heroic age" of Antarctic exploration began in 1897 with the new goal of reaching the South Pole. The 1901–4 expedition under the Englishman Robert F. Scott penetrated farther south than any previous explorer; during the same years Antarctic expeditions were mounted by Germany, Sweden, Scotland, and France. The pole would be reached by the Norwegian Roald Amundsen in 1911.

367.21   One of the last visits I made in Florence . . . was to Mrs. Wilkes] Born Mary H. Lynch, Mrs. Wilkes was first married to William Compton Bolton, who at the time of his death in 1849 was a commodore in the U.S. Navy. In 1854 she married Wilkes—whose first wife had died in 1848—and they had one child. According to his notebook, Clemens met with Mrs. Wilkes on 4 April 1904 (Notebook 47, TS p. 8, CU-MARK).

367.33–34   article which you wrote once . . . about my grandfather, Anson Burlingame] Clemens eulogized Burlingame in February 1870 in a Buffalo *Express* article (SLC 1870a; see "My Debut as a Literary Person," note at 128.30–32).

368.43–369.3   Potter, (that is the name, I think,) the Congressional bully . . . laughter of the nation ringing in his ears] Clemens misremembered the name of Preston S. Brooks (1819–57), known in the North as "Bully" Brooks. A representative from South Carolina, in 1856 he brutally beat Senator Charles Sumner in the Senate chamber in retaliation for perceived insults to his state and kin. Anson Burlingame, then a representative from Massachusetts, denounced Brooks's assault in a House speech. Brooks promptly challenged him to duel; Burlingame accepted, naming the Canadian side of Niagara Falls as the place and rifles as the weapon. Brooks, who could not with safety travel across the Northern states, declined to pursue the matter (Nicolay and Hay 1890, 2:47–55; "The Brooks Affair; Examination of the Controversy between Mr. Brooks and Mr. Burlingame," New York *Times,* 25 July 1856, 2).

369.14   I have already told the rest in some book of mine] Clemens alludes to "My Debut as a Literary Person," written in 1898, and included in the Preliminary Manuscripts and Dictations section of this volume.

369.19   Mr. Burlingame's son—now editor of *Scribner's Monthly*] Edward L. Burlingame (1848–1922) left his studies at Harvard University to travel to China as his father's secretary. He later earned a Ph.D. at Heidelberg. He took a position at the New York *Tribune* in 1871, forming a lifelong friendship with John Hay. In 1872–79 he was one of the editors of the *American Encyclopedia,* and in 1879 began to work for Charles Scribner's Sons, becoming the editor of *Scribner's Monthly* from its first number in 1887. After his resignation in 1914, he became a general editorial adviser for the publisher ("Edward Burlingame, Editor, Dead at 74," New York *Times,* 17 Nov 1922, 16).

369.25–26   "If a man compel thee to go with him a mile, go *with* him Twain."] Matthew 5:41, "And whosoever shall compel thee to go a mile, go with him twain."

Autobiographical Dictation, 21 February 1906

370.32–33   E. Bliss, junior . . . a later chapter] Elisha P. Bliss, Jr. (1821–80), was born in Massachusetts. He worked in the dry goods business until becoming secretary of the American Publishing Company of Hartford (1867–70, 1871–73), and then its president (1870, 1873–80). During his tenure this subscription house published all of Clemens's major books from *The Innocents Abroad* (1869) to *A Tramp Abroad* (1880). For the "later chapter" see the Autobiographical Dictation of 23 May 1906 (2 Dec 1867 to Bliss, *L2,* 120 n. 1; Hill 1964, 15).

370.34–40   I told him my terms . . . I showed him letters . . . what they could get out of the book as an advertisement] Clemens's extant correspondence for that time does not support his contention here that other firms offered him half profits, or more. When Bliss visited Clemens at Elmira in mid-July 1870 to discuss terms for the publication of *Roughing It,* Clemens claimed only to have been offered "*ten* per cent" by an unnamed publisher (2 Aug 1870 to Bliss, *L4,* 179–80; see *RI 1993,* 806–8).

371.13   contract . . . had nothing in it about half profits] See "A Call with W. D. Howells on General Grant," note at 71.36–37.

371.22–23   He published that book . . . the next two at 10 per cent] Clemens recounted his royalty arrangements correctly, allowing for a slight shuffling of the books' publication order. By "that book and the next one" he meant *Roughing It* (1872) and *Mark Twain's Sketches, New and Old* (1875c); by "the next two" he meant *The Gilded Age* (1873–74, 10 percent shared with coauthor Charles Dudley Warner) and *Tom Sawyer* (1876, 10 percent) (*RI 1993,* 806–8; *ET&S1,* 435–36; "Contract for the American Publishing Company *Gilded Age,*" *L5,* 635–36; royalty statement in Scrapbook 10:77, CU-MARK).

371.35–372.2   he wanted to leave and set up for himself . . . we signed the contract . . . Those are the terms. Take them or leave them] Although in 1879 Elisha Bliss, Jr., did contemplate leaving the American Publishing Company "by & by," it was actually Francis (Frank) Bliss (1843–1915), Elisha's son and the treasurer of the company, who resigned and established his own subscription house (Bliss to SLC, 13 Feb 1879, CU-MARK). Before leaving for Europe in 1878, Clemens had signed a contract with Frank—without Elisha's knowledge—for a proposed travel book (ultimately *A Tramp Abroad,* published in 1880), stipulating a royalty of 10 percent. Frank agreed to keep detailed records of his costs in order to calculate the "gross profits," and "if at the end of the first year one half of said gross profits exceeds the amount of said royalty for said year," Clemens was to receive "the amount of such excess in addition to said royalty" (contract dated 8 Mar 1878, CU-MARK). Frank Bliss's company did not thrive, however, and in November 1879, when the book was in production, Clemens agreed to transfer the contract to the American Publishing Company. A year later he claimed that "as a consideration for the book," Elisha Bliss "required them to allow him one-half of the *company's* entire profits for 3 years!—& they were exceedingly glad to comply. For it saved the company's life & set them high on their pins & free of debt" (24 Oct 1880 to OC, *Letters 1876–1880;* Hill 1964, 127–32, 142–43; for a somewhat different account see AD, 23 May 1906).

372.16–17 Newton Case] Case, a Hartford neighbor, was part owner of a printing and publishing establishment—the Case, Lockwood and Brainard Company—as well as a director of the American Publishing Company (*N&J3,* 203 n. 67, 456 n. 161).

372.25–27 J. R. Osgood . . . "Old Times on the Mississippi,"] James R. Osgood first solicited a publication in 1872 from Clemens, who could not comply because of his prior contracts with the American Publishing Company. Osgood was likewise unable to publish *Sketches, New and Old,* and had to settle for the little book *A True Story, and the Recent Carnival of Crime* (SLC 1877a). For his part, Clemens was eager for the prestige of Osgood's imprint, and published *The Prince and the Pauper* with him in 1881—requiring, however, that it be sold by subscription, an approach entirely unfamiliar to Osgood. The next year Osgood issued *The Stolen White Elephant, Etc.* He traveled with Clemens down the Mississippi, and in 1883 published the book that resulted from that trip, *Life on the Mississippi* (31 Mar 1872 to Osgood, *LS,* 72–73 nn. 2–3; *ET&S1,* 619–20; *P&P,* 9–11).

372.29–30 these industries of his had cost me fifty-six thousand dollars] Clemens wrote to Osgood on 21 December 1883, "The Prince & Pauper & the Mississippi are the only books of mine which have ever failed. The first failure was not unbearable—but this second one is so nearly so that it is not a calming subject for me to talk upon. I am out $50,000 on this last book—that is to say, the sale which should have been 80,000 . . . is only 30,000" (21 Dec 1883 to Osgood, MH-H, in *MTLP,* 164). The total cost of the plates, paper, and binding of *Life on the Mississippi* came to $39,458.78 by Osgood's mid-March 1884 account. Clemens also paid the cost of renting Osgood's New York office during this period. His figure of "fifty-six thousand dollars" may include that expense as well (10 Mar 1884 to Webster, CU-MARK; SLC notes on handwritten sheet of printing costs for *Life on the Mississippi,* NPV).

372.38 check for fifty-four thousand five hundred dollars] Clemens's figure is not inconsistent with the high sales figures for *Adventures of Huckleberry Finn.* Less than three months after publication, it had sold fifty-one thousand copies at prices ranging from $2.75 to $5.50 a volume (Webster to Moffett, 6 May 1885, CU-MARK; *HF 2003,* 660–61).

Autobiographical Dictation, 22 February 1906

373.9–10   Aunt Susy] Susan Crane.

373.15   to-day's report of General Grant] The newspapers closely followed Grant's battle with cancer. On 16 April 1885 the New York *Times* described "the General . . . serenely conversing with his family, his voice good, his appearance indicative of returning health, walking about with as firm steps as in bygone months, and the family free from worry about him" ("A Day of Hopefulness," 16 Apr 1885, 4).

373.16   Judge Smith] H. Boardman Smith, an attorney with Smith, Robertson and Fassett of Elmira, was a witness to the will, not an executor. Presumably he later became a judge. The executors included Clemens himself, Theodore Crane, Charles J. Langdon, John D. F. Slee, and Langdon's widow, Olivia L. Langdon (Boyd and Boyd 1872, 195; "Last Will and Testament of Jervis Langdon," photocopy in CU-MARK).

373.28   Mr. Atwater] Dwight Atwater (1822–90) was born in a rural area near Ithaca, New York. He engaged in the lumber business in New York and Pennsylvania before settling in Elmira. In later years he owned a boot and shoe factory there ("Death of Dwight Atwater," Elmira *Advertiser,* 2 Jan 1890, unknown page).

375.2   Norman Hapgood's palace up-town] Hapgood (1868–1937), a writer and journalist, had been editor of *Collier's Weekly* since 1903. His house was on East 73rd Street, off Park Avenue.

375.7   He said "David Gray."] David Gray, Jr. (1870–1968), graduated from Harvard in 1892, wrote for several Buffalo newspapers, and was admitted to the bar in 1899. In World War I he served in the American Expeditionary Force, receiving the Croix de Guerre. From 1940 to 1947 he was the U.S. minister to Ireland ("David Gray Dies; Former Envoy, 97," New York *Times,* 13 Apr 1968, 25).

375.23   Ned House] Edward H. House (1836–1901) was a staff journalist on the New York *Tribune* when he met Clemens in January 1867. In 1870 he went to Japan to teach English at the University of Tokyo and to serve as the *Tribune*'s "regular correspondent." He also corresponded for the New York *Herald* on Japan's 1874 incursion into Formosa, turning his reportage into a book-length monograph, *The Japanese Expedition to Formosa,* which he printed in Tokyo in 1875. He founded the Tokyo *Times,* an English-language weekly funded by the Japanese government. He returned permanently to the United States in 1880, subsequently publishing a travel volume, *Japanese Episodes* (House 1881), and an illustrated novel, *Yone Santo: A Child of Japan* (House 1888) (3 May 1871 to Bliss, *L4,* 389 n. 1; 20 Jan 1872 to OLC, *L5,* 30 n. 2; *L6:* 10 Apr 1875 to Bliss, 445 n. 1; link note following 10 Nov 1875 to Seaver, 591–92 n. 1). In 1889–90 House and Clemens quarreled over a dramatization of *The Prince and the Pauper.* The adaptation for the stage was done by Abby Sage Richardson; House claimed Clemens had given him the dramatic rights to the novel in 1886, and filed an injunction to prevent performance. The controversy estranged House and Clemens permanently. House spent his last years in Japan (9 June 1870 to Bliss, *L4,* 149–50 n. 3; *N&J3,* 542–43 n. 183).

375.31   railway disaster, at night] The accident occurred on the Delaware, Lackawanna, and Western Railroad near Binghamton, New York, early on the morning of 16 March 1888. Gray suffered a head injury and died two days later (New York *Times:* "Overturned in the Snow," 17 Mar 1888, 5; "Editor Gray Dead," 19 Mar 1888, 1).

Autobiographical Dictation, 23 February 1906

376.4–7   Mr. Talmage Brown, who was an annex of the family by marriage . . . yielded a large loss] Brown (d. 1891), a Des Moines, Iowa, attorney, real estate developer, and paving contractor, was married to Olivia's first cousin, the former Anna Marsh. In 1869 Langdon brought suit against the city of Memphis, which owed him five hundred thousand dollars. After Brown's death, Clemens preserved three obituary clippings from Des Moines newspapers that eulogized him for his generosity, business acumen, devotion to family, and religious enthusiasm. In the notebook he was using at the time, Clemens indicated that these tributes made him question his own negative view (*N&J3,* 635; *L4:* link note following 28–31 Jan 1870 to Twichell, 43; 6 July 1870 to OLC, 165 n. 1; see also AD, 26 Mar 1906).

377.14   Mr. Henry W. Sage, of Ithaca] Sage (1814–97) was a highly successful businessman whose lumber enterprises made him one of the largest landholders in the state. He was a generous benefactor of Cornell University, and built and endowed many libraries, churches, and schools. His son, Dean Sage, was a good friend of Clemens's (*L6:* 28 Mar 1875 to Sage, 431 n. 1; 22 Apr 1875 to Sage, 453 n. 5).

377.37   Mr. Arnot] John Arnot (1793–1873) emigrated with his family from Scotland in 1801. He was an Elmira merchant and foundry owner before taking a position as cashier at the Chemung Canal Bank, becoming president in 1852 (Peirce and Hurd 1879, 284; Boyd and Boyd 1872, 41).

378.25–27   bulky manuscript, an autobiography of my brother Orion . . . from Keokuk, Iowa] Clemens suggested to Orion two possible plans of writing a ruthlessly honest memoir in a letter of 26 February 1880. Orion, excited rather than insulted by the prospect of writing "The Autobiography of a Coward" or "Confessions of a Life that was a Failure" (Clemens's suggested titles), went straight to work, and by June 1880 Clemens was able to offer Howells a sample for publication in the *Atlantic Monthly.* Howells declined: "It wrung my heart, and I felt haggard after I had finished it. . . . But the writer's soul is laid *too* bare: it is shocking" (Howells to SLC, 14 June 1880, CU-MARK, in *MTHL,* 1:315). Orion sent his brother the finished manuscript of 2,523 pages, retitled "The Autobiography of a Crank," on 18 January 1882; but it would never see print. Here Clemens claims that Orion's manuscript was "in the other room"; in the Autobiographical Dictation of 6 April 1906, he claims to have "destroyed a considerable part" of it at an early date. The manuscript, whether whole or fragmentary, was apparently lost by Paine in Grand Central Station on 11 July 1907. After Clemens's death, Paine gave inconsistent accounts of the fate of the autobiography, claiming variously that it had been deposited in a vault, lost, or destroyed at Clemens's behest; Paine quotes from it, however, in *Mark Twain: A Biography,* saying there that the earliest chapters had been preserved. Apart from those quotations, Orion's autobiography is extant only as a few stray leaves in the Mark Twain Papers, and some items of correspondence that Orion annotated for inclusion (*Letters 1876–1880:* 26 Feb 1880 to OC, 9 June 1880 to Howells; OC to SLC: 29 Feb and 1 Mar 1880, 18 Jan 1882, 19 Jan 1882, CU-MARK; *MTB*, 1:24, 44, 85, 2:674–77; MS fragments in DV 391, CU-MARK; Orion's note on 6 Feb 1861 to OC and MEC, NPV; Schmidt 2008b).

378.32–34   Benvenuto tells a number of things . . . Rousseau and his "Confessions."] The autobiography of Benvenuto Cellini was for Clemens the "most entertaining of books" (*N&J2*, 229); he referred to it in his letters and notebooks as well as in chapter 35 of *Huckleberry Finn*, and in chapter 17 of *A Connecticut Yankee*. In his letter of 26 February 1880 he told Orion that "Rousseau confesses to masturbation, theft, lying, shameful treachery" (*Letters 1876–1880;* the letter is quoted more fully in the Introduction, p. 6).

379.1–13   I think perhaps I have already mentioned . . . My brother tells that incident in his autobiography] See "My Autobiography [Random Extracts from It]," 209.24–33 and note. Orion's account, in which he rather than Samuel is left behind, is less dramatic; he was fourteen (1839–40) and his "abandonment" was brief: "The wagon had gone a few feet when I was discovered and invited to enter" (*MTB*, 1:24).

Autobiographical Dictation, 26 February 1906

380.9–20   In Germany once . . . our friend and excursion-comrade—American Consul at a German city] This accident occurred at Worms in July 1878. The "friend and excursion-comrade" was probably Edward M. Smith, U.S. consul at Mannheim (*N&J2*, 46, 125 n. 22, 248 n. 68).

380.28–29   Clara Spaulding . . . has a son who is a senior in college, and a daughter who is in college in Germany] John B. Stanchfield, Jr. (1889–1946), and Alice Spaulding Stanchfield (1887–1941), who later married Arthur M. Wright.

381.9–10   "Adonis" (word illegible) acted] This musical burlesque starring comedian Henry E. Dixey was a record-setting Broadway hit, with more than six hundred performances from 1884 to 1886 (New York *Times:* "Amusements," 5 Sept 1884, 4; "A Great Day for Dixey," 8 Jan 1886, 1). The parenthetical comment was Clemens's substitute for what appears to be "the pals": "We went to the theater and enjoyed 'Adonis,' the pals acted very much" (OSC 1885–86, 17). Susy may have meant to write "the play acted."

381.14   Major Pond] James B. Pond (1838–1903) was born in Allegany County, New York. First apprenticed to a printer, he became a journalist, and worked at several newspapers. During the Civil War he served in the Third Wisconsin Cavalry and was commissioned major at the end of the conflict. He joined the Boston Lyceum Bureau of lecture manager James Redpath, and bought out Redpath's share of the business in 1875. Pond opened his own bureau in 1879. He managed Clemens's 1884–85 tour of public readings with George Washington Cable, and arranged Clemens's 1895–96 lecture trip around the world. Over the next years Pond made lavish offers for further tours, which Clemens declined (13 Sept 1897 to Rogers, 6–7 Nov 1898 to Rogers, 21 July 1900 to Rogers, Salm, in *HHR*, 300, 374, 448).

381 *footnote*   *I was his publisher] See "About General Grant's Memoirs."

382.14–18   General Hood . . . Sherman . . . was perfectly free to proceed . . . through Georgia] John B. Hood (1831–79) attended West Point, and served in the Union army until he resigned and joined the Confederacy in April 1861. He was promoted to major general in October 1862. Grant gave substantially the same account of Sherman's march to the sea in his *Personal Memoirs* (Grant 1885–86, 2:374–76).

383.10–11   new and devilish invention—the thing called an Authors' Reading] The event described here took place on Wednesday, 29 April 1885, at Madison Square Theatre, and was the second of two readings benefiting the American Copyright League. Clemens read his oft-repeated "A Trying Situation," from chapter 25 of *A Tramp Abroad;* the other readers included Howells and Henry Ward Beecher. "Devilish" though he may have found them, the new fashion for authors' readings (as opposed to recitations from memory) had been initiated by Clemens himself. The Washington *Post* noted that "the Cable-Twain reading venture of last winter may be made the beginning of a new kind of entertainment. The lecture is obsolescent . . . but for an author . . . to read from his own writings is a new idea and an attractive one" ("News Notes in New York," 3 May 1885, 5). Clemens's Vassar lecture was on 1 May (*N&J3*, 112, 140–41 n. 48; "Listening to the Authors," New York *Times,* 30 Apr 1885, 5; "Authors' Readings," *Life* 5 [30 Apr 1885]: 248; "The Authors' Readings," *The Critic,* 2 May 1885, 210).

383.37–38   I went to Boston to help . . . memorial to Mr. Longfellow] The Longfellow Memorial Association was formed in 1882 to raise funds for a monument honoring the late poet. The authors' reading benefiting the association was held at the Boston Museum (a theater) on 31 March 1887 (Longfellow Memorial Association 1882; "The Authors' Readings in Boston," *The Critic,* 9 Apr 1887, 177; see *MTHL,* 2:589–90 n. 1).

384.15   We got it arranged at last . . . fifteen minutes, perhaps] Howells read a selection from *Their Wedding Journey* (Howells 1872; *MTHL,* 2:589–90 n. 1).

384.18   I think that that was the occasion when we had sixteen] There were nine speakers at the Boston event ("Authors' Readings for the Longfellow Memorial Fund," printed program, CLjC).

384.18–20   If it wasn't then it was in Washington, in 1888 . . . in the afternoon, in the Globe Theatre] Clemens was confusing two readings: the one in Boston, in 1887, and another in Washington, in March 1888, at the Congregational Church (not the Globe Theatre); see the note at 385.1–3.

384.24   That graceful and competent speaker, Professor Norton] Author and reformer Charles Eliot Norton (1827–1908) presided at the 1887 Boston reading. According to Howells, "he fell prey to one of those lapses of tact" when he introduced Clemens, claiming that Darwin habitually read his books at bedtime in order to feel "secure of a good night's rest" (Howells 1910, 51).

384.27–33   Dr. Holmes recited . . . "The Last Leaf," . . . until silence had taken the place of encores] According to a contemporary account, Holmes read only "The Chambered Nautilus" (1858) and "Dorothy Q." (1871). Holmes "gave himself completely to the spirit of the poetry, tingling and vibrating with life, rising on his toes and ending with a dash and sparkle which made his hearers beside themselves with delight" ("The Authors' Readings in Boston," *The Critic,* 9 Apr 1887, 177).

384.35–38   third place on the program . . . did my reading in the ten minutes] Clemens was first on the program, reading selections from "English as She Is Taught," which appeared in the April 1887 issue of the *Century Magazine* (SLC 1887).

385.1–3   At the reading in Washington . . . Thomas Nelson Page . . . all due at the White House] Clemens read at two benefits for the American Copyright League at the Congregational Church, on 17 and 19 March 1888. He had not been scheduled to read at the first one, but as an "unexpected treat" he substituted for Charles Dudley Warner (delayed by a snowstorm), reading "How I Escaped Being Killed in a Duel" ("Authors as Readers," Washington *Post,* 18 Mar 1888, 5; SLC 1872a). Here he describes the second event, at which there were ten speakers; he read "An Encounter with an Interviewer" (SLC 1875b). Page (1853–1922), best known for his sympathetic and idealized depiction of the antebellum South, read two pieces in the "peculiar dialect of the Virginia negro." Afterward the authors and their guests were given a lavish reception and supper in the Blue Parlor of the White House (Washington *Post:* "Local Intelligence," 20 Mar 1888, 3; "Society," 20 Mar 1888, 4).

385.11–13   I think that it was upon the occasion . . . prepared me for my visit . . . could look after me herself] See the next Autobiographical Dictation (5 Mar 1906).

Autobiographical Dictation, 5 March 1906

385.28–30   upon the occasion referred to . . . Authors' Reception at the White House] That is, referred to at the end of the previous Autobiographical Dictation (26 Feb 1906). After his first reading at a matinee on 17 March 1888, which Olivia did not attend, Clemens went to a tea at the White House. Olivia joined him in Washington in time for his second reading on 19 March, and accompanied him to the reception afterward (16 Mar 1888 to OLC, CU-MARK, in *LLMT,* 249–51; Rosamond Gilder 1916, 195–96).

385.35–36   President Cleveland's first term. I had never seen his wife . . . the fascinating] Cleveland served two terms, in 1885–89 and 1893–97. He married Frances Folsom (1864–1947) in the White House on 2 June 1886. She became known for her beauty, her advocacy of women's education, her Saturday receptions for working-class women and the poor, and her liveliness and wit. The anecdote Clemens recounts here must have occurred on 17 March 1888, at the tea after his first Washington reading.

386.8–9   I asked her to sign her name below those words] The card, now in the Mark Twain Papers, is reproduced here.

386.25–27   During 1893 and '94 we were living in Paris . . . other side of the Seine] The Clemens family stayed at the Hotel Brighton from November 1893 until June 1894, when they left the city to travel elsewhere in France, returning to Paris in the fall. There they again stayed at the Hotel Brighton until mid-November, when they relocated to the house at 169, rue de l'Université, where they remained until the end of April 1895.

386.28   Pomeroy, the artist] The English sculptor Frederick William Pomeroy (1856–1924) won the gold medal and traveling scholarship from the Royal Academy Schools in London in 1885, and subsequently studied in Paris and in Italy. He was associated with the "New Sculpture" movement, which depicted ideal figures drawn from mythology and literature. Nothing is known of his association with Clemens.

386.42–387.1   Mammoth Cave] An enormous cave in Kentucky, which by the 1890s was thought to be about one hundred seventy-five miles long; it is now known to be over twice that size (Baedeker 1893, 318; National Park Service 2008).

387.6   Four or five years ago, when we took a house . . . at Riverdale] In early July 1901 the Clemenses toured William H. Appleton's house in Riverdale-on-the-Hudson, New York, and arranged to rent it from 1 October. They remained there through July 1903. Clemens called it "the pleasantest home & the pleasantest neighborhood in the Republic" (30 June 1903 to Perkins, NRivd2; Stein 2001, B1; 9 July 1901 to Rogers, CU-MARK, in *HHR,* 465; Wave Hill 2008).

388.13   Buck Fanshaw's riot, it broke up the riot before it got a chance to begin] In chapter 47 of *Roughing It,* "Scotty" Briggs tells how Buck Fanshaw had an election riot "all broke up and prevented nice before anybody ever got a chance to strike a blow" (*RI 1993,* 314).

388.17–20   The Cleveland family . . . passed away] Ruth ("Baby Ruth," 1891–1904), who died at twelve of heart failure during a bout of diphtheria, was the first of five Cleveland children, followed by sisters Esther (1893–1980) and Marion (1895–1977), and brothers Richard (1897–1974) and Francis (1903–95) ("Ruth Cleveland Dead," New York *Times,* 8 Jan 1904, 7). Clemens wrote to her on 3 November 1892, when she was one year old, just before her father's election to his second term (DLC):

> Dear Miss Cleveland:
>   If you will read this letter to your father, or ask your mother to do it if you are too busy, I will do something for you someday—anything you command. For I mean to come & see you in the White House before the four years are out. I am going to have Congress enlarge it, for you will take up a good deal of room, probably. And I am writing a book for you to practice your gums on—the very thing, for I know, myself, it is a very tough book. I shall bring my arctics, but that is all right—I know what to do with them now. . . .
>   No Administration could be more creditable than your father's & mother's last one was—& yet it ain't agoing to begin with this one, now that you are on deck.
>   You have my homage, & I am
>
> Affectionately Yours
S. L. Clemens.

388.29–30 kindly send a sealed greeting under cover to me ... South to him] Clemens complied with Gilder's request the following day. See the Autobiographical Dictation of 6 March 1906 for the text of his letter, which Gilder sent to Cleveland in Stuart, Florida. Gilder had first met President Cleveland in the White House before Cleveland's marriage in 1886, but their friendship began in 1887 (Richard Watson Gilder 1910, 7; Rosamond Gilder 1916, 142; Lynch 1932, 533).

388.36–39 Mason, an old and valued friend ... Frankfort in '78] Clemens first became acquainted with Frank H. Mason (1840–1916), his wife, Jennie V. Birchard Mason (1844?–1916), and their son, Dean B. Mason (b. 1867), in Cleveland in 1867–68. Mason worked as reporter, editorial writer, and finally managing editor of the Cleveland *Leader* from 1866 to 1880, when he was appointed U.S. consul at Basel, Switzerland. Clemens must be misremembering when he "spent a good deal of time" with Mason, since neither family sojourned in Frankfurt in 1878. The families did socialize, however, during the summer of 1892 in Bad Nauheim: Mason wrote in 1905 that his family had "kept you all in the same old warm corner of our hearts," and recalled, "We were at the Hotel Kaiserhof, in the suite of rooms just above the ones in which Mrs. Clemens and you and the girls lived during that happy summer" (Mason to SLC, 30 July 1905, CU-MARK; "Mrs. Frank H. Mason Dead," Washington *Post,* 26 Nov 1916, 2).

389.1 ignorant, vulgar, and incapable men ... political heelers] Heelers, or ward heelers, were apparently so called because they followed at the heels of a political boss, sometimes acting unscrupulously in the hope of future reward.

389.4–5 Mason, in '78, had been Consul General in Frankfort several years ... He had come from Marseilles with a great record] Although Clemens's account of Mason's career is essentially correct, his dates are not. In early 1884, Mason was appointed U.S. consul at Marseilles, where within months a cholera epidemic broke out, followed by a widespread panic and flight from the city. During the ensuing year he distinguished himself by his detailed dispatches about the origins, treatment, and social effects of the disease (which was complicated by a concurrent outbreak of typhus and typhoid fever), and by his efforts to prevent its spread. By late August 1885 he reported that the panic of 1884 had subsided somewhat, but the death rate in the "reeking city" was still a "frightful record." From 1889 through 1898 he served as consul general at Frankfurt, and from 1899 to 1905 as consul general at Berlin; his next post was in Paris (Washington *Post:* "The Cholera at Marseilles," 8 Sept 1885, 4; "Capt. Frank H. Mason Dead," 25 June 1916, ES11; New York *Times:* "The Cholera Panic in France," 4 July 1884, 1; "Origin of the Epidemic," 1 Aug 1884, 3; Department of State 1911).

389.10–15 This great record of Mason's ... save him from destruction] Mason's letter is not known to survive. For Clemens's response to his request, see the next Autobiographical Dictation (6 Mar 1906).

Autobiographical Dictation, 6 March 1906

390.2–12 I wrote the little child ... to keep Mason in his place would be a benefaction to the nation] Clemens made his plea for Mason in a second letter to one-year-old Ruth Cleveland, probably written in January or early February 1893, before the formal beginning of her father's second term:

> My dear Ruth,—
> I belong to the Mugwumps, & one of the most sacred rules of our order prevents us from asking favors of officials or recommending men to office, but there is no harm in writing a friendly letter to you & telling you that an infernal outrage is about to be committed by your father in turning out of office the best Consul I know (& I know a great many) just because he is a Republican and a Democrat wants his place. . . .
> I can't send any message to the President, but the next time you have a talk with him concerning such matters I wish you would tell him about Captain Mason & what I think of a Government that so treats its efficient officials. (1 Jan–15 Feb 1893 to Ruth Cleveland, *MTB,* 2:864)

390.14   I received a letter from the President] In reply—probably after Cleveland's 4 March 1893 inauguration—Clemens received a "tiny envelope" with a note in President Cleveland's hand:

> Miss Ruth Cleveland begs to acknowledge the receipt of Mr. Twain's letter and say that she took the liberty of reading it to the President, who desires her to thank Mr. Twain for her information, and to say to him that Captain Mason will not be disturbed in the Frankfort Consulate. The President also desires Miss Cleveland to say that if Mr. Twain knows of any other cases of this kind he will be greatly obliged if he will write him concerning them at his earliest convenience. (Cleveland to SLC, *MTB,* 2:864)

Mason remained consul general at Frankfurt through 1898.

390.19–27   beginning of Mr. Cleveland's second term . . . Mason wrote me again . . . wrote Ruth Cleveland once more] Mason's second letter requesting Clemens's aid is also lost. But Clemens replied on 25 February 1893, promising to "inquire after that letter I sent to Mr. Cleveland" (IaDmE). If he wrote a third letter, it has not survived.

390.39–391.5   Honored Sir . . . March 18/06] The manuscript of this letter—written to honor Cleveland's birthday on 18 March—survives in the Cleveland Papers at the Library of Congress (DLC). The text of the letter in this dictation, however, was transcribed by Hobby from Clemens's own security copy (now in NN-BGC), which omits the original's letterhead ("21 Fifth Avenue"), the date and salutation ("March 6, 1906. | Grover Cleveland, Esq. | Ex-President"), and the complimentary close ("With the profoundest respect").

391.6–20   When Mr. Cleveland . . . his part] The incident Clemens describes has not been identified. On another occasion, however, Cleveland refused an offer from the New York Central Railroad that his Buffalo law partner, Wilson S. Bissell (1847–1903), wanted to accept. In about 1880 Chauncey M. Depew, president of the railroad, tried to persuade the firm to become its general counsel in western New York. Cleveland claimed that "if they accepted they would . . . practically be at the disposal of the railroad with its many interests and its large volume of work—acquiring land, defending damage suits, representing it in all its dealings with the city and, of course, with the other cities and towns of western New York" (Tugwell

1968, 47; Depew 1922, 124–25, 227). After Cleveland took up his post as mayor of Buffalo in 1882, he became known as the "veto mayor" for his refusal to adopt civic bills and award contracts whose overriding purpose was to enrich a ring of corrupt politicians, companies, and contractors at the expense of the city (Tugwell 1968, 53–61; Lynch 1932, 74, 85–95).

391.20   in Buffalo in '70 and '71, Mr. Cleveland was sheriff] From 1871 through 1872 Cleveland was sheriff of Erie County, New York, of which Buffalo was the county seat.

392.6–8   There was a cluster of sixteen bell-buttons . . . I came to hatch out those sixteen clerks] While Clemens was on his 1884–85 reading tour with Cable, he wrote about this incident to his wife:

> On the train, Dec. 3/84.
> We arrived at Albany at noon, & a person in authority met us & said Gov. Cleveland had expressed a strong desire to have me call, as he wanted to get acquainted with me. So as soon as we had fed ourselves the gentleman, with some additional escort, took us in two barouches to the Capitol, & we had a quite jolly & pleasant brief chat with the President-elect. He remembered me easily, hav[ing] seen me often in Buffalo, but I didn't remember him, of course, & I didn't say I did. He had to meet the electors at a banquet in the evening, & expressed great regret that that must debar him from coming to the lecture; so I said if he would take my place on the platform I would run the banquet for him; but he said that that would be only a one-sided affair, because the lecture audience would be so disappointed. Then I sat down on four electrical bells at once (as the cats used to do at the farm,) & summoned four pages whom nobody had any use for. (CU-MARK)

392.11–18   Abbott Thayers . . . knew Miss Lyon, my secretary, very well] Clemens's neighbors were the artists Abbott Handerson Thayer (1849–1921) and his second wife, Emeline (Emma) Beach Thayer (1850–1924), and his three children by his first marriage, Mary (b. 1876), Gerald (1883–1939), and Gladys (1886–1945). Emma Beach Thayer was Clemens's old shipmate and friend from the *Quaker City* voyage in 1867. Witter Bynner (1881–1968), who later won fame as a poet, had been an editor for S. S. McClure, publisher of the muckraking *McClure's Magazine,* since his graduation from Harvard in 1902. Barry Faulkner (1881–1966), an artist and former classmate of Bynner's at Harvard, was a cousin and student of Abbott Thayer's. (Clemens evidently misremembered his first name.) They had first introduced themselves to Isabel Lyon at Ceccina's Restaurant in New York City on 3 May 1905 (link note following 2?–7 Feb 1867 to McComb, *L2,* 15; AskART 2008a, 2008b, 2008c, 2008d; Patricia Thayer Muno, personal communication, 30 July 2008; Lyon 1905, 108–9, 123, 276).

Autobiographical Dictation, 7 March 1906

392 *title*   Wednesday, March 7, 1906] The first page of this dictation is reproduced in facsimile in the Introduction (figure 16).

392.29   next day] Susy described the morning of 30 April 1885 in New York City, the day after Clemens's participation in an Authors' Reading (see AD, 26 Feb 1906, note at 383.10–11).

393.34–35   Liebes Geshchenk . . . Susy's spelling, not mine] Correctly spelled, it should read, "Liebes Geschenk an die Mama," which can be roughly translated as "Loving gift to Mama."

393.43   went to see the Brooklyn Bridge] The Brooklyn Bridge had been open to the public for less than two years, since 24 May 1883, after nearly fourteen years of construction.

394.12   O heilige . . . Jesus!] "O holy Mary mother of Jesus!"

394.15–18   that pretty little German girl . . . knew no English] Jean's young German nurse with a penchant for cursing first came to work for the Clemenses on 16 August 1883, replacing Rosina Hay, who left that day to prepare for her wedding. Clemens wrote his mother the same day, "We like the new girl exceedingly, & she speaks a good clean German, as easy to understand as English" (16 Aug 1883 to JLC, CU-MARK).

394.30   Gott sei Dank . . . Haar!] "Thank God I'm really finished with the God damned hair!"

394.41   lady principal] Abby F. Goodsell was the lady principal of Vassar, "chief executive aid of the President in the direction of the Teachers, and in the government of the students" in 1875–77 and 1881–91. Among other duties she offered "maternal supervision" of the students, provided housing, and oversaw public and social events (Vassar College 2008a).

395.12   He read "A Trying Situation" and "The Golden Arm,"] Both "A Trying Situation," taken from chapter 25 of *A Tramp Abroad,* and "The Woman with the Golden Arm" (which Clemens sometimes called "A Ghost Story") were regularly on the program for the 1884–85 "Twins of Genius" tour with George Washington Cable (*N&J3,* 69; see "My Autobiography [Random Extracts from It]," note at 217.25–27).

395.29–42   President of the College . . . I detest his memory] Samuel L. Caldwell (1820–89), a Baptist minister, had been president of Vassar College since 1878. Caldwell wrote Clemens on 3 April 1885, thanking him for his willingness to speak and inviting him and Olivia to stay, and again on 9 April 1885, assuring him that they had sufficient guest chambers for him and Susy and that "the Lady Principal, I am sure, can make your daughter happier than she will be at a hotel" (CU-MARK). Clemens immediately accepted (11 Apr 1885 to Caldwell, NPV). Caldwell was an inexperienced administrator, and in 1884 the alumnae became especially dissatisfied with his inadequate efforts to attract students. They were backed by the Board of Trustees, and on 9 June 1885, five weeks after Clemens gave his readings in honor of Founder's Day, they accepted Caldwell's resignation (Vassar College 2008b; Daniels 2008).

Autobiographical Dictation, 8 March 1906

396.13–19   Miss Taylor . . . Mrs. (Professor) Lord . . . Miss Russell . . . Miss Hill] Miss Taylor was probably Virginia Taylor of the senior class, who had recently participated in the Barnard Union's senior debate and appeared as the Earl of Leicester in the undergraduate play, Sheridan's *The Critic.* Mrs. Lord was the wife of Herbert Lord, professor of philosophy. Isabelle (Belle) K. Russell of the senior class was chairman of the Barnard Union. The dean of Barnard College, since 1901, was Laura Drake Gill (1860–1926). She received her bachelor's degree in mathematics from Smith College in 1881, and her master's in 1885. She interrupted her subsequent teaching career for advanced studies at the universities of Leipzig and Geneva and at the Sorbonne. She joined the Red Cross in 1898 after the outbreak of the Spanish-American War and managed a Red Cross hospital in Cuba. After the war she took charge of the Cuban Orphan Society and helped organize Cuban schools (*Barnard Bulletin:* "Departmental Changes," 4 [24 Mar 1902]: 3; Belle K. Russell, "Barnard Union," 10 [15 Jan 1906]: 1; "Undergraduate Play," 10 [21 Mar 1906]: 1; "Dr. Laura Drake Gill," 30 [12 Feb 1926]: 4; Barnard College 2008a, 2008b; "Dr. Laura Gill Dies," New York *Times,* 5 Feb 1926, 19).

396.22–25   I lectured upon Morals . . . never knew so grave a subject to create so much noise before] The *Barnard Bulletin* described Clemens's talk:

> He said he had nothing to talk about, but that he did have some fine illustrations he was going to get in somehow. "The Caprice of Memory," he thought, would be a good subject, though he might just as easily talk on morals. For it is better to teach than to practice them; better to confer morals on others than to experiment too much with them on one's self. As his first illustration, Mr. Clemens told how he once had in his possession a watermelon—a Missouri melon, and therefore large and luscious. Most people would have said he had stolen it. But the word "steal" was too much for him, a good boy; in fact, the best boy in his town. He said he had *extracted* it from a grocer's cart, for "extract" refers to dentistry, and more accurately expresses how he got that melon; since as the dentist never extracts his own teeth, so this wasn't his own melon. But the melon was green, and because it was so, Mark Twain began to reflect. And reflection is the beginning of morality. It was his duty to take it back and to admonish that grocerman on the evil of selling green melons. The moral, Mr. Clemens said, was that the grocer repented of his sins and soon was perched on the highest pinnacle of virtue.
>
>   In the course of another equally good illustration of a moral, Mark Twain said that in his family there had been a prejudice against going fishing unless you asked permission, and it was bad judgment to ask permission. ("Mark Twain at Barnard," *Barnard Bulletin* 10 [14 Mar 1906]: 2)

The full text of the talk was published in the New York *World* ("'We Wanted You Because We Love You,' Said the Barnard Girls to Mark Twain," 11 Mar 1906, M1; reprinted in Fatout 1976, 495–502).

397.1   "HUCKLEBERRY FINN" DEAD] The article was from the Los Angeles *Times* of 3 February 1906; the original clipping that Hobby transcribed has not been found.

397.13   I have replied that "Huckleberry Finn" was Tom Blankenship] Clemens wrote the same day to Alexander (Aleck) Campbell Toncray (1837–1933), half-brother of the deceased Addison Ovando Toncray (1842–1906) (8 Mar 1906 to Toncray *per* Lyon, photocopy in CU-MARK):

> Dear Mr. Toncray:
>   It is plain to me that you knew the Hannibal of my boyhood, the names you quote prove it. This is an unusual circumstance in my experience. With some frequency letters come from strangers reminding me of old friends & early episodes, but in almost every case these strangers have mixed me up with somebody else, and the names and incidents are foreign to me.
>   Huckleberry Finn was Tom Blankenship. You may remember that Tom was a good

boy, notwithstanding his circumstances. To my mind he was a better boy than Henry
Beebe & John Reagan put together, those swells of the ancient days.

Sincerely Yours,
S. L. Clemens

Alexander (born in Rushville, Illinois) and Addison (born in Fort Madison, Iowa) were the
sons of John Goodson Toncray (1810–60), who emigrated to Hannibal in the mid-1840s and
opened the Virginia Hotel and Saloon on the levee. Alexander worked as a steamboat and
forwarding agent in 1860 in Hannibal, and as a sign painter in Los Angeles after 1912. After
what he claimed was a stint as captain on the steamboat *Key West,* Addison moved West as
well. In 1880 he was listed in the census as a farm hand in Red Bluff, Montana, and by 1884
he had moved to Murray, Idaho. There, though "Capt. Tonk" was known as a habitual drunk,
he was well liked and lived by odd jobs and hand-me-downs (Brainard [n.d.]; Sellers 1972;
James R. Toncray, personal communications, 17 Dec 2008, 20 Dec 2008; *Marion Census* 1850,
307; Fotheringham 1859, 57).

397.14–15 Tom's father was at one time Town Drunkard] Tom Blankenship (b. 1831?)
was one of eight children of Woodson and Mahala Blankenship. Woodson Blankenship (b.
1799?) was listed in the 1850 census as a laborer from South Carolina (*Marion Census* 1850,
308, 309).

397.20–26 In "Huckleberry Finn" I have drawn Tom Blankenship exactly . . . more of
his society than of any other boy's] Clemens's description here of Tom Blankenship, who was
perhaps four years his senior, closely reflects his characterizations of Huckleberry Finn in
numerous works. In chapter 6 of *Tom Sawyer,* for example, Huck is "the juvenile pariah of
the village . . . son of the town drunkard" who is "cordially hated and dreaded by all the
mothers of the town, because he was idle, and lawless, and vulgar and bad—and because all
their children admired him so" (SLC 1982, xvii, 47). After hearing this chapter read aloud,
Clemens's sister, Pamela Moffett, said, "Why, that's Tom Blankenship!" (*MTBus,* 265). In
1899, Blankenship's sister, apparently "little impressed with the distinction conferred on the
family," recognized Tom and perhaps her other older brother in Huck: "Yes, I reckon it was
him. Sam and our boys run together considerable them days, and I reckon it was Tom or Ben,
one; it don't matter which, for both of 'em's dead" (Fielder 1899, 10). Huckleberry Finn also
appears in *Adventures of Huckleberry Finn, Tom Sawyer Abroad* (SLC 1894a), and "Tom
Sawyer, Detective" (SLC 1896c), as well as in several unfinished works: "Huck Finn and Tom
Sawyer among the Indians" (SLC 1884), "Tom Sawyer's Conspiracy" (SLC 1897–?1902),
"Schoolhouse Hill" (SLC 1898c), and the fragmentary "Huck Finn" (*Inds,* 260–61, 302–3;
see also Clemens's 1895 draft introduction for a reading from chapter 16 of *Huckleberry Finn*
in *HF 2003,* 619).

397.26–27 I heard, four years ago, that he was Justice of the Peace in a remote village in
Montana, and . . . greatly respected] Blankenship, who remained in Hannibal, was arrested
repeatedly for stealing food (Hannibal *Messenger,* 21 Apr 1861, and "At His Old Business," 4
June 1861, reprinted in Lorch 1940, 352). No evidence has been found that he went to Montana.
In 1889 Clemens was informed of his death from cholera, and confirmed it when visiting

Hannibal in 1902 (Wetzel 1985, 33; "He Returns," undated clipping from the Hannibal *Journal,* enclosed in Coontz to SLC, 18 Apr 1889, CU-MARK; Fielder 1899, 10; "Good-Bye to Mark Twain," Hannibal *Courier-Post,* 3 June 1902, 1).

398.12–15   my nephew, by marriage, Edward Loomis . . . carried him there still oftener] Edward Eugene Loomis (1864–1937) married Julia Olivia Langdon (1871–1948), Charles Langdon's eldest daughter, in 1902. After his graduation from Utica Commercial College in the early 1880s, Loomis worked for a succession of railway companies in Denver and in New York, by 1894 serving as superintendent responsible for overseeing the bituminous coal and lumber interests of the Erie Railroad Company. In June 1899, he became manager of the anthracite coal properties of the Delaware, Lackawanna and Western Railroad Company. He was responsible for several innovations in the company's anthracite mines, and in 1902 was elected first vice-president, member of the board of managers, and director and officer of all the railroad's subsidiary corporations.

398.20   Mr. Buckly] Unidentified.

399.17–18   Mr. Dawson's school] John D. Dawson (b. 1812?), a native of Scotland and veteran of fourteen years' teaching, announced the opening of his school for young ladies and boys "of good morals, and of ages under 12 years," on Third Street in Hannibal, in April 1847. He ran the school until 1849, when he left for California, where he became a miner in Tuolumne County. Dawson's was the last school Clemens attended. The character Dobbins in *Tom Sawyer* is based on Dawson (Wecter 1952, 132–34; *Inds,* 317).

399.18   Sam and Will Bowen] See AD, 9 Mar 1906, note at 402.16–33.

399.18   Andy Fuqua] Anderson (Andy) Fuqua (1829?–97) was one of the six children of Nathaniel Fuqua, a tobacco merchant and a town councilman in 1845 when Hannibal was incorporated. In the 1860s Anderson worked at a livery stable and then became a tobacconist and commercial boat owner (*Marion Census* 1860, 122–23; Fotheringham 1859, 26, 33; Ellsberry 1965a, 5; Holcombe 1884, 900; *MTBus,* 83).

399.22–23   I remember Dawson's schoolhouse perfectly. If I wanted to describe it I could save myself the trouble by conveying the description of it . . . from "Tom Sawyer."] Clemens described Dawson's school in chapters 6–7 and 21 of *Tom Sawyer* and again in chapter 1 of the unfinished "Schoolhouse Hill" manuscript, where the Scottish schoolmaster is based on Dawson (*Inds,* 317).

399.25   Cardiff Hill, (Holliday's Hill,)] For Clemens's memories of Cardiff Hill (his fictional name for Holliday's Hill) see "Scraps from My Autobiography. From Chapter IX."

399.27–28   Nannie Owsley, a child of seven] Anna (Nannie) B. Owsley (b. 1840?) was one of six children of William Perry Owsley (b. 1813) and Almira Roberts Owsley. She and her sister Elizabeth (b. 1839?) attended Dawson's school with Clemens. Nannie, who later married William M. Johnson, had six children of her own. It was William Owsley who shot Sam Smarr on a street in Hannibal (see "Scraps from My Autobiography. From Chapter IX," note at 158.5; *Marion Census* 1850, 323; *Marion Census* 1860, 121; Owsley 1890, 28, 29, 133).

399.28–29   George Robards, eighteen or twenty years old, the only pupil who studied

Latin] George C. Robards (1833–79) was the eldest of six children born to Amanda Carpenter Robards (1808–65) and Captain Archibald S. Robards (1787–1862), a former Kentucky plantation and slave owner (*Marion Census* 1860, 133; Holcombe 1884, 992; *Robards Family Genealogy* 2009, part 14:65). The spelling of the family name was later changed to RoBards by George's younger brother, John L. RoBards (see AD, 9 Mar 1906).

399.34   Arch Fuqua—the other one's brother] Archibald (b. 1833?) Fuqua, Anderson's brother, worked as a tobacco roller, and served with Clemens in the Marion Rangers. The character of Archy Thompson in "Boy's Manuscript" (SLC 1868e) is based on him (*Marion Census* 1860, 122–23; Fotheringham 1859, 26; Ellsberry 1965a, 5; *Inds,* 268, 319).

399.40–400.1   Theodore Eddy, who could work his ears like a horse] Theodore Eddy (b. 1836?) was the eldest of five children of Martha J. Eddy (b. 1818?) and William Eddy (b. 1804?), a carpenter and builder and one of Hannibal's first town councilmen in 1845 (*Marion Census* 1850, 323; Holcombe 1884, 900).

Autobiographical Dictation, 9 March 1906

400.20   My hair was a dense ruck of short curls, and so was my brother Henry's] See the photograph of Henry at age eight or nine, following page 204.

400.26–27   George . . . and Mary Moss were sweethearts and pledged to eternal constancy . . . But Mr. Lakenan arrived] Mary Moss (b. 1832) was one of six children of Mary Moss (b. 1816) and Russell W. Moss (b. 1810?), who with William Samuel owned a pork and beef packing plant on the levee, reputed to be the second largest in the United States. Mary, remembered as "the *belle* of Hannibal," was a frequent visitor to the Clemens home. Robert F. Lakenan (1820–83), of Virginia, moved to Hannibal soon after his admission to the bar in 1845. He helped to found the Hannibal and St. Joseph Railway in the late 1840s, acting as its director attorney and later as its general attorney. His first wife, Lizzie Ayres, died in 1850 after less than a year of marriage. He married Mary Moss in 1854. They retired to his farm in Shelby County from 1861 to 1866, thereafter returning to Hannibal. He was elected state senator in 1876, and then state representative in 1882. They had six children (*Inds,* 328–29, 336; Holcombe 1884, 608–10; Brashear 1935). Clemens told the story of their unhappy marriage in "Villagers of 1840–3," written in 1897:

> Mary, very sweet and pretty at 16 and 17. Wanted to marry George Robards. Lawyer Lakenan the rising stranger, held to be the better match by the parents, who were looking higher than commerce. They made her engage herself to L.   L. made her study hard a year to fit herself to be his intellectual company; then married her, shut her up, the docile and heart-hurt young beauty, and continued her education rigorously. When he was ready to trot her out in society 2 years later and exhibit her, she had become wedded to her seclusion and her melancholy broodings, and begged to be left alone. He compelled her—that is, commanded. She obeyed. Her first exit was her last. The sleigh was overturned, her thigh was broken; it was badly set. She got well with a terrible limp, and forever after stayed in the house and produced children. Saw no company, not even the mates of her girlhood. (*Inds,* 94)

400.38–401.1   George went away, presently, to some far-off region and there he died—of a broken heart] In "Villagers of 1840–3" Clemens remembered that George, after the failure of his courtship, was "disappointed, wandered out into the world, and not heard of again for certain. Floating rumors at long intervals that he had been seen in South America (Lima) and other far places. Family apparently not disturbed by his absence. But it was known that Mary Moss was" (*Inds,* 93, 344–45). In fact, Robards was living in Hannibal and working as a farmer in 1860, and thereafter served as a captain in the Confederate Army throughout the war. He worked in Hannibal as a real estate and insurance agent in the 1870s, and was elected county assessor in 1876 (*Robards Family Genealogy* 2009, part 14:65).

401.4–6   Mary still lives . . . Missouri University] For Clemens's honorary degree, see the Autobiographical Dictation of 12 February 1906. Upon arrival in Hannibal in 1902, Clemens wrote to his wife about the trip from St. Louis to Hannibal (where he stopped for several days before proceeding to Columbia, Missouri, to receive his degree): "In the train was accosted by a lady who required me to name her. I said I was *sure* I could do it. But I had the wit to say that if she would tell me her name I would tell her whether I had guessed correctly or not. It was the widow of Mr. Lakenan. I had known her as a child. We talked 3 hours" (31 May 1902 to OLC, CU-MARK, in *LLMT,* 337; Holcombe 1884, 610; Hagood and Hagood 1985, 46; *Boone Census* 1900, 212; "Farewell to Hannibal," St. Louis *Globe-Democrat,* 3 June 1902, 2).

401.7–16   John Robards . . . He had been in ships] In 1849, John Lewis RoBards (1838–1925) left for Mariposa, California, with his father, Archibald, and a party of fifteen men, for whom his father furnished "at his own expense ample vehicles, provisions, stock, etc., for the entire expedition" (Holcombe 1884, 991). Letters to the local newspapers helped Hannibal's citizens keep track of the Robards party, who took the route through New Mexico, prospecting in the Taos Mountains in July 1849 but finding only "small quantities" of gold and moving on ("The Emigrants," Hannibal *Courier,* 23 Aug 1849, unknown page). John RoBards remembered that "about 1,200 hostile Pimo Indians surrounded the camp, and, with arrows presented, demanded the surrender of the itinerant strangers. Except for the remarkable presence of mind of his father the company would have been massacred" (Holcombe 1884, 992). Other adventures included a Mexican fandango in Santa Barbara, after which the hosts, childless, offered his father $1,000 in silver for John. By the middle of 1850, a local newspaper reported that "Capt. Robards is at Stockton—his men all left him," and in early January 1851, another reported the return to Hannibal of "Capt. A. S. Robards and Son" on the steamer *Wyoming* ("California Letter," Hannibal *Courier,* 27 June 1850, unknown page; "Returned Californians," Hannibal *Western Union,* 9 Jan 1851, unknown page; RoBards 1909, 71–74). RoBards attended the University of Missouri and Jefferson School of Law in Kentucky, and in 1861 returned to Hannibal, where he set up his law practice and married Sara (Sallie) Crump Helm (1842–1918), with whom he had seven children, only three of whom survived until adulthood. In 1861, RoBards, along with Clemens and others, organized the Marion Rangers, a company in the Missouri State Guard. In "The Private History of a Campaign That Failed" Clemens mocked RoBards's spelling of his name by portraying his character as "d'Un Lap" (formerly

Dunlap), which later he "was ashamed of" (SLC 1885b; 19? Apr 1887 to Davis, ViU, in Wecter 1952, 298 n. 13; *Robards Family Genealogy* 2009, part 14:65; *Inds,* 345–46).

401.23–29   his granddaughter, twelve years old . . . her brief life came to a close a few days later] Sara Ellen Richardson (1890–1902) was the only child of RoBards's daughter Mary L. RoBards Richardson (b. 1864) and her husband, Elisha A. Richardson (b. 1860) of Louisville, Kentucky (*Jefferson Census* 1900, 8A, 8B; *Portrait* 1895, 144–45). At the news of her death, Clemens wrote: "My dear old playmate & friend, the tidings you send me are inexpressibly distressing, & my heart goes out to you in your sorrow. Good-bye—I grieve with you" (3 June 1902 to RoBards, MoHM and MoCoJ).

401.30–34   John Garth . . . Helen Kercheval . . . John's tomb] John H. Garth (1837–99), one of Clemens's close childhood friends, was the younger son of John Garth (1784–?1857), a tobacco and grain merchant, and his wife, Emily Houston Garth (d. 1844?). He attended the University of Missouri, then returned to Hannibal to work in the family tobacco business. In 1860 he married Helen Kercheval (1838–1923), and in 1862 they moved to New York City, where he worked alongside his brother David J. Garth (1822–1912) at the newly established Garth, Son and Company, a nationwide chain of tobacco warehouses. In the early 1870s he returned to Hannibal, where he became one of the town's most prominent and prosperous citizens (*Portrait* 1895, 776–77; *Inds,* 320). Helen V. Kercheval (1838–1923) was the daughter of Anna M. and William E. Kercheval, manager of a Hannibal dry goods firm called the "People's Store" ("'The People's Store' Once More," Hannibal *Courier,* 15 Apr 1852, unknown page; *Inds,* 328). In May 1882, while visiting old friends in Hannibal, Clemens stayed with the Garths at "Woodside," their six-hundred-acre estate: "It has been a moving time. I spent my nights with John & Helen Garth, three miles from town, in their spacious & beautiful house. They were children with me, & afterwards school-mates" (17 May 1882 to OLC, CU-MARK, in *MTL,* 1:419). John Garth died of Bright's disease; Clemens saw his tomb at Mount Olivet cemetery when Helen Garth and her daughter took him there during his 1902 visit to Hannibal. In his working notes for "Schoolhouse Hill," Clemens planned characters named Jack Stillson and Fanny Brewster modeled on John and Helen, but only Jack Stillson appears in the unfinished manuscript (31 May 1902 to OLC, CU-MARK, in *LLMT,* 338; Hagood and Hagood 1985, 29).

401.36–402.2   Mr. Kercheval, had an apprentice . . . and he had also a slave woman . . . I was saved again] The apprentice has not been identified. The "slave woman," who must have been about forty-four years old when she rescued Clemens, is identified only by Kercheval's name in the 1850 census, which describes her as a female mulatto (*Marion Census* 1850 ["Slave Inhabitants"], 615).

402.2–4   I was drowned seven times . . . once in Bear Creek and six times in the Mississippi] Clemens elsewhere claimed that he had survived drowning nine times: "As a small boy I was notoriously lucky. It was usual for one or two of our lads (per annum) to get drowned in the Mississippi or in Bear Creek, but I was pulled out in a $\frac{2}{3}$ drowned condition 9 times before I learned to swim, & was considered to be a cat in disguise" (2 Jan 1895 to Rogers, CU-MARK, in *HHR,* 115; see also SLC 1899a).

402.8–12   Another schoolmate was John Meredith . . . devastations and sheddings of blood] John D. Meredith (1837–70) was one of five children of the Clemens family's old friend and doctor, Hugh Meredith, and his wife, Anna D. Meredith (b. 1813?) (see "Something about Doctors," note at 188.19–20). John worked as a printer at the Hannibal *Messenger* office in 1859. Despite Clemens's memory of John as a Confederate guerrilla, official records show that Hugh, John, and his younger brother, Henry H. Meredith (b. 1840), all served in the Union army. Hugh served as a captain surgeon in 1861 and 1862 in the Twenty-second Regiment Infantry Volunteers; between 1863 and 1865 John served as a captain in the Fifty-third Regiment of the Enrolled Missouri Militia, then in the Second Regiment of the Provisional Enrolled Missouri Militia, and finally in the Thirty-ninth Regiment Infantry Volunteers. Henry, who enlisted in 1861, served in 1864 under his brother John in the Enrolled Missouri Militia (*Marion Census* 1850, 326; *Marion Census* 1860, unknown page; *Marion Census* 1870, 690; Fotheringham 1859, 41; *Marion Veterans Census* 1890, 1; Missouri Digital Heritage 2009b, reels s794, s817, s852, s863, s895; *Inds,* 310, 335; Wecter 1952, 55).

402.16–33   Will Bowen was another schoolmate, and so was his brother, Sam . . . Death came swiftly to both pilots] William Bowen (1836–93) and Samuel Adams Bowen, Jr. (1838?–78), were the two youngest boys of seven children born to Samuel Adams Bowen, Sr., and Amanda Stone Bowen (1802–81). Will and Sam (and their older brother Bart) became pilots on the Mississippi, operating on the same route as Clemens, between St. Louis and New Orleans. Clemens was Sam's copilot on the *John H. Dickey* during the summer of 1858, and twice Will's copilot on the *A. B. Chambers* and the *Alonzo Child* between 1859 and 1861 (*Inds,* 303–5). Clemens told the story of Sam's marriage, using fictional names, in chapter 49 of *Life on the Mississippi;* the character based on Sam was a "shiftless young spendthrift, boisterous, good-hearted, full of careless generosities, and pretty conspicuously promising to fool his possibilities away early, and come to nothing." Clemens retold the story in "Villagers of 1840–3," noting that Sam "slept with the rich baker's daughter, telling the adoptive parents they were married," and describing Sam's character and death: "Sam no account and a pauper. Neglected his wife; she took up with another man. Sam a drinker. Dropped pretty low. Died of yellow fever and whisky on a little boat with Bill Kribben the defaulting secretary" (*Inds,* 97). William J. (Bill) Kribben (d. 1878), who had embezzled the Western Boatmen's Benevolent Association Fund when he was secretary and treasurer during the Civil War, was Sam Bowen's copilot on the *Molly Moore* when they caught yellow fever and died. "Island 82" was just above Greenville, Mississippi, and Columbia, Arkansas. In 1882, when Clemens revisited the Mississippi Valley, he noted that Bowen had been buried in Arkansas at "Jackson's point" (or "Parker's Bend") at the head of Island 65. "The river has cut away the banks & Bowen is washed into the river." Island 65 had completely disappeared by 1884 (*N&J2,* 527, 561; Bragg 1977, 105–9, 130; Clabaugh to SLC, 19 July 1890, CU-MARK; *Inds,* 328).

Autobiographical Dictation, 12 March 1906

403.12–15   A tribe of Moros, dark skinned savages . . . bitter against us because we have been trying for eight years to take their liberties away . . . a menace] In December 1898, after the battle of Manila in the Spanish-American War, Spain ceded the Philippines to the United States. Rather than granting independence to the Filipinos as had been expected, the United States established military rule. What had been a war of independence against Spain soon became a war of independence against the United States, concentrated in the primarily Tagalog north. The Moros, a collection of thirteen cultural-linguistic groups sometimes at war with one another but united by their adherence to Islam, lived primarily in the south, in the Sulu Archipelago, where Jolo Island is located, and in the southern half of Mindanao (Byler 2005, 1–3). In 1899, in what was later admitted to be solely a "temporary expedient," the American administrative authority signed a treaty with the sultan of Sulu promising governing autonomy in return for recognizing U.S. sovereignty. In the succeeding years it increasingly attempted to assert social and military control of the south, resulting in a series of battles with the Moros, whom the U.S. army many times overpowered in battle but did not defeat (Kho 2009, 1–5). In March 1904, President Roosevelt and Secretary of War Taft decided to abrogate the treaty, which "provided salaries for the Sultan and certain of his dattos and at the same time, it is said, sustained polygamy and slavery" on the grounds that it had simply been "a modus vivendi and an executive agreement" ("America Abrogates Treaty with Moros," New York *Times,* 15 Mar 1904, 5). Although they soon reinstated payments to the sultan and his tribal chiefs, the war continued unabated. Before the present action, the Moros had retreated to their fortress in the bowl of the extinct volcano on Mount Dajo ("The Troops in Action," New York *Tribune,* 10 Mar 1906, 3; Bacevich 2006).

403.15   Our commander, General Leonard Wood] Major General Leonard Wood (1860–1927) earned his medical degree at Harvard Medical School in 1883 and thereafter worked as an army contract surgeon, participating in the last battle against Geronimo in 1886. He served as personal physician to President William McKinley, and he became friends with McKinley's assistant secretary of the navy, Theodore Roosevelt. In 1898, at the outbreak of the Spanish-American War, he assumed command of the First Volunteer Cavalry—the Rough Riders—to Roosevelt's second in command, and led his men at the battle of San Juan Hill. For the remainder of the war he led the Second Cavalry Brigade, and from 1900 to 1902 served as military governor of Cuba, instituting various reforms but also arousing controversy. In 1902 he became commander of the Philippines Division, and from 1903 to 1906, after President Roosevelt appointed him major general, he served as governor of Moro Province. After attempting to force reforms and impose taxes, he took charge of the military campaign against the Moros (Fort Leonard Wood 2009; *Boston Medical Journal* 1899, 973). Wood was a controversial figure in his time and remains so. His career, considered stellar and full of well-deserved high honors by some contemporary chroniclers and modern historians, was seen very differently by others, including Clemens, who had watched Wood's rise to high office, and had in December 1903 written a scathing essay, "Major General Wood, M.D.," about his character and the machinations to appoint him major general (SLC 1903e; see AD, 14 Mar 1906, note at 409.1–17).

403.28   General Wood's order was "Kill or capture the six hundred."] The New York *Times* reported on 10 March that Wood "directed Col. Joseph W. Duncan to attack the Moros in the crater and capture or kill them. This was accomplished after repeated demands to surrender" ("15 Americans, 600 Moros Slain in 2 Days' Fight," 10 Mar 1906, 1).

403.31–33   probably with brickbats . . . Heretofore the Moros have used knives and clubs mainly; also ineffectual trade-muskets when they had any] The New York *Times* reported that the "600 fanatical Moros" were armed with "rifles and knives and supported by native artillery" ("15 Americans, 600 Moros Slain in 2 Days' Fight," 10 Mar 1906, 1). The Moros' "weapon of choice was the kris, a short sword with a wavy blade; the Americans toted Springfield rifles and field guns" (Bacevich 2006).

404.5–11   The official report quite . . . minutely and faithfully described the nature of the wounds . . . by cable, at one dollar and fifty cents a word] Wood's cable named seven of the thirty-two wounded, including Coxswain Gilmore, "severely wounded in the elbow" (according to the New York *Globe and Commercial Advertiser*), and three with "slight" wounds in the thigh, right hand, and left eye ("15 Americans, 600 Moros Slain in Two-Day Fight," 9 Mar 1906, 1). None of the accounts in the New York newspapers (*Herald, Globe and Commercial Advertiser, Evening Post, Evening Sun, Times, Tribune,* or *World*) specified a nose injury.

404.15–25   In one of the great battles of the Civil War . . . Waterloo . . . the pathetic comedy called the Cuban war . . . crippled on the field] Clemens may have had in mind the Appomattox campaign, in which the casualties equaled about 10 percent of the 163,000 men who fought on both sides. According to modern historians, most of the major battles in the Civil War had a far greater percentage of casualties (Home of the American Civil War 2009; American Civil War 2009b; Fox 1889). His estimate of the number of combatants at Waterloo (on 18 June 1815) is high. By one estimate, only about 141,000 men engaged in the battle; French casualties were about 54 percent, and Allied casualties about 33 percent. Troop strength and casualty figures for the Cuban battles of the Spanish-American War also differ, but Clemens's statistics are substantially correct. A far greater number of Americans, perhaps 90 percent, died in hospitals of yellow fever, malaria, dysentery, and food poisoning than died in action (Veteran's Museum and Memorial Center 2009; Library of Congress 2009). Clemens's source for Spanish casualty figures is uncertain, but it is known that they also lost a greater number to tropical disease than to battle (Bollet 2005).

404.32–41   The splendid news appeared . . . on Friday morning . . . nobody said a word about the "battle."] The dispatch from General Wood reporting the "severe action between troops," dated Friday, 9 March, was first published or excerpted the same day in at least three New York newspapers, the *Evening Post, Evening Sun,* and the *Globe and Commercial Advertiser,* and the next day, the morning of Saturday, 10 March, in the *Times, Tribune, World,* and others. Only two, the New York *Evening Post* and the *World,* had an editorial comment. The *Post* wrote: "Congress would make no mistake if it should rigidly inquire into the latest 'battle' in the Philippines. . . . What possible military excuse was there for charging up a mountain cone, 2,100 feet high, to attack an almost impregnable fort? Was there no possibility of forcing these Moros to surrender by starving them out?" ("The Latest Moro Slaughter," New York *Evening Post,* 10 Mar 1906, 4).

405.13–17   Washington . . . (Signed) Theodore Roosevelt] Roosevelt's congratulatory cable of 10 March was widely published on 11 March, with no direct commentary ("Special to the New York Times," New York *Times,* 1; "President Congratulates Wood," New York *Tribune,* 1; "President Congratulates Wood upon the Massacre," New York *World,* 1).

405.28 WOMEN SLAIN IN MORO SLAUGHTER] This headline and the others quoted below through 406.22 were from the New York *Herald* of 11 March.

406.23 Lieutenant Johnson has pervaded the cablegrams] Lieutenant Gordon Johnston (1874–1934) was the son of Confederate General Robert Daniel Johnston and nephew of Joseph F. Johnston, governor of Alabama, 1896–1900. His injury was followed closely in the newspapers because of his connection to Roosevelt. (Many newspapers erroneously called him Johnson, the name Clemens uses.) On 10 March the New York *Tribune* published two stories, headlined "Lieutenant Johnston Formerly in Rough Riders" and "Lieut. Johnston Not Badly Hurt," and the *Globe and Commercial Advertiser* published "Moro Fight Hero. Lieut. Johnson, Princeton Graduate, Is Badly Wounded in Leading a Charge." On 11 March the *World* noted that his wounds "are severe, a slug having passed through his right shoulder. He performed a gallant deed when he scaled the wall of the Rio crater and was blown off the parapet by the force of exploding artillery" ("900 Moros Slain, It Is Now Said, in Fatal Crater," 1). On 12 March, the New York *Times* reported Roosevelt's telegram and Johnston's answer in a story headlined, "Fine, Cables Johnston, Answering Roosevelt" (12 Mar 1906, 6; Arlington National Cemetery 2009).

406.25–26 Gillette's comedy farce of a few years ago, "Too Much Johnson."] William Gillette's comedy, based on the French comic operetta *La Plantation Thomassin* by Maurice Ordonneau and Albert Vizentini, opened on Broadway on 26 November 1894 and ran until June 1895 ("The Theatrical Week," New York *Times,* 2 Dec 1894, 10; Broadway League 2009).

Autobiographical Dictation, 14 March 1906

407.13–14 hardly a ghost of a whisper . . . in the editorial columns of the papers] Although comment about the Jolo massacre was at first sparing or nonexistent in several New York newspapers, as early as 10 March the *World* began publishing daily or almost daily editorials and editorial cartoons, which became more disapproving as new information reached the press. The 10 March editorial concluded: "There will be many Americans who will regret, along with the death of almost a score of our brave men, that so crushing a blow should fall by our arms upon a people who have never appealed to us to extend to them the 'blessings of civilization,' but are willing to rule themselves" (New York *World:* "The Slaughter in Jolo," 10 Mar 1906, 6; "Peace in Jolo," 12 Mar 1906, 6; "The Soldier Dead," 13 Mar 1906, 6; "The Jolo Massacre," 14 Mar 1906, 8). The *Tribune's* editors, convinced that these Moros were "plain, ordinary, everyday outlaws and brigands," were on 11 March regretful but approving: "It was not a question of submission to American rule but a question of regard for any rule at all and for the peace of the Moro people. [¶] The manner of doing the work was undoubtedly severe. There are cases in which severity is humanity" ("Suppressing Crime in Jolo," New York *Tribune,* 11 Mar 1906, 6). On 12 March the *Times* reported official criticism of General

Wood "for bringing on such a struggle. It is contended that he might have accomplished enough by laying siege to the fort and starving the Moros into submission" and similarly reported "no little criticism" of Roosevelt's congratulatory message, "on the ground that it was entirely uncalled for. . . . The fight at Fort Dajo is compared frequently with that of Wounded Knee, in January, 1891, when the Sioux ghost dancers were shot down, squaws and children with the braves" ("Not All Praise for Wood. Officials Believe His Policy Caused the Needless Killing of Moro Women and Children," 12 Mar 1906, 6). But on the same day, the *Times* published an editorial justifying the action: "Lamentable as it is to hear of the enforced slaughter of 600 inhabitants of the islands where we established peace some five years ago, there is yet consolation in the knowledge that these last rebels against our undoubtedly beneficent rule are men who, if nothing except extermination can reduce them to order, can be exterminated with exceptional facility" ("Extermination or Utilization," 12 Mar 1906, 8). And on the following day, the *Times* published another editorial defending General Wood ("Finding Fault with Gen. Wood," 13 Mar 1906, 8; see also "Fighting Fuzzy-Wuzzies," New York *Globe and Commercial Advertiser,* 12 Mar 1906, 6, and "The Battle of the Crater," New York *Evening Sun,* 13 Mar 1906, 6).

408.5–7 "no wanton destruction of . . . used them as shields in the hand-to-hand fighting."] Here and at 408.17–18 Clemens quoted from "No Wanton Massacre" in the New York *Evening Post* (13 Mar 1906, 1).

408.30–42 Colonel Funston had penetrated to the refuge of the patriot, Aguinaldo . . . disgracing the uniform, the flag, the nation, and himself] Emilio Aguinaldo (1869–1964) was the leader of the fight for Filipino independence, first against Spain and then against the United States. Frederick Funston (1865–1917), nicknamed the "scrapper" and known as a "dare-devil sort of soldier," participated as a volunteer in more than twenty battles in the Cuban war, where he had been seriously wounded three times, captured by the Spanish and sentenced to death, liberated or escaped, and barely survived a bout of "Cuban fever." He thereafter joined the Twentieth Kansas Volunteers to fight in the Philippines as a colonel, and had been promoted to brigadier general in 1899 after swimming across the Rio Grande under "galling fire from Aguinaldo's men." In February 1901, McKinley considered him for promotion to the regular army, but concluded that he was "not a man of proper temperament for any rank higher than that of Lieutenant in the regulars" ("Gen. Funston's Career," New York *Times,* 28 Mar 1901, 2). Although by that time the Filipino fight for independence was essentially over, "largely due to the patient, indefatigable, constant efforts of officers whose names are barely known to the public and whose personalities are almost unknown," Funston proceeded, in late March, to capture Aguinaldo by treachery and deceit. Despite his reluctance to reward Funston and thereby seem to overlook the more important efforts of other officers, McKinley promoted him to brigadier general in the regular army on 30 March 1901 ("The President's Dilemma. To Reward Funston Would Be to Slight Hard Work of Other Officers in the Philippines," New York *Times,* 30 Mar 1901, 2). Clemens's bitterly satiric "A Defence of General Funston," published in the *North American Review* in May 1902, scathingly criticized Funston for the "forgeries and falsehoods" and "ingratitudes and amazing treacheries" he had employed (SLC

1902c, 620, 622). Clemens also wrote a critical book review (SLC 1902a), which he left un-published, of Edwin Wildman's *Aguinaldo: A Narrative of Filipino Ambitions* (1901).

409.1–17   Wood was an army surgeon . . . the Senate hadn't spirit enough to repudiate it]
Clemens's commentary on Wood and Roosevelt reflected his 1903 "Major General Wood,
M.D.," a "pretty pison article" which he originally planned to submit for publication in the
North American Review or *Harper's Weekly*, but suppressed (30 Dec 1903 to Duneka, MoSW).
In it he pretended to advocate for Wood's elevation to major general:

> I think that the President's delight in the history of him and the character of him and the
> smell of him ought to be considered; I think that Dr. Wood's distinguished "expectations,"
> and spurious medals, and shady silver-plate, and furtive insubordinations, and clandestine
> libels, and frank falsehoods, pimping for gambling hells, and destitution of honor and
> dignity, taken together with his devoted and diligent labors in seeking a great place which
> has not sought him, have earned it and entitled him to it. (SLC 1903e, TS p. 3)

On 7 December 1903 the Senate "had two legislative days, one in the expiring session and one
in the new session," and in the interval between them Roosevelt reappointed Wood and 167
other officers, considering them to be "recess appointments." On 18 March, Wood was confirmed as a major general by the Senate (New York *Times:* "Special Session Is Merged into
Regular. President Roosevelt Decides for 'Constructive Recess,'" 8 Dec 1903, 1; "Wood's
Nomination Is Confirmed by Senate," 19 Mar 1904, 5).

Autobiographical Dictation, 15 March 1906

409.18   Monday, March 5, 1906] The events discussed in this dictation on 15 March had
been reported in the newspapers ten days earlier.

409.27   POLICE HUSTLE CROWD AWAITING MARK TWAIN] This article from
the New York *Times* of 5 March was pasted into the typescript of the dictation.

410.29   Rev. Dr. Charles P. Fagnani] Fagnani (1854–1941) held degrees in arts, science and
law. In 1882 he was ordained a Presbyterian minister, and since 1892 had taught Hebrew at the
Union Theological Seminary in New York, later becoming associate professor of Old Testament
literature ("Dr. Fagnani, 86, Dies in Occupied France," New York *Times*, 7 Jan 1941, 25).

410.40–41   Mark Twain . . . was greeted with a storm of applause] Clemens's talk, entitled
"Reminiscences," was preceded by a lengthy program of several other speakers, a singer (Anna
Taylor Jones, contralto), a "mixed string-and-piano-band" (the Misses Kleckhoefer), and a
Bible reader, causing him to cut his planned talk by half an hour (see AD, 3 Apr 1906;
"Y.M.C.A. Meetings," New York *Globe and Commercial Advertiser,* 3 Mar 1906, 15). Versions
of the speech were published under the title "Layman's Sermon" (*MTS* 1910, 136–39; *MTS*
1923, 281–83; see also Fatout 1976, 492–95).

411.4   Dr. Russell spoke of organization] After the audience was seated and the police
had dispersed the remaining crowd outside, Rev. Dr. Howard H. Russell (1855–1946), superintendent of the national Anti-Saloon League,

denounced the affair from the platform as a police outrage, and said that respectable citizens had been jabbed in the ribs with night sticks to make them move on, when there was no opportunity to move on.

An impromptu indignation meeting was held on the platform, and there was much talk of resolutions passed against the police. They would have passed, but Mark Twain killed them. He began to talk about the individual's duty as a citizen.

"Don't try to infringe on other people's rights," he said, "or take responsibilities on your shoulders that you should not. But if others should try to trample on you, then assert your citizenship. When you resolve to do a thing, do it, but I heard Dr. Russell speak of resolutions about the police. I don't believe in denouncing the whole police force for the fault of one man." ("Fight to See Twain," New York *Tribune,* 5 Mar 1906, 1; "Hurt in Crush to Hear Mark Twain," New York *Morning Telegraph,* 5 Mar 1906, 1)

411.5–6   When they say 'Step lively,' remember it is not an insult from a conductor to you personally] In 1892, the *Railroad Gazette* noted: "On the Manhattan Elevated the injunction of the trainmen to 'step lively' has become a by-word, and they doubtless find the duty of reiterating it thousands of times very irksome, but it is only by this constant spurring at all points that a great passenger movement can be accomplished with punctuality" ("Step Lively," New York *Times,* 27 Dec 1892, 3).

411.11–12   I was traveling from Chicago with my publisher and stenographer . . . and engaged a stateroom on a certain train] Other reports of this speech make clear that Clemens said that he was "in Chicago . . . about to depart for New York" and that the publisher was James R. Osgood. The "stenographer" was Roswell H. Phelps. The three men traveled together in 1882, when Clemens gathered material for *Life on the Mississippi* ("Ten Thousand Stampede at a Mark Twain Meeting," New York *Herald,* 5 Mar 1906, 1).

411.25   Mr. Thomson of the Pennsylvania] Between 1882 and 1899, Frank Thomson (1841–99) served as second vice-president, first vice-president, and president of the Pennsylvania Railroad.

412.7–10   I think it damaged my speech for Miss Lyon . . . I knew that she knew it] Isabel Lyon recorded her impressions that evening; Clemens's young friend Gertrude Natkin also attended:

Today we went up to the Majestic Theatre[,] Mr. Clemens & mother & I . . . But the main thing is that Gertrude was there, "that darling child." We went in the stage door & for a very long time Gertrude didn't arrive. Mr. Clemens's look of disappointment made me heartsick & feebly I tried to find the child in that vast crowd. It was a Christian crowd; but as I turned away from a big burly young man who had tried to gain admittance & had failed, I heard him say: "Just my God damn luck!" . . . Mr. Clemens's talk was lovely & brave & strong & instructive & humorous. No one else in all the world can combine all those qualities with such great wonderful personal charm. . . . He seems never to be aware of himself. (Lyon 1906, 63)

412.16   letter from William Dean Howells] Howells's letter was dated 28 February 1906 (CSmH, in *MTHL,* 2:801–2).

412.39–40   So may I be courteous . . . the path I trod] Clemens paraphrased the final lines of "A Song" by Clarence Urmy (1858–1923), which was printed in the March 1906 issue of *Harper's Bazar* and quoted many times subsequently, often without attribution (Urmy 1906):

> I shall not pass this way again,
> May I be courteous to men,
> Faithful to friends, true to my God,
> A fragrance on the path I trod.

412.41–42   At the funeral I saw Patrick's family . . . The children were men and women] Clemens attended McAleer's funeral at the Cathedral of St. Joseph on Farmington Avenue in Hartford on the morning of 28 February, and "took his place" with the pallbearers "going in and coming out." The McAleers' four surviving children (out of nine)—Michael, William, Alice, and Anne—attended the funeral with their families (Twichell 1874–1916, entry for 27 Feb 1906, 7:126; Hartford *Courant:* "Coachman Many Years for Mark Twain," 26 Feb 1906, 6; "Mark Twain Pays Tribute to Servant," 28 Feb 1906, 3; *Hartford Census:* 1880, 117; 1900, 8B; 1910, 7B; see AD, 1 Feb 1906, note at 322.31–42).

413.4   John, our old gardener] John O'Neil (b. 1848) took care of the grounds and greenhouse at the Clemenses' Hartford house during the 1880s, and from 1891 to 1900, when the family was in Europe (*Hartford Census* 1900, 1A).

413.6–9   at the Hartford Club I met, at a luncheon, eleven of my oldest friends . . . Welch] The Hartford Club, which Clemens joined in 1881, was organized in 1873 for "the promotion of social intercourse, art and literature" (Hartford Club 2009). Before he left New York for the funeral, Clemens asked Charles H. Clark to "assemble some Cheneys & Twichells & other friends at Hartford Club Thursday & lunch them & me at my expense" (26 Feb 1906 to Clark, TxU). In addition to Clark, the guests were Judge William Hamersley, Colonel Frank W. Cheney, Samuel G. Dunham, Rev. Joseph H. Twichell, Rev. Dr. Edwin Pond Parker, Charles E. Perkins, Archibald A. Welch, Rev. Dr. Francis Goodwin, Franklin G. Whitmore, and Dr. E. K. Root ("Mr. Clemens Lunches with Friends," Hartford *Courant,* 14 March 1906, 4). Frank Woodbridge Cheney (1832–1909), a lieutenant colonel in the Civil War who had been wounded at Antietam, served as head of Cheney Brothers silk manufacturers, as a director of the Connecticut Mutual Life Insurance Company for more than thirty years, and as a director of the New York, New Haven, and Hartford Railroad for seven years (*Connecticut Biography* 1917, 277–80; "Death of Colonel Cheney," Hartford *Courant,* 5 June 1909, 5). Archibald Ashley Welch (1859–1935), prominent in many civic organizations, was in 1906 second vice-president of the Phoenix Mutual Life Insurance Company (Burpee 1928, 3:1062–65). Dr. Edward K. Root (b. 1856), a Hartford physician and Charles Clark's brother-in-law, served on the Hartford Board of Health, the State Board of Health, and as medical director of the Connecticut Mutual Life Insurance Company ("Dr. Edward K. Root," Hartford *Courant,* 24 Oct 1899, 8; *Hartford Census* 1900, 8B).

413.12   Rev. Dr. McKnight] Clemens probably refers to the Rev. Dr. George H. McKnight (b. 1830) of Elmira's Episcopal Trinity Church, who earned his A.M. degree at Hobart College in 1851 and his D.D. at Hamilton College in 1873. McKnight performed the marriage cere-mony for Charles J. Langdon (Olivia's brother) and Ida B. Clark in October 1870 (Towner 1892, 287–88; *Chemung Census* 1900, 14B; 13 Oct 1870 to Fairbanks, *L4*, 208–9).

413.33–35   when Sir Thomas Lipton came . . . to race for the America cup, I . . . Mr. Rogers and half a dozen other worldlings] On 3 October 1901, Clemens and Twichell joined Henry H. Rogers and his other guests on the *Kanawha*, which left Sandy Hook, New Jersey, to follow the second race of the series between the American yacht *Columbia* and Sir Thomas Lipton's *Shamrock II.* Lipton (1850–1931), knighted by Queen Victoria in 1898, was famous for his grocery chain, tea shops, and charitable works. This was his second challenge (out of five) for the America's Cup between 1899 and 1930 (*HHR*, 474; "Sir Thomas Gives Up Hope," New York *Times*, 4 Oct 1901, 1; Twichell 1874–1916, entry for 2–3 Oct 1901, 7:105–6).

414.8–9   name of Richard Croker, the celebrated Tammany leader] Croker (1843–1922), acknowledged as Tammany boss after 1884, had brought about the elections of the subsequent three New York Democratic mayors. In September 1901, when Croker had just returned from ten months abroad, the newspapers were filled with stories and speculation about his influence on the upcoming mayoral election, and two recently published books were reviewed in the New York *Times:* a complimentary biography of Croker by Alfred Henry Lewis, and a book by Gustavus Myers that included two chapters on Croker and was highly critical of Tammany Hall's unbroken record of corruption and graft ("About Tammany Hall," 7 Sept 1901, BR3; Alfred Henry Lewis 1901; Myers 1901; "Richard Croker Met by Tammany Leaders," New York *Times*, 15 Sept 1901, 10).

414.11–26   I knew his father very well indeed . . . do you take me for a God damned papist?] The Croker forebears, originally English and Protestant, had gone to Ireland with Cromwell. Twichell evidently assumed that the Crokers were Catholic because of their Irish ancestry. Richard Croker's father, Eyre Coote Croker, a Presbyterian, emigrated to the United States with his family in 1846. He found work as a blacksmith and veterinary horse surgeon, and joined the Union army at the outbreak of the Civil War (Alfred Henry Lewis 1901, 5, 13–14; Lothrop Stoddard 1931, 2, 260–61; see AD, 17 Jan 1906, for Clemens's remarks about General Sickles and the regiment in which Twichell and Croker served).

417.5   dog let out a howl of anguish that could be heard beyond the frontier] The occasion on which Twichell's Decoration Day (Memorial Day) speech was interrupted by the howling dog probably took place in the mid-1870s. In his notebooks, Clemens reminded himself several times in 1878 and after to make use of the incident (jotting down both "Joe Twichell's Deco-ration-day prayer—'G-d d—n that dog'" and an explanation for its howls, "He had a rat!"), and he did use it in chapter 27 of *Huckleberry Finn*, which one Hartford newspaper recognized when the book was published: "The 'He had a rat' story put into a funeral scene, where it actu-ally occurred in this city, will be recognized by a number of Hartford people, who have had many hearty laughs at it in its chrysalis period" ("New Publications," Hartford *Evening Post*, 17 Feb 1885, 3; *HF 2003*, 232–33, 443; *N&J2*, 58, 343; *N&J3*, 16, 92).

Autobiographical Dictation, 16 March 1906

417.19–23 I recall Mary Miller . . . this sorrow did not remain with me long] Clemens's classmate Mary Miller (b. 1835?), who regularly competed with him for the spelling medal, was the eldest daughter of lumber merchant Thomas S. Miller (1807?–60) and Mary E. Miller (1812?–49). She was about the same age as Clemens, according to census records. She married Clemens's friend and classmate John B. Briggs (Hannibal *Courier:* "Obituary," 30 Aug 1849, unknown page; "Look Out for the Old Lumber Yard," 4 Mar 1852, unknown page; *Marion Census* 1850, 307; *Marion Census* 1870, 447; "Good-Bye to Mark Twain," Hannibal *Courier-Post,* 3 June 1902, 1).

417.24–27 I soon transferred my worship to Artimisia Briggs . . . pestered by children] Artemissa (also spelled Artimissa, Artimisia, Artemesia, and Artemissia) Briggs (1832–1910), the elder sister of Clemens's friend and classmate John B. Briggs, was the second of eight children of Rhoda Briggs (b. 1811?) and William Briggs (b. 1799?) (*Marion Census* 1850, 315–16; *Marion Census* 1860, 145; death certificate for Artemissia Briggs, Missouri Digital Heritage 2009a; *Inds,* 306–7).

417.28–32 Mary Lacy . . . was a schoolmate . . . Four years ago she was still living, and had been married fifty years] Most likely, Clemens was confusing Mary Lacy with another schoolmate, Mary Nash. Mary Elizabeth Lacy (b. 1838?) was the daughter of John L. Lacy (1808?–83), who in 1850 worked as a pork packer to support his large family. She married Leonard Mefford in Hannibal on 31 May 1854 and by 1860 had two children (*Marion Census* 1850, 319; *Marion Census* 1860, 149; "Missouri Marriage Records, 1805–2002" 2009). In 1898 Clemens sketched a plan in his notebook to use her as a character in "Schoolhouse Hill," the version of "The Mysterious Stranger" set in the fictional Hannibal, St. Petersburg. When Satan arrives on earth he finds that his son, little Satan, "has been rejected by Mary Lacy, who took him for crazy & who is now horribly sorry she didn't jump at the chance, since she finds that the Holy Family of Hell are not disturbed by the fire, but only their guests. Satan is glad his boy didn't marry beneath him—he is arranging with the shade of Pope Alexander VI to marry him to a descendant" (Notebook 40, TS pp. 51–52, CU-MARK). Mary Nash (b. 1832?) was the half-sister of Clemens's friend Tom Nash. She married John Hubbard of Frytown in January 1851. In 1901, a year before Clemens's Hannibal trip, he responded to an announcement of her fiftieth anniversary, "I remember the wedding very well, although it was 50 years ago; & I wish you & your husband joy of this anniversary of it" (13 Jan 1901 to Hubbard, MoHM). He planned to (but ultimately did not) use her as the model for two literary characters: in his working notes for "Tom Sawyer's Conspiracy" he named her Mary Benton and characterized her as "wild"; and in his working notes for "Schoolhouse Hill" he called her Louisa Robbins and characterized her as "Mary Nash, *bad.*" He may have based the independent Rachel Hotchkiss, the title character in "Hellfire Hotchkiss," on her as well (*Inds,* 214–59, 287–88, 134–213, 337; *HH&T,* 383; *MSM,* 431).

417.33–34 Jimmy McDaniel was another schoolmate . . . His father kept the candy shop] James W. (Jimmy) McDaniel (1833–1911) was the son of William McDaniel (b. 1811?), who ran the confectionary and variety store in Hannibal, which advertised that the "*Confectionary*

Department consists in all the finest varieties of Candy, Nuts, Raisins, Prunes, Dates, Figs, Currants, Citrons, fig Paste, Jellies, Preserves and many other articles too tedious to mention" ("Confectionary and Fancy Goods," Hannibal *Courier*, 7 Oct 1852, unknown page). Jimmy worked as a bookseller at fifteen, a tobacconist before he was twenty, a salesman at his father's store at thirty, and later a packer and manager of the Holmes-Dakin cigar company (Fotheringham 1859, 40; Honeyman 1866, 37; Hallock 1877, 100; Stone, Davidson, and McIntosh 1885, 118, 150; *Marion Census* 1850, 310; death certificate for James W. McDaniel, Missouri Digital Heritage 2009a).

418.2   Jim Wolf and the cats] See "Scraps from My Autobiography. From Chapter IX."

418.5   I saw him four years ago when I was out there] In 1902, the Hannibal newspaper reported that as Clemens

> was driving up Main street he espied James W. McDaniel, the old confectioner and greeted him with "Hello Jim, I'm truly glad to see you. Let me see that scalp of yours; what's become of your hair?" Mr. Clemens and Mr. McDaniel used to be old chums and . . . although they had not met before in nearly forty years they recognized each other on sight. ("See[s] Points of Interest," Hannibal *Morning Journal,* 30 May 1902, reprinted in the Hannibal *Evening Courier-Post,* 6 Mar 1935, 4B, transcript in CU-MARK)

418.11–12   Artimisia Briggs . . . married Richmond . . . my Methodist Sunday-school teacher] In March 1853, at the age of twenty-one, Artemissa Briggs married the local bricklayer, William J. Marsh (b. 1815?), not Joshua Richmond (b. 1816?), the stone mason. Richmond married Angelina Matilda Cook (b. 1829?) in January 1849; he taught Clemens's earliest Sunday school class at Hannibal's Methodist Old Ship of Zion Church, on the public square (*Marion Census* 1860, 145; Fotheringham 1859, 39; Ellsberry 1965b, 1:10; Wecter 1952, 183, 305 n. 15; *Inds,* 95, 344; "Married," Hannibal *Missouri Courier,* 18 Jan 1849, unknown page).

418.24   five foolish virgins] Matthew 25:1–13.

418.29–30   Twenty years ago Mr. Richmond had become possessed of Tom Sawyer's cave . . . made a tourist-resort of it] The limestone cave that Clemens called "McDougal's cave" in *Tom Sawyer* was during his childhood at first called Simms Cave for the brothers who discovered it, then Saltpetre Cave for the mineral found there (potassium nitrate, thought to be derived from bat guano), and finally McDowell's Cave (see "My Autobiography [Random Extracts from It]," note at 214.3–4; Sweets 1986b, 1–2). After the publication of *Tom Sawyer* in 1876, it began to be called Mark Twain Cave or Tom Sawyer's Cave. Joshua Richmond was evidently one of several owners in or after 1886, when the cave formally opened to the public. Evan T. Cameron, guide to the cave since 1886 and later manager, established a "permanent tour route through the cave's maze of passageways, built a small ticket building near the entrance, purchased lanterns that people could carry for lighting, hired cave guides, and advertised the attraction as Mark Twain Cave" (Weaver 2008, 15–16, 97). The current public entrance to the Mark Twain Cave "was blasted out of the hillside to make an easy, comfortable entrance" for the tourist, as the original "was a steep climb up the hill" (George Walley to John Lockwood, 21 Sept 2005, photocopy in CU-MARK).

418.42–419.4   they make the finest kind of Portland cement there now . . . being ground into cement] In August 1901 the Atlas Portland Cement Company began construction of the "largest Portland cement plant in the United States and the first cement plant west of the Mississippi," in Cave Hollow, where many of the entrances to the cave were situated (Sweets 1986a, 3). The telegram Mark Twain received has not been found.

419.9–11   Reuel Gridley attended that school of ours . . . Then came the Mexican war and he volunteered] Reuel Colt Gridley (1829–70), who must have been about seventeen or eighteen years old when he attended Dawson's school, enrolled in the Third Regiment Missouri Mounted Volunteers at the age of eighteen on 5 May 1847 in New London, Missouri, was mustered into service the following month, and was honorably discharged on 28 October 1848 (Missouri Digital Heritage 2009b, reel s912).

419.11–21   A company of infantry was raised . . . and Mr. Hickman . . . was made captain of it . . . Hickman is dead—it is the old story] Philander A. Hickman (b. 1824) was born in Virginia. Unlike Gridley, he did not join the Missouri Volunteers. He enrolled in the infantry as a first lieutenant on 5 March 1847, was mustered into the Fourteenth Regiment on 9 April, and became a captain on 22 October. He married Sarah M. Brittingham (1828–89) on 11 May 1848, and was honorably discharged from the infantry on 25 July (*Marion Census* 1850, 309; Heitman 1903, 1:528; Robarts 1887, 30). After the discovery of gold in California, Hickman and two of his in-laws emigrated, but he returned to Hannibal in the 1850s and established a store which sold stoves and hardware. In the 1870s, he became a representative in the state legislature. Clemens had last seen him in Hannibal in 1882: "Lieutenant Hickman, the spruce young han[d]somely-uniformed volunteer of 1846, called on me—a grisly elephantine patriarch of 65, now, his graces all vanished" (17 May 1882 to OLC, CU-MARK, in *MTL,* 1:429). He was dead within three years ("The Emigration," unidentified clipping in Meltzer 1960, 15; Fotheringham 1859, 30; Honeyman 1866, 26; Hallock 1877, 79, 178; Stone, Davidson, and McIntosh 1885, 115).

419.21–22   As Susy said, "What is it all for?"] See the Autobiographical Dictation of 2 February 1906.

419.23–420.3   Reuel Gridley went away to the wars . . . dead these many, many years—it is the old story] After he was discharged from the Volunteers in 1848, Gridley returned to Hannibal, where he worked as a carpenter and attempted but failed to learn piloting on the Mississippi River from steamboat captain Bart S. Bowen, who found him "so much given to larking, that he couldn't learn" ("River News," Cincinnati *Commercial,* 13 Feb 1865, 4). In September 1850 he married Susannah L. Snider (b. 1832?), and in 1852 left for California, where he operated an express mail service in Oroville; his wife joined him two years later. Before 1863, he moved to the Reese River area in Nevada and opened another store—Gridley, Hobart and Jacobs—in a mining camp that later became the town of Austin. Gridley, who described himself to Clemens as "Union to the backbone, but a Copperhead in sympathies," made a bet on the Democratic candidate for mayor and lost to Dr. H. S. Herrick, who backed the Republican candidate. Gridley had agreed to give Herrick a fifty-pound sack of flour, "and carry it to him on his shoulder, a mile and a quarter, with a brass band at his heels playing 'John

Brown.'" If Gridley had won, Herrick was to have carried the flour "to the tune of 'Dixie'" (17 May 1864 to JLC and PAM, *L1,* 282, 285–86 n. 11). After a year spent selling and reselling the flour sack around the country, in the summer of 1865 Gridley took the sack and his proceeds to the St. Louis Fair, which the Western Sanitary Commission held to raise funds for "the relief of sick and wounded Union soldiers" (*L1,* 284 n. 3). He found it was illegal in Missouri to repeatedly resell the same item, but "it was suggested that the flour be baked into cakes which could be sold. That Gridley refused to do for he felt that the flour came from the west and that was where it belonged. Thus the tour ended on a sour note and he headed home" (Elizabeth H. Smith 1965, 16). The total amount raised by Gridley is uncertain. In 1872, Clemens estimated $150,000; other estimates range from $40,000 to $275,000. When Gridley returned home in July 1865, he was almost bankrupt and his health was "completely broken down" (Tinkham 1921, 66). After he died on 24 November 1870 in Paradise City, California, Clemens eulogized him in a letter to the editor of the New York *Tribune* (11 Dec 1870, *L4,* 270–71; see *RI 1993,* 294–98, 660–64; *Marion Census* 1850, 310; "Missouri Marriage Records, 1805–2002" 2009; *Butte Census* 1860, 574; Elizabeth H. Smith 1965, 11–13).

420.4–11   first Jews I had ever seen . . . "Twice Levin—twenty-two."] The Levin family apparently lived in Hannibal for a short time during the 1840s. Something of the towns-people's attitude toward the boys is revealed in Clemens's 1897 notes for a planned novel, "New Huck Finn" (Notebook 41, TS pp. 59–60, CU-MARK; the boy who drowned was Clint Levering):

> *The Lev'n boys—the first Jew family ever seen there—an awful impression among us—it *realized* Jews, they had been creatures of vanished ages, myths, unrealities—the shudder visited every boy in the town—under breath the boys discussed them & were afraid of them. "Shall we crucify them?"
>
> It was believed that the drowning of Writer Levering was a judgment on him & his parents because his great-grandmother had given the 11 boys protection when they were being chased & stoned.
>
> All this feeling against Jews had been bred by the German youth who got so many verses by heart, *before* the 11ˢ appeared. The ground was all prepared, & yet the Jew was a surprise at last when he came—as explained* above. . . .
>
> Instead of 11, call them 9 (Nein) & 18.
>
> Tom stands by them & has fights.

420.12–13   Irving Ayres—but no matter, he is dead] Ayres (b. 1837?), another of Clemens's schoolmates, was the younger son of Thomas J. Ayres (b. 1816?), Hannibal postmaster and tavern keeper, who in 1836 established the Brady House, a downtown hotel in a double-log house with hogs beneath the floor, "crowded with boarders" and fleas that "hopped upstairs, downstairs, into the parlors, bed-rooms, beds, and indeed every nook and cranny" (Holcombe 1884, 202, 896). In his 1897 notebook, Clemens listed Irving and his elder brother Tubman (b. 1829?) as characters in notes for his planned "New Huck Finn" (Notebook 41, p. 61, CU-MARK).

420.13–16   George Butler . . . was a nephew of General Ben Butler . . . dead, long and long ago] Clemens's schoolmate George H. Butler (1839?–86) was the son of Andrew Jackson Butler (1815–64) and nephew of Andrew's brother, Major General Benjamin Franklin Butler (1818–93), the controversial Civil War general and Massachusetts congressman and governor who was known both for his brutality during the war and for his progressive politics afterwards. After working as an engineer in California, George joined the Union army Tenth Infantry in May 1861 and served as a first lieutenant during the battle of Ball's Bluff on 21 October 1861, in Loudoun County, Virginia. The catastrophic battle resulted in a Confederate victory when Union forces attempted to cross the Potomac to capture Leesburg, Virginia; caught in a Confederate counterattack, they were driven over a high bluff into the river and suffered heavy casualties. Butler served as regimental quartermaster from late 1862 until his resignation from the army in June 1863 (*Marion Census* 1850, 313; NNDB 2009; American Civil War 2009a; Missouri Digital Heritage 2009b, box 13; Heitman 1903, 1:269; *Sonoma Census* 1860, 649).

420.17   Will Bowen (dead long ago)] Bowen died on 19 May 1893 of sudden heart failure while on a business trip to Waco, Texas (Hornberger 1941, 8). See the Autobiographical Dictation of 9 March 1906, 402.16–33 and note.

420.17   Ed Stevens (dead long ago)] Clemens's classmate and friend Edmund C. Stevens (b. 1834?) by the age of sixteen had learned the trade of watchmaking from his father, Thomas B. Stevens (b. 1791?), the town jeweler. As a child he led a classroom "rebellion" against their stern teacher, Miss Newcomb, and was one of the gang who rolled a giant boulder down Holliday's Hill. He was a corporal to Clemens's second lieutenant in the Marion Rangers; Clemens described him in "The Private History of a Campaign That Failed": "trim-built, handsome, graceful, neat as a cat; bright, educated, but given over entirely to fun. There was nothing serious in life to him. As far as he was concerned, this military expedition of ours was simply a holiday" (SLC 1885b, 194). Clemens wrote Stevens's brother in 1901: "We were great friends, warm friends, he & I. He was of a killingly entertaining spirit; he had the light heart, the carefree ways, the bright word, the easy laugh, the unquenchable genius of fun, he was a friendly light in a frowning world—he should not have died out of it" (28 Aug 1901 to Stevens, CU-MARK). Clemens recalled him in "Villagers of 1840–3" and planned to use him as Jimmy Steel in "Tom Sawyer's Conspiracy" and as Ed Sanders, watchmaker, in "Schoolhouse Hill" (*Inds*, 96, 134–213, 214–59, 349; *HH&T*, 383; *MSM*, 432).

420.17–18   John Briggs . . . is still living] In 1902 Clemens said of John B. Briggs (1837–1907), with whom he had shared many childhood scrapes, "We were like brothers once," and in his notebook reminded himself to "draw a fine character of John Briggs. Good & true & brave, & robbed orchards tore down the stable stole the skiff " ("Friendship of Boyhood Pals Never Waned," Hannibal *Evening Courier-Post*, 6 Mar 1935, 5C; Notebook 45, TS p. 13, CU-MARK). Briggs joined the Cadets of Temperance with Clemens in 1850, and in 1860 served with Clemens in the Marion Rangers. "Briggs and I," Clemens said in 1902, "were the best retreaters in the company" (Love 1902, 5). Briggs later worked in a tobacco factory and became a farmer. He was almost certainly one of three boys upon whom Clemens based the "composite" character of Tom Sawyer, and perhaps of Ben Rogers as well, in *Tom Sawyer*. In 1902 notes for "New Huck Finn," Clemens contemplated using an incident from Briggs's childhood, in which Briggs's father sold a young slave boy down the river, evidently believing he had struck John, when in fact John had struck the boy, "something so shameful that he could never bring himself to confess" (SLC 1902b; SLC 1982, 270; *Inds,* 134–213, 307; *HH&T,* 383). See the notes at 417.19–23 and 417.24–27 above and the Autobiographical Dictation of 8 May 1908.

420.19–421.12   In 1845, when I was ten years old, there was an epidemic of measles . . . vain of it] The deadly epidemics of measles that occurred in the 1840s were called "black" or "virulent" measles. In the spring of 1844, when Clemens was nine years old, the measles broke out in Hannibal "with uncommon virulence. Nearly 40 citizens died. . . . There were seven deaths in one day, all from measles" (Holcombe 1884, 900). Paine wrote that "in later life Mr. Clemens did not recollect the precise period of this illness. With habitual indifference he assigned it to various years, as his mood or the exigencies of his theme required" (*MTB,* 1:29). In "The Turning Point of My Life," Clemens said that it was the cause of his mother's apprenticing him to a printer: "I can say with truth that the reason I am in the literary profession is because I had the measles when I was twelve years old" (SLC 1910, 118–19).

421.13   Dr. Cunningham] Unidentified.

Autobiographical Dictation, 20 March 1906

421.22–38   John D. Rockefeller, junior's, Bible Class . . . as are his son's] John D. Rockefeller, Sr. (1839–1937), president of Standard Oil, was generally recognized as the world's richest man, with a personal fortune estimated in 1901 as over $900 million. He served as superintendent of the Sunday school of Cleveland's Euclid Avenue Baptist Church from 1872 until 1905. His son, John D. Rockefeller, Jr. (1874–1960), graduated from Brown University and became his father's business associate, eventually taking charge of his philanthropic enterprises. He expounded the Scriptures at the Sunday school of the Fifth Avenue Baptist Church in New York. Clemens was acquainted with both Rockefellers through a mutual friend, Standard Oil executive Henry H. Rogers. Both men's Bible lessons were regularly reported in the press, provoking much objection and ridicule (Chicago *Daily Tribune:* "Church and Clergy," 29 Oct 1893, 12; "How J. D. Rockefeller, Jr., Teaches Bible Class," 10 Feb 1901, 36; New York *Times:* "Rockefeller to His Pupils," 12 Oct 1903, 1; "Story of Mr. Rockefeller," 15 June 1903, 1, and letters to the editor in the editions of 8 Feb 1906 [8], 9 Feb 1906 [8], and 13 Feb 1906 [6]; Case Western Reserve University 2008).

422.17   young John is using no new whitewash upon Joseph] See the note at 423.11–16.

422.22–25   exposition, three years ago . . . "Sell all thou hast . . . poor."] This verse occurs in slightly different versions in three of the Gospels: Matthew 19:21, Mark 10:21, and Luke 18:22. Rockefeller made it part of his 11 January 1903 Bible class talk, during which he argued that Jesus's teachings are not to be taken literally ("Rockefeller Would Keep His Wealth," Washington *Times,* 12 Jan 1903, 3).

422.38   Three years ago I went with young John to his Bible Class and talked to it] Clemens recalled his 28 January 1902 appearance "at the regular monthly meeting" of Rockefeller's Bible class. The New York *Times* reported:

> Mark Twain attempted to teach the class how to reach a person of great eminence, an Emperor, for instance. At 9:20 he stopped short and informed the young men that he would have to go.
> "I'm a farmer now," he said. "Not a very good farmer yet, but a farmer just the same. So I'll have to go now to be up early in the morning to take care of my crop. I don't know yet what the crop will be, but I think from present indications it will be icicles." ("Mr. Rockefeller's Class," 29 Jan 1902, 9)

Before his facetious abortive ending, Clemens read from his "Two Little Tales," comprising "The Man with a Message for the Director-General" and "How the Chimney-Sweep Got the Ear of the Emperor," published in the *Century Magazine* for November 1901 (SLC 1901; "Mark Twain at Bible Class," New York *Sun,* 29 Jan 1902, 2, cited in Schmidt 2008a).

422.41–423.4   Some days ago a Bible Class official sent me word . . . letter which could be read to those people? . . . following letter] Dr. Edward M. Foote (1866?–1945), chairman of the "Entertainment Committee" of the Fifth Avenue Baptist Church, wrote on 9 March, inviting Clemens to "speak a few words upon some topic" to the Bible class on March 22, or send a "written message" instead (CU-MARK). Isabel Lyon noted his reply on the bottom of the letter, "I daren't be with them. I'd like to mighty well." The letter to Foote inserted below was transcribed from a manuscript draft in the Mark Twain Papers; it is not known whether any letter was actually sent to Foote, or "privately to young John himself," as Clemens claims (425.19) ("Dr. Edward M. Foote, Retired Surgeon, 79," New York *Times,* 15 Feb 1945, 19).

423.11–16   Eight years ago I . . . explained Joseph . . . to say about him] In "Concerning the Jews," Clemens summarized chapter 47 of Genesis and explained Joseph as follows:

> We have all thoughtfully—or unthoughtfully—read the pathetic story of the years of plenty and the years of famine in Egypt, and how Joseph, with that opportunity, made a corner in broken hearts, and the crusts of the poor, and human liberty—a corner whereby he took a nation's money all away, to the last penny; took a nation's live-stock all away, to the last hoof; took a nation's land away, to the last acre; then took the nation itself, buying it for bread, man by man, woman by woman, child by child, till all were slaves; a corner which took everything, left nothing; a corner so stupendous that, by comparison with it, the most gigantic corners in subsequent history are but baby things, for it dealt in hundreds of millions of bushels, and its profits were reckonable by hundreds of millions of dollars, and it was a disaster so crushing that its effects have not wholly disappeared from Egypt to-day, more than three thousand years after the event.

The essay was actually published in *Harper's New Monthly Magazine* for September 1899 (SLC 1899b, 530). Mark Twain's "Collected Works" were issued in numerous editions published both by the American Publishing Company and by Harper and Brothers, beginning in 1899. "Concerning the Jews" was included in volume 22, *How to Tell a Story and Other Essays* (SLC 1900a, 250–75; *HHR,* 540; see *BAL,* 2:3458, and Johnson 1935, 150–53).

423.16–21   by the newspapers I lately saw . . . published estimate of Joseph differs from mine] Rockefeller discussed Joseph in his Bible class meetings on 4, 18, and 25 February 1906. He called Joseph a "grand young man" and "a splendid example of a young business man," and argued that in cornering the corn market Joseph had served the people by giving them "a market for their product," by making them tenants but not slaves, by letting them "have corn on their own terms," and by saving them from famine. "The people seemed to be pleased, for we have no record of censure. He did not lose their confidence, but was regarded with gratitude by them. According to the usages of his time, I believe he acted commendably" (New York *Times:* "Avoid All Temptation, Says Rockefeller, Jr.," 5 Feb 1906, 9; "Faith Is Essential, Says Rockefeller, Jr.," 19 Feb 1906, 4; "Young Mr. Rockefeller Again Praises Joseph," 26 Feb 1906, 9).

423.30–31   Sunday before last the very learned and able Dr. Silverman was thus reported in the *Times*] Joseph Silverman (1860–1930) was the chief rabbi of Temple Emanu-El, at Fifth Avenue and Forty-third Street in New York. To provide the text of Silverman's speech and the Bible passage following it, Clemens pasted clippings from the New York *Times* of 4 March 1906 into his manuscript letter ("Young Mr. Rockefeller and Joseph's Corn 'Corner,'" SM2).

424.8   This is the Bible's statement] Genesis 47:13–26.

425.29   I have treated this matter in one of my books] Clemens alludes to "On the Decay of the Art of Lying" (SLC 1880b), which he read at the Hartford Monday Evening Club on 5 April 1880 and published in *The Stolen White Elephant* two years later (SLC 1882a; Howell Cheney 1954, 35).

425.35–36   I can't go . . . the doctor has forbidden it] On 20 March, Clemens wrote Rockefeller (*per* Isabel Lyon):

> I am very sorry that, after all, I cannot meet the honorary membership Thursday Evening. I am not sick—I have merely *been* sick, & the doctor requires me to keep my room three or four days longer. In answer to my protest, he says, "Risks which a younger person might venture are forbidden the Methuselah of American literature." Do you suppose that that clumsy remark is meant as a compliment? If so, I shall find it where a doctor's compliments are always to be found—in the bill. There should be a law against this kind of graft. (NN-BGC)

Clemens also telephoned his regrets (see AD, 26 Mar 1906, 440.24).

426.5   My first appearance . . . was forty years ago, in San Francisco] See "Notes on 'Innocents Abroad,'" 226.41–227.1.

426.13–15   General Fred Grant . . . Robert Fulton Memorial Association . . . and I Vice-President] Frederick D. Grant (son of Ulysses S. Grant) and Clemens were among the incorporators of the Robert Fulton Memorial Association, organized in January 1906, which intended to erect a monument in New York to the designer of the first commercially viable steamboat. Grant had agreed to serve as temporary president. Clemens was a member of the "Executive and General Committee" and served as first vice-president as well. He also contributed at least a thousand dollars to the monument fund. Although the Fulton Memorial Association envisioned a grandiose monument consisting of a tomb, boat landing, and exhibition hall on Riverside Drive from 114th Street to 116th Street, it was never constructed. Clemens's appearance was initially planned for 10 April, but was postponed until 19 April (New York *Times:* "For a Monument to Fulton," 18 Jan 1906, 8, and 18 Feb 1906, 20; "Fulton Watergate Designs Selected," 10 Apr 1910, 6; "New York's $3,000,000 Robert Fulton Memorial," 22 May 1910, SM5; Miller to SLC, 28 Mar 1906, CU-MARK).

426.20–21   I wrote the correspondence at once . . . and I here insert it] The concocted correspondence with Grant and with Hugh Gordon Miller, secretary of the Fulton Memorial Association, was in fact used to generate publicity. The New York *Times,* for example, paraphrased and excerpted the letters liberally on 15 April 1906 ("Mark Twain Tells How to Manage Audiences," 9). On 19 April, at the benefit for the association, Clemens made a comical speech in which he credited Fulton with inventing the "electric telegraph" and the "dirigible balloon," and then digressed into a few of his standard set pieces. Striking a serious note, he then appealed for charitable assistance for the victims of San Francisco's devastating earthquake of 18 April ("Mark Twain Appeals for the 'Smitten City,'" New York *Times,* 20 Apr 1906, 11; for a text of the speech, see Fatout 1976, 515–18).

427.29–30   Paul Jones . . . Horace Porter] John Paul Jones (1747–92), the American naval hero, and Horace Porter (1837–1921), Union brigadier general, Congressional Medal of Honor winner, and former U.S. ambassador to France (1897–1905).

427.32   gems of the very first water] At this point in his manuscript, Clemens deleted the following paragraph: "I am getting a lot of information about Fulton out of the Barnard students—mainly the freshmen. They tell me everything they know. Do you like freshmen?—that kind, I mean. I do." Clemens had spoken at Barnard on 7 March (see AD, 8 Mar 1906).

Autobiographical Dictation, 21 March 1906

429.6   mental telegraphy] This was Clemens's term for thought transference or mind-to-mind communication, the possibility of which had fascinated him at least since 1875, when he attributed it to "mesmeric sympathies" (29 Mar and 4 Apr 1875 to Wright, *L6, 434*). He had explored the phenomenon in two *Harper's Monthly* articles: "Mental Telegraphy" in December 1891 and "Mental Telegraphy Again" in September 1895 (SLC 1891b; SLC 1895).

429.7–8   A few weeks ago when I was dictating something about Dr. John Brown] See the Autobiographical Dictations of 2 and 5 February 1906.

429.12–13   article about him and about Marjorie Fleming . . . and yesterday I began the article] "Marjorie Fleming, the Wonder Child," published in the December 1909 number of *Harper's Bazar* (SLC 1909d).

429.14   his son Jock] John ("Jock") Brown (b. 1846), whom Clemens had met in Scotland in 1873 (22 and 25 Sept 1873 to Brown, *L5,* 441 n. 4; John Brown 1907, 60).

429.22–25   7 GREENHILL PLACE ... Dear Mr Clemens] Hobby transcribed Brown's original typed letter, now in the Mark Twain Papers, into the typescript of this dictation.

429.27–29   Dr J. T. Brown ... made no use of the letters] John Taylor Brown (1811–1901), a Scottish newspaper editor, was Dr. John Brown's cousin and biographer. He wrote the entry on Brown for the *Dictionary of National Biography* and also *Dr. John Brown: A Biography and a Criticism,* published in 1903 (John Taylor Brown 1903).

429.35–36   I enclose letters from yourself and Mrs Clemens which I should like to use] Brown included six letters from Samuel and Olivia Clemens, written between 1874 and 1882, in *Letters of Dr. John Brown,* published in 1907 (John Brown 1907, 351, 353–54, 357–58, 360–61). Elizabeth T. McLaren wrote the biographical introductions as well as the notes for the volume. She also wrote *Dr. John Brown and His Sister Isabella,* published in 1889, two copies of which Jock Brown sent to the Clemenses (McLaren 1889; Brown to SLC, 28 Dec 1889 and 25 Jan 1890, CU-MARK; Gribben 1980, 1:444).

429.39   yours. ...] Clemens omitted the rest of Brown's letter, which mentioned his marriage to his cousin, "M. McKay," and their two children, aged twelve and fourteen, whose photographs he enclosed (Brown to SLC, 8 Mar 1906, CU-MARK).

430.4–6   During our ten years' absence ... we shall find them yet] In June 1891, partly as a result of Clemens's losses on the Paige typesetter, which made upkeep of the family house in Hartford difficult, and partly to allow Olivia Clemens to seek treatment for heart strain, the Clemenses left for what became a nine-year exile in Europe (*N&J3,* 574). The letters from John Brown were found. Seventeen of them, dated between 1873 and 1879, survive in the Mark Twain Papers.

430.9   Harmony, his wife] Twichell married Julia Harmony Cushman (1843–1910) in 1865 (18 Oct 1868 to OLL, *L2,* 269 n. 2).

430.12   Magician of the North] While anonymously publishing the string of popular novels that began with *Waverley* in 1814, Sir Walter Scott (1771–1832) was referred to as "the Wizard of the North" and "the Great Magician." It was not until 1827 that Scott admitted his authorship.

430.29–30   at Petersburg ... in the Civil War] On 30 July 1864, while Petersburg, Virginia (which protected the southern approaches to Richmond), was under siege by Ulysses S. Grant's forces, a large mine was exploded beneath the Confederate emplacements. Twichell, serving as a Union chaplain, was near Petersburg in June and July 1864, but finished his tour of duty about three weeks before the explosion (Twichell 2006, 306–9).

430.40–431.7   Joe's picture is different ... the file ... did not march away martially erect and stiff-legged] In a letter of 14 and 16 June 1863 to his stepmother, Jane Walkley Twichell, Twichell described one such execution, of a deserter to whom he had ministered:

> They seated him on his coffin, tied his elbows behind him, bound a handkerchief over his eyes and opened his shirt front so that his bosom was bared. ... At a signal six muskets were raised, cocked and aimed—the distance was about 10 paces. Another signal and the

dread suspense was broken. He swayed a little forwards, then with a single convulsive straitening of his body, fell back over the coffin. Then a Sergeant and one man stepped up and discharged their pieces through his head, although five bullets had already pierced his breast. This is a custom—dictated by humanity—in all military executions. They lifted the body into the coffin—a plain pine box. It was over. . . . The scene on the field now changed from one of utter stillness to one of noise and motion. Orders were shouted along the lines of troops, and the march was resumed as if nothing had happened. (CtY-BR, in Twichell 2006, 239, 241–42)

431.12–28   Daly's Theatre . . . vote in its favor was unanimous] Daly's letter was tran-scribed into this dictation from his original manuscript, now in the Mark Twain Papers. In 1888 Daly's Theatre, at Broadway and 30th Street, was one of New York's leading theaters, featuring a resident company of well-known actors in elaborate productions of Shakespeare, as well as popular plays of the day ("Amusements," New York *Times,* 1 Jan 1888, 3, 7). In *Talks in a Library with Laurence Hutton,* first published in 1905 and reprinted several times, Hutton gave this account of the naming of The Players:

> Booth had long desired to do something in a tangible and in an enduring way for the good of his profession; and various schemes were fully discussed during a fortnight's cruise on the steam-yacht *Oneida* in the summer of 1886. The party consisted of Mr. E. C. Benedict, the owner of the beautiful vessel, Mr. Thomas Bailey Aldrich, Lawrence Barrett, Mr. William Bispham, Booth, and myself. . . . The notion of a club for actors was then proposed. Mr. Aldrich with a peculiarly happy inspiration suggested its name, "The Players," and the general plan of the organisation was gradually outlined. (Hutton 1909, 86–87)

Another account of Aldrich's "happy inspiration" confirmed that it occurred aboard the *Oneida,* but put the date as 27 July 1887 (Lanier 1938, 18–19). Clemens replied to Daly's in-vitation to the 6 January 1888 organizational luncheon, "Schon güt! I'll be there"; it was probably on that occasion that he heard a reprise of the naming anecdote (3 Jan 1888 to Daly, TS in MH-H). For further discussion of The Players club see the Autobiographical Dictation of 10 January 1906 and notes.

431.31–34   Magonigle . . . he retired from his position superannuated] John Henry Ma-gonigle (1830–1919), Edwin Booth's longtime friend and business manager, was the brother-in-law of Booth's wife. He was the superintendent, but never the secretary, of The Players club, and also, from 1906 to 1919, a member. Letters from Magonigle to Clemens and to Franklin Whitmore dated 16 February 1891 and 6 May 1891, respectively, both attempting to collect unpaid dues, survive in the Mark Twain Papers. They were part of the dispute that Clemens describes in this dictation ("John Henry Magonigle Dies at 89," New York *Times,* 23 Dec 1919, 9; Winter 1893, 47 n. 1; Lanier 1938, 358, 376).

432.10–11   Robert Reid . . . put themselves in communication with me] Reid, for example, wrote to Clemens on 19 January 1903, a week after the expulsion: "Dont desert us on account of the dead-but-doesnt know-it-manager-& janiter of the office   We need you—be good forgive & forget!" (CU-MARK).

Autobiographical Dictation, 22 March 1906

433.2   Our tripp to Vassar] See the Autobiographical Dictation of 7 March 1906.

433.3–4   after Miss Emma Nigh died] See the Autobiographical Dictation of 15 February 1906, 362.21–28 and note.

433.19–21   his trouble prooved to be diptheeria . . . burried . . . at Elmira, New York] Langdon Clemens, born prematurely, was never robust and was slow to develop. He died in Hartford from diphtheria, on 2 June 1872, at the age of nineteen months. After funeral services in Hartford, he was buried in the Langdon family plot at Woodlawn Cemetery, in Elmira, near Olivia's father, Jervis Langdon. Clemens must have "confessed" more than once, for in 1911 his sister-in-law, Susan L. Crane, remarked that "Mr Clemens was often inclined to blame himself unjustly" (*L5:* Crane to Paine, 25 May 1911, photocopy in CU-MARK, in link note following 26 May 1872 to Bliss, 99–101; 13 Feb 1872 to Fairbanks, 44; 22 Apr 1872 to the Warners, 79; 15 May 1872 to OC and MEC, 86).

433.21–23   After that . . . with a great deal of good care she recovered] Olivia had wished to accompany Langdon's body to Elmira, but because of "her poor state of health," and because she could not leave infant Susy, she stayed behind in Hartford. Clemens remained there with her, entrusting the body to Susan and Theodore Crane (Lilly Warner to George Warner, 3 and 5 June 1872, CU-MARK, in link note following 26 May 1872 to Bliss, *L5,* 98).

433.27–35   Mr. Charles Kingsley . . . They are all dead except Sir Charles Dilke and Mr. Tom Hughes] Charles Kingsley (1819–75), minister, canon of Westminster, Cambridge history professor, novelist, poet, and essayist; Henry M. Stanley (1841–1904), journalist and explorer, whom Clemens first met in St. Louis in 1867; Sir Thomas Duffus Hardy (1804–78), deputy keeper of the Public Records, but not a descendant of Sir Thomas Masterman Hardy (1769–1839), who witnessed Lord Nelson's death at Trafalgar in October 1805; actor Sir Henry Irving (1838–1905); poet Robert Browning (1812–89); Sir Charles Wentworth Dilke (1843–1911), liberal member of Parliament and proprietor of the *Athenaeum,* a weekly journal of literary and artistic criticism; novelist and dramatist Charles Reade (1814–84); journalist and novelist William Black (1841–98); Richard Monckton Milnes (1809–85), first Baron Houghton, statesman, poet, and writer, and editor of Keats; Francis Trevelyan Buckland (1826–80), physician and prominent natural historian and pisciculturist; novelist Anthony Trollope (1815–82); Tom Hood (1835–74), poet, journalist, anthologist, and son of poet and humorist Thomas Hood (1799–1845); poet, novelist, and children's author George MacDonald (1824–1905), his wife, Louisa (1822–1902), and their eleven children; and journalist and historical novelist William Harrison Ainsworth (1805–82). Clemens was unaware that novelist, biographer, journalist, and member of Parliament Thomas Hughes (1822–96), best known for *Tom Brown's School Days* (1857), was also dead. When an excerpt from this dictation was published in the *North American Review* of 16 November 1906, his name had been removed from this sentence, presumably not by Clemens (NAR 6, 970). Presumably it was Olivia who furnished Susy with an account of the 1873 trip to Great Britain. For details of the Clemenses' contacts with most of these individuals, see Clemens's letters for 1872–73 (*L5,* passim).

433.36–38   We met . . . Lewis Carroll, author of the immortal "Alice" . . . "Uncle Remus."]
The meeting with Lewis Carroll (Charles L. Dodgson, 1832–98) came at the home of George
and Louisa MacDonald, the "Retreat" in Hammersmith, but on Saturday, 26 July 1879, not
in 1873. Carroll noted in his diary that day: "Met Mr. Clements (Mark Twain), with whom I
was pleased and interested." The MacDonald family gave a dramatic performance, as they had
also done when the Clemenses visited on 16 July 1873 (Dodgson 1993–2007, 194–95; 11 July
73 to Smith, *L5*, 414). Clemens had been familiar with the "Uncle Remus" stories by Joel
Chandler Harris since 1880 (see "My Autobiography [Random Extracts from It]," note at
217.25–27).

434.1   At a dinner at Smalley's we met Herbert Spencer] George Washburn Smalley
(1833–1916) was in charge of the New York *Tribune*'s European correspondence from 1867
to 1895 and was himself the paper's London correspondent. From 1895 to 1905 he was U.S.
correspondent of the London *Times*. Philosopher Herbert Spencer (1820–1903) and the
Clemenses were among the dinner guests at Smalley's home on 2 July 1873 (*L5*: 11 June 1873
to Miller, 377–78 n. 2; 1 and 2 July 1873 to Miller, 395–96 n. 1).

434.2–3   we met Sir Arthur Helps . . . is quite forgotten now] Sir Arthur Helps (1813–75)
was clerk of the privy council, a personal adviser to Queen Victoria, and a popular writer of
the day, producing numerous volumes of fiction, history, and biography.

434.3–4   Lord Elcho . . . was talking earnestly about Godalming] Francis Wemyss-
Charteris-Douglas (1818–1914), eighth earl of Wemyss, sixth earl of March, and Lord Elcho,
was a member of Parliament and a lord of the treasury. Godalming is an ancient town in Surrey, thirty miles southwest of London.

434.7   Lady Houghton] The former Annabella Hungerford Crewe (1814–74) married
Richard Monckton Milnes (Lord Houghton) in 1851.

434.12–13   I will insert here one or two of the letters . . . copied into yesterday's record]
All three of the letters Clemens inserted below were included by Jock Brown in his edition of
his father's letters (John Brown 1907, 354, 357–58, 360–61). The texts were transcribed into
this dictation from the typescripts Brown had sent from Scotland.

434.14   June 22, 1876] The letter sent to Brown in 1876 was written by both of the Clemenses; in this dictation Clemens inserted only the part that Olivia had written, which followed
his (for the full text see SLC and OLC to Brown, 22 June 1876, *Letters 1876–1880*).

434.20–21   farm . . . where my sister spends her summers] Quarry Farm, near Elmira.

434.23–24   Mr. J. T. Fields . . . we talked most affectionately of you] Author and retired
Boston publisher James T. Fields and his wife, Annie, had visited the Clemenses in Hartford
from 27 to 29 April 1876. Fields and Clemens were parties to the 1876 campaign to raise a
retirement fund for Dr. John Brown (see 17 Mar 1876 to Redpath, n. 2, *Letters 1876–1880*,
and the Introduction, p. 7). Annie Adams Fields (1834–1915), a poet, biographer, and social
reformer, was known for her hospitality. She entertained a wide circle of literary acquaintances
at her Boston home, recording personal anecdotes of famous authors in her diaries; some of
them were published in *Memories of a Hostess* (Howe 1922).

434.25   your sister] Isabella Cranston Brown (see AD, 5 Feb 1906, note at 328.30–33).

434.29   (1875)] This letter was undated, and when Hobby transcribed it into this dictation, she typed merely "(18   )." The date now assigned to it is 25–28 October 1875 (for the text as it was sent, and the letter from Brown that it answered, see OLC and SLC to Brown, 25–28 Oct 1875, *L6,* 570–72).

434.39–41   Mr. Clemens is hard at work on a new book now . . . some few are new] The "new book" may have been one of a number of unidentified works Clemens had in mind or in progress in the fall of 1875 (see 4 Nov 1875 to Howells, *L6,* 585 n. 9). The sketchbook was *Mark Twain's Sketches, New and Old* (1875c), which he had his publisher send to Brown on 6 December 1875 (11 Jan 1876 to Bliss, *Letters 1876–1880*).

435.3–5   nurse that we had with us . . . quiet lady-like German girl] Ellen (Nellie) Bermingham and Rosina Hay, respectively ("Contract for the Routledge *The Gilded Age,*" *L5,* 641 n. 4; SLC and OLC to Brown, 4 Sept 1874, *L6,* 226 n. 8).

435.20–21   I was three thousand miles from home . . . sorrowful news among the cable dispatches] Brown died on 11 May 1882, at which time Clemens was in New Orleans gathering material for *Life on the Mississippi.*

435.35   Our Susy is still "Megalopis." He gave her that name] In 1873 Brown gave the nickname to seventeen-month-old Susy because, Clemens later explained, her "large eyes seemed to him to warrant that sounding Greek epithet" (SLC 1876–85, 3).

435.36–37   one taken in group with ourselves] See the photograph following page 204.

436.6–8   courier in service until we got back to Liverpool . . . be done with him] Clemens seems to have confused the two couriers he employed during the family's 1878–79 European sojourn. George Burk, a German, worked for the Clemenses in Germany, Switzerland, and Italy from early August until 1 October 1878, when he was discharged for incompetence. Joseph Verey, a Pole, worked for them in France, Belgium, the Netherlands, and probably briefly in England from 8 July until around 20 July 1879, when they reached London, giving great satisfaction during that time. The Clemenses arrived in Liverpool on 21 August and sailed for the United States two days later (*N&J2,* 48, 52 n. 16, 121 n. 17, 197–98 n. 71, 210–11, 327 n. 67).

Autobiographical Dictation, 23 March 1906

436.25–30   Doctor was guessing at our address . . . Near Boston, U.S.A.] Brown sent two letters to Clemens in early 1874 that were returned to Scotland "Unclaimed." According to a complaint about the post office that Clemens wrote to the editor of the Boston *Advertiser* on 16 June 1874, one was addressed "Hartford, State of New York." In his complaint Clemens also mentioned another letter, addressed to him in "Hartford, Near Boston, New York," which did reach him "promptly" from England (16 June 1874 to the Editor of the Boston *Advertiser, L6,* 162–63).

437.3   Menzies, the publisher] John Menzies (1808–79) was an Edinburgh publisher, bookseller, and newsagent, whose company was one of Scotland's principal book, magazine, and newspaper distributors. The firm continues in business today and despite diversification still derives much of its revenue from newspaper and magazine distribution (Clan Menzies 2009; John Menzies plc 2009).

437.12   I think Postmaster-General Key was in office then] The postmaster general at the time John Brown's letters were mishandled was John A. J. Creswell (1828–91), a Republican congressman and senator from Maryland (1863–65, 1865–67, respectively), who served from March 1869 until July 1874. He is considered to have been exceptionally effective, responsible for sweeping reforms that reduced costs and increased speed and efficiency of delivery of both domestic and foreign mail. David McKendree Key (1824–1900), a lawyer, Confederate soldier, and Democratic senator from Tennessee (1875–77), was postmaster general from March 1877 to June 1880.

437.19–31   Key suddenly issued some boiler-iron rules . . . the letter must go to the Dead Letter Office] Clemens alludes to the United States Postal Laws and Regulations issued by Postmaster General Key on 1 July 1879, and to supplementary orders regarding misdirected letters issued by him in September and October of that year. Postmasters and postal employees could not on their own authority change a letter's "direction to a different person or different office or different state." Misdirected matter received at any post office for delivery had to be returned to the sender if his name and address were on it, and if not, the item had to be sent to the dead-letter office. Letter addresses were required to include both city and state, making "New York, N.Y." the acceptable form, with letters addressed merely to "New York City" consigned to the dead-letter office. These rules occasioned much complaint and criticism. Clemens added his voice to the protests in a letter of 22 November 1879 and two letters of 8 December 1879, all to the Hartford *Courant* (*Letters 1876–1880*; Bissell and Kirby 1879, 2, 117; New York *Times*: "Notes from the Capital," 10 Oct 1879, 2; "Orders to Postmasters," 12 Oct 1879, 2; "The Post Office . . . ," 15 Oct 1879, 4; "Imperfectly-Directed Letters," 31 Oct 1879, 3).

438.11–12   Mark Twain, God knows where] Clemens was in London, in 1896, when he received the letter thus addressed, which had been sent (according to Paine) by Brander Matthews and Francis Wilson of The Players club (*MTB*, 2:565–66). Clemens replied:

> I glanced at your envelope by accident, and got several chuckles for reward—and chuckles are worth much in this world. And there was a curious thing; that I should get a letter addressed "God-Knows-Where" showed that He did know where I was, although I was hiding from the world, and no one in America knows my address, and the stamped legend "Deficiency of address supplied by the New York P.O.," showed that He had given it away. In the same mail comes a letter from friends in New Zealand addressed, "Mrs. Clemens (care Mark Twain), United States of America," and again He gave us away—this time to the deficiency department of the San Francisco P.O. (24 Nov 1896 to The Players, New York *Tribune*, 31 Dec 1896, 6)

438.20–30 It comes from France … Washington postmark of yesterday] The envelope, but not the letter itself, survives in the Mark Twain Papers, and was once pinned to the typescript of this dictation (see the envelope with the redirected address, below).

438.31–32 In a diary which Mrs. Clemens kept … mentions of Mrs. Harriet Beecher Stowe] A diary that Olivia used sporadically between 21 October 1877 and 19 June 1902, with only twenty-five of its leaves bearing her writing, survives in the Mark Twain Papers. Just one entry mentions Harriet Beecher Stowe. Dated 7 June 1885, it describes how Stowe appeared that afternoon

> carrying in her hand a bunch of wild flowers that she had just gathered. She asked if I would like some flowers, of course I said that I should. She handed them to me thanking me most heartily for taking them. Said she could not help gathering them as she walked but that when she took them home the daughters would say "Ma what are you going to do with them, everything is full" meaning with those that she had already gathered. Mrs Stowe is so gentle and lovely. (OLC 1877–1902)

439.11 Reverend Charley Stowe's little boy] Charles Edward Stowe's son was author and editor Lyman Beecher Stowe (1880–1963) ("Charles E. Stowe" in "Hartford Residents" 1974; "Lyman Beecher Stowe Dead," New York *Times,* 26 Sept 1963, 35).

Autobiographical Dictation, 26 March 1906

439.27 ROCKEFELLER, JR., ON WEALTH] Clemens had a clipping of this article, from the New York *Times* of 26 March 1906, pasted into the typescript of his dictation.

440.22–23   I missed his . . . Bible Class last Thursday night] See the Autobiographical Dictation of 20 March 1906.

440.29   BABY ADVICE IN A CAR] Clemens had a clipping of this article, from the New York *Times* of 26 March 1906, pasted into the typescript of his dictation.

442.1–16   Day before yesterday . . . that reporter . . . did his work well] This "happy literary" effort has not been identified. The incident occurred on the morning of 23 March 1906, as confirmed by a detailed account—not the one that Clemens saw, however—that appeared on the same day in the New York *Evening Sun* ("A Girl's Despair," 6), and by brief reports on the following day in the New York *Herald* ("No Finery, Takes Poison," 5) and the New York *Tribune* ("City News in Brief," 10).

442.20   what the Vanderbilts are doing] The activities and pastimes of the descendants of financier and railroad promoter Cornelius Vanderbilt (1794–1877) and their families, were, as Clemens says, regular grist for the news and society columns.

442.21–22   John D. Rockefeller . . . testify about alleged Standard Oil iniquities] In March 1906 Rockefeller was in retreat at his country estate in Lakewood, New Jersey, to avoid a New York subpoena requiring his testimony in an ongoing investigation of Standard Oil. At one point, in response to inquiries about Rockefeller's whereabouts, his family physician responded, "Mr. Rockefeller is on Mars. That's a planet, you know, near Jupiter. He's up there playing golf. One might have heard the whacks quite plainly. One of the golf balls went clear over to Jupiter" (New York *Times:* numerous articles, 9–25 Mar 1906, especially "Rockefeller on Mars," 11 Mar 1906, 1).

442.23   Mr. Carnegie's movements and sayings] Clemens's friend Andrew Carnegie was much in the news at this time for his charitable works, and especially for his funding of a Simplified Spelling Board, whose membership included Clemens and was committed to controversial orthographic reform (New York *Times:* numerous articles, 12–26 Mar 1906; Clemens discusses Carnegie and simplified spelling in AD, 10 Dec 1907).

442.30–31   they got married and went under cover and got quiet] Alice Lee Roosevelt (1884–1980), the oldest of Theodore Roosevelt's six children, married Nicholas Longworth (1869–1931), Republican congressman from Ohio (1903–13, 1915–31), on 17 February 1906 in an elaborate White House wedding ("Alice Roosevelt Longworth Dies; She Reigned in Capital 80 Years," New York *Times,* 21 Feb 1980, 1). The official announcement of the wedding that Clemens received from the White House survives in the Mark Twain Papers. On the back of it Isabel Lyon wrote: "We ought to drop them a note & say we'd heard it." No such note has been discovered.

443.4   The Swangos] Clemens had a clipping of this article, from the New York *Times* of 26 March 1906, pasted into the typescript of his dictation.

443.22   CAPT. E. L. MARSH] Clemens had a clipping of this unidentified article pasted into the typescript of his dictation; the wording suggests that it was from an Elmira newspaper (not a Des Moines newspaper, as claimed at 444.1). It may have been sent either by Charles J. Langdon, Clemens's brother-in-law, or by another member of the Langdon family.

443.41 General Charles J. Langdon] Langdon's title derived from his 1880 service as commissary general on the New York gubernatorial staff (Towner 1892, 615).

444.4–7 in his Company of the Second Iowa Infantry was Dick Higham . . . in my brother's small printing-office in Keokuk] On 4 May 1861 Marsh enlisted as a corporal in Company D of the Second Regiment of the Iowa Volunteer Infantry, and Higham (1839–62) enlisted as a private in Company A. Marsh rose to the rank of captain before his resignation on 23 May 1864 (Guy E. Logan 2009; Youngquist 2001). In 1856 Higham had been an apprentice in the Ben Franklin Book and Job Office, which Orion Clemens owned while living in Keokuk, Iowa, from June 1855 until June 1857. Both Samuel Clemens and Henry Clemens worked for Orion as well (*L1:* link note following 5 Mar 1855 to the Muscatine *Tri-Weekly Journal,* 58–59; 10 June 1856 to JLC and PAM, 63, 65 n. 3; 5 Aug 1856 to HC, 67, 69 n. 13; 9 Mar 1858 to OC and MEC, 79 n. 11; 2 Apr 1862 to JLC, 184 n. 6).

444.14–24 Second Iowa . . . Dick fell with a bullet . . . furled in disgrace] The Second Regiment of the Iowa Volunteer Infantry gave important service both before and after the engagement at Fort Donelson, in Tennessee, its first great battle, where it distinguished itself as "the bravest of the brave" and was given "the honor of leading the column" that entered the conquered stronghold (Guy E. Logan 2009). The regiment had been disgraced by general order for having failed to prevent vandals from stealing taxidermic specimens from McDowell College in St. Louis, which was being used as a prison. Higham died at Fort Donelson, on 16 February 1862. After learning of his death, Clemens, in a letter from Carson City, recalled the prankish "musket drill" he put Higham through in the Ben Franklin Book and Job Office in Keokuk (2 Apr 1862 to JLC, *L1,* 181–82; Ingersoll 1866, 36–37).

445.4–13 my ancient silver-mining comrade, Calvin H. Higbie . . . Captain John Nye . . . too late to save our fortune from the jumpers] Higbie (1831?–1914) was Clemens's cabinmate for a time in 1862 in Aurora. He not only figures in chapters 37 through 42 of *Roughing It,* including the "blind lead" episode and the hunt for "the marvelous Whiteman cement mine," but was the "Honest Man . . . Genial Comrade, and . . . Steadfast Friend" to whom the book was dedicated (*RI 1993,* 637). John Nye, the brother of Nevada Territorial Governor James W. Nye, was a mining, timber, and railroad entrepreneur in Nevada in 1861–62, when Clemens first knew him, and then for many years was a San Francisco real estate agent. He appears in chapters 35 and 41 of *Roughing It,* in the latter of which Clemens reported nursing him through nine days of "spasmodic rheumatism" (*RI 1993,* 644).

445.20 Greenville, Plumas co. California] Higbie's letter and the letter from Miner that follows were transcribed into this dictation from Higbie's original manuscript and transcript, now in the Mark Twain Papers.

446.16–17 Geo. R. Miner, Sunday Editor] Miner (1862–1918) had been a reporter and editor for several newspapers before becoming the New York *Herald*'s Sunday editor, a post he held from 1902 until 1908.

446.18 I have written Higbie] Clemens dictated and sent the following letter (CU-MARK):

March 26. 1906
New York.

Dear Higbie:

I went down to Aurora about midsummer of '62. I suppose it must have been toward the end of October, '62 that I went to Walker River to nurse Capt. John Nye. I crossed the Sierras into California for the first time along about the middle of '64, I should say.

Send me your manuscript. I shall be as competent as anybody to sit in judgment upon its value and arrive at a verdict. Then I will ask the New York Herald to name a price & come to my house and talk with me, in case he finds that your narrative comes up to his expectations. If he should decide that he doesn't want it—but that is further along. If you have told your story with your pen in the simple unadorned & straightforward way in which you would tell it with your tongue, I think it cannot help but have value.

I was very glad to hear from you, old comrade, & shall be also glad to be of service to you in this matter if I can.

Sincerely Yours,
S L. Clemens.

Clemens nursed John Nye in late June 1862. He first left Nevada for California in May 1863, on a two-month visit to San Francisco, and then moved to San Francisco almost exactly a year later (see *L1:* 9 July 1862 to OC, 224, 226 n. 1; 11 and 12 Apr 1863 to JLC and PAM, 250 n. 7; 18? May 1863 to JLC and PAM through 20 June 1863 to OC and MEC, 252–59; and the link note following 28 May 1864 to Cutler, 302–3). Clemens continues the story of Higbie's literary ambition in the Autobiographical Dictation of 10 August 1906.

Autobiographical Dictation, 27 March 1906

447.4–5   silver-mining claim . . . in partnership with Bob Howland and Horatio Phillips] For Howland, see the Autobiographical Dictation of 19 January 1906, note at 295.20. Clemens probably first met Phillips in Carson City in August 1861. Shortly afterward they became partners in several claims in the Esmeralda mining district. Among them were the Horatio and Derby ledges, in which Howland was also a partner. Clemens and Phillips lived together in Aurora, in the Esmeralda district, in the spring of 1862 (*L1:* 29 Oct 1861 to Phillips, 140–43; 8 and 9 Feb 1862 to JLC and PAM, 156, 161 n. 2; 13 Apr 1862 to OC, 186; 11 and 12 May 1862 to OC, 207; 30 July 1862 to OC, 232–33 n. 2).

447.9   I secured a place in a near-by quartz mill] Clemens described his experience at the quartz mill in chapter 36 of *Roughing It*.

447.25   Pioneer] The Pioneer Mill, erected in June 1861, was the first in Aurora (13 Apr 1862 to OC, *L1,* 188 n. 8).

449.3–7   I parted from Higbie . . . told all about this in "Roughing It."] Clemens arrived in Virginia City, to take up his new post on the *Territorial Enterprise,* by late September 1862 (see AD, 9 Jan 1906, note at 251.32–38). He told about his experiences there in chapters 42–49, 51–52, and 54–55 of *Roughing It*.

450.13–19 This young man wrote me two or three times a year . . . any more] Clemens recalled William James Lampton (1851?–1917), a second cousin, who wrote on 20 May 1875 from St. Louis, where he was a bookkeeper for a dealer in pig iron, introducing himself and asking for Clemens's assistance in getting a position as a reporter. Clemens's reply survives only as a notation he made on the envelope of Lampton's letter: "Told him to serve an apprentice-ship *for nothing* & when worth wages he would get them." Contrary to the account in this dictation, however, Lampton did not take Clemens's advice, but in 1877 instead made his entry into journalism by using his father's money to start his own newspaper. In February 1882 he became city editor of the Louisville (Ky.) *Courier-Journal*. It seems unlikely that he wrote Clemens "two or three times a year." Only two additional letters from Lampton survive, dated 26 June 1876 and 18 February 1882, neither of them reporting encouragingly on Clemens's employment "scheme" and neither of them received with enthusiasm (see 22? May 1875 to Lampton, *L6*, 484–85). Just one letter from Clemens to Lampton is known to survive. Written in 1901, evidently in March, it is a sarcastic response to Lampton's patriotic poem, "Ready If Needed."

450.20–21 my nephew, Samuel E. Moffett . . . lost his inherited property] Moffett (1860–1908) had an inheritance left by his father, William (1816–65), a St. Louis commis-sion merchant, consisting of stocks and U.S. savings bonds totaling about eight thousand dollars and a one-third interest in some "unproductive land" in Missouri ("Estate of S.E. Moffett at the beginning of the administration of P.A. Moffett as Guardian in 1870," 23 Nov 1881, CU-MARK). His mother, Clemens's sister Pamela, managed it until November 1881, when he turned twenty-one and she transferred control to him, along with a detailed account-ing of earnings and expenditures over the years. By August 1882 Moffett had drawn on his inheritance to finance the purchase of a ranch in Kingsburg, California, near Fresno, where he tried raising wheat, fruit, and livestock. Within three years, however, he was attempting to sell the property. In January 1886, having failed to find a buyer, he was instead offering, without success, to rent it. How he finally disposed of this ranch is not presently known, but he evidently was unable to recoup his investment. He also owned a ranch in San Diego that he was prepar-ing to sell for $3,000 in April 1886 (Pamela A. Moffett–Samuel E. Moffett correspondence, 1881–86, especially 23 Nov 1881, 15 June 1885, 25 Apr 1886; Goodman to Moffett, 14 Jan 1886, 23 Jan 1886, 31 Jan 1886; all in CU-MARK).

450.22–23 A nervous malady had early unfitted him for attending school] Moffett's unidentified disorder and an eye condition that prevented reading troubled the Clemens and Moffett families in the early 1870s (*L4*: 17 Feb 1871 to JLC and family, 332–33; 11 June 1871 to JLC, 403; 21 June 1871 to OC and MEC, 411; MEC and SLC to JLC and PAM, 26 Nov 1872, *L5*, 230, 232 n. 6; 28 Aug 1874 to Belknap, *L6*, 212). Clemens also discusses the maladies, and Moffett's compensation for them, in his Autobiographical Dictation of 16 August 1908.

450.23 he had come up without a school education] Moffett eventually was able to acquire formal education. In 1881 and 1882 he was a student at the University of California in Berkeley before completing his undergraduate education at Columbia University. In 1901 he earned an

A.M. degree from Columbia, and in 1907 a Ph.D. ("Editor Moffett Dies, Struggling in Surf," New York *Times,* 2 Aug 1908, 1; "Samuel E. Moffett," *Collier's* 41 [15 Aug 1908]: 23; "Vita," Moffett 1907, 125–26).

450.31   built the whole game out of his memory] In his Autobiographical Dictation of 16 August 1908, Clemens dates this incident in 1870, when Moffett was ten years old. This history game anticipated the game Clemens conceived of in the spring of 1883 and first worked out in rudimentary fashion in July of that year. His assistants in subsequently researching historical facts and devising the game board were Orion Clemens and Charles L. Webster. Clemens patented the resultant game in August 1885, but it was 1891 before he tried to market it, as "Mark Twain's Memory-Builder." He was not successful (see *N&J3,* 19–20 n. 37).

450.33–35   he wrote me from San Francisco . . . I wrote back] None of this correspondence is known to survive.

450.41   he had married] Moffett married Mary Emily Mantz, of San Jose, California, on 13 April 1887 ("Genealogies of the Clemens and Langdon families," *L6,* 613; "Samuel E. Moffett" 1908).

451.15–16   Moffett remains with Collier] Moffett died of a stroke on 1 August 1908 while swimming in the ocean. In its tribute *Collier's* magazine gave this summary of Moffett's career:

> For a brief period during his early life Mr. Moffett was a farmer in California. Practically all his mature years, however, he was engaged in newspaper work. In 1885 he was chief editorial writer of the San Francisco "Evening Post." In 1891 he was sent to Washington and remained two years as correspondent of the San Francisco "Examiner." For the four years following he was the chief editorial writer on that paper. The late nineties he spent as an editorial writer on the New York "Journal." In 1902, while Mr. John Brisben Walker was the owner of the "Cosmopolitan Magazine," Mr. Moffett was his managing editor. The following two years he was a writer of editorials on the New York "World," where he was the especial reliance of Mr. Pulitzer. His work for COLLIER'S was begun with the issue of January 14, 1905. He announced it as "a weekly review of current history, under the title 'What the World is Doing.'" ("Samuel E. Moffett," *Collier's* 41 [15 Aug 1908]: 23)

Autobiographical Dictation, 28 March 1906

451.27–36   Orion Clemens was born in Jamestown . . . Benjamin, who died in 1843 aged ten or twelve] See the Appendix "Family Biographies" (p. 655) and "My Autobiography [Random Extracts from It]," note at 206.2–6.

452.17–18   Edward Bates, who was afterwards in Mr. Lincoln's first cabinet] Bates (1793–1869) was Lincoln's first attorney general, serving from March 1861 until November 1864. It was Bates who, soon after taking his cabinet office, secured Orion's appointment as Nevada territorial secretary (6 Feb 1861 to OC and MEC, *L1,* 114 n. 9; see *RI 1993,* 574, for Bates's letter of recommendation to William Seward, dated 12 Mar 1861).

453.22–23   Dr. Meredith] See the Autobiographical Dictation of 9 March 1906, note at 402.8–12.

454.32   the dishonest act of one Ira Stout] See "The Tennessee Land," note at 62.41–63.1.

454.33–38   My father had just been elected County Judge . . . to be sworn in, about the end of February] This account of John Clemens's career is not entirely accurate: see the Appendix "Family Biographies" (p. 654).

455.1–2   I became a bankrupt through . . . Charles L. Webster] The 1894 failure of Clemens's own publishing house, Charles L. Webster and Company, was a critical element in his bankruptcy. Clemens unfairly blamed Webster for the firm's collapse, although much of its decline came after his 1888 retirement as manager. See the note at 79.21–22 in "About General Grant's Memoirs," the Autobiographical Dictations of 2 June and 6 August 1906, and *N&J3,* passim.

455.10–11   In Florence, Italy, June 5, 1904] See "Villa di Quarto," Clemens's account of the family's sojourn in Florence.

455 *footnote*   *Inventor of a type-setting machine . . . Cornell University] See "The Machine Episode." Paige built two prototypes. His 1887 machine survives at the Mark Twain House and Museum in Hartford. His 1894 machine went to Cornell University, which eventually donated it for scrap metal during World War II (Rasmussen 2007, 2:828).

Autobiographical Dictation, 29 March 1906

455.22–23   Orion . . . was a journeyman printer and earning wages] Orion lived in St. Louis, working as a typesetter in the printing house of Thomas Watt Ustick, from about 1842 until mid-1850, when he returned to Hannibal (*Inds,* 311, 351). See the note at 459.22–23.

455.25   My sister Pamela helped . . . by taking piano pupils] Paine reported that Pamela Clemens, "who had acquired a considerable knowledge of the piano and guitar, went to the town of Paris, in Monroe County, about fifty miles away, and taught a class of music pupils, contributing whatever remained after paying for her board and clothing to the family fund" (*MTB,* 1:75–76).

455.27–28   placed in the office of the Hannibal *Courier* . . . Mr. Ament, the editor and proprietor of the paper] Clemens was apprenticed to Henry La Cossitt, editor and owner of the Hannibal *Gazette,* in 1847, and then, probably in May 1848, to Joseph P. Ament (1824–79), who had just moved his *Missouri Courier* from Palmyra to Hannibal. Clemens remained in school part-time until at least 1849, however (6 Feb 1861 to OC and MEC, *L1,* 113–14 n. 5; Gregory 1976, 1).

455.34–456.2   There were two other apprentices . . . Wales McCormick . . . was delightful company] McCormick had left Hannibal by 1850 and in 1885 was living in Quincy, Illinois, where Clemens visited him while on a lecture tour. Clemens was in touch with McCormick, and assisted him financially, at least as late as 1888. He was the inspiration for the handsome and charming printer Doangivadam in "No. 44, The Mysterious Stranger" (*MSM,* 221–405, 489–92; see *Inds,* 332–33). There were two apprentices in addition to McCormick: William T.

League (see the note at 459.40–41) and Dick Rutter, of nearby Palmyra, Missouri. In December 1907 Clemens recalled the names of all three of his colleagues (3? Dec 1907 to Powell, MoHM; see *Inds,* 331).

456.9   Ralph] Unidentified.

456.25–26   Emperor . . . tried to pretend that he was not shocked and outraged] This incident occurred in Vienna on 20 February 1892, at a banquet given by Clemens's third cousin Alice Clemens von Versen (1850–1912), whose husband, Maximilian (1833–93), was an officer on the Imperial German general staff. Despite Clemens's blunder, Wilhelm II (1859–1941), emperor of Germany and king of Prussia, was complimentary. In his Autobiographical Dictations of 6 December 1906 and 10 February 1907, Clemens reported that Wilhelm praised *A Tramp Abroad* and called "Old Times on the Mississippi" (that is, *Life on the Mississippi*) his "best and most valuable book" (Notebook 31, TS pp. 21, 31, CU-MARK; Selby 1973, 75, 146; Maximilian von Versen biographical information in CU-MARK).

456.35   Pet McMurry] In 1885 Clemens recalled T. P. (Pet) McMurry (d. 1886) as "a dandy, with plug hat tipped far forward & resting almost on his very nose; dark red, greasy hair, long & rolled under at the bottom, down on his neck; red goatee; a most mincing, self-conceited gait—the most astonishing gait that ever I saw—a gait possible nowhere on earth but in our South & in that old day" (23 Jan 1885 to OLC, CU-MARK, in *LLMT,* 232–33). McMurry later became a merchant; he was probably the model for the title character of "Jul'us Caesar," a sketch Clemens wrote in the mid-1850s but left unpublished (SLC 1855–56; *Inds,* 334–35).

456.36–37   Mrs. Ament was a bride . . . after waiting a good part of a lifetime for it] Ament's wife, Sarah, was only nineteen in 1850; Clemens was probably recalling his fifty-year-old mother, Judith D. Ament (Gregory 1976, 2).

457.10–11   new and wide-spread sect called Campbellites] The Disciples of Christ, also called Campbellites after their leaders, Thomas Campbell (1763–1854) and his son Alexander (1788–1866), originated in America early in the nineteenth century. The sect advocated individual interpretation of the Bible as the basis of faith. Clemens's father, John Marshall Clemens, was a Campbellite sympathizer, though never a church member. Clemens's sister Pamela was a member in her early teens (*Inds,* 288).

459.22–23   About 1849 or 1850 Orion . . . bought a weekly paper called the Hannibal *Journal*] Orion returned to Hannibal in mid-1850 and started a weekly paper, the *Western Union.* Within a year he purchased the Hannibal *Journal,* and on 4 September 1851 first published the consolidated Hannibal *Journal and Western Union,* which six months later became just the Hannibal *Journal* (*Inds,* 311).

459.40–41   Finally he handed it over to Mr. Johnson, and . . . acquired a small interest in a weekly newspaper there] In fact, on 22 September 1853 Orion sold the Hannibal *Journal* to William T. League, Samuel Clemens's former fellow apprentice on the Hannibal *Courier.* League already was proprietor of the Hannibal *Whig Messenger* at the time. Orion then moved with his brother Henry and their mother to Muscatine, Iowa, where he purchased an interest in the Muscatine *Journal.* He published his first issue in Muscatine on 30 September 1853 (*Inds,* 311, 331; *L1:* 3? Sept 1853 to PAM, 15 n. 5; 8 Oct 1853 to PAM, 18 n. 3).

460.8–9   Then he married the Keokuk girl and they began a struggle for life] Orion married Mary Eleanor (Mollie) Stotts (1834–1904) on 19 December 1854. For details of his varied and futile struggles to earn a living, some of which Clemens alludes to later in this dictation, see *Inds,* 311–13.

460.12–13   He bought a little bit of a job printing-plant] After selling the Muscatine *Journal* in June 1855, Orion bought the Ben Franklin Book and Job Office, in Keokuk, Iowa (link note following 5 March 1855 to the Muscatine *Tri-Weekly Journal, L1,* 58).

460.16–29   I disappeared one night and fled to St. Louis . . . didn't wake again for thirty-six hours] In June 1853 Clemens escaped Hannibal to work as a typesetter in St. Louis, New York, and Philadelphia, and to visit Washington, D.C. He returned to St. Louis briefly in the spring of 1854, then went to Muscatine, where he worked on Orion's *Journal* for several months, before taking work in St. Louis again by August 1854. (For the best account of this period, see the link note preceding 24 Aug 1853 to JLC through the link note preceding 16 Feb 1855 to the Editors of the Muscatine *Tri-Weekly Journal, L1,* 1–46.)

460.31   I worked in that little job office in Keokuk as much as two years] Except for a few brief interruptions, Clemens lived in Keokuk, working as Orion's assistant at the Ben Franklin Book and Job Office, from mid-June 1855 until October 1856 (see the link note following 5 Mar 1855 to the Muscatine *Tri-Weekly Journal* through the link note following 5 Aug 1856 to HC, *L1,* 58–69).

460.35   One day in the mid-winter of 1856 or 1857] Other than the present account, relatively little detail is available about Clemens's activities between his departure from Keokuk in October 1856 (not in "mid-winter") and the beginning of his steamboat piloting apprenticeship in April 1857. For a reconstruction of the period, see *L1* (link note following 5 Aug 1856 to HC, 69–71).

461.5–6   the printing-office of Wrightson and Company] Clemens worked at T. Wrightson and Company, one of Cincinnati's leading printers, from late October 1856 until 16 February 1857, when he left Cincinnati aboard the *Paul Jones* (Branch 1992, 2).

461.6–7   Herndon's account of his explorations of the Amazon] Volume one, by William Lewis Herndon, of *Exploration of the Valley of the Amazon, Made under Direction of the Navy Department* (Herndon and Gibbon 1853–54). In 1910 in "The Turning Point of My Life," Clemens recalled that Herndon told "an astonishing tale" about the "miraculous powers" of coca, instilling in him "a longing to ascend the Amazon" and "open up a trade in coca with all the world" (SLC 1910).

461.10   One of the pilots of that boat was Horace Bixby] Bixby (1826–1912) was a leading Mississippi River steamboat pilot and later captain.

461.16–17   He said he would do it for a hundred dollars cash in advance] In 1910, after Clemens's death, Bixby recalled telling Clemens "that I would instruct him till he became a competent pilot for $500." This fee was considered exorbitant and Clemens evidently ended up paying only $300 or $400, including his down payment of $100 (see *L1:* link note following 5 Aug 1856 to HC, 70–71; 25 Oct 1861 to PAM and JLC, 134–35 n. 5).

461.21–22   I became a competent pilot, and I served that office until . . . the Civil War]
Clemens received his pilot's license on 9 April 1859, after a nearly two-year apprenticeship. He
made his last trip as a pilot in early May 1861, about three weeks after the outbreak of the Civil
War. For details of his time on the Mississippi, see the link note following 5 Aug 1856 to HC
through the link note following 26 Apr 1861 to OC, *L1,* 70–121, and *Life on the Mississippi,*
chapters 6–21 (1883).

461.29   Blackstone] *Commentaries on the Laws of England,* by Sir William Blackstone
(1723–80), an exhaustive treatise on English law, was crucial to the teaching and study of law
in England and the United States (Blackstone 1765–69).

461.38–39   Orion and I cleared for that country . . . I paying the fares] The Clemens
brothers left St. Louis, on the first leg of their journey to Nevada Territory, on 18 July 1861.
The fare for the two of them was $400 (link note following 26 Apr 1861 to OC, *L1,* 121–22).
Clemens devoted the first twenty chapters of *Roughing It* to an account of the journey (see *RI
1993,* 574–612).

462.4   Noah Webster] Webster (1758–1843), an educator and editor as well as a lexicog-
rapher, published his landmark *American Dictionary of the English Language* in 1828.

Autobiographical Dictation, 30 March 1906

462.12   a neighbor brought the celebrated Russian revolutionist, Tchaykoffsky] Nikolai
Vasilievich Chaykovsky (1850–1926), founder and leader of the Socialist Revolutionary Party,
was in New York to appeal for weapons for the Russian revolutionary struggle ("Russian Here
for Firearms," New York *Times,* 21 Mar 1906, 4). The neighbor was Charlotte Teller (1876–
1953), a writer and socialist who lived nearby. Teller later explained that when Chaykovsky
arrived he was

> much depressed because he did not know how to reach Mark Twain, whom he wanted as
> chairman for a big mass meeting. Although I did not know Mark Twain myself, I offered
> to see what could be done. I went to 21 Fifth Ave. and asked for Mr. Clemens' secretary.
> She said to bring Tschaikowsky back at 2 o'clock in the afternoon. (Teller 1925, 5)

Clemens developed a friendship with Teller and treated her as a sort of protégée. Their relationship later became problematic, when rumors circulated that she was a fortune hunter who
sought to marry him (see Schmidt 2009a).

462.19   McKinleys] William McKinley (1843–1901) was the twenty-fifth president of
the United States, elected in 1896 and again in 1900, but was assassinated in September 1901,
whereupon he was succeeded by his vice-president, Theodore Roosevelt. The Spanish-American
War (1898), which left the United States in control of Cuba and the Philippines, was fought
during his term of office.

462.33–36   when our windy and flamboyant President . . . new Angel of Peace . . . peace
between Russia and Japan] The Russo-Japanese War, fought over control of Manchuria and

Korea, lasted from February 1904 until September 1905. On 30 March 1905, exactly a year before the present dictation, it was first reported that the combatant nations had chosen Theodore Roosevelt as mediator. Roosevelt's sustained efforts eventually resulted in the Treaty of Portsmouth (New Hampshire), signed on 5 September. His peacemaking received lavish praise, at home and abroad, including a tribute from Cardinal James Gibbons (1834–1921), the ranking Catholic prelate of the United States, who called him "an angel of peace to the world." As a result of the conflict, Russia, which had lost several major battles and had seen its entire fleet destroyed, was forced to recognize Korea's independence and to make major concessions in Manchuria, while Japan emerged as the strongest power in East Asia (New York *Times:* numerous articles, 31 Mar–7 Sept 1905, especially "Roosevelt May End War in Far East," 31 Mar 1905, 1, and "Roosevelt 'Angel of Peace,'" 18 June 1905, 2).

462.36–37   no one . . . except Dr. Seaman and myself uttered a public protest] Surgeon Louis L. Seaman (1851–1932), a highly decorated army major and expert on military sanitation who had spent six months in Manchuria during the Russo-Japanese War, proclaimed on 30 August 1905 that the peace mediated by Roosevelt would "prove detrimental to the Japanese and to the rest of the world," that "in fifteen years Russia will have recuperated sufficiently for another struggle," and that the war should have been allowed to continue "until the Russians had been driven away entirely from the Pacific Coast" ("Thinks Peace a Mistake," New York *Times,* 31 Aug 1905, 3). Clemens's own "public protest" came in a letter of 29 August 1905 to the editor of the Boston *Globe:*

> Russia was on the high road to emancipation from an insane and intolerable slavery. I was hoping there would be no peace until Russian liberty was safe. I think that this was a holy war in the best and noblest sense of that abused term, and that no war was ever charged with a higher mission; I think there can be no doubt that that mission is now defeated and Russia's chains re-riveted, this time to stay.
>
> I think the czar will now withdraw the small humanities that have been forced from him, and resume his medieval barbarisms with a relieved spirit and an immeasurable joy. I think Russian liberty has had its last chance, and has lost it.
>
> I think nothing has been gained by the peace that is remotely comparable to what has been sacrificed by it. One more battle would have abolished the waiting chains of billions upon billions of unborn Russians, and I wish it could have been fought.
>
> I hope I am mistaken, yet in all sincerity I believe that this peace is entitled to rank as the most conspicuous disaster in political history. (SLC 1905d)

463.2   Roosevelt had given the Russian revolution its death-blow] Clemens's conviction that Roosevelt's peacemaking had enabled the Tsarist government to concentrate on suppressing domestic political reform was widely shared. Government violence against the populace in fact had been extreme in 1905 following the peace (see AD, 10 Jan 1906, note at 257.18–21), and again during the first three months of 1906 (New York *Times:* "Russians Are Skeptical," 13 June 1905, 2; "Gorky Not Coming Here," 6 July 1905, 2; "John Bigelow Condemns Peace of Portsmouth," 3 Dec 1905, SM4; "Roosevelt and Russia," 13 Feb 1906, 6, and numerous articles, 1 Jan–30 Mar 1906).

463.4   I came across Dr. Seaman last night] Probably at the meeting of the New York State Association for Promoting the Interests of the Blind (see the note at 464.17–19).

463.9–10   only two or three months ago . . . You raised two millions of dollars in a breath] In early December 1905 it was reported that in only eighteen days, American Jews had raised $1 million for the relief of Jews being massacred in Russia, with contributions from Germany and Great Britain bringing the total to $2.475 million. Clemens assisted in the fundraising by speaking at an 18 December benefit matinee at the Casino Theatre at which several prominent actors, including Sarah Bernhardt, performed:

> Mark Twain, who followed Mme. Bernhardt, spoke of the wonderful French language, which he always felt as if he were "just going to understand."
> "Mme. Bernhardt is so marvelously young," he added. "She and I are two of the youngest people alive."
> Then the humorist told a story of how when Mme. Bernhardt was playing in Hartford some years ago three charitable old ladies decided to deny themselves the pleasure of seeing the great actress and to send the money instead to some needy friends.
> "And the needy friends," concluded Mr. Clemens drily, "gratefully took the money and bought Bernhardt tickets with it." ("Mark Twain Speaks After Bernhardt Acts," New York *Times,* 19 Dec 1905, 9)

By late December, the total raised in America and Europe, from Jews and Gentiles, exceeded $3 million (New York *Times:* "Fund Exceeds $1,000,000, Still More to Come," 3 Dec 1905, 8; "Asks $1,000,000 More for Jewish Relief," 5 Dec 1905, 6; "$935,000 Already Sent to Aid Russian Jews," 7 Dec 1905, 6; "Amusements," 18 Dec 1905, 14; "Relief Fund over $3,000,000," 29 Dec 1905, 2).

463.23   ARMS TO FREE RUSSIA, TCHAYKOFFSKY'S APPEAL] Clemens had a clipping of this article, from the New York *Times* of 30 March 1906, pasted into the typescript of his dictation.

464.17–19   Chairman at the first meeting of the Association . . . in the interest of the adult blind. Joseph H. Choate and I had a very good time there] Clemens presided at the meeting of the New York State Association for Promoting the Interest of the Blind, held in the ballroom of the Waldorf-Astoria Hotel on 29 March 1906. As an instance of a time when he was himself momentarily blind, Clemens told about his hunt for a lost sock in a darkened German inn, which he had originally described in 1880 in chapter 13 of *A Tramp Abroad* (for a text of the speech, see Fatout 1976, 506–11). Choate, a leader in humanitarian causes, made a humorous appeal for contributions to the association ("Twain and Choate Talk at Meeting for Blind," New York *Times,* 30 Mar 1906, 9; for Choate see AD, 23 Jan 1906, note at 303.2–10).

464.34–35   Blackwell's Island] An island in the East River, named for Robert Blackwell (d. 1717?), its onetime owner, which housed a penitentiary for men and women, a workhouse for the drunken and disorderly, an almshouse and hospitals for some of New York City's poor, and America's first municipal insane asylum. Its name was changed to Welfare Island in 1921, then to Roosevelt Island, in honor of Franklin D. Roosevelt, in 1973. Soon after that it became largely residential (Moses King 1893, 496–500; NYC10044 2009; Roosevelt Island Historical Society 2009).

465.6–7 She was to be at Laurence Hutton's house . . . Henry Rogers and I went together] In 1929 Keller devoted a chapter of *Midstream: My Later Life* to her long friendship with Mark Twain, recalling its beginning at Hutton's home on a Sunday in 1894, when she was fourteen and Clemens "was vigorous, before the shadows began to gather":

> During the afternoon several celebrities dropped in, and among them Mr. Clemens. The instant I clasped his hand in mine, I knew that he was my friend. He made me laugh and feel thoroughly happy by telling some good stories, which I read from his lips. I have forgotten a great deal more than I remember, but I shall never forget how tender he was.

Keller also wrote fondly of Henry H. Rogers, whom she first met that same day and afterward saw frequently, and who financed her college education (Keller 1929, 47–48, 71, 288–89).

465.9 Miss Sullivan] Annie Sullivan (1866–1936), herself only partially sighted, had become Keller's teacher in 1887. Her groundbreaking technique for educating Keller was based on a system of touch teaching. The two remained lifelong companions, even after Sullivan's 1905 marriage to writer and literary critic John Macy, and together worked for increased opportunities for the blind.

466.7 Miss Holt] Winifred T. Holt (1870–1945), a sculptor, was the principal founder of the New York State Association for Promoting the Interests of the Blind. In early 1906 she was the organization's treasurer pro tem and secretary, retaining the latter post until at least 1920. She later wrote numerous books and papers on blindness and worked extensively for the education and rehabilitation of the blind both in the United States and abroad (Holt to SLC, 24 Jan 1906, CU-MARK).

466.26 Wrentham, Mass., March 27, 1906] Keller's letter was transcribed into this dictation from her original typed and signed letter, now in the Mark Twain Papers. She later published it in *Out of the Dark* (Keller 1913, 208–12).

APPENDIXES

SAMUEL L. CLEMENS: A BRIEF CHRONOLOGY

1835   Born 30 November in Florida, Mo., the sixth child of John Marshall and Jane Lampton Clemens. Of his six siblings, only Orion, Pamela, and Henry lived into adulthood. (For details, see the next appendix, "Family Biographies.")

1839–40   Moves to Hannibal, Mo., on the west bank of the Mississippi River; enters typical western common school in Hannibal (1840).

1842–47   Spends summers at his uncle John Quarles's farm, near Florida, Mo.

1847   On 24 March his father dies. Leaves school to work as an errand boy and apprentice typesetter for Henry La Cossitt's Hannibal *Gazette.*

1848   Apprenticed to Joseph P. Ament, the new editor and owner of the Hannibal *Missouri Courier.* Works for and lives with Ament until the end of 1850.

1851   In January joins Orion's newspaper, the Hannibal *Western Union,* where he soon prints "A Gallant Fireman," his earliest known published work.

1853–57   After almost three years as Orion's apprentice, leaves Hannibal in June 1853. Works as a journeyman typesetter in St. Louis, New York, Philadelphia, Muscatine (Iowa), Keokuk (Iowa), and Cincinnati.

1857   On 16 February departs Cincinnati on the *Paul Jones,* piloted by Horace E. Bixby, who agrees to train him as a Mississippi River pilot.

1858   Henry Clemens dies of injuries from the explosion of the *Pennsylvania.*

1859   On 9 April officially licensed to pilot steamboats "to and from St. Louis and New Orleans." By 1861 has served as "a good average" pilot on at least a dozen boats.

1861   Becomes a Freemason (resigns from his lodge in 1869). Works as a commercial pilot until the outbreak of the Civil War. Joins the Hannibal Home Guard, a small band of volunteers with Confederate sympathies. Resigns after two weeks and accompanies Orion to Nevada Territory, where Orion will serve until 1864 as the territorial secretary. Works briefly for Orion, then prospects for silver.

1862   Prospects in the Humboldt and Esmeralda mining districts. Sends contributions signed "Josh" (now lost) to the Virginia City *Territorial Enterprise,* and in October becomes its local reporter.

1863–64   On 3 February 1863 first signs himself "Mark Twain." While writing for the *Enterprise* he becomes Nevada correspondent for the San Francisco *Morning*

Call. To escape prosecution for dueling, moves to San Francisco about 1 June 1864 and for four months works as local reporter for the *Call.* Writes for the *Californian* and the *Golden Era.* In early December visits Jackass Hill in Tuolumne County, Calif.

1865   Visits Angels Camp in Calaveras County, Calif. Returns to San Francisco and begins writing a daily letter for the *Enterprise.* Continues to write for the *Californian.* "Jim Smiley and His Jumping Frog" published in the New York *Saturday Press* on 18 November.

1866   Travels to the Sandwich Islands (Hawaii) as correspondent for the Sacramento *Union*, to which he writes twenty-five letters. In October gives his first lecture in San Francisco.

1867   His first book, *The Celebrated Jumping Frog of Calaveras County, and Other Sketches,* published in May. Gives first lecture in New York City. Sails on *Quaker City* to Europe and the Holy Land. Meets Olivia (Livy) Langdon in New York on 27 December. In Washington, D.C., serves briefly as private secretary to Senator William M. Stewart of Nevada.

1868   Lectures widely in eastern and midwestern states. Courts and proposes to Livy, winning her consent in November.

1869   *The Innocents Abroad* published. With Jervis Langdon's help, buys one-third interest in the Buffalo *Express.*

1870   Marries Olivia on 2 February; they settle in Buffalo in a house purchased for them by Jervis Langdon. Son, Langdon, born prematurely on 7 November.

1871   Sells *Express* and the house and moves to Hartford, Conn. For the next two decades the family will live in Hartford and spend summers at Quarry Farm, in Elmira.

1872   Daughter Olivia Susan (Susy) Clemens born 19 March; son Langdon dies 2 June. *Roughing It* published in London (securing British copyright) and Hartford. Visits London to lecture in the fall.

1873   Takes family to England and Scotland for five months. Escorts them home (Livy is pregnant) and returns to England alone in November. *The Gilded Age,* written with Charles Dudley Warner, published in London and Hartford.

1874   Returns home in January; daughter Clara Langdon Clemens born 8 June. The family moves into the house they have built in Hartford.

1875–76   *Mark Twain's Sketches, New and Old* (1875) and *The Adventures of Tom Sawyer* (1876) published.

1878–79   Travels with family in Europe.

1880   *A Tramp Abroad* published. Daughter Jane (Jean) Lampton Clemens born 26 July.

1881   Begins to invest in Paige typesetting machine. *The Prince and the Pauper* published.

1882   Revisits the Mississippi to gather material for *Life on the Mississippi,* published 1883.

1884–85   Founds publishing house, Charles L. Webster and Co., named for his nephew by marriage, its chief officer. Reading tour with George Washington Cable (November–February). *Adventures of Huckleberry Finn* published in London (1884) and New York (1885). Publishes Ulysses S. Grant's *Memoirs* (1885).

1889   *A Connecticut Yankee in King Arthur's Court* published.

1891–94   Travels and lives in France, Switzerland, Germany, and Italy, with frequent business trips to the United States. Henry H. Rogers, vice-president of Standard Oil, undertakes to salvage Clemens's fortunes. In 1894 Webster and Co. declares bankruptcy, and on Rogers's advice Clemens abandons the Paige machine. *The Tragedy of Pudd'nhead Wilson* published serially and as a book in 1894.

1895   In August starts an around-the-world lecture tour to raise money, accompanied by Olivia and Clara; lectures en route to the Pacific Coast and then in Australia and New Zealand.

1896   Lectures in India, Ceylon, and South Africa. *Personal Recollections of Joan of Arc* published. On 18 August Susy dies from meningitis in Hartford. Jean is diagnosed with epilepsy. Resides in London.

1897   *Following the Equator* published in London and Hartford. Lives in Weggis (Switzerland) and Vienna.

1898   Pays his creditors in full. Lives in Vienna and nearby Kaltenleutgeben.

1899–   Resides in London, with stays at European spas. The family returns to the
1901   United States in October 1900, living at 14 West 10th Street, New York, then in Riverdale in the Bronx. Publishes "To the Person Sitting in Darkness" (February 1901).

1902   Makes last visit to Hannibal and St. Louis. Olivia's health deteriorates severely. Isabel V. Lyon, hired as her secretary, is soon secretary to Clemens.

1903   Moves family to rented Villa di Quarto in Florence. Harper and Brothers acquires exclusive rights to all Mark Twain's work.

1904   Begins dictating autobiography to Lyon; Jean types up her copy. Olivia dies of heart failure in Florence on 5 June. Family returns to the United States. Clemens leases a house at 21 Fifth Avenue, New York.

1905   Spends summer in Dublin, New Hampshire, with Jean. Writes "The War-Prayer."

1906   Begins Autobiographical Dictations in January. Selections from them will appear in the *North American Review,* 1906–7. Commissions John Mead Howells to design a house to be built at Redding, Conn. *What Is Man?* printed anonymously for private distribution.

1907   *Christian Science* published. Hires Ralph W. Ashcroft as business assistant. Travels to England to receive honorary degree from Oxford University.

1908   Moves into the Redding house ("Innocence at Home," then "Stormfield").

1909   Dismisses Lyon and Ashcroft. Jean rejoins Clemens at Stormfield. Clara marries

Ossip Gabrilowitsch, pianist and conductor, on 6 October. Jean dies of heart failure on 24 December.

1910   Suffers severe angina while in Bermuda; with Paine leaves for New York on 12 April. Dies at Stormfield on 21 April.

For a much more detailed chronology, see *Mark Twain: Collected Tales, Sketches, Speeches, and Essays, 1852–1890* (Budd 1992a, 949–97).

FAMILY BIOGRAPHIES

Biographies are provided here only for Clemens's immediate family—his parents, siblings, wife, and children. Information about other relatives, including Olivia Clemens's family, may be located through the Index.

John Marshall Clemens (1798–1847), Clemens's father, was born in Virginia. As a youth he moved with his mother and siblings to Kentucky, where he studied law and in 1822 was licensed to practice. He married Jane Lampton the following year. In 1827 the Clemenses relocated to Jamestown, Tennessee, where he opened a store and eventually became a clerk of the county court. In 1835 he moved his family to Missouri, settling first in the village of Florida, where Samuel Clemens was born. Two years later he was appointed judge of Monroe County Court, earning the honorific "Judge," which young Clemens unwittingly exaggerated into a position of great power. In 1839 he moved the family to Hannibal, where he kept a store on Main Street and was elected justice of the peace, probably in 1844. At the time of his death, he was a candidate for the position of clerk of the circuit court, but died some months before the election. He was regarded as one of the foremost citizens of the county, scrupulously honest, but within his family circle he was taciturn and irritable. A contemporary reference to John Clemens's "shattered nerves," together with his extensive use of medicines, may point to some chronic condition. His sudden death from pneumonia in 1847 left the family in genteel poverty. When his father died Clemens was only eleven; he later wrote that "my own knowledge of him amounted to little more than an introduction" (*Inds,* 309–11; 4 Sept 1883 to Holcombe, MnHi).

Jane Lampton Clemens (1803–90), Clemens's mother, was born in Adair County, Kentucky. Her marriage to the dour and humorless John Marshall Clemens was not a love match: late in life she confided to her family that she had married to spite another suitor. She bore seven children, of whom only four (Orion, Pamela, Samuel, and Henry [1838–58]) survived at the time of her husband's death in 1847. The widowed Jane left Hannibal, Missouri, and between 1853 and 1870 lived in Muscatine, and possibly Keokuk, Iowa, and in St. Louis, Missouri, initially as part of Orion Clemens's household and then with her daughter, Pamela Moffett. After Clemens married and settled in Buffalo, New York, in 1870, Jane set up house in nearby Fredonia with the widowed Pamela. In 1882 she moved to Keokuk, Iowa, where she lived with Orion for the rest of her life. She was buried in Hannibal's Mount Olivet Cemetery, alongside her husband and her son Henry. Her Hannibal pastor called her "a woman of the sunniest temperament, lively, affable, a general favorite" (Wecter 1952, 86). She was the model for Aunt Polly in *Tom Sawyer* (SLC 1876),

Huckleberry Finn (SLC 1885), and other works. After her death in 1890 Clemens wrote a moving tribute to her, "Jane Lampton Clemens" (*Inds*, 82–92, 311).

Orion (pronounced O'-ree-ən) Clemens (1825–97), Clemens's older brother, was born in Gainesboro, Tennessee. After the Clemens family's move to Hannibal, Missouri, he was apprenticed to a printer. In 1850 he started the Hannibal *Western Union,* and the following year became the owner of the Hannibal *Journal* as well, employing Clemens and Henry, their younger brother, as typesetters. In 1853, shortly after Clemens left home to travel, Orion moved with his mother and Henry to Muscatine, Iowa. There he married Mary (Mollie) Stotts (1834–1904), who bore him a daughter, Jennie, in 1855. He campaigned for Lincoln in the presidential election of 1860, and through the influence of a friend was rewarded with an appointment as secretary of the newly formed Nevada Territory (1861). Mollie and Jennie joined him there in 1862; Jennie died in 1864 of spotted fever. That year Nevada became a state, and Orion could not obtain a post comparable to his territorial position. Over the next two decades he struggled to earn a living as a proofreader, inventor, chicken farmer, lawyer, lecturer, and author. From the mid-1870s until his death in 1897, Orion was supported by an amused and exasperated Clemens, who said that "he was always honest and honorable" but "he was always dreaming; he was a dreamer from birth" (*Inds*, 311–13; see AD, 28 Mar 1906 and notes).

Pamela (pronounced Pə-mee'-la) A. (Clemens) Moffett (1827–1904), also known as "Pamelia" or "Mela," was Clemens's older sister. Born in Jamestown, Tennessee, after the Clemens family's move to Hannibal she attended Elizabeth Horr's school and in November 1840 was commended by her teacher for her "amiable deportment and faithful application to her various studies." Pamela played piano and guitar, and in the 1840s helped support the family by giving music lessons. In September 1851, she married William Anderson Moffett (1816–65), a commission merchant, and moved to St. Louis. Their children were Annie (1852–1950) and Samuel (1860–1908). From 1870 Pamela lived in Fredonia, New York. Clemens called Pamela "a lifelong invalid"; she was probably the model for Tom's cousin Mary in *Tom Sawyer, Huckleberry Finn,* and other works (*Inds*, 313).

Olivia Louise Langdon Clemens (1845–1904), familiarly known as "Livy," was born and raised in Elmira, New York, the daughter of wealthy coal merchant Jervis Langdon (1809–70) and Olivia Lewis Langdon (1810–90). The Langdons were strongly religious, reformist, and abolitionist. Livy's education, in the 1850s and 1860s, was a combination of home tutoring and classes at Thurston's Female Seminary and Elmira Female College. Always delicate, her health deteriorated into invalidism for a time between 1860 and 1864. "She was never strong again while her life lasted," Clemens said in 1906. Clemens was first introduced to the shy and serious Livy in December 1867; he soon began an earnest and protracted courtship, conducted largely through letters. They married in February 1870 and settled in Buffalo, New York, in a house purchased for them by Livy's father; their first child, Langdon Clemens, was born there in November. In 1871 they moved, as renters, to the Nook Farm neighborhood of Hartford, Connecticut, and quickly became an integral part of the social life of that literary and intellectual enclave. They purchased land and built the distinctive house which was their home from 1874 to 1891. Young Langdon died in 1872, but three daughters were born: Olivia Susan (Susy) in 1872, Clara in 1874, and Jane (Jean) in 1880. Clara later recalled her mother's "unselfish, tender nature—combined with a complete understanding, both intellectual and human, of her husband"; she took "care of everything pertaining to house and home, which included hospitality to many guests," and made "time for lessons in French and German as well as hours for reading aloud to my sisters and me" (CC 1931, 24–25). To her adoring husband, whom she addressed fondly as "Youth," Livy was "my faithful, judicious, and painstaking editor" (AD, 14 Feb 1906; see also AD, 13 Feb 1906). In June 1891, with their expenses mounting and Clemens's investments draining his earnings as well as Livy's personal income, they permanently closed the Hartford house and left for a period of retrenchment in Europe; thenceforth Livy's life was spent in temporary quarters, hotel suites, and rented houses. When Clemens was forced to declare bankruptcy in April 1894, the family's financial future was salvaged by the expedient of giving Livy "preferred creditor" status and assigning all Clemens's copyrights to her. In 1895–96 she and Clara accompanied Clemens on his round-the-world lecture tour. The death of her daughter Susy in 1896 was a blow from which she never recovered. She died of heart failure in Italy in June 1904.

Olivia Susan Clemens (1872–96), known as "Susy," was Clemens's eldest daughter. Her early education was conducted largely at home by her mother and, for several years starting in 1880, by a governess. Her talents for writing, dramatics, and music were soon apparent. At thirteen, she secretly began to write a biography of Clemens, much of which he later incorporated into his autobiography; it is a charming portrait of idyllic family life. Susy accompanied her parents to England in 1873 and for a longer stay abroad in 1878–79. In the fall of 1890 she left home to attend Bryn Mawr College in Pennsylvania, but completed only one semester. In June 1891, the Clemenses closed the Hartford house, and the family, including Susy, left for a period of retrenchment in Europe that would last until mid-1895. Susy attended schools in Geneva and Berlin and took language and voice lessons, but increasingly she suffered from physical and nervous complaints for which her parents sought treatments including "mind cure" and hydrotherapy. After the European sojourn Susy chose not to go with her father, mother, and sister Clara on Clemens's lecture trip around the world (1895–96); she and her sister Jean stayed at the Elmira, New York, home of their aunt Susan Crane. In August 1896, while visiting her childhood home in Hartford, Susy came down with a fever, which proved to be spinal meningitis. She died while her mother and sister were making the transatlantic journey to be with her. "The cloud is permanent, now," Clemens wrote in his notebook (Notebook 40, TS p. 8, CU-MARK; see AD, 2 Feb 1906).

Clara Langdon Clemens (1874–1962), called "Bay," was Clemens's second daughter. Born in Hartford, Connecticut, she was mostly educated at home by her mother and governesses. During the family's sojourn in Europe between 1891 and 1895, Clara enjoyed more independence than her sisters, returning alone to Berlin to study music. She was the only one of Clemens's daughters to go with him and Livy on their 1895–96 trip around the world. The death of her sister Susy, and the first epileptic seizure of her other sister, Jean, both came in 1896: "It was a long time before anyone laughed in our household," Clara recalled (CC 1931, 179). The family settled in Vienna in 1897. Clara aspired to be a pianist, studying under Theodor Le-schetizky, through whom she met the young Russian pianist Ossip Gabrilowitsch (1878–1936). By 1898 Clara's vocation had changed from pianist to singer, a career in which she found more indulgence than acclaim. After her mother's death in 1904 Clara suffered a breakdown and was intermittently away from her family at rest cures in 1905 and 1906. She was financially dependent on her father but spent less and less time in his household, traveling and giving occasional recitals. Increasingly suspicious of the control exerted by Isabel V. Lyon and Ralph Ashcroft over her father and his finances, Clara convinced Clemens to dismiss the pair in 1909. She married Gabrilowitsch in 1909; their daughter, Nina Gabrilowitsch (1910–66) was Clemens's last direct descendant. Between 1904 and 1910 Clara lost her mother, her sister Jean, and her father; at the age of thirty-five, she was sole heir to the estate of Mark Twain, which was held in trust for her, not to be disposed in its entirety until her own death. For the rest of her life she used her influence to control the public representation of her father. Gabrilowitsch died in 1936; in 1944 Clara married Russian conductor Jacques Samossoud (1894–1966). Her memoir of Clemens, *My Father, Mark Twain,* was published in 1931. She spent the last decades of her life in Southern California. Clara's bequest of Clemens's personal papers to the University of California, Berkeley, in 1962, formed the basis of the Mark Twain Papers now housed in The Bancroft Library.

Jean (Jane Lampton) Clemens (1880–1909), Clemens's youngest daughter, was named after his mother but was always called Jean. Like her sisters, she was educated largely at home. In 1896, however, she was attending school in Elmira, New York, when she suffered a severe epileptic seizure. Sedatives were prescribed, and for the next several years her anxious parents tried to forestall the progress of her illness, even spending the summer of 1899 in Sweden so that she could be treated by the well-known osteopath Jonas Kellgren. Her condition, which worsened after her mother's death in 1904, and the household's frequent relocations, gave Jean little chance to develop an independent existence. In late 1899 she began teaching herself how to type so that she could transcribe her father's manuscripts. She also loved riding and other outdoor activities, and espoused animal and human-rights causes. In October 1906 Jean was sent to a sanatorium in Katonah, New York, and remained in "exile" until April 1909, when she rejoined her father at Stormfield, in Redding, Connecticut. Over the next months she enjoyed a close, happy relationship with him and took over Isabel Lyon's duties as secretary. Jean died at Stormfield on 24 December 1909, apparently of a heart attack suffered during a seizure. Over the next few days Clemens wrote a heart-breaking reminiscence of her entitled "Closing Words of My Autobiography" (SLC 1909).

SPEECH AT THE SEVENTIETH BIRTHDAY DINNER, 5 DECEMBER 1905

This text of Clemens's speech at his seventieth birthday celebration was printed in *Harper's Weekly* on 23 December 1905 with the title "Mark Twain's 70th Birthday: Souvenir of Its Celebration" (SLC 1905g; see AD, 12 Jan 1906). It is likely that the *Harper's* text was based on a manuscript that Clemens provided. No manuscript has been found, however, and the source of the magazine text has not been determined.

Clemens was introduced by William Dean Howells, who commented:

> Mr. Clemens has always had the effect on me of throwing me into a poetic ecstasy. (Laughter.) I know it is very uncommon. Most people speak of him in prose, and I dare say there will be a deal of prosing about him to-night; but for myself, I am obliged to resort to metre whenever I think of him.

Howells then read his own "Sonnet to Mark Twain" in which the "American joke"—personified as a "Colossus"—expounded his role as the bringer of joy and freedom and announced, "Mark Twain made me." Howells concluded with the toast, "I will not say, 'Oh King, live forever,' but 'Oh King, live as long as you like!'"

————————

Well, if I made that joke, it is the best one I ever made, and it is in the prettiest language too. I never can get quite to that height. But I appreciate that joke and I shall remember it,—and I shall use it when occasion requires. (Laughter.)

I have had a great many birthdays in my time. I remember the first one very well (laughter), and I always think of it with indignation (renewed laughter); everything was so crude, unaesthetic, primeval. Nothing like this at all. (Laughter.) No proper appreciative preparation made; nothing really ready. (Prolonged laughter.) Now, for a person born with high and delicate instincts,—why, even the cradle wasn't whitewashed,—nothing ready at all. I hadn't any hair (laughter), I hadn't any teeth (laughter), I hadn't any clothes (laughter), I had to go to my first banquet just like that. (Prolonged laughter.) Well, everybody came swarming in. It was the merest little bit of a village,—hardly that, just a little hamlet, in the backwoods of Missouri, where nothing ever happened, and the people were all interested (laughter), and they all came; they looked me over to see if there was anything fresh in my line. Why, nothing ever happened in that village—I—why, I was the only thing that had really happened there (laughter) for months and months and months; and although I say it myself that shouldn't, I came the nearest to being a real event that had happened in that village in more than two years. (Laughter.) Well, those people came, they came with that curiosity which is so provincial, with that frankness which also is so provincial, and they examined me all around and gave their opinion. Nobody asked them, and I shouldn't have minded if anybody had paid me a compliment, but nobody did. Their opinions were all just green with prejudice, and I feel those opinions to this day. (Laughter.) Well, I stood that as long as—well, you know I was born courteous (laughter), and I stood it to the limit. I stood it an hour and then the worm turned. I was the worm; it was my turn to turn, and I turned. (Laughter.) I knew very well the strength of my position; I knew that I was the only spotlessly pure and innocent person in that whole town (laughter), and I came out and said so. And they could not say a word. It was so true. They blushed, they were embarrassed. Well, that was the first after-dinner speech I ever made (laughter). I think it was after dinner. (Renewed laughter.)

It's a long stretch between that first birthday speech and this one. That was my cradle-song, and this is my swan-song, I suppose. I am used to swan-songs; I have sung them several times.

This is my seventieth birthday, and I wonder if you all rise to the size of that proposition, realizing all the significance of that phrase, seventieth birthday.

The seventieth birthday! It is the time of life when you arrive at a new and awful dignity; when you may throw aside the decent reserves which have oppressed you for a generation and stand unafraid and unabashed upon your seven-terraced summit and look down and teach—unrebuked. You can tell the world how you got there. It is what they all do. You shall never get tired of telling by what delicate arts and deep moralities you climbed up to that great place. You will explain the process and dwell on the particulars with senile rapture. I have been anxious to explain my own system this long time, and now at last I have the right.

I have achieved my seventy years in the usual way: by sticking strictly to a scheme of life which would kill anybody else. (Laughter.) It sounds like an exaggeration, but that is really the common rule for attaining to old age. When we examine the programme of any of these garrulous old people we always find that the habits which have preserved them would have decayed us; that the way of life which enabled them to live upon the property of their heirs so long, as Mr. Choate says, would have put us out of commission ahead of time. I will offer here, as a sound maxim, this: That we can't reach old age by another man's road.

I will now teach, offering my way of life to whomsoever desires to commit suicide by the scheme which has enabled me to beat the doctor and the hangman for seventy years. (Laughter.) Some of the details may sound untrue, but they are not. I am not here to deceive; I am here to teach.

We have no permanent habits until we are forty. Then they begin to harden, presently they petrify, then business begins. Since forty I have been regular about going to bed and getting up—and that is one of the main things. I have made it a rule to go to bed when there wasn't anybody left to sit up with; and I have made it a rule to get up when I had to. (Laughter.) This has resulted in an unswerving regularity of irregularity. It has saved me sound, but it would injure another person.

In the matter of diet—which is another main thing—I have been persistently strict in sticking to the things which didn't agree with me until one or the other of us got the best of it. Until lately I got the best of it myself. (Laughter.) But last spring I stopped frolicking with mince pie after midnight; up to then I had always believed it wasn't loaded. (Laughter.) For thirty years I have taken coffee and bread at eight in the morning, and no bite nor sup until 7.30 in the evening. Eleven hours. That is all right for me, and is wholesome, because I have never had a headache in my life, but headachy people would not reach seventy comfortably by that road, and they would be foolish to try it. And I wish to urge upon you this—which I think is wisdom—that if you find you can't make seventy by any but an uncomfortable road, don't you go. When they take off the Pullman and retire you to the rancid smoker, put on your things, count your checks, and get out at the first way station where there's a cemetery. (Laughter.)

I have made it a rule never to smoke more than one cigar at a time. I have no other restriction as regards smoking. I do not know just when I began to smoke, I only know that it was in my father's lifetime, and that I was discreet. He passed from this life early in 1847, when I was a shade past eleven; ever since then I have smoked publicly. As an example to others, and not that I care for moderation myself, it has always been my rule never to smoke when asleep, and never to refrain when awake. (Laughter.) It is a good rule. I mean, for me; but some of you know quite well that it wouldn't answer for everybody that's trying to get to be seventy.

I smoke in bed until I have to go to sleep; I wake up in the night, sometimes once, sometimes twice, sometimes three times, and I never waste any of these opportunities to smoke. This habit is so old and dear and precious to me that I would feel as you, sir, would feel if you should lose the only moral you've got—meaning the chairman—if you've got one: I am making no charges. (Laughter.) I will grant, here, that I have stopped smoking now and then, for a few months at a time, but it was not on principle, it was only to show off; it was to pulverize those critics who said I was a slave to my habits and couldn't break my bonds. (Laughter.)

To-day it is all of sixty years since I began to smoke the limit. I have never bought cigars with life-belts around them. (Laughter.) I early found that those were too expensive for me. I have always bought cheap cigars—reasonably cheap, at any rate. Sixty years ago they cost me four dollars a barrel, but my taste has improved, latterly, and I pay seven now. (Laughter.) Six or seven. Seven, I think. Yes, it's seven. But that includes the barrel. (Laughter.) I often have smoking-parties at my house; but the people that come have always just taken the pledge. I wonder why that is? (Laughter.)

As for drinking, I have no rule about that. When the others drink I like to help; otherwise I remain dry, by habit and preference. (Laughter.) This dryness does not hurt me, but it could easily hurt you, because you are different. (Laughter.) You let it alone.

Since I was seven years old I have seldom taken a dose of medicine, and have still seldomer needed one. But up to seven I lived exclusively on allopathic medicines. (Laughter.) Not that I needed them, for I don't think I did; it was for economy; my father took a drug-store for a debt, and it made cod-liver oil cheaper than the other breakfast foods. (Laughter.) We had nine barrels of it, and it lasted me seven years. Then I was weaned. (Laughter.) The rest of the family had to get along with rhubarb and ipecac and such things, because I was the pet. I was the first Standard Oil Trust. (Laughter.) I had it all. By the time the drug-store was exhausted my health was established, and there has never been much the matter with me since. But you know very well it would be foolish for the average child to start for seventy on that basis. It happened to be just the thing for me, but that was merely an accident; it couldn't happen again in a century. (Laughter.)

I have never taken any exercise, except sleeping and resting, and I never intend to take any. Exercise is loathsome. And it cannot be any benefit when you are tired; I was always tired. (Laughter.) But let another person try my way, and see where he will come out.

I desire now to repeat and emphasize that maxim: We can't reach old age by another man's road. My habits protect my life, but they would assassinate you.

I have lived a severely moral life. But it would be a mistake for other people to try that, or for me to recommend it. Very few would succeed: you have to have a perfectly colossal stock of morals; and you can't get them on a margin; you have to have the whole thing, and put them in your box. Morals are an acquirement—like music, like a foreign language, like piety, poker, paralysis—no man is born with them. I wasn't myself, I started poor. I hadn't a single moral.

There is hardly a man in this house that is poorer than I was then. (Laughter.) Yes, I started like that—the world before me, not a moral in the slot. Not even an insurance moral. (Laughter.) I can remember the first one I ever got. I can remember the landscape, the weather, the—I can remember how everything looked. It was an old moral, an old second-hand moral, all out of repair, and didn't fit anyway. But if you are careful with a thing like that, and keep it in a dry place, and save it for processions, and Chautauquas, and World's Fairs, and so on, and disinfect it now and then, and give it a fresh coat of whitewash once in a while, you will be surprised to see how well she will last and how long she will keep sweet, or at least inoffensive. When I got that mouldy old moral she had stopped growing, because she hadn't any exercise; but I worked her hard, I worked her Sundays and all. Under this cultivation she waxed in might and stature beyond belief, and served me well and was my pride and joy for sixty-three years; then she got to associating with insurance presidents, and lost flesh and character, and was a sorrow to look at and no longer competent for business. (Laughter.) She was a great loss to me. Yet not all loss. I sold her—ah, pathetic skeleton, as she was—I sold her to Leopold, the pirate King of Belgium; he sold her to our Metropolitan Museum, and it was very glad to get her, for, without a rag on, she stands 57 feet long and 16 feet high, and they think she's a brontosaur. (Laughter.) Well, she looks it. They believe it will take nineteen geological periods to breed her match.

Morals are of inestimable value, for every man is born crammed with sin microbes, and the only thing that can extirpate these sin microbes is morals. Now you take a sterilized Christian—I mean, you take *the* sterilized Christian (laughter), for there's only one. Dear sir, I wish you wouldn't look at me like that. (Laughter.)

Threescore years and ten!

It is the Scriptural statute of limitations. After that, you owe no active duties; for you the strenuous life is over. You are a time-expired man, to use Kipling's military phrase: You have served your term, well or less well, and you are mustered out. You are become an honorary member of the republic, you are emancipated, compulsions are not for you, nor any bugle-call but "lights out." You pay the time-worn duty bills if you choose, or decline if you prefer—and without prejudice—for they are not legally collectable.

The previous-engagement plea, which in forty years has cost you so many twinges, you can lay aside forever; on this side of the grave you will never need it again. If you shrink at thought of night, and winter, and the late home-coming from the banquet and the lights and the laughter through the deserted streets—a desolation which would not remind you now, as for a generation it did, that your friends are sleeping, and you must creep in a-tiptoe and not disturb them, but would only remind you that you need not tiptoe, you can never disturb them more—if you shrink at thought of these things, you need only reply, "Your invitation honors me, and pleases me because you still keep me in your remembrance, but I am seventy; seventy, and would nestle in the chimney corner, and smoke my pipe, and read my book, and take my rest, wishing you well in all affection, and that when you in your turn shall arrive at pier No. 70 you may step aboard your waiting ship with a reconciled spirit, and lay your course toward the sinking sun with a contented heart." (Prolonged applause.)

SPEECH AT THE PLAYERS, 3 JANUARY 1906

On 3 January 1906 Clemens spoke at a dinner at The Players club, held to celebrate his renewed membership; his text was a version of the "Wapping Alice" story (SLC 1981; see AD, 10 Jan 1906, and the note at 256.5–6). The text reproduced here is from a book published in 1943 by the club's majordomo, Walter Oettel, entitled *Walter's Sketch Book of the Players* (Oettel 1943, 54–57). The source of Oettel's text is not known. The mention of Clemens's "slow drawling way" suggests that someone at the dinner took down the speech in shorthand, but it is also possible that Clemens gave Oettel his manuscript.

———————

"She was," he said, in his slow drawling way, "an English importation of Mrs. Clemens. She came well-recommended, and was duly installed as cook in our household. She was a prepossessing maiden of thirty years, well-liked by all the family.

"During the summer months the family went abroad. I and a few of the servants, including English Mary, remained at home. The house underwent renovation that summer, and among other improvements, a burglar alarm system was installed—the annunciator of the alarm being placed in my bedroom.

"One night, shortly after the system was completed, the alarm sounded. It was repeated three nights in succession, but no trace of an intruder could be found. Each time the indicator showed that a window in the basement had been tampered with. Believing it to be of little or no importance, I thought no more of it until the alarm was repeated on the fourth night. I then decided to investigate thoroughly. Putting on my robe and slippers, I quietly descended the stairs. On reaching the basement I found that Mary had company—a big strapping young fellow about twenty-five years of age. Of course I apologized for intruding, and returned to my room. The next morning I sent for Mary, to give her a mild scolding, and likewise to lend her a key to the basement door so that her evening caller might enter without causing a commotion in my room.

"It was a few months later that English Mary came to me one morning with tears in her eyes. She asked me for advice, informing me that her young friend, the handsome young Swede, was about to leave her. She confessed that circumstances made it imperative that he marry her at once. They loved each other devotedly, and she had long expected to become his wife. I told her to cheer up, I would do what I could. She was to advise me when he called that night.

"The servants were told to be in readiness to help me out of any particular difficulty. I telephoned my friend, the Chief of Police, to have a man shadow the young Romeo, to allow him to enter the house but not to leave it. Also, he must have an officer at my door at ten o'clock. In addition, I secured the services of a clerical friend for the evening.

"I stationed the police officer at the right of my library door, and told him to enter if I rang the bell three times. The clergyman hid himself in a little room on the side of my bedroom. (This was, by the way, the hottest place in the whole house.) I explained to my friend that I expected a wedding party, and wanted him to tie the knot. I had ordered good things to eat and drink to celebrate the event—for I anticipated a victory.

"The young man arrived very early, to say good-bye. Mary persuaded him to come up to speak to me also. He entered my room, carrying himself in a most flippant manner. I liked the fellow, however. Despite his self-assurance, he had an open countenance which a woman of Mary's type could not resist.

"First, I asked his name, and he told me. As to his prospects in life, he said he expected to earn a good living at his trade, carpentering. I told him that he owed it to Mary to propose an immediate marriage. He said he would think it over.

"'Well,' said I, 'you have exactly five minutes to think it over. You have your choice of two things, marriage or prison.' I pulled out my watch and put it on the table beside me, and lit a fresh cigar.

"He said that he was going then, but he would let me know his decision the next day. 'One minute,' I said. 'When you entered this room I locked the door and put the key in my pocket. You have now three minutes to think. In the meantime let me tell you that an indictment for housebreaking is hanging over you for entering my house, night after night. Five years in prison is the penalty for that offense. There is a police officer in the next room, waiting to take you into custody. Now, I want you and Mary to be happy. She loves you, and she is soon to be the mother of your child. She has a good home here, and I want you to share it with her. You may have the best room in the house until the family comes back. Mary will make a good wife to you. A clergyman is waiting in the next room, the servants are ready to witness your marriage, and everything is ready for a fine wedding. We can all have a big time.'

"Well, the fellow made a number of excuses, but I disposed of them all. Finally he consented to be married peaceably. I called Mary, the rest of the servants, and the minister. English Mary became a bride that night. The policeman stood up with her, and we all had a jolly time after the ceremony.

"The couple lived with us for three months before starting their own home. We left Hartford the next year, and it was not until two years later that I returned to the city. I was walking from the depot when I saw a man driving a team of spirited horses. He seemed to be gazing at me. Suddenly he drew up near me and asked: 'Don't you know me, Mr. Clemens? I am Frank, Mary's husband.' I expressed my gladness at seeing him, and inquired about Mary and the baby.

"'Mr. Clemens,' he said, 'it was the best thing you ever did—to make me marry Mary. She has been a fine wife to me. She had a little money saved and with that she started me in business. This is my rig; I am a contractor and builder now. You must come to see us . . . As to my *family*—there was never a baby, or any suspicion of any.'"

PREVIOUS PUBLICATION

Below is a list of each piece in this volume and its publication history. All works cited by an abbreviation such as *MTA,* by SLC and a date, or by NAR (*North American Review*) and an installment number are fully defined in References. The term "partial publication" indicates that the text may be merely an excerpt, or be nearly complete. Charles Neider, the editor of

The *Autobiography of Mark Twain (AMT),* reordered and recombined excerpts to such an extent that all publication in his volume is considered partial. At the end of this appendix is a list of the "Chapters from My Autobiography" published in NAR installments between 7 September 1906 and December 1907. Except for the subtitle "Random Extracts from It" (which Clemens himself enclosed in brackets), bracketed titles have been editorially supplied for works that Clemens left untitled.

Preliminary Manuscripts and Dictations, 1870–1905

[The Tennessee Land]: *MTA,* 1:3–7, partial; *AMT,* 22–24.
[Early Years in Florida, Missouri]: SLC 1922a, 274–75; *MTA,* 1:7–10; *AMT,* 1–3.
[The Grant Dictations]
    The Chicago G.A.R. Festival: *MTA,* 1:13–19; *AMT,* 241–45.
    [A Call with W. D. Howells on General Grant]: *MTA,* 1:24–27.
    Grant and the Chinese: *MTA,* 1:20–24.
    Gerhardt: previously unpublished.
    About General Grant's Memoirs: *MTA,* 1:27–57, 57–68, partial.
    [The Rev. Dr. Newman]: *MTA,* 1:68–70.
The Machine Episode: *MTA,* 1:70–78, partial.
Travel-Scraps I: previously unpublished.
[Four Sketches about Vienna]
    [Beauties of the German Language]: *MTA,* 1:164–66.
    [Comment on Tautology and Grammar]: *MTA,* 1:172–74.
    [A Group of Servants]: SLC 2009, 61–69.
    [A Viennese Procession]: *MTA,* 1:166–71.
My Debut as a Literary Person: SLC 1899d; SLC 1900b, 84–127; SLC 1903a, 11–47.
Horace Greeley: *MTE,* 347–48.
Lecture-Times: *MTA,* 1:147–53, partial; *AMT,* 161, 166–69.
Ralph Keeler: *MTA,* 1:154–64; *AMT,* 161–62, 163–66.
Scraps from My Autobiography. From Chapter IX: NAR 2, 453–56, partial; NAR 17, 4–12,
    partial; *MTA,* 1:125–43; *AMT,* 37–43, 44–47; SLC 2004, 157–60, partial.
Scraps from My Autobiography. Private History of a Manuscript That Came to Grief:
    MTA, 1:175–89, partial.
[Reflections on a Letter and a Book]: SLC 1922c, 312–15, partial.
[Something about Doctors]: previously unpublished.
[Henry H. Rogers]: *MTA,* 1:250–56, partial.
[Anecdote of Jean]: previously unpublished.

Autobiography of Mark Twain

An Early Attempt: previously unpublished.
My Autobiography [Random Extracts from It]: NAR 1, 322–30, partial; NAR 13, 449–63,

partial; SLC 1922a, 275–76, partial; *MTA,* 1:81–115, partial; *AMT,* 1, 3–21, 24–25; SLC 2004, 61–62, 97–99, partial.

The Latest Attempt: *MTA,* 1:193.

The Final (and Right) Plan: SLC 1922a, 273; *MTA,* 1:xviii.

Preface. As from the Grave (section I): *MTA,* 1:xv–xvi; *AMT,* xxviii.

Preface. As from the Grave (sections II and III): previously unpublished.

[The Florentine Dictations]

   [John Hay]: NAR 12, 344–46, partial; *MTA,* 1:232–38.

   Notes on "Innocents Abroad": NAR 20, 465–71; *MTA,* 1:238–46; *AMT,* 143, 147–51.

   [Robert Louis Stevenson and Thomas Bailey Aldrich]: NAR 2, 456–59; *MTA,* 1:246–50; *AMT,* 288–90.

   [Villa di Quarto]: *MTA,* 1:195–232, partial; *AMT,* 314–22.

Note for the Instruction of Future Editors and Publishers of This Autobiography: *AMT,* xi.

Autobiographical Dictations, January–March 1906

9 January: *MTA,* 1:269–78, partial.

10 January: *MTA,* 1:278–91.

11 January: NAR 25, 481–89, partial.

12 January: NAR 16, 785–88, partial; *MTA,* 1:291–303, partial.

13 January: NAR 16, 788–92, partial; *MTA,* 1:303–12; *AMT,* 98–101.

15 January: NAR 16, 792–93, partial; *MTA,* 1:312–26, partial; *AMT,* 101–2.

16 January: *MTA,* 1:326–35.

17 January: NAR 14, 570–71, partial; *MTA,* 1:335–45, partial.

18 January: *MTA,* 1:345–50.

19 January: NAR 8, 1217–24, partial; NAR 22, 13–17, partial; *MTA,* 1:350–61, partial; *AMT,* 112–18.

23 January: *MTA,* 2:1–13, partial.

24 January: *MTA,* 2:13–23.

1 February: NAR 3, 577–80, partial; *MTA,* 2:23–33; *AMT,* 183, 185–86, 322.

2 February: NAR 3, 580–85, partial; *MTA,* 2:33–44, partial; *AMT,* 190–95, 322–24.

5 February: NAR 3, 585–89, partial; *MTA,* 2:44–59; *AMT,* 195–201.

6 February: *MTA,* 2:59–64, partial.

7 February: NAR 4, 705–10, partial; *MTA,* 2:64–73, partial; *AMT,* 201–3, 274–75.

8 February: NAR 4, 710–16; *MTA,* 2:73–83, partial; *AMT,* 204–10; SLC 2004, 173–76, partial.

9 February: NAR 5, 833–38; *MTA,* 2:83–91, partial; *AMT,* 210–13; SLC 2004, 15–19, partial.

12 February: NAR 5, 838–44; *MTA,* 2:91–99, partial; *AMT,* 33–37, 213–14.

13 February: *MTA,* 2:99–105; *AMT,* 43–44, 183–85.

14 February: *MTA,* 2:106–12; *AMT,* 186–90.

15 February: *MTA,* 2:112–17, partial; *MTE,* 249–52, partial.

16 February: *MTA,* 2:117–19, partial; *MTE,* 77–81, partial.

20 February: *MTA,* 2:120–26.

21 February: *MTA,* 2:126–28, partial.

22 February: *MTA,* 2:128–34.

23 February: *MTA,* 2:135–39, partial.

26 February: NAR 6, 961–64, partial; *MTA,* 2:139–51, partial.

5 March: NAR 7, 1089–91, partial; *MTA,* 2:151–60; SLC 2004, 20–22, partial.

6 March: NAR 7, 1092–95, partial; *MTA,* 2:160–66, partial.

7 March: NAR 6, 964–69; *MTA,* 2:166–72, partial.

8 March: NAR 21, 691–95, partial; *MTA,* 2:172–80, partial; *AMT,* 67–70.

9 March: NAR 23, 161–63, partial; *MTA,* 2:180–86, partial; *AMT,* 70–73.

12 March: *MTA,* 2:187–96.

14 March: *MTA,* 2:196–200, partial.

15 March: *MTA,* 2:200–212, partial.

16 March: *MTA,* 2:212–21, partial; *AMT,* 73–78.

20 March: *MTL,* 2:790–94, partial; *MTE,* 83–91, partial.

21 March: *MTA,* 2:221–29, partial.

22 March: NAR 6, 969–70, partial; *MTA,* 2:229–37; *AMT,* 190.

23 March: NAR 7, 1094–95, partial; *MTA,* 2:237–43, partial.

26 March: NAR 1, 321–22, partial; *MTA,* 2:243–56, partial; *AMT,* 107–9.

27 March: *MTA,* 2:256–68; *AMT,* 109–12.

28 March: NAR 10, 113–18, partial; *MTA,* 2:268–75, partial; *AMT,* 84–88.

29 March: NAR 10, 118–19, partial; NAR 11, 225–29, partial; *MTA,* 2:275–91, partial; *AMT,* 88–95, 98, 102–3.

30 March: *MTA,* 2:291–303, partial.

"Chapters from My Autobiography" in the *North American Review,* 1906–1907

The texts listed below in italic type were published in full or nearly so—that is, with no more than a paragraph or occasional sentence omitted.

Installment	Published	Contents
NAR 1	7 Sept 1906	AD, 26 Mar 1906 (Introduction); My Autobiography [Random Extracts from It] (first part)
NAR 2	21 Sept 1906	AD, *21 May 1906;* Scraps from My Autobiography. From Chapter IX (first part); *[Robert Louis Stevenson and Thomas Bailey Aldrich];* AD, 3 Apr 1906
NAR 3	5 Oct 1906	ADs, 1 Feb 1906, 2 Feb 1906, 5 Feb 1906
NAR 4	19 Oct 1906	ADs, 7 Feb 1906, *8 Feb 1906*
NAR 5	2 Nov 1906	ADs, *9 Feb 1906, 12 Feb 1906*
NAR 6	16 Nov 1906	ADs, 26 Feb 1906, *7 Mar 1906,* 22 Mar 1906

NAR 7	7 Dec 1906	ADs, 5 Mar 1906, 6 Mar 1906, 23 Mar 1906
NAR 8	21 Dec 1906	AD, 19 Jan 1906
NAR 9	4 Jan 1907	ADs, *13 Dec 1906, 1 Dec 1906, 2 Dec 1906*
NAR 10	18 Jan 1907	ADs, 28 Mar 1906, 29 Mar 1906
NAR 11	1 Feb 1907	ADs, 29 Mar 1906 (misdated 28 Mar in the NAR), 2 Apr 1906
NAR 12	15 Feb 1907	[John Hay]; ADs, 5 Apr 1906, 6 Apr 1906
NAR 13	1 Mar 1907	My Autobiography [Random Extracts from It] (second part)
NAR 14	15 Mar 1907	ADs, *6 Dec 1906,* 17 Dec 1906, 11 Feb 1907 (misdated 10 Feb in the NAR), 12 Feb 1907, 17 Jan 1906
NAR 15	5 Apr 1907	ADs, *8 Oct 1906, 22 Jan 1907*
NAR 16	19 Apr 1907	ADs, 12 Jan 1906, 13 Jan 1906, 15 Jan 1906
NAR 17	3 May 1907	AD, 15 Oct 1906; Scraps from My Autobiography. From Chapter IX (second part)
NAR 18	17 May 1907	ADs, 21 Dec 1906, *28 Mar 1907*
NAR 19	7 June 1907	ADs, 21 Dec 1906 (with note dated 22 Dec), 19 Nov 1906, 30 Nov 1906, 28 Mar 1907, *5 Sept 1906*
NAR 20	5 July 1907	*Notes on "Innocents Abroad"*; AD, *23 Jan 1907*
NAR 21	2 Aug 1907	ADs, 8 Nov 1906, 8 Mar 1906, *6 Jan 1907*
NAR 22	Sept 1907	ADs, *10 Oct 1906,* 19 Jan 1906 (dated 12 Mar 1906 in the NAR, with note dated 13 May 1907), *20 Dec 1906*
NAR 23	Oct 1907	ADs, 9 Mar 1906, *16 Mar 1906,* 26 July 1907, 30 July 1907
NAR 24	Nov 1907	ADs, *9 Oct 1906, 16 Oct 1906,* 11 Oct 1906, *12 Oct 1906, 23 Jan 1907*
NAR 25	Dec 1907	ADs, 11 Jan 1906, *3 Oct 1907*

NOTE ON THE TEXT

The Introduction traces the history of Clemens's work on his autobiography, from the preliminary manuscripts and dictations he produced between 1870 and 1905 through the Autobiographical Dictations that he began in early 1906. It also gives an explanation of his final plan for the *Autobiography of Mark Twain,* based largely on an analysis of various typescripts and manuscripts created in 1906. These source documents are summarized here, and the summary is followed by a description of the editorial policy that has been used to create the critical text of this edition.

THE DOCUMENTS

Manuscripts and typescripts (before 1906)

The source documents for the texts collected in the section entitled Preliminary Manuscripts and Dictations include manuscripts in the author's hand as well as a diverse assortment of typescripts made from his dictation by James Redpath, Jean Clemens, or Josephine Hobby. Redpath took down Clemens's words in an unidentified shorthand and typed the translation himself on an all-capitals typewriter. Jean Clemens, a novice at the typewriter, transcribed Isabel Lyon's longhand notes. Hobby was a skilled stenographer and her own typist. Her typescripts are the most reliable, with Redpath's and Jean's somewhat less so. The manuscripts are the most straightforward record of the author's intention, but even they sometimes contain errors. The editorial policy discussed below has been applied to each work, with adjustments as needed to accommodate its particular textual history, which is always described in detail in the Textual Commentary at *Mark Twain Project Online* (*MTPO*).

TS1 (1906–1909)

Produced between 1906 and 1909, TS1 is the first of three distinct, sequentially paginated typescripts for the final plan of the autobiography as conceived by Clemens in 1906, now in the Mark Twain Papers. Typed by Hobby, it begins with the dictation of 9 January 1906 and ends with the dictation of 14 July 1908, extending far beyond the other sequences. Two later typists, Mary Louise Howden and William Edgar Grumman, produced an additional hundred or so pages of typescript, numbering each dictation separately. TS1 and the typescripts of Howden and Grumman, transcribed by each typist from his or her shorthand notes, are the primary record of Clemens's dictated text. Together they are the *only* text for the roughly one hundred and seventy dictations made between late August 1906 and 1909. Clemens revised many of the pages of TS1 for publication in the *North American Review,* adjusting the wording to accommodate omissions and suppressing or altering text that he considered "written in too independent a fashion for a magazine."[1] Only in TS1 is the date of dictation close to the date the typescript was created. Many pages of TS1 were marked by Paine as the printer's copy for his 1924 edition of the autobiography; he discarded some of the material he chose not to include, and those pages are now missing.

TS2 and TS4 (1906)

The page numbers on TS2 (made by Hobby) and TS4 (made by an unidentified typist) differ from those on TS1 and from each other because both typescripts begin with material not present in TS1 (everything before the 9 January 1906 dictation). Together TS2 and TS4 total over twenty-five hundred pages. Begun in mid-June, they provide conclusive evidence of exactly which of his accumulated drafts and false starts Clemens decided to include in his final plan for the autobiography. TS2 and TS4 begin with "My Autobiography [Random Extracts from It]," but omit the preface ("An Early Attempt") that was written to introduce it. The second (three-part) preface—"The Latest Attempt," "The Final (and Right) Plan," and "Preface. As from the Grave"—is fully present in TS4, which also includes four Florentine Dictations, but in TS2 the five pages on which the three-part preface was typed, as well as the pages containing the third and fourth Florentine Dictations, are lost. Both typescripts continue with the 1906 Autobiographical Dictations that were begun on 9 January; TS2 ends with the dictation of 7 August, and TS4 ends with that of 29 August. Both typescripts incorporate the revisions that Clemens wrote on TS1. He further revised much of TS2, making improvements in wording as well as softening and censoring the texts for publication in the *North American Review.* He made no changes on TS4. Whenever TS1 is extant for a given dictation, TS4 is derivative and does not affect the critical text. When TS1 is missing, however, both TS2 and TS4 are relied on to recreate its text, since both derive from it, so that either one may contain authoritative readings that are not found in the other. When TS2 and TS4 do not vary from each other, they confirm the reading of the missing TS1.

TS3 and the NAR Extracts (1906–1907)

Typed by Hobby between early August 1906 and late January 1907, TS3 comprises fewer than one hundred and fifty pages. Prepared as printer's copy for six installments in the *North American Review,* it reproduces the first section of "Scraps from My Autobiography. From Chapter IX," one Florentine Dictation ("Robert Louis Stevenson and Thomas Bailey Aldrich"), and excerpts from the Autobiographical Dictations through 21 May 1906. It consists of four batches, each beginning with page 1. Three of the batches include the text for a single *Review* installment (NAR 2, NAR 3, and NAR 16), and one batch encompasses three install-

1. 10 Oct 1898 to Bok, ViU. See "Revisions for magazine publication," below.

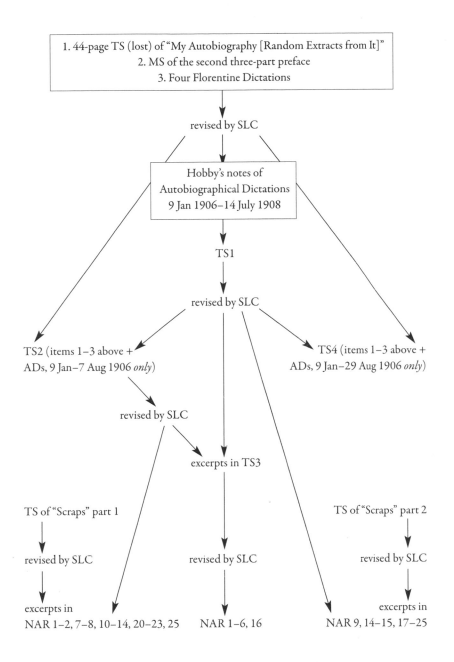

1. 44-page TS (lost) of "My Autobiography [Random Extracts from It]"
2. MS of the second three-part preface
3. Four Florentine Dictations

revised by SLC

Hobby's notes of
Autobiographical Dictations
9 Jan 1906–14 July 1908

TS1

revised by SLC

TS2 (items 1–3 above +
ADs, 9 Jan–7 Aug 1906 *only*)

TS4 (items 1–3 above +
ADs, 9 Jan–29 Aug 1906 *only*)

revised by SLC

excerpts in TS3

TS of "Scraps" part 1

TS of "Scraps" part 2

revised by SLC

revised by SLC

revised by SLC

excerpts in
NAR 1–2, 7–8, 10–14, 20–23, 25

NAR 1–6, 16

excerpts in
NAR 9, 14–15, 17–25

ments (NAR 4, NAR 5, and NAR 6). TS3 was typed primarily from TS1, incorporating its revisions, and includes further changes made to accommodate magazine publication.

Above is a diagram of the textual relationships between TS1, TS2, TS3, and TS4 of the 1906–9 Autobiographical Dictations and the twenty-five NAR installments that published excerpts from them (and from one other typescript). The "Early Attempt" preface is not present in either TS2 (now incomplete) or TS4 (complete), but both typescripts include "My Autobiography [Random Extracts from It]," followed by the second three-part preface ("The Latest Attempt," "The Final [and Right] Plan," and "Preface. As from the Grave") and four Florentine

Dictations. TS3 was typed from the revised TS1 for all but one installment, NAR 16, which was typed from the revised TS2. The first and second parts of "Scraps from My Autobiography. From Chapter IX" were published in NAR installments 2 and 17, respectively, typeset directly from a typescript made by Jean Clemens in 1902. See the Appendix "Previous Publication" (pp. 366–67) for a list of the contents of each NAR installment.

Handwriting on the typescripts

Throughout the pages of TS1, TS2, and TS3 there are revisions, corrections, and editorial instructions in two colors of ink, in lead pencil, and in blue, purple, and red pencil. These were made not only by Clemens himself, but also by the following people: his typists, chiefly Hobby; his secretary, Isabel V. Lyon; Albert Bigelow Paine; George Harvey and David Munro, editors for the *North American Review;* Clara Clemens Gabrilowitsch; Paine's successor as literary executor, Bernard DeVoto; and DeVoto's assistant, Rosamond Hart Chapman. There are also specific instructions to omit this or that passage, each signed "ABP" by Paine and (though also in Paine's hand) "CG" for Clara Clemens Gabrilowitsch, who along with Paine had been charged with deciding which of her father's papers to publish.

Paine felt free to alter the typescripts (and some manuscripts) by writing his changes on them, and even to hand some of them to the printer to set up his 1924 edition. Markings by Paine and DeVoto have been especially problematic. Paine's handwriting can be difficult to distinguish from Clemens's, especially in small verbal changes or punctuation. But he clearly renumbered many pages, styled the texts for his publications, annotated and "corrected" them in large and small ways, and occasionally scissored out passages he intended to suppress. Paine's blue crayon printer's-copy page numbers and his typesetter's galley numbers (in plain lead pencil) for his 1924 edition are scattered throughout, and many typescript pages are smudged with printer's ink and pierced by a spindle hole, both signs that they literally served as setting copy. In preparing copy for *Mark Twain in Eruption,* DeVoto also wrote (in pencil) on the original typescript pages. He inscribed editorial notes to himself, to Rosamond Chapman, and to his typist, Henry Beck; he struck through whole sections of text; and he was so irritated by the typed punctuation that he canceled much of it, penciling through the offending marks so emphatically that it is sometimes difficult to recover the original reading.

THE CRITICAL TEXT

Authorial intention

This edition of the *Autobiography of Mark Twain* offers the reader an unmodernized, critically constructed text, both of the preliminary manuscripts and dictations and of the final text that Clemens intended his "heirs and assigns" to publish after his death. The editorial construction adheres to his intention as it is manifest in the most authoritative documents available, or can be reliably inferred from them, and aims at presenting the texts exactly as he would have published them, so far as that is possible—that is, as they were when he ceased to make changes in them. Except for the revisions the author made for magazine publication (discussed below), all of his revisions and corrections are adopted, whether inscribed on a surviving typescript or detected by collation when the revised typescript is missing. Every decision to adopt (or not) is reported in the Textual Commentaries at *MTPO*, which also record every alteration that the editors have made in the source texts.[2]

Revisions for magazine publication

Many of the changes that Clemens made on TS1, TS2, and TS3 were aimed at shortening, taming, or softening the texts selected for publication in the *North American Review*. These changes are *not* accepted into the edited text, on the grounds that Clemens was clear that they were temporary concessions to propriety, not permanent alterations to the text. Other changes were corrections or revisions made for purely literary reasons, and these *are* adopted. Very occasionally the two kinds of changes are intermixed, and in those cases we err on the side of caution, retaining the original uncensored version.

Dictated texts

Wherever works like the *Autobiography* were created solely by dictation, they pose all the usual problems of textual transmission plus some additional ones not native to manuscripts in the author's hand. In a dictated text, unless the author has specified more than words while or before dictating ("use a semicolon not a period after that word"), the punctuation, spelling, emphasis, paragraphing, and many other small details simply *never existed*—only the inflections, gestures, and pauses of the author speaking and the grammatical structure of his sentences. It makes no sense to say that the author "intended" to spell a word in a certain way, since in speaking the word he may not have been thinking of any particular spelling at all. For some kinds of punctuation, like end-of-sentence periods and question marks, the speaker is more constrained by "rules" and probably comes a little closer to actually intending terminal punctuation, whereas the intended placement of commas, semicolons, colons, dashes, and so forth is less clear.

Of course Clemens did not dictate his autobiography in order to produce a text *without* punctuation. Unlike a public speech, where the authorially intended form is actually an oral performance, dictation was intended to result in a written record, in this case a double-spaced typescript that could be reviewed and corrected and ultimately published in the normal way. So to what extent should we accept the spelling, punctuation, and other details as typed by the stenographer who, we must assume, produced such details without specific instructions from the author? Clemens's review and correction of the typescript made from Hobby's stenographic notes (TS1) is some assurance that whatever he found wrong or misleading he corrected, but such assurance only goes so far, and his ability or willingness to scrutinize the transcript for such details was limited.

2. Only nontextual changes, such as the typographic style of titles, are omitted from this record. But all such "silent" changes are still listed by category at *MTPO*.

A dictating author and his stenographer collaborate to produce a text, and their respective contributions cannot easily be pried apart after the fact. To take a simple example, nowhere do Hobby's typescripts record the kind of hesitation, reiteration, and self-correction that must have occurred even in Clemens's slow and deliberate speech. By mutual though tacit agreement, such things were no doubt omitted, or silently repaired and smoothed over by the stenographer. Fortunately, in the case of Hobby, the collaboration was highly satisfactory to Clemens. Her stenographic notes are presumed lost, but the accuracy of her work can to some extent be judged from the resulting typescripts. They are double spaced (leaving room for revision and correction) and unfailingly neat; the rare typing errors are discreetly erased and corrected by her, with occasional doubtful spellings likewise identified by a lightly penciled question mark. And the number of corrections (as distinct from revisions) inscribed by Clemens is very small. There is some evidence that he trained Hobby to punctuate as he liked. Twenty months after dictation began, a journalist who visited Clemens reported that he "dictates slowly, using the semicolon mark, of which he is particularly fond, as frequently as possible. When the copy is handed to him by the stenographer it is almost always ready for the press, so few are the corrections to be made."[3] It is easy to find passages in the dictations that exemplify this pattern, in which the typist used semicolons where full stops would, to an uninstructed listener, seem the more natural punctuation.[4] There is other evidence that Clemens actually dictated punctuation and other details. Almost forty years after his death, Lyon remembered that "Paine used to say when he was dictating he'd walk slowly up & down and say 'period' or 'paragraph.'" And in 1908, when Hobby left Clemens's employment and he had to break in a new stenographer, Mary Louise Howden, he took even more explicit control of these details. Howden herself recalled in 1925 that Clemens "put in the punctuation himself. His stenographer was never allowed to add so much as a comma."[5]

Whether Clemens literally expressed the punctuation, described his preferences to Hobby, or expected her to learn his style more or less osmotically makes little difference: her punctuation of the typescripts is remarkably close to the use patterns found in Clemens's holograph manuscripts. We know Hobby did learn from his corrections on the typescripts, eventually spelling "Twichell" and "Susy" correctly, for instance. Inevitably, when expanding her shorthand she sometimes mistyped slightly unusual words: "silver boring" for "silver bearing," "visited" for "billeted," and "driveling" for "drizzling."[6] But the author and the stenographer were remarkably well attuned to one another. As a result, Hobby's spelling, punctuation, paragraphing, and so forth on TS1 (made directly from her notes), as well as her rare corrections of these details on any subsequent typescript, whether marked in her hand or introduced

3. "A Day with Mark Twain," Chicago *Tribune,* 29 Sept 1907, F6. It is not clear whether the reporter observed Clemens at work or was repeating remarks by Isabel Lyon.

4. See AD, 30 Mar 1906, p. 462.

5. Notes made by Doris Webster for Dixon Wecter about an interview with Isabel Lyon, ca. March 1948, CU-MARK; Howden 1925. Typescripts prepared by Howden show that she typed some punctuation, presumably because Clemens spoke it aloud, but that he supplied the vast bulk of it by hand—as in the AD of 6 Oct 1908, for example. Clemens's practice with Hobby does not show this same kind of after-the-fact punctuation of the typescript, suggesting that she, more than Howden, had learned what was expected.

6. Each of these errors is identified by Clemens's correction of them on the ADs of 9 Jan, 13 Jan, and 14 Feb 1906.

while typing, command assent. So, if TS1 lacks a paragraph break which was then supplied by Hobby when she created TS2, we adopt her change as a correction of the original typescript. On the other hand, when TS2 shows a change in wording not initiated by Clemens on TS1, the change is *not* accepted unless it is a necessary correction, one that would have been made by the editors whether or not Hobby made it. Most such small verbal differences between typescripts were obviously inadvertent.

Incomplete revision

Because Clemens never prepared any of the texts for actual typesetting and publication, it is not always possible to follow his instructions. For instance, to the dictation of 20 February 1906 Clemens added a note: "Insert, here my account of the 'Hornet' disaster, published in the 'Century' about 1898 as being a chapter from my Autobiography"—a reference to "My Debut as a Literary Person."[7] But if that bald instruction were carried out, the resulting text would be both self-contradictory, because it would still include the remark "I will go no further with the subject now," and deeply puzzling, because it would contain a very long and rather irrelevant digression. Similarly, he noted in the dictation of 12 January 1906, "(Here paste in the proceedings of the Birthday Banquet)"—referring to the thirty-two-page illustrated issue of *Harper's Weekly* commemorating his seventieth birthday.[8] The length and nature of this publication make it impractical to carry out his instruction in a printed volume. Indeed both instructions are more plausibly construed as instructions to himself rather than to his editors. In such cases, Clemens's intention can be described and—wherever possible—the reader directed to the relevant text. In the case of "My Debut," the text is already included with the preliminary manuscripts and dictations in this volume. The impracticality of including the *Harper's Weekly* issue is overcome by directing the reader to a scanned copy at *MTPO,* and the elastic boundaries of the website may be used for other, similar cases, the rationale for which is always explained in the Textual Commentary. In general, such rough edges are an inevitable part of works that were not set into type and published by the author. On the other hand, if informal remarks can be rendered intelligibly in their own right ("I will ask Miss Lyon to see—but I will go on and dictate the dream now") they are included in the edited text, even though the author would doubtless have removed them had he carried out the revision he planned.[9]

Errors of external fact

Clemens's misstatements of fact are almost always allowed to remain uncorrected in the text. For example, when he gave the year of his first meeting with Ulysses S. Grant as 1866

7. This essay was written in 1898 and published as a magazine article in 1899, but without any indication that it came from the autobiography.

8. Clemens referred to "Mark Twain's 70th Birthday: Souvenir of Its Celebration" (SLC 1905g). In the dictation of 16 December 1908 he again said, "I think I will insert here (if I have not inserted it in some earlier chapter of this autobiography) the grand account of the banquet which . . . appeared in Harper's Weekly a week later."

9. AD, 13 Jan 1906, p. 274.

(rather than the correct year, 1868), the error is merely pointed out in the explanatory notes, because it is clear that his memory (not the typist) was at fault. Likewise, in a paragraph of reminiscence about his family in the dictation of 28 March 1906, Clemens said that his sister Margaret died at the age of "ten, in 1837" when she in fact died at the age of nine in 1839, and that his brother Orion was "twelve and a half years old" at the time of the family's move to Hannibal, when he was actually fourteen. In the dictation of 8 March 1906 he mistakenly referred to a "Miss Hill," dean of Barnard College, whose name was actually "Gill." And in the dictation of 12 March 1906 he relied on a New York *Times* article that misnamed someone "Johnson" instead of "Johnston." In all these cases the text is permitted to stand as Clemens left it, and its factual errors are addressed only in the notes.

On the other hand, if Clemens indicated that he wanted something checked, and by implication made accurate, the text has been corrected. For example, in the dictation of 5 March 1906 Clemens described a room in the Villa Viviani as "forty-two feet square and forty-two feet high," but added a query in the margin of the typescript: "42? or was it 40? See previous somewhere." He had used the lower number in the manuscript about the Villa Viviani inserted into "Villa di Quarto," so that number has been adopted in the text. Errors introduced by the stenographer or typist have also been corrected, since they cannot have been intended by Clemens. For example, in TS2 and TS4 of the dictation for 11 January 1906 (TS1 is lost), Clemens appears to say that he was in Venice in "1888," when in fact the year was 1878. It is extremely unlikely that the error was his, since he did not travel in Europe in the 1880s. But the difference of one digit could easily have been a transcription error, and it is therefore corrected.

Errors of form: spelling, syntax, and punctuation

Factual errors apart, it is naturally the case that publishing the autobiography texts as Clemens intended does sometimes require the correction of trivial spelling errors and lapses such as omitted words. We take it as given that he did not intend his published works to contain such obvious errors: there can be no doubt that he would want "monotonous" substituted for manuscript "monotous," and "initiated" printed instead of manuscript "iniated." Nor could he have expected phrases such as "look her" or "either us" to remain uncorrected, and they have therefore been altered to "look at her" and "either of us." Simple errors in the typescripts (such as "publsher") or in printed texts being quoted by Clemens (such as "yaung" for "young" in the New York *Times*) are likewise corrected. If the name of a real person is correct but misspelled, it is mended, whether the error originated with Clemens or with his stenographer ("Greeley" instead of "Greely," for example).[10]

We approach the task of correction with caution, always bearing in mind Clemens's well-documented attitude toward misguided interference with his text. Whenever seeming errors were in fact *intended* (dialect spellings, for instance), we of course make no change. Small

10. See the Textual Commentaries at *MTPO* for "Travel-Scraps I," "Ralph Keeler," the ADs of 17 Jan 1906 and 15 Mar 1906, and "Horace Greeley."

grammatical quirks deemed more or less peculiar to spoken language are also preserved intact. Clemens himself was highly appreciative of this aspect of dictated narrative, "the subtle something which makes good talk so much better than the best imitation of it that can be done with a pen."[11] For that reason (among others) we do not alter sentences like the following: "To-day she is suing for a separation from her shabby purchase, and the world's sympathy and compassion are with her, where it belongs." Or, "A careful statement of Mr. Langdon's affairs showed that the assets were worth eight hundred thousand dollars, and that against them was merely the ordinary obligations of the business."[12] And although there is evidence that Clemens sometimes welcomed corrections of his grammar (see the letter to Ticknor quoted below), errors that are common in spoken language, like "who" for "whom," have been retained.

It is well known that Clemens wanted his punctuation respected, and not altered by anyone else. "Yesterday Mr. Hall wrote that the printer's proof-reader was improving my punctuation for me," he once wrote to Howells, "& I telegraphed orders to have him shot without giving him time to pray."[13] He was equally alert to the well-intentioned "corrections" of the various typists he hired to copy his manuscripts. In revising the typescript for chapter 25 of *Connecticut Yankee* (where one of the knights applies for a position in the Yankee's standing army), Clemens added the following remark: "Try to conceive of this mollusk gravely applying for an official position, of any kind under the sun! Why, he had all the ear-marks of a type-writer copyist, if you leave out the disposition to contribute uninvited emendations of your grammar and punctuation."[14]

His objection to "uninvited emendations of . . . grammar and punctuation" was, however, somewhat less absolute than those words might suggest. To the publisher Benjamin H. Ticknor, then overseeing the typesetting of *The Prince and the Pauper,* he wrote in mid-August 1881:

> Let the printers follow my punctuation—it is the one thing I am inflexibly particular about. For corrections turning my "sprang" into "sprung" I am thankful; also for corrections of my grammar, for grammar is a science that was always too many for yours truly; but I like to have my punctuation respected. I learned it in a hundred printing-offices when I was a jour. printer; so it's got more real variety about it than any other accomplishment I possess, & I reverence it accordingly.[15]

And to Chatto and Windus in 1897 he complained about the proofreader of *More Tramps Abroad* (the English edition of *Following the Equator*):

> Conceive of this tumble-bug interesting himself in my punctuation—which is none of his business & with which he has nothing to do—& then instead of correcting misspelling, which *is* in his degraded line, striking a mark under the word & silently confessing

11. 16 Jan 1904 to Howells, MH-H, in *MTHL,* 2:778. This letter is quoted more fully in the Introduction, pp. 20–21.
12. In the ADs of 16 Feb and 23 Feb 1906.
13. 21 Aug 1889 to Howells, MH-H, in *MTHL,* 2:610.
14. *CY,* 292.
15. 16–22 Aug 1881 to Ticknor, Ticknor 1922, 140.

that he doesn't know what the hell to do with it! The damned half-developed foetus!
But this is the Sabbath Day, & I must not continue in this worldly vein.[16]

The punctuation in Clemens's manuscripts, as well as in the typescripts, is faithfully reproduced *except* where it is deemed defective—for example, in the rare instances when he omitted
a closing quotation mark or the second comma in an appositional clause. Dictated texts, in
which the punctuation is somewhat less authorial than in the manuscripts, have received a few
additional corrections, to accord with Clemens's consistent manuscript usage. The following
examples illustrate the three categories in which punctuation has been added: 1. "Mr. Twichell,
do you take me for a God damned papist?" (comma supplied); 2. "Yes," I said, "that is my position" (second comma supplied); 3. "and we said, [¶] 'That is a very good thing to do'" (comma
supplied before a paragraph break).

Uniformity

It is well established that throughout his career Clemens strove to avoid spelling, capitalizing, or abbreviating the same word in more than one way within a given work, and the extraordinary consistency of his manuscripts in this respect is itself strong testimony to that
intention. But he also knew that he required the cooperation of the typesetter to achieve and
maintain uniformity of this kind in print. In 1897 we find him complaining, again on the
proofs for *More Tramps Abroad*, that this "proof-reader doesn't even preserve uniformity."
And on the first manuscript page of "A Horse's Tale" he addressed himself to the "composing-
room," asking it to "ignore my capitalization of military titles, & apply its own laws—the which
will secure uniformity, & that is the only essential thing."[17]

To fall short of "uniformity" in this sense meant to Clemens that unintended, pointless,
and therefore potentially misleading variation in spelling, capitalization, and the rendering of
numbers and abbreviations (expanded or not) would mar the published text. Variation in these
formal elements within a single work has therefore been treated as an error and corrected in
all parts of the text, except where Clemens is quoting someone else. The preliminary manuscripts and dictations, written or dictated over a period of thirty-five years, are each made
uniform within themselves; the final text of the *Autobiography* is made uniform throughout.
In cases where the stenographer spelled or capitalized a word consistently, that form has been
retained. Where the typescripts vary, however, Clemens's preferred forms have been adopted.

16. 25 July 1897 to Chatto and Windus, ViU. The proofreader had made half a dozen changes in the punctuation (which Clemens corrected) and he had struck a line under the word "drouths" (which was exactly as Clemens
had spelled it in the manuscript). Clemens made the correction himself to "droughts" on the proof of chapter 25,
page 147, of *More Tramps Abroad* (SLC 1897b). The proof with these changes is bound with the manuscript for the
book at NN-BGC, part 2, following MS page 473.

17. In the first example the typesetter had set "FROM DIARY" instead of "From Diary" (as in the manuscript)
on the proof of page 147 of *More Tramps Abroad* (NN-BGC). There Clemens explained: "Lower-case, as always
before," referring to his consistent practice with "From Diary" earlier in the text. In the example from "A Horse's
Tale" (SLC 1906c, MS at NN-BGC), he simply realized he was incapable of capitalizing the military titles consistently
(and correctly). The typesetters did as he asked.

These have been identified through a wide-ranging search of all available manuscripts, whose results are recorded in a 125-page document in the Mark Twain Papers (1,456 entries, from "acoming" to "zig-zag") that lists every variant form in the Autobiographical Dictations, as well as the form or forms found in Clemens's handwritten additions to the typescripts and in hundreds of other manuscripts. The result is that the rendering of these details is brought into uniformity, while the form adopted is as completely authorial as the evidence permits.

Inserted documents

Into the typescripts of his dictations, Clemens frequently inserted not only his own earlier manuscripts, but also newspaper clippings, letters he had received, and other documents. His own inserted manuscripts have been treated in accord with the editorial policy already described. In the case of other texts, simple errors (typographical and otherwise) are corrected, but they are not altered to achieve uniformity of spelling, capitalization, and so forth. If we have the document that Hobby transcribed into the text, we retranscribe it as the primary source. Her transcription tells us how detailed or inclusive Clemens wanted such a text to be (in other words, what he instructed her to leave out). If the document from which she worked cannot be found, we of course rely on her transcription, correcting only manifest errors. Inserted texts can on occasion be very complex and require exceptions to these rules of thumb.[18] In all such cases the rationale for changing the readings of the source documents in any way is fully spelled out in the Textual Commentary available online for each text.

H.E.S.

18. See, for example, the Textual Commentary for AD, 11 Jan 1906 *(MTPO),* in which Clemens inserted a text of his Whittier dinner speech (1877).

WORD DIVISION IN THIS VOLUME

The following compound words that could be rendered either solid or with a hyphen are hyphenated at the end of a line in this volume. For purposes of quotation each is listed here with its correct form.

121.17–18	hall-mark
124.6–7	over-full
157.16–17	grand-daughter
193.32–33	outworks
215.25–26	grandfather
298.16–17	stage-coach
318.18–19	common-sense
321.19–20	death-bed
324.4–5	thunder-stroke
336.38–39	schoolroom
341.16–17	mantelpiece
373.39–40	common-sense
395.3–4	dining-room
398.2–3	window-panes
425.16–17	whitewashing
438.4–5	chain-mail
440.32–33	uptown
452.13–14	midnight
465.30–31	hand-shake

REFERENCES

This list defines the abbreviations used in this volume and provides full bibliographic information for works cited by an author's name and a date, a short title, or an abbreviation. Works by members of the Clemens family may be found under the writer's initials: SLC, OLC, OSC, and CC.

AD. Autobiographical Dictation.

Adams, Alton D. 1903. "New England Gas and Coke." *The Journal of Political Economy* 11 (March): 257–72.

Agassiz, Louis. 1886. *Louis Agassiz: His Life and Correspondence.* Edited by Elizabeth Cary Agassiz. Boston: Houghton, Mifflin and Co.

American Civil War.

    2009a. "Ball's Bluff, Harrison's Landing, Leesburg, Civil War, Virginia." http://american civilwar.com/statepic/va/va006.html. Accessed 2 April 2009.

    2009b. "Civil War Battle Statistics, Commanders, and Casualties." http://americancivilwar. com/cwstats.html. Accessed 28 April 2009.

AMT. 1959. *The Autobiography of Mark Twain.* Edited by Charles Neider. New York: Harper and Brothers.

Andrews, Gregg. 1996. *City of Dust: A Cement Company Town in the Land of Tom Sawyer.* Columbia: University of Missouri Press.

Andrews, Kenneth R. 1950. *Nook Farm: Mark Twain's Hartford Circle.* Cambridge: Harvard University Press.

Angel, Myron, ed. 1881. *History of Nevada.* Oakland, Calif.: Thompson and West. Index in Poulton 1966.

Annual Cyclopaedia 1883. 1884. *Appletons' Annual Cyclopaedia and Register of Important Events of the Year 1883.* Vol. 23 (n.s. vol. 8). New York: D. Appleton and Co.

Annual Cyclopaedia 1884. 1885. *Appletons' Annual Cyclopaedia and Register of Important Events of the Year 1884.* Vol. 24 (n.s. vol. 9). New York: D. Appleton and Co.

Annual Cyclopaedia 1885. 1886. *Appletons' Annual Cyclopaedia and Register of Important Events of the Year 1885.* Vol. 25 (n.s. vol. 10). New York: D. Appleton and Co.

Annual Cyclopaedia 1901. 1902. *Appletons' Annual Cyclopaedia and Register of Important Events of the Year 1901.* Vol. 41 (3d ser. vol. 6). New York: D. Appleton and Co.

"Antarctic Discoveries." 1840. *Monthly Chronicle of Events, Discoveries, Improvements and Opinions* 1 (July): 210–19.

Applegate, Debby. 2006. *The Most Famous Man in America: The Biography of Henry Ward Beecher.* New York: Doubleday.

Arlington National Cemetery. 2009. "Gordon Johnston." http://arlingtoncemetery.net/gjohnstn .htm. Accessed 27 May 2009.

Ashcroft, Ralph W. 1904. "Plasmon's Career in America: As Recounted by R. W. Ashcroft." TS in CU-MARK.

AskART.

2008a. "Barry Faulkner." http://www.askart.com/artist.aspx?artist = 21782. Accessed 30 July 2008.

2008b. "Emma Beach Thayer." http://www.askart.com/AskART/artists/biography. aspx?artist = 80017. Accessed 30 July 2008.

2008c. "Gerald Handerson Thayer." http://www.askart.com/AskART/artists/biography. aspx?artist = 19926. Accessed 29 July 2008.

2008d. "Gladys Thayer (Mrs. David) Reasoner." http://www.askart.com/AskART/artists/ biography.aspx?artist = 86887. Accessed 30 July 2008.

2008e. "Karl Gerhardt." http://www.askart.com/AskART/artists/biography.aspx?artist = 116168. Accessed 28 August 2008.

Austen, Roger. 1991. *Genteel Pagan: The Double Life of Charles Warren Stoddard.* Edited by John W. Crowley. Amherst: University of Massachusetts Press.

Austin, James C.

1953. *Fields of "The Atlantic Monthly": Letters to an Editor, 1861–1870.* San Marino, Calif.: Huntington Library.

1965. *Petroleum V. Nasby (David Ross Locke).* Twayne's United States Authors Series, edited by Sylvia E. Bowman, no. 89. New York: Twayne Publishers.

Bacevich, Andrew J. 2006. "What Happened at Bud Dajo: A Forgotten Massacre—and Its Lessons." Boston *Globe,* 12 March, C2.

Badeau, Adam.

1868–81. *Military History of Ulysses S. Grant, from April, 1861, to April, 1865.* 3 vols. New York: D. Appleton and Co.

1887. *Grant in Peace.* Hartford: S. S. Scranton and Co.

Baedeker, Karl.

1880. *The Rhine from Rotterdam to Constance. Handbook for Travellers.* 7th remodelled ed. Leipzig: Karl Baedeker.

1893. *The United States, with an Excursion into Mexico.* Leipzig: Karl Baedeker.

1903. *Italy: Handbook for Travellers. First Part: Northern Italy.* Leipzig: Karl Baedeker.

Baetzhold, Howard G. 1970. *Mark Twain and John Bull: The British Connection.* Bloomington: Indiana University Press.

Bailey, Hugh C. 2009. "Edgar Gardner Murphy." *Encyclopedia of Alabama.* http://www .encyclopediaofalabama.org/face/Article.jsp?id = h-1183. Accessed 4 September 2009.

BAL. 1955–91. *Bibliography of American Literature.* Compiled by Jacob Blanck. 9 vols. New Haven: Yale University Press.

Barnard College.

2008a. "The Making of Barnard. From Madison to Morningside." http://beatl.barnard. columbia.edu/barnard/timelines/bc1889.htm. Accessed 3 September 2008.

2008b. "Past Barnard Leaders." http://www.barnard.columbia.edu/president/search/
leaders.html. Accessed 3 September 2008.

Beecher, William C., and Rev. Samuel Scoville, assisted by Mrs. Henry Ward Beecher. 1888.
A Biography of Rev. Henry Ward Beecher. New York: Charles L. Webster and Co.

Beers, Ethel Lynn. 1861. "The Picket-Guard." *Harper's Weekly* 5 (30 November): 766.

Bell, Raymond Martin. 1984. "The Ancestry of Samuel Clemens, Grandfather of Mark Twain."
413 Burton Avenue, Washington, Pa.: Raymond Martin Bell. Mimeograph.

Bierce, Ambrose. 1868. "The Pi-Ute Indians of Nevada." *Golden Era* 16 (4 July): 2–3.

Biographical Review. 1898. *Biographical Review, Containing Life Sketches of Leading Citizens
of New London County, Connecticut.* Atlantic States Series of Biographical Reviews, Vol. 26.
Boston: Biographical Review Publishing Company.

Bishop, William Henry.

    1877–78. "Detmold: A Romance." *Atlantic Monthly* 40 (December 1877): 732–43, 41
(January–June 1878): 76–87, 189–201, 273–85, 409–20, 553–65, 697–710.

    1879. *Detmold: A Romance.* Boston: Houghton, Osgood and Co.

Bissell, Arthur H., and Thomas B. Kirby, comps. and eds. 1879. *The Postal Laws and Regulations of the United States of America, Published in Accordance with the Act of Congress Approved March 3, 1879.* Washington, D.C.: Government Printing Office.

Blackstone, William. 1765–69. *Commentaries on the Laws of England.* 4 vols. Oxford: Clar-
endon Press.

Bollet, Alfred Jay. 2005. "Military Medicine in the Spanish-American War." *Perspectives in
Biology and Medicine* 48 (Spring): 293–300.

Boone Census. 1900. *Population Schedules of the Twelfth Census of the United States, 1900. Roll
T623. Missouri: Boone County.* Photocopy in CU-MARK.

Boothby, H. E. 1919. "Up from Idolatry." *Hawaiian Almanac and Annual for 1920,* 53–78.

Boston Medical Journal. 1899. "Major-General Leonard Wood, M.D." *Boston Medical Journal*
(22 April): 973.

Bowditch, Nathaniel. 1854. *The New American Practical Navigator.* New York: E. and G. W.
Blunt.

Boyd, Andrew, and W. Harry Boyd, comps. 1872. *Boyds' Elmira and Corning Directory: Containing the Names of the Citizens, a Compendium of the Government, and Public and Private
Institutions . . . 1872–73.* Elmira, N.Y.: Andrew and W. Harry Boyd.

Bragg, Marion. 1977. *Historic Names and Places on the Lower Mississippi River.* Vicksburg,
Miss.: Mississippi River Commission.

Brainard, Wendell. [n.d.]. "Tonk." Undated clipping from the Shoshone County, Idaho *News-
Press,* photocopy in CU-MARK.

Branch, Edgar Marquess.

    1985. *Men Call Me Lucky: Mark Twain and the "Pennsylvania."* Oxford, Ohio: Friends of
the Library Society, Miami University.

    1992. "Bixby vs. Carroll: New Light on Sam Clemens's Early River Career." *Mark Twain
Journal* 30 (Fall): 2–22.

Brashear, Minnie M. 1935. "Mark Twain's Niece, Daughter of His Sister, Pamela, Taking Keen Interest in Centennial." Hannibal *Evening Courier-Post,* 6 March, 11.

Briggs, Charles A., ed. 1890. *How Shall We Revise the Westminster Confession of Faith? A Bundle of Papers.* New York: Charles Scribner's Sons.

Briggs, Emily Edson. 1906. *The Olivia Letters: Being Some History of Washington City for Forty Years as Told by the Letters of a Newspaper Correspondent.* New York: The Neale Publishing Company.

Brigidi, E. A. 1885. *La Nuova Guida di Siena.* 2d ed. Siena: E. Torrini.

British Census. 1881. *Census Returns of England and Wales, 1881. Kew, Surrey, England.* RG11/649. The National Archives of the United Kingdom: Public Records Office. PH in CU-MARK.

Broadway League. 2009. *Internet Broadway Database.* http://www.ibdb.com/production .php?id = 7246. Accessed 4 May 2009.

Brooks, Noah. 1898. "Mark Twain in California." *Century Magazine,* n.s. 57 (November): 97–99.

Brougham, John, and John Elderkin, eds. 1875. *Lotos Leaves.* Boston: William F. Gill and Co.

Brown, Alexander Crosby. 1974. *Longboat to Hawaii: An Account of the Voyage of the Clipper Ship Hornet of New York Bound for San Francisco in 1866.* Cambridge, Md.: Cornell Maritime Press.

Brown, Curtis. 1899. "Mark Twain Talks." Buffalo *Express,* 30 July, 1. Reprinted in Scharnhorst 2006, 340–45.

Brown, John.

1863a. "Pet Marjorie: A Story of Child Life Fifty Years Ago." *North British Review* 39 (November): 379–98.

1863b. *Marjorie Fleming, a Sketch. Being the Paper Entitled "Pet Marjorie: A Story of Child Life Fifty Years Ago."* Edinburgh: Edmonston and Douglas.

1907. *Letters of Dr. John Brown. With Letters from Ruskin, Thackeray, and Others.* Edited by John Brown and D. W. Forrest. With biographical introductions by Elizabeth T. McLaren. London: Adam and Charles Black.

Brown, John Taylor. 1903. *Dr. John Brown: A Biography and a Criticism.* Edited, with a Short Sketch of the Biographer, by W. B. Dunlop. London: Adam and Charles Black.

Budd, Louis J.

1962. *Mark Twain: Social Philosopher.* Bloomington: Indiana University Press.

1977. "A Listing of and Selection from Newspaper and Magazine Interviews with Samuel L. Clemens, 1874–1910." *American Literary Realism* 10 (Winter): iii–100.

1981. "Color Him Curious about Yellow Journalism: Mark Twain and the New York City Press." *Journal of Popular Culture* 15 (Fall): 25–33.

1992a. *Mark Twain: Collected Tales, Sketches, Speeches, & Essays, 1852–1890.* The Library of America. New York: Literary Classics of the United States.

1992b. *Mark Twain: Collected Tales, Sketches, Speeches, & Essays, 1891–1910.* The Library of America. New York: Literary Classics of the United States.

1999. *Mark Twain: The Contemporary Reviews.* Cambridge: Cambridge University Press.

Burke, Bernard. 1904. *A Genealogical and Heraldic Dictionary of the Peerage and Baronetage, the Privy Council, Knightage and Companionage.* Edited by Ashworth P. Burke. 66th ed. London: Harrison and Sons.

Burns, Robert. 1969. *Complete Poems and Songs.* Edited by James Kinsley. Oxford: Oxford University Press.

Burpee, Charles W. 1928. *History of Hartford County, Connecticut, 1633–1928.* 3 vols. Chicago: S. J. Clarke Publishing Company.

Burton, Nathaniel J. 1888. *Yale Lectures on Preaching, and Other Writings.* New York: Charles L. Webster and Co.

Butte Census. 1860. *Population Schedules of the Eighth Census of the United States, 1860. Roll M653. California: Butte County.* Photocopy in CU-MARK.

Byler, Charles. 2005. "Pacifying the Moros: American Military Government in the Southern Philippines, 1899–1913." *Military Review* (May–June). http://findarticles.com/p/articles/mi_mOPBZ/is_3_85/ai_n14695890. Accessed 20 April 2009.

C. California State Library, Sacramento.

Cadets of Temperance. [1850]. "The Property of Cadets of Temperance Hannibal Mo." MS of two pages containing the membership roster, MoHM.

Campbell, William Wilfred. 1891. "Love." *Century Magazine* 42 (October): 910.

Cardwell, Guy A. 1953. *Twins of Genius.* [East Lansing]: Michigan State College Press.

Case Western Reserve University. 2008. "The Euclid Ave. Baptist Church." *The Encyclopedia of Cleveland History.* http://ech.cwru.edu/ech-cgi/article.pl?id=EABC. Accessed 15 March 2008.

CC (Clara Langdon Clemens, later Gabrilowitsch and Samossoud). 1931. *My Father, Mark Twain.* New York: Harper and Brothers.

Cellini, Benvenuto. 1896. *The Life of Benvenuto Cellini.* Translated by John Addington Symonds. London: John C. Nimmo.

Chemung Census. 1900. *Population Schedules of the Twelfth Census of the United States, 1900. Roll T623. New York: Chemung County.* PH in CU-MARK.

Cheney, Howell, ed. 1954. *The List of Members of the Monday Evening Club Together with the Record of Papers Read at Their Meetings, 1869–1954.* Hartford: Privately printed.

Cheney, Mary Bushnell. 1880. *Life and Letters of Horace Bushnell.* New York: Harper and Brothers.

Child, Theodore. 1887. "Duelling in Paris." *Harper's New Monthly Magazine* 74 (March): 519–35.

Clan Menzies. 2009. "Menzies of Interest." http://www.menzies.org/history/menziesofinterest.htm. Accessed 23 February 2009.

Clemens, Clara Langdon. See CC.

Clemens, Olivia Susan [Susy]. See OSC.

Clemens, Samuel Langhorne. See SLC.

CLjC. James S. Copley Library, La Jolla, Calif.

Coe, Michael D. 1999. *Breaking the Maya Code.* Rev. ed. New York: Thames and Hudson.

CofC. 1969. *Clemens of the "Call": Mark Twain in San Francisco.* Edited by Edgar M. Branch. Berkeley and Los Angeles: University of California Press.

Connecticut Biography. 1917. *Encyclopedia of Connecticut Biography.* Compiled by Samuel Hart et al. Boston: The American Historical Society.

Connecticut Light and Power. 2008. "The Hartford Electric Light Company." http://www.cl-p .com/companyinfo/helcohistory.asp. Accessed 9 July 2008.

Connecticut State Historical Society. 2005. "Hamersley, William." http://www.chs.org/ library/msscoll.htm. Accessed 8 March 2005.

Connecticut State Library.

    2006. "Obituary Sketch of William Hamersley." *Memorials of Connecticut Judges and Attorneys as Printed in the Connecticut Reports* 120:704–6. http://www.cslib.org/memorials/ hamersleyw.htm. Accessed 9 October 2006.

    2008a. "Obituary Sketch of Henry C. Robinson." http://www.cslib.org/memorials/robin sonh.htm. Accessed 9 July 2008.

    2008b. "Wethersfield Prison Records." http://www.cslib.org/wethers.asp. Accessed 27 June 2008.

Cotton, Michelle L. 1985. *Mark Twain's Elmira, 1870–1910.* Elmira, N.Y.: Chemung County Historical Society.

Courtney, Steve. 2008. *Joseph Hopkins Twichell: The Life and Times of Mark Twain's Closest Friend.* Athens: University of Georgia Press.

Cox, J. Randolph. 2000. *The Dime Novel Companion: A Source Book.* Westport, Conn.: Greenwood Press.

Cox, James M. 1966. *Mark Twain: The Fate of Humor.* Princeton: Princeton University Press.

CSmH. Henry E. Huntington Library, Art Collections and Botanical Gardens, San Marino, Calif.

CtHMTH. Mark Twain House and Museum, Hartford, Conn.

CtHSD. Stowe-Day Memorial Library and Historical Foundation, Hartford, Conn.

CtMyMHi. G. W. Blunt White Library, Mystic Seaport Museum, Inc., Mystic, Conn.

CtY-BR. Yale University, Beinecke Rare Book and Manuscript Library, New Haven, Conn.

CU-MARK. University of California, Mark Twain Collection, Berkeley.

CY. 1979. *A Connecticut Yankee in King Arthur's Court.* Edited by Bernard L. Stein, with an introduction by Henry Nash Smith. The Works of Mark Twain. Berkeley and Los Angeles: University of California Press.

Daniels, Elizabeth. 2008. "Vassar History, 1871–1890." *History of Vassar College.* http:// historian.vassar.edu/chronology/1871_1890.html. Accessed 28 August 2008.

Davidson, Cathy N. 1988. "Ambrose Bierce." *Dictionary of Literary Biography, Volume 74: American Short-Story Writers Before 1880.* Edited by Bobby Ellen Kimbel with the assistance of William E. Grant. Detroit: Gale Research Company.

Dawson, N. E. 1902. "Ten-Year-Old Filipinos." Letter to the editor. Washington *Post,* 28 April, 10.

Debrett, John. 1980. *Debrett's Peerage and Baronetage.* Edited by Patrick Montague-Smith. London: Debrett's Peerage.

Dempsey, Terrell. 2003. *Searching for Jim: Slavery in Sam Clemens's World*. Columbia: University of Missouri Press.

Dennett, Tyler. 1933. *John Hay: From Poetry to Politics*. New York: Dodd, Mead and Co.

Department of State. 1911. *Register of the Department of State*. Washington, D.C.: U.S. Government Printing Office.

Depew, Chauncey M. 1922. *My Memories of Eighty Years*. New York: Charles Scribner's Sons.

Derby, George H. [John Phoenix, pseud.].
  1856. *Phoenixiana; or, Sketches and Burlesques*. New York: D. Appleton and Co.
  1865. *The Squibob Papers*. New York: G. W. Carleton.

DLC. United States Library of Congress, Washington, D.C.

DNDAR. Daughters of the American Revolution, National Society Library, Washington, D.C.

Dodge, Richard Irving. 1883. *Our Wild Indians: Thirty-three Years' Personal Experience among the Red Men of the Great West*. Hartford: A. D. Worthington.

Dodgson, Charles Lutwidge [Lewis Carroll, pseud.]. 1993–2007. *Lewis Carroll's Diaries: The Private Journals of Charles Lutwidge Dodgson*. With notes and annotations by Edward Wakeling. 10 vols. Clifford, Herefordshire: The Lewis Carroll Society.

Dolby, George. 1887. *Charles Dickens as I Knew Him: The Story of the Reading Tours in Great Britain and America (1866–1870)*. London: T. Fisher Unwin.

Dolmetsch, Carl. 1992. *"Our Famous Guest": Mark Twain in Vienna*. Athens: University of Georgia Press.

Driscoll, Kerry. 2005. "'How Much Higher and Finer Is the Indian God': Mark Twain and Native American Religion." TS in CU-MARK.

Dunham, Isaac Watson, comp. 1907. *Dunham Genealogy: English and American Branches of the Dunham Family*. Norwich, Conn.: Bulletin Print.

Eddy, Richard. 1887. *Alcohol in History: An Account of Intemperance in All Ages*. New York: National Temperance Society and Publication House.

Edgar, Neal L. 1986. "James R. Osgood and Company (Boston: 1871–1878; 1880–1885); Houghton, Osgood and Company (Boston: 1878–1880); Ticknor and Company (Boston: 1885–1889)." *Dictionary of Literary Biography, Volume 49: American Literary Publishing Houses, 1638–1899. Part 2: N–Z*. Edited by Peter Dzwonkoski. Detroit: Gale Research Company.

Ellis, W. T. 1939. *Memories: My Seventy-two Years in the Romantic County of Yuba, California*. Eugene: University of Oregon.

Ellsberry, Elizabeth Prather, comp.
  1965a. "Will Records of Marion County, Missouri, 1853–1887." Box 206, Chillicothe, Mo.: Elizabeth Ellsberry. Mimeograph.
  1965b. "Will Records of Ralls County, Missouri." 2 vols. Box 206, Chillicothe, Mo.: Elizabeth Ellsberry. Mimeograph.

ET&S1. 1979. *Early Tales & Sketches, Volume 1 (1851–1864)*. Edited by Edgar Marquess Branch and Robert H. Hirst, with the assistance of Harriet Elinor Smith. The Works of Mark Twain. Berkeley and Los Angeles: University of California Press.

ET&S2. 1981. *Early Tales & Sketches, Volume 2 (1864–1865)*. Edited by Edgar Marquess

Branch and Robert H. Hirst, with the assistance of Harriet Elinor Smith. The Works of Mark Twain. Berkeley and Los Angeles: University of California Press.

Eubank, Marjorie Harrell. 1969. "The Redpath Lyceum Bureau from 1868 to 1901." Ph.D. diss., University of Michigan, Ann Arbor.

Farnie, Henry Brougham. 1858. *Pet Marjorie: A Story of Child Life Fifty Years Ago*. Edinburgh, n.p.

Fatout, Paul.

    1960. *Mark Twain on the Lecture Circuit*. Bloomington: Indiana University Press.

    1976. *Mark Twain Speaking*. Iowa City: University of Iowa Press.

Fentress County Deeds. 1820–48. *Fentress County Register of Deeds, Vols. A–D, November 1820 to October 1848. Roll 7*. Tennessee State Library and Archives, Nashville, Tennessee.

Fentress County Land Grants. 1841–45. *Mountain District Land Grants. Roll 144*. Tennessee State Library and Archives, Nashville, Tennessee.

Ferguson, Henry. 1866. "Journal of Henry Ferguson." MS in CtY-BR. Published in Ferguson and Ferguson 1924 and in Alexander Crosby Brown 1974.

Ferguson, Henry, and Samuel Ferguson. 1924. *The Journal of Henry Ferguson, January to August 1866*. Hartford: Privately printed by the Case, Lockwood and Brainard Co.

Ferguson, Samuel. 1866. "Journal of Samuel Ferguson." MS in CtMyMHi. Published in Ferguson and Ferguson 1924 and in Alexander Crosby Brown 1974.

Field, Kate.

    1868. *Pen Photographs of Charles Dickens's Readings*. Boston: Loring.

    1996. *Kate Field: Selected Letters*. Edited by Carolyn J. Moss. Carbondale: Southern Illinois University Press.

Fielder, Elizabeth Davis. 1899. "Familiar Haunts of Mark Twain." *Harper's Weekly* 43 (16 December): 10–11.

Fischer, Victor. 1983. "*Huck Finn* Reviewed: The Reception of *Huckleberry Finn* in the United States, 1885–1897." *American Literary Realism* 16 (Spring): 1–57.

Fleming, Marjory. 1935. *The Complete Marjory Fleming: Her Journals, Letters and Verses*. Transcribed and edited by Frank Sidgwick. New York: Oxford University Press.

Fort Leonard Wood. 2009. "Major General Leonard Wood." http://www.wood.army.mil/MGLeonardwood.htm. Accessed 17 April 2009.

Fotheringham, H. 1859. *Hannibal City Directory, for 1859–60*. Hannibal, Mo.: H. Fotheringham.

Fox, William F. 1889. *Regimental Losses in the American Civil War, 1861–1865*. Albany, N.Y.: Albany Publishing Company. Chapter 5, "Casualties Compared with Those of Foreign Wars," at http://www.civilwarhome.com/foxs.htm. Accessed 27 April 2009.

Fulton, Joe B.

    2005. "The Lost Manuscript Conclusion to Mark Twain's 'Corn-Pone Opinions': An Editorial History and an Edition of the Restored Text." *American Literary Realism* 37 (Spring): 238–58.

    2006. *The Reverend Mark Twain: Theological Burlesque, Form, and Content*. Columbus: Ohio State University Press.

Gale, Robert L. 1978. *John Hay.* Twayne's United States Authors Series, edited by Sylvia E. Bowman, no. 296. Boston: Twayne Publishers.

Geer, Elihu, comp.

1882. *Geer's Hartford City Directory and Hartford Illustrated; for the Year Commencing July 1st, 1882: Containing a New Map of the City; New Street Guide; General Directory of Citizens, Corporations, Etc.* Hartford: Elihu Geer.

1886. *Geer's Hartford City Directory; July 1, 1886: Being a Fifteen-Fold Directory of Hartford.* Hartford: Elihu Geer.

GEU. Emory University, Atlanta, Ga.

Gilder, Richard Watson. 1910. *Grover Cleveland: A Record of Friendship.* New York: The Century Company.

Gilder, Rosamond. 1916. *Letters of Richard Watson Gilder.* Boston: Houghton Mifflin Company.

"Glossary of Steamboat Terms." 2008. http://www.steamboats.org/history-education/glossary .html. Accessed 10 July 2008.

Goldhurst, Richard. 1975. *Many Are the Hearts: The Agony and the Triumph of Ulysses S. Grant.* New York: Reader's Digest Press.

Goodman, Joseph T.

1897. *The Archaic Maya Inscriptions.* London: Taylor and Francis.

1898. *The Maya Graphic System: Reasons for Believing It to Be Nothing but a Cipher Code.* London: Taylor and Francis.

1905. "Maya Dates." *American Anthropologist,* n.s. 7 (October–December): 642–47.

Grant, Julia Dent. 1975. *The Personal Memoirs of Julia Dent Grant (Mrs. Ulysses S. Grant).* Edited by John Y. Simon. New York: G. P. Putnam's Sons.

Grant, Ulysses S.

1885a. "The Battle of Shiloh." *Century Magazine* 29 (February): 593–614.

1885b. "The Siege of Vicksburg." *Century Magazine* 30 (September): 752–67.

1885c. "Personal Memoirs of U. S. Grant: Chattanooga." *Century Magazine* 31 (November): 128–46.

1885–86. *Personal Memoirs of U. S. Grant.* 2 vols. New York: Charles L. Webster and Co.

1886. "Personal Memoirs of U. S. Grant: Preparing for the Wilderness Campaign." *Century Magazine* 31 (February): 573–82.

Gregory, Ralph. 1976. "Joseph P. Ament—Master-Printer to Sam Clemens." *Mark Twain Journal* 18 (Summer): 1–4.

Gribben, Alan. 1980. *Mark Twain's Library: A Reconstruction.* 2 vols. Boston: G. K. Hall and Co.

Gudde, Erwin G. 1962. *California Place Names: The Origin and Etymology of Current Geographical Names.* 2d ed., rev. and enl. Berkeley and Los Angeles: University of California Press.

Hagood, J. Hurley, and Roberta Hagood. 1985. *A List of Deaths in Hannibal, Missouri, 1880–1910, from City of Hannibal Records. Also a Partial List of Burials from Other Years in the Old Baptist Cemetery and Other Miscellaneous Related Materials.* Mimeograph.

Hallock, W.S. 1877. *Hallock's Hannibal Directory for 1877–78.* Hannibal, Mo.: W.S. Hallock.

Halstead, Murat. 1897. *The Story of Cuba: Her Struggles for Liberty . . . The Cause, Crisis and Destiny of the Pearl of the Antilles.* Akron, Ohio: The Werner Company.

Harlow, Barbara, and Mia Carter. 1999. *Imperialism and Orientalism: A Documentary Sourcebook.* Malden, Mass.: Blackwell Publishers.

Harris, Joel Chandler. 1880. *Uncle Remus: His Songs and Sayings.* New York: D. Appleton and Co.

Harris, Julia Collier. 1918. *The Life and Letters of Joel Chandler Harris.* Boston and New York: Houghton Mifflin Company.

Harrison, John M. 1969. *The Man Who Made Nasby, David Ross Locke.* Chapel Hill: University of North Carolina Press.

Harrison, Lynde. 1890. "The Connecticut Secret Ballot Law." *New Englander and Yale Review* 242 (May): 401–9.

Hart, James D. 1987. *A Companion to California.* Rev. ed. Berkeley and Los Angeles: University of California Press.

Hartford Census.

    1880. *Population Schedules of the Tenth Census of the United States, 1880. Roll T9. Connecticut: Hartford County.* Photocopy in CU-MARK.

    1900. *Population Schedules of the Twelfth Census of the United States, 1900. Roll T623. Connecticut: Hartford County.* Photocopy in CU-MARK.

    1910. *Population Schedules of the Thirteenth Census of the United States, 1910. Roll T624. Connecticut: Hartford County.* Photocopy in CU-MARK.

Hartford Club. 2009. "The Hartford Club: The Heart of Hartford Since 1873." http://www.hartfordclub.com/fw/main/Club-History-19.html. Accessed 14 May 2009.

"Hartford Residents." 1974. Unpublished TS by anonymous compiler, CtHSD.

Hartford Seminary Record. 1910. *The Hartford Seminary Record. Issued under the Auspices of the Faculty of Hartford Theological Seminary.* Vol. 20. Hartford: Hartford Seminary Press.

Harvey, George. 1906. "The Editor's Diary." *North American Review* 183 (7 September): 433–48.

Hawthorne, Julian.

    1876. *Saxon Studies.* London: Strahan and Co.

    1885. *Nathaniel Hawthorne and His Wife: A Biography.* 2 vols. Boston: James R. Osgood and Co.

HC. Henry Clemens.

Heitman, Francis B. 1903. *Historical Register and Dictionary of the United States Army, from Its Organization, September 29, 1789, to March 2, 1903.* 2 vols. Washington, D.C.: Government Printing Office.

Herndon, William Lewis, and Lardner Gibbon. 1853–54. *Exploration of the Valley of the Amazon, Made under Direction of the Navy Department.* 2 vols. Washington, D.C.: Robert Armstrong.

HF 2003. 2003. *Adventures of Huckleberry Finn.* Edited by Victor Fischer and Lin Salamo, with the late Walter Blair. The Works of Mark Twain. Berkeley and Los Angeles: University of California Press. Also online at *MTPO*.

HH&T. 1969. *Mark Twain's Hannibal, Huck & Tom.* Edited by Walter Blair. The Mark Twain Papers. Berkeley and Los Angeles: University of California Press.

HHR. 1969. *Mark Twain's Correspondence with Henry Huttleston Rogers.* Edited by Lewis Leary. The Mark Twain Papers. Berkeley and Los Angeles: University of California Press.

Hibbert, Christopher. 2001. *Queen Victoria: A Personal History.* New York: Da Capo Press.

Hill, Hamlin. 1964. *Mark Twain and Elisha Bliss.* Columbia: University of Missouri Press.

Holcombe, Return I. 1884. *History of Marion County, Missouri.* St. Louis: E. F. Perkins. [Citations are to the 1979 reprint edition, Hannibal: Marion County Historical Society.]

Holmes, Oliver Wendell. 1862. *The Poems of Oliver Wendell Holmes.* Boston: Ticknor and Fields.

Home of the American Civil War. 2009. "The Price in Blood! Casualties in the Civil War." http://www.civilwarhome.com/casualties.htm. Accessed 28 September 2009.

Honeyman, Samuel H., comp. 1866. *Hannibal City Directory for 1866.* Hannibal, Mo.: Winchell, Ebert and Marsh.

Hood, Tom, ed.

    1872. *Tom Hood's Comic Annual for 1873.* With Twenty-three Pages of Illustrations by the Brothers Dalziel. London: Published at the Fun Office.

    1873. *Tom Hood's Comic Annual for 1874.* With Twenty-three Pages of Illustrations by the Brothers Dalziel. London: Published at the Fun Office.

Hornberger, Theodore. 1941. *Mark Twain's Letters to Will Bowen.* Austin: University of Texas.

Horner, Charles F. 1926. *The Life of James Redpath and the Development of the Modern Lyceum.* New York: Barse and Hopkins.

Horowitz, Johannes. 1898. "What Vienna Talks About." New York *Times,* 3 April, 7.

Horr, Elizabeth. 1840. MS of one page, a school certificate commending "Miss Pamelia Clemens," 27 November, CU-MARK. Published in *MTB,* 1:39.

Hotten, John Camden, ed. 1872. *Practical Jokes with Artemus Ward, Including the Story of the Man Who Fought Cats.* London: John Camden Hotten. [Includes several pieces erroneously attributed to Clemens.]

House, Edward H.

    1881. *Japanese Episodes.* Boston: James R. Osgood and Co.

    1888. *Yone Santo: A Child of Japan.* Chicago: Belford, Clarke and Co.

Houston, Edwin J. 1898. *A Dictionary of Electrical Words, Terms and Phrases.* 4th ed. New York: The W. J. Johnston Company.

Howden, Mary Louise. 1925. "Mark Twain as His Secretary at Stormfield Remembers Him." New York *Herald,* 13 December, section 7: 1–4. Available at http://www.twainquotes.com/howden.html.

Howe, M. A. DeWolfe. 1922. *Memories of a Hostess: A Chronicle of Eminent Friendships Drawn Chiefly from the Diaries of Mrs. James T. Fields.* Boston: Atlantic Monthly Press.

Howells, William Dean.

    1869. "Reviews and Literary Notices." *Atlantic Monthly* 24 (December): 764–66.

    1872. *Their Wedding Journey.* Boston: James R. Osgood and Co.

    1874a. "Ralph Keeler." *Atlantic Monthly* 33 (March): 366–67.

    1874b. "Recent Literature." *Atlantic Monthly* 33 (March): 368–76.

    1885. *The Rise of Silas Lapham.* Boston: Ticknor and Co.

    1886. *Tuscan Cities.* Boston: Ticknor and Co.

    1890. *A Hazard of New Fortunes.* 2 vols. New York: Harper and Brothers.

    1891. "Editor's Study." *Harper's New Monthly Magazine* 82 (February): 478–83.

    1900. *Literary Friends and Acquaintance: A Personal Retrospect of American Authorship.* New York: Harper and Brothers.

    1910. *My Mark Twain: Reminiscences and Criticisms.* New York: Harper and Brothers.

    1979. *W. D. Howells, Selected Letters, Volume 2: 1873–1881.* Edited and annotated by George Arms and Christoph K. Lohmann. Textual editors Christoph K. Lohmann and Jerry Herron. Boston: Twayne Publishers.

    1980. *W. D. Howells, Selected Letters, Volume 3: 1882–1891.* Edited and annotated by Robert C. Leitz III, with Richard H. Ballinger and Christoph K. Lohmann. Textual editor Christoph K. Lohmann. Boston: Twayne Publishers.

Hoxie, Charles DeForest. 1910. *Civics for New York State.* New ed. New York: American Book Company.

Hutchinson, Joseph. 1910. "Two Opinions of Twain." San Francisco *Morning Call,* 24 April, 36.

Hutton, Laurence. 1909. *Talks in a Library with Laurence Hutton, Recorded by Isabel Moore.* New York: G. P. Putnam's Sons.

IaDmE. Iowa State Education Association, Des Moines.

Inds. 1989. *Huck Finn and Tom Sawyer among the Indians, and Other Unfinished Stories.* Foreword and notes by Dahlia Armon and Walter Blair. The Mark Twain Library. Berkeley and Los Angeles: University of California Press. Also online at *MTPO.*

Ingersoll, Lurton Dunham. 1866. *Iowa and the Rebellion.* Philadelphia: J. B. Lippincott and Co.

InU-Li. Indiana University Lilly Rare Books, Bloomington.

Irvine, Leigh H. 1900. "The Lone Cruise of the 'Hornet' Men." *Wide World Magazine* 5 (September): 571–77.

James, George Wharton. 1911. "Charles Warren Stoddard." *National Magazine* 34 (August): 659–72.

JC. Jean Lampton Clemens.

Jefferson Census. 1900. *Population Schedules of the Twelfth Census of the United States, 1900. Roll T623. Kentucky: Jefferson County.* Photocopy in CU-MARK.

JLC. Jane Lampton Clemens.

"John Menzies plc." 2009. http://www.fundinguniverse.com/company-histories/John-Men zies-plc-Company-History.html. Accessed 23 February 2009.

Johnson, Merle. 1935. *A Bibliography of the Works of Mark Twain, Samuel Langhorne Clemens.* 2d ed., rev. and enl. New York: Harper and Brothers.

Johnson, Robert U. 1923. *Remembered Yesterdays.* Boston: Little, Brown and Co.

Johnson, Robert U., and C. C. Clough Buel, eds. 1887–88. *Battles and Leaders of the Civil War.* 4 vols. New York: The Century Company.

Joshi, S. T., and David E. Schultz. 1999. *Ambrose Bierce: An Annotated Bibliography of Primary Sources.* Westport, Conn.: Greenwood Press.

Keeler, Ralph.

    1869a. *Gloverson and His Silent Partners.* Boston: Lee and Shepard.

    1869b. "Three Years as a Negro Minstrel." *Atlantic Monthly* 24 (July): 7–86.

    1870a. "The Tour of Europe for $181 in Currency." *Atlantic Monthly* 26 (July): 92–105.

    1870b. *Vagabond Adventures.* Boston: Fields, Osgood and Co.

    1874. "Owen Brown's Escape from Harper's Ferry." *Atlantic Monthly* 33 (March): 342–65.

Keith, Clayton. 1914. *Sketch of the Lampton Family in America, 1740–1914.* N.p.

Keller, Helen.

    1913. *Out of the Dark: Essays, Letters, and Addresses on Physical and Social Vision.* Garden City, N.Y.: Doubleday, Page and Co.

    1929. *Midstream: My Later Life.* Garden City, N.Y.: Doubleday, Doran and Co.

    2003. *The Story of My Life.* Edited by Roger Shattuck and Dorothy Herrmann. New York: W. W. Norton and Co.

Kelly, J. Wells, comp. 1863. *Second Directory of Nevada Territory.* San Francisco: Valentine and Co.

Kho, Madge. 2009. "The Bates Treaty." http://www.philippineupdate.com/Bates.htm. Accessed 20 April 2009.

Kielbowicz, Richard B. 1989. *News in the Mail: The Press, Post Office, and Public Information, 1700–1860s.* New York: Greenwood Press.

King, Grace. 1932. *Memories of a Southern Woman of Letters.* New York: Macmillan.

King, Joseph L. 1910. *History of the San Francisco Stock and Exchange Board.* San Francisco: Jos. L. King.

King, Moses. 1893. *King's Handbook of New York City: An Outline History and Description of the American Metropolis.* 2d ed. Boston: Moses King.

Krauth, Leland. 1999. *Proper Mark Twain.* Athens: University of Georgia Press.

L1. 1988. *Mark Twain's Letters, Volume 1: 1853–1866.* Edited by Edgar Marquess Branch, Michael B. Frank, and Kenneth M. Sanderson. The Mark Twain Papers. Berkeley and Los Angeles: University of California Press. Also online at *MTPO.*

L2. 1990. *Mark Twain's Letters, Volume 2: 1867–1868.* Edited by Harriet Elinor Smith, Richard Bucci, and Lin Salamo. The Mark Twain Papers. Berkeley and Los Angeles: University of California Press. Also online at *MTPO.*

L3. 1992. *Mark Twain's Letters, Volume 3: 1869.* Edited by Victor Fischer, Michael B. Frank, and Dahlia Armon. The Mark Twain Papers. Berkeley and Los Angeles: University of California Press. Also online at *MTPO.*

L4. 1995. *Mark Twain's Letters, Volume 4: 1870–1871.* Edited by Victor Fischer, Michael B. Frank, and Lin Salamo. The Mark Twain Papers. Berkeley and Los Angeles: University of California Press. Also online at *MTPO.*

L5. 1997. *Mark Twain's Letters, Volume 5: 1872–1873.* Edited by Lin Salamo and Harriet Elinor Smith. The Mark Twain Papers. Berkeley and Los Angeles: University of California Press. Also online at *MTPO.*

L6. 2002. *Mark Twain's Letters, Volume 6: 1874–1875.* Edited by Michael B. Frank and Harriet Elinor Smith. The Mark Twain Papers. Berkeley and Los Angeles: University of California Press. Also online at *MTPO.*

Letters 1876–1880. 2007. *Mark Twain's Letters, 1876–1880.* Edited by Victor Fischer, Michael B. Frank, and Harriet Elinor Smith, with Sharon K. Goetz, Benjamin Griffin, and Leslie Myrick. *Mark Twain Project Online.* Berkeley and Los Angeles: University of California Press. [To locate a letter text from its citation, select the Letters link at http://www.mark twainproject.org, then use the "Date Written" links in the left-hand column.]

Lampton, Lucius Marion. 1990. *The Genealogy of Mark Twain.* Jackson, Miss.: Diamond L. Publishing.

Lanier, Henry Wysham, ed. 1938. *The Players' Book: A Half-Century of Fact, Feeling, Fun and Folklore.* New York: The Players.

Lawson, Thomas W. 1905. *Frenzied Finance: The Crime of Amalgamated.* New York: Ridgway-Thayer Company.

Leary, Lewis, ed. 1961. *Mark Twain's Letters to Mary.* New York: Columbia University Press.

Lee, Judith Yaross. 1987. "Anatomy of a Fascinating Failure." *Invention and Technology* 3 (Summer): 55–60.

Legros, Lucien Alphonse, and John Cameron Grant. 1916. *Typographical Printing-Surfaces: The Technology and Mechanism of Their Production.* London: Longmans, Green and Co.

Lewis, Alfred Henry. 1901. *Richard Croker.* New York: Life Publishing Company.

Lewis, Oscar.

1947. *Silver Kings: The Lives and Times of Mackay, Fair, Flood, and O'Brien, Lords of the Nevada Comstock Lode.* Ashland, Ore.: Lewis Osborne.

1971. *The Life and Times of the Virginia City "Territorial Enterprise": Being Reminiscences of Five Distinguished Comstock Journalists.* Ashland, Ore.: Lewis Osborne.

Library of Congress.

2008. "When Johnny comes marching home again." http://lcweb2.loc.gov/diglib/ihas/loc .natlib.ihas.200000024/default.html. Accessed 8 April 2008.

2009. "The World of 1898: The Spanish-American War." http://www.loc.gov/rr/hispanic/ 1898/intro.html. Accessed 29 April 2009.

Lincoln, Abraham. 1894. *Abraham Lincoln: Complete Works, Comprising His Speeches, Letters, State Papers, and Miscellaneous Writings.* Edited by John G. Nicolay and John Hay. 2 vols. New York: The Century Company.

LLMT. 1949. *The Love Letters of Mark Twain.* Edited by Dixon Wecter. New York: Harper and Brothers.

Lloyd, B. E. 1876. *Lights and Shades in San Francisco.* San Francisco: A. L. Bancroft and Co.

Logan, Guy E. 2009. "Historical Sketch: Second Regiment Iowa Volunteer Infantry." Volume 1 of *Roster and Record of Iowa Troops in the Rebellion.* 6 vols. In "Iowa in the Civil War Project." http://iagenweb.org/civilwar/books/logan/mil302.htm. Accessed 19 March 2009.

Logan, Olive. 1870. *Before the Footlights and Behind the Scenes.* Philadelphia: Parmelee and Co.

Longfellow Memorial Association. 1882. "Longfellow Memorial Association. [Circular.]" *Literary World* 13 (20 May): 160.

Lorch, Fred W.

    1940. "A Note on Tom Blankenship (Huckleberry Finn)." *American Literature* 12 (November): 351–53.

    1968. *The Trouble Begins at Eight: Mark Twain's Lecture Tours.* Ames: Iowa State University Press.

Lord, Eliot. 1883. *Comstock Mining and Miners.* Washington, D.C.: U.S. Government Printing Office. [Citations are to the 1959 reprint edition, introduction by David F. Myrick, Berkeley: Howell-North.]

Love, Robertus. 1902. "Mark Twain Takes a Drive with His Schoolmate's Pretty Daughter." St. Louis *Post-Dispatch,* 2 June, 5.

Lyceum.

    1870. *The Lyceum: Containing a Complete List of Lecturers, Readers, and Musicians for the Season of 1870–71.* Boston: Redpath and Fall.

    1871. *The Lyceum Magazine: Edited by the Boston Lyceum Bureau, and Containing Its Third Annual List. For the Season of 1871–1872.* Boston: Redpath and Fall.

    1883. *The Redpath Lyceum Magazine. An Annual Publication Issued by the Redpath Lyceum Bureau, Sole Agents for the Principal Lecturers, Readers and Musical Celebrities of the Country. Season of 1883–84. Fifteenth Year.* Boston and Chicago: [Redpath's Lyceum Bureau].

Lynch, Denis Tilden. 1932. *Grover Cleveland: A Man Four-Square.* New York: Horace Liveright.

Lyon, Isabel V.

    1903–6. Journal of seventy-four pages, with entries dated 7 November 1903 to 14 January 1906, CU-MARK.

    1905. Diary in *The Standard Daily Reminder: 1905.* MS notebook of 368 pages, CU-MARK.

    1906. Diary in *The Standard Daily Reminder: 1906.* MS notebook of 368 pages, CU-MARK.

    1907. Diary in *Date Book for 1907.* MS notebook of 368 pages, CU-MARK.

Lystra, Karen. 2004. *Dangerous Intimacy: The Untold Story of Mark Twain's Final Years.* Berkeley and Los Angeles: University of California Press.

Macpherson, John, ed. 1881. *The Westminster Confession of Faith.* Edinburgh: T. and T. Clark.

Manley, R. M.

    1897. "The Criticism of Mr. Savage." New York *Times,* 25 December, 6.

    1903. [Hilary Trent, pseud.] *Mr. Claghorn's Daughter.* New York: J. S. Ogilvie Publishing Company.

Marchman, Watt P. 1957. "David Ross Locke ('Petroleum V. Nasby.')" *Museum Echoes* 30 (May): 35–38.

Marion Census.

1850. *Population Schedules of the Seventh Census of the United States, 1850. Roll 406. Missouri: Marion, Mercer, Miller, and Mississippi Counties.* National Archives Microfilm Publications, Microcopy no. 432. Washington, D.C.: General Services Administration.

1860. *Population Schedules of the Eighth Census of the United States, 1860. Roll 632. Missouri: Maries and Marion Counties.* National Archives Microfilm Publications, Microcopy no. 653. Washington, D.C.: General Services Administration.

1870. *Population Schedules of the Ninth Census of the United States, 1870. Roll M593. Missouri: Marion County.* Photocopy in CU-MARK.

Marion Veterans Census. 1890. "Special Schedule. Surviving Soldiers, Sailors, and Marines, and Widows, etc." *Special Schedules of the Eleventh Census Enumerating Union Veterans and Widows of Union Veterans of the Civil War. Roll 31. Missouri: Marion County.* Photocopy in CU-MARK.

Marsh, Andrew J., Samuel L. Clemens, and Amos Bowman. 1972. *Reports of the 1863 Constitutional Convention of the Territory of Nevada.* Edited by William C. Miller, Eleanore Bushnell, Russell W. McDonald, and Ann Rollins. Reno: Legislative Counsel Bureau, State of Nevada.

Massachusetts Historical Society. 2008. "Twentieth Century Association Records, 1894–1964." http://www.masshist.org/findingaids/doc.cfm?fa = fa0022. Accessed 9 April 2008.

Mathews, Mitford M., ed. 1951. *A Dictionary of Americanisms on Historical Principles.* 2 vols. Chicago: University of Chicago Press.

Matthews, Brander.

1917. *These Many Years: Recollections of a New Yorker.* New York: Charles Scribner's Sons.

1922. "Memories of Mark Twain." In *The Tocsin of Revolt and Other Essays,* 253–94. New York: Charles Scribner's Sons.

Maudslay, Alfred P., and Joseph T. Goodman. 1899–1902. *Archaeology.* 6 vols. London: R. H. Porter and Dulau and Co.

MB. Boston Public Library and Eastern Massachusetts Regional Public Library System, Boston.

McClellan, George B. 1887. *McClellan's Own Story.* Edited by William C. Prime. New York: Charles L. Webster and Co.

McFeely, William S. 1981. *Grant: A Biography.* New York: W. W. Norton and Co.

McLaren, Elizabeth T. 1889. *Dr. John Brown and His Sister Isabella: Outlines.* Edinburgh: David Douglas.

McNulty, John Bard. 1964. *Older than the Nation: The Story of the Hartford Courant.* Stonington, Conn.: Pequot Press.

MEC. Mary E. (Mollie) Clemens.

Meltzer, Milton. 1960. *Mark Twain Himself.* New York: Thomas Y. Crowell Company.

MFai. Millicent Library, Fairhaven, Mass.

MH-H. Harvard University, Houghton Library, Cambridge, Mass.

MHi. Massachusetts Historical Society, Boston.

Missouri Digital Heritage.

    2009a. "Missouri Birth and Death Records Database, pre-1910" and "Missouri Death Certificates 1910–1958." Missouri State Archives. http://www.sos.mo.gov/archives/resources/birthdeath. Accessed 4 March 2009.

    2009b. "Soldiers' Records: War of 1812–World War I." Missouri State Archives. http://www.sos.mo.gov/archives/soldiers. Accessed 13 February 2009.

"Missouri Marriage Records, 1805–2002." 2009. http://www.ancestry.com/search/locality/dbpage.aspx?tp = 2&p = 28. Accessed 5 March 2009.

Mitchell, Josiah A.

    1866. "Diary of Capt. J. A. Mitchell of the Ship *Hornet* for the Year 1866." MS in C. Published in Mitchell 1927 and in Alexander Crosby Brown 1974.

    1927. *The Diary of Captain Josiah A. Mitchell, 1866.* Hartford: Privately printed by the Case, Lockwood and Brainard Company.

MiU-H. University of Michigan, Michigan Historical Collection, Ann Arbor.

MnHi. Minnesota Historical Society, St. Paul.

MoCoJ. Western Historical Manuscript Collection, Columbia, Mo.

Moffett, Samuel E.

    1899. "Mark Twain: A Biographical Sketch." *McClure's Magazine* 13 (October): 523–29. Reprinted with revisions in SLC 1900a, 314–33.

    1907. *The Americanization of Canada.* Ph.D. diss., Columbia University. N.p.

MoHM. Mark Twain Museum, Hannibal, Mo.

Monk, John. 2003. "Bitter S.C. Feud Led to 1903 'Crime of the Century.'" http://www.latinamericanstudies.org/gonzales/ng-murder.htm. Accessed 18 September 2008. Reprinted from Columbia (South Carolina) *State,* 12 January 2003.

MoPlS. School of the Ozarks, Point Lookout, Mo.

MoSW. Washington University, St. Louis, Mo.

Mott, Frank Luther.

    1938. *A History of American Magazines, 1850–1865.* Cambridge: Harvard University Press.

    1957. *A History of American Magazines, 1865–1885.* 2d printing [1st printing, 1938]. Cambridge: Belknap Press of Harvard University Press.

MS. Manuscript.

MSM. 1969. *Mark Twain's Mysterious Stranger Manuscripts.* Edited by William M. Gibson. The Mark Twain Papers. Berkeley and Los Angeles: University of California Press.

MTA. 1924. *Mark Twain's Autobiography.* Edited by Albert Bigelow Paine. 2 vols. New York: Harper and Brothers.

MTB. 1912. *Mark Twain: A Biography.* Edited by Albert Bigelow Paine. 3 vols. New York: Harper and Brothers. [Volume numbers in citations are to this edition; page numbers are the same in all editions.]

MTBus. 1946. *Mark Twain, Business Man.* Edited by Samuel Charles Webster. Boston: Little, Brown and Co.

MTE. 1940. *Mark Twain in Eruption.* Edited by Bernard DeVoto. New York: Harper and Brothers.

MTEnt. 1957. *Mark Twain of the "Enterprise."* Edited by Henry Nash Smith, with the assistance of Frederick Anderson. Berkeley and Los Angeles: University of California Press.

MTH. 1947. *Mark Twain and Hawaii.* By Walter Francis Frear. Chicago: Lakeside Press.

MTHL. 1960. *Mark Twain–Howells Letters.* Edited by Henry Nash Smith and William M. Gibson, with the assistance of Frederick Anderson. 2 vols. Cambridge: Belknap Press of Harvard University Press.

MTL. 1917. *Mark Twain's Letters.* Edited by Albert Bigelow Paine. 2 vols. New York: Harper and Brothers.

MTLP. 1967. *Mark Twain's Letters to His Publishers, 1867–1894.* Edited by Hamlin Hill. The Mark Twain Papers. Berkeley and Los Angeles: University of California Press.

MTMF. 1949. *Mark Twain to Mrs. Fairbanks.* Edited by Dixon Wecter. San Marino, Calif.: Huntington Library.

MTN. 1935. *Mark Twain's Notebook.* Edited by Albert Bigelow Paine. New York: Harper and Brothers.

MTPO. *Mark Twain Project Online.* Edited by the Mark Twain Project. Berkeley and Los Angeles: University of California Press. [Launched 1 November 2007.] http://www.mark twainproject.org.

MTS 1910. 1910. *Mark Twain's Speeches.* Edited by Albert Bigelow Paine. New York: Harper and Brothers.

MTS 1923. 1923. *Mark Twain's Speeches.* Edited by Albert Bigelow Paine. New York: Harper and Brothers.

MTTB. 1940. *Mark Twain's Travels with Mr. Brown.* Edited by Franklin Walker and G. Ezra Dane. New York: Alfred A. Knopf.

Murphy, Edgar Gardner. 1904. *Problems of the Present South.* New York: Macmillan.

Myers, Gustavus. 1901. *The History of Tammany Hall.* New York: The author. [Second edition published in 1917 by Boni and Liveright.]

N&J1. 1975. *Mark Twain's Notebooks & Journals, Volume 1 (1855–1873).* Edited by Frederick Anderson, Michael B. Frank, and Kenneth M. Sanderson. The Mark Twain Papers. Berkeley and Los Angeles: University of California Press.

N&J2. 1975. *Mark Twain's Notebooks & Journals, Volume 2 (1877–1883).* Edited by Frederick Anderson, Lin Salamo, and Bernard Stein. The Mark Twain Papers. Berkeley and Los Angeles: University of California Press.

N&J3. 1979. *Mark Twain's Notebooks & Journals, Volume 3 (1883–1891).* Edited by Robert Pack Browning, Michael B. Frank, and Lin Salamo. The Mark Twain Papers. Berkeley and Los Angeles: University of California Press.

NAR 1. 1906. "Chapters from My Autobiography.—I. By Mark Twain." *North American Review* 183 (7 September): 321–30. Galley proofs of the "Introduction" only (NAR 1pf) at ViU.

NAR 2. 1906. "Chapters from My Autobiography.—II. By Mark Twain." *North American Review* 183 (21 September): 449–60. Galley proofs (NAR 2pf) at ViU.

NAR 3. 1906. "Chapters from My Autobiography.—III. By Mark Twain." *North American Review* 183 (5 October): 577–89. Galley proofs (NAR 3pf) at ViU.

NAR 4. 1906. "Chapters from My Autobiography.—IV. By Mark Twain." *North American Review* 183 (19 October): 705–16. Galley proofs (NAR 4pf) at ViU.

NAR 5. 1906. "Chapters from My Autobiography.—V. By Mark Twain." *North American Review* 183 (2 November): 833–44. Galley proofs (NAR 5pf) at ViU.

NAR 6. 1906. "Chapters from My Autobiography.—VI. By Mark Twain." *North American Review* 183 (16 November): 961–70. Galley proofs (NAR 6pf) at ViU.

NAR 7. 1906. "Chapters from My Autobiography.—VII. By Mark Twain." *North American Review* 183 (7 December): 1089–95. Galley proofs (NAR 7pf) at ViU.

NAR 8. 1906. "Chapters from My Autobiography.—VIII. By Mark Twain." *North American Review* 183 (21 December): 1217–24. Galley proofs (NAR 8pf) at ViU.

NAR 9. 1907. "Chapters from My Autobiography.—IX. By Mark Twain." *North American Review* 184 (4 January): 1–14. Galley proofs (NAR 9pf) at ViU.

NAR 10. 1907. "Chapters from My Autobiography.—X. By Mark Twain." *North American Review* 184 (18 January): 113–19. Galley proofs (NAR 10pf) at ViU.

NAR 11. 1907. "Chapters from My Autobiography.—XI. By Mark Twain." *North American Review* 184 (1 February): 225–32. Galley proofs (NAR 11pf) at ViU.

NAR 12. 1907. "Chapters from My Autobiography.—XII. By Mark Twain." *North American Review* 184 (15 February): 337–46. Galley proofs (NAR 12pf) at ViU.

NAR 13. 1907. "Chapters from My Autobiography.—XIII. By Mark Twain." *North American Review* 184 (1 March): 449–63. Galley proofs (NAR 13pf) at ViU.

NAR 14. 1907. "Chapters from My Autobiography.—XIV. By Mark Twain." *North American Review* 184 (15 March): 561–71.

NAR 15. 1907. "Chapters from My Autobiography.—XV. By Mark Twain." *North American Review* 184 (5 April): 673–82. Galley proofs (NAR 15pf) at ViU.

NAR 16. 1907. "Chapters from My Autobiography.—XVI. By Mark Twain." *North American Review* 184 (19 April): 785–93.

NAR 17. 1907. "Chapters from My Autobiography.—XVII. By Mark Twain." *North American Review* 185 (3 May): 1–12. Galley proofs (NAR 17pf) at ViU.

NAR 18. 1907. "Chapters from My Autobiography.—XVIII. By Mark Twain." *North American Review* 185 (17 May): 113–22.

NAR 19. 1907. "Chapters from My Autobiography.—XIX. By Mark Twain." *North American Review* 185 (7 June): 241–51. Galley proofs (NAR 19pf) at ViU.

NAR 20. 1907. "Chapters from My Autobiography.—XX. By Mark Twain." *North American Review* 185 (5 July): 465–74.

NAR 21. 1907. "Chapters from My Autobiography—XXI. By Mark Twain." *North American Review* 185 (2 August): 689–98. Galley proofs (NAR 21pf) at ViU.

NAR 22. 1907. "Chapters from My Autobiography.—XXII. By Mark Twain." *North American Review* 186 (September): 8–21.

NAR 23. 1907. "Chapters from My Autobiography.—XXIII. By Mark Twain." *North American Review* 186 (October): 161–73.

NAR 24. 1907. "Chapters from My Autobiography.—XXIV. By Mark Twain." *North American Review* 186 (November): 327–36. Galley proofs (NAR 24pf) at ViU.

NAR 25. 1907. "Chapters from My Autobiography.—XXV. By Mark Twain." *North American Review* 186 (December): 481–94. Galley proofs (NAR 25pf) at ViU.

National Park Service. 2008. "Mammoth Cave National Park. Frequently Asked Questions." U.S. Department of the Interior. http://www.nps.gov/maca/faqs.htm. Accessed 2 July 2008.

Newton, A. E. 1879. *The Modern Bethesda, or the Gift of Healing Restored. Being Some Account of the Life and Labors of Dr. J. R. Newton, Healer.* New York: Newton Publishing Company.

NIC. Cornell University, Ithaca, N.Y.

Nicolay, John G., and John Hay. 1890. *Abraham Lincoln: A History.* 10 vols. New York: The Century Company.

NjWoE. Rutgers, The State University of New Jersey, Thomas A. Edison Papers Project.

NMh. Library of Poultney Bigelow, Bigelow Homestead, Malden-on-Hudson, N.Y.

NNAL. American Academy of Arts and Letters, New York, N.Y.

NN-BGC. New York Public Library, Albert A. and Henry W. Berg Collection, New York, N.Y.

NNC. Columbia University, New York, N.Y.

NNDB. 2009. "Benjamin Franklin Butler." http://www.nndb.com/people/171/000102862. Accessed 2 April 2009.

NNPM. Pierpont Morgan Library, New York, N.Y.

NNWH. Walter Hampden Memorial Library, New York, N.Y.

"Nook Farm Genealogy." 1974. TS by anonymous compiler, CtHSD.

NPV. Vassar College, Poughkeepsie, N.Y.

NRivd2. Wave Hill House, Riverdale, Bronx, N.Y.

NYC10044. 2009. "Roosevelt Island: Timeline of Island History." http://nyc10044.com/timeln/timeline.html. Accessed 13 May 2009.

Ober, K. Patrick. 2003. *Mark Twain and Medicine: "Any Mummery Will Cure."* Columbia: University of Missouri Press.

OC. Orion Clemens.

ODaU. University of Dayton, Roesch Library, Dayton, Ohio.

Oettel, Walter. 1943. *Walter's Sketch Book of The Players.* [New York]: Privately printed by the Gotham Press.

Ohio County Public Library. 2008. "The Wheeling Stogie." http://wheeling.weirton.lib.wv.us/history/bus/stogie79.htm. Accessed 27 June 2008.

OKeU. Kent State University, Kent, Ohio.

OLC (Olivia [Livy] Langdon Clemens). 1877–1902. Diary of twenty-five leaves, written intermittently between 1877 and 1902, CU-MARK.

OLL. Olivia (Livy) Louise Langdon.

OSC (Olivia Susan [Susy] Clemens).
   1885–86. Untitled biography of her father, MS of 131 pages, annotated by SLC, ViU.

Published in OSC 1985, 83–225; in part in *MTA,* vol. 2, passim; and in Salsbury 1965, passim.

———. 1985. *Papa: An Intimate Biography of Mark Twain.* Edited by Charles Neider. Garden City, N.Y.: Doubleday and Co.

Owsley, Harry Bryan. 1890. "Genealogical Facts of the Owsley Family in England and America from the Time of the 'Restoration' to the Present." TS of 105 pages, DNDAR.

PAM. Pamela Ann Moffett.

Panama Canal Authority. 2008. "Frequently Asked Questions: History." http://www.pancanal .com/eng/general/canal-faqs/index.html. Accessed 28 February 2008.

P&P. 1979. *The Prince and the Pauper.* Edited by Victor Fischer and Lin Salamo with the assistance of Mary Jane Jones. The Works of Mark Twain. Berkeley and Los Angeles: University of California Press.

Pasko, Wesley Washington. 1894. *American Dictionary of Printing and Bookmaking.* New York: Howard Lockwood and Co. [Citations are to the 1967 reprint edition, Detroit: Gale Research Company.]

Peirce, Henry B., and D. Hamilton Hurd. 1879. *History of Tioga, Chemung, Tompkins and Schuyler Counties, New York.* Philadelphia: Everts and Ensign.

Pond, James B. 1900. *Eccentricities of Genius: Memories of Famous Men and Women of the Platform and Stage.* New York: G. W. Dillingham Company.

Portrait. 1895. *Portrait and Biographical Record of Marion, Ralls and Pike Counties, with a Few from Macon, Adair, and Lewis Counties, Missouri.* Chicago: C. O. Owen and Co. [Citations are to the 1982 revised reprint edition, edited by Oliver Howard and Goldena Howard. New London, Mo.: Ralls County Book Company.]

Poulton, Helen J. 1966. *Index to History of Nevada.* Reno: University of Nevada Press.

Prime, William C. 1857. *Tent Life in the Holy Land.* New York: Harper and Brothers.

Quicherat, Jules. 1841–49. *Procès de la Condamnation et de Réhabilitation de Jeanne d'Arc, dite la Pucelle.* Paris: Société de l'Histoire de France.

Ralls Census. 1850. *Population Schedules of the Seventh Census of the United States, 1850. Roll 411. Missouri: District 73, Ralls County.* Photocopy in CU-MARK.

Ramsay, Robert L., and Frances G. Emberson. 1963. *A Mark Twain Lexicon.* New York: Russell and Russell.

Rasmussen, R. Kent. 2007. *Critical Companion to Mark Twain: A Literary Reference to His Life and Work.* 2 vols. New York: Facts on File.

Raymond, R. W. 1881. *A Glossary of Mining and Metallurgical Terms.* Easton, Pa.: American Institute of Mining Engineers.

"Rev. Dr. Buckley and Newton the Healer." 1883. *The Medical Record* 24 (10 November): 519–20.

RI 1993. 1993. *Roughing It.* Edited by Harriet Elinor Smith, Edgar Marquess Branch, Lin Salamo, and Robert Pack Browning. The Works of Mark Twain. Berkeley and Los Angeles: University of California Press. [This edition supersedes the one published in 1972.]

RoBards, John L. 1909. "How a Boy of Eleven Years Crossed the Plains in Forty-Nine. Recollections of Col. John L. Robards of Hannibal, Missouri, Whose Trip to California Made Him the Wonder of Other Boys." Newspaper interview dated 6 November 1909. In *Genealogy of the RoBards Family (1910)*. Part 15, 70–77. http://dgmweb.net/genealogy/7/Robards/Genealogies/RoBardsFamily1910-Pt15-JohnLewisRobards.htm. Accessed 2 February 2009.

Robards Family Genealogy. 2009. *History and Genealogy of the RoBards Family (1910)*. James Harvey Robards, comp. 18 parts; http://dgmweb.net/genealogy/7/Robards/Genealogies/RoBardsFamily1910-Pt01-PrefaceEtc.htm. Accessed 2 February 2009.

Robarts, William Hugh. 1887. *Mexican War Veterans: A Complete Roster of the Regular and Volunteer Troops in the War between the United States and Mexico, from 1846 to 1848*. Washington, D.C.: Brentano's.

Robinson, Forrest G. 2007. *The Author-Cat: Clemens's Life in Fiction*. New York: Fordham University Press.

Robinson, William S. 1869. "Letter from 'Warrington.'" Springfield (Mass.) *Republican,* 13 November, 2.

Roosevelt, Theodore. 1906. *A Square Deal*. Allendale, N.J.: Allendale Press.

Roosevelt Island Historical Society. 2009. "The Roosevelt Island Story." http://www.correctionhistory.org/rooseveltisland. Accessed 13 May 2009.

Ross, Janet. 1912. *The Fourth Generation: Reminiscences by Janet Ross*. London: Constable and Co.

RPB-JH. Brown University, John Hay Library of Rare Books and Special Collections, Providence, R.I.

Salm. Collection of Peter A. Salm.

Salsbury, Edith Colgate, ed. 1965. *Susy and Mark Twain: Family Dialogues*. New York: Harper and Row.

S&B. 1967. *Mark Twain's Satires & Burlesques*. Edited by Franklin R. Rogers. Berkeley and Los Angeles: University of California Press.

Satre, Lowell J. 1982. "After the Match Girls' Strike: Bryant and May in the 1890s." *Victorian Studies* 26 (Autumn): 7–31.

Sayre, Paul L. 1932. Review of W. P. Barrett, *The Trial of Jeanne d'Arc. Harvard Law Review* 45 (June): 1449–51.

Scharnhorst, Gary.

2004. "Kate Field and the *New York Tribune*." *American Periodicals: A Journal of History, Criticism, and Bibliography* 14 (2):159–78.

2006. *Mark Twain: The Complete Interviews*. Tuscaloosa: University of Alabama Press.

Schmidt, Barbara.

2008a. "Chronology of Known Mark Twain Speeches, Public Readings, and Lectures." http://www.twainquotes.com/SpeechIndex.html. Accessed 24 October 2008.

2008b. "The Lost Autobiography of Orion Clemens." http://www.twainquotes.com/oc.html. Accessed 10 July 2008.

2009a. "Mark Twain's Angel-Fish Roster and Other Young Women of Interest." http://www.twainquotes.com/angelfish/angelfish.html. Accessed 20 May 2009.

2009b. "Mark Twain's Illustrated Autobiography." http://www.twainquotes.com/IllustratedAutobio.html. Accessed 21 September 2009.

2009c. "Mark Twain and Karl Gerhardt." http://www.twainquotes.com/Gerhardt/gerhardt.html. Accessed 25 September 2009.

2009d. "Works of Karl Gerhardt." http://www.twainquotes.com/Gerhardt/grantbustdetails.html. Accessed 27 September 2009.

Scientific American. 1901. "Mark Twain, James W. Paige and the Paige Typesetter." *Scientific American* 84 (9 March): 150.

Scott, Arthur L. 1963. "*The Innocents Adrift* Edited by Mark Twain's Official Biographer." *PMLA* 78 (June): 230–37.

Selby, P. O., comp. 1973. *Mark Twain's Kinfolks.* Kirksville, Mo.: Missouriana Library, Northeast Missouri State University.

Sellers, Ruth Aulbach. 1972. "Captain Tonk Was Clown Prince of Murray, Idaho." Kellogg (Idaho) *Evening News,* 22 December, unknown page.

Shapiro, Fred R., ed. 2006. *The Yale Book of Quotations.* New Haven, Conn.: Yale University Press.

Shaw, Henry Wheeler [Josh Billings, pseud.]. 1869. *Josh Billings' Farmer's Allminax for the Year of Our Lord 1870.* New York: G. W. Carleton.

Sheridan, Philip H. 1888. *Personal Memoirs of P. H. Sheridan, General, United States Army.* 2 vols. New York: Charles L. Webster and Co.

Sherman, William T. 1875. *Memoirs of General William T. Sherman.* 2 vols. New York: D. Appleton and Co.

Skandera-Trombley, Laura E. 1994. *Mark Twain in the Company of Women.* Philadelphia: University of Pennsylvania Press.

SLC (Samuel Langhorne Clemens).

1851. "A Gallant Fireman." Hannibal *Western Union,* 16 January, 3. Reprinted in *ET&S1,* 62.

1855–56. "'Jul'us Caesar.'" MS of fourteen pages on four folios, NPV. Published in *ET&S1,* 110–17.

1864a. "Doings in Nevada." Letter dated 4 January. New York *Sunday Mercury,* 7 February, 3. Reprinted in *MTEnt,* 121–26.

1864b. "Those Blasted Children." New York *Sunday Mercury,* 21 February, 3.

1865. "Jim Smiley and His Jumping Frog." New York *Saturday Press* 4 (18 November): 248–49. Reprinted in *ET&S2,* 282–88.

1866a. "Captain Montgomery." San Francisco *Golden Era* 14 (28 January): 6.

1866b. "Scenes in Honolulu—No. 13." Letter dated 22 June. Sacramento *Union,* 16 July, 3. Reprinted in *MTH,* 328–34.

1866c. "Letter from Honolulu." Letter dated 25 June. Sacramento *Union,* 19 July, 1. Reprinted in *MTH,* 335–47.

1866d. "Forty-three Days in an Open Boat." *Harper's New Monthly Magazine* 34 (December): 104–13.

1867a. *The Celebrated Jumping Frog of Calaveras County, and Other Sketches.* Edited by John Paul. New York: C. H. Webb.

1867b. "The Winner of the Medal." New York *Sunday Mercury,* 3 March, 3.

1867c. "A Curtain Lecture Concerning Skating." New York *Sunday Mercury,* 17 March, 3.

1867d. "Barbarous." New York *Sunday Mercury,* 24 March, 3.

1867e. "From Mark Twain. Explanatory." St. Louis *Missouri Republican,* 24 March, 1.

1867f. "Female Suffrage." New York *Sunday Mercury,* 7 April, 3.

1867g. "Official Physic." New York *Sunday Mercury,* 21 April, 3.

1867h. "Letter from 'Mark Twain.'[No. 14.]" Letter dated 16 April. San Francisco *Alta California,* 26 May, 1. Reprinted in *MTTB,* 141–48.

1867i. "Letter from 'Mark Twain.'[No. 18.]" Letter dated 18 May. San Francisco *Alta California,* 23 June, 1. Reprinted in part in *MTTB,* 180–91.

1867j. "A Reminiscence of Artemus Ward." New York *Sunday Mercury,* 7 July, 3.

1867k. "Jim Wolf and the Tom-Cats." New York *Sunday Mercury,* 14 July, 3. Reprinted in Budd 1992a, 235–37.

1867l. "The Mediterranean Excursion." Letter dated 23 June. New York *Tribune,* 30 July, 2. Reprinted in *TIA,* 10–18.

1867m. "The Mediterranean Excursion." New York *Tribune,* 6 September, 2. Reprinted in *TIA,* 72–74.

1867n. "Americans on a Visit to the Emperor of Russia." Letter dated 26 August. New York *Tribune,* 19 September, 1. Reprinted in *TIA,* 142–50.

1867o. "A Yankee in the Orient." Letter dated 31 August. New York *Tribune,* 25 October, 2. Reprinted in *TIA,* 128–32.

1867p. "The American Colony in Palestine." Letter dated 2 October. New York *Tribune,* 2 November, 2. Reprinted in *TIA,* 306–9.

1867q. "The Holy Land Excursion. Letter from 'Mark Twain.' Number Twenty-one." San Francisco *Alta California,* 3 November, 1. Reprinted in *TIA,* 137–42.

1867r. "The Holy Land. First Day in Palestine." New York *Tribune,* 9 November, 1. Reprinted in *TIA,* 209–13.

1867s. "The Cruise of the Quaker City." Undated letter written 19 November. New York *Herald,* 20 November, 7. Reprinted in *TIA,* 313–19.

1867t. "Interview with Gen. Grant." MS of nine leaves, datelined "Washington, Dec. 6," NPV.

1868a. "Mark Twain in Washington. Special Correspondence of the *Alta California.*" Letter dated 10 December 1867. San Francisco *Alta California,* 15 January, 1.

1868b. "General Washington's Negro Body-Servant. A Biographical Sketch." *Galaxy* 5 (February): 154–56.

1868c. "Mark Twain in Washington. Special Correspondent of the *Alta California.*" Letter dated 11 January. San Francisco *Alta California,* 5 February, 2.

1868d. "Letter from Mark Twain." Letter dated 31 January. Chicago *Republican,* 8 February, 2.

1868e. "Boy's Manuscript." MS of fifty-eight leaves, written in October–November, CU-MARK. Published in *Inds,* 1–19.

1869a. *The Innocents Abroad; or, The New Pilgrims' Progress.* Hartford: American Publishing Company.

1869b. "Letter from Mark Twain." Letter dated July. San Francisco *Alta California,* 25 July, 1.

1870a. "Anson Burlingame." Buffalo *Express,* 25 February, 2. Reprinted in SLC 1923, 17–23.

1870b. "The Facts in the Case of the Great Beef Contract." *Galaxy* 9 (May): 718–21. Reprinted in Budd 1992a, 367–73.

1870c. "The Late Benjamin Franklin." *Galaxy* 10 (July): 138–40.

1870d. "Fortifications of Paris." Buffalo *Express,* 17 September, 2.

1870e. "Riley—Newspaper Correspondent." *Galaxy* 10 (November): 726–27.

1871a. *Mark Twain's (Burlesque) Autobiography and First Romance.* New York: Sheldon and Co.

1871b. "The Facts in the Case of George Fisher, Deceased." *Galaxy* 11 (January): 152–55. Reprinted in Budd 1992a, 500–506.

1871c. "An Autobiography." *Aldine* 4 (April): 52.

1872. *Roughing It.* Hartford: American Publishing Company.

1873–74. *The Gilded Age: A Tale of To-day.* Charles Dudley Warner, coauthor. Hartford: American Publishing Company. [Early copies bound with 1873 title page, later ones with 1874 title page: see *BAL* 3357.]

1874a. *Colonel Sellers. A Drama in Five Acts. By Samuel L. Clemens. Mark Twain. Elmira N. Y. Entered in the Office of the Librarian of Congress. July 1874.* A dramatization of *The Gilded Age.* Three manuscripts survive: one in DLC, and two in CU-MARK.

1874b. "A True Story, Repeated Word for Word as I Heard It." *Atlantic Monthly* 34 (November): 591–94. Reprinted in Budd 1992a, 578–82.

1875a. "Old Times on the Mississippi." *Atlantic Monthly* 35 (January–June): 69–73, 217–24, 283–89, 446–52, 567–74, 721–30; *Atlantic Monthly* 36 (August): 190–96.

1875b. "Encounter with an Interviewer." In Brougham and Elderkin 1875, 25–32. Reprinted in Budd 1992a, 583–87.

1875c. *Mark Twain's Sketches, New and Old.* Hartford: American Publishing Company.

1876. *The Adventures of Tom Sawyer.* Hartford: American Publishing Company.

1876–85. "A Record of the Small Foolishnesses of Susie & 'Bay' Clemens (Infants)." MS of 111 pages, ViU.

1877a. *A True Story, and the Recent Carnival of Crime.* Boston: James R. Osgood and Co.

1877b. "Autobiography of a Damned Fool." MS of 115 leaves, written March–May, with minor revisions after 1880, CU-MARK. Published in *S&B,* 136–61.

1880a. *A Tramp Abroad.* Hartford: American Publishing Company.

1880b. "On the Decay of the Art of Lying." Paper presented at the Hartford Monday Evening Club on 5 April. Published in SLC 1882a, 217–25. Reprinted in Budd 1992a, 824–29.

1880c. "The Shakspeare Mulberry." MS of twelve pages, written on 23 November, CtHMTH.

1881. *The Prince and the Pauper: A Tale for Young People of All Ages.* Boston: James R. Osgood and Co.

1882a. *The Stolen White Elephant, Etc.* Boston: James R. Osgood and Co.

1882b. "The McWilliamses and the Burglar Alarm." *Harper's Christmas: Pictures and Papers Done by the Tile Club and Its Literary Friends* (December): 28–29. Reprinted in Budd 1992a, 837–43.

1883. *Life on the Mississippi.* Boston: James R. Osgood and Co.

1884. "Huck Finn and Tom Sawyer among the Indians." MS originally of 228 pages, written beginning in July, primarily in MiD (some of the MS is at other institutions, some is missing: see *Inds,* 372–73). Published in *HH&T,* 81–140, and *Inds,* 33–81.

1885a. *Adventures of Huckleberry Finn.* New York: Charles L. Webster and Co.

1885b. "The Private History of a Campaign That Failed." *Century Magazine* 31 (December): 193–204. Reprinted in Budd 1992b, 863–82.

1887. "English as She Is Taught." *Century Magazine* 33 (April): 932–36.

1889. *A Connecticut Yankee in King Arthur's Court.* New York: Charles L. Webster and Co.

1891a. "The Innocents Adrift." MS of 174 pages, CU-MARK. Published in part as "Down the Rhone" in SLC 1923, 129–68.

1891b. "Mental Telegraphy." *Harper's New Monthly Magazine* 84 (December): 95–104.

1892. *The American Claimant.* New York: Charles L. Webster and Co.

1893. "The Back Number: A Monthly Magazine." MS of five leaves, NNPM.

1894a. *Tom Sawyer Abroad.* New York: Charles L. Webster and Co.

1894b. *The Tragedy of Pudd'nhead Wilson and the Comedy Those Extraordinary Twins.* Hartford: American Publishing Company.

1895. "Mental Telegraphy Again." *Harper's New Monthly Magazine* 91 (September): 521–24.

1896a. *Personal Recollections of Joan of Arc.* New York: Harper and Brothers.

1896b. *Tom Sawyer Abroad, Tom Sawyer, Detective and Other Stories Etc., Etc.* New York: Harper and Brothers.

1896c. "Tom Sawyer, Detective." *Harper's New Monthly Magazine* 93 (August–September): 344–61, 519–37.

1896–1906. "Memorial to Susy." MS of 104 leaves, various drafts and parts, CU-MARK.

1897a. *Following the Equator: A Journey around the World.* Hartford: American Publishing Company.

1897b. *More Tramps Abroad.* London: Chatto and Windus.

1897c. Untitled MS of thirty-nine leaves concerning Wilhelmine, Margravine of Bayreuth, CU-MARK.

1897d. "England's Jubilee Pageant to Be the Greatest in History." San Francisco *Examiner,* 20 June, 13. Reprinted in SLC 1923, 193–206.

1897e. "His Jubilee Art." San Francisco *Examiner,* 20 June, 13–14.

1897f. "All Nations Pay Homage to Victoria." San Francisco *Examiner,* 23 June, 1, 4. Reprinted in SLC 1923, 206–10.

1897g. "Villagers of 1840–3." MS of forty-three leaves, written in July–August, CU-MARK. Published in *Inds,* 93–108.

1897–?1902. "Tom Sawyer's Conspiracy." MS of 241 pages, CU-MARK. Published in *HH&T,* 152–242, and *Inds,* 134–213.

1898a. "Dueling." MS of sixteen pages, written on 8 March, CU-MARK.

1898b. "At the Appetite-Cure." *Cosmopolitan* 25 (August): 425–33.

1898c. "Schoolhouse Hill." MS of 139 pages, written in November–December, CU-MARK. Published in *MSM,* 175–220, and *Inds,* 214–59.

1899a. "Samuel Langhorne Clemens." MS of fourteen leaves, notes written in March for Samuel E. Moffett to use in preparing a biographical sketch, NN-BGC.

1899b. "Concerning the Jews." *Harper's New Monthly Magazine* 99 (September): 527–35. Reprinted in SLC 1900a, 250–75.

1899c. "Christian Science and the Book of Mrs. Eddy." *Cosmopolitan* 27 (October): 585–94.

1899d. "My Début as a Literary Person." *Century Magazine* 59 (November): 76–88.

1899e. "My First Lie and How I Got Out of It." New York *World,* 10 December, Supplement, 1–2. Reprinted in Budd 1992b, 439–46.

1900a. *How to Tell a Story and Other Essays.* The Writings of Mark Twain. Édition de Luxe. Volume 22. Hartford: American Publishing Company.

1900b. *The Man That Corrupted Hadleyburg and Other Stories and Essays.* New York: Harper and Brothers.

1901. "Two Little Tales." *Century Magazine* 63 (November): 24–32.

1902a. "Aguinaldo." MS of sixty-two leaves and TS of twenty-one leaves, CU-MARK. Published as "Review of Edwin Wildman's Biography of Aguinaldo" in Zwick 1992, 86–108.

1902b. "Huck." MS of one page, probably written in 1902, CU-MARK.

1902c. "A Defence of General Funston." *North American Review* 174 (May): 613–24. Reprinted in Zwick 1992, 119–32.

1902d. "Christian Science." *North American Review* 175 (December): 756–68.

1903a. *My Début as a Literary Person with Other Essays and Stories.* Hartford: American Publishing Company.

1903b. "Christian Science—II." *North American Review* 176 (January): 1–9.

1903c. "Christian Science—III." *North American Review* 176 (February): 173–84.

1903d. "Mrs. Eddy in Error." *North American Review* 176 (April): 505–17.

1903e. "Major General Wood, M.D." MS of ten leaves, written 15 December, and TS of five leaves, typed and revised before 28 December, CU-MARK. Published in Zwick 1992, 151–55.

1904a. "The Countess Massiglia." MS of thirty-six leaves, CU-MARK.

1904b. "Saint Joan of Arc." *Harper's Monthly Magazine* 110 (December): 3–12.

1905a. *King Leopold's Soliloquy: A Defense of His Congo Rule.* Boston: P. R. Warren Company.

1905b. "Concerning Copyright: An Open Letter to the Register of Copyrights." *North American Review* 180 (January): 1–8. Reprinted in Budd 1992b, 627–34.

1905c. "From My Unpublished Autobiography." *Harper's Weekly* 49 (18 March): 391. Reprinted as "Mark Twain Was Pioneer in Use of Typewriter," Atlanta *Constitution,* 3 April, 6.

1905d. "'Russian Liberty Has Had Its Last Chance,' Says Mark Twain." Letter to the editor dated 29 August. Boston *Globe,* 30 August, 4 (morning edition), 11 (evening edition). Also known as "The Treaty of Portsmouth."

1905e. "John Hay and the Ballads." *Harper's Weekly* 49 (21 October): 1530.

1905f. "'Mark Twain' Talks Peace." Chicago *Tribune,* 5 November, 1. Text of speech available online at http://www.twainquotes.com/Peace.html.

1905g. "Mark Twain's 70th Birthday: Souvenir of Its Celebration." Supplement to *Harper's Weekly* 49 (23 December): 1883–1914. Facsimile available at *MTPO.*

1906a. "A Family Sketch." MS of sixty-five pages, CLjC.

1906b. *What Is Man?* New York: De Vinne Press.

1906c. "A Horse's Tale." *Harper's Monthly Magazine* 113 (August–September): 327–42, 539–49.

1906d. "Hunting the Deceitful Turkey." *Harper's Monthly Magazine* 114 (December): 57–58.

1909a. "To Rev. S. C. Thompson." MS of seventeen pages, written 23 April, CU-MARK. Published in part in *MTB,* 1:482–83.

1909b. "Ashcroft-Lyon Manuscript." MS of 464 leaves, written May–September, CU-MARK.

1909c. "H. H. Rogers." MS of twenty pages, consisting of several pagination sequences, written between August and December, CU-MARK. Published in *MTA,* 1:256–65.

1909d. "Marjorie Fleming, the Wonder Child." *Harper's Bazar* 43 (December): 1182–83, 1229.

1909e. "Closing Words of My Autobiography." MS of forty-four pages, written on 24, 25, and 26 December, CU-MARK. Published as "The Death of Jean" in *Harper's Monthly Magazine* 122 (January 1911): 210–15.

1910. "The Turning Point of My Life." *Harper's Bazar* 44 (February): 118–19. Reprinted in Budd 1992b, 929–38, and *WIM,* 455–64.

1917. *What Is Man? And Other Essays.* New York: Harper and Brothers.

1922a. "Unpublished Chapters from the Autobiography of Mark Twain: Part I." *Harper's Monthly Magazine* 144 (February): 273–80.

1922b. "Unpublished Chapters from the Autobiography of Mark Twain: Part II." *Harper's Monthly Magazine* 144 (March): 455–60.

1922c. "Unpublished Chapters from the Autobiography of Mark Twain." *Harper's Monthly Magazine* 145 (August): 310–15.

1923. *Europe and Elsewhere.* With an Appreciation by Brander Matthews and an Introduction by Albert Bigelow Paine. New York: Harper and Brothers.

1981. *Wapping Alice: Printed for the First Time, Together with Three Factual Letters to Olivia Clemens; Another Story, the McWilliamses and the Burglar Alarm; and Revelatory Portions of the Autobiographical Dictation of April 10, 1907. . . .* Berkeley: Friends of The Bancroft Library.

1982. *The Adventures of Tom Sawyer.* Foreword and notes by John C. Gerber; text established by Paul Baender. The Mark Twain Library. Berkeley and Los Angeles: University of California Press.

1990. *Mark Twain's Own Autobiography: The Chapters from the* North American Review. With an introduction and notes by Michael J. Kiskis. Madison: University of Wisconsin Press.

1996. *Chapters from My Autobiography.* With an introduction by Arthur Miller and an afterword by Michael J. Kiskis. The Oxford Mark Twain, edited by Shelley Fisher Fishkin. New York: Oxford University Press.

2004. *Mark Twain's Helpful Hints for Good Living: A Handbook for the Damned Human Race.* Edited by Lin Salamo, Victor Fischer, and Michael B. Frank. Berkeley and Los Angeles: University of California Press.

2009. *Who Is Mark Twain?* Edited, with a note on the text, by Robert H. Hirst. New York: HarperStudio.

Smith, Elizabeth H. 1965. "Reuel Colt Gridley." *Tales of the Paradise Ridge* 6 (June): 11–18.

Smith, Henry Nash.

1955. "That Hideous Mistake of Poor Clemens's." *Harvard Library Bulletin* 9 (Spring): 145–80.

1962. *Mark Twain: The Development of a Writer.* Cambridge: Belknap Press of Harvard University Press.

Smith, Jean Edward. 2001. *Grant.* New York: Simon and Schuster.

Smith, Stephanie. 2006. *Former Presidents: Federal Pension and Retirement Benefits.* CRS Report for Congress. http://www.senate.gov/reference/resources/pdf/98–249.pdf. Accessed 13 July 2006.

Sonoma Census. 1860. *Population Schedules of the Eighth Census of the United States, 1860. Roll M653. California: Sonoma, Sonoma County.* Photocopy in CU-MARK.

Soria, Regina. 1964. "Mark Twain and Vedder's Medusa." *American Quarterly* 16:602–6.

StEdNL. National Library of Scotland, Edinburgh [formerly UkENL].

Stein, Bernard L. 2001. "Life on the Hudson: A Mark Twain Idyll." *Riverdale Press* 52 (25 October): A1, B1, B4.

Stewart, A. A., comp. 1912. *The Printer's Dictionary of Technical Terms.* Boston: School of Printing, North End Union.

Stoddard, Charles Warren.

1867. *Poems.* San Francisco: A. Roman.

1873. *South-Sea Idyls.* Boston: James R. Osgood and Co.

1885. *A Troubled Heart and How It Was Comforted at Last.* Notre Dame, Ind.: Joseph A. Lyons.

1903. *Exits and Entrances: A Book of Essays and Sketches.* Boston: Lothrop Publishing Company.

Stoddard, Lothrop. 1931. *Master of Manhattan: The Life of Richard Croker.* New York: Longmans, Green and Co.

Stone, H. N., D. M. Davidson, and W. R. McIntosh. 1885. *Stone, Davidson & Co.'s Hannibal City Directory.* Hannibal: Stone, Davidson and Co.

Streamer, Volney, comp.

    1897. *Voices of Doubt and Trust.* New York: Brentano's.

    1904. *In Friendship's Name.* 14th ed. New York: Brentano's.

Strong, Leah A. 1966. *Joseph Hopkins Twichell: Mark Twain's Friend and Pastor.* Athens: University of Georgia Press.

Sweets, Henry H., III.

    1986a. "Cave's Fun Disguised Inherent Commercial Wealth." *The Fence Painter* 6 (Summer): 3.

    1986b. "Hannibal's Great Cave Is Steeped in History." *The Fence Painter* 6 (Summer): 1–2.

Teller, Charlotte. 1925. *S.L.C. to C.T.* New York: Privately printed.

Thayer, William Roscoe. 1915. *The Life and Letters of John Hay.* 2 vols. Boston: Houghton Mifflin Company.

TIA. 1958. *Traveling with the Innocents Abroad: Mark Twain's Original Reports from Europe and the Holy Land.* Edited by Daniel Morley McKeithan. Norman: University of Oklahoma Press.

Ticknor, Caroline. 1922. *Glimpses of Authors.* Boston: Houghton Mifflin Company.

Tinkham, George H. 1921. *History of Stanislaus County, California.* Los Angeles: Historic Record Company.

Tooke, Thomas. 1838–57. *A History of Prices, and of the State of the Circulation, from 1793 to 1837; Preceded by a Brief Sketch of the State of the Corn Trade in the Last Two Centuries.* 6 vols. London: Longman, Orme, Brown, Green, and Longmans.

Towner, Ausburn [Ishmael, pseud.]. 1892. *Our County and Its People: A History of the Valley and County of Chemung from the Closing Years of the Eighteenth Century.* Syracuse, N.Y.: D. Mason and Co.

Tozzer, Alfred M. 1931. "Alfred Percival Maudslay." *American Anthropologist,* n.s. 33 (July–September): 403–12.

Trumbull, James Hammond, ed. 1886. *The Memorial History of Hartford County, Connecticut, 1633–1884.* 2 vols. Boston: Edward L. Osgood.

TS. Typescript.

TS1. First typescript, in CU-MARK, made in 1906–8 by Josephine Hobby from her stenographic notes of Clemens's dictation; it includes the Autobiographical Dictations of 9 January 1906 through 14 July 1908 and was revised by Clemens.

TS2. Second typescript, in CU-MARK, made in 1906 by Josephine Hobby; it includes "My Autobiography [Random Extracts from It]" and four Florentine Dictations ("John Hay," "Notes on 'Innocents Abroad,'" "Robert Louis Stevenson and Thomas Bailey Aldrich," and "Villa di Quarto"), plus the Autobiographical Dictations of 9 January 1906 through 7 August 1906, incorporating the revisions on TS1, and was revised by Clemens.

TS3. Third typescript, in CU-MARK, made in 1906–7 by Josephine Hobby from the revised TS1 or the revised TS2, to serve as printer's copy for several installments of "Chapters from My Autobiography" in the *North American Review;* it consists of four independently paginated batches of selections from pre-1906 writings and the Autobiographical Dictations of January–May 1906, and was revised by Clemens.

TS4. Fourth typescript, in CU-MARK, made in 1906 by an unidentified typist; it includes the same pre-1906 pieces as TS2, plus the Autobiographical Dictations of 9 January 1906 through 29 August 1906 and incorporates the revisions on TS1, but was not further reviewed by Clemens.

Tugwell, Rexford G. 1968. *Grover Cleveland.* New York: Macmillan Company.

Twichell, Joseph Hopkins.

1874–1916. "Personal Journal." MS, Joseph H. Twichell Collection, CtY-BR.

2006. *The Civil War Letters of Joseph Hopkins Twichell: A Chaplain's Story.* Edited by Peter Messent and Steve Courtney. Athens: University of Georgia Press.

TxU. University of Texas, Austin.

TxU-Hu. Harry Ransom Humanities Research Center, University of Texas, Austin.

Urmy, Clarence. 1906. "A Song." *Harper's Bazar* 40 (March): 124.

U.S. National Archives and Records Administration.

1907–9. *Fentress Land Co. et al. v. Bruno Gernt et al.* Civil Case No. 967, Circuit Court of the United States for the Southern Division of the Eastern District of Tennessee, Southeast Region Archives, Morrow, Georgia.

1950–54. "Massiglia, Frances Paxton." Department of State General Records, Record Group 59, Central Decimal Files, 1950–54, 265.113, 4–1863, Box 1101, National Archives, Washington, D.C.

Varble, Rachel M. 1964. *Jane Clemens: The Story of Mark Twain's Mother.* Garden City, N.Y.: Doubleday and Co.

Vassar College.

2008a. "Lady Principals." http://vcencyclopedia.vassar.edu/index.php/Lady_Principals. Accessed 29 August 2008.

2008b. "Samuel L. Caldwell." http://vcencyclopedia.vassar.edu/index.php/Samuel_L._Caldwell. Accessed 28 August 2008.

Veteran's Museum and Memorial Center. 2009. "Spanish-American War, 1898." http://veteranmuseum.org/spanish-american.html. Accessed 29 April 2009.

Victoria, Empress, consort of Frederick III. 1913. *The Empress Frederick: A Memoir.* London: James Nisbet and Co.

ViU. University of Virginia, Charlottesville.

Walker, Franklin. 1969. *San Francisco's Literary Frontier.* Rev. ed. Seattle: University of Washington Press.

Wave Hill. 2008. "A Brief History of Wave Hill: 1843–1903." http://www.wavehill.org/about/history.html-print = true. Accessed 18 June 2008.

Weaver, H. Dwight. 2008. *Missouri Caves in History and Legend.* Columbia: University of Missouri Press.

Webster, Noah. 1828. *An American Dictionary of the English Language.* 2 vols. New York: S. Converse.

Wecter, Dixon. 1952. *Sam Clemens of Hannibal.* Boston: Houghton Mifflin Company, Riverside Press.

Wetzel, Betty. 1985. "Huckleberry Finn in Montana: One of Twain's Last Jokes?" *Montana Magazine* (November–December): 33–35.

White, Edgar. 1924. "The Old Home Town." *The Mentor* 12 (May): 51–53.

White, Horatio S. 1925. *Willard Fiske, Life and Correspondence: A Biographical Study.* New York: Oxford University Press.

Whitney, William Dwight, and Benjamin E. Smith, eds. 1889–91. *The Century Dictionary: An Encyclopedic Lexicon of the English Language.* 6 vols. New York: The Century Company.

Wildman, Edwin. 1901. *Aguinaldo: A Narrative of Filipino Ambitions.* Boston: Lothrop Publishing Company.

Wilhelmine, Margravine, consort of Friedrich, Margrave of Bayreuth. 1877. *Memoirs of Frederica Sophia Wilhelmina, Princess Royal of Prussia, Margravine of Baireuth, Sister of Frederick the Great.* Boston: James R. Osgood and Co. SLC copy in CU-MARK.

WIM. 1973. *What Is Man? And Other Philosophical Writings.* Edited by Paul Baender. The Works of Mark Twain. Berkeley: University of California Press.

Winship, Michael. 1995. *Literary Publishing in the Mid-Nineteenth Century: The Business of Ticknor and Fields.* Cambridge: Cambridge University Press.

Winter, William. 1893. *Life and Art of Edwin Booth.* New York: Macmillan and Co.

Wright, William [Dan De Quille, pseud.]. 1893. "Reminiscences of the Comstock," in "The Passing of a Pioneer." San Francisco *Examiner,* 22 January, 15. Reprinted as "The Story of the Enterprise" in Lewis 1971, 5–10.

Young, John Russell. 1879. *Around the World with General Grant: A Narrative of the Visit of General U.S. Grant, Ex-President of the United States, to Various Countries in Europe, Asia, and Africa, in 1877, 1878, 1879.* New York: American News Company.

Youngquist, Sally. 2001. "Iowa Second Infantry, Lee County Iowa." *Iowa in the Civil War Project.* http://iagenweb.org/lee/military/cw2ndinfantry.htm. Accessed 19 March 2009.

Yung, Wing. 1909. *My Life in China and America.* New York: Henry Holt and Co.

Zwick, Jim. 1992. *Mark Twain's Weapons of Satire: Anti-Imperialist Writings on the Philippine-American War.* Syracuse: Syracuse University Press.

INDEX

Boldfaced page numbers indicate principal identifications or short biographies. Clemens's frequently mentioned works are listed in main entries; his other writings are listed only under "Clemens, Samuel Langhorne, WORKS." Place names are indexed only when they refer to locations that Clemens lived in, visited, or commented upon. Newspapers are listed by city, other periodicals by title. Entries for Clemens's family members, friends, and employees do not include references to their photographs, which may be found following page 204.

Clemens, Jean (Jane Lampton), 242, 322, 339; "Anecdote of Jean," 23, 199, 524; biography, **657**; birth, 480, 652, 656; childhood and youth, 333, 339, 341, 345, 349, 361, 387–88, 394; Clemens family plays and charades, 336–37, 580; "Closing Words of My Autobiography," 4, 24, 657; death, 1, 4, 24, 57, 656; death of Susy Clemens, 323–25; German nursemaid, 394, 607; health, 339, 653, 656; letters from, 321, 324, 325; love of animals, 199; travel, 12, 19, 25, 28, 322, 500, 540, 654; typewriting and SLC typescripts, 18–19, 20, 22, 155, 192, 513, 539, 669

Clemens, Jeremiah (1732–1811), **526**

Clemens, Jeremiah (1814–65), 205, 349, 526, **527**, 588

Clemens, John Marshall: biography, 651, **654**; as county judge, 61, 62, 454, 470, 644; death, 274, 454, 659; financial problems, 62–63, 470; as justice of the peace, 11, 62, 514; marriage, 205–6, 528; religion, 645; slaves owned or hired, 65, 212, 471, 528; Tennessee land, 61–62, 63, 206, 208–9, 469, 530; undemonstrative nature, 274, 321

Clemens, Langdon: birth and death, 323, 361–62, 433, 634, 652, 655–56; health, 433, 592, 634; infant habits, 363

Clemens, Margaret, 206, 451, 528

Clemens, Mary Eleanor Stotts (Mrs. Orion Clemens), 460, 646, 655

Clemens, Olivia Louise Langdon (Livy): biography, 652–53, **655–56**; birth of Clara Clemens, 434, 480, 652, 656; birth of Jean Clemens, 480, 652, 656; birth and death of Langdon Clemens, 361–62, 433, 592, 634, 652; birth and death of Susy Clemens, 323–25, 480, 652, 656; Clemens family plays and charades, 335–37; courtship, engagement, and wedding, 320–22, 355, 357–59, 508, 577–78, 591–92; diary, 438, 638; as editor of SLC's books, 349, 359; family history, 355–56; father's final illness, 360–61; financial matters, 192, 455, 578; health, 19, 328, 356, 361, 362, 500, 590–91, 632, 634; illness and death, 20, 23, 25, 192, 239, 242, 243, 320, 359, 429, 455; letters from, 385–86, 434–35, 632, 635; letters to, 146, 373, 386, 430, 474, 554, 637; relationship with daughters, 326–27, 330–31, 332–33, 382; relationship with SLC, 342, 343, 344–45, 346–48, 385–86, 387–88; servants, 118, 270, 322, 335, 394, 662; SLC's description, 320–21, 361; spelling ability, 333–34, 583; travel, 12, 19, 385, 392, 486, 516, 540, 581, 602, 604, 634

Clemens, Olivia Susan (Susy): biography, **656**; birth, 323, 480, 652; childhood and youth, 325–28, 329, 330–33, 375, 393, 395, 434, 579–81, 582–83; Clemens family plays and charades, 327, 335–37, 580, 583; compared to Marjory Fleming, 328, 581; compassion for animals, 331; illness and death, 12, 323–25, 382–83, 579, 653; nicknames (Megalopis, Wee Wifie), 329, 435, 636; play *A Love-Chase,* 327, 580; poem misattributed, 325, 579; relationship with Dr. Brown, 329, 434–35; relationship with mother, 326–27, 330–31, 382; relationship with sisters, 327–28, 330–31, 333, 581; Sarah Bernhardt imitations, 337, 584; spelling ability, 333, 338, 393, 584, 606; travel, 12, 516, 581; visit to Grant with SLC, 335, 381–82; "What is it all for?" question, 326, 375, 419, 580

SUSY'S BIOGRAPHY OF SLC, 9, 49, 337–38, 369, 584, 587; *Adventures of Huckleberry Finn,* 348; Clemens family history, 349; excerpts, 339–40, 342, 345–46, 348–50, 353, 355, 357, 359, 361, 363, 373, 379, 381–83, 392, 394–95, 433; Jervis Langdon, 373, 360; Langdon Clemens, 361–62, 363, 433; Langdon family, 355–56; *The Prince and the Pauper,* 348; SLC and OLC's first house, 360; SLC and OLC's first meeting, 355; SLC and OLC's marriage, 357; SLC's appearance, 341; SLC's childhood antics, 350; SLC's drinking and swearing, 346, 353; SLC's early adulthood, 355; SLC's failures to comprehend, 342–43; SLC's gait, 345; SLC's love letters, 359–60; SLC's names for cats, 345; SLC's not going to church, 346; trip to New York, 379, 381, 382, 383, 392, 393–95, 606; trip to England and Scotland, 433, 634, 652

Hannibal *Journal,* 521; Orion Clemens buys and combines with *Western Union,* 459, 470, 645, 655

Hannibal *Missouri Courier:* SLC apprenticed to Joseph P. Ament, 455–59, 515, 644–45, 651

Hannibal *Western Union,* 515, 651; Orion Clemens starts, 470, 645, 655

Hapgood, Norman, 375, **598**

Hardy, Samuel F., **504**

Hardy, Thomas Duffus, 433, **634**

Hardy, Thomas Masterman, **634**

Harper, Henry, 127

Harper and Brothers, 19, 29, 49, 56, 557, 564, 629, 653

Harper's Bazar, 621, 631

Harper's Monthly, 547; SLC's first contribution, 127–28, 501, 503, 504; SLC's other contributions, 145, 181, 629, 631

Harper's Weekly, 22, 51, 542, 547, 553, 557, 619; SLC's birthday issue, 558, 657, 675

Harris, Joel Chandler (Uncle Remus), 217, **532–33,** 635

Harrison, Carter Henry, Sr., 68, **473**

Harrison, Henry B., 482

Harrison, Katharine I., 193, 194, 522

Harte, Bret, 23, 146, 150, 229, **509,** 516, 539

Hartford Club, 413, 621

Hartford *Courant,* 93, 491, 525, 637; on Cleveland-Blaine election, 316–17, 319, 577; owners and editors, 319, 413, 481, 576, 577

Hartford Monday Evening Club, 269–70, 318, 558–60

Harvey, George Brinton McClellan, **557,** 564, 574, 672; handwriting on typescripts, 48, 52, 672; posthumous publication of the autobiography, 19, 57–58; publication of excerpts from the autobiography, 51–54, 56, 155; on U.S. massacre of Moros, 407; SLC's birthday dinner, 267–68

Hawaii. *See* Sandwich Islands

Hawkes, Forbes Robert, 286, **565**

Hawkins, John, 203, **526**

Hawley, Harriet Foote, 579

Hawley, Joseph Roswell, 205, 317, 528, **576,** 577

Hay, Clara L. Stone (Mrs. John Milton Hay), 223, **534–35**

Hay, John Milton, 145, 363; as assistant and biographer of Lincoln, 224, 535; conversation with SLC about autobiography, 7–8, 64, 223–24, 535; French novel incident, 392–93; friend of Burlingame, 596; friend of Gray, 363, 375; friend of Greeley, 145, 222; "John Hay," 22, 32, 46n86, 54, 222–24, **534–35**

Hay, Rosina, 65, 435, 581, 607, 636

Hayes, Isaac I., 146, 149, 151, **509,** 511

Hayes, Rutherford B., 528

Hearst, George, 315–16, **576**

Hearst, William Randolph, 219, 315, 450–51, 501, **576**

Helps, Arthur, 434, **635**

Henry, Hubert-Joseph, 302, **571**

"Henry H. Rogers," 22, 192–98, 522–24

Herndon, William Lewis, 461, **646**

Herrick, H. S., 625–26

Hickman, Philander A., 419, **625**

Hickman, Sarah M. Brittingham (Mrs. Philander A. Hickman), **625**

Higbie, Calvin H., 445–49, **640–41**

Higginson, Thomas W., 555

Higham, Dick, 444, 460, **640**

Hobby, Josephine S.: oral transmission of Susy's biography, 584; skill, 1, 25, 27–29, 669, 671; as stenographer for Autobiographical Dictations, 23–29, 48, **543,** 564, 584, 669, 672–75, 710; transcribes earlier autobiographical writings, 31n81, 155, 192, 525, 574; transcribes inserted documents, 572, 605, 608, 632, 636, 679; types TS2, 31n81, 32, 46, 670–71, 675, 710; types TS3, 52, 54, 670–72, 710

Hofer, Andreas, 126, **500**

Holland, 581

Holmes, Oliver Wendell, 150, **510;** Authors' Reading, 384, 601–2; SLC's alleged plagiarism, 225–26, 535–36; Whittier birthday dinner, 260, 261–65, 553–56

Holmes, Oliver Wendell, Jr., 475

Holt, Winifred T., 466, **650**

Homer, 465

Hood, John B., 382, **601**

Hood, Thomas, 433, **634**

Hood, Tom, 162, 433, **517,** 634

"Horace Greeley," 16, 145, 506

Hornet (clipper ship), 127–44, 501–6

reporter for the San Francisco *Morning Call*, 226, 509, 536, 552, 568, 651–52; SLC's residence, 295, 472, 507–9, 543, 552–53, 641, 652; writing of *Innocents Abroad*, 225. *See also* Clemens, Samuel Langhorne, JOURNALISM; Sandwich Islands, SLC's lecture

San Francisco *Alta California*, 473, 532, 538, 563, 585; SLC as Washington, D.C., correspondent, 563, 508–9, 585; SLC's *Quaker City* letters, 226–28, 472, 532, 536–38; SLC's review of Dickens, 508–9; SLC's review of Nasby, 146, 507

San Francisco *Chronicle*, 516, 544

San Francisco *Evening Mirror*, 544, 568

San Francisco *Evening Post*, 643

San Francisco *Examiner*, 450–51, 576, 643

San Francisco *Herald*, 538

San Francisco *Ledger*, 538

San Francisco *Morning Call*: SLC as local reporter, 226, 509, 536, 552, 568, 651–52

Sanger, Frank W., 547

Schieffelin, William Jay, 304, **573**

Scotland. *See* Edinburgh

Scott, Walter, 24, 228, 430, 581, **632**

"Scraps from My Autobiography. From Chapter IV," 17–18

"Scraps from My Autobiography. From Chapter IX," 17, 18, 52, 54n102, 155–63, 513–17, 670–72

"Scraps from My Autobiography. Private History of a Manuscript That Came to Grief," 17, 164–80, 188, 518–20

Scribner's Monthly, 369, 487, 596

Seaman, Louis L., 462–63, **648**–49

Seckendorff, Count Goetz von, 204–5, **527**

Sellers, Eschol, 207, 529

Servants: wages, 65. *See also* Bermingham, Ellen; Charlotte; Cord, Mary Ann; Elise; English Mary; Griffin, George; "A Group of Servants"; Hay, Rosina; Leary, Katy; McAleer, Patrick; O'Neil, John; White, Ellen; Wuthering Heights (servant)

Seward, Clarence A., 80, 81, 91, **486**

Seward, William, 492

Shakespeare, William, 165–66, 196, 209, 523, 633; people compared to, 102, 172, 465; SLC's editorial for birthday, 296, 569–70

Shaw, Henry Wheeler (Josh Billings), 148, 151, **508**, 511

Sheppard, John Morris, 280, **562**

Sheridan, Philip H., 67, 69, **472**, 473

Sheridan, Richard Brinsley, 607

Sherman, William Tecumseh, 68, 382, 431, **473**, 601

Sickles, Daniel Edgar, 287–91, 414, **565–66**

Sikes, William Wirt, 152, 512

Silverman, Joseph, 423–24, **630**

Slavery, 65, 203, 305, 611; abolitionists, 69, 147, 349, 414, 453, 474, 506, 507, 512–13, 576, 588; Burns, 267, 556; Cord, 189, 521; cruelty witnessed by SLC, 158, 514, 627–28; Daniel (Uncle Dan'l), 211–12, 217, 531, 533; Douglass helped by Jervis Langdon, 578; Griffin, 269–70, 316, 335, 583; Hannah (Aunt), 211; Jenny, 471; Sandy, 155–56, 212, 513, 531; Uncle Remus tales (Joel Chandler Harris), 217, 532–33, 635; Washington on, 302–9, 572; woman who saves SLC from drowning, 401, 613

Slee, John D. F., 376–77, 578, 598

Smalley, George Washington, 434, **635**

Smarr, Sam, 158, **514**, 610

Smith, Edward M., 380, 600

Smith, H. Boardman, 373, **598**

Smith, Roswell, 80, 92, **487**, 489, 490

Smith, Sidney, 190, 522

Smith College, 396, 607

"Something about Doctors," 188–91, 520–22

South Africa, 653

Spaulding, Clara L. (Mrs. John B. Stanchfield; Aunt Clara), 363, 379–81, 395, **593–94**, 600

Spencer, Herbert, 434, 635

Spofford, Ainsworth Rand, 282, **563–64**, 593

Springfield (Mass.) *Republican*, 94–95, 490–92, 509, 557

Stanchfield, Alice Spaulding (Mrs. Arthur M. Wright), 600

Stanchfield, John Barry, 586, 594

Stanchfield, John Barry, Jr., 600

Standard Oil Corporation, 422, 425, 660; Rogers as vice-president, 192–95, 425, 497, 522–24, 628, 653; lawsuits and investigations, 192–95, 257, 442, 549, 639

Stanford, Leland, 99, **493**

The Mark Twain Project is housed within the Mark Twain Papers of The Bancroft Library at the University of California, Berkeley. The Papers were given to the University by Mark Twain's only surviving daughter, Clara Clemens Samossoud, and form the core of the world's largest archive of primary materials by and about Mark Twain. Since 1967 the Mark Twain Project has been producing volumes in the first comprehensive critical edition of everything Mark Twain wrote, as well as readers' editions of his most important texts. More than thirty-five volumes have been published, all by the University of California Press.

The Mark Twain Papers and *The Works of Mark Twain* are the ongoing comprehensive editions for scholars. Full list of volumes in the Papers at http://www.ucpress.edu/books/series/mtp.php Full list of volumes in the Works at http://www.ucpress.edu/books/series/mtw.php

The Mark Twain Library is the readers' edition that reprints texts and notes from the Papers and Works volumes for the benefit of students and the general reader. Full list of Library volumes at http://www.ucpress.edu/books/series/mtl.php

Mark Twain Project Online is the electronic edition for the Mark Twain Project. *Autobiography of Mark Twain, Volume 1,* is now published there. All volumes in the Papers and Works as well as the Library will eventually be made available at http://www.marktwainproject.org

Jumping Frogs: Undiscovered, Rediscovered, and Celebrated Writings of Mark Twain brings to readers neglected treasures by Mark Twain—stories, tall tales, novels, travelogues, plays, imaginative journalism, speeches, sketches, satires, burlesques, and much more. Full list of Jumping Frogs volumes at http://www.ucpress.edu/books/series/jf.php

Editorial work for all volumes in the Mark Twain Project's Papers, Works, and Library series has been supported by grants from the National Endowment for the Humanities, an independent federal agency, and by donations to The Bancroft Library, matched equally by the Endowment.

DESIGNER: SANDY DROOKER
TEXT: 10/14 ADOBE GARAMOND
DISPLAY: AKZIDENZ GROTESK
COMPOSITOR: INTEGRATED COMPOSITION SYSTEMS, INC.
PRINTER AND BINDER: THOMSON-SHORE, INC.